FOURTH EDITION

SOCIAL WORK TREATMENT

INTERLOCKING THEORETICAL APPROACHES

EDITED BY

FRANCIS J. TURNER

THE FREE PRESS

NEW YORK   LONDON   TORONTO   SYDNEY   SINGAPORE

THE FREE PRESS
A Division of Simon & Schuster Inc.
1230 Avenue of the Americas
New York, NY 10020

Designed by Michael Mendelsohn of MMDesign 2000, Inc.

Manufactured in the United States of America

10 9 8 7 6 5 4 3 2 1

Note to Readers of *Social Work Treatment*

A revised chart that compares the twenty-seven theories discussed herein along a series of fifty variables, measuring approximately 35 by 40 inches, constitutes an efficient resource for practitioners, students, and teachers. It has proven to be a useful supplement to the book and can be ordered from:

Dr. Francis J. Turner
186 Claremont Avenue
Kitchener, Ontario
Canada N2M 2P8

Price (including postage): $35.00

Library of Congress Cataloging-in-Publication Data

Social work treatment: interlocking theoretical approaches / edited
    by Francis J. Turner. — 4th ed.
        p.   cm.
    Includes bibliographical references and index.
    ISBN 0–684–82994–0
    1. Social service.   I. Turner, Francis J. (Francis Joseph)
HV37.S579   1996
361—dc20   96–30360
                                               CIP

ISBN 0–684–82994–0

CONTENTS

FOREWORD TO
THE FIRST EDITION

To many social work educators and practitioners the development of a usable, expanding and internally consistent theory of social work practice is both urgent and long delayed. To others it is an exercise in beating our breasts which fills a good deal of paper but is remote from the daily demands of practice. Is it then an exercise primarily engaged in by academics in their struggle to keep up with other academic Joneses? Or is it so crucial for the improvement of practice that we are rightly to be taken to task for elevating assumptions into theories or concentrating on practice without analyzing the common factors that could be discerned in that practice or testing the fruitful application of theory to it?

Probably the only useful way to resolve this debate is to ask what is the use of theory. The first point is that it must be a good theory, based not only on observation but also on hypothesis in which alternative possible explanations have been ruled out. For instance, an observer in the early nineteenth century noted that men who wore top hats did not die of starvation, and a society to provide free top hats was about to be launched, so it is said, before further observation ruled out the hypothesis. Similarly, in social work the enormous complexity of the scene with which social workers engage, the "big, buzzing confusion," to quote William James, may well have a good deal to do with our failure to develop theories of the right size, i.e., neither so comprehensive that they are of little use for every day purposes or so one-track that they leave most of the real world out of account. To produce usable theories of the right size over a sufficient range of commonly encountered persons in their major life experience is a formidable task. But once again "what is the point of it?" The first thing to be said is that theory is not an end in itself but a means to an end. That end is the objectives or goals of social work; however these may be expressed at any given time they are essentially concerned with enabling people to make a better go of it with themselves and others and to achieve or have provided for them more elbow room in their social circumstances. The hallmark of a good theory is, of course, its capacity to predict the outcome of any given action. It also provides a guide to what is the same and what is different in a range of similar situations, and it should thus be a springboard for the development of further theory that sheds light on fresh interconnections. The point of a good theory is thus that it works in practice and in the very working generates more comprehensive, more powerful theory. The other overwhelming advantage of theory applied and tested in practice is that it is transmissible to other practitioners and is testable by them in a way that does not hold for wisdom acquired through practice or for assumptions.

The present study is significant, indeed a landmark, because it contributes to and springs from the new impetus to pioneer for social work the application of theory in practice without which it cannot advance as a profession—or, what is more important, in its capacity to deliver the goods—at this point in its development. The two-pronged attempt to elucidate theory and to study rigorously what actually happens in practice is now going forward, even if spasmodically, in several different countries. This is important, because we need to discover not only what theories reliably predict outcome within a given culture and circumstances but what in these is directly relayed to universals in human nature and is thus applicable, even by different modes of operation, in different cultures or in cultures within certain similar traditions. All the authors have illustrated from practice the theories they each discuss. This adds greatly to the values of the study from an international point of view. Other countries and continents where the practice of social work, and education for it, has spread rapidly in the last quarter century are greatly in need of studies like those which Dr. Turner and his collaborators have brought together here. It is to be hoped that this book will be widely read, not to be slavishly learned and regurgitated, but for use as a further stimulus to the well-planned study which must go ahead in other situations where social work is practiced. This is essential for the much needed cross-fertilization of well recorded and tested theories. In short, we must develop the attitude of mind that inspired this book, not only for the improvement of practice, but also for the vastly better education of social work students which is so urgently needed in the world as a whole.

Dame Eileen L. Younghusband
Former Honorary President
International Association of Schools of Social Work

PREFACE

It is particularly satisfying to me that the time has come do a fourth edition of *Social Work Treatment*. It is also highly surprising that it is already almost ten years since the last edition. Trite as it must sound, it really does seem a short time ago that I worked on the third edition during my sabbatical at Hunter College. I am pleased that the interest in the book continues strong and increasingly widespread. Dame Younghusband hinted at the important correlation between theoretical diversity and a multicultural-oriented profession when she wrote the Foreword to the first edition in 1974. As the years go by and I have more opportunity to meet colleagues from all corners of the world, I am increasingly convinced of the wisdom of her suggestion.

In preparing to write this Preface, I first reread those of the earlier three editions. Several things struck me. First, the original intent or goal of the book remains the same. It is aimed principally at practitioners and students in social work. Thus, its main objective is to produce a highly pragmatic volume that will bring together in one place the rich range of theories found to have significant utility in contemporary social work practice. This is not only to ensure that our frontline colleagues have ready access to the theoretical richness that is the mark of contemporary social work, but, more important, to provide a resource book that can enrich practice. Its goal thus is to ensure that clients receive the most theoretically sound and diverse treatment that is available.

However, as I continue to study this fascinating topic of theoretical diversity and its relevance for practice I find that my own thinking has changed in several ways. It is clear that the trend to diversity continues. We are not, as I earlier predicted, moving to any type of uni-theory or general theory. Rather, the reverse is true. Diversity is continuing to expand. And with this, considerably less interest is being given to the idea of a general theory for the profession. But an important part of this expanding diversity is that there is much more comfort with it.

As well, the idea of an interlocking approach to practice built on a wide spectrum of distinct theories is rapidly expanding. Thus, although I had thought there would be a slowing in the emergence of new theories, this has not occurred. In fact, six new theories have been added to this edition.

I have also observed that some of the systems I thought might well be coming together, such as ego psychology, psychosocial, and psychoanalytic, indeed remain distinct although strongly interlocking. These systems, which over the decades have powerfully impacted on the profession, continue to stand clearly as separate viewpoints, each of which gives us a different view or searchlight on practice.

Some of the new additions to this edition were anticipated. For example, in the introduction to the third edition I suggested that we would probably have a chapter on empowerment theory, which we do, and one on deviance theory, which we do not. The decision about which new approaches to add was based on the assessment as to whether the system in question had developed to the point where at least some significant component of the profession saw it as contributing something new to practice, broadly speaking.

It is this latter point that led me to omit the chapter on family theory. I have long recognized that there is something illogical in having a chapter on family theory and not one of individuals, dyads, groups, and community. No doubt when the first edition was first being prepared it was at a time when family theory and family practice had achieved a high profile. Of course, in no way has this importance diminished; indeed, it is a form of practice that each theory must consider.

In this regard, it has become evident to me that all social work practice theories have to address all modalities of intervention. Indeed, each of them does, but differentially. There is, of course, a rich spectrum of professional literature addressing each of our modalities of intervention. In this volume, we are looking beyond individual methodologies at systems that have applicability to all methods. Certainly, different authors and different systems have developed applications for different theories more strongly in one area than in others. However, as social work as a profession has finally become essentially multimethod in its practice, so too must each and every theory that it espouses. As a result, in inviting each author to participate, I stressed the need to discuss the application of her or his particular system to all methods.

I am pleased that many of the authors from earlier editions have once again agreed to contribute. This lends the necessary strength of continuity to the ongoing development of our theoretical base. However, some are no longer with us or no longer write or no longer practice, and new colleagues have been asked to contribute. These, too, I welcome with enthusiasm.

A concern that I have is that the book is still totally North American in its authorship. As our profession becomes more internationally aware of its common identity and concomitantly aware of the paradox of a unifying quality to theoretical diversity, we need to become much more comfortable in drawing on the wisdom of colleagues in other parts of the world. In this regard, we still have a long way to go. It is my fond hope that the next edition of this book will indeed reflect many different cultures and countries with contributions from colleagues in other parts of the world as well as from those previously involved. I have already begun this search.

Pleased as we have been with the book's reception, there have been criticisms leveled against it. There are three in particular. The first is related to the inclusion of meditation as a suitable therapy for social work. The argument has been made that social work is essentially Judeo-Christian in its origins, and that these origins are in conflict with the origins of meditation. The second criticism was related to the chapter in the chapter on psychoanalytic theory, where issue was taken with the relevance of the research discussed. The third criticism was that one of the cases in the chapter on cognitive thinking reflected an inappropriate pathologizing of a homosexual young man.

In addition, as mentioned in the Preface to the third edition some have suggested that equal time be given to "masculine therapy" along with feminist therapy. In my own view, this body of thought has not yet developed to a point where it can be viewed as a social work practice theory, although this may well occur in the next few years.

I have taken each of these questions seriously and appreciate their being raised by colleagues. Clearly, I do not agree with some of them, as is reflected in what I have decided to continue with in this edition, but just as clearly have I taken action on some of the others.

What has been especially useful is that these concerns have clearly brought to the fore the awareness that one of the ways in which theories differ is in their value base. This is an important strength of theories, but it can also be a source of difference and stress between and among strong adherents of different theories.

As before, it is my strong hope and ambition that this fourth edition of *Social Work Treatment* will assist our profession in its worldwide commitment to addressing the spectrum of systemic problems that exist in society and to serving more effectively the individuals, dyads, families, groups, and communities that turn to us for ethical, accountable, value-sensitive, and effective treatment.

As I have found before, it is difficult to identify all the persons who have assisted both directly and indirectly in this project. Certainly, Anne Marie, Sarah, and Francis, though more distant now and pursuing their own careers and lives, still serve as critically important agents of encouragement and interest. As the project neared completion, I was able to draw on Sarah's much-needed expertise, and this was most helpful and appreciated.

Joanne, as always, was steadfast, supportive, and understanding throughout, even with middle-of-the-night faxed messages from colleagues in other parts of the world.

Clearly, the ongoing attention that has been given to earlier editions by students and colleagues in many countries has stimulated me to produce yet another edition. There is much less dogmatism and more of the restless seeking of the scientist among us; this spurs me on.

What has been of particular help is the questioning, discussion, and examination of concepts and ideas with colleagues and students on many campuses. In particular, the doctoral students at the Mandell School at Case Western Reserve have existentially both supported and challenged.

Colleagues who have shared in the writing are, of course, the major sources of inspiration. From them I have learned much in working through the various drafts of the manuscript. In a highly pragmatic way, Susan Arellano and the Free Press gang continue to show support for this undertaking and hold me to the task through the idiosyncrasies of the U.S. post, Her Majesty's Mail, and the wonders of technology.

I am truly grateful to all!

F.J.T
Collingwood, Ont.
February 1996

To Joanne
(Ph.D with congratulations)

About the Contributors

Dan Andreae, MSW, CSW, is president of the Ontario Association of Social Workers. Previous positions include the first executive director of the Alzheimer Society for Metropolitan Toronto. Dan is currently pursuing his doctoral degree at the Ontario Institute for Studies in Education, and has authored several publications on social and health care policy issues. In 1994, Dan was awarded a Governor General's Commemorative Medal for his contributions to social services.

G. Brent Angell, PhD, is assistant professor in the School of Social Work, East Carolina University, where he is the lead professor of the graduate program's mental health specialization. He is in private practice and conducts training in neurolinguistic programming. His interests include multicultural practice approaches, particularly as they relate to North American First Nations, public school systems, interregional migration, and professional values and ethics.

Steve Burghardt, MSW, PhD, is an associate professor of urban policy and practice at Hunter College School of Social Work in New York. A longtime activist in various forms of political organizing since the 1960s, he is the author of *The Other Side of Organizing: Resolving the Personal Dilemmas and Political Demands of Daily Practice, Organizing for Community Action,* and numerous articles on policy and practice.

Donald E. Carpenter, PhD, is social work professor emeritus, Lakehead University, Thunder Bay, Ontario. He is currently on the faculty of the Department of Psychology at the University of Minnesota, Duluth.

Elaine P. Congress, DSW, is an associate professor and director of the doctoral program at Fordham University Graduate School of Social Service, New York. She is the author of the forthcoming *Multicultural Perspectives in Working with Families,* as well as of many book chapters and articles.

Marlene Cooper, PhD, ACSW, is an assistant professor at Fordham University Graduate School of Social Service, New York. An earlier co-authored chapter on transactional analysis was published in the nineteenth edition of the *Encyclopedia of Social Work.* Together with Sandra Turner, she has co-authored several articles, including "Obsessive-Compulsive Disorder and Alcoholism," which was recently accepted for publication in *The Alcoholism Treatment Quarterly.*

Au-Deane S. Cowley, PhD, is a professor and associate dean of curriculum and student affairs at the Graduate School of Social Work, University of Utah. She is the author of several publications including two books, and has maintained a small clinical practice for over two and a half decades.

Liane Vida Davis, MSW, PhD, is an assistant professor at the School of Social Welfare, Nelson A. Rockefeller College of Public Affairs and Policy, State University of New York at Albany.

Katie M. Dunlap, PhD, ACSW, is a professor in the MSW program at the University of North Carolina at Charlotte. She has extensive experience in substance abuse, family counseling, school social work, and medical social services. Her research interests include adult and early childhood education, homelessness, community organization, and family empowerment using a strengths perspective.

Kathleen Ell, DSW, is a professor at the University of Southern California School of Social Work. She recently served as the executive director of the Institute for the Advancement of Social Work Research in Washington, DC, and has published extensively in the health field.

Alex Gitterman, DSW, is a professor and former associate dean at the Columbia University School of Social Work. Currently editor of a series for Columbia University Press on the subject "Helping Empower the Process," he also directs a federally funded project to train social workers for leadership in the field of maternal and child health.

Gilbert J. Greene, PhD, ACSW, LISW, is associate professor in the College of Social Work at The Ohio State University. He has previously held faculty positions in the Schools of Social Work at Michigan State University and the University of Iowa. He teaches courses on clinical social work with individuals, couples, families, and crisis intervention.

Eda Goldstein, DSW, is professor and chairperson of the social work practice curriculum area at the New York University Shirley M. Ehrenkranz School of Social Work. She is consulting editor to several social work journals and maintains a private practice. She has authored over thirty publications, including two editions of *Ego Psychology and Social Work Practice* and *Borderline Disorders: Clinical Models and Techniques.*

Rose Marie Jaco, PhD, is professor emeritus with a long career of teaching in the BSW program at King's College, University of Western Ontario. She has been an active board member of several community social agencies, promoting the development and delivery of counseling services, particularly in the area of bereavement.

Thomas Keefe, DSW, is a professor and head of the Department of Social Work at the University of Northern Iowa. His research and theoretical articles address empathy, meditation, and practice. His most recent book is *Realizing Peace: An Introduction to Peace Studies,* written with Ron E. Roberts.

Patricia Kelley, PhD., is a professor and director of the School of Social Work at the University of Iowa. In addition to her numerous articles on the subject of clinical social work and family theory and therapy, she is the author of *Uses of Writing in Psychotherapy* and *Developing Healthy Stepfamilies: Twenty Families Tell Their Stories.*

Donald Krill, MSW, has been a professor at the University of Denver's Graduate School of Social Work since 1967. He developed the Family Therapy Training

Centre of Colorado, in Denver, and is the leading writer on existential social work. His publications include *Existential Social Work, The Beat Worker,* and *Practice Wisdom.*

Jim Lantz, PhD, is an associate professor at The Ohio State University's College of Social Work and is co-director of Lantz and Lantz Counseling Associates.

Judith A.B. Lee, DSW, is a professor of social work at the University of Connecticut School of Social Work. Formerly chair of the group work sequence at New York University, she has also taught at Columbia University. She is the author of *The Empowerment Approach to Social Work Practice* and the editor of *Group Work with the Poor and Oppressed.*

Anne-Marie Mawhiney, PhD, is a professor of social work and director of the Institute of Northern Ontario Research and Development at Laurentian University. She is the author of *Towards Aboriginal Self-Government* and editor of *Rebirth: Political, Economic and Social Development in First Nations.*

Herb Nabigon (*Maangiins*—Little Loon), PhD, is assistant professor and former coordinator of the Native Human Service Program at Laurentian University. He is a pipe carrier and traditional teacher who was taught Cree healing methods by several elders from western Canada. He has written chapters for *Rebirth: Political, Economic and Social Development in First Nations* and *Schooling and Employment in Canada.*

William Nugent, PhD, is an associate professor at the College of Social Work at the University of Tennessee, Knoxville. His areas of interest include aggressive and antisocial children and adolescents. He has received extensive training in hypnosis and has been recognized as a fellow in hypnotherapy by the American Association of Professional Hypnotherapists.

William J. Reid, DSW, is a professor at the School of Social Welfare, Rockefeller College of Public Policy and Affairs, University at Albany, State University of New York. His most recent books are *Qualitative Research in Social Work* (co-edited with Edmund Sherman) and *Generalist Practice: A Task-centered Approach* (with Eleanor Tolson and Charles Garvin).

Howard Robinson, MA, MSW, is assistant director of the post-masters certificate program in child and adolescent social work and instructor of social work at Fordham University Graduate School of Social Services, New York. He maintains a private clinical practice with individuals and families.

William Rowe, DSW, is a professor and director of the School of Social Work at McGill University. He contributes to the social work and medical literature in HIV and the sexuality of disabled persons.

Herbert S. Strean, DSW, is distinguished professor emeritus at Rutgers University and director emeritus at the New York Centre for Psychoanalytic Training. He is the author of over thirty books and 100 professional papers.

Barbara Thomlison, PhD, is associate professor of social work at the University of Calgary, where she directs a pilot practice evaluation project to examine family reunification for children in long-term care. As a current recipient of a Killam Resident Fellow Award, she is working on *The Practice of Family Assessment* *and Planning for Social Workers.* She is actively involved in treatment foster care and community-based service models of child welfare and foster care, and serves on numerous child welfare committees and research advisory boards.

Ray Thomlison, PhD, is dean and professor of social work at the University of Calgary, Canada. As an educator, he is actively interested in international social work education and practice. He serves on numerous local, national, and international social work boards and committees. He is the author of numerous books, book chapters, and articles on behavior modification, social work practice, child sexual abuse, employee assistance, and social welfare.

Francis J. Turner, DSW, is professor emeritus and former dean of the School of Social Work, Wilfrid Laurier University. Currently he is the editor of the *Journal of International Social Work.* He is the author and editor of several books on practice, including *Differential Diagnosis and Treatment in Social Work.*

Joanne C. Turner, PhD, is associate professor, School of Social Work at King's College, University of Western Ontario. She is a consultant and private practitioner, specializing in clinical practice with individuals and families. Her current research examines the relationship between quality of life and case management for developmentally handicapped persons. She is a past chairperson of the Ontario College of Certified Social Workers and co-editor of *Canadian Social Welfare.*

Sandra Turner, PhD, is associate professor, Fordham University Graduate School of Social Service, New York. An earlier co-authored chapter on transactional analysis was published in the nineteenth edition of the *Encyclopedia of Social Work.* Together with Marlene Cooper, she has co-authored several articles, including "Obsessive-Compulsive Disorder and Alcoholism," which was recently accepted for publication in *The Alcoholism Treatment Quarterly.*

Mary Valentich, PhD, is a professor in the Faculty of Social Work at the University of Calgary. Formerly the advisor to the president of the University of Calgary on women's issues, she has been extensively involved in community and university activism since the early 1970s. She has co-edited two books on social work practice in sexual problems, in addition to numerous articles; as well, she has written a self-help manual, *Acting Assertively at Work,* with her partner, Dr. Jim Gripton.

Mary E. Woods, MSW, recently retired as adjunct associate professor, Hunter College of Social Work, New York, and from clinical practice with individuals and families. She co-authored, with Florence Hollis, the third and fourth editions of *Casework: A Psychosocial Therapy.*

CHAPTER 1

THEORY AND SOCIAL WORK TREATMENT

FRANCIS J. TURNER

E"*verybody has won and all must have prizes.*" I am certain that Lewis B. Carroll was not thinking of social work and social work theories when he penned these words from *Alice in Wonderland* in Oxford many years ago. However, their theme reflects accurately my viewpoint as I continue to wrestle with the ever-expanding reality of our profession's rich theory base. For me, each of our several theories stands as an important contribution to the field if it gives us a better way of helping even one client. And whether or not one or another of these theories fits our individual view of the world and how we believe our practice is to be conducted, each deserves a prize and each needs to be a part of our practice treasury.

THE GOAL

This book has three principal goals. As in earlier editions, its principal objective is to provide our colleagues, be they the inquiring student, the conscientious practitioner, the searching professor, or the harried administrator, with a readily available overview of the principal theories currently influencing social work practice around the world. Second, it aspires to achieve this goal based on the assumption that to fully appreciate and make effective use of these theories they must be understood both as individual conceptual constructs and as bodies of thought that are interinfluencing, interconnecting, and *interlocking*. Last, the volume seeks to identify the teaching, practice, and research challenges that our theoretical diversity presents. This to ensure that we make optimum use of them for the efficacy of our clients, for whom we are responsible, be they individuals, dyads, groups, or communities.

Underlying this threefold objective is a strongly held assumption that theory and practice are inexorably interconnected. Few would deny this in public discussion of the profession, although in the private world of collegial interaction, there are clearly other viewpoints. Even though we argue strongly that theory is critical to practice, it is still difficult to demonstrate that these two factors are closely intertwined. The days

1

of exhortations that we must make our practice more theory based are well over. The challenge now is how to do so.

In addressing this challenge we can no longer decry a paucity of theory, for now we have a well-established richness of old and new theories, as well as theories in the making. Accompanying this reality is a growing acceptance of, interest in, and indeed excitement about the implications and challenges for practice of this diversity. A part of this altered perspective is the growing understanding of, and commitment to, the need to ensure that accountable practice is based on a firm knowledge base (Carew, 1979; Reid & Hanrahan, 1982; Thomlison, 1984). However, whether this move to accountability has been enhanced by our richness of theories, or whether this plurality only serves to disillusion and confuse, is still open to question.

The position, reflected in this volume, is that this diversity has been an exciting step forward. It has strengthened our understanding of the importance of tested theory. As well, it has demonstrated the pitfalls of practice devoid of theory or overdependent on a single theory. Further, it has helped us add precision to the growing complexities of our practice by providing us with tools to better understand its scope and dimensions.

However, in order to tap the potential of the differential use of specific theories, each of us must be familiar with all of them. Many theories exist in contemporary social work. Others continue to emerge. All have an impact on some components of practice. We believe strongly that what we do is closely connected to what we know. As yet, though, we still have difficulty in demonstrating the validity of this concept.

But even if this is so, it does not mean that practitioners function irresponsibly, or ineffectively. The evidence of day-to-day practice dramatically disproves this (Rubin, 1985; Thomlison, 1984). Our challenge is to build a rigorous conceptual base for drawing on this wealth of knowledge to make practice even more effective and accountable.

To take some further steps in this necessary direction we will present an overview of each of the major theories currently affecting practice. As a preliminary to these presentations we will first address six topics. They are: What is theory? What is the place of theory in social work history? What is the place of theory in contemporary practice? What are the uses of theory in practice? What is the potential harm of theory? How can we classify the current range of theories?

WHAT IS THEORY?

One of the difficulties of defining the word *theory* in a social work practitioner-oriented text stems from the various ways in which this term is used in our day-to-day practice. Most of us can recall from our research courses that the more precise meaning of this term is a model of reality appropriate to a particular discipline. Such a model helps us to understand what is, what is possible, and how to achieve the possible (Hearn, 1958; Siporin, 1989). Four associated terms are considered essential to the definition of theory: concepts, facts, hypotheses, and principles.

Concepts are abstractions representing logical descriptions of reality that a discipline develops to describe the phenomena with which it is dealing. Concepts are thus the labels by which we communicate with others within a discipline, and increasingly in today's practice, in other disciplines. They are the agreed-upon terms that describe our practice world. Within a discipline there is a constant thrust to try and make concepts increasingly precise to ensure clear and effective communication between colleagues. A concept is not a phenomenon. Rather, it is a formulation about a phenomenon that is derived from abstractions based on our experiences. As we all remember from our research classes, one of the mistakes of researchers and practitioners is to treat such abstractions as concrete realities. Examples of concepts in social work practice are relationship, personality strengths, crisis, homeostasis, self-identity, and defense mechanisms.

Facts are concepts that can be empirically verified, that is, they are testable observations related to the concepts with which we deal. What constitutes adequate empirical evidence for a concept to be a fact is an involved and challenging issue. The history of the search for knowledge over the centuries is replete with examples of accepted "facts" subsequently supplanted by other facts.

Theory emerges from the process of ordering facts in a meaningful way. That is, a certain relationship between facts is posited through observation or through deduction, induction, speculation, inspiration, or experience and then subjected to testing.

These relationships between facts are described in statements called hypotheses, which are tested for accuracy though the methods of disciplined observation employed in the varied processes of research. When a hypothesis has been found to be supported, the theory can be said to have advanced a step.

Principles are statements about fundamental laws or rules that emerge from tested hypotheses. They become the bases on which theory-based action is taken. In social work practice, the statement from systems theory that a change in one part of a system results in change in the entire system would be an example of a theory-based principle.

Clearly, this is a highly summarized description of the involved and ongoing efforts of all disciplines, including our own, to develop bodies of tested facts in a manner that helps us understand and predict some aspect of the reality with which we deal and so provide us with guidelines for effective action. Hence, the development of any theory, especially in all of the helping professions, is an ongoing process. We can never say when a theory is fully developed.

This raises the complex and often debated question of when an evolving body of concepts can be designated a theory. When are we talking about some interesting new ideas from which a theory may or may not develop? When are we talking about a developing theory? When are we talking about a body of thought that is sufficiently well developed to be called a theory? This is not the place to answer this question definitively. Such debates go on, and need to go on, among those who study the development of thought. However, since I have made decisions about what to include and what to exclude from this volume, I need to answer the question as to what criteria I used for the selection of topics. Indeed, it is a question that has frequently been put to me (Goldstein, 1990).

For me, the answer has been and will continue to be a highly pragmatic, practitioner-based one. In my judgment, we have a new practice theory in social work when the following eight criteria have been met:

1. The ideas are indeed new and are not restatements of earlier knowledge using new terminology.
2. The ideas generated by the thought system give us new insights into a significant aspect of the human condition, into a significant group of clients, or into some aspect of relevant social and environmental systems.
3. The system has been found to be demonstrably useful by a significant component of the profession.
4. There is a beginning body of empirically tested knowledge that supports the new ideas.
5. The interventions emerging from the theory are ethical.
6. The interventions and concepts can be learned, understood, and utilized by a significant component of the profession.
7. The system addresses a broad spectrum of practice and methodologies.
8. The theory is beginning to be accepted by the profession.

Obviously, there is a range of judgments involved in this paradigm. Further, since theory is an evolving dynamic process, there will probably never be (nor should there be) full consensus on this point. For example, a chapter on meditation included in the second edition of this book provoked severe criticism by some segments of the profession. Now there is a much broader acceptance and understanding of its relevance to social work, and meditation is viewed by many as an important resource.

What we have said thus far applies to the formal meaning of the term "theory." However, we are not always consistent in the way terminology is used. One does not have to go far to find two very different yet equally powerful meanings of the word. One is the popular but very imprecise meaning that is far from the idea of a tested hypothesis. Thus, one frequently hears the word *theory* used almost as a synonym for a hunch or personal opinion. We see this in such phrases as "What's your theory about this situation?" or "I've got a theory about what's going on here." Rarely does the meaning conveyed by this usage relate to the idea of concepts, facts, or findings; rather, it describes something more like a gut reaction.

We also tend to use the term in various collegial ways, some of which are pejorative. Hence, another popular but incorrect use of theory is in reference to something distant, unreal, and impractical, as in "He is much too theoretical" or "Don't let theory get in the way of being practical." Unfortunately, these popular uses of the word frequently result in a minimizing and even disparagement of this important treatment concept, and hence in a turning away from the powerful reservoir of helpful knowledge that is available.

THE PLACE OF THEORY IN SOCIAL WORK HISTORY

As befits any responsible profession, the search for a strong theoretical base has been a continuing theme throughout the history of social work practice. We have been constant and enduring in this quest, and we have approached the challenge from a variety of perspectives. To date, *thirteen* such approaches can be identified in the literature. Their presentation in the list that follows is not to imply that they arose sequentially. Rather, many of them continue to be employed simultaneously and independently.

1. The first approach describes what is best described as the pre-theory period in our theoretical development, when our early colleagues were attempting to conceptualize practice, to formulate definitions, and to classify interventive procedures and methods. Examples of these are Mary Richmond's *Social Diagnosis* and Gordon Hamilton's classic *Theory and Practice of Social Casework*, a book that for a long time was the basic text for clinicians (Hamilton, 1951; Richmond, 1917). Despite the title, *Theory and Practice of Social Casework*, Hamilton rarely uses the word theory and makes little reference to the process of theory building and the place of research in the process. Rather than discussing concepts and tested hypotheses, she refers to "basic assumptions which cannot be proved" and uses such terms as axioms, values, attitudes, and exhortations. She speaks authoritatively and comfortably from her knowledge of and competence in practice. Her book is more prescriptive than theory based. These early writings are not to be disparaged, for they were the essential first steps in bringing together in a scholarly manner the practice wisdom of the profession, which is the base from which theory evolves.

2. A second approach to theory building, which predates the work of Hamilton but follows that of Mary Richmond, can be found in an important but largely unknown book by Frank J. Bruno, written in 1936 and entitled *The Theory of Social Work* (Bruno, 1936). In spite of its title, it is not about social work theory. Rather, it is about the theoretical bodies of thought that social work practice of the time drew upon. The author argues strongly against a search for a unitheory, stating that any answer that pretends to explain social events in a single formula must be viewed with strong suspicion (p. 585). In criticizing the search for a single theory, he gives particular attention to the strong influence of Freudian thinking on the practice of his day. He is challenged by the complexity of the social work task and reviews the bodies of knowledge from which, in his view, social work needs to draw. Interestingly, in addition to emphasizing the need to understand the physical bases of some of the problems we encounter, he discusses the importance of psychoanalysis, functionalism, Gestalt and Adlerian thinking, Jungian thought, and the work of Marx. Quoting Tennyson—"Our little systems have their day; They have their day and cease to be"—he warns of the danger of faddism.

3.   The third approach to theory building is seen in that rich cluster of writings based on an accepted body of theory, specifically, psychodynamic theory. The authors built their works on a strong adherence to one or another school of psychodynamic thought and then postulated the implications of the relevant concepts for social work practice. Two influential examples of this work are Howard Parad's two books, *Ego Psychology and Dynamic Casework* and *Ego-Oriented Casework,* co-authored with Roger Miller (Parad, 1958b; Parad & Miller, 1963). These writings do not attempt to develop a new or different theory but to apply existing theory to practice.

4.   A fourth approach to theory building, again from the clinical arm of the profession, may be found in the work of authors who begin to formulate a distinct theory base, again drawing on their own experience and that of others with whom they have practiced. In most instances, the theory that has evolved is not totally unique but builds on other thought systems, to which are added a conceptual framework that does represent a new understanding of practice. Florence Hollis's psychosocial system and Helen Harris Perlman's "problem solving approach" are well-known examples (Hollis, 1964; Perlman, 1957; Woods & Hollis, 1990). From the perspective of group practice, Gisela Konopka's *Social Group Work: A Helping Process* also represents this approach (Konopka, 1963). Both Hollis and Konopka state the conceptual bases of their approach, and Perlman presents a series of axioms or principles that underlie each of their approaches to a theory of practice. These systems are based on well thought out conceptual systems and each contains the foundation for the development of a theory. However, as they were first formulated, these systems did not meet the criteria for a theory, although later formulations did emerge as standalone practice theories. These were and remain major contributions to our profession, albeit often underestimated in our current commitment to modernity. One consequence of the emergence of different theories for social work was the tendency to take an either/or position: if you were drawn to one system you had to reject the other. This, of course, was the situation during the diagnostic-functional schism of an earlier day, and the division was similar, though not as intense, between the viewpoints of Perlman and Hollis.

5.   A fifth approach to theory building is the early custom of dividing practice and the emerging theories of practice along methods lines. This was done initially with casework and group work, but later family therapy was also separated out. The historical reasons for this separation are complex and related to the way in which these different methodologies emerged. The tendency helped foster the perception that our profession needed a pluralistic theoretical base, one for each practice method. It has only been in the last three decades that attention has been drawn to the theoretical commonalities across methods, and hence to the possibility of multimethod practitioners.

6.   Prior to the 1950s, the majority of clinical theoretical writing was based on either some form of psychodynamic thinking or small group theory. In the early sixties, we began to see a growing acceptance of theoretical plurality, which

led to a series of important writings based on a range of other theoretical systems. Hence, we find Perlman writing a book from a role theory perspective, Parad editing a work on crisis theory, Harold Werner publishing on cognitive theory, and Derick Jehu and Edwin Thomas each producing major writings from a learning theory and behavioral approach (Jehu, 1967; Parad, 1958a; Perlman, 1968; Thomas, 1967; Werner, 1965). Similarly, there were writings related to systems theory by Werner Lutz and Gordon Hearn, among others (Hearn, 1958; Lutz, 1956). More recently, we have seen a large number of writings from both feminist and constructivist perspectives. The exciting aspect of this development is the awareness and acceptance that there is much more to be learned and that there are many sources of learning.

7. The next identifiable approach to theory building is the search for interconnectedness between systems, both old and new. As practice began to develop a diverse theoretical base, the question arose of how these various approaches did or did not fit together. The concept of separate methodologies remained in force, and thus these comparisons of theories were made along methodological lines. In this way, Joan Stein and her associates compared the various emerging theories related to family therapy (Stein, 1969). Roberts and Nee, and later Strean, wrote about diverse theories of casework (Roberts & Nee, 1970; Strean, 1971). Hollis and later Hollis and Wood showed how some of these theories could be incorporated into the psychosocial approach (Hollis & Woods, 1981; Strean, 1971; Woods & Hollis, 1990). In the group treatment field, we find Schwartz and Zalba doing a similar study of the differential theoretical bases of group practice (Schwartz & Zalba, 1971). Although there was a strong hope that by comparing the various systems a unified theory would emerge, this did not take place.

8. The next observable component of theory development flowed from the growing acceptance of, and enthusiasm for, the potential of plurality. Thus, once at least some segments of the profession had broken away from the tradition of staying close to one or two theories, there was a growing interest in searching widely for new ideas and less concern about their interconnection. In this way, we moved rapidly from the six systems described in the Roberts and Nee book to the fourteen in the first edition, nineteen in the second edition, twenty-two in the third, and twenty-nine in the current edition (Roberts & Nee, 1970; Turner, 1976; Turner, 1979; Turner, 1986b). Thus, colleagues began to look at such things as Transactional Analysis and Gestalt, to wonder about other systems such as meditation and existentialism, and to develop systems of our own, such as task-centered and the Life Model. This trend was declared by some to be a confounding outcome of faddism, while others saw it as a mature and commendable search for better ways of serving clients.

9. With the rapid growth in the number of theories and the return of a close identification with the interests and disciplines of the social sciences, more attention began to be paid to the process of theory building and the nature and characteristics of theory (Merton, 1957). Examples include the work of Lutz

and Hearn, and more recently that of Paley (Hearn, 1958; Lutz, 1956; Paley, 1987). Much of this early work was influenced by systems theory and the wish to understand how theoretical systems and practice systems interfaced (Nugent, 1987). Although this process did not lead to the enrichment of practice, it did cause us to reexamine the concept of theory and to be more precise in the use of theoretical terminology.

10. The next theory building activity is related to the very essence of theory, that is, the testing of it through research. As theory almost became equivalent to dogma for many colleagues who followed it unquestioningly, and as the risks of this were recognized, there was increasing interest in and commitment to testing various components of the theories being practiced. This is an area in which a considerable amount of work still needs to be done. In this mode, various concepts from different theories are operationally defined and tested through the formulation of hypotheses and the publication of the resultant data. Lillian Ripple's studies using the concepts of motivation, capacity, and opportunity are an excellent example, as are William Reid and Anne Shyne's work on short-term treatment, which led to the development of task-centered theory (Reid & Shyne, 1969; Ripple et al., 1964). Hollis's work testing her paradigm of treatment methods and Fisher's work on cognitive and behavioral principles, as well as recent work on crisis theory, are further examples (Fischer, 1978; Hollis, 1972; Ripple et al., 1964). However, this type of research does not seem as prevalent now as it was a few years ago, in spite of the vast amount of material yet to be examined. Nonetheless, the amount of practice-based research has expanded greatly. This is reflected in the recent decision to divide the very important *Journal of Social Work Research and Abstracts* into two separate publications, one of which is devoted entirely to research.

11. A contemporary approach to the plurality of practice theories, frequently employed and with much potential to strengthen practice theory, is eclecticism. (Koglevzon & Maykrznz, 1982). In this approach, concepts are adopted from various theories and an amalgam is formed, which is used as the basis of practice.

There appear to be two forms of eclecticism. In the first, choices are made based on the preferences of the particular practitioner or the nature of the practice setting. This strategy appears to be strongly influenced by the person's own value base and his or her perception of practice rather than on an analysis of all the theories from which a conceptual framework might be developed (Latting, 1990).

The second form of eclecticism is best explicated by Joel Fischer, who argues that only those elements of a theory that have been demonstrated to be effective should be used (Fischer, 1978). Our knowledge base thus should be built on the findings of research, not on preference. This approach fosters a process in which theory is developed in an ongoing, selective, and incremental manner.

12. A more recent approach to theory building is reflected in the increasing number of articles in the professional literature that address highly discrete components of selected theories. Rather than attempting to address a system in its entirety and its application in practice, these authors are more targeted. In some instances, they are looking at a specific application of a theory, such as the use of crisis theory in a particular practice situation such as physical assault. In other instances, they are concerned with practice applications of a discrete concept, such as the concept of homeostasis in work with couples (Turner, 1986a). Both of these strategies reflect the growing appreciation that progress in the more precise use of theoretical concepts will take place in a step-by-step manner.

13. Another approach to theory building is represented by the present work. Here, theories of significance in contemporary practice are brought together in a single source. Each author has been asked to write against a common framework, one that considers the application of the theory to all modalities of direct practice. It is hoped that this will not only provide information about the use of each theory, but will also assist in the important task of examining how these various systems interact, interinfluence, and interlock.

Overall, these various approaches show that we have always been committed to the search for a strong theoretical base. Just as our theoretical base is diverse, so too are the various strategies we have used to foster it. It is our position that all theories should be seen as having equal value in themselves, and as having differential value only in their proper or improper use. Similarly, we argue that all the various approaches to strengthening our theoretical base that have been taken over the last six decades are valuable in themselves. No one is better than the other. We should cherish each of them as each has helped us move forward. Above all, we should avoid recriminations and competitiveness. The important thing is that we continue to differentially develop theories, just as we are learning how to differentially use them.

As we begin to understand and become more interested in the need for strong and selectively effective theories to cope with the demands of our complex practice, longstanding academic-clinical and theoretical-practical dichotomies will hopefully continue to blur, and one day disappear. We are beginning to understand the close connection between practice and theory building. We understand better than before that the process of assessment and diagnosis is very much akin to the process of hypothesis formulation and testing, which is the heart of theory building. Harold Lewis (1982) describes this well:

Every practitioner should know that her observations are not simply casual scannings; they involve a conceptually ordered search for evidence. Her eyes and ears are trained to help her select evidence relative to some framework that will permit inferences to be drawn, order revealed, meanings surmised, and an exploratory guide for action planned. The organizing frameworks are theories (p. 6).

The discussion thus far has assumed that effective, accountable practice needs to be founded on solid theory. This is the primary premise of this work. For many, this statement is axiomatic. However, we frequently meet colleagues for whom it is not so evident. In recent years, I have met a number of senior clinicians—persons for whom I have considerable respect—who view theory as antithetical to effective practice. For them, effective treatment consists of a warm, understanding, respectful, responsive, empathetic reaching out to another, who is perceived and treated as an equal. Quantifying, classifying, qualifying, analyzing, testing, experimenting—the regular scholarly components of an academic approach to theory—are looked on with suspicion (Timms, 1970). Such activities are viewed as depersonalizing the clinical encounter. Initially, I had considerable difficulty with this point of view, which seemed unethical and irresponsible. However, having met so many experienced, renowned, and highly effective practitioners whose position is atheoretical, I must conclude that they have much to teach us.

It is easy to be critical of our past record of theory development, but we should not be. Instead, we ought to be grateful to those who preceded us and who helped move us from a thin theoretical base to our current situation, where the challenge is how to deal with an overwhelming body of knowledge.

WHAT ARE THE USES OF THEORY IN PRACTICE?

The principal thesis of this work is that responsible, ethical practice needs to be built on strong theory. But what are the functions of theory for the practitioner? Why is it so important?

Clearly, the most essential function of theory is its ability to explain and hence predict phenomena. The answers to two questions are sought in practice: What will happen if I do nothing in this situation? And what will happen if I respond in a particular way or ways? Theory helps us to recognize patterns, relationships, and significant variables that assist in bringing order to the complexities of contemporary practice. It helps us to "compare, evaluate and relate data" (Siporin, 1975).

In consciously formulating a treatment plan based on assessment and diagnosis, a practitioner is involved in either a theory-building or a theory-testing activity. A treatment plan presumes sufficient understanding of a situation that actions can be taken with predictable outcomes. Without such an understanding, practice remains in the realm of guesswork and impressionistic response. This is not to say that we are close to having a high level of certainty in all aspects of our practice, only that we need to draw on what we know to advance our certitude (Siporin, 1979).

Theory also aids the practitioner in anticipating outcomes and speculating about unanticipated relationships between variables. That is, theory should help us to recognize, understand, and explain new situations. If we understand sufficiently the phenomena with which we are dealing and their interrelationships, we should have the conceptual tools for dealing with unexpected or unanticipated behaviors. To the extent that our theory is sound, we should meet with fewer surprises in our practice and be better able to solve problems.

Theory also helps us carry knowledge from one situation to the next, by helping us recognize what is similar or different in our ongoing practice experiences. This in no way detracts from our individuality or self-determination; in fact, it can enhance these by helping us see not only how the client or situation resembles other clients and situations, but how each is unique. Theory helps us to expand our horizons as we follow the implications of some observation or fact that does not appear to fit what we know or have experienced before. In these situations, we are led to speculate about other ways of viewing reality. This, in turn, can lead to an enriched perspective on clients and situations.

A sound and logically consistent theoretical structure and mind-set permit us to explain our activity to others, to transfer our knowledge and skills in a testable and demonstrable way, and to have our activities scrutinized and evaluated by others. If we have sound theories, others can profit by our experience by applying those theories on the basis of how action was been taken in particular situations.

Further, theory helps us to recognize when we encounter new situations that indicate gaps in our knowledge. For example, when the application of a theoretical concept does not have the expected outcome, we have either misunderstood or our knowledge is not sufficient to deal with the situation at hand. After meeting with a difficult or new practice situation, practitioners frequently blame themselves, assuming that if they had been more aware they would have coped more effectively. In fact, there may have been no available theoretical construct to explain the presenting phenomena. It is just as important to know what is not known as it is to know what is!

Theory also provides the practitioner with assurance. We have all experienced the awesome responsibility of practice and endured the loneliness it brings. Theory will never completely dispel these feelings, but a firm theoretical orientation gives us a base on which to organize what we do know. A set of anchoring concepts can help us avoid the aimless wandering with the client that occurs when we do not know what we are doing (Pllalls, 1986).

Theory brings some order to our practice by helping to put into perspective the mass of facts, impressions, and suppositions developed in the process of therapeutic contact with an individual, dyad family, group, or community. A cynic might even suggest that theory, whether sound or not, gives a sense of security to the therapist, thus increasing effectiveness, even when the theory has little to do with the treatment employed.

In addition, reliance on one theory permits us to assess other theories. If we are clear about which of our concepts are empirically verifiable and connected, we are in a much better position to evaluate emerging ideas in light of what we know. In our field, there can be several theoretical explanations for a single phenomenon. Determining which of these is most useful requires constant testing. Theoretical explanations different from our own help us to better understand and modify our own theoretical stance.

Finally, a strong and inquiring theoretical mind-set helps us look with some objectivity at new ideas and emerging developments, and to find a middle way between the dismissiveness of the cynic who has heard it all before and the overeagerness of those who leap on every bandwagon that passes by.

OTHER ROLES OF THEORY

It is also important to understand the role that theory plays in the dynamics, sociology, and politics of our profession, and its interaction with other professions.

The increased interest in theory has strengthened our commitment to research, which, in turn, has raised our profile with scholars in other disciplines. Implied in the very nature of theory is an essential commitment to testing, experimentation, and conceptual and empirical development. Following the era in which theory was treated by many as dogma, the essential role of research came to be accepted and was given a much higher profile in the profession. Thus, in addition to the great expansion of research activities, we have seen in recent years the establishment of research centers, the rapid expansion of professional journals whose primary interest is research, the strengthening of the research component of curricula, and an enriched perception of the essential interface between research, practice, and theory. These have greatly enhanced the status of and respect for the profession on many fronts.

Thus, there is now within the profession a very strong commitment to the essential place of theory. However, this commitment is far from total. There is still a strong perception among many that the development of theory is something to be carried out by academics and graduate students, and by professional researchers at research centers. We still do not seem to have built a strong practice-theory link, and hence maintain an unfortunate chasm between these two essential components of any professional endeavor.

Another interesting phenomenon related to the plurality of theories is that each is recognized and prized to differing degrees at different times, in different parts of the profession, and at different stages in the lives of colleagues. Theories thus become the basis of many family fights within the profession. Since theories are value driven, they are respected, rejected, or ignored depending on how the values of the practitioner. These preferences can be seen within agencies indeed even within particular departments within agencies (Specht, 1990).

As a theory takes on a high status it acquires a corresponding power base, becoming the measuring stick for the awarding of position and recognition. As political correctness has caused the popularity of theories to ebb and flow, clients have been deprived of available knowledge. This is a serious problem, with serious ethical implications.

Changing preferences for particular theories also create challenges in the design and implementation of curricula at schools of social work at all levels. Virtually all curricula at the university level now include courses that address one or two discrete theories or the theoretical base of practice in a general way. In the face of an expanding diversity of theories, the approaches to the problem of what and how to teach about a theory are numerous. The pedagogical challenge becomes even more complex given the changing status of different theories. We are not suggesting that every theory needs to be taught in the same manner and afforded the same emphasis. But students need to be taught to respect each theory and to be given the tools with which to learn about and incorporate each into their theoretical base of available resources.

WHAT HARM CAN THEORY DO?

There are several ways in which theory can be a detriment to practice. The harm that this can do is to define clients' help based on knowledge rather than responding on an ad hoc basis: That is, the negative perception of theory becomes an agent of harm. When theory becomes overly cerebral and mechanistic, stressing labeling and classifying rather than on the individuality of each client and situation, it can become an end in itself. Then the ability to predict, explain, and even control becomes the goal, rather than the optimizing of human potential and the facilitating of growth. In such an ethos, the practitioner's commitment to empathy is minimized or devalued. Hence, the search for a theory of human behavior can lead away from the primary values of human freedom and autonomy.

Theory can also be self-fulfilling, especially if we become strongly attached to a particular system. We begin to see the world only from our chosen theoretical perspective and tend to interpret all phenomena in a way that fits that conceptual framework. This can, of course, be very limiting, preventing us from taking into account alternative explanations of situations.

Similarly, theory that takes on the form of dogma ceases to be living, self-examining, and dynamic. This often happens when a particular system is identified with a charismatic founder, group, or movement. When this occurs, the theory is used to close out other explanations and to dismiss those who offer them as heretics. Such a mind-set has a chilling effect on the development of new and possibly more useful and powerful ideas.

A final misuse of theory, as mentioned before, is its politicization. When a particular theory gains power within professional circles, agencies or practitioners can be granted or deprived of status depending on their adherence to the "official truth." This can have a powerful influence on what kinds of client goals are served, what services are offered, what problems are addressed, and who is considered worthy to act in the prescribed therapeutic role.

Finally, some suggest that the search for a theory is futile and should be eschewed. They argue that the subjects of our professional practice are so complex, individualized, and mobile that they cannot be understood or influenced in terms of any theory, and efforts to do so only diminish the uniqueness of the individual client. Clearly, we will never fully understand everything about our profession's areas of interest. But the history of humankind has made it abundantly clear that the quest to do so can only help us to become more effective.

THE CLASSIFICATION OF THEORY

One of the challenges presented by each edition of this book is how to classify or order the spectrum of theories addressed. Since a major thesis of this work is that these theories need to both stand alone and interlock and interinfluence, it is important to consider different organizational methods and their implications.

For example, theories could be ranged along various continua, from the most abstract to the most concrete, from the most particular to the most general, from the most internally to the most externally oriented, or from the most individualistically to the most socially oriented. It is important to note that no one of these is better or more correct than any of the others. Each is useful and could lead to a better understanding of the various theories, of what they add to each other and to our pool of knowledge.

The theories could also be organized into clusters, such as foundation theories that provide a general orientation and practice theories that are more action-specific. Or they could be clustered into three groups: highly general, midrange specific, and highly focused. Siporin's suggestion is clustering according to those that are assessment oriented by nature and those that are intervention oriented. In his view, there are theories that help us understand phenomena but do not provide much help in knowing what to do, while others are more action oriented than conceptual (Siporin, 1975). Golan calls some theories transitional and suggests that this is a basis for clustering theories into those that can be connected with other theories and those that can stand alone (Turner, 1986b). Another way of clustering is according to value bases. One way of doing this is according to a relational value base. Here, some theories are more individualistically oriented, some more group oriented, some more family oriented, and some more community focused. Many other approaches to clustering could be also considered (Fischer, 1971).

We have employed yet another method of clustering, examining each theory from the perspective of its focus on a particular aspect of the human condition. Since a major postulate of this work is that each of these therapeutic systems is differentially effective in different situations, we concluded that focusing on each theory's perceived emphasis would be a useful means of clustering. This approach led to the development of the following table, first discussed in the third edition. We use two variables, the person and the person's various relationships with him- or herself, significant others, and society as a whole. Several systems have been added to this edition, and the paradigm still appears useful.

However, I have not in this edition used this table as the basis for the order of presentation. At this point, I am not satisfied that it is sufficiently conceptually compelling to serve as such. Instead, I have presented the chapters in alphabetical order so as not to overemphasize a preconceived structure, and offer the chart as a possible way to develop a classification of theories.

One of the inherent challenges of any classification scheme is the risk that it will be seen as more definitive than it really is, causing differences to be overstressed and similarities to be minimized. In regard to our spectrum theories, it needs to be emphasized that each system needs to look at similar variables. This table highlights the identified bases from which each system begins, from the perspective that all systems are interlocking and interinfluencing.

Table 1–1

Classification of Selected Social Work Practice Theories From the Perspective of the Primary Human Activity Focus*

Distinguishing Area of Focus	Relevant Theories[†]
The Person and His or Her Attributes	
Person as a biological being	Neurolinguistic Programming
Person as a psychological being	Functional Psychoanalytic
Person as a learner	Behavioral theory
Person as thinker	Cognitive
	Constructivism
	Narrative
Person's Use of Attributes	
Person as contemplator	Meditation
Person as experiential being	Existential
	Gestalt
	Hypnosis
Person as communicator	Communication
Person as doer	Empowerment
	Problem solving
	Task
Person and Society	
Person as individual	Ego psychology
	Client centered
	Crisis
Person as communal being	Feminist Psychosocial
	Transactional Analysis
Person as societal being	Aboriginal
	Role
Person in relation to the universe	Life Model
	Systems

*See *Social Work Treatment,* 3d ed., p. 15.

†As a social work theory, each system needs to address the entire spectrum of a person's bio-psycho-social reality. The differences between and among systems relate to emphasis on focus of the system on discrete aspects of the human condition.

First presented for discussion at a faculty symposium, Columbia University, School of Social Work, Feb. 25, 1985.

SUMMARY

From our earliest days, we have been cognizant of the nature and critical importance of theory. We have not always been precise in our use of the term, nor are we yet. However, we are now much more prepared to acknowledge our diversity.

In the following chapters, each of the systems identified as a component of our current theory base will be presented and discussed from the perspective of its present place in the profession, its implications for practice, and the challenges it presents.

In the final chapter, we will discuss some of the interlocking components of the various approaches, examine some research challenges, and speculate on possible further developments for theory building in the decade ahead.

BIBLIOGRAPHY

Bruno, F. J. (1936). *The Theory of Social Work.* New York: D. C. Heath and Co.

Carew, R. (1979). The Place of Knowledge in Social Work Activity. *British Journal of Social Work* 9, 349–364.

Fischer, J. (1971). A Framework for the Analysis and Comparison of Clinical Theories of Induced Change. *Social Service Review* 45(4), 440–454.

Fischer, J. (1978). *Effective Casework Practice: An Eclectic Approach.* New York: McGraw-Hill.

Goldstein, H. (1990). The Knowledge Base of Social Work Practice: Theory, Wisdom, Analogue, Craft? *Families in Society* 71(1), 32–43.

Hamilton, G. (1951). *Theory and Practice of Social Casework* (2nd ed.). New York: Columbia University Press.

Hearn, G. (1958). *Theory Building in Social Work.* Toronto: University of Toronto Press.

Hollis, F. (1964). *Casework: A Psychosocial Therapy.* New York: Random House.

Hollis, F. (1972). *Casework: A Psychosocial Therapy* (2nd ed.). New York: Random House.

Hollis, F., & Woods, Mary E. (1981). *Casework: A Psychosocial Therapy* (3rd ed.). New York: Random House.

Jehu, D. (1967). *Learning Theory and Social Work.* London: Routledge.

Koglevzon, M., & Maykrznz, J. (1982). Theoretical Orientation and Clinical Practice: Uniformity versus Eclecticism. *Social Service Review* 56(1), 120–129.

Konopka, G. (1963). *Social Group Work: A Helping Process.* Englewood Cliffs, NJ: Prentice-Hall.

Latting, J. K. (1990). Identifying the "Isms": Enabling Social Work Students to Confront Their Biases. *Journal of Social Work Education* 26(1), 36–44.

Lewis, H. (1982). *The Intellectual Base of Social Work Practice.* New York: Haworth Press.

Lutz, W. (1956). *Concepts and Principles Underlying Casework Practice.* Washington, DC: National Association of Social Workers.

Merton, R. K. (1957). *Social Theory and Social Structure.* Glencoe, IL: Free Press.

Nugent, W. R. (1987). Use and Evaluation of Theories. *Social Work Research and Abstracts* 23(1), 14–19.

Paley, J. (1987). Social Work and the Sociology of Knowledge. *The British Journal of Social Work* 17(2), 169–186.

Parad, H. J. (ed.). (1958a). *Crisis Intervention: Selected Readings.* New York: Family Service Association of America.

Parad, H. J. (1958b). *Ego Psychology and Dynamic Casework.* New York: Family Service Association of America.

Parad, H. J., & Miller, R. (eds.). (1963). *Ego-Oriented Casework: Problems and Perspectives.* New York: Family Service Association of America.

Perlman, H. H. (1957). *Social Casework: A Problem Solving Process.* Chicago: University of Chicago Press.

Perlman, H. H. (1968). *Persona: Social Role and Responsibility.* Chicago: University of Chicago Press.

Pllalls, J. (1986). The Integration of Theory and Function: A Reexamination of a Paradoxical Expectation. *The British Journal of Social Work* 16(1), 79–96.

Reid, W. J., & Hanrahan, P. (1982). Recent Evaluations of Social Work: Grounds for Optimism. *Social Work* 27(4), 328–340.

Reid, W. J., & Shyne, A. W. (1969). *Brief and Extended Casework.* New York: Columbia University Press.

Richmond, M. (1917). *Social Diagnosis.* New York: Russell Sage Foundation.

Ripple, L., Alexander, E., & Polemis, B. (1964). *Motivation, Capacity and Opportunity: Social Service Monographs.* Chicago: University of Chicago Press.

Roberts, R. W., & Nee, R. H. (1970). *Theories of Social Casework.* Chicago: University of Chicago Press.

Rubin, A. (1985). Practice Effectiveness: More Grounds for Optimism. *Social Work* 30, 469–476.

Schwartz, W., & Zalba, S. R. (1971). *The Practice of Group Work.* New York: Columbia University Press.

Siporin, M. (1975). *Introduction to Social Work Practice.* New York: Macmillan.

Siporin, M. (1979). Practice Theory for Clinical Social Work. *Clinical Social Work Journal* 7(1), 75–89.

Siporin, M. (1989). Metamodels, Models and Basics: An Essay Review. *Social Service Review* 63(3), 474–480.

Specht, H. (1990). Social Work and the Popular Psychotherapies. *Social Service Review* 64(3), 345–357.

Stein, J. W. (1969). *The Family as a Unit of Study and Treatment.* Seattle: Regional Rehabilitation Research Institute, University of Washington, School of Social Work.

Strean, H. F. (ed.). (1971). *Social Casework: Theories in Action.* Metuchen, NJ: Scarecrow Press.

Thomas, E. J. (1967). *Behavioral Science for Social Workers.* New York: Free Press.

Thomlison, R. J. (1984). Something Works: Evidence from Practice Effectiveness Studies. *Social Work* 29 (Jan.–Feb.), 51–56.

Timms, N. (1970). *Social Work.* London: Routledge.

Turner, F. J. (1976). Interlocking Theoretical Approaches to Clinical Practice: Some Pedagogical Perspectives. *Canadian Journal of Social Work Education* 2(2), 6–14.

Turner, F. J. (ed.). (1979). *Social Work Treatment: Interlocking Theoretical Approaches* (3rd ed.). New York: Free Press.

Turner, F. J. (ed.). (1986a). *Differential Diagnosis and Treatment* (3rd ed.). New York: Free Press.

Turner, F. J. (ed.). (1986b). *Social Work Treatment: Interlocking Theoretical Perspectives* (3rd ed.). New York: Free Press.

Werner, H. (1965). *A Rational Approach to Social Casework.* New York: Association Press.

Woods, M. E., & Hollis, F. (1990). *Casework: A Psychosocial Therapy* (4th ed.). New York: McGraw Hill.

CHAPTER 2

ABORIGINAL THEORY
A CREE MEDICINE WHEEL GUIDE FOR HEALING
FIRST NATIONS

HERB NABIGON AND ANNE-MARIE MAWHINEY

INTRODUCTION

In this chapter, the authors introduce an aboriginal approach to healing individuals, groups, and communities. The approach is a holistic one based on Cree traditional teachings* in existence in North America for many centuries. It is only recently that First Nations ways of helping people have become visible to those working from a Western worldview. However, aboriginal people all over the world have been practicing their traditional ways of healing for many years before contact with westerners. In this chapter, only one of many such traditional aboriginal approaches is described, using the ancient Cree oral teachings of the medicine wheel, the four directions, and the hub. These teachings help describe ways of healing and growing spiritually by interpreting symbols. The Cree teachings provide a spiritual map to heal people and help them maintain balance.

For many First Nations and other aboriginal social workers, this chapter will provide a summary of concepts and traditional practices with which they may already be familiar. For others working with traditional healing practices, it will provide an interesting point of comparison with their own traditional healing methods. For non-aboriginal social workers, the chapter can provide an introduction to a holistic First Nations approach to helping others that is successful with many First Nations individuals, families, and communities. While this introduction cannot provide sufficient detail to develop skills in the application of the approach, interested and motivated social workers may choose to engage in a long-term learning process guided by an

---

*The authors would like to acknowledge the teachings of Eddy Bellrose, Michael Thrasher, Rebecca Martel (*Kakegee Sikaw Wapestak,* "Keeper of the Dawn"), the late Abe Burnstick, and one other senior elder who prefers to remain anonymous. Their teachings have guided and shaped this chapter.

elder or a traditional teacher. For other social workers, this chapter will provide enough of an overview that they can learn to understand, respect, and support the use of the approach by others, especially First Nations colleagues and clients. For still others, this chapter will present some basic concepts and practices, such as the hub, that can be incorporated into their day-to-day practice. In all these cases, the hope is that this chapter can help build a bridge between First Nations and those with other worldviews, and show that while the healing paths may be different, the intent is the same: to recreate harmony and oneness with ourselves and our surroundings.

OVERVIEW OF THE APPROACH

Aboriginal teachings from North America provide a way to frame our experiences.* Its simple analogies and natural-world symbolism are a means to connect all creation. Life itself is sacred and a Great Mystery, but these teachings help us accept the interrelation of all parts of creation. Traditionally, First Nations people did not see nature as being apart from us, but rather as an extension of our being. The natural world was not something separate from our emotional and mental life, and so could not be dominated or mastered[1] (Colorado & Collins, 1987). Nature was part of us and we were a part of the natural world. Unlike westerners, who see themselves as dominating other parts of nature, First Nations people viewed our relationship with nature as an equal one; humility is to know ourselves as a sacred part of Creation, no better and no worse than other parts.

The teachings assume that all humans can exist in balance with themselves, their families, communities, and their natural surroundings. Where alcoholism, violence, abuse, or any kind of dysfunction exist there is imbalance: the dark side dominates. When the dark side dominates, people who act out rage, anger, or any strong emotion in destructive ways are out of harmony within themselves—a form of spiritual disease. What is needed is for these people to find their way back to a balance. In other words, problems occur when people focus or act out of the dark side. A person who is functioning well feels balanced, in touch with self and others, including nature; the person is in touch with reality. The dark and light sides are in balance.

The Cree teachings, which include the medicine wheel, the hub, and the four directions, provide a map to restore an individual's spiritual balance. Symptoms such as greed, materialism, low self-esteem, and other kinds of problems can be healed by incorporating Native teachings into our way of thinking and living.

PATH INTO SOCIAL WORK

The spiritual masters say it is time to share our teachings with the world, because of the pain and environmental damage that exist in the world today. The teachings from

---

*The authors have chosen to refer to First Nations people in the first person plural to highlight that this chapter focuses on a worldview that is separate from the dominant one. The senior author is Anishnabe from Northern Ontario.

the five colors and the dark sides provide a method for healing the pain and the environment. An old grandmother, Elizabeth (now deceased), always said, "The sun shines for everyone, not just for Indians, and we all need sun for our survival." This simple teaching applies to all of Creation.

There is only one race of people, but four colors of people are represented: red, yellow, white, and black, and there are only four blood types amongst humans. For that reason we can reproduce, and we are all part of the human family. Spiritual knowledge helps to diminish racism and we strive to build healthier communities. We were given the teachings a long time ago, to solve our problems. The elders also say that the time to revisit the teachings has arrived again, and we need the spiritual teachings to improve our social and environmental conditions.

At the same time that elders are empowering younger First Nations people to share traditional teachings, some social work educators have started to look beyond Western worldviews for alternate ways of helping. In Canada, schools of social work at the University of Regina, Laurentian University, the University of Victoria, and Dalhousie University initiated social work education for Native students in the mid-1980s. While each of these programs, as well as the ones that followed, was established and taught in different ways, all were guided by the ideas of local First Nations people. As some schools started to hire First Nations professors, teaching, research, and program structures started to reflect these new professors' worldviews, and some students and faculty have started to be heavily influenced by these ways of thinking.

SOCIAL WORK LITERATURE

First Nations traditional teachings exist in many forms, many oral, some written, many kept hidden from outsiders to maintain their sacredness. The first written forms of the traditions and ways of living were descriptions by early visitors to North America, including explorers, missionaries, and early anthropologists (see, for example, Spence, 1914; Jamieson, 1990). Some of these writings have been interpreted more recently by academics and others (Anderson, 1985; Milloy, 1983; Nazar, 1987; Tobias, 1983) in order to regain some of the traditional knowledge that was lost as a result of colonialism and eurocentrism. Most literature of immediate relevance to social work focuses on social policy (Weaver, 1981; McKenzie & Hudson, 1985; Mawhiney, 1994), including the history of relations between First Nations and the government of Canada, self-government, and self-determination (Boldt & Long 1985; Penner, 1983). Many of these were written by nonaboriginal authors, and as a first generation of materials for teaching about First Nations and social work have been useful. Since 1985, the literature has started to expand to include writing by aboriginal authors and co-authors on themes related to social work and helping (Antone et al., 1986; Brown et al., 1995; Mussell et al., 1993; Nabigon, 1993; McKenzie & Morrisette, 1993).

BASIC ASSUMPTIONS

PRESUPPOSITIONS OF THE CREE MAP

Traditionally, First Nations teachings suggest that all humans need healing and that the means to grow spiritually are incorporated into every aspect of life. Healing is a lifelong journey and individuals strive constantly to create and recreate balance and harmony. Spiritual life is not separate from everyday life. Every aspect of existence is spiritual. Emphasis is on *being* rather than *doing*. Our traditional teachings tell us that all things *are* related. There is no sense of object and subject; all is one. Mind, body, emotions, and spirit are not separate, and humans are not separate from the earth and everything on and in it.

The First Nations philosophy of life helps people understand the relationship among all things. Understanding necessitates acceptance and putting into practice a way of life that promotes healing. Healing reconnects us with our innermost self and our surroundings. This, in turn, shapes our surroundings. All aspects of life may be improved, whether we are seeking help because of dysfunction, change, or a desire for a greater awareness of life and self.

Cree ways of helping offer us ways to balance our inner selves by listening to ourselves, our surroundings, and others. When we listen to our inner self, we get in touch with our inner spiritual fire. Facing the pain and understanding takes courage. Most people do not consciously start a journey of personal growth unless the pain of not growing is greater than the pain of growing. However, once the journey is started, it is virtually impossible to return to the old ways of relating, and the journey is a constant, ongoing process of change.

NATURE OF PERSONALITY

There are two parts of life that each person needs to pay attention to or risk imbalance: the external self and the inner self. The external self is the image we project to the outside world in our day-to-day interactions. We cultivate our external self to fit into the current culture and times. This takes many forms, including our dress, language, education, likes, and dislikes. We take care of our inner life by personal reflection. Personal reflection can make use of the hub, medicine wheel, sweet grass, and the sacred pipe. Through reflection we change and grow spiritually.

A way to present the Cree understanding of the personality is by using a conceptual device called the hub. The hub consists of three circles, one inside the other. The outer circle represents the negative, or dark side of life. The second circle represents the positive or light side, and the center represents the spiritual fire at the core of one's being. The center circle has light and dark sides, also. Balance of the three parts is the ideal to strive for. The circles are divided into four directions: north, south, east, and west. All aspects of a person's psychological and emotional life can be placed on the hub, which provides a means of understanding problems. The hub and the medicine wheel are the basic components in the Cree approach to healing.

FIGURE 2–1 THE HUB

The inner circle represents positive values, while the outer circle represents negative values. Native people who walk the red road attempt to balance their lives between positive and negative cycles of life.

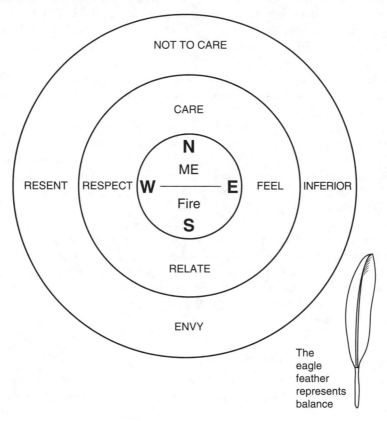

The eagle feather represents balance

Outer circle east.

Feelings of inferiority and shame are represented on the outer circle, in the east. A person who feels inferior does not feel equal to the next person. This often starts when children, who are small, feel that big people have all the power. Unless children are allowed to feel they have some power of choice over their own lives as they grow up, they are likely to feel they are victims, or at the very least, they will fear people they perceive as having authority over them. This perception is often carried over into adulthood and can lead to a sense of powerlessness, feelings of being trapped, depression, and other psychological problems. Let us not forget that we co-create our lives with our souls (minds), and so we must learn how to empower ourselves so that we can create the kind of life we really want.

Feelings of inferiority and shame very often lead to the pretense that we are better than we feel. Western families, schools, and religion often teach this to children. The competitive nature of our society causes people to compare themselves to others, contributing to this condition. On the other hand, feelings of inferiority and shame are broken as we begin to shed our inner pain in the face of unconditional acceptance and love. Denial becomes more and more difficult when we see ourselves in so many others.

Outer circle south.
Elders explain that when a person feels inferior, he or she begins to envy other people. Envy is represented on the outer circle of the hub in the south. Envy is simply wanting what other people have but not being willing to do the work necessary to get it. Envy can range from the material to the spiritual.

Envy can reinforce feelings of inferiority by providing evidence that one does not have what it takes in comparison with others. Envy promotes discontent, unhappiness, and greed. Envious thoughts produce nothing but feelings of helplessness, which in turn prevent action. However, many who feel envy do not know how to change. It is when the techniques for change are known and are not used that laziness also results. Envy may also serve to prod us into looking for methods to change.

We are often taught to compare ourselves to others by competitive values throughout society. However, success should be defined only by the individual, in relation to her or his personal goals and journey's path. Cree teachings promote self-empowerment and responsibility for ourselves and our actions.

Outer circle west.
An envious person more often than not harbors resentment. Resentment means refeeling unexpressed negative or dark feelings from the past. In other words, the emotion was not expressed at the time and was held in the body. These build up and cause a sickness called resentment that permeates a person's attitude. Repression of positive feelings can also lead to resentment. This can be seen in unemotional people. They usually go around with stony faces that are unlined, impenetrable masks. A resentful person can only focus on the dark side and is unable to look twice at her or his personal dilemma.

Outer circle north.
The attitude of uncaring is represented in the north. Apathy and disregard for our well-being signify an attitude of uncaring. Many misunderstand this concept. Many will say they care. They go out of their way to help family, friends, and neighbors, and do not think twice about themselves and their needs. They do this in the belief that they are being selfless, good, and kind. They forget that real caring starts with self; no one can really care about another until she or he has learned to care about self. Conversely, we cannot receive caring from another unless we already care about ourselves.

Center circle.

There is no doubt that a person who feels inferior, envious, resentful, and uncaring harbors jealousies as well. Jealousy is represented as the negative side of the center circle. A jealous person does not know how to listen to self and cannot share self. This often leads to possessiveness and unfulfillment.

The inability to listen to self, to be quiet long enough to listen for feelings and let them be useful guides to action, can in extreme cases lead to suicide. Elders say that people who commit suicide did not listen. At the very least, not listening will cause a person to be out of touch with feelings and therefore not know what to pay attention to. Listening to our bodies is also very important. Many illnesses could be treated sooner if the patient listened to his or her body before the symptoms got really serious.

Middle circle east.

The middle circle represents the positive side. A number of positive aspects are represented in the east, such as good feelings, food, and vision in the sense of representing in the mind. To have a clear mind and feelings of well-being, one needs good food. Both physical and spiritual food are represented here, and both are essential. Appropriate sharing of feelings, not minimizing them or exaggerating them no matter what they are, is very important because when we choose not to share our feelings, those old inferiority feelings come up again. Sometimes it helps to just tell a trusted friend who can keep calm.

Sharing of positive feelings is also necessary for mental health. Sharing laughter with friends and family has extraordinary healing value. Awareness of the language of feeling is essential to spiritual growth for how does one know who one is without feeling? Appropriate expression of feeling provides energy and reduces stress.

Middle circle south.

A good feeling from within usually leads to good relationships with self and others. The ability to relate is represented in the south on the hub. Here it means to relate to self, which is closely connected to listening to self. If we do not listen to ourselves we feel alienated from ourselves. When this happens, people refer to feeling lost or to having lost their way. Relationship with self and others requires an inner quietness and an inner peace that are gained by listening.

Developing relationships with ourselves is always a lifelong journey. Time is a dimension of our reality, and we often wish to hurry it along so that we can be there sooner. However, taking the time to prepare properly, experience nuances, and savor the present moment often requires patience. The hub and medicine wheel show us what is. We cannot be other than we are at the present moment so what is the rush? Where are we going that we have to get there so fast? And where is "there" anyway?

Middle circle west.

Respect is represented in the west on the middle circle. The literal meaning of respect is to look twice. Developing a good relationship with ourselves eventually leads to self-respect. Nonjudgmental attitudes are also important in developing self-respect *and* respect for others. The power of reason is placed in the west door. With reasoning power we can think twice before thinking inappropriate thoughts or saying something that might be harmful to ourselves or others. Respect has to do with honoring ourselves by allowing appropriate expression of feeling. Integrity comes with honoring ourselves.

Middle circle north.

Caring is represented at the north door on the middle circle. Caring is more than a feeling. It is action. It is important to remember the reasons for caring as well. Taking risks on behalf of ourselves, being willing to change, and keeping the focus on ourselves rather than what others do are the keys to action and are all important aspects to caring. This always involves persistence.

Some cultures say it is selfish to think of ourselves first. This is a misunderstanding of the dynamics involved. Providing space to care about ourselves allows others the space to start caring for themselves without being overly dependent.

Center circle (light side).

Cree elders teach that spiritual fire is symbolized in the center circle, opposite the dark side of not listening. The mystery of life, the spark of energy that gives life, is situated at the core of being. It is the core of being that must be contacted to live a happy, successful, productive life. It is also the place from which intuitive knowledge and understanding spring. Compassion flows freely from the spiritual fire if all is in balance because love flows through one's whole nature.

PROCESS OF CHANGE

The tools, or conceptual frameworks, that guide the healing process are very different from Western approaches. The hub and medicine wheel are used in healing circles and sweat lodge ceremonies. The hub can be applied to one's inner life and used orally, guided by an elder as in the Cree tradition, or used introspectively on one's own. It is used to guide our thoughts about ourselves and how we understand the world as we are experiencing it. The healing journey starts with looking inward and dealing with internal conflicts. No one is an island, however. The immediate environment of family, friends, and community influences a person, as does the greater environment—the earth. We, as individuals and collectively, influence these things, too. In fact, we cannot be separated from them, nor can we be separated from our ancestors, as we see time as a spiral connecting our past through our present to our future, not only as individuals but also as peoples.

There are many paths to growth, and although everyone has different experiences along the way, there are commonalities in human spirituality that make it possible to create methods that many can use. The ancients developed some tools that are as applicable today as they were before Caucasians came to the shores of North America.

The relationship between those seeking help and the helper is not so different from that in many of the Western helping approaches. A person—or people—unable to deal with his or her own concerns or pain seeks help from someone who has some wisdom or knowledge that might help in improving the situation. In the case of healing using Cree approaches, the guide or helper is most often an elder or elderly teacher. In approaching the teacher or elder, we are asking for help in a process that integrates our mind, body, and spirit through traditional ceremonies and healing practices.

The hub is used to sort out confusion and decipher the aspects of human thought, feeling, and behavior. The hub shows how the parts can relate to each other in a coherent format that is easy to understand. It is a simple, concrete map that helps people decipher parts of their being and points the way to healing of mind, body, and spirit. This, in turn, helps people to live more wholesome, balanced lives.

The process starts with taking a look at one's inner self and changing that before going on to look at one's environment. In fact, there is a ripple effect that starts at the center of our being and flows outward to make a difference in all aspects of our lives. The medicine wheel is used to guide the healing process.

Sweet grass, sage, cedar, and tobacco are traditional sacred plants. Each has spiritual properties and is used for specific purposes. Sweet grass, sage, and cedar are used for smudging, among other things, and tobacco is well known as an offering during prayer. The elders braid sweet grass and ignite the end, allowing it to smoulder. The smoke smells pleasant and sweet. They use the smoke of the burning sweet grass to clean the mind, body, and spirit by smudging the body with it. The ritual of cleansing with sweet grass smoke represents simple honesty and simple kindness, the kind of honesty and kindness we have as children. When we burn sweet grass we are smudging our minds, body, and spirit to remind ourselves of the importance of honesty and kindness, to wash away the darkness, to cleanse our inner self.

IMPORTANCE OF THE EXTERNAL WORLD

The Cree approach is used with individuals, groups—including families, and communities. However, it is impossible to separate one of these elements from another; we cannot separate any person from his or her context, nor can we separate a community from the people who live in it. The hub is useful in showing the interconnectedness of people and their external world, which includes ancestors, family, friends, community, and natural environment. Traditional healing, at times, has meant that those who have done harm to others, and therefore to their community and natural environment, are part of the healing process for those affected.

In addition to those aspects of our lives that we can observe, we also consider our spiritual world, including our grandfathers, as being an extension of the external world. The grandfathers can be understood in terms of universal spirit guides who possess all the knowledge of the universe. They are available to everyone. Sometimes they may plant thoughts in our minds to give us direction and guidance. These thoughts always make the utmost sense in light of their purpose, which is to help us in our spiritual evolution. The term "grandfather" was coined eons ago when the traditions were being laid down, because it was a word people connected with wisdom.

VALUE BASE OF THE CREE APPROACH

We see time as a spiral, where everything that went before is behind us, leading us through the present toward the future (Dumont, 1989). The past time includes that of our ancestors and all that they did to set us on our present path, as individuals and as peoples. As we live the present, we need to be constantly mindful not only of the immediate results of our actions but also of the consequences for future generations; our teachings tell us that everything we do today will have an impact on the next seven generations.

We use sweet grass to put us in touch with our past, present, and future and to reintroduce traditional Cree concepts to those who are interested in reexamining traditional values and applying them to today's problems. The Ojibwa and Cree cultures embrace universal values that are treasured by all peoples of the world. Honesty and kindness are central to all major cultures and religions. However, the traditional Native culture expresses these values in a unique way. All of our values are expressed through nature, and nature teaches us how to behave and how to conduct our lives. The trick is to learn how to read and understand nature. It takes a long time to get close to nature. The Teachings of the Seven Grandfathers show the traditional values that shape the healing process. These are wisdom, love, respect, bravery, honesty, humility, and truth (Benton-Benai, 1988).

The tree is the symbol of honesty in our traditions. If you take a walk in the forest you will notice there are many kinds of trees. There are white trees, yellow trees, black trees, red trees and many shades in between. Trees symbolize the four races of the world. The different shades symbolize the products of intermarriage among the four races. Also, if you walk in the bush, you will see trees of different shapes, different sizes. Some are tall, some are crooked, some are twisted. They represent all the people of the world. Walking the sweet grass road helps me be tall and straight like a tall, straight tree. Long straight trees symbolize honesty.

The Cree also believe that the rock and the tree have a spirit. Grass and animals have a spirit too; all the living things that the Creator made in our garden have a spirit. This is what the elders teach.

Animals teach affection. A little house dog is a very affectionate animal. If you call him, he will always come to you wagging his tail. He will rub his body against your legs. If you get angry with him, a few seconds later he will forgive you. Animals teach us not to abuse sex. For instance, loons mate for life. They are loyal to each other. Animals can teach us many things if we have the courage to admit our weaknesses. The elders teach that animals are equal to us and can teach us if we know how to observe and understand their behavior. Animals can also teach us companionship. Their companionship is a model of how we should relate to companions and friends. Finally, animals can teach about sacrifice. Our collective relationship with animals is such that they die so that we can live. The animal makes the ultimate sacrifice and teaches us that we, also, should sacrifice. In this way, animals are key to our survival. We need to maintain the well-being of animals for our own well-being; this is a basic teaching of our elders.

The Cree map has been used for many generations of Crees. It has the most direct importance for the Cree and other First Nations.

TREATMENT

PRINCIPAL THERAPEUTIC GOAL

The goal of treatment is to promote balance and harmony within individuals and groups of people, including communities, and to assist in taking action to relieve pain in the communities and nations of the world.

PRACTICE MODEL

In our Native culture, we relate to and learn much by observing nature over a long period of time. The First Nation worldview is divided into the four sacred directions. These directions are used to search for harmony and peace from within. The Cree and other North American aboriginal cultures use the medicine wheel to heal individuals, communities, and nations. The medicine wheel uses the compass points of the four directions to help each person to rediscover and find the way back to his or her path. In Cree teachings, the healer starts the helping process in the east.

East.
It is believed that the creator began life in the east, symbolized by the color red. In the spring, when the east wind blows a soft breeze, the earth, our mother, begins to get warmer. Plants, especially the roots and the alder shoots, turn a reddish brown. Spring is symbolized by the color red because the roots are renewing themselves as the earth renews herself. The earth cleans herself every spring like a woman's womb is cleansed once a month. Spring is a healing season. Everything is healed and all life is reborn during the spring months. New life and new feeling come to all living things in the springtime.

Aboriginal people are represented in the east, and the Creator bestowed the gifts of food, feelings, and vision on the people. In the spring, the animals have their young and we use those animals for food. In the Ojibwa culture, the symbols for food are the moose and whitefish. Historically, the moose provided us with meat, clothes, and tools. The moose and fish were great providers. Without food we would not live very long. Food is medicine; it doctors us and it heals us. There is a strong relationship between food and feelings. Good food brings us good feelings. When we feel good about ourselves, we enjoy vision. In this sense, vision means purpose and direction. Feelings of inferiority also come from this direction. Today, many people ex-

FIGURE 2–2 THE MEDICINE WHEEL
© 1990

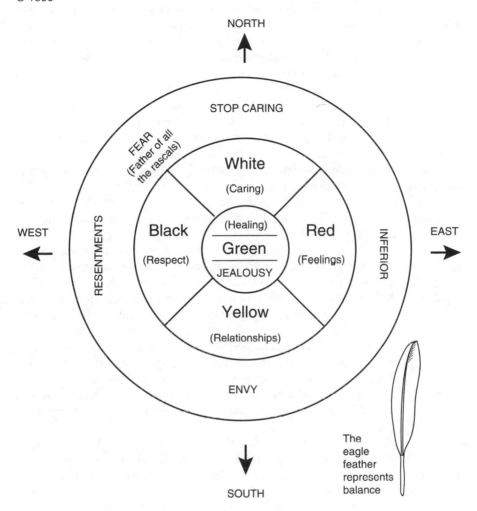

perience inferior feelings and strong anger comes from the east. Anger from the east can be translated into many of our domestic problems, which are signs of inappropriately expressed anger. Traditional teachings from this direction bring a message of peace and harmony into our communities. The turtle clan and the fish clan are also represented in the east. Traditionally, these clans were poets and orators.

In the east door, elders and traditional teachers help the person to look at her or his aspirations; the person reflects on where she or he is heading and what is to be accomplished.

South.

The color yellow is a symbol of summer, time, relationships, and the sun. At midday, the sun is facing south. The heat of summer teaches us patience because it is too hot to move very quickly. Patience helps us in our relationships with others and with ourselves. When we sit quietly, we become aware of our feelings, thoughts, and spiritual ways; we become aware of our mind, body, and spirit; there is power in silence.

We are helped to understand self through our relationships with family, extended family, friends, and community. It takes time to understand our identity as human beings. We learn and understand self by interacting with peers, and values are transmitted through our parents and institutions like school and church.

Puberty is a time of change for all young people. Adolescence is often a time of crisis. For young Natives, it is a time to define their Nativeness. The process of defining cultural heritage takes precedence over all activities, including education. It is during this period of self-exploration that a young person's academic grades may begin to decline. Educators and some parents forget to take this factor into consideration when there is a crisis at school. Elders and traditional teachers can help to understand and defuse the crisis.

The opposite of a good relationship is envy. Envy can be defined as wanting what someone else has, but not willing to work for it. Envy needs to be diffused in sacred healing circles. Late in the summer the leaves start to turn yellow. Yellow reminds us of patience which is essential to any relationship. Oriental people, represented in the south, bring the gifts of time, patience, and relationships because these are so highly valued in their cultures.

The Ginoo (golden eagle) is represented in the south. The eagle is a very sacred bird, traditionally. Because the eagle flies so high in the sky it is considered to be able to deliver messages for the Great Mystery. An eagle's feather is held in great respect.

In the south door, the person reflects on his or her relationship to family and community, seeking to build on existing strengths and overcoming barriers and problems.

West.

The color black is a symbol of respect, reason, water, and fall. When the west wind comes, fall is around the corner. In the fall, everything turns black. Leaves and other living things, especially the green things, turn black. The quality of our inner life is enhanced when we understand and implement the word *respect*. If a person thinks twice before making a decision or taking some action, her or his reasoning is good.

Many adolescents have a difficult time reviewing their inner life because of change and crisis. Native spiritual leaders have an intimate understanding of adolescence and healing ceremonies are made available. There are times when dysfunctional families overburden their older children with the responsibility for taking care of younger siblings. This practice creates hostility and resentment. Elders and traditional teachers conduct sacred ceremonies to defuse resentment, which destroys any self-respect we may have.

Black in the fall also reminds us of the Black people, who understand humility.

Humility is the recognition of our place within nature. We have much to learn about respect.

Black clouds appear in the spring and they bring rain showers and the thunderbirds. The thunderbirds' purpose is to shed light on our inner life. Water, brought by rain showers, is a very important source of energy for every being. Water is used in many different ways. But, like everything else, we can have too much water. We can bloat up, or drown in a lake.

In the west door, the person reflects on intimate relationships and her or his own behavior. Showing respect for others and for one's self is central to balance in relationships with others.

North.

White is the symbol of winter, caring, movement, and air. Caring can be defined by our level of interaction, within family, school, community, and nation. Isolation usually indicates that problems exist and they need to be dealt with accordingly. "All human beings are capable of using common sense," said a grandmother a long time ago. For her it was common sense to care. Care is as necessary as the air we breathe. Infants die if they are not cared for or touched in a caring way. If we are not taught to care for ourselves we will always be dependent, compulsively needing others to nurture us. Our belief is that caring is given to us in the north.

When the strong north wind blows, everything turns white and we have the season of winter. The north wind is a great mover. It is a master of movement. It can move trees, houses, almost anything that gets in its way. So air moves everything on our planet, Mother Earth. This is a reminder that every action has a consequence, either a caring one or one that promotes fear. Also, everyone makes a difference either in a caring way or an uncaring way. Some methods of natural healing are yelling, laughing, sweating, crying, yawning, and shaking. These can help a person move through fear.

White also symbolizes the white race. Caring is being moved. Have you noticed how the white race has moved, or spread, all over the world? When caring was not considered during their movement, many peoples of other races were displaced.

In the north door, the person builds on his or her understanding of the ways that his or her behavior affects the family and community.

Center.

Green is a healing color and is the symbol of Mother Earth, which is at the center of all things. The earth nurtures the four races of humankind and all living things. Thus, green and Mother Earth are in the center circle on the medicine wheel. When we are in balance we are in touch with our inner spiritual fire. Green is a symbol of balance and listening. Spiritual leaders emphasize that we should listen and pay attention to the dark side of life so that we can learn and heal. The dark side can be denied by the five little rascals of inferiority feelings, envy, resentment, not caring, and jealousy. The dark side of green means we stop listening. The first step toward healing is to learn how to listen to the dark side. Listening helps to make the appropriate changes from negative to positive behavior. The underlying assumption at the center of the wheel is that the ability to listen is needed in the healing process.

The four sacred directions help people to balance themselves and to know their place in the world. The importance of a balanced diet cannot be overemphasized. Food is one of the sacred gifts. A long time ago, a grandmother said that the earth is our garden—the Creator made this garden for us and it was up to us to live in harmony with it. When we take from Mother Earth to feed ourselves, we should always thank Mother Earth and the animals and put something back. The principle that whenever you take, you must also give was what our grandmother was teaching.

The white race has improved technology for harvesting food from nature, which makes it easier for us. But we should always remember that without nature, human beings are nothing. Our dependency on nature should never be forgotten. Nature's diversity—the different colors and smells of nature, the sound of animals—are very good things. They remind us of our dependency on nature. They also remind us of the gifts that the Creator has provided for us to live on this earth.

Another tool that is used in helping people regain inner balance and well-being is fasting in natural surroundings. Fasting is a purification ritual or vision quest that facilitates one's spiritual growth. It is very sacred within the Anishinabe context. We abstain from food and water while living in the forest for four days and nights. Food is a symbol of the animals and the east door. We use animals for food. Anishinabe honors that relationship and we are grateful for that life support. Red is a symbol for the aboriginal people of renewal. Fasting is a time of renewal. Just as life begins in the east we experience a time of renewal during the fast. When we honor the spirits in this way, they honor us by giving us the power of understanding.

BASIC ASSESSMENT QUESTIONS*

The following questions can be used as guides in using the medicine wheel to help people develop a basic understanding of their own behavior, their environment, the ways in which they are influenced by and influence this environment.

EAST DOOR—ASPIRATIONS

1. Why do you think you were sent here?
2. What is your understanding of your problems?
3. Where do you hope to be one year from now?
4. What do you want to be doing for the rest of your teen years?
5. What do you want to be doing when you are an adult?

---

*This section is based on an assessment framework developed by Barbara Waterfall and Herb Nabigon (1995) for adolescents seeking help from Weechi-it-te-win Family Services in Fort Francis, Ontario. The questions were pretested for six months and then changed to better fit the language and ways of thinking of this adolescent client group. Used with the permission of Weechi-it-te-win.

SOUTH DOOR—RELATIONSHIPS AND TIME

1. Describe your relationship with your family or caregiver.
2. Have you been with your family since birth?
3. Are there happy times in your family?
4. Describe what you like most about your family.
5. Describe what you like least about your family.
6. Do you have a girlfriend/boyfriend? (Further questions may be needed; for example, Are you sexually active?)

WEST DOOR—RESPECT AND REASON

1. What would you say is positive about your community?
2. Is there any alcohol, drug abuse, or sniffing in your family?
3. Describe the good parts of your family.
4. Describe what happens when there is alcohol, drug abuse, or a party in your family.
5. Do you personally drink alcohol, use drugs, or sniff?
6. Did anyone ever touch you in a way that made you feel uncomfortable?

NORTH DOOR—BEHAVIOR

1. How would you describe your own behavior in the family?
2. What do you like most about yourself?
3. Is there something that you don't like about yourself?
4. Would you describe your behavior in your family as gentle or harsh?
5. Describe your interaction with family when you seek to relieve your pain or hurt. (Further questions may be needed, for instance, about withdrawing behavior.)

CENTER HEALING STRATEGIES

1. How important is listening to you?
2. Why is listening important?
3. Do you believe listening teaches us how to be good? Give some examples.
4. What are some things you must do to heal yourself from pain?
5. Is there someone you can talk to regarding your pain?

ORIGINAL TEACHINGS

According to the original teachings, the Sacred Sweat Lodge was given to us by the Creator through a little boy. The Creator took the boy into his home and he taught him the meaning of the lodge.

The sweat lodge is a purification ceremony, and within the lodge there are four sacred doors we use to heal ourselves. The actual ceremony provides an inner body experience, which helps individuals to understand the spirit realm. The lodge is built in the form of our Mother's womb, and inside it is totally dark. We return to her womb in order to remind ourselves of our humble beginnings; we all come from her womb. The powerful and the poor are equal in the eyes of the Creator.

According to the spiritual masters, life begins in the east. At sunrise, the sky turns red. Dawn signifies a new beginning. The gifts from the east are vision, animals, and feelings. In the beginning, tobacco was given by the Creator. We offer tobacco when we pray for strength and guidance. Animals including the bear, wolf, moose, fish, and water fowl are born in the spring and sit in the east. We use animals for food, and when we eat properly, our feelings and vision improve. In our society, we often eat poorly and our vision and feelings suffer as a result. We develop inferior feelings and poor vision.

OUR CHILDREN AND FAMILIES

The Creator gave the animals instructions on the proper ways to use sex. For example, the loon mates for life and there is no physical or sexual abuse among the loons. Perhaps we can take some lessons from loons on how to behave when it comes to taking care of our families.

The sun moves from left to right across the sky and at midday the sun faces the south. The south door represents summer, the color yellow, time, relationships, and patience. Everything takes time. For example, it takes time to understand the mysteries of life. Yellow people remind us how important it is to practice patience in our relationships. Patience is very important to maintain and sustain relationships. Time is given by the Creator without condition, and how we use time in our lifetime is our own choice to make. The golden eagle, in Ojibwa called Ginoo, delivers all our thoughts and prayers to the Creator. The eagle has powerful eyesight and her invisible helpers will visit our lodges: they come in the form of little blue lights and the sound of flapping wings. The lodge is the home of the Creator and the grandfathers.

The west is the door of reflection. It is a door we use to heal the pain from yesterday. The spiritual master says you must look back in order to move forward. Denial plays a major role in this door. So many people refuse to look back and they block their feelings. The color in the west is black or blue, depending on the First Nation. Some people use the hub in the west door as a method of looking inward and it is used to heal the inner life. The grandfather who sits in the west is the thunderbird. The thunderbird brings us water in early spring; clean water is a strong medicine.

The north wind represents the north. When it is cold in winter a white blanket covers our part of Turtle Island (Earth). Many people find peace by taking a walk in the bush during the winter. For our people, white represents peace. Air is a life giver. Without air nothing moves; air is the master of movement. The white people through their technology move things around. For example, you can travel anywhere and find pop cans. The red, yellow, or black races did not make or move the cans to remote places, it was the white race with its commerce and technology. We say that the white race is the master of movement. Harmful technology is destroying our Mother Earth and the human race. The white race needs to build technology to support life, not destroy it.

The grandfather who sits in the north is the bear. We see the bear as a healer. Unlike all the other animals, the bear is a meat eater and a vegetarian; she carries all these good medicines and all the other animals go to her for healing. She also represents peace. We pray to the grandfathers to send us messengers of peace. Mother Teresa is a good example of such a messenger. She knows the sacredness of life and for that reason she feeds the poor of India. In many ways, she represents what is good about our white sisters and brothers.

According to our traditional teachings, there are four levels of knowledge that help us understand the natural laws of balance. The first level is understanding self; without this knowledge there can be no balance. The second level is understanding others through our understanding of self. The third level is understanding and appreciating the Creator. The fourth level provides us with a deep understanding of balance. When we can integrate all four levels of knowledge we are in balance not only within ourselves but also with those around us and with our environment. When we miss one or more levels of understanding, we and those around us are not in balance. To those of us from the east door, many people from the north door seem to be missing this balance because they do not integrate all four levels of knowledge. As we look at the world around us, this sense of imbalance is shown by the ways that Mother Earth has been exploited for the benefit of a few people. By regaining understanding and balance in all things, we can start to improve our natural environment.

The four directions form a sacred circle and invite the four colors of women and men to join us and build a strong sacred circle of life. To make the invitation possible, the spiritual masters say we must empty our hearts of all our credentials and material possessions and make room for the spirit. We must make room in our hearts and enter the world of the sacred. The north door in the lodge has enormous responsibilities for promoting peace and building technologies that support life, instead of destroying it.

VIGNETTES

LOON

A long time ago a loon was badly hurt. He lived on a lake of firewater. He, and many other loons who lived there with him, drank the water of this lake, which made them all very sick. The loon's spirit was broken, and his mind and body were confused because he drank too much firewater. The lake was polluted and the surroundings of the lake were ugly to look at because all the loons that lived on the lake drank too much.

One day the loon met two other loons from a different lake. The confused loon, the one with the broken spirit, began to talk with the visiting loons. The two loons called Eddy and Michael took time to talk with the loon. They talked and walked the sweet grass road. They told him that only through simple honesty and simple kindness are we able to build our fire. If we cannot build this fire we eventually die. Imagine dying on this lake, alone and forlorn, never knowing love. The two loons said that love embraces everything. Love does not exclude anything, or anyone. If we cannot accept love ourselves, they told him, then we can never experience loving someone else.

"How can I love when there is so much cruelty and injustice?" said the loon with the broken spirit. He felt self-pity, which is not good because it leaves no room for healing due to narrowing of vision. The loon did not feel he had the strength to follow the sweet grass road. He did try for many months, however, but he kept stumbling and falling down.

Then one winter he met another loon called John. John showed the broken-spirited loon what the two other loons had been telling him. The wise old loon took him and showed him how to pray in a Native way. So the three strong loons—Eddy, Michael, and John—taught the loon with the broken spirit how to pray the Native way.

Gradually, the loon with the broken spirit began to feel his fire and he left the lake of confusion, pain, and violence. He didn't want any more water from this lake, the lake that was full of poison. The three strong loons carried the loon with the broken spirit on their backs and they flew through the sky until they found a quiet spot on the ground, and they taught him the old ways. The loon with the broken spirit slowly began to feel good about himself. He no longer desired to take a drink of poison. The compulsion left him entirely. He did not want to drink any more. He never wanted to touch that firewater again.

SUE WHITE

Sue is an Anishnabekwe (an Ojibwa woman) living in Manitou Reserve in Northern Ontario. She has three children, aged four, seven, and sixteen. Her husband was killed in a car accident three years ago. Manitou Reserve is an isolated First Nation accessible by plane or, in the summer months only, by an old lumber road. Sue spends her winters going out to her trap line and fishing to support her family, including her mother and a sister who has one child. Her seven-year-old son, Adam, goes to school in the community, and her sixteen-year-old daughter, Brenda, is living with a cousin in an urban community 300 miles away and attending a high school there. Her cousin has called concerned about Brenda's social activities on the weekends, which include drinking with her friends and staying out late at parties. Brenda has done very well in school but her grades have recently been dropping. Sue is very concerned but doesn't have the money to pay for a trip to visit Brenda, nor can she take the time away from the trap line. Brenda may be implicated in an incident in which a group of students were drinking and driving. Brenda's education counselor has advised the cousin that Brenda may be suspended because of this incident.

SUMMARY

The Cree medicine wheel, as it is described here, presents an overview of one First Nation's healing process. Training to become an elder is a very long process, one that is not undertaken lightly and one that elders do not confer on just anyone. It is our intention in presenting this overview to guide the reader through an initial journey, in order to promote respect for an alternative treatment approach—one that is from another worldview than those found in the rest of this book.

REFERENCES

Anderson, K. (1985). "Commodity, exchange and subordination: Montagnais and Huron women 1600 to 1650." *Signs: Journal of Women in Culture and Society.* Chicago: University of Chicago Press, 48–62.

Antone, R., Miller, D., & Meyers, B. (1986). *The Power within People.* Deseronto, Ont.: Peace Trees Technologies Inc.

Benton-Banai, E. O. (1988) *The Mishomis Book.* Hayword, WI: Indian Country Comm and Company.

Boldt, M., & Long, J. A. (1985). *The Quest for Justice: Aboriginal Peoples and Aboriginal Rights.* Toronto: University of Toronto Press.

Brown, I., Jamieson, C., & Kovach, M. (1995). "Feminism and First Nations: Conflict or Concert?" *Canadian Review of Social Policy,* 35, 68–78.

Colorado, P., & Collins, D. (1987). "Western scientific colonialism and the reemergence of native science," *Practice: The Journal of Politics, Economics, Psychology, Sociology and Culture,* Vol. V, no. 3 (Winter), 50–65.

Dumont, J. (1989). *Culture, Behaviour and the Identity of the Native Person.* Course manual for NATI 2105 EZ. Sudbury: Centre for Continuing Education, Laurentian University.

Jameson, Anna, 1990, Winter studies and summer rambles in Canada (1838) Toronto: McLellan Stewart.

Mawhiney, A. (1994). *Towards Aboriginal Self-Government.* New York: Garland Publishing.

McKenzie, B., & Hudson, P. (1985). "Native children, child welfare and the colonization of Native people." In K. L. Levitt and B. Wharf (eds.), *The Challenge of Child Welfare.* Vancouver: University of British Columbia Press.

McKenzie, B., & Morrisette, L. (1993). "Cultural empowerment and healing for aboriginal youth in Winnipeg." In A. Mawhiney (ed.), *Rebirth.* Toronto: Dundurn Press.

Milloy, J. (1983). "The early Indian acts: Developmental strategy and constitutional change." In I. A. L. Getty and A. S. Lussier (eds.), *As Long as the Sun Shines and Water Flows.* Toronto: University of Toronto Press.

Mussel, W., Nicholls, W., & Adler, M. (1993). *Making Meaning of Mental Health: Challenges in First Nations.* Chiliwack, British Columbia: Salt'shan Institute.

Nabigon, H. (1993). "Reclaiming the spirit for First Nations self-government." In A. Mawhiney (ed.), *Rebirth.* Toronto: Dundurn Press.

Nabigon, H. and Waterfall, B. (1995). "As assessment tool for First Nations individuals and families." Used with the permission of Weech-it-te-win Family Services, Training and Learning Centre, Fort Francis, Ontario. Unpublished.

Nazar, D. (1987). *The Jesuits and Wikwemikong, 1840–1880.* Unpublished manuscript.

Penner, K. (1983). *Report of the Special Committee on Indian Self-Government.* Ottawa: Ministry of Supply and Services.

Spence, L. (1914). *Myths and Legends of the North American Indians.* London: George G. Harrap.

Tobias, J. L. (1983). "Protection, civilization, and assimilation: an outline history of Canada's Indian policy." In I. A. L. Getty and A. S. Lussier (eds.), *As Long as the Sun Shines and Water Flows*. Toronto: University of Toronto Press.

Weaver, S. (1981). *Making Canadian Indian Policy: The Hidden Agenda*. Toronto: University of Toronto Press.

CHAPTER 3

BEHAVIOR THEORY AND SOCIAL WORK TREATMENT

BARBARA THOMLISON AND RAY THOMLISON*

Behavioral social workers practice in nearly every type of organization and environment and with a variety of populations, problems, and issues requiring change. Extensive behavioral literature illustrates the compatibility of behavior theory with social work values and treatment. Most important, the outcome research studies demonstrate the effectiveness of behavior therapy in contemporary social work problems and practice. A review of the empirical research in social work and related fields of service identifies behavioral elements in social work interventions with individuals, couples, families, small groups, and communities (Thomlison, 1984a). As well, the application of single-system research designs to the evaluation of social work practice has taken on significant prominence (Thyer & Boynton Thyer, 1992). These developments suggest that the impact of behavior therapy on social work practice has been more than a passing interest of the past two decades. The literature addresses the theory, application, monitoring, and practice of behavior therapy in social work. This chapter is therefore written with two primary objectives in mind: (1) to inform social work practitioners of the origins and development of behavioral social work and of its basic assumptions, conceptual framework, procedures, and techniques and (2) to illustrate common applications of behavioral theory to social work practice. As well, the writers hope to inspire social workers to integrate social learning theory and behavioral therapy into their social work treatment model.

DEVELOPMENT OF BEHAVIORAL SOCIAL WORK

Behavior therapy† refers to the systematic application of techniques intended to facilitate behavioral changes that are based principally, but not exclusively, on the con-

*The authors wish to thank Cathryn Bradshaw for her invaluable research assistance in the preparation of this chapter.
†Some argue that the concepts of behavior therapy and behavior modification are differentially applied (Wilson, 1990). For the purposes of this chapter we prefer behavior therapy but the concepts will be used synonymously.

ditioning theories of learning. It may be argued that it is more appropriate to refer to the behavior therapies than to imply that a single method of behavior therapy exists. Behavior therapy is, however, characterized by multiple theories and techniques, in the same way as other "therapies" such as psychotherapy, marital therapy, and family therapy.

Behavioral practice traces its beginnings to the first quarter of this century in the work of Ivan Pavlov on respondent or classical conditioning; of Thorndike, Hull, Watson, and B. F. Skinner on operant conditioning; and of Bandura on social learning theory (Franks et al., 1990). The contributions of Pavlov and Skinner are well documented in both the behavioral and social work literature and need only be mentioned here. It is important to recognize that these two founders of modern behavior therapy identified and studied two distinct behavioral processes.

Pavlov's studies of the salivation reflex of dogs are familiar to most students of human behavior. The basic experimental procedure for the learning process involved placing food within the view of the dog. Salivation was elicited and the relationship between the unconditioned stimulus (food) and the unconditioned response (salivation) was established. An arbitrary event for example, a bell, was then established to occur at the same time as the presentation of the food. Over a number of such pairings, the bell (the conditioned stimulus) took on the power to elicit the response of salivation (the conditioned response). This behavioral learning process is referred to as respondent conditioning and remains the fundamental theoretical explanation for a variety of anxiety and phobic disorders in contemporary behavior therapy (Thomlison, 1984b).

Skinner's contribution to behavior therapy was initially motivated by a different set of objectives than those of Pavlov. Skinner was dedicated to the scientific study of human behavior. While he did not deny the possibility of the internal mechanisms postulated by other theorists, he argued that human behavior could be empirically investigated only through the measurement of observable behavior. He expressed the belief underlying his approach as follows: "If we are to use the methods of science in the field of human affairs, we must assume that behavior is lawful and determined. We must expect to discover that what an individual does is the result of specifiable conditions and that once these conditions have been discovered, we can anticipate and to some extent determine one's actions" (Skinner, 1953, p. 6). It is necessary to understand that this commitment to science set relatively stringent requirements on the pursuit of knowledge within the behavioral school, not the least of which was the need to develop techniques of measurement compatible with the exploration of human behavior.

True to his commitment, Skinner evolved one of the most empirically based theories of human behavior and set the foundation for contemporary behavior therapy. At the heart of this Skinnerian theory was the concept of reinforcement. The operant (or voluntary) behavior of an individual could be increased in frequency if it was positively or negatively reinforced. Alternatively, the frequency of a behavior could be decreased by either administering punishment or withholding reinforcement; this latter process was referred to as extinction. In other words, the essence of the Skinnerian or operant model of human behavior relied heavily upon an understanding of the environmental (behavioral) events that preceded and/or followed the behavior(s) under scrutiny. This theoretical explanation of human behavior has been refined and elaborated as a result of clinical experience and research. Importantly, however, the interaction between behavior and the events the precede and follow it remains the foundation of most contemporary behavior therapy.

Cognitive behavioral approaches are also regarded as part of the behavioral paradigm and are illustrated by the contributions of Beck (1976), Ellis (1989), and Meichenbaum (1977). Cognitive approaches have developed directly from behavior theory, but because they are considered to contain distinct ideas, they are discussed in a separate chapter in this textbook (see chapter 5).

It was not until the late 1960s, when psychodynamic theories came under attack, that behavioral approaches appeared in social work. Much of the impetus for the development of behavior therapy as applied to social work was provided by the practice and research contributions of Bruce Thyer (1987a, 1988, 1989, 1990, 1991, 1992). Other significant initial contributors were Ray Thomlison (1972, 1981, 1982, 1984a, 1984b), for work on the applications of behavior theory to marital problems and phobic disorders and on its effectiveness for clinical social work practice; Richard Stuart (1971, 1977), for work on the application of behavior theory to delinquency, marital problems, and weight management; Sheldon Rose (1981), for behavior therapy conducted in groups; and Eileen Gambrill (1977, 1983, 1994), for work with clinical problems. Current contributors to the single-system research designs are identified in a bibliography compiled by Thyer and Boynton Thyer (1992).

BASIC ASSUMPTIONS AND PRINCIPAL CONCEPTS

Several assumptions about behavior underlie behavior therapy. All behavior is assumed to be learned and can be both defined and changed. Problems are formulated as undesirable behavior that can be understood through systematic exploration and modified through specific behavioral techniques. Thus, personal and social problems are translated into behavior that is observable, measurable, and changeable. Change occurs by rearranging "contingencies of reinforcement," that is, by altering what happens before and after the specified behavior. Behaviorists believe that behavioral change is brought about by changing environmental events and reinforcement by significant others in the environment, as well as by the enhanced perception of self that comes from acquiring new behavior. Behavior therapy acknowledges that there are a large number of reinforcing and aversive events that can be operative in any given behavioral exchange. Identifying current and alternative stimuli is essential. By changing the contingencies of reinforcement, the behavior that needs to be changed can be extinguished or other behavior can be conditioned to replace it. The learning and changing of behavior can be understood using social learning theory.

ELEMENTS OF SOCIAL LEARNING THEORY

Social learning theory comprises three major elements: target behaviors, antecedents, and consequences (Bandura, 1976). First are those behaviors that are the focus of the behavioral analysis. These are often identified during the period of assessment as undesirable, problematic, or a behavior that needs to be changed. When behaviors become the focus for change they are referred to as the "target behaviors." The other elements are those behaviors or environmental events that precede the problematic or target behaviors. These are referred to as "antecedent behaviors" or "events." Events that follow behavior are called "consequences." They are often identified as the controlling or maintaining conditions for the problem behaviors. These behaviors serve as the focus of the behavioral assessment. The interaction of these three elements is described in the ABC behavior therapy paradigm and is represented in Figure 3–1.

It must be noted that this paradigm serves to label one exchange in an ongoing sequence of exchanges between people. In order for the social worker to determine the antecedents and consequences, a decision as to the problem or target behavior must first be made. With this target behavior in mind, the social worker identifies those events or behaviors that precede or follow the target behavior. This identification process is usually done by direct observation by the social worker or by client self-report. This process is known as "behavioral analysis" and is considered essential to effective behavior therapy.

A common parent–child behavioral exchange can serve to illustrate the application of this social learning paradigm to a behavior therapy assessment and change program. Mr. S. complains that his child, Josh, will "never do what he is told." One of the concerns is that Josh will not come to the dinner table when he is called. The presenting situation, as explained by Mr. S., is shown in Table 3–1.

In order to assess the behavior further, it is generally necessary to examine the nature of the consequences that might be provided for Josh. Behavioral consequences differ in terms of quality and purpose. Some are of a positive (pleasing) nature, while others are of a negative (displeasing) variety. The former category is referred to as "positive consequence" and is employed to increase the occurrence of a behavior. The latter category is usually referred to as "punishment" and is frequently observed when a parent attempts to prevent the recurrence of an undesired behavior by spanking the child, that is, by physical punishment. While the use of physical punishment as a consequence is acknowledged as a means of decreasing the frequency of a behavior, it is viewed among behavioral social workers as an unacceptable means of altering behavior. In addition to humanitarian reasons, physical punishment is generally considered unacceptable because in many instances it suppresses a behavior without providing an alternative, more desirable behavior. Behavior therapy requires that any

FIGURE 3–1 THE A-B-C BEHAVIOR THERAPY PARADIGM

Antecedent Event(s) ⟶ Behavior ⟶ Consequence(s)

(A)   (B)   (C)

Table 3–1
Illustration of A-B-C Paradigm

	Antecedents (A)	Behavior (B)	Consequences (C)
Behavioral Analysis of Presenting Situation	Mr. S. calls Josh several times to the table. There is an escalation of threats and yelling when Josh does not immediately respond	Josh ignores his father's first requests but eventually presents himself angrily at the table and begins to eat	Father is silent and appears angry
Behavior Change Contract	Mr. S. makes one verbal request in a pleasant tone for Josh to come to the table	Josh comes to the table when called	When Josh arrives at the table as requested, Mr. S. verbally praises Josh and places a check mark on Josh's tally sheet
			If Josh chooses not to respond to his father's request, Mr. S. will begin eating alone, ignoring Josh's absence. Josh will forego the opportunity for his father's praise and tangible, positive acknowledgment for this dinner time

agreed-upon behavioral change must be defined in terms of desired increased frequency by the participants. This requires that all parties to a behavioral change define what behaviors are desired, not simply what is undesired. This is often a difficult requirement, as it is almost always easier to tell someone to stop doing something that is undesirable than to ask them to engage in a desired behavioral alternative. The use of positive consequences to increase desirable behavior is the strength of the social learning approach to behavior therapy. The research in the clinical arena strongly supports the use of positive consequences as a means of facilitating desired behavior. Few would find this an unacceptable research finding and, indeed, might see it as axiomatic. Interestingly, however, it is not always easy to put this principle into practice. For example, Mr. S. may feel that if Josh would do what he was told, then all would be okay, but until Josh changes Mr. S. feels he cannot give Josh any positive messages or praise. Unfortunately, Josh and his father have reached a stalemate such that, even if they agree that change is desirable, it is difficult because they are into a "coercive exchange" (Patterson & Reid, 1970).

Attempting to control another person's behavior by command and threat is familiar to most of us. In many instances, however, it has the effect demonstrated by Josh and his father. The commands and threats escalate until finally the child complies in order to terminate the threats and/or yelling. By the time the child obeys the parent's command, the parent has become agitated enough to lose any motivation to acknowledge, in positive terms, the child's compliance. This coercive process can be conceptualized using the following Skinnerian notions: a "negative reinforcement process," that is, the termination of a behavior (threats) upon occurrence of the desired behavior (compliance); an "extinction process," that is, the withholding of a positive reinforcer upon the occurrence of the desired behavior (compliance); and a "positive reinforcement process," that is, Mr. S. achieves what he set out to get (compliance).

In other words, when Josh did do as he was asked, for example, sit down at the table, his father chose to ignore his compliant behavior. On the other hand, Mr. S. achieved his objective and to some degree was positively reinforced, except for the feelings of frustration and anger. The difficulty is that one person (Josh) is being negatively reinforced and the other (Mr. S.) is being positively reinforced. This behavioral exchange will therefore be strengthened and can be predicted to increase in frequency unless an alternative exchange can be identified and practiced by both.

In order to help Josh and his father alter their undesirable interaction, the social worker will need to devise a program by which the father can give a clear cue, or instruction, to Josh and positive consequences if Josh complies by arriving at the dinner table at the desired time. Intervention requires that a target behavior for desired change be clearly identified. In this case, such a target might be labelled "Josh coming to the table when called." New antecedents or instructions would be identified, as well as new consequences for this new target behavior. An agreement to change might well be formalized as a contractual statement detailing the new behavioral target, its antecedents, and its consequences (see Table 3–1).

This brief example serves to demonstrate the basic procedures of assessment and intervention in accordance with the A-B-C paradigm. While the overall behavior therapy program would require a more detailed assessment and a more comprehensive intervention strategy, behavior and its controlling antecedents and consequences remain the focus of this approach.

ELEMENTS OF COGNITIVE THEORY

Returning briefly to the developmental history of behavior therapy, there has always been some question raised, both within and outside the behavioral school, regarding the place of human "internal mental" or cognitive processes. Essentially, there is considerable interest in the role of cognition in shaping behavior. For example, the relatively potent technology of systematic desensitization used in the treatment of anxiety reactions and phobic disorders has always depended heavily on a classical learning theory explanation. However, the actual procedures of desensitization developed by Joseph Wolpe require the anxiety-ridden client to learn a relaxation response that is then called forth in association with mental images of the client's anxiety-provoking situations. Simply speaking, the client is instructed to imagine a hierarchy of increasingly anxiety-provoking scenes while in a state of relaxation. This reliance on visual imagery to facilitate the therapeutic process has lent considerable support to the exploration of the place of cognition in behavioral change. An analysis of the literature since 1979 demonstrates an increasing emphasis on cognitions within the behavioral field (Dobson et al., 1992). For some, this seems to be the next logical phase of development for behavior therapy, while for others it represents a basic violation of the principles underlying empirically based behavior therapy.

The debate regarding the place of cognitions in behavior therapy centers on several assertions by traditional behaviorists. Some theorists, such as Skinner (1988) and Wolpe (1989), argue that behavior therapy has been sidetracked through the inclusion of cognitively based techniques and principles. They propose that a reliance on cognitions in behavior therapy has led to a general abandonment of individualized behavior analysis in favor of treating classes of problems. It has also been stated that the empirical nature of behavior therapy has been eroded through the inclusion of feelings and thoughts that are inaccessible to direct, external observation. Finally, analysis of research data comparing behavior therapy and cognitive and/or cognitive-behavioral therapy outcomes indicate that, in general, outcomes are not improved through the addition of cognitive components to behavior therapy (Sweet & Loizeaux, 1991; Wolpe, 1989). For example, Sweet and Loizeaux (1991) reported that eighty-three percent of the forty clinical outcome studies used in their analysis demonstrated that "no more beneficial outcome was achieved by adding therapy modules that specifically attended to cognitive-semantic variables" (p. 176). However, the efficacy of treatment methods tended to vary according to type of problem. When follow-up versus immediate post-treatment results were considered, cognitive-behavior interventions seemed to offer longer-lasting results.

Whatever the final resolution of this debate, there is no doubt that a cognitively based behavior therapy has developed, one that is quite compatible with social work practice. In its broadest definition, cognition incorporates many of the elements of human thought processes characteristically of concern to social work. These include the processes by which information (input) from the environment is translated, considered, integrated, stored, retrieved, and eventually produced as some form of personal activity (output). Cognitive-behavior practitioners have selected and explored certain cognitive elements in behavior change. In a consideration of cognitive-behavior modification, Robert Schwartz (1982) identified the following elements of cognitive theory used in behavior modification:

1. *information processing:* the acquisition, storage and utilization of information; encompassing attention, perception, language and memory;
2. *beliefs and belief systems:* ideas, attitudes and expectations about self, others and experience;
3. *self statements:* private monologues that influence behavior and feelings; and
4. *problem-solving and coping:* conceptual and symbolic processes involved in arriving at effective responses to deal with problematic situation (Schwartz, 1982, p. 269).

Cognitive-behavior therapy is the result of a concerted effort to integrate two important theories of human functioning: behavior and cognitive. It should offer a viable alternative to those social workers who have been attracted to the behavioral focus of behavior therapy but have felt that it did not adequately deal with the individual's internal processes.

BEHAVIORAL SOCIAL WORK PRACTICE

Behavioral approaches to assessment, intervention, implementation, and evaluation share a number of characteristics with the basic social work problem-solving process. The goals of behavioral social work treatment are to increase desirable behaviors and reduce undesirable behaviors in order that the client can improve his or her day-to-day and moment-to-moment functioning. Relationship skills form the foundation of work with clients, just as it does in other areas of social work treatment. The basic behavioral assessment method is used to analyze the client's problem and assist in a plan of change by developing appropriate behavioral change goals. Behavioral interventions have been applied and evaluated with increasing sophistication and success and provide the most effective strategies for dealing with common client problems. The selection of a specific intervention is based on the assessment process, during which presenting problems are translated into observable behaviors. Then, specification of behavior techniques and strategies to be followed are detailed in a treatment contract that addresses the client's problems and circumstances.

Conducting a behavioral assessment requires a focus on the here and now of the problem, as well as on current environmental factors related to the problem behavior. Also, a clear description of the intervention is provided, along with concrete ways to measure progress. Building on client strengths while developing new skills and increasing the knowledge base is another characteristic of behavioral intervention. Generally, the etiology of the behavior is not investigated, nor is the provision of a diagnostic label pursued. Both of these are deemed stigmatizing and uninformative (Gambrill, 1994). Much of the behavioral research literature utilizes diagnostic labels (for example, agoraphobia, attention deficit disorder, post-traumatic stress syndrome) in describing the problem behavior under investigation. This has resulted from the integration of behavior assessment methods with traditional psychiatric diagnostic classifications. This practice has been criticized as promoting a neglect of individual differences (Gambrill, 1994; Wolpe, 1989) and potentially masking outcome differences between types of intervention (Eifert et al., 1990).

The major behavior therapy techniques include: (1) cognitive-behavioral procedures such as cognitive restructuring, self-instructional training, thought stopping, and stress inoculation training; (2) assertiveness training; (3) systematic desensitization and variants of this procedure such as eye-movement desensitization, procedures involving strong anxiety evocation (e.g., flooding and paradoxical intention), and operant-conditioning methods (e.g., extinction and positive or negative reinforcement); and (4) aversion therapy. Each of these approaches deserves a depth of exploration that space does not permit here. However, texts on behavior therapy and practice provide descriptions of the application of these procedures and their effectiveness (Franks et al., 1990; Granvold, 1994; Sundel & Sundel, 1993; Thomlison, 1984b, 1986; Thyer, 1992; Wolpe, 1990). These methods can be applied to practice with individuals, couples, families, groups, and communities. The choice of a specific intervention method should be based on a careful assessment of client needs and the empirically determined effectiveness of specific procedures.

GENERAL APPROACH TO BEHAVIORAL ASSESSMENT AND INTERVENTION

Behavior therapy provides a planned systematic approach to social work intervention. Indeed, there are specific stages through which all behavior therapy must proceed. While there are a range of activities that are specific to each of the different behavior therapy approaches, there is also a basic set of general procedures that serve as a framework. It is important to remember, however, that this framework is essentially a summary of a behavior therapy approach and is based primarily on the social learning paradigm. The following procedural outline is based on the authors' practice and research with married couples, children, and families. Since much of clinical social work practice is carried out within the context of the family, the outline is presented as an approach to working with the family system.

Beyond the procedural steps identified here, it is important to emphasize that behavioral social workers bring a strong sense of importance to building a positive therapeutic relationship early in the contact with the client system and actively involving the client as much as possible in each step of the assessment and intervention. The importance of this relationship building is not to be underestimated as it establishes trust, rapport, and necessary support to the analysis and management of problem behavior. Once the client system is engaged through the relationship, behavioral procedures can occur. A behavioral assessment to determine the client's problem is the next step.

ASSESSMENT PROCEDURES

This section outlines ten procedures during a behavioral assessment. The objective is to define as clearly as possible the problems or events for change and the desired outcome.

1. Compilation of the problematic behavior inventory.
   (a) Begin by asking one member of the family group to identify the perception of the problems that have resulted in the meeting.
   (b) Clarify these perceived problems by asking for behaviorally specific examples. Most perceived problems can be translated into statements of who does what to whom within what context.
   (c) As each family member offers his or her perception of the problem, there is a high probability that the ensuing discussion will stimulate disagree-

ments among family members. It is important to observe who disagrees with whom, and over what behavioral statements. Therefore, these interchanges must be allowed to occur; however, they can become counterproductive to the objective of the assessment. When this occurs, the social worker should intervene, requesting the family members to terminate the debate yet acknowledging that differences of opinion are expected. Assure all family members that their perceptions of the problems are important and that each member will have an opportunity to present personal views.

2. Identify priority behavioral problems and their maintaining conditions.
    (a) Attempt to identify the antecedent events of at least those behaviors that arouse the highest level of intensity of feeling among family members. Antecedent events are those conditions existent immediately prior to the occurrence of the target behavior (e.g., what other members of the family are doing or not doing prior to the occurrence of an undesired behavior).
    (b) Identify the consequences of those problem behaviors that elicit the more intense family feelings. Identify the consequences of those events that occur after a target behavior (e.g., what other family members do after one of the problem behaviors has occurred).

3. Identify the contingencies existent for the provision of consequences, that is, what rules appear to govern the conditions under which these consequences are provided (e.g., when a child is or is not reprimanded, or when privileges are or are not withdrawn.

4. Identify recurrent behavior patterns in the exchanges among family members. Observe and record behavioral exchanges (e.g., coercive exchanges, shouting, avoidance responses, excessive demands, etc.).

5. Secure a commitment from all members of the family system, ensuring that they wish to work toward change. This commitment should state clearly: (a) that they will work as a unit on these family problems and (b) that they, as individuals, will work toward behavioral change. At this point in the assessment procedure, the social worker should be able to demonstrate to the family the interconnections among their individual behaviors: when one individual behaves, all family members respond in some manner. That is, behaviors do not occur in isolation. For example, when the adolescent repeatedly violates a curfew, the resultant parent-youth conflict affects all members of the family.

6. Begin to identify possible behavior targets for change. The target behaviors should be desirable behaviors and the objective to increase their frequency. This identification is often assisted by asking each family member to answer two questions: How could you behave differently to make this a happier family? How would you like to see others behave to make this a happier family? These questions may be given as homework assignments, with each family member asked to provide as many answers as possible to each question. The social worker should point out that this assignment is a challenge, as it requires the identification of desired behaviors. Individuals are more often accustomed to identifying what behaviors they do not like to see, as opposed to those they prefer.

7. On the basis of the family's homework assignment, discuss possible appropriate behavioral targets for change.

   (a) Select behaviors that are to be increased in frequency in order to maximize the opportunities for positive consequences.

   (b) Select behaviors that appear to be most relevant to this family's definition of its own happiness.

   (c) Select behaviors that are incompatible with undesirable (problematic) behaviors.

   (d) For each child, select at least one behavior that is "low risk" for change. A "low-risk behavioral target" is one that can be easily attained by the child and that, if performed without positive reinforcement (a violation of the change contract), will not jeopardize the growing trust of the child. An example of a child's low-risk target behavior change might be combing the hair in the morning or cleaning up after dinner each evening.

   (e) Attempt to select behaviors that are commonly identified by family members (e.g., mealtime behavior, family get-togethers, tidying up cooperatively, playing with all siblings).

   (f) Remember that a behavior must be observable to all. It is therefore necessary to explicate the indicators of some behaviors in order to minimize debate over whether they have actually occurred. For many parents, the behavior called "cleaning up her room" is a desired behavior change objective. Interestingly, what appears to be a very clear behavior leaves a great deal open to individual interpretation. It is therefore necessary to pinpoint specific behaviors such as picking up clothes, placing them in the appropriate locations, making the bed, placing trash in appropriate containers, etc.

8. Allow time for all family members to present their concerns and their support for the target behaviors. Certain behavior choices will elicit strong feelings from some family members. Negotiation must take place before selected behaviors are settled upon and must always take place within the spirit of the agreement or commitment to change. If one or more family members wishes to reevaluate this commitment in light of the selected targets for change, this request must be honored. Such reevaluation may have to take place within the context of the consequences of no change; that is, all persons have a right not to be required to change. There are, however, certain consequences of not changing. What are they for the individual and the family?

9. When target behaviors have been agreed upon, set the conditions for a baseline measure.

   (a) Before instructing the family to change, request that the parents monitor the frequency of occurrence of the target behaviors. This will allow for some baseline behavior frequency measures. These measures should be recorded and can be used at a later date to assess ongoing behavioral changes within the family.

   (b) Appoint the parents monitors of the behavior targets. Give them a tally sheet and instructions to record the frequency of each target behavior.

10. During the assessment phase, the social worker may identify problems with an individual or with the couple that require specific attention. On occasion, the assessment may indicates that the change process should be focused on the couple rather than on the child. Behavioral intervention is compatible with the assessment in progress. With the couple's agreement, the intervention may be temporarily suspended in light of the recognized need to concentrate on the couple's problems.

IMPLEMENTATION PROCEDURES

The implementation phase of a behavioral therapy program is marked by the identification of new contingencies between identified behaviors and their consequences. To this point the focus has been on the appropriate targeting of behaviors for change. When a program for change is to be implemented, a "contingency contract" might be formulated in order to facilitate a systematic, cooperative effort on the part of the family.

1. Clearly identify the target behaviors that have been agreed upon as the focus for change.
2. Establish new antecedent events for each of these target behaviors.
3. Establish new consequences that are to be provided for each occurrence or nonoccurrence of a targeted behavior.
4. Formulate a written contract specifying the following:
    (a) The target behaviors for change and their pinpointed elements.
    (b) New antecedents; if these are to be instructions, specify by whom they are to be given.
    (c) New positive consequences; these might include check marks and/or tokens provided upon behavioral occurrence, as well as social reinforcers such as affection and praise.
    (d) Specify what is to happen if there is a violation of the contract; that is, if a behavior does not occur or an undesired behavior occurs, it must be clear what others in the family are to do. For example, if a target behavior focuses on good dinner table behavior and one or more of the children violate this agreement, all family members must be clear about what is to happen.
    (e) Specify those positive consequences that are to act as bonus reinforcers, particularly when certain behavioral objectives are accomplished. For example, it is often helpful to include special privileges, such as family outings, as bonus reinforcers of a designated behavioral achievement, such as a target behavior that occurs at the desired level for a period of one week or more.
    (f) Specify those in the family unit who are to be responsible for recording the frequency of behavioral occurrences. This is usually one or both of the parents. These tally records are important in communicating to family members the degree and intensity of change.

(g) Contracts may be written in a variety of ways, but they must all state who does what to whom under what conditions. Many different examples of contracts may be found in the literature.

5. It is necessary to follow up with a series of telephone calls to ensure that the program has been implemented. In addition, these telephone calls provide the opportunity for members of the family, particularly the parents, to ask any questions that might have arisen as a result of implementing the program for change. These calls need not take long and should be limited to the pragmatics of the program implementation. Any conflict among family members reported at this time should be directed back to the family for resolution. If resolution is not possible, the persons in charge of recording should make note of the nature of the conflict and the context in which it occurs. This will be dealt with at the next meeting with the social worker.

6. Difficulties in implementing the program are inevitable. These problems usually pertain to such things as tally recording, differences in target behavior definition, and lack of "cooperation" on the part of certain family members. In order to deal with these problems, the social worker must remember that the contract is the reference point. Once agreed to, all problems must relate back to the original document. Changes in the contract must be negotiated by all members of the family. Remember that all problems related to implementation of and adherence to a contract for family interactional modification may eventually have to be related back to the original commitment to change agreed to by the family during the assessment period.

7. Each interview with the family after implementation should begin with an examination of the tally recording provided by the family members. Where change is evident in these data, the social worker must provide positive reinforcement by acknowledging the change and the hard work of all family members.

8. Discussion must then shift to problems arising between sessions. These discussions may address more general aspects of the family's functioning, and special techniques such as role playing, modelling, and behavioral rehearsal may be introduced in an effort to assist the family in dealing with these problems.

9. Since much of the family's energy goes into problem-solving and conflict resolution, the social worker must spend time on these areas of family life. One of the advantages of having required the family to negotiate a contingency contract is that they have experienced successful problem solving and negotiation. Examples derived from that process can be utilized in the ongoing problem-solving and conflict resolution training.

10. Where the monitoring of change indicates that little if any change is taking place, it is necessary to examine certain aspects of the program design. Depending on the area in which the program is failing, it will be necessary to consider changes in target behavior, consequences, or violations. It is often necessary to assess whether people are in fact following through on the re-

quirements of the contract. For example, it might be that a parent has agreed to read a bedtime story for successful achievement of a behavioral objective during the day, but fails to deliver.

11.   When target behaviors have been achieved at the desired level of frequency, identify new behaviors for change or move toward termination of the behavioral therapy program.

TERMINATION PROCEDURES

1.   Together with the family system, evaluate progress in relation to the objectives of the contract.
2.   If the decision is to terminate, set the conditions for behavioral maintenance.
3.   Behavioral maintenance requires the social worker to review with the family the basic learning principles identified during the modification of the target behavior (e.g., positive consequences versus punishment).
4.   Instruct the family to continue the tally recording over the next four weeks but without the regularly scheduled appointments.
5.   Set up an appointment for four weeks from the last interview for the purposes of termination and follow-up.

FOLLOW-UP PROCEDURES

The follow-up interview should assess whether or not the behavioral changes have been maintained. If they have not been maintained at a level consistent with the expectations of the social worker and/or the family, it will be necessary to reinstitute the program structure. If, on the other hand, the social worker and family feel that the behavioral changes have been maintained within desired parameters, termination may take place. Termination, of course, does allow for the family to contact the social worker at any point in the future when they feel the necessity.

From the perspective of clinical evaluation, it is important that the social worker analyze the results of the behavioral change program. Further, it is helpful for the social worker to contact family members at three-month and six-month intervals to ascertain the degree to which the behavioral changes have been maintained.

PRINCIPAL APPLICATIONS IN SOCIAL WORK TREATMENT

The diverse applications of behavior theory in social work practice can only be briefly highlighted in this chapter. Given the quantity of behavioral articles in social work journals and textbooks, behavioral social work has been characterized as a "major school of practice" (Thyer, 1991, p. 1). In a survey of clinical social workers, one-third of the practitioners who participated preferred a behavioral approach in their practice (Thyer, 1987a). Social workers have found behavioral interventions most influential when applied to disorders such as anxiety, depression, phobias, addictions, sexual dysfunction, and relationship distress. A number of misconceptions about behavior therapy continue to persist and may account for why some social workers do not employ behavioral strategies in their practice. A few of the most common myths held by social workers and other professionals about behavior therapy are that it ignores client feelings and is applicable to simple rather than complex problems, and that it overrelies on aversive techniques and is limited to symptom alleviation rather than treatment of root problems (Acierno et al., 1994b; Franks et al., 1990; Thyer, 1991).

Because behavior therapy has been applied to clients who have severely debilitating or difficult-to-treat conditions, ethical considerations play a prominent role in behavior therapy. Many programs have established protective mechanisms, such as treatment review processes, to address the issues of utilizing aversive procedures, determining appropriate individualized assessment and intervention, as well as keeping written records and assessment checklists and questionnaires (Sundel & Sundel, 1993).

During the past two decades, one of the most important areas of behavioral practice to emerge has been that of dealing with parenting, parent training, and child management and skill acquisition. With the help of the basic A-B-C paradigm, many childhood problems have been reconceptualized as behavioral problems resulting from interactional exchanges between children and parents. By systematically altering these exchanges in the context of behavior therapy, it has repeatedly been demonstrated that both parental and child behavior can be altered toward their desired objectives (Dangel et al., 1994; Graziano & Diament, 1992; Sundel & Sundel, 1993).Typical child problems addressed using behavioral techniques include noncompliance, chore completion, enuresis, eating disorders, interrupting, fire setting, sleep problems and bedtime anxieties, and hyperactivity (Butterfield & Cobb, 1994). Conduct disorders or antisocial behaviors in children have received considerable clinical and research attention in the past decade. Behavioral techniques have been demonstrated as effective in changing these behaviors (Christophersen & Finney, 1993; Doren, 1993; Jensen & Howard, 1990; Kazdin, 1990). It has been estimated that three to five percent of school-age children have attention deficit-hyperactivity disorder (ADHD), which has been identified as a risk factor in conduct disturbance and antisocial behavior (DuPaul et al., 1991). Social workers encounter these children and adolescents within the program contexts of child welfare, foster care, incarceration, therapeutic day programs, and residential and school-based programs (Meadowcroft et al., 1994).

Home-based interventions with families and children have developed as the preferred treatment setting for many multifactor child and parent-related problems. The focus is on family interaction supported by the social learning model. Maltreatment or risk of maltreatment of children by primary caretakers has become a focus of in-home intervention. Problem-solving and skills training for parents usually include child management skills, anger management, and parent issues involving substance abuse, communication difficulties, and social isolation (Gambrill, 1994; Hodges, 1994).

Since the late 1950s, the treatment of choice for many professionals working with anxiety- and phobic-disordered clients has been Joseph Wolpe's systematic desensitization (1990). Clients suffering the inhibitory effects of phobic disorders have been the subjects of a great deal of effective intervention by behavior social workers. Combined with the basic systematic desensitization, new cognitive-behavioral approaches are promising even more effective outcomes. In fact, it is now to the point where a social worker would be hard-pressed to make an argument for an alternate treatment method for any of the phobic disorders.

Couple counselling is another area where social workers frequently utilize a behavioral approach. Jacobson (1992) asserts that behavioral interventions are the most widely investigated treatment for couple problems. Communication, conflict management, and problem-solving skills building are the most common behavioral interventions used. Behavioral procedures have been demonstrated to be effective with a multitude of problems, circumstances, and populations in diverse settings. Indeed, behavioral social work treatments have been found to be superior to other treatment approaches to social skills training, phobias, hyperactivity and, developmental problems of children and adults.

EDUCATION AND TRAINING FACTORS

Training for behavior therapy occurs in a variety of educational contexts. The content, format, and objectives of behavior training vary widely (Alberts & Edelstein, 1990). Social work curricula generally provide an overview of behavioral change principles and techniques but not detailed training (Thyer & Maddox, 1988). There are some social work educational programs that offer electives in behavioral social work practice. Thyer (1991) reports there over sixty published textbooks on behavioral social work and most social work textbooks present practice information on behavioral social work treatment. Many organizations, treatment settings, and programs offer behavioral training to social workers, foster parents, and in-home family support workers. Given the efficacy of behavioral methods and their extensive application to social work practice, an argument can be made for the inclusion of behavioral social work practice in the core curriculum in social work education.

CULTURALLY COMPETENT BEHAVIORAL PRACTICE

It is only relatively recently that concern for the needs of culturally different groups has received attention among behavior therapists. Behavior theory, like many contemporary practice theories, draws on Western cultural values, assumptions, and philosophy. In reality, both clients and behavioral social workers are racially diverse. Efforts to offer culturally competent therapy are very much affected by the political, social, and economic power and status of each group. Additionally, barriers exist in terms of access to and participation in therapy for different racial and ethnic groups. Barriers include philosophical and value differences, language, as well as individual and organizational structures associated with Western helping systems (Corcoran & Vandiver, 1996).

Working with culturally different individuals involves recognizing diversity in the perspectives and behavior of individuals. Different cultural groups develop their own patterns of coping strategies. Many of the techniques used by Western trained behavioral social workers may employ strategies that conflict with the values, beliefs, and family traditions of a particular cultural group. For example, the understanding of time is critical to the concept of shaping, reinforcement schedules, and extinction. This concept may be understood differently by those who view time in other ways. As well, what constitutes problematic behavior, help-seeking behavior, and inappropriate behavior is interwoven with the Western perspective on the person and what behaviors, thoughts, and feelings make up the person. Many behavioral social workers argue, however, that the principles underlying behavior cross the boundaries of culture. The main concern is whether the assumptions underlying the principles of learning are universally accepted. This needs further exploration. For example, the definition of a positive reinforcer, as an event that increases behavior frequency, does not appear to be culturally determined, but a specific positive reinforcer, such as TV watching, may work in one culture but not in another.

It is therefore very important for behavioral social workers at the beginning of assessment to understand how family and the individuals who constitute family are defined in a given culture, and to recognize that individuals make different choices based on the culture. If social workers mislabel behavioral interactions, their interventions can compound rather than resolve parenting dilemmas or other problematic behaviors. Therefore, interventions should be carefully sculpted to the client's cultural orientation and preferences. It requires modification of existing interventions and understandings of behavior, so that they are grounded in local understandings (Landrine & Klonoff, 1995).

Many social workers are beginning to ask what the cultural determinants and parameters of behavior therapy are. It is suggested that organizations in culturally specific and diverse communities should ensure that the social work staff be diverse and have a high level of self-awareness and openness. The ability to do a cultural self-assessment is also essential. Behavioral social workers must keep in mind that individuals develop problem-solving styles that fit their culture and values, and therefore solutions must fit the cultural attributes of culturally different populations. Most of the existing knowledge about diversity has not been developed by behavior therapists. Therefore, the creation of multicultural interventions is only beginning. In summary, research on the relationship between cultural competencies, behavior theory, and outcomes is largely absent or inappropriate for culturally specific situations.

SELECTED CONCERNS IN BEHAVIORAL PRACTICE

The social work literature once reflected numerous concerns about the use of behavior therapy in social work practices. Many of these earlier concerns appear to have abated. For illustrative purposes, the following concerns reflect the current practice literature.

1. For those who want "insight" or a "talking" psychotherapy, this approach is not appropriate. It is action oriented and leans heavily on an educative focus for client change.
2. The focus is on behavior/cognitive change and generally requires a structured approach to change by both client and therapist. Some social workers feel this is inappropriate or restrictive.
3. Some nonprofessionals and professionals misunderstand or misrepresent the approach, seeing it as very simple and as a quick fix for complex problems. The usual sources of such misunderstanding are inappropriately designed child management programs that rely on aversive methods of "punishment" for undesired behavior, often coupled with the unsystematic use of "rewards" for compliant behavior. Such interventions are devoid of the elements of behavior analysis and the systematic use of behavioral techniques essential for successful behavioral change.
4. The behavior therapies are often thought to be derived from a homogeneous theory, when in fact they are made up of numerous theories of behavior with an array of optional intervention strategies and techniques. Many social workers fail to understand that differential approaches are often available for specific problems identified through the process of behavioral assessment. Such matching of technique to problem is criticized by some therapists as contrived and as treating the symptom rather than the cause. Differential applications relate to the problem and are guided by the behavioral analysis of the conditions under which the problem behavior occurs.
5. Some behavioral techniques appear on the surface to be insensitive to the client. For example, the use of imagery and/or confrontation with fear-producing events is viewed as causing undue anxiety and discomfort to the client.

EMPIRICAL BASE

In general, the effectiveness of the various strategies is increasingly a concern for social work practitioners. Much of the literature supporting the relative success of various therapies depends on anecdotal material from the case reports of social workers. Many of these accounts are unidimensional and relatively few are based on empirical findings that use before and after measures and that establish clear relationships between the therapeutic intervention and client change.

In contrast, behavior therapies have a built-in opportunity for data collection by both social workers and clients. Behavioral procedures involve the systematic application of specific techniques intended to facilitate observable behavior change. Measurement of change is therefore an integral part of behavior therapy. This emphasis on problem assessment and concrete indicators of progress has led to the extensive development and use of standardized measures. One example of a widely utilized behavioral measure is the Achenbach Child Behavior Checklist (Achenbach, 1991). The empirical literature reports extensive research data demonstrating the effectiveness of behavioral approaches to many client problems. Indeed, behavior therapy has championed the use of single-system research design (Gambrill, 1994; Hersen, 1990; Thyer & Boynton Thyer, 1992), as well as studies in group outcome research (Barrios, 1990; Kazdin, 1989).

Many behavioral treatments have progressed to the advanced stage where they can be implemented on a presciptive basis with children and adults. This is a highly desirable opportunity for improving social work clinical practice. Prescriptive interventions are standardized treatments that have been empirically validated for use with precisely defined populations and problems under clearly defined conditions. This maturity and richness in the empirical literature is the result of decades of clinical application of behavioral interventions and rigorous research in such areas as anxiety disorders, phobic disorders, and marital problems. The development of behavioral interventions for other problematic behaviors is still in its infancy and as yet has not developed strong empirical validation. It should be noted that for some problems, behavior therapy is routinely and effectively used in conjunction with pharmacotherapy (e.g., some depressions, attention deficit-hyperactivity disorder, obsessive-compulsive disorder). The *Handbook of Behavior Therapy with Children and Adults* (Ammerman & Hersen, 1993) includes pharmacological approaches commonly combined with behavioral approaches. Table 3–2 provides a selective sampling of research studies and literature reviews that appraise the effectiveness of behavior therapy in producing individual change for a wide range of problems.

Behavior approaches to group work have a recognized place in social work primarily due to the excellent ongoing work of Rose (1981). Gambrill (1983), Tolman and Molidor (1994), and others. (Gambrill, 1983) have used the behavioral approach successfully with a variety of groups including adults and children (Gamble et al., 1989; Tallant et al., 1989; Thyer, 1987b; Van Der Ploeg-Stapert & Van Der Ploeg, 1986). Group work often focuses on teaching assertive behaviors and other interpersonal skills. It has been utilized extensively in the treatment of depression, eating disorders, parent and child skills training, and addictions. Tolman and Molidor (1994) reviewed group work within social work practice throughout the 1980s. They note that 69 percent of the articles reviewed had a cognitive-behavioral orientation. Child social skills training and other behavior problems of children and adolescents were the most frequently targeted fields of social work practice research utilizing behavioral group work (Jenson & Howard, 1990; Zimpfer, 1992).

Finally, applications of behavior therapy principles to community practice have been somewhat more limited but have not been ignored. Importantly, however, there are numerous examples of community projects based on behavioral principles reported in the literature (Mattaini, 1993; O'Donnell & Tharpe, 1990; Rothman & Thyer, 1984). The behavioral interventions employed are the same as those utilized for individual change (for example, modelling, feedback, contingency management).

Table 3–2
Selective Summary of Behavior Therapy Effectiveness

Problem Area	Effectiveness Research*
Addictions	Acierno, Donohue, & Kogan, 1994; Goldapple & Montgomery, 1993; Hall, Hall, & Ginsberg, 1990; Lipsey, & Wilson, 1993; Peyrot, Yen, & Baldassano, 1994; Polansky & Horan, 1993; Sobell, Sobell, & Nirenberg, 1988
Anxiety disorders	Acierno, Hersen, & Van Hasselt, 1993; Beck & Zebb, 1994; Emmelkamp & Gerlsma, 1994; Lipsey & Wilson, 1993; Rachmann, 1993; Van Oppen, De Haan, Van Balkom, Spinhoven, Hoogdin, & Van Dyck, 1995
Autism	Celiberti & Harris, 1993; Ducharme, Lucas, & Pontes, 1994; McEachin, Smith, & Lovaas, 1993; Scheibman, Koegel, Charlop, & Egel, 1990
Child maltreatment	Gambrill 1983; Finkelhor & Berliner, 1995; Gaudin, 1993; Meadowcroft, Thomlison, & Chamberlain, 1994; Wekerle & Wolfe, 1993; Wolfe, 1990; Wolfe & Wekerle, 1993
Conduct disorders	Bramlett, Wodarski, & Thyer, 1991; Christophersen & Finney, 1993; Dumas, 1989; Kazdin, 1990; Lochman & Lenhart, 1993; Maag & Kotlash, 1994; Magen & Rose, 1994; Raines & Foy, 1994
Couple problems	Granvold, 1994; Epstein, Baucom & Rankin, 1993; Halford, Sanders, & Behrens, 1994; Hahlweg & Markman, 1988; Lipsey & Wilson, 1993; Montang & Wilson, 1992; O'Farrell, 1994; Thomlison, 1984a
Depression	Beach, Whisman, & O'Leary, 1994; Frame & Cooper, 1993; Hoberman & Clarke, 1993; Norman & Lowry, 1995; Rohde, Lewinsohn, & Seeley, 1994
Developmental disabilities	Feldman, 1994; Hile & Derochers, 1993; Kirkham, 1993; Nixon & Singer, 1993; Thomlison, 1981; Underwood & Thyer, 1990
Eating disorders	Garner & Rosen, 1990; Isreal, 1990; Kennedy, Katz, Neitzert, Ralevski, & Mendlowitz, 1995; Lipsey & Wilson, 1993; Morin, Winter, Besalel, & Azrin, 1987; Saunders & Saunders, 1993; Smith, Marcus, & Eldridge, 1994; Wilson, 1994
Family violence	Edleson & Syers, 1990; 1991; Faulkner, Stoltenberg, Cogen, Nolder, & Shooter, 1992; Peled & Edleson, 1992; Tolman & Bennett, 1990
Gerontology	Fisher & Carstensen, 1990; Hersen & Van Hasselt, 1992; Nicholson & Blanchard, 1993; Widner & Zeichner, 1993
Juvenile delinquency	Bank, Marlowe, Reid, Patterson, & Weinrott, 1991; Hagan & King, 1992; Hawkins, Jensen, Catalano, & Wells, 1991; Lipsey & Wilson, 1993; Meadowcroft, Thomlison, & Chamberlain, 1994; Zimpfer, 1992
Pain management	Biederman & Schefft, 1994; Gamsa, 1994; Holroyd & Penzien, 1994; Lipsey & Wilson, 1993; Subramanian, 1991; 1994
Phobic disorders	Donohue, Van Hasselt, & Hersen, 1994; King, 1993; Mersch, 1995; Newman, Hofman, Trabert, Roth, & Taylor, 1994; Turner, Beidel, & Cooley-Quille, 1995
Post-traumatic stress	Caddell & Drabman, 1993; Corrigan, 1991; Foy, Resnick, & Lipovosky, 1993; Richards, Lovell & Marks, 1994; Saigh, 1992
Psychosis	Liberman, Kopelowicz, & Young, 1994; Lipsey & Wilson, 1993; Morrison & Sayers, 1993; Scotti, McMorrow, & Trawitzki, 1993; Tarrier, Beckett, Harwood, Baker, Yusupoff, & Ugarteburu, 1993
Sexual deviance	Camp & Thyer, 1993; Hanson, Steffy, & Gauthier, 1993; Marshall, Jones, Ward, Johnston, & Barbaree, 1991; Kaplan, Morales, & Becker, 1993; Marques, Day, Nelson, & West, 1994
Sleep disturbances	Lichstein & Riedel, 1994; Minde, Popiel, Leos, & Falkner, 1993
Stress management	Dubbert, 1995; Lipsey & Wilson, 1993

*When possible, review articles and research directly applicable to social work practice were selected.

Some of the problem areas addressed in behavioral community practice have been increasing the level and quality of community participation and decreasing undesirable community practices (Mattaini, 1993).

Overall, and relative to other approaches, behavior therapy has an attractive record of success with a wide variety of human problems. However, several gaps in knowledge and research of behavior therapy are noted in the literature. These gaps include maintaining and generalizing behavioral changes and determining which behavioral approaches work most effectively with which kind of problem in what context. Maintenance refers to the durability of the behavioral change over time; generalization refers to behavioral change in contexts different from the one in which the intervention took place. Strategies to enhance both maintenance and generalization need to become part of any behavioral change program and to be validated through empirical research (Gambrill, 1994; Kendall, 1989; Whisman, 1990). Critical variables that predict which clients will benefit from which intervention procedures can be identified not only by looking at those clients for whom a specific behavioral procedure is effective but also by considering those clients who fail to improve from the treatment (Goldfried & Castonguay, 1993; Steketee & Chambless, 1992). The quality of prediction will improve if a number of common methodological problems are addressed.

PROSPECTUS

Behavior therapy, as it has been presented here, comprises a variety of distinctly different approaches to facilitating behavioral and, in some cases, cognitive changes. It has been developed from a strong commitment to planned and systematic assessment, a distinct strength over other therapeutic models of change. Intervention strategies evolve from the prescriptive approach to assessment within a context of empirical inquiry, primarily utilizing nominal and ratio level of measurement to establish frequency and duration of problems. Its impact on social work practice continues to be felt both directly in clinical practice and indirectly in practice areas such as task-centered approaches, as well as single-system designs in research. Behavior therapy has been demonstrated to be effective in most areas of social work practice. For some large and complex problems such as those of crack addicts and autistic children, the theory is considered underdeveloped (Jordan & Franklin, 1995, p. 21). However, for the majority of problems encountered by social workers, empirical support for behavior therapy as an effective therapeutic intervention is well established and most argue behavior theory is the most advisable therapeutic option. There is little doubt that its place within social work practice has been assured. It is our sincere hope that social workers will understand the contribution behavior theory will make to quality assurance in social work practice.

APPENDIX

BASIC ASSUMPTIONS AND PRINCIPLES

Contingencies of reinforcement

Target behaviors

Consequences

Coercive exchange

Positive reinforcement process

A-B-C paradigm

Beliefs and belief systems

Problem solving and coping

Reinforcing and aversive stimuli

Antecedent behaviors

Behavioral analysis

Negative reinforcement process

Extinction process

Information processing

Self statements

BEHAVIORAL ASSESSMENT AND INTERVENTIONS

Behavior inventory

Contingencies

Homework assignments

Observable

Commitment to change

Contingency contract

Social reinforcers

Recording

Role playing

Behavioral rehearsal

Conflict resolution

Evaluate progress

Maintaining conditions

Behavioral exchanges

Low-risk behavioral target

Negotiation

Baseline measure

Tokens

Bonus reinforcers

Tally records

Modelling

Problem-solving activity

Monitoring of change

Behavioral maintenance
    clinical evaluation

REFERENCES

Achenbach, T. M. (1991). Manual for the child behavior checklist/4-18 and 1991 profile. Burlington, VT: Department of Psychiatry, University of Vermont.

Acierno, R., Donohue, B., & Kogan, E. (1994a). Psychological interventions for drug abuse: A critique and summation of controlled studies. *Clinical Psychology Review 14,* 417–440.

Acierno, R., Hersen, M., & Van Hasselt, V. (1993). Interventions for panic disorder: A critical review of the literature. *Clinical Psychology Review 13,* 561–578.

Acierno, R., Hersen, M., Van Hasselt, V., & Ammerman, R. (1994b). Remedying the Achilles heel of behavior research and therapy: Prescriptive matching of intervention and psychopathology. *Journal of Behavior Therapy and Experimental Psychiatry 25,* 179–188.

Alberts, G. M., & Edelstein, B. A. (1990). Training in behavior therapy. In A. Bellack, M. Hersen, and A. Kazdin (Eds.), *International Handbook of Behavior Modification and Therapy* (pp. 213–226). New York: Plenum Press.

Ammerman, R. T., & Hersen, M. (Eds.) (1993). *Handbook of Behavior Therapy with Children and Adults: A Developmental and Longitudinal Perspective.* Boston: Allyn and Bacon.

Bandura, A. (1976). *Social Learning Theory.* Englewood Cliffs, NJ: Prentice-Hall.

Bank, L., Marlowe, J. H., Reid, J. B., Patterson, G. R., & Weinrott, M. R. (1991). A comparative evaluation of parent-training interventions for families of chronic delinquents. *Journal of Abnormal Child Psychology 19,* 15–33.

Barrios, B. (1990). Experimental design in group outcome research. In A. Bellack, M. Hersen, and A. Kazdin (Eds.), *International Handbook of Behavior Modification and Therapy* (pp. 151–174). New York: Plenum Press.

Beach, S. R., Whisman, M. A., O'Leary, K. D. (1994). Marital therapy for depression: Theoretical foundation, current status, and future directions. *Behavior Therapy 25,* 345–372.

Beck, A. (1976). *Cognitive Therapy and the Emotional Disorders.* New York: International Universities Press.

Beck, J. G., & Zebb, B. J. (1994). Behavioral assessment and treatment of panic disorder: Current status, future directions. *Behavior Therapy 25,* 581–612.

Biederman, J. J., & Schefft, B. K. (1994). Behavioral, physiological, and self-evaluative effects of anxiety on the self-control of pain. *Behavior Modification 18,* 89–105.

Bramlett R., Wodarski, J. S., & Thyer, B. A. (1991). Social work practice with antisocial children: A review of current issues. *Journal of Applied Social sciences 15,* 169–182.

Butterfield, W. H., & Cobb, N. H. (1994). Cognitive-behavioral treatment of children and adolescents. In D. K. Granvold (Ed.), *Cognitive and Behavioral Treatment: Methods and Applications* (pp. 63–89). Pacific Grove, CA: Brooks/Cole Publishing Company.

Caddell, J. M., & Drabman, R. S. (1993). Post-traumatic stress disorder in children. In R. Ammerman and M. Hersen (Eds.), *Handbook of Behavior Therapy with Children and Adults: A Developmental and Longitudinal Perspective* (pp. 219–235). Boston: Allyn and Bacon.

Camp, B. H., & Thyer, B. A. (1993). Treatment of adolescent sex offenders: A review of empirical research. *Journal of Applied Social Sciences 17,* 191–206.

Celiberti, D. A., & Harris, S. L. (1993). Behavioral interventions for siblings of children with autism: A focus on skills to enhance play. *Behavior Therapy 24,* 573–599.

Christophersen, E. R., & Finney, J. W. (1993). Conduct disorder. In R. Ammerman and M. Hersen (Eds.), *Handbook of Behavior Therapy with Children and Adults: A Developmental and Longitudinal Perspective* (pp. 251–262). Boston: Allyn and Bacon.

Corcoran, K., & Vandiver, V. (1996). *Maneuvering the Maze of Managed Care.* New York: Free Press.

Corrigan, P. W. (1991). Social skills training in adult psychiatric populations: A meta-analysis. *Journal of Behavior Therapy and Experimental Psychiatry 22,* 203–210.

Dangel, R. F., Yu, M., Slot, N. W., & Fashimpar, G. (1994). Behavioral parent training. In D. K. Granvold (Ed.), *Cognitive and behavioral treatment: Methods and applications* (pp. 108–122). Pacific Grove, CA: Brooks/Cole Publishing Company.

Dobson, K. S., Beamish, M., & Taylor, J. (1992). Advances in behavior therapy: The changing face of AABT conventions. *Behavior Therapy 23,* 483–491.

Donohue, B. C., Van Hasselt, V. B., & Hersen, M. (1994). Behavioral assessment and treatment of social phobia: An evaluative review. *Behavior Modification 18,* 262–288.

Doren, D. M. (1993). Antisocial personality disorder. In R. Ammerman and M. Hersen (Eds.), *Handbook of Behavior Therapy with Children and Adults: A Developmental and Longitudinal Perspective* (pp. 263–276). Boston: Allyn and Bacon.

Dubbert, P. M. (1995). Behavioral (lifestyle) modification in the prevention of hypertension. *Clinical Psychology Review 15,* 187–216.

Dumas, J. E. (1989). Treating antisocial behavior in children: Child and family approaches. *Clinical Psychology Review 9,* 197–222.

Ducharme, J. M., Lucas, H., & Pontes, E. (1994). Errorless embedding in the reduction of severe maladaptive behavior during interactive and learning tasks. *Behavior Therapy 25,* 489–502.

DuPaul, G. J., Guevremont, D. C., & Barkley, R. A. (1991). Attention deficit-hyperactivity disorder in adolescence: Critical assessment parameters. *Clinical Psychology Review 11,* 231–245.

Edleson, J. L., & Syers, M. (1990). Relative effectiveness of group treatments for men who batter. *Social Work Research and Abstracts 26,* 10–17.

Edleson, J. L., & Syers, M. (1991). The effects of group treatment for men who batter: An 18-month follow-up study. *Research on Social Work Practice 1,* 227–243.

Eifert, G. H., Evans, I. M., & McKendrick, V. G. (1990). Matching treatments to client problems not diagnostic labels: A case for paradigmatic behavior therapy. *Journal of Behavior Therapy and Experimental Psychiatry 21,* 163–172.

Ellis, A. (1989). Overview of the clinical theory of rational-emotive therapy. In R. Grieger & J. Boyd (Eds.), *Rational-Emotive therapy: A Skills Based Approach.* New York: Van Nostrand Reinhold.

Emmelkamp, P. M., & Gerlsma, C. (1994). Marital functioning and the anxiety disorders. *Behavior Therapy 25,* 407–430.

Epstein, N., Baucom, D. H., & Rankin, L. A. (1993). Treatment of marital conflict: A cognitive-behavioral approach. *Clinical Psychology Review 13,* 45–57.

Faulkner, K., Stoltenberg, C. D., Cogen, R., Nolder, M., & Shooter, E. (1992). Cognitive-behavioral group treatment for male spouse abusers. *Journal of Family Violence, 7,* 37–55.

Feldman, M. A. (1994). Parenting education for parents with intellectual disabilities: A review of outcome studies. *Research in Developmental Disabilities 15,* 299–302.

Finkelhor, D., & Berliner, L. (1995). Research on the treatment of sexually abused children: A review and recommendations. *Journal of the American Academy of Child and Adolescent Psychiatry 34,* 1–16.

Fisher, J. E., & Carstensen, L. L. (1990). Behavior management of the dementias. *Clinical Psychology Review 10,* 611–629.

Foy, D. W., Resnick, H. S., & Lipovsky, J. A. (1993). Post-traumatic stress disorder in adults. In R. Ammerman and M. Hersen (Eds.), *Handbook of Behavior Therapy with Children and Adults: A Developmental and Longitudinal Perspective* (pp. 236–248). Boston: Allyn and Bacon.

Frame, C. L., & Cooper, D. K. (1993). Major depression in children. In R. Ammerman and M. Hersen (Eds.), *Handbook of Behavior Therapy with Children and Adults: A Developmental and Longitudinal Perspective* (pp. 57–72). Boston: Allyn and Bacon.

Franks, C. M., Wilson, G. T., Kendall, P. C., & Foreyt, J. P. (1990). *Review of Behavior Therapy: Theory and Practice.* Vol. 12. New York: Guilford Press.

Gamble, E. H., Elder, S. T., & Lashley, J. K. (1989). Group behavior therapy: a selective review of the literature. *Medical Psychotherapy An International Journal 2,* 193–204.

Gambrill, E. D. (1977). *Behavior Modification: A Handbook of Assessment, Intervention, and Evaluation.* San Francisco: Jossey-Bass.

Gambrill, E. D. (1983). Behavioral intervention with child abuse and neglect. In M. Hersen, R. Eisler, and P. Miller (Eds.), *Progress in Behavior Modification* (pp. 1–56). New York: Academic Press.

Gambrill, E. D. (1994). Concepts and methods of behavioral treatment. In D. K. Granvold (Ed.), *Cognitive and Behavioral Treatment: Methods and Applications* (pp. 32–62). Pacific Grove, CA: Brooks/Cole Publishing Company.

Gamsa, A. (1994). The role of psychological factors in chronic pain. Part I: A half century of study. *Pain 57,* 5–15.

Garner, D. M., & Rosen, L. W. (1990). Anorexia nervosa and bulimia nervosa. In A. Bellack, M. Hersen, and A. Kazdin (Eds.), *International Handbook of Behavior Modification and Therapy* (pp. 805–817). New York: Plenum Press.

Gaudin, J. M., Jr. (1993). Effective interventions with neglectful families. *Criminal Justice and Behavior 20,* 66–89.

Goldapple, G. C., & Montgomery, D. (1993). Evaluating a behaviorally based intervention to improve client retention in therapeutic community treatment for drug dependency. *Research on Social Work Practice 3,* 21–39.

Goldfried, M. R., & Castonguay, L. G. (1993). Behavior therapy: Redefining strengths and limitations. *Behavior Therapy 24,* 505–526.

Granvold, D. K. (Ed.). (1994). *Cognitive and Behavioral Treatment: Methods and Applications.* Pacific Grove, CA: Brooks/Cole Publishing Company.

Graziano, A. M., & Diament, D. M. (1992). Parent behavioral training: An examination of the paradigm. *Behavior Modification 16,* 3–38.

Hagan, M., & King, R. P. (1992). Recidivism rates of youth completing an intensive treatment program in a juvenile correctional facility. *International Journal of Offender Therapy and Comparative Criminology 36,* 349–358.

Hahlweg, K., & Markman, H. J. (1988). Effectiveness of behavioral marital therapy: Empirical status of behavioral techniques in preventing and alleviating marital distress. *Journal of Consulting and Clinical Psychology 56,* 440–447.

Halford, K. K., Sanders, M. R., & Behrens, B. C. (1994). Self-regulation in behavioral couples' therapy. *Behavior Therapy 25,* 431–452.

Hall, S. M., Hall, R. G., & Ginsberg, D. (1990). Cigarette dependence. In A. Bellack, M. Hersen, and A. Kazdin (Eds.), *International Handbook of Behavior Modification and Therapy* (pp. 437–448). New York: Plenum Press.

Hanson, R. K., Steffy, R. A., & Gauthier, R. (1993). Long-term recidivism of child molesters. *Journal of Consulting and Clinical Psychology 61,* 646–652.

Hawkins, J. D., Jenson, J. M., Catalano, R. F., & Wells, E. A. (1991). Effects of a skill training intervention with juvenile delinquents. *Research on Social Work Practice 1,* 107–121.

Hersen, M. (1990). Single-case experimental designs. In A. Bellack, M. Hersen, and A. Kazdin (Eds.), *International Handbook of Behavior Modification and Therapy* (pp. 175–212). New York: Plenum Press.

Hersen, M., & Van Hasselt, V. B. (1992). Behavioral assessment and treatment of anxiety in the elderly. *Clinical Psychology Review 12,* 619–640.

Hile, M. G., & Derochers, M. N. (1993). The relationship between functional assessment and treatment selection for aggressive behavior. *Research in Developmental Disabilities 14,* 265–274.

Hoberman, H. M., & Clarke, G. N. (1993). Major depression in adults. In R. Ammerman and M. Hersen (Eds.), *Handbook of Behavior Therapy with Children and Adults: A Developmental and Longitudinal perspective* (pp. 73–90). Boston: Allyn and Bacon.

Hodges, V. G. (1994). Home-based behavioral interventions with children and families. In D. K. Granvold (Ed.), *Cognitive and Behavioral Treatment: Methods and Applications* (pp. 90–107). Pacific Grove, CA: Brooks/Cole Publishing Company.

Holroyd, K. A., & Penzien, D. B. (1994). Psychosocial interventions in the management of recurrent headache disorders. Part I: Overview and effectiveness. *Behavioral Medicine 20,* 53–63.

Isreal, A. C. (1990). Childhood obesity. In A. Bellack, M. Hersen, and A. Kazdin (Eds.), *International Handbook of Behavior Modification and Therapy* (pp. 819–830). New York: Plenum Press.

Jacobson, N. S. (1992). Behavioral couple therapy: A new beginning. *Behavior Therapy 23,* 493–506.

Jenson, J. M., & Howard, M. O. (1990). Skills deficits, skills training, and delinquency. *Children and Youth Services Review 12,* 213–228.

Jordan, C., and Franklin, C. (1995). *Clinical Assessment for Social Workers: Quantitative and Qualitative Methods.* Chicago: Lyceum.

Kaplan, M. S., Morales, M., & Becker, J. V. (1993). The impact of verbal satiation of adolescent sex offenders: A preliminary report. *Journal of Child Sexual Abuse 2,* 81–88.

Kazdin, A. E. (1989). *Behavior Modification in Applied Settings* (4th ed.). Homewood, IL: Dorsey.

Kazdin, A. E. (1990). Conduct disorders. In A. Bellack, M. Hersen, and A. Kazdin (Eds.), *International Handbook of Behavior Modification and Therapy* (pp. 669–706). New York: Plenum Press.

Kendall, P. C. (1989). The generalization and maintenance of behavior change: Comments, considerations, and the "no-cure" criticism. Behavior Therapy 20, 357–364.

Kennedy, S. H., Katz, R., Neitzert, C. S., Ralevski, E., & Mendlowitz, S. (1995). Exposure with response treatment of anorexia nervosa-bulimic subtype and bulimia nervosa. *Behaviour Research and Therapy 33,* 685–689.

King, N. J. (1993). Simple and social phobias. *Advances in Clinical Child Psychology 15,* 305–341.

Kirkham, M. A. (1993). Two-year follow-up of skills training with mothers of children with disabilities. *American Journal on Mental Retardation 97,* 509–520.

Landrine, H., & Klonoff, E. (1995). Cultural diversity and the silence of behavior therapy. *The Behavior Therapist 18*(10), 187–189.

Liberman, R. P., Kopelowicz, A., & Young, A. S. (1994). Biobehavioral treatment and rehabilitation of schizophrenia. *Behavior Therapy 25,* 89–107.

Lichstein, K. L., & Riedel, B. W. (1994). Behavioral assessment and treatment of insomnia: A review with an emphasis on clinical applications. *Behavior Therapy 25,* 659–588.

Lipsey, M. W., & Wilson, D. B. (1993). The efficacy of psychological, educational, and behavioral treatment. *American Psychologist 48,* 1181–1209.

Lochman, J. E., & Lenhart, L. A. (1993). Anger coping intervention for aggressive children: Conceptual models and outcome effects. *Clinical Psychology Review 13,* 785–805.

Maag, J. W., & Kotlash, J. (1994). Review of stress inoculation training with children and adolescents. *Behavior Modification 18,* 443–469.

Magen, R. H., & Rose, S. D. (1994). Parents in groups: Problem solving versus behavioral skills training. *Research on Social Work Practice 4,* 172–191.

Marques, J. K., Day, D. M., Nelson, C., & West, M. A. (1994). Effects of cognitive-behavioral treatment on sex offender recidivism: Preliminary results of a longitudinal study. Special Issue: The assessment and treatment of sex offenders. *Criminal Justice and Behavior 21,* 28–54.

Marshall, W. L., Jones, R., Ward, T., Johnston, P., & Barbaree, H. E. (1991). Treatment outcome with sex offenders. *Clinical Psychology Review 11,* 465–485.

Mattaini, M. A. (1993). Behavior analysis and community practice: A review. *Research on Social Work Practice 3,* 420–447.

McEachin, J. J., Smith, T., & Lovaas, O. I. (1993). Long-term outcome for children with autism who receive early intensive behavioral treatment. *American Journal on Mental Retardation 97,* 359–372.

Meadowcroft, P., Thomlison, B., & Chamberlain, P. (1994). A research agenda for treatment foster family care. *Child Welfare* (special issue) *(73)5,* 565–581.

Meichenbaum, D. (1977). *Cognitive Behavior Modification.* New York: Plenum Press.

Mersh, P. P. A. (1995). The treatment of social phobia: The differential effectiveness of exposure *in vivo* and the integration of exposure *in vivo,* rational emotive therapy and social skills training. *Behavioural Research and Therapy 33,* 259–269.

Minde, K., Popiel, K., Leos, N., & Falkner, S. (1993). The evaluation and treatment of sleep disturbances in young children. *Journal of Child Psychology and Psychiatry and Allied Disciplines 34,* 521–533.

Montang, K. R., & Wilson, G. L. (1992). An empirical evaluation of behavioral and cognitive-behavioral group marital treatments with discordant couples. *Journal of Sex and Marital Therapy 18,* 255–272.

Morin, C. M., Winter, B., Besalel, V. A., & Azrin, N. H. (1987). Bulimia: A case illustration of the superiority of behavioral over cognitive treatment. *Journal of Behavior Therapy and Experimental Psychiatry 18,* 165–169.

Morrison, R. L., & Sayers, S. (1993). Schizophrenia in adults. In R. Ammerman and M. Hersen (Eds.), *Handbook of Behavior Therapy with Children and Adults: A Developmental and Longitudinal Perspective* (pp. 295–310). Boston: Allyn and Bacon.

Newman, M. G., Hofman, S. G., Trabert, W., Roth, W. T., & Taylor, C. B. (1994). Does behavioral treatment of social phobia lead to cognitive changes? *Behavior Therapy 25,* 503–517.

Nicholson, N. L., & Blanchard, E. B. (1993). A controlled evaluation of behavioral treatment of chronic headache in the elderly. *Behavioral Therapy 24,* 395–408.

Nixon, C. D., & Singer, G. H. (1993). Group cognitive-behavioral treatment for excessive parental self-blame and guilt. *American Journal on Mental Retardation 97,* 665–672.

Norman, J., & Lowry, C. E. (1995). Evaluating inpatient treatment for women with clinical depression. *Research on Social Work Practice 5,* 10–19.

O'Donnell, C., & Tharpe, R. (1990). Community intervention guided by theoretical development. In A. Bellack, M. Hersen, and A. Kazdin (Eds.), *International Handbook of Behavior Modification and Therapy* (pp. 251–266). New York: Plenum Press.

O'Farrell, T. J. (1994). Marital therapy and spouse-involved treatment with alcoholic patient. *Behavior Therapy 25,* 391–406.

Patterson, G., & Reid, J. (1970). Reciprocity and coercion: Two facets of social systems. In C. Neuringer and J. Michael (Eds.), *Behavior Modification in Clinical Psychology* (pp. 133–177). New York: Appleton-Century-Crofts.

Peled, E., & Edleson, J. L. (1992). Multiple perspectives on group work with children of battered women. *Violence and Victims 7,* 327–346.

Peyrot, M., Yen, S., & Baldassano, C. A. (1994). Short-term substance abuse prevention in jail: A cognitive behavioral approach. *Journal of Drug Education 24,* 33–47.

Polansky, J., & Horan, J. J. (1993). Psychoactive substance abuse in adolescents. In R. Ammerman and M. Hersen (Eds.), *Handbook of Behavior Therapy with Children and Adults: A Developmental and Longitudinal Perspective* (pp. 351–360). Boston: Allyn and Bacon.

Rachmann, S. (1993). A critique of cognitive therapy for anxiety disorders. *Journal of Behavior Therapy and Experimental Psychiatry 24,* 279–288.

Raines, J. C., & Foy, C. W. (1994). Extinguishing the fires within: Treating juvenile firesetters. *Families in Society 75,* 595–607.

Richards, D. A., Lovell, K., & Marks, I. M. (1994). Evaluation of a behavioral treatment program. *Journal of Traumatic Stress 7,* 669–680.

Rohde, P., Lewinsohn, P. M., & Seeley, J. R. (1994). Response of depressed adolescents to cognitive-behavioral treatment: Do differences in initial severity clarify the comparison of treatments? *Journal of Consulting and Clinical Psychology 62,* 851–854.

Rose, S. (1981). Cognitive behavioural modification in groups. *International Journal of Behavioural Social Work and Abstracts 1*(1), 27–38.

Rothman, J., & Thyer, B. A. (1984). Behavioral social work in community and organizational settings. *Journal of Sociology and Social Welfare 11,* 294–326.

Saigh, P. A. (1992). The behavioral treatment of child and adolescent posttraumatic stress disorder. *Advances in Behaviour Research and Therapy 14,* 247–275.

Saunders, R. I., & Saunders, D. N. (1993). Social work practice with a bulimic population: A comparative evaluation of purgers and nonpurgers. *Research on Social Work Practice 3,* 123–136.

Scheibman, L., Koegel, R. L., Charlop, M. H., & Egel, A. L. (1990). Infantile autism. In A. Bellack, M. Hersen, and A. Kazdin (Eds.), *International Handbook of Behavior Modification and Therapy* (pp. 763–789). New York: Plenum Press.

Schwartz, R. (1982). Cognitive-behavior modification: A conceptual review. *Clinical Psychology Review 2,* 267–293.

Scotti, J. R., McMorrow, M. J., & Trawitzki, A. L. (1993). Behavioral treatment of chronic psychiatric disorders: Publication trends and future directions. *Behavior Therapy 24,* 527–550.

Skinner, B. F. (1953). *Science and Human Behavior.* New York: Macmillan.

Skinner, B. F. (1988). The operant side of behavior therapy. *Journal of Behavior Therapy and Experimental Psychiatry 19,* 171–179.

Smith, D. E., Marcus, M. D., & Eldredge, K. L. (1994). Binge eating syndromes: A review of assessment and treatment with an emphasis on clinical application. *Behavior Therapy 25,* 635–658.

Sobell, L. C., Sobell, M. B., & Nirenberg, T. D. (1988). Behavioral assessment and treatment planning with alcohol and drug abusers: A review with an emphasis on clinical application. *Clinical Psychology Review 8,* 19–54.

Steketee, G., & Chambless, D. L. (1992). Methodological issues in prediction of treatment outcome. *Clinical Psychology Review 12,* 387–400.

Stuart, R. B. (1971). Behavioral contracting with families of delinquents. *Journal of Behavior Therapy and Experimental Psychiatry 2,* 1–11.

Stuart, R. B. (Ed.). (1977). *Behavioral Self Management: Strategies, Techniques, and Outcomes.* New York: Brunner/Mazel.

Subramanian, K. (1991). Structured group work for the management of chronic pain: An experimental investigation. *Research on Social Work Practice 1,* 32–45.

Subramanian, K. (1994). Long-term follow-up of a structured group treatment for the management of chronic pain. *Research on Social Work Practice 4,* 208–223.

Sundel, S., & Sundel, M. (1993). *Behavior Modification in the Human Services* (3rd ed.). Newbury Park, CA: Sage.

Sweet, A. A., & Loizeaux, A. L. (1991). Behavioral and cognitive treatment methods: A critical comparative review. *Journal of Behavior Therapy and Experimental Psychiatry 22,* 159–185.

Tallant, S., Rose, S. D., & Tolman, R. M. (1989). New evidence for the effectiveness of stress management training in groups. Special Issue: Empirical research in behavioural social work. *Behavior Modification 13,* 431–446.

Tarrier, N., Beckett, R., Harwood, S., Baker, A., Yusupoff, L., & Ugarteburu, I. (1993). A trial of two cognitive-behavioral methods of treating drug-resistant residual psychotic symptoms in schizophrenic patients. Part I: Outcome. *British Journal of Psychiatry 162,* 524–532.

Thomlison, R. J. (1972). *A Behavioral Model for Social Work Intervention with the Marital Dyad.* Unpublished doctoral dissertation. Toronto: University of Toronto.

Thomlison, R. J. (1981). Behavioral family intervention with the family of a mentally handicapped child. In D. Freeman and B. Trute (Eds.), *Treating Families with Special Needs* (pp. 15–42). Ottawa: Canadian Association of Social Workers.

Thomlison, R. J. (1982). Ethical issues in the use of behavior modification in social work practice. In Shankar Yelaja (Ed.), *Ethical Issues in Social Work.* Springfield, IL: Charles B. Thomas.

Thomlison, R. J. (1984a). Something works: Evidence from practice effectiveness studies. *Social Work 29,* 51–56.

Thomlison, R. J. (1984b). Phobic disorders. In Francis Turner (Ed.), *Adult Psychopathology: A Social Work Perspective* (pp. 280–315). New York: Free Press.

Thomlison, R. J. (1986). Behavior therapy in social work practice. In Francis Turner (Ed.), *Social Work Treatment: Interlocking Theoretical Approaches* (pp. 131–155). New York: Free Press.

Thyer, B. A. (1987a). Behavioral social work: An overview. *Behavior Therapist 10,* 131–134.

Thyer, B. A. (1987b). Community-based self-help groups for the treatment of agoraphobia. *Journal of Sociology and Social Welfare 14,* 135–141.

Thyer, B. A. (1988). Radical behaviorism and clinical social work. In R. Dorfman (Ed.), *Paradigms of Clinical Social Work* (pp. 123–148). New York: Guilford Press.

Thyer, B. A. (1989). Introduction to the special issue. *Behavior Modification 13*(4), 411–414.

Thyer, B. A. (1990). Single-system research designs and social work practice. In L. Sherman and W. J. Reid (Eds.), *Advances in Clinical Social Work Research* (pp. 33–37). Silver Spring, MD: National Association of Social Workers Press.

Thyer, B. A. (1991). Behavioral social work: It is not what you think. *Arete 16,* 1–9.

Thyer, B. A. (1992). Behavior therapies for persons with phobias. In K. Corcoran (Ed.), *Structuring Change. Effective Practice for Common Client Problems* (pp. 31–71). Chicago: Lyceum.

Thyer, B. A., and Boynton Thyer, K. (1992). Single-system research designs in social work practice: A bibliography from 1965 to 1990. *Research on Social Work Practice, 2,* 99–116.

Thyer, B. A., & Maddox, M. K. (1988). Behavioral social work: Results of a national survey on graduate curricula. *Psychological Reports 63,* 239–242.

Tolman, R. M., & Bennett, L. W. (1990). A review of quantitative research on men who batter. *Journal of Interpersonal Violence 5,* 87–118.

Tolman, R. M., & Molidor, C. E. (1994). A decade of social work group work research: Trends in methodology, theory, and program development. *Research on Social Work Practice 4,* 142–159.

Turner, S. M., Beidel, D. C., & Cooley-Quille, M. R. (1995). Two-year follow-up of social phobics with social effectiveness therapy. *Behaviour Research and Therapy 33,* 553–555.

Underwood, L., & Thyer, B. A. (1990). Social work practice with the mentally retarded: Reducing self-injurious behaviors using non-aversive methods. *Arete 15,* 14–23.

Van Der Ploeg-Stapert, J. D., & Van Der Ploeg, H. M. (1986). Behavioral group treatment of test anxiety: An evaluation study. *Journal of Behavior Therapy and Experimental Psychiatry 17,* 255–259.

Van Oppen, P., De Haan, E., Van Balkom, A., Spinhoven, P., Hoogduin, K., & Van Dyck, R. (1995). Cognitive therapy and expose *in vivo* in the treatment of obsessive compulsive disorder. *Behaviour Research and Therapy 33,* 379–390.

Wekerle, C., & Wolfe, D. A. (1993). Prevention of child physical abuse and neglect: Promising new directions. *Clinical Psychology Review 13,* 501–540.

Whisman, M. A. (1990). The efficacy of booster maintenance sessions in behavior therapy: Review and methodological critique. *Clinical Psychology Review 10,* 155–170.

Widner, S., & Zeichner, A. (1993). Psychologic interventions for elderly chronic patients. *Clinical Gerontologist 13,* 3–18.

Wilson, G. T. (1994). Behavioral treatment of obesity: Thirty years and counting. *Advances in Behavior Research and Therapy 16,* 31–75.

Wolf, M., Philips, E., Fixsen, D., Braukmann, C., Kirigin, K., Willner, A., & Schumaker, J. (1976). Achievement Place: The teaching family model. *Child Care Quarterly 5,* 92–103.

Wolfe, D. A., & Wekerle, C. (1993). Treatment strategies for child physical abuse and neglect: A critical progress report. *Clinical Psychology Review 13*, 473–500.

Wolfe, V. V. (1990). Sexual abuse of children. In A. Bellack, M. Hersen, and A. Kazdin (Eds.), *International Handbook of Behavior Modification and Therapy* (pp. 707–730). New York: Plenum Press.

Wolpe, J. (1989). The derailment of behavior therapy: A tale of conceptual misdirection. *Journal of Behavior Therapy and Experimental Psychiatry 20*, 3–15.

Wolpe, J. (1990). *The Practice of Behavior Therapy* (4th ed.). New York: Pergamon Press.

Zimpfer, D. G. (1992). Group work with juvenile delinquents. *Journal for Specialists in Group Work 17*, 116–126.

CHAPTER 4

CLIENT-CENTERED THEORY: A PERSON-CENTERED APPROACH

WILLIAM ROWE

INTRODUCTION

A number of significant events have occurred since this chapter was written for the third edition of *Social Work Treatment*. The term "client-centered" has been primarily replaced with "person-centered," and while there are historical and research variances, for most purposes the terms are interchangeable. Carl Rogers passed away in 1987 after a rich and varied life that saw the development, expansion, and globalization of his theories. Rogers himself, just prior to his death, had continued to test and develop his theories by applying them to some of the more complex social dilemmas and exploring areas of convergence with other significant thinkers in psychology and human behavior (Rogers, 1986). One of the things that has changed very little since 1986 is that the vast majority of literature in person-centered theory continues to be developed outside of social work, even though the parallels with social work thinking and social work activity remain constant.

Many of the tenets of client-centered theory have been hallmarks of the social work profession since its beginnings. The term "client" as opposed to "patient" was in popular use by social workers long before the field of psychology embraced client-centered theories. In addition, the values espoused by client-centered theorists were established and accepted by the earliest of workers, including Octavia Hill and Mary Richmond (1917).

The fact that most of the theory and research in the client-centered approach has developed outside of the social work profession is somewhat of a historical anomaly. Carl Rogers developed many of the original principles of client-centered theory via the influence and observation of social work practitioners (Rogers, 1980). The following pages present the historical origins and basic principles of client-centered theory, explore its confluence with and divergence from social work practice, and reflect on new developments in and uses for person-centered theory.

HISTORICAL ORIGINS

Client-centered theory and Carl Rogers have been all but synonymous for over four decades. When an individual is so central to a thought system, biographical data tend to illuminate the theory as well as the person (Seeman, 1990). What is unique about Rogers's influence on client-centered theory is that even though he was its parent and chief proponent, his force was derived more from the integration and organization of existing concepts than from the generation of new ideas. This may account for the lack of authoritative rigidity and dogma that is characteristic of client-centered theory. Therefore, the persons and ideas that shaped Rogers's early development also influenced the formulation of client-centered theory. Rogers's ideas were both an expression of and a reaction to the suburban, upper-middle-class Protestant family to which he was born in 1902. His experience on the family farm, to which they moved when he was fourteen, led to an interest in agriculture and to scientific methodology and empiricism, which later became an important feature of client-centered theory (Rogers, 1961b). However, after studying agriculture at the University of Wisconsin, Rogers decided to pursue a career in the ministry and attended Union Theological Seminary in New York.

Rogers later applied the liberal religious outlook that he found at UTS to client-centered theory by stressing the importance of individuality, trust in feeling and intuition, and nonauthoritarian relationships (Sollod, 1978). Even though Rogers was at UTS for a short time, he helped organize a study group that was reminiscent of later encounter groups.

After deciding that the ministry was too constrictive for his own professional growth and development, Rogers elected to pursue an M.A. in education and psychology at Columbia University. It was here that Rogers was significantly influenced by the pragmatic philosophy of John Dewey and the educational wisdom of William Kilpatrick. Kilpatrick, as a leader of the progressive education movement, stressed learner-focused education and redefined education as a process of continuous growth (Kilpatrick, 1926). The connection between Kilpatrick's ideas and what was later articulated as client-centered theory is by no means coincidental.

Rogers began his professional career as a psychologist at the Rochester Child Guidance Clinic while continuing to work on his doctorate at Columbia. The academic and professional isolation he experienced in Rochester allowed him to develop his approach to working with clients in a relatively unencumbered manner. In this pragmatic creative environment, Rogers first became interested in effective therapeutic methods as opposed to psychological ideologies. After attending a two-day seminar led by Otto Rank, he found that his practice was similar to that of the Rankians. Rogers learned even more about Rank's theories from a social worker at the Rochester Clinic who had been trained at the Philadelphia School of Social Work (Rogers, 1980).

In 1939, Rogers published *The Clinical Treatment of the Problem Child,* a book that drew heavily on the work of Jessie Taft and relationship therapy. Many aspects of Rankian-based relationship therapy, as expressed in this book, show up later as tenets of client-centered theory. Among these are an emphasis on present experiences and circumstances, a positive valuation of the expression of feelings, a focus on individual growth and will, and a devaluation of the authority relationship in therapy. Relationship therapy continued to be developed in psychology by Rank, Taft, and C. H. Patterson and in social work by the functional school led by Taft, Virginia Robinson, and Ruth Smalley. In "relationship therapy," Rogers found the practical affirmation of the progressive educational concepts that he had embraced earlier. There can be no mistaking the similarity between client-centered theory and the following description of therapist attitude by Taft:

> It is not so easy as it sounds to learn to ignore content and to go through it to the fundamental attitude and emotions behind it, but it is possible, if one has no need for the patient to be or feel one thing rather than another and then is free to perceive and accept what is happening even if it means rejection of the therapeutic goal. The analyst in this view has no goal, has no right to one. He is passive in the sense that he tries to keep his own ends out of the situation to the extent of being willing to leave even the "cure" so-called, to the will of the patient. (1951).

Rogers's definition and articulation of the essential elements of the counseling and psychotherapy he had practiced for a decade began at Ohio State University, where he received an appointment in 1940. In the same year he attended a symposium at Teachers College at Columbia that was presided over by Goodwin Watson, who at the time was attempting to discover the essential elements of effective therapy. The model of therapy articulated by Watson at this time was similar to the nondirective model that was to be the basis for Rogers's ideas in *Counseling and Psychotherapy*. Rogers identified this as an emerging viewpoint for which there was a "sizable core of agreement" (1942).

During his tenure at Ohio State University, Rogers reaffirmed his earlier commitment to empiricism. In his own work and the work he did with his graduate students, he attempted to operationalize and study the process of psychotherapy. The recording and analysis of interviews and outcome research were significant innovations for the time. Those activities brought Rogers's ideas into the mainstream of psychology.

In 1945, Rogers accepted an invitation to head a new counseling center at the University of Chicago. The twelve years he spent there resulted in his wide recognition as a leading therapist, theorist, teacher, and researcher. This period also signaled the shift from the theoretical period described as nondirective to the period described as reflective or client-centered. It was during this period that interest in Rogers's ideas developed in an ever-widening circle. As Rogers described it later, "To me, as I try to understand the phenomenon, it seems that without knowing it I had expressed an idea whose time had come. It is as though a pond had become utterly still so that a pebble dropped into it sent ripples out farther and farther and farther having an influence that could not be understood by looking at the pebble" (1980, p. 49). Theoreticians and practitioners from various fields, who gravitated to the principles that

Rogers espoused, advanced client-centered theories in their own disciplines. Rogers's flexibility and nonauthoritarian stance helped characterize him as the benign parent of client-centered theory in a variety of areas to be described later in this chapter.

In 1957, Rogers moved to the University of Wisconsin, where he helped bridge the gap between psychology and psychiatry through the completion of his work on schizophrenics and the loosening of the psychiatric monopoly on the practice of psychotherapy.

In 1964, Rogers moved to California, where he was able to fully develop the work with encounter groups that he had begun in Chicago. In 1968, Rogers and several staff members left to found the Center for Studies of the Person at La Jolla, California. Through the center, Rogers was able to apply the person-centered approach to perplexing problems in Northern Ireland, South Africa, Warsaw, Venezuela, and many other areas. With the publication of *Carl Rogers on Personal Power* (1977) and *A Way of Being* (1980), Rogers moved person-centered theory into the realm of politics and philosophy.

Rogers continued to be an extraordinary philosopher and scientist up to his passing in 1987. He attended the Evolution of Psychotherapy conference at Phoenix in 1986, where he presented a paper that compared his person-centered theory with the work of Kohut and Erikson (Rogers, 1986). This author was fortunate to take part in some "conversation" and "demonstration" sessions that illustrated Rogers's personification of the theories he developed and espoused. In his eighties, Rogers retained the clarity, honesty, personal warmth, and therapeutic effectiveness that had set the standard for an entire field of psychology. Even after Rogers's passing, person-centered theories continue to be debated and advanced in the literature, in terms of both fundamental theory (Moreira, 1993; Purton, 1989) and practical application (Quinn, 1993; Lambert, 1986).

PRINCIPAL PROPONENTS OF CLIENT-CENTERED THEORY

COUNSELING AND CLINICAL PSYCHOLOGY

By far, client-centered theory has had its greatest impact on the field of counseling and clinical psychology. From the outset, it was clear that this approach represented a third force in American psychology. Many therapists embraced it as a desirable alternative to orthodox analysis or rigid behaviorism. The term "client," as opposed to "patient" or "subject," suggested the person's active, voluntary, and responsible participation. The process, or "how to," of psychotherapy was described for the first time, allowing students to study and become proficient in observable counseling skills. A second attractive feature for counselors was the attention to the expression of positive humanistic values in a pragmatic approach to therapy. Finally, the continuing concern with effectiveness and outcome in the client-centered approach added to the credibility of the worker.

Many of the individuals who were influenced by Rogers and client-centered theory developed orientations of their own. Eugene Gendlin furthered the concept of "focusing" as a significant tool for change (1978). Robert Carkhuff (1969), along with Bernard Berenson (Carkhuff & Berenson, 1977), and C. B. Truax (Truax, 1967), advanced the client-centered principles in greater depth and with greater precision. Numerous others have incorporated the essential elements of client-centered theory, which will likely ensure that it will continue to be a major component of the theory base of both counseling and clinical psychology.

PSYCHIATRY

Rogers was for some time engaged in a struggle to get the field of psychiatry to recognize the value of client-centered theory to psychotherapy. Psychiatry to that point had retained a virtual stranglehold on the practice of psychotherapy. It was not until the results of his work with schizophrenics were published that psychiatry as a whole began to recognize the value of his approach (Gendlin, 1962; Rogers 1961a). Currently, client-centered theory is an accepted, if not widely practiced, orientation in psychiatry. Even though recent studies have reaffirmed the effectiveness of Rogerian counseling with patients diagnosed as paranoid schizophrenic (Gerwood, 1993), the approach does not appear to have been developed or expanded in psychiatry. After Rogers turned his attention to working with "nonpathological" clients in nontraditional or nonstructured settings, psychiatry as a whole appeared to lose interest in this form of counseling.

Some encounter group principles are still utilized in psychiatric settings in group psychotherapy and therapeutic communities. But, as psychiatry has increased its concern with the organic etiology of the more severe psychological impairments, there has been a diminishing interest in client-centered theory and much greater emphasis on psychopharmacology.

Coincidently, a body of literature has surfaced in family medicine and general practice that is referred to as patient-centered (Stewart, Weston, Brown, McWhinney, McWilliam & Freeman, 1995). The parallels are obvious and physicians appear to be embracing the concepts as they are increasingly faced with a diverse patient body that is informed, empowered, and demanding of a more equal helping relationship.

ADMINISTRATION AND LEADERSHIP

The whole field of administration and leadership training has been noticeably affected by client-centered theory. Client-centered principles found easy application in conflict resolution, organizational behavior, and employer-employee relations. Many of the practices were utilized and expanded by those involved with the National Training Laboratories in Bethel, Maine, and the numerous T-groups and sensitivity training sessions that were organized to help groups work more effectively and meaningfully (Lewin, 1951; Maslow, 1971). Helen MacGregor's "Y theory" and Abraham Maslow's "Z theory" of management are both clearly reflective of the application of client-centered principles to this area (Maslow, 1971).

These ideas have lost some of their allure in today's highly competitive workplace, which is increasingly less concerned with the person as an entity in favor of a set of skills that serve the corporate purpose and can be discarded when necessary. As people adapt to the modern workplace, their need for personal fulfillment, interrelatedness, and community building will likely be expressed in a different form. Hence, there may be an even greater role for person-centered theory in the workplace of the future.

SOCIAL WORK

Client-centered theory was highly acceptable to social workers from its inception. This is partly due to the fact that in its infancy, client-centered theory was more or less a conceptualization of many of the practices of relationship therapy, which was the central force of the functional school of social casework. Many of the values that are expressed in client-centered theory are fundamental to social work practice. Rogers found himself closely aligned with the social work profession in the early part of his career, and in fact held office in social work organizations at both the local and national levels while in Rochester (Rogers, 1961b). In the 1940s, Rogers and client-centered theory became identified with the field of psychology. Since social work had become entangled in the debate between the diagnostic and functional schools of casework, client-centered theory as a separate entity received less attention. Many of the principles of client-centered theory continued to be applied by social workers, but relatively little of this was reported or researched.

In the 1950s and 1960s, the profession turned its attention to the development of a unified theory of social work based on the person–environment continuum. Client-centered theory to this point had appeared too person-centered to be of much use in this effort. Barrett-Lennard's description of client-centered theory and its usefulness in social work practice theory was the first major reference in social work literature to Rogers's contribution (Barrett-Leonard, 1979).

In the 1970s, an increased concern with effectiveness and accountability sent theorists and investigators in search of methods that could be demonstrated and evaluated. As a result, there was a resurgence of interest in client-centered theory and its utility in social work, since it was one of the few demonstrably effective treatment approaches. It was followed up by investigations into the value of client-centered principles in training social workers (Keefe, 1976; Larsen, 1975; Rowe, 1981; Wallman, 1980). Today, most interpersonal skills training takes place in the undergraduate curriculum, and it is increasingly difficult to discern client-centered principles from good basic interviewing skills. At this point, practice skills texts utilize client-centered theory and practice, but as part of a set of generic or eclectic skills that are framed in a social work context. Social work educators would be wise to incorporate some of the person-centered ideas that are related to complex social and political problems into the macro and international spheres curricula.

THEORETICAL PERSPECTIVES AND BASIC CONCEPTS

THEORY BUILDING

As noted earlier, Rogers was more a coordinator than a generator of the principles that are associated with person-centered theory. Because he essentially followed a deductive line of reasoning in his early investigations, his personality theory emerged ex post facto. Epistemologically, his work is best described by the term "humanistic phenomenology" (Nye, 1975). Rogers's "humanism" is related to his belief that humans are essentially growth-oriented, forward moving, and concerned with fulfilling their basic potentialities. He assumes that basic human nature is positive, and that if individuals are not forced into socially constructed molds but are accepted for what they are, they will turn out "good" and live in ways that enhance both themselves and society.

Phenomenology is concerned with the individual's perceptions in determining reality. Rogers believes that knowledge of these perceptions of reality can help to explain human behavior. Objective reality is less important than our perception of reality, which is the main determinant of our behavior. The phenomenological approach guided Rogers's approach to both therapy and research as he struggled with the difficulty of perceiving reality through another person's eyes.

As a scientist, Rogers sees determinism as "the very foundation stone of science" (1969), and hence he is committed to objective study and evolution. He sees this approach as incomplete in fostering an understanding of the "inner human experience," and embraces freedom as critical to effective personal and interpersonal functioning.

BASIC (KEY) CONCEPTS

Rogers gave a detailed presentation of his theories of therapy, personality, and interpersonal relationships in volume three of *Psychology: A Study of a Science* (1959). The following are nine propositions that outline the personality theory underlying this approach.

1. "All individuals exist in a continually changing world of experience of which they are the center." The "phenomenal field," as it is sometimes called, includes all that the individual experiences. Only the individual can completely and genuinely perceive his experience of the world.
2. "Individuals react to their phenomenal field as they experience and perceive it." The perceptual field is reality for the individual. Individuals will react to reality as they perceive it, rather than as it may be perceived by others.
3. "The organism has one basic tendency and striving to actualize, maintain and enhance the experiencing organism." Rogers suggests that all organic and psychological needs may be described as partial aspects of this one fundamental need.
4. "Behaviour is basically the goal-directed attempt of individuals to satisfy their needs as experienced in their phenomenal field as perceived." Reality for any given individual is that individual's perception of reality, whether or not it has

been confirmed. There is no absolute reality that takes precedence over an individual's perceptions.

5. "The best vantage point for understanding behaviour is from the internal frame of reference of the individual." This includes the full range of sensations, perceptions, meanings, and memories available to the conscious mind. Accurate empathy is required to achieve this understanding.

6. "Most ways of behaving adopted by the individual are consistent with the individual's concept of self." The concept of self is basic to client-centered theory. Self-concept is an organized internal view consisting of the individual's perceptions of himself alone, himself in relation to others, and himself in relation to his environment and to the values attached to these perceptions. Self-concept is seen as an ever-evolving entity.

7. "The incongruence that often occurs between an individual's conscious wishes and his behaviour is the result of a split between the individual's self-concept and his experiences." As the individual gains an awareness of self, he develops a need for positive regard and positive self-regard. When the individual feels loved or not loved by significant others, he develops positive or negative self-regard.

8. "When there is incongruence between the individual's self-concept and experiences with others, a state of anxiety results." This anxiety is often the result of the incongruence between the ideal and real self. To lower an individual's anxiety, the self-concept must become more congruent with the individual's actual experiences.

9. "The fully functioning individual is open to all experiences, exhibiting no defensiveness." Such a person fully accepts himself and can exhibit unconditional positive regard for others. The self-concept is congruent with the experiences and the individual is able to assert his basic actualizing tendency.

With regard to motivation, Rogers believed the organism to be active initiator that exhibits a directional tendency (Rogers, 1977). He agreed with White's description of motivation as more than simple stasis: "Even when its primary needs are satisfied and its homeostatic chores are done, an organism is alive, active and up to something" (White, 1959). Rogers affirmed that there is a central source of energy in the organism that is concerned with enhancement as well as maintenance (Rogers, 1977).

The following are some of the most significant assumptions of Rogers's personality theory from the perspective of therapy:

We behave in accordance with our perception of reality. In light of this, in order to understand the client's problem, we must fully understand how she perceives it.

We are motivated by an innate primary drive to self-actualization. The individual will automatically develop her potential under favorable conditions. These conditions can be established in therapy and the stance of the therapist must, as a result, be nondirective.

The individual has a basic need for love and acceptance. This translates into a focus on relationship and the communication of empathy, respect, and authenticity by the therapist.

The individual's self-concept is dependent upon the nature of the acceptance and respect she experiences from others. The client's self-concept can be changed by her experiencing unconditional positive regard in therapy.

VALUES

The valuing process has been discussed at some length in client-centered theory. Rogers hypothesized that "there is an organismic commonality of value directions" and that "these common value directions are of such kinds as to enhance the development of the individual himself or others in his community and to make for the survival and evolution of his species" (Rogers, 1964). This positive and hopeful view of human beings is by and large acceptable to a profession like social work that is dedicated to the enhancement of social relationships and functioning.

In addition to being concerned with the "organismic valuing process," client-centered theory professes both general and specific attitudinal values. In its early stages, client-centered theory was essentially neutral regarding values. Over the years, it has progressed to the point where person-centered or humanistic values are asserted (Carkhuff & Berenson, 1967). These include the following (Boy & Pine, 1982; Rogers, 1964, 1977):

1. The counselor who intends to be of service to a client must value the client's integral worth as a person.
2. Responsible action occurs within the context of respect for the dignity and worth of others.
3. The counselor who values the client has a fundamental respect for the client's freedom to know, shape, and determine personal attitudes and behavior.
4. The client possesses free will; she can be the determiner of a personal destiny.
5. A person's free functioning not only tends toward development of the self, but also includes a responsibility to other persons.
6. The client enhances the self by fulfilling obligations to herself and others.
7. The client begins to relate to others with a sense of personal responsibility and ethical behavior.
8. Love and peace are basic strivings and must be advanced during one's lifetime.

These values are universally expressed and professed in social work. A belief in the fundamental dignity and worth of an individual is similar to 1 and 2. Social work's commitment to self-determination is captured in 3 and 4. The importance of social responsibility and reciprocity has also become a more broadly accepted value (Compton & Gallaway, 1979; Siporin, 1975) and is reflected in 5, 6, and 7. Number 8 (a commitment to the advancement of love and peace) is a value that few social workers would reject, although it is not articulated and asserted by the mainstream in the profession as yet.

The major values of the person-centered approach appear to be closely aligned with those expressed in social work. This is partly because of the similarity of historical roots, but it is also due to the cross-cultural, time-tested effectiveness of these values. In other words, they appear to be functional as well as philosophical.

SOCIOCULTURAL SENSITIVITY

Person-centered theory, especially that characterized by Rogers's early work, has come under criticism for placing too much emphasis on individualism and independence, although dependency on family, friends, and authority figures is considered appropriate and necessary in many cultures (Usher, 1989). Rogers recognized the importance of a client's natural support systems and traditional healing methods in his later writings, and others have managed to find significant points of convergence in cross-cultural settings (Hayashi et al., 1992). It is notable that person-centered theory has received more attention and generated more interest in multicultural settings outside of North America in the past decade than in its historical stronghold.

TREATMENT

The basic goal of client-centered therapy is to release an already existing capacity for self-actualization in a potentially competent individual. The underlying assumptions are as follows:

1. The individual has the capacity to guide, regulate, direct, and control himself providing certain conditions exist.
2. The individual has the potential to understand what is in his life that is related to his distress and anxiety.
3. The individual has the potential to reorganize himself in such a way as not only to eliminate his distress and anxiety, but also to experience self-fulfillment and happiness.

In 1957, Rogers postulated the following elements that he believed were necessary and sufficient for a positive outcome in therapy.

1. The therapist is genuine and congruent in the relationship.
2. The therapist experiences unconditional positive regard toward the client.
3. The therapist experiences empathic understanding of the client's internal frame of reference.
4. The client perceives these conditions at least to a minimal degree.

These core conditions, as they came to be known, have been linked with positive outcomes in therapy for a wide variety of clients in various settings (Carkhuff, 1971; Carkhuff & Berenson, 1967; Truax & Mitchell, 1971). Additional dimensions of the therapist, such as concreteness, confrontation, self-disclosure, and immediacy, have been recognized as important (Carkhuff, 1969).

Quinn (1993) has argued for an expansion of the concept of genuineness to include a developmental-interactional component, and Natiello (1987) has suggested that the therapist's personal power is so crucial that it should be treated as a fourth condition.

The process of therapy and counseling in the client-centered approach is basically the following:

1. The therapist and client establish a mutual counseling contract.
2. The therapist presents an attitude in the relationship characterized by the core conditions.
3. The client's greatest capacity for problem solving is released because he is free from the anxiety and doubts that were blocking his potential.

It is difficult to make a comprehensive statement about person-centered therapy because, true to its basic philosophy, it has been changing, evolving, and actualizing since its inception. Table 4-1, adapted from David Cole (1982) and J. T. Hart (1970), illustrates some of the major points associated with those changes over the past forty years.

The person-centered developments referred to in the table are more indicative of Rogers's orientation since 1970. Some proponents of person-centered theory have continued to develop and refine the microlevel counseling aspects. Carkhuff and his associates have developed specific training programs in which the novice counselor first learns how to discriminate between high-level responses (understanding and direction) and low-level responses (little understanding or direction). Second, the student counselor learns how to communicate high levels of accurate empathy, authenticity, and positive regard. The following dialogue exemplifies this process:

CLIENT: I don't know if I'm right or wrong feeling the way I do, but I find myself withdrawing from people. I don't seem to socialize and play their stupid little games any more.

COUNSELOR'S RESPONSE

(Low level): Friendships like this are precarious at best.

(Medium level): You're really down because they won't let you be yourself.

(High level): You feel really bad because you can't be yourself and you want to be. The first thing you might do is spend a little time exploring who you are without them.

Table 4-1
The Development of Client-Centered Therapy

Therapy	Therapist Goals	Therapist Roles
Nondirective cognitive orientation (insight) 1940–1950	1. Create an atmosphere of permission and acceptance 2. Help client clarify thoughts and feelings rather than interpret for him 3. Help client increase knowledge of self	1. Passive, nonjudgmental listening 2. Empathic 3. Nonconfronting 4. Nonsharing of self 5. Feedback objective, rephrasing, repeating, clarifying
Client-centered or reflective emotional orientation (self-concept) 1950–1957	1. Develop the conditions necessary and sufficient for constructive personality change 2. Communicate to client • empathy, • unconditional positive regard • genuineness	1. Active listening 2. Accurate, emphatic 3. Nonconfronting 4. Sharing of self 5. Noninterpretive 6. Feedback, subjective indicating how therapist believes client feels
Experiential existential/encounter orientation (humanistic) 1957–1970	1. Establishing therapeutic relationship 2. Reflecting client experiencing 3. Expressing therapist experiencing 4. Client as a unique individual and as a group member	1. Active listening 2. Accurate empathy 3. Confronting 4. Sharing an authentic friendship 5. Interpreting, if appropriate 6. Feedback is subjective prizing, loving, caring
Person-centered • community • institution • political orientation (militant humanism) 1970 to present	Humanize and facilitate the actualization of communities, institutions, and political systems	1. Apply effective components of person-centered approach to such organizations 2. Assert humanistic values 3. Quiet revolutionary

CLIENT: Sometimes I question my adequacy raising three boys, especially the baby. Well, I call him the baby because he's the last. I can't have any more, so I know I kept him a baby longer than the others. He won't let anyone else do things for him. Only Mommy!
COUNSELOR'S RESPONSE
(Low level): Could you tell me, have you talked with your husband about this?
(Medium level): You feel concern because your son is so demanding.
(High level): You're disappointed in yourself because you haven't helped him develop fully and you really want to. Now a first step might be to design a little program for you and for him (Carkhuff, 1976).

Person-centered theory can no longer be described or evaluated in a singular fashion. So many individuals and groups have embraced the approach that the underlying philosophy and principles are evident even in approaches that are not specifically identified as client-centered. For the beginning counselor or therapist, person-centered theory still appears to offer a comprehensive approach. In a refinement of this approach, Angelo Boy and Gerald Pine offered the following reasons for utilizing person-centered theory in counseling (Boy & Pine, 1982):

Possesses a positive philosophy of the person

Articulates propositions regarding human personality and behavior

Possesses achievable human goals for the client

Possesses a definition of the counselor's role within the counseling relationship

Has research evidence supporting its effectiveness

Is comprehensive and can be applied beyond the one-to-one counseling relationship

Is clear and precise regarding application

Has an expansive intellectual and attitudinal substance

Focuses on the client as a person rather than on the client's problem

Focuses on the attitudes of the counselor rather than on techniques

Provides the counselor with a systematic response pattern

Provides flexibility for the counselor to go beyond reflection of feelings

Can be individualized to the particular needs of a client

Enables client behavior to change in a natural sequence of events

Can draw from the process components of other theories of counseling and human development

Not surprisingly, person-centered theory is most often identified with the person end of the person–environment continuum. The concept of self is so important to Rogers's view of personality that it is often referred to as self-psychology or self-theory. Rogers viewed human nature as growth-oriented and positive and believed that maladaptation is generally more a problem in the environment than in the person. In most cases, client-centered therapy is predicated on the belief that the client's innate self-actualizing tendencies will flourish if the conditions are right. This view recognizes the importance of the environment and places the locus of change in that area. Essentially, the environment should be altered or adjusted to suit humans, rather than the reverse.

This view has received limited acceptance in social work. Most social work approaches afford equal importance to both aspects of the person–environment continuum, at least in theory. In practice, a great deal of social work activity is directed toward helping the individual adjust to society. Person-centered theory is at odds with both of these.

SOCIAL WORK WITH INDIVIDUALS

Person-centered theory has found both acceptance and expression in social work with individuals, or "social casework." Person-centered theory is most closely aligned with the functional approach to social casework, although there are areas of convergence with and divergence from the other major approaches. This is understandable given Rogers's involvement with social work and the functional school in the 1930s.

Psychosocial History

The place of a psychosocial history in casework, firmly established by Mary Richmond (1917), for the most part has been broadly accepted by the profession. Person-centered theory has historically placed little emphasis on this aspect of the helping process. In applying the person-centered approach narrowly, workers would only concern themselves with history-taking to the degree the client was willing. A broader interpretation of person-centered theory would also promote history-taking, since a full appreciation and credible acceptance of the client can be better realized when the worker is cognizant of both the past and the present. History-taking is one of the areas that has become more acceptable to person-centered therapists in its more eclectic form.

Diagnosis

Another area of traditional divergence has been the place of diagnosis in casework. Person-centered theory has been fundamentally opposed to diagnostic classification. This theory's belief in the uniqueness of the person disallows the categorization, classification, and dehumanized labeling of individuals. Diagnosis has been and continues to be an important concept in social casework (Hollis, 1972: Turner, 1968, 1976), where it is generally viewed as a dynamic and functional process. Smalley's approach, in which the worker and client are both fully considered in the diagnosis, is most reminiscent of the person-centered approach.

Rogers and others have demonstrated that the person-centered approach is effective with a variety of diagnostic categories including schizophrenics and psychotics (Gerwood, 1993; Rogers, 1980; Rogers et al., 1967). This research, coupled with the person-centered philosophy, has established some of the rationale for rejecting the concept of diagnosis. The person-centered approach in social work need not reject this concept wholly, and may indeed discover that person-centered theory applied within the diagnostic framework can increase its effectiveness. This latter approach would undoubtedly be more acceptable to social caseworkers.

The Helping Interview

By far the greatest contribution person-centered theory has made to social casework has been the helping interview. Most approaches to social casework recognize the utility of the "core conditions of helping." These conditions of communicating accurate empathy, authenticity, and positive regard in the helping interview have been demonstrated as effective by Truax, Carkhuff, and Mitchell. In the 1970s, social work educators introduced training in the core conditions to the social work curriculum (Fischer, 1978; Hammond et al., 1978; Wells, 1975).

The core conditions appear to be a good base from which to begin skill development in the helping interview. In order to be more broadly useful and acceptable to social caseworkers, they need to be expanded and adapted to fit the wide variety of casework situations and circumstances.

SOCIAL WORK WITH FAMILIES

Person-centered principles have had a wide impact on the whole area of work with children and families. Rogers (1939), in his doctoral dissertation and his first book, focused on therapy with children and found it necessary to include the entire family. A few years after Rogers published *Counseling and Psychotherapy* (1942), Virginia Axline presented a work that drew from his nondirective principles and from the relationship therapy orientation of Taft (1951) and Allen (1942). Axline's approach to nondirective play therapy included the basic principles of acceptance, relationship, freedom of expression, and freedom of behavior. Others, like Clark Moustakas (1953), expanded and developed these principles to help make the person-centered approach a significant force in child therapy.

By the late 1950s, therapists were increasingly including parents and family members in the counseling context and applying person-centered principles to work with families. Guerney described a process of filial therapy in which parents were taught person-centered skills so they could deal with their children themselves (Guerney, 1964; Guerney & Andronico, 1970). Some explored the development of self-concept in families (Van der Veen et al., 1964), while others used person-centered principles in working with couples (Rogers, 1972a).

While the person-centered approach to working with families has by and large been found useful and philosophically acceptable by social workers, it has essentially been overshadowed by concurrent developments in the application of systems theory to both family work and social work. These two schools of thought appear to be fundamentally divergent in terms of basic assumptions, but some have attempted to establish a dialogue between the two. For example, O'Leary has written: "Family members need to be received as subjects while being encouraged to face their reality as part of a system with patterns not entirely in their consciousness or control. They need to be acknowledged as mysteries as well as confronted with the limits and unacknowledged potential in their interpersonal living" (1989).

SOCIAL WORK WITH GROUPS

Group work in the person-centered tradition has received sporadic acceptance in social work circles. Social work had a rich history in group work long before person-centered principles were applied to this area. The major application of person-centered principles to group work has been in the form of the encounter group or T-group, as developed by Rogers (1970). The encounter group began in the 1940s at the University of Chicago with Rogers, and in Bethel, Maine, with Kurt Lewin. Rogers viewed the intensive group experience as an important vehicle for therapeutic growth and attitudinal change, whereas Lewin focused on the improvement of human relations and interpersonal interaction.

Rogers (1970) noted the following as central to the process of change in intensive group experience:

Climate of safety

Expression of immediate feelings and reactions

Mutual trust

Change in attitudes and behavior

Understanding and openness

Feedback

Innovation, change, and risk

Transfer of learning to other situations

Many of the above are seen as essential elements of mutual aid in social group work (Shulman, 1979). As well, the following description of the goals of the therapist leader (Beck, 1974) are not incompatible with the orientation of many social group workers:

1. the facilitation of group members to take responsibility for themselves in whatever way is realistically possible
2. the clarification and solution of problems and conflicts by a process of self-understanding and the development of an empathic understanding of others
3. recognition of the client as she is and recognition of her reality as she sees it
4. attempts to offer an attitude that is nonjudgmental in order to facilitate exploratory and self-reflective behavior in the client, and
5. recognition of the significance of maintaining as high a degree as possible of clarity about the leader's own views, feelings, and reactions while he is in the therapeutic relationship

The expression of the core conditions by group leaders has been shown to have a positive impact on increasing client self-exploration (O'Hare, 1979).

Given the therapeutic aim of encounter groups and their focus on the individual in group, they are most readily identified with the remedial model of social group work. However, many of the underlying principles and some of the techniques are more reminiscent of the reciprocal model of social group work. Some aspects, such as adherence to democratic principles, are aligned with social group work in general. Recently, some researchers have argued that there may be points of compatibility between structuring group process and nondirectiveness (Coughlan & McIlduff, 1990). This opens the door for a much wider use of person-centered group work with, for example, low functioning or involuntary clients (Foreman, 1988; Patterson, 1990).

SOCIAL WORK WITH COMMUNITIES

The more recent developments in person-centered theory have included an interest and involvement in the concept of community. Rogers applied the fundamental principles of person-centered theory to both community concerns and community development. Much of this was initiated at the Center for Studies of the Person in workshops and learning laboratories. Some concurrent efforts continued at the University of Chicago, where Gendlin and others established a therapeutic community called Changes, which was based on person-centered principles (Rogers, 1980). The experiments in community have included work with a wide variety of neighborhoods, cultures, religions, and political situations.

In the tradition of the person-centered orientation, writers have first concerned themselves with establishing propositions that describe the basic assumptions concerning communities. Barrett-Lennard (1979) has postulated that "a well functioning community would be an open system in interface with other systems . . . continually in process . . . and characterized by an organismic egalitarianism." William Rogers (1974) suggests that, from the person-centered viewpoint, "individuals seek a community of belonging, understanding and mutual support that will enhance the actualization of life," and that "persons within a community are potentially better able to understand and articulate the identity and hopes of that community than are persons from outside." William Rogers moves to the next phase by considering the necessary steps in the process of social change. Some of the person-centered principles contained in his approach are:

The importance of listening deeply to the needs and concerns of individuals and groups within the constituent communities

The facilitation of community self-perception

The recognition and encouragement of indigenous leadership

The facilitation of the communication among divergent groups

The identification of community goals.

In work with communities, person-centered theory is most clearly aligned with the principles of locality development. The person-centered approach to community development articulated by William Rogers is both astute and pragmatic. As such, it is generally more acceptable to social workers than the more esoteric, unstructured offerings developed at such places as the Center for Studies of the Person and Changes. Many community workers in social work find the community-building techniques developed and experimented with in the person-centered approach to be useful in conjunction with their own theories. To this end, the person-centered approach affords an important laboratory for exploring different aspects of community building. Curiously, it is possible that the person-centered approach as it has evolved may be too value laden and prescriptive for most social work community organizers to embrace.

SOCIAL WORK ADMINISTRATION

For many years, Rogers viewed the tenets of person-centered theory as applicable to all human interaction. In *Carl Rogers on Personal Power* (1977), he described how these features have been successfully applied to agencies and organizations. Rogers provided examples of how person-centered approaches resulted in greater productivity, as well as greater career and personal satisfaction. In this approach, leadership is characterized by influence and impact, rather than power and control. The person-centered administrator, where possible, gives autonomy to persons and groups, stimulates independence, facilitates learning, delegates responsibility, encourages self-evaluation, and finds rewards in the development and achievements of others (Rogers, 1977).

Person-centered theories of administration did not originate with Rogers, but were articulated in administration circles since the early part of this century (Schatz, 1970). The major contribution of Rogers has once again been the operationalization and application of the concepts within an organized framework.

Social workers have found many aspects of person-centered administration to be compatible with their values. There has been a great deal of interest in and experimentation with participatory management approaches (McMahon, 1981; Schatz, 1970) and equality-based supervisory practices (Mandell, 1973). Rogers's approach to administration, with its antiauthoritarianism, is limited in its broad application in social work. As they are applied and refined, however, the principles may mature into an acceptable, coherent, and functional administrative orientation.

EMPIRICAL BASE

Investigators received a new impetus from the study of client-centered theory. Rogers's personal commitment to empiricism and to outcome-and-evaluation research opened new avenues in research that had previously not been considered. Rogers's objective observations of the subjective experience of counselors and clients through hypothesizing and testing were clearly innovative. While his initial interest was in the systematic description of the process of psychotherapy, his attention later turned to effectiveness and outcome measures, and finally, to attempts to substantiate his theoretical postulates.

John Shlien and Fred Zimring identified four stages in the development of research methods and directives in client-centered theory (1970). In stage one, the emphasis was on the client in the context of therapy. In stage two, the emphasis expanded to cover the phenomenological aspects of perception and personality. In stage three, the emphasis shifted to the study of the therapist, and in stage four, all three elements merged into a process conception of psychotherapy. An extraordinary number of studies have been generated in all of these areas. Although many support the original claims, some challenge both the original assumptions and the external validity of some of the findings. Investigators such as Charles B. Truax and Robert Carkhuff further refined, expanded, and substantiated the basic principles of client-centered theory.

The research on the core conditions of therapy is especially notable. There is considerable agreement across a number of professions, including psychology, psychiatry, social work, and nursing, that the core conditions are demonstrably linked with effective counseling practices. As such, the core conditions remain one of the only substantive elements of effective counseling, and are supported by numerous studies.

With the possible exception of behavior therapy, no other approach has had such an intensive research orientation. This is in part attributable to the fact that, unlike most schools of therapy, client-centered theory was developed primarily in the university setting. As Rogers remarked, "Client-centered therapy will at least be remembered for its willingness to take a square look at the facts" (1960), and this emphasis has been embraced by most of those associated with the client-centered orientation. The methods employed in client-centered research appear to be particularly adaptable to the needs of social work research. The stages of development in client-research are closely aligned with social work concerns.

The first level of development in client-centered research was the recording of cases, the definition of concepts, the development of objective measures of the concepts, the application of the concepts, and the establishment of relationships among the concepts. This is similar to attempts in social work research to quantify and evaluate practice, as in Larry Shulman's study on casework skill (1978). It is widely acknowledged that much of what is considered to be practice wisdom in social work would be better understood and utilized if it were subjected to this kind of rigor (Siporin, 1975).

Another stage of research in client-centered theory that is directly useful to social work is outcomes research. Numerous effectiveness and outcome studies have been done using creative investigative techniques such as the Q-sort. Social work researchers are increasingly concerned with the same issues in light of increased demands for accountability. As social workers become better able to define and operationalize their objectives, these research techniques have proven useful.

In the past decade, social work research has increased significantly and social workers have expanded their repertoire of research methods. Heuristic models and qualitative research methods are finding increasing usage in social work and their congruence with the empirical base in person-centered theory is clear (Barrineau & Bozarth, 1989). As direct practice becomes more eclectic in nature, the challenge is to establish how person-centered approaches are more or less useful, under what conditions, and with what particular disorders or needs (Lambert, 1986).

PROSPECTUS

There are numerous areas of convergence and compatibility between person-centered theory and social work practice. Given the similarities in philosophy and practice, it is in some ways curious that person-centered theory is not more accepted by the profession. For example, not long ago, Howard Goldstein (1983) published an article entitled "Starting Where the Client Is," in which he competently articulated the value of his longstanding social work adage. It is odd that he made only passing reference to Rogers and person-centered theory, considering the amount of theory and research available to support his thesis.

Rogers presents what many believe is a naive and one-sided view of human nature. Many social workers support this positive view of humanity in theory, but decades of practice with some of the more disturbing problems in society (poverty, child abuse and neglect, family violence) diminish enthusiasm for such beliefs. Much of person-centered theory was developed in controlled university settings, whereas the social worker's practice environment is often far more unpredictable. Much of the work done in the past decade has advanced the use of person-centered methods with difficult-to-serve clients (Gerwood, 1993; Patterson, 1990) and should help to bridge this gap.

Most of the research validating the concepts takes the expressions of the clients at face value and gives little attention to unconscious processes. Many social workers firmly believe in the importance of understanding unconscious motivations and have experienced the usefulness of this understanding in both assessment and intervention. Some of the theory bridging begun by Rogers (1986) and furthered by others (Purton, 1989; Quinn, 1993) will allow for more convergence on these issues in the future.

Another area of divergence between person-centered theory and social work pertains to the concept of authority. Rogers took an extreme position against authority and saw it as an essentially destructive component of relationships. While many social workers deemphasize authority, the major concern is more often how to make positive use of it, as opposed to simply denying its existence. Not all person-centered therapists are as adamant about this issue as Rogers was, and some of the more recent contributors have included rather than rejected the concept of authority relationships (Boy & Pine, 1982; Coughlan & McIlduff, 1990; O'Leary, 1989).

The development of person-centered theory in many ways has been a microcosm of the development of the social work profession. Both began with the worker-client interaction and progressed to include groups, families, organizations, communities, and political systems. Person-centered theory has matured along with social work theory to the point where Orlov (1990) made reference to "person-centered politics"—a concept that would have been unthinkable a short time ago. Soloman (1990), in a work entitled "Carl Rogers's Efforts for World Peace," demonstrated advances in the application of person-centered theory that have significant ramifications for international work.

Many social work students, upon their first introduction to person-centered concepts, dismiss them as simplistic and unsophisticated. It is only when workers have had significant experience that they are in a position to rediscover person-centered theory, with its many layers of depth and meaning. Miriam Polster (1987) captured this well when she referred to Rogers's work as "informed simplicity," not unlike a Picasso painting (Zeig, 1987, p. 198).

The term "person-centered" is highly appropriate for both theory and practice in a profession that has traditionally attempted to encompass both science and compassion. In essence, both the emphasis on the person and the research practices of person-centered theory are valuable to social work. It is essential that, as professional boundaries become less distinct and multidisciplinary practice becomes more the norm, we re-embrace person-centered theory and all that it has to offer in its old and new forms.

REFERENCES

Allen, F.H. (1942). *Psychotherapy with Children.* New York: Norton.

Axline, V.M. (1947). *Play Therapy.* Boston: Houghton Mifflin.

Barrett-Leonard, G.T. (1979). The person-centered system unfolding. In Francis J. Turner (Ed.), *Social Work Treatment* (2nd ed.). New York: Free Press.

Barrineau, P., & Bozarth, J. (1989). A person-centered research model. *Person-Centered Review 4* (4), 465–474.

Beck, A.M. (1974). Phases in the development of structure in therapy and encounter groups. In D.A. Wexler & L.M. Rice (Eds.), *Innovations in Person-centered Therapy.* New York: Wiley.

Boy, A.V., & Pine, G.J. (1982). *Person-centered Counseling: A Renewal.* Boston: Allyn and Bacon.

Carkhuff, R.R. (1969). *Helping and Human Relations.* Vols. 1 and 2. New York: Holt, Rinehart and Winston.

———. (1971). *The Development of Human Resources.* New York: Holt, Rinehart and Winston.

———. (1976). *Counselor-Counselee and Audio-tape Handbook.* Amherst, MA: Human Resource Development Press.

Carkhuff, R.R., & Berenson, B.G. (1967). *Beyond Counseling and Therapy.* New York: Holt, Rinehart and Winston.

———. (1976). *Teaching as Treatment.* Amherst, MA: Human Resource Development Press.

———. (1977). *Beyond Counseling and Therapy* (2nd ed.). New York: Holt, Rinehart and Winston.

Cole, D.R. (1982). *Helping.* Toronto: Butterworths.

Compton, B., & Gallaway, B. (1979). *Social Work Processes* (rev. ed.). Homewood, IL: Dorsey Press.

Coughlan D., & McIlduff, E. (1990). Structuring and nondirectiveness in group facilitation. *Person-Centered Review 5* (1), 13–29.

Fischer, J. (1974). Training for effective therapeutic practice. *Psychotherapy: Theory, Research, and Practice 12,* 118–123.

———. (1978). *Effective Casework Practice.* New York: McGraw-Hill.

Foreman, J. (1988). Use of person-centered theory with parents of handicapped children. *Texas Association for Counseling and Development Journal 16* (2), 115–118.

Gendlin, E.T. (1962). Person-centered developments and work with schizophrenics. *Journal of Counseling Psychology 9* (3), 205–211.

———. (1978). *Focusing.* New York: Everest House.

Gerwood, J. (1993). Nondirective counseling interventions with schizophrenics. *Psychological Reports 73,* 1147–1151.

Goldstein, H. (1983). Starting where the client is. *Social Casework 64* (May), 267–275.

Gordon, T. (1970). *Parent Effectiveness Training.* New York: Wyden.

——— & Burch, N. (1974). *T.E.T. Teacher Effectiveness Training.* New York: Wyden.

Guerney, B.G. (1964). Filial therapy: description and rationale. *Journal of Consulting Psychology 28,* 304–310.

———, Guerney, L.F., & Andronico, M.P. (1970). Filial therapy. In J.T. Hart and T.M. Tomlinson (Eds.), *New Directions in Person-centered Therapy.* Boston: Houghton Mifflin, 372–386.

Hammond, D.C., Hepworth, D.H., & Smith, V.G. (1978). *Improving Therapeutic Communication.* San Francisco: Jossey-Bass.

Hart, J.T. (1970). The development of person-centered therapy. In J.T. Hart and T.M. Tomlinson (Eds.), *New Directions in Person-centered Therapy.* Boston: Houghton Mifflin.

Hayashi, S., Kuno, T., Osawa, M., Shimizu, M., & Suetake, Y. (1992). The client-centered therapy and person-centered approach in Japan. *Journal of Humanistic Psychology 32* (2), 115–136.

Hollis, (1972). *Casework: A Psychosocial Therapy* (2nd ed.). New York: Random House.

Keefe, T. (1976). Empathy: the critical skill. *Social Work 21,* 10–14.

Kilpatrick, W.H. (1926). *Foundation of Method.* New York: Macmillan.

Lambert, M. (1986). Future directions for research in client-centered psychotherapy. *Person-Centered Review 1* (2), 185–200.

Larsen, J.A. (1975). *A Comparative Study of Traditional and Competency-based Methods of Teaching Interpersonal Skills in Social Work Education.* Doctoral dissertation. University of Utah.

Lewin, K. (1951). *Field Theory in Social Science.* New York: Harper.

Mandell, B. (1973). The equality revolution and supervision. *Journal of Education for Social Work* (Winter).

Maslow, A. (1971). *The Farther Reaches of Human Nature.* New York: Viking.

McMahon, P.C. (1981). *Management by Objectives in the Social Services.* Ottawa: Canadian Association of Social Workers.

Moreira, V. (1993). Beyond the person: Marleau-Penty's concept of "flesh" as (re)defining Carl Rogers' person-centered theory. *The Humanistic Psychologist 21* (2), 138–157.

Moustakas, C.E. (1953). *Children in Play Therapy.* New York: McGraw-Hill.

Natiello, P. (1987). The person-centered approach. *Person-Centered Review 2* (2), 203–216.

Nye, R.D. (1975). *Three Views of Man.* Monterey, CA: Brooks/Cole Publishing.

O'Hare, C. (1979). Counseling group process: Relationship between counselor and client behaviours in the helping process. *The Journal for Specialists in Group Work.*

O'Leary, C. (1989). The person-centered approach and family therapy. *Person-Centered Review 4* (3), 308–323.

Orlov, A. (1990). Carl Rogers and contemporary humanism. (Karl Rodzhers i sovremennyi gumanizm). *Vestn. Mosk, un-ta.,* Ser. 14, *Psikhologiia,* (2), 55–58.

Patterson, C. (1990). Involuntary clients. *Person-Centered Review 5* (3), 316–320.

Pfeiffer, J., & Jones, J.A. (1971). *Handbook of Structured Experiences for Human Relations Training.* Iowa City, IA: University Assoc.

Purton, C. (1989). The person-centered Jungian. *Person-Centered Review 4* (4), 403–419.

Quinn, R. (1993). Confronting Carl Rogers: A developmental-interactional approach to person-centered therapy. *Journal of Humanistic Psychology 33* (1), 6–23.

Richmond, M.E. (1917). *Social Diagnosis.* New York: Russell Sage Foundation.

Rogers, C.R. (1939). *The Clinical Treatment of the Problem Child.* Boston: Houghton Mifflin.

———. (1942). *Counseling and Psychotherapy.* Boston: Houghton Mifflin.

——— (1957). The necessary and sufficient conditions of therapeutic personality change. *Journal of Counseling Psychology 21,* 95–103.

———. (1959). A theory of therapy, personality and interpersonal relationships, as developed in the person-centered framework. In S. Koch (Ed.), *Psychology: A Study of Science.* Vol. 3. New York: McGraw-Hill, 184–256.

———. (1960). Significant trends in the person-centered orientation. *Progress in Clinical Psychology 4,* 85–99.

———. (1961a). A theory of psychotherapy with schizophrenics and a proposal for its empirical investigation. In J.G. Dawson, H.K. Stone, and N.P. Dellis (Eds.), *Psychotherapy with Schizophrenics.* Baton Rouge: Louisiana State University Press, 3–19.

———. (1961b). *On Becoming a Person.* Boston: Houghton Mifflin.

———. (1964). Toward a modern approach to values: the valuing process in the mature person. *Journal of Abnormal and Social Psychology 68* (2), 160–167.

——— (Ed.). (1967). *The Therapeutic Relationship and Its Impact: A Study of Psychotherapy with Schizophrenics.* Madison: University of Wisconsin Press.

———. (1969). *Freedom to Learn.* Columbus, OH: Merrill.

———. (1970). *Carl Rogers on Encounter Groups.* New York: Harper and Row.

———. (1972a). *Becoming Partners: Marriage and Its Alternatives.* New York: Delacorte.

———. (1972b). My personal growth. In Arthur Burton et al. (Eds.), *Twelve Therapists.* San Francisco: Jossey-Bass, 28–77.

———. (1974). Person-centered and symbolic perspectives on social change: A schematic model. In D.A. Wexler and L.M. Rice (Eds.), *Innovations in Person-centered Therapy.* New York: Wiley.

——— (1977). *Carl Rogers on Personal Power.* New York: Dell.

———. (1980). *A Way of Being.* Boston: Houghton Mifflin.

———. (1986). Rogers, Kohut and Erikson. *Person-Centered Review 1* (2), 125–140.

Rogers, C.R., Gendlin, E.J., Kiesler, D.J., & Truax, C.B. (Eds.). (1967). *The Therapeutic Relationship and Its Impact: A Study of Psychotherapy with Schizophrenics.* Madison: University of Wisconsin Press.

Rogers, C.R., & Stevens, D. (1975). *Person to Person.* New York: Pocket Books.

Rogers, W.R. (1974). Person-centered and symbolic perspectives on social change: A schematic model. In D.A. Wexler and L.N. Rice (Eds.), *Innovations in Person-centered Therapy.* New York: Wiley.

Rowe, W. (1981). Laboratory training in the baccalaureate curriculum. *Canadian Journal of Social Work Education 7* (3), 93–104.

———. (1983). An integrated skills laboratory. *Review '83,* 161–169.

Schatz, H.A. (1970). Staff involvement in agency administration. In Harry A. Schatz (Ed.), *Social Work Administration.* New York: Council on Social Work Education.

Seeman, J. (1990). Theory as autobiography. *Person-Centered Review 5* (4), 373–386.

Shlien, J.M., & Zimring, F.M. (1970). Research directives and methods in person-centered therapy. In J.T. Hart and T.M. Tomlinson (Eds.), *New Directions in Person-centered Therapy.* Boston: Houghton Mifflin.

Schulman, L. (1978). A study of practice skills. *Social Work 23* (4), 274–281.

———. (1979). *The Skills of Helping.* Itasca, IL: Peacock.

Siporin, M. (1975). *Introduction to Social Work Practice.* New York: Macmillan.

Smalley, R.E. (1967). *Theory for Social Work Practice.* New York: Columbia University Press.

Sollod, R.N. (1978). Carl Rogers and the origins of person-centered therapy. *Professional Psychology 4* (1), 93–104.

Solomon, L. (1990). Carl Rogers's efforts for world peace. *Person-Centered Review 5* (1), 39–56.

Stewart, M.A., Weston, W.W., Brown, J.B., McWhinney, I.E., McWilliam, C., & Freeman, T.R. (1995). *Patient-Centered Medicine.* Thousand Oaks, CA: Sage Publications.

Taft, J. (1951). *The Dynamics of Therapy in a Controlled Relationship.* New York: Harper.

Truax, C.B., & Carkhuff, R.R. (1967). *Toward Effective Counseling and Psychotherapy: Training and Practice.* Chicago: Aldine.

Truax, C.B., & Mitchell, K.J. (1971). Research on certain therapist interpersonal skills in relation to process and outcome. In A.E. Bergin and S.L. Garfield (Eds.), *Handbook of Psychotherapy and Behavior Change: An Empirical Analysis.* New York: Wiley, 299–344.

Turner, F.J. (1968). *Differential Diagnosis and Treatment in Social Work.* New York: Free Press.

——— (Ed.), (1974). *Social Work Treatment.* New York: Free Press.

——— (Ed.). (1979). *Social Work Treatment* (2nd ed.). New York: Free Press.

Usher, C. (1989). Recognizing cultural bias in counseling theory and practice: The case of Rogers. *Journal of Multicultural Counseling and Development 17* (2), 62–71.

Van der Veen, F., et al. (1964). Relationships between the parents' concept of the family and family adjustment. *American Journal of Orthopsychiatry 34* (January), 45–55.

Wallman, G. (1980). *The Impact of the First Year of Social Work Education on Student Skill in Communication of Empathy and Discrimination of Effective Responses.* Doctoral dissertation. Adelphi University, New York.

Wells, R.A. (1975). Training in facilitative skills. *Social Work 20,* 242–243.

Wexler, D.A., & Rice, L.M. (Eds.). (1974). *Innovations in Person-centered Therapy.* New York: Wiley.

White, R.W. (1959). Motivation reconsidered: The concept of competence. *Psychological Review 66,* 315.

Zeig, J.K. (Ed.). (1987). *The Evolution of Psychology.* New York: Brunner/Mazel.

ANNOTATED LISTING OF KEY REFERENCES

Boy, Angelo V., & Pine, Gerald J. (1982). *Person-centered Counseling: A Renewal.* Boston: Allyn and Bacon. The authors focus on the current application of person-centered theory to individual and group counseling. Boy and Pine recognize the shift of most person-centered authors to applications in teaching, administration, community building, race relations, and conflict resolution. They offer a refinement of the original person-centered counseling principles and renewed possibilities for individual and group application. In addition, Boy and Pine critically discuss the counseling concerns of personality theory, values, accountability, evaluation, and counselor education.

Carkhuff, Robert R., & Berenson, Bernard G. (1977). *Beyond Counseling and Therapy* (2nd ed.). New York: Holt, Rinehart and Winston. Carkhuff and Berenson have significantly advanced person-centered theory through both clinical and research efforts. This book supplies a comprehensive statement of the research and clinical observations that support their view of the person-centered model of helping. The authors compare the person-centered approach with other major helping theories and show the rationale for their particular beliefs. In addition, the philosophy, values, and content of a training approach for counselors are outlined.

Fischer, J. (1978). *Effective Casework Practice.* New York: McGraw-Hill. Fischer presents an approach to casework that bridges the gap between research and practice. He describes an eclectic approach that consists of empirically validated helping models. Fischer's "integrative model" includes components of behavior modification, cognitive procedures, and the core conditions of helping. A model for training and learning the core conditions is presented. Fisher's book represents one of the few significant references to person-centered theory in social work literature.

Rogers, Carl R. (1961). *On Becoming a Person.* Boston: Houghton Mifflin. This is a classic work that helped establish Rogers and person-centered theory as a major force in American psychology. Rogers articulates the culmination of three decades of theory development, clinical practice, and clinical research as a cohesive approach to helping and personal growth. As such, it is an excellent first reading for individuals interested in the person-centered approach.

Rogers, Carl R. (1977). *Carl Rogers on Personal Power.* New York: Dell. Rogers describes the impact of the person-centered approach on relationships, education, administration, and political systems. He reiterates the theoretical foundation of this approach and shows how it translates into a base for political activity and what he terms the "quiet revolution." Rogers details the principles of the person-centered approach and describes a number of examples of these principles in practice, in the workplace and in the political arena. In conclusion, Rogers offers some humanistic alternatives to polarized conflict and entrenched political structures.

CHAPTER 5

COGNITIVE THEORY AND SOCIAL WORK TREATMENT

JIM LANTZ

OVERVIEW OF THEORY

A cognitive approach to social work practice is based upon the idea that a person's thinking is the principal determinant of emotions and behavior.[46] As a result, cognitive theorists and cognitive social work practitioners believe that good social work treatment will include considerable effort directed toward helping the client identify, challenge, and change thinking patterns that result in dysfunctional forms of emotion, behavior, and problem solving.[20,21,44,45,46] As Werner[44,45] has noted, cognitive theory is not a system of ideas created by one or two individuals. Cognitive theory is rather a consistent and coherent orientation to understanding human functioning and human change that includes the ideas and contributions of many different individuals.[18,21,22]

HISTORICAL ORIGINS

The first cognitive therapist and practitioner was Alfred Adler.[1,2] Adler worked with Sigmund Freud and was initially an important member of the psychoanalytic movement in Vienna. Adler separated from Freud for a number of reasons. Adler believed that the personality is a unified whole and that it does not make sense to split the personality into the id, ego, and super-ego, as did Freud. Adler[1] also did not agree with Freud's understanding of human motivation. Adler believed that people are primarily motivated by social drives rather than by sexual drives. Adler[1,2] also believed that human cognition is of much greater importance than was suggested by Freud. For Adler,[2] a person's behavior is shaped by what Adler called the "life-style." For Adler,[2] the life-style consists of a person's ideas and beliefs about the self, self-ideal expectations, as well as the person's "picture of the world."[1,2] For Adler,[1,2] the life-style also includes cognitive ideas about how to "correctly" solve problems and to exist in the world. For Adler,[1,2] psychotherapy and human service should include rigorous examination of the client's life-style assumptions as a way to initiate change.[22] Alfred Adler[2] is considered by many to be the first cognitive theorist in the mental health professions.[22,23,39]

IMPORTANT PRACTITIONERS AND PROPONENTS

Alfred Adler[1,2] was the first major cognitive theorist and practitioner, but there have been many other cognitive theorists and mental health practitioners. In 1954, Joseph Furst[12] reported that neurosis is a distortion and/or limitation of consciousness and that treatment should be considered to be "rational psychotherapy" that helps a client change cognitive distortions and expand conscious awareness.

In the late 1950s and the early 1960s, Albert Ellis[10] reported that dysfunctional emotion is reactive to a strongly evaluative kind of thinking. For Ellis,[10] dysfunctional emotion results from irrational self-talk cognitions. Ellis[10] believes that effective psychotherapy and counseling include help from a service provider who focuses the client upon identifying, challenging, and changing dysfunctional thinking and distorted cognitions. In 1962, Ellis[10] published his classic work, *Reason and Emotion in Psychotherapy,* which has served as a bible for many cognitive counselors and/or psychotherapists since that time.

William Glasser's[16] approach to psychotherapy, which he calls "reality therapy," has also been a popular approach to cognitive psychotherapy and mental health intervention. For Glasser,[16] there are two basic human needs: to give and receive love and to behave in a way that enables one to feel worthwhile to self and others. For Glasser,[16] effective psychotherapy helps the client find the courage needed to change, to use thought to identify responsible goals and responsible actions, and to use cognitive evaluation processes to identify opportunities for responsibility and the responsible awareness of reality.

Maxie Maultsby[38] is another mental health professional who has made significant contributions to cognitive theory and cognitive mental health practice. Maultsby's[38] major book, *Help Yourself to Happiness,* outlines his approach to "rational behavior therapy." Some of Maultsby's contributions include his use of cognitive theory in group psychotherapy, his promotion of cognitive self-help groups, his descriptions of the use of rational behavior therapy with adolescents, and his integration of hypnosis as a cognitive treatment strategy.[39]

Arnold Lazarus[32] published the extremely influential *Practice of Multimodal Therapy,* which is often considered the most systematic, comprehensive, and useful description of the use of cognitive theory in facilitating human change. In the Lazarus model,[32] the helping professional is first encouraged to assess seven modes of the client's functioning: behavior, affect, sensation, imagery, cognition, interpersonal living, and drugs-biology. Lazarus[32] calls this the "basic id" of assessment and intervention. For Lazarus,[32] it is important for the helper to use the basic id to outline a comprehensive treatment plan that will help in all areas of social functioning. For Lazarus,[32] the basic id is a way to tailor treatment to meet the specific and concrete treatment needs of the client who comes for help.

Arnold Lazarus[32] is a bit different from other cognitive psychotherapists in his ideas about the "sequence" of thinking, feeling, and human behavior. For Ellis,[10] Beck,[3] Maultsby,[38] and many other cognitive theorists, thinking almost always triggers and/or creates feeling and behavior. For Lazarus,[32] thinking is often reactive to feeling and behavior. For Lazarus,[32] an important part of assessment is to determine the sequence of cognition, affect, and behavior for each individual client requesting service. For Lazarus,[32] every client has a unique sequence of thinking, feeling, and behavior that needs to be assessed.

Don Tosi[42] is a cognitive psychotherapist who has made major contributions in the integration of hypnosis and cognitive therapy. The approach developed by Tosi[42] is called "rational stage directed hypnotherapy" and uses the stages of awareness, exploration, commitment, skill development, skill refinement, and redirection to focus hypnotic imagery in a way that helps the client change cognitions and "picture" thinking in a healthy direction.

Victor Raimy[39] is a psychotherapist who has used cognitive theory to understand self-concept and self-concept change. In Raimy's[39] classic work, *Misunderstandings of the Self,* he shows how the relationship between client and therapist can be used to help the client challenge and change cognitive misunderstandings of the self.

Rollo May[36,37] has not been listed consistently as a cognitive theorist or cognitive psychotherapist in most articles, books, or chapters on cognitive theory, yet his existential work does include significant cognitive elements. May[36,37] defines the unconscious as "unactualized being." For May,[36] an important part of psychotherapy is to help the client use freedom and responsibility to review his or her life, identify unactualized being, and "think" about ways that freedom and responsibility can be used to actualize being.

Like Rollo May, Viktor Frankl[13,14,15] is an existential psychotherapist who has not been identified consistently as either a cognitive theorist or a cognitive psychotherapist. In spite of this omission, it is this author's opinion that Frankl[14,15] should be understood as both an existential and a cognitive practitioner. In Frankl's[13,15] view, an important aspect of the treatment process is to utilize Socratic questions in a way that facilitates the client's thinking about the meanings and meaning potentials in his or her life. For Frankl,[14,15] the core of the treatment process is to help the client identify these meanings and meaning potentials through cognitive reflection. Frankl[13,14,15] calls this cognitive reflection on meanings and meaning potentials "existential analysis" or *"existenzanalysis."*

A final non–social work practitioner who has made significant contributions in cognitive treatment is Aron Beck. Beck is a psychiatrist who has utilized cognitive theory in the treatment of depression,[3] anxiety disorders,[4] and personality problems[5] with excellent results. In this author's opinion, Beck's[3,4,5] major contributions include "refining" cognitive treatment processes in a systematic and concrete way with a variety of psychiatric and mental health problems, and demonstrating through his research efforts and evaluation research studies[3] that cognitive therapy is effective with a wide variety of human problems. In recent years, Beck's daughter, Judy Beck,[6] has continued to expand the theory and practice of cognitive psychotherapy by building upon and refining her father's work.

PATH INTO SOCIAL WORK

Over the past three decades, numerous social work practitioners have made significant contributions to the theory of cognitive practice and the use of cognitive theory in the social work profession. Significant social work contributions have been made by Berlin,[7] Chatterjee,[8] Combs,[9] Epstein,[11] Goldstein,[17,18] Krill,[19] Lantz,[21] Reid,[40] Snyder,[41] Weiner and Fox,[43] Werner,[44,45,46] Witkin,[47] and Zastrow.[50] In spite of the excellent contributions to cognitive theory made by many of these social workers, this author will pay specific attention to the contributions of Werner, Goldstein, and Lantz.

Harold Werner[44,45,46] must be given credit for being the pioneer social worker in the use of cognitive theory in social work practice. Werner has contributed two outstanding books on the use of cognitive therapy in social work practice. In 1965, Werner published the classic *A Rational Approach to Social Casework*.[44] In 1983, he published another outstanding book, *Cognitive Therapy: A Humanistic Approach*.[45]

Although Werner is now recognized as a pioneer social work theorist,[46] he has not always received great respect in the social work profession. At the time of his early contributions, Werner was severely attacked by psychoanalytically oriented social workers who made very little effort to understand his work and to discuss it with him in a professional manner. In spite of this experience, Werner continued to publish and present his ideas. It is a tribute to Werner's efforts and vision that cognitive theory is so widely accepted and utilized in the social work profession today.

A second important pioneer in the use of cognitive therapy in social work practice is Howard Goldstein, who also produced a body of significant writings. He is the author of *A Cognitive Approach to Human Services*[17] and *Creative Change: A Cognitive-Humanistic Approach to Social Work Practice*.[18] Both books should be considered classics in the field. In addition to these two excellent books, Goldstein is the author of many articles that outline the creative and humanistic use of cognitive theory in social work.

The author of this chapter is responsible for the development of a cognitive-existential approach to social work practice.[24,25,26,27,28,29,30] Starting out as a classically trained cognitive practitioner,[20,21,22,23,31] this author was significantly influenced by the existential concepts of the Viennese psychiatrist Viktor Frankl[13,14,15] and the French philosopher Gabriel Marcel,[33,34,35] and as a result developed a treatment system that integrates cognitive theory with existential philosophy. This author's approach to cognitive-existential treatment is presented in his book *Existential Family Therapy: Using the Concepts of Viktor Frankl*,[27] as well as in numerous book chapters and journal articles.[24,25,26,28,29,30]

PRINCIPAL CONCEPTS AND ASSUMPTIONS

In a cognitive approach to social work practice, the central concept is that most human emotion is the direct result of what people think, tell themselves, assume, or believe about themselves and their social situation.[6,10,21] Albert Ellis[10] formulated a cognitive "ABC" theory of emotion based upon this primary cognitive concept. In the Ellis[10] framework, A represents the activating event; B represents what people believe, think, and tell themselves about themselves or the activating event; and C represents the emotional consequence of such beliefs, cognitions, and self-talk. According to Ellis,[10] when people's beliefs, thoughts, and self-talk are rational, they feel emotions that are functional. When their beliefs, thoughts, and self-talk are disturbed or irrational, however, people develop dysfunctional emotions, affect, and behavior. In cognitive social work practice, it is the social worker's responsibility to help clients change the disturbed and/or irrational cognitions, beliefs, and self-talk that create dysfunctional emotions and behavior.[21,44]

Raimy[39] has stated this primary premise of cognitive theory in a somewhat different way. In Raimy's[39] view, most dysfunctional human emotions and behaviors are a direct result of "misconceptions" that people hold about themselves or about various environmental situations. Raimy[39] also believes that most dysfunctional emotions can be changed when the person feeling the emotion is able to correct the misconceptions creating it.

A second basic concept in cognitive social work practice is that many misconceptions, irrational thinking, erroneous beliefs, and distributed cognitions are outside of a person's conscious awareness.[20,21,22,31] As a result, in many instances, the social work client does not know just what thoughts, ideas, beliefs, and misconceptions are creating his or her unpleasant or dysfunctional emotion. Maultsby[38] uses the example of learning to drive a car to describe this phenomenon. When a person first learns to drive a car, he or she engages in a great deal of active thinking and self-talk (i.e., a message from the self to the self) about driving. The person will actively tell him- or herself to step on the brake or to turn the steering wheel in order to stop or turn. After a period of time, this self-talk or thinking becomes so well learned that it becomes automatic and generally outside the person's awareness. A similar process occurs in the development of most dysfunctional human emotion. The person practices and learns misconceptions and irrational self-talk so well that these cognitive beliefs become "automatic" and create dysfunctional emotion without the person's conscious awareness of the specific content of his or her misconceptions, irrational beliefs, and irrational self-talk.[6,10,21,42,46] As a result, to help a client learn to change dysfunctional emotions, it is important that the social work practitioner help him or her to bring into active awareness the thoughts, beliefs, and misconceptions that are creating and maintaining dysfunctional emotions.[21,46]

Although cognitive social work practitioners consider most dysfunctional emotional states to be a direct result of the individual's misconceptions and irrational beliefs, a third cognitive concept is that there are exceptions to this rule. Some dysfunctional emotions may be the result of organic, physiological, neurological, or chemical problems.[21] Examples of such problems include thyroid imbalance, blood sugar imbalance, brain tissue damage, malnutrition, intake of toxic substances, aging, prolonged exposure to the elements, some forms of depression and schizophrenia, and any physical problem that can create an imbalance in brain chemistry.[21]

A fourth concept central to cognitive social work practice is that not all unpleasant emotions are dysfunctional and not all pleasant emotions are functional.[21] Maultsby[38] illustrates this point with the example of a person who feels very happy about being close to a rattlesnake. An individual who sees a rattlesnake that is set to bite and tells him- or herself that the rattlesnake is not dangerous is engaging in irrational self-talk. This misconception will result in a pleasant emotional state that is dysfunctional because it does not provide the person with the experience of fear that would motivate him or her to move away from the dangerous snake. In this situation, the happy feeling is dysfunctional because it is based upon a cognitive misconception that the rattlesnake is not dangerous.[38]

Because most cognitive social work practitioners base their opinion of the functionality of any emotional state on the rationality of the cognitive self-talk that produces it, practitioner and client can benefit from a basic definition of a rational thought as opposed to a misconception.[20,21,31] Maultsby[38] provides a definition of a rational thought that has proved helpful to many clients and practitioners of cognitive treatment. Maultsby[39] defines a rational cognition as any thought, idea, belief, attitude, or statement to the self that is based upon objective reality, is life preserving and productive for achieving one's goals, and that will decrease significant internal conflict and conflict with others. Although this definition of a rational thought does not "perfectly" solve the definitional problem, it is helpful and useful for many clients.[20]

NATURE OF PERSONALITY

In cognitive social work practice, it is believed that the human personality is flexible and can be influenced by both physical and social factors. Although cognitive practitioners recognize the influence of physical and environmental factors upon the manifestation of personality, most accept that people can decide to shape and change their external and internal environments.[1,5,10] Adler,[2] Ellis,[10] and Werner[44] all note that although people are not complete masters of their lives or fates, they can choose the posture they adopt toward life and fate. Adler's [1,2] cognitive view of the individual's ability to shape the personal life is described by Viktor Frankl[13,14,15] as being a "forerunner" to existential psychiatry and existential psychotherapy.

VIEW OF PEOPLE

In contrast to Freudian theory, which stresses the competitive nature of people, cognitive theorists and practitioners have consistently described people as collaborators, equals, fellow human beings, and cooperators in life.[2,10,22] The cognitive model of social work practice generally views people as neither good nor bad but as creative beings who can decide how to live their life.[22] Cognitive theorists and social work practitioners are highly impressed by the individual's ability to utilize thought to identify personal goals and actions and to use these to change the self and the social environment surrounding the self.[18,22,44,45,48,49]

THE PROCESS OF CHANGE

In a cognitive theory approach to social work practice, human change occurs when the social work helper is able to facilitate a cognitive reflection process in which the client identifies, challenges, and changes misconceptions, faulty beliefs, distorted cognitions, and irrational self-talk that have created dysfunctional emotions and behavior.[20,21,23,44,45,50] In most cognitive theory approaches to social work treatment, emotional support given by the helper to the client is considered useful and important but it is not the core aspect of treatment. Also, in a cognitive approach to social work treatment, advocacy and environmental modifications are considered important and useful, but helping the client to identify, challenge, and change cognitive misconceptions remains the central agent of change.[20,45]

In a cognitive approach to social work treatment, the process of helping the client is primarily educational.[20,21] The purpose of treatment is to help the client learn to be his or her own counselor and to use cognitive theory concepts to consistently understand the self and control dysfunctional emotions and behavior.[31] As a result, cognitive practitioners seriously attempt to "empower" their clients by giving them cognitive theory tools for the purpose of mastery, control, and self-help.[6,10,20,38,42,44] Ellis,[10] Beck,[6] and Maultsby[38] outline in detail group-educational programs to supplement casework, counseling, and psychotherapy and specifically address the client's need to learn cognitive intervention skills for self-mastery, empowerment, and control.

SIGNIFICANT OTHERS AND SIGNIFICANT ENVIRONMENTS

Cognitive theorists and cognitive practitioners have a mixed record in terms of understanding the importance of the client's family, significant others, and the social environment. For some early cognitive theorists, it was considered most important to emphasize the human capacity to use rational thinking to overcome problems in the social environment or in the family. As a result, many cognitive theory practitioners have not emphasized social action, environmental modification, family treatment, and/or network interventions. This deficiency in the cognitive theory tradition is not, however, a problem in the Adlerian[1,2] approach to cognitive theory practice.

In the Adlerian approach to cognitive theory practice, the human "life-style" is understood as a set of cognitive beliefs, conceptions, and/or misconceptions that a person accepts about the world, about the self, and about problem-solving in the world.[1,2,22] Life-style cognitions may be understood as cognitive beliefs about the person's self-concept, self-ideal expectations, picture of the world, and ethical conceptions.[1,2,22] In the Adlerian approach to cognitive theory, beliefs, conceptions, misconceptions, and self-talk are learned primarily through a person's social experiences and interactions with his or her family and family of origin.[22] As a result, the family and the social environment often are targets for intervention in Adlerian treatment.[22]

TIME IN COGNITIVE THEORY PRACTICE

For most cognitive theorists and cognitive theory practitioners, the past is not extremely important. For Ellis,[10] Beck,[6] Maultsby,[38] and Tosi,[42] the present moment is the most important part of time because it is when change can and does occur. For Ellis,[10] Tosi,[42] and Maultsby,[38] it is a technical mistake to spend a great deal of time with a client reflecting on the past. For these cognitive practitioners,[10,38,42] what matter most are the self-talk, misconceptions, and cognitive distortions that the client is using in the present to create dysfunctional emotions and behavior, and the healthier ideas, beliefs, and self-talk that could be used in the here and now to improve affect and behavior.

Adlerian cognitive theory practitioners have a somewhat different idea about time and its importance in the treatment process. For Adler[1,2] and many Adlerian practitioners,[22] it is helpful to talk about the past with a client because it gives the practitioner insight into the cognitions, thoughts, beliefs, and/or misconceptions used by the client in the present to create problematic feelings and behavior. This Adlerian view of time resulted in one of the first projective tests (the Early Recollection Test) developed in the mental health professions.[22]

A third view of time is held by cognitive-existential practitioners.[30] In the cognitive-existential view,[28,29,30] the future, the present, and the past are all important. In the cognitive-existential approach to the helping process, it is the function of the practitioner to help the client use cognition and reflection to find and make use of the meanings and meaning potentials in life.[13,14,15,27] Specifically, the cognitive-existential practitioner facilitates client thought and reflection in a way that helps the client to "notice" meaning potentials in the future, to "actualize" such meaning potentials in the present moment, and to recollect, remember, and "honor" meaning potentials previously actualized and deposited in the past.[13,14,15,27,28,29,30,48,49]

SOCIOCULTURAL AND ETHNIC SENSITIVITY

Cognitive theory practitioners have consistently noted that irrational beliefs, self-talk, and misconceptions are generally learned and reactive to social and cultural experiences.[10] As a result, cognitive practitioners understand that race, class, and gender experience may well have an impact upon client beliefs and cognitions. Still, as Ellis,[10] Maultsby,[38] and Tosi[42] all note, there is no demonstrated association or correlation between race, class, gender, and irrational thinking. Most cognitive practitioners agree that all classes, races, and genders are capable of irrational thinking rather equally.[10,38,42] The cognitive treatment tradition would be improved by the implementation of research studies focusing upon race, class, and gender in the cognitive theory treatment process.

COGNITIVE THEORY TREATMENT

As noted previously, the principal therapeutic goal in cognitive theory social work practice is to help the client identify, challenge, and change the misconceptions, faulty beliefs, disturbed thinking, and irrational self-talk that create dysfunctional feelings and behavior. In a recent publication, Judith Beck[6] summarizes ten useful treatment principles of the cognitive approach to social work treatment:

1. Cognitive treatment is based upon an evolving formulation of the client and client problems in cognitive terms.
2. Cognitive treatment requires a sound therapeutic treatment relationship.
3. Cognitive treatment is based upon collaboration with the helper and active participation by the client.
4. Cognitive treatment is problem focused and goal oriented.
5. Cognitive treatment emphasizes the present.
6. Cognitive treatment is educational and hopes to teach the client to be his or her own helper.
7. Cognitive treatment attempts to be time limited when possible.
8. Cognitive treatment interviews are structured.
9. Cognitive treatment teaches clients to identify, evaluate, and respond effectively to dysfunctional thoughts and beliefs.
10. Cognitive treatment uses a variety of treatment techniques to help the client change thinking, feelings, and behavior.[6]

THE TREATMENT RELATIONSHIP IN COGNITIVE SOCIAL WORK PRACTICE

In cognitive theory practice, the relationship between client and helper is an important part of the treatment process.[6] The treatment relationship allows the client to learn and gives him or her an opportunity to view the self and the world in different ways.[6,29,39]

The treatment relationship can be used in two major ways as a powerful tool for helping the client change cognitive misconceptions that result in dysfunctional emotions and behavior. First, the supportive element in the treatment relationship gives the client a message about the social worker's opinion of his or her capacity for growth, ability to function in a healthy way, and value as a human being. When the social worker takes time to be with the client, shows interest in the client as a person, and responds to the client with empathy and concern, the social worker is frequently giving the client quite a different message regarding his or her importance as a person than the client usually receives from him- or herself or from others. According to Raimy,[39] low self-esteem is an emotional response resulting primarily from the client's negative misconceptions about the self. This cognitive process can be challenged or interrupted when the social worker demonstrates the belief that the client is important by providing respect, support, and encouragement during the treatment process. Raimy[39] has labeled such behavior "positive regard" and has shown that such feelings, actions, and beliefs on the part of the professional helper are often a primary curative factor in the process of human change.

A second way in which the treatment relationship can be used to help the client change misconceptions is by focusing on and examining distortions in the relationship between the client and the worker. As Raimy[39] and others have noted, during the treatment process the client may often begin to ascribe to the professional helper many attitudes, ideas, feelings, and motivations that do not, in reality, originate with the worker. Such distortions are often a result of the client's misconceptions about how a significant other "should" think, feel, and behave toward him or her. If the client has positive feelings about the self, he or she will expect others to act accordingly. If the client's idea of self is negative, he or she will project negative feelings, thoughts, and behaviors about him- or herself onto others. Examining the relationship between the worker and the client can bring into the client's awareness many of his or her misconceptions about the self and how he or she expects to be treated by others. Such misconceptions are then subject to the possibility of change through cognitive review. This can often be facilitated either by teaching the client how to check out such assumptions with significant others, such as the caseworker, as they occur in the present, or by helping the client identify how such patterns of distortion and misconception began, through a discussion of the client's developmental experiences.[28,29,39] Cognitive theory practitioners do not generally use the terms "transference" and "countertransference." Cognitive theory practitioners view such phenomena as cognitive distortions that disrupt encounter and the treatment relationship.[6,10,24,39] The Freudian view of transference and countertransference is not accepted by most cognitive practitioners.[31,46]

The following section will provide an overview of many of the treatment techniques that can be used in cognitive social work practice. All of the following treatment techniques depend upon a good treatment relationship in order to be useful and effective.

CLARIFYING INTERNAL COMMUNICATION

Clarification of internal communication is a frequently used procedure in cognitive theory social work that is effective, in this author's opinion, primarily because it provides feedback to the client about what the client is thinking and telling the self. In this way, the social work helps the client develop a better understanding of many of the misconceptions and irrational beliefs that are hidden in the client's verbalizations both to him- or herself and to others. Again, when such misconceptions are brought to the client's awareness, they become available for change through cognitive review.

In the following illustration, a social worker uses clarification of internal communication to help the mother of a ten-year-old boy develop insight into a hidden assumption that prevents her from providing more effective direction to her son.

MOTHER: He's terrible.

CASEWORKER: In what specific way is he terrible?

MOTHER: He won't do what I say. I want him to pick up his toys, and he starts screaming.

CASEWORKER: Then what do you say?

MOTHER: Sometimes nothing. I get upset.

CASEWORKER: What does your silence mean in that situation? What could it mean?

MOTHER: I don't know. I guess I feel guilty.

CASEWORKER: Guilty?

MOTHER: Yes. I don't know. . . . I don't feel . . . It's hard for me to punish him. I've made a lot of mistakes and it hasn't been easy for him. So, you know . . . I feel guilty about punishing him.

CASEWORKER: What kind of people make mistakes?

MOTHER: [Silence] *Failures.*

CASEWORKER: You think you are a failure?

MOTHER: [Silence] Yes. Often.

EXPLANATION

Explanation is another treatment procedure that can be used to help the client change misconceptions. In cognitive social work treatment, "explanation" is a term used for a set of treatment techniques aimed at teaching the client Ellis's[10] ABC model of how emotions work. They help the client to identify and discover the misconceptions he or she is using to create dysfunctional emotions, and to challenge and change misconceptions and irrational ideas. The following illustration gives a more specific idea of how explanation can be used by cognitive social work practitioners to help the client change.

Mrs. Smith was referred for mental health services by her caseworker at a child welfare agency. Mrs. Smith was listless, slept a great deal during the day, felt depressed, had periodic outbursts of anger, and was becoming phobic about leaving her house. The referring caseworker was considering temporarily removing Mrs. Smith's only child from the home.

In their first interview, the clinical social worker and Mrs. Smith were able to develop some initial trust. The client stated that her goal for treatment was to stop feeling so depressed. The worker explained to Mrs. Smith that probably one of the reasons she was not able to stop feeling depressed was that she did not know much about how emotions worked and about what might help. The worker and Mrs. Smith agreed to a contract whereby the worker would teach the client how emotions worked and some strategies she could use to decrease her depression. Mrs. Smith agreed to attend treatment sessions regularly and to do the homework that the worker assigned.

The clinical worker then began explaining the ABC emotional analysis model. Part of the conversation was as follows:

SOCIAL WORKER: If I told you a bomb was under your chair, how would you feel?

MRS. SMITH: I'd laugh.

SOCIAL WORKER: You wouldn't be afraid?

MRS. SMITH: No, because I wouldn't believe you.

SOCIAL WORKER: Good. You see, it's what you believe or think that causes how you feel. A is what I told you about the bomb, the event. B is what you believed and told yourself about the event. C, how you feel, depends on B, what you believe.

Once Mrs. Smith realized that, "in theory," emotions are caused by thoughts and beliefs, the social worker explained how to use a written homework form to help discover and challenge the misconceptions that she frequently used to create and maintain her depression.

WRITTEN HOMEWORK

Written homework is often a useful way for clients who can read and write to learn how to use the Ellis[10] ABC theory of emotions to identify, challenge, and change misconceptions and irrational self-talk. The following written homework form was developed by Maultsby[38] and is often a helpful part of the cognitive theory practice process.

A: What is the event?

B: What are my misconceptions about the event, or what could I be thinking to cause my feelings?

C: How do I feel?

D1: Is my description of A accurate?

D2: Are my Bs rational? If not, challenge them.

E: What new emotion will result from D1 and D2?

This form is used both as part of the explanation treatment procedure and as a format for emotional fractionalization, that is, it helps the client break down a complex emotional sequence into a more understandable problem.[10,20,21,23,38]

EXPERIENTIAL LEARNING

Experiential learning used as a procedure for challenging and changing cognitive misconceptions is best explained by the cognitive dissonance principle. Cognitive dissonance refers to human beings' tendency to change attitudes and beliefs that do not seem congruent with their behavior, actions, or style of life.[21] When using the principle of cognitive dissonance as a way of changing misconceptions, the cognitive practitioner attempts to set up a treatment situation that will help the client engage in specific behaviors that are incongruent with the client's misconceptions. As the client engages in such behaviors, he or she will tend to change the misconceptions.[21] Many common treatment techniques may be based in part on the use of experiential learning and the principle of cognitive dissonance, including assertiveness training, group therapy socialization experiences, role prescription, psychodrama, modeling, role playing, and task assignments.[10]

PARADOXICAL INTENTION

Paradoxical intention is a cognitive restarting technique developed by Viktor Frankl.[13,14,15] The technique is used most appropriately when the client has developed a specific unpleasant behavior that is often triggered by anxiety about the possible occurrence of the same behavior. For example, one of this author's clients, a usually medically stabilized epileptic, would frequently worry about having a seizure at a business meeting in front of his peers. The client's anxiety about this possibility would, in fact, trigger a seizure. Using paradoxical intention, the author instructed the client to try to have a seizure at the beginning of every business meeting to get it out of the way. The fact that the client was then unable to do so helped him stop thinking about how awful a seizure would be, and as a result, no further seizures occurred in this situation. The prescription of the symptom challenged the client's misconceptions about having no way to control it, decreasing the anticipatory anxiety that triggered the seizures.

In this author's view, it is important to use paradoxical intention only in situations of anticipatory anxiety.[27] The technique should never be used to challenge suicidal ideation and should not be used when symptoms have a physical basis.[13,27] It is also this author's view that paradoxical intention should be used "with" the client, not "on" the client, and that the client should be fully informed about this treatment technique before it is used.[27]

DYNAMIC AND EXISTENTIAL REFLECTION TREATMENT ACTIVITIES

Dynamic and existential reflection treatment activities are cognitive restructing activities[27,28,29,30] based upon Lantz's understanding of the philosophical concepts of Gabriel Marcel.[33,34,35] They are used in a cognitive-existential approach to social work practice to help the client notice, actualize, and honor the meanings and meaning potentials in his or her life.[27,28,33,34,35]

Gabriel Marcel[33,34,35] distinguishes two kinds of human thought, "dynamic" and "existential" reflection. In Marcel's view,[33,34] both kinds of thought are necessary and valid when properly used. Dynamic reflection (which predominates in science and technology) should be used to focus upon problems and problem solving, and existential reflection (which is more characteristic of philosophy, religion, art, meditation, and prayer) is the means by which we facilitate the discovery of meanings and meaning potentials in human life.[27,28,29,30,33,34,35]

Dynamic reflection is problem-solving reflection that aims at knowledge that is verifiable, objective, experimental, and abstract.[33,34] An important feature of dynamic reflection is the separation of the reflector from the object of reflection.[34,35] In dynamic reflection, thought is directed at confronting, reducing, and breaking down problems.

Because dynamic reflection is directed toward the development of knowledge that is objective and verifiable, it is abstract and includes a "minimized" relationship between the thinker and the object of thinking.[27,28,33,34] Dynamic reflection puts the material world in a spotlight and "pushes" the world to answer questions.[27,34] Dynamic reflection is different from existential reflection in that it is directed at breaking down and solving problems, whereas existential reflection is the way to discover connection, unity, wholeness, meanings, and meaning potentials.[27,28,35] In cognitive-existential social work practice, dynamic reflection is best utilized to help clients develop problem-solving strategies that can help them actualize and make use of the meanings and meaning potentials discovered through existential reflection.[27,28,29,30]

Gabriel Marcel[33,34,35] does not criticize dynamic reflection but is adamant in his criticism of its misuse. For Marcel,[33,34] dynamic reflection has allowed and encouraged us to use technology and abstraction to manipulate our world, gain knowledge, and solve many problems. Marcel's[33,34,35] critical observations about the misuse of dynamic reflection highlight the moral and meaning confusions that result when dynamic reflection is "imperialistic" and "judges" all knowledge and truth only by objective and abstract criteria.

For Marcel,[33,34,35] dynamic reflection is used to gain clarity about problems through verification and objectification, whereas existential reflection is used to gain a deeper, richer, wider, and more inclusive understanding of the meanings and meaning potentials of human existence. Existential reflection is the path toward the awareness of meanings and meaning potentials in life.[33,34,35]

The specific mechanics of existential reflection are difficult to present in an exact and systematic fashion.[28] One aspect of existential reflection is "disbelief" in the complete adequacy of dynamic reflection, which then results in an attempted "recovery" of meanings and of the unity of experience that is distorted by abstract and dynamic thought.[24,25,26,28,29,30,33,34] Here, Marcel[33,34,35] is pointing out that abstract thought and the manipulative and experimental aspects of dynamic reflection are "reductionistic" and can cloud the meanings of human existence. Marcel[33,34] believes that whenever dynamic reflection reduces loves, life, friendship, faith, prayer, commitment, fidelity, encounter, courage, joy, and other manifestations of meaning to experiences that can be understood "clearly" or "systematically" or "experimentally," existential reflection must and will "rise up" to correct the "blindness" of dynamic reflection.

A second aspect of existential reflection is its capacity to help us discover and participate in the "unmeasurable" meanings and meaning potentials of life in a serious, sensitive, and "rigorous" fashion.[24,27,33,34] Existential reflection includes discovery through participation instead of distant observation, encounter instead of the subject-object split, and concrete involvement in daily life rather than distant and disengaged abstraction.[27,30,33,34,35] Existential reflection is practiced in the presence of meaning potentials, during participation in what is being contemplated, and with personal connection to what is being recollected and experienced.[27,33,34] Existential reflection allows us to discover the meanings and meaning potentials to be found in friendship, love, art, literature, drama, meditation, recollections, celebration, poetry, music, testimony, and the "I-Thou" dialogue.[27,33,34,35] In this author's view, existential reflection is the way to rediscover and recollect meaning potentials that have been deposited in the past and to discover those in the future that can be actualized in the here and now.[24,25,26,27,28] Existential reflection recollects meanings deposited in the past and notices meaning potentials available in the future, while dynamic reflection helps us actualize meaning potentials in the present.[25,29,30]

CASE VIGNETTES

The following two case illustrations are provided to give the reader a taste of how cognitive theory can be used in the practice of social work. The first case illustrates a rather classical, Ellis–Beck style of using cognitive theory, with an adult man worried about his mother. The second case provides a clinical example of how the Adlerian approach to cognitive theory social work practice was helpful to a graduate student.

MR. A

Mr. A was referred to the mental health center by a caseworker at the Welfare Department, where he had applied for a nursing home placement for his mother. In an interview with the department caseworker, the client talked about his depression, his difficulty sleeping, and how terrible he felt about having to apply for assistance. The caseworker accurately assessed Mr. A's acute reactive depression and referred him to the mental health center for cognitive theory social work treatment.

INTERVIEW ONE:

At the same interview, Mr. A, who was fifty-two, employed, and married with five children, said his family doctor had told him his mother needed to be placed in a nursing home because she required twenty-four-hour nursing care. Mr. A had then appealed to the Welfare Department. He felt terrible. He felt that receiving welfare was "bad" and a son should never "put his mother out." He felt guilty and depressed about taking such a step, as he was "the first person in the family to ever do such a thing." Mr. A said he was worried, had started missing work, and was drinking too much.

The social worker at the mental health center helped Mr. A to realize that his mother did need nursing home care, that he did need to apply for assistance, and that it was doubtful that these things would change. The worker asked Mr. A whether he wanted to feel better even if things didn't change. Mr. A said that he needed to get over this because he had "a wife and children to take care of," and that he would do whatever was necessary. The worker then told the client that he felt it might take about ten interviews for Mr. A to get over his depression, and that Mr. A would have to "work at it very hard." The worker asked whether he could tape record the rest of the session, and Mr. A agreed. At this point, the worker explained to Mr. A how emotions work, using the Ellis[10] ABC emotional analysis framework, with examples different from Mr. A's situation. When the worker was sure the client understood the theory, he explained that Mr. A's depression was the result of what he was telling himself (that he was "bad," a "terrible person," "the first rotten egg in the family," and "a failure as a son, as a man should live up to all of his financial responsibilities"). The worker challenged each of Mr. A's irrational ideas and beliefs. At the end of the interview, Mr. A said that he felt better, and that he had been telling himself some "crazy stuff." The worker told Mr. A he would probably slip back into the irrational self-talk, and suggested that at least ten times a day, Mr. A should go over the rational self-analysis (RSA) homework sheet that the worker had filled out. The worker also asked Mr. A to take the tape-recorded interview with him and play it several times a day. Mr. A was asked to return in three days. The initial interview lasted two hours.

INTERVIEW TWO:

At the second interview, Mr. A said he felt "a lot better." On a couple of occasions, he had begun to feel low, but had gone over his homework sheet and had repeated the rational thoughts to himself. He had listened to the tape of the previous interview and found it helpful. The rest of the session was spent reviewing and repeating the discussion in the first session, and reviewing the homework.

INTERVIEW THREE:

Mr. A came to the third interview somewhat depressed. He had made plans to move his mother into a nursing home the next day and was worried about how she would react. He hoped she wouldn't cry or "make a scene." The worker helped Mr. A to complete an RSA homework sheet using his mother's crying as the event section. At the end of the interview, Mr. A thought he would be able to handle the nursing home move. An appointment was set for the next week.

INTERVIEW FOUR:

Mr. A said that the move had gone well and he had realized that his mother had a right to cry if she wanted to. He believed he had done the right thing for her; he felt sad that it had to happen, but not depressed. He was going to work every day, had stopped drinking, and no longer believed he was a failure. The worker suggested that Mr. A start applying his new insights and ideas in other areas of his life, and asked him to do homework on problems other than his mother's situation and to bring the homework sheets with him the next week.

INTERVIEWS FIVE, SIX, AND SEVEN:

The next three interviews were spent on rational principles to help Mr. A in other areas of his life. He said he often "got down on himself" about bills and tended to take responsibility for all family problems onto his own shoulders. As a result of his new insights, he was able to ask his wife and children for more help. His children started earning money for their own minor expenses, and Mr. A started requiring the children to do more around the house. He no longer was afraid of "emotional reactions" from his family.

TERMINATION INTERVIEW:

Mr. A said that he felt things were much better and that he no longer needed to come for social work treatment. The worker explained that because Mr. A had a long-term habit of putting himself down, it would help if he continued to do written homework.

The worker called Mr. A six months after termination. Mr. A said that "everything was fine" and that he was still doing homework.

FRED

Fred was a thirty-two-year-old graduate student of business administration who requested social work treatment after the termination of a relationship with a girlfriend whom he had wanted to marry. His major complaints included depression, problems with sleep, poor appetite, studying difficulties, and the development of an obsessive-compulsive hand-washing ritual. Fred stated that he was frightened that he would "lose his mind." He was worried that his present "condition" would cause him to "drop out of school." Fred and the worker agreed that the initial goals for treatment would be to help Fred overcome his depression, remain in graduate school, and function effectively as a student.

PSYCHOSOCIAL HISTORY:

Fred was the eldest of three children, and the only boy, born to a doctor and his wife. He was eight when the first of his two sisters was born. Fred graduated from high school and college, worked for a period of time, and then returned to graduate school. He was married for approximately two years but had no children. After he and his wife divorced, Fred "felt like a failure" and experienced depression.

Fred viewed his father as "demanding perfection and excellence." He did well in high school and college, but believed that his father was not proud of him. Fred remembered feeling "cheated" when his first sister was born. One of Fred's early recollections was of helping his father to paint a fence and being told to stop because, as Fred recalled, "I wasn't doing it right."

Life-style Assessment:

One way of understanding Fred is to view him as a young man who experiences strong feelings of inferiority. These feelings seem to stem from three major life-style themes. The first could be called the "living for a dominant other" theme. In this style of life, the individual accepts the evaluations of significant others as the total evidence upon which his or her own evaluation of the self is based. This often results in severe depression. Fred seemed to live for his father, his teachers, and the women in his life.

Fred's second major life-style theme was a low self-concept and high expectations as a part of the self-ideal. Fred seemed to have accepted that his father viewed him as inadequate and as not living up to "standards." Whether or not Fred's father actually communicated this message was not as important as the fact that Fred believed that he did, and had internalized that message.

Fred's third major life-style theme was the development of obsessive-compulsive compensation mechanisms to fend off feelings of inferiority. Over the years, Fred had developed a compulsive style of working and studying to fend off the possibility of failure. Unfortunately, this had also prevented him from enjoying study or work. After the breakup with his girlfriend, Fred developed an obsessive hand-washing ritual. This ritual served to provide Fred with a reason to avoid people and his work at school. The ritual may be understood as a sort of "side show"[12] that gave Fred a reason to avoid continued functioning. It protected him from additional inferiority feelings by providing an excuse for failure ("I couldn't do my work because of my symptoms, but I could have done this work if I did not have symptoms").

Treatment Approach:

During the first ten weeks of treatment, Fred was seen by the social worker twice a week. This was to maximize support and encourage Fred, who was grieving over the loss of his girlfriend, to continue in graduate school even though he felt depressed. Fred was also encouraged to do a half-hour of strenuous physical exercise before he went to bed. This, combined with the worker's support, helped Fred to sleep at night.

During the fourth social work treatment session, the worker said that he considered the hand-washing ritual to be a very intelligent way for Fred to protect himself from further damage to his self-esteem by providing an excuse for his failure at school (Fred was not going to classes because he could not wash his hands in class). The worker presented this interpretation as evidence of Fred's creativity, intelligence, and coping ability, and he wondered out loud whether Fred really needed or wanted to use this approach. This interpretation "made sense" to Fred; the "unconscious use" of the symptom stopped, and Fred returned to classes.

During the initial sessions, the worker helped Fred put into words the attitudes, beliefs, and assumptions that he had about himself as a result of the breakup with his girlfriend. Putting such assumptions into words creates a feedback loop that can help the client to recognize misconceptions and reorganize his or her thinking. As his attitudes were put into words, Fred was able to start reorganizing his thinking. A significant decrease in anxiety and depression occurred. By the tenth week of treatment, Fred was working well in school, was no longer feeling depressed, and wanted to discuss termination.

During the termination discussion, the social worker said that termination seemed appropriate because Fred had achieved the goals agreed upon during the initial treatment interview. The worker also said that Fred could benefit from continued treatment by trying to change his tendency to rely on others for his self-esteem and to set up unrealistic expectations for himself in his daily life. Fred was asked to return in three weeks to give the worker his decision about whether to stop or continue treatment. Fred opted for long-term social work treatment that focused upon helping to change some of his basic life-style patterns. Family assessment, early recollections, and dream interpretations were utilized to help Fred understand and reorganize his cognitive life-style assumptions and to help him develop more social interests. At the follow-up evaluation two years later, Fred reported no depression. He felt more comfortable with himself and had learned to take it easy and enjoy the "little things." He had married, had a baby, done well at his job, and was on the board of directors of a social service organization.

TREATMENT MODALITIES

The two previous clinical illustrations demonstrate the use of cognitive theory during individual social work treatment. In addition to individual treatment,[1,3,6,10,17,20,21,32,38,39,42,46,50] cognitive theory has been used in group treatment,[2,3,6,10,16,38,42] marital treatment,[2,3,6,10,25,27,28,29,32] and family treatment.[2,3,6,10,27,28,32] According to Judy Beck,[6] cognitive theory has had good results in all treatment modalities. Cognitive theory is especially useful in support groups in theme-centered groups in which the educational aspect of the treatment theory can be enhanced by group process.[6,22] Lantz[27] has presented considerable evaluation data demonstrating that cognitive-existential treatment is effective in marital and family treatment.

INDICATIONS AND CONTRAINDICATIONS

Cognitive treatment practice has been extremely well researched in a variety of treatment settings and with a variety of clients and clinical problems. According to Judy Beck,[6] cognitive theory has been shown to be especially useful in the treatment of depression, anxiety, substance abuse, and personality disorders. Cognitive theory practice is most effective with clients who have learned cognitive misconceptions and irrational thoughts.[6,10] Cognitive theory can also be used with good results as an adjunctive, existential treatment when the client is suffering with schizophrenia, biochemical depression, and/or organic mental conditions.[21] Cognitive theory should not be used as the only treatment for victims of violence. In such situations, cognitive theory is used "after" the victim of violence has been protected from the abusive person.[27]

PRACTICE APPLICATIONS

Cognitive theory can be utilized in a great number of social work practice settings. Cognitive theory social work practice has been found useful in mental health, crisis intervention, child welfare, public assistance, family service, health care, substance abuse, settlement house, and private practice settings.[6,7,9,17,20,21,22,27,31,41,43,44,47,50] Cognitive theory is compatible with social work values and can be adapted for use with a wide variety of client service requests.[6,21,32,46]

PROSPECTS

The future is hard to predict. Still, it is this author's prediction that cognitive theory will be found to be more and more useful by social work practitioners as the years go by. Cognitive theory is a flexible theory that can be adapted for use in a variety of social work settings. It can also be utilized in either short-term or long-term treatment.[6] As a result, cognitive theory practitioners often adjust well in the managed care environment.[6] Cognitive theory is compatible with existential social work, feminist social work, constructionist social work, narrative social work, and communication theory social work practice. Cognitive theory should continue to provide the social work profession with excellent practice principles and treatment activities that many generations of young social workers looking for a service orientation that is flexible and that works will appreciate, value, and use.

REFERENCES

1. Adler, A. (1959). *Understanding Human Nature*. New York: Premier Books.
2. Adler, A. (1963). *The Practice and Theory of Individual Psychology*. Patterson, NJ: Littlefield.
3. Beck, A. (1976). *Cognitive Theory and the Emotional Disorders*. New York: International Universities Press.

4.   Beck, A. (1988). *Love is Never Enough.* New York: Harper and Row.
5.   Beck, A., & Greenberg, R. (1974). *Coping with Depression.* Bala Cynwyd, PA: Beck Institute for Cognitive Therapy and Research.
6.   Beck, J. (1995). *Cognitive Therapy: Basics and Beyond.* New York: Guilford Press.
7.   Berlin, S. (1980). "A Cognitive-Learning Perspective for Social Work." *Social Service Review* 54, 537–555.
8.   Chatterjee, P. (1984). "Cognitive Theories and Social Work Practice." *Social Service Review* 58, 63–80.
9.   Combs, T. (1980). "A Cognitive Therapy for Depression: Theory, Techniques and Issues." *Social Casework* 61, 361–366.
10.   Ellis, A. (1962). *Reason and Emotion in Psychotherapy.* New York: Stuart.
11.   Epstein, L. (1980). *Helping People: The Task-Centered Approach.* St. Louis: Mosby.
12.   Furst, J. (1954). *The Neurotic—His Inner and Outer Worlds.* New York: Citadel Press.
13.   Frankl, V. (1955). *The Doctor and the Soul.* New York: Vintage.
14.   Frankl, V. (1959). *Man's Search for Meaning.* New York: Simon and Schuster.
15.   Frankl, V. (1969). *The Will to Meaning.* New York: New American Library.
16.   Glasser, W. (1965). *Reality Therapy.* New York: Harper and Row.
17.   Goldstein, H. (1981). *Social Learning and Change: A Cognitive Approach to Human Services.* Columbia: University of South Carolina Press.
18.   Goldstein, H. (1984). *Creative Change: A Cognitive-Humanistic Approach to Social Work Practice.* New York: Methuen.
19.   Krill, D. (1978). *Existential Social Work.* New York: Free Press.
20.   Lantz, J. (1975). "The Rational Treatment of Parental Adjustment Reaction to Adolescence." *Clinical Social Work Journal* 3, 100–108.
21.   Lantz, J. (1978). "Cognitive Theory and Social Casework." *Social Work* 23, 361–366.
22.   Lantz, J. (1980). "Adlerian Concepts, A Caseworker's Review." *Clinical Social Work Journal* 8, 188–197.
23.   Lantz, J. (1981). "Depression and Social Interest Tasks." *Journal of Individual Psychology* 31, 113–116.
24.   Lantz, J. (1989). "Meaning in Profanity and Pain." *Voices* 25, 34–37.
25.   Lantz, J. (1990). "Existential Reflection in Marital Therapy with Vietnam Veterans." *Journal of Couples Therapy* 1, 81–88.
26.   Lantz, J. (1993). "Existential Reflection and the Unconscious Ought." *Voices* 29, 50–55.
27.   Lantz, J. (1993). *Existential Family Therapy: Using the Concepts of Viktor Frankl.* Northvale, NJ: Jason Aronson, Inc.
28.   Lantz, J. (1994). "Primary and Secondary Reflection in Existential Family Therapy." *Contemporary Family Therapy* 16, 315–327.
29.   Lantz, J. (1994). "Marcel's Availability in Existential Psychotherapy with Couples and Families." *Contemporary Family Therapy* 16, 489–501.
30.   Lantz, J. (1995). "Frankl's Concept of Time: Existential Psychotherapy with Couples and Families." *Journal of Contemporary Psychotherapy* 25, 135–144.
31.   Lantz, J., and Werk, K. (1976). "Short Term Casework: A Rational-Emotive Approach." *Child Welfare* 55, 29–38.
32.   Lazarus, A. (1981). *The Practice of Multimodal Therapy.* Baltimore: John Hopkins University Press.
33.   Marcel, G. (1951). *Homo Viator.* Chicago: Henry Regnery Press.
34.   Marcel, G. (1956). *The Philosophy of Existence.* New York: Citadel Press.
35.   Marcel, G. (1963). *The Existential Background of Human Dignity.* Cambridge: Harvard University Press.
36.   May, R. (1979). *Psychology and the Human Dilemma.* New York: W. W. Norton.
37.   May, R. (1983). *The Discovery of Being.* New York: W. W. Norton.

38. Maultsby, M. (1975). *Help Yourself to Happiness.* New York: Institute for Rational Living.
39. Raimy, V. (1975). *Misunderstandings of the Self.* San Francisco: Jossey-Bass.
40. Reid, W. (1978). *The Task Centered System.* New York: Columbia University Press.
41. Snyder, V. (1975). "Cognitive Approaches in the Treatment of Alcoholism." *Social Casework* 56, 480–498.
42. Tosi, D. (1974). *Youth Towards Personal Growth: A Rational-Emotive Approach.* Columbus, OH: Charles C. Merrel.
43. Weiner, H., and Fox, S. (1982). "Cognitive-Behavioral Therapy with Substance Abusers." *Social Casework* 63, 564–567.
44. Werner, H. (1965). *A Rational Approach to Social Casework.* New York: Association Press.
45. Werner, H. (1982). *Cognitive Therapy: A Humanistic Approach.* New York: Free Press.
46. Werner, H. (1986). "Cognitive Therapy." In Turner, F. (ed.), *Social Work Treatment.* New Yokr: Free Press.
47. Witkin, S. (1982). "Cognitive Clinical Practice." *Social Work* 27, 389–395.
48. Yalom, I. (1980). *Existential Psychotherapy.* New York: Basic Books.
49. Yalom, I. (1989). *Love's Executioner.* New York: Basic Books.
50. Zastrow, C. (1981). "Self-Talk: A Rational Approach to Understanding and Treating Child Abuse." *Social Casework* 62, 182–185.

CHAPTER 6

COMMUNICATION THEORY AND SOCIAL WORK TREATMENT

GILBERT J. GREENE

Communications theory is very relevant to social workers because successful practice depends on our ability to communicate effectively with clients. It is a basic tenet in social work practice that clients need to feel comfortable with the worker in order to communicate openly with her or him. The social worker must know how to communicate skillfully with the client in order for the type of relationship to develop in which open client communication can occur. In addition, a common dynamic operating in clients' lives involves communication problems with significant others. Often a desired outcome of social work practice is the improvement of clients' communication skills in their everyday lives. Human communication, however, is complex and multifaceted and social workers must go beyond focusing only on their ability to develop a "helping relationship" and facilitating improved client communication skills with significant others.

Communications theory, as will be discussed in this chapter, focuses on identifying the redundant communicational patterns that are involved when the client's presenting problem is present. These redundant patterns are the *rules* governing interactions. Since these problematic patterns integrally involve the client's communications, the social worker must know how to skillfully communicate with the client in a way that interrupts these patterns, which then allows the client to develop and/or rediscover more effective ways of feeling/thinking/behaving especially in relation to other people.

The discussion is this chapter is based on the communications theory of the Mental Research Institute (MRI) in Palo Alto, California (Watzlawick, Beavin & Jackson 1967; Watzlawick & Weakland, 1977; Jackson, 1968a, b). The communications theory of the MRI grew out of the work of the anthropologist Gregory Bateson and his team of researchers based at the Veterans Administration (VA) Hospital in Palo Alto, California, beginning in 1952. The original team consisted of John Weakland, a chemical engineer and anthropologist, Jay Haley, a communications specialist, and

William Fry, a psychiatrist. Don D. Jackson, a psychiatrist, joined them in 1954, followed by Jules Riskin, also a psychiatrist, in 1957.

Bateson's work in Palo Alto, California, began as a result of a grant from the Rockefeller Foundation for a project titled "The Significance of the Paradoxes of Abstraction in Communication." Initially, the project involved anthropological research on paradoxes of abstraction in communication with nonclinical subjects and situations including communication between animals and between animals and humans (Weakland, Watzlawick, & Riskin, 1995). It was only after a couple of years of the project that Bateson and his research team started observing, filming, and studying the interactions of schizophrenics and their family members at the Palo Alto Veterans Hospital and focusing entirely on human communication, especially in regard to problematic behavior and its treatment. One of the first published papers by the members of the Bateson project (1956), "Toward a Theory of Schizophrenia," was also probably their most influential one because it introduced the concept of the *double-bind theory* as a significant factor in human relationships (this will be discussed in more detail later in this chapter). Other publications followed over the next several years as the Bateson project continued until 1962.

In 1959 Don D. Jackson left the Bateson project and started the Mental Research Institute along with Jules Riskin and Virginia Satir, a social worker; the MRI staff and members of the Bateson project continued to collaborate for several more years. Paul Watzlawick came to MRI in 1960 and Jay Haley and John Weakland in 1961 as the Bateson project was winding down (Weakland et al., 1995). After a few years at MRI, Haley and Satir left and eventually set up clinical training programs of their own. Watzlawick and Weakland continued their association with MRI. In addition, Lynn Segal, a social worker, has been closely associated with the MRI for many years.

Initially, the members of the MRI made the communications theory underpinnings of their work explicit (Watzlawick et al., 1967; Weakland, 1976; Segal & Bavelas, 1983) while also referring to their work as "the interactional view" (Watzlawick & Weakland, 1977). Communications theory is the major underpinning of the various forms of *strategic therapy*. The primary versions of strategic therapy include what has become known as the MRI approach (Segal, 1991a), the approaches of Jay Haley (1984, 1987) and Cloe Madanes (1981, 1984), and the approach of the group in Milan, Italy (the Milan approach) (Selvini Palazzoli, Boscolo, Cecchin, & Prata, 1978). The focus of this chapter, therefore, will be communications theory–based strategic therapy, especially the MRI approach.

Though there has been a significant amount of writing in social work on communication, there is only a small amount of literature on communications theory as an explicit approach to social work practice. Judith Nelsen is the person best known in the literature for using communications theory as an explicit approach to social work practice (Nelsen, 1978, 1980, 1986). There are a number of social workers, however, who have contributed to the development and practice of strategic therapy who have published in the family therapy literature rather than the social work literature. Many of these social workers include the following: Allon Bross (1982), Brian Cade (1980), David Grove (1993), Lynn Hoffman (1981), Peggy Papp (1983), Lynn Segal (1980), Olga Silverstein (1986), and Andrew Solovey (1989). In fact, Braverman (1986) has pointed out how some of the original developers of social casework utilized techniques and approaches that are consistent with the present-day practice of strategic therapy.

BASIC ASSUMPTIONS

PRAGMATICS OF HUMAN COMMUNICATION

The early work of the MRI (Watzlawick, Beavin, & Jackson, 1967) focused on the *pragmatics* of human communication; that is, how communication affects behavior. Watzlawick et al. posited that ". . . all behavior, not only speech, is communication, and all communication—even the communicational clues in an impersonal context—affects behavior" (1967, p. 22). These authors were especially concerned with how interactants mutually affect each other and not just that of a sender of a message on its receiver.

INFORMATION

One cannot discuss communication without mentioning *information*. According to Bateson (1979), information is "a difference that makes a difference" (p. 99). Information is a result of contrasting phenomena and noticing distinctions between them. This view distinguishes information from new facts. A new fact may not be information if it fits one's existing assumptions about oneself and the world. Information occurs when a communication is different from any of one's current assumptive categories. Such a communication is truly "news of difference" or "a difference that makes a difference"; it is considered to be *novelty* in view of one's current assumptive categories.

Information affects how social systems behave. Social systems and their environment mutually affect each other through feedback. Feedback involves part of a system's output being reintroduced into the system as information about the output (Watzlawick, et al., 1967, p. 31). According to Watzlawick et al. (1967), a single unit of communication is a *message* and an *interaction* is the exchange of a series of messages between two people. Over time, communicational feedback processes become redundant and patterned and these *patterns of interactions* become the *rules* (assumptions) of the system. According to Bateson (1979), systems cannot change without *information*; that is, new or *novel* input acts as a catalyst for systems to go beyond their current rules or assumptions.

THE AXIOMS OF HUMAN COMMUNICATION

At the heart of the interactional view of the MRI are their five axioms of communication. The first of these is: *One cannot* not *communicate"* (Watzlawick et al., 1967,

p. 51). In the presence of another person one cannot *not* behave nor can one not *not* communicate. Even when one is silent in the presence of another person, she or he may be communicating to the other that she or he is not interested in having a conversation at that time. The other person may give additional meaning to the situation such as deciding that the silent person may be arrogant, socially inept, or mentally ill. Problems can occur in relationships when people do not commit to making their communications clearly understood to others. One can reject, accept, or disqualify another's communication. Communications must be clear for there to be a mutual understanding of rejection or acceptance. Disqualifying a communication, however, leaves the situation ambiguous. Disqualifying communications invalidates one's own or other's communications and this can be done by a variety of ways, such as "self-contradictions, inconsistencies, subject switches, tangentializations, incomplete sentences, misunderstandings, obscure style or mannerisms of speech, the literal interpretations of metaphor and the metaphorical interpretation of literal remarks, etc." (Watzlawick et al., 1967, p. 76). One can also avoid committing to clear communication by means of symptomatic behavior which gives the responsibility to the symptom rather than the individual for not committing to clearly communicating.

The second axiom of human communication is: *"Every communication has a content and a relationship aspect such that the latter classifies the former and is therefore a metacommunication"* (Watzlawick et al., 1967, p. 54). When people communicate with each other, they are not only conveying a substantive message but they are also making a statement about the definition of the relationship (Haley, 1963); this involves communicating about the communication (Watzlawick et al., 1967). According to Haley (1963), people not only communicate substantive messages to each other, but they also communicate about their communication. Communicating about one's communication is referred to as *metacommunication* (Haley, 1963). Metacommunication involves the qualifying of messages. Communication is qualified by other verbal messages, the nonverbal communication of bodily movements, paralinguistic patterns, or the context of the communication (Haley, 1963). Problems can develop in relationships when the individuals disagree at the relationship level but they try to resolve their differences at the content level; this may result only in temporary peace in the relationship because the real differences still have not been solved.

The third axiom of communications states: *"The nature of a relationship is contingent upon the punctuation of the communicational sequences between the communicants"* (Watzlawick et al., 1967, p. 59). This axiom involves the issue of cause and effect, or blame, in relationships. Just as punctuation marks are used to break up a series of written words on a page to make sense of them, for example by indicating the beginning and ending of sentences, people break up the ongoing stream of communicating between them in order to make sense of their meaning. For instance, when a couple have an argument, they often put considerable energy into attributing blame to each other for having started it. Each person is truly convinced about the correctness of his or her view of reality. This situation occurs because each person is punctuating the sequence of events in their relationship differently. They have different but equally valid ways of "chopping up" the communicational stream in their relationship and giving meaning to them, finding a beginning (who started it) and ending to interactions.

The fourth axiom of communication holds that people communicate both *digitally and analogically*. Digital communication consists of words, which are "arbitrary signs that are manipulated according to the logical syntax of language" (Watzlawick et al., 1967, p. 61). Analogical communication, on the other hand, involves all nonverbal communication in the broadest sense, such as "posture, gesture, facial expression, voice inflection, the sequence, rhythm, and cadence of the words themselves" (Watzlawick et al., 1967, p. 62) as well as the context in which the communication takes place. This axiom is related to axiom number two in that content of messages is usually conveyed digitally and the relationship aspect of messages is conveyed analogically.

Axiom number five states: *"All communicational interchanges are either symmetrical or complementary, depending on whether they are based on equality or difference"* (Watzlawick et al., 1967, p. 70). In symmetrical communication people interact in ways that define their relationship as one between equals. In complementary communication, on the other hand, individuals interact in ways that define one person in the "one-up" position and the other in the "one-down" position. Difficulties in communications and relationships can occur when the individuals interact in ways that reflect disagreement about how the relationship is to be defined but lack *rules* for successfully metacommunicating and, thus, effectively negotiating the definition of the relationship (Watzlawick et al., 1967).

From these five axioms, it is evident that human communication occurs at different levels. Given that there are different levels, it is quite easy for confusion and ambiguity to exist in human communication and interpersonal relationships. People in relationships need to be willing and able (to be committed) to openly and directly communicate with each other (to metacommunicate) when such confusion and ambiguity inevitably arises. Failure to do so can lead to difficulties for the interactants and their relationship.

THE DOUBLE BIND

Difficulties in relationships arise in the case of the *double-bind* situation. According to Abeles (1976), "[d]ouble bind theory is about relationships, and what happens when important basic relationships are chronically subjected to invalidation through paradoxical interaction" (pp. 115–116). Watzlawick et al. (1967) define *paradox* as a "contradiction that follows correct deduction from consistent premises" (p. 188). The classic example of this is the liar's paradox where, for example, in response to the social worker's question as to the presenting problem a man replies: "I am a liar." In this case the man is telling the truth if he is lying and lying if he is telling the truth. It is a "no-win situation" for the social worker in trying to definitively decide which is true.

The double-bind situation becomes especially problematic when it characterizes the nature of the ongoing relationship between a child and his or her parents. Child development occurs in a learning context in which individuals come to answer important questions such as "who am I?" "what is expected and acceptable behavior?" or even "what is real?" In a double-bind learning context the child can never get straight answers from the parents to these all-important questions. Bateson et al. (1956) presented the "essential ingredients" of the double bind and others later elaborated on them (Sluzki, Beavin, Tarnopolsky, & Veron, 1967; Sluzki & Veron, 1971). The common elements (essential ingredients) of the double bind are the following:

1. An intense relationship involving two or more persons with one person being in a one-up position and the other person in the one-down position. Because it is an intense relationship, it is necessary for the person in the one-down position to be able to accurately interpret the messages the one-up person is giving her or him. The usual context for a person to learn a double-bind view of the world is the family of origin with a child in the one-down position and at least one parent in the one-up position. The double-binding situation may involve others such as the other parent, siblings, or a grandparent. If only one parent and a child are involved, then for the double bind to have lasting impact, it requires that no one else regularly intervene to neutralize the impact of the double-binding situation.

2. Double-binding dynamics involve the person in the one-up position (the parent) giving the child in the one-down position messages (injunctions), usually verbal, about how to feel, think, or behave appropriately (what to do or not do). In order to "motivate" the child, the parent consistently uses punishment or threats of punishment and never rewards, thus creating a learning context based on avoidance of punishment rather than reward seeking. In regard to this, Bateson et al. (1956) state "that the punishment may be either the withdrawal of love or the expression of hate or anger—or most devastating—the kind of abandonment that results from the parent's expression of extreme helplessness" (p. 253).

3. At the same time the parent is giving the child verbal messages, he or she is also sending another message, usually nonverbal, that conflicts with the verbal message. The nonverbal message may be communicated by means of "[p]osture, gesture, tone of voice, meaningful action, and the implications concealed in verbal comment" (Bateson et al., 1956, p. 254).

4. All parents sometimes give conflicting messages and are inconsistent. What makes a situation a double bind is the inability of the child to escape the situation or get clarity about the conflicting messages by metacommunicating. A very young child may not be able to escape because of dependency on the parent for survival. For someone older the escape may be made impossible "by certain devices which are not purely negative, e.g., capricious promises of love, and the like" (Bateson et al., 1956, p. 254). Also in the double-bind situation, if the child comments on the conflicting messages and/or tries to gets clarification from the parent about their communications (he or she metacommunicates), the parent will deny he is giving conflicting messages and/or verbally attack the child for even questioning him. Because the child can never get a straight an-

swer, she or he is in an impossible, paradoxical, no-win situation—the child is "damned if she or he does and damned if she or he doesn't."

5. For the child to learn to perceive the world through a double-bind lens in a lasting way, double-bind experiences must be repeated and pervasive.

The double-binding situation is confusing and disorienting for the person, resulting in his being very prone to experiencing anxiety, panic, and rage (Bateson et al., 1956). After a person learns to experience the world in double-bind communicational patterns, he is then hypersensitive to experiencing double-binding communications from others even when such messages are not present. Consequently, the person comes to distrust most communication from other people, even when it is direct, clear, and consistent. A result of the person in the "one-down" position developing such a double-bind view of the world is that now the person in the "one-up" position will get double-bind messages from the person in the "one-down" position. Consequently, a pattern of reciprocal double-bind messages between the two or more people is now set. No longer is one person in the one-up position and the other in the one-down position—they are now stuck in this pattern together (Elkaim, 1990).

In illustrating the double bind, Bateson et al. (1956, pp. 256–258) provide an example of a parent having strong feelings, such as hostility or affection, toward the child and also feeling a strong need to withdraw from the child. But instead of the parent saying something like "Go away, I need some alone time," she says, "Go to bed, you're tired and I want you to get your sleep." This loving statement may disguise the parent's true feelings of "Get out of my sight because I'm sick of you." If the child is able to accurately perceive the parent's true feelings, then he or she would have to accept the fact that his or her parent does not want him or her around and is using a loving statement to deceive him or her. If the child takes the parent's "loving" statement at face value, he or she might seek more closeness with the parent and this in turn might provoke the parent to withdraw even more. If the child withdraws, the parent might interpret this as the child seeing the parent as unloving, which is unacceptable to the parent, who then might get angry with the child. If the child were to comment on what is going on or ask for clarification from the parent as to what he or she really means, the parent might accuse the child of being unloving or bad or somehow deficient for even questioning the parent. The child, then, might find it easier to just accept the parent's definition of how the child is feeling. The child, therefore, is punished for accurately discriminating what the parent is expressing but also punished for inaccurately discriminating and, thus, is in a double bind (Bateson et al., 1956, 256–258).

PROBLEMS AND SYMPTOMS

A usual result of a child growing up in an ongoing double-bind situation is symptomatic behavior of various forms. Though it was originally conceptualized as significantly contributing to the etiology of schizophrenia, Sluzki and Veron (1971) see the double-bind situation as a significant contributing factor in the etiology of all clinical disorders. According to Haley (1963), problematic symptoms are likely to develop when a person's behavior has extreme influence on another person and the symptomatic person indicates that she or he cannot help it; that is, the person exhibits the symptomatic behavior "involuntarily." From the communications theory perspective, symptomatic behavior involves incongruence between levels of messages. In this situation the symptomatic person "does something extreme, or avoids doing something, and indicates that he is not doing it because he cannot help himself" [sic] (Haley, 1963, p. 5). Symptomatic behavior, therefore, is very likely to occur in relationships in which the individuals are not able to establish a mutual definition of their relationship through direct communication (Haley, 1963). Developing symptoms is a way for one person to control the definition of the relationship while at the same time denying that he or she is doing so (Haley, 1963).

A by-product of symptomatic behavior is that it makes the social world of the symptom-bearer and her or his significant others more predictable (Haley, 1963). Another significant by-product of symptomatic behavior is it "protects" significant others of the symptom bearer from having to face their own issues such as depression, anxiety, insecurity, incompetence, low self-esteem, and so on (Haley, 1963). This situation is not something the symptom bearer has consciously decided or openly discussed with his or her significant other(s) but is an unspoken *quid pro quo* (Haley, 1963; Jackson, 1965). At the same time, however, having symptoms is usually very unpleasant not only for the person with the symptoms but for the significant people in his or her social world.

FIRST- AND SECOND-ORDER CHANGE

Because of the unpleasantness of the situation, the person with the problem usually will make various efforts to solve the problem and get rid of the symptoms; significant others, out of caring and concern, or a need for relief themselves, will do likewise. However, the attempts by the person with the problem and/or the significant others often do not result in the desired changes. In an effort to bring about change in the situation, the problematic person and/or the significant others often will increase their efforts to make changes. Often these increased attempts to solve the problem still do not result in the desired changes. When such a situation occurs, many people will try even harder to make change using even more of the same ineffective solutions, still resulting in no change. After a while, those involved in the problematic situation find themselves stuck in a "vicious cycle" whereby, unknown to them, the attempts to solve the problem are maintaining the problem such that now "the solution is the problem." The MRI approach refers to their repetitive pattern of using even "more of the same" ineffective solutions to a problem as *first-order change* (Watzlawick, & Fisch, 1974).

First-order change is change that is attempted according to the rules or assumptions a client system has about change. These attempts at change are logical and commonsensical to the client system because they are in keeping with one's assumptions about change. Consequently, the problematic person and/or the significant others assume that if a little of an attempted solution does not get results, then "more of the same" needs to be applied to the problem, and if this does not get results, then one should try even harder at making change but by using even more of the same attempted solutions. Frequently, first-order change involves applying the opposite of the problem. For example, a person experiencing insomnia may consciously and willfully try to make himself go to sleep or parents may use rational appeals to teenagers to change when they think the teenagers are thinking irrationally and behaving irresponsibly. Some other common attempts that result in first-order change are giving advice, nagging, punishing, appealing to another logically and rationally, lecturing and teaching, and so on. The result is that "things change but everything remains the same" (Watzlawick et al., 1974, p. 1).

Attempts at first-order change introduce no novelty into the client system and, thus, they are assimilated according to one's assumptions about the world, usually resulting in no change occurring (Dowd & Pace, 1989). Client systems get stuck in the vicious cycle of first-order change when they do not have enough flexibility to allow themselves to step outside their situation to look at it from a new perspective. What they are lacking is a rule for changing the rules (a metarule) regarding problem solving. In order to change the rules, those within the problematic situation must be able to communicate about their communication (metacommunicate) and, thus, the rules. Without a metarule (the ability to metacommunicate), change cannot be generated by those operating within the assumptive world (the rules) of that system. To break such an impasse, the client system needs to experience *second-order change* (Dowd & Pace, 1989; Watzlawick et al., 1974).

Second-order change is change that is outside the client system's current rules (assumptions); it results in an expansion and increasing complexity in the rules (assumptions). The catalyst for such change is the introduction of novelty (a difference that makes a difference) to the client from his or her environment to which the client has to accommodate (Dowd & Pace, 1989). Because second-order change is beyond the client's current assumptive world, she or he will usually initially experience it as illogical, uncommonsensical, perhaps even weird and/or radical, resulting in some degree of disequilibrium. Once the client successfully accommodates to the novelty, he or she will experience growth, development, and change (Dowd & Pace, 1989).

TREATMENT

The various approaches to strategic therapy focus on resolving the presenting problem as defined by the client. A more important focus for intervention is the pattern of attempted solutions that are maintaining the problem. Therefore, the clinician needs to develop and implement interventions that will interrupt these rigid problem-maintaining patterns and this in turn opens the door for clients to try something new and different. The pragmatic orientation of the MRI approach posits that if what one is doing is not getting results, then one needs to stop doing it and try something different (Fisch et al., 1982). This pragmatic position holds very true for the social worker using a strategic approach to practice and is quite different from most other theoretical approaches (Dowd & Pace, 1989).

Dowd and Pace (1989) state that most approaches to treatment use first-order change interventions in trying to bring about client change. They are first-order interventions in that they: are logical and commonsensical, try to bring about the opposite of the problem, focus primarily on making change in the problem, and tend to utilize more of the same ineffective interventions when clients do not respond to or are noncompliant with (resist) treatment. What is needed, according to Dowd and Pace (1989), is the use of interventions that will result in second-order change. Second-order interventions focus on making changes in the attempted solutions rather than the presenting problem. Of course, if the client, his or her significant others, or the social worker use very different types of solutions to the problem, then resolution of the problem should result.

THE STAGES OF TREATMENT

In keeping with its pragmatic orientation, MRI strategic therapy organizes treatment in a stepwise approach. The following is an adaptation of the MRI stages of treatment (Nardone & Watzlawick, 1993): (1) join the client system; (2) define the problem; (3) define the outcome goal; (4) identify attempted solutions; (5) develop and implement change strategies; (6) termination.

Joining the client system is analogous to developing the therapeutic relationship. A social worker must know how to communicate so that the client feels comfortable with the social worker and experiences him or her as trustworthy. The development of joining is facilitated when the social worker demonstrates empathy, acceptance, support, and genuineness, and maintains a focus. Joining is enhanced when the social worker "matches" the client nonverbally and "uses the client's language" (Nardone & Watzlawick, 1993); this involves initially adopting the clients' verbal and nonverbal styles of communicating. In using the client's language the social worker must observe and listen carefully for the client's metaphors, figures of speech, and concepts of reality. This approach to practice is quite different from most others which usually require the client to learn to speak the language of whatever theoretical approach the clinician is using. According to Nardone and Watzlawick (1993), research has consistently found that people are made to feel most comfortable by things familiar and/or similar to them. Initially adopting the client's verbal and nonverbal communication style communicates such familiarity and similarity.

Defining the problem involves getting a concrete and specific definition and description from the client. Problems can fall within three general categories: (1) a person's relationship with herself or himself, (2) a person's relationship with others, and (3) a person's relationship with the world, which involves "the social environment, the values and norms of the social context within which the person lives" (Nardone & Watzlawick, 1993, p. 49). Eliciting a concrete and specific definition of the problem involves the social worker obtaining the following information from the client:

(1) how does the client define the problem? (2) how is the problem manifested? (3) who is involved when the problem appears, worsens, or does not appear? (4) where does the problem usually appear? (5) in what situations does the problem occur? (6) how and how often does the problem manifest itself? (7) whom or what does the problem benefit? (8) what would be the negative consequences if the problem disappeared? (Nardone & Watzlawick, 1993, p. 50). In other words, the problem needs to be defined from the client's perspective as concretely and specifically as possible in terms of who, what, where, when, how, and how often.

Defining the outcome goal also needs to be done as concretely and specifically as possible and from the client's perspective. In defining the goal the social worker is asking the client to describe a future in which the problem no longer exists or at least has been significantly reduced to the client's satisfaction. In addition, outcome goals should be defined in the positive rather than the absence of something. The goal provides a specific focus for treatment and provides a basis for evaluating practice (Greene, 1989; Nardone & Watzlawick, 1993). Setting a specific outcome goal also is an indirect use of visualization in that the client, in describing a future without the problem, must imagine what this will be like for him or her and significant others. In addition, the worker and client mutually discussing and agreeing upon the focus of treatment can increase the client's cooperation in and commitment to successfully achieving the outcome goal (Nardone & Watzlawick, 1993).

To achieve as much specificity and concreteness as possible in defining an outcome goal, the MRI approach advocates asking the client what she or he would consider to be the first minimal indicator of change. To obtain this the worker could ask the client: "What, if it were to happen, would you see as a first sign that a significant—though maybe small—change had occurred? (Fisch, Weakland, & Segal, 1982, p. 79)" or "What would be the first minimal change to occur that would indicate you were starting to turn the corner towards some meaningful change?" Such a question breaks down the problem and goal further and increases the likelihood of the client achieving and experiencing some success early in the treatment.

Identifying attempted solutions indicates how the client and/or significant others are caught up in a vicious cycle of first-order change. At this point the social worker wants to know what the client and significant others have been doing in attempting to solve the presenting problem and reach the desired goal. By identifying the attempted solutions of first-order change the clinician initially learns what types of interventions to avoid using; Fisch et al. (1982) refer to this as the "mine field" (p. 114). The MRI approach assumes that the problem-maintaining patterns of the vicious cycle may have nothing to do with what got the entire process going in the first place. Therefore, it is not necessary to investigate a client's intrapsychic world or past history (Nardone & Watzlawick, 1993, p. 52).

The *development and implementation of change strategies* follows from the assessed problem, goal, and attempted solutions. For a client system stuck in a vicious cycle, the change strategies usually must be of a second-order nature to bring about lasting positive change. Second-order change strategies tend to be the opposite of the problem-maintaining attempted solutions involved in the vicious cycle; conse-quently, interventions focus primarily on interrupting the attempted solution(s) (Fisch et al., 1982). Strategic therapy assumes that clients have the resources to make desired changes once the vicious cycle is disrupted. As a general rule, the clinician's initial intervention(s) should seek only small change (Fisch et al., 1982). Clients are much more likely to comply with requests for small change and this can set change processes in motion which gets the momentum going toward larger change (Fisch et al., 1982). Some specific second-order change interventions will be discussed below.

A strategic approach to treatment tends to be *briefer* than most other approaches because it is problem- and goal-focused and the primary interventions are tasks clients carry out in their everyday lives. The treatment relationship, therefore, is viewed as important in facilitating client compliance with the tasks rather than being the primary vehicle for client change. Consequently, *termination of treatment* is not a significant issue as it is in many other therapeutic approaches (Fisch et al., 1982). Given that the clinician and client keep a focus on resolving the presenting problem and achieving the outcome goal throughout treatment, the stage is set for terminating treatment when this has been accomplished (Fisch et al., 1982). When a presenting problem and outcome goal are concretely and specifically defined by the client, then both the clinician and client will more likely be aware of when this has been achieved and treatment is no longer necessary.

THE TECHNIQUES AND STRATEGIES

A strategic approach to treatment is a way of thinking and, thus, provides more than just a list of interventions. In this section of the chapter, however, some commonly used strategic interventions will be reviewed. A strategic approach to treatment has generated numerous interventions over the years. The interventions of a strategic approach to treatment can be grouped into four categories: (1) reframing; (2) restraint from change; (3) positioning; and (4) behavioral prescriptions (Dowd & Pace, 1989).

Reframing

Reframing involves the clinician offering a plausible, alternative meaning to some aspect of the "facts" of the client's presenting problematic situation. Therefore, the "facts" of the situation do not change but rather the meaning attributed to them by the client and/or significant others (Watzlawick et al., 1974). Most of the reframing involves the clinician taking the "facts" of the presenting situation the client and/or significant others have defined negatively and providing a positive meaning to them; this has also been referred to as positive connotation (Selvini Palazzoli et al., 1978). It is important that the clinician offer the plausible, alternative meaning in a tentative manner in order to avoid an unnecessary power struggle with the client over its rightness or wrongness. When reframing is successful, clients cannot return to their previous narrow view of reality that contributed to the problem-maintaining vicious cycles (Watzlawick et al., 1974). The suggested positive reframe may introduce enough novelty to the client's assumptive world that it will start to put a small "chink" in the client's habitual problem maintaining patterns (Nardone & Watzlawick, 1993).

An example of reframing used in family therapy would be suggesting that a six-year-old child's acting out could be a result of caring for and protecting a depressed parent. When the child acts out, the parent gets angry at him or her and, thus, the child's misbehavior mobilizes the parent out of his or her depression. The parent being angry is also reassuring to the child, since usually children would rather have their parents angry at them than see them depressed.

Restraint from Change

Restraining clients from changing can be useful in the initial sessions and later when positive change is beginning to occur. Restraint from change interventions can take several forms with some of the more commonly used ones involving the clinician suggesting to the client that "she or he, for now, should probably go slowly in trying to make changes" or "it might not be a good idea to try to make too many changes too quickly." Restraining interventions can be helpful with compliant clients who present problems that are at least partially maintained by the attempts to keep them from happening such as obsessive thinking, anxiety, and insomnia (Teenen, Eron, & Rohrbaugh, 1991, p. 197); complying with such restraints will short-circuit the problem-maintaining patterns.

Restraining interventions are also useful with clients who tend to be oppositional and noncompliant (resistant) in that one way they can oppose the clinician is by taking some steps in the direction from which the clinician is restraining them. For clients who have not complied with homework tasks and/or are ambivalent about changing, it might be helpful for the clinician to restrain change by discussing with them "the possible dangers of improvement" and/or the "possible benefits of not changing." An intervention such as this is the opposite of the clients' significant others who have been trying to get the clients to change by focusing only on the benefits of changing.

Restraint from change is helpful when clients have high expectations from themselves or others for change. Frequently clients respond with relief when the clinician uses a restraint from change intervention. Clients can experience the clinician as accepting and nonjudgmental when the clinician, unlike themselves and others, will not be putting high expectations on them for immediate change; this can also facilitate the joining process and client cooperation with treatment. Clinicians often have a tendency to have expectations for even more change once clients start to make some positive changes. Sometimes change, even small change, needs time to stabilize; restraint from change allows such stabilization to occur. In addition, if clients tend to be oppositional, they may make even more positive changes, which is what one wants to have occur in treatment in the first place.

Positioning

Often the problem-maintaining pattern involves the client's friends, family members, and others consistently communicating their optimism that the client can and will get better. The client's response to such optimism is pessimism. However, the more optimistic the significant others are, the more the client responds with pessimism, resulting in an ongoing, spiraling vicious cycle. One way to begin to disrupt this vicious cycle is for the clinician to take an even more pessimistic position than the client. The clinician can do this after listening to the client's story about his or her interventions with significant others about the problem and then responding with something like "Instead of being all that optimistic about your situation, Mr. Jones, actually I'm surprised that things aren't really worse than you say they are." In situations in which the client has experienced a number of "treatment failures," the clinician might want to add that "perhaps all we might realistically be able to accomplish in our work together is for you to learn to live with your situation." The clinician's communication of pessimism greater than the client's then invites the client to challenge the clinician's pessimism with optimism. Positioning can be especially helpful with oppositional clients who are "help-rejecting complainers" (those who play the "Yes, but" game with helpers).

Behavioral Prescriptions
Many approaches to practice believe that clients will make desired changes if they understand "why" they currently behave as they do (develop insight). Strategic therapy, on the other hand, believes that insight is not necessary for change to occur and if the client does develop insight he or she will do so after having made some desired behavioral changes (Nardone & Watzlawick, 1993). To bring about these changes, the strategic approach advocates using behavioral prescriptions (Nardone & Watzlawick, 1993), which are also referred to as directives (Haley, 1987).

Clinicians can use prescriptions *directly* by giving the client good advice and information in order to try to bring about desired change. Offering advice to clients about how to change usually will be ineffective because by the time they enter treatment other people have already given them a lot of advice which the clients have not followed (Haley, 1987). Giving advice usually involves telling clients how they can stop having the problem and symptoms. Such advice and information are first-order change interventions which most theoretical approaches emphasize in one form or another (Dowd & Pace, 1989). Though the advice and information may be correct, many clients do not comply because they experience it as being critical and judgmental of them. Clients may not comply with such advice and information as a way to maintain some dignity and self-esteem (Green, 1996). In addition, clients may not comply with such direct interventions as a result of the double-binding communications they received during their developmental years in the family of origin. They have learned to perceive the world through double-binding lenses and thus tend not to trust direct communications; they tend to be on guard against the "hidden message."

Behavioral prescriptions can also involve second-order change and are considered to be *paradoxical.* A therapeutic paradox (double bind) is the mirror image of the pathological paradox (double bind) (Hoffman, 1981). In the pathological paradox the client when growing up was given prescriptions in the family of origin about how to feel, think, and behave appropriately. However, when the client did what was ap propriate, he or she was ignored, criticized, or punished for not performing in the right way or not having the right motivations. Therefore, in the family of origin, the child was told verbally to "change" but the nonverbal context said "don't change." In the therapeutic paradox, the client, in so many words, receives the message of "don't change" in a context for change (Hoffman, 1981).

Therapeutic paradox involves prescribing a change in either the usual pattern and/or sequence around the exhibition of the presenting problem or the frequency or intensity of the problem itself. The clinician does not explicitly focus on trying to improve the presenting problem but rather focuses on just changing some small aspect of the Gestalt of the problematic situation. In doing so, the clinician asks the client to go ahead and have the problem/symptom but to modify its performance in some way. Therefore, instead of directly trying to get the client to stop having the problem, the clinician "goes with the resistance" and utilizes the problem (symptom) in the service of the changes the client desires. A properly designed therapeutic paradox (double bind) results in the following: if the client complies with the prescription, the problem-maintaining pattern will be interrupted and thus change will begin occurring; however, if the client does not follow the clinician's prescription, then the only way he or she can resist is by making some changes in the desired direction. In the therapeutic paradox (double bind) the client is "changed if she or he does or changed if she or he doesn't," which is contrary to the pathological paradox (double bind) in which the client is "damned if she or he does or damned if she or he doesn't." Such a prescription can also contribute to change because the client is now asked to voluntarily perform an aspect of the presenting problem which previously had been defined as being entirely "involuntary" (Haley, 1987; Nardone & Watzlawick, 1993).

Cade and O'Hanlon (1993), in discussing designing paradoxical prescriptions, listed several general ways to do so (taken from O'Hanlon, 1987, pp. 36–37):

- Changing the frequency/rate of the symptoms/symptom-pattern.
- Changing the duration of the symptom/symptom-pattern.
- Changing the time (of day/week/month/year) of the symptom/symptom-pattern.
- Changing the location (in the body or [geographically]) of the symptom/symptom-pattern
- Changing the intensity of the symptom/symptom-pattern
- Changing some other quality or circumstance of the symptom.
- Changing the sequence (order) of events around the symptom.
- Creating a short-circuit in the sequence (i.e., a jump from the beginning of the sequence to the end).
- Interrupting or otherwise preventing all or part of the sequence from occurring ("derailing").
- Adding or subtracting (at least) one element to or from the sequence.
- Breaking up any previously whole element into smaller elements.
- Having the symptom performed without the symptom-pattern.
- Having the symptom-pattern performed minus the symptom.

- Reversing the pattern.
- Linking the occurrence of the symptom-pattern to another pattern—usually an undesired experience, an avoided activity, or a desirable but difficult-to-attain goal ("symptom-contingent task").

Most therapeutic paradoxes involve prescribing some change in the patterns and sequences around the problem. Such second-order change prescriptions are considered to be *indirect*, since change in the presenting problem occurs because of first focusing on making some change in the problem-maintaining patterns (Nardone & Watzlawick, 1993). There is no limit to the types of indirect prescriptions. The indirect prescriptions that can be used are limited to the nature of clients' presenting problems, problem-maintaining patterns, and the creativity of clinicians. Additional indirect prescriptions have been developed and some are briefly described below.

Advertising instead of concealing: Some problems are made worse by individuals trying to conceal them. For instance, it is not unusual for someone with an anxiety or phobia to try to conceal and control it when in the presence of other people. However, one can become more anxious worrying about whether the anxiety will become evident. In other words, one gets anxious about being anxious (anticipatory anxiety). Consequently, such a person can become so anxious that the feared event happens anyway. One way to deal with this situation is for the person to announce the existence of the anxiety and fears one has about it right off to others, to deliberately perform the very thing she or he fears. One example given by Watzlawick et al. (1974) is anxiety about public speaking. The more one tries to relax and conceal anxiety about speaking publicly, the more tense and anxious one becomes and the less effective the speaking becomes. An opposite approach would be for the person to say something (very calm and straight-faced) like the following: "Before I start my speech there is one thing I would like to tell the group. I get very anxious when I give a speech. I just want to forewarn you that I could get so anxious that I might faint and pass out. But don't worry, I usually recover quickly and give an even better speech from that point on." The audience is very likely to laugh at this and so will the speaker, thus becoming more relaxed. By performing this prescription, the client is able to make voluntary what previously had been considered involuntary, thus allowing the client to gain some control over the "uncontrollable." Even if a person does not follow through on this prescription, just suggesting it to a client can be therapeutic because she or he most likely will be thinking of this suggestion and chuckling inside and feeling more relaxed when preparing for and giving a speech.

The great effects of small causes: Another way a person can escalate anxiety is by being "perfectionistic." This can be problematic on the job whereby a person constantly worries that he or she will make a mistake, be considered incompetent, and be fired from the job. The more the client worries about this, the more tense and anxious he or she becomes and the less he or she likes the job. Eventually, worry and anxiety about job performance can occupy most of the client's nonworking time as well. One way of helping the client deal with this "no win" situation is to suggest that he or she purposely make one small, inconsequential mistake every day on the job. Again, the client deliberately performs voluntarily what heretofore had been defined as being involuntary and thus the client is able to have some control over the "uncontrollable" (Watzlawick et al., 1974).

A version of this intervention can be applied to clients who are underachieving academically. A dynamic in this situation is a perfectionistic client who procrastinates in studying and doing course assignments. Students such as this often have exceptionally high standards and pressure themselves for nothing less than "A" work. Because of the pressure and fear of doing less than "A" work, the student puts off doing the schoolwork until the last possible minute and ends up doing mediocre work. In this situation, the clinician can instruct the student for his or her next assignment to deliberately try to do only "C" work. Aiming for a grade of only "C" takes the pressure off the student and allows her or him to actually enjoy doing the assignment. Following this prescription usually results in the student decreasing procrastination and increasing his academic performance.

The devil's pact: An underlying issue involved in clients' staying stuck is their unwillingness to take risks necessary for change to occur. It could be said that always playing it safe is the attempted solution maintaining the problem. This dynamic is often seen in clients who are "help-rejecting complainers." Nothing a clinician suggests seems appropriate for them. Sometimes they may have agreed to a homework assignment but did not follow through on it. Despite their resistance, they are still reporting unhappiness with the status quo and a strong desire for relief. In the devil's pact, clients are asked to agree to carry out a task that is guaranteed to bring about change but they must agree to do it before the clinician will tell them what it is. If the clients make such an agreement, then some change has already occurred since they now have taken the risk of agreeing to an intervention before knowing what it is. In this instance they did not play it safe. After they make this agreement, the task the clinicians asks them to do can be any number of possibilities. It is best to use the devil's pact toward the end of a session, thus not telling them what the sure-fire intervention is, and suggest they think about it between sessions to ensure they are making the right decision. This heightens their anticipation and, thus, willingness to change.

Odd-day/even-day ritual: In this prescription, the client is asked to perform one behavior on one day and another behavior, usually the opposite, on another day. With an individual client, the clinician asks him or her to perform the problematic behavior on odd-numbered days and the desired outcome behavior on even-numbered days. This prescription helps to reduce client resistance and increase risk taking in that she or he is asked to make desired changes in half-steps rather than full-steps (Bergman, 1983). In addition, clients are more likely to comply since change is requested to last for no more than one day (Bergman, 1983).

A version of this prescription can be used in family therapy, in which a child is getting contradictory (double binding) messages from parents and the parents are making no efforts to reconcile their inconsistencies (Selvini Palazzoli, Boscolo, Cecchin, & Prata, 1978). In this case one parent is instructed that on even days of the week (Tuesdays, Thursdays, and Saturdays) she or he is to be completely in charge of parenting and the other parent is to behave as if she or he were not there. On odd days of the week the other parent is to be completely in charge of parenting and the first parent is to behave as if he or she is not there. On Sundays, everyone in the family must spontaneously do what they usually do. This prescription can be adapted for use with single-parent families when a grandparent is giving the child messages that contradict the parent. Another adaptation of this can be used when a single parent is giving the child inconsistent messages. For example, the single parent can be asked to be strict and firm with the child on even days and lenient on odd days.

Two other skills the clinician can use throughout working with clients are "taking a one-down position" and "using qualifying language" (Fisch et al., 1982). In the treatment situation the clinician is inherently in a one-up, authority position and the client feels in a one-down position by the very nature of having a problem(s) necessitating professional help. Such an arrangement may increase client resistance and decrease cooperation since people often resent experts and authorities (Fisch et. al., 1982), especially while feeling one-down. In order to counter this barrier, it is helpful for the clinician to take a *one-down position*. The one-down position is often subtly conveyed and can be expressed in a variety of ways. An example of taking a one-down position is: "I'm sorry but I'm a fairly concrete kind of person in my thinking, so please bear with me while I ask some questions which may seem to be nitpicky." The one-down position can also be used at those times when the client asks the clinician early in treatment what he or she should do in a particular situation. The clinician can respond with. "I really can't say right now. I am still getting to know you and you are the expert on you. You know more about yourself than anyone else, so I need your help in getting to know you better."

In *using qualifying language* the clinician refrains from taking a definitive position, thus preventing an unnecessary power struggle with the client (Fisch et al., 1982). In qualifying comments and suggestions, the clinician uses such words as "may," "depends upon," "if," and so on. By using such qualifying words, the clinician can introduce novel ideas or behaviors so that the client cannot reject them outright just because they came from the clinician. Clients are much more likely to consider the ideas or try the suggestions if they feel that they have the freedom to reject them. An example of using qualifying language is: "I have some ideas about your situation which may or may not be true or helpful. I have found what I am about to say and suggest to be true and helpful for some clients I have worked with who have had problems similar to yours, but this may not be the case in your situation—it is just food for thought at this time." Another example is: "I have a suggestion to make, but I'm not sure how much it will accomplish. It will depend on your ability to use your imagination and, perhaps, on your readiness to take a step toward improvement." (Fisch et al., 1982, p. 31).

PRINCIPAL APPLICATIONS IN SOCIAL WORK PRACTICE

Strategic therapy provides a way of viewing problem formation and problem resolution involving both clinician and nonclinical situations. In regard to use with various client configurations, the MRI/strategic approach has been used extensively in clinical practice with individuals (Fisch, Weakland, & Segal, 1982), couples (Coyne, 1986; Green & Bobele, 1988), and families in general (Hansen & L'Abate, 1928; Segal, 1980, 1991; Segal & Bavelas, 1983) and single-parent families in particular (Bray & Anderson, 1984; Morawitz & Walker, 1984). The discussion of the use of the strategic approach in working with organizations and communities has not been as extensive. In two early books, the members of MRI used a number of organizational and community examples to explain and illustrate various concepts (Watzlawick, Beavin, & Jackson, 1967; Watzlawick, Weakland, & Fisch, 1974).

Some specific strategic therapy concepts and interventions have been used in assessing and intervening in organizations and communities. Reframing has been systematically applied as a skill in leading and managing organizations (Bolman & Deal, 1991; Fairhurst & Sarr, 1996). The double-bind concept has been used to examine intra- and interorganizational dynamics (Markowitz & Nitzberg, 1982) and the dynamics of community change (Andelson, 1981). Bartunek and Moch (1987) have added the notion of third-order change to first- and second-order change in facilitating organizational development. In addition, strategic therapy has been used to effect changes in individuals within organizations as well as in the organizations themselves (Brandon, 1985; Morrissette, 1989; Schindler-Zimmerman, Washle, & Protinsky, 1990; Woodruff & Engle, 1985).

There is not an extensive literature on the application of the strategic approach to larger systems and communities. The concepts of first- and second-order change have been adapted and applied in discussions of first-, second-, and third-order reality (Greene, 1996; Keeney, 1987; Keeney & Silverstein, 1986). First-order reality deals with discrete behaviors of individuals; second-order reality is the interactional pattern in which discrete behaviors are a part; and, third-order reality is the larger social ecology in which the interactional pattern is one of several patterns. What is involved here are levels of reality that are increasingly complex; the communicational patterns at the higher levels can override what takes place at the lower levels. The implication for social work treatment is that if interventions at a lower level are not effective, then interventions at the next higher level may be necessary. Therefore, first-order reality involves intervening with individuals, second-order reality involves treatment of couples and the nuclear family, and third-order reality involves intervening with extended family and/or the parts of the larger community impinging upon the client system. Keeney's model as well as MRI/strategic therapy have considerable potential for macro-level social work practice. For instance, Allen (1987) has pointed out how a strategic perspective can be used in viewing and bringing about large-scale change.

The strategic approach has been used successfully with a variety of presenting problems and types of clients social workers often treat: depression (Chubb, 1982), poststroke depression (Watzlawick & Coyne, 1980), suicidal behavior (Aldridge & Rossiter, 1983), anxiety-related somatic complaints (Greene & Sattin, 1985), chronic pain (Shutty & Sheras, 1991), chronic physical illness (Norfleet, 1983), alcoholism (Fisch, 1986; Potter-Efron & Potter-Efron, 1986), chemical dependency (McGarty,

1986), adolescent substance abuse (Heath & Ayers, 1991), vague medical problems (Weakland & Fisch, 1984), child protective services (Weakland & Jordan, 1992), severe mental disability (Bergman, 1982; Haley, 1980; Soo-Hoo, 1995), children (Chubb, 1983; Efron, 1981; Zimmerman & Protinsky, 1990), older adults (Herr & Weakland, 1979), crisis intervention (Fraser, 1986), eating disorders (Moley, 1983), marital problems (Madanes, 1980), school behavior problems (Amatea, 1989), and psychosis (Haley & Schiff, 1993). Because strategic therapy focuses on interrupting problem-maintaining patterns rather than treating diagnoses, it has wide application. Therefore, if used properly, the strategic approach is not contraindicated for use with any type of client problem. With some presenting problems such as suicidal ideation or substance abuse, however, one needs to be careful to not prescribe the symptom but rather a change in some aspect of the problem-maintaining pattern or context. Changing some aspect of the pattern/context of drinking might introduce enough novelty to the client that small, positive change occurs.

ADMINISTRATIVE AND TRAINING FACTORS

One must be able to use a number of skills and techniques with a high degree of competence and finesse in order to do strategic therapy competently. To develop such competence, one needs specific training in and supervision on strategic therapy. The MRI group (Fisch, 1988), Haley and Madanes (Mazza, 1988), and the Milan group (Pirrotta & Cecchin, 1988) have been providing systematic training and supervision in their approaches to strategic therapy for many years. Many graduates of these programs have gone on and established training and supervision programs of their own. Though these three training programs differ in various ways, they all have the following in common: (1) required reading; (2) role play; (3) watching videotapes of the clinical work of others; (4) observing the clinical work of others from behind a one-way mirror; (5) having their own clinical work observed by others from behind a one-way mirror; (6) interrupting sessions to give the trainee suggestions and corrective feedback; and (7) having videotapes of one's own clinical work viewed and critiqued.

Other learning activities can be used if one does not have the time or money to receive training and supervision at one of these strategic therapy programs. A person can receive training and supervision at the place of employment if there is a supervisor who is competent in strategic therapy. Also, one can do cotherapy and/or form a peer supervision group with other social workers who want to learn strategic therapy and are at a similar level of competence (Rabi, Lehr, & Hayner, 1984). This peer supervision group can view and critique videotapes of each other's clinical work and/or once or twice a month take turns observing from behind a one-way mirror. In addition, one can attend workshops on strategic therapy as well as rent or purchase videotapes developed by the experts. Finally, of course, one should read as much as possible on the topic of strategic therapy.

As mentioned previously, strategic therapy has been used in a wide variety of practice settings with a wide variety of clients and client problems. However, a social worker who is the only one using strategic therapy in an agency can expect some fall-out and reaction from co-workers, supervisors, and administrators (Held, 1982). A strategic approach is such a different paradigm than other theoretical approaches that our professionals in the agency may have no idea what *you* the clinician is doing and, therefore, may criticize the clinician's work. One can feel isolated and frustrated if he or she is the only strategic therapist in an agency. This is one reason that being in a strategic therapy training program or having a peer supervision group is important. Keeping in mind the basic tenet of the MRI approach of "doing what works" is help-ful as well as consistently having good results with difficult clients; others in the agency are then likely to leave you alone and some might even start asking questions about what you are doing.

EMPIRICAL BASE

There are many published case examples and anecdotes that illustrate the effective-ness of strategic therapy. However, there are not many well-designed empirical stud-ies on the effectiveness of this approach. The MRI group frequently makes three-month follow-up calls to clients to obtain their self-evaluation of the success of treatment. In a report on 148 cases, Segal (1991b) stated that thirty-eight percent ex-perienced no improvement, twenty-six percent had significant improvement, and thirty-six percent had complete success in that they achieved all their treatment goals; however, there was no control or comparison group.

Chubb and Evans (1990) compared the efficiency of an HMO that used only the MRI approach to an HMO that used a traditional eclectic-psychodynamic approach. The MRI HMO had no waiting list whereas the comparison HMO had an average waiting period of twenty-two weeks. In addition, the MRI HMO clients had many fewer sessions than the comparison HMO and, thus, the MRI therapists were able to see considerably more clients over a two-year period than the therapists at the com-parison HMO. Also, the MRI HMO had many fewer hospital admissions and much shorter average lengths of stay than the comparison condition. Well over ninety per-cent of the clients of the MRI HMO reported they were satisfied with the services and, according to Chubb (1990), this is quite comparable to client satisfaction ratings reported in other studies. The findings of this study are supportive of the efficiency of the MRI approach in an HMO setting, but the findings were not statistically analyzed nor were results on effectiveness reported.

Throughout the history and development of strategic therapy, its use in marital and family therapy has been emphasized. Analyses of marital and family therapy re-search have generally found all the various theoretical approaches, including strate-gic, to be effective, with no on approach being more effective than any other (Hazelrigg, Cooper, & Borduin, 1987; Shadish, Montgomery, Wilson, Wilson, Bright & Okwumabua, 1993). A therapeutic approach combining the techniques of MRI and the strategic therapy of Haley/Madanes was found to be effective in a family ap-proach to psychiatric crises (Langsley, Machotka, & Flomenhaft, 1971). In addition, strategic therapy has been found effective when integrated with other approaches for specific problems, such as with structural family therapy in treating substance abuse (Stanton, Todd, et al., 1982) and behavioral family therapy in treating delinquents (Alexander, Barton, Schiavo, & Parsons, 1976). In regard to the effectiveness of the Milan Family Systems Approach, Carr (1991) in a review of ten studies found it resulted in significant improvement in presenting symptoms in approximately two-thirds to three-fourths of all cases.

The effectiveness of some of the key interventions of strategic therapy has also been examined. In a review of research on the use of paradox with various symptoms and problems, Kim, Poling, and Ascher (1991) found it to be effective with insomnia, agoraphobia, obsessive disorders, and disorders of elimination (urinary frequency/retention and encopresis). The studies reviewed by Kim et al. used single-subject or group designs. In the group designs, paradoxical interventions were consistently found to be more effective than no-treatment control conditions and equally effective as and sometimes more effective than various comparison treatments. These findings are consistent with meta-analyses of studies on the effectiveness of paradoxical interventions with such problems as insomnia, depression, agoraphobia, procrastination, and stress (Hill, 1987; Shoham-Salomon & Rosenthal, 1987). In addition, Shoham-Salomon and Rosenthal concluded that paradoxical interventions resulted in more durable positive outcomes and were more effective with clients presenting more severe problems and resistance to treatment than nonparadoxical interventions.

Positive reframing and the restraining from change intervention of discussing "the dangers of improvement" were both found to be effective in the treatment of depression, with reframing being more effective than restraining (Swoboda, Dowd, & Wise, 1990). Other studies have also found positive reframing to be very effective in the treatment of depression (Shoham-Salomon & Rosenthal, 1987). In a study of treatment for social phobia, Akillas and Efran (1995) found symptom prescription to be effective but a combination of symptom prescription with reframing together was even more effective.

The research on the effectiveness of strategic marital and family therapy is mounting. In addition, a growing body of research is finding that the specific strategic therapy interventions of reframing and paradoxical prescriptions are effective. However, more well-designed, controlled studies still need to be done on the effectiveness of strategic therapy generally and its component interventions specifically, and not just reframing and therapeutic paradox.

CONCLUSIONS AND FUTURE PROSPECTS

As mentioned previously, communications theory and strategic therapy have not been discussed very much in social work literature. However, social workers have discussed the clinical use of communications theory and strategic therapy elsewhere, primarily in the family therapy literature. One reason for this may be the perceived conflict between social work values and the practice of strategic therapy. For example, social work treatment generally places great emphasis on the importance of the therapeutic relationship, and the worker dealing with the client's feelings is central to this endeavor. Strategic therapy has been criticized for focusing only on behaviors and cognitions and ignoring feelings. This criticism may have had some validity in the early days of strategic therapy; however, it has been emphasized in more recent years that the effective use of strategic therapy requires clinicians to be empathic with clients and validate their feelings (Cade & O'Hanlon, 1993; Kleckner, Frank, Bland, Amendt, & Bryant, 1992).

Strategic therapy has also received considerable criticism for being manipulative primarily because of its indirectness and use of paradox (Hoffman, 1985). Therapist manipulation and being in a one-up position are seen as being disrespectful and disempowering to clients. It is true that early in its development, the proponents of strategic therapy placed considerable emphasis on the therapist being in control of treatment and "tricking" clients out of their symptoms. A basic tenet in the use of paradox has been that it works best when concealed from clients. However, it has been pointed out (Haley, 1987; Strupp, 1977) that regardless of theoretical orientation, clinicians must use some concealment in that they cannot completely reveal all their thoughts to the client, and, therefore, all therapy involves some manipulation.

In recent years, however, strategic therapy has been modified in ways that minimize its manipulative qualities (Greene, Jones, Frappier, Klein, & Culton, in press; Solovey & Duncan, 1992). These modifications include: (1) Designing indirect, paradoxical techniques that are plausible explanations for the client's situation. For instance, when restraining change by suggesting that "the client should go slowly and not change too much too quickly" it may very well be that doing so is in the client's best interest in the short run; the decision for making any changes resides with the client (Greene et al., in press; Solovey & Duncan, 1992). (2) The clinician suggestion, not prescribing, to the client both direct and indirect interventions (sometimes three or more interventions) but prescribing none (Greene et al., in press). This introduces novel ideas to the client but still leaves it up to the client to accept or reject any of them. (3) Discussing and designing paradox openly with clients (Hill, 1992). In this way, the client is an active participant in the construction and implementation of paradoxical interventions. This is consistent with some research that suggests that openly discussing paradox with clients does not hinder its effectiveness (Kim, Poling, & Ascher, 1991). In addition, research evidence indicates that therapeutic paradox, even when concealed, is not deleterious to the clinician-client relationship (Kim et al., 1991).

A basic assumption of strategic therapy is that clients already have the strengths and resources they need in order to make the changes they want. This posture of the clinician lends itself to a positive therapeutic relationship and client empowerment (Coyne, 1987; Jacobson, 1983). Coyne (1987) and Jacobson (1983) discuss how major strategic therapy interventions allow clients to discover solutions to their problems on their own and, thus, clients are able to give themselves, and not the clinician, credit for positive change (Stanton, 1980). An empowering approach such as this also lends itself to use with diverse client populations such as women (Terry, 1992) and minorities (Boyd-Franklin, 1987; Ho, 1989; Kim, 1985; Lemon, Newfield, & Dobbins, 1993) who have been targets of discrimination and denied access to power in this country. In addition, the use of strategic therapy has not been restricted only to the United States. For example, strategic therapy has been effectively used in other countries such as India (Appasamy, 1995), Argentina (Weyland, 1995), Sweden (Pothoff, 1995), and, of course, Italy (Selvini Palazzoli et al., 1978).

Several newer approaches to practice have evolved out of the communications theory/strategic therapy tradition in recent years which place major emphasis on the clinician-client relationship being nonhierarchical and collaborative. These newer approaches are: solution-focused therapy (de Shazer, 1985; Berg, 1994), narrative therapy (White & Epston, 1990), and constructivist therapy (Hoffman, 1988). These newer approaches also deemphasize the use of indirectness, concealment, and paradox. The primary originators of these newer approaches are all social workers.

Another trend is the integration of strategic therapy and its various techniques with other approaches (Case & Robinson, 1990; Duncan & Solovey, 1989; Held, 1984; Seaburn, Landau-Stanton, & Horwitz, 1995). The integration of strategic therapy with structural family therapy and with behavioral therapy was referred to earlier in this chapter. In addition, reframing is now used in cognitive therapy (Schuyler, 1991) and paradox is used in both cognitive therapy (Dattilio & Freeman, 1992) and task-centered treatment (Reid, 1990). The integration of strategic therapy, solution-focused therapy, narrative therapy, and constructivist therapy in various combinations has also been discussed in the literature (Durrant, 1995; Quick, 1996; Selekman, 1993). Such integrations are natural for these approaches since they come out of the communications theory tradition which emphasizes "using what works" in bringing about client change as quickly as possible. Because of this emphasis, strategic therapy and its derivative approaches of solution-faced therapy, narrative therapy, and constructivist therapy lend themselves to brief treatment.

Another major trend impacting social work practice in significant ways is managed health care. Because of managed care's emphasis on limiting the number of treatment sessions to which a person is entitled every year, social service and mental health agencies are starting to use brief treatment approaches almost exclusively, always searching for the most effective and efficient interventions. This trend toward the use of brief treatment approaches, however, makes a lot of sense given that there has been an accumulation of a considerable amount of research which has consistently found brief treatment to be equally effective when compared to long-term treatment (Koss & Shiang, 1993). The practice context of managed care means that social service and mental health agencies will be seeking to hire and promote social workers skilled in using strategic therapy and its derivative approaches. Consequently, graduate schools of social work need to modify their curricula to prepare students for the realities of current practice. It is very likely, therefore, that communications theory–based strategic therapy and its derivatives will become the predominant treatment models for many years to come.

REFERENCES

Abeles, G. (1976). Researching the unresearchable: Experimentation on the double bind. In C.E. Sluzki & D.C. Ransom (Eds.), *Double bind: The foundation of the communicational approach to the family* (pp. 113–149). New York: Grune & Stratton.

Akillas, E., & Efran, J.S. (1995). Symptom prescription and reframing: Should they be combined? *Cognitive Therapy and Research, 19,* 263–279.

Aldridge, D., & Rossiter, J. (1983). A strategic approach to suicidal behavior. *Journal of Strategic and Systemic Therapies, 2,* 49–62.

Alexander, J.F., Barton, C., Schiavo, R.S., & Parsons, B.V. (1976). Systems-behavioral intervention with families of delinquents: Therapists characteristics, family behavior, and outcome. *Journal of Consulting and Clinical Psychology, 44,* 656–664.

Allen, J.R. (1987). The use of strategic techniques in large systems: Mohandas K. Gandhi and the Indian independence movement. *Journal of Strategic and Systemic Therapies, 6,* 57–64.

Amatea, E.S. (1989). *Brief strategic intervention for school behavior problems.* San Francisco: Jossey-Bass.

Andelson, J.G. (1981). The double bind and social change in communal Amana. *Human Relations, 34,* 111–125.

Appasamy, P. (1995). Doing brief therapy in India. In J.H. Weakland & W.A. Ray (Eds.), *Propagations: Thirty years of influence from the Mental Research Institute* (pp. 157–173). New York: Haworth Press.

Bartunek, J.M., & Moch, M.K. (1987). First-order, second-order, and third-order change and organization development interventions: A cognitive approach. *Journal of Applied Behavioral Science, 23,* 483–500.

Bateson, G. (1979). *Mind and nature: A necessary unity.* New York: E.P. Dutton.

Bateson, G., Jackson, D.D., Haley, J., & Weakland, J. (1956). Toward a theory of schizophrenia. *Behavioral Science, 1,* 251–264.

Berg, I.K. (1994). *Family-based services: A solution-focused approach.* New York: W.W. Norton.

Bergman, J.S. (1982). Paradoxical interventions with people who insist on acting crazy. *American Journal of Psychotherapy, XXXVI,* 214–222.

Bergman, J.S. (1983). On odd days and even days: Rituals used in strategic therapy. In L. Wolberg & M. Aronson (Eds.), *Group and family therapy 1983* (pp. 273–281). New York: Brunner/Mazel.

Blotcky, A.D., Tittler, B.I., & Friedman, S. (1982). The double-bind situation in families of disturbed children. *Journal of Genetic Psychology, 141,* 129–142.

Bolman, L.G., & Deal, T.E. (1991). *Reframing organizations: Artistry, choice, and leadership.* San Francisco: Jossey-Bass.

Boyd-Franklin, N. (1987). The contribution of family therapy models to the treatment of black families. *Psychotherapy, 24,* 621–629.

Brandon, J. (1985). Some applications of a strategic family therapy perspective in the practice of OD. *Journal of Strategic and Systemic Therapies, 4,* 15–24.

Braverman, L. (1986). Social casework and strategic therapy. *Social Casework,* April, 234–239.

Bray, J.H., & Anderson, H. (1984). Strategic interventions with single-parent families. *Psychotherapy, 21,* 101–109.

Bross, A. (Ed.) (1982). *Family therapy: Principles of strategic practice.* New York: Guilford Press.

Cade, B. (1980). Strategic therapy. *Journal of Family Therapy, 2,* 89–99.

Cade, B., & O'Hanlon, W.H. (1993). *A brief guide to brief therapy.* New York: W.W. Norton.

Carr, A. (1991). Milan systemic family therapy: A review of ten empirical investigations. *Journal of Family Therapy, 13,* 237–263.

Case, E.M., & Robinson, N.S. (1990). Toward integration: The changing world of family therapy. *American Journal of Family Therapy, 18,* 153–160.

Chubb, H., & Evans, E.L. (1990). Therapist efficiency and clinic accessibility with the Mental Health Research Institute brief therapy model. *Community Mental Health Journal, 26,* 139–149.

Chubb, H. (1982). Strategic brief therapy in a clinic setting. *Psychotherapy: Theory, Research and Practice, 19,* 160–165.

Chubb, H. (1983). Interactional brief therapy: Child problems in an HMO clinic. *Journal of Strategic and Systemic Therapies, 2,* 70–76.

Coyne, J.C. (1986). Strategic marital therapy for depression. In N.S. Jacobson & A.S. Gurman (Eds.), *Clinical handbook of marital therapy* (pp. 495–512). New York: Guilford Press.

Coyne, J.C. (1987). The concept of empowerment in strategic therapy. *Psychotherapy, 24,* 539–545.

Dattilio, F.M., & Freeman, A. (1992). Introduction to cognitive therapy. In A. Freeman & F.M. Dattilio (Eds.), *Comprehensive casebook of cognitive therapy* (pp. 3–11). New York: Plenum Press.

de Shazer, S. (1985). *Keys to solution in brief therapy.* New York: W.W. Norton.

Dowd, E.T., & Pace, T.M. (1989). The relativity of reality: Second-order change in psychotherapy. In A. Freeman et al. (Eds.), *Comprehensive handbook of cognitive therapy* (pp. 213–226). New York: Plenum Press.

Duncan, B.L., & Solovey, A.D. (1989). Strategic-brief therapy: An insight-oriented approach. *Journal of Marital and Family Therapy, 15,* 1–9.

Durrant, M. (1995). *Creative strategies for school problems.* New York: W.W. Norton.

Efron, D.E. (1981). Strategic therapy interventions with latency-age children. *Social Casework,* November, 543–550.

Elkaim, M. (1990). *If you love me, don't love me: Constructions of reality and change in family therapy.* New York: Basic Books.

Fairhurst, G.T., & Sarr, R.A. (1996). *The art of framing: Managing the language of leadership.* San Francisco: Jossey-Bass.

Ferreira, A. (1960). The double bind and delinquent behavior. *Archives of General Psychiatry, 3,* 359–367.

Fisch, R. (1986). The brief treatment of alcoholism. *Journal of Strategic and Systemic Therapies, 5,* 40–49.

Fisch, R. (1988). Training in the brief therapy model. In H.A. Liddle, D.C. Breulin, & R.C. Schwartz (Eds.), *Handbook of family therapy training and supervision* (pp. 79–92). New York: Guilford Press.

Fisch, R., Weakland, J.H., & Segal, L. (1982). *The tactics of change: Doing therapy briefly.* San Francisco: Jossey-Bass.

Fraser, J.S. (1986). The crisis interview: Strategic rapid intervention. *Journal of Strategic and Systemic Therapies, 5,* 71–87.

Green, S., & Bobele, M. (1988). An interactional approach to marital infidelity: Including the "other woman" in therapy. *Journal of Strategic and Systemic Therapies, 7,* 35–47.

Greene, G.J. (1989). Using the written contract for evaluating and enhancing practice effectiveness. *Journal of Independent Social Work, 4,* 135–155.

Greene, G.J. (1996). An integrative dialectical-pragmatic approach to time-limited treatment: Working with unemployed clients as a case in point. In A.R. Roberts (Ed.), *Managing crisis and brief treatment* (pp. 160–194). Chicago: Nelson-Hall.

Greene, G.J., Jones, D.H., Frappier, C., Klein, M., & Culton, B. (in press). School social workers as family therapists: A dialectical-systemic-constructivist model. *Social Work in Education.*

Greene, G.J., & Sattin, D.B. (1985). A paradoxical treatment format for anxiety-related somatic complaints: Four case studies. *Family Systems Medicine, 3,* 197–204.

Grove, D., & Haley, J. (1993). *Conversations on therapy: Popular problems and uncommon solutions.* New York: W.W. Norton.

Haley, J. (1963). *Strategies of psychotherapy.* New York: Grune & Stratton.

Haley, J. (1980). *Leaving home: The therapy of disturbed young people.* New York: McGraw-Hill.

Haley, J. (1984). *Ordeal therapy.* San Francisco: Jossey-Bass.

Haley, J. (1987). *Problem-solving therapy* (2nd ed.). San Francisco: Jossey-Bass.

Haley, J., & Schiff, N.P. (1993). A model therapy for psychotic young people. *Journal of Systemic Therapies, 12,* 74–87.

Hansen, J.C., & L'Abate, L. (1982). The communications theory of Paul Watzlawick. In J.C. Hansen & L. L'Abarte, *Approaches to family therapy* (pp. 85–100). New York: Macmillan.

Hazelrigg, M.D., Cooper, H.M., & Borduin, C.M. (1987). Evaluating the effectiveness of family therapies: An integrative review and analysis. *Psychological Bulletin, 101,* 428–442.

Heath, A.W., & Ayers, T.C. (1991). MRI brief therapy with adolescent substance abusers. In T.C. Todd & M.D. Selekman (Eds.), *Family therapy approaches with adolescent substance abusers* (pp. 49–69). Boston: Allyn & Bacon.

Held, B.S. (1982). Entering a mental health system: A strategic-systemic approach. *Journal of Strategic and Systemic Therapies, 1,* 40–50.

Held. B.S. (1984). Toward a strategic eclecticism: A proposal. *Psychotherapy, 21,* 232–240.

Herr, J.J., & Weakland, J.H. (1979). *Counseling elders and their families: Practical techniques for applied gerontology.* New York: Springer.

Hill, K.A. (1987). Meta-analysis of paradoxical interventions. *Psychotherapy, 24,* 266–270.

Hill, M. (1992). A feminist model for the use of paradoxical techniques in psychotherapy. *Professional Psychology, 23,* 287–292.

Ho, M.K. (1989). Applying family therapy theories to Asian/Pacific Americans. *Contemporary Family Therapy, 11,* 61–70.

Hoffman, L. (1981). *Foundations of family therapy.* New York: Basic Books.

Hoffman, L. (1985). Beyond power and control: Toward a second-order family systems therapy. *Family Systems Medicine, 3,* 381–396.

Hoffman, L. (1988). A constructivist position for family therapy. *Irish Journal of Psychology, 9,* 110–129.

Jackson, D.D. (1965). Family rules: Marital *quid pro quo. Archives of General Psychiatry, 12,* 589–594.

Jackson, D.D. (1968a). *Communication, family, and marriage: Human communication (Vol. 1).* Palo Alto, CA: Science and Behavior Books.

Jackson, D.D. (1968b). *Therapy, communication, and change: Human communication (Vol. 2).* Palo Alto, CA: Science and Behavior Books.

Jacobson, A. (1983). Empowering the client in strategic therapy. *Journal of Strategic and Systemic Therapies, 2,* 77–87.

Keeney, B.P. (1983). *Aesthetics of change.* New York: Guilford Press.

Keeney, B.P. (1987). The construction of therapeutic realities. *Psychotherapy, 24,* 469–476.

Keeney, B.P., & Silverstein, O. (1986). *The therapeutic voice of Olga Silverstein.* New York: Guilford Press.

Kim, R.S., Poling, J., & Ascher, L.M. (1991). An introduction to research on the clinical efficacy of paradoxical intention. In G.R. Weeks (Ed.), *Promoting change through paradoxical therapy* (Rev. ed.) (pp. 216–250). New York: Brunner/Mazel.

Kim, S.C. (1985). Family therapy for Asian Americans: A strategic-structural framework. *Psychotherapy, 22,* 342–348.

Kleckner, T., Amendt, J.H., Frank, L., Bland, C., & Bryant, R. (1992). The myth of the unfeeling strategic therapist. *Journal of Marital and Family Therapy, 18,* 41–51.

Koss, M.P., & Shiang, J. (1993). Research on brief psychotherapy. In A.E. Bergin & S.L. Garfield (Eds.), *Handbook of psychotherapy and behavior change* (pp. 664–700). New York: Wiley.

Langsley, D.G., Machotka, P., & Flomenhaft, K. (1971). Avoiding mental hospital admissions: A follow-up study. *American Journal of Psychiatry, 127,* 1391–1394.

Lemon, S.D., Newfield, N.A., & Dobbins, J.E. (1993). Culturally sensitive family therapy in Appalachia. *Journal of Systemic Therapies, 12,* 8–26.

Madanes, C. (1980). Marital therapy when a symptom is presented by a spouse. *International Journal of Family Therapy, 2,* 120–136.

Madanes, C. (1981). *Strategic family therapy.* San Francisco: Jossey-Bass.

Madanes, C. (1984). *Behind the one-way mirror: Advances in the practice of strategic therapy.* San Francisco: Jossey-Bass.

Markowitz, M.A., & Nitzberg, M.L. (1982). Communication in the psychiatric halfway house and the double bind. *Clinical Social Work Journal, 10,* 176–189.

Mazza, J. (1988). Training strategic therapists: The use of indirect techniques. In H.A. Liddle, D.C. Breunlin, & R.C. Schwartz (Eds.), *Handbook of family therapy training and supervision* (pp. 93–109) New York: Guilford Press.

McGarty, R. (1986). Use of strategic and brief techniques in the treatment of chemical dependency. *Journal of Strategic and Systemic Therapies, 5,* 13–19.

Molcy, V. (1983). Interactional treatment of eating disorders. *Journal of Strategic and Systemic Therapies, 2,* 10–28.

Morawitz, A., & Walker, G. (1984). *Brief therapy with single-parent families.* New York: Brunner/Mazel.

Morrissette, P.J. (1989) Benevolent restraining: A strategy for interrupting various cycles in residential care. *Journal of Strategic and Systemic Therapies, 8,* 31–35.

Nardone, G., & Watzlawick, P. (1993). *The art of change. Strategic therapy and hypnotherapy without trance.* San Francisco: Jossey-Bass.

Nelsen, J. (1978). Use of communications theory in single-subject research. *Social Work Research and Abstracts, 4,* 12–19.

Nelsen, J. (1980). *Communications theory and social work practice.* Chicago: University of Chicago Press.

Nelsen, J. (1986). Communication theory and social work treatment. In F.J. Turner (Ed.), *Social work treatment: Interlocking theoretical approaches* (3rd ed.) (pp. 219–243). New York: Free Press.

Norfleet, M.A. (1983). Paradoxical interventions in the treatment of chronic physical illness. *Journal of Strategic and Systemic Therapies, 2,* 63–69.

O'Hanlon, W.H. (1987). *Taproots: Underlying principles of Milton H. Erickson's therapy and hypnosis.* New York: W.W. Norton.

Papp, P. (1983). *The process of change.* New York: Guilford Press.

Pirrotta, S., & Cecchin, G. (1988). The Milan training program. In H.A. Liddle, D.C. Breulin, & R.C. Schwartz (Eds.), *Handbook of family therapy training and supervision* (pp. 38–61). New York: Guilford Press.

Pothoff, K. (1995). A Swedish experience. In J.H. Weakland & W.A. Ray (Eds.), *Propagations: Thirty years of influence from the Mental Research Institute* (pp. 197–198). New York: Haworth Press.

Potter-Efron, P.S., & Potter-Efron, R.T. (1986). Promoting second order change in alcoholic systems. *Journal of Strategic and Systemic Therapies, 5,* 20–29.

Quick, E.K. (1996). *Doing what works in brief therapy: A strategic solution focused approach.* New York: Academic Press.

Rabi, J.S., Lehr, M.L., & Hayner, M.L. (1984). The peer consultation team: An alternative. *Journal of Strategic and Systemic Therapies, 3,* 66–71.

Reid, W.J. (1990). An integrative model for short-term treatment. In R.A. Wells & V.J. Giannetti (Eds.), *Handbook of the brief psychotherapies* (pp. 55–77). New York: Plenum Press.

Schindler-Zimmerman, T., Washle, W., & Protinsky, H. (1990). Strategic intervention in an athletic system. *Journal of Strategic and Systemic Therapies, 9,* 1–7.

Schuyler, D. (1991). *A practical guide to cognitive therapy.* New York: W.W. Norton.

Seaburn, D., Landau-Stanton, J., & Horwitz, S. (1995). Core techniques in family therapy. In R.H. Mikesell, D.D. Lusterman, & S.H. McDaniel (Eds.), *Integrating family therapy: Handbook of family psychology and systems theory* (pp. 5–26). Washington, DC: American Psychological Association.

Segal, L. (1980). Focused problem resolution. In E.R. Tolson & W.J. Reid (Eds.), *Models of family therapy* (pp. 199–223). New York: Columbia University Press.

Segal, L. (1991a). Brief therapy: The MRI approach. In A.S. Gurman and D.P. Kniskern (Eds.), *Handbook of family therapy, Vol. II*. New York: Brunner/Mazel.

Segal, L. (1991b). Brief family therapy. In A.M. Horne & L. Passmore (Eds.), *Family counseling and therapy* (2nd ed.) (pp. 179–206). Itasca, IL: F.E. Peacock Publishers.

Segal, L., & Bavelas, J.B. (1983). Human systems and communication theory. In B.B. Wolman & G. Stricker (Eds.), *Handbook of family and marital therapy* (pp. 61–76). New York: Plenum Press.

Selekman, M.D. 1993). *Pathways to change: Brief therapy solutions with difficult adolescents.* New York: Guilford Press.

Selvini Palazzoli, M., Boscolo, L., Cecchin, G., & Prata, G. (1978a). A ritualized prescription in family therapy: Odd days and even days. *Journal of Marriage and Family Counseling, 4,* 3–9.

Selvini Palazzoli, M., Boscolo, L., Cecchin, G.F., & Prata, G. (1978b). *Paradox and counterparadox: A new model in the therapy of the family in schizophrenic transaction.* New York: Jason Aronson.

Shadish, W.R., Montgomery, L.M., Wilson P., Wilson, M.R., Bright, I., & Okwumabua, T. (1993). The effects of family and marital psychotherapies: A meta-analysis. *Journal of Consulting and Clinical Psychology, 61,* 992–1002.

Shoham-Salomon, V., & Rosenthal, R. (1987). Paradoxical interventions: A meta-analysis. *Journal of Consulting and Clinical Psychology, 55,* 22–28.

Shutty, M.S., & Sheras, P. (1991). Brief strategic psychotherapy with chronic pain patients: Reframing and problem resolution. *Psychotherapy, 28,* 636–642.

Sluzki, C.E., Beavin, J., Tarnopolsky, A., & Veron, E. (1967). Transactional disqualification: Research on the double bind. *Archives of General Psychiatry, 16,* 494–504.

Sluzki, C.E., & Veron, E. (1971). The double bind as a universal pathogenic situation. *Family Process, 10,* 397–410.

Solovey, A., & Duncan, B.L. (1992). Ethics and strategic therapy: A proposed ethical direction. *Journal of Marital and Family Therapy, 18,* 53–61.

Soo-Hoo, T. (1995). Implementing brief strategic therapy within a psychiatric residential/daytreatment center. In J.H. Weakland & W.A. Ray (Eds.), *Propagations: Thirty years of influence from the Mental Research Institute* (pp. 107–128). New York: Haworth Press.

Stanton, M.D. (1980). Who should get credit for change which occurs in therapy? In A.S. Gurman (Ed.), *Questions and answers in the practice of family therapy*. New York: Brunner/Mazel.

Stanton, M.D., Todd, T.C., et al. (1982). *The family therapy of drug abuse and addiction.* New York: Guilford Press.

Strupp, H.H. (1977). A reformulation of the dynamics of the therapist's contribution. In A.S. Gurman & A.M. Razin (Eds.), *Effective psychotherapy: A handbook of research* (pp. 3–22). New York: Pergamon Press.

Swoboda, J.S., Dowd, E.T., & Wise, S.L. (1990). Reframing and restraining directives in the treatment of clinical depression. *Journal of Counseling Psychology, 37,* 254–260.

Tennen, H., Eron, J.B., & Rohrbaugh, M. (1991). Paradox in context. In G.R. Weeks (Ed.), *Promoting change through paradoxical therapy* (Rev. Ed.) (pp. 187–215). New York: Brunner/Mazel.

Terry, L.L. (1992). I want my old wife back: A case illustration of a four-stage approach to a feminist-informed strategic/systemic therapy. *Journal of Strategic and Systemic Therapies, 11,* 27–41.

Watzlawick, P., Beavin, J.H., & Jackson, D.D. (1967). *Pragmatics of human communication: A study of interactional patterns, pathologies, and paradoxes.* New York: W.W. Norton.

Watzlawick, P., & Coyne, J.C. (1980). Depression following stroke: Brief, problem-focused family treatment. *Family Process, 19,* 13–18.

Watzlawick, P., & Weakland, J.H. (1977). *The interactional view: Studies at the Mental Research Institute Palo Alto 1965–1974.* New York: W.W. Norton.

Watzlawick, P., Weakland, J.H., & Fisch, R. (1974). *Change: Principles of problem formation and problem resolution.* New York: W.W. Norton.

Weakland, J.H. (1976). Communication theory and clinical change. In P.J. Guerin (Ed.), *Family therapy: Theory and practice* (pp. 111–128). New York: Gardner Press.

Weakland, J.H., & Fisch, R. (1984). Cases that "Don't make sense": Brief strategic treatment in medical practice. *Family Systems Medicine, 2,* 125–136.

Weakland, J.H., & Jordan, L. (1992). Working briefly with reluctant clients: Child protective services as an example. *Journal of Family Therapy, 14,* 231–254.

Weakland, J.H., Watzlawick, P., & Riskin, J. (1995). Introduction: MRI—A little background music. In J.H. Weakland & W.A. Ray (Eds.), *Propagations: Thirty years of influence from the Mental Research Institute.* New York: Haworth Press.

Weyland, D. (1995). From the dictatorship of Lacan to the democracy of short-term therapies. In J.H. Weakland & W.A. Ray (Eds.), *Propagations: Thirty years of influence from the Mental Research Institute* (pp. 189–195). New York: Haworth Press.

White, M., & Epston, D. (1990). *Narrative means to therapeutic ends.* New York: W.W. Norton.

Woodruff, A.F., & Engle, T. (1985). Strategic therapy and agency development: Using circular thinking to turn the corner. *Journal of Strategic and Systemic Therapies, 4,* 25–29.

Zimmerman, T., & Protinsky, H. (1990). Strategic parenting: The tactics of changing children's behavior. *Journal of Strategic and Systemic Therapies, 9,* 6–13.

CHAPTER 7

CONSTRUCTIVISM AND SOCIAL WORK TREATMENT

DONALD CARPENTER

INTRODUCTION

Constructivism as a conceptual framework for social work treatment is relatively new. Constructivist ideas, however, have a long history, having found expression in such diverse fields as art, mathematics, literary criticism, philosophy, and, more recently, in the social and behavioral sciences and related helping professions. Any exhaustive examination of constructivism for its relevance to human behavior alone would lead to the complex deliberations of philosophers on metaphysics, epistemology, and ontology, as well as to the studies of psychologists on the nature of perception, cognition, learning, and behavior. While an investigation of this scale is obviously beyond the scope of this chapter, areas of these fields of inquiry will be visited in formulating a constructivist framework for social work theory and treatment.

In classifying the various theory development approaches taken by social work, Turner (1986) identifies one as the introduction of "new thought systems," for example, role theory, ego psychology, and systems theory (p. 8). In this vein, constructivism can be viewed as a new thought system for social work theory. While various practice perspectives and treatment approaches in social work have historically reflected constructivist ideas and concepts, not until recently have these been recognized as such.

In the interest of specificity but at the expense of linguistic economy, constructivism can be viewed as a *philosophical-behavioral-methodological thought system* for social work practice. Philosophically, constructivism is concerned with the nature of reality and being (metaphysics and ontology) and the nature and acquisition of human knowledge (epistemology). The behavioral aspect pertains to certain understandings of human perception and cognition, personal and interpersonal dynamics, and the nature and execution of change. From the philosophical and behavioral components, methodological (practice) implications emerge for social work theory and treatment.

It should be clarified that constructivism is not a practice theory but a conceptual framework that can inform given practice approaches in the sense that ecological systems theory informs the life model of practice, for instance. *General* practice principles may be inferred, however, from the basic postulates of constructivism. While *specific* practice guidelines on strategy and technique levels can also be inferred from constructivist principles, these are more properly dealt with in discussions of practice models as such. For this, the reader is referred to a volume on *narrative therapy,* which is based in constructivist principles. Several contemporary psychological and psychosocial treatment approaches in the human service disciplines are based in the constructivist framework to varying degrees. Labels such as "solution-focused," "dialogic," "discursive," and "narrative" designate treatment approaches (or, in the case of the dialogic and other approaches, "families" of treatment approaches") that employ constructivist ideas to a greater or lesser extent.

HISTORICAL FOUNDATIONS

EARLY BEGINNINGS

The roots of constructivism are in the soil of antiquity. The Greek Sophist philosopher Protagoras (c.490–c.420 B.C.) maintained that "humans are the measure of all things—of things that are, that they are, of things that are not, that they are not." For Protagoras, there was no "objective" world and no perception any more true than another, although some were more useful and should be followed (Ide, 1995, p. 752). The Italian philosopher Giambattista Vico (1668–1744) was the first to make an organized case for the constructive processes in human perception and knowing. He maintained that humans order their experience with mental categories projected onto the unfamiliar. The German philosopher Immanuel Kant (1724–1804), in his *Critique of Pure Reason* (1781), argued that the human mind has an inherent structure that it imposes on both thought and experience, and that *a priori* knowledge (knowledge independent of or prior to experience) is possible and in fact occurs. Kant maintained that the mind is not a passive slate upon which experience is written but a proactive organ molding experience. The Kantian epistemological tradition concerning the nature and acquisition of knowledge, frequently cited as a major foundation block of constructivism, maintained that human knowledge is ultimately a function of the interaction of the world of experience (empirical) and the basic nature (*a priori* state) of the human mind. Another major constructivist, Hans Vaihinger (1852–1933), emphasized the importance of cognitive processes in determining behavior. Vaihinger formulated the philosophy of "As if," which postulates that we hold concepts and beliefs "as if" they were true because of their utility. (Mahoney, 1991, pp. 97–99).

The epistemological position of these philosophers is in direct opposition to that of the Lockean empiricists. John Locke (1632–1704) maintained that knowledge is imparted to the human mind from an external objective world by way of the senses and that, contrary to what philosophers like Vico and Kant had said, *a priori* knowledge is *not* possible (Wolterstorff, 1995, pp. 437–440).

MODERN CONTRIBUTIONS

In more recent times, the developmental psychologist Jean Piaget (1896–1980), from his studies in child development, formulated a theory of *developmental epistemology.* Piaget concluded that the newborn comes equipped with mental regulatory mechanisms (evolutionary in origin), which, in interaction with the child's environment, result in the development of intelligence (1929, 1950, 1970). The cognitive psychologist George Kelly has contributed significantly to constructivism with his theory of *personal constructs.* Personal constructs are the means by which an individual construes, perceives, interprets, understands, predicts, and controls his/her world (1955). For Kelly, mental constructs are imposed on the world and not vice versa. Another psychologist, Paul Watzlawick (1976, 1984), must also be cited as a major contributor to modern constructivist theory, especially to constructivist epistemology, in his examination of our assumed "realness" of an "objective" world and of the possibility of constructing more desirable individual worlds. Two other theoreticians, Ernst von Glaserfeld (1984) and Heinz von Foerster (1984), must be credited for significant contributions to constructivism. Each has made important formulations of that aspect of constructivist epistemology concerned with the nature of reality as observer-dependent.

Two Chilean neurobiologists, Humberto Maturana and Francisco Varela, have exerted perhaps the most basic influence on modern constructivist thought in the biological, social, and behavior sciences, an influence that has most recently found its way into the behavioral helping professions. From their experimentation with animals have come some rather astounding conclusions about the basic organization of living systems and the nature of the influence of perception on behavior (Maturana, 1980; Maturana & Varela, 1987). According to Maturana and Varela, living systems are *autopoietic* or self-organizing. The behaviors of organisms are not directly influenced by their mediums (environments), but are determined by their structure (neurophysiological makeup). According to Maturana and Varela, organisms are *structure determined* (1987, pp. 95–97). The biological contributions of Maturana and Varela to constructivist theory hold important implications for social work practice theory and will be drawn on throughout the formulation here of a constructivist framework for social work practice.

PATH INTO SOCIAL WORK

Constructivism has been making its way quietly along the path into social work for some time but only recently has its identity been recognized. All theoretical frameworks that stress the importance of the individual's internal processes, especially perception and cognition, for understanding human behavior have kinship with constructivism. Some of these will be discussed in a later section comparing constructivist-based treatment approaches with others having constructivist elements that have not been labeled as such.

From the social work literature, two major works, *An Introduction to Constructivism for Social Workers* by Fisher (1991) and *Revisioning Social Work Education: A Social Constructionist Approach* edited by Laird (1993), have contributed significantly to practice theory and professional education. An increasing number of social work journal articles on constructivism are also in evidence (see, for example, Dean & Fenby, 1989; Dean & Fleck-Henderson, 1992; Hartman, 1991).

PRESUPPOSITIONS OF CONSTRUCTIVISM

PHILOSOPHICAL RELATIVISM

The philosophical component of constructivism reflects the basic conceptions of a school of thought in Western philosophy known as *epistemological relativism*. This position holds that nothing is universally true and that the world cannot be attributed intrinsic characteristics: there are only different ways of interpreting it (Pojman, 1995, p. 690). "Cognitive [epistemological] relativism is the view that truth and logic are always formulated in the framework of, and are relative to, a given thought-world with its own language" (Elkana, 1978, p. 312). The relativist position denies certain ties, absolutes, and permanence. In this vein, the philosopher Nelson Goodman (1972), a proponent of philosophical relativism, writes:

> There are very many different equally true descriptions of the world and their truth is the only standard of their faithfulness. And when we say of them that they all involve conventionalizations, we are saying that no one of these different descriptions is *exclusively* true, since the others are also true. None of them tells us *the* way the world is, but each of them tells us *a* way the world is (pp. 30–31).

In opposition to the position of relativism lies that of philosophical *realism,* which maintains essentially opposite notions about the "realness" and "objective" existence of the world:

> Reality is a singular, stable order of events and objects external to and independent of mind and mental processes. . . . the senses and other technical methods of observation are said to reveal, albeit imperfectly, regularities and principles of reality (Mahoney, 1991, p. 36).

While realists hold the position of an ontologically existing world that is not observer-dependent for its reality, relativists contend that such a world, while seeming to exist, is actually observer-dependent relative to the nature of the perceptual and cognitive apparatus of human beings, which reveal not *a* world, but, as Goodman says, *versions* of a world (1984, pp. 29–34). It is the *relativist* position that is the philosophical bedrock of constructivism.

Constructivist Epistemology

An age-old problem for philosophers pertains to what is knowable by humans and the means by which knowledge is acquired. In constructive epistemology, knowledge is not composed of impressions of an objective world or "reality" existing independently of the knower, but instead is the creation of individual knowers, resulting in as many worlds or "realities" as there are world reality observers. If this is so, how do individuals seem to experience a common world? Von Glaserfeld (1984) says, "To appreciate this, it is necessary to keep in mind the most fundamental trail of constructivist epistemology, that is, that the world which is constructed is an experiential world that consists of experiences and makes no claim whatsoever about 'truth' in the sense of correspondence with an ontological reality" (p. 29). In other words, what we experience in common does not depend on the existence of a single objective "real" world. Constructivists maintain that what we refer to as common human experiences are based on a consensual world of language, thought, and experience.

To appreciate the constructivist view of the nature of human knowledge and its acquisition requires a willingness to set aside some very basic beliefs about the phenomenon we call knowledge. It requires suspending notions of certainty, realness, objectivity, and externality, and the belief that these are indeed the anchors of human experience. In constructivism, ". . . the phenomenon of knowing cannot be taken as though there were 'facts' or objects out there that we grasp and store in our head. The experience of anything out there is validated in a special way by the human structure, which makes possible 'the thing' that arises in the description. . . . *every act of knowing brings forth a world*" (Maturana & Varela, 1987, pp. 25–26).

Knowledge can be viewed as both process and product. In distinguishing the problem of what we know from that of how we know, Watzlawick (1984) writes:

> How we know is a far more vexing problem. To solve it, the mind needs to step outside itself, so to speak, and observe itself at work; for at this point we are no longer faced with facts that apparently exist independently of us in the outside world, but with mental processes whose nature is not at all self-evident. . . . For if *what* we know depends on *how* we came to know it, then our view of reality is no longer a true image of what is the case outside ourselves, but is inevitably determined also by the processes through which we arrived at this view (p. 9).

The major contributions to epistemological theory have traditionally come from philosophy and psychology. The development of constructivist epistemology, however, has seen foundation contributions from the experimental work and theoretical formulations of Maturana and Varela as biologists. Much of what they have contributed runs counter to traditional realist epistemology. The following, pertaining to the nature of the functional relationship between the brain and the environment, is an example:

> The nervous system does not "pick up information" from the environment, as we often hear. On the contrary, it brings forth a world by specifying what patterns of the environment are perturbations [stimuli] and what changes trigger them in the organism. The popular metaphor of calling the brain an "information-processing device" is not only ambiguous but patently wrong (Maturana & Varela, 1987, p. 169).

In other words, the brain, by virtue of its structure, "decides" how it will allow itself to be stimulated (perturbed) by the environment, and on the neurophysiological level is in no sense of the word at the mercy of the environment.

THE CONCEPTUAL FRAMEWORK

VARIANTS OF CONSTRUCTIVISM

While the whole of constructivism is clearly rooted in philosophical relativism, at least two major versions can be identified. Mahoney (1991) has made a useful distinction between the two while citing some of the major contributors to each:

> *Radical constructivism* is on the idealist end of the spectrum and has been differentially endorsed and expressed by Heinz von Foerster, Ernst von Glaserfeld, Humberto Maturana, Francisco Varela, and Paul Watzlawick. This perspective is most elegantly expressed in theory and research on *autopoiesis* (self-organizing systems). . . . In its most extreme expressions, radical constructivism comes close to the classical position of ontological idealism, arguing that *there is no (even hypothetical) reality beyond our personal experience* [emphasis added].
>   *Critical constructivists*, on the other hand, do not deny the existence and influence of an unknowable but inescapable real world. They are, instead, critical or hypothetical realists, admitting that the universe is populated with entities we call "objects" but denying that we can ever "directly" know them. Representatives of modern critical constructivism include Guidano, Hayek, Kelly, myself [Mahoney], Piaget, and Weimer. For critical constructivists, the individual is not a self-sufficient, sole producer of his or her own experience. Rather, the individual is conceived as a "co-creator" or "co-constructor" of personal realities, with the prefix *co* emphasizing an interactive interdependence with their social and physical environments (p. 111).

The radical variety of constructivism is so termed because of its assumptions about the nature of reality. It questions certain basic beliefs, the validity of which most take for granted. For example, it questions our "common sense" notion that reality is obviously what all competent observers know is "real" or "true" about the world we live in. It maintains that instead of there being only one reality, there are as many realities as there are perceivers of reality (Goodman, 1984, pp. 31–32; Watzlawick, 1990, pp. 131–151). Common sense would have us believe with Gertrude Stein, for instance, that "a rose is a rose is a rose" because all competent observers agree that a certain kind of flower *is* a rose and not an elephant. Radical constructivists would maintain, however, that greater accuracy is achieved in saying that there are as many "rose realities" as there are individuals who experience roses. Each individual will experience a rose in some different way and derive a somewhat different meaning from the experience than all other individuals; but each will still call it a rose. By the same token, a therapist treating a mother, father, and three children is not in the presence of *a* family but of as *many* families as there are family observers (the family members plus the therapist). For the radical constructivist, the roses and families that we talk about are products of our nervous system. Radical constructivism moves sharply away from the Newtonian-Cartesian certainty of a single reality and a knowable, objective world.

In contrast to radical constructivism, critical constructivism does not deny the existence of an objective external world to which we all react. It does maintain, however, that we cannot "know" this world directly, but only indirectly through the filtering mechanisms of perception, cognition, affect, and belief systems.

The conceptual framework for practice formulated here draws on both radical and critical versions of constructivism and the neurobiological view of perception, cognition, and behavior developed by Maturana and Varela.

Principal Concepts

Structure Determinism

The concept of *structure determinism* represents the cornerstone of constructivism as formulated here. In pursuit of his notion of organisms as closed systems, Maturana and his associates conducted several biological experiments out of which emerged the concept of structure determinism. One of these experiments, cited by Bell (1985), is representative of the nature and general outcome of the experiments:

> [Maturana] demonstrated that no correlation could be established between colors (as defined by spectral energies and the relations of activity of retinal ganglion cells of either pigeons or human beings) (Maturana, Uribe & Frenk, 1968). Instead, he found that the nervous system demonstrated its own *internal* correlations: the relations of activity of retinal ganglion cells correlated with color-naming behavior of the organism (but did not correlate with the actual colors as defined by spectral energies). The implication of this finding is that the nervous system functions as a closed, internally consistent system and does *not* contain representations or coded transforms of the environment.

Efran, Lukens, and Lukens (1990) further elaborate on this radically different conception of the relationship between the neurophysiological makeup of the individual and the environment:

> People are brought up to believe they perceive the outside world. The visual system, for example, appears to provide direct and immediate access to our surroundings. The eyes are said to be our windows on the world. However, although the eyelids open, the neurons of the retina do not. Energy waves bump up against the retinal surface . . . but outside light cannot get in. Obviously, experiences we attribute to light—as well as all our other experiences—are created entirely within our own system. . . . This is evident in dreams, in response to sharp blows (when we "see" stars), when neurons are directly touched with electrical probes, and when chemical substances are ingested. At a fireworks display, there may be a lot going on outside, but nevertheless the sparkling colors we see are internal creations.

Based on this conception then, in a so-called "visual experience," what one actually "sees" is not an "outside" world but his/her nervous system itself, which is, to say the least, a counterintuitive conception of visual experience.

An important consequence of the structure-determined state of organisms is immunity to the reception of "information." Contrary to prevalent views in communications and systems theory, it is held by Maturana and Varela that structure-determined systems are *informationally closed*. What Maturana and Varela call *instructive interaction*, which is the *direct* influence of one person on another, is held to be impossible. Mahoney (1991) explains:

> The ongoing structural changes (and exchanges) that living systems undergo are the result of "perturbations," which can arise from interactions with their medium [environment] or, recursively, with themselves. These perturbations "trigger" structural changes in the organism but do not automatically convey information about the nature or properties of the perturbing entity. They are not, in other words, "instructive" in the traditional sense of that term. Perturbations do not "cause" changes in the organism by putting something into it (like "information"); they simply trigger changes of state that are structure-determined by the organism. From this perspective, "information" is not something transferred or processed. Instead, "information" is literally translated from its Latin origin: *in formare*, "that which is formed from within" (p. 392).

Another important aspect of constructivist epistemological theory pertains, again, to neurobiological considerations and distinguishes *feedback* (information processing model) from the constructivist concept of *feedforward,* in which the elements comprising a human "experience" are characterized predominately by an "inside-in" process (informationally closed system) rather than an "outside-in" process, as represented by feedback in the information processing model. Mahoney (1991) provides an example of feedforward:

> On the assumption that visual experience is highly correlated with neuro-chemical activity in the visual cortex, only about 20 percent of that activity can be attributed to impulses from the retina . . . impulses from the retina can influence—but do not specify—activity in the visual cortex. On the average, as much as 80 percent of what we "see" may be a tacit construction "fed forward" from the superior colliculus, the hypothalamus, the reticular formation, and the visual cortex itself (p. 101).

Mince (1992), recognizing the importance of the contributions of Maturana and Varela to an understanding of the neurobiological basis of human experience and behavior, makes reference to them as significant figures in the *new biology,* which has shifted from the traditional concern of biology with the evolution and classification of life forms to the nature of organization within living things (p. 327). Mince provides a pertinent description of Maturana and Varela's contribution to the new biology, with their concept of structure determinism and its implication for shifting the basis for understanding human behavior from philosophical assumptions to neurobiology:

> The new biologists [Maturana and Varela] eventually realized [from their experiments] that the nervous system of living things operates in its connections to the organism's receptors and effectors as a closed system. That is, the structure of the nervous system is such that it cannot know about external reality in any direct manner. It is a closed system which operates through a series of electrochemical structural changes to inform itself about the outside world. *The closing of the nervous system was necessary for the eventual development of constructivist theory, and provided a scientific rigor for concepts which had long been discussed in the philosophical community* [emphasis added] (p. 372).

Autopoiesis

Because they are structure-determined and organizationally closed, living systems are said to be *autopoietic,* or self-organizing, entities. Autopoietic entities are autonomous in the sense that they survive, prosper, or perish under the "self-law" of their own makeup (Mahoney, 1991, p. 393). In contrast to a state of autopoiesis is that of *allopoiesis,* which is the essential principle of systems theory. A number of parts interrelate among themselves to produce a specified outcome. An example is an automobile composed of a number of interrelated parts that work in unison to propel it down the road; but it has no capacity to produce and maintain itself as an autopoietic system does.

Autopoietic entities, because of the way they are structurally organized, are engaged in the process of producing more of themselves. This process is manifest at every level of organization, from the cell to the colony. Cells grow and split, forming additional like-structured cells. Parents have offspring, perpetuating the family line . . . Living, from the ingestion of food to the excretion of waste, consists of cycles of self-production. For a living system there is a unity between product and process: In other words, the major line of work for a living system is creating more of itself (Efran et al., 1990, p. 47).

Structural Coupling

It is the constructivist principle of structural coupling that makes it possible for structure-determined autopoietic individuals to interact with entities other than themselves and their own nervous systems. The principle of structural coupling also allows constructivist theory to avoid the epistemological pitfall of solipsism, or a state of complete self-reference. Structural coupling corresponds roughly to the more traditional concept of "interpersonal interaction" in an ongoing "relationship," with the important difference that the interaction is seen to be between *closed,* not open, systems.

Episodes of interaction between individuals and their environment are instigated through mutual *perturbations,* or triggering stimuli. These perturbations form the *basis* for changes in each (person and environment) but do not *determine* those changes, which are instead brought about by the nature of their respective structures. One person does not "cause" another person to do anything; this would be *instructive interaction,* or direct influence, which, according to Maturana and Varela, is not possible because of the closed nature of each person's system.

In structural coupling, what interacts are the mutual perturbations (stimuli) of the entities involved. The dynamics of this are different than in the usual conception of interpersonal dynamics in two ways. First, it is the qualities and configurations of the reciprocal stimuli of person and environment that actually interact and *not* the structures of each; *interaction is an external, not an internal phenomenon.* Second, it is each person's *structure,* or internal dynamics, that determines what environmental stimulus configurations can trigger changes in each (Maturana & Varela, 1987, p. 135–136). Tom and Mary Jones can attain a state of structural coupling by initiating a verbal conversation (auditory mutual perturbation), and the state of structural coupling will last as long as the verbal perturbations do not exceed the linguistic structure (ability to deal with the language being used and its meanings) of one or both of them, making the episode intolerable or unprofitable. When this happens, they will become "structurally uncoupled" and the interaction will end.

Constructivism obviously poses some quite nontraditional views of human nature, human functioning, and, indeed, "the world." Based on its epistemology, which blurs subject-object distinctions and questions notions of objectivity and reality, constructivism shifts us to a "many worlds" frame of reference and away from normative views of truth and falsehood, right and wrong, functional and dysfunctional. Significant practice implications arise from the "many worlds" constructivist way of thinking about human behavior. Several of these are examined in the following section and are focused primarily on practice-principle implications for the practitioner.

IMPLICATIONS FOR ASSESSMENT, DIAGNOSIS, AND TREATMENT

IMPLICATIONS FOR ASSESSMENT

The case assessment process involves the knottiest of all problems in understanding human behavior—that of causality. Positivist causal explanations have assumed that a great deal of both individual and aggregate behavior is the direct result of identifiable "external" influences. Constructivist causal assumptions, however, are based on a view of the human nervous system and its relationship to the environment that maintains that the nervous system can only be "perturbed" or "bumped up against" but not "entered" by external stimuli, indicating a closed system. What, then, are some constructivist implications for assessment if the individual is viewed as a structure-determined closed system?

Perhaps the most basic implication is that practitioners can only assess the functioning of *individual* clients. In constructivist theory, "aggregate" units such as family, group, and community are viewed as reifications existing only in language and thought and devoid of ontological existence. While the constructivist practitioner may think in terms of working with a "system," he/she continually keeps in mind that the number of systems is always equal to the number of system observers he/she is dealing with at any given time. A major implication of this for assessment is that the practitioner must bring to each client case a "many worlds mind-set," which mandates a dedication to learning as much as possible about each client's views, understandings, and beliefs (the client's "world") about the problem(s) at hand. It is the client's sense that the main concern of the practitioner *is,* in fact, to learn about him/her as an individual, with the right to be the person he/she is at that time, that translates into feelings of being highly respected and valued by the practitioner. This, in turn, frees the client from the need to self-defend and makes possible reconstructions of his/her problematic life situation and experimentation with new solutions. Constructivist theory supports the time-honored assessment principle in social work of starting (and staying) where the client is.

Essentially, what is assessed in a constructivist-based approach is the client's frame of reference, pertaining to the problems being discussed, and the nature of reciprocal perturbations between the client and relevant aspects of his/her medium (environment). This is a process representing close collaboration between practitioner and client, in which the client is made to feel that it is the practitioner who is learning and he/she who is teaching.

IMPLICATIONS FOR DIAGNOSIS

Diagnosis, in the sense that it has been used in the so-called medical model by the behavioral helping professions, is not supported by constructivist theory. "What's wrong" is not seen as an entity in the same sense that the physician views a fractured leg or appendicitis as entities, i.e., as having ontological existence. The principle of structure determinism negates the validity of externally imposed predetermined categories and labels. In the approach represented by the *Diagnostic and Statistical Manual of Mental Disorders,* for example, diagnostic expertise in a case lies with the practitioner and his/her skill in use of the classification system. The client's role becomes that of passive recipient of the practitioner's expertise. A constructivist-based approach to developing ideas about the nature of problems stresses the need for practitioner-client collaboration and mutuality, with the "expert" role assigned to the client, not the practitioner. This will be explained later in more detail.

TREATMENT IMPLICATIONS

Treatment Focus

In a constructivist-based practice approach, treatment focus is on the *client's* problem reality, i.e., his/her perceptions, understandings, and definitions of the problem as this reality interacts with characteristics of his/her medium (environment). In more traditional practice approaches, especially psychodynamic ones, uncovering the "real problem" in a case has been seen as an essential job for the practitioner. The "real problem" concept implies that there is an objective pathological/dysfunctional condition of the client that can be discovered through the clinical skills of the practitioner, as when the physician finds malignant cells and diagnoses cancer—the real problem underlying the patient's pain and other symptoms. In constructivist-based assessment and treatment, however, no real problem is assumed to exist (which is not to say that *no* problem exists). Constructivists maintain that "psychosocial problems" do not exist in the ontological sense but only in language and thought. It is the *nature* of the client's verbalizations and thinking about the problem, interacting with relevant sociocultural values, norms, and definitions, that constitute the reality of the problem and hence the focus of treatment. Contrary to a widespread practice among practitioners in the behavioral helping professions, the constructivist practitioner would not try to get the client to "own his problem" but to cognitively divest him/herself of it instead. For some cases dealt with in a narrative approach to treatment, for example, separating the problem from the person is seen to be essential. A technique called "externalizing the problem" is frequently used, often with dramatic positive results (see, for example, White, 1989; O'Hanlon, 1994, p. 24). It is believed that externalizing the problem (essentially a process of giving it a name as apart from the client) helps free the client to view the problem as an adversary outside instead of inside the self, thus freeing him/her to develop alternative problem versions and solutions. This is thought to be especially helpful in cases where the client has seemed to incorporate the problem with his/her identity, for example, in anorexia.

Client Self-determination

The principle of client self-determination has been held as a major, if not *the* major, value in social work from the beginnings of the profession. It is supported not only as a value in constructivism, but is identified as a "natural" state of the person by virtue of his/her structure-determined nature and exists whether or not it is "valued." If the responses of individuals are determined by their structure, they are by definition self-determining. The practitioner has no option of respecting or not respecting this practice principle. As with individualizing clients, the only option is in doing it consciously or unknowingly. A practitioner could *believe* that he/she was executing a controlling technique of some kind, e.g., giving a client paradoxical instructions; however, the client's response would not be *determined* by the paradoxical instructions but only *selected* by them, i.e., they would "trigger" *some* response but would not determine *what* response—that being brought about by the individual's neurophysiological structure and psychological makeup. For the practitioner to realize this state of affairs settles the issue of whether or not the client should be "allowed" to be self-determining in a given situation—he/she *will* be in *all* situations. It should be pointed out, however, that acknowledging the client's mandatory self-determination does not mean accepting everything the client might want to do. "While accepting that there are multiple versions of reality, we may choose not to accept versions that are congruent with the perpetuation of racism, domestic violence, school dropouts, runaway teenagers, and other destructive interactions. We may still try to change uglier versions of reality" (Colapinto, 1985, p. 30).

Practitioner Demands

It may be well to point out that because of the level of counterintuitiveness inherent in constructivist theory, a certain tolerance for ambiguity is required on the part of the practitioner—this making it possible to embrace the "many worlds" perspective of constructivism on the one hand and, on the other, to interact with the client as though he or she shared the same work as theirs. As Vaihinger would say, the practitioner has to act "as if" there is an objective world "because it is useful." Some may feel uncomfortable with such a paradoxical professional mind-set, while others will have no difficulty.

CASE EXAMPLE

Perhaps one of the most difficult aspects of constructivism to comprehend pertains to its epistemology, which deemphasizes traditional normative perceptions and understandings of an objective world and stresses instead the importance of the individual's subjective idiosyncratic world as the primary basis for behavior. The following case vignette, described by Harlene Anderson as cited by M. Sykes Wylie (1992), illustrates a practice implication of the constructivist epistemological stance.

A family came to therapy after the children had been removed from their home and the mother had gone to a shelter because the father had so severely beat them. The mother came in looking disheveled, wearing house slippers and missing several teeth. The father—a huge man, barefoot, weighing probably 300 pounds and wearing denim, bib-front overalls with no shirt on underneath—began shouting as soon as he was in the room that he was poor, white trash, he'd never be anything, but he would not be told what to do by anybody, he would handle his family the way he saw fit and the only reason he was there was because "the fuckers downtown" [legal authorities] had made him come. He also announced, rather mysteriously, that he "hated niggers."

At that point, says Anderson, "everyone behind the mirror instinctively moved their chairs back," except Harriet Roberts, a consultant to the clinic, and a black woman. She got up, walked into the therapy session, calmly introduced herself and with apparently complete sincerity said she wanted to learn more about what he was saying and why he disliked blacks.

Roberts continued the therapy, seeing both husband and wife separately and together (the wife had gone back to live with him, as she always had in the past), bringing in the man's mother, and the staff from the shelter where the woman had stayed, and consulting with the child protective agency. Gradually, as he became more human in therapy, his behavior outside improved; after the first session, he stopped beating his wife, and when his children were eventually returned, he did not beat them again, either (p. 28).

The practice principle applied here, derived from constructive epistemology, was in evidence from the therapist's obvious assumption of the role of learner with the client—a client who at the moment was potentially dangerous to her and had proven himself dangerous to his family.

According to Anderson, the therapists [referring to other therapists subsequently involved] entered therapy with an attitude that they did *not* know, objectively, better than the man or his wife or the children or any of the other people involved in the case, what constituted universal truths about good and bad families, emotional pathology and health. They did not feel that their professional expertise allowed them to "write the story" for the family. Instead, they believed that in conversation, all these participants together could come up with a better, more humane story that locked nobody out of the process of creating it.

What seems to have happened is that a man who has felt ignored, ostracized and generally loathed for most of his life, meets a therapist who is unafraid of his hostility, uninsulted by his bigotry and unoffended by his repulsive persona. . . . He says that for the first time in his life he feels he has been listened to and understood (pp. 28–29).

On first consideration, what the consultant did here might only seem like reframing, a commonly used technique in which the practitioner redefines the meaning of a problem situation from negative to positive, changing the client's view accordingly.

However, it was more than that. The consultant, by walking calmly into the client's presence, saying she wanted to understand more about why he disliked blacks, demonstrated her respect and unconditional positive regard for him in the face of his anger and implied threats, and made it possible for him to *reconstrue* his constructive world.

Through her actions, the consultant recognized the client's structure-determined nature as reflected in his insistence that he would handle his family as he wanted and that he had the right to hate black people. In acknowledging his very "being" as the only person he could be at the moment, he then became free to begin to reconstrue his meanings closer to those of his medium (environment). This was not an episode of simple *adjustment* on the client's part but of *adaptation,* because an aspect of his medium, the consultant, moved toward him and he toward her, and it became a two-way process in which *structural coupling* occurred.

ADMINISTRATIVE AND TRAINING FACTORS

AGENCY ACCEPTANCE

Being a newcomer to social work, constructivist-based treatment approaches are not yet widely recognized as such. Psychodynamic, cognitive, behavioral, and systems theories remain predominant as the foundation theories of social work practice, and are also the main ingredients of the eclecticism professed by many practitioners. Social workers interested in constructivism may be successful in stimulating the interest of fellow practitioners, supervisors, and administrators. Most current social workers were not exposed to constructivist ideas as such in their professional training and may find constructivist conceptions foreign to their way of thinking about working with clients. However, opportunities to learn about this conceptual framework for practice are becoming more numerous, with an increasing number of relevant publications, workshops, and courses in some schools of social work. "Official" agency recognition and acceptance of constructivist-based treatment approaches should increase as practitioners successfully experiment with these ideas in working with clients.

FORMAL TRAINING

In some schools of social work, constructivist ideas are beginning to find their way into the HBSE curriculum, practice theory courses, field instruction, and research courses. Apparently rare, however, is course content dealing with constructivist implications for social policy, which would in general be concerned with factors related to improving the fit between the needs of clients as self-determining agents and various elements of socioeconomic and political environments through the application of constructivist concepts such as autopoiesis and structural coupling.

To help insure a thorough grounding in the principles of constructivism, students should have course work pertaining to all three aspects of constructivism as a thought system—philosophical, theoretical, and methodological. For the philosophical aspect, students should have an introductory exposure to the basics of epistemology in order to compare realist and constructivist epistemologies. Study of the theoretical aspect of constructivism should expose students to topics in psychology such as sensation, perception, and cognition, as well as elementary physiological psychology. For the methodology aspect, the basic concepts and postulates of constructivism would be translated into assessment/treatment principles, techniques, and strategies, with opportunities provided for students to learn practice applications in their field experiences. For an excellent source of information on some of the ways constructivist ideas are currently being incorporated into social work curricula, the reader is referred to *Revisioning Social Work Education: A Social Constructionist Approach* (Laird, 1993).

EMPIRICAL BASE

ATTITUDE TOWARD THE EMPIRICAL STANCE

Constructivist treatment approaches do not attempt to validate their effectiveness through the same means as those submitting themselves to empirical studies. "Constructivists do not believe that empirical evidence plays a significant role in evaluation, and therefore the question of whether their position can be empirically supported would be taken by them only as evidence of naïveté (Cole, 1992, p. 252).

For constructivists, denial of the positivist notion of a single objective reality also negates the usefulness of "measures" of objective reality as employed in empirical research. The epistemological position of constructivism locates it within the camp of those advocating the need for a switch in the behavioral sciences and related helping professions from the investigative model of the natural sciences to another approach. Smith, Harre, and Van Langenhove (1995), in a critical review of the positivistic-based research model, suggest its replacement with a *hermeneutic* (interpretative) model:

> The problem with such a view [positivistic] is thus that it does not take into account that human behavior is meaningful behavior that involves active agents with intentions and expectations and able to communicate with other equally active agents. . . . the natural sciences model is aimed at seeking causality, favors quantitative forms of analysis in so-called "extensive" designs that generate universal knowledge, and is related to positivist philosophy of science. The hermeneutic model is aimed at the search for meaning, favors qualitative analysis that generates knowledge of particulars, and is related to non-positivist philosophies of science (p. 15).

Neimeyer (1993), in considering constructivist-based psychotherapies and existing methods of research, indicates that an appropriate approach for research on such therapies might require a fundamental reappraisal of inquiry (p. 229):

The resulting mode of inquiry might bear little resemblance to the apparently objective, nomothetic orientation of most psychotherapy research. Instead, its goal would be the articulation of deeply personal meanings and the construction of possible worlds through imaginative participation in conversation with the client. Ultimately, such a discipline of discourse would blur the line between basic research and clinical application altogether, suggesting a form of encounter between therapist and client that is simultaneously interrogative and therapeutic (p. 230).

Because of the relatively recent appearance in social work of constructivist-based treatment approaches, the development of a research base is in the early stages. As this base develops, it will most likely be fed from both quantitative and qualitative studies. Charmaz (1995) indicates that *grounded theory* holds promise for addressing the central investigative concerns of both the interpretative (constructionist) and realist (positivist) camps (pp. 30–32). "By offering a set of systematic procedures, grounded theory enables qualitative researchers to generate ideas that may later be verified through traditional logico-deductive methods" (p. 48).

EFFECTIVENESS

Evidence of the effectiveness of constructivist-based treatment approaches is largely anecdotal at this point, as might be expected in view of their relative newness and the inevitable search for the most efficacious approach to researching practice outcomes. While not in themselves proof of effectiveness, practitioner enthusiasm and client acceptance run high for constructivist approaches. Work needing to be done toward developing appropriate investigative methods includes the formulation of criteria for judging positive treatment outcomes that are acceptable to both practitioners and researchers and the development of procedures for applying these criteria.

CONNECTIONS TO OTHER THEORIES

Constructivism and constructivist-based treatment approaches are difficult to compare to other frameworks. This is because there are similarities and differences with any given perspective or practice approach. For example, most other approaches view the practitioner as the expert in the helping process. The constructivist approach, however, views the client as the expert and the practitioner in the role of learner, thus creating an important difference with most other approaches. Possible exceptions are the phenomenological/humanistic-based approaches such as client-centered and existential approaches. At the same time, constructivist-based approaches have a kinship with some others that do view the practitioner as the expert. Notable are the psychodynamic approaches, which emphasize the importance of perception, meaning making, and idiosyncratic subjective experience, e.g., the psychosocial model and psychoanalytically oriented approaches. There are, of course, clear connections with approaches based in cognitive theory, with its emphasis on the "knowing" process and mentation, and this would be another example where the practitioner would tend to be viewed as the expert, not the client. Clear agreements are also to be found between the feminist perspective and constructivism. Both maintain that reality is socially constructed and that each person has his/her own reality of equal worth with all others. Both emphasize the oppressive influence that certain sociocultural norms can exert on individuals, families, groups, and organizations and the contribution of these toxic norms to the development of psychosocial problems on all levels.

While space does not permit a detailed comparison of the constructivist approach with all others, in general it is most akin to those placing a high degree of importance on internal dynamics, client self-determination, respect for client individuality, and the importance of language and communication. Those emphasizing "objective" definitions of "adjustment," the concept of diagnosis, and the practitioner as change agent (expert) would tend have the least in common with the constructivist approach.

While its simultaneous similarities and differences with other approaches make comparison a complex task, the task may be well worth the effort. The constructivist framework would seem to hold promise for bridging some seeming differences and strengthening the total enterprise of social work theory development. An example would be that of the similarities and differences between the psychoanalytic concept of transference and the constructivist principle of structure determinism. Efran et al. (1990) make the comparison:

> Freud . . . was correct in placing transference at the heart of his theory of treatment. Transference affects us all. It isn't just an affliction of the neurotic or a set of reactions specific to the psychotherapy setting. It isn't even necessarily a product of psychopathology or defense systems. It is an inevitable byproduct of how the nervous system is structured. *All* our reactions are tied to internal workings. When people react to us, they are really reacting to aspects of themselves. Because Freud was working within an objectivist framework, he conceptualized transference reactions as departures from reality. We prefer to think about transference in terms of the *relative* fit between a person's judgments and prevailing community standards. *Reality is not the anchor—consensus is* [emphasis added] (p. 72).

LIMITATIONS AND PROBLEMS

As is always the case with any new theory (and old ones too), controversies and various concerns have arisen about constructivism and its implications for explaining and changing human behavior.

On the conceptual side, it can be difficult to know if there are substantive differences with nonconstructivist concepts that are seemingly essentially similar. For example, consider Bell's (1985) comment on Maturana's view of interpersonal causation:

When Maturana says that causality is impossible, he means that the professor's lecture did not determine the response of his students (that would be instructive interaction). The professor's lecture *selected* the students' responses, but their structure *determined* their responses . . . Maturana is claiming that our everyday use of the word "cause" always implies or threatens to imply a determining in the sense of instructive interaction—whereas "causation" is always only a selecting. Thus, he says causality is impossible (p. 8).

Perhaps what Maturana means by "select" and "determine" is essentially similar to "necessary" and "sufficient" causes in models of linear causality. Is the distinction, then, between the constructivist conception of "select/determine" and the realist conception of "necessary/sufficient" a distinction with a difference? if one is a constructivist, the answer is yes, but if a realist the answer is no. The constructivist bears the burden of convincing the realist of the unreality of *the* world—one in which the realist believes that happenings are cause and effect phenomena. The realist, on the other hand, must try to persuade the constructivist that he/she is, in fact, in *the* world and not just in *a* world as his epistemic delusions would have him believe. And so the argument would go, the essence of which may be the basis on which one likes or dislikes constructivist theory, i.e., whether one is at heart a believer in philosophical relativism or realism.

Other concerns about conceptual and practical aspects of constructivism have been expressed by Mahoney (1991):

Beyond the heuristic abstractions of "structure determination," "organizational closure," and "structural coupling," what is it that determines an organism's adaptations to/of its environment? What are the parameters of "congruence" between the structures of a living system and its medium? Why are some systems capable of much wider ranges of self-restructuring than others, and what are the explicit implications for parent, education, and psychological services?

Another way of expressing this reservation is to say that . . . current autopoietic theory pays too little attention to the world in which the living system lives, not to mention the mentation involved and the processes by which that system learns, changes, or develops. . . . As many cognitive therapists have learned over the last two decades, psychotherapy clients can be urged to "restructure" their perceptions and beliefs about self and world, but the self-perpetuating aspects of that self and the everyday constraints imposed by that world are not always conducive to that undertaking (p. 396).

CONCLUSIONS

The selective use of an ever-expanding body of knowledge and theory in social work becomes an increasing necessity as the complexity of social work practice continues to grow. Constructivism as a conceptual framework for practice and constructivist-based treatment approaches have recently added to the profession's available technology. The future for constructivism in the profession will undoubtedly unfold according to he "laws of nature," i.e., the extent to which it is found to be compatible with social work values, its usefulness to practitioners and effectiveness with clients, its attractiveness to the academic community for further conceptual development, and its compatibility with the priorities of the social welfare bureaucracy. Payne (1991) writes:

> New ideas within social work theory arise in various ways and go through a process of *naturalization* by which they become adjusted to the conventional framework of social work. Some theories have not fully naturalized, because they do not deal well with some of the important features of social work within the period in which they become important. Theories which do naturalize affect the common features of social work (p. 37).

Cole (1992) has distinguished between "core" knowledge in a discipline and "frontier" knowledge. The core knowledge, including a relatively small number of theories, is the "given" or "starting point" for that discipline. The frontier component is composed of that knowledge which is in the early stages of being developed and about which substantial consensus is still lacking (p. 15). Constructivism as a framework for social work treatment fits into the frontier category at this point. Further use by practitioners and testing by researchers will be necessary for constructivism to arrive at a point where it may slip over into the core of social work knowledge.

It has been shown in this chapter how some of the basic postulates of constructivism are not only compatible with major social work practice principles but provide them with additional support. Constructivist-based practice clearly addresses current major concerns of the profession such as the need to empower clients, the right of racial, cultural, ethnic, gender, and age groups to be self-determining, and the need to enhance the degree of dignity and respect accorded to all people.

The formulations of constructivism set forth here as a conceptual framework for social work treatment have drawn substantially on the conceptions of Maturana and Varela. These conceptions are rooted in neurobiology instead of the social and behavioral sciences that social work has traditionally drawn on for foundational theory. In pondering the theory-development usefulness of constructivism for social work, it should also be noted that constructivism supports and may give added meaning to long-held values and ethical positions of the profession.

> If we know that our world is necessarily the world we bring forth with others, every time we are in conflict with another human being *with whom we want to remain in coexistence,* we cannot affirm what for us is certain (an absolute truth) because that would negate the other person. If we want to coexist with the other person, we must see that *his certainty—however undesirable it may seem to us—is as legitimate and valid as our own* because, like our own, that certainty expresses his conservation of structural coupling in a domain of ex-

istence—in which both parties fit in the bringing forth of a common world. A conflict is always a mutual negation. It can never be solved in the domain where it takes place if the disputants are "certain." A conflict can go away only if we move to another domain where coexistence takes place. The knowledge of this knowledge constitutes the social imperative for a human-centered ethics (Maturana & Varela, 1987, pp. 245–246).

Would this not seem to be the knowledge of which the consultant was in command who successfully engaged the enraged client whose hostility she sincerely wanted to learn about and, in so doing, saw the client's anger and abusive behavior toward his family dissolved? Would it stretch the imagination too far to believe that if that client had possessed the necessary linguistic sophistication, he might have expressed something similar to Maturana's words after his encounter with the consultant?

Every human being, as an autopoietic system, stands alone. Yet let us not lament that we must exist in a subject-dependent reality. Life is more interesting like this, because the only transcendence of our individual loneliness that we can experience arises through the consensual reality that we create with others, that is, through love (1978, p. 63).

BIBLIOGRAPHY

Bell, P. (1985). Understanding Batten and Maturana: towards a biological foundation for the social sciences. *Journal of Marital and Family Therapy 11* (1), p. 6.
Charmaz, K. (1995). Grounded theory. In J. Smith, R. Harre, and L. Van Langenhove (Eds.), *Rethinking Methods in Psychology*. London: Sage Publications.
Colapinto, J. (1985). Maturana and the ideology of conformity. *The Family Therapy Networker,* May-June.
Cole, S. (1992). *Making Science: Between Nature and Society.* Cambridge. MA: Harvard University Press, p. 11.
Dean, R., & Fenby, D. (1989). Exploring epistemologies: Social work action as a reflection of philosophical assumptions. *Journals of Social Work Education 25* (1), pp. 46–54.
Dean, R., & Fleck-Henderson, A. (1992). Teaching clinical theory and practice through a constructivist lens. *Journal of Teaching in Social Work 6* (1), pp. 3–20.
Efran, J. & Lukens, M., (1985). The world according to Humberto Maturana. *The Family Therapy Networker,* May-June.
———, Lukens, M. & Lukens, R. (1990). *Language, Structure and Change: Frameworks of Meaning in Psychotherapy.* New York: W.W. Norton.
Elkana, Y. (1978). Two-tier thinking: philosophical realism and historical relativism. *Social Studies of Science 8.* pp. 309–326.
Fisher, D.D.V. (1991). *An Introduction to Constructivism for Social Workers.* New York: Praeger.
Goodman, N. (1972). in The Way the World Is. In *Problems and Projects.* New York: Bobbs-Merrill, pp. 30–31.
———. (1984). *Of Mind and Other Matters.* Cambridge, MA: Harvard University Press.
Grossman, Dean R. (1993). Teaching a constructivist approach to clinical practice. *Journal of Teaching in Social Work 8,* (1/2), pp. 55–75.

Hartman, A. (1991). Words create worlds. *Social Work 36* (1), pp. 275–276.

Ide, H. (1995) Sophists. In R. Audi (Ed.), *The Cambridge Dictionary of Philosophy,* New York: Cambridge University Press.

Kant, I. (1938) [1781]. *The Critique of Pure Reason.* Trans., N.K. Smith. New York: Macmillan.

Kelly, G. (1955). *The Psychology of Personal Constructs* (2 vols). New York: W.W. Norton.

Laird, J. (Ed.). (1993). *Revisioning Social Work Education: A Social Constructionist Approach.* New York: Haworth Press.

Mahoney, M. (1991). *Human Change Processes: The Scientific Foundations of Psychotherapy.* New York: Basic Books.

Maturana, H. (1975). The organization of the living: A theory of the living organization. *The International Journal of Man-Machine Studies 7,* pp. 313–332.

———. (1978). Biology of language: the epistemology of reality. In G.A. Miller and E. Lenneberg (Eds.), *Psychology and Biology of Language and Thought.* New York: Academic Press.

———. (1980). Biology of cognition. In H. Maturana and F. Varela (Eds.), *Autopoiesis and Cognition: The Realization of the Living.* Boston: Reidel.

———, Uribe, G., & Frenk, S. (1968) A biological theory of relativistic color coding in the primate retina. *Arch. Biologica y Med. Exp.,* Sjupplemonto No. 1, pp. 1–30.

——— & Varela, F.J. (1987). *The Tree of Knowledge: The Biological Roots of Human Understanding.* Boston: Shambhala Publications.

Neimeyer, R. (1993). An appraisal of constructivist psychotherapies. *Journal of Consulting and Clinical Psychology 61* (2), p. 230.

O'Hanlon, B. (1994). The third wave. *The Family Therapy Networker 18* (6).

Payne, M. (1991). *Modern Social Work Theory: A Critical Introduction.* Chicago: Lyceum Books.

Piaget, J. (1929). *The Child's Conception of the World.* New York: Harcourt, Brace.

———. (1950). *The Psychology of Intelligence.* New York: Harcourt, Brace.

———. (1970). *Towards a Theory of Knowledge.* New York: Viking.

Pojman, L. (1995). Relativism. In R. Audi (Ed.), *The Cambridge Dictionary of Philosophy.* New York: Cambridge University Press.

Smith, J., Harre, R., & Van Langenhove, L. (1995). (Eds.). *Rethinking Psychology.* London: Sage Publications.

Sykes Wylie, M. (1992). The evolution of a revolution. *The Family Therapy Networker 18* (6), p. 48.

Turner, F.J. (1986). Theory in social work practice. In F.J. Turner (Ed.), *Social Work Treatment: Interlocking Theoretical Approaches* (3rd ed.). New York: Free Press

Van Langenhove, L. (1995). The theoretical foundations of experimental psychology and its alternatives. In J. Smith, R. Harre, and L. Van Langenhove (Eds.), *Rethinking Psychology.* London: Sage Publications.

von Foerster, H. (1984). On constructing a reality. In P. Watzlawick (Ed.), *The Invented Reality.* New York: W.W. Norton.

von Glaserfeld, E. (1984). An introduction to radical constructivism. In P. Watzlawick (Ed.), *The Invented Reality.* New York: W.W. Norton.

Watzlawick, P. (1976). *How Real is Real?* New York: Random House.

——— (Ed.). (1984). *The Invented Reality.* New York: W.W. Norton.

———. (1990). *Munchhausen's Pigtail or Psychotherapy and Reality.* New York: W.W. Norton.

White, M. (1989). The externalizing of the problem and the re-authoring of lives and relationships. *Dulwhich Centre Newsletter,* Summer, pp. 5–12.

Wolterstorff, N. (1995). Locke, John. In R. Audi (Ed.), *The Cambridge Dictionary of Philosophy.* New York: Cambridge University Press.

CHAPTER 8

CRISIS THEORY AND SOCIAL WORK PRACTICE

KATHLEEN ELL

OVERVIEW

CRISIS THEORY

Stressful life events can precipitate a state of "crisis," wherein people experience temporary feelings of severe acute distress and of being overwhelmed or unable to cope in ways that reduce the discomfort or the hazardous circumstances. For some people, particularly when the event is traumatic or catastrophic and outside of their expected life experiences, the resulting crisis may become a significant risk factor for subsequent dysfunctional behavior, impaired physical and social functioning, and acute and prolonged mental disorder. The best way to prevent negative outcomes following exposure to hazardous events is to provide people with immediate emotional, informational, and environmental aid.

These central propositions underlie emerging theories about human crisis experience as well as a broad range of crisis interventions by social workers, psychologists, physicians, nurses, teachers, clergy, lawyers, police, and emergency and disaster workers.

While exposure to stressful life events is ubiquitous in human experience, the response to stressful events varies considerably. Few people, if any, escape major stressful life events, but not all, or even most, of them experience levels of distress or dysfunction that require professional intervention. Whether or not people will experience a crisis following normal stressful events (and how severe the distress will be and how long it will last) varies depending on the nature of the event, its perceived meaning, and the perceived adequacy of personal and environmental resources to meet the demands posed by the event.

Traumatic and catastrophic events (perceived to be outside of normal life experience) are likely to precipitate severe distress for most people and significantly increase their risk for subsequent negative outcomes. Unfortunately, more people are exposed to traumatic events than was once believed, particularly family violence and abuse, and crime in the community, schools, and workplace. Even natural disasters now place more people at risk as high-density communities develop in flood plains, beach fronts, and seismically active locations where the chance of severe devastation is high.

Additional crises are those precipitated by social-structural changes such as economic downturns and those made worse by impoverished environments. Moreover, an individual or family crisis can occur when a discrete event or series of events is piled on top of chronically stressful lives.

Crisis interventions for people distressed by "normal" life events are frequently provided at the initiation of the individual or family. In contrast, the high degree of risk associated with exposure to traumatic events, and the fact that at-risk individuals are often identifiable at the time of exposure (an exception being family violence), has spurred the development of crisis interventions that reach out to targeted individuals instead of waiting for them to seek help themselves (Brom & Kleber, 1989). For example, critical incident debriefing interventions are increasingly provided by social workers through outreach programs (Bell, 1995; Wollman, 1993). People experiencing a crisis on top of chronically stressful lives usually need crisis interventions that include environmental intervention, tangible assistance, and access to longer-term treatment or rehabilitative or maintenance services.

Crisis Theory

It is important to note from the outset that although the term "theory" is used throughout this chapter and is commonly used in the crisis literature, many of the elements of crisis theory are only beginning to be formulated and few have been rigorously tested (Parad & Parad, 1990). Definitions of crisis and its distinguishing characteristics remain general, and the term is widely applied to a variety of circumstances.

In this chapter, crisis "theory" refers to a general set of assumptions and propositions rather than to a systematically verified formal theoretical system that delineates predictive and causal interactions. From this perspective, crisis theory refers to "a work-in-progress" rather than to an established formal theory (Hobfoll & Shlomo, 1986).

Insofar as crisis theory posits a rationale for preventive action, important overarching questions are raised. What is a crisis? How do we know it when we see it? How does it differ from other types of psychological problems? What risk and protective factors predict a crisis and, most important, its negative effects on functional status? What negative outcomes are produced by a crisis and what is their prevalence in the general and clinical population? What types of preventive interventions should be undertaken, under what circumstances, for which individuals, and at what cost and what benefit? Throughout this century, these and related questions have increasingly preoccupied both stress researchers and health and human service practitioners. Although important questions remain, much has been learned.

What Is a Crisis?

A crisis is defined as an acute emotional upset in an individual's usual steady state, accompanied by a perceived breakdown in his or her usual coping abilities. The acute upset is manifested by physical, psychological, cognitive, and relational distress and symptoms. A crisis can be experienced by an individual independent of others or by groups of individuals within families, organizations, and communities. A crisis is preceded by an identifiable stressful life event that evokes the perception of loss, threat of loss, or a challenge. A crisis state is time-limited, taking weeks or months for an adaptive or maladaptive resolution to be reached.

Early crisis theorists and practitioners emphasized the universal elements in crises induced by "normal" life events (Parad, 1971; Parad & Parad, 1990). A crisis was viewed as a normal time-limited reaction to a significant life stressor. Attention was focused on the maturational opportunity inherent in crisis experience; successful mastery of the crisis could enhance self-esteem and expand coping repertoires. According to the pioneering research of Lindemann (1944), an archetypical crisis was bereavement. Over time, attention focused on crises that were precipitated by a perceived loss or threat of loss during universal life transitions such as premature birth, physical illness, adolescence, divorce, and retirement.

In contrast, current literature on crisis and crisis intervention reflects greater emphasis on people with severe crisis symptomatology, and on the "casualties" of crises induced by traumatic events. For example, experience with Vietnam veterans during the 1970s produced a distinct literature on what came to be called posttraumatic stress disorder (PTSD). Grounded in earlier experience with combat stress, Holocaust survivors, and prisoners of war, the clinical and research literature on traumatic and catastrophic life events has expanded to include natural and technological disasters, and family, school, workplace, and community violence. Pathological crisis states and their aftermath are now codified in the *Diagnostic and Statistical Manual of Mental Disorders* (DSM-IV) as acute stress disorder and PTSD.

Prevalence of Negative Outcomes

Exposure to traumatic events of individuals in the United States is high, with estimates of as much as sixty-nine percent of the population (Green, 1984). Studies indicate that people who suffer serious psychological impairment following exposure to a traumatic event number from one-third to one-half of the population (Green, 1994; Green & Lindy, 1994). A significant proportion of identified mental health patients report past exposure to a major stressful event (Green, 1994). PTSD is often associated with other disorders such as depression and substance abuse (Davis & Breslau, 1994; Green, 1994), and for many individuals, PTSD is a chronic mental disorder (Green, 1994). Crime victimization and domestic violence account for many negative outcomes (Foa & Riggs, 1995), but recent studies document acute PTSD among burn, cardiac, accident, and cancer patients (Blanchard et al., 1995; Green, 1994; Kelly et al., 1995; Vrana & Lauterbach, 1994).

Risk and Protective Factors

Research has identified factors that place individuals at risk for experiencing a severe crisis and factors that protect them from becoming severely impaired following a crisis. These data are used to identify at-risk groups and to aid in designing interventions that enhance protective factors. The primary risk factor for PTSD is the severity of exposure (Green, 1994). Other risk factors include socioeconomic status, previous psychiatric symptoms, child abuse, youth, and previous multiple events (Breslau et al., 1995; Green, 1994). Research on the effects of exposure to serious stressors among children is more sparse, but growing evidence documents their vulnerability (Pitcher & Poland, 1992). While studies of PTSD have retrospectively identified risk factors, little is known about factors that influence the course of PTSD over time.

Other research identifies protective personal and environmental resources in stress response. Primary among these is an extensive body of research confirming the powerful salutary effects of social support in mitigating stress and its negative outcomes (Coyne et al., 1990). Characteristics of resilient families have been identified that help explain why some families successfully cope with life stress and tragedies, while others break down (McCubbin et al., 1988).

During the past decade, researchers have also begun to identify factors that characterize "resilient" children. Studies of children exposed to chronic poverty, parental psychopathology, family breakdown, neglect, and war have found that up to one-third develop into healthy adults (Werner, 1995). Protective factors that help to explain these positive outcomes include personal, family, and community characteristics such as effective coping patterns, close bonds with at least one competent caring person, and caring educational and community programs (Werner, 1995).

Crisis Interventions

The quest to understand and ultimately attempt to prevent long-term human suffering precipitated by stressful life events spurred the work of early crisis theorists (Caplan, 1964; Parad, 1971). Working together, pioneering researchers and practitioners spawned a series of action-research programs. In the process, they identified the human costs of exposure to traumatic and normative life stressors and developed, implemented, and evaluated interventions to prevent, reduce, and ameliorate its harmful effects (Golan, 1978; Parad & Parad, 1990).

Today, an extensive range of practice principles guide practitioners on interventions that provide immediate aid aimed at reducing people's feelings of distress and helplessness, activating social resources, and supporting effective coping strategies. Similar practice principles are applied across a broad spectrum of modalities and service delivery systems, including individual, group, and family brief treatments, twenty-four-hour crisis response programs, and disaster teams.

The natural inclination of social workers and other helping professionals might be that, because of the risks associated with crisis, crisis intervention should be provided to all affected individuals. Given the large numbers of people exposed to major traumatic events, however, and the fact that many cope successfully without professional assistance, this would not be practical. It is essential, therefore, to use assessment and screening methods to identify as early as possible those individuals who are likely to require professional intervention. Recent attempts to classify and define criteria for pathological crisis states are consistent with this aim.

Unfortunately, recent rigorous examination of the effectiveness of interventions and treatments has been relatively sparse. This critical task remains to challenge both practitioners and researchers.

ORIGINS OF THE THEORY

During this century, practitioners, researchers, and theorists have jointly contributed to crisis and crisis intervention theory. Knowledge about human crisis experience has been heavily influenced by human stress and coping theory and epidemiological and clinical research on pathological crises and dysfunctional outcomes. Health and human service practitioners have responded and contributed to this advancing knowledge base by developing a range of interventions to prevent crises from occurring and to "treat" crises and thereby prevent acute or prolonged psychological disorder or family breakdown.

Early Clinical Research.

Grounded in the seminal research by Lindemann on acute grief reactions following the Coconut Grove fire (1944) and subsequently advanced by the preventive psychiatry research program of psychiatrist Gerald Caplan (1965) and social worker Howard Parad (Parad, 1971; Parad & Parad, 1990), crisis intervention theory and practice grew rapidly during the 1960s and 1970s, particularly in social work.

An early forerunner of today's theorists who focus on traumatic events, Tyhurst (1958) described the reactions of previously healthy people to severe stress and advocated prompt intervention soon after the traumatic experience in order to effect a positive outcome. Defining a crisis as a temporary upset in the emotional homeostasis of the individual produced by hazardous events, Caplan emphasized that crises were unique opportunities for the individual to achieve a better or worse emotional balance. Therefore, he became a leading advocate for community-based preventive crisis intervention services (Caplan, 1964).

Sociological constructions of family stress are based on the seminal work of Reubin Hill (1949). Hill's theoretical model of family crisis grew from research on families during war-induced separations and reunions. Briefly stated, Hill's model proposes that:

> A (the event)—interacting with B (the family's crisis-meeting resources)—interacting with C (the definition the family makes of the event)—produces X (the crisis). The second and third determinants—the family resources and definitions of the event—lie within the family itself and must be seen in terms of the family's structures and values. The hardships of the event, which go to make up the first determinant, lie outside the family and are an attribute of the event itself (Hill, 1958).

Influenced by the general systems paradigm, Hill's formulation of family stress theory underpins contemporary family stress literature as well as family crisis intervention theory (Boss, 1988; McCubbin & Patterson, 1982). Hill's work spawned decades of research on family stress response, including attempts to explain and predict dysfunctional family behavior and family breakdown (McCubbin & McCubbin, 1992).

Stress and Illness

Crisis theory has been strongly influenced by extensive research on physiological responses to stress (Parad, 1971; Golan, 1987). During a lifetime of research, Selye (1956) identified the natural state of the organism as equilibrium with its environment. Change in one part of the organism results in disequilibrium among all parts. Selye proposed that the struggle to reestablish homeostasis involved an alarm phase, in which the organism mobilizes for fight or flight, and a resistance phase, in which it copes with the change. If the organism fails over time to overcome the threat, a state of exhaustion occurs, eventually resulting in illness.

Stress and Coping

Shifting the emphasis away from the physiological elements in stress response, Lazarus (1966) proposed a psychologically focused model that includes potential mediating factors in stress response, such as the individual's cognitive appraisal of the meaning of the event and of the threats or challenges presented by the event and the resources available to meet them. Coping theory assumes that people are rarely passive in the face of life events, but instead actively seek to change the stressor or to influence the personal meaning of the event or their own emotional response to it.

Ecologically oriented conceptualizations of stress and coping (Pearlin, 1989; Aneshensel, 1992; Mirowsky & Ross, 1989) emphasize the importance of chronic role strains that, over time, produce stress. While little attention has been paid to the ways in which crises vary depending on people's social position, gender, racial/ethnic status, age, and marital status (Pearlin, 1989; Aneshensel, 1992), the evidence that illness rates—including psychological disorder—are higher among people of lower socioeconomic status is formidable (Anderson & Armstead, 1995).

CRISIS THEORY AND SOCIAL WORK

Social work practice is characterized by frequent encounters with people who have been exposed to potentially hazardous life events or who are in crisis. Indeed, providing crisis intervention services is an everyday experience for most social workers, and for many of them, people in crisis make up all or most of their practice. It is not surprising, therefore, that references to crises, crisis theory, and crisis intervention pervade social work literature. A consequence of the widespread use of these terms has been a blurring of the distinctions between the unique theoretical, empirical, and practical components of crisis intervention and the interventions and services provided by social workers.

The historical development of crisis theory and its refinement into an accepted social work practice method is well documented in social work literature (Golan,

1978; 1987; Parad, 1971; Parad & Parad, 1990). Influenced by developments in stress and coping theory, social workers were prominent in formulating and refining the elements of crisis intervention theory and in promoting crisis intervention services in the community (Parad, 1971; Golan, 1987). Social workers in community mental health programs, suicide prevention centers, family service agencies, and medical care systems made major contributions to the early development and promotion of crisis intervention. Currently, social workers in child welfare systems, schools, rape treatment centers, crisis response teams, and employee assistance programs are expanding the use of crisis interventions.

The early crisis intervention literature within social work was characterized by extensive conceptual, definitional, and practice debates about 1) what constituted a crisis (as distinct from a life stress); 2) what was actually meant by time-limited crises; 3) what were the unique components of crisis intervention; 4) what distinguished it from other forms of brief treatment; 5) whether it was a legitimate practice approach or a poor substitute for more effective longer-term approaches; and 6) who was qualified to provide crisis intervention services (Parad & Parad, 1990).

Over the past decade, however, there is less evidence in social work literature of the stimulating intellectual climate that characterized the early work. Perhaps the general acceptance of the initial propositions, and their intuitive logic and practical utility, have thwarted intellectual ferment. Particularly disturbing is the current lack of a rigorous program of effectiveness and outcome research to build on the preliminary research of Parad and others (Parad & Parad, 1990).

Current social work literature reflects three general tendencies: 1) the widespread application by social workers of remarkably similar general practice principles for providing emotional aid to people who are experiencing acute situational distress; 2) the emergence of subspecialties that delineate specific interventions for people suffering from specific types of traumatic or catastrophic life events; and 3) the development of integrated service models that combine emotionally and environmentally focused crisis intervention to meet the multiple needs of vulnerable people coping with acute stress and chronically stressful lives.

BASIC ASSUMPTIONS

Social workers act to ameliorate human suffering and, if possible, to prevent it. Crisis theory provides practitioners with a basic set of assumptions to guide decisions about whether to intervene, for whom, and in what ways.

PRESUPPOSITIONS OF CRISIS THEORY

Emphasizing the emotional, cognitive, physiological, and functional elements of human crisis, crisis theory makes the following basic assumptions: 1) it is not uncommon for individuals to experience a state of acute emotional disequilibrium, social disorganization, cognitive impairment, and physical symptomatology in the face of immediate situational stress or hazardous life events; 2) acute situational distress is a normative life experience, an upset in a usually steady emotional, cognitive, and physical state that is not pathological, that can happen to anyone, and that, indeed, is likely to happen to most people at some time in their lives; 3) specific life events will be universally devastating; 4) during a state of disequilibrium, people will automatically strive to regain homeostasis or balance within their lives, a process that involves an appraisal of the meaning of the event within the overall context of the individual's life and of the personal and social resources available to cope with it; 5) while struggling to regain emotional equilibrium, the individual is in an intense, time-limited state of psychological (and in some cases, physiological) vulnerability; 6) during this heightened state of vulnerability, the individual is particularly amenable to psychological intervention; 7) the crisis response is characterized by universal stages toward adaptive or maladaptive crisis resolution; and 8) crises afford an opportunity for growth and development as well as for negative outcomes (Golan, 1987; Slaikeu, 1990).

The rapidly growing literature on traumatic life events retains these general assumptions while highlighting characteristic symptom patterns at the pathological end of the continuum. The neurobiologic response to stress that contributes to the prolonged symptoms reported by patients with PTSD has been identified (Southwick et al., 1994). A few patients with PTSD have been found to grow from the experience (Tomb, 1994); however, many PTSD patients experience prolonged distress and dysfunction.

Propositions about the ecological dimensions of crises are less clearly delineated (Ell, 1995). However, the environmental context in which a crisis occurs is recognized as influencing the severity of distress as well as the availability of resources to meet its demands. Therefore, people who are already vulnerable because of socioeconomic status, chronically stressful lives, or inadequate support systems are presumed to be at greater risk for the negative effects of crisis.

Crisis "contagion" and positive and negative impacts on environmental resources are also assumed to influence crisis response when groups of people are affected at the same time (Kaniasty & Norris, 1995). For example, the shooting of a student or teacher precipitates a crisis for the entire student-body and faculty (Pitcher & Poland, 1992). Similarly, a hurricane simultaneously impedes and enhances the exchange of social support, producing community altruism and solidarity while disrupting social support networks as a result of death, injury, or relocation (Kaniasty & Norris, 1993).

PRINCIPAL CONCEPTS

In arguing that acute psychological upsets were frequently triggered by external events, early formulators of crisis theory moved beyond the psychoanalytic tradition, which addressed human crisis as solely an intrapsychic experience (Hobfoll, 1988). Crisis theory views personality characteristics as important primarily insofar as they affect individual coping resources. Individual history is relevant as it pertains to previous or repeated event exposure. Two key elements of crisis theory are the character of the precipitant event and the symptom patterns that identify an acute or prolonged crisis.

Stressful Events

As implied above, a key factor in determining the response to stressful events is the nature of the event. Attesting to the ubiquitous nature of human stress experience (Lukton, 1982), two categories of life events are likely to precipitate a state of crisis: universal life experiences and extraordinary life experiences (Baldwin, 1978; Slaikeu, 1990). The former include normal maturational experiences such as childbirth, adolescence, marriage, menopause, and retirement. For most people, normal developmental stressful life events are accompanied by temporary feelings of severe upset that eventually respond to usual coping resources and strategies. For a minority of people, these events trigger a crisis that precipitates more serious acute psychological and functional impairment or that requires professional intervention.

In contrast, traumatic life events (particularly those that are viewed as outside of normal human experience) are far more likely to produce severe distress, in some cases leading to long-term impaired psychological, social, and physical status. Traumatic life events include life-threatening illness or trauma, the death of a loved one, natural and man-made disasters (such as fire, floor, or war), and violent crimes (a rape or mugging).

In some cases, stressful events refer to chronic stressors (Scott & Stradling, 1994). For example, repeated exposure to the same event, as in child abuse, or exposure to a series of events over time can lead to a crisis. Similarly, chronically stressful lives make people more vulnerable to crisis-producing events by wearing down their adaptive coping resources and increasing the likelihood that they will feel overwhelmed and powerless. Social workers are familiar with each of these pathways into crisis and the high degree of risk that they carry for negative outcomes. For example, chronic exposure to trauma such as repeated sexual abuse (McLeer et al., 1994) and domestic violence (particularly without crisis intervention) is a known risk factor for subsequent serious dysfunction (Pelcovitz et al., 1994) and mental disorder.

The Crisis State

As already mentioned, a crisis is a severe emotional upset, frequently accompanied by feelings of confusion, anxiety, depression, and anger and by impaired social functioning and physical symptoms (Halpern, 1973; Parad & Parad, 1990). During a crisis, individuals experience heightened psychological vulnerability, reduced defensiveness, and a severe breakdown in coping and problem-solving ability (Slaikeu, 1990). The acute crisis state is generally thought to be time-limited, although recent research indicates that its duration, originally thought to be six to eight weeks, can be considerably longer and is likely to vary depending on the nature of the precipitating event, its meaning to the individual, and the coping resources and life circumstances of the individual or family (Slaikeu, 1990).

The crisis sate is not inherently pathological (Hobbs, 1984). Phases or stages from the acute onset of the crisis state through its eventual resolution include the mastery of developmental and coping tasks specific to the event (Lukton, 1982), a reduction in the intensity of the psychological upset, and a renewed state of emotional equilibrium after a relatively brief period. Successful adaptation to crisis enhances people's ability to cope with future events.

The response to traumatic events frequently involves intense fear, helplessness, or horror, and in children may be expressed by disorganized or agitated behavior (DSM-IV, 1994). Traumatic events can shatter basic assumptions and beliefs about personal vulnerability and the social fabric. Most people will experience symptoms following exposure to a traumatic event and should be considered to be in severe crisis. For example, individuals frequently report reexperiencing, avoidance, and arousal symptoms (Ulman, 1995).

PATHOLOGICAL OUTCOMES

Crisis outcomes include restoration to previous, to better, or to worse functioning. While pathological response to traumatic events has long been recognized, the line between it and normal response is somewhat arbitrary. As already said, most people will experience symptoms, and specific criteria for acute stress disorder and PTSD are included in the DSM-IV (1994). While research on the processes involved in the progression between normal symptoms and disorder has been sparse, practitioners are able to observe the protective influence of personal and social resources and intervene to strengthen them.

According to the DSM-IV (1994), acute stress disorder and posttraumatic stress disorder are precipitated by exposure to an "extreme traumatic stressor involving direct personal experience of an event that involves actual or threatened death or serious injury, or other threat to one's physical integrity; or witnessing an event that involves death, injury, or a threat to the physical integrity of another person; or learning about unexpected or violent death, serious harm or threat of death or injury experienced by a family or other close associate" (p. 424). Traumatic events include being diagnosed with a life-threatening illness, severe transportation accidents, personal assaults (a sexual assault, physical attack, robbery, or mugging), incarceration as a prisoner of war or in a concentration camp, natural or man-made disasters, military combat, and being kidnapped, taken hostage, or subjected to terrorism or torture.

A person is diagnosed as having an acute disorder if he or she develops, within one month of exposure, and experiences for at least two days but for less than one month, at least three of the characteristic anxiety, dissociative, and other symptoms (including a subjective sense of numbing, detachment, or absence of emotional responsiveness; a reduction in awareness of surroundings; derealization; depersonalization; dissociative amnesia; persistent reexperience of the event; marked avoidance of stimuli that arouse recollection; and marked anxiety and arousal) (DSM-IV, 1994; Koopman et al., 1995; Lundin, 1994).

Posttraumatic stress disorder features seventeen symptoms (DSM-IV, 1994) divided into three clusters: 1) reexperiencing of the traumatic event (e.g., nightmares, flashbacks); 2) avoidance and numbing (e.g., avoiding trauma reminders, detachment from other people); and 3) increased arousal (e.g., hypervigilance, irritability). Individuals experiencing at least one reexperiencing symptom, three avoidance-numbing symptoms, and two arousal symptoms for at least one month are defined as meeting symptom criteria for PTSD. The disorder is labeled "acute" if symptoms persist for less than three months, "chronic" if they last more than three months, and "delayed" if symptoms first appear six months or more after the traumatic event.

It was noted earlier that bereavement is generally regarded as a normal crisis for most people. According to the DSM-IV (1994), the presence of the following symptoms are not characteristic of a "normal" grief reaction: "1) guilt about things other than actions taken or not taken by the survivor at the time of the death; 2) thoughts of death other than the survivor feeling that he or she would be better off dead or should have died with the deceased person; 3) morbid preoccupation with worthlessness; 4) marked psychomotor retardation; 5) prolonged and marked functional impairment; and 6) hallucinatory experiences other than thinking that he or she hears the voice of, or transiently sees the image of, the deceased person" (pp. 684–85). These reactions should alert the practitioner to consider specific interventions, including the use of medication.

Crises besides PTSD that are precipitated by traumatic events are found to be associated with a full range of negative outcomes. These include depression, substance abuse, antisocial personality disorder, sexual dysfunction, phobias, obsessive compulsive disorder, physical illness and somatization, higher health service utilization, relationship problems, impaired social functioning, homelessness, criminal behavior, and suicide (Burton et al., 1994; Kramer et al., 1994; North et al., 1994).

Neglected in the early crisis literature, the effects of crisis events on children's lives are receiving increasing attention (Fink et al., 1995; Giaconia et al., 1994; Shannon et al., 1994). In fact, there is a growing body of research that documents a strong relationship between behavioral problems in school and crisis events such as divorce, severe physical illness, and death of a significant other (Kovacs et al., 1995; Pitcher & Poland, 1992). Sexually abused children are found to have high rates of psychiatric disorder (Merry & Andrews, 1994). Fortunately, there is also evidence that, over time, children recover from traumatic exposure (Green et al., 1994).

CRISIS INTERVENTIONS

Of primary concern to social workers is the opportunity to reduce the risks of event exposure through crisis intervention (Armstrong et al., 1995; Bell, 1995; Danish & D'Augelli, 1980; Golan, 1987; Parad & Parad, 1990). Crisis intervention refers to a broad spectrum of interventions that vary with respect to principal goals, modalities used, populations served, and the service delivery system and programs through which they are provided. Therefore, classifying crisis interventions is difficult and the boundaries between classifications by goal, modality, population, and delivery system will inevitably be blurred.

PRINCIPAL THERAPEUTIC GOAL

Prevention is the overarching goal of crisis intervention. To prevent means to keep something from happening, but the something in the case of crisis intervention refers to more than one circumstance. Public health prevention nomenclature identifies three types of prevention: primary, secondary, and tertiary. Applied to crisis intervention, primary prevention seeks to decrease the number of people who experience a state of crisis. Secondary prevention refers to interventions to minimize the severity of the crisis state and to reduce the number of people for whom the crisis results in prolonged functional impairment and psychological disorder. Tertiary prevention aims at reducing the degree of impairment or disability that resulted from the original crisis or preventing an impaired level of functioning from worsening. An example of the latter, crisis intervention for the severely and persistently mentally ill, is aimed at preventing hospitalization or further family breakdown. Taken together, crisis interventions aim to prevent, restore, improve, or maintain.

An alternative prevention classification system was recently used in a landmark study by the Institute of Medicine on preventive intervention research on reducing risks for mental disorders (Mrazek & Haggerty, 1994). Originally developed by Gordon (1983), the system consists of three categories: universal, selective, and indicated. The first refers to preventive interventions that are deemed desirable for everybody in specific populations. For example, preventive crisis interventions in this category would include stress inoculation programs for all military personnel (Armfield, 1994), problem-solving skill training for adolescents in a school system (Pitcher & Poland, 1992), and new-parent support groups. These crisis interventions aim to reduce the number of people who experience an overwhelming crisis.

A selective preventive intervention is targeted at groups or individuals immediately following their exposure to a potentially crisis-producing event. Examples include critical incident debriefing interventions and open-ended support groups for people with newly diagnosed life-threatening illness. Indicated preventive interventions are provided for people who are experiencing symptoms indicating that they are at risk for acute stress disorder, PTSD, or family breakdown.

PRINCIPLES OF CRISIS INTERVENTION

Crisis intervention practice principles are remarkably similar despite variations in the event, the population served, the methods used, and the delivery system (Golan, 1978; 1987; Parad & Parad, 1990; Smith, 1978, 1979; VandenBos & Bryant, 1987). Interestingly, similar practice guidelines have been formulated for other than traditional mental health service providers, including the clergy, lawyers, police, teachers, and emergency and disaster personnel (Hendricks, 1991; Slaikeu, 1990).

Hallmark principles of crisis intervention include the following: 1) aid is provided as quickly as possible, often through outreach programs; 2) interventions are time-limited and brief; 3) the practitioner role is active; 4) symptom reduction is a primary goal; 5) practical information and tangible support are provided; 6) social support is mobilized; 7) expression of feelings, symptoms, and worries is encouraged; 8) effective coping is supported to restore a sense of competency as early as possible; and 9) cognitive issues about reality testing and confronting the experience are addressed.

Individuals with acute stress disorder require supportive and behavioral treatments to reduce symptoms. For individuals diagnosed with PTSD, the use of cognitive treatments is recommended, at times in combination with medication for associated depression and anxiety. Similar practice guidelines for critical incident debriefing have been developed for use with primary and secondary victims (Armstrong et al., 1995; Bell, 1995). The latter include individuals who have observed the trauma, such as family members, fellow employees or students, and emergency workers.

THE FOCI OF CRISIS INTERVENTION

Crisis intervention may be psychological, educational, environmental, or pharmacological. Psychologically focused crisis intervention for individuals and families continues to be widely used by social workers, particularly for individuals with readily accessible social and community service resources. Combining psychological and informational elements is also common in practice.

When social workers encounter people in crisis whose lives are characterized by chronically stressful environments, they provide interventions targeted to the socioenvironmental context. Examples include an individual or family crisis precipitated by a severe breakdown in the social environment (including repeated domestic and neighborhood violence, homelessness, and chronic unemployment) or a "normative" crisis among people whose daily lives are characterized by poverty, discrimination, impaired physical and mental health, and inadequate community service systems.

Assessment Tools
Clinically administered assessment tools have been developed to assist in identifying childhood trauma (Fink et al., 1995) and PTSD (Hendrix et al., 1994; Neal et al., 1994). Social workers are also using computerized assessment methods (Franklin et al., 1993).

EFFECTIVENESS AND OUTCOMES RESEARCH

Early crisis theory and practice were well grounded in basic and applied research (Lindemann, 1944; Parad & Parad, 1990). During the 1960s, crisis intervention program evaluations provided evidence of the utility of this approach, as well as of other short-term therapies (Parad & Parad, 1990). However, few methodologically rigorous studies of crisis interventions have been conducted in recent years (Slaikeu, 1990).

The need for studies of the cost benefits of crisis intervention is underscored by ongoing considerations about whether mental health services will be provided by managed care and other human service systems, and, if so, what type. There is an urgent need, therefore, for comparative outcome studies of different crisis intervention methodologies (Eggert et al., 1990; Nelson et al., 1990). Research is also needed to answer critical questions about what type of crisis intervention (e.g., individually focused, family-based, environmentally targeted) is most effective for which groups of clients experiencing which type of crisis. Studies of both the short- and long-term effects of crisis intervention are needed (Viney et al., 1985).

Outcome research is particularly needed to advance the scientific knowledge base for crisis intervention with socioculturally diverse populations (Bromley, 1987; Weiss & Parish, 1989). To date, crisis intervention research on the validity of theoretical assumptions and practice principles for diverse sociocultural groups has been rare. As a result, questions remain about the ways in which crises, as well as practice guidelines and principles, might vary by gender, age, and socioeconomic, racial, and ethnic status. Indeed, there is evidence that crisis intervention may not be effective in all cases. For example, adverse effects on outcome were found when gender differences were not considered in the design of the crisis intervention (Viney et al., 1985). Furthermore, even when they are under presumed severe stress, such as when facing life-threatening illness, ethnic minorities and individuals from lower socioeconomic groups are less likely to participate in crisis support groups, raising questions about the design of the intervention and access to the service (Taylor et al., 1988).

To enhance the effectiveness of interventions targeted at the most vulnerable in society, there is a need to conceptualize the ecological dimensions of crisis theory (Ell, 1995). Crisis theory is frequently cited as the basis for the broad range of environmental interventions and strategies widely used by social workers. However, there are important gaps in existing knowledge about the effects of chronic stress on acute crises (Ell, 1995). For example, crisis intervention by family preservation programs has yet to be proven effective for dysfunctional families under extreme chronic environmental stress (Rossi, 1992). Integrating knowledge from research on the interactional, social-structural, and ecological dimensions of stress, social support, and coping is likely to advance the utility of crisis intervention for vulnerable multiproblem individuals and families (Coyne et al., 1990; Hobfoll, 1988; Moos, 1976; Eckenrode, 1991).

An ecological perspective also raises questions about the utility and practicality of primary and universal preventive interventions. Can coping skills be taught that enhance people's coping skills and social resources and so prevent stressful events such as divorce, interpersonal violence, and family breakdown? Do social policies that result in fewer economic and social resources for the most vulnerable members of society increase the number of people experiencing crises precipitated or exacerbated by a lack of adequate and readily accessible community services? Community settings such as churches, mutual help groups, and senior centers have been found to buffer life stress (Maton, 1989), whereas chronically stressful environments have been shown to erode supportive resources (Lepore et al., 1991). Designing, implementing, and evaluating primary preventive interventions will continue to be a responsibility of social workers and other human service professionals (Anderson & Armstead, 1995).

PTSD Research

To date, few studies have evaluated the effectiveness of interventions for persons suffering from PTSD (Richards et al., 1994) and little is known about gender and cultural influences on the assessment of PTSD (Allen, 1994). There is also evidence that many patients remain symptomatic, and that exposure techniques and cognitive reworking of PTSD memories are critical elements in effective treatment (McFarlane, 1994).

PRINCIPAL APPLICATIONS IN SOCIAL WORK PRACTICE

Spurred by growing concerns about cost and declining mental health and social service resources, social workers increasingly provide brief episodic treatment and services such as crisis intervention (Parad & Parad, 1990). The ubiquitous nature of human crisis and the variation in its manifestations have spawned interventions designed for different populations along the continuum of crisis experience. References to a wide spectrum of interventions, including emergency treatment, crisis debriefing, crisis support, crisis intervention, brief treatment, and environmental crisis intervention, are found in social work literature.

Caplan's seminal research (1964; 1974) emphasized the critical role of environmental resources (particularly the community service system) in crisis resolution and subsequent adaptation. However, early crisis intervention practice emphasized individually- and family-focused clinical approaches (Parad, 1971). During the past decade, a resurgence in community-based crisis interventions is evidenced by the growth of critical-incident stress management teams, by the crisis models of family preservation programs, and by the growth of school-based programs, mobile crisis units, crisis intervention centers, hotlines, and crisis intervention training programs for community emergency and disaster personnel.

Individually Focused Treatments

All types of psychoeducational, brief psychotherapies, stress inoculation, emotional debriefing, and pharmacological treatments (Sutherland & Davidson, 1994) are used by social workers in conducting individually focused crisis intervention. Cognitive-behavioral treatments, including those that use live and imaginal exposure techniques, are increasingly used to treat PTSD (Mancoske et al., 1994; Richards et al., 1994).

Crisis Intervention Groups

Crisis intervention groups for adults and children undergoing similar crises are widely used across practice settings (Gambe & Getzel, 1989; Gilbar, 1991; Haran,

1988; Northen, 1989; Schopler & Galinsky, 1993) and the use of groups for families undergoing crises is increasing (Gutstein, 1987; Halpern, 1986; Holmes-Garrett, 1989; Kilpatrick & Pippin, 1987; McPeak, 1989; Silverman, 1986; Taylor, 1986; Van Hook, 1987). In critical incident stress debriefing, crisis intervention groups are the method of choice (Wollman, 1993).

Family Crisis Intervention
Use of family crisis intervention methods is also widely reported by social workers (Allen & Bloom, 1994; Pardeck & Nolden, 1985; Sugarman & Masheter, 1985). Examples are found for a wide range of crises, such as those precipitated by marital separation (Counts & Sacks, 1985), family care giving (Walker et al., 1994), adolescent suicide attempts (Rotherman-Borus et al., 1994), and serious physical trauma (Silverman, 1986).

Multimodal Strategies
Mainly because of the growth of poverty, the lives of increasing numbers of children and adults are characterized by poor physical and mental health, community and family violence, repeated exposure to class and racial/ethnic discrimination, and increasing deficiencies in social and human service systems (including child welfare, education, health and mental health, and the justice system) (Mirowsky & Ross, 1989; National Research Council, 1993).

To confront the human problems that result from deteriorating social and physical environments, social workers deliver crisis interventions through programs that aim to mobilize environmental resources and thereby reduce crisis-producing events or ameliorate their severity. In these circumstances, psychologically focused crisis intervention is provided in combination with other interventions in multimodal and multitargeted service programs for individuals, families, groups, and communities (Hunner, 1986; Paschal & Schwahn, 1986).

There are many examples of crisis intervention provided in this way. Residential treatment programs use structural environmental interventions in combination with intensive psychologically focused crisis therapy (Weisman, 1985). Community programs for the severely and persistently mentally ill provide twenty-four-hour crisis intervention in addition to environmental resources (Kerson, 1989; Newhill, 1989). In response to gangs and teen offenders, crisis intervention has been combined with street surveillance (Spergel, 1986) and other services (Stewart et al., 1986). In the face of imminent family crisis, multiple interventions are aimed at activating or creating social system resources to reduce the immediate crisis and restore and improve precrisis family functioning (Michael et al., 1985; Nelson et al., 1990; Wells & Biegel, 1992).

Population-Based Preventive Interventions
Critical-incident debriefing, open-ended support groups, stress inoculation, and psychoeducational and coping-skill training interventions are examples of strategies

used by social workers to enhance people's ability to respond to stressful life events and to reduce the likelihood of their experiencing an overwhelming crisis or PTSD. These interventions generally include outreach to targeted populations in schools, workplaces, hospitals, and community disaster sites.

Population-based interventions assume that while not everyone needs treatment, most would benefit from immediate information and support. In the case of critical-incident stress debriefings, interventions are frequently provided by social workers in teams. Communitywide intervention programs are used in the face of natural disasters (Kaniasty & Norris, 1993; Wright et al., 1990). Debriefing interventions are provided for victims and for observers, such as members of a military unit who have witnessed the death or severe injury of a colleague and fire fighters, police, and other emergency personnel (Bell, 1995; Brom & Kleber, 1989; Smith & deChesney, 1994).

Service Delivery Systems

Crisis intervention services are provided throughout the health and human service system. They are delivered under a broad range of administrative and organizational auspices, including crisis teams (West et al., 1993), mobile intervention units (Geller et al., 1995), hotlines, individual and family counseling and therapy groups (Berger, 1984), and rape crisis treatment centers (Edlis, 1994). They are provided in general emergency rooms (Lambert, 1995), in-patient units (Anthony, 1992), workplaces (Mor-Barak, 1988; Sussal & Ojakian, 1988), schools (Steele & Raider, 1991), and the juvenile justice system (Hendricks, 1991). In general, population-based preventive interventions can be provided by nonmental health professionals, whereas other forms of intervention are better provided by trained mental health professionals. Social workers are prominent among crisis intervention providers.

PROSPECTUS

Crisis intervention will continue to be a primary social work intervention. The utility of enhancing people's ability to cope with life stressors and of providing immediate aid to those with severe disabling distress is unquestioned. However, advancing knowledge about the effectiveness (and cost) of alternative crisis intervention methods and services for different types and manifestations of crises must be high on the profession's knowledge-building agenda, challenging both social work practitioners and researchers. In fact, in the future, only crisis interventions with proven effectiveness are likely to be publicly or privately financed. Perhaps most daunting is the task of effectively assisting people whose emotional crises are exacerbated by social contexts of severe chronic environmental stress and inadequate community resources.

REFERENCES

Allen, S.N. (1994). Psychological assessment of post-traumatic stress disorder. Psychometrics, current trends, and future directions. *Psychiatric Clinics of North America* 17(2) 327–349.

Allen, S.N., & Bloom, S.L. (1994). Group and family treatment of post-traumatic stress disorder. *Psychiatric Clinics of North America* 17(2) 425–427.

Anderson, N.B., & Armstead, C.A. (1995). Toward understanding the association of socioeconomic status and health: A new challenge for the biopsychosocial approach. *Psychosomatic Medicine* 57, 213–225.

Aneshensel, C.S. (1992). Social stress: Theory and research. *Annual Review of Sociology* 18, 15–38.

Anthony, D.J. (1992). A retrospective analysis of factors influencing successful outcomes on an inpatient psychiatric crisis unit. *Research on Social Work Practice* 2(1), 56–64.

Armfield, F. (1994). Preventing post-traumatic stress disorder resulting from military operations. *Military Medicine* 159(12), 739–746.

Armstrong, K.R., Lund, P.F., McWright, L.T., & Tichener, V. (1995). Multiple stressor debriefing and the American Red Cross: The East Bay Hills fire experience. *Social Work* 40(1), 83–90.

Baldwin, B.A. (1978). A paradigm for the classification of emotional crises: Implications for crisis intervention. *American Journal of Orthopsychiatry* 48(3), 538–551.

Bell, J.L. (1995). Traumatic event debriefing: Service delivery designs and the role of social work. *Social Work* 40(1), 36–43.

Berger, J.M. (1984). Crisis intervention. *Social Work in Health Care* 10(2), 81–92.

Bertalanffy, L. von. (1968). *General System Theory: Foundations, Development, Applications.* New York: George Braziller.

Blanchard, E.B., Hickling, E.J., Taylor, A.E., Forneris, C.A., Loos, W., & Jaccard, J. (1995). Short-term follow-up of post-traumatic stress symptoms in motor vehicle accident victims. *Behavior Research Theory* 33(4), 369–377.

Boss, P. (1988). *Family Stress Management.* Newbury Park, CA: Sage Publications.

Breslau, N., Davis, G.C., & Andreski, P. (1995). Risk factors for PTSD-related traumatic events: A prospective analysis. *American Journal of Psychiatry* 152(4), 529–535.

Brom, D., & Kleber, J.R. (1989). Prevention of post-traumatic stress disorders. *Journal of Traumatic Stress* 2(3), 335–351.

Bromley, M.A. (1987). New beginnings for Cambodian refugees—or further disruptions? *Social Work* 32(3), 236–239.

Burton, D., Foy, D., Bwanausi, C., Johnson, J., & Moore L. (1994). The relationship between traumatic exposure, family dysfunction, and post-traumatic stress symptoms in male juvenile offenders. *Journal of Traumatic Stress* 7(1), 83–93.

Caplan, G. (1964). *Principles of Preventive Psychiatry,* New York: Basic Books.

Caplan, G. (1974). *Support Systems and Community Mental Health.* New York: Basic Books.

Counts, R.M., & Sacks, A. (1985). The need for crisis intervention during marital separation. *Social Work* 30(2), 146–150.

Coyne, J.C., Ellard, J.H., & Smith, D. (1990). Social support, interdependence, and the dilemmas of helping. In B.R. Sarason, E.N. Shearin, G. Pierce, & I.G. Sarason (eds.), *Social Support: An Interactional View.* New York: John Wiley.

Danish, S.J., & D'Augelli, A.R. (1980). Promoting competence and enhancing development through development intervention. In L.A. Bond, & J.C. Rosen (eds.), *Competence and Coping During Adulthood.* Hanover, NH: University Press of New England.

Davis, G.C., & Breslau, N. (1994). Post-traumatic stress disorder in victims of civilian trauma and criminal violence. *Psychiatric Clinics of North America* 17(2), 289–299

Diagnostic and Statistical Manual of Mental Disorders, 4th ed., (1994). Washington, DC: American Psychiatric Association.

Eckenrode, J. (ed.) . (1991). *The Social Context of Coping.* New York: Plenum Press.

Edlis, N. (1994). Rape crisis: development of a center in an Israeli hospital. *Social Work in Health Care* 18(3/4), 169–178.

Eggert, G.M., Friedman, B., & Zimmer, J.G. (1990). Models of intensive case management. *Journal of Gerontological Social Work* 15(3/4), 75–101.

Ell, K. (1995) Crisis intervention: Research needs. In R. Edwards (ed.), *Encyclopedia of Social Work* (19th ed.), Vol. 1. Washington, DC: National Association of Social Workers, 660–666.

Fink, L.A., Bernstein, D., Handelsman, L., Foote, J., & Lovejoy, M. (1995). Initial reliability and validity of the childhood trauma interview: A new multidimensional measure of childhood interpersonal trauma. *American Journal of Psychiatry* 152(9), 1329–1335.

Foa, E.B., & Riggs, D.S. (1995). Posttraumatic stress disorder following assault: Theoretical considerations and empirical findings. *New Directions in Psychological Science* 4(2), 61–65.

Franklin, C., Nowicki, J., Trapp, J., Schwab, A.J., & Petersen, J. (1993). A computerized assessment system for brief, crisis-oriented youth services. *Families in Society: The Journal of Contemporary Human Services* 74(10), 602–616.

Gambe, R., & Getzel, G.S. (1989). Group work with gay men with AIDS. *Social Casework* 70(3), 172–179.

Geller, J.L., Fisher, W.H., & McDermeit, M. (1995). A national survey of mobile crisis services and their evaluation. *Psychiatric Services* 46(9), 893–284.

Giaconia, R.M., Reinherz, H.Z., Silverman, A.B., Pakiz, B., Frost, A.K., & Cohan, E. (1994). Ages of onset of psychiatric disorders in a community of older adolescents. *Journal of the American Academy of Child Adolescent Psychiatry* 33(5), 706–717.

Gilbar, O. (1991). Model for crisis intervention through group therapy for women with breast cancer. *Clinical Social Work Journal* 19(3), 293–304.

Golan, N. (1978). *Treatment in Crisis Situations.* New York: Free Press.

Golan, N. (1987). Crisis intervention. In A. Minahan (ed.), *Encyclopedia of Social Work* (18th ed.), Vol 1. Washington, DC: National Association of Social Workers, 360–372.

Gordon, R. (1983). An operational classification of disease prevention. In J.A. Steinberg & M.M. Silverman (eds.), *Preventing Mental Disorders.* Rockville, MD: DHHS, 20–26.

Green, B.L. (1994). Psychosocial research in traumatic stress: An update. *Journal of Traumatic Stress* 7(3), 341–362.

Green, B.L., Grace, M.C., Vary, M.G., Kramer, T.L., Gleser, G.C., & Leonard, A.C. (1994). Children of disaster in the second decade. *Journal of the American Academy Child Adolescent Psychiatry* 33(1), 71–79.

Green, B.L., & Lindy, J.D. (1994). Post-traumatic stress disorder in victims of disasters. *Psychiatric Clinics of North America* 17(2), 301–309.

Gutstein, S. (1987). Family reconciliation as a response to adolescent crises. *Family Process* 26, 475–491.

Halpern, H.A. (1973). Crisis theory: A definitional study. *Community Mental Health Journal* 9, 342–349.

Halpern, R. (1986). Home-based early intervention: Dimensions of current practice. *Child Welfare* 115(4), 387–398.

Haran, J. (1988). Use of group work to help children cope with the violent death of a classmate. *Social Work with Groups* 11(3), 79–92.

Hendricks, J.E. (ed.). (1991). *Crisis Intervention in Criminal Justice/Social Service.* Springfield, IL: Charles C. Thomas.

Hendrix, C.C., Anelli, L.M., Gibbs, J.P., & Fournier, D.G. (1994). Validation of the Purdue Post-Traumatic Stress Scale on a sample of Vietnam veterans. *Journal of Traumatic Stress* 7(2), 311–318.

Hill, R. (1949). *Families Under Stress.* New York: Harper and Brothers.

Hill, R. (1958). Social stresses on the family: Generic features of families under stress. *Social Casework* 39, 139–150.

Hobbs, M. (1984). Crisis intervention in theory and practice: A selective review. *British Journal of Medical Psychology* 57, 23–34.

Hobfoll, S.E. (1988). *The Ecology of Stress.* New York: Hemisphere Publishing.

Hobfoll, S. E., & Shlomo, W. (1986). Stressful events, mastery, and depression: An evaluation of crisis theory. *Journal of Community Psychology* 14, 183–195.

Holmes-Garret, C. (1989). The crisis of the forgotten family: A single session group in the ICU waiting room. *Social Work with Groups* 12, 141–157.

Hunner, R.J. (1986). Reasonable efforts to prevent placement and preserve families: Defining active and reasonable efforts to preserve families. *Children Today* 15(6), 27–30.

Kaniasty, K., & Norris, F.H. (1993). A test of the social support deterioration model in the context of natural disaster. *Journal of Personality and Social Psychology* 64(3), 395–408.

Kaniasty, K., & Norris, F.H. (1995). Mobilization and deterioration of social support following natural disasters. *Current Directions in Psychological Science* 4(3), 94–98.

Kelly, B.B., Raphael, B., Smithers, M., Swanson, C., Reid, C., McLeod, R., Thomson, D., & Walpole, E. (1995). Psychological responses to malignant melanoma: An investigation of traumatic stress reactions to life-threatening illness. *General Hospital Psychiatry* 17, 126–134.

Kerson, T.S. (1989). Community housing for chronically mentally ill people. *Health and Social Work* 14, 293–294.

Kilpatrick, A.C., & Pippin, J.A. (1987). Families in crisis: A structured meditation method for peaceful solutions. *International Social Work* 30(2), 159–169.

Koopman, C., Classen, C., Cardena, E., & Spiegel, D. (1995). When disaster strikes, acute stress disorder may follow. *Journal of Traumatic Stress* 8(1), 29–46.

Kovacs, M., Ho, V., & Pollock, M.H. (1995). Criterion and predictive validity of the diagnosis of adjustment disorder: A prospective study of youths with new-onset insulin-dependent diabetes mellitus. *American Journal of Psychiatry* 152(4), 523–528.

Kramer, T.L., Lindy, J.D., Green, B.L., Grace, M.C., & Leonard, A.C. (1994). The comorbidity of post-traumatic stress disorder and suicidality in Vietnam veterans. *Suicide & Life Threatening Behavior* 24(1), 58–67.

Lambert, M. (1995). Psychiatric crisis intervention in the general emergency service of a veterans affairs hospital. *Psychiatric Services* 46(3), 283–284.

Lazarus, R.S. (1966). *Psychological Stress and the Coping Process.* New York: McGraw-Hill.

Lepore, S.J., Evans, G.W., & Schneider, M.L. (1991). Dynamic role of social support in the link between chronic stress and psychological distress. *Journal of Personality and Social Psychology* 61(6), 899–909.

Lindemann, E. (1944). Symptomatology and management of acute grief. *American Journal of Psychiatry* 101, 141–148.

Lukton, R.C. (1982). Myths and realities of crisis intervention. *Social Casework: The Journal of Contemporary Social Work* 63(May), 276–284.

Lundin, T. (1994). The treatment of acute trauma: Post-traumatic stress disorder prevention. *Psychiatric Clinics of North America* 17(2), 385–391.

Mancoske, R.J., Standifer, D., & Cauley, C. (1994). The effectiveness of brief counseling services for battered women. *Research on Social Work Practice* 4(1), 53–63.

Maton, K.I. (1989). Community settings as buffers of life stress? Highly supportive churches, mutual help groups, and senior centers. *American Journal of Community Psychology* 17(2), 203–232.

McCubbin, H., & Patterson, J.M. (1982). Family adaptation to crisis. In H.I. McCubbin, A. E. Cauble, & J. M. Patterson (eds.), *Family Stress, Coping and Social Support.* Springfield, IL: Charles C. Thomas, 26–47.

McCubbin, H., Thompson, A., Priner, P., & McCubbin, M. (1988). *Family Types and Family Strengths: A Life-span and Ecological Perspective.* Edina, MN: Burgess International.

McCubbin, H., & McCubbin, M. (1992). Research utilization in social work practice of family treatment. In A.J. Grasso & I. Epstein (eds.), *Research Utilization in the Social Services: Innovations for Practice and Administration.* New York: Haworth Press, 149–192.

McFarlane, A.C. (1994). Individual psychotherapy for post-traumatic stress disorder. *Psychiatric Clinics of North America* 17(2), 393–408.

McLeer, S.L., Callaghan, M., Henry, D., & Wallen, J. (1994). Psychiatric disorders in sexually-abused children. *Journal of the American Academy for Child Adolescent Psychiatry* 33(3), 313–319.

McPeak, W.R. (1989). Family intervention models and chronic mental illness: New implications from family systems theory. *Community Alternatives: International Journal of Family Care* 1(2), 53–63.

Merry, S.N., & Andrews, L.K. (1994). Psychiatric status of sexually abused children 12 months after disclosure of abuse. *Journal of the American Academy of Child Adolescent Psychiatry* 33(7), 939–944.

Michael, S., Lurie, E., Russell, N., & Unger, L. (1985). Rapid response mutual aid groups: A new response to social crises and natural disasters. *Social Work* 30, 245–252.

Mirowsky, J., & Ross, C.E. (1989). *Social Causes of Psychological Distress.* New York: Aldine de Gruyter.

Moos, R.H. (ed.). (1976). *Human Adaptation: Coping with Life Crises.* Lexington, MA: D.C. Heath.

Mor-Barak, M.E. (1988). Support systems intervention in crisis situations: Theory, strategies and a case illustration. *International Social Work* 31(4), 285–304.

Mrazek, P.J., & Haggerty, R.J. (1994). *Reducing Risks for Mental Disorders.* Washington, DC: National Academy Press.

National Research Council. (1993). *Losing Generations: Adolescents in High-risk Settings.* Washington, DC: National Academy Press.

Neal, L.A., Busuttil, W., Herapath, R., & Strike. P.W. (1994). Development and validation of the computerized clinician administered post-traumatic stress disorder scale-1-revised. *Psychological Medicine* 24(3), 701–706.

Nelson, K.E., Landsman, M.J., & Deutelbaum, W. (1990). Three models of family-centered placement prevention services. *Child Welfare* 69(1), 3–21.

Newhill, C.E. (1989). Psychiatric emergencies: overview of clinical principles and clinical practice. *Clinical Social Work Journal* 17(3), 245–258.

North, C.S., Smith, E.M., & Spitznagel, E.L. (1994). Violence and the homeless: An epidemiologic study of victimization and aggression. *Journal of Traumatic Stress* 7(1) 95–110.

Northen, H. (1989). Social work practice with groups in health care. *Social Work with Groups* 12(4), 7–26.

Parad, H.J. (1971). Crisis intervention. In R. Morris (ed.), *Encyclopedia of Social Work,* (16th ed). Vol. 1. New York: National Association of Social Workers.

Parad, H.J., & Parad, L.G. (1990). *Crisis Intervention.* Milwaukee: Families International.

Pardeck, J.T., & Nolden, W.L. (1985). An evaluation of a crisis intervention center for parents at risk. *Family Therapy* 12(1), 25–33.

Paschal, J.H., & Schwahn, L. (1986). Intensive crisis counseling in Florida. *Children Today* 15(6), 12–16.

Pearlin, L.I. (1989). The sociological study of stress. *Journal of Health and Social Behavior* 30(September), 241–256.

Pelcovitz, D., Kaplan, S., Goldenberg, B., Mandel, F., Lehane, J., & Guarrera, J. (1994). Post-traumatic stress disorder in physically abused adolescents. *Journal of the American Academy for Child Adolescent Psychiatry* 33(3), 305–312.

Pitcher, G.D., & Poland, S. (1992). *Crisis Intervention in the Schools.* New York: Guilford Press.

Richards, D.A., Lovell, K., & Marks, I.M. (1994). Post-traumatic stress disorder: Evaluation of a behavioral treatment program. *Journal of Traumatic Stress* 7(4), 669–680.

Rossi, P.H. (1992). Assessing family preservation programs. *Children and Youth Services Review* 14, 77–92.

Rotherman-Borus, M. J. Piacentini, J., Miller, S., & Graae, F. (1994). Brief, cognitive behavioral treatment for adolescent suicide attempters and their families. *Journal of the American Academy of Child and Adolescent Psychiatry* 33(4), 508–517.

Schopler, J.H., & Galinsky M.J. (1993). Support groups as open systems: A model for practice and research. *Health & Social Work* 18(3), 195–207.

Scott, M.J., & Stradling, S.G. (1994). Post-traumatic stress disorder without the trauma. *British Journal of Clinical Psychology* 33(1), 71–71.

Selye, H. (1956). *The Stress of Life*. New York: McGraw-Hill.

Shannon, M.P., Lonigan, C.J., Finch, A.J., & Taylor, C.M. (1994). Children exposed to disaster. *Journal of the American Academy of Child Adolescent Psychiatry* 33(1), 80–93.

Silverman, E. (1986). The social worker's role in shock-trauma units. *Social Work* 31(4), 311–313.

Slaikeu, K.A. (1990). *Crisis Intervention: A Handbook for Practice and Research* (2nd ed.). Boston: Allyn and Bacon.

Smith, C.L., & deChesney, M. (1994). Critical incident stress debriefings for crisis management in post-traumatic stress disorders. *Medicine Law* 13(1-2), 185–191.

Smith, L.L. (1978). A review of crisis intervention theory. *Social Casework* 59, 396–405.

Smith, L.L. (1979). Crisis intervention in practice. *Social Casework: The Journal of Contemporary Social Work* 60, 81–88.

Southwick, S.M., Bremmer, D., Krystal, J.H., & Charney, D.S. (1994). Psychobiologic research in post-traumatic stress disorder. *Psychiatric Clinics of North America* 17(2), 251–264.

Steele, W., & Raider, M. (1991). *Working with Families in Crisis: School Based Intervention*. New York: Guilford Press.

Stewart, M.J., Vickell, E.L., & Ray, R.E. (1986). Decreasing court appearances of juvenile status offenders. *Social Casework* 67, 74–79.

Sugarman, S., & Masheter, C. (1985). The family crisis intervention literature: What is meant by "family"? *Journal of Marital & Family Therapy* 11(2), 167–177.

Sussal, M., & Ojakian, E. (1988). Crisis intervention in the workplace. *Employee Assistance Quarterly* 4(1), 71–85.

Sutherland, S.M., & Davidson, J.R. (1994). Pharmacotherapy for post-traumatic stress disorder. *Psychiatric Clinics of North America* 17(2), 409–423.

Taylor, S.E. (1986). Social casework and the multimodal treatment of incest. *Social Casework* 67, 451–459.

Taylor, S.E., Folkes, R.L., Mazel, R.M., & Hilsberg, B.L. (1988). Sources of satisfaction and dissatisfaction among members of cancer groups. In B. Gottlieb (cd.), *Creating Support Groups: Formats, Processes, and Effects*. Beverly Hills, CA: Sage Publications, 187–208.

Tomb, D.A. (1994). The phenomenology of post-traumatic stress disorder. *Psychiatric Clinics of North America* 17(2), 237–250.

Tyhurst, J.S. (1958). The role of transitional states—including disaster—in mental illness. In Walter Reed Army Institute of Research, *Symposium on Preventive and Social Psychiatry*. Washington, DC: U.S. Government Printing Office.

Ulman, S.E. (1995). Adult trauma survivors and post-traumatic stress sequelae: An analysis of reexperiencing, avoidance and arousal criteria. *Journal of Traumatic Stress* 8(1), 151–159.

VandenBos, G.R., & Bryant, B.K. (eds.). (1987). *Cataclysms, Crises and Catastrophes: Psychology in Action*. Washington, DC: American Psychological Association.

Van Hook, M.P. (1987). Harvest of despair: Using the ABCX model for farm families in crisis. *Social Casework* 68, 273–278.

Viney, L.L., Benjamin, Y.N., Clarke, A.M., & Bunn, T.A. (1985). Sex differences in the psychological reaction of medical and surgical patients to crisis intervention and counseling: Sauce for the goose may not be sauce for the gander. *Social Science and Medicine* 20, 1199–1205.

Vrana, S., & Lauterbach, D. (1994) Prevalence of traumatic events and post-traumatic psychological symptoms in a nonclinical sample of college students. *Journal of Traumatic Stress* 7(2), 289–302.

Walker, B.A., & Mehr, M. (1983). Adolescent suicide—a family crisis: A model for effective intervention by family therapists. *Adolescence* 18(70), 285–292.

Walker, R.J., Pomeroy, E.C., McNeil, J.S., & Franklin, C. (1994). A psychoeducational model for caregivers of patients with Alzheimer's. *Journal of Gerontological Social Work* 22(1/2), 75–91.

Weisman, G.K. (1985). Crisis-oriented residential treatment as an alternative to hospitalization. *Hospital and Community Psychiatry* 36(12), 1302–1305.

Weiss, B.S., & Parish, B. (1989). Culturally appropriate crisis counseling: Adapting an American method for use with Indochinese refugees. *Social Work* 34(3), 252–254.

Wells, K., & Biegel, D. (1992). Intensive family preservation services research: Current status and future agenda. *Social Work Research & Abstracts* 8(1), 21–27.

Werner, E. E. (1995). Resilience in development. *Current Directions in Psychological Science* 4(3), 81–85.

West, L., Mercer, S.O., & Altzheimer, E. (1993). Operation Desert Storm: The response of a social work outreach team. *Social Work in Health Care* 19(2), 81–98.

Wollman, D. (1993). Critical incident stress debriefing and crisis groups—a review of the literature. *Groups* 17(2), 70–83.

Wright, K.M., Ursano, R.J., Bartone, P.T., & Ingraham, L.H. (1990). The shared experience of catastrophe: An expanded classification of the disaster community. *American Journal of Orthopsychiatry* 60, 35–42.

CHAPTER 9

EGO PSYCHOLOGY THEORY

EDA GOLDSTEIN

OVERVIEW

Ego psychology is the biopsychosocial theory of human behavior that underpins ego-oriented treatment. It also has influenced many other intervention models. Ego psychological theory consists of a related set of concepts about human development that focus on the executive arm of the personality—the ego—and its relationship to other aspects of the personality and to the external environment.

HISTORICAL ORIGINS
AND PRINCIPAL PROPONENTS

In the 1923 publication *The Ego and the Id,* Freud proposed what became known as structural theory and initiated ego psychology. Structural theory permitted greater understanding of the individual's negotiations with the external world and led to an appreciation of the impact of the environment and interpersonal relationships on behavior.

Structural theory described the ego as one of three structures of the mental apparatus of the personality, along with the id (the seat of the instincts) and the superego (the conscience and ego-ideal). Freud defined the ego by its functions: mediating between the drives (id) and external reality; moderating conflict between the drives (id) and the internalized prohibitions against their expression (superego); instituting mechanisms (defenses) to protect the ego from anxiety; and playing a crucial role in development through its capacity for identification with external objects.

Anna Freud's 1936 publication, *Ego and the Mechanisms of Defense,* put forth the first important extension of structural theory. She identified the adaptiveness of defensive behavior, described a greater repertoire of defenses, and linked the origin of defenses to specific developmental phases.

A second important development in ego psychology was introduced by Heinz Hartmann in *Ego Psychology and the Problem of Adaptation* (1939). He originated the concept of the autonomy of the ego, proposing that both the ego and the id have their own energy source and originate in an "undifferentiated matrix" at birth. The individual is born "preadapted" to an "average expectable environment" for the species. The ego matures on its own and thus, many ego functions are "conflict-free" and have a "primary autonomy" from the drives.

A third crucial development in ego psychology is reflected in the work of Erik Erikson. In *Childhood and Society* (1950) and *Identity and the Life Cycle* (1959), Erikson described ego development as psychosocial in nature, involving progressive mastery of developmental tasks in each of eight successive stages of the human life cycle. Erikson called attention not only to biological and psychodynamic factors but also to interpersonal, environmental, societal, and cultural influences in the developmental process. He was among the first theorists to view adulthood as a period for growth and change.

Unlike Erikson, Robert White (1959, 1963) broke away from the Freudian psychoanalytic tradition. He postulated that the individual is born with not only innate and autonomous ego functions that give pleasure in their own right, but also with a drive toward mastery and competence. According to White, the ego actively seeks opportunities in the environment in which the individual can be "effective." In turn, the ego is strengthened by successful transactions with the environment.

Grounded in classical psychoanalytic theory and ego psychology, Rene Spitz (1945, 1965), Margaret Mahler (1968; Mahler et al., 1975), M.D.S. Ainsworth (1973), and John Bowlby (1958) generated crucial data and theory from their observational studies of children. Each delineated the child's unique development as a function of his or her interactions with the caretaking environment. More recently, Daniel Stern's (1985) research has shed new light on early development that challenges prevailing views.

Studies of children also have contributed to the understanding of the interaction between innate personality features and the environmental conditions during early childhood that lead to the development of coping capacity on the one hand and vulnerability on the other (Escalona, 1968; Murphy & Moriarity, 1976).

Cognitive theory relies on a different set of assumptions about personality development, human problems, and their treatment than does ego psychology. Nevertheless, selected aspects of the former can be integrated into ego-oriented approaches. For example, Piaget's theory of intelligence (1951, 1952) and Kohlberg's theory of moral development (1966) offer concepts that complement those of ego psychology. Others have contributed to the development of cognitive theory and its application to the treatment of many types of dysfunction (Beck et al., 1979, 1990).

Stress and crisis theory also add to our knowledge of ego functioning. There are many studies of how the ego copes with various types of biological, psychological, and environmental stress (Grinker & Spiegel, 1945; Hill, 1958; Lazarus, 1966; Lindemann, 1944; Selye, 1956). Crisis theory describes the ego's capacity to restore equilibrium after a major disruption.

Family systems theories, theories of small-group behavior, and organizational theories all contribute to understanding the impact of the social context on individual development. These theories also have been enriched by ego psychological concepts.

NEWER AREAS OF INQUIRY AND THEORETICAL LINKAGES

Attempting to correct what they argued was a male bias in traditional theories, feminist writers such as Jessica Benjamin (1988), Nancy Chodorow (1978), Dorothy Dinnerstein (1977), Carol Gilligan (1982), and Jean Baker Miller (1977) and her colleagues at the Stone Center for Developmental Services and Studies at Wellesley College in Massachusetts (Jordan, 1991) proposed new perspectives on women's victimization in society (Abarbanel & Richman, 1990; Berlin, 1981; Faria & Belohlavek, 1984; Simon, 1988; Star et al., 1981) and suggested more gender-sensitive treatment models that can be integrated with ego-oriented intervention (Bricker-Jenkins et al. 1991; Collins, 1986; Greenspan, 1983; Howell & Bayes, 1981; Norman & Mancuso, 1980).

Likewise, more affirmative views of gays and lesbians, greater understanding of people of color and other culturally diverse and oppressed groups, and increased awareness of the impact of childhood trauma have modified and enriched ego psychology and resulted in more sensitive interventions (Abarbanel & Richman, 1990; Bowker, 1983; Coleman, 1982; Colgan, 1988; Comas-Diaz & Greene, 1994; Cornett, 1995; Courtois, 1988; Davies & Frawley, 1994; de la Cancela, 1986; Espin, 1987; Falco, 1991; Gutierrez, 1990; Hetrick & Martin, 1988; Hirayama & Cetingok, 1988; Lee & Rosenthal, 1983; Lewis, 1984; Montijo, 1985; Pinderhughes, 1983; Robinson, 1989; Ryan, 1985; Schlossberg & Kagan, 1988; Tully, 1992; Weille, 1993).

Personality theories that have linkages to, but also some important differences from, ego psychology have become popular. For example, the work of Melanie Klein (1948), W.R.D. Fairbairn (1952), D.W. Winnicott (1965), Harry Guntrip (1969, 1973), the British object relations theorists, and Otto Kernberg (1984) and Heinz Kohut (1984) have complemented and in some instances modified our understanding of the developmental process, human problems, and their treatment.

PATH INTO SOCIAL WORK AND MAJOR SOCIAL WORK AUTHORS

Beginning in the late 1930s, but especially in the post–World War II period, numerous individuals became associated with attempts to assimilate ego psychological concepts into social casework. Prominent among these were Lucille Austin (1948), Louise Bandler (1963), Eleanor Cockerill & Colleagues (1953), Annette Garrett (1958), Gordon Hamilton (1940, 1958), Florence Hollis (1949, 1964), Isabell Stamm (1959), and Charlotte Towle (1949).

Ego psychology embodied a more optimistic and humanistic view of human functioning and potential than that reflected in classical psychoanalytic theory, which had dominated casework in many circles previously. It viewed environmental and sociocultural factors as important in shaping behavior and in providing opportunities for the development, enhancement, and sustainment of ego functioning.

Ego psychological concepts were used to refocus the study and assessment process on (1) the client's person-environment transactions in the here and now, and particularly the degree to which he or she is coping effectively with major life roles and tasks; (2) the client's adaptive, autonomous, and conflict-free areas of ego functioning, as well as his or her ego deficits and maladaptive defenses and patterns; (3) the key developmental issues affecting the client's current reactions; and (4) the degree to which the external environment is creating obstacles to successful coping.

Ego psychology provided the rationale for improving or sustaining adaptive ego functioning by means of work with both the individual and the environment. A repertoire of techniques for working with the ego was systematized. Ego psychological concepts recognized the reality of the client-worker relationship, rather than focusing exclusively on its transference or distorted aspects, and moved beyond an exclusive emphasis on insight as the mechanism for individual change.

Ego psychological concepts helped to transform the casework process from a never-ending, unfocused exploration of personality difficulties to a more deliberate and focused use of the phases of the casework process. Ego psychological concepts underscored the importance of the client's responsibility for directing treatment and his or her own life.

Efforts to incorporate ego psychology and related behavioral and social science theories also led to the distinctive problem-solving casework model developed by Helen Perlman (1957). She attempted to bridge the lingering dispute between diagnostic (psychoanalytic) and functional (Rankian) caseworkers, as well as to offer correctives for practices that she viewed as dysfunctional for the client. Perlman evolved a casework model that was based on the premise that all human living is effective problem solving.

Despite ego psychology's potential to bridge person and environment in theory and practice, casework practice often was criticized for its focus on the inner life of the individual at the apparent expense of attention to the environmental component of intervention, particularly as clients seemed "harder to reach" and "multiproblemed."

The push toward equality, social justice, and freedom from oppression on the part of people of color, women, and gays and lesbians also constituted a challenge to psychodynamic theory and individual treatment. A general distrust of the medical model and its view that people who encountered difficulties in coping were afflicted with diseases that could be diagnosed and treated gathered momentum. Followers of ego psychology were criticized for blaming the victim rather than the effects of oppression, poverty, and trauma and for "pathologizing" the behavior of women, gays and lesbians, and those who are culturally diverse rather than respecting their unique characteristics and strengths.

The 1960s ushered in an emphasis on large-scale social programs financed by the federal government that aimed to ameliorate if not eradicate the increasing social problems in society. The social work profession emphasized social change or "macrosystems" intervention rather than direct practice or "microsystems" intervention. Dissatisfaction with expensive and lengthy approaches to treatment in the face of increasing demand for services and budgetary cutbacks mounted.

Because the concepts and associated practices of ego psychology were not operationalized and studied, evidence supporting their efficacy was not forthcoming. This became increasingly important as whatever research did begin to accumulate on casework effectiveness was negative or equivocal and as casework came under attack. Moreover, the accretion of knowledge in the behavioral and social sciences fostered the development of new practice models at this time. While ego psychology informed a variety of these approaches, its significance waned as attention turned to competing theories and models and away from psychodynamic theory and practice itself.

Direct practice reasserted its importance during the 1970s, 1980s, and 1990s for numerous reasons. Disillusionment with government and feelings of powerlessness about influencing social policy set in as a consequence of political assassinations, the intense struggle over the Vietnam War, the failure of the Great Society programs, increasing political conservatism, harsher attitudes toward those who were economically disadvantaged, and severe economic cutbacks. Concurrently, the awareness of the pressing needs of clients for individualized services led to renewed attention to microsystems intervention and generated creative approaches in work with special populations. Experimentation with emerging intervention models increased (Turner, 1986). As a profession, social work began to press for more status through licensing and vendorship, and the number of practitioners entering private practice on at least a part-time basis grew.

Along with the resurgence of direct practice, ego psychology has enjoyed a renaissance of interest. With its emphasis on ego functioning and defenses, normal coping strategies, the need for mastery and competence, cognitive processes, person-environmental transactions, biopsychosocial factors in development, growth in adulthood, and stress and crisis, ego psychology addresses the needs of a broad range of clients. Refinements and extensions addressing internalized object relations and self-development provide an "in-depth" dimension to understanding human behavior, maladaptation, and severe personality difficulties. The integration of knowledge regarding cultural diversity, female development, trauma, and the impact of oppression on certain populations has broadened its applicability. Ego-oriented intervention extends to many diverse populations and provides the conceptual underpinnings to a variety of practice models, including the psychosocial, problem-solving, crisis intervention, and life models. It has important linkages to family and group theories and approaches, as well as to the design of service delivery, large-scale social programs, and social policy.

BASIC ASSUMPTIONS

The following seven propositions characterize ego psychology's view of human functioning (Goldstein, 1995).

1. Ego psychology views people as born with an innate capacity to function adaptively. Individuals engage in a lifelong biopsychosocial development process in which the ego is an active, dynamic force for coping with, adapting to, and shaping the external environment.
2. The ego is considered to be a mental structure of the personality that is responsible for negotiating between the internal needs of the individual and the outside world. While the ego has the capacity for functioning autonomously, it is only one part of the personality and must be understood in relation to "inter" and outer factors.
3. The ego contains the basic functions essential to the individual's successful adaptation to the environment. Ego functions are innate and develop through maturation and the interaction among biopsychosocial factors.
4. Ego development occurs sequentially as a result of constitutional factors, the meeting of basic needs, identification with others, interpersonal relationships, learning, mastery of developmental tasks, effective problem solving, and successful coping.
5. The ego not only mediates between the individual and the environment but also mediates internal conflict among various aspects of the personality. It can elicit defenses that protect the individual from anxiety and conflict and that serve adaptive or maladaptive purposes.
6. The social environment shapes the personality and provides the conditions that foster or obstruct successful coping. Cultural factors, racial, ethnic, and religious diversity, gender, age, sexual orientation, and the presence or absence of physical challenges affect ego development.
7. Problems in social functioning must be viewed in relation both to possible ego deficits and to the fit between needs and capacities and environmental conditions and resources.

MAIN CONCEPTS

Ego psychology contains four main sets of concepts: ego functions; defenses; ego mastery and adaptation; and object relations.

EGO FUNCTIONS

Ego functions are the means by which the individual adapts to the world. The most comprehensive effort to study ego functions can be found in the work of Bellak and his colleagues (1973), who identified twelve major ego functions.

Reality Testing

This involves the accurate perception of the external environment, of one's internal world, and of the differences between them. The most severe manifestations of the failure of reality testing are seen in delusions and hallucinations (false beliefs and perceptions that cannot be objectively validated).

Judgment

This involves the capacity to identify certain possible courses of action and to anticipate and weigh the consequences of behavior in order to take action that achieves desired goals with minimal negative consequences.

Sense of Reality About the World and the Self

It is possible to *perceive* inner and outer reality accurately but to *experience* the world and the self in distorted ways. A good sense of reality involves the ability to feel or to be aware of the world and one's connection to it as real, to experience one's own body as intact and belonging to oneself, to feel a sense of self, and to experience the separation or boundaries between oneself and others as distinct organisms. An individual may experience himself or herself as estranged from the world (derealization), as if there were an invisible screen between the self and others. In depersonalization, one feels estranged from one's own body, as if one were apart from it and looking at it, as at a separate object. Parts of one's body may seem disconnected. Certain distortions of body image also involve disturbances in the sense of reality.

Regulation and Control of Drives, Affects, and Impulses

This involves the ability to modulate, delay, inhibit, or control the expression of impulses and affects (feelings) in accord with reality. It also entails the ability to tolerate anxiety, frustration, and unpleasant emotions such as anger and depression without becoming overwhelmed, impulsive, or symptomatic.

Object (or Interpersonal) Relations

This refers both to the quality and patterning of one's interpersonal relationships and to the level of development of one's internalized sense of self and others. It will be discussed in more detail below.

Thought Processes

Primary process thinking follows the pleasure principle in that it is characterized by wishful fantasies and the need for immediate instinctual discharge irrespective of its appropriateness. Wishes and thoughts are equated with action. In contrast, secondary process thinking follows the reality principle. It is characterized by the ability to postpone instinctual gratification or discharge until conditions are appropriate and available; it replaces wish-fulfillment with appropriate action upon the outside world. Wishes and thoughts alone are not sufficient to obtain gratification. Secondary process thinking is goal-directed, organized, and oriented to reality.

Adaptive Regression in the Service of the Ego

This connotes the ability to relax one's hold on and relationship to reality, to experience aspects of the self that are ordinarily inaccessible when one is engaged in concentrated attention to reality, and to emerge with increased adaptive capacity as a result of creative integrations.

Defensive Functioning

The individual develops unconscious, internal mechanisms called defenses for protection from the painful experience of anxiety or from fear-inducing situations. Adaptive defenses safeguard the individual from anxiety while simultaneously fostering effective coping. Maladaptive defenses also protect the individual from anxiety, but often at the expense of optimal functioning. The types of defense will be described later in this chapter.

Stimulus Barrier

Each individual appears to have a different threshold for stimulation. An important aspect of the stimulus barrier is the degree to which an individual is able to maintain his or her level of functioning or comfort amid increases or decreases in the level of stimulation to which he is exposed.

Autonomous Functions

Certain ego functions such as attention, concentration, memory, learning, perception, motor functions, and intention have a primary autonomy from the drives and thus are conflict-free, that is, they do not arise in response to frustration and conflict. They can lose their autonomy by becoming associated with conflict in the course of early childhood development. Other capacities of the individual that originally develop in association with frustration and conflict later undergo a "change of function" and acquire autonomy from the conflict with which they were associated. Thus, certain interests originally may develop as a way of coping with stress but later are pursued in their own right.

Mastery-Competence

The individual's capacity to interact successfully with the environment is his or her actual competence; his or her subjective feelings about that capacity is termed the "sense of competence."

Synthetic/Integrative Function

The synthetic function binds or fits all the disparate aspects of the personality into a unified structure that acts upon the external world. It is responsible for personality integration and the resolution of splits, fragmentation, and conflicting tendencies within the person.

EGO STRENGTH

The term "ego strength" implies a composite picture of the internal psychological equipment or capacities that an individual brings to his or her interactions with others and with the social environment. Within the same individual, certain ego functions may be better developed than others and may show more stability. That is, they tend to fluctuate less from situation to situation, or over time, and are less prone to regression or disorganization under stress. Further, even in individuals who manifest ego strength, regression in selected areas of ego functioning may be normal in certain types of situations, for example, illness, social upheavals, crises, and role transitions, and does not necessarily imply ego deficiencies. It is important to note that it is possible for the same individual to have highly variable ego functioning, although in cases of the most severe psychopathology, ego functions may be impaired generally.

THE CONCEPT OF DEFENSE

Defenses are part of the ego's repertoire of mechanisms for protecting the individual from anxiety by keeping intolerable or unacceptable impulses or threats from conscious awareness. Defenses operate unconsciously. All people use defenses, but their exact type and extent vary from individual to individual. All defenses falsify or distort reality to some extent, although in individuals who function more effectively such distortions are minimal or transient and do not impair the person's ability to test reality. When such defenses enable the person to function well without undue anxiety, they are said to be effective.

Efforts directed at modifying defenses create anxiety and are often unconsciously resisted by the individual. The person does not deliberately seek to maintain his or her defenses. This resistance, however, creates obstacles to achieving the very changes that the person desires. While it may seem desirable to try to lessen or modify certain maladaptive defenses in a given individual because they interfere with effective coping, such mechanisms serve an important protective function. In many cases they should be respected, approached with caution, and even strengthened.

Under acute or unremitting stress, illness, or fatigue, the ego's defenses, along with the other ego functions, may fail. When there is a massive defensive failure, the person becomes flooded with anxiety. This can result in a severe and rapid deterioration of ego functioning, and in some cases the personality becomes fragmented and chaotic, just as in a psychotic episode. When defenses are rigid, an individual may appear exceedingly brittle, taut, and driven; his or her behavior may seem increasingly mechanical, withdrawn, or peculiar.

Common defenses are described below (Laughlin, 1979).

> *Repression.* A crucial mechanism, repression involves keeping unwanted thoughts and feelings out of awareness, or unconscious. What is repressed may once have been conscious (secondary repression) or may never have

reached awareness (primary repression). Repression may involve loss of memory for specific incidents, especially traumatic ones or those associated with painful emotions.

Reaction formation. Like repression, reaction formation involves keeping certain impulses out of awareness by replacing the unwanted impulse with its opposite.

Projection. When the individual attributes to others unacceptable thoughts and feelings of his or her own that are not conscious, he or she is using projection.

Isolation. Sometimes the mechanism of isolation is referred to as isolation of affect, for there is a repression of feelings associated with particular items, or of ideas connected with certain affects. Often this is accompanied by the experience of the feelings in the context of a different situation.

Undoing. This involves symbolically nullifying or voiding an unacceptable or guilt-provoking act, thought, or feeling.

Regression. Regression involves the return to an earlier developmental phase, level of functioning, or type of behavior in order to avoid the anxieties of the present.

Introjection. Introjection involves taking another person into the self, psychologically speaking, in order to avoid the direct expression of powerful emotions such as love or hate. When the object (person) of the intense feelings is introjected, the feelings are experienced toward the self, which has now become associated with or a substitute for the object.

Reversal. Reversal is a general mechanism for the process of turning a feeling or attitude into its opposite.

Sublimation. Sublimation is considered to be the highest-level or most mature defense. It involves converting an impulse from a socially objectionable aim to a socially acceptable one while still retaining the original goal of the impulse.

Intellectualization. The warding off of unacceptable affects and impulses by thinking about them rather than experiencing them directly is intellectualization. It is similar to isolation.

Rationalization. This involves the use of convincing reasons to justify certain ideas, feelings, or actions so as to avoid recognizing their true underlying motive, which is unacceptable.

Displacement. Shifting feelings or conflicts about one person or situation onto another is called displacement.

Denial. This mechanism involves the negation or nonacceptance of important aspects of reality or of one's own experience, even though they may actually be perceived.

Somatization. In somatization, intolerable impulses or conflicts are converted into physical symptoms.

Idealization. The overvaluing of, for example, person, place, family, or activity beyond what is realistic is idealization. To the degree that idealized figures inspire or serve as models, idealization is not necessarily defensive. When used defensively, idealization protects the individual from anxiety associated with aggressive or competitive feelings toward a loved or feared person.

Compensation. A person using compensation tries to make up for what he or she perceives as deficits or deficiencies.

Asceticism. Often used in adolescence, this defense involves the moral renunciation of certain pleasures in order to avoid the anxiety and conflict associated with impulse gratification.

Altruism. In altruism, one obtains satisfaction through self-sacrificing service to others or through participation in causes. It is defensive when it serves as a way of dealing with unacceptable feelings and conflicts.

Splitting. Characteristic of borderline conditions, this defense involves the keeping apart of two contradictory ego states such as love and hate. Those who utilize splitting cannot integrate in consciousness contradictory aspects of their own feelings or identity or the contradictory characteristics of others. People are seen in black or white terms.

Ego Mastery and Adaptation

A mastery drive or instinct (Hendrick, 1942; White, 1959, 1963) has been postulated by theorists who believe there is an inborn, active striving toward interaction with the environment, leading to the individual's experiencing a sense of competence or effectiveness. White (1959) described the ego as having independent energies that propelled the individual to gain pleasure through manipulating, exploring, and acting upon the environment. White called these energies "effectance" and suggested that feelings of efficacy are the pleasure derived from each interaction with the environment.

In White's view, ego identity results from the degree to which one's effectance and feelings of efficacy have been nurtured. It affects present and future behavior, because it reflects basic attitudes such as self-esteem, self-confidence, trust in one's own judgment, and belief in one's decision-making capacities, all of which shape the way one deals with the environment.

Erik Erikson viewed optimal ego development as resulting from the mastery of stage-specific developmental tasks and crises. He argued that the successful resolution of each crisis from birth to death leads to a sense of ego identity and may be said to constitute the core of one's sense of self.

The term "crisis" refers to the state of tension or disequilibrium at the beginning of each new stage. Each crisis is described in terms of extreme positive and negative solutions, although in any individual the resolution of the core developmental crisis may lie anywhere on a continuum from best to worst outcome. This developmental scheme implies that the ideal resolution of one phase depends on earlier ones.

According to Erikson, resolution of each successive crisis depends as much on those with whom the individual interacts as on his or her own innate capacities. Similarly, crisis resolution is dependent upon the impact of culture and environment, which shape child-rearing practices and provide opportunities or obstacles to optimal adaptation.

Erikson was among the first theorists to suggest that adulthood is dynamic rather than a static time, and that ego development continues throughout adulthood. There is mounting interest in, and evidence for, the idea that personality change occurs in adult life. Adulthood is seen to contain elements of the past as well as its own dynamic processes, which lead to change. Neugarten (1964; 1968), Butler (1963), Vaillant (1977), Gould (1978), Levinson (1978), Benedek (1970), and Colarusso and Nemiroff (1981) are among those who have made seminal contributions to the understanding of adult developmental processes.

Feminists have criticized Erikson for overemphasizing biological differences and underemphasizing cultural factors and socialization in personality development. They have also pointed out that his theory of the life cycle is based on male experience and male examples.

New conclusions about women's attributes have been reached as a result of studies of females in comparison to males. For example, Robert Stoller's (1977) studies lent support to the view that parental attitudes and behavior in the child's first five years of life are more important in determining gender identity (that is, whether the child regards him- or herself as male or female) than actual biological sex at birth. Carol Gilligan (1982) showed that women's capacity for relatedness, emotionality, and nurturing are essential to their identity development. She proposed a different standard for evaluating women's moral development, based on the relationship between caring for oneself and caring for others. In her view, women have a different way of thinking in which conflicting responsibilities in the context of relationships are paramount in influencing judgments. Women's moral judgments begin at a primarily egocentric or premoral level; at the next level, such judgments are based mainly on concern for others, and at the most advanced stage on a balanced concern for oneself and others. Gilligan further noted that many women might be at a disadvantage in achieving success in the world as a result of their morality, which does not easily permit them to show self-concern.

OBJECT RELATIONS

One usage of the term "object relations" refers to the quality of external interpersonal relationships, but a second usage refers to specific intrapsychic structures, an aspect of ego organization (Horner, 1979). Rather than viewing object relations as a single ego function, some authors view it as providing the context in which all ego functions develop. The infant is thought to be innately object-seeking from birth, and to develop a sense of self and others as a result of experiences with others. The inner representations of self and others, once developed, affect all subsequent interpersonal relations.

The separation-individuation process described by Mahler comprises a series of chronologically ordered phases, each of which leads to major achievements in the areas of separation, individuation, and internalized object relations (Mahler et al., 1975).

The Autistic Phase

The newborn infant generally is unresponsive to external stimuli for a number of weeks and is dominated by physiological needs and processes. The infant's primary autonomous ego apparatuses are still somewhat undifferentiated and are not yet called into play to act upon the environment. The infant literally exists in its own world or in what has been termed an autistic state, although gradually he or she becomes responsive, if only fleetingly, to external stimuli. In terms of object relations, the child is in a preattachment phase.

The Symbiotic Phase

Gradually the protective shell around the child gives way, and he or she begins to perceive the "need-satisfying object." However, this object is experienced within the infant's ego boundary and lacks a separate identity. In the symbiotic state, the mother's ego functions for the infant, and it is the mother who mediates between the infant and the external world. This period marks the beginning of the capacity to invest in another.

Separation-Individuation: The Differentiation Subphase

Differentiation beings at about four or five months. The child's attention shifts from being inwardly directed or focused within the symbiosis to being more outwardly directed. The infant literally begins to separate self-representations from representations of the caretaker (the object).

Separation-Individuation: The Practicing Subphase

The practicing subphase continues the process of separation of self and object representations and accelerates the individuation process, as the infant's own autonomous ego functions assume more importance. The first part of the practicing period, when the infant is approximately eight to ten or twelve months old, is characterized by attempts to move away from the mother physically, for example, through crawling. The infant expands his or her world and the capacity to maneuver within it autonomously, optimally always in close proximity to the maternal figure, who is there to provide support and encouragement.

In the early practicing subphase, the child experiences the simultaneous pull of the outside world and of the mother, and separation anxiety may increase until the child is reassured that the mother will remain despite his or her movement away from her. One can observe the initial efforts on the part of the child to keep track of the mother. Gradually, the child is able to be on its own for longer periods of time.

During the second part of the practicing period, the child's ability to get around by himself or herself seems to lead to a "love affair with the world." At times, the child appears oblivious to the mother's temporary absence. The child consolidates his or her separateness during this period and acquires a more stable internal self-representation that is distinct from the object representation. The child's "all-good" self and object experiences, however, are separated from "all-bad" ones. Thus, when the mother is frustrating she is experienced as all bad; when she is experienced as loving she is all good.

Separation-Individuation: The Rapprochement Subphase

In the rapprochement subphase, the child sheds his or her belief in the mother's omnipotence and begins to want to act independently. However, the child also becomes frightened of being alone and seeks the mother's presence actively, wanting her to share everything and provide constant reassurance. There is a back-and-forth movement between autonomy and dependence.

Separation-Individuation: On the Road to Object Constancy

In this phase, the child again seems able to be on his or her own without undue concern about the mother's whereabouts. The child's internalization of the mother, which remains fluid for some time, begins to permit him or her to individuate more fully and to function independently without experiencing or fearing separation, abandonment, or loss of love. The final achievement of object constancy implies the capacity to maintain a positive mental representation of the object in the object's absence or in the face of frustration. The normal splitting is overcome in the later reapprochement subphase, when the good and bad self and the good and bad object both begin to be integrated.

Blos (1975) has suggested a second separation-individuation phase occurring in adolescence. The healthy adolescent has an internalized sense of self and others but must disengage from the more infantile aspects of these inner representations in order to acquire a more realistically based sense of self and others. This disengagement also requires the discovery of new love objects outside the orbit of the family.

Even adults who show optimal functioning may relive sparation-individuation themes throughout the life cycle, particularly at life transitional points or during more acute stresses. Those who do not successfully complete this key developmental process will show serious interpersonal difficulties (Blanck & Blanck, 1974).

An account of the developmental process that challenges Mahler's views is continued in the work of Daniel Stern (1985), who systematically studied child-mother interactions. In contrast to Mahler, he provides evidence that the infant is born with an innate sense of separateness from others, and that over time, the child's self evolves as a consequence of complex interpersonal transactions. Stern does not regard development as demarcated by distinct, time-bound phases, nor does he believe that the individual grows out of any particular stage. Instead, each stage becomes a distinct form of experience that becomes further elaborated over time as the individual deals with increasingly advanced developmental tasks.

Stern delineated four phases of self-development, or "domains of relatedness": the sense of emergent self, the sense of core self, the sense of subjective self, and the sense of verbal self. Stern views each domain as codetermined by the growing infant's innate maturational capacities and by the nature and degree of caretaker attunement.

The Stone Center group, including Jean Baker Miller, Judith Jordan, Alexandra Kaplan, Irene Stiver, and Janet Surrey (Jordan, 1991), also criticize the view implicit in Mahler's theory that the healthy person is individuated, autonomous, and separate with clear boundaries. They regard women's self-development as evolving in the context of relatedness, and argue that enhanced connection rather than increased self-object differentiation and separateness is women's major goal.

Social and cultural factors greatly affect identity development. It has been recognized that the achievement of a stable and integrated identity is more difficult when, at an early age, the individual does not know where he or she belongs culturally, or when the individual learns early in life that he or she is a member of a group that is stigmatized by and excluded from society. Such experiences engender low self-esteem, self-hatred, negative self-concepts, feelings of powerlessness, and alienation. Attuned parenting and the presence of other familial and environmental supports will cushion some but not all individuals from the negative impact of discrimination, racism, and homophobia. African-Americans, Latinos, Asians, Native Americans, and gays and lesbians are examples of groups within society who are vulnerable in this regard.

Greater understanding of women's development and of the individualization of culturally diverse and oppressed populations has contributed to more awareness and respect for the strengths and special characteristics of both groups and has enriched our understanding of their coping capacities. For example, in discussing male machismo, de la Cancela (1986) points out its adaptive significance in the context of the socioeconomic realities of Puerto Ricans and cautions against "blaming the victim." Instead, he advocates a more respectful and attuned approach in work with Puerto Rican men and their families. Wilson (1989) describes the socioeconomic factors that have given rise to the prevalence of the extended family in the African-American community and highlights its value and positive effects. Likewise, Ryan (1985) shows how the teachings of Confucius, Laotze, and Buddha continue to influence the way Chinese-Americans live, think, and communicate.

More affirmative views of gay and lesbian life have emerged. In summarizing the results of several decades of research, numerous authors point out that gay men and lesbians cannot be reliably differentiated from heterosexuals in their personality characteristics, family background, gender identity, defenses, or ego and object relations development (Falco, 1991; Friedman, 1986; Gonsiorek, 1982).

Another significant influence on self-development is early childhood trauma, which undermines security, safety, and connection. It involves violence, danger, threats to the body or to life itself, and causes terror, fear, helplessness, and loss of control. Long after the traumatic events themselves, survivors may exhibit characteristic symptoms that interfere with their optimal functioning and are extremely debilitating.

TREATMENT

GOALS

The goal of intervention is (1) nurturing, maintaining, enhancing, or modifying inner capacities; (2) mobilizing, improving, or changing environmental conditions, or (3) improving the fit between inner capacities and external circumstances. Goals should be arrived at with the client.

THE NATURE AND IMPORTANCE OF ASSESSMENT

Assessment is biopsychosocial in nature and focuses on the client's current and past functioning and life circumstances. It considers the client's needs, problems, gender, ethnicity, race, life-stage, social roles, characteristic ego functioning and coping patterns, relationships, environmental stressors, and social supports. The use of clinical or medical diagnoses may provide important information but should be augmented by a broader and individualized assessment. Thus, the conclusion that a client has a learning disability, medical problem, emotional disorder, or substance abuse problem would have important implications but would not be sufficient for the purposes of assessment and the planning of intervention.

The following questions are important guides to the practitioner in the assessment process (Goldstein, 1995).

1. To what extent is the client's problem a function of stresses imposed by current life roles or developmental tasks?
2. To what extent is the client's problem a function of situational stress or a traumatic event?
3. To what extent is the client's problem a function of impairments in ego capacities or developmental difficulties or dynamics?
4. To what extent is the client's problem a function of a lack of environmental resources or supports or a poor fit between inner capacities and external circumstances?
5. What inner capacities and environmental resources does the client have that can be mobilized to improve coping?

THE FOCUS OF INTERVENTION

The focus and nature of intervention follow from the assessment, and the client should be involved in establishing the treatment plan. Generally, ego-oriented approaches can be grouped according to whether their goals are ego-supportive or ego-modifying (Hollis, 1972). Ego-supportive intervention aims at restoring, maintaining, or enhancing the individual's adaptive functioning, as well as strengthening or building ego where there are deficits or impairments. In contrast, ego-modifying intervention aims at changing basic personality patterns.

THE NATURE OF CHANGE

In an ego-supportive approach, change results from: (1) the exercise of autonomous ego functioning in the service of mastering new developmental, life transitional, crisis, or other stressful situations; (2) a greater understanding of the impact of one's behavior on others; (3) the learning and positive reinforcement of new behavior, skills, attitudes, problem-solving capacities, and coping strategies; (4) the utilization of conflict-free areas of ego functioning to neutralize conflict-laden areas; (5) the use of relationships and experiences to correct for previous difficulties and deprivations; and (6) the use of the environment to provide more opportunities and conditions for the use of one's capacities.

THE NATURE AND IMPORTANCE OF THE HELPING RELATIONSHIP

The worker conveys certain key attitudes and values irrespective of the client. These include acceptance of the client's worth, a nonjudgmental attitude toward the client, appreciation of the client's individuality or uniqueness, respect for the client's right to self-determination, and adherence to the rule of confidentiality. In contrast to earlier views that stressed the importance of worker neutrality and objectivity, there is now greater emphasis on the worker's ability to show empathy for clients, to engage in controlled involvement, to convey genuineness, and to encourage mutuality.

Ego-supportive intervention emphasizes the more realistic as well as the transference aspects of the helping relationship. Consequently, the worker in the ego-supportive approach may encourage the client's accurate perception of the worker as a helping agent rather than as a transference figure. The worker provides a human and genuine experience in the helping relationship. In many instances, however, the worker uses the positive transference and becomes a benign authority or parental figure who fosters the client's phase-appropriate needs and development. In some instances, the worker becomes a "corrective" figure to the client. A client may develop intense reactions to the worker of an unrealistic kind even in an ego-supportive approach. Such reactions do need to be worked with, but the aim, in most cases, is to restore the positive relationship (Garrett, 1958; Hollis, 1972; and Perlman, 1957).

Another important aspect of the use of relationship in an ego-supportive approach is the worker's willingness to function outside of the client-worker relationship in a variety of roles on behalf of the client. It may be important for the worker to be an advocate or systems negotiator for the client or to meet with family members (Grinnell et al., 1981).

SPECIFIC TECHNIQUES

Among the psychological techniques used in ego-supportive intervention are those that are sustaining, directive, educative, and structured, in contrast to those that are nondirective, reflective, confronting, and interpretive. Hollis (1972) described six main groups of psychological techniques that are important in ego psychological intervention: sustaining; direct influence; exploration, description, and ventilation; person-situation reflection; pattern-dynamic reflection; and developmental reflection. Other important techniques are education and structuring techniques.

Environmental intervention is critical to intervention within an ego-psychological perspective. For example, it may be important to mobilize resources and opportunities that will enable the individual to use his or her inner capacities, or to restructure the environment so that it nurtures or fits better with the individual's needs and capacities.

APPROPRIATE CLIENT POPULATIONS

Ego-supportive treatment approaches can be utilized with a broad range of clients whose ego functioning has been disrupted by current stresses or who show severe and chronic problems in coping, including moderate to severe emotional disorders. Ego-modifying approaches on an outpatient basis usually require that the client have sufficient ego strength to tolerate the anxiety associated with ego-modifying procedures. Otherwise, the client may need hospitalization or other types of environmental structuring as well.

DURATION OF INTERVENTION

While ego psychology often has been associated with long-term psychotherapy, it also has been used to guide crisis and short-term intervention. The use of briefer forms of intervention requires somewhat different skills than those involved in more extended forms of treatment, since faster assessments and more active and focused interventions are required.

THE M CASE

Ms. M is a single, thirty-year-old unemployed commercial artist who receives unemployment insurance. She has no close friends, rarely sees her parents, and is reluctant to seek full-time employment because of its demands. Several months ago, she became acutely psychotic and was hospitalized briefly. She recovered quickly, was discharged from the hospital, and began seeing a social worker at an outpatient clinic.

Among Ms. M's major difficulties are her extreme suspiciousness and her tendency to merge with others in close relationships. At her last job, she began to feel that her female employer wanted to have a sexual relationship with her, merely because she was friendly and supportive. Ms. M became fearful and withdrew, to the point of being unable to work. At times she thinks others can read her mind and often attributes her own thoughts to others. While she tells herself that she is imagining these things, she is never fully convinced and expends a great deal of energy trying to contain her anxiety. She rarely asks directly for reassurance, nor does she question people about their intentions or about statements they make that she does not understand.

When asked at the first session how she was experiencing the meeting with the worker, Ms. M responded that she felt the worker was sympathetic but wondered if she was tape-recording her words. When asked what gave her that idea, Ms. M pointed to a dictating machine on the worker's desk. The worker let Ms. M check to see if the dictating machine was running, and Ms. M seemed satisfied that it was not. Then she said that she guessed it was a ridiculous idea, but it just seemed to her for a moment that the worker might be recording the session. The worker commented that it was good that Ms. M had asked about the machine so that she could clear up her confusion. Ms. M acknowledged that she lived with this kind of confusion most of the time and that it was a problem for her. They agreed that this was something they could work on together.

The worker met with Ms. M weekly, and they used the sessions to identify what Ms. M was feeling, to help her sort out her feelings from the worker's. This was done to help her expand her understanding of the possible motivations of the worker that did not relate to Ms. M. specifically, to help her find ways of recognizing when her perceptions might be distorted, and to find ways of correcting them before she became overwhelmed by anxiety. Simultaneously, the worker helped Ms. M think through ways in which she could pursue both work and interpersonal relationships gradually, without exposing herself to too much stress at once. They decided together that free-lancing was a good option for Ms. M, since it would permit her to work by herself. The worker also suggested that Ms. M attend a weekly discussion group at a local church. The group addressed a specific topic each night, followed by a coffee hour during which people could socialize. Because of its structured nature, this seemed a less threatening way for Ms. M to begin to involve herself in activities and to meet others. The worker discussed what happened at these meetings with Ms. M in order to help her find new ways of coping with stressful situations and to reinforce her good handling of situations that arose. After a year, Ms. M felt much less fearful and insecure. She was able to venture out to a greater extent, was able to work as a free-lancer, and had enhanced self-esteem.

DISCUSSION

In this example, the worker engaged in ego-building efforts with Ms. M, whose severe ego deficits were hampering her ability to use her capacities. The worker used the client-worker relationship as a testing ground on which Ms. M could identify and overcome the difficulties she had in perceiving others and communicating with them. The worker used Ms. M's observing ego in this process and tapped her motivation to improve. The worker helped Ms. M to understand her needs and capacities and to learn to structure her external life. The worker also provided a forum in which Ms. M could discuss her everyday problems and learn to cope more effectively.

APPLICATION TO FAMILY AND GROUP INTERVENTION

Although family and group modalities generally draw on theoretical systems other than ego psychology and follow intervention principles different from those governing individual intervention, ego psychological concepts can be applied to family and group intervention.

The family has its own life cycle and various family systems theories, rather than ego psychology, usually are utilized to describe its internal processes and relationship to the environment (Carter & McGoldrick, 1980; Nichols, 1984). Nevertheless, the family is a potent force in personality development, both creating and reinforcing adaptive or maladaptive characteristics and patterns. It also is profoundly affected by the problems encountered by individual members and can be a crucial resource for them at times of stress. Thus, assessment of the family's systemic processes and its needs and problems can complement ego-oriented assessment. Likewise, there are times when family intervention can be used alongside of individual treatment. Within an ego psychological framework, family intervention can focus on educating families about the developmental and ongoing needs of its members and on how family life fosters or obstructs their functioning; supporting the family at times of stress; enhancing the family's coping skills; facilitating the family's positive participation in the treatment of, or ability to be a resource to, a family member; and enabling the family to cope with the impact of the illness or disability of one of its members (Anderson et al., 1980; Goldstein, 1979, 1981).

Groups are a potent force in offering clients acceptance, reassurance, and encouragement; in promoting problem solving; in developing ego capacities; in teaching skills and promoting a sense of competence; in providing information; in changing attitudes and behavior; in mobilizing people for collective action; in fostering collaboration with others; and in overcoming client discomfort with accepting help (Lee, 1981; Middleman, 1981).

IMPLICATIONS FOR COMMUNITY INTERVENTION, SERVICE DELIVERY, AND SOCIAL POLICY

While ego psychology's greatest contribution is to the understanding of human behavior and to the shaping of direct-practice models, it also has important implications for service delivery and social policy. Ego psychology's emphasis on the importance of developmental stages, role and life transitions, and stress and crisis in human functioning alerts us to the times and conditions during the life cycle when such help is needed.

Ego psychology can be particularly useful in directing service delivery toward primary prevention rather than only remediation (Roskin, 1980). The understanding of the factors that promote healthy development or effective coping is invaluable in establishing services that prevent problems from occurring or worsening. High-risk populations or individuals can be identified and reached before problems escalate.

At the same time, ego psychology's view of the significance of the acute or chronic impairments in ego capacity that some individuals bring to their life transactions points to the need for a range of remedial, rehabilitative, or sustaining services, many of which need to be offered on an ongoing basis.

Ego-oriented practice views the social and environmental context as a proper locus of intervention if it is creating obstacles to the intervention's growth and functioning. Clearly, the goal of making the social environment and social policy more responsive to client needs requires that social workers actively engage in social and political action.

EMPIRICAL BASE

Over the years, ego psychology as a body of theory has been enriched by research. Greater sophistication in research methodology and design, and more willingness on the part of theorists to subject their ideas to investigation, have led to more systematic study of child and adult development and the ways in which people cope with stress, crisis, and various types of life demands and events. Tools for assessing normal and pathological ego functioning and adaptive and maladaptive coping also have evolved.

In contrast to these developments, systematic research on the nature and effectiveness of practice based on ego psychological principles has been lacking, and research findings often are not integrated by practitioners.

When social casework and its ego psychological base came under attack in the 1960s, the studies of social work intervention that were conducted were disheartening (Mullen et al., 1972). Upon closer analysis, however, it is clear that the goals, processes, and outcomes studied were not well selected (Perlman, 1972). In the years since these studies, outcome studies have yielded more positive results (Rubin, 1985; Thomlison, 1984). Yet the task of operationally defining psychosocial variables, interventions, and outcomes remains difficult.

It is critical that the rich knowledge base for social work practice provided by ego psychology receive more research attention from social work practitioners. More diverse research strategies that move beyond the use of large experimental or single-case designs also are important. Practitioners must become an ally rather than an enemy of research and researchers need to become more practice friendly.

PRESENT STATUS AND FUTURE DIRECTIONS

Important factors that affect the training of social workers in ego psychology include the diminishing amount of curriculum space in MSW programs allocated to teaching human behavior and practice, the dearth of advanced or doctoral programs in advanced practice, and the lack of experienced practitioners on their faculties. There is a compelling need for educational programs in social work that address the needs of practitioners by making clinical content a higher priority and by recruiting faculty who are experienced practitioners within a biopsychosocial perspective that encompasses ego psychology.

In competition with other theories and practice models, ego psychology continues to have a major impact on social work practice. In a survey of the 1982 NASW Register of Clinical Social Workers (Mackey et al., 1987), fifty-one percent "identified ego psychology as being the most instrumental to their approach" (p. 368). While this study was conducted over ten year ago, the popularity of the approach does not seem to have waned. The literature on ego psychology and its practice applications is voluminous and continues to grow. Despite its person-in-situation focus, its broad applicability, and its continuing evolution, however, some still criticize ego psychology for being too narrow or too clinical and for not being relevant in today's practice arena.

Changes in society have focused greater attention on the application of ego-oriented intervention to different client problems and populations (Goldstein, 1995); AIDS (Dane & Miller, 1992; Lopez & Getzel, 1984); rape and other forms of violent assault (Abarbanel & Richman, 1990; Lee & Rosenthal, 1983); child abuse (Brekke, 1990); domestic violence (Bowker, 1983); substance abuse (Chernus, 1985; Straussner, 1993); borderline and other types of character pathology (Goldstein, 1990); homelessness and chronic mental illness (Belcher & Ephross, 1989; Harris & Bergman, 1987); and the effects of childhood sexual abuse on adults (Courtois, 1988; Faria & Belohlavek, 1984). Likewise, ego psychology addresses the special needs of culturally diverse and oppressed populations. In the future, there must be a continuing effort to articulate the application of ego psychological principles to the problems of diverse, oppressed, economically disadvantaged, and special populations in today's practice arena. Further, in the present climate of managed care and cutbacks in service delivery, and the resultant emphasis on very brief and often mechanistic interventions, ego-oriented short-term models need to be developed, utilized, disseminated, and studied to a greater degree than previously. As a biopsychosocial theory, it can help us in designing more holistic and meaningful treatment plans and in establishing guidelines for clients who need more extensive and differential services.

BIBLIOGRAPHY

Abarbanel, G., & Richman, G. (1990). The rape victim. In H.J. Parad & L.G. Parad (eds.), *Crisis Intervention: The Practitioner's Sourcebook for Brief Therapy.* Vol. 2. Milwaukee, WI: Family Service Association of America, 93–118.

Ainsworth, M.D.S. (1973). The development of mother-infant attachment. In B. Caldwell & H. Ricciuti (eds.), *Review of Child Development Research.* Vol. 3. Chicago: University of Chicago Press, 1–94.

Anderson, C., Hogarty, G. E., & Reiss, D. J. (1980). Family treatment of adult schizophrenic patients: A psychoeducational approach. *Schizophrenia Bulletin* 6, 490–505.

Austin, L. (1948). Trends in differential treamtent in social casework. *Social Casework* 29, 203–11.

Bandler, L. (1963). Some aspects of ego growth through sublimation. In H.J. Parad & R. Miller (eds.), *Ego-oriented Casework*. New York: Family Service Association of America, 27–44.

Beck, A.T., Freeman, A., & Associates (1990). *Cognitive Therapy of Personality Disorders.* New York: Guilford Press.

Beck, A.T., Rush, A.J., Shaw, B.F., & Emery, G. (1979). *Cognitive Therapy of Depression.* New York: Guilford Press.

Belcher, J.R., & Ephross, P.H. (1989). Toward an effective practice model for the homeless mentally ill. *Social Casework: Journal of Contemporary Social Work* 70, 421–27.

Bellak, L., Hurvich, M., & Gediman, H. (1973). *Ego Functions in Schizophrenics, Neurotics, and Normals.* New York: John Wiley & Sons.

Benedek, T. (1970). Parenthood during the life cycle. In J. Anthony & T. Benedek (eds.), *Parenthood—Its Psychology and Psychopathology.* Boston: Little, Brown, 185–208.

Benjamin, J. (1988). *The Bonds of Love: Psychoanalysis, Feminism, and the Problem of Domination.* New York: Panthcon.

Berlin, S., & Kravetz, D. (1981). Women as victims: A feminist social work perspective. *Social Work* 26, 447–49.

Blanck, G., & Blanck, R. (1974). *Ego Psychology in Theory and Practice.* New York: Columbia University Press.

Blos, P. (1975). The second individuation process of adolescence. In A. Esman (ed.) *The Psychology of Adolescence; Essential Readings.* New York: International Universities Press, 156–77.

Bowlby, J. (1958). The nature of the child's tie to the mother. *International Journal of Psychoanalysis* 39, 350–73.

Bowker, L. H. (1983). Marital rape: A distinct syndrome. *Social Casework: The Journal of Contemporary Social Work* 64, 347–52.

Brekke, J. (1990). Crisis intervention with victims and perpetrators of spouse abuse. In H.J. Parad & L.G. Parad (eds.), *Crisis Intervention: The Practitioner's Sourcebook for Brief Therapy.* Vol. 2. Milwaukee, WI: Family Service Association of America, 161–78.

Bricker-Jenkins, M., Hooyman, N.R., & Gottlieb, N. (eds.). (1991). *Feminist Social Work Practice in Clinical Settings.* Sage Sourcebook for the Human Services Series, 19. Newbury Park, CA: Sage Publications.

Butler, R.N. (1963). The life review: An intrepretation of reminiscence in the aged. *Psychiatry* 26, 65–76.

Carter, E. A., & McGoldrick, M. (eds.). (1980). *The Family Life Cycle: A Framework for Family Therapy.* New York: Gardner Press.

Chernus, L.A. (1985). Clinical issues in alcoholism treatment. *Social Casework* 66, 67–75.

Chodorow, N. (1978). *The Reproduction of Mothering.* Berkeley: University of California Press.

Cockerill, E., & Colleagues. (1953). *A Conceptual Framework of Social Casework.* Pittsburgh: University of Pittsburgh Press.

Colarusso, C., & Nemiroff, R.A. (1981). *Adult Development.* New York: Plenum Press.

Coleman, E. (1982). Developmental stages of the coming out process. In J.C. Gonsiorek (ed.), *Homosexuality and Psychotherapy: A Practitioner's Handbook of Affirmative Models.* New York: Haworth Press, 31–44.

Colgan, P. (1988). Treatment of identity and intimacy issues in gay males. In E. Coleman (ed.), *Integrated Identity: Gay Men and Lesbians.* New York: Harrington Park Press, 101–23.

Collins, B.G. (1986). Defining feminist social work. *Social Work* 31, 214–20.

Comas-Diaz, L., & Greene, B. (1994). *Women of Color.* New York: Guilford Press.

Cornett, C. (1995). *Reclaiming the Authentic Self.* New York: Jason Aronson.

Courtois, C.A. (1988). *Healing the Incest Wound: Adult Survivors in Therapy.* New York: W.W. Norton.

Dane, B.O., & Miller, S.O. (1992). *AIDS: Intervening with Hidden Grievers.* Westport, CT: Auburn House.

Davies, J.M., & Frawley, M.G. (1994). *Treating the Adult Survivors of Childhood Sexual Abuse: A Psychoanalytic Perspective.* New York: Basic Books.

de la Cancela, V. (1986). A critical analysis of Puerto Rican machismo: Implications for clinical practice. *Psychotherapy* 23, 291–96.

Dinnerstein, D. (1977). *The Mermaid and the Minotaur.* New York: Harper Colophon.

Erikson, E. (1959). Identity and the life cycle. *Psychological Issues* 1, 50–100.

Erikson, E. (1950). *Childhood and Society.* New York: W.W. Norton.

Escalona, S.K. (1968). *The Roots of Individuality: Normal Patterns of Development in Infancy.* Chicago: Aldine

Espin: O.M. (1987). Psychological impact of migration on Latinas. *Psychology of Women Quarterly* II, 489–503.

Fairbairn, W.R.D. (1952). *Psychoanalytic Studies of the Personality.* London: Routledge & Kegan Paul.

Falco, K. L. (1991). *Psychotherapy with Lesbian Clients: Theory into Practice.* New York: Brunner/Mazel.

Faria, G., & Belohlavek, N. (1984). Treating female adult survivors of childhood incest. *Social Casework: The Journal of Contemporary Social Work* 65, 465–71.

Freud, A. (1936). *The Ego and the Mechanisms of Defense.* New York: International Universities Press.

Freud, S. (1923). The Ego and the Id. In J. Strachey (ed.), *The Standard Edition of the Complete Psychological Works of Sigmund Freud.* Vol. 19. London: Hogarth, 1961.

Friedman, R.M. (1986). The psychoanalytic model of male homosexuality: A historical and theoretical critique. *Psychoanalytic Review* 73, 483–519.

Garrett, A. (1958). Modern casework: The contributions of ego psychology. In H.J. Parad (ed.), *Ego Psychology and Dynamic Casework.* New York: Family Service Association of America, 38–52.

Gilligan, C. (1982). *In a Different Voice: Psychological Theory and Women's Development.* Cambridge, MA: Harvard University Press.

Goldstein, E.G. (1995). *Ego Psychology and Social Work Practice* (2nd ed.). New York: Free Press.

Goldstein, E.G. (1981). Promoting competence in families of psychiatric patients. In A. N. Malluccio (ed.), *Promoting Competence in Clients: A New/Old Approach to Social Work Practice.* New York: Free Press, 317–42.

Goldstein, E.G. (1979). Mothers of psychiatric patients revisited. In C.B. Germain (ed.), Social Work Practice: People and Environments. New York: Columbia University Press, 150–73.

Gonsiorek, J.C. (ed.). (1982). *Homosexuality and Psychotherapy: A Practitioner's Handbook of Affirmative Models.* New York: Haworth Press.

Gould, R.L. (1978). *Transformations: Growth and Change in Adult Life.* New York: Simon & Schuster.

Greenspan, M. (1983). *A New Approach to Women in Therapy.* New York: McGraw-Hill.

Grinker, R.R., & Spiegel, J.D. (1945). *Men Under Stress.* Philadelphia: Blakiston.

Grinnell, R.M., Kyte, N.S., & Bostwick, G.J. (1981). Environmental modification. In A.N. Malluccio (ed.), *Promoting Competence in Clients: A New/Old Approach to Social Work Practice.* New York: Free Press, 152–84.

Guntrip, H. (1973). *Psychoanalytic Theory, Therapy, and the Self.* New York: Basic Books.

Guntrip, H. (1969). *Schizoid Phenomena, Object Relations, and the Self.* New York: International Universities Press.

Gutierrez, L.M. (1990). Working with women of color: An empowerment perspective. *Social Work* 35, 149–54.

Hamilton, G. (1958). A theory of personality: Freud's contribution to social casework. In H.J. Parad (ed.), *Ego Psychology and Dynamic Casework*. New York: Family Service Association of America, 11–37.

Hamilton, G. (1940). *Theory and Practice of Social Casework*. New York: Columbia University Press.

Harris, M., & Bergman, H.C. (1987). Case management with the chronically mentally ill: A clinical perspective. *American Journal of Orthopsychiatry* 56, 296–302.

Henrick, I. (1942). Instinct and the ego during infancy. *Psychoanalytic Quarterly* II, 33–58.

Hetrick, E.S., & Martin, D.A. (1988). Developmental issues and their resolution for gay and lesbian adolescents. In E. Coleman, (ed.), *Integrated Identity: Gay Men and Lesbians*. New York: Harrington Park Press, 25–43.

Hill, R. (1958). Generic features of families under stress. *Social Casework* 39, 139–50.

Hirayama, H., & Cetingok, M. (1988). Empowerment: A social work approach for Asian immigrants. *Social Casework: The Journal of Contemporary Social Work* 69, 41–47.

Hollis, F. (1972). *Casework: A Psychosocial Therapy*. (2nd ed.). New York: Random House.

Hollis, F. (1964). *Casework: A Psychosocial Therapy*. New York: Random House.

Hollis, F. (1949). The techniques of casework. *Journal of Social Casework* 30, 235–44.

Horner, A. (1979). *Object Relations and the Developing Ego in Therapy*. New York: Jason Aronson.

Howell, E., & Bayes, M. (eds.). (1981). *Women and Mental Health*. New York: Basic Books.

Jordan, J.V., et al., (1991). *Women's Growth In Connection*. New York: Guilford Press.

Kernberg, O.F. (1984). *Severe Personality Disorders*. New Haven, CT: Yale University Press.

Klein, M. (1948). *Contributions to Psychoanalysis: 1921–1945*. London: Hogarth Press.

Kohlberg, L. (1966). A cognitive-developmental analysis of childrens' sex-role concepts and attitudes. In E.E. Macoby (ed.), *The Development of Sex-Differences*. Stanford, CA: Stanford University Press, 83–173.

Kohut, H. (1984). *How Does Analysis Cure?* Chicago: University of Chicago Press.

Laughlin, H.P. (1979). *The Ego and Its Defenses* (2nd ed.) New York: Jason Aronson.

Lazarus, R.S. (1966). *Psychological Stress and the Coping Process*. New York: McGraw-Hill.

Lee, J.A.B. (1981). Promoting competence in children and youth. In A.N. Maluccio (ed.), *Promoting Competence in Clients: A New/Old Approach to Social Work Practice*. New York: Free Press, 236–63.

Lee, J.A.B., & Rosenthal, S.J. (1983). Working with victims of violent assault. *Social Casework: The Journal of Contemporary Social Work* 64, 593–601.

Levinson, D.J. (1978). *The Seasons of a Man's Life*. New York: Alfred A. Knopf.

Lewis, L.A. (1984). The coming-out process of lesbians: Integrating a stable identity. *Social Work* 29, 464–69.

Lindemann, E. (1944). Symptomatology and management of acute grief. *American Journal of Psychiatry* 101, 7–21.

Lopez, D., & Getzel, G.S. (1984). Helping gay AIDS patients in crisis. *Social Casework: The Journal of Contemporary Social Work* 65, 387–94.

Mackey, R.A., Urek, M.B., & Charkoudian, S. (1987). The relationship of theory to clinical practice. *Clinical Social Work Journal* 15, 368–83.

Mahler, M.S. (1968). *On Human Symbiosis and the Vicissitudes of Individuation*. New York: International Universities Press.

Mahler, M.S., Pine, F., & Bergman, A. (1975). *The Psychological Birth of the Human Infant*. New York: Basic Books.

Middleman, R.R. (1981). The pursuit of competence through involvement in structured groups. In A.N. Maluccio (ed.), *Promoting Competence in Clients: A New/Old Approach to Social Work Practice*. New York: Free Press, 185–212.

Miller, J.B. (1977). *Toward a New Psychology of Women.* Boston: Beacon Paperback.

Montijo, J.A. (1985). Therapeutic relationships with the poor: A Puerto Rican perspective. *Psychotherapy* 22, 436–40.

Mullen, E.J., Dumpson, J.R., & Associates (eds.). (1972). *Evaluation of Social Intervention.* San Francisco: Jossey-Bass.

Murphy, L.B., & Moriarity, A.E. (1976). *Vulnerability, Coping and Growth from Infancy to Adolesence.* New Haven: Yale University Press.

Neugarten, B.L. (1968). Adult personality: Toward a psychology of the life cycle. In W.E. Vinacke (ed.), *Readings in General Psychology.* New York: American Book, 332–43.

Neugarten, B.L., & Associates (eds.). (1964). *Personality in Middle and Late Life.* New York: Atherton Press.

Nichols, M. (1984). *Family Therapy: Concepts and Methods.* New York: Gardner Press.

Norman, E., & Mancuso, A. (eds.). (1980). *Women's Issues and Social Work Practice.* Itasca, IL: Peacock.

Perlman, H.H. (1972). Once more with feeling. In E.J. Mullen, J.R. Dumpson, & Associates (eds.), *Evaluation of Social Intervention.* San Francisco: Jossey-Bass, 191–209.

Perlman, H.H. (1957). *Social Casework: A Problem-Solving Process.* Chicago: University of Chicago Press.

Piaget, J. (1952). *The Origins of Intelligence in Children.* New York: International Universities Press.

Piaget, J. (1951). *The Child's Conception of the World.* London: Routledge & Kegan Paul.

Pinderhughes, E.G. (1983). Empowerment for our clients and for ourselves. *Social Casework: The Journal of Contemporary Social Work* 64, 331–38.

Robinson, J.B. (1989). Clinical treatment of black families: Issues and strategies. *Social Work* 34, 232–29.

Roskin, M. (1980). Integration of primary prevention in social work. *Social Work* 25, 192–97.

Rubin, A. (1985). Practice effectiveness: More grounds for optimism. *Social Work* 30, 469–76.

Ryan, A.S. (1985). Cultural factors in casework with Chinese Americans. *Social Casework: The Journal of Contemporary Social Work* 66, 333–40.

Schlossberg, S.B., & Kagan, R.M. (1988). Practice strategies for engaging chronic multi-problem families. *Social Casework: The Journal of Contemporary Social Work* 69, 3–9.

Selye, H. (1956). *The Stress of Life.* New York: McGraw-Hill.

Simon, B.L. (1988). The feminization of poverty: A call for primary prevention. *Journal of Primary Prevention* 9, 6–17.

Spitz, R. (1965). *The First Year of Life: A Psychoanalytic Study of Normal and Deviant Development of Object Relations.* New York: International Universities Press.

Spitz, R. (1945). Hospitalism: An inquiry into the genesis of psychiatric conditions in early childhood. *Psychoanalytic Study of the Child* 2, 313–42.

Stamm, R. (1959). Ego psychology in the emerging theoretical base of social work. In A.J. Kahn (ed.), *Issues in American Social Work.* New York: Columbia University Press, 80–109.

Star, B., et al. (1981). Psychosocial aspects of wife-battering. In E. Howell & M. Bayes (eds.), *Women and Mental Health.* New York: Basic Books, 426–39.

Stern, D. (1985). *The Interpersonal World of the Infant: A View from Psychoanalysis and Developmental Psychology.* New York: Basic Books.

Stoller, R. (1977). Primary femininity. In H. Blum (ed.), *Female Psychology: Contemporary Psychoanalytic Views.* New York: International Universities Press, 59–78.

Straussner, S.L.A. (1993). Assessment and treatment of clients with alcohol and other drug abuse problems: An overview. In S.L.A. Straussner (ed.), *Clinical Work with Substance-Abusing Clients.* New York: Guilford Press, 3–32.

Thomlison, R.J. (1984). Something works: Evidence from practice effectiveness studies. *Social Work* 29, 51–56.

Towle, C. (1949). Helping the client to use his capacities and resources. *Proceedings of the National Conference of Social Work, 1948*. New York: Columbia University Press, 259–79.

Tully, C. (1992). Research on older lesbian women: What is known, what is not known, and how to learn more. In N.J. Woodman (ed.), *Gay and Lesbian Lifestyles: A Guide for Counseling and Education*. New York: Irvington Publishers, 235–64.

Turner, F. J. (1986). *Social Work Treatment*. New York: Free Press.

Vaillant, G. E. (1977). *Adaptation in Life*. Boston: Little, Brown.

Weille, K.L.H. (1993). Reworking developmental theory: The case of lesbian identity formation. *Clinical Social Work Journal* 21, 151–60.

White, R.F. (1963). Ego and reality in psychoanalytic theory. *Psychological Issues*. Vol. 2, New York: International Universities Press.

White, R.J. (1959). Motivation reconsidered: The concept of competence. *Psychological Review* 66, 297–33.

Wilson, M.N. (1989). Child development in the context of the black extended family. *American Psychologist* 44, 380–85.

Winnicott, D.W. (1965). *Maturational Processes and the Facilitating Environment*. New York: International Universities Press.

CHAPTER 10

THE EMPOWERMENT APPROACH TO SOCIAL WORK PRACTICE

JUDITH A.B. LEE

> In the ghetto
> we stand
> What we see?
> Misery
> falling like rain.
> —Sudeka Linda Harrison
> (Thomas, 1978)

OVERVIEW

These are the words of a fifteen-year-old African-American girl living in urban poverty whose brave and tragic story ends in suicide (Lee, 1994; Thomas, 1978). Her story, the lives of the many people of poverty, color, and difference whom I have known in three decades of social work practice and teaching, and my own life experiences of difference and marginalization convinced me of the need for an approach to social work practice that addresses both personal and political empowerment in working with oppressed groups.

As we approach the year 2000, little has changed for the Sudekas of the world except that the ranks of the poor are fuller. In 1991, almost thirty-six million Americans lived in poverty. At least one-fifth of America's children are poor. The poverty of Black and Hispanic children approaches fifty percent. Forty-four percent of poor two-parent families have at least one full-time worker (*New York Times,* Sept. 4, 1992; Brazelton, 1990). The elderly and children are pitted each against other in the competition for survival resources (Ozawa, 1989). Contemporary code words like "welfare reform" are the new battle cry for war on the poor (Katz, 1989). For poor and working-class Americans and for many members of the middle class, these are the hardest times in three decades.

The empowerment approach to social work practice enables practitioners to coinvestigate reality with the poor, the working poor, people of color, women, and those who are oppressed by virtue of sexual orientation, physical or mental challenges, youth, or age and to help them confront the obstacles imposed by class, race, and difference. Practice with people who are pushed to the edge of American or global society necessitates a joining with and validation of that experience and a dual focus on people's potential and on political/structural change. The synthesis of a wide range of theories and skills is needed for effective empowerment practice. The empowerment approach provides an overarching conceptualization that links the personal and political levels of empowerment.

Theorist William Schwartz elaborated on C. Wright Mills's notion that the "personal troubles of milieu and public issues of structure must be stated in terms of the other, and of the interaction between the two . . . There can be no choice or even a division of labor between serving individual needs and social problems . . ." (1974b:75). Integrating these in theory and practice is the dual focus of the empowerment approach. Despite polarization in the profession throughout history, the recent focus on a simultaneous concern for people and environments has guided social work past falsely dichotomizing individual growth and social change (Bartlett, 1958; Germain, 1979; Germain and Gitterman, 1980; Gordon, 1968, 1996; Middleman and Goldberg, 1974; Schwartz, 1974a,b). But even this dual view of function needs an additional component: that people/clients themselves actively work to change the oppressive environment and mitigate the effects of internalized oppression. A side-by-side stance of worker and client is needed. As bell hooks, the African-American feminist writer, notes: "Radical post modernism calls attention to those shared sensibilities which cross the boundaries of class, gender, race, etc., that could be fertile ground for the construction of empathy—ties that would promote recognition of common commitments and serve as a base for solidarity and coalition" (1990:26–27). Such empathy is the sine qua non of the empowerment process. It enables bridges to be made and crossed so client and worker can stand together to confront personal blocks to empowerment and injustice.

EMPOWERMENT CONCEPTS

The empowerment approach makes connections between social and economic justice and individual pain and suffering. Utilizing empowerment theory as a unifying framework, it presents an integrative, holistic approach to meeting the needs of members of oppressed groups.

This approach adopts the ecological perspective advanced by *Carel Germain,**† which helps us to see the interdependence of all living and nonliving systems and the transactional nature of relationships (Germain, 1979, 1991; Germain & Gitterman,

---

*The names of primary contributors to empowerment thinking in social work practice will be italicized in the text discussion for emphasis.

† This chapter is dedicated to the memory of Carel B. Germain, cherished friend, challenging mentor, and extraordinarily empowered woman.

1980). Yet it does not deny the possibility of conflict as a means of releasing the potentialities of people and environments (Germain, 1979, 1980; Germain & Gitterman, 1980, 1996). Potentialities are the power bases that are developed in all of us when there is a "goodness of fit" between people and environments. By definition, poor people and oppressed groups seldom have this "fit," as injustice stifles human potential. To change this unfavorable equation, people must examine the forces of oppression, name them, face them, and join together to challenge them as they have been internalized and encountered in external power structures. The greatest potentiality to tap is the power of collectivity, people joining together to act, reflect, and act again in the process of praxis. This process is fueled by mutual caring and support.

FIFOCAL VISION

Five perspectives are used to develop an empowerment practice framework. This multifocal, or "fifocal," vision also determines the view of the client. It comprises the following:

- A historical perspective: learning a group's history of oppression, including a critical-historical analysis of related social policy.
- An ecological perspective, including a stress-coping paradigm and other concepts related to coping (a transactional view of ego functioning that takes oppression into account, problem solving, and cognitive restructuring of the false beliefs engendered with internalized oppression).
- Ethclass and feminist perspectives, which appreciate the ceilings and lowering floors imposed by class and race and gender, the concept that power may be developed and the unity of the personal and political. A critical perspective, analyzing the status quo.

Imagine a pair of glasses with five lenses ground in (not trifocals but fifocals). There is a good deal of overlap, so it will not take long to get used to five foci. Our vision is sharpened in particular areas yet clearly focused. In addition to this fifocal perspective, the empowerment approach is based on values, principles, processes, and skills integrated into an overall conceptual framework. Helping processes include supporting strengths and ego functioning, challenging false beliefs, challenging external obstacles and unjust systems, developing pride in peoplehood, problem solving and problem posing, consciousness raising and dialogue, and building collectivity. These are used in the one-to-one, family, small group, and wider community, including the political arena. The group, in particular the "empowerment group," is the heart of the empowerment practice. The uniqueness of this approach is the integration of the personal/clinical and the political in a direct-practice approach relevant to poor and oppressed people.

EMPOWERMENT'S PATH INTO SOCIAL WORK: HISTORICAL PRECEDENTS AND CONTEMPORARY TRENDS

The most important historical precedents for empowerment practice in social work history are the settlement movement, particularly the work of Jane Addams and her cohorts; the generally unrecognized women's clubs and social reform work of nineteenth-century African Americans and other minority groups; early group work theorists, particularly Grace Coyle; and the work of Bertha C. Reynolds, the radical psychoanalytic social caseworker.

JANE ADDAMS—SETTLEMENT MOVEMENT

Social work methodology experienced an early split relating to "cause" (social goals or activist movements) and "function" (direct practice method). Yet Jane Addams's life and work were a testimony to the unity of social work purpose

Addams had a talent for dealing with "baffling complexity" and seeing things whole. The development of Hull House in Chicago (1889) in association with her life partner, Mary Rozet Smith, and her leadership in domestic reform movements gained her a national reputation by 1900 (Pottick, 1989). Her international work on behalf of women and peace won her the Nobel Peace Prize in 1931. She also authored nine books, several on settlement method and work.

The beginnings of the empowerment approach may be found in the work of great women. These women did not have the right to vote, to live alone or unmarried without scandal, to attend universities of their choice, or to freely enter the professions as they built the profession of social work. From Jane Addams and her cohorts, the empowerment tradition in social work also inherits a passion for social equality, social justice, and social reform; a respect for difference and the richness of diverse cultures; and a sense of world consciousness and responsibility (Addams, 1922, 1930; Simon, 1994). At Hull House, outstanding and ordinary women and men gave their lives to living and working side by side with oppressed groups so that "reciprocity and a fair share of resources might flow between the classes" (Addams, 1910). Group work methodology, discussion, and dialogue and global and local action are building blocks for an empowerment approach.

AFRICAN-AMERICAN WOMEN'S CLUBS

Addams was dedicated to racial justice established in dialogue with the African-American community. Blacks were forced to develop their own helping institutions due to rigid segregation laws (Solomon, 1976). Robenia and Lawrence Gary have documented the social welfare leadership of fifty-six Black women (1975). Noting that the "Black church, mutual aid and fraternal organizations were the major social welfare institutions of the Black community," they emphasize that Black women played important roles in these organizations. Some Black women's clubs also worked cooperatively with white women, including Jane Addams.

By the turn of the century, African Americans were included in a separate and un-equal service system. COS, for example, served almost entirely white families (Solomon, 1976). Most settlement houses were segregated as were the communities they served. Blacks entering white communities were usually met with violence and sometimes death (Berman-Rossi & Miller, 1992; Katz, 1986). Hull House served large numbers of Mexican Americans despite negative neighborhood sentiment (Addams, 1930).

Many Black women activists were instrumental in promoting social reform. Some, like Ida B. Wells-Barnett, spoke out at rallies, at political events, and through journalism. African-American women founded local organizations such as neighborhood improvement clubs, women's clubs, houses for the aged, and children's homes. The women's clubs offered services similar to settlement house programs (Gary & Gary, 1975). Leading Black social reformers who, among their many leadership roles, also developed women's clubs and settlement houses during the Progressive Era were Janie Porter-Barrett, Sarah A. Collins-Fernandis, Mary Eliza Church Terrell, and Ida Bell Wells-Barnett (Lee, 1994).

The legacy of the settlement house movement and the Black women's clubs is a legacy of social action (Addams, 1910, 1930; Lee, 1994). As Ben-Zion Shapiro notes:

> The pioneers in social work with groups shared a concern for the development of a democratic society within the United States and internationally. Their work can be traced in the association between Jane Addams and John Dewey in Chicago in the 1890s and in a more organized affiliation among Dewey, Mary Parker Follett, Eduard Lindeman, Grace Coyle and others in a group called The Inquiry in the 1920s and in the early 30s (1991:8,9).

The Inquiry used political, social, and economic analysis as tools in building theory that emphasized harnessing group processes for social change goals. Grace Coyle translated much of this thinking for social group workers. She saw groups as tapping the "great molten stream of social discontent and social injustice underlying present conditions" and as providing direct education on social questions and social action (Shapiro, 1991:11).

By the 1940s, this passion for democracy was transmuted into a concern for "social responsibility" and the development of methodology that displaced social action as the central concern of group work (Shapiro, 1991). The 1960s saw a short-lived revival of social action groups (Weiner, 1964) and the heyday of grass-roots community organizing (Brager & Specht, 1973; Lewis, 1991). It met its demise with the War on Poverty of the Johnson administration and the onslaught of reactionary politics.

BERTHA CAPEN REYNOLDS: A RADICAL PSYCHIATRIC CASEWORKER WHO STOOD BETWEEN CLIENT AND COMMUNITY

A turning point in the American social welfare system was the period of the Great Depression and the New Deal, which provided a small measure of social security for working Americans. Yet few social workers made connections between major socioeconomic events and social work. Bertha C. Reynolds (1885–1978) was an exception. Influenced by teaching experience with W.E.B. DuBois at Atlanta University in 1910, Reynolds graduated in 1918 from Smith College School of Social Work (she served as its associate director from 1925–38). She combined the day's psychoanalytically oriented casework practice with a progressive, democratic-socialist and social action worldview that gave her unparalleled depth and an integrated perspective.

Bertha Reynolds asserted that social work had a mandate to work with the "plain people," to be "ever and always a go-between profession" (1964:17). She saw social work as having a "meditating function." Politically, her vision included the highest ideals of democracy, full citizen participation, and equity in the distribution of resources more common to socialism. The vision placed social work in the arena where people work and live. It offered "penetrating social appraisal" of how people cope in order to "meet their reality or change it" (1951:131).

Reynolds took social work to task:

> Social work . . . has tried to deny incurable poverty, illness and social maladjustment, first by assuming that the solution lies in the treatment of unconscious conflict within the person, instead of in society itself. Then, in self-protection, social agencies have moved away from contact with cases in which poverty, illness and friction were too obviously beyond the reach of a change in the clients' feelings . . . (1951:130).

She emphasized that "our practice is in the world of social living, whether we like it or not, and whether or not our theories correspond with it" (1951:ix). Reynolds urged social work's cooperation with existing progressive forces: "It was not we, a handful of social workers, against a sea of human misery. It was humanity itself building dikes, and we were helping in our own peculiarly useful way" (1964:184). Empowered people themselves are the builders. We are fellow workers, and neighbors with special expertise in the struggle for social living and social justice.

CURRENT INFLUENCES

In the current time, political science, psychology, sociology, economics, and religion, especially liberation theology, have contributed to social work's synthesis of empowerment theory for social work practice (Lee, 1994; Simon; 1994). For some, the term "liberation" more accurately describes the process and objectives of empowerment. Although liberation is a social movement that, by definition, cannot be the domain of any one profession (Germain, 1980), social work can assist people in empowering themselves to work toward liberation.

There are two strong streams that feed into empowerment theory for social work practice. The first is such social/political/economic movements as decolonization, the African liberation movements, the women's movement, the gay rights movement, and the Black power and poor people's power movements (Simon, 1994). The second human development/clinical theories from the helping professions related to releasing human potentialities. The empowerment approach seeks to channel the two streams into one mighty flow.

Personal and political power are interrelated. *Barbara Bryant Solomon* (1976) was the first major thinker to develop the concept of empowerment for the social work profession. Solomon identifies direct and indirect blocks to power. Indirect power blocks represent internalized negative valuations (of the oppressor), which are "incorporated into the developmental experiences of the individual as mediated by significant others." Direct power blocks "are applied directly by some agent of society's major social institutions (1976). Powerlessness is based on several factors, including economic insecurity, absence of experience in the political arena, absence of access to information, lack of training in critical and abstract thought, physical and emotional stress, learned helplessness, and the aspects of a person's emotional or intellectual makeup that prevent him or her from actualizing possibilities that do exist (Cox, 1989). The actual and perceived ability to use available resources contributes to a sense of power that is directly connected to self-esteem (Parsons, 1989). Society "blames the victim" for power deficits even as power is withheld and abused by dominant groups (Ryan, 1971). Victim blaming can be blatant or subtle, as in the popular concept of co-dependency. (Pence, 1987). *Jeffry Galper*'s radical casework approach, which seeks to unite the personal and political, is an important forerunner of empowerment thinking (1980), while *Helen Northen*'s clinical social work text is particularly sensitive to issues of oppression (1994). The empowerment approach weaves clinical and political thinking into one fabric.

EMPOWERMENT DEFINED

Empowerment "deals with a particular kind of block to problem-solving: that imposed by the external society by virtue of a stigmatized collective identity" (Solomon, 1976:21). Webster's definition of the word *empower* is "to give power or authority to; to give ability to, enable, permit," which implies that power can be given to another. This is rarely so. Staples sees empowerment as the process of gaining power, developing power, taking or seizing power, or facilitating or enabling power (Parsons, 1991). As *Barbara Simon*, who has documented the empowerment tradition in social work practice (1994), stresses:

> Empowerment is a reflexive activity, a process capable of being initiated and sustained only by (those) who seek power or self-determination. Others can only aid and abet in this empowerment process (1990:32).

The empowerment process resides in the person, not the helper.

There are three interlocking dimensions of empowerment: (1) the development of a more positive and potent sense of self; (2) the construction of knowledge and capacity for more critical comprehension of social and political realities of one's environment; and (3) the cultivation of resources and strategies, or more functional competence, for attainment of personal and collective social goals, or liberation. As we partialize and operationalize the concept of empowerment, it can be the keystone of social work (Beck, 1983).

Ron Mancoske and *Jeanne Hunzeker,* distinctive forerunners of the empowerment approach, define empowerment as "using interventions which enable those with whom we interact to be more in control of the interactions in exchanges . . . and the capacity to influence the forces which affect one's life space for one's own benefit" (1989:14,15). They state, and I agree, that Carel B. Germain and *Alex Gitterman*'s life model of social work practice (1980) fits well with an empowerment approach, as it allows for multilevel examinations and interventions that may be clinical or political, it is almost by definition a praxis model, and the empowerment perspective gives direction to life model practice (Mancoske & Hunzeker, 1989). The specialized assessment and interventive methods used in the empowerment approach incorporate and build on the categories and the spirit of the life model.

Critical consciousness and knowledge of oppression is power. Power also comes from healthy personality development in the face of oppression, which fuels the ability to influence others. This includes self-esteem/identity; self-direction; and competence and relatedness (Germain, 1991). Clinical and political interventions must challenge the external and internal obstacles to the development of these attributes. Transformation, or throwing off oppression in personal and community life, occurs as people are empowered through consciousness raising to see and reach for alternatives (Harris, 1993). It requires anger at injustice and the dehumanization of poverty, negative valuations, and the culture of personal greed (Mancoske & Hunzeker, 1989). The strengths perspective of *Dennis Saleebey* (1992) and the structural approach of *Gale Wood-Goldberg* and *Ruth Middleman* (1989) are also compatible with the empowerment approach.

Social work practice must decide whether it will opt to work with the oppressed, building on community and not on self-interest and broadening the possibility of the imaginable as it goes beyond immediate problem solving to the promulgation of hope (Mancoske & Hunzeker, 1989). Two conditions are needed for empowerment: a worker with a raised consciousness and a client who seeks to be empowered.

Empowerment practice addresses: direct and indirect power blocks; individual, familial, and organizational resource problems (multiple dimensions of poverty); problems of asymmetrical exchange relationships; problems of powerlessness, constraining, and inhibiting or hindering power structures; and problems related to arbitrary social criteria or values (Staub-Bernasconi, 1991). Powerlessness is low social attractiveness due to poor resources (material and emotional resources and knowledge). To help empower, we must first learn to speak openly about power with clients and then engage in examination of power bases stemming from personal resources and articulation power, symbolic power, value power, positional power, or authority and organizational power. Unfair social stratification and unfair distribution of goods are the most difficult issues facing world society. Education and a guaranteed basic income are imperative. International social work can help link different groups/cultures together to claim a fair share of power resources and resist domination (Staub-Bernasconi, 1992).

Paulo Freire

A major contributor to empowerment thinking in social work is Brazilian educator *Paulo Freire* (1973, 1990, 1994). It is the translation of Freire's critical thinking into social work theory that marks the uniqueness of this empowerment approach.

The "radical pedagogy" and "dialogic process" of Freire (1973) is clearly a relevant method for empowerment in social work (Breton, 1989; Freire, 1990; Gutiérrez, 1990; Lee, 1989, 1991; Mancoske & Hunzeker, 1989; Parsons, 1989; Pence, 1987). Freire's group and community oriented methods of dialogue promote critical thinking and action:

> Every human being is capable of looking critically at his world in a dialogical encounter with others . . . in this process . . . Each man wins back his own right to say his own word, to name the world (1973: 11–13).

Liberation theology, with its notions of base communities serving as units of social and political change and its use of consciousness raising, is particularly pertinent to social work thinking (Breton, 1992; Evans, 1992; Germain, 1991; Lee, 1994; Lewis, 1991; Mancoske & Hunzeker, 1989). Freire defines conscientization as "learning to perceive social, political and economic contradictions and to take action against the oppressive elements of reality" (1973:20). Critical consciousness raising and dialogue are the key methods that help people to think, see, talk, and act for themselves (Freire, 1973).

Lorraine Gutiérrez cites consciousness raising as goal, process, and outcome in empowerment work (1989, 1990). She notes:

> It is not sufficient to focus only on developing a sense of personal power or developing skills or working toward social change. These three elements combined are the goal of empowerment in social work practice (1989).

Gutiérrez sees developing critical consciousness, reducing self-blame; assuming personal responsibility for change, and enhancing self-efficacy as critical to empowerment (1989). She sees group work as central to empowerment practice, based on research on the effective use of ethnic identity and consciousness-raising groups with Latino college students (Gutiérrez & Ortega, 1989). Gutiérrez has also written on empowering women of color (1990). *Ruth Parsons, James Jorgensen, and Santos Hernandez* (1994) have developed specific goals and change principles for working with the disempowered.

Empowerment Theory and Groups

Empowerment theory applied to group work was first introduced in 1983 by *Ruby Pernell* at the Fifth Annual Symposium of the Association for the Advancement of

Social Work With Groups. She noted that group work is a natural vehicle for empowerment as its historic goals include "growth towards social ends" (1986).

Noting that Black Americans have borne the lion's share of power insufficiency and inequities, Pernell emphasized that empowerment practice can not remain politically neutral:

> . . . Empowerment as a goal is a political position, as it challenges the status quo and attempts to change existing power relationships . . . It goes beyond "enabling." It requires of the worker the ability to analyze social processes and interpersonal behavior in terms of power and powerlessness . . . and . . . to enable group members to . . . develop skills using their influence effectively (1986:111).

The skills of working with indigenous leadership; knowing resources—where the power lies and how to get it; and enabling group members to do for themselves are important in attaining empowerment. Shapiro notes:

> The recent work of Hirayama and Hirayama (1986), Pernell (1986), Lee (1986), Wood and Middleman (1989), Lewis (1989), and Breton (1989a,b) using the language of competence, consciousness-raising and empowerment, is suggestive of theory which goes beyond the conceptualizations of the "social goals" model and its proponents (1991:16).

Exhaustive work on ethnic sensitive social work practice, particularly that of *Devore* and *Schlesinger* (1991); *Lum* (1986), *Davis* (1984), and *Chau* (1990), made knowledge of culture and race critical to empowerment practice. DeCrescenzo (1979) discussed group work with gay adolescents, but there is little in most social work journals regarding the empowerment of lesbians and gay men. The work of *Hilda Hidalgo, Trans Peterson*, and *Nathalie Woodman* (1985) has made a significant contribution to filling this gap in social work literature.

Margot Breton and *Elizabeth Lewis* have been major contributors to the integration of humanism, liberation theology, and community group work into empowerment practice. Groups that seek change in the environment are empowering to the degree that group members (not organizers) have actually brought about and reflected upon the change. According to Lewis (1983), face-to-face grass-roots (or "adult community") groups in neighborhoods and communities bridge an "interstitial area" between group work and community organization practice. Political empowerment is the purpose but personal satisfaction, growth, community or ethnic pride, and heightened self-esteem may be by-products of these experiences. Breton (1992) stresses the importance of community action and coalition building to human liberation.

The Interactionist Approach and the Mutual Aid Group

The interactionist approach of *William Schwartz* (1974a) is a stepping stone to the empowerment approach. The group is a microcosm of social interaction. The worker's role is to mediate the process through which individuals and their systems reach out to each other, particularly "when the ties are almost severed." This approach appreciates reciprocity and the strength of the group itself as a mutual aid and self-empowering system (Berman-Rossi, 1994). *Catherine Papell* and *Beulah Rothman*'s (1980) conceptualization of the "mainstream model" of social work with groups draws on the interactionist approach. Formed or natural groups can encompass a variety of empowerment purposes. A blending of critical education and conscientization group methods with the interactionist and mainstream models forms a foundation for the empowerment group (Lee, 1994).

Ruth Parsons (1989) emphasizes the importance of the group. Empowerment is an outcome and an process that comes initially from the validation of peers and a perception of commonality:

> The idea of building collectivity is central to the helping process. Collectivity involves the process of merging energy of individuals into a whole . . . It goes beyond treatment in a group. It contains Schwartz' notion of the provision of a mediating or third force function.

Groups may have consciousness raising, help to individuals, social action, social support, and the development of skills and competence as overlapping foci to help members facing oppression gain equality and justice (Garvin, 1985). *Beth Reed* and *Charles Garvin* have more important contributions regarding the empowerment of women through groups (1983). *Audrey Mullender* and *Dave Ward* (1991), major British theorists, stress that empowerment group work must be a self-directed (not worker-directed) process. Parsons (1989, 1991) identifies empowerment as a developmental process that begins with individual growth and may culminate in social change, as a psychological state marked by heightened feelings of self-esteem, efficacy, and control, and as liberation. The conceptual framework presented here integrates these three kinds of empowerment into a unified approach.

BASIC ASSUMPTIONS

A basic assumption of the empowerment approach is that oppression is a structurally based phenomenon with far-reaching effects on individuals and communities. These effects range from physical death (infant or child mortality and the death of adolescents and young adults from gang violence, drugs, other forms of homicide, and suicide) to incarceration and the death of hope. Hopelessness leads to destruction of self and others, despair, apathy, internalized rage, and false beliefs about the worth of the self (Harris, 1993). When the efforts of oppression become internalized, the maintenance of oppression may become a transactional phenomenon. Two societal institutions militate against the individual's succumbing to or internalizing the oppressor's view of the self: a strong family unit and a strong community (Chestang, 1976). Hence, strong support networks and good human relatedness and connections are essential to developing a positive sense of identity and self-direction. The assumption is that self is found in community with others (Swenson, 1992). Building pride in peoplehood and community is both a preventive and a remedial measure. However, the problems caused by oppression almost always necessitate a dual focus on changing the environment and strengthening the self.

The assumption about people in this approach is that they are fully capable of solving immediate problems and moving beyond them to analyze institutionalized oppression and the structures that maintain it, as well as its effect upon themselves. They are able to strengthen internal resources and work collaboratively in their families, groups, and communities to change and empower themselves in order to challenge the very conditions that oppress. The basic principle of this approach is that people empower themselves through individual empowerment work, empowerment-oriented group work, community action, and political knowledge and skill. The approach sees people as capable of praxis: action-reflection and action, action-in-reflection, and dialogue.

A unitary conception of person: environment prevents us from victim blaming on the one hand and naivete regarding the panacea of environmental change on the other. It leads toward the development of helping "technologies" (strategies, methods, knowledge, and skills) that are both clinical and political. It necessitates "both and" conceptualizations of practice (Bricker-Jenkins & Hooyman, 1986; Bricker-Jenkins et al., 1991; Van Den Bergh & Cooper, 1986). People can and must take themselves and their environments in hand to attain empowerment. To envision social change that comes about without the full efforts of oppressed people is to envision a Machiavellian Utopia. To envision oppressed people making this effort without changing themselves—by refusing oppression, actualizing potentialities, and actively struggling to obtain resources—is to negate the effects of oppression in the lives of the oppressed. Both changed societies and changed people who will work toward this are the nature of the sought-for change. The ultimate goal of empowerment work goes beyond meeting individual needs for growth and power to empowering communities and developing a strong people. The goals are collective more than individual and yet these two are inseparable. The assumption here is that both the oppressor and the oppressed, as well as those who seemingly stand by or pass by on the other side, are damaged by oppression and in need of liberation. This view seeks unity and harmony among oppressed groups. Yet it does not shy away from nonviolent confrontation and conflict, which may be a necessary part of liberation.

VALUE BASE OF THE EMPOWERMENT APPROACH

Most practice models or approaches that serve "all people" neglect to pay adequate attention to poor people, people of color, women, and people who are otherwise oppressed (Lum, 1986). The NASW Code of Ethics and the ethical principle of impartiality entreat us to cultivate our knowledge and skill in order to reach out to those clients who face bias and discrimination and act (with them) to challenge oppression. Poor people, women, people of color, gay men, and lesbians come to a variety of agencies where they may meet with worker or institutional bias as well as a lack of knowledge regarding who they are and what special issues they may bring. Attempts at equanimity minimize central aspects of people's lives that necessitate exceptional coping abilities. Color, class, gender, stigma, or difference "blindness" is not useful to clients (Lum, 1986). Empowerment means that both workers and clients draw strength from working through the meaning of these different statuses, enabling them to be who they are: persons with a rich heritage. The value base and the conceptual framework that underpin this empowerment approach are summarized in Table 10–1.

Table 10–1
A Conceptual Framework

The Empowerment Approach to Social Work Practice

Professional Purpose: Based on a simultaneous concern for people and environments, to assist people who experience poverty and oppression in their efforts to empower themselves to enhance their adaptive potentials and to work toward changing environmental and structural arrangements that are oppressive.

Value Base: Preference for working with people who are poor, oppressed, and stigmatized to strengthen individual adaptive potentials and promote environmental/structural change through individual and collective action; preference for social policies and programs that create a just society with equal opportunity and access to resources.

Knowledge Base and Theoretical Foundations: Theory and concepts about person:environment transactions in situations of oppression. This includes "fifocal vision": the history of oppression; ecological, ethclass, feminist, and critical theory perspectives; knowledge about individual adaptive potentialities, unique personhood, and the ways people cope—ego functioning, social and cognitive behavioral learning and problem solving in the face of oppression; empowering individual, family, group and community helping processes; and larger systems and structural change processes in order that we may assist people in empowering themselves on the personal, interpersonal, and political levels.

Method—Principles, Processes and Skills: The empowerment method rests on empowerment values and purposes and the eight principles that undergird the approach. The method may be used in the one-to-one, group, or community relational systems. It depends on a collaborative relationship that encompasses mutuality, reciprocity, shared power, and shared human struggle; the use of empowerment groups to identify and work on direct and indirect power blocks toward personal, interpersonal, and political power; and collective activity that reflects a raised consciousness regarding oppression. The method uses specific skills in operationalizing the practice principles to address and promote action at all levels of living.

THE ROLES, PROCESSES, AND SKILLS OF THE EMPOWERMENT APPROACH

Processes and Skills to Promote Coping and Adaptation/ Social Change

In the empowerment approach, the worker promotes reflection, thinking, and problem solving on person:environment transactions, including the client's role in them and the experience of oppression. Along with the client's self-defined problem focus, oppressive conditions and proposed solutions are the content of reflective procedures. Sustaining skills, particularly the use of well-attuned empathy born of fifocal vision and listening, make the difficult work of empowerment possible (Germain & Gitterman, 1980; Northen, 1994; Shulman, 1994; Woods & Hollis, 1990, 1996). The worker also assesses ego functioning and provides ego-supportive intervention to bolster clients' strengths (Goldstein, 1984, 1994; Lee, 1994). Client and worker together then seek to change oppressive conditions using a range of skills.

According to Carel Germain (1984), people must develop certain attributes in order to cope and adapt. The attributes achieved by adequate person:environment transactions are: motivation, which corresponds to the incentives and rewards provided by the environment; problem-solving skills, which correspond to the strengths and efficacy of society's socializing institutions (including the family and schools); maintenance of psychic comfort (including managing feelings) and self-esteem, which corresponds to the emotional and other support provided by the environment; and self-direction, which corresponds to the provision of information, choices, and adequate time and space (Germain, 1984, 1991; Mechanic, 1974; White, 1974).

Empowering Skills to Bolster Motivation

Motivation can only be sustained if basic needs for housing, food, clothing, and financial and emotional support are met. As these needs are met by client and worker through gaining resources and opportunities and attending to presenting problems, the worker can help to keep hope alive. Encouraging the client's own words about his or her problems and life and accepting the client's problem definition also provide motivation. The worker can also reach for and convey understanding of feelings of difference, isolation, alienation, and being misunderstood, as well as experiences of discrimination at the hands of systems needed to sustain life and growth. In partializing the stressful demands into workable segments with the client, the worker also encourages the client to share how he or she has dealt before with similar problems. The skill of having the client name and own his or her strengths also provides motivation to continue. Hope of changing the oppressive systems must also be offered through the worker's skills of lending a vision and beginning to enlist the client's energy in this thinking. The worker may also use skills of appropriate self-disclosure around dealing with oppressive conditions to build bridges to the client's experiences and to offer further hope of change. The worker should also use skills of system negotiation so that the client gains expertise in this area.

TO MAINTAIN PSYCHIC COMFORT AND SELF-ESTEEM

In helping the client to maintain psychic comfort, manage feelings, and attain an optimal level of self-esteem, the worker has the additional tasks of externalizing the sources of oppression in order to reduce self-blame and foster pride in peoplehood. Here the role is one of co-teacher and critical educator as the worker helps the client identify and own his or her group's achievements and heightens awareness and appreciation of the client's own culture.

The worker uses family and group skills to help members share and validate each other's experiences with oppression (Hartman & Laird, 1983; Wood & Middleman, 1989). As members discover they share a common experience, self-deprecatory feelings may diminish. Here also the worker co-teaches about the oppressed group's achievements against the odds, which builds communal and self-esteem. Giving information helps clients gain familiarity with how systems work, diminishes fear, and adds to feelings of competence. The worker also helps to mobilize natural helping networks and structures and focuses on changing systemic inequities that promote the clients' discomforts and anxiety.

TO ENHANCE PROBLEM SOLVING AND PROMOTE SELF-DIRECTION

The skills of problem solving are especially important in the empowerment approach. Ultimately, the aim is to help people to think differently and act differently, not only in solving personal problems but in dealing with the connected problems of oppression. *Sharon Berlin* (1983) suggests a nine-step cognitive behavioral problem-solving process that moves from awareness of the problem to taking action. Germain (1984) adds the dimension of teaching the skills needed for achieving the solutions, providing group experiences for such learning, and working with the environment to offer the options and services needed.

PARTICULAR SKILLS NEEDED TO SOLVE PROBLEMS IN THE EMPOWERMENT APPROACH

These skills includes *consciousness raising, praxis,* and *critical education.* Skills of *maintaining equality in the problem-solving process* are critical. This includes *observing the rules of symmetry and parity* in communication. The worker who is directive and lectures, or who filibusters or interprets frequently in the process, is not providing the conditions necessary for empowerment.

Consciousness raising is the process of developing heightened awareness and knowledge about situations of oppression, which leads to new ways of thinking about the social order. As with all skills and processes discussed here, it may be done on the one-to-one or family level or on the group or community level. This is a tall order.

The four attributes (motivation, psychic comfort, problem solving, and self-direction) are interdependent and must be sustained throughout the helping process. A raised consciousness provides motivation, but motivation and psychic comfort are necessary to raise consciousness because ultimately it means change in thinking and doing. To view the world differently may initially be both a frightening and a freeing experience. The worker's skill in working with feelings will include hearing, naming, staying with, validating, and helping clients to express the pain, anger, and sadness that come with consciously realizing that they have been oppressed and victimized socially and economically. The use of "codes" developed by the clients and of their own experiences—for example, using books, art, music, poetry, and other ways of reaching people's level of conscious awareness—can be extremely helpful. A facilitator who worked with a group of battered women reflects on the painful unbinding of women's feet in China in the 1920s:

> It was so painful that they could peel only a few layers of binding off at a time . . . Now when I facilitate a women's group I've become aware of how gentle with each other we must be in unbinding our minds. (Pence, 1987:20).

The skills of gently sharing information in the co-teaching role are critical here as well. Knowledge is power. To be kept from knowledge is oppression. The skills of cognitive restructuring (Berlin, 1983) are needed to raise consciousness about being oppressed. The worker helps clients to identify thinking patterns; revise false beliefs; devise more adaptive ways of dealing with internalized and external oppression; and to talk and think healthier about themselves, their group, and their situation. The worker than encourages clients to rename and recreate their own reality in their own words.

The worker's skills of guiding in the process of praxis are extremely important. As noted, praxis (action-reflection and return to action) involves a sometimes painful unpeeling of awareness and feeling that takes place over time. The ability to promote competence and action is critical. This is also a good time for the worker to share his or her own struggles in challenging such obstacles.

It is as important to be a problem poser as it is to facilitate problem solving. The skills of critical education are central to the empowerment process. This includes the skill of posing critical questions that help people think about the oppressive situation in new ways. This is combined with the skills of information giving noted above. For example, in one agency staff group, I used a newspaper article entitled "Steep Pay Difference Found For Educated Whites, Blacks" (*Hartford Courant*, Sept. 20, 1991) as a code. Sandwiched in the article were two lines regarding those with a high school education, noting only that both Black and white men earned $10,000 more than Black and white women, whose pay scales were close. Asking why these facts are so makes for excellent dialogue and consciousness raising on both race and gender issues.

As noted, Freire's method of critical education (Freire, 1973); Mancoske & Hunzeker, 1989; Pence, 1987) is an important set of processes and skills social workers can learn and utilize. It has five steps, which are taken with a team of representative persons called a culture circle. First, a survey is conducted. The team listens to what is on people's minds, assessing what people talk about and what emotions are linked to. This work must include emotionally cathectic concerns. Second, a theme is chosen and problems are posed in question form. Themes broaden the base of an issue. For example, a theme in Pence's battered women's group was, What is the effect of abusive behavior on women? (Pence, 1987). Third, the problem is analyzed from three perspectives: the personal, the institutional, and the cultural. Questions are asked about each perspective. Fourth, a code is developed. A code is chose to focus the work when a theme generates work on all three levels. Finally, options for action are generated on all three levels. When actions are taken, a process of praxis is used to consolidate and deepen the work of developing critical understanding and a vision of social change.

Ultimately, work that promotes motivation, problem solving, and psychic comfort contributes to a client's self-direction and empowerment.

SKILLS TO PROMOTE SOCIAL CHANGE

Beyond the gains to the self, empowering work can empower communities. Group- and community-centered skills are essential. Much of the above-noted work is done most effectively in small groups, which then may build coalitions with other groups and forces in the community to effect social change (Breton, 1991). Empowerment group skills include making a clear mutual contract that bridges the personal and the political and include a social change focus (Lee, 1991), establishing the common ground and common cause among members, challenging the obstacles to the group's work, lending a vision, and reaching for each member's fullest possible participation in the process. These are a variation on Schwartz's skills and tasks of the group worker (1974a). The worker will also skillfully pose critical questions and develop codes to focus the group's work as discussed above (Freire, 1973b). Combined, these become "empowerment group" method. Community skills incorporate these group skills but include coalition building and the skills of task-oriented action. Here, one wants to help members choose initial tasks at which they can achieve success. Wider political skills include lobbying and testifying at legislative hearings, as well as organizing meetings, protests, and nonviolent-resistance activities. These are skills for workers and clients to develop together (Lee, 1994; Richan, 1991; Staples, 1984).

ROLES AND STANCE OF THE WORKER

Above all, the worker in the empowerment approach is a real person who has awareness of her or his own experiences of oppression and/or membership in the oppressor group. This awareness begins with self-awareness, including issues of counter-transference, but goes beyond this to having a raised consciousness about oppression itself and an ability to share this in the helping process through appropriate self-disclosure. There is no mysticism about the helper or the helping process. The stance is "side-by-side" and an authentic presentation of self. The helping process itself is shared with the client initially and as the process unfolds.

Assessment is important in this approach. The worker must gain an understanding of who the client is and what tolls oppression has taken on the client's well-being currently or in the past. In individual and family work and in empowerment group work, it is helpful to make an assessment based on the client's story. The concept of "the client's story" includes the presenting problem as primary, but it often goes beyond that to the client's view of historical material that is relevant to the problem at hand. This is both a narrative and oral history approach that seeks to unearth the strengths of individuals and their people over historical time (Martin, 1995). While principles of good clinical assessment are utilized, this assessment process differs from "purely" clinical approaches in two important ways: the level of mutuality of the process as the worker shares his or her thinking openly while seeking to comprehend how the client makes sense of the situation, and the explicit inclusion of eth-class, race, gender, and other areas where oppression and power shortages or power deficits may have been experienced by the client. Hence, the assessment is of the client in transaction with oppression and of the oppressive environment, not of the client as if he or she existed in a vacuum.

The contract or mutually derived working agreement explicitly includes looking at the experience of oppression as one of the foci of the work. Of course, as in any approach, immediate and material problems have priority. The client may choose, after being made aware of his or her options, to focus only on immediate problem solving. This approach assumes that poor people and other oppressed groups already have a point of view on their oppression and the ability to reflect on, challenge, and take action to rid themselves and their cohorts of oppression. Many clients already have a raised consciousness and may in fact be surprised that a social worker shares this consciousness. Some, however, have become so accustomed to living in oppression that the anger or despair at victimization and discrimination has been unconsciously repressed. This illuminates another level of consciousness raising.

The length of intervention may vary, but extremely brief treatment focused only on the immediate problem is not the goal in empowerment practice. However long it takes to both solve the issue(s) at hand and raise consciousness in order to challenge immobilizing oppression is the optimal time frame. Very often, as individual or family problems are relieved, the client is motivated to join with others in an empowerment group. Sometimes the intervention can start with the empowerment group experience, and then individual work or personal political work can be added. Such groups may also be building blocks for empowered communities. They may join with other community groups for larger change efforts. It is important to note that this work is not open-ended and forever. At some point in the process, the client feels empowered enough to continue the work without the worker. The worker, in effect, does him- or herself out of a job as empowered people stand ready with awareness, resources, and knowledge to pursue their own goals. Table 10–2 illustrates the steps in developing an assessment for empowerment.

Table 10–2

Outline: Assessment for Empowerment

---

1. Basic Information
   Briefly state age, ethnicity (ethclass), relational status, work, living situation.
2. Life Transitions
   Highlight developmental, status/role, crisis issues, relevant developmental history (if child, include actual school performance, IQ testing, etc.).
3. Health and Mental Health
   Highlight physical and mental challenges; include psychiatric and substance abuse history and ego functioning (assess 10 to 13 functions).
4. Interpersonal
   Be specific about family members, significant relationships, social networks, patterns of communication and roles in group; determine the nature and quality of relationships.
5. Physical and Socioeconomic Environment
   Describe and evaluate impact on client.
6. Manifestations of Oppression
   In areas of basic survival; in facing discrimination and direct blocks to resources and opportunities; in internalized oppression; inequalities in power, rank, or value as a result of oppression.
7. Areas of Powerlessness or Power Shortages
   In what knowledge, skill, attitudes, consciousness, or resources does the client experience deficits?
8. What are the specific strengths in the person and in the environment?
9. Weigh and make a statement of assessment.
10. State the initial working agreement and next steps in intervention.

WORKER TRAINING WITHIN THE EMPOWERMENT APPROACH

Workers need both clinical and political knowledge and expertise to do the job. They need to be what Armando Morales called "generalist-specialists," both broad and deep (1977). They need to be individual and family clinicians, group workers, and community workers and they need to know how to use political process to effect change. Some undergraduate and graduate programs already aim at developing this kind of worker. Others are over-specialized at one or the other end of the spectrum of roles. It may take some shifting of the curriculum as well as postgraduate training and supportive supervision to develop this kind of social worker. Team approaches may also help practitioners to deliver the breadth of empowerment-oriented services. This kind of work may begin in agencies that are constrained by managed-care guidelines, but probably most come to fruition where there is greater flexibility in the way workers may approach services. Empowerment work is appropriate for anyone facing issues of oppression. It is not possible to do it when clients are active drug or alcohol abusers, as all cognitive and emotional abilities must be harnessed to do the work. Such persons must be helped to enter recovery, though part of the motivation to do so may be a frank discussion of the slavery that addiction imposes (Lee, 1994).

Persons with mental illness or other mental or physical challenges benefit from empowerment work. Clinical awareness of the nature of mental illness helps workers do more effective work with this group.

The vocabulary of empowerment work includes a few new words that we have defined in this chapter. These include consciousness raising, praxis, dialogue, and codes. The usual vocabulary of the clinically and politically astute practitioner has been used and explained as well throughout this chapter. As in all empowerment, as we use different words to describe our thoughts we begin to think differently. The tried-and-true approaches to personal/clinical work and to group, community, and political work and the newer strategies of empowerment are grafted in an approach that is therefore both old and new. Hence, the practitioner is empowered with a new yet not unfamiliar level of knowledge to share in working with oppressed groups.

We will conclude this chapter with case vignettes exemplifying empowerment practice and the discussion of its status in the professional lexicon of approaches.

CASE VIGNETTES

To illustrate the empowerment approach in action, I will present excerpts of empowerment group work, political activities, and individual and family-oriented empowerment practice at My Sisters' Place (MSP), a four-tiered program for homeless and formerly homeless women and children in Hartford, Connecticut. Most homeless women with children are young women of color, aged eighteen to the early thirties (Johnson & Lee, 1994). Asking why this is so is an important critical question. Clearly the answer speaks to multiple oppression of race, gender, class, age, and difference. My work with homeless women in New York City (Lee, 1986, 1990, 1994) and in Hartford grounded the empowerment approach in practice reality (Lee, 1991). All of these women, especially Judith Beaumont (1987)—executive director, activist, and my partner in life and in empowerment group work—and the staff of My Sisters' Place "co-authored" the empowerment approach.

THE SUCCESSFUL WOMEN'S GROUP

FORMATION

Membership in an empowerment group is a matter of personal choice based on knowledge of the experience. A "try it and see" philosophy helps members who share common ground understand what it is like to be in such a group. In forming an empowerment group for women who had "graduated" from the services of MSP, the co-workers began by inviting large groups of "alumnae" to six evening get-togethers. This approximated Freire's culture circle. The codes and themes for the empowerment work would emerge from these six meetings, as would a nucleus of women interested in pursuing empowerment together. The format of the evening, which took place in the homey atmosphere of the shelter, included a dinner where introductions and an informal style of sharing mutual concerns could take place and a formal period of group discussion when empowerment notions were introduced. National and local protest activities regarding affordable housing that many attended coincided with these meetings. Seven African-American women, ages twenty-two to thirty-four, decided to become the Alumnae Empowerment Group.

The co-workers started off as central to the process of helping the group develop a structure and maintain a focus on issues of empowerment, but they soon took on a more advisory role. Within four months, the group developed a club-style structure with a president who called the meetings and maintained the work focus. The group chose the meeting nights, time, frequency (biweekly), outreach to new members, and the content of the meetings. The workers bolstered the leadership structure and continued to contribute information and to assist in guiding praxis and reflecting on feelings and facts to deepen the work. The group existed for two years, though members continue to be there for each other. This is an excerpt from a meeting nine months into the life of the group in which they name themselves.

> Tracey, the President, said, "Alumnae" just don't get it. Who are we? asked Vesalie. We are successful women, said Tracey. Yeah, said Latoya, "The Successful Women's Group." No, said Vesalie, we can't call ourselves that. Why? Shandra asked. Vesalie strongly replied, it implies too much power, that we are powerful. The worker asked if they felt powerful. Vesalie said, yes we are more powerful now—we've got good jobs, we're good mothers, we help others who are homeless, we are meeting our goals, but we haven't gotten there yet. The worker asked, when you get there, then you have the power? Tracey replied, but that's just it, we need that power to get there, and we're on our way. Let's convey that we are powerful women, we are successful women. Let's take that name and make it ours. We deserve to walk with that name! The others strongly agreed. Vesalie thoughtfully accepted this and the name Successful Women was enthusiastically adopted.

Names mean a great deal. The worker's questions here were consciousness-raising questions. This renaming after nine months of meeting represented a 180-degree turnaround in self-esteem, group pride, and conscientization. The use of codes helped the group achieve this new image.

CODIFICATION

In the Successful Women's Group, two themes were codified. These were "barriers to success" and "African-American womanhood." Addressing the first theme, the worker asked the group members to define success. It was defined as personal achievement and "people-centered" accomplishments (giving back to the community). The "wall of barriers" was the code.

The members were asked to imagine and dramatically act out climbing and pulling bricks down from a wall, which represented barriers. The worker asked, What are the barriers to young African-American women getting over the wall to success for themselves and their people? Amika was first to try to dramatize it. She said: The wall is over there, I'm going toward it. Oops, she said as she slipped and fell with a great thud, they greased the ground, I can't even get to the wall. Forget it! Everyone roared as Amika, a large, heavily built woman, dramatized falling down in disarray. Tracey said, It isn't really funny. Amika is right, some of us can't even get to the wall. The grease is prejudice and racism. And sexism, Ves added, don't forget that. Shandra said, Yeah, but determination makes you try and you reach the wall. Like you finish high school and you think you're somewhere, but you didn't take the right courses or go to college so you got to start all over again. Tracey said, I was angry too when I found out my diploma meant so little.

Shandra got up and started using a hammer and a chisel, saying, And this one you got to strike at, it's prejudice on the job. You get the job, but they treat you like you're stupid just because you're Black. She told of how she was treated by a nurse she worked with. She unwedged the brick and threw it down hard. Everyone applauded. Ves said, OK, watch out! I'm driving this bulldozer right into the wall. Later for brick-by-brick or climbing, the whole thing is coming down. Slam, crash. Everyone cheered her on. Wait, said Latoya, a brick hit me, I'm hurt. She wiped imagined blood from her head. It's the brick of hating myself because I believed if you're black stand back, and I stood back and didn't go for even what you all went for, a real job and all. But I survived and stand here to tell it, I'm going to get me some too! Everyone encouraged her.

The use of humor by African Americans and other oppressed groups is an adaptive mechanism. But no one should mistake the seriousness of the meanings in this dramatic enactment, which was at once therapeutic and political, leading to a variety of actions.

Their next codification on African-American womanhood was the reading together of Ntozake Shange's choreopoem, *For Colored Girls Who Have Considered Suicide When the Rainbow Is Enuf* (1977). After several readings of selected poems and their discussion, Tracey, who had committed some to memory, concluded:

These are our lives. It could have gone either way for us, we too could have died, or chosen paths that lead to death of our spirits and our bodies. But we didn't because we found other women who was feeling what we were feeling and living what we was living. I will always see myself in Shandra. I will always be there for her. We found true shelter and we found each other, and we found God in ourselves, like the poem says. Yes, said Ves, and we found the truth about our struggles too. And we are free, no turning back.

SHANDRA LOYAL

Shandra, a member of the Successful Women's group, is a twenty-five-year-old African-American woman whose story of empowerment was initially told in detail in *The Empowerment Approach to Social Work Practice* (Lee, 1994). Here I will briefly present and update the assessment and summarize the individual work that took place at the time of that writing and the additional growth toward empowerment that Shandra accomplished more recently.

Shandra is a pretty, dark-skinned, intelligent, somewhat overweight young woman who began her empowerment work at MSP five years ago, when she entered the shelter during her seventh month of pregnancy. Although she had worked full time since graduating from vocational high school, she was sleeping on the floor at her grandmother's home. Her mother was struggling with depression and her own recovery from drugs. Shandra wisely chose not to live with the baby's father and his family, as he was drug dealing and physically abusive to her, although she did not disclose this at the time. By the time her daughter was a month old, Shandra had moved into subsidized housing, established her household, and returned to work.

Several months later she became a founding member of the Successful Women's Group. Some of her work in the group is shown in the two excerpts above. She developed a close bond with another group member and with the group's co-workers. Group members did work on physically abusive relationships, but in retrospect, I think we needed to work harder at drawing her into this work. We were aware of her depression and generally low self-esteem, but assumed that we knew her whole story. The more vocal members also drew our attention.

While she tended to be a quiet yet thoughtful participant, Shandra did work on speaking up more in all aspects of her life. An ongoing area of growth for her was balancing the culturally appropriate but sometimes excessive demands of an African-American daughter, sister, grandchild, partner, mother, and person with her own needs. It is remarkable that Shandra remained drug- and alcohol-free, thereby also assuming a highly responsible role in her family. She had also learned well to keep discussion of serious trouble within the family. Going to counseling was not acceptable in her family, and her life as a working mother and caretaker was all consuming. At twenty-two, her strengths were many, but so were her burdens.

About a year later, she contacted me from the inpatient unit of the local psychiatric facility, where she had been admitted for uncontrollable crying on the job and suicidal ideation. It was then that she shared the history of Thomas's violent abuse, for which he had been incarcerated at length on two occasions, also in conjunction with drug charges. During those periods, she said, she "forgot what she was like." But this first and very frightening psychiatric hospitalization was on the eve of Thomas's release from prison. There were several other stressors: an increase in her migraine headaches; the difficulties of managing two-year-old, Tomika; an overload of family responsibilities; a cut in her job hours so she could barely make ends meet; and racial tension in the job setting. Shandra was discharged from this facility in one week, with only monthly medication monitoring as the service plan.

It was not clear if this was a major depressive episode, or an acute situational depression precipitated by extremely high stress levels, topped off by the imminence of Thomas's return. Given her mother's history of depression, only time would tell. But it was extremely important to lower the stress levels dramatically, ensure proper medical follow-up, work with her on the safety factors related to Thomas's return, and teach problem-solving skills. As this was accomplished with a social worker from MSP, and consciousness-raising activities were continued. The manifestations of oppression in Shandra's life were obvious: battering by Thomas, racial and gender prejudice on the job, economic cutbacks and hardship, and second-rate service offered by the health system. Oppression as well as depression were defined as the problem foci and part of the agreed-upon contract. As social workers, we had to tolerate, however, that once safety plans were in place (EWAR, 1992), the relationship with Thomas would have to proceed according to Shandra's timetable, not ours.

The worker here was Gail Bourdon, program director of MSP III, a program serving women with serious mental health problems. The work took several months to accomplish, as Thomas initially had Shandra convinced that he had "reformed" in jail. It became clear that she was attached to him and that repression of abuse was a lifelong pattern. When Thomas refused to see a counselor and began to engage in violent behavior in the community, Shandra finally became frightened and took her key away from him.

The worker supported Shandra's action and willingness to involve the police. Then the worker suggested that she and Shandra look together at the Power and Control Wheel, a pie-shaped chart that shows eight levels and types of physical and sexual violence (Pence, 1987). Shandra did this with much interest, revealing that her stepfather had used many of the same tactics with her mother and herself. Shandra wrote her own response to each of the eight categories, and later her responses formed the substance of the work.

Under Using Coercion she wrote, "He threatened to kill me and pushed me around when I was pregnant. I felt safer when he was in jail." Under Using Intimidation she wrote, "Makes me afraid by mean looks and threatens to trash my apartment to get me evicted—like punching holes in the walls. And his friends also fear him." Under Emotional Abuse she wrote, "He says I'm a big baby . . . He says I'm fat and humiliates me in front of others." Under Using Isolation she added, "He uses jealousy to justify anything he does to keep me away from others." Under Economic Abuse she noted, "I pay all the bills, he has a free ride," and under Using the Children she wrote, "He uses Tomika to get to see me."

The worker records:

After the work on the chart, I picked up on the part where she said she felt safer when Thomas was in jail. (Focusing on her safety.) She described how on one occasion Thomas tried to shoot two people but missed them and hit two other people instead, one in the head and one in the neck. I noted how serious an incident that was and that he could have murdered people. (Affirming her perceptions, putting it into words.) She described how he pushed her several times when she was four months pregnant and threatened to kill her . . . He's like that again but she hasn't let herself see it until now. I affirmed her ability to see it now. (Strengthening her reality testing, encouraging the lowering of her defenses.) She said it makes her angry that he checks up on her and tells her who she can talk to, what to do and how to do it. She said his friends fear his anger and she is afraid that she will experience much worse than what she has. I seriously agreed, adding she is such a good person and I would not want to see anything like that happen to her or Tomika. (Conveying empathy and reinforcing her judgment.) She paused and agreed, stating that is why she needs to make a change now . . . I said Thomas presents a threat of physical danger and that he possesses physical power which she does not have. She agreed. I added that using the police is a way of changing that power balance. I said she should not have to live with that fear in her own home. (Empathizing and naming her feelings.) She agreed, noting he is not even on the lease.

When Shandra was ready, the worker was able to use this code to skillfully help her own up, describe in her own words, and reflect on her oppression, her safety, and her actions. In time, Shandra was able to end the relationship with Thomas, move to another town, complete a cosmetology course, work out of her home, and enter college. With the help of a new MSP worker, she also obtained state-of-the-art medical care for migraines and connected with support systems in her new town, including a group for women of color where she continues empowerment work. Although she also mourned the death of her beloved grandmother during this time, she had no recurrence of depression, nor has she needed antidepression medication. When her mother faced a crisis related to the grandmother's death, Shandra was helpful in connecting her to MSP's services, where she too is pursuing her empowerment.

BRENDA: THE PERSONAL/POLITICAL EMPOWERMENT OF A WOMAN WITH MENTAL ILLNESS

Brenda Gray, a thirty-nine-year-old African-American woman with multiple physical problems and chronic paranoid schizophrenia, experienced periods of intermittent homelessness for five years. Leaving her children with relatives, she moved cyclically from the streets to the hospital to several shelters. Then she entered MSP's residential support program, which set her up in her own apartment and offered daily support and empowerment services. For the first time since the onset of her illness, Brenda experienced inner peace. Brenda's appearance is marred by skin eruptions but she radiates a quiet joy. She is not spontaneous, but when she is called on, her good intellect is revealed. Recently Brenda volunteered to testify at public hearings on proposed state cutbacks of mental health programs. This is an excerpt:

> We need our programs to keep us aware of life's possibilities. No matter what you want to be it's possible. These programs kept me on track and looking forward to life. If the state cuts those programs, the state also cuts the good that they do . . . we have a women's group every week. We talk about what goes on in our lives—the problems we experience and solutions to them by getting feedback from each other.

To get Brenda and her peers to this point, the worker, Gail Bourdon, prepared the empowerment group to understand the issues and the process of testifying before asking for their participation. First, she shared specific details of the proposed cuts and elicited the group members' reactions. She proposed that they might want to learn how to testify at the hearings and speak up for themselves. Then, when interest was high, she took two volunteers (Brenda and Vicky) and the staff to a workshop on the legislative process. Two weeks later, during an empowerment meeting, a summary of the legislative process was given to the group by the worker and the members who went to the workshop. Brenda volunteered to speak and composed her testimony that night.

> Early the next evening we went to testify. Brenda patiently waited two hours in line and an additional 2½ hours before testifying. The testimony was presented in the Hall of the House of Representatives. Brenda and I presented our testimony. It was a striking image to see Brenda, in her woolen hat, speaking so well from the seat of the minority leader. One senator thanked Brenda for her testimony. Brenda was clearly the group leader that night.

The group then reflected on their actions in the next meeting. The worker invited praxis, the members' reflections on the process of testifying and going to the legislative hearing.

> Group members read the entire *Hartford Courant* article to each other. I asked what the women thought and felt about attending the hearings. Brenda smiled and proudly stated she felt good about having spoken. I asked Vicky how she felt about attending the hearing. Vicky said, I was happy. It was one of the happiest times in my life. I saw and heard things I never thought I'd even learn about. The entire group cheered . . . I asked Brenda if she thought her message was heard. Brenda said she thought so because they did not ask her unfriendly questions. They accepted her

word and even thanked her. I asked the group members who went how it was for them and each replied affirmatively. Vicky added, I feel that I could do that sometime . . . I feel the strength. The entire group agreed, noting that they had a voice and were heard. Ida said that those who simply sat there also brought support and power in numbers, so they had a presence as well as a voice . . . Brenda added, it's good to know what I can accomplish things even with a mental illness. Sometimes people think you can't do things because you have a mental illness. I live with the illness, but this does not mean I am not able to take care of business. The other members thoughtfully agreed.

The careful preparation paid off in the group members' confident action. The skills of guiding praxis helped the members own their gains and expand their understanding and political skill as well as their self-esteem and self-direction.

In all of these examples, one can see that personal and political empowerment are part of the same process and outcome.

STATUS IN THE PROFESSION

Empowerment practice is gaining in momentum as the oppression of many groups, especially those who are poor, escalates in a reactionary political climate. As noted, many contemporary thinkers are researching and conceptualizing empowerment-oriented practice. Hence, there is a growing empirical base to anchor empowerment in the professional lexicon of social work approaches. Yet, it is difficult to study and measure a concept that is transactionally based and both clinical and political. Perhaps in some ways such measurement is a moot point, for the power that people develop on the personal, interpersonal, and political levels ultimately makes up a whole that may defy quantification and oversimplification. At best, the separate aspects of the approach will be empirically documented. The empowerment approach is grounded in practice and conceptualized from qualitative data which, I believe, is a prerequisite to quantification of such complex ideas (Lee, 1991, 1994). Further grounding in such qualitative data would be helpful.

The empowerment approach provides a conceptual framework for empowerment-oriented social work practice. It brings social work into the dialogue between sociology, political science, and religion. It is relevant in education, ministry, community work, and a range of helping professions. It is both old and new, both clinical and political. It is also a paradigm for international social work practice, as it offers social workers a way to challenge oppression with people throughout the world.

REFERENCES

Addams, Jane (1910). *Twenty Years at Hull House.* New York: Macmillan, 1961.

Addams, Jane (1922). *Peace and Bread In Time of War.* New York: Macmillan.

Addams, Jane C. (1930). *The Second Twenty Years at Hull House.* New York: Macmillan.

Bartlett, Harriet M. (1958). "Toward Clarification and Improvement of Social Work Practice." *Social Work* 3 (April):5–9.

Beaumont, Judith A. (1987). "Prison Witness: Exposing the Injustice." In Arthur J. Laffin and Anne Montgomery (eds.), *Swords Into Plowshares: Nonviolent Direct Action for Disarmament.* New York: Harper & Row, 80–85.

Beck, Bertram M. (1983). "Empowerment: A Future Goal for Social Work." Paper presented at the National Association of Social Workers Annual Conference.

Berlin, Sharon (1983). "Cognitive Behavioral Approaches." In Allan Rosenblatt and Diana Waldfogel (eds.), *The Handbook of Clinical Social Work.* San Francisco: Jossey-Bass, 1095–1119.

Berman-Rossi, Toby, & Miller, Irving (1992). "Racism and The Settlement Movement." Paper presented at the 14th Annual Symposium for the Advancement of Social Work with Groups, Atlanta, Georgia.

Berman-Rossi, Toby, ed. 1994. *Social Work: The Collected Writings of William Schwartz.* Ithasca, IFE Peace Publishers.

Brager, George, & Specht, Harry (1973). *Community Organizing.* New York: Columbia University Press.

Brazleton, T. Berry (1990). "Is America Failing Its Children?" *New York Times Magazine* (September 9): 40–43, 50–51, 90.

Breton, Margot (1989). "The Need for Mutual Aid Groups in a Drop-in For Homeless Women: The Sistering Case." In Judith A.B. Lee (ed.), *Group Work with the Poor and Oppressed.* New York: Haworth Press, 47–59.

Breton, Margot (1991). "Toward a Model of Work Groupwork Practice with Marginalized Populations." *Groupwork* 4(1): 31–47.

Breton, Margot (1992). "Liberation Theology, Group Work, and the Right of the Poor and Oppressed to Participate in the Life of the Community." In James A. Garland (ed.), *Group Work Reaching Out: People Places, and Power.* New York: Haworth Press, 257–270.

Bricker-Jenkins, Mary, & Hooyman, Nancy (1986). *Not for Women Only: Social Work Practice For a Feminist Future.* Silver Spring, MD: NASW.

Bricker-Jenkins, Mary, Hooyman, Nancy, & Gottlieb, Naomi (eds.). (1991). *Feminist Social Work Practice in Clinical Settings.* Newbury Park, CA: Sage.

Chau, Kenneth (ed.) (1900). *Ethnicity and Biculturalism: Emerging Perspective of Social Group Work.* New York: Haworth Press.

Chestang, Leon (1976). "Environmental Influences on Social Functioning: The Black Experience." In P. San Juan Cafferty and Leon Chestang (eds.), *The Diverse Society: Implications for Social Policy.* Washington, DC: NASW, 59–74.

Cox, Enid O. (1989). "Empowerment of the Low Income Elderly Through Group Work." In Judith A.B. Lee (ed.), *Group Work With the Poor and Oppressed.* New York: Haworth Press, 111–125.

Coyle, Grace L. (1930). *Social Process in Organized Groups.* Hebron, CT: Practitioner's Press, 1979.

Davis, Larry E. (1984). *Ethnicity in Social Group Work Practice.* New York: Haworth Press.

De Crescenzo, Theresa (1979). "Group Work with Gay Adolescents." *Social Work with Groups* 2(1): 35–44.

Devore, Wynetta, & Schlesinger, Elfriede (1991). *Ethnic Sensitive Social Work Practice* (3rd ed.). Columbus, OH: Merrill.

Estes, Richard (1991). "Social Development and Social Work With Groups." Plenary speech presented at the Thirteenth Annual Symposium of AASWG, Akron, Ohio. *Proceeding.* New York: Haworth Press, 1995.

Evans, Estella N. (1992). "Liberation Theology, Empowerment Theory and Social Work Practice with the Oppressed." *International Social Work,* 35: 3–15.

EWAR Project (1992). "A Handbook for Empowering Women in Abusive and Controlling Relationships: Facilitating Critical Thinking in Groups." Arcata, CA: Humboldt University.

Freeman, Edith M. (1990). "The Black Family's Life Cycle: Operationalizing a Strengths Perspective." In Sadye Logan, Edith Freeman, and Ruth McRoy (eds.), *Social Work Practice with Black Families.* New York: Longman Publishing, 55–72.

Freire, Paulo (1973). *Pedagogy of the Oppressed.* New York: Seabury.

Freire, Paulo (1990). "A Critical Understanding of Social Work." *Journal of Progress Human Services.* 1(1): 3–9.

Freire, Paulo (1994). *Pedagogy of Hope: Reliving Pedagogy of the Oppressed.* New York: Continuum Publishing.

Galper, Jeffry H. (1980). *Social Work Practice: A Radical Perspective.* Englewood Cliffs, NJ: Prentice-Hall.

Garvin, Charles (1987). *Contemporary Group Work* (2nd ed.). Englewood Cliffs, NJ: Prentice-Hall.

Gary, Robenia B., & Gary, Lawrence E. (1975). "Profile of Black Female Social Welfare Leaders During the 1920s." National Institute of Mental Health. Grant #MH-25551-02, 9–13.

Germain, Carel B. (1979). *Social Work Practice: People and Environments.* New York: Columbia University Press, 1–22.

Germain, Carel B. (1984). *Social Work Practice in Health Care.* New York: Free Press.

Germain, Carel B. (1987). "Ecological Perspective." In *The Encyclopedia of Social Work* (18th ed.). Silver Spring, MD: NASW, 488–499.

Germain, Carel B. (1990). "Life Forces and the Anatomy of Practice." Smith College Studies in Social Work 60 (March 2).

Germain, Carel B. (1991). *Human Behavior in the Social Environment: An Ecological View.* New York: Columbia University Press.

Germain, Carel B., and Gitterman, Alex (1980). *The Life Model of Social Work Practice.* New York: Columbia University Press.

Germain, Carel B., and Gitterman, Alex (1996). *The Life Model of Social Work Practice: Advanced Theory and Practice.* New York: Columbia University Press.

Goldstein, Eda (1994). *Ego Psychology and Social Work Practice* (2nd ed.). New York: Free Press.

Gutiérrez, Lorraine M. (1989). "Empowerment in Social Work Practice: Considerations for Practice and Education." Paper presented at the annual meeting of the Council on Social Work Education, Chicago, IL.

Gutiérrez, Lorraine (1990). "Working with Women of Color: An Empowerment Perspective." *Social Work* 35:149–155.

Gutiérrez, Lorraine, & Ortega, Robert (1989). "Using Group Work to Empower Latinos: A Preliminary Analysis." Proceedings of the Eleventh Annual Symposium of the Association for the Advancement of Social Work with Groups.

Harris, Forrest E., Sr. (1993). *Ministry for Social Crisis: Theology and Praxis in the Black Church Tradition.* Macon, GA: Mercer University Press.

Hartman, Ann, and Laird, Joan (1983). *Family Centered Social Work Practice.* New York: Free Press.

Hidalgo, Hilda, Peterson, Travis L., & Woodman, Natalie Jane (eds.). (1985). *Lesbian and Gay Issues: A Resource Manual For Social Workers.* Silver Spring, MD: National Association of Social Workers.

hooks, bell (1990). *Yearning: Race, Gender and Cultural Politics.* Boston, MA: South End Press.

Hopps, June G. (1982). "Oppression Based on Color." *Social Casework* (Jan.) 27:3–6.

Hopps, June G. (1987). "Minorities of Color." In *The Encyclopedia of Social Work* (18th ed). Silver Spring, MD: National Association of Social Workers, 161–170.

Johnson, Alice K., & Lee, Judith A.B. (1994). "Empowerment Work with Homeless Women." In Marsha M. Pravder (ed.), *Women In Context: Toward A Feminist Reconstruction of Psychotherapy.* New York: Guilford Press.

Katz, Michael B. (1986). *In the Shadow of the Poorhouse: A Social History of Welfare in America.* New York: Basic Books.

Katz, Michael B. (1989). *The Undeserving Poor: From the War on Poverty to the War on Welfare.* New York: Pantheon.

Konopka, Gisela (1988). *Courage and Love.* Edina, MN: Burgess Printing Co.

Konopka, Gisela (1991). "All Lives Are Connected to Other Lives: The Meaning of Social Group Work." In Marie Weil, Kenneth Chau, and Dannia Southerland (eds.), *Theory and Practice in Social Group Work: Creative Connections.* New York: Haworth Press, 29–38.

Lang, Norma (1986). "Social Work Practice in Small Social Forms: Identifying Collectivity." In Norma Lang and Joanne Sulman (eds.), *Collectivity in Social Group Work: Concept and Practice.* New York: Haworth Press.

Lee, Judith A.B. (1986). "No Place To Go: Homeless Women." In Alex Gitterman and Lawrence Shulman (eds.), *Mutual Aid Groups and the Life Cycle.* Itasca, IL: F.E. Peacock, 245–262.

Lee, Judith A.B. (ed.). (1989). *Group Work with the Poor and Oppressed.* New York: Haworth Press.

Lee, Judith A.B. (1990). "When I Was Well, I Was a Sister: Social Work with Homeless Women." *The Jewish Social Work Forum* 26, Spring 1990: 22–30.

Lee, Judith A.B. (1991). "Empowerment Through Mutual Aid Groups: A Practice Grounded Conceptual Framework." *Groupwork* 4(1):5–21.

Lee, Judith A.B. (1992). "Teaching Content Related to Lesbian and Gay Identity Formation." In Natalie J. Woodman (ed.), *Lesbian and Gay Lifestyles: A Guide for Counseling and Education.* New York: Irvington Press.

Lee, Judith A.B. (1994). *The Empowerment Approach to Social Work Practice.* New York: Columbia University Press.

Lewis, Elizabeth (1983). "Social Group Work in Community Life: Group Characteristics and Worker Role." *Social Work With Groups* 6(2) Summer: 3–18.

Lewis, Elizabeth (1991). "Social Change and Citizen Action: A Philosophical Explanation for Modern Social Group Work." In Abe Vinik and Morris Levin (eds.), *Social Action in Group Work.* New York: Haworth Press, 23–34.

Logan, Sadye M.L., Freeman, Edith M., & McRoy, G. Ruth (1990). *Social Work Practice with Black Families: A Culturally Specific Perspective.* New York: Longman Publishing.

Lum, Doman (1986). *Social Work Practice and People of Color.* Monterey, CA: Brooks/Cole.

Mack, John E., & Hickler, Holly (1981). *Vivienne.* Boston: Mentor.

Mancoske, Ronald J., & Hunzeker, Jeanne M. (1989) *Empowerment Based Generalist Practice: Direct Services With Individuals.* New York: Cummings and Hathaway.

Mann, Bonnie (1987). "Working with Battered Women: Radical Education or Therapy." In Ellen Pence, *In Our Best Interest—A Process for Personal and Social Change.* Duluth, MN: Program Development, Inc.

Martin, Ruth. R (1995). Oral History In Social Work: Research, Assessment and Intervention. Thousand Oaks, CA: Sage.

Mechanic, David (1974). "Social Structure and Personal Adaptation." In George V. Coelho, David A. Hamburg, and John E. Adams (eds.) *Coping and Adaptation.* New York: Basic Books, 32–46.

Middleman, Ruth R., & Goldberg, Gale (1974). *Social Service Delivery: A Structural Approach to Social Work Practice.* New York: Columbia University Press.

Morales, Armando (1977). "Beyond Traditional Conceptual Frameworks." *Social Work: A Profession of Many Faces* (3rd ed.). Boston: Allyn & Bacon.

Mullender, Audrey, & Ward, Dave (1991). *Self-Directed Groupwork: Users Take Action for Empowerment.* London: Whiting and Birch.

New York Times (1992). "Poverty In America." Sept. 4, 1992: A1, 14.

Northen, Helen (1994). *Clinical Social Work* (2nd ed.). New York: Columbia University Press.

Ozawa, Martha N. (1989). "Nonwhite and the Demographic Imperative in Social Welfare Spending." In Ira C. Colby (ed.), *Social Welfare Policy.* Chicago: Dorsey Press, 437–454.

Papell, Catherine P., & Rothman, Beulah (1980). "Relating the Mainstream Mode of Social Work With Groups to Group Psychotherapy and the Structural Group Approach." *Social Work With Groups* (Summer) 3:5–22.

Parsons, Ruth J. (1989). "Empowerment for Role Alternatives for Low-Income Minority Girls: A Group Work Approach." In Judith A.B. Lee (ed.), *Group Work with the Poor and Oppressed.* New York: Haworth Press, 27–46.

Parsons, Ruth J. (1991). "Empowerment: Purpose and Practice Principles in Social Work." *Social Work With Groups* 14(2):7–21.

Parsons, Ruth J., Jorgensen, James D., & Hernandez, Santos H. (1994). *The Integration of Social Work Practice.* Pacific Grove, CA: Brooks/Cole Publishing.

Pence, Ellen (1987). *In Our Best Interests: A Process for Personal and Social Change.* Duluth, MN: Minnesota Program Development, Inc.

Pernell, Ruby B. (1986). "Empowerment and Social Group Work." In Marvin Parnes (ed.), *Innovations in Social Group Work.* New York: Haworth Press, 107–118.

Pottick, Kathleen (1989). "Jane Addams Revisited: Practice Theory and Social Economics." In Judith A.B. Lee (ed.), *Group Work With the Poor and Oppressed.* New York: Haworth Press, 11–26.

Reed, Beth G., & Garvin, Charles D. (eds.). (1983). *Groupwork with Women/Groupwork with Men: An Overview of Gender Issues in Social Groupwork Practice. Social Work with Groups,* Special Issue, 6 (3/4).

Reynolds, Bertha C. (1934). *Between Client and Community: A Study in Responsibility in Social Casework.* New York: Oriole Editions, 1973.

Reynolds, Bertha C. (1951). *Social Work and Social Living Explorations in Philosophy and Practice.* Silver Spring, MD: First National Association of Social Workers Classic Edition, 1975.

Reynolds, Betha C. (1964). *An Uncharted Journey: Fifty Years of Growth in Social Work.* Hebron, CT: Practitioner's Press.

Richan, Willard C. (1991). *Lobbying for Social Change.* New York: Haworth Press.

Ryan, William (1971). *Blaming the Victims.* New York: Vintage.

Saleebey, Dennis (1992). *The Strengths Perspective in Social Work Practice.* New York: Longman Publishing.

Schwartz, William (1974a). "The Social Worker in the Group." In Robert W. Klenk and Robert W. Ryan (eds.), *The Practice of Social Work* (2nd ed.). Belmont, CA: Wadsworth Publishing, 208–228.

Schwartz, William (1974b). "Private Troubles and Public Issues: One Social Work Job or Two?" In Robert W. Klenk and Robert W. Ryan (eds.), *The Practice of Social Work* (2nd ed.). Belmont, CA: Wadsworth Publishing, 62–81.

Shange, Ntozake (1977). *For Colored Girls Who Have considered suicide When the Rainbow is Enuf.* New York: Macmillan.

Shapiro, Ben-Zion (1991). "Social Action, the Group and Society." *Social Work With Groups* 14(3/4): 7–22.

Shulman, Lawrence (1992). *The Skills of Helping Individuals, Families and Groups* (3rd ed.). Itasca, IL: F.E. Peacock.

Simon, Barbara Levy (1990). "Rethinking Empowerment." *Journal of Progressive Human Services* 1(1):29

Simon, Barbara (1994). *The Empowerment Tradition in American Social Work.* New York: Columbia University Press.

Solomon, Barbara B. (1976). *Black Empowerment: Social Work in Oppressed Communities.* New York: Columbia University Press.

Staples, Lee (1984). *Roots to Power.* New York: Praeger.

Staub-Bernasconi, Silvia (1991). "Social Action, Empowerment, and Social Work: An Integrating Theoretical Framework." *Social Work with Groups* 14(3/4):35–52.

Swenson, Carol (1992). "Clinical Practice and the Decline of Community." Paper Presented at the Council on Social Work Education Conference, March 1992, Kansas City, Missouri.

Thomas, Ianthe (1978). "Death of a Young Poet." *Village Voice* (March 20): 2, 26–27.

Van Den Bergh, Nan, & Cooper, Lynne B. (eds.). (1986). *Feminist Visions For Social Work.* Silver Spring, MD: National Association of Social Workers.

Weiner, Hyman J. (1964). "Social Change and Group Work Practice." *Social Work,* 9(3): 106–112.

White, Robert (1974). "Strategies of Adaptation: An Attempt at Systematic Description." In George Coelho, David A. Hamburg, and John E. Adams. (eds.), *Coping and Adaptation.* New York: Basic Books, 47–68.

Wood, Gale, and Middleman, Ruth R. (1989). *The Structural Approach to Direct Practice in Social Work.* New York: Columbia University Press.

Woodman, Natalie J. (ed.). (1992). *Lesbian and Gay Lifestyles: A Guide for Counseling and Education.* New York: Irvington Press.

CHAPTER 11

EXISTENTIAL SOCIAL WORK

DONALD F. KRILL

The impact of existential philosophy upon the social work profession remains unclear. While the first article on the subject appeared in social work literature in 1962, and three books by social workers delineated existential perspectives in 1969, 1970, and 1978, the topic of existentialism has seldom been raised at the National Conference of Social Workers.

Those social workers familiar with the existential viewpoint emphasize that this perspective speaks to the profession's most pressing needs: for more effective treatment of the poor and minorities; for the present-focused, experiential, task-oriented work with families and individuals; for a more flexible and eclectic use of varied treatment techniques; for a lessening of categorization of people and of paternalistic efforts by therapists to adjust the values of clients to those of their families or those of the established society. The existential perspective is even seen as providing an important humanizing effect on social workers' present experimentation with social change.

The reasons for the failure of the existentialists to attract major attention among social work professionals may be twofold. In the first place, writings of this type by philosophers, psychologists, theologians, and social workers tend to employ a terminology that seems foreign to the average practitioner (Being, Nothingness, the Absurd, Dread, I-Thou, Bad Faith, etc.). Social workers have intended to be doers rather than theoreticians, and even the theorists tend to be pragmatic rather than philosophical. Second, existential social work writers have tended to propose a more philosophical perspective rather than specific working techniques. This is primarily because there does not really seem to be an existential psychotherapy per se. To be more accurate, one might say there is an existential philosophical viewpoint on how one sees oneself, one's client system, and what can happen between them. Various theoretical approaches may then be used to provide techniques compatible with this philosophical perspective.

THE EXISTENTIAL STANCE

Modern existentialism was born in the ruins, chaos, and atmosphere of disillusionment of Europe during and following World War II. Earlier existential writers, such as Kierkegaard and Dostoevsky, had reacted against what they believed to be false hopes for the salvation of men and the world through the contemporary philosophy and politics of rationalism. In the United States, with its boundless faith in achieving the good life through economic productivity and scientific advancement, interest in existentialism was slower in coming.

The disillusioning events of the sixties (assassinations, the generation gap, protest movements, the Vietnam War) continued into the early seventies (Watergate, economic instability, mounting divorce and crime rates, the failure of psychotherapy). These troubling occurrences opened the minds of many Americans to the existential themes that had previously only interested Beatniks, artists, and a smattering of intellectuals.

Existentialism has been termed a "philosophy of despair," partly because it seems to emerge from disillusionment. But we may view this emergence as the origin of existentialism and a turning away from a primary allegiance to those idols and values that have fallen. Where it goes beyond this point depends upon which particular writer, theologian, philosopher, or film director one chooses to follow.

In most of the philosophical literature on existentialism, four themes seem to recur: the stress upon individual freedom and the related fundamental value of the uniqueness of the person; the recognition of suffering as a necessary part of the ongoing process of life—for human growth and the realization of meaning; the emphasis upon involvement in the immediate moment as the most genuine way of discovering one's identity and what life is about (not in any finalized sense but, rather, in an ongoing, open way); and the sense of commitment that seeks to maintain a life of both discipline and spontaneity, contemplation and action, egolessness and an emerging care for others. In all of these there is an obvious emphasis upon turning inward in contrast to the "organizational" or "outer-directed" person of the 1950s.

The existentialists disagree with those who hold human beings to be either essentially impulse-driven animals or social animals of learned conditioning. Both of these ideas deny what is, for the existentialists, the individual's source of dignity: the absolute value of individual uniqueness. A person discovers her uniqueness in the way she relates to her own objective experience of life. Jean-Paul Sartre points out that this subjectivity is a person's freedom; it is something that is there; it cannot be escaped from or avoided; one can only deny one's own responsibility for choices made within this freedom. From the existential point of view, psychoanalytic theory is sometimes misused by encouraging the individual's denial of responsibility on the basis of impulsiveness forces; similarly, sociological and learning theory may be misused by excusing a person on the basis of totally determining social forces.

Characters from fiction, drama, mythology, and philosophical tradition have portrayed the existential posture. Stoicism, courage, and individualism are common attributes. The existentialist hero is often characterized as living on the edge of the traditions, values, and enticements of his society, prizing the preservation of his own uniqueness and authenticity above all else. He is tough-minded in holding to his own code, evaluating it and preserving its integrity. He refuses to be "put down" by dehumanizing social forces through conformity or by selling himself out to their rewards.

He is against system efforts to suppress the individuality of others in his society. His values are concrete and inseparable from situations: certain arising social or political issues, loyalty to friends, unfolding creative potentials, honesty and sincerity in relationships. His interaction with life defines who he is rather than the acceptance of some definition of himself imposed by an outside authority, such as family, church, or economic system. The rhythm of responsive life-swinging-in-situation is his sole guide.

Existentialism is rejected by many as a narcissistic withdrawal from life when disappointments arise. At first glance, this might appear true as we hear the existentialist proclaim her own consciousness, subjectivity, uniqueness as the sole absolute: "truth is subjectivity," said Kierkegaard. The existentialist does reject the world, in one sense, in her new commitment to her own deepest self. What she rejects, however, is not life—its conditions, limits, joys, and possibilities—but the mistaken hopes and expectations she had held about life, which, under closer examination, failed to fit with the reality of her life.

SUBJECTIVITY

What is this subjectivity, this freedom, that holds the devotion and loyalty of a person? To Sartre, freedom is "nothingness." For Kierkegaard, it is the human encounter with the transcendent one's moment before God. Buber sees this as the "I" meeting the "Thou" of life. Kazantzakis speaks of the cry from deep within the human personality. To respond to it is our sole possibility of freedom.

Yet this subjectivity, while termed by some as an encounter with the transcendent, should not be mistaken for a direct expression of the divine. Each of us is all too soon aware of the finite nature of subjectivity. It is not all-knowing, and subjectivity is different in each person and constantly in the process of change within the same person. Subjectivity exists as a unique responsive relation to the world. Its primary activity is the conveyance of meaning through thought and feeling, intuition and sensation, and the assertion of this unique perspective through creative acts. Some would term this the activity of spirit, a divine possibility available to human beings. Yet divine and human remain intertwined.

It is this relationship between one's own subjectivity and the outside world that is the basis for responsible freedom instead of narcissistic caprice. One's inner objectivity encounters other realities again and again in the form of limits set up by life that challenge certain beliefs and meanings one has concluded about oneself. One experiences failures, misjudgments, hurt of others, neglect of self, conflict, and guilt. There is inevitable death, uncertainty, and suffering. These limiting situations, this suffering, becomes a revealing, guiding force of one's life. In a similar way, one realizes one's potentials. A person senses that the world wants and needs some response from her. She feels called upon to choose, to act, to give, and to imprint herself on the world. This awareness of both limits and potentials is the foundation upon which one can judge one's own unique perspective and readjust it when necessary. The ongoing encounter between subjectivity and the outside world may be looked upon as a continuing dialogue, dance, responsive process of inner and outer reality, continually affecting and being affected by the uniqueness of all forms involved.

We fail, finally, in our resurging hopes, the existentialist might say, but then we are a brotherhood in this—not only with others, but with all of nature. For there is a striving everywhere, a fight, and, in the end, only the remnants of our struggles—and a little later there are no longer even the remnants. Our loyalty is to the thrust behind this struggle in all things. What is this thrust? A mystery! A meaningful silence! Can we be sure it is meaningful? Who is to know? The questions of salvation or an afterlife must be held in abeyance. They can no longer be certainties. For many, these very uncertainties become the springboard to religious faith.

The mystical flavor of life is shared by existential believers and nonbelievers alike. It affirms life as meaningful, not because it has been clearly revealed as such through science or scripture, but rather because one has sensed a deeper or clearer experience of reality in certain moments. Such experiences as love, beauty, creative work, rhythm, awe, and psychic phenomena suggest seeing "through a glass darkly." Those followers of religious faiths may find a "rebirth," an adult reorientation to the message of revelation in religious writings. Yet the revelation of ultimate significance must be made personal.

THE BOND WITH OTHERS

If subjectivity and its uniqueness, development, and expression is valued in oneself, it must be valued in others as well. Since there is no absolute subjective perspective, each person's unique view and contribution contains an intrinsic value. The existentialist feels a bond with others and is responsive to their needs and to friendship, for she respects their subjectivity as being as valid as her own. She also knows that the assertion of courage is difficult and often impossible without occasional affirmation from others. Human love is the effort to understand, share, and participate in the uniqueness of others. It is validating in others that which one also values within oneself. Love is sometimes an act of helping, at other times a passive compassion. At times it reaches a total merging that takes one beyond the fundamental awareness of isolation.

The existentialists realize, too, the dangers in human relationships. Just as one guards against self-deceptions that tempt one toward a narcissistic idolization of oneself, so one remains on guard in relation to the institutions of society. The assertion of individual uniqueness is often a threat to others and to a smoothly functioning social group. This is because such assertion will frequently defy those rules, patterns, habits, and values that are sources of defined security for others, or a group. Thus, society and subgroups within a society will again and again attempt to suppress arising individual uniqueness out of a sense of threat or an inability to comprehend. Conformity is urged. It happens with family, friends, neighborhoods, church, professional, and political groups. The existentialist often finds himself estranged from others because of his own creativity and authenticity. Even when there is a relationship of mutual respect, with moments of unity through love, there will also come the moments of threat and misunderstanding because of the impossibility of one person's subjectivity fully comprehending that of another.

Yet conflict and threat in relationships do not move the existentialist into a schizoid withdrawal. She may display a touch of cynicism as she hears others identify themselves wholly with some group effort or as they proclaim the hope of humanity to be in her sensitive and loving interchange with her fellow man. But she knows that her own growth depends upon both affirmation from others and their occasional disagreement with her. The same interchanges are true for their growth. She believes in the beauty and warmth of love even though it is momentary. She knows that people must stand together in respecting and validating the uniqueness of one another and resisting those who believe themselves blessed with an absolute truth that justifies their using other people as things instead of as valued, unique personalities.

The philosophical position described stresses both faith and commitment to a perspective deemed valid as a result of one's direct and sensitive involvement in the life process. It is in opposition to establishing a life perspective by accepting some theoretical explanation of life as defined by some outside authority—whether parental, religious, scientific, or political.

The subjective involvement of the whole person is essential to the life perspective one finally concludes is reality. This perspective is also in opposition to those who use fragmented life experiences as the ground for a total life perspective (as is sometimes found in the superficial assessments of the meaning of a weekend sensitivity group experience). Human life is highly complex and one must seek an openness to its totality of experiences if the search is to be legitimate. This sort of array should not neglect an opening up of oneself to the meaning of experience as described by others as well.

What becomes apparent is a movement in personal awareness—from egotistical striving to self-understanding; then to I-thou relationships with one's immediate surroundings; and finally, in the incorporation of some overall principle where humanity and universe are joined. Both discipline and spontaneity are societal elements on this road of increasing awareness. Disillusionment, freedom, suffering, joy, and dialogue are all important happenings along the way. The end of this process does not really arrive until death. It is a continuing way that requires again and again the reaffirmation of that personal perspective called "truth." A transcendent view of existential freedom might be that of an illuminating light seeking understanding, compassion, and sometimes protective action in the surrounding world. This luminosity may also recognize that this very awareness is shared by all other humans whether they know and validate it or not.

PROFESSIONAL CONTRIBUTIONS

Existential philosophy as we know it today had its initial comprehensive presentation by Soren Kierkegaard (1813–55), whose writings were a passionate reaction to the all-embracing system of Hegelian philosophy. Later developments included the thought of Friedrich Nietzsche and Henri Bergson. Modern-day existential philosophers include Martin Heidegger, Jean-Paul Sartre, Albert Camus, Simone de Beauvoir, Miguel de Unamuno, Ortega y Gasset, Nicholas Berdyaev, Martin Buber, Gabriel Marcel, and Paul Tillich.

Much of existential psychology had its ideological rooting among the phenomenologists, most notably Edmund Husserl. Two European analysts, Ludwig Binswanger and Medard Boss, were constructing an existential psychology during Freud's lifetime.

Viktor Frankl, a Viennese psychiatrist, developed his "logo therapy" following his imprisonment in a German concentration camp during World War II. Logo therapy is based upon existential philosophy, and Frankl remains of the most lucid writers in conveying existential thinking to members of the helping professions.

Rollo May's monumental work *Existence*,[57] published in 1958, was the first major exploration of the impact of existential psychology upon American psychiatry and psychology. May presented translations of the works of existential psychologists and psychiatrists from Europe, where such thinking had become popular and in many places had replaced psychoanalytic thought. There was a readiness in America for existential thinking, evidenced by two journals devoted specifically to existential psychology and psychotherapy that began quarterly publication in the United States in the early 1960s, and it quickly became part of the third force, or humanistic psychology movement. This group included people such as Karen Horney, Carl Jung, Clark Moustakas, Carl Rogers, Abraham Maslow, Gordon Allport, Andras Angyal, and Prescott Lecky.

Existential thought was related to Gestalt therapy (Frederick Perls), the encounter movement (Carl Rogers and Arthur Burton), rational-emotive psychotherapy (Albert Ellis), and R.D. Laing's provocative writings labeled "antipsychiatry." Thomas Szasz pursued a similar attack upon psychiatry, particularly in relation to the "therapeutic state," the insanity plea, and the dehumanizing use of clinical diagnostic categories. Ernest Becker and Irvin Yalom presented challenging reappraisals of psychoanalytic thinking from existential postures. The most intense descriptions of the existential therapists' use of self are found in the works of Thomas Hora and William Offman.

Perhaps the earliest social work writings with a decidedly existential flavor were by Jessie Taft of the functional school, which had its roots in the psychology of Otto Rank. In his Pulitzer Prize–winning book, *The Denial of Death*, Becker produced a monumental integration of the thought of Rank and Freud.[5] Social workers, who once avidly debated the "dynamic" versus the "functional" schools of social work theory, appear to have totally ignored Becker's incisive thought as to how these two systems of thought could be effectively wedded. A welcome scholarly exception to this is Robert Kramer's work which links Rank with Carl Rogers and Rollo May[43].

In 1962, David Weiss's article appeared in *The Social Worker*[88] and Gerald Rubin's paper in *Social Work*.[70] Andrew Curry was publishing articles in the existential psychiatry journals. In the late 1960s, several articles appeared in various social work journals written by John Stretch, Robert Sinsheimer, David Weiss, Margery Frohberg, and Krill. These papers were specifically related to the application of existential philosophy in social work thought and practice.

There were also several social work papers published during this period that did not specifically emphasize existentialism but were related to similar concerns of the existential social work group. These writers included Elizabeth Salomon, Mary Gyarfas, and Roberta Wells Imre.

The first book on the subject of existentialism in social work was published in 1969 by Exposition Press: Kirk Bradford's *Existentialism and Casework*.[10] Its subtitle expresses its intent: *The Relationship Between Social Casework and the Philosophy and Psychotherapy of Existentialism*, and it should be considered an introductory and integrative work rather than a comprehensive or prophetic book. In 1970, Alan Klein related existential thinking to social group work in his book *Social Work Through Group Process*.[42] A second, more comprehensive work applying existential thought to various aspects of social work practice was published in 1975 by Dawson College Press of Montreal: David Weiss's *Existential Human Relations*. In 1974, James Whittaker's *Social Treatment* legitimized existential thinking as one of the four major theories contributing to social work practice. An effort to clarify both spiritual and systemic ideas for social workers was Krill's *Existential Social Work*.[48] Two subsequent books in practical application were *The Beat Worker*[49] and *Practice Wisdom*.[50] The former focused upon psychotherapy and the latter upon teaching the integration of self-awareness, philosophical thinking, and the therapeutic relationship to graduate students. Other social work writers related the existential view to child abuse,[11] to social work education,[79] and to cross-cultural counseling.[86]

While there appears to be a rising, if somewhat limited, interest in existential philosophy in social work literature, it would seem that the interest is far more widespread among social work students and younger professionals. Many of the newer therapeutic approaches are closely akin to the existential view of the therapeutic process. Such points of emphasis as choice and action, here-and-now problem orientation, dispensing with the use of diagnostic categories, stressing the worker as a vital, human person, and recognizing the connection of personal identity with the quality of significant-other relationships all have their existential linkages.

THERAPEUTIC CONCEPTS

The philosophical perspective discussed earlier suggests five organizing concepts of existential thought: disillusionment, freedom of choice, meaning in suffering, the necessity of dialogue, and a stance of responsible commitment. These same concepts can provide a way of viewing the therapeutic process.[47]

DISILLUSIONMENT

In existential thinking, one can move from a life of "bad faith" to one of authenticity. To do this, one must risk the pain of disillusionment. Similarly, in psychotherapy, change can be viewed as a result of relinquishing those very defensive beliefs, judgments, symptoms, or manipulations that interfere with the natural growth process. This growth process are seen as the emergence of unique personhood through responsive acts in relation to one's surroundings. Realistic needs and potentials begin to be the source of choice and action instead of neurotic, self-deceptive security needs.

An important therapeutic task, then, is to help a client experience disillusionment with those various security efforts that block his own growth. Disillusionment will seldom result from a rational exploration of one's past in order to realize causal factors of present defensive behavior. It is rare that one gives up security patterns because they are viewed as irrational, immature, or no longer applicable. Disillusionment occurs through the pain of loneliness and impotence. On the far side of such despair arises the possibility of new values and beliefs. It is the therapist's concern that these be more human values than those abandoned. The therapist acts as a midwife for the release of the natural growth energies within personality so that what is wholly and individually unique may emerge. Any tampering with this natural direction, once begun, is likely to do more harm than good.

FREEDOM OF CHOICE

Sartre characterizes consciousness as "no-thing-ness," for it is an awareness of oneself that transcends any fixed identity one might have concluded about oneself. Personality is always emerging. To view it as static or secure is our act of self-deception (bad faith). This conception of consciousness as freedom is a break with conception that personality is totally ruled by "unconscious" or by early learned behavior.

Despite a person's past, despite any diagnostic label pinned upon him, he always has the capacity to change himself. He can choose new values, or a new life-style. This does not always necessitate years or months of "working something through"; it may occur within days or weeks.

Choice is for action and differs from intellectual meandering or good intentions. Chosen actions occur in the present. Therapy is, therefore, present-focused and task- or action-oriented. People learn from experience, not from reason alone, although the very process of understanding how one's current belief and value system operates (and its consequences) can itself lead to new choices.

The critical ingredient for change is the client's wish to change. Therapy must, therefore, be designed to clarify quickly the nature of change sought by the client, and the therapist must be able to work within this framework, rather than seek to convince or seduce the client into redefining his problems and aiming for some type of change goal that pleases the therapist but is only vaguely understood by the client.

A therapist's belief in the client's capacity for change is a message of positive affirmation conveyed throughout treatment. There is no question but that a therapist's focus upon unraveling the intricacies of past relationships conveys a deterministic message that is a commentary upon the weakness and helplessness of a client.

MEANING IN SUFFERING

Just as existentialists see suffering as an inherent part of a life of authenticity based upon responsibility and freedom, so, too, does the existential therapist not seek to discredit or eliminate anxiety and guilt in her clients. She, instead, affirms such suffering as both necessary and directional for a person. She will help reveal what real anxiety and guilt may lie disguised behind neurotic (unrealistic) anxiety and guilt. But she does not seek to minimize or eradicate realistic anxiety and guilt. Such efforts would themselves be dehumanizing, unless used to prevent decompensation. In many cases, the normalizing of pain or a problem as a natural consequence of one's valued conclusions about adjusting to life can enhance one's sense of responsibility and the potential for changing one's orientation.

NECESSITY OF DIALOGUE

A person does not grow from within herself alone. Her emergence happens in responsive relation to her surroundings. She creates her own meaning in response to situations, and these meanings become the basis for choices and actions. However, her own meanings are no more absolute than those of any other person. Her own growth has to do with the continued reassessment of personal meanings, and she depends upon feedback from her environment (particularly human responses) for this reassessment activity. In order to gain honest feedback, one must allow others to be honest and free in their own expression. In therapy, therefore, it is critical to help a person open herself to relationships with others wherein she gives up her manipulative or "game" efforts in order to invite free responses from others. In doing this, she not only allows herself experiences of intimacy, but she also realizes that her own emerging sense of self requires such honest transactions with others.

COMMITMENT

A client's recognition of and commitment to his own inner emerging unique lifestyle is a hope of the existential therapist. The client realizes this commitment through his experience of the therapist's own affirmation of the client's worldview. This unique worldview is affirmed from the beginning in the therapist's acceptance of how the client perceives his symptoms, problems, conflicts—how he perceives change and what he wants changed. His uniqueness is also affirmed during the course of treatment by the way a therapist relates to "where a client is" in each interview. The theme of a session comes as an emerging force from the client, rather than as a rationally predicted starting point made in advance by the therapist. Both the goal-setting process and the activity of entering upon and working with an interview theme are therefore client-centered rather than therapist-centered. This in no way cramps the therapist's operation as a skilled professional with expertise, but he acts out of this expertise rather than displaying it in a manner that inhibits the process of therapy. A useful axiom, here, is the idea that it is who one is, as a person, rather than the amount of knowledge one has, theoretically, that is most important in helping people.

The client's awareness of and respect for his own unique life-style might be described as a turning away from self-pity and impotence. Rather than complaining about his lot in life, he discovers that he is intricately involved in the life process itself. He learns to listen to what life says to him and finds meaning in the response that is unique to himself. This is what is meant by the existential concept of dialogue and commitment.

RELATED THERAPEUTIC APPROACHES

As suggested earlier, there are obvious differences among those therapists claiming the existential label. This becomes more understandable if we consider the above therapeutic principles and note how they may be activated in a number of differing ways. A consideration of the range of techniques that may fit with the principles outlined will also clarify how other treatment theories tend to be compatible with the existential view.

Existentialism claims no technique system of its own and needs none. Its affirmation of the uniqueness of each client results in a perspective of each treatment situation being also unique. whatever techniques can be used, from whatever treatment theory, become the tools toward accomplishment of the unique goal chosen. In this sense existentialism is thoroughly eclectic. Techniques are always secondary to the uniqueness of the client and the puzzle he presents to the therapist.

Several therapeutic systems are compatible with existential thinking; some are not, and these will be considered later. The reality-oriented therapists (Glasser, Ellis, O. Hobart Mowrer, and Frankl) all stress choice and specific behavior change. William Reid, Laura Epstein, and Harold Werner have described similar cognitive-oriented approaches in social work literature. They are present-focused and commonly propose specific tasks for clients wherein the client is expected to put into immediate practice a decision for change. They tend to use reason to aid the decision for change, but then stress action. The action is usually expected to occur outside of the therapy interview (often as homework assignments) but its results are brought back for further discussion. The reality therapist focuses upon the disillusionment process by clearly identifying "faulty or irrational beliefs" that are responsible for problematic behavior. She affirms the client's freedom to choose and encourages a value shift through action.

Gestalt therapy, psychodrama, client-centered therapy, and provocative therapy techniques all stress a heightening of the client's awareness through action in the here and now. They seek the immediacy of experience as a thrust for change rather than a rational process of analyzing causal connections. They differ from the reality therapies in that the stress is upon choice and action that is more immediate; it is to occur in the here and now of the therapy meeting itself. Whether the client seeks to make use of this experience in his outside daily life is usually left up to him. There is less effort to deal rationally with the disillusionment process of beliefs and manipulations. These are dealt with experientially as group members are encouraged to give direct and open feedback to the attitudes and behavior expressed by others. The activity of dialogue is stressed.

Family systems approaches, like those of Virginia Satir, Salvador Minuchin, and Murray Bowen, combine awareness heightening with choices and tasks yet add the ingredient of activating the significant-other system in the helping process. Here the dimension of dialogue and intimacy is at last addressed within its daily living context. Bowen and Satir emphasize individuation, while Minuchin focused more upon action tasks.

There are few therapists to whom the term "existential" fits more accurately than any other: Carl Whittaker, Frank Farrelly, Lester Havens, William Offman, Walter Kempler, Irvin Yalom, Sydney Jourard, and Thomas Hora. Their common attribute is an intense, often surprising use of their personal self-expression combined with a general disdain for conceptualization about clients from theory. Here the subjective emphasis of existentialism reaches its height of therapeutic expression. When these therapists are paradoxical in their actions, it is seldom as a result of planned strategy. Paradox results from their intuitive response to the client and often expresses the paradoxical life stance of the therapist himself.

From the foregoing comparisons of therapeutic approaches, as they relate to existential thought, several areas of existential theory become more clearly delineated. We shall look at these in more detail, considering the therapeutic relationship, nature of personality, concept of change, use of historical data and diagnosis, and treatment methods.

THE THERAPEUTIC RELATIONSHIP

One might conclude that all psychotherapies value theory, techniques, and the therapeutic relationship; nevertheless, the priority of importance varies. Ego psychology clearly elaborates theory in its maze of complexities. Behaviorism delineates a vast variety of techniques, matched to specific symptoms. Humanistic psychology, and especially the existential worker, stresses the relationship itself, its transparency, spontaneity, and intensity. The therapist's use of himself and the type of relationship he seeks to foster with a client will be considered from two vantage points: first, the attitude of the therapist toward the client and her problems; and second, the behavior of the therapist as he interacts with the client—his use of himself as a unique person in his own right.

There is a critical difference between a therapist who sees the client as a complex of defenses or learned behaviors that are dysfunctional and a therapist who views the client as a unique, irreplaceable worldview that is in the process of growth, emergence, and expansion. The latter is an existential position. It views the problems and symptoms of a client as her own efforts to deal with the growth forces within herself and the risks these pose to her in relation to her self-image, relationship with significant others in her life, and her role in society.

The writings of R.D. Laing are aimed at clarifying the critical differences between the two types of therapists.[53] He points out that the therapist who sees the client as a mass of complexes, defenses, and dysfunctional learnings sees himself as the authority. His task is to diagnose the nature of these "dynamics" and convey these insights to the client either through verbal commentary or through specific behavioral tasks he gives the client. But in doing so, he also acts as another societal force that seeks to adjust the client to someone's definition of the functional personality. Such a therapist tends to support the view that the client's symptoms and problems identify her as ill (even "dysfunctional" implies that she is out of step with her surroundings). The therapist often becomes another dehumanizing force in the client's life in the sense of urging the "patient" to adjust to her family, her instincts, her needs, society's needs, etc. In contrast to this position, the existential therapist has no prescriptions for how the client should live. He sees his task as that of a midwife, an agent who has knowledge and skills to aid in the unblocking process that will allow the client to resume her own unique growth and emergence—whether or not this puts her in further conflict with her family, friends, and society. While the therapist may point out the potential risks and consequences of an emerging life-style, he will not negate its potential value.

The existential therapist's attitude affirms the inherent value of the client as a unique person with a very special worldview or life-style that is hers alone to charter. The client is also aware that the therapist sees in her the power of free choice. Instead of being helplessly at the mercy of forces beyond her consciousness, she can see the significant choices in her present life situation and has the power to decide which way she will proceed in the shaping of her life.

In one sense, the existential therapist does stand for a particular life-style, but it is one based upon his belief in the nature of humanness rather than a cultural viewpoint on how a person should pursue her role in her family or her society. The values conveyed by the existential therapist are these: human beings have the capacity for free choice; they are of fundamental worth in their own unique perspective on life and their assertion of this perspective; they require an open interaction with their surroundings in order to grow—emergence is a responsive and interactive process; suffering is an inevitable part of the growth process for emergence involves risks and unknowns; and self-deception is a potent force.

These values are in opposition to several values supported by society at large: that an individual is a helpless creature both at the mercy of an unknown unconscious and of utter insignificance in the complex mechanisms called society; that one can, and should, find happiness through avoidance of suffering and pain and by means of the distractions and pleasures offered at every turn; that a person is what he is, so he should fulfill his role in his family or social system as best he can and be satisfied with his already finished identity; and that since there are groups of people considered ultimately wise in politics, universities, at the executive level of business and in the military, in churches, and in medical buildings, the citizen should essentially consider a conforming obedience to what these soothsayers say is best for him.

The existential value perspective of the worker also differs significantly from "value life models" all too often conveyed by "therapist gurus." These models have been described by the author in three forms: the hope of enlightening reason, the hope of flowering actualization, and the hope of satisfying mediocrity.[49]

The therapist guru enjoys a priestly role of telling people how to attain happiness, enlightenment, or maturity. While the existential worker sometimes addresses value issues as they relate to the presenting problems, she is unwilling to represent a value life model, or ideal, to the client. She prefers that the client seek such ultimate definitions and commitments through his own significant others and/or support groups. Counseling is neither a truth search (guru model) nor an exercise in symptom alleviation (technician model). Problems are addressed in such a manner as to invite the client to consider the relationship of his current value framework and life-style as possibly problem-related. Problems are not merely annoyances to be discarded, but may be signposts for self-examination. There is an exception to the discussion of value life models. When the worker shares the same religious or philosophical belief system as the client she may freely discuss belief understandings as a peer (not as an expert).

The behavior of the existential therapist reflects her philosophical-psychological attitudes toward the client. Another useful axiom regarding the therapeutic relationship is this: what facilitates change in people most powerfully are the values of the worker, not spoken but demonstrated in her response to the client's concerns. If she is not the authority with the answers, what is she? The therapist does see herself as an expert, but her expertise has to do with her skills and talents of empathy; understanding; appreciation of and compassion for individual human beings and their struggles; experience in the process of self-deception, having struggled with growth-defensive process within herself; affirmation of the value of the unique soul, having herself been disillusioned with all the society-made authorities who offer solutions, happiness, etc.; and an open honesty that offers the client the possibility of genuine dialogue, if the client seeks to engage in such. The worker, then, seeks to normalize the problems of the client by reference to the struggles of the human situation. She avoids paternalistic conclusions about the client, viewing both problem and person exploration as a mutual process. Another way the worker avoids paternalism is by being honest and clear, rather than hidden and deceptive, in relation to the strategies utilized.

She may exhibit a type of detachment. But this detachment is not the cool aloofness of the objective mechanist who is dissecting and reforming the patient. The detachment of the existential therapist is an expression of her profound belief in the freedom of the client. The client has a right to his own life-style. If he chooses not to follow a direction of personal growth, but chooses to maintain his defensive posture for security or other reason, so be it. The therapist's sense of worth is not in the client's hands but within herself. Her detachment is from results, even though her actual activity in the helping process will be quite open and involved.

Detachment must not impair vitality and therefore cannot take the form of intellectual aloofness, analyzing the client from afar. Vital engagement through spontaneity, surprise, and unsettling responses is one of the valued methods of the existential worker. Genuine dialogue calls for an immediacy of feedback in many cases, and considered responses in others. Habitual mind-sets and communication patterns of clients require interruption and jostling, on occasion, in order for the new, the creative, to be brought to awareness. The use of vitality, lightness, spontaneity, and humor will often unbalance a client's defensive posturing. He becomes engaged emotionally and released from a fixed role or value position. At such moments he is more free to experiment with new possibilities.

The relationship between therapist and client is seen by many existential writers as the essential ingredient of change. The concepts of individual growth and genuine encounter with others are interdependent in the thought of Martin Buber. David Weiss emphasizes this same connectedness in his discussion of healing and revealing.[93] This I-Thou relation need not be seen as mystical. Carl Rogers's description of this activity suggests that the therapist provide an atmosphere for growth by means of a nonthreatening, affirming, understanding responsiveness.[68] But this does not mean the therapist remains passive. On the contrary, Rogers emphasizes the importance of the therapist's being himself in the expression of important arising feelings. To offer a dialogue is at least to present one side of it in an open, honest fashion. The therapist reveals himself in another manner at times, in that he shares some of his own struggles, disillusionment, and experiences wherein he, too, sought growth in the face of pain. In both these examples of the therapist's openness, we see that the therapist sees his own unique world view as an important experience to share with his client—not in a "go and do likewise" spirit, but rather showing himself as a *fellow traveler on the rocky road of human existence.*

HUMAN PERSONALITY

Freudian theory proposes the ego as a balancing, organizing, controlling, harmonizing agent among the demands of the superego, the pressures of the "outside world," and the cravings of the id. Behavior theory suggest a passive psyche that is primarily molded by outside forces. What one learns from others is what one is. Both roles render the individual practically helpless to resist the many forces that work upon him.

Two key concepts differentiate the existential view from those above. The first is the idea of an integrating, creative force for growth at the core of the personality. The second is the belief that every individual has the capacity to shift his style of life radically at any moment.

In terms of the human dynamo, the existentialists would not disagree with Freud's formulation of the id as a composite of Eros and Thanatos, or the life and death instincts. To this is added, however, the notion of a force that moves one toward meaning and toward relations with one's surroundings on the basis of meanings concluded. There is an integrative, unifying, creative force within a person that synthesizes his experiences, potentials, and opportunities and provides him with clues for his own direction of growth. No matter how emotionally disturbed a patient may seem, there is this integrative core within him that prompts him in the direction of experiencing and expressing his own uniqueness (realistic needs and potentials). He may shut himself off from such integrative promptings; he may refuse to listen or mislabel such messages as dangerous. But they are with him always.

The existential idea of a core integration and creation suggests a conflict-free portion of personality that survives and transcends any dysfunctioning that may possess a person. Such a force toward integration and meaning need not be considered separate from id. It is an expression of id activity. Teilhard de Chardin posits such a force as existing in all forms of existence: animals, plants, and even inanimate matter. Chardin sees in man the fruition of this drive toward complexity, and it is experienced in man's need for meaning and for love.

Martin Buber, too, suggests a force in man that permits him to enter the realm of relation with nature, ideas, other men, and God. This is a force that transcends what otherwise appears to be his limited, finite, individual self. This thinking helps distinguish the existential view of the creative force in man from what the ego psychologists have attempted to add to basic Freudian theory to explain creative functioning through certain basic powers of the ego.

The second major distinction has to do with the power of free choice possessed by every person. Even the most disturbed individual is not solely at the mercy of chaotic, irrational, destructive forces—an id gone wild. Nor is he at the total mercy of environmental forces that seek to identify, coerce, dehumanize, conform, or destroy him. The individual personality is always in the process of change and emergence. Sartre defined human consciousness as a "nothingness." Since it is always in the process of becoming, it is never fixed and completed. This no-thing-ness is an openness to the new, the unknown; it is forever moving beyond whatever identity one has concluded about oneself. Sartre sees this as an essential human construct. One may deny one's freedom and find ways of avoiding responsibility for this very process of change and emergence, but the process itself goes on. Pathology is not the arresting of growth but the self-chosen distortion of growth.[3]

Human consciousness is itself freedom—for it is a force that moves forever beyond whatever one has become as a fulfilled identity. As such, it is the power within man to change, to alter his life-style, his direction, and his sense of identity. It is an ever-present potential for a conversion experience. "To find one's self, one must lose one's self."

If one has the capacity for free choice and also some awareness of integrative promptings toward growth from the very core of one's psyche, why should one choose dysfunctioning, defensive symptomatology, or madness?

Freud's concept of the superego and his view of defense mechanisms and pathological symptomatology are seen by the existentialist in a more holistic manner. The existential idea of bad faith is a person's denial of freedom and emergence for the sake of a sense of security and identity. He deceives himself by a set of beliefs that define specifically who he is and what he can expect from others. This belief system contains both positive and negative judgments about himself and suggests how he must relate to other people. It is the center of his defensive control efforts, of his symptomatology, of his manipulations of relationships, and of his fostering myths about who he is. He chooses to believe certain notions about himself when he is quite young and undergoing the socialization process with his parents, teachers, peers, etc.

The beliefs he holds are used to maintain a sense of secured identity. He is tempted somehow to reassure himself of the solidity of his identity whenever he feels threatened. This he can do through manipulations of others, physical or psychological symptomatology, and reassuring beliefs about himself. The belief pattern may change over the years, so that ideas implanted by parents may become more personalized beliefs, but it is the rigidity and response to threat that characterize his security image, rather than the nature of the beliefs themselves.

This defensive belief system, or security image configuration, has its values, too. It helps the young, developing ego with limited experience and judgment conclude a manner of survival in a family constellation. The beliefs concluded about self and others provide habit patterns that furnish a sense of security so that one can use one's energy for their achievements as well. Even the adult ego is occasionally on the verge of exhaustion and needs to resort to the security image patterns of reassuring contentment. One will at times choose security image behavior, even when one knows it to be irrational and defensive, simply as a means of enduring and managing under considerable stress.

Security image patterns take the form of outer identifications, as well as inner passions. Outer identification includes all ways by which a person uses others to conclude who she is as a fixed identity—using her parents, spouse, children, friends, employer, profession, politics, church, race, social norms, etc. Inner passions have to do with feeling responses to life's situations that slow fulfill a sense of identity, so that certain feelings become fanned into possessing passions. For the self identified as "top dog," irritation can become rage. For the self-identified Don Juan, sensual excitement can become lust. In the outer identifications, one identifies with beliefs and roles; in the inner passions, one identifies with specific feelings. In either case, the sense of self is experienced as fixed, solidified, defined, rather than flowing, free, and emerging.

The defensive belief system or security image configuration is sometimes referred to as one's world design, composed of self-concluded value positions. These are seldom the idealized values thought to be one's "ego ideal" but rather the everyday pragmatic values related to security-based hopes and fears.

THE PROCESS OF CHANGE

If you want to know who you are, don't conceptualize upon it. Look at your actions, your behavior, your choices. Existentialism is a philosophy rooted in personal experience. "Truth is subjectivity," Kierkegaard's slogan, and "existence precedes essence," Sartre's assertion, are both ways of rooting identity in personal experience—one's active and unique response in a situation. Being-in-the-world is a concept of Heidegger's that asserts the same notion.

There are two components commonly accepted as necessary for the change process, one rational and the other experiential. Almost every form of psychotherapy includes both these components, despite their occasional assertions to the contrary.

The experiential component has to do with the client's experiencing herself in a new and different way. She may discover that she is being dealt with differently by a significant other in her life. She may also find new kinds of feelings or symptoms arising within herself. The rational component has to do with self-understanding through the process of reflecting and conceptualizing about oneself—the cause-effect relationships in her background, evaluating how she handled recent situations, etc.

The existentialists see value in both components of change—one reinforces the other when both occur. The existentialists, however, are particularly wary of the common self-deception of intellectualizing about oneself—of dwelling on self-evaluation and introspection in a manner that negates any action or choice in the here and now. The self-understanding of importance is that of one's world design, its orienting values and the negative consequences that naturally accompany this. William Offman [61] stresses that an emphasis upon change agrees with the client's self-criticism (get rid of my problem), whereas a normalizing of the problem as an expression of the client's world design affirms the client while at the same time stressing her personal responsibility for the problem. There are no problem-free value positions, so the client may simply accept her problems as inevitable consequences or consider some alternate value position.

Here are some therapeutic activities that promote both clarified self-understanding and emotion-inducing experiences:

1. The attitude of the therapist toward the client can present a new type of affirmation by a significant other that the client has never experienced.
2. The therapist's skill with empathy may provide the client with an experience of being understood more intensely than by others in his life.
3. The openness of the therapist about himself as a revealing, engaging person provides an invitation for the client to the dialogical experience. It can also offer an experience of an authority figure as human and of equal status. Such openness by a therapist may constructively take the form of provocative, negative, feedback to the client about his appearance, attitudes, feelings, and behavior. Here the client experiences a candid honesty that may be otherwise denied him in his everyday world of interactions.
4. Techniques designed for here-and-now heightening of awareness, such as in Gestalt, psychodrama, and encounter groups, or the dealing with "transference" interactions between therapist and client, are obviously aimed primarily at the experiential component of change. Similarly, efforts to vitalize new interactions between group or family members quickly stir new areas of individual awareness.
5. Action tasks for the client to perform outside of therapy sessions provide new behavioral experiences.

Compatible with the existential therapist's emphasis upon experiential change is his lack of interest in historical data. Some history may be of value in the early interviews to help the therapist see the client in a more human, rounded perspective, so that the therapist is less inclined to make superficial judgments about the client in response to the stereotype the client usually presents to other people. But the therapist often does not even need this aid. It is far more important to understand the dynamics of the client's present struggle, and what her symptoms or complaints reveal about her efforts to grow and meet her own needs (the present beliefs and activities of her defensive belief system).

If the client herself brings up historical material, the existential therapist will often seek to make it immediately relevant. He may do this by relating the past experience to present choices, or else (using Gestalt techniques) by asking the client to bring the early parent figure into the present interview session by role playing the past interaction that the client is describing.

History sometimes serves a useful purpose in relation to understanding a client's world design. When the client is able to recall patterns of thinking, feeling, and behavior that have reoccurred time and again, the power of his determining value positions, or conclusions, becomes more poignant.

WORLD DESIGN AND DIAGNOSIS

Clinical diagnosis has its value as a shorthand way of communicating to peers about clients, in terms of areas of conflict and types of defenses. Other than this, it is of questionable value in the eyes of the existential therapist and commonly results in more harm than good. The danger of diagnosis is the categorization of a client, so as to provide the therapist some "objective" way of defining prognosis, goals, the role she must play as she interacts with the client, and her decision about termination. Such objective efforts based upon generalizations about clients with a similar history-symptomatology-mental status constellation miss what is unique about a particular client. A further danger described by Laing is that diagnosis is often used as a way of agreeing with the family that this client is "sick" and in need of readjustment to the demands and expectations of the family.

This depreciation of the value of clinical diagnosis, however, does not suggest a disregard for understanding the nature of a client's present struggles, conflicts, strivings, and fears. World design understanding remains of key importance. Here the existentialist differs with the behavioral modifier who relates himself only to a specific symptom without regard for its meaning and the client's present life-style.

It is critical to understand the unique worldview of the client. This consists of patterns of relating to meaningful others and expectations of them. It also includes beliefs about oneself, both positive and negative judgments, and assumptions about oneself and how these affect the way one meets one's own needs and handles one's frustrations of need satisfaction. It is important to see how the client is interfering with his own growth, and this includes both the beliefs he holds about the sort of person he is and the notions he has about how he must deal with the significant people in his life. It may even include how he evaluates forces of society that play upon him and attempt to conform his behavior into some stereotype that is useful to society's needs (employers, church, racial attitudes, etc.). Normalization in the assessment phase conveys this message: given your special way of viewing the world and your patterns of affecting it and responding to it, your problem is perfectly understand-able—it is a natural expression of you. This is not to say that he created the problem; nor, on the other hand, is he a total victim of it.

This type of self-understanding in relation to orienting value conclusions stresses the here-and-now life-style—the client's present being-in-the-world. How he gets this way is of questionable significance. The values of identity formulations are twofold. First, they provide the therapist with an understanding of her unique client and how his present symptoms are ways of handling a particular stress or conflict area. Second, world design gives the therapist somewhat of a guideline to assess her own work with the client, particularly when she discovers that her therapeutic efforts are bringing no results.

The world design understanding of an existential social worker will often em-phasize family dynamics (interactions, scapegoating, alliances, etc.). These usually make up the most significant area of the client's life-style functioning. Intervention efforts will frequently involve other family members for the same reason. The exis-tential understanding of the person as "being-in-the-world" is wholly compatible with the dual focus model of social work. The personal, unique truth of the individ-ual is known best through his relation with others and forces beyond his own ego— usually social but at times, perhaps, transcendental in nature.

Even when the problem is not set forth as family or marital in nature, the thera-pist will tend to see the presenting symptom as a means of dealing with significant others in the person's life. An interpersonal appraisal of symptoms is attuned to the absence, loss, breakdown, or dysfunctioning of important human relationships in his life. Therapeutic work will commonly be addressed to the creation, the restoration, or the improvement of such relationships. This interpersonal focus upon symptomatol-ogy need not neglect the individual's subjective experience of attitudes, values, and feelings. The two are obviously interdependent. However, the existential therapist sees catharsis and self-understanding as a vehicle for altering the person's world of human relationships, which is the fundamental goal. This interpersonal emphasis dis-tinguishes the existential social worker from most existential psychiatrists and psy-chologists.

TREATMENT METHODS

It is difficult to talk of treatment methods without first considering the types of clients and problems for which the methods are used. In one sense, the existential perspective is loyal to no particular treatment system. It is eclectic and uses whatever techniques will best meet the needs of a particular client. In another sense, the exis-tential therapist may be considered best equipped to work with clients whose prob-lem involves a loss of direction, a value confusion, a shaken identity in a swirling world of anomie. For these clients, certain techniques have been developed to focus precisely on such difficulties. However, it should be clearly understood that the existentialist works out of his unique philosophical perspective with all clients, and he should not be viewed only as a specialist with clients experiencing personal alienation.

There are three principles of treatment that clarify the therapeutic approach of the existentialist. These are:

1. A client-centered orientation.
2. An experiential change emphasis.
3. A concern with values and philosophical or religious perspectives.

CLIENT-CENTERED ORIENTATION

The client-centered focus has already become apparent in our introductory comments on the existentialist's antiauthoritarian stance. Client-centeredness: goal formulations and work with an emerging theme in any given interview.

Goal formulation involves the therapist and client working out a mutual agreement in the early interviews as to the purpose of future treatment. What must be guarded against here is the type of therapeutic dogmatism that seeks to convince the client as to the "true implications" of her symptoms or problem, so that she will work in the manner the therapist wishes. The most important initial step in treatment, following the age-old social work principle, is to "start where the client is." This adage refers to focusing on how the client is experiencing her problem, what it is she wants changed, and other ideas as to the type of help she is seeking.

The mode of therapy used (individual, couple, group, family) or the types of techniques (reality, behavioral modification, encounter, psychoanalytic ego, Gestalt, etc.) will vary, of course, in accordance with the interest of the client, the skills of the therapist, and the nature of the treatment setting itself. However, certain techniques are obviously more appropriate for certain goals. Behavior modification would be particularly useful with the goals of provocative contact and specific behavior (symptom) change. The core conditions elaborated by Carl Rogers will be most useful in providing a sustaining relationship for a client. Social work literature provides many useful approaches to accomplishing the goal of environmental change. The goal of relationship change can be dealt with using communications theory (Satir, Haley, Jackson) and other family and marital therapy models. Directional change can be effected by techniques described by Rogers, Farrelly, the Gestaltists, reality therapy, cognitive therapy, task-centered casework, and psychoanalytic psychotherapy. The critical point here is that the therapeutic approach must fit the unique goal and needs of a client rather than fitting clients into some pet system of psychotherapy, and dismissing the misfits as "unmotivated."

What is important to understand in this goal framework is that it provides a starting point for treatment in a manner that recognizes the unique experience of the client as valid. The goal may change during treatment as the client begins to experience her problems in some other light. The goal must also be tested out in early interviews so as to ascertain whether the goal agreed upon is merely a verbalized goal of the client, or whether it is indeed the way in which the client experiences the need for help and hope for change. With this framework, the therapist engages the client in a manner by which they can both "talk the same language" and have similar expectations for what is to follow.

There would appear to be a contradiction between some of the above-mentioned goals and what has previously been described as the existential focus upon disillusionment, freedom of choice, finding meaning and suffering, discovering the growth value of dialogue, and coming to a sense of personal commitment in relation to one's future. Such a focus seems most applicable to the goal category of directional change. The existential therapist, however, is not bound to pursue such a focus, if it does not seem appropriate. The existentialist's concern with client-centered treatment and emphasis upon experiential change enable him to assert his philosophical perspective to a degree in all goal categories described.

The other client-centered activity deals with the interview theme of any given session. The client is not a problem to be solved, a puzzle to be completed. She is a person who is undergoing constant change from week to week, day to day. Change occurs in her life for both the good and the bad apart from what happens during her therapy sessions. For the therapist to preplan an interview, picking up where the last one ended or getting into what the therapist considers to be an area of increasing importance, is often presumptuous.

The interview begins and the therapist listens to both verbal and nonverbal expressions of the client. He is alert to possible inconsistencies among what the client says, her feeling state, and behavior. The therapist's most important listening tool is his capacity for empathy. In the initial stages of the interview, the therapist must free himself of preconceptions about the client and preoccupations with himself in order to open himself to the whole person before him.

How the theme is made known as well as how it is dealt with are related to the goal of therapy (thinking in terms of the goal framework described earlier) and what particular therapeutic approach a therapist favors for work on such a goal. The therapist and client work together from the point of theme clarity.

AN EXPERIENTIAL CHANGE EMPHASIS

The experiential emphasis has already been discussed. The activities encouraging experiential change include: attitude of therapist, empathy, therapist's openness or transparency, heightening of here-and-now awareness, tasks for choice, and action. In the earlier discussion of how various theories of therapy reflect existential points of emphasis, it was apparent that techniques could be tapped from many theoretical sources.

It is clear by now that the existentialist is radically concerned with the here-and-now encounter between a person and his world. For it is in this moment of responsiveness, of being-in-the-world, that the person experiences her freedom of choice and meaning making. Who she is stems from what she does—the choice she activates—and does not stem from the intellectual conceptualization she holds about herself, nor from any dogmas or groups to which she holds allegiance in exchange for some bestowed identity.

A CONCERN WITH VALUES AND PHILOSOPHICAL OR RELIGIOUS PERSPECTIVES

The concern with pinpointing, challenging, and clarifying values, and with philosophical or religious perspectives is also dealt with by various writers. There are strong similarities between the rational-emotive psychotherapy of Albert Ellis and the Morita therapy of Japan. Both pinpoint "irrational" or "unrealistic" beliefs that specifically propose other more realistic and human beliefs in substitution for the dysfunctional beliefs. Hobart Mowrer's integrity therapy follows a similar course, where the emphasis is upon helping the client see his guilt as a contradiction between the values he holds in common with his significant others and his behavior or actual life-style. Frankl has developed two techniques, dereflection and paradoxical intention, that are designed to help a client reexamine and alter his philosophical perspective so as to affirm a new way of viewing himself in relation to his symptoms, choices, and life direction.

These "reality-oriented" approaches include four common ingredients:

1. Pinpointing specific values (attitudes, beliefs, judgments about self and others) manifested by the client's life-style.
2. Clarifying how these very values may be interfering with his own growth and intimacy needs or efforts.
3. Helping him consider more realistic human values and beliefs instead of the dysfunctional ones so his realistic growth and intimacy needs might achieve more direct satisfaction.
4. Encouraging decisions, choices, and actions (often as homework assignments) in order to activate the new values concluded to be more valid.

Thomas Hora [35] discusses values by distinguishing between two versions of reality: "the way it seems" and "the way it is." The first of these describes the distorted and limited views the client has about his life-style and its related value perspectives. The second view of reality is that expanded by the therapist as he highlights other values in the client's life-style that are being ignored or minimized. Like Offman, Hora will also clarify negative consequences in relation to some of the client's value positions and pose alternative possibilities for the client's consideration. Hora emphasizes the personal stance of the therapist to be one of a "benevolent presence" through which he may convey peace, assurance, gratitude, and love as important human realities.

This therapeutic emphasis upon values and a philosophical perspective is designed for certain types of clients—those whose working goal is directional change. There is a growing recognition of the effects of anomie in modern culture with resulting personal alienation from the roots of human needs and human strivings. Jung reported this phenomenon forty years ago and existential novelists, philosophers, and psychologists have been emphasizing the extent of alienation ever since.

In relation to religion and spirituality, the existential teacher would strongly endorse a recent development in graduate social work programs across the country. Related to the emphasis on diversity, schools are developing courses on religion and spirituality in order for students to address their own prejudices and appreciate the varied religious resources in the lives of their clients.

American culture has finally felt the same impact of alienation that shook Europe during and after World War II. In America, this awareness was helped along by the revolt of the youth, minority groups, and poor people. At this point, it is unclear whether alienation is a problem of a particular client population or whether it is really at the root of all emotional distress. The writing of Laing, Becker, and, recently, Irvin Yalom are certainly weighted toward the latter view.

Considering the three therapeutic principles discussed (the client-centered orientation, focus upon experiential change, and concern for values and philosophical perspectives), it becomes clear that the existential caseworker seeks to work with all types of clients and human problems and that she could function with any kind of social agency or therapeutic setting, provided she was given the administrative approval to work as she wished. It is also clear that the existential position is in opposition to those therapeutic practices that seek to adjust clients to family and social norms or to those prognostic norms stemming from the rigid use of diagnostic categories. The authoritative misuse of behavior modification and psychoanalytic theory is a major concern of the existential social worker.

The existential social worker is also concerned with how monetary preoccupations of insurance companies and funding sources of agencies are dictating therapeutic approaches. The popular emphasis on short-term, symptom-relief therapies ignores the existentialist's view that a presenting problem is commonly a warning sign of more troubling value issues of the client's life-style. This Band-Aid, patchwork approach simply reinforces the inclination of many clients to view themselves in a superficial manner.

Considering the eclectic use of treatment approaches suggested by the existential perspective, it is also apparent that social workers can make more creative and varied use of the existential perspective than can psychiatrists, psychologists, ministers, or nurses. This is because of the wide-ranging problem activities that engage the efforts of social workers, necessitating a manner of work that includes multiple skills. While there is still a lack of research verification, it appears that work with a middle-class clientele will commonly involve techniques aimed at heightening here-and-now awareness, as well as dealing with values and philosophical perspectives. Clients from the lower classes, who are considered unresponsive to traditional treatment approaches, would appear most responsive to task-oriented techniques emphasizing choice and action in the context of a present focus of problem understanding.

The modes of therapy (individual, couple, family, and group) are all effective ways of conducting an existential-oriented treatment. Application to individual counseling has been elaborated upon, particularly by Rogers, Farrelly, May, Frankl, and Perls. Work with groups with an existential perspective has been described by Helen Durkin, Carl Rogers, Arthur Burton, and Irvin Yalom. Social work writer Alan Klein relates the group work approach to existential thinking. Family therapists whose approaches are highly compatible with the existential perspective include Jay Haley, Virginia Satir, John Bell, and Carl Whittaker.

The existential approach fulfills two major needs of modern social work practice. First, it is the only social work approach the emphasizes value issues related to the client's problem. With the apparent increase of alienation and anomie, social work may require methods of response to value questions. Second, the emphasis upon the human ingredients of the therapeutic relationship coupled with an "atheoretical" understanding of the client as a person result in a restoration of humanitarian helping. Self-aware workers are better able to appreciate all clients as more like themselves and less as objects for diagnostic categorization and manipulation.

CASE EXAMPLE

The following could be considered an example of the existential social work approach. The case described is short-term casework with an individual from the goal framework of specific behavior change. It should be clear from the previous discussion about differing goals and the eclectic use of treatment techniques, that other case examples would take much different forms from the one described. The three existential principles of client-centered focus, experiential change, and value focus are illustrated in this case.

> An attractive Spanish-American woman, aged thirty-four, came to me complaining of a severely inhibiting depression. In the course of the evaluation, it appeared that she had little interest or sensitivity for seeing any connection of her symptoms to her past or present living situation. She was somewhat troubled over a divorce of a year ago. There was also a problem with her mother (living across the street) who tried to dominate her and provoke her guilt, and who often took care of her two teenage daughters. Some rebellion in the older teenage daughter was apparent. She also believed herself "hexed" by her mother-in-law. These were areas of complaints, yet she saw no prospects for changing them. Her concerns for change were very concrete: she could not do her housework or cook the meals or discipline the children, for she would usually go to bed soon after she returned from work. In bed, she would either sleep or fantasize about how bad off she was,

and the running of the house was left to the children, particularly the rebellious older one. She feared losing her job as a nurse's aide at the local hospital and had already missed several days of work because of feeling too tired. She had given up going out with her boyfriend and felt extremely alone and worthless.

Within ten interviews, occurring on alternate weeks, the depression had lifted. She managed her housework well; disciplined the children—the older one was much less rebellious; she could stand up to her mother on a realistic basis; she was dating again; and she was taking a training course to become a practical nurse. The goal was specific behavioral change although its successful accomplishment resulted in a broadening of this woman's constructive activity in several areas of her life. My techniques dealt primarily with the symptoms of depression and helplessness. In the second interview, I emphasized what I sensed to be her inhibited potential: I said that she could make herself get out of bed (or refuse to enter it) by performing the tasks of her housework and by going to her hospital work every day, no matter how tired she felt. I recognized that feelings of depression were strong within her, but pointed out that they represented a part of herself that seemed to be trying to convince her that she was no good. She could go on believing this or she could challenge this idea. In the third interview, I dealt actively with another belief, challenging its power and questioning her need to be dominated by it. She thought the depression resulted from being hexed. I told her I had doubts about the magic of hexing and if there was anything to it, it probably had to do with her own reaction to the notion that she had been hexed. I linked this belief with the part of her that was trying to convince her that she was helplessly useless and inadequate. As sessions went on, she did bring up material about her mother, husband, children, job, and relatives, but this was more from the standpoint of content for discussion in what she felt to be a positive, affirming relationship. The actual therapeutic effort, in terms of pinpointing her problem and a way of dealing with it, was primarily in relation to the depressive symptom described. The techniques used were my ways of responding to her area of concern and view of change. We could communicate through the goal of specific behavior change. She was able to see the depression as being a self-defeating part of her. This freed her from the belief that the depressive symptom was a condemnation and failure of her whole personality, which had been implied in her notion of being hexed. While this was a limited shift in the belief system of this woman, it could still be a significant one. Furthermore, her resumption of responsibility in the family had its rewarding feedback responses from the children, as well as from her own mother who was closely involved with her family.

Note the three principles involved: a client-centered focus in terms of goal selection and interview management; emphasis upon experiential change through use of task assignment as well as through the attitude of the therapist regarding the client's potential strengths; and finally, an effort to deal with the woman's value system, specifically suggesting that she did have some capacity for free choice and need not identify herself completely with her symptom (feelings of fated helplessness).

This case raises an interesting cultural issue in relation to the client's view of the change process and how she views change as possibly occurring. An alternative approach might have been a referral of this woman to a *curandero* to handle the "hexed" issue. Had she been unresponsive to my rational efforts to deal with her belief about being hexed, I would have considered such a referral. Since she had sought out my help, I chose to deal with this belief issue in this more personal, challenging way.

EXISTENTIALISM AND COMMUNITY

Existentialism is sometimes criticized as an individualistic philosophy lacking a social ethic. This is a misnomer. Philosophers such as Camus, Berdyaev, Tillich, and Buber have written extensively on the application of existential thinking to social issues. Members of the helping professions have also related existential philosophy to social concerns. Edward Tiryakian, a sociologist, compares existential thought with that of Durkheim. Lionel Rubinoff's critique of modern philosophical, psychological, and sociological thought addresses the subject of the individual and his relationship to society. Rubinoff's basic premises are existential. R.D. Laing also uses an existential framework in his critique of society and of the helping professions as dehumanizing extensions of society's values.

Beginning with the existential belief that truth is not found in an objective fashion, within a doctrine or within a group of people, we find some implications for a view of society and social change. In the first place, the existentialist stands against tyranny in any form not only by politically conservative, status quo-oriented leaders, but also by the rational social engineers who would seek to establish the utopian society necessitating many controls and committed to adjustment of individuals to a "properly functioning" society. The existentialists are a prime opponent of Skinner in his appeal for a society that meets humanity's needs by limiting freedom and nonconformity.

The existentialists know that power corrupts and that much of the evil perpetrated is unpredictable at the moment of its inception. If, on the other hand, there is an effort to decondition evil-producing behavior, this effort itself, if successful, would result in the most profound evil of all: the dehumanization of people by depriving individuals of freedom—the only valid source of their sense of personal meaning and dignity.

On the other hand, an appeal for a completely free and open society, such as proposed in Charles Reich's *Greening of America,* [64] is again a naive position founded upon a disregard for the self-defeating, aggressive, and evil-producing behavior of people. Spontaneous "doing one's own thing" is too simple a commitment. We can be defeated by our own instincts and self-deceptions as easily as by our efforts to organize and construct the happy state.

The direction for a society's emergence stems from the sufferings and potentials of its people, and not from an elite group of rebels or social organizers. Eric Hoffer was right in saying that the most creative and innovative shifts in a society stem from its outcasts, nonconformists, and those who experience the failures of its present functioning. The existential model for social change would be one wherein the very people who suffer from dehumanizing social forces would be the indicators of what sorts of changes are needed. The community organization social worker would have a facilitating, clarifying, enabling role here, perhaps, and once a direction is clear she may use her knowledge of power structure and change tactics in order to mobilize the social change effort.

The "antiexistential" community organizer would be one who decides for himself what change other people really need and then uses his knowledge and skills to "educate," seduce, and pressure a disadvantaged group into deciding what its problems are and the change indicated. The worker's basic notions of change, here, come either from his own needs, or his rational, analytical conclusions of what this group or community lacks in comparison with some ideal he holds about how people should live. The impetus for change is worker-oriented rather than community-oriented.

The opposite extreme, also antiexistential, is sometimes seen in community mental health clinics. Although such clinics are committed, by their very purpose (and federal funding), to a community outreach stance, there is little genuine effort at dialogue with those needy members of the community who do not enter the portals of the clinic itself requesting some specific help. In contrast, the genuinely committed community mental health clinic is actively seeking contact with those groups in its community who are known through police, welfare, and schools to have problems but who are not availing themselves of any helping services. Primary prevention at times of family or neighborhood crisis becomes a major way of help, and this most often takes the form of consultation with police, welfare workers, teachers, nurses, ministers, and doctors.

As discussed earlier, the existentialists see many of the forces of society as being in opposition to the individual's effort at an authentic life-style establishing her unique direction out of an awareness of her own freedom, responsibility, and what she learns through personal suffering. Modern society encourages anomie and personal alienation by its forces of seduction and oppression. Insofar as the economic-political system uses people as objects in order to preserve its own efficient functioning, it may be said to be dehumanizing. Various social institutions combine their efforts to achieve this goal. Certain roles in the system are rewarded with status, financial remuneration, and prestige while others are ignored. Happiness is defined in such a way as to keep the public at large an active consumer of economic goods. An attunement to personal suffering is discouraged through the various tranquilization forms of drugs, alcohol, treadmill activities, and a work ethic that implies a solution to all of one's problems with the purchase of the next automobile, house, or packaged vacation plan. Such writers as Erich Fromm [28] and Henry Winthrop [98] have elaborated upon the multiple forms of social dehumanization that are too numerous and complex to mention here.

The helping professional is faced with a critical choice in relation to social dehumanization. He can become a part of this system that is a purveyor of anomie by the very way he performs his helping role. Or, on the other hand, he can be a member of a vanguard actively in touch with many of society's victims, who can help bring individuals and groups to an active awareness of themselves as free and responsible beings despite the negative forces bestowed upon them by society. Beyond such awareness, he will help them toward personal direction and action that affirms human dignity in the face of tyrannical and dehumanizing social forces.

The institutions of society can and do provide constructive, affirming forces for individuals and groups, of course, through education, employment, protection, health, and welfare care as well as valued traditions, a sense of history, and a national spirit that affirms a set of values that is generally accepted and may be quite compatible with the freedom, responsibility, and valuing of uniqueness and personal dignity that characterize existentialism. The existential helping professional realizes, however, that the constructive forces of society cannot in themselves bring an individual to authenticity. The matter of personal choice and acceptance of responsibility for one's own worldview and life-style remain essential. The existentialist is, therefore, cynical in response to social utopians who seek to construct a society of need-met, happy people.

RESEARCH AND KNOWLEDGE GAPS

The existential approach eludes research. Its lack of a specific theory of personality, its emphasis upon subjectivity and uniqueness, its eclectic use of multivaried techniques, and its concern about values are all factors that make structured studies difficult. On the other hand, the existential perspective extends the hand of gratitude to the numerous research studies that have clearly unseated dogmatic authoritative assumptions proselytized by "sophisticated" adherents to the varied theories of personality. When it comes to practice, the existential worker tends to agree with the behaviorist: we should utilize what was proven effective in practice to avoid forcing clients to submit to our favored (though ineffective) methods. Research indicates that effective treatment can occur with the following conditions: client-worker liking of one another; use of placebo effect in structuring the treatment process; core conditions (warmth, genuineness, empathy) combined with attitude change; attitude change accompanied with emotional change as well as task assignments; and the use of significant others in the assessment and treatment process wherever possible.[49]

Another important conclusion from practice research has been that no theory of treatment has proven itself superior to any other mode. The existentialist sees this as a crucial statement about the place of theory in practice. Theory does not seem to be the important ingredient in helping people, and is therefore considered of secondary (informative) value. While it is not clear what then is the magic ingredient, the existential worker would suggest it to be human sensitivity as developed over time through both self-awareness and learning from many experiences with clients. The better one comes to know oneself, the more clearly is one able to see oneself within the client's experiences as well. This a most important area for future research study.

In conclusion, the existential stance provides a philosophical perspective that can be related to the many avenues of social work practice. One does not need a profound acquaintance with existential philosophy in order to benefit from the perspective. One might, instead, view the existentialists as emphasizing a sense or direction and a style of working that are primarily concerned with a greater humanization of the social work profession. From their emphasis upon the value of the uniqueness of the individual there comes an affirmation of a client-centered focus and an awareness of the dangers of anomie in a mechanistic society. From their view of growth through choice and action there comes a primary effort aimed at experiential change with clients. From their model of man as a meaning-making being there comes a recognition of the importance of values, philosophy, and religion as ingredients of the casework process. From their emphasis upon dialogue there comes the concern for therapist transparency and authenticity as well as the valuing of a participatory democracy. And from their appreciation of the powers of self-deception at work with human beings, there comes an emphasis upon personal commitment in the face of suffering and uncertainty, as well as a suspicion about any authority that establishes itself as knowing how other people should live their lives.

REFERENCES

1. Allport, G. (1965). *Letters from Jenny.* New York: Harcourt, Brace and World.
2. Angyal, A. (1965). *Neurosis and Treatment.* New York: Wiley.
3. Barnes, H. (1959). *The Literature of Possibility: A Study of Humanistic Existentialism.* Lincoln: University of Nebraska Press.
4. Barrett, W. (1958). *Irrational Man.* New York: Doubleday.
5. Becker, E. (1958). *The Denial of Death.* New York: Free Press.
6. Berdyaev, N. (1944). *Slavery and Freedom.* New York: Scribner.
7. Binswanger, L. (1963). *Begin in the World.* New York: Basic Books.
8. Borowitz, E. (1966). *A Layman's Guide to Religious Existentialism.* New York: Delta.
9. Boss, M. (1963). *Psychoanalysis and Daseinsanalysis.* New York: Basic Books.
10. Bradford, K.A. (1969). *Existentialism and Casework.* Jericho, NY: Exposition Press.
11. Brown, J.A. (1980). Child abuse: An existential process. *Clinical Social Work Journal 8* (2), pp. 108–111.
12. Buber, M. (1955). *Between Man and Man.* Boston: Beacon Press.
13. ———. 1965. *The Knowledge of Man.* New York: Harper & Row.
14. Burton, A. (Ed.), (1969). *Encounter.* San Francisco: Jossey-Bass.
15. Camus, A. (1969). *The Rebel.* New York: Knopf.
16. Curry, A. (1967). Toward a phenomenological study of the family. *Existential Psychiatry 6* (27), Spring, pp. 35–44.
17. Dorfman, R.A. (1988). *Paradigms of Clinical Social Work.* New York: Brunner/Mazel.
18. Durkin, H. (1964). *The Group in Depth.* New York: International Universities Press.
19. Edwards, D. (1982). *Existential Psychotherapy.* New York: Gardner Press.
20. Ellis, A. (1962). *Reason and Emotion in Psychotherapy.* New York: Stuart.
21. *Farber, L.* (1966). *The Ways of the Will.* New York: Harper Colophon Books.
22. Farrelly, F. (1974). *Provocative Therapy.* Madison, WI: Family, Social & Psychotherapy Services.

23. Ford, D., & Urban, H. (1964). *Systems of Psychotherapy* (Chapter 12). New York: Wiley.
24. Frankl, V.E. (1962). *Man's Search for Meaning: An Introduction to Logo Therapy.* Boston: Beacon Press.
25. ———.(1965). *The Doctor and the Soul: From Psychotherapy to Logo Therapy.* New York: Knopf.
26. ——— . (1967). *Psychotherapy and Existentialism: Selected Papers on Logo Therapy.* New York: Simon & Schuster.
27. Frohberg, M. (1967). Existentialism: An introduction to the contemporary conscience. *Perceptions 1*(1), Spring, School of Social Work, San Diego State College, pp. 24–32.
28. Fromm, E. (1955). *The Sane Society.* New York: Rinehart.
29. Glasser, W. (1965). *Reality Therapy.* New York: Harper & Row.
30. Gyarfas, M. (1960). Social science, technology and social work: A caseworker's view. *Social Sevice Review 43*(3), September, pp. 259–273.
31. Haley, J. (1963). *Strategies of Psychotherapy.* New York: Grune and Stratton.
32. ——— . (1976). *Problem-Solving Therapy.* San Francisco: Josscy-Bass.
33. Heinecken, M.J. (1956). *The Moment before God.* Philadelphia: Muhlenberg Press.
34. Hoffer, E. (1951). *The True Believer.* New York: Harper.
35. Hora, T. (1977). *Existential Metapsychiatry,* New York: Seabury Press.
36. Imre, R.W. (1971). A theological view of social casework. *Social Casework 52*(9), November, pp. 578–585.
37. James, M., & Jongeward, D. (1971). *Born to Win: Transactional Analysis with Gestalt Experiments.* Reading, MA: Addison-Wesley.
38. Jourard, S. (1964). *The Transparent Self.* Princeton, NJ: Van Nostrand.
39. Jung, C.G. (1933). *Modern Man in Search of a Soul.* New York: Harcourt, Brace.
40. Katz, R. (1963). *Empathy.* New York: Free Press.
41. Kazantzakis, N. (1960). *The Saviors of God.* New York: Simon & Schuster.
42. Klein, A.F. (1970). *Social Work Through Group Process.* Albany, NY: School of Social Welfare, State University of New York.
43. Kramer, R. (1995). Carl Rogers meets Otto Rank: The discover of relationship. In T. Pauchant (Ed.), *In Search of Meaning: Managing the Health of Our Organizations, Our Communities and the Natural World* (pp. 197–223). San Francisco: Jossey-Bass.
44. Krill, D.F. (1965). Psychoanalysis, Mowrer and the existentialists. *Pastoral Psychology 16,* October, pp. 27–36.
45. ——— . (1966). Existentialism: A philosophy for our current revolutions. *Social Service Review 40* (3), September, pp. 289–301.
46. ——— . (1968). A framework for determining client modifiability. *Social Casework, 49*(10) December, pp. 602–611.
47. ——— . (1969). Existential psychotherapy and the problem of anomie. *Social Work 14* (2), April, pp. 33–49.
48. ——— . (1978). *Existential Social Work.* New York: Free Press.
49. ——— . (1986). *The Beat Worker.* Lanham, MD: University Press of America.
50. ——— . (1990). *Practice Wisdom.* Newbury Park, CA: Sage.
51. Kuckelmans, J.J. (1967). *Phenomenology: The Philosophy of Edmund Husserl and its Interpretation.* New York: Doubleday.
52. Laing, R.D. (1964). *The Divided Self.* Baltimore: Penguin.
53. ——— . (1967). *The Politics of Experience.* Baltimore: Penguin.
54. Maslow, A.H. (1962). *Toward a Psychology of Being.* Princeton, NJ: Van Nostrand.
55. May, R. (Ed.). (1961). *Existential Psychology.* New York: Random House.
56. ——— . (1967). *Psychology and the Human Dilemma.* Princeton, NJ: Van Nostrand.
57. May, R., Angel, E., & Ellenberger, H.F. (Eds.). (1958). *Existence: A New Dimension in Psychiatry and Psychology.* New York: Basic Books.
58. Moustakas, C. (Ed.). (1956). *The Self: Explorations in Personal Growth.* New York: Harper & Row.

59. Mowrer, O.H. (1961). *The Crisis in Psychiatry and Religion.* Princeton, NJ: Van Nostrand.
60. Nuttin, J. (1962). *Psychoanalysis and Personality.* New York: Mentor-Omega.
61. Offman, W.V. (1976). *Affirmation and Reality.* CA: Western Psychological Services.
62. Perls, F.S. (1969). *Gestalt Therapy Verbatim.* Lafayette, CA: Real People Press.
63. Picardie, M. (1980). Dreadful moments: Existential thoughts on doing social work. *British Journal of Social Work 10,* pp. 483–490.
64. Reich, C. (1970). *The Greening of America.* New York: Random House.
65. Reid, W. (1979). *The Task-centered System.* New York: Columbia University Press.
66. Reinhardt, K.F. (1952). *The Existentialist Revolt.* New York: Unger.
67. Reynolds, D. (1984). *Playing Ball on Running Water.* New York: Quill.
68. Rogers, C. (1961). *On Becoming a Person.* Boston: Houghton Mifflin.
69. ———. (1969). The group comes of age. *Psychology Today 3*(7), December, p.29.
70. Rubin, G.K. (1962). Helping a clinic patient modify self-destructive thinking. *Social Work 7*(1), January, pp. 76–80.
71. Rubinoff, L. (1969). *The Pornography of Power.* New York: Ballantine.
72. Ruesch, J., & Bateson, G. (1968). *Communication: The Social Matrix of Psychiatry.* New York: Norton.
73. Salomon, E. (1967). Humanistic values and social casework. *Social Casework 48* (1), January, pp. 26–32.
74. Satir, V. (1964). *Conjoint Family Therapy.* Palo Alto, CA: Science and Behavior Books.
75. Sinsheimer, R. (1969). The existential casework relationship. *Social Casework 50*(2), February, pp. 67–73.
76. Skinner, B.F. (1971). *Beyond Freedom and Dignity.* New York: Knopf.
77. Stretch, J. (1967). Existentialism: A proposed philosophical orientation for social work. *Social Work 12*(4), October, pp. 97–102.
78. Sutherland, R. (1962). Choosing as therapeutic aim, method, and philosophy. *Journal of Existential Psychiatry 2*(8). Spring, pp. 371–392.
79. Swaine, R.L., & Baird, V. (1977). An existentially based approach to teaching social work practice. *Journal of Education for Social Work 13*(3), Fall, pp. 99–106.
80. Szasz, T. (1984). *The Therapeutic State.* New York: Prometheus Books.
81. Taft, J. (1950). A conception of the growth underlying social casework practice. *Social Casework 21*(5), pp. 311–316.
82. Teilhard de Chardin, P. (1959). *The Phenomenon of Man.* New York: Harper & Row.
83. Tillich, P. (1952). *The Courage to Be.* New Haven: Yale University Press.
84. ———. (1960). *Love, Power, and Justice.* New York: Oxford.
85. Tiryakian, E.A. (1962). *Sociologism and Existentialism.* Englewood Cliffs, NJ: Prentice-Hall.
86. Vontess, C.E. (1979). Cross-cultural counselling: An existential approach. *Personnel and Guidance Journal 58* (2), pp. 117–122.
87. Watzlawick, P., Weakland, J., & Fisch, R. (1974). *Change: Principles of Problem Formation and Problem Resolution.* New York: W.W. Norton.
88. Weiss, D. (1962). Ontological dimension—Social casework. *Social Worker,* June, C.A.S.W.
89. ———. The existential approach to social work. *Viewpoints,* Spring 1967, Montreal.
90. ———. (1968). Social work as authentication. *Social Worker,* February, C.A.S.W.
91. ———. (1969). Self-determination in social work—An existential dialogue. *Social Worker,* November, C.A.S.W.
92. ———. (1970). Social work as encountering. *Journal of Jewish Communal Service,* Spring.
93. ———. (1970). Social work as healing and revealing. *Intervention 50,* Summer.
94. ———. (1971). The existential approach to fields of practice. *Intervention 55,* Fall.
95. ———. (1972). The living language of encountering: Homage to Martin Buber, 1878–1965. *Intervention 57,* Spring.

96. Wheelis. A. (1958). *The Quest for Identity.* New York: W.W. Norton.
97. Wilber, K. (1981). *No Boundary,* Boulder, CO: Shambhaala.
98. Winthrop, H. (1967). Culture, mass society, and the American metropolis; high culture and middlebrow culture: An existential view. *Journal of Existentialism 8* (27), Spring, p. 371.
99. Whittaker, J.K. & Tracey, E.M. (1989). *Social Treatment: An Introduction to Social Work Practice.* New York: Aldine de Gruyte.
100. Yalom, I. (1980). *Existential Psychotherapy.* New York: Basic Books.

CHAPTER 12

FEMINIST THEORY AND SOCIAL WORK PRACTICE

MARY VALENTICH

INTRODUCTION

Feminist social work practice has developed tremendously in the decade since this subject was discussed in the 3rd edition (Valentich, 1986). Then, the existence of a full-fledged feminist social work practice was debatable—but no longer. In company with other disciplines, feminist social work practitioners still use feminist counseling and feminist therapy as overarching designations of practice by women for women (Russell, 1984). But a distinctive social work perspective on such practice is now very much evident in texts such as *Not for Women Only: Social Work Practice for a Feminist Future* (Bricker-Jenkins & Hooyman, 1986); *Feminist Visions for Social Work* (Van Den Bergh & Cooper, 1986); *Feminist Social Work* (Dominelli & McLeod, 1989); *Women and Social Work: Towards a Woman-centered Practice* (Hanmer & Statham, 1989); *Women in Therapy and Counseling* (Walker, 1990); *Feminist Social Work Practice in Clinical Settings* (Bricker-Jenkins, Hooyman, & Gottlieb, 1991); and *Feminist Practice in the 21st Century* (Van Den Bergh, 1995). This is not to suggest that our feminist pioneers kept their social work hats hidden. On the contrary: but the Women's Movement provided new ways of understanding women's situations and working for change, and it involved women from grassroots groups and several helping professions (Gilbert & Osipow, 1991; Marecek & Hare-Mustin, 1991). Our commonalities as feminist counselors and therapists were prominent as we sought support for an approach that challenged traditional ways of practicing with women.

We have not lost our connections with the many manifestations of the Women's Movement (Simon, 1988) and other disciplines, and we continue to draw on the burgeoning literature on feminism. We have, however, greater confidence in the congruence of social work values and feminist practice (Collins, 1986) and can build on our own foundation. As Jimenez and Rice (1990) state:

> Feminism and social work share a commitment to the unique nature and essential dignity of all people. . . . Furthermore, social work's emphasis on the

person-in-environment is congruent with the central methodological theme of feminism—the personal is the political—and the feminist value of personal empowerment is a key underlying theme of social work intervention. (Collins, 1986, pp. 8–9)

This chapter updates developments in feminist theory and feminist social work practice. Space limitations have made inevitable the oversight of important strands of theory and the contributions of some scholar/practitioners who have applied a feminist perspective to a particular problem or population. Feminist social work practice has blossomed too profusely to be fully captured in one chapter. Further, simply to summarize the emergence of feminist social work practice during the 1970s and 1980s would be giving short shrift to those who embarked on a revolutionary venture during what Taylor and Whittier (1983) have identified as the first two stages of the contemporary wave of feminism—resurgence (1966–71) and the feminist heyday (1972–1982). The earlier chapter provides details of the first decade of feminist social work practice (1970–1980) and the period from 1980 to 1985 when feminist social work practice began to mature. In this chapter, we will follow that process of maturing as feminist perspectives are applied to an increasing number of problems and groups.

OVERVIEW OF DEVELOPMENTS

Despite the greater presence of feminist perspectives in social work, feminist theory has not yet fully established itself within the discipline. Nevertheless Sancier (1987, p. 6) states: "Now, the body of feminist work is so large and so impressive that it can no longer be ignored in the field as a whole." Further, there are indicators that consideration of women's issues is more firmly established in the profession. Since the 1980s, accrediting bodies in the United States and Canada have expected that social work education curricula include content on women. The social work journal *Affilia,* initiated in 1986, continues to provide a forum for feminist contributions. Although Nichols-Casebolt, Krysik, and Hamilton (1994) found that articles focusing on women's issues comprised only ten percent of all articles published in selected social work journals between 1982 and 1991, several have devoted special issues to women. Most social work conferences now include papers or sections of the program addressing feminist perspectives or practice.

In 1973, the Council on Social Work Education established a Women's Commission on the Role and Status of Women in Social Work Education. In Canada, the Women's Caucus has met annually since 1975 at the Learned Societies Conference to promote a feminist voice within social work education. The mission of the Association for Women in Social Work, founded in the United States in 1984, has been the infusion of a feminist perspective into the profession (FYI, 1986). In 1995, led by the National Committee on Women's Issues, the National Association of Social Workers proposed forming a section for members interested in improving practice with women, enhancing education about women's issues, developing and advocating for national initiatives related to women's needs, and exploring feminist models of practice (NASW forming, January 1995, p. 5). Finally, in 1988 Mary Bricker-Jenkins called together fifteen women who organized the first gathering of the Women's Community for Feminist Social Work—FemSchool '94 held in Kentucky. The setting for FemSchool '95 was Indianapolis. FemSchool's vision statement, open to on-going revision, includes developing and teaching methods of practice that are grounded in and advance feminist world views and commitments (Sohng et al., 1996).

The wellspring for developments in feminist social work practice remains the Women's Movement (Adamson, Briskin, & McPhail, 1988; Backhouse & Flaherty, 1992; Katzenstein & Mueller, 1987). When fourteen women at the University of Montreal's school of engineering were gunned down on December 6, 1989 (Malette & Chalouh, 1991), feminists throughout Canada responded by intensifying their efforts to address the problems of violence against women. The national consciousness is growing: witness the clear-cut feminist perspective adopted by the Canadian Panel on Violence Against Women (1993):

> . . . we will demonstrate how looking through a feminist lens enables us to see how gender, race and class oppress women and how these forms of oppression are interrelated and interconnected. . . . Violence against women, both now and in the past is the outcome of social, economic, political, cultural inequality. (p. 13)

We are not, however, tied only to events in our own nation. A global feminism has evolved (Bunch, 1993) and events around the world from femicide (Caputi & Russell, 1993), to rape (Valentich, 1994) and genital mutilation (Berg, 1995) have captured the attention and engaged the energies of feminist practitioners who, nonetheless, may be working in one domain of feminist practice. The feminist social work practice literature comes primarily from Australia, Canada, Great Britain, and the United States, but feminist practitioners are increasingly aware of the oppression of women around the world and of women's heroic efforts to altar their circumstances (Taylor & Daly, 1995).

World assemblies such as the United Nations conference held in Beijing in September 1995 foster this global perspective, which has a trickle-down effect on practice everywhere. As well, disruptions in the lives of women and men throughout the world caused by war and epidemics have resulted in more refugees coming to Canada and the United States. These refugees, along with a changing immigrant population, have prompted the helping professions in general, and feminist practitioners in particular, to consider women's problems from a multicultural perspective (Jagger & Rothenberg, 1993). The 1990s have witnessed increasing sensitivity by feminist practitioners to sociocultural, ethnic, and racial diversity.

Feminist perspectives will be considered in the next section, which examines feminism as theory as well as specific theoretical developments relevant to feminist social work practice.

A CONCEPTUAL BASE FOR PRACTICE

Qualitative research is the foundation for much emergent theory, more so than positivistic research. Feminist theory development takes several forms: the revision of existing ideological frameworks to reflect the diversity of women's experience; incorporation of relevant thought systems; formulation of new theories about women; and the critique of concepts and traditional theories about women. Despite the diversity of feminist theory, there are key concepts that pertain to most practice models.

Feminist Frameworks.

Since the chapter that appeared in the previous edition, there has been considerable rethinking about the nature of feminist theory. As Jagger and Rothenberg (1993) note, much was asked of feminist frameworks in the 1970s and 1980s:

> . . . feminist frameworks were integrated theories of women's place both in our present society and in the new society that feminists were struggling to build. We saw feminist frameworks as including descriptive, explanatory, and normative elements, offering both comprehensive analyses of the nature and causes of women's subordination and correlated sets of proposals for ending it. (p. xv)

These frameworks have been considered ideological perspectives and are still employed (Adamson, Briskin, & McPhail, 1988; Freeman, 1990; Sancier, 1990).

Jagger and Rothenberg currently present feminist frameworks through the metaphor of lenses; they identify women's subordination through the lens of sex as conservatism; through gender as liberalism; through class as classical Marxism; through sex/gender and sexuality as radical feminism; and through sex/gender, sexuality, and class as socialist feminism. To reflect changes in theory, in particular, contemporary feminists' dismay with the treatment of race and ethnicity, they offer two new frameworks: multicultural feminism, which views women's subordination through the lens of sex/gender, sexuality, class, and race; and global feminism, which incorporates all the social forces that divide women such as race, class, sexuality, colonialism, poverty, religion, and nationality. All of these forces are seen as integral to the struggle against male domination.

While it was commonplace in the 1970s to characterize the women's movement in terms of liberal, socialist, and radical feminism (Ryan, 1989; Buechler, 1990), Taylor and Whittier (1993) summarize the current situation as follows:

> Feminist ideology today continues to be a mix of several orientations that differ in the scope of change sought, the extent to which gender inequality is linked to other systems of domination, especially class, race/ethnicity, and sexuality, and the significance attributed to gender differences. (p. 534)

Feminism as a mode of analysis involves "certain ways of thinking and of acting that are designed to achieve women's liberation by eliminating the oppression of women in society" (Freeman, 1990, p. 74). Contemporary feminists, however, are less concerned with arguing the root cause of women's subordination, or whether subordination on the basis of sex or gender or some other variable is the most urgent problem facing women. There is mistrust of grand theorizing pertaining to "women" with more attention being given to complex conceptualizations of sex, gender, race, and class. Within social work practice, this type of theory development is exemplified by *Race, Gender & Class* in which Davis and Proctor (1989) present guidelines for practice with individuals, families, and groups based on the research findings relevant to these variables.

New Paradigms

Current developments in feminist theory challenge what may appear as the emergence of more categories. In particular, the growing prominence of poststructuralism and postmodernism within social work warrants recognition. Ann Hartman's (1992) editorial, "In Search of Subjugated Knowledge," drew on the work of Foucault to alert us that knowledge and power are one and that as practitioners and researchers "we must abandon the role of expert, the notion that we are objective observers and our clients are passive subjects to be described and defined" (p. 484). Pardeck, Murphy, and Choi (1994) elaborated on the implications of postmodernism for social work practice, namely, that neither individuals nor systems should be targets for intervention, but rather communities, that is, domains where certain assumptions about reality are acknowledged to have validity. Chambon and Irving (1994) and Pozatek (1994) also consider the linkages between postmodernism and social work. Sands and Nuccio (1992), Brown (1994) as well as Van Den Bergh (1995) make explicit connections between postmodern feminist theory and social work.

Van Den Bergh (1995) considers feminism an epistemological framework that can employ standpoints (Swigonski, 1994), that is, truths or knowledge that derives from the multiplicity of experiences of women. Based on her review of feminist and feminist postmodern literature, she identifies four standpoints that enable practitioners to be more responsive to clients—knowing, caring, connecting, and multiplicity. She concludes that:

> A practice informed by listening to many ways of knowing, centered and located within diverse client life experiences and co-created through relationships that are reflexive and intersubjective, can provide a context for caring, connecting, partnering and community building. (pp. xxxiv–xxxv)

It is difficult to predict how strongly postmodernism will influence feminist theory. Even understanding the nature of this complex set of ideas is a challenge because postmodern feminism is rooted in poststructuralism, postmodernism, postmodern philosophy, and French feminist theory, all of which emerged spontaneously around the same time (Sands & Nuccio, 1992, p. 490). Further, theorists are not easily classified because the boundaries among these schools are problematic, themes overlap, and there are contradictions within schools.

While Sands and Nuccio (1992) present material clearly, that is not the case generally in this literature, with the result that the ideas are not easily accessible and likely far removed from the consciousness of the troubled client. Jagger and Rothenberg (1993, p. 77) state, "Epistemological relativism is not conducive to social activism, and for this reason some feminists have concluded that postmodernism is actually dangerous to feminist political projects." Their view is that feminists have given postmodernism a mixed reception, recognizing some of its features as congruent with feminism, such as its attention to diversity, and yet being concerned about various aspects, such as its language.

Within the context of such debates, feminist scholars have considerably developed the theoretical foundations of feminist practice over the past decade. However, because women's experience of the world is always changing, "feminist theory and values are, by definition, ever tentative, never absolute, and always becoming" (Bricker-Jenkins & Hooyman, 1986, p. 8).

As stated in the earlier chapter, social psychological and sociological theories are more congruent with feminism. Because of the lack of attention to social factors and location of the problem within the client, traditional psychoanalytic formulations are not favored (Lerman, 1986), although there are feminist practitioners who see promise in pursuing psychoanalytic ideas (James, 1992; Marecek & Hare-Mustin, 1991, pp. 529–530). Worell and Remer (1992, pp. 115–121) propose that a psychological theory may be gender-biased if its content and constructs are androcentric, gendercentric, ethnocentric, heterosexist, intrapsychic, or deterministic; a feminist theory would be gender-free, flexible, interactionist, and life-span in its scope. They also demonstrate a process for theory transformation with two selected theories—cognitive behavioral and psychodrama—to a format more suited to feminist practice.

New Theory
Self-in-relation theory (Miller, 1986; Surrey, 1985), derived from the study of women and focusing on women's capacity to connect with others and to speak in a different voice, has many adherents in social work (Berzoff, 1989; Rubenstein & Lawler, 1990). Thus Gillespie (1992, p. 113) in her review of *Women's Growth in Connection* (Jordan, Kaplan, Miller, Stiver, & Survey, 1991) notes:

> The center's [Stone Center] relational psychology is indispensable, a mainstay for any mental health professional who works with women. Whether one agrees with these psychologists' psychoanalytic framework, one simply cannot do without their contributions to the psychology of women. (p. 113)

Similarly, the work of Belenky, Clinchy, Goldberger, and Tarule (1986) on women's different ways of knowing has been well received, in part, because it offers women a range of legitimate learning styles, not simply the option of viewing themselves as less competent than men in employing a rational, logical approach.

A conception of women as oriented to caring, responsibility, and connectedness has had much resonance within social work (Baines, Evans, & Neysmith, 1992;

Grimwood & Popplestone, 1993). While these new theories of women's psychological and moral development are seen "as providing normative models of social work practice that are sensitive to the nature of women's moral development" (Freedberg, 1993, p. 538), they are also subject to criticism. Gould (1988) suggests that Gilligan's (1982) recasting of social and moral development is dominated by a white, middle-class Western conception of adulthood, filtered through a psychological voice. Gilligan is seen as being totally person-oriented in judging moral maturity, rather than taking into account the oppressive circumstances of women's lives. Gould fears that the wholehearted adoption of Gilligan's work might "once again lead to the adoption of a deficiency model that might hinder, rather than help, a disadvantaged group" (p. 414).

Tensions between psychologically and sociologically oriented perspectives are not unique to feminist social work practice. For feminist practitioners, the feminist principle—the personal is the political—still rings true, despite the increasing prominence of conservatism and biologically oriented perspectives.

Critique of Concepts and Theories

A major contribution of feminist theories has been to offer critiques of concepts and perspectives that have not recognized social structural factors as accounting for women's problems. Thus Gould (1987b) suggests that a major flaw in the life model is its reliance on a transactional framework and its underestimation of the power of societal factors. Gould argues that a conflict model might be more useful for promoting advocacy actions to remove structural barriers that have impeded women's participation in society. While a systems perspective does account for the relevant factors influencing a client's situation, it is seen as oriented to the status quo. In general, feminist practitioners seek theories that incorporate institutional change.

The idea of women gaining power to challenge oppressive conditions in their lives contrasts with the image of women as codependent, that is, as somehow involved in being responsible for her own pain (Frank & Golden, 1992). The concept of codependence has become very popular in the self-help literature and refers to "a disease that originates in 'dysfunctional' families where children come to overcompensate for parental inadequacies and develop an excessive sensitivity to the needs of others" (Haaken, 1993, p. 322). While codependence is often described as a feminine malady and seems to support feminist concerns regarding destructive aspects of the patriarchal family, it has received sharp criticism from feminist social workers (Anderson, 1994; Collins, 1993; Frank & Golden, 1992) who sees it as pathologizing women's difficulties. Collins believes that the self-in-relation theorists at the Stone Center provide an alternative perspective on women as seeking connections while asserting their own needs, with the central issue being how to create societal contexts within which growth-producing relationships can flourish.

Key concepts

Gender and related concepts (Richmond-Abbott, 1992) remain central to feminist social work practice, with the important distinction between sex and gender firmly in place. A gender analysis (Ferree, 1993) refers to women using their own experiences, needs, concerns, and realities as women to understand and interpret and issue:

> Through consultations, meetings, readings and discussions, we try to incor-
> porate the experiences of lesbians, native women, women with disabilities,
> young women, older women, poor women, immigrant women, in short,
> women whose life experiences may be the same or different from our own. A
> gender analysis also makes a distinction between sex differences, which are
> those things which physically characterize us as women, and gender differ-
> ences, those things which society has developed and imposed upon us a
> women. (Muzychka, 1995, p. 2)

The complexities of a gender analysis are evident when one reviews the amount of research related to gender that Davis and Proctor (1989) consider with respect to individual, family, and group treatment. Worell and Remer (1992), in their discussion of the psychology of women and gender, also reveal the range of research pertaining to sex-related comparisons, situational contexts, and women's lives. They define gender as "culturally-determined cognitions, attitudes, and belief systems about females and males" (p. 8) and make the point that gender is socially constructed and thus varies across culture, through historical time, and in terms of who makes the observations and judgments.

Not only are we all subject to gender stereotypes, but there may be bias in terms of an "essentialist" position that emphasizes differences between women and men and the contrasting position that ignores or minimizes differences. In Worell and Remer's view, either bias may be problematic with respect to practice with clients. They do, however, present a useful model for understanding gender role functioning as influenced by a range of life development events, psychological processes, and societal forces (p. 13), a conceptualization congruent with a person-in-environment perspective.

The concept that best embodies the sought-for change is empowerment (Hartman, 1993) for the purpose of self-actualization (Bricker-Jenkins, 1991, p. 273). Lazzari (1991, p. 72) notes that empowerment as a goal, a state of being, a process, a specific program, an approach, or a world view is fundamental to both social work and feminism. For Bricker-Jenkins and Hooyman (1986), empowerment is a central feminist ideological theme and the core of feminist social work practice.

McWhirter (1991) notes that empowerment has been used with increasing frequency in social work and other literature, but that there is no consensus on its meaning. Her analysis focuses on empowerment as a process affecting not just the individual, but the individual in relation to others, to the community, and to the society. Her definition captures the process of change.

> Empowerment is the process by which people, organizations, or groups who
> are powerless (a) become aware of the power dynamics at work in their life
> context; (b) develop the skills and capacity for gaining some reasonable con-

trol over their lives, (c) exercise this control without infringing upon the rights of others, and (d) support the empowerment of others in their community. (p. 224)

With respect to the empowerment of women of color, Gutiérrez (1991) proposes that movement from apathy to action involves four psychological stages—from increasing self-efficacy to developing a group consciousness, to reducing self-blame and the assumption of personal responsibility.

VALUE BASES OF THEORY

Feminist social work practice is guided by theories of human behavior that vary in the extent of their attention to the past. Feminist analysis often focuses on the more recent or contemporary social forces that influence the conditions of the client's life. The time orientation is primarily present and future directed. Human nature is considered inherently good or neutral rather than negative (McWhirter, 1991, p. 224) and humanity is seen as relating to the environment in an independent manner, not in terms of "power over" or domination (Collins, 1986, p. 216). Eco-feminism (Adams, 1991; Mies & Shiva, 1993) involves feminists examining their relationships with animals and the environment and respect to exploitation.

The concern with possible exploitation, even inadvertently, pervades feminist practitioners' views regarding the dynamics of the relationship between practitioner and client. The helping relationship has been intensively scrutinized with respect to power differentials and possible abuse. For some, this has meant refusing to play the expert role as practitioner and adopting a range of measure to lessen the distance between client and practitioner; others have not denied their knowledge and skills, but have recognized the client's expertise in her life, and also have taken measures to engage the client in a collaborative, understandable process, for example, judicious self-disclosure and avoidance of diagnostic labels.

NATURE OF PRACTICE

Feminist social work practice is a diverse enterprise, in part, because of the varying theoretical perspectives within feminism, the groups and problems that comprise one's work, and the setting for practice with its particular mandate. Thus, a social worker in private practice may have little need for psychiatric labels and view them as antithetical to her client's well-being (Marecek & Hare-Mustin, 1991, pp. 524–525); yet another social worker in a mental health setting cannot avoid using these categories. Both practitioners may feel strongly committed to their feminist stance. The commonalities for feminist practitioners include the following ideological themes: "an end to patriarchy, empowerment, process, the personal is the political, unity-diversity, validation of the non-rational, and consciousness raising/praxis" (Bricker-Jenkins & Hooyman, 1986, p. 8). These themes or principles are not understood identically by all feminists, nor is there agreement on all the elements presented, but they represent anchoring points for most feminist practitioners.

While the goal of the encounter is empowerment of the client, this may mean individual or social change; that is, the intervention may be at the level of the individual, couple, family, organizations, the community, or institutions. All these foci will not necessarily receive attention in any one helping relationship, but feminist social work practice is committed to promoting change in any oppressive system.

PRACTICE MODELS

Because feminist practice is an ever-evolving system, there is not just *one* practice model. The major approaches will be identified by principal authors.

Bricker-Jenkins and Hooyman

Practitioners, in a 1983 study, described their approach as generalist; incorporating consciousness raising and educational techniques to foster empowerment of the client as well as engagement of the client and sometimes, the practitioner in social action; and utilizing a collaborative working relationship that relies heavily on groups and support networks, and coalitions in political work (Bricker-Jenkins & Hooyman, 1986, p. 29). Bricker-Jenkins and Hooyman assert that ideology is the core of feminist practice and that feminist practitioners seek congruence of all aspects of their work with feminist ideology.

Bricker-Jenkins, Hooyman, and Gottlieb (1991) state that feminist practice is a "work in progress," the principal author of feminist practice theory is the feminist practitioner, and the "chief currency of practice is made up of case studies and personal reflections" (p. 6). Thus, they present case studies and discussions from practitioners in hospital, mental health, day-care, and rural settings to illustrate core concepts of feminist analysis—the personal is the political, empowering women, and celebrating the strengths of women as survivors.

In the final chapter, Bricker-Jenkins (1991) discusses how feminist practitioners enable clients to achieve self-actualization. The assessment process includes "a mutual examination of constraints and opportunities in personal, interpersonal and political power dynamics" (p. 290), with special attention given to basic, concrete needs and to physical and psychological safety. Methods and techniques for personal/political transformation include validation of the client's reality and consciousness raising as a problem-posing dialogue. Mobilizing resources and creating nurturing relationships and validating environments is an important component of practice. The action that results is transformative: the client knows herself, in community, to be capable of and responsible for the creation of reality.

Van Den Bergh and Cooper

There is considerable comparability between Bricker-Jenkins and Hooyman's feminist principles and those outlined by Van Den Bergh and Cooper (1986). The latter include "eliminating false dichotomies and artificial separations, reconceptualizing power, valuing process as equally as product, validating renaming, and believing that the personal is political" (p. 4).

In their summary of *feminist visions for social work,* Van Den Bergh and Cooper (1986) argue that, by eliminating false dichotomies such as direct and indirect services, social work could move toward more of a generalist model. Individuals would still have their areas of expertise, but the "overall training and practice model would be more integrated and generalist; and social work practice would be more holistic, ecological, and preventive" (p. 13). The remainder of their book illustrates the comprehensive nature of a feminist perspective that may be applied to research, mental health, social development, and community organizing.

In *Feminist Practice in the 21st Century,* Van Den Bergh (1995) adopts a postmodern perspective and reviews the implications for social work practice of continuing to pursue gender-associated bifurcated thinking. That is, rather than ascribing certain traits to men and others to women, thereby fostering the dominion of men over women, she believes that it would be more useful for social workers to practice in a society that values human dignity and worth as well as collaborative efforts to provide care for its members. Professional relationships would be characterized as partnerships, a more valid description of what transpires in feminist practice, rather than assumptions about the "equality" of client-worker relationships. Van Den Bergh argues for local rather than universal truths with knowledge in narrative form, based on an individual's perceptions of reality and its meanings, within a context; a practice venue that is community-based, with its members perceiving reality in a similar fashion; and deconstructed knowledge base that "can be altered by reconstructing truth through inclusion of the voices of disempowered people" (p. xix).

Van Den Bergh favors social work's person-in-environment (PIE) model and ecological perspectives as they seem syntonic with the postmodern precept that "truth" is a function of one's ontological experience: thus client's problems are contextually based in the client's history and life space and may be conceptualized as "paralyzing narratives" or stories that limit possibilities (p. xx). If knowledge is socially constructed, and knowledge and power are linked, Van Den Bergh asks which of our practice models and theories that guide our interventions have been derived by listening to the voices of our clients. She proposes that standpoint perspectives (Davis, 1993; Stanley & Wise, 1983, 1990; Swigonski, 1994) that assume that all people see the world in terms of their own sociocultural context can have great value for informing feminist social work research and practice.

The standpoints most evident to Van Den Bergh portrayed "action as well as values and represent social work . . . as the operationalization of activism and caring on behalf of client advocacy and empowerment" (p. xxx). She sees feminism as moving beyond the five principles previously elaborated by herself and Cooper (1986) with the following standpoints articulating an awareness of the multiplicity of women's experiences and hence the diversity of their ways of knowing: (1) knowing, (2) connecting, (3) caring, and (4) diversity. She concludes that "a practice informed by listening to many ways of knowing, centered and located within diverse client life experiences and co-created through relationships that are reflexive and intersubjective, can provide a context for caring, connecting, partnering, and community building" (pp. xxxiv–xxxv).

In the remainder of *Feminist Practice in the 21st Century,* various authors examine methods including clinical, family-centered practice and group work; fields of practice (five); and special populations (eight). Thus, Land (1995, pp. 3–19) describes feminist clinical social work as empowerment practice and a philosophy of psychotherapeutic intervention rather than a set of techniques. She notes that feminist social workers practice with a range of theoretical orientations including cognitive-behavioral, psychodynamic, psychosocial, problem-solving, family systems, constructivist, or interpersonal approaches, and they may use treatment modalities of the individual, couple, family, or group to achieve goals that may include intrapsychic, interpersonal, behavioral, and sociocultural change.

Land summarizes what various authors since the 1970s have identified as basic components of feminist practice: validating the social context; revaluing positions enacted by women; recognizing difference in male and female experience; rebalancing perceptions of normality and deviance; an inclusive stance; attention to power dynamics in the therapeutic relationship; recognizing how the personal is the political; a deconstructive stance; and a partnering stance. Inclusive scholarship that values a variety of scholarly traditions as well a challenge to reductionistic models that restrict male and female behavior are contributions of feminist practice to knowledge development.

Worell and Remer

A detailed presentation of empowerment feminist therapy is offered by Worell and Remer (1992) for all clinicians practicing feminist therapy. Based on a radical feminist ideology that focuses on power differences in societal conditions of men and women, the model views women's low social power as the basis for their problems and argues for both social and individual changes. Worell and Remer present the now-familiar principles of the personal is political, egalitarian relationships (to the extent possible), and valuing the female perspective. For each principle, they suggest a number of appropriate counseling goals, with the majority focused on individual rather than social change goals, although the former may be necessary for action toward the two social goals mentioned—"acquire skills for enacting environmental change and restructure institutions to rid them of discriminatory practices" (p. 94).

For each of their principles, Worell and Remer identify several techniques, two of which are unique to feminist therapy—sex role analysis and power analysis. Although the authors recognize that sex roles are socially constructed and that gender role is a frequent designation, they have chosen to use "sex roles" (p. 12). In addition, they discuss assertiveness, consciousness-raising groups, bibliotherapy, reframing and relabeling, and therapy-dymystifying strategies.

In Worell and Remer's (1992) view, three types of feminist therapy—radical, gender-role and woman-centered—are integrated into empowerment feminist therapy. While the radical approach is most commonly espoused in Canada and the

United States, adherents of the other approaches can be found. The second group focuses on the differences in gender role socialization and works primarily toward individual change. The third, according to Worell and Remer, is "composed of both cultural feminists and psychodynamic therapists, and believes that there are fundamental differences in the psychological make-up of women and men" (p. 88). The counseling goals in this approach are to assist clients to value their female characteristics such as cooperation, empathy, and altruism.

Russell

Worell and Remer's model is congruent with Russell's (1984) work on feminist counseling presented in the earlier chapter and still applicable:

> What is unique is the constellation of skills, their avowed feminist purpose, and their interaction in the counseling encounter, which gives feminist counseling its special character. The net result of skill interactions is a counseling mode that is active, direct, externally oriented, present focused, behaviorally oriented, and egalitarian. (p. 53)

The skills Russell presents range from straightforward to complex and include behavior feedback, self-disclosure, positive evaluation of women, social analysis, and encouragement of total development. Her discussion of skills focus on work with the individual client, with collective action a possibility in the termination phase of counseling.

Hanmer and Statham

A woman-centered practice is proposed by Hanmer and Statham (1989) in *Women and Social Work*. Adopting a gendered perspective, the authors draw on the experiences of social workers and clients in Great Britain to reveal their commonalities and differences. They examine women and poverty, the labor market, women's careers as caregivers, relationships with men, identity and esteem issues, and strategies for the workplace.

In their chapter on practice, Hanmer and Statham note that the focus is on enhancing women's sense of control and coping, and that all social work approaches are available to workers, although approaches must be adapted so that they are women-affirming (pp. 128–129). They recommend women-only groups, linking women with agencies addressing women's needs, increasing resources for women, involving women in decision-making and policy processes in agencies, and drawing up a code for feminist practice. The code provides useful directives to agency-based social workers for altering agency practices and behavior with clients, but does not directly address the need for social change or how to achieve it. This aspect of woman-centered practice may be implicit in their restating that women's problems are multidimensional and require the use of the full range of social work methods: individual, group, and community work.

White's (1995) exploratory study of ten social workers in England revealed that they were reluctant to categorize their practice in terms of various feminist perspectives. Commonality with service users, beyond the occasional empathetic feelings, was regarded as either impossible or deeply problematic; and gender as the basis for commonality of experiences and interests between social workers and clients was questioned. Finally, social workers' identities as feminists were not a given, but depended on the contingencies of their statutory role. This study points to the importance of more systematic and larger-scale study of the nature of feminist practice in different contexts.

Laidlaw and Malmo

A practice model that differs somewhat from those presented above is based on healing. Laidlaw and Malmo (1990), two psychologists, present work of feminist therapists, some of whom are social workers, who employ techniques oriented to the intuitive, nonverbal, and imaginative (Richardson, Donald, & O'Malley, 1985/86). The following techniques are described: guided imagery, role playing, storytelling, music, hypnosis, massage, consciousness raising, and visualization. Each chapter includes the voice of a client relating how she has experienced the therapy. Laidlaw and Malmo and the other therapists consider the healing process as transformative in that it is more than cumulative or cognitive, and they also recognize how past events influence present feelings, thoughts, and behavior. The therapists help their clients "reclaim and heal their lost and damaged childhood selves, [and] the healing they refer to involves an inner change made up of two parts: the identification and expression of feelings and the reframing of destructive and unhealthy beliefs (p. xiv)."

THE RELATIONSHIP

The above practice models rely on a worker-client relationship of partnership or sisterhood, although the latter term is not used. The particular theoretical orientation employed by practitioners influences the extent to which there is acknowledgement and use of transference. Thus, several authors in *Healing Voices* (Laidlaw et al., 1990), drawing on psychodynamic traditions, recognize that women's healing may involve a journey to childhood where the traumas occurred; the transference becomes central to the reparenting of reclaiming of the inner child. More typically, there is concern registered about the risk of abuse when the power of the worker is accentuated through use of the transference as well as other powerful techniques such as paradoxical injunction or mysterious prescriptions such as rituals (Valentich & Anderson, 1989). Hartman (1993, p. 504) voices this concern by suggesting that the effort should be "to keep transference to a minimum and to foster independence, competence, strengths, and confidence."

With respect to all other aspects of the helping process, the choice of theoretical orientation will be critical. The past as embodied in the history will be more important in approaches that are psychodynamically oriented and less important in others.

ASSESSMENT

In developing a shared understanding of either the distant or more immediate past, the practitioner and client will focus on the social conditions of the woman's life. There have been concerns regarding assessment procedures or instruments that appear to be more oriented to traditionally masculine ways of perceiving the world (Handy, Valentich, Cammaert, & Gripton, 1985). The feminist critique within psychology has been quite severe (Lewin & Wild, 1991) as many measures were designed to test only males in stereotypical settings. Some feminist social work practitioners do make use of tests, for example, the Hudson scales (1982), and occasionally social work authors refer to the use of instruments for assessment and evaluation (Lundy, 1993; Rathbone-McCuan, Tebb, & Harbert, 1991).

LANGUAGE

The language of feminist practice is a political language employing terms such as "advocacy," "empowerment," "liberation," and "transformation" (Bricker-Jenkins, 1991, p. 284). Terms such as "therapy" and "treatment" that suggest pathology are viewed with caution. The bifurcation of professional activity into separate domains, for example, micro and macro, is also seen as detracting from an integrated feminist practice approach that offers personal and social transformation to its clients.

LENGTH OF ENCOUNTER

There is no predetermination of the duration of feminist helping approaches; again, theoretical orientations as well as factors related to the setting will be influential. Generally, except for psychodynamically oriented models, lengthy contact tends not to be favored because of concerns regarding the increased dependence that might ensue. Yet, it is recognized that personal and social transformations will not occur overnight. Hence, a periodic case strategy, which involves the client's returning when she sees fit, is in keeping with a principle of self-directed growth (Valentich & Gripton, 1985).

SPECIFIC METHODS APPLICATION

Individuals and Groups

Individual and group work are, in a sense, the givens in feminist practice approaches. It is assumed that women will be seen individually and, if at all possible, in a group. As noted in the earlier chapter, consciousness-raising groups have been the primary vehicle for awakening women's sense of themselves as actors in a patriarchal social system and these groups, in modified form, are used in the practice situation.

The special issue of *Journal of Social Work with Groups* entitled "Groupwork with Women/Groupwork with Men" (Garvin & Reed, 1983) heralded social work's awareness of the impact of gender in work with all kinds of groups. A later special issue focused on "Violence: Prevention and Treatment in Groups" (Getzel, 1988). Articles addressed family violence, work with abusive men, child abuse victims, children coping with the violent death of a classmate, rape survivors, and battered women. Lewis (1992), however, believes that the practice of social group work "has succumbed to the pressures for containment and management of symptoms and to the definition of participants (clients) not as equal partners and members in a common endeavor but as somehow damaged and defective beings" (p. 273). She argues for the application of feminist perspectives to social group work to regain group work's promise of "developing the full range of human potential, not discarding spirituality, nurturance or emotion, but adding capacities for assertiveness, conflict resolution, decision making, cooperation and accomplishment of important social public tasks" (p. 277).

   Feminist Groupwork is a social group work text by Butler and Wintram (1991) based on their experiences with working-class rural and urban women's groups in England. Home's (1993) review is favorable although she notes that empowerment is dealt with mainly on an individual level, with only some attention to how collective empowerment of women can be accomplished. In Gutiérrez' (1991, pp. 205–206) view, small group work is the ideal modality for empowering women or changing institutions because other techniques can be integrated within it. Garvin and Reed (1995) present a useful analysis of group work models with implications for a feminist model that will enable social worker to use groups to achieve social justice and empowerment in all types of practice with individuals, organizations, and communities.

Couples

Work with couples is a method that receives relatively light treatment in the feminist literature, except within the context of family social work (Nelson-Gardell, 1995), marital and family counseling (Enns, 1988), or feminist family therapy (Goodrich, Rampage, Ellman, & Halstead, 1988; Ellman, Rampage, & Goodrich, 1989). The occasional article is found that incorporates a feminist perspective, for example, Basham's (1992) review of resistance in work with couples. There is, however, an abundant literature that criticizes existing family therapy models and proposes the application of feminist principles (Avis, 1989b).

Families

While social work practice with couples and families predates the emergence of several family therapy schools, social work was relegated to a secondary role in family therapy during the 1970s. Criticisms of the patriarchal structure of family therapy units and theory that posited father as the head of the family were voiced softly. It was not until Hare-Mustin's (1978) article that a stream of criticism began. Now a mighty river flows.

   It is beyond the scope of this chapter to detail the history of the evolution of feminist family therapy (Carter, 1992), the trends (Goldner, 1992; Piercy & Sprenkle, 1990); or the contributions from members of several disciplines (Avis, 1989b; Leslie

& Clossick, 1992). Major players include Lois Braverman (1988a,b) and the numerous members of the editorial board of *Feminist Family Therapy,* which was established in 1986. Nor is the development of feminist family therapy solely a North American enterprise; key contributors include social workers Laurie MacKinnon (1985, 1987, 1993), originally from Canada, and her Australian colleague, Kerrie James (1983, 1984, 1989, 1990, 1992), who with Dusty Miller and Deborah McIntyre, in various combinations, have published numerous articles significantly influencing the evolution of feminist family therapy. There are several classic texts (Ault-Riché, 1986; Walter, Carter, Papp, & Silverstein, 1988) and special issue of journals as well as review articles that identify the range of criticisms questioning concepts such as circularity and neutrality, decrying woman blaming, the emphasis on the system as opposed to the individual, and the ignoring of power dynamics within the family or the social context (Nelson-Gardell, 1995; Paterson & Trathen, 1994). Suffice to say that feminist family therapy is alive and well.

Laird (1995) notes that are least three other perspectives, overlapping to some extent—postmodernism, social construction, and cultural metaphors—have contributed to the evolution of family therapy as a more mutual venture. Feminist practitioners are no longer hesitant to welcome long-ignored clients—single mothers, and lesbian couples and their children—into their practice. Gender questions (Sheinberg & Penn, 1991) and a feminist family therapist behavior checklist (Chaney & Piercy, 1988) have been developed; and techniques involving the cocreation of narratives (Gorman, 1993) are being employed. Cautionary notes are, however, sounded (Laird, 1995): "Client stories are privileged or constrained by such factors as gender, age, race, sexual orientation, skin color, and social class, depending on how such factors are 'storied' in the large surround" (p. 29). Feminist family therapy, however, is moving to address issues of power related to race, class, gender, culture, and sexual orientation (Almeida, 1994).

Community

While feminist practice clearly entails work at the community level, the literature tends to consist of case studies on changing organizations, working with women's groups to change policies and services, and practice within a specific community such as a rural setting. Empowerment, however, is a theme that is central to group and community work (Breton, 1994; Zippay, 1995). In her analysis of a feminist approach to community organizing, Weil (1986) details how feminist issues and roles can be incorporated into social policy, community liaison, community development, and planning, participation, and political empowerment.

PRINCIPAL APPLICATIONS IN SOCIAL WORK PRACTICE

RANGE OF APPLICATIONS

Feminist perspectives have been applied in numerous areas of social work practice. Thus *Feminist Practice in the 21st Century* (Van Den Bergh, 1995) considers fields of practice such as the world of work, rural women's work, the political arena, the peace movement, and women's well-being throughout the world; and special populations such as women of color, poor women, homeless women, women with substance abuse problems, lesbian and gay clients, women with HIV/AIDS, women who have been abused and who have abused, and elderly women. *Feminist Social Work Practice in Clinical Settings* (Bricker-Jenkins et al., 1991) offers articles relating to practice in hospital, mental health, day-care, rural, and organizational settings. The range of applications is bounded only by the energy and creativity of the practitioners.

ISSUES OF DIVERSITY

During the 1970s and, to some extent the 1980s, feminist practice concerned itself with the issues relevant to the lives of the dominant group in the Women's Movement in Canada and the United States, namely, white and middle-class women. Just as the Women's Movement has become more diversified and representative of women of color, so has feminist practice begun to address the concerns not of the generic "woman," but of women in their diversity with respect to color, ethnicity, sexual orientation, age, and class.

The journal *Women and Therapy* has recognized this diversity and the desire of feminist practitioners to become more culturally competent by publishing two special issues—"The Politics of Race and Gender in Therapy" (Fulani, 1987) and "Jewish Women in Therapy: Seen but Not Heard" (Cole & Rothblum, 1991). Overall, increased attention has been given no concerns of women of all ethnic and racial groups by psychologists (Comas-Diaz, 1987; Ho, 1990; Sieber & Cairns, 1991; Skodra, 1992) and social workers (Bernard, Lucas-White, & Moore, 1993; Gold, 1993; Gould, 1987a). Feminist social work practice is becoming increasingly ethnic-sensitive and thereby better suited for practice with all women.

WORK WITH MALE CLIENTS

There have been applications of feminist practice perspectives to work with men (Collins, 1992; Tolman, Mowry, Jones, & Brekke, 1986) as well as discussion of the implications of sexism for men (Thompson, 1995). With the occasional exception (Sancier, 1987; Walter et al., 1988), the feminist literature remains silent on the role of men with respect to a feminist future or whether or how feminist social work practitioners can engage men. Laidlaw and Malmo (1990) suggest the applicability of their healing approach to work with men; the other practice models omit consideration of this question. Given that many social workers do not limit their practice to women clients, the omission is serious. Gender-sensitive practice (Valentich, 1992) draws on feminist and masculinist perspectives for purposes of developing a unified framework for practice that attends to women and men as clients and that promotes institutional changes to achieve equality of women and men. The mainstream feminist social work practice literature leaves the "men question" in the air.

CLIENT TYPES

Since feminist practice models tend not to use diagnostic categories or other typologies, one cannot readily identify diagnostic types for which feminist practice is more or less appropriate. Given that feminist clients will tend to seek feminist practitioners, such clients will likely be favorably disposed toward this form of practice. By the same token, clients with conservative ideologies relating to family and gender roles might be uncomfortable with some aspects of feminist approaches. This is not to suggest that feminist practitioners would be imposing their values on clients. A counterindication for engagement of a client by a feminist practitioner would be the client's expressed distaste for feminism as a philosophy or movement.

PROBLEM AREAS

There are several prominent problem areas where feminist social work practice has become established and the literature is extensive. Additionally, there are numerous problems where there is some documentation regarding application of a feminist practice approach. A commentary follows on the major problem areas with literature drawn from social work and other disciplines

Sexual Assault

Since the 1970s the Women's Movement has vigorously drawn societal attention to the pervasive social problem of rape or sexual assault of women, the latter term being the legal designation in Canada. Research into the nature of sexual assault, its effects, and effective services has continued unabated (Burgess, 1991). Controversy still exists about the nature of the programs that agencies should offer—from crisis to longer-term counseling, to education, and social action—by whom, and under what auspices (Ignagni, Parent, Perreault, & Willatar, 1988; Valentich & Gripton, 1984). There is research support for feminist helping approaches to women who initially are victimized, but move to the survivor status (Hutchinson & McDaniel, 1986).

It is now recognized that men and boys can be victims of sexual assault and also require services (Isely, 1991). Marital and acquaintance sexual assault or date rape are viewed as problems (Bergman, 1992; Yegidis, 1988), as is sexual harassment in the workplace (Kaplan, 1991) and sexual exploitation by helping professionals (Gripton & Valentich, 1991). There is increased attention to services for offenders (Warren, Gripton, Francis, & Green, 1994), some of whom will be women. How to help persons who have been sexually assaulted and are at risk of HIV or other sexually transmitted diseases has also become a practice focus (Laszlo, Burgess, & Grant, 1991; Ledray, 1991). Finally, there is greater awareness of sexual assault in war as part of a systematic policy of ethnic cleansing (Valentich, 1994).

Sexual Abuse

The 1980s was the decade during which helping professionals, researchers, and the public recognized the pervasiveness of sexual abuse of children, first girls and then boys, both by relatives and by strangers (Avis, 1992; Bagley & King, 1990; Gelles & Conte, 1990; Kelly & Lusk, 1992). The practice literature, feminist and otherwise, is enormous (Everstine & Everstine, 1989; Gavey, Florence, Pezaro, & Tan, 1990; Maddock & Larson, 1995; Trepper & Barrett, 1989).

The long-term effects of sexual abuse of girls (Anderson, Yasenik, & Ross, 1993; Bagley & Ramsay, 1986; Kilpatrick, 1992) have been studied, as well as the effectiveness of the services offered to adult women (Alexander, Neimeyer, Follette, Moore, & Harter, 1989; Gold & Anderson, 1994; Jehu, Klassen, & Gazan, 1986; 1988; Lundy, 1993; Mennen, 1990; Westerland, 1992). Satanic and ritual abuse has been identified (McShane, 1993) as well as the debate regarding its nature (Ross, 1995). The complexity of interlocking emotional, physical, and sexual abuse as causing psychiatric problems for women has also received attention (Bagley, in press; Moeller, Bachmann, & Moeller, 1993).

The 1990s have also seen the development of sharp disagreements concerning repressed memories of child sexual abuse survivors. Feminists have long argued that children should be believed when they report sexual abuse, and by extension, feminists have believed adult women regarding their reported abuse histories. Unfortunately, some professionals may unwittingly foster the expression of stories of abuse. Resolution of this controversy, involving professionals and laypersons on all sides, in the near future seems unlikely.

Woman Battering

Just as the Women's Movement raised social awareness of sexual assault and sexual abuse, it also identified the dangers of the family with respect to the physical, emotional, and other abuse directed by men toward their female partners (Dobash & Dobash, 1979; Dutton, 1988; Kurz, 1993; Valentine, 1986). Research and practice in this field occurs within two competing frameworks, one being the feminist and the other, the family violence perspective as exemplified by the work of Straus, Gelles, and Steinmetz (1980). *Physical Violence in American Families* (1990) is a comprehensive account of the research of Straus and Gelles and their collaborators.

While the feminist perspective places female-male relations at the center of its analysis, the family or domestic violence perspective does not see aggression as a gender-specific problem (Kurz, 1993). Rather, violence is reported as being initiated at the same rate within families by men and women, albeit with more serious physical consequences for women, and the violence between male and female partners is seen as part of a pattern of violence occurring among all family members. Both perspectives hold that the subordination of women is a factor in creating violence; feminist, however, view it as a central factor as opposed to one of several contributing factors (Kurz, 1993). Carlson's reviews (1991, 1992) are helpful in sorting out the nature of violence between men and women as reported in family violence studies and abuse as experienced primarily by female victims of their male partners.

The implications for practice are dependent on the perspective employed. Thus, in her review of social work literature dealing with battered women, Gutiérrez (1987) found that "authors with a psychological perspective were apt to suggest individual responses, authors with a sociological view tend to suggest individual or community responses, and authors with a feminist orientation were likely to suggest community or societal interventions" (p. 43). An example of the latter are the recommendations of the Canadian Panel on Violence against Women (1993) that aim to achieve equality of women and to eliminate violence against women through measures directed to key sectors of the society.

The predominant measure has been the establishment of shelters for women and children who are seeking safety, after deciding to leave an abusive situation (Tutty, 1993). A continuing concern for feminists (Prieur, 1995; Davis & Hagen, 1992) has been that violence against women has been reconstituted into a professional psychiatric or counseling problem with the "battered wife" concept (Zetlin, 1989) substituted for the political analysis of violence by men against women. Backhouse (1992) expresses similar concerns regarding the intrusion of professionalized social services into a political issue.

Professional social workers, however, have been involved in offering feminist oriented services that have included a time-limited safe setting with individual and group work (Cantin & Rinfret-Raynor, 1993; Davis & Hagen, 1992; Mancoske, Standifer, & Cauley, 1994; Shepard, 1991). Pâquet-Deehy, Rinfret-Raynor, and Larouche (1992, p. 5) describe a feminist model that includes an initial interview to reduce emotional tensions and support the women's decision to return to or break with her spouse; short-term therapy focusing in the women's self-esteem and autonomy; medium- to long-term intervention to reduce victim behavior through assertiveness training, expression of anger, reclaiming of emotions, acquiring information on violence, and social conditioning; and participation in a group in order to break through her isolation. The woman is enabled to grow through a variety of means in order to renegotiate a contract with her partner. The intervention model draws on structural, psychosocial, and sociobehavioral paradigms and employs several sociobehavioral and cognitive techniques as well as postulating "the need for a denunciation of sexist socialization and violence" (p. 7).

Programs for men who batter developed during the 1980s and often focused on anger management, sometimes with little or no contact with the partner (Carlson, 1991; National Clearinghouse, 1994). Groups are the primary vehicle for helping men who abuse (Kaufman, 1992; Russell, 1995), with feminist, cognitive-behavioral, and psychoeducational approaches widely used (National Clearinghouse, 1994). Group approaches seem to offer the best hope for changing the behavior of some men who abuse (Dutton, 1995).

The most controversial aspect of professional services to deal with women battering pertains to marital and family counseling or therapy. There is extensive literature on the various approaches to working with families in which violence has occurred (Hansen & Harway, 1993; Lupton & Gillespie, 1994; Pressman, Cameron, & Rothery, 1989). Since the 1980s, traditional marital and family therapy approaches have been subjected to an onslaught of feminist criticism. The gist of the feminist critique is that various forms of family therapy were slow to acknowledge the existence of wife or partner abuse and then ignored the power dynamics within families as well as access of the partners to other societal resources. Women have, therefore, been seen as contributing to their own abuse (Avis, 1992).

Golden and Frank (1994) argue against couple counseling, family systems therapy, mediation, and any other approach that does not recognize the power difference between men and women in a family. From their perspective, men may best be helped by arrest and "strong, confrontive, educational counseling that isolates men from their partners, defines the spectrum of abuse, and holds abusers solely responsible for their actions" (p. 637). A comprehensive, unified approach (Dwyer, Smokowski, Bricourt, & Wodarski, 1995; Pennell, 1995; Pressman, 1989) based on a system of mutual caring, and involving a range of resources, protections, and services, seems to be a desirable route.

Mental Health

The above problem areas as well as others have sometimes been considered under the umbrella of women's mental health. Witness the scope of the special issue of the *Canadian Journal of Community Mental Health* entitled "Women and Mental Health" (McCannell, 1986). Similarly, two major conferences sponsored by the Canadian Mental Health Association, in Banff, Canada, in 1989 and 1991, with the latter involving approximately 1000 people, engaged laypersons, professionals, consumers, and providers of services in discussing the many forms of violence against women, the harm caused by some of the traditional services, and the nature of feminist approaches.

Feminist practice also concerns itself with various forms of what has traditionally been referred to as mental illness. For example, a serious problem for women is depression (Jensen, 1993). There are also issues pertaining to women caring for mentally ill relatives (Scheyett, 1990) and to the classification of mental illnesses (Wetzel, 1991). Concerns regarding the medical model are still pervasive in the feminist practice literature (Penfold & Walker, 1986).

Health

Milner and Widerman (1994) shed light on the application of feminist perspectives to women's health issues. They found thirty-six articles in the professional journals from 1985 to 1992, with over half addressing issues of reproduction and sexuality including pregnancy, family planning, abortion, substance abuse in pregnancy, and fetal protection policies. The remaining articles dealt with medical diagnoses including HIV/AIDS/STDs, cancer, illnesses associated with aging, PMS, Turner's syndrome, and chronic fatigue syndrome. The authors note that many serious diseases are not examined and that the content of the articles suggests that women are still considered primarily in terms of their reproductive and sexual functioning. In their view, the overall number of articles is small, and the majority deal with practice implications only on the individual or group level, not the family, community, or society levels. Only one-fourth of the articles were written from a feminist perspective and most of these were found in *Affilia*.

A welcome addition to the literature in this area is the special issue of *Social*

Work in Health Care entitled "Women's Health and Social Work: Feminist Perspectives" (Olson, 1994). Within the broad topic of women's health, the new reproductive technologies are gaining attention (Carter, 1992; CRIAW, 1989; Moss, 1988; Walther & Young, 1992), as is substance abuse (Turner, 1992; Nelson-Zlupko, Kauffman, & Dore, 1995) and disability (Quinn, 1994).

Other Problem Areas

Numerous other problem areas have been considered from a feminist social work practice perspective—child welfare (Costin, 1985); sexual problems (Keystone, 1994; Valentich & Gripton, 1992); adolescent girls (D'Haene, 1995); adolescent single mothers (Freeman, Logan, & Gowdy, 1992); various subgroups of elderly women (Browne, 1995; Butler & Weatherley, 1992; Carlton-LaNey, 1992; Perkins, 1992); lesbians (Morrow, 1993; Swigonski, 1995; special issue of *Smith College Studies in Social Work* (Laird, 1993) and *Women & Therapy* (Rothblum, 1988); and homeless women (Brown & Ziefert, 1990).

ADMINISTRATIVE TRAINING FACTORS

TEACHING FEMINIST PRACTICE

The preparation of feminist social work practitioners is ripe for examination. On the one hand, there is the position presented by Bricker-Jenkins et al., (1991) that they know no one who learned feminist practice in a school of social work because feminist practice is not the progeny or property of academics:

> Rather, this new approach evolved from the efforts of feminist social workers to reconcile and integrate their feminist perspectives and commitments with the conventional theories and methods in which they were trained. (p. 6).

Walker (1990) holds a similar view of feminist counseling as a perspective, not a technique to be learned in a workshop:

> It reflects, rather, a way of being, believing and understanding . . . that arises from many sources that flow into, and feed, one another. It is essentially a perspective that allows fluidity, acknowledges interconnectedness, and encourages exploration. (p. 73)

Curriculum Developments

On the other hand, within academe, there are questions being raised and actions taken that do impinge on the development of feminist practice competence. First, there is the question of how well schools are responding to the requirements of accreditation bodies to include content on women in their curricula. Presumably well enough, given the successful accreditation of programs since the mid-1980s. There is, however, a concern regarding the knowledge base: Nichols-Casebolt et al. (1994) found that the articles focusing on women's issues comprised less than ten percent of all articles published in the sampled journals during the decade ending in 1991. Additionally, how well have students and practitioners incorporated the knowledge regarding women's issues (Marshall, Valentich, & Gripton, 1991)?

Finally, should the content on women be in a separate course or infused throughout the curriculum? Vinton's (1992) research on the knowledge and attitudes of 70 undergraduate majors suggest that those students who had taken a separate course had greater knowledge of female biological processes and the historical processes affecting women. Freeman's (1990) research on social work educators' views of women's problems indicates that feminist theory does provide a lens for viewing women's problems and that a "women's issues" component in the curriculum cannot be assumed to be equivalent to a component on feminist theory.

There are other curriculum developments that focus on how to infuse more relevant content into the curriculum. A very comprehensive proposal to integrate women's issues into an MSW curriculum is offered by female faculty at Arizona State University's School of Social Work (Carter et al., 1994). Additionally, Pennell, Flaherty, Gravel, Milliken, and Neuman (1993) report on the results of teaching feminist content in three classes of predominantly white students and one class of native Canadian and immigrant students.

Attention has also been given to how feminist and related perspectives might be addressed in field education (Rogers, 1995; Lazzari, 1991) and research education (Krane, 1991). Avis (1989a) offers a proposal for integrating gender into a family therapy curriculum with attention to course formats, the organization and process of training, the impact of gender training on students, and the different processes experienced by men and women.

Feminist Pedagogy
There is considerable interest in feminist pedagogy with respect to teaching social work practice (Dore, 1994), social work practice with groups (Cramer, 1995); feminist practice (Bartlett, Tebb, & Chadha, 1995), feminist counseling skills (Russell, 1986); feminist identification (Parnell & Andrews, 1994), and ways in which women and men in social work communicate and engage in learning (De Lange, 1995).

How well prepared are social workers for feminist practice? It is premature to comment, but there are promising developments within the schools as well as opportunities for updates on practice at most social work conferences. Elective courses on feminist practice, sessions at conferences, and workshops are typically much sought after; and although the numbers are small, FemSchool is being offered for the third year in 1996.

SUPERVISION

There is some commentary on the nature of supervision with respect to feminist practice (Ault-Riché, 1988; Chernesky, 1986). It is recognized that the process of acquiring knowledge regarding women and the identification with women's causes is emotionally both invigorating and draining (Kirst-Ashman, 1992). While some settings will foster opportunities for increasing one's identification with women's issues, others will constrain social workers who wish to speak out, advocate, lobby, and engage in social action with clients and other practitioners (Pâquet-Deehy et al., 1992). Hence, guidance during this process is critical. Given that many feminist social work practitioners choose private practice, traditional forms of supervision are less available; occasionally, practitioners form consultative groups or relationships.

ETHICAL ISSUES

There are questions deriving from feminism about the realities of practice with respect to valuing diversity of cultures, presenting feminist values when clients have "self-determined" patriarchy, and social workers addressing sexism in their own family and work spheres (Glassman, 1992). Discussion of these issues in some forum, if not hierarchically organized supervision, would be welcome, especially to practitioners in an early phase of their careers.

Given the range of feminist dilemmas in practice, including issues pertaining to dual relationships (Gripton & Valentich, 1991; Kagle & Giebelhausen, 1994; Valentich & Gripton, 1992, 1994), it is not surprising that resolution of ethical issues is an important training factor. As Margolies (1990) notes, feminist practitioners have had a difficult time practicing within the confines of the traditional ground rules of therapy and have experimented with respect to setting time limits, fee arrangements, and contact outside of the professional relationship. Two excellent resources for reviewing the complexities of ethical issues within feminist practice are *Feminist Ethics in Psychotherapy* by Lerman and Porter (1990) and *Ethical Decision Making in Therapy: Feminist Perspectives* by Rave and Larsen (1995).

In resolving ethical dilemmas, the practitioner is advised to record both the decision and action (Valentich & Gripton, 1994). Recording, an important administrative requirement, gets minimal attention in feminist practice literature. Undoubtedly, practitioners must meet the reporting requirements of their settings; yet, concerns about labeling and its harmful effects remain. Further, since the early days of grassroots feminist organizations, feminist practitioners have been concerned about the confidentiality of their clients' records and have taken various precautions, including a "bare bones" approach to recording, especially if the courts wished to have access to the sexual and other histories of clients.

EMPIRICAL BASE OF PRACTICE

In Kravetz' (1986) examination of women and mental health, she observes that "because the emergence and development of family therapy are relatively recent, there has been little empirical investigation of its processes and outcomes" (p. 117). She reviews the few available studies and finds that the results give some indication of the benefits of family therapy. One cannot claim that feminist social work practice is still in its infancy, but the empirical base is only modestly developed, although some areas of application include considerable research-oriented literature. This situation should be understood in the context of the extensive feminist critique of research, in particular, of the positivistic tradition. Thus, Davis and Srinivasan (1995), in noting the dearth of research on working with battered women, state:

> Most research published in academic and professional journals is patriarchal and androcentric (see Davis, 1986; Eichler, 1988; and Reinharz, 1992). This bias is seen most clearly in research on intervention models that are designed to maintain existing role relationships. It is also reflected in the choice of the research methods themselves. (p. 50).

The problems of sexist research identified by Eichler (1988) and others—androcentricity, overgeneralization, gender insensitivity, double standards, and familism—may be overcome, in particular, as feminist researchers develop designs intended to empower the participants in a research process. The research can be collaborative or participatory and may include an action component (Richardson & Taylor, 1993).

A feminist perspective can even be applied to empirical clinical practice with its single-case or group research methodologies (Ivanoff, Robinson, & Blythe, 1987). Further, the two texts, *Race, Gender and Class* (Davis & Proctor, 1989) and *Feminist Perspectives in Therapy* (Worell & Remer, 1992) rely on research to support their models of practice. Occasionally, research using a comparative treatment groups design (Mancoske, Standifer, & Cauley, 1994) has produced results that warrant further study with larger samples. Nonetheless, because of a mistrust of "male-dominated" research approaches, the empirical base is modest. This may change as feminist practitioners increasingly turn to qualitative approaches and/or other designs and methodologies that engage the participants in the research endeavor in a beneficial fashion.

THE FUTURE

The developments in feminist social work practice since the mid-1980s suggest that feminist perspectives will become more influential for all social work practitioners and their clients. These perspectives show promise of resolving some of the divisions in practice, for example, between micro and macro practice, or between those who practice in mainstream as opposed to alternative settings. Feminism promotes women's voices being heard about the diverse nature of their personal and professional experiences, with the expectation that this will lead to individual and institutional change, even within the worlds of social work education and practice.

Nor is social work the only helping profession giving considerable attention to feminist perspectives (Gilbert & Osipow, 1992; Marecek & Hare-Mustin, 1991). This gathering of forces means that developments in feminist theory and practice will accelerate. However, the overall political climate in countries where feminist practice thrives in increasingly conservative; hence, there will be no easy route to equality of women and men, and an end to the oppressions related to color, class, region, age, and health. In short, feminist social work practitioners, in company with like-minded individuals, will face opposition and challenge, but in pursuing individual and collective change, they may find fulfillment and liberation.

REFERENCES

Adams, C.J. (1991). Ecofeminism: Anima, animus, animal. In L. Richardson & V. Taylor (Eds.), *Feminist frontiers III* (pp. 522–524). New York: McGraw-Hill.

Adamson, N., Briskin, L., & McPhail, M. (1988). *Feminist organizing for change: The contemporary women's movement in Canada.* Toronto: Oxford University Press.

Alexander, P., Neimeyer, R., Follette, V., Moore, M., & Harter, S. (1989). A comparison of group treatments of women sexually abused as children. *Journal of Consulting and Clinical Psychology, 57* (4), 479–483.

Almeida, R.V. (Ed.) (1994). *Expansions of feminist family theory through diversity.* Binghamton, NY: Haworth Press.

Anderson G., Yasenik, L., & Ross, C. (1993). Dissociative experiences and disorders among women who identify themselves as sexual abuse survivors. *Child Abuse and Neglect, 17*(5), 677–686.

Anderson, S.C. (1994). A critical analysis of the concept of codependency. *Social Work, 39*(6), 677–685.

Ault-Riché, M. (1986). *Women and family therapy.* Rockville, MD: Aspen Systems.

Ault-Riché, M. (1988). Teaching an integrated model of family therapy: Women as students, women as supervisors. In L. Braverman (Ed.). *Women, feminism and family therapy.* Binghamton, NY: Haworth Press.

Avis, J.M. (1982). Current trends in feminist thought and therapy: Perspectives on sexual abuse and violence within families in North America. *Journal of Feminist Family Therapy, 4*(3/4), 87–99.

Avis, J.M. (1989a). Integrating gender into the family therapy curriculum. *Journal of Feminist Family Therapy, 1*(2), 3–26.

Avis, J.M. (1989b). Reference guide to feminism and family therapy. *Journal of Feminist Family Therapy, 1*(1), 93–100.

Avis, J.M. (1992). Where are all the family therapists? Abuse and violence within families and family therapy's response. *Journal of Marital and Family Therapy, 18*(3), 225–232.

Backhouse, C. (1992). The contemporary women's movements in Canada and the United States: An introduction. In C. Backhouse & D.H. Flaherty (Eds.). *Challenging times: The women's movement in Canada and the United States* (pp. 3–15). Montreal & Kingston: McGill-Queen's University Press.

Backhouse, C., & Flaherty, D.H. (Eds.). (1992). *Challenging times: The women's movement in Canada and the United States* (pp. 3–15). Montreal & Kingston: McGill-Queen's University Press.

Bagley, C. (in press). A typology of child sexual abuse: Addressing the paradox of interlocking emotional, and physical and sexual abuse as cause of adult psychiatric sequels in women. *The Canadian Journal of Human Sexuality.*

Bagley, C., & King, K. (1990). *Child sexual abuse: The search for healing.* London: Tavistock/Routledge.

Bagley, C., & Ramsay, R. (1986). Sexual abuse in childhood: Psychosocial outcomes and implications for social work practice. In J. Gripton & M. Valentich (Eds.). *Social work practice in sexual problems* (pp. 33–47). New York: Haworth Press.

Baines, C.T., Evans, P.M., & Neysmith, S.M. (Eds.). (1991). *Women's caring: Feminist perspectives on social welfare.* Toronto: McClelland & Stewart.

Baines, C.T., Evans, P.M., & Neysmith, S.M. (1992). Confronting women's caring: Challenges for practice and policy. *Affilia, 7*(1), 21–44.

Bartlett, M., Tebb, S., & Chadha, J. (1995). Teaching feminist practice: Support, transition, change. *Affilia 10*(4), 442–457.

Basham, K. (1992). Resistance and couple therapy. *Smith College Studies in Social Work, 62*(3), 245–264.

Belenky, M.F., Clinchy, B.M., Goldberger, N.R., & Tarule, J.M. (1986). *Women's ways of knowing: The development of self, voice, and mind.* New York: Basic Books.

Berg, K.C. (1995). *Issues surrounding female genital mutilation and immigrant and refugee women in Canada.* Unpublished manuscript.

Bergman, L. (1992). Dating violence among high school students. *Social Work, 37*(1), 20–27.

Bernard, W.T., Lucas-White, L., & Moore, D.E. (1993). Triple jeopardy: Assessing life experiences of Black Nova Scotian women from a social work perspective. In M. Valentich, M. Russell, & G. Martin (Eds.), Women and social work: Celebrating our progress [Special Issue]. *Canadian Social Work Review, 10*(2), 256–274.

Berzoff, J. (1989). From separation to connection: Shifts in understanding women's development. *Affilia, 4*(1), 45–58.

Braverman, L. (Ed.). (1988a). *A guide to feminist family therapy.* New York: Harrington Park Press.

Braverman, L. (Ed.). (1988b). *Women, feminism and family therapy.* Binghamton, NY: Haworth Press.

Breton, M. (1994). On the meaning of empowerment and empowerment-oriented social work practice. *Social Work with Groups, 17*(3), 23–37.

Bricker-Jenkins, M. (1991). The propositions and assumptions of feminist social work practice. In M. Bricker-Jenkins, N.R. Hooyman, & N. Gottlieb (Eds.), *Feminist social work practice in clinical settings* (pp. 271–303). Newbury Park, CA: Sage.

Bricker-Jenkins, M., & Hooyman, N.R. (Eds.). (1986). *Not for women only: Social work practice for a feminist future.* Silver Spring, MD: National Association of Social Workers.

Bricker-Jenkins, M., Hooyman, N.R., & Gottlieb, N. (Eds.). (1991). *Feminist social work practice in clinical settings.* Newbury Park, CA: Sage.

Brown, C. (1994) Feminist postmodernism and the challenge of diversity. In A.S. Chambon & A. Irving (Eds.), *Essays on postmodernism and social work* (pp. 33–46). Toronto: Canadian Scholars Press.

Brown, K.S., & Ziefert, M. (1990). A feminist approach to working with homeless women. *Affilia, 5*(1), 6–20.

Browne, C.V. (1995). Empowerment in social work practice with older women. *Social Work, 40*(3), 358–364.

Buechler, S.M. (1990). *Women's movements in the United States.* New Brunswick, NJ: Rutgers.

Bunch, C. (1993). Women's subordination worldwide: Global feminism. In A.M. Jaggar & P.S. Rothenberg (Eds.). *Feminist Frameworks* (3rd ed). New York: McGraw-Hill.

Burgess, A.W. (Ed.). (1991). *Rape and sexual assault III.* New York: Garland Press.

Butler, S.S., & Weatherley, R.A. (1992). Poor women at midlife and categories of neglect. *Social Work, 37*(6), 510–515.

Butler, S., & Wintram, C. (1991). *Feminist groupwork.* Newbury Park, CA: Sage.

Canadian Panel on Violence Against Women. (1993). *Changing the landscape: Ending violence–achieving equality.* Ottawa: Minister of Supply and Services Canada.

Cantin, S., & Rinfret-Raynor, M. (1993). Battered women using social services: Factors associated with dropouts. In M. Valentich, M. Russell, & M. Martin (Eds.). Women and social work: Celebrating our progress [Special issue]. *Canadian Social Work Review, 10*(2), 202–219.

Caputi, J., & Russell, D.E.H. (1993). In L. Richardson & V. Taylor (Eds.), *Feminist frontiers III* (pp. 424–431). New York: McGraw-Hill.

Carlson, B.E. (1991). Domestic Violence. In A. Gitterman. *Handbook of social work practice with vulnerable populations* (pp. 471–502). New York: Columbia University Press.

Carlson, B.E. (1992). Questioning the party line on family violence. *Affilia, 7*(2), 94–110.

Carlton-LaNey, I. (1992). Elderly black farm women: a population at risk. *Social Work, 37*(6), 517–523.

Carter, B. (1992). The evolution of feminist family therapy in the United States. *Journal of Feminist Family Therapy, 4*(3/4), 53–58.

Carter, C., Coudrouglou, A., Figueira-McDonough, J., Lie, G.Y., MacEachron, A.E., Netting, F.E., Nichols-Casebolt, A., Nichols, A.W., & Risley-Curtiss, C. (1994). Integrating women's issues in the social work curriculum: A proposal. *Journal of the Council on Social Work Education, 30*(2), 200–216.

Chambon, A.S., & Irving, A. (Eds.). (1994). *Essays on postmodernism and social work.* Toronto: Canadian Scholars' Press.

Chaney, S.E., & Piercy, F.P. (1988). A feminist family therapist behaviour checklist. *American Journal of Family Therapy, 16*(4), 305–318.

Charter, N. (1991). Unexamined history repeats itself: Race and class in the Canadian reproductive rights movement. *Fireweed, 33,* 44–59.

Chernesky, R.H. (1986). A new model of supervision. In N. Van Den Bergh & L.B. Cooper (Eds.), *feminist visions for social work* (pp. 128–148). Silver Spring, MD: National Association of Social Workers.

Cole, E., & Rothblum, E.D. (Eds.). (1991). Jewish women in therapy: Seen but not heard. [Special issue]. *Women & Therapy, 10*(4).

Collins, B.G. (1986). Defining feminist social work. *Social Work, 31*(3), 214–219.

Collins, B.G. (1993). Reconstructing codependency using self-in-relation theory: A feminist perspective. *Social Work, 38*(4), 470–476.

Collins, D. (1992). Thoughts of a male counsellor attempting a feminist approach. *Journal of Child and Youth Care, 7*(2), 69–74.

Comas-Diaz, L. (1987). Feminist therapy with mainland Puerto Rican women. *Psychology of Women Quarterly, 11*(4), 461–474.

Costin, L.B. (Ed.). (1985). Toward a feminist approach to child welfare [Special edition]. *Child Welfare, LXIV*(3).

Cramer, E.P. (1995). Feminist pedagogy and teaching social work practice with groups: A case study. *Journal of Teaching in Social Work, 11*(1/2), 192–215.

CRIAW/ICREF Working Group on Reproductive Technologies. (Eds.). (1989, October). *Reproductive technologies and women: A research tool.* Ottawa: CRIAW/CREF.

Davis, L. (1986). A feminist approach to social work research. *Affilia, 1*(1), 32–47.

Davis, L. (1993). Feminism and constructivism: Teaching social work practice with women. In J. Laird (Ed.), *Revisionary social work education: A social constructionist approach* (pp. 147–163). New York: Haworth Press.

Davis, L., & Hagen, J.L. (1992). The problem of wife abuse: The interrelationship of social policy and social work practice. *Social Work, 37*(1), 15–20.

Davis, L., & Proctor, E.K. (1989). *Race, gender and class: Guidelines for practice with individuals, families and groups.* Englewood Cliffs, NJ: Prentice Hall.

Davis, L.V., & Srinivasan M. (1995). Listening to the voices of battered women: What helps them escape violence. *Affilia, 10*(1), 49–69.

De Lange, J. (1995). Gender and communication in social work education: A cross-cultural perspective. *Journal of Social Work Education, 31*(1), 75–81.

D'Haene, M.T. (1995). Evaluation of feminist-based adolescent group therapy. *Smith College Studies in Social Work, 56*(2), 153–166.

Dobash, R.E., & Dobash, R. (1979). *Violence against wives.* New York: Free Press.

Dominelli, L., & McLeod, E. (1989). *Feminist social work.* Chicago: Lyceum.

Dore, M.M. (1994). Feminist pedagogy and the teaching of social work practice. *Journal of Social Work Education, 30*(1), 97–106.

Dutton, D.G. (1988). *The domestic assault of women: Psychological and criminal justice perspectives*. Newton, MA: Allyn & Bacon.

Dutton, D.G. (1995). *The batterer: A psychological profile*. New York: Basic Books.

Dwyer, D.C., Smokowski, P.R., Bricout, J.C., & Wodarski, J.S. (1995). Domestic violence research: Theoretical and practice implications for social work. *Clinical Social Work Journal, 23*(2), 185–198.

Eichler, M. (1988). *Nonsexist research methods: A practical guide*. Winchester, MA: Allen & Unwin.

Ellman, B., Rampage, C., & Goodrich, T.J. (1989). A feminist family therapy approach towards "A standard pair." *Journal of Feminist Family Therapy, 1*(1), 45–60.

Enns, C.Z. (1988). Dilemmas of power and equality in marital and family counseling: Proposals for a feminist perspective. *Journal of Counseling and Development, 67*(4), 242–248.

Everstine, D.S., & Everstine, L. (1989). *Sexual trauma in children and adolescents*. New York: Brunner/Mazel.

Ferree, M.M. (1993). Beyond separate spheres: Feminism and family research. In L. Richardson, & V. Taylor (Eds.), *Feminist frontiers III* (pp. 237–257). New York: McGraw-Hill.

Frank, P.B., & Golden, G.K. (1992). Blaming by naming: Battered women and the epidemic of co-dependence. *Social Work, 37*(1), 5–6.

Freedberg, S. (1993). The feminine ethic of care and the professionalization of social work. *Social Work, 38*(5), 535–540.

Freeman, E.M., Logan, S.L., & Gowdy, E.A. (1992). Empowering single mothers. *Affilia, 7*(2), 123–141.

Freeman, M.L. (1990). Beyond women's issues: Feminism and social work. *Affilia, 5*(2), 72–89.

Fulani, L. (Ed.). (1987). The politics of race and gender in therapy [Special issue]. *Women & Therapy, 6*(4).

F.Y.I. (1986). Association for women in social work. *Affilia, 1*(4), 64.

Garvin, C.D., & Reed, B.G. (Eds.). (1983). Groupwork with women/groupwork with men [Special Issue]. *Journal of Social Work with Groups, 6*(3/4).

Garvin, C.D., & Reed, B.G. (1995). Sources and visions for feminist group works: Reflective processes, social justice, diversity, and connection, in N. Van den Bergh (Ed.), *Feminist practice in the 21st century* (pp. 41–43). Washington, DC. NASW Press.

Gavey, N., Florence, J., Pezaro, S., & Tan, J. (1990). Mother-blaming, the perfect alibi: Family therapy and the mothers of incest survivors. *Journal of Feminist Family Therapy, 2*(1), 1–26.

Gelles, R.J., & Conte, J.R. (1990). Domestic violence and sexual abuse of children: A review of research in the eighties. *Journal of Marriage and the Family, 52*(4), 1045–1058.

Getzel, G.S. (1988). Violence: Prevention and treatment in groups [Special issue]. *Social Work with Groups, 11*(3).

Gilbert, L.A., & Osipow, S.H. (1991). Feminist contributions to counseling psychology. *Psychology of Women Quarterly, 15*(4), 537–547.

Gillespie, D. (1992). [Review of the book *Women's growth in connection*]. *Affilia, 7*(3), 113–114.

Gilligan, C. (1982). *In a different voice*. Cambridge: Harvard University Press.

Glassman, C. (1992). Feminist dilemmas in practice. *Affilia, 7*(2), 160–166.

Gold, K., & Anderson, L. (1994). On feminism in action: Developing resources for incest survivors through a training project for service providers. *Affilia, 9*(2), 190–199.

Gold, N. (1993). On diversity, Jewish women, and social work. In M. Valentich, M. Russell, & M. Martin (Eds.), Women and social work: Celebrating our progress [Special issue]. *Canadian Social Work Review, 10*(2), 240–255.

Golden, G.K., & Frank, P.B. (1994). When 50-50 isn't fair: The case against couple counseling in domestic abuse. *Social Work, 39*(6), 636–637.

Goldner, V.I. (1992). Current trends in feminist thought and therapy: U.S.A. *Journal of Feminist Family Therapy, 4*(3/4), 73–80.

Goodrich, T.J., Rampage, C., Ellman, B., & Halstead, K. (1988). *Feminism and family therapy: A case book.* New York: W.W. Norton.

Gorman, J. (1993). Postmodernism and the conduct of inquiry in social work: *Affilia, 8*(3), 247–264.

Gould, K.H. (1987a). Feminist principles and minority concerns: Contributions, problems, and solutions. *Affilia, 2*(3), 6–19.

Gould, K.H. (1987b). Life models versus conflict models: A feminist perspective. *Social Work, 32*(4), 346–351.

Gould, K.H. (1988). Old wine in new bottles: A feminist perspective on Gilligan's theory. *Social Work, 33*(5), 411–415.

Grimwood, C., & Popplestone, R. (1993). *Women, management and care.* London: Macmillan.

Gripton, J., & Valentich, M. (1991). Sexual exploitation of clients by counsellors: The Canadian scene. *SIECANN Journal, 6*(4), 33–38.

Gutiérrez, L.M. (1987). Social work theories and practice with battered women: A conflict-of-values analysis. *Affilia, 2*(2), 36–52.

Gutiérrez, L.M. (1991). Empowering women of color: A feminist model. In M. Bricker-Jenkins, N. Hooyman, & N. Gottlieb (Eds.), *Feminist social work in clinical settings* (pp. 199–214). Newbury Park, CA: Sage.

Haaken, J. (1993). From Al-Anon to ACOA: Codependence and the reconstruction of caregiving. *Signs, 18*(2), 321–345.

Handy, L.C., Valentich, M., Cammaert, L.P., & Gripton, J. (1985). Feminist issue in sex therapy. In M. Valentich & J. Gripton (Eds.), *Feminist perspectives on social work and human sexuality* (pp. 69–80). New York: Haworth Press.

Hanmer, J., & Statham, D. (1989). *Women and social work: Towards a woman-centered practice.* Chicago: Lyceum Books.

Hansen, M., & Harway, M. (Eds.). (1993). *Battering and family therapy: A feminist perspective.* Newbury Park, CA: Sage.

Hare-Mustin, R.T. (1978). A feminist approach to family therapy. *Family Process, 17*(2), 181–194.

Hartman, A. (1992). In search of subjugated knowledge. *Social Work, 37*(6), 483–484.

Hartman, A. (1993). The professional is political. *Social Work, 38*(4), 365–366, 504.

Ho, C.K. (1990). An analysis of domestic violence in Asian American communities: A multicultural approach to counseling. *Women & Therapy, 9*(1–2), 129–150.

Home, A.M. (1993). (Review of the book *Feminist groupwork*]. *Social Work with Groups, 16*(4), 125–128.

Hudson, W.W. (1982). *The clinical measurement package: A field manual.* Chicago: Dorsey Press.

Hutchinson, C.H., & McDaniel, S.A. (1987). The social reconstruction of sexual assault by women victims: A comparison of therapeutic experiences. *Canadian Journal of Community Mental Health, 5*(2), 17–33.

Ignagni, E., Parent, D., Perreault, Y., & Willats, A. (1988, Winter/Spring). Around the kitchen table. *Fireweed, 26,* 69–81.

Isely, P. (1991). Adult male sexual assault in the community: A literature review and group treatment model. In A. Burgess (Ed.), *Rape and sexual assault III* (pp. 161–193). New York: Garland Press.

Ivanoff, A., Robinson, E.A.R., & Blythe, B.J. (1987). Empirical clinical practice from a feminist perspective. *Social Work, 32*(5), 417–423.

Jagger, A.M., & Rothenberg, P.S. (Eds.). (1993). *Feminist frameworks.* New York: McGraw-Hill.

James, K. (1984). Breaking the chains of gender. *Australian Journal of Family therapy, 5*(4), 241–248.

James, K. (1992). Why feminists have become interested in psychoanalysis–Or "la plus ça change . . ." *Journal of Feminist Family Therapy, 4*(3/4), 81–85.

James, K., & MacKinnon, L. (1990). The "incestuous family" revisited: A critical analysis of family therapy myths. *Journal of Marital and Family Therapy, 16*(1), 71–88.

James, K., & McIntyre, D. (1983). The reproduction of families: The social role of family therapy? *Journal of Marital and Family Therapy, 9*(2), 119–129.

James, K., & McIntyre, D. (1989). "A momentary gleam of enlightenment": Towards a model of feminist family therapy. *Journal of Feminist Family Therapy, 1*(3), 3–24.

Jehu, D. (1988). *Beyond sexual abuse: Therapy with women who were childhood victims.* Chichester, UK: John Wiley.

Jehu, D., Klassen, C., & Gazan, M. (1986). Cognitive restructuring of distorted beliefs associated with childhood sexual abuse. In J. Gripton & M. Valentich (Eds.), *Social work practice in sexual problems* (pp. 49–69). New York: Haworth Press.

Jensen, C.C. (1993). Treating major depression. *Affilia, 8*(2), 213–222.

Jimenez, M.A., & Rice, S. (1990). Popular advice to women: A feminist perspective. *Affilia, 5*(3), 8–26.

Jordan, J.V., Kaplan, A.G., Miller, J.B., Stiver, I.P., & Surrey, J.L. (1991). *Women's growth in connection.* New York: Guilford Press.

Kagle, J.D., & Giebelhausen, P.N. (1994). Dual relationships and professional boundaries. *Social Work, 39*(2), 213–220.

Kaplan, S.J. (1991). Consequences of sexual harassment in the workplace. *Affilia, 6*(3), 50–65.

Katzenstein, M.F., & Mueller, C.M. (Eds.). (1987). *The women's movements of the United States and western Europe.* Philadelphia: Temple University Press.

Kaufman, Jr. G. (1992). The mysterious disappearance of battered women in family therapists' offices: Male privilege colluding with male violence. *Journal of Marital and Family Therapy, 18*(3), 233–243.

Kelly, R., & Lusk, R. (1992). Theories of pedophilia. In W. Donohue & J. Geer (Eds.), *The sexual abuse of children: Theory and results* (Vol. 1) (pp. 168–203). Hillsdale, NJ: Lawrence Erlbaum Associates.

Keystone, M. (1994). A feminist approach to couple and sex therapy. *Canadian Journal of Human Sexuality, 3*(4), 321–326.

Kilpatrick, A. (1992). *Long-range effects of child and adolescent sexual experiences: Myths, mores and menaces.* Hillsdale, NJ: Lawrence Erlbaum Associates.

Kirst-Ashman, K.K. (1992). Feminist values and social work: A model for educating nonfeminists. *Areté, 17*(1), 13–25.

Krane, J. (1991). Teaching social work research. *Affilia, 6*(4), 53–70.

Kravetz, D. (1986). Women and mental health. In N. Van Den Bergh & L. Cooper (Eds.), *feminist visions for social work* (pp. 100–127), Silver Spring, MD: National Association of Social Workers.

Kurz, D. (1993). Social science perspectives on wife abuse: Current debates and future directions. In P.B. Bart, & E.G. Moran (Eds.). *Violence against women: The bloody footprints* (pp. 252–269). Newbury Park, CA: Sage.

Laidlaw, T., Malmo, C., & associates. (1990). *Healing voices: Feminist approaches to therapy with women.* San Francisco: Jossey-Bass.

Laird, J. (Ed.). (1993). Lesbians and lesbian families: Multiple reflections [Special issue]. *Smith College Studies in Social Work, 63*(3).

Laird, J. (1995). Family-centered practice: Feminist, constructionist, and cultural perspectives. In N. Van Den Bergh (Ed.), *Feminist practice in the 21st century* (pp. 30–39). Washington, DC: NASW Press.

Land, H. (1995). Feminist social work in the 21st century. In N. Van Den Bergh, (Ed.), *Feminist practice in the 21st century* (pp. 3–19). Washington, DC: NASW Press.

Laszlo, A.T., Burgess, A., & Grant, C.A. (1991). HIV counseling issues and victims of sexual assault. In A.W. Burgess (Ed.), *Rape and sexual assault III* (pp. 221–232). New York: Garland Press.

Lazzari, M.M. (1991). Feminism, empowerment, and field education. *Affilia, 6*(4), 71–87.

Ledray, L.E. (1991). Sexual assault and sexually transmitted disease: The issues and concerns. In A.W. Burgess (Ed.). *Rape and sexual assault III* (pp. 181–193). New York: Garland Press.

Lerman, H. (1986). From Freud to feminist personality theory: Getting here from there. *Psychology of Women Quarterly, 10*(1), 1–18.

Lerman, H., & Porter, N. (Eds.). (1990). *Feminist ethics in psychotherapy.* New York: Springer.

Leslie, L.A., & Clossick, M.L. (1992). Changing set: teaching family therapy from a feminist perspective. *Family Relations, 41*(3), 256–263.

Lewin, M., & Wild, C.L. (1991). The impact of the feminist critique on tests, assessment, and methodology. *Psychology of Women Quarterly, 15*(4), 581–596.

Lewis, E. (1992). Regaining promise: Feminist perspectives for social group work practice [Special issue, Group work reaching out: People, places, and power]. *Social Work with Groups, 15*(2–3), 271–284.

Lundy, M. (1993). Explicitness: The unspoken mandate of feminist social work. *Affilia, 8*(2), 184–199.

Lupton, C., & Gillespie, T. (Eds.). (1994). *Working with violence.* London: Macmillan.

MacKinnon, L. (1993). Systems in settings: The therapist as power broker. *Australia and New Zealand Journal of Family Therapy, 14*(3), 117–122.

MacKinnon, L., & Miller, D. (1985). The sexual component in family therapy: A feminist critique. In M. Valentich & J. Gripton (Eds.), *Feminist perspectives in social work and human sexuality* (pp. 81–101), New York: Haworth Press.

MacKinnon, L., & Miller, D. (1987). The new epistemology and the Milan approach: Feminist and socio-political considerations. *Journal of Marital and Family Therapy, 13*(2), 139–155.

Maddock, J.W., & Larson, N.R. (1995). *Incestuous families: An ecological approach to understanding and treatment.* Dunmore, PA: Norton Professional Books.

Malette, L., & Chalouh, M. (Eds.). (1991). *The Montreal massacre.* Charlottetown, PEI: Gynergy Books.

Mancoske, R.J., Standifer, D., & Cauley, C. (1994). The effectiveness of brief counseling services for battered women. *Research on Social Work Practice, 4*(1), 53–63.

Marecek, J., & Hare-Mustin, R.T. (1991). A short history of the future: Feminism and clinical psychology. *Psychology of Women Quarterly, 15*(4), 521–536.

Margolies, L. (1990). Cracks in the frame: Feminism and the boundaries of therapy. *Women & Therapy, 9*(4), 19–35.

Marshall, C., Valentich, M., & Gripton, J. (1991). Development of a "knowledge about women" scale. *Canadian Social Work Review 8*(1), 28–39.

McCannell, K. (Ed.). (1986). Women and mental health [Special issue]. *Canadian Journal of Community Mental Health, 5*(2).

McShane, C. (1993). Satanic sexual abuse: A paradigm. *Affilia, 8*(2), 200–212.

McWhirter, E.H. (1991), Empowerment in counseling. *Journal of Counseling and Development, 69*(3), 222–227.

Mennen, F.E. (1990). Dilemmas and demands: Working with adult survivors of sexual abuse. *Affilia, 5*(4), 72–86.

Miles, M., & Shiva, V. (1993). *Ecofeminism.* London: Zed Books.

Miller, J.B. (1986). *Toward a new psychology of women* (2nd ed.). Boston: Beacon.

Milner, L., & Wilderman, E. (1994). Women's health issues: A review of the current literature in the social work journals, 1985–1992. *In Women's Health and Social Work: Feminist Perspectives* (pp. 145–172). New York: Haworth Press.

Moeller, T., Bachmann, G., & Moeller, J. (1993). The combined effects of physical, sexual and emotional abuse during childhood: long-term mental-health consequences for women. *Child Abuse and Neglect, 17*(5), 623–640.

Morrow, D.F. (1993). Social work with gay and lesbian adolescents. *Social Work, 38*(6), 655–660.

Moss, K.E. (1988). New reproductive technologies: Concerns of feminists and researchers. *Affilia, 3*(4), 38–50.

Muzychka, M. (1995). *Women matter: Gender, development and policy.* St. John's, NF: Provincial Advisory Council on the Status of Women, Newfoundland and Labrador.

NASW forming women's issues section (1995, January). *Connection: The Association for Women in Social Work Newsletters,* p. 5.

National Clearinghouse on Family Violence. (1994). *Canada's treatment programs for men who abuse their partners.* Ottawa: National Clearinghouse on Family Violence, Family Violence Prevention Division, Health Canada.

Nelson-Gardell, D. (1995). Feminism and family social work. *Journal of Family Social Work, 1*(1), 77–95.

Nelson-Zlupko, L., Kauffman, E., & Dore M.M. (1995). Gender differences in drug addiction and treatment: Implications for social work intervention with substance-abusing women. *Social Work, 40*(1), 45–54.

Nichols-Casebolt, A., Krysik, J., & Hamilton, B. (1994). Coverage of women's issues in social work journals: Are we building an adequate knowledge base? *Journal of Social Work Education, 30*(3), 348–362.

Olson, M.M. (Ed.). (1994). Women's health and social work: Feminist perspectives [Special issue]. *Social Work in Health Care, 19*(3/4).

Pâquet-Deehy, A., Rinfret-Raynor, M., & Larouche G. (1992). *Training social workers in a feminist approach to conjugal violence.* Ottawa: National Clearinghouse on Family Violence, Health and Welfare Canada.

Pardeck, J.T., Murphy, J.W., & Choi, J.M. (1994). Some implications of postmodernism for social work practice. *Social Work, 39*(4), 343–346.

Parnell, S., & Andrews, J. (1994). Complementary principles of social work and feminism: A teaching guide. *Areté, 19*(2), 60–64.

Paterson, R., & Trathen, S. (1994). Feminist in(ter)ventions in family therapy. *Australia and New Zealand Journal of Family Therapy, 15*(2), 91–98.

Penfold. S.P., & Walker, G.A. (1986). The psychiatric paradox and women. In K. McCannell (Ed.), Women and mental health [Special issue]. *Canadian Journal of Community Mental Health 5*,(2), 9–15.

Pennell, J. (1995). Encountering or countering women abuse. In P. Taylor & C. Daly, *Gender dilemmas in social work: Issues affecting women in the profession* (pp. 89–106). Toronto: Canadian Scholars' Press.

Pennell, J., Flaherty, M., Gravel, N., Milliken, E., & Neuman, M. (1993). Feminist social work education in mainstream and nonmainstream classrooms. *Affilia, 8*(3), 317–338.

Perkins, K. (1992). Psychosocial implications of women and retirement. *Social Work, 37*(6), 526–532.

Piercy, F.P., & Sprenkle, D.H. (1990). Marriage and family therapy: A decade review. *Journal of Marriage and the Family Therapy, 52*(4), 1116–1126.

Pozatek, E. (1994). The problem of certainty: Clinical social work in the postmodern era. *Social Work, 39*(4), 396–403.

Pressman, B. (1989). Wife-abused couples: The need for comprehensive theoretical perspectives and integrated treatment models. *Journal of Feminist Family Therapy, 1*(1), 23–44.

Pressman, B., Cameron, G., & Rothery, M. (Eds.). (1989). *Intervening with assaulted women: Current theory, research and practice.* Hillsdale, NJ: Lawrence Erlbaum Associates.

Prieur, D. (1995). Wife assault: Reclaiming the feminist agenda. *Vis-à-vis, 12*(4), 1, 4.

Quinn, P. (1994). America's disability policy: Another double standard? *Affilia, 9*(1), 45–59.

Rathbone-McCuan, E., Tebb, S., & Harbert, T.L. (1991). Feminist social work with older women caregivers in a DVA setting. In M. Bricker-Jenkins, N.R. Hooyman, & N. Gottlieb (Eds.), *Feminist social work practice in clinical settings* (pp. 35–57). Newbury Park, CA: Sage.

Rave, E.J., & Larsen, C.C. (Eds.). (1995). *Ethical decision making in therapy: Feminist perspectives.* New York: Guilford Press.

Reinharz, S. (1992): *Feminist methods in social research.* New York: Oxford University Press.

Richardson, L., & Taylor, V. (Eds.). (1993). *Feminist frontiers III.* New York: McGraw-Hill.

Richardson, S.A., Donald, K.M., & O'Malley, K.M. (1985/86). Right brain approaches to counseling: Tapping your "Feminine" Side. *Women & Therapy, 4*(4), 9–21.

Richmond-Abbott, M. (1992). *Masculine and feminine: Gender roles over the lifecycle.* New York: McGraw-Hill.

Rogers, G. (1995). Practice teaching guidelines for learning ethnically sensitive, antidiscriminatory practice: A Canadian application. *British Journal of Social Work, 25*(4), 441–457.

Ross, C. (1995). *Satanic ritual abuse: Principles of treatment.* Toronto: University of Toronto Press.

Rothblum, E.D. (Ed.) (1988). Lesbianism: Affirming nontraditional roles [Special issue]. *Women & Therapy, 8*(1/2).

Rubenstein, H., & Lawler, S.K. (1990). Toward the psychosocial empowerment of women. *Affilia, 5*(3), 27–38.

Russell, M. (1984). *Skills in counseling women—The feminist approach.* Springfield, IL: Charles C Thomas.

Russell, M. (1986). Teaching feminist counselling skills: An evaluation. *Counselor-Education-and-Supervision, 25*(4), 320–331.

Russell, M. (1995). *Confronting abusive beliefs.* Thousand Oaks, CA: Sage.

Ryan, B. (1989). Ideological purity and feminism: The U.S. women's movement from 1966 to 1975. *Gender and Society, 3*(2), 239–257.

Sancier, B. (Ed.). (1987). Women, men and Affilia. *Affilia, 2*(4), 3–6.

Sancier, B. (Ed.). (1990). Feminist paradoxes and the need for new agendas. *Affilia, 5*(2), 5–7.

Sands, R.G., & Nuccio, K. (1992). Postmodern feminist theory and social work. *Social Work, 37*(6), 489–494.

Scheyett, A. (1990). The oppression of caring: Women caregivers of relatives with mental illness. *Affilia, 5*(1), 32–48.

Sheinberg, M., & Penn, P. (1991). Gender dilemmas, gender questions, and the gender mantra. *Journal of Marital and Family Therapy, 17*(1), 33–44.

Shepard, M. (1991). feminist principles for social work intervention in wife abuse. *Affilia, 6*(2), 87–93.

Sieber, J.A., & Cairns, K.V. (1991). Feminist therapy with ethnic minority women. *Canadian Journal of Counselling, 25*(4), 567–580.

Simon, B.L. (1988). Social work responds to the women's movement. *Affilia, 3*(4), 60–68.

Skodra, E.E. (1992). Ethnic/immigrant women and psychotherapy: The issue of empowerment. *Women & Therapy, 13*(4), 81–97.

Sohng, S., Porterfield, S., Langston, S., Kehle, L., Cramer, L., Chang, V.N., Bryson, B.J., & Bricker-Jenkins, M. (in press). FemSchool: A work in progress. *Affilia.*

Stanley, L. & Wise, S. (1983). *Breaking out: Feminist consciousness and feminist research.* London: Routledge & Kegan Paul.

Stanley, L. & Wise, S. (1990). Method, methodology and epistemology in feminist research process. In L. Stanley (Ed.), *Feminist praxis: Research, theory, and epistemology in feminist sociology* (pp. 20–60). Boston: Routledge & Kegan Paul.

Straus, M.A., & Gelles, R.J. (1990). *Physical violence in American families.* New Brunswick, NJ: Transaction.

Straus, M.A., Gelles, R.J., & Steinmetz, S.K. (1980). *Behind closed doors: Violence in the American family.* New York: Doubleday/Anchor.

Surrey, J.L. (1985). *Self-in-relation: A theory of women's development* (Work in Progress Series, No. 13). Wellesley, MA: Wellesley College, Stone Center for Developmental Services and Studies.

Swigonski, M.E. (1994). The logic of feminist standpoint theory for social work research. *Social Work, 39*(4), 387–393.

Swigonski, M.E. (1995). Claiming a lesbian identity as an act of empowerment. *Affilia, 10*(4), 413–425.

Taylor, P., & Daly, C. (1985). Women's status, global issues and social work. In P. Taylor & C. Daly (Eds.), *Gender dilemmas in social work: Issues affecting women in the profession* (pp. 141–148). Toronto: Canadian Scholars' Press.

Taylor, V., & Whittier, N. (1993). The new feminist movement. In L. Richardson & V. Taylor (Eds.), (1993). *Feminist frontiers III* (pp. 533–548). New York: McGraw-Hill.

Thompson, N. (1995). Men and anti-sexism. *British Journal of Social Work, 25*(4), 459–475.

Tolman, R.M., Mowry, D.D., Jones, L.E., & Brekke, J. (1986). Developing a profeminist commitment among men in social work. In N. Van Den Bergh & L.B. Cooper (Eds.). *feminist visions for social work* (pp. 61–79). Silver Spring, MD: National Association of Social Workers.

Trepper, T.S., & Barrett, M.J. (1989). *Systemic treatment of incest: A therapeutic handbook.* New York: Brunner/Mazel.

Turner, S. (1992). Alcoholism and depression in women. *Affilia, 7*(3), 8–22.

Tutty, L.M. (1993). After the shelter: Critical issues for women who leave assaultive relationships. In M. Valentich, M. Russell, & G. Martin (Eds.), Women and social work: Celebrating our progress [Special issue]. *Canadian Social Work Review, 10*(2), 183–201.

Valentich, M. (1986). Feminism and social work practice. In F.J. Turner (Ed.), *Social work treatment: Interlocking theoretical approaches* (3rd ed.) (pp. 564–589). New York: Free Press.

Valentich, M. (1992). Toward gender-sensitive clinical social work practice. Areté, 17(1), 1–12.

Valentich, M. (1994). Rape revisited: Sexual violence against women in the former Yugoslavia. *Canadian Journal of Human Sexuality 3*(1), 53–64.

Valentich, M., & Anderson, C. (1989). The rights of individuals in family treatment of child sexual abuse. *Journal of Feminist Family Therapy, 1*(5), 51–66.

Valentich, M., & Gripton, J. (1984). Ideological perspectives on the sexual assault of women. *Social Service Review, 58*(3), 448–461.

Valentich, M., & Gripton, J. (1985). A periodic case strategy for helping people with sexual problems. *Journal of Sex Education and therapy, 11*(2), 24–29.

Valentich, M., & Gripton, J. (1992a). Dual relationships: Dilemmas and doubts. *Canadian Journal of Human Sexuality, 1*(3), 153–166.

Valentich, M., & Gripton, J. (1992b). Gender-sensitive practice in sexual problems. *Canadian Journal of Human Sexuality, 1*(1), 11–18.

Valentich, M., & Gripton, J. (1994, October). Making decisions about dual relationships. Paper presented at the Conference on Sexual Exploitation by Health Professionals and Clergy, Toronto, Ontario, Canada.

Valentine, D. (1986). Family violence: An expanded perspective. *Affilia, 1*(3), 6–16.

Van Den Bergh, N. (Ed.). (1995). *Feminist practice in the 21st century.* Washington, DC: NASW Press.

Van Den Bergh, N., & Cooper, L.B. (Eds.) (1986). *feminist visions for social work.* Silver Spring, MD: National Association of Social Workers.

Vinton, L. (1992). Women's content in social work curricula: Separate but equal? *Affilia, 7*(1), 74–89.

Walker, M. (1990). *Women in therapy and counseling: Out of the shadows.* Milton Keynes, England: Open University Press.

Walter, M., Carter, B., Papp, P., & Silverstein, O. (1988). *The invisible web: Gender patterns in family relationships.* New York: Guilford Press.

Walther, V.N., & Young A.T. (1992). Costs and benefits of reproductive technologies. *Affilia, 7*(2), 111–122.

Warren, R., Gripton, J., Francis R., & Green, M. (1994). Transformative treatment of adult sex offenders. *Canadian Journal of Human Sexuality, 3*(4), 349–358.

Weil, M. (1986). Women, community, and organizing. In N. Van Den Bergh & L. Cooper (Eds.), *Feminist visions for social work.* Silver Spring, MD: National Association of Social Workers.

Westerland, E. (1992). *Women's sexuality after incest.* New York: W.W. Norton.

Wetzel, J.W. (1991). Universal mental health classification systems: Reclaiming women's experience. *Affilia, 6*(3), 8–31.

White, V. (1995). Commonality and diversity in feminist social work. *British Journal of Social Work, 25*(2), 143–156.

Wood, G.G., & Middleman, R.R. (1992). Groups to empower battered women. *Affilia, 7*(4), 82–95.

Worell J., & Remer, P. (1992). *Feminist perspectives in therapy: An empowerment model for women.* New York: John Wiley & Sons.

Yegidis, B.L. (1988). Wife abuse and marital rape among women who seek help. *Affilia, 3*(1), 62–68.

Zetlin, P.A. (1989). A proposal for a new diagnostic category: Abuse disorder. *Journal of Feminist Family Therapy, 1*(4), 67–84.

Zippay, A. (1995). The politics of empowerment. *Social Work, 40*(2), 263–267.

CHAPTER 13

FUNCTIONAL THEORY AND SOCIAL WORK PRACTICE

KATHERINE M. DUNLAP

INTRODUCTION

The principles of functional theory were first developed by Otto Rank, a German psychoanalyst and erstwhile student of Sigmund Freud. Functional theory was subsequently adapted for social work practice by Jessie Taft and the faculty of the School of Social Work at the University of Pennsylvania. Although only a few schools and agencies ultimately endorsed this approach, functional methods were applied to individual, group, and community practice as well as to supervision, administration, research, and social work education, particularly on the east coast of the United States.

Functional social work is a therapeutic approach derived from psychoanalytic theory. Three characteristics differentiate functional social work from the Freudian or diagnostic school, the only other clearly formulated approach extant in the early 1920s, when functionalism was developed (Smalley, 1971). First, functional theory is predicated on a psychology of growth that replaces the concept of treatment with that of helping. Second, functional theory assumes that the structure of the agency defines the focus, direction, content, and duration of service. Third, functional theory stresses the concept of process. Through the therapeutic relationship, the client and the clinician work together to discover what can be done with the help that is offered.

Functional theories have had a dramatic impact on contemporary social work, yet most educators and practitioners possess limited knowledge about the functional roots of modern methods. This chapter recapitulates the historic conditions from which the functional school emerged, explains major tenets and reviews applications of the functional approach, and examines the future of a once powerful agenda.

Following the lead of Yelaja (1986), the term "theory" is defined loosely, not scientifically, as a "scheme for practice based on a set of identified principles that are interrelated and derive from a common basis in relevant knowledge" (p. 47).

HISTORICAL ANTECEDENTS

Functional theory was incorporated into social work practice in the United States during the turbulent 1920s and 1930s, but its roots must be traced to three antecedents: the emergence of the field of psychiatry during the first decades of this century, concomitant changes in scientific thought, and the influence of Otto Rank, who worked with Freud in Germany before the First World War. The following sections summarize the contributions of Freud, review scientific changes, and explore the life and work of Rank.

PSYCHOANALYTIC THEORY

Sigmund Freud revolutionized the study of human behavior by developing the first systematic, scientific theory of personality. Today, Freud's contributions are well known. When first proposed, however, psychoanalytical theory was considered radical and controversial. Although Freudian methods were initially rejected by some, this theory offered hope to others seeking effective treatment for troubled people.

Freud's work was based on principles of scientific determinism. He and his disciples assumed that present behavior has meaning that can be understood through intense examination of past events. To garner meaning, they focused on the inner world of the self—thoughts, feelings, impulses, and fantasies.

Using case study methods, Freud and his followers engaged in a process of diagnosis. Their primary goal was to discover the cause of present difficulties. They assumed that by removing cause they could remove symptoms, as in medical practice.

One of the keystones of Freud's personality structure was the concept of the unconscious mind, which he claimed to have discovered through his experiments in hypnosis and the study of dreams. To produce "unconscious" material without hypnosis, Freud proposed the technique he called "free association." To elicit material, the analyst was instructed to maintain an attitude of dynamic passivity. Freud declared that these techniques would enable the analyst to uncover the underlying motives that prompt behavior. Tentative hypotheses were confirmed by interpretation, a process through which the analyst shared insights gained "through the careful weighing of evidence and critical comparison" (Aptekar, 1955, p. 9). By analyzing the progress of people treated with these new methods, Freud identified several patterns of predictable responses, including resistance, blocking, and transference. The goal of psychoanalysis was understanding, not change.

A number of Freud's theories have gained wide exposure, including the epigenetic process of psychosexual development; the organization of personality into three structures that together govern knowledge, emotion, and behavior; the creation and maintenance of defense mechanisms; and the presence of instinctive drives toward pleasure and death. As the following sections indicate, many of these theories were embraced by the diagnostic school of social work.

A SCIENTIFIC REVOLUTION

As Freud reached his maturity in the early decades of this century, the entire arena of scientific thought experienced what Kuhn (1970) might call a paradigm shift. Drucker (1959) explains that there was "a philosophical shift from the Cartesian universe of mechanical cause to the new universe of pattern, purpose, and process" (p. XI). Scientists abandoned the deterministic search for irreversible causes as they faced the realization that the only thing predictable is unpredictability itself. Researchers in diverse fields began to explore the concept of growth as an orderly process with a universally recognizable purpose (Corner, 1944; Sinnott, 1950). Yelaja (1986) summarized four assumptions first articulated during this period: 1) the goal-directed whole of an organism transcends the sum of its parts; 2) despite common patterns, each being is unique; 3) the observer affects the observed; and 4) will and freedom exist and impel individual growth. These presumptions had profound implications, particularly for theorists in the field of services (Mead, 1936).

INNOVATIONS OF OTTO RANK

Freud was surrounded by an inquisitive, dedicated circle of disciples who worked with him to elaborate and refine psychoanalytic theory, as the new school of thought came to be called. One of the most dedicated and brilliant of this circle was Otto Rank, and it was Rank who devised the concepts that led to functional social work. Because Rank is less well known, his life and work are recapitulated here.

Otto Rank was born Otto Rosenfeld in 1884, the third child of an alcoholic jeweler. According to Rudnytsky (1991), the family was economically and emotionally deprived. Rank's older brother Paul received academic training and a law degree, but Otto Rank was forced to attend trade school and work long hours in a machine shop. He still found time to attend the theater, and he read voraciously (Taft, 1958). Rank charted his own intellectual development in diaries and daybooks containing quotations, references, cryptic scribbles, personal notes, and theories. His ambition was to live fully and creatively (Lieberman, 1985).

When Rank was twenty-one, Alfred Adler introduced him to Sigmund Freud. This was a dream come true for Rank (Rudnytsky, 1984). Freud readily accepted Rank into the circle of disciples, for he enriched the medical group with his discerning understanding of history and culture. Freud brought Rank to the center of the group by making him secretary, and for many years Rank prepared the minutes of the weekly meetings of the Vienna Psychoanalytic Society (Klein, 1981).

Recognizing Rank's creative capacities, Freud helped him publish his first book, *Der Künstler (The Artist),* in 1907. Freud also financed Rank's studies at the University of Vienna, where he obtained the doctorate in 1912 for his thesis on the Lohengrin legend. Rank was the first to employ psychoanalytic methodology in a doctoral thesis, and he was also the first in psychodynamic literature to explore death symbolism and relate it to birth symbolism (Lieberman, 1985).

This was a period of great productivity for Rank. Under Freud's guidance and with his support, Rank engaged in theoretical research, edited journals, wrote monographs, organized the psychoanalytical movement, and practiced lay analysis for two decades (Progoff, 1956). However, as psychoanalysis began to harden into a standardized procedure, Rank reassessed and rejected many of Freud's notions and continued to experiment with innovative ideas of his own (Karpf, 1953).

Rank was surprised by the storm of controversy generated by the publication of *Trauma of Birth* in 1924. Although the book was dedicated to Freud, it posited new, innovative concepts and was not well received by Freud or his followers.

The criticisms of the Vienna circle were sharp and bitter. With his subsequent departure for Paris, Rank dissociated himself from the official psychoanalytical group and continued to formulate his own theory and approach. His physical move to the United States was followed by an emotional breach with Freud that was never repaired. What began as a theoretical disagreement between two people grew into a vendetta persisting to this day (Menaker, 1982). The two met for the last time in April 1926 to say good-bye. Rank was forty-two, and Freud was nearing seventy.

In *Art and Artist,* written in 1932, Rank explained his view of the human condition. Rank was not a feminist, but he respected women's freedom of choice, and he recognized the significant power in the mother/child bond (Sward, 1980–81). Using the metaphor that "life is a loan, death the repayment," Rank presented life as a series of separations beginning with a painful birth. He focused on the importance of living fully—with creativity, humor, and joy—in the limited time available between beginnings and endings.

Rank believed that people oscillate between their need to merge with a larger entity and their desire for separation. To achieve a unique identity and live an abundant life, the individual must exercise personal will (Menaker, 1984).

The concept of will is elaborated in *Will Therapy* and *Truth and Reality,* written in 1928 and 1929, respectively, and translated by Jessie Taft into English in 1936. Rank explains will as a complex, organizing element that delineates the total personality of the person, including creative ideas, feelings, and the energy of action. Will arises from counter-will, or the oppositional stance of "not wanting to," a condition readily observed in young children. While others claim that behavior can be reduced to a primary cause, Rank maintains that people appropriately use will to adapt situations to their own unique needs. The situation may be external, as in an unhappy childhood, or internal, as in a counterproductive attitude. Regardless, individuation is achieved through active acceptance.

As an analyst, Rank viewed each therapeutic hour as a microcosm of life, a time with its own beginning and end. In his therapy sessions, he emphasized the present, rather than the past or future. He encouraged patients to "experience" rather than to analyze the thoughts, feelings, and behaviors arising from the therapeutic process. He focused on recurring interactions and patterns instead of isolated events (Taft, 1958).

Rank is perhaps most famous for setting time limits. He used this device to help clients crystallize their conflicts regarding continuation or termination of therapy. Within this context, the conscious use of will becomes a therapeutic agent. For example, Rank noted that people must consciously chose to accept a course of action, even if there appears to be no other choice. By making ambivalence explicit, Rank enabled clients to mobilize their will. In the preface to his last book, *Beyond Psychology* (1941), Rank explains, "Man (sic) is born beyond psychology and he dies beyond it but he can live beyond it only through vital experience of his own" (p. 16).

Relationship is the determining element in this therapeutic process. Rank rejected the stance of dynamic passivity. For him, the helping relationship is marked by mutuality, as in teaching and learning, but not by reciprocity, as in friendship. The therapist first establishes a setting in which the client can discover and use the strength that arises from vulnerability. Then the therapist becomes the tool that enables the client to explore and expand will. Finally, the therapist precipitates termination by setting limits so that the client can achieve autonomy and avoid dependency.

Rank saw psychotherapy as an art as well as a science. Since every person is different, every therapeutic encounter will be different. The therapeutic alliance is characterized by spontaneity and creativity, for the analyst must fabricate conditions for growth in every session. It is this intense, emotional process that produces change.

Rank frequently lectured in the United States. Although he scrupulously guarded the identity of his clients, it is now known that he worked with many famous individuals, including Henry Miller and Anäis Nin. He led courses at the University of Pennsylvania School of Social Work, New York School of Social Work, and at the Graduate School for Jewish Social Work (Lieberman, 1985). Until his untimely death in 1939 at age fifty-six, Rank continued to develop and revise his theories about the human condition.

Although he has had a major impact on the development of personality theory and psychotherapy, Rank's list of publications is not large, and his material is not widely read. There are several reasons for this. First, not all his books are available in any one language; some, originally written in German, have not been translated into English, while others, written in English, have not been translated into German. Second, Rank's complex, Germanic style has made translation into English difficult. And third, his lack of precision has frustrated many scholars.

ADVENT OF TWO SCHOOLS

In psychology, the two great poles during the 1920s were psychoanalysis and behaviorism (Lieberman, 1985). In social work, the primary focus was also on the internal problems of the individual (Kadushin, 1959). This epoch was characterized by relative indifference to social reform and social problems (Meyer, 1970). Social work paid little attention to behaviorism. Instead, the profession became deeply committed to the medical model, which in turn embraced psychoanalytical theory. The pace toward professionalism accelerated as two factions, the diagnostic and the functional schools, endorsed and adapted psychoanalytic methods.

The Diagnostic School

Like the early Otto Rank, most social workers in the United States were enamored of the theories of Sigmund Freud. As the new theory swept through the profession, a major branch absorbed Freudian methods (Hollis, 1970). This group, first called the diagnostic and later the psychosocial school of social work, found in Freudian theory "the first great opportunity in history to break through to an understanding of the hitherto hidden mysteries" (Bartlett, 1970).

The diagnostic school has since evolved and expanded (Hollis & Woods, 1981), but in its early forms, diagnostic social work was based on scientific determinism, or the assumption that people are products of their past. The emphasis was on the past, for proponents maintained that only an understanding and acceptance of previous experiences can bring relief. The goal of treatment was to overcome blocks to normal, healthy functioning by bringing unconscious thoughts to mind (Hamilton, 1937a, b). Research was conducted through the meticulous analysis of case material (Hollis, 1939).

This approach assigned well-defined roles to social workers and clients. The client was presumed to be psychologically ill and in need of services. It was the worker's responsibility to collect information through the social history, to diagnose the illness, and to provide treatment. Usually, the presenting problem was viewed as a symptom of a deeper, all-pervading psychological problem (Hamilton, 1936).

The worker treated the client over an indefinite period of time, assuming sole responsibility for the goals and direction of the treatment. As Hamilton (1940) explains, "Not everyone is equally capable of self-help, and the amount we must do for people is directly inverse to what they can do for themselves" (p. 171).

To avoid counter-transference, the worker operated from a stance of dynamic passivity. The client was encouraged to expose deep-seated emotions that the worker subsequently interpreted. Hamilton (1940) explains that the effect of past influences was regarded as irreversible, so that the goal of treatment was not change, but adjustment or mitigation of "the crippling effects of deprivations or pathological exposures" (p. 168). She adds, "Case work is less often able to free its clients from disabilities than to help them live within their disabilities through social compensations" (p. 168).

Treatment rarely reached the termination stage in those early days. Hamilton (1940) recalled, "When social studies were being worked out, case workers carried on so much investigation that they scarcely got around to treatment. In the twenties case workers became so interested in the psychogenetic causes of difficulty that long histories were a major activity and often the treatment did not progress, stagnating in a dead center of diagnosis" (p. 141).

THE GREAT SCHISM

For many years, the diagnostic and functional schools competed for supremacy (Hamilton, 1941). Each group defended its stance with evangelistic fervor, for each believed it had found the way to end psychic pain and mental illness. The polemic was public and painful; and the subject of casework became a contentious one for social workers and others (Kasius, 1950; Murphy, 1933).

In trying to integrate the two disparate schools of thought, Aptekar (1955) prepared a comparison of the primary tenets of each:

Summing up, we might say that the chief conceptions of Freud which have been taken over and widely used by caseworkers are as follows:

1. Unconscious mind as a determinant of behavior.
2. Ambivalence in feeling and attitude.
3. Past experience as a determinant of present behavior.
4. The transference as essential to therapy.
5. Resistance as a factor to be dealt with in all helping.

The chief conceptions of Rankian thinking, taken over by the functional school and substituted for the above, are:

1. The will as an organizing force in personality.
2. The counter-will as a manifestation of the need of the individual to differentiate himself.
3. Present experience as a source of therapeutic development.
4. The significance of separation.
5. The inherent creativity of man (1955, p. 35)

The principles and presuppositions of functional social work are explored more fully in the following sections.

PATH INTO SOCIAL WORK

While the majority of social workers espoused Freudian theory, a small group adopted the approach of Otto Rank. Led by Jessie Taft and the faculty of the School of Social Work at the University of Pennsylvania, this group came to be called the Rankians or functionalists, a term coined by Taft to describe the controls imposed by agency parameters. (The term "functional" in this context bears no relationship to the same term used in sociology.)

A child psychologist by training, Taft attained the doctorate from the University of Chicago in 1913. She was a supervisor of the Foster Home Department of the Children's Aid Society of Pennsylvania, when she met Rank. Their first contact occurred on June 3, 1924, at a meeting of the American Psychoanalytical Association where Rank discussed the ideas contained in *Trauma of Birth*. Two years and many letters later, Taft began analysis with Rank in New York (Robinson, 1962).

At first, Taft was ignorant of Rank's feud with Freud, but it was not long before she realized that she would have to "face Freudian difference, painful as it was, not merely through Rank but in my own thinking, reading, and use of the therapeutic relationship" (Robinson, 1962, p. 126). Taft immersed herself in Rank's philosophy and methods as she translated *Will Therapy* and *Truth and Reality* (1964). In addition to her agency employment, she concentrated on her psychoanalytical practice, studied the new theories, supervised others, and taught at the University of Pennsylvania School of Social Work. It was through these activities that Taft introduced the ideas of Otto Rank to social work.

EVOLUTION OF FUNCTIONAL THEORY

Rank was a catalyst. After his break with the established psychoanalytical community, he lectured at the University of Pennsylvania School of Social Work, but he never related his theory to the profession of social work. In his later years, he did not even recognize the term "functional" (Smalley, 1971). The evolution of Rankian theory into functional social work was precipitated by others.

Virginia Robinson was one of the leaders. A lifelong colleague and companion of Taft, Robinson participated in therapy with Rank in 1927. At the time, Robinson was head of the casework department at the University of Pennsylvania School of Social Work. She was impressed by her brief experience with analysis. Like Taft, she adopted and applied Rank's ideas.

Colleagues of Taft and Robinson, and those who followed them—including Aptekar, Dawley, de Schweinitz, Faatz, Gilpin-Wells, Hofstein, Phillips, Pray, Lewis, Smalley, and Wessel—elaborated and expanded Rankian concepts into functional social work (Smalley, 1970). Taft (1937) added the pivotal concepts regarding agency function.

While functional theory was predicated on Rankian philosophy, it also incorporates material from George Herbert Mead, W. I. Thomas, James Tufts, and John Dewey—masters whom Taft and Robinson had encountered in Chicago (Robinson, 1978). Functionalism accepted the scientific changes of the time and embraced the propositions elucidated by Corner (1944) and Sinnott (1950), to wit, that "human growth expresses *purpose* and constitutes a *process*" (Smalley, 1970, p. 86).

The functionalists read widely in diverse fields, including philosophy, education, science, art, and literature, as a cursory perusal of the *Journal of the Otto Rank Society* attests. As Smalley (1967) reports, many assumptions were imported from psychology. From Gordon Allport (1955) came the confirmation that people have autonomy, the ability to reason, and the capacity to make choices in a free society. Kurt Lewin (1935) added an understanding for the dynamic nature of change and the importance of environment; Erik Erikson (1940) contributed his early notions predicating an epigenetic unfolding of the human life cycle replete with psychosocial crises, or challenges, and opportunities for revitalization. Helen Merrel Lynd (1961) posited a psychology of abundance to replace what she saw as the psychology of economic scarcity.

In addition, Maslow (1937) delineated the concept of self-actualization, and Karen Horney (1939) portrayed anxiety and inner strivings as the positive sign of a continuously maturing individual. Moustakas summarized the contributions of Lecky, Angyal, Goldstein, Rank, and others in *The Self: Explorations in Personal*

Growth (1956). All of these theorists were expanding on the same themes: the human capacity for positive growth and change; the uniqueness of the individual; and the ability of people to shape their destiny.

Basic Assumptions of the Functional School

Increasingly dissatisfied with the restrictive, pessimistic Freudian view of people, the early functionalists eagerly endorsed the proposition that people are purposeful, change-oriented masters of their own fate. Biological and environmental forces are not ignored in Rankian thought, but they are relegated to a secondary position.

Optimistic Underpinnings

Robinson's milestone work, *A Changing Psychology in Social Casework* (1930), introduced Rankian philosophy to the broader social work community. Robinson presents a positive and hopeful view of individuals creatively using inner and outer experiences and resources to determine their own lives. The functionalists replace the psychology of illness with a belief in human growth, and they replace the obligation to treat with a mandate to serve (Lewis, 1966).

Ruth Elizabeth Smalley (1970), dean of the School of Social Work at the University of Pennsylvania, summarizes the optimistic underpinnings of the functional approach:

> The functional school sees the push toward life, health, and fulfillment as primary in human beings, and the human as capable throughout his life of modifying both himself and his environment, in accordance with his own changing purposes with the limitations and opportunities of his own capacity and his own environment (p. 90).

The holon is the individual, "the central, active figure" in the process (Faatz, 1953, p. 47). Functional caseworkers embrace the view that basic human nature is inherently good. Consequently, in a move considered revolutionary, they abandon "judgmental standards of approval or condemnation of behavior" (Faatz, 1953, p. 22). Caseworkers presume that change is not only possible, but inevitable, since each individual is endowed with an innate push toward psychological growth and a fuller, more integrated self. As Smalley (1960) suggests, the view sees people "as not only responsible for [their] own future evolution but capable of it" (p. 107).

Role of Will

The primary tenet of functional theory is Rank's revolutionary concept of will and self-determination. This new concept established the foundation on which all else rests. As Taft (1932) explains:

> The anxious parent, the angry school teacher, the despairing wife or husband, must bear their own burdens, solve their own problems. I can help them only

in and for themselves, if they are able to use me. I cannot perform a magic on the bad child, the inattentive pupil, the faithless partner, because they want him made over in their own terms. . . . Here is a beloved child to be saved, a family unity to be preserved, an important teacher to be enlightened. Before all these problems in which one's reputation, one's pleasure in utilizing professional skill, as well as one's real feeling for the person in distress are perhaps painfully involved, one must accept one's final limitation and the right of the other,—perhaps his necessity,—to refuse help or to take help in his own terms, not as therapist, friends or society might choose. My knowledge and my skill avail nothing unless they are accepted and used by the other (p. 369).

Caseworkers realize that even when change is wanted, it comes with a price—the sacrifice of certainty and security. Accordingly, functionalists understand that people resist change even as they reach for growth. As Taft (1950) explains, "Only at points of growth crisis, where the pressure for further development becomes strong enough to overcome the fear of change and disruption, is the ordinary individual brought to the necessity of enlarging his hard-won integration" (p. 5).

The Value Base of Functionalism

As the preceding quotation illustrates, casework implies a collateral relationship marked by mutuality. Further, functionalists maintain that people cannot change others, for others are also endowed with will. Early writers did not specifically address issues related to sociocultural or ethnic sensitivity, for they considered each person as a unique human being with distinct needs and particular gifts to contribute to the casework experience.

Putsch (1966), recounting her participation in the Civil Rights Movement in Georgia, affirms this philosophy. Her agency had worked hard to develop an atmosphere in which people of many different colors and convictions could work out a more satisfying way of living together. Putsch reflects, "As I had learned from my own experience, when we know too surely what is right we are impatient of difference and miss the opportunity for attaining full understanding through considering different viewpoints" (p. 95).

Significant others and environmental resources are considered from a Lewinian (1951) perspective; that is, they are elements in the topography of an individual's life space. They are part of the problem if they inhibit growth, and they are part of the solution if they promote change. Although the functionalists accepted the common premise that people are subject to the physical laws of nature, their belief in growth suggests that a harmony with nature is possible and desirable. People are encouraged to use natural resources that are available and accessible, but individual responsibility is stressed.

The functionalists always focus on the present time. In fact, this orientation is a hallmark of functional theory. The past is explored only to the extent that it impinges on current concerns. The future is projected only as a guide for present activities. Aware that the future is always uncertain, caseworkers help people learn to live in the present, making the best of themselves with the resources that are currently available.

The overarching goal of casework is the exercise of free will moderated by responsibility; however, functional caseworkers never speculate on the type of change anticipated or desired, for setting goals is considered the prerogative of the client. The role of the caseworker is to help the client obtain and use whatever tools are needed to forge the future. Recognizing the limitations inherent in the situation, only the client can determine what that future can and should be.

MAJOR CONCEPTS OF FUNCTIONAL SOCIAL WORK PRACTICE

Smalley (1970) summarizes three basic assumptions that, when combined with the concept of self-determination, describe functional social work practice. These three concepts, paraphrased below, were derived from Rankian methods, but they have been modified and expanded. They are applicable in private and public settings.

Understanding the Nature of Humanity
The functional group works from a psychology of growth, which occurs in the context of relationship. The center for change lies with the client, not the worker. Taking social and cultural factors into account, the worker helps clients release their own potential for choice and growth through the power of the relationship. The functionalists use the term "helping" rather than "treatment" to describe their method.

Understanding the Purpose of Social Casework
The agency gives focus, direction, and content to the worker's practice. By so doing the agency protects both the worker and the client. Casework is not a form of psychosocial treatment, but is a method for administering a specific social service.

Understanding the Concept of Process in Social Casework
Casework is a helping process through which agency services are made available. Workers take the lead in initiating, sustaining, and terminating the process; however, they enter the relationship without classifying the client, prescribing a particular treatment, or assuming responsibility for an anticipated outcome. Together, the worker and client discover what can be done with the help offered (pp. 79–81).

TREATMENT THROUGH FUNCTIONAL SOCIAL WORK METHODS

Functional social work is an insight-oriented therapy. Although its primary method is colloquy, proponents focus on the casework relationship, which offers an opportunity to reject old patterns in favor of new ones that promote growth. In addition to the basic presuppositions listed above, Smalley (1967) captures the mature tenets of the functional school in the five generic principles paraphrased here:

1. *Diagnosis* should be related to the use of agency services. It should be developed jointly, modified as needed, and shared with the client.
2. *Time* phases in the social work process—beginnings, middles, and endings—should be fully exploited for the use of the client.
3. *Agency function* gives focus, content, and direction to social work processes, ensures accountability by society, and engages the client in the process characterized by partialization, concreteness, and differentiation.
4. The *conscious use of structure* furthers the effectiveness of social work processes by using a myriad of elements such as application forms, agency policy, and the physical setting to define and delimit service.
5. All effective social work processes take place within *relationship*. The purpose of the relationship is to help clients make propitious choices.

The functional approach to therapy flows directly from these key tenets. Because they are so vital in the helping process, each is described and examined in greater detail.

Diagnosis

Functionalists eschew diagnosis as an objective of data collection (Austin, 1938). Diagnosis is considered important when naming a condition helps a client to modify it. In the same vein, history is important only as it encroaches on the present, and early childhood experiences are analyzed only when the client and caseworker agree that they may be contributing to the current difficulty. The assessment process is a joint endeavor (Dawley, 1937), and it constitutes the first phase of therapy.

Relationship and the Process of Change

Instead of focusing on diagnosis, the functionalists stress relationship and the process of change. These two are considered to be inseparable, for all change takes place within the context of relationship. The act of giving and taking help is a dynamic process that occurs over time (Hofstein, 1964). Further, the process is "never static, never finished, always chiefly significant for its inner quality and movement, for its meaning to those it engages, rather than for its form or status or outcome at any instance of time" (Pray, 1949, p. 238).

Since every human being is unique, each person develops a distinct pattern for handling critical experiences. The pattern is initiated during the first separation, or beginning, which Rank called the birth trauma; it is reinforced through subsequent opportunities for change. The nature of the relationship with others determines whether an experience will be growth producing or growth limiting. For example, when early relationships with the mother are positive and constructive, the will learns to accept the inevitability of separation and to adapt to the limitations of reality. If early experiences with the mother are negative or destructive, the will develops a pattern of refusing to accept separation. This usually results in repeated and futile attempts to complete the self through the other person in the relationship.

The concepts of will, counter-will, and resistance are, to the functionalists, not only inevitable but also necessary for "movement," a functional term connoting change or growth. Conflict is inherent in human growth as individual wants and needs clash with the wants and needs of other people and with society. The counter-will, or negative aspect of will, opposes the will of others and resists reality as presented by society. The counter-will carries with it a connotation of guilt. Resistance, a natural attempt to maintain the self, is inevitable in the beginning casework relationship. Resistance is not seen as a problem or deficit, it is considered a sign of strength indispensable to new growth.

The term "transference" is rarely used in functional literature. Taft (1933/1962) explains, "Transference, like resistance, is accepted for what it is, a stage in the growth process, in taking over of the own will into the self" (p. 97). Caseworkers assume that clients want to make themselves known and the only way they can do this is to project their desires, fears, and conflicts onto the worker (Robinson, 1942). A competent worker must be sensitive enough to identify with these projections without getting lost in them (Aptekar, 1941). Throughout the course of therapy, the caseworker establishes and maintain sufficient separateness from the client that neither confuses the self with the other. The worker's identification with agency function helps preserve this necessary separation.

Regardless of how negative previous experiences may have been, people have an opportunity to embrace growth and attain potential through the casework relationship. The process consists of a beginning, a middle, and an ending phase. From the beginning, the caseworker displays a consistent attitude of respect and an unwavering belief that clients can change. The worker also creates an atmosphere in which clients feel safe and free to be themselves. The worker presents both reality and acceptance, creating for the client a "situation so safe, so reassuring that none of his defenses is needed and, therefore, fall away, leaving his underlying fears, loves and jealousies free to express themselves" (Robinson, 1962, p. 113).

During the middle phase of therapy, movement occurs as clients take increasing responsibility for their own actions. Caseworkers offer something new—either a new view of the situation or a new grip on it (Lewis, 1966), and relationships deepen as caseworkers continue to build on client strengths. Clients practice new behaviors with the caseworker and through this rehearsal gain a heightened sense of accomplishment and power.

Endings are fears and welcomed, for they embody both the emptiness of loss and the pride of accomplishment. During termination, the client and therapist recapitulate goals, assess movement, and summarize gains. When therapy has been successful, endings signal a rebirth of the client, now armed with courage, confidence, and a capacity for other healthy unions. Yet, termination also signals the end of the powerful alliance that gave the client this new life. Thus, the ending is marked by both sadness and joy, emptiness and fullness, security and challenge.

Some terminations are established by agency function, as when a patient leaves the hospital. More often, however, endings are precipitated by the caseworker to help the client consolidate gains and move along independently. The technique of setting time limits is a hallmark of the functional approach.

Use of Time

Time is a critical element in functional casework, for it is the only medium through which help can be offered and received. Faatz (1953), who has written extensively about the nature of choice in casework, emphasizes the importance of the immediate present—the here and now—as the only setting in which change can actually occur. In this, Faatz anticipates systems theory, noting that emotions and events experienced during the therapeutic hour can influence and change the remainder of a client's life.

As Taft (1932) writes, "Time represents more vividly than any other category the necessity of accepting limitation as well as the inability to do so, and symbolizes therefore the whole problem of living" (p. 375). Taft elaborates on this precept with examples from therapy. She explains that the person who arrives very early bears responsibility for the self and other, while the person who arrives very late is abdicating responsibility. By addressing these problems in the therapeutic hour, the therapist enables the client to live that one hour fully and thus conquer the secret of all hours.

There is no predetermined or ideal duration of treatment. For some people, a few sessions may suffice, while for others, therapy may continue for an extended period of time. Functional therapists frequently establish time limits in order to facilitate movement, a technique that has been misunderstood. Time limits may be derived from natural time periods, such as a school year or a season. The limits may be recommended by agency function, or they may evolve from therapeutic needs. Regardless of the origin, appropriate limits are never rigid or arbitrary; instead, they are derived from the situation. Appropriate time limits become an incentive to use the present productively and wisely.

Agency Function and the Conscious Use of Structure

The concept that may be the most relevant to social work involves the use of agency function and structure in the helping process. It was Taft (1937), not Rank, who first identified the importance of agency function. Taft viewed therapy as too unreal and public relief as too real. The concept of agency function enabled early caseworkers to find a productive place "between pure therapy and public therapy" (p. 11). Taft's introduction of agency function as the unifying theme in social work practice gave functional social work its moniker.

The principle is simple: the creative, positive acceptance of agency parameters can have significant philosophical and psychological benefits for both caseworker and client (Taft, 1937). In the conscious decision to work within the parameters of a specific agency, the worker accepts a circumscribed area of service. The caseworker's responsibility is mediated by what the agency can and cannot do. Worker attitude is important. The caseworker must not sink into resignation, chafe at limitations, revolt, or secretly resolve to overlook rules. When caseworkers recognize, accept, and use limitations, agency function becomes one of their most valuable tools.

Agency function is also a valuable tool for clients. When clients choose to accept agency limitations, they identify with the social purpose of the agency. Personal risk is minimized, for clients need not submit to an entire personality reconstruction.

Rather, they can ask for help with specific concerns and know that their request will be respected. Through the casework relationship, clients learn to use limits to deal responsibly with reality in the pursuit of personal goals.

The structure and form of service arise from the function of the agency. Agency policy is the primary authority that determines all other forms and structures. As we have seen, time is used deliberately. All forms and structures are consciously designed for the maximum effectiveness of social work processes. Every item—from intake procedures, application forms, and assessment tools to termination rituals—is planned (Bellet, 1938). Even the setting—the structure of place—is considered important in defining and delimiting agency function. Because change is constant, forms and structures are reassessed regularly to ensure congruence with intent.

The relationship between freedom of choice and agency function is clear when a client voluntarily applies for service and then freely chooses to accept or reject the help that is offered. This relationship is less clear when client participation is involuntary. Pray (1949), whose experience was primarily in the field of corrections, has written extensively about this apparent dilemma, and he argues that freedom and authority are not mutually exclusive. Pray identifies two conditions essential for success in an authoritarian setting. First, the authority must reflect a social will, not the will of an individual. Second, within that setting, the captive client must be free to reject the service that is offered. Only by being free to reject can a client be free to accept and find fulfillment within the bounds (Yelaja, 1971).

PRINCIPAL APPLICATIONS OF FUNCTIONAL SOCIAL WORK

Functional methods were initially limited to work with individuals. In fact, when the University of Pennsylvania School of Social Work hired its first group worker, Helen Phillips, in the 1940s, the two areas were kept entirely separate (Robinson, 1960). Over time, their similarities became more apparent than their differences (Phillips, 1957). After World War II, the number of opportunities for group work expanded dramatically (Eisen, 1960).

In her definitive summary, Smalley (1967) indicates that functional methods are effective with many types of groups and a wide variety of problems. Smalley cites case materials from a leisure-time group of adult women being served by a Jewish community center and from a therapy group of chronically mentally ill men in a psychiatric hospital. Although she acknowledges that specific knowledge and skill are required in these applications, she combines these dissimilar examples with case notes from a community organization to affirm the five generic principles previously listed.

Eisen (1960) reiterates the commonalities between group work and casework, adding that the group worker must also possess not only special knowledge about the impact of group process on the individual but also special skill in using group interaction. Eisen underscores the range of services that can be provided in functional groups, listing four types of groups that might be formed in a mental hospital: special-purpose groups, such as an orientation for new patients; a ward group for patient governance; peer groups for support and leisure activities; and community-focused programs.

The power in the group or community is essentially the same as the power in the individual (Smalley, 1967). Each is in process, striving toward self-fulfillment or purpose. Whether the goal is personal adjustment or social agitation, the worker facilitates the process though a helping relationship that is clearly delimited by agency controls. As Eisen (1960) explains, "Our service should be geared to helping patients overcome their disabilities, enhancing their capacity for group and self direction. Toward this end the group process becomes an individual experience" (p. 114).

The earliest writings acknowledge the importance of families (Taft, 1930) and address parent/child interactions, especially as related to abuse, neglect, and incompetence (Mayer, 1956). However, functional principles were not systematically applied to the family as a unit until the early 1960s. The process was initially called family casework.

Rappaport (1960) was an early proponent of family-focused service. Recognizing that family problems are often rooted in the problems of society, she calls for "more vibrant and vital ways of helping" families with multiple problems, and she recommends social action and coordination of resources as well as the application of functional principles to family practice (p. 86).

Berl (1964) also affirms the relationship between family and society and notes that the major challenges of family casework involve a dynamic balance between the elements necessary for successful functioning, the integration of knowledge and practice, and systematic progress toward health and growth. He recommends the application of functional methods to prevention and crisis intervention, to treatment settings and educational institutions, and to society at large. The field of family casework evolved slowly, however, for in 1967 Smalley presents generic principles for functional casework, group work, and community organization, but she does not mention family work.

Whether practiced with individuals, dyads, families, groups, or communities, functional social work is most appropriate for client systems seeking solutions to problems they have identified and embraced. Functional casework is especially effective for people seeking personal growth. It provides an insight-oriented process appropriate for children and adults (Taft, 1930). Neither formal education nor a high intelligence quotient are prerequisites, and individuals with cognitive limitations can benefit if they have the capacity for reflection. The only qualifications needed to benefit from this method are an ability and willingness to engage in the process of change.

Because the worker and client explore the process of change together, functional methods are applicable whether the participants have similar or dissimilar backgrounds. The first tasks of the worker are to establish rapport and acquire a rich understanding of the situation from the perspective of the client. Through this exploration, the worker comes to appreciate and value both similarities and differences in heritage, background, tradition, and experience. The recognition and affirmation of difference is reinforced in supervision, a process that scrutinizes client/worker differences so that workers can maintain appropriate roles and separate their needs and goals from those of the client.

Proponents identify few limitations or contraindications; however, functional methods alone are not sufficient for clients who also require medical or pharmaceutical intervention. Functional practice is also less effective with people who have psychotic disorders; dementia; or antisocial, paranoid, schizoid, or borderline personality disorders. With specific populations or problems, functional methods may require adaptations to be developed by the worker (Smalley, 1970).

Since participation is entirely voluntary, risks are few. When a client's problems lie outside the purview of an agency's function, workers are obliged to refer the client to a more appropriate facility where help can be obtained.

This method can be successfully applied to even the most complex problems, including psychosocial crises and introspective concerns, interpersonal conflicts, and environmental issues and social strife.

ADMINISTRATIVE AND TRAINING FACTORS

The University of Pennsylvania School of Social Work developed the first master's degree program around 1934 under the leadership of Taft (Robinson, 1960). From this point forward, caseworkers were expected to obtain the master's degree before they were allowed to provide therapy to clients. Educators assumed that these professional social workers would become leaders and administrators in their employing agencies (Pray, 1938), but no requisite knowledge or skill—other than those of the functional method—is identified.

Supervision is a critical element in training students and overseeing experienced workers (Faith, 1960), for before workers can help others, they must become aware of and manage their own inner and outer conflicts. Intrapersonal material, in addition to case content, constitutes the substance of supervision (Robinson, 1936).

The supervisory relationship is considered a special derivative of the therapeutic relationship, for it includes all the controls of the therapeutic alliance plus the needs of a third system. Sometimes the third entity is the agency, sometimes it is the client (Robinson, 1949). In either case, effective supervision is indispensable, for it binds people to agency function. It also prevents the condition now called "burnout."

Hughes (1938) acknowledged that not all agency employees have professional training. In functional agencies, paraprofessional workers and volunteers are still required to uphold functional principles. As Hughes explains, "Lack of skill in knowing how to use our function helpfully is costly to the agency in time, in money, and in human misery" (p. 73).

EMPIRICAL BASE

It is clear that functional principles are drawn from a substantive scientific base (Marcus, 1966), and it appears that casework students were consistently trained in research methods (Smalley, 1962, 1967). Nevertheless, the empirical base for this approach is limited.

De Schweinitz (1960) urged the university community to collaborate with practitioners. Lewis (1962) exhorted agencies to add the function of research analysis to agency services. Both Lewis and Smalley (1967) suggested engaging a research specialist, as Mencher (1959) recommended. Sprafkin (1964) accepted this challenge but reported on the process, not the outcome.

Single case studies have been conducted using agency records, which often contain only idiosyncratic process recordings. These investigations focus more on process than product, since by definition goals are set by the client and can change during the course of therapy. They add little information about the overall effectiveness of functional methods.

PROSPECTUS

This chapter describes the lively and dramatic debate that shaped social work practice during the first half of this century. At its zenith, functional social work was practiced and taught at the universities of Pennsylvania, North Carolina, and Southern California; the Graduate School for Jewish Social Work; and, briefly, at the New York School of Social Work (Robinson, 1978). The sixteenth edition of the *Encyclopedia of Social Work* devoted twelve pages to the functional method (Smalley, 1971), and the seventeenth edition allotted eleven pages (Smalley & Bloom, 1977).

Today, a few historians and psychoanalysts have rediscovered Otto Rank (Lieberman, 1985; Menaker, 1982; Rudnytsky, 1991), but functional social work has received only a few passing references in more recent editions of the *Encyclopedia*. No graduate schools of social work in the United States promulgate functional methods as a unitary approach, and few explore the historical roots of this tradition.

In fact, the revolutionary concepts that engendered such controversy have been modified and adapted, and ultimately subsumed in the major theories of social work today. Theorists have incorporated once-heretical ideas—such as freedom of choice and self-determination, the human potential for change, and the use of time as a treatment element—without reference to their stormy origins in the functional school. For example, self-help groups stress personal choice and responsibility in the notions of "hitting bottom" and co-dependency, and the importance of the present is captured by the slogan "One day at a time." Realty therapists regularly promote the functional limits of an agency, and the newly emerging empowerment movement is built on client strengths and capacities for change within the context of neighborhood. However, few proponents of these theoretical approaches would recognize the functional roots undergirding these popular techniques.

As the end of the century draws near, economic and political conditions resemble those found in the 1920s and 1930s. As then, economic necessities compel agencies to maintain services strictly within budget realities. Communities wish to avert suffering, especially for children, but they intend to conserve scarce resources. To this end, elected officials are reviewing mandates, setting limits on allotments, and demanding personal responsibility. An understanding and intentional use of agency function can ensure accountability to society and the attainment of social work objectives (Smalley, 1967). A deeper awareness of historical antecedents can enable the profession to meet the needs of a changing environment with greater efficiency and increased effectiveness.

ACKNOWLEDGMENT

This chapter is dedicated to my teacher and mentor, Dr. Alan Keith-Lucas (2/5/10–8/5/95). A graduate of Western Reserve University in the diagnostic tradition, Dr. Keith-Lucas was brought to the University of North Carolina to "clean up that functional mess." Instead, he joined forces with the functionalists, and for more than fifty years his ideas and influence shaped social work services and group child care in North Carolina and the Southeast.

REFERENCES

Allport, G.W. (1955). *Becoming*. New Haven: Yale University Press.

Aptekar, H.H. (1941). *Basic Concepts in Social Case Work*. Chapel Hill: University of North Carolina Press.

Aptekar, H.H. (1955). *The Dynamics of Casework and Counseling*. Boston: Houghton Mifflin.

Austin, L.N. (1938). Evolution of our case-work concepts. *Proceedings of the National Conference of Social Work*. Chicago: University of Chicago Press, 99–111).

Barlett, H.M., with Saunders, B.N. (1970). *The Common Base of Social Work Practice*. Washington, DC: National Association of Social Workers.

Bellet, I.S. (1938). The Application Desk. *Journal of Social Work Process* 2(1) Philadelphia: University of Pennsylvania Press, pp. 32–43.

Berl, F. (1964). Family casework—Dialectics of problem, process, and task. *Journal of Social Work Process 14*, 55–76.

Corner, G.W. (1944). *Ourselves Unborn*. New Haven: Yale University Press.

Dawley, A. (1937). Diagnosis—The dynamic of effective treatment. *Journal of Social Work Process, 1*(1), 19–31.

De Schweinitz, K. (1960). The past as a guide to the function and pattern of social work. In W.W. Weaver (ed.), *Frontiers for Social Work: A Colloquium on the Fiftieth Anniversary of the School of Social Work of the University of Pennsylvania*. Philadelphia: University of Pennsylvania Press, 59–94.

Drucker, P. (1959). *Landmarks of Tomorrow*. New York: Harper & Row.

Eisen, A. (1960). Utilization of the group work method in the social service department of a mental hospital. *Journal of Social Process 11*, 106–114.

Erikson, E.H. (1940). Problems of infancy and early childhood. *Cyclopedia of Medicine*. Philadelphia: Davis, 714–30.

Faatz, A.J. (1953). *The Nature of Choice in Casework Process*. Chapel Hill: University of North Carolina Press.

Faith, G.B. (1960). Facing current questions in relation to supervision—How shall we value the uses of supervision. *Journal of Social Work Process*. 11, 122–129.

Hamilton, G. (1936). *Social Case Recording*. New York: Columbia University Press.

Hamilton, G. (1937a). Basic concepts in social case work. *The Family 43*(5), 147–156.

Hamilton, G. (1937b). Basic concepts in social case work. *Proceedings of the National Conference of Social Work*. Chicago: University of Chicago Press, 138–49.

Hamilton, G. (1940). *Theory and Practice of Social Case Work.* New York: Columbia University Press.

Hamilton, G. (1941). The underlying philosophy of social case work. *The Family 22*(5), 139–147.

Hofstein, S. (1964). The nature of process: Its implication for social work. *Journal of Social Process 14,* 13–53.

Hollis, F. (1939). *Social Case Work in Practice: Six Case Studies.* New York: Family Welfare Association of America.

Hollis, F. (1970). The psychosocial approach to the practice of casework. In R.W. Roberts & R.H. Nee (eds.), *Theories of Social Casework.* Chicago: University of Chicago Press, 33–75.

Hollis, F., & Woods, M.E. (1981). *Casework: A Psychosocial Therapy* (3rd. ed.). New York: Random House.

Horney, K. (1939). *New Ways in Psychoanalysis.* New York: W.W. Norton.

Hughes, S.S. (1938). Interpreting function to the visitor. *Journal of Social Work Process 2*(1), 61–73.

Kadushin, A. (1959). The knowledge base of social work. In A.J. Kahn (ed.), *Issues in American Social Work.* New York: Columbia University Press.

Karpf, F.B. (1953). *The Psychology and Psychotherapy of Otto Rank: An Historical and Comparative Introduction.* Westport, CT: Greenwood Press, 1970.

Kasius, C. (ed.). (1950). *A Comparison of Diagnostic and Functional Casework Concepts.* New York: Family Service Association of America.

Klein, D.B. (1981). *Jewish Origins of the Psychoanalytic Movement.* New York: Praeger.

Kuhn, T.S. (1970). *The Structure of Scientific Revolutions* (2nd ed.). Chicago: University of Chicago Press.

Lewin, K. (1935). *A Dynamic Theory of Personality* (D.K. Adams and K.E. Zener, trans.). New York: McGraw-Hill.

Lewin, K. (1951). *Field Theory in Social Science* (D. Cartwright, Ed.). New York: Harper & Row.

Lewis, H. (1962). Research analysis as an agency function. *Journal of Social Work Process 13,* 71–85.

Lewis, H. (1966). The functional approach to social work practice—A restatement of assumptions and principles. *Journal of Social Work Process 15,* 115–133.

Lieberman, E.J. (1985). *Act of Will: The Life and Work of Otto Rank.* New York: Free Press.

Lynd, H.M. (1961). *On Shame and the Search for Identity.* New York: Harcourt, Brace and World.

Marcus, G. (1966). The search for social work knowledge. *Journal of Social Work Process 15,* 17–33.

Maslow, A.H. (1937). Personality and patterns of culture. In R. Stagner, *Psychology of Personality.* New York: McGraw-Hill, 408–428.

Mayer, E.R. (1956). Some aspects of casework help to young retarded adults and their families. *Journal of Social Work Process 7,* 29–48.

Mead, G.H. (1936). *Movements of Thought in the Nineteenth Century.* Chicago: University of Chicago Press.

Menaker, E. (1982). *Otto Rank: a Rediscovered Legacy.* New York: Columbia University Press.

Menaker, E. (1984). The ethical and the empathic in the thinking of Otto Rank. *American Imago 41*(4), 343–351.

Mencher, S. (1959). *The Research Method in Social Work Education.* A Project Report of the Curriculum Study, Vol. 9. New York: Council on Social Work Education.

Meyer, C.H. (1970). *Social Work Practice: A Response to the Urban Crisis.* New York: Free Press.

Moustakas, C.E. (Ed.). (1956). *The Self-Explorations in Personal Growth.* New York: Harper & Row.

Murphy, J.P. (1933). Certain philosophical contributions to children's case work. *Proceedings of the National Conference of Social Work.* Chicago: University of Chicago Press, 75–90.

Phillips, H.U. (1957). *Essentials of Social Group Work Skill.* New York: Association Press.

Pray, K.L.M. (1938). New emphasis in education for public social work. *The Journal of Social Work Process* 2(1), 88–100.

Pray, K.L.M. (1949). *Social Work in a Revolutionary Age.* Philadelphia: University of Pennsylvania Press.

Progoff, I. (1956). *The Death & Rebirth of Psychology: An Integrative Evaluation of Freud, Adler, Jung and Rank and the Impact of Their Insights on Modern Man.* New York: McGraw-Hill.

Putsch, L. (1966). The impact of racial demonstrations on a social agency in the deep south. *Journal of Social Process* 15, 81–100.

Rank, O. (1924). *The Trauma of Birth.* New York: Harper & Row, 1973.

Rank, O. (1925). *Der Künstler (The Artist).* (4th Ed.). (E. Salomon and E.J. Lieberman, trans.). *Journal of the Otto Rank Association* 15(1), 1–63.

Rank, O. (1928). *Will Therapy* (J.J. Taft, trans.). New York: Alfred A. Knopf, 1964.

Rank, O. (1930). *Literary Autobiography. Journal of the Otto Rank Society* 16(1–2), 1–38.

Rank, O. (1932). *Art and Artist: Creative Urge and Personality Development.* (C.F. Atkinson, trans.). New York: Agathon Press.

Rank, O. (1936). *Truth and Reality* (J.J. Taft, trans.). New York: Alfred A. Knopf, 1964.

Rank, O. (1941) *Beyond Psychology.* Philadelphia: Privately published. (Printed by Haddon Craftsmen, Camden, NJ).

Rappaport, M.F. (1960). Clarifying the service to families with many problems. *Journal of Social Work Process 11,* 77–87.

Roberts, R.W., & Nee, Robert H. (eds.) (1970). *Theories of Social Casework.* Chicago: University of Chicago Press.

Robinson, V.P. (1930). *A Changing Psychology in Social Casework.* Chapel Hill: University of North Carolina Press.

Robinson, V.P. (1936). *Supervision in Social Case Work.* Chapel Hill: University of North Carolina Press.

Robinson, V.P. (1942). The meaning of skill. *Journal of Social Work Process 4,* 7–31.

Robinson, V.P. (1949). *The Dynamics of Supervision under Functional Controls: a Professional Process in Social Casework.* Philadelphia: University of Pennsylvania Press.

Robinson, V.P. (1960). University of Pennsylvania School of Social Work in Perspective: 1909–1959. *Journal of Social Work Process 11,* 10–29.

Robinson, V.P. (ed.). (1962). *Jessie Taft: Therapist and Social Work Educator.* Philadelphia: University of Pennsylvania Press.

Robinson, V.P. (1978). *The Development of a Professional Self: Teaching and Learning in Professional Helping Processes. Selected Writings, 1930–1968.* New York: AMS Press.

Robinson, V.P. (1978). The influence of Rank in social work: A journey into a past. In V.P. Robinson (ed), *The Development of a Professional Self: Teaching and Learning in Professional Helping Processes. Selected Writings, 1930–1968.* New York: AMS Press, 3–30.

Rudnytsky, P.L. (ed.). (1984). Otto Rank: A Centennial Tribute. *American Imago* 41(4).

Rudnytsky, P.L. (1991). *Rank, Winnicott, and the Legacy of Freud.* New Haven: Yale University Press.

Sinnott, E.W. (1950). *Cell and Psyche.* New York: Harper & Row.

Smalley, R.E. (1960). Today's frontiers in social work education. In W.W. Weaver (ed.), *Frontiers for Social Work: A Colloquium on the Fiftieth Anniversary of the School of Social Work of the University of Pennsylvania.* Philadelphia: University of Pennsylvania Press, 95–125.

Smalley, R.E. (1962). The advanced curriculum in the University of Pennsylvania School of Social Work. *Journal of Social Work Process, 7* 1–16.

Smalley, R.E. (1967). *Theory for Social Work Practice.* New York: Columbia University Press.

Smalley, R.E. (1970). The functional approach to casework. In R.W. Roberts and R.H. Nee (eds.), *Theories of Social Casework.* Chicago: University of Chicago Press, 77–128.

Smalley, R.E. (1971). Social casework: The functional approach. In R.E. Morris (ed.), *Encyclopedia of Social Work* (16th ed.). Vol. 2. New York: National Association of Social Workers, 1195–1206.

Smalley, R.E., & Bloom, R. (1977). Social casework: The functional approach. In J.B. Turner (ed.), *Encyclopedia of Social Work* (17th ed). Vol. 2. Washington, DC: National Association of Social Workers, 1280–1290.

Sprafkin, B.R. (1964). Introducing research into a family service agency. *Journal of Social Work Process 14,* 117–132.

Sward, K. (1980–81). Self-actualization and women: Rank and Freud contrasted. *Journal of the Otto Rank Association 15*(2), 49–63.

Taft, J.J. (1930). The "catch" in praise. *Child Study 7*(8), 133–135, 150.

Taft, J.J. (1932). The time element in mental hygiene therapy as applied to social case work. *Proceedings of the National Conference of Social Work.* Chicago: University of Chicago Press, 368–381.

Taft, J.J. (1933). *The Dynamics of Therapy in a Controlled Relationship.* New York: Macmillan.

Taft, J.J. (1937). The relation of function to process in social case work. *The Journal of Social Work Process 1*(1) 1–18.

Taft, J.J. (1962). *The Dynamics of Therapy in a Controlled Relationship.* New York: Dover. (Original work published in 1933)

Taft, J.J. (1950). A conception of the growth process underlying social casework practice. *Social Casework 31*(8), 311–318.

Taft, J.J. (1958). *Otto Rank: A Biographical Study Based on Notebooks, Letters, Collected Writings, Therapeutic Achievements and Personal Associations.* New York: Julian Press.

Yelaja, S.A. (1971). *Authority and Social Work: Concept and Use.* Toronto: University of Toronto Press.

Yelaja, S.A. (1986). Functional theory for social work practice. In F.J. Turner (ed.), *Social Work Treatment: Interlocking Theoretical Approaches* (3rd ed.). New York: Free Press, 46–67.

CHAPTER 14

GESTALT THEORY AND SOCIAL WORK TREATMENT

ELAINE P. CONGRESS

OVERVIEW

OVERVIEW OF THEORY

While many view Gestalt theory as primarily a collection of techniques, this model is firmly rooted in existential philosophy (Perls, 1992). Derived from a German word denoting wholeness, Gestalt refers to the holistic nature of human experience. A Gestalt is seen as much more than its collected parts. Although Gestalt therapy focuses on the "figure," the experience of the individual in current context, there is also consideration of the "ground," the present as well as past background of the individual. While the here and now is stressed, past experiences and relationships are examined in the present in order for the client to gain greater understanding about his/her current situation.

HISTORICAL ORIGINS

First developed in the late forties, Gestalt theory presented an alternative to psychoanalytic theory about the nature of personality, human development, and therapy. The founder and principal proponent of Gestalt theory and therapy, Frederick (Fritz) Perls, disagreed with the Freudian lineal approach, which stressed the past, the focus on individual pathology stemming from oedipal conflicts, and a treatment method that fostered dependency on the therapist. An early book, *Ego, Hunger, and Aggression: A Revision of Freud's Theory and Method* (Perls, 1947), presents the initial development of Gestalt theory.

While Perls disagreed with traditional psychoanalytic theory, he embraced existential philosophy and Gestalt psychology. Perls was greatly influenced by the existential focus on individual responsibility for one's experience within the present. The Gestalt therapeutic relationship is likened to the I-thou relationship described by Buber (1958) in which the therapist accepts the unique personality of the client unconditionally. In the I-thou relationship the barrier between self and others is minimized and each person connects on a human level. From Gestalt psychology Perls derives his focus on the total person who is more than his/her separate parts. In contrast to the psychoanalytic theory, which presents sex and aggression as primary drives, Gestalt theory sees the basic human drive as that of self-actualization.

Gestalt therapy was most popular in the sixties when Fritz Perls conducted many workshops and seminars to disseminate his theory. It has been suggested that Gestalt therapy, which focused on here-and-now experiential methods, was particularly suitable to the radical revolutionary nature of the sixties (Miller, 1989). Gestalt therapy, however, is not only a collection of dated dramatic techniques designed to bring about rapid personality change, but presents a philosophical world view and a therapeutic method which has continued to have relevance and following into the 1990s.

EXTENT OF LITERATURE IN GENERAL

In the beginning Frederick Perls was the principal author of literature on Gestalt theory. Important books by Perls which outline theoretical and treatment concepts of this model include *Gestalt Therapy Verbatim* (1969), *In and Out of the Garbage Pail* (1969), *The Gestalt Approach and Eye Witness to Therapy* (1973), and with R. F. Hefferline and P. Goodman, *Gestalt Therapy* (1951). Other authors on Gestalt therapy include Polster (1992), Polster, Polster, and Smith (1990), Harman (1990), Korb, Gorrell, and VanDeRiet (1989), Clarkson (1989), Smith (1992), and Nevis (1992). Gestalt therapy has been linked to psychoanalytic models in the work of Yontef (1987), to transactional analysis and redecision theory in Goulding (1989), to self psychology in Breshgold and Zahm (1992), and to insight-oriented therapy in the work of Scanlon (1980). The *Gestalt Journal* also includes timely articles on Gestalt theory and practice.

PATH INTO SOCIAL WORK

Although Gestalt theory was originally developed by a psychiatrist, Fritz Perls, and his wife, a psychologist, Laura Perls, and the majority of literature has been written by psychologists, there are many tenets that seem particularly pertinent to the social work perspective. Both Gestalt and social work focus on beginning where the client is. What Gestalt therapists describe as the figure/ground experience is similar to the social work focus on the person in environment ecological perspective. The social work concern about the total person, including the physical, cognitive, behavioral, and emotional, verbal and nonverbal, resembles the Gestalt therapy focus on wholeness. Both the Gestalt therapist and the social worker emphasize increasing self-awareness for client and therapist, as well as the positive use of self (Lammert, 1986).

EXTENT OF SOCIAL WORK LITERATURE

Social work literature on Gestalt theory has been limited, as a review of *Social Work Abstracts* from 1977 to March 1995 yields nine journal articles, only five of which have appeared in social work journals. In Levenson (1979) differences between Gestalt therapy and psychoanalytic psychotherapy are considered. Other social work authors have focused on the application of Gestalt therapy to clinical practice (Lammert and Dolan, 1983), to groups for chronic schizophrenics (Potocky, 1993), to marriage counseling (Hale, 1978), and to training groups in Gestalt therapy (Napoli & Walk, 1989). In an earlier edition of this book Blugerman discussed the usefulness of Gestalt theory for social work practice and research (Blugerman, 1986).

BASIC ASSUMPTIONS

PRINCIPAL CONCEPTS

Gestalt theory presupposes a belief in the wholeness of human experience and the value of each person. Six main concepts in Gestalt therapy include wholeness, awareness, contact, figure/ground, here and now, and self-regulation (Smith, 1992). They are described as follows:

1. Wholeness
Gestalt theory stresses the wholeness of the person without separation between mind and body, thought, emotion, and action. The problems or symptoms presented by clients are viewed as integral parts of their experience.

2. Awareness
The Gestalt therapist seeks to help the client become more aware of internal feelings and processes, as well as others in the external environment. As children, all human beings have the capacity for awareness and growth, but are often encouraged to minimize certain thoughts and behaviors as inappropriate. For example, a young girl may be taught that girls should never be assertive and should always be passive and accepting. This may lead to conflicts as an adult when a boss places unreasonable demands on her. A Gestalt therapist would help this client become aware of her feelings of anger which she had not been able to express as a child. By becoming more aware of both inner and outer experiences as a child and now as an adult, she can move toward developing more appropriate assertive behavior in the here and now.

3. Contact
The focus of Gestalt therapy is to expand the range and scope of contact between a person's inner and outer self and environment, as well as between client and environment. The Gestalt therapist views transference as a contact boundary disturbance and tries to increase the client's awareness of this distortion (Frew, 1990).

4. Figure/Ground
This concept, which stems from Gestalt psychology, alludes to the human person in relation to the environment (Perls, Hefferline, & Goodman, 1951). A Gestalt therapist helps the client to increase awareness of figure as a unified personality at the

point of contact between the external and internal world, while the ground becomes everything which is not the focus of attention at the experienced moment.

5. Self-Regulation

Pursuant to the existentialist focus on personal responsibility, Gestalt therapists believe that each person has the capacity to regulate his or her own actions. Contrary to Freudian-determined drives of aggression and sexuality, Gestalt therapists believe that human beings can self-regulate their own needs, as well as self-support and self-actualize. This process is enhanced when clients increase self-awareness at contact points and view themselves in a more unified way.

6. Here and Now

The Gestalt therapist's focus on the here and now represents the most radical departure from psychoanalytic theory. While a Gestalt therapist is primarily concerned with increasing a client's self-awareness at the current contact point between client and external environment, it is assumed that the past does affect the present experience of the client. The Gestalt therapist, however, does not dwell on past experiences and instead is more likely to use exercises to help clients understand past experiences in the context of the here and now. When the client is able to assume new roles or become aware of previously unarticulated feelings, the client learns how past experiences impact on the here and now and can begin to work thorough "unfinished business" from the past.

NATURE OF PERSONALITY

Gestalt theorists define personality as "the relatively stable or predictable ways in which one person will behave differently from another, under the same external conditions" (Wheeler, 1992, p. 115). This theory of personality departs markedly from psychoanalytic theory which postulates that all people progress through certain well-defined developmental stages. The diversity of individual personality is stressed. Also in contrast to the Freudians, Gestalt therapists stress the unity, the total Gestalt of personality. Freudians emphasize the structural theory of personality and psychodynamic therapy focuses on helping clients gain insight into different structural parts and making the ego dominate. While Perls in early Gestalt writings spoke of the ego, superego, and id and in *Gestalt Therapy Verbatim* (1969) even added an infraego, Gestalt therapists in general do not focus on the divisions of personality structure, but rather the totality and integration of different parts of the personality.

NATURE AND PROCESS OF CHANGE

Unlike most other psychotherapies, the focus of Gestalt theory is not to produce change in the client, but rather to produce increased awareness. Consistent with an existential approach, the Gestalt therapist accepts the client as a unified whole without judgment or criticism (Cole, 1994). The therapist does not seek to change the client according to the former's evaluation of the client's problems and/or pathology. Therapeutic change is defined as increased awareness of inner self and outer self as a unified whole. The client has the capacity to change, grow, and self-actualize, while the therapist only serves as a facilitator in this process.

IMPORTANCE OF SIGNIFICANT OTHERS

Gestalt therapists minimize the role of significant others in contributing to a client's move toward change and self-actualization. In fact, the Gestalt prayer, "I do my thing, and you do your thing. I am not in this world to live up to your expectations and you are not in this world to live up to mine," which Perls includes in the introduction to *Gestalt Therapy Verbatim* (1969), stresses the focus on the individual without regard for either support or hindrance of others. Other Gestalt therapists, however, have recognized the importance of significant others and Gestalt techniques have been used in marital counseling (Hale, 1978). With Gestalt marital therapy each partner is encouraged to develop basic awareness of the other and of the effect of the partner on the self during each here-and-now moment.

IMPORTANCE OF RESOURCES

Similar to other psychological theories, Gestalt theory focuses primarily on the person of the client, rather than on environmental resources which may or may not be available to the client. Although Gestalt therapy may not concentrate on concrete resources in the client's environment or teach client's skills to access them, a Gestalt therapist does acknowledge the importance of the totality of a client's experience, which includes environmental resources, as well as psychological resources.

VALUE BASES OF THEORY

Time Orientation.

The focus of Gestalt theory is most clearly on the present, the here and now. Yet Gestalt therapists acknowledge that past experiences often influence the perception and behavior of clients in the present. Past relationships with significant others, especially parental figures, are often reenacted in the present to help clients develop greater understanding of how the perceptions and distortions of these relationships are impacting on the here and now. Contrary to the Freudian deterministic belief that the past has inextricably influenced the present, Gestalt therapists believe that a client can revisit the past to reshape the present and future. The future, as well as the past, is not the primary focus of Gestalt therapy. Gestalt therapy is not goal directed. The current existential moment is the most important, the way the client experiences the world with increasing self-awareness. The future in terms of client or therapist goals is unknown and not considered as important as the current process of Gestalt therapy.

Basic Human Nature.
Gestalt theory presents an optimistic view of human nature. Each person is viewed as capable of self-actualization and increasing self-awareness. Each has the ability to see himself or herself as a unified whole. Gestalt theorists do not see people as bad or sick. Consequently, focus on social problems and/or psychological dysfunctions is minimized.

Relationship.
A key relationship within Gestalt theory is the therapeutic relationship between therapist and client. This relationship resembles Buber's I-thou relationship in which power differentials do not exist. Other positive relationships within a person's here and now should follow a similar format. The nature of activity for Gestalt therapy is primarily emotional experience, rather than behavioral change. The goal is to help the client understand his/her Gestalt rather than change behavior. Gestalt theory views people as existing in harmony with nature, rather than in conflict or as dominant. By increasing self-awareness a human being can become more aware of the impact of nature on the total Gestalt.

SOCIAL, CULTURAL, AND ETHNIC SENSITIVITY

Nowhere in Perls or other Gestalt theorists is there a focus on cultural and ethnic differences. Most of the early Gestalt clients were from white, middle-class, American or Western European backgrounds. Gestalt therapy is thought to foster an American individualistic perspective (Saner, 1989). Yet the focus on self-actualization, acceptance of diverse perspectives, and concentration on the whole seems particularly relevant for work with ethnically and culturally diverse people. It has been suggested that the Gestalt focus on emotional experience may not be helpful for some culturally diverse clients (Corey, 1991).

TREATMENT

PRINCIPAL THERAPEUTIC GOALS

Although Gestalt therapists avoid specific goal setting with individual clients, the following general goals are relevant to Gestalt therapy:

1. increase the variety of behaviors used by clients. Often clients have a very limited repertoire of behaviors. Gestalt therapy encourages them to expand their use of different behaviors.
2. encourage clients to take more responsibility for their lives. While clients may initially blame others for their life situations, Gestalt therapy helps clients to accept their own role in creating their Gestalt.
3. maximize experiential learning. Gestalt therapy encourages clients to rely not only on cognition, but to integrate this type of thinking with their emotions.

4. complete unfinished business from the past and integrate these experiences into their present Gestalt. Clients with disturbing past experiences which detrimentally affect their current functioning will be encouraged to bring these experiences into the here and now. By reliving and reworking through these experiences clients become more receptive to new life experiences.

5. increase opportunities for clients to feel and act stronger, more competent, and self supported through conscious and responsible choices, thereby facilitating-good contact (Korb, Gorrell, & VanDeRiet, 1989, p. 95).

PRINCIPAL THERAPEUTIC CONCEPTS

These goals are achieved through the nature of the therapeutic relationship and the variety of techniques employed by the Gestalt therapist. In Gestalt therapy the focus is always on the client. It is assumed that clients have all the tools required to make any desired personal changes (Korb, Gorrell, & VanDeRiet, 1989, p. 69). The therapist functions as a facilitator who aids in the client's discovery of what the client is doing, how the client is doing it, and explores the underlying processes that influence the behavior. The client is helped to accept responsibility for his/her behavior, not for the situation or other people's actions. The therapist enables the client to explore and take responsibility for his/her actions.

NATURE OF THERAPEUTIC RELATIONSHIP

The nature of the therapeutic relationship is crucial in Gestalt therapy. The most important quality for a Gestalt therapist is authenticity, that is, to have achieved good self-awareness and be open and honest with the client. The therapist must be able to enter into the client's world. Gestalt therapists must develop a close, personal relationship with clients, rather than an "aloof, distant, or totally objective" interaction (Korb, Gorrell, & VanDeRiet, 1989, p. 110). The Gestalt therapist minimizes the power differential which occurs between therapist and client. The establishment of an authoritarian relationship between therapist and client wherein the therapist knows best for the client is avoided, as the Gestalt therapist respects the client's desire to change as well as desire to remain the same (Cole, 1994). The client's reality is considered paramount and is seen to possess the capacity to grow and change with minimal assistance from the therapist. The therapeutic relationship is likened to Buber I-thou dialogue, which implies complete acceptance and respect for the other.

Role and Importance of Transference.

Unlike psychoanalytic approaches the Gestalt therapist does not foster the development of a transference relationship. Yet Gestalt therapists acknowledge that clients come into therapy with expectations that the therapist will relate to them in ways similar to what they experienced in childhood. The I-thou position of the therapist, however, "chips away at the client's expectation of trauma in the client relationship" (Cole, 1994, p. 84). The Gestalt therapist may present himself as the good parent, but only to facilitate the growth and change of the client. Transference in Gestalt therapy only functions as a means to an end, not as an end goal as in psychoanalytic treatment.

PERCEPTION OF AND IMPORTANCE OF HISTORY

Although the main focus of Gestalt therapy is on the here and now, it is a mistake to think of Gestalt therapy as ahistorical. A person's history is very crucial as all that is unfinished from the past manifests itself in the here and now (Huckabay, 1992). In contrast to the psychoanalytic model, which encourages clients to talk about past experiences, the Gestalt therapist uses exercises to help clients relive past events and relationships in the here and now.

PERCEPTION OF AND IMPORTANCE OF ASSESSMENT

A Gestalt therapist's assessment of a client differs significantly from a social worker's psychosocial assessment. Neither a discussion of the physical, psychological, intellectual, cognitive, and emotional characteristics of the client nor an analysis of familial, social, and environmental resources can be found in the Gestalt therapist's assessment of a client. In terms of diagnosis, Gestalt therapy does not focus on pathology. Diagnosis according to DSM-IV, symptom description, defense mechanisms, and even client "problems" are not relevant to a Gestalt therapist's "assessment" of a client (Yontef, 1987). Statements such as "This is a manic-depressive, single parent, or welfare recipient" are avoided. While psychoanalysts see the defense mechanism of resistance as a negative force to be eliminated, Gestalt therapists see the need "to enliven the resistances to awareness, so as to give them new flexibility and contact with the realities of the self and the social world" (Cole, 1994, p. 72).

While Gestalt therapy does not recognize assessment and diagnosis according to the psychoanalyst, psychiatric DSM-IV, or social work psychosocial model, problems that occur at the point of contact, dysfunctional boundary disturbances *confluence, introjection, projection,* and *retroflection* can be identified in clients and become the focus of treatment. Even the word *disturbances* has been considered too judgmental for Gestalt therapists and it has been suggested that "processes" would be a better descriptive word (Swanson, 1988).

SPECIFIC THERAPEUTIC VOCABULARY

The four disturbances (processes) that occur between person and environment can be described as follows:

Confluence involves the denial of differences and an unrealistic focus on similarities. It is similar to the psychological phenomenon of accommodation and generalization. For example, if one places a hand on a wall, at first the person is very aware of temperature and textural differences, but these differences blur within a short period. Similarly, in some marriages differences between the partners are denied and a false sense of togetherness ensues. Gestalt therapy helps couples to examine ambivalent feelings about each other, as well as the "shoulds" and expectations of their relationships (Hale, 1978). Couples become more aware of individual needs apart from their confluent relationship.

A second contact disturbance, *introjection,* refers to the inappropriate intake of information from others, especially significant historical figures. Often parental messages become internalized with the result that the client is plagued by commands of "I should," "I ought to," or "I have to." When introjection is a client's disturbance, the Gestalt therapist may encourage the client to assume a voice apart from the introjected parent and carry on a dialogue in the here-and-now. The purpose of this exercise is to help the client differentiate himself/herself from the parental introject. While psychoanalysts would assess introjection as an ego defense against anxiety, Gestalt therapists perceive introjection as a disturbance between person and environment which can be readily be remedied in the here and now.

A third contact disturbance, *projection,* describes the process of disavowing parts of oneself and projecting these parts upon others. Ego psychologists consider this phenomenon a defense mechanism in which unacceptable parts of one's own personality are rejected and attributed to another. This defense mechanism is considered a lower level type of ego defense which is used most frequently by the severely mentally ill. Gestalt therapists, on the other hand, do not consider that clients who use this process are more mentally ill, but rather that these clients have lost a significant part of themselves. This behavior takes away power from themselves and gives the environment more control than warranted. Gestalt therapists would help clients reclaim lost parts of themselves. For example, a client who thought all men were angry at her might be helped to acknowledge her own feelings of anger toward significant men past and present.

A final disturbance of contact, *retroflection,* describes the process during which individuals do to themselves what they would like to do to someone else or to have someone else do to them. This behavior sometimes is a very healthy response, as when an angry mother very actively cleans the kitchen rather than abuse her child or a woman rejected by a boyfriend buys herself a new suit (Polster & Polster, 1973). Retroflection can be overused and a person may not be able to function in the current here and now because of powerful forces from the past. For example, clients rejected by their parents as children may not reach out to others as adults and only depend on themselves for support. A Gestalt therapist would work with clients to help them understand that they no longer have to be the primary source of their support and that they can connect with others in their current environment.

The assessment of contact point disturbances occurs at the very beginning of treatment. Assessment is not viewed as a prerequisite to treatment. The integration of assessment and treatment from the very beginning serves to bring the Gestalt therapist and client together immediately, thus avoiding the professional distance created by a more formal, diagnostic assessment process.

SPECIFIC TECHNIQUES AND STRATEGIES

Gestalt therapists often use a variety of strategies or techniques in working with clients. Respect for the personhood of the client as well as flexibility are main principles that govern the choice of specific techniques to use with clients. The choice of techniques depends on the health and readiness of the client. Therapy often creates the safe emergency in which the client learns that it is acceptable to be angry, elated, or unhappy (Stevens, 1975). Translating this safe emergency into action is often accomplished through the use of an experiment (Polster & Polster, 1973). A Gestalt experiment has been described as "an attempt to counter the aboutist deadlock by bringing the individual's action system right into the room" (Polster & Polster, 1973, p. 234). In general, experiments help clients to understand themselves better through acting out problems and feelings, rather than only talking about them. While an important role for the Gestalt therapist is facilitator, the therapist often assumes the role of director in introducing and carrying through the following experiments. Some of the main classic experiments can be summarized as follows (Korb, Gorrell, & VanDeRiet, 1989):

Dialogue, the most well recognized of Gestalt therapy techniques, is commonly referred to as the empty chair technique. Although this technique is often criticized as being overly dramatic, it should be remembered that it was originally designed to teach others about Gestalt therapy, as well as to facilitate growth in an individual client (Blugerman, 1986). When a client has conflict with another person past or present or with a part of his/her personality, the Gestalt therapist asks the client to imagine that this person or personality aspect is in the empty chair. By promoting this separation the client is often able to achieve greater understanding of and insight into what is frequently an area of conflict. For example, a client who is very demanding and a perfectionist in his behavior may benefit from the experience of having his imagined father sit in the empty chair and having the opportunity of "talking" with his father about the latter's multiple demands for perfection.

Enactment of dreams often permits clients to become aware of issues and conflicts about which they are not aware. In contrast to psychoanalytic theorists, who encourage clients to discuss their dreams to provide greater understanding of the unconscious, Gestalt therapists see dreams as "existential messages" about the current situations in the client's life (Latner, 1992, p. 51). While psychoanalysts stress interpretation of dreams as most important, Gestalt therapists encourage clients to act out their dreams as an expression of their current Gestalt.

Exaggeration occurs when the Gestalt therapist asks the client to exaggerate some motion or speech pattern. This exercise may help the client get in touch with feelings about which there was no previous awareness. For example, a Gestalt therapist noted that a client frowned when she discussed an impending visit by her in-laws. After the client was encouraged to exaggerate her frown, she became more aware of her negative feelings about her in-laws' visit.

Reversal involves suggesting that a client reverse a statement which has been made. Polarities are common in human experience, and encouraging clients to state the opposite often leads to greater awareness and acceptance of integrated feelings toward significant others. For example, a mother who was having a difficult time separating from her latency-aged son stated that she did not want her child to go to summer camp as he was too young to take care of himself away from home. When the client was asked to reverse the statement, she became more in touch with part of herself which really wanted to encourage her child to be more independent.

Rehearsal serves to prepare the client before seeking any change. Clients often lack a self-support system and fear there will be dire consequences if they try a new experience. Practicing words beforehand often gives the client confidence to approach a new situation. For example, the client who is fearful of asking the boss for a raise may benefit from the opportunity to rehearse this experience with the therapist. It should be noted that many cognitive behavior therapies also make use of this rehearsal technique.

Making the rounds is a Gestalt group work technique which provides an opportunity for the client to rehearse and receive feedback from other group members. By introducing the environment of other members, the client is helped to become clearer about his/her own experience. For example, a group member struggling with his plans to separate from his wife was asked to rehearse this discussion within the group and hear group members' reactions.

Exposing the obvious describes a technique in which Gestalt therapists are encouraged to follow up on a client's initial statements and movements which are often indicative of deeper processes. This technique is familiar to social workers who learn it to follow up on both verbal and nonverbal communication. An example of this occurred in Gestalt therapy when the therapist noted to the client that he had been yawning repeatedly since he came into the session.

Directed awareness experiments help clients establish contact with different inner and outer experiences. Gestalt therapists use these techniques to help clients gain a clearer picture of sensory as well as internal body sensations.

In *Creative Process in Psychotherapy* Zinker outlines the following steps in a Gestalt therapy session:

1. Laying the groundwork
2. Negotiating a consensus between client and therapist
3. Grading (assessing that an experiment is challenging, not frustrating)
4. Surfacing the client's awareness
5. Locating the client's energy
6. Generating self-support for both client and therapist
7. Generating a theme
8. Choosing an experiment by mutual process
9. Enacting the experiment
10. Insight and completion

Reorientation is necessary after the use of a Gestalt experiment (Heikkinen, 1989).

PERCEPTION OF LENGTH OF TREATMENT

Gestalt therapy, like other therapies, delineates the following four stages: (1) establishing a relationship, (2) exploring a problem in depth, (3) determining steps for the client to take, and (4) providing support and encouragement for growth (Egan, 1986). Gestalt therapists believe that for some clients all four stages may occur in the first session whereas with other clients the process may span several years. The average client often falls somewhere in between (Korb, Gorrell, & VanDeRiet, 1989). Flexibility in duration of treatment is consistent with Gestalt theory, which supports a client-centered focus on treatment. The client, not the therapist, makes decisions about the length of treatment. Allowing the client to make decisions about the length of treatment seems to contradict both the traditional psychoanalytic model, which favors long-term treatment, and current managed-care model of brief treatment.

In general, however, Gestalt therapy is not usually considered a long-term model. Because the focus is on flexibility and acceptance of each client, the duration of Gestalt therapy is often short-term. This factor increases the usefulness of Gestalt therapy for those who practice in a managed-care environment.

IMPORTANCE OF SPECIFIC METHODS

Work with Individuals and Groups.

The founder of Gestalt therapy, Fritz Perls, was primarily an individual therapist. Even when he led groups he worked primarily with one individual at a time with little interaction from other group members (Nevis, 1992). Groups were seen to provide an excellent opportunity to demonstrate Gestalt theory and practice to others. An early Perls group would consist of placing one individual in the "hot seat" and exploring a particular topic with the other group members as spectators. Other members might be asked to contribute in a structured way about the client in the hot seat. A client usually stayed in the hot seat about ten to thirty minutes, and in a two- to three-hour session two to four participants took the hot seat (Korb, Gorrell, VanDeRiet, 1989).

Currently the most frequently used Gestalt group therapy model is the Gestalt group process model (Zinker, 1977; Huckabay, 1992). With this model the therapist continues as the director of experimentation, but is more receptive to interventions from other group members (Korb, Gorrell, & VanDeRiet, 1989). Group interaction and the development of cohesiveness are encouraged. With this model one group member may express awareness of a particular theme which is shared by other group members. The group leader may lead the group in an activity related to this issue.

Although Gestalt therapy began as an individual model and is still used as an individual model, four features of Gestalt therapy are particularly suitable to work with groups: self-regulation, contact and the contact boundary, awareness, and an emphasis on the here and now (Frew, 1988). Groups, like individuals, demonstrate their own tendency to self-regulate and seek wholeness. The possibilities of contact between different group members, different subgroups, and the group leader are manifold in group process. Awareness or focused attention is even more important in group work than individual work. Finally, a focus on the here and now is paramount in group work. With this focus Gestalt group therapy is short-term, which is particularly advantageous in the current managed-care mental health environment.

Work with Dyads.

In addition to individual and group work, Gestalt therapy has also been applied to work with couples. Treatment of couples, however, may be difficult for the Gestalt therapist who has been trained to focus on the individual and his/her boundary in relation to the external world. (Zinker, 1992). The Gestalt therapist must focus on the couple as a system, a Gestalt and the boundary of the couple as they relate to the outside world. Couple therapy consists of prescribing certain exercises for the couple to increase their awareness and interaction with each other (Hale, 1978; Zinker, 1992).

Work with Families.

While not initially developed as a family therapy model, Gestalt theory has been used in family therapy. Kempler, a Gestalt family therapist, applied Gestalt theory and techniques in his work with troubled families (Kempler, 1974). Other family therapists including Satir adopted an experiential, existentialist approach in working with families and developed Gestalt-like family therapy techniques such as family posturing and family sculpture (Satir, 1983).

Work with Community.

Gestalt therapy as it was originally developed was intended primarily for micro practice with individuals and other small systems including couples, groups, and families. Although not directing their change efforts toward the community, Smith, a contemporary Gestalt therapist, writes, "My power to influence social change resides in my person and the effect of my person on others through intimate contacting" (Smith, 1992, p. 294). Others have seen Gestalt therapy as being more socially and community focused in contrast to American individualism (Brown, Lichtenberg, Lukensmeyer, & Miller, 1993). Gestalt therapy has been used to study macro organizational patterns (Critchley & Casey, 1989) as well as in therapeutic milieu settings such as psychiatric hospitals, group homes, day treatment centers, and sheltered workshops.

PRINCIPAL APPLICATIONS TO SOCIAL WORK PRACTICE

Uses in Practice—Range of Applications

Gestalt therapy was first developed for use with depressed, phobic, and obsessive clients with adjustment to neurotic disorders. Most clients are and have been of white, middle-class background. Yet the existential focus of Gestalt therapy which stresses the uniqueness and value of each client's experience seems particularly well suited to the diverse economic, social, cultural, and racial clients with whom social workers work.

Gestalt therapy has been used primarily with young and middle-aged adults, but has also been applied successfully in work with children (Oaklander, 1992) and older persons (Crouse, 1990). Other clients who have benefitted from Gestalt therapy include abused women (Little, 1990), abused children (Sluckin, Weller, & Highton, 1989), amputees (Grossman, 1990), people with AIDS (Klepner, 1992; Siemens, 1993), clients with family members who have committed suicide (Bengesser & Sokoloff, 1989), and alcoholics (Shore, 1978; Carlock, O'Halloran, Glaus, & Shaw, 1992).

KNOWN RISKS

A prevailing belief has been that Gestalt therapy is inappropriate for clients with severe personality disorders or psychoses (Shepard, 1970). Clients who have difficulty differentiating reality from fantasy may become more disoriented during guided fantasies, a frequent experiment used in Gestalt therapy. It has been suggested that Gestalt therapy can be modified for work with people who are borderline (Greenberg, 1989), groups of people diagnosed as chronic schizophrenic (Potocky, 1993), and individuals hospitalized for psychoses (Harris, 1992). There is greater risk, however, in using Gestalt therapy with people who have a tenuous grasp of reality and sense of self, as they may not be able to return easily from fantasy to the real world.

KNOWN LIMITATIONS

While Gestalt therapy presents risks for many clients with severe psychotic disorders, this model of therapy also may not be appropriate for poor clients for whom environmental advocacy and securing of resources is needed. Most successful with middle-class or working-class clients with neurotic or adjustment disorders, Gestalt therapy seems particularly to differ from case management, a current treatment model for work with the chronic mentally ill and others who require therapist activity in securing and coordination of community resources.

ADMINISTRATIVE AND TRAINING FACTORS

REQUIRED LEVEL AND EXTENT OF TRAINING

Importance of Supervision

Gestalt therapy is often briefly covered in graduate social work or psychology programs and most Gestalt therapists receive their training in postgraduate training centers located in many large cities. There are no universal guidelines for the extent of training, but most educators in the Gestalt therapy field believe that the three main areas to be covered in Gestalt training are (1) theoretical grounding, (2) intense personal Gestalt work, and (3) extended supervision (Korb, Gorrell, & VanDeRiet, 1989). Educators believe that beginning students must study extensively the theoretical orientation of Gestalt therapy in order to have an understanding of this method as more than a collection of techniques. Because of the importance of the therapeutic relationship in Gestalt work, the therapist must have a good understanding of self as explored through his/her own Gestalt therapy. Finally, ongoing supervision is considered essential for students studying the Gestalt method.

IMPORTANCE AND FUNCTION OF RECORDING

Recording for Gestalt therapists focuses on the verbal and nonverbal process of the interview, similar to the process recordings of social work students. Diagnosis, history taking, and psychosocial assessment are usually absent from Gestalt recordings because these areas are not part of Gestalt therapist work with clients. Instead Gestalt literature on practice with clients often focuses on the initial awareness/contact phase with clients. What is stressed is the process that occurs between therapist and client.

ROLE OF SETTING

Although the agency context is certainly part of a client's total Gestalt, Gestalt therapists minimize the role of agency setting. Most Gestalt therapy occurs within Gestalt training institutes or in private practice, although many professionals may use some Gestalt techniques with their clients in a variety of mental health settings.

CASE VIGNETTES

The following case vignettes present a Gestalt therapist's initial sessions with an individual client suffering from depression and with a group of people who are HIV-positive.

Susan, a twenty-five-year-old married woman, had been referred for therapy because of recurring symptoms of depression characterized by feelings of low self-esteem and crying spells. The therapist introduced herself as Jane Smith. Immediately the therapist noted that Susan seemed to sink into the chair and did not make any comments until asked. In this first session the therapist asked Susan to describe how she was feeling, to which Susan responded "terrible," but she did not understand why she felt this way as her husband was very supportive, she had a good job, a nice home. The therapist was careful to stay with the original feeling she had expressed and asked the client to describe in more detail the experience of feeling terrible. After some encouragement, the client indicated that she felt like a piece of garbage. The therapist asked the client to explore what being a piece of garbage felt like. The client described herself as feeling dirty, unclean, and rejected. She remembered that once as an adolescent she had cooked dinner and her mother had said the food tasted like garbage, and that her room had been compared to a garbage dump. It became apparent that Susan was very angry at her mother for such criticism, but had turned this anger inward. As a Gestalt therapist Jane saw that her client was suffering from retroflection, a process by which a client turns back on him/herself what he/she would like to do to another and decided to use a Gestalt exercise of the empty chair to help Jane get in touch with and verbalize some of her previously unexpressed angry feelings toward her mother. It should be noted that with Gestalt therapy the past is not ignored, but brought into the present. Susan was able to express angry feelings toward her mother (sitting in the empty chair) and after the exercise reported that she felt better than she had in a long time.

The second case vignette focuses on Gestalt work with a group whose members had recently been diagnosed as HIV-positive. This group follows a Gestalt group process model rather than the original Perls individual in group model.

This group consisted of six homosexual men ranging in age from twenty to thirty-five who had learned of their HIV status within the last month. Group members were each asked to introduce themselves and tell what they expected to get out of the group. Most group members were in a state of denial as to their illness. Several made no reference to having HIV; one said he was sure he was misdiagnosed; another indicated that a cure was just around the corner. The Gestalt group leader was supportive of where each member was. When one member mentioned how hopeless and helpless he felt, the group leader again was able to support this member's awareness. The focus was on the here-and-now feelings of group members, not historical events.

In the beginning, the group leader related to each member individually, but was very encouraging when another group member reported that he too had felt powerless when he learned of his diagnosis. He reported that he had last felt this powerless when his mother died when he was sixteen. At this point the client started to cry; the other members were very supportive, as was the group leader. The group leader tried to facilitate this interaction by asking if others had experienced losses. Reliving this loss in the here-and-now was an important experience because it allowed the client to work through issues of loss which had never been completely resolved. This interaction also served to promote group cohesiveness as many group members reached out to this client while before they had all been quite isolated. Also, this sadness over a past loss led to a discussion about current losses, health and impending disability, and fears of future losses, that is, death. Finally, this incident demonstrated a Gestalt therapist's concern about the whole person, that each group person is not only just a person who is HIV-positive but also has a history and current Gestalt of which HIV is only one part.

After each member had the opportunity to express himself and some initial group cohesiveness was developed, the group leader introduced a Gestalt experiment. Group members were asked to imagine that they had a treasure box in which they could store all that was most precious to them. One member spoke very concretely that he would use this box to store T cells for a time he might need them in fighting his illness. Another expressed concern about his younger brother and visualized that he would store him in this box to prevent him from being harmed. Another would store in his box all his successes in life such as when he was selected to give the graduation address in college and when he was named director of his division at work. A group member saved sunsets and the first day of spring. This exercise served to create connection between the men, as well as help them begin to confront the present reality of their illness.

EMPIRICAL BASE

EXTENT OF RESEARCH BASE—KNOWN OVERALL EFFECTIVENESS

Because Gestalt theory focuses on the experiential rather than the empirical nature of treatment, single subject case studies greatly outnumber large research studies on Gestalt therapy. Some of the many reports of clients who benefitted from Gestalt therapy can be found in Harman (1989), Smith (1992), and Nevis (1992). There had been clinical research on Gestalt methods (Clarke & Greenberg, 1988), "Good moments in psychotherapy," including extratherapy behavior change, acceptance of problem, and increased general well-being, have been linked with specific Gestalt treatment methods (Mahrer, White, Howard, & Gagnon, 1992). Research on Gestalt therapy has demonstrated effectiveness in resolving decisional conflict (Greenberg & Webster, 1982), in groups (O'Leary & Page, 1990; Anderson, 1978), and in teaching (Napoli & Walk, 1989).

ATTITUDE TO RESEARCH AND GAPS IN KNOWLEDGE AND RESEARCH

In general, empirical research on Gestalt therapy has been limited and the need for more research to substantiate its effectiveness as a treatment method continues to exist. There are difficulties, however, in conducting empirical research on an experiential, highly individualistic form of treatment and most Gestalt therapists minimize the need for research of this type.

PROSPECTUS

PRESENT STATUS AND INFLUENCE ON CURRENT PRACTICE

In a different political and social climate than that of the sixties during which Perls developed and taught others about his model, Gestalt therapy has declined in popularity (Miller, 1989). Yet many Gestalt therapy institutes exist around the country and the *Gestalt Journal* continues to publish articles of current interest to Gestalt therapists. While Gestalt therapy has frequently been accused of relying too extensively on techniques, current Gestalt therapists have argued that Gestalt therapy is more philosophical than technical (Perls, 1992) and that creativity, not technical skill, is essential for Gestalt therapists (Zinker, 1991). Also, Gestalt therapy groups have changed over the years from the therapist's focus on individual clients in the group to the current stress on increasing client interactions with each other (Harman, 1989; Frew, 1988).

CONTRIBUTIONS TO THE PROFESSION

Many aspects of Gestalt therapy are particularly pertinent for the social work profession. First, the Gestalt focus on the point of contact between person and environment suggests social work's attention to person in situation. Also, the Gestalt figure/ground concept relates to the profession's use of the systems approach. While Gestalt stresses the I-thou relationship, social work speaks to the importance of developing an empathic helping relationship with the client. Both Gestalt therapist and social work professionals see much importance in increasing self-awareness and use of self. Gestalt therapists, as well as social workers, focus on clients' strengths. Also, Gestalt therapists and social workers agree on self-actualization as a primary treatment goal. Finally, the Gestalt therapy's concern with the total Gestalt resembles the social work focus on the total person including physical, cognitive, behavioral, emotional, verbal, and nonverbal.

IMPLICATIONS FOR PRACTICE

Current social work practice includes clients from very different social, economic, and cultural backgrounds. Gestalt therapy, which begins with the acceptance of the client and his/her Gestalt, would seem very useful for social workers in working with very diverse clients.

Gestalt therapy, however, may not be an effective treatment modality for all social workers in all settings. Social workers who treat clients with severe psychiatric or socioeconomic problems may not be able to use this model. Also, the I-thou relationship of Gestalt therapist and client may be difficult for social workers who define their primary role as that of professional expert. Furthermore, the Gestalt therapist's lack of emphasis on history taking, diagnosis, psychosocial assessment, and goal setting may not be acceptable to social workers and their agencies who have been schooled in a more psychodynamic or psychosocial approach.

CONNECTION TO OTHER MODELS

In terms of treatment modalities, Gestalt therapy, which stresses the here-and-now, resembles current treatment modalities of brief treatment, problem solving, and crisis intervention which are often used by social workers. Also, since most Gestalt therapy is brief, this treatment modality works within a managed-care environment, which introduces many time constraints into treatment.

FUTURE OF THEORY FOR THE PROFESSION

Currently a number of social workers are involved in Gestalt training institutes. Social workers often learn little about this treatment modality during their graduate education, and those who wish to develop their expertise in this area usually attend a Gestalt therapy institute for postgraduate training. For social workers interested in this model Gestalt therapy will continue to be a significant practice method for use in social work treatment.

Gestalt therapy's focus on and acceptance of the individual person-in-environment points to its current, as well as future, value in social work treatment. The clients we serve are becoming increasingly diverse. The applicability of this model in working with clients from different cultural and socioeconomic backgrounds suggests that social workers can make greater use of Gestalt theory and therapy in their treatment of clients.

REFERENCES

American Psychiatric Association (1994). *Diagnostic and statistical manual of mental disorders* (4th ed.) Washington, DC: APA Press.

Anderson, J. (1978). Growth groups and alienation: A comparative study of Rogerian encounter, self-directed encounter, and Gestalt. *Group and Organization Studies, 3*(1), 85–107.

Bengesser, G., & Sokoloff, S. (1989). After suicide—postvention. *European Journal of Psychiatry, 3*(2), 116–118.

Blugerman, M. (1986). Contributions of Gestalt theory to social work treatment. In Francis Turner (Ed.), *Social work treatment* (3rd ed.) (pp. 69–90). New York; Free Press.

Breshgold, E. (1989). Resistance in Gestalt therapy: An historical theoretical perspective. *Gestalt Journal, 12*(2), 73–102.

Breshgold, E., & Zahm, S. (1992). A case for the integration of self psychology developmental theory into the practice of Gestalt therapy. *Gestalt Journal, 15*(1), 61–93.

Brown, J., Lichtenberg, P., Lukensmeyer, C., & Miller M. (1993) The implications of Gestalt therapy for social and political change. *Gestalt Journal, 16*(1), 7–54.

Buber, M. (1958). *I and thou* (2nd ed.). New York: Scribner and Sons.

Carlock, J., O'Halloran, Glaus, K., & Shaw, K. (1992). The alcoholic: A Gestalt view. In Edwin Nevis (Ed.), *Gestalt therapy: Perspectives and applications* (pp. 191–237). New York: Gardner Press.

Clarke, K., & Greenberg, L. (1988). Clinical research on Gestalt methods. In Fraser N. Watts. (Ed.), *New developments in clinical psychology* (pp. 5–19). New York: John Wiley and Sons.

Clarkson, P. (1989). *Gestalt counselling in action.* London: Sage Publications.

Cole, P. (1994). Resistance to awareness: A Gestalt therapy perspective. *Gestalt Journal, 17*(1), 71–94.

Corey, G. (1991). *Theory and practice of counseling and psychotherapy* (4th ed.). Pacific Grove, CA: Brooks/Cole.

Critchley, B., & Casey, D. (1989). Organizations get stuck too. *Leadership and Organization Development Journal, 10*(4), 3–12.

Crouse, R. (1990). Reviewing the past in the here and now: Using Gestalt therapy techniques with life review. *Journal of Mental Health Counseling, 12*(3), 279–287.

Egan, G. (1986). *The skilled helper* (3rd ed.) Pacific Grove, CA: Brooks/Cole.

Frew, J. (1988). The practice of Gestalt therapy in groups. *Gestalt Journal, 11*(1), 77–96.

Frew, J. (1990). Analysis of transference in Gestalt group psychotherapy *International Journal of Group Psychotherapy, 40*(2), 189–202.

Frew, J. (1992). From the perspective of the environment. *Gestalt Journal, 15*(1), 39–60.

Goulding, R. (1989). Teaching transactional analysis and redecision therapy. *Journal of Independent Social Work, 3*(4), 71–86.

Greenberg, E. (1989). Healing the borderline. *Gestalt Journal, 12*(2), 11–55.

Greenberg, L., & Webster, M. (1982). Resolving decisional conflict by Gestalt two-chair dialogues relating process to outcome. *Journal of Counseling Psychology, 29*(5), 468–477.

Grossman, E. (1990). The Gestalt approach to people with amputations. *Journal of Applied Rehabilitation Counseling, 21*(1), 16–19.

Hale, B. (1978). Gestalt techniques in marriage counseling. *Social Casework, 59*(7), 428–433.

Harman, R. (1989). *Gestalt therapy with groups, couples, sexually dysfunctional men, and dreams.* Springfield, IL: Charles C Thomas.

Harman, R. (1990). *Gestalt therapy: Discussions with the masters.* Springfield, IL: Charles C Thomas.

Harris, C. (1992). Group work with psychotics. In E. Nevis (Ed.), *Gestalt therapy* (pp. 239–261). New York: Gardner Press.

Heikkinen, C. (1989). Reorientation from altered states: Please, move carefully. *Journal of Counseling and Development, 67*(9), 520–521.

Huckabay, M. (1992). An overview of the theory and practice of Gestalt group process. In E. Nevis (Ed.), *Gestalt therapy* (pp. 303–330). New York: Gardner Press.

Jacobs, L. (1992). Insights from psychoanalytic self-psychology and intersubjectivity theory for Gestalt therapists. *Gestalt Journal, 15*(2), 25–60.

Kempler, W. (1974). *Principles of Gestalt family therapy.* Costa Mesa, CA: The Kempler Institute.

Klepner, P. (1992). AIDS/HIV and Gestalt therapy. *Gestalt Journal, 15*(2), 5–24.

Korb, M., Gorrell, J., & VanDeRiet, V. (1989). *Gestalt therapy: Practice and theory.* New York: Pergamon Press.

Lammert, M. (1986). Experience as knowing: Utilizing therapist self-awareness. *Social Casework, 23*(1), 369–376.

Lammert, M. & Dolan, M. (1983). Active intervention in clinical practice: Contribution of Gestalt therapy. *Adolescence, 18*(69), 43–50.

Latner, J. (1992). Theory of Gestalt therapy. In E. Nevis (ed.), *Gestalt therapy* (pp. 13–56). New York: Gardner Press.

Levenson, J. (1979). A comparison of Robert Lang's psychoanalytic psychotherapy and Erving Polster's Gestalt therapy. *Smith College Studies in Social Work, 49*(2), 146–157.

Little, L. (1990). Gestalt therapy with females involved in intimate violence. In S. Smith, M. Williams, & K. Rosen (Eds.), *Violence hits home: Comprehensive approaches to domestic violence* (pp. 47–65). New York: Springer Publishing Company.

Mahrer, A., White, M., Howard, T., & Gagnon, R. (1992). How to bring some very good moments in psychotherapy sessions. *Psychotherapy Research, 2*(4), 252–265.

Meyer, L. (1991). Using Gestalt therapy in the treatment of anorexia nervosa. *British Review of Bulimia and Anorexia Nervosa, 5(1),* 7–16.

Miller, M. (1989). Introduction to Gestalt therapy verbatim. *Gestalt Journal, 12*(1), 5–24.

Napoli, D., & Walk, C. (1989). Circular learning: Teaching and learning Gestalt therapy in groups. *Journal of Independent Social Work, 27*(1), 57–70.

Nevis, E. (Ed.). (1992). *Gestalt therapy.* New York: Gardner Press.

Oaklander, V. (1992). Gestalt work with children: Working with anger and introjects. In E. Nevis (Ed.), *Gestalt therapy* (pp. 263–284). New York: Gardner Press.

O'Leary, E., & Page, R. (1990). An evaluation of a person-centered Gestalt group using the semantic differential. *Counseling Psychology Quarterly, 3*(1), 13–20.

Perls, F. (1947). *Ego, hunger, and aggression: A revision of Freud's theory and method.* London: Allen & Unwin.

Perls, F. (1969a). *Gestalt therapy verbatim.* Moab, UT: Real Person Press.

Perls, F. (1969b). *In and out of the garbage pail.* Moab, UT: Real Person Press.

Perls, F. (1973). *The gestalt approach and eye witness to therapy.* Palo Alto, CA: Science and Behavior Books.

Perls, F.S., Hefferline, R.F., & Goodman, P. (1951). *Gestalt therapy.* New York: Julian Press.

Perls, L. (1992). Concepts and misconceptions of Gestalt therapy. *Journal of Humanistic Psychology, 32*(3), 50–56.

Polster, E, (1992). The self in action: A Gestalt outlook. In J. Zeig (Ed.), *The evolution of psychotherapy: The second conference* (pp. 143–154). New York: Brunner/Mazel.

Polster, E., & Polster, M. (1973). *Gestalt therapy integrated: Contours of theory and practice.* New York: Brunner/Mazel.

Polster, E., Polster, M., & Smith, E. (1990). Gestalt approaches. In J. Zeig & M. Munion, (Eds.), *What is psychotherapy?: Contemporary perspectives* (pp. 103–111). San Francisco: Jossey-Bass Publishers.

Potocky, M. (1993). An art therapy group for clients with chronic schizophrenia. *Social Work with Groups, 16*(3), 73–82.

Saner, R. (1989). Culture bias of Gestalt therapy: Made in USA. *Gestalt Journal, 12*(2), 57–71.

Satir, V. (1983). *Conjoint family therapy.* Palo Alto, CA: Science and Behavioral Books.

Scanlon, P. (1980). A Gestalt approach to insight-oriented treatment. *Social Casework, 61*(7), 407–415.

Shepard, I. (1970). Limitations and cautions in Gestalt approach. In J. Fagan & I. Shepard (Eds.), *Gestalt therapy now.* Palo Alto, CA: Science and Behavioral Books.

Shore, J. (1978). The use of self-identity workshop with recovering alcoholics. *Social Work with Groups, 1*(3), 299–307.

Siemens, H. (1993). A Gestalt approach in the care of persons with HIV. *Gestalt Journal, 16*(1), 91–104.

Sluckin, A., Weller, A., & Highton, J. (1989). Recovering from trauma: Gestalt therapy with an abused child. *Maladjustment and Therapeutic Education, 7*(3), 147–157.

Smith, E. (1992a). *Gestalt voices.* Norwood, NJ: Ablex Publishing Company.

Smith, E. (1992b). Personal growth and social influence. In *Gestalt voices* (pp. 294–295). Norwood, NJ: Ablex Publishing Company.

Stevens, J. (1975). *Gestalt is.* Moab, UT: Real People Press.

Swanson, J. (1988). Boundary processes and boundary states: A proposed revision of the Gestalt theory of boundary disturbances. *Gestalt Journal, 11*(?), 5–24.

Wheeler, G. (1992). Gestalt ethics. In E. Nevis, (Ed.), *Gestalt therapy* (pp. 113–128). New York: Gardner Press.

Yontef, G. (1987). Gestalt therapy 1986: A polemic. *Gestalt Journal, 10* (1), 41–68.

Zinker, J. (1977). *Creative process in Gestalt therapy.* New York: Vintage Books.

Zinker, J. (1991). Creative process in Gestalt therapy: The therapist as artist. *Gestalt Journal 14*(2), 71–88.

Zinker, J. (1992). The Gestalt approach to couple therapy. In Edwin Nevis (Ed.), *Gestalt therapy* (pp. 285–302). New York: Gardner Press.

CHAPTER 15

THE USE OF HYPNOSIS IN SOCIAL WORK PRACTICE

WILLIAM NUGENT

Hypnosis has a long and controversial history. From time immemorial humans have used hypnotic and suggestive procedures for magical, religious, and other purposes. Hypnotic procedures have been used at least since the late 1700s as a method of healing (Shor, 1979). Recently an independent panel of the National Institutes of Health endorsed hypnosis as an alternative treatment for several problems. The panel further recommended that hypnosis be used by social workers [though not all agree with this position—see Cournoyer (1996) and the author's response (Nugent, 1996)] as a means of providing this intervention to clients at lower costs than if physicians or psychologists provide it.

Hypnosis is best thought of as an approach to intervention, or, in Fischer's (1978) terms, an intervention model as opposed to a causal-developmental model. As such, hypnosis can be used as an intervention procedure by social workers approaching their practice from nearly any theoretical perspective. For example, social workers operating within traditional psychodynamic models or within behavioral models of practice can readily incorporate hypnosis (Coe, 1980). There are numerous theories of hypnosis (see, for example, Hilgard, 1979; Fromm, 1979) and its exact nature is still controversial (Coe, 1980; Cournoyer, 1996). Rather than focus on theories of what hypnosis might be, the author intends in this chapter to give the reader an introduction to one model of hypnotherapy that can be used in practice by social workers: Milton Erickson and Ernest Rossi's *utilization model*. The first part of the chapter gives a brief historical overview that will provide a context for understanding Erickson and Rossi's model. Next is a presentation of their model and a brief review of some of the forms of *indirect suggestion* that are critical components of this model. An illustrative case example is then presented, followed by a presentation of some research that bears on the use of hypnosis as an intervention procedure, with a focus on both effectiveness and potential harm. The chapter concludes with a discussion of the need for appropriate training and supervision.

A BRIEF HISTORY OF HYPNOSIS

Franz Anton Mesmer, a healer in the late eighteenth century, began what may have been the first scientific study of hypnotic and suggestive phenomena. While Mesmer's theory of hypnosis combined astrological and mystical concepts, he also framed his teachings in two major concepts of the physics of his time, electricity and magnetism. In Mesmer's view, health involved the balance in mind and body of a life force, or fluid, similar to magnetism, that permeated the universe. The effect of this fluid on living beings was called "animal magnetism." Disease was caused by an imbalance of the life force. Mesmer conceived of this fluid as being controllable by human will and theorized that a critical first step in healing was to cause some of his own stored life fluid to flow into an ill person, thereby provoking an even greater imbalance. This increased imbalance would instigate a crisis in the ill person and lead to a violent seizure. The seizure would lead to a restoration of life force equilibrium and restored health. His techniques combined the laying on of hands, exorcism, and the use of magnets. He would pass magnets over his clients' bodies or, perhaps, have them sit in a tub of water surrounded by magnetized rods, though he found that he could obtain results without the use of magnets. Mesmer's methods came to be called "mesmerism" (Shor, 1979; Coe, 1980; Lankton & Lankton, 1983).

Mesmer's work was controversial, and in 1784 a team was sent from the French Academy of Science to investigate mesmerism. This team included Benjamin Franklin, the chemist Antoine-Laurent Lavosier, and Joseph Guillotin (the inventor of the guillotine) from the French Academy. They ended up denying the existence of animal magnetism and declared Mesmer's work fraudulent. In that same year Armand Chastenet, Marquis de Puysegur, announced the discovery of what he called "artificial somnambulism." This was an induced, sleeplike state in which a person could speak, open his eyes and walk around, respond to the hypnotist's commands, and then awaken with an amnesia for some, or all, events that had occurred during the sleeplike state. Many others working within the mesmeric tradition had observed these phenomena but had deemed them immaterial. The critical element in the mesmeric tradition was the production of the convulsions seen as necessary for regained health (Shor, 1979).

Puysegur's discovery led to new theoretical developments. The concepts of animal magnetism and a physical, external life fluid were dropped in these new conceptualizations. There was instead the development of the notion of a highly personalized will power. Puysegur and his followers conceived of a curative fluid that flowed from the hypnotist's brain in response to his or her will power. The transmission of this fluid depended in an important manner on the hypnotist's self-confidence in her/his powers of domination over the patient. Hypnosis was seen as a phenomenon in which the hypnotist controlled, to some extent, the person with whom he was working (Shor, 1979; Coe, 1980).

Numerous phenomena were reported by investigators of mesmeric or hypnotic procedures. These phenomena included those referred to today as "classical hypnotic phenomena": amnesia, anesthesias and analgesias, positive and negative hallucinations, posthypnotic phenomena, and individual differences in hypnotic responsiveness. Other phenomena were also reported, including foretelling the future, mediumship, and other mystical powers and parapsychological phenomena. Some linked hypnosis with Satan and evil. These parapsychological claims were investigated in another special inquiry made by the French Academy of Sciences in the 1820s. The failure to observe any parapsychological events led to another rejection of hypnosis by the Academy. At about this time Phineas Quimby came to Portland, Maine, advertising himself as a "mental healer," and further associated mesmerism with the spiritual realm. Quimby's association of mesmerism with spiritualism further discouraged serious scientific investigation of hypnotic phenomena (Alexander & Selisnick, 1966; Shor, 1979).

In spite of these events, other practitioners and theoreticians took up the use and investigation of hypnosis. James Braid created a theory of mesmerism based on physiological concepts. He theorized that the fixed staring at some object induced fatigue in the eyelids, leading to a type of exhaustion. This exhaustion led to a special sleep in which the activity of the central nervous system decreased (Braid, 1843). This condition Braid termed "neuro-hypnotism," "nervous sleep," or "hypnotism." Braid later revised his model to focus on psychological as opposed to physiological factors. In this new formulation, Braid viewed the "nervous sleep" as a special case of a more fundamental psychological principle he called "monoidesim" (Braid, 1847). This work was an important factor in bringing the study of hypnosis back into the realm of respectable scientific research. At about the same time as Braid, James Esdaile, using techniques similar to those of Braid, worked in Calcutta, India. He successfully used hypnosis as an anesthetic in over 100 medical operations, including such procedures as amputations, in which patients were reportedly free from pain. He also reported that the death rate from surgical shock in these patients was greatly reduced (Shor, 1979; Coe, 1980; Edmonston, 1981; Lankton & Lankton, 1983).

Ambroise Auguste Liebeault also developed a psychological model of hypnosis (Liebeault, 1866). Hippolyte Marie Bernheim strongly endorsed this model, thereby drawing considerable attention to healing procedures based on verbal suggestion. Hypnosis was conceptualized as resulting from, and as being a part of, a suggestibility created by having a person focus on the idea of sleep. During the special sleep of hypnosis the person was in a unique rapport with the hypnotist. Critical mental faculties were seen to be temporarily abandoned, resulting in increased amenability to suggestions made by the hypnotist. The hypnotized person *had* to obey the requests of the hypnotist, as would an automaton. Hypnotic treatment in this tradition consisted of the induction of hypnotic sleep, followed by verbal suggestions given in a tone of supreme authority and confidence. This approach to hypnosis has been called the "authoritarian approach" (Shor, 1979; Rossi, 1989a).

It was while visiting Liebeault and Bernheim's clinic in France in 1889 that Sigmund Freud observed that a suggestion given during hypnosis, though forgotten upon awakening, was often carried out posthypnotically. Freud (1925) wrote that this was his first inkling of the possibility of unconscious processes. Freud and Josef Breuer experimented with hypnosis as a treatment for hysteria, though Freud rejected hypnosis in favor of free association and dream interpretation when he later began his development of psychoanalytic theory (Lankton & Lankton, 1983).

The work of Freud stimulated renewed interest in hypnosis. Many investigators around the world conducted inquiries on hypnosis, including Pavlov in Russia, Piere Janet in France, and Morton Prince in the United States (Lankton & Lankton, 1983; Edmonston, 1981). Milton H. Erickson, while an undergraduate premed student at the University of Wisconsin, conducted a series of investigations into hypnosis and, in 1923, conducted a graduate seminar, at the request of Clark L. Hull (the American behaviorist), on his research. Erickson's research was an important element in the beginning of his career as a hypnotherapist (Erickson, 1964a, 1967; Rossi, 1989a), and probably influenced Hulls's contributions to hypnosis (Shor, 1979; Edmonston, 1981).

Erickson has been called one of the most influential and creative of modern hypnotherapists (Zeig, 1982). It is the model explicated by Erickson (Erickson & Rossi, 1979) that we will study in some detail in this chapter. Erickson's approaches differ significantly from the authoritarian methods developed by earlier practitioners and researchers. Erickson's approach made use of the client's presenting problems and behavior and involved indirect, as opposed to direct, suggestion. In this approach the response the client makes to the hypnotist's suggestions come exclusively from the client's innate abilities, expectations, and life experiences. Gone is the notion of the client responding as an automaton to the authoritative suggestions of the hypnotist. Instead, the hypnotherapist might be thought of as merely providing the conditions within which the client is able to access from within her or himself the resources needed to resolve their problems. Erickson has been called the "Einstein of intervention" and it has been said by some that his influence is equal to that of Freud (Lankton & Lankton, 1983).

This history is necessarily brief and leaves out many important persons involved in the evolution of the methods and theories of hypnosis currently in use. However, it will give the reader an idea of the historical context from which the hypnotic methods described below have arisen. The reader is referred to historical accounts by Bramwell (1956), Hilgard (1965), Sarbin and Coe (1972), Shor (1979), and Edmonston (1981).

MODEL ASSUMPTIONS

As mentioned earlier, Erickson and Rossi's (1979) model is best thought of as an intervention model. The model presents an approach to conducting hypnotherapeutic interventions for any type of problem presented by a client. The author has never seen assumptions associated with Erickson and Rossi's (1979) model explicitly stated, though Lankton and Lankton (1983) enumerate a number of what they call "principles of treatment." Nonetheless, there are some assumptions that seem implicit in Erickson and Rossi's (1979) model:

1. Unconscious mental processes exist in human beings;
2. Information can be communicated to human beings in such a manner that it is received and processed unconsciously;
3. These unconscious processes can initiate creative change in the individual without the individual's conscious awareness of what has transpired;
4. Human problems involve learned limitations; and
5. All human experience contains aspects that can be used as strengths in problem resolution. These aspects of a person's experiential history can be taken out of the original context in which they were experienced and used in a new, problematic context.

There is research evidence that supports the validity of assumptions (1) through (3). There is research evidence that humans do, in fact, receive and process information outside of conscious awareness (MacLeod, Mathews, & Tata, 1986; Derryberry & Rothbart, 1984; Mandler & Shebo, 1983; Mandler, Nakamura, & Van Zandt, 1987; Barlow, 1988). Further, there is evidence that cognitive changes can occur without conscious awareness of the processes involved (Horton & Kjeldergaard, 1961; Nisbett & Wilson, 1977; Foa & Kozack, 1991). Some research has suggested that the human brain, when we are questioned, continues an exhaustive search throughout our entire memory system, on an unconscious level, even after a satisfying answer has been given consciously (Sternberg, 1975).

Behavioral models are based, in part, on variations of assumption number (4), and behavioral research supports the validity of this notion (see, for example, Bandura, 1969; Nay, 1976; Kanfer & Goldstein, 1980). The validity of the last assumption above must be inferred from anecdotal case studies and research conducted by Erickson himself (see Rossi, 1989a,b,c,d). These studies contain numerous clinical examples of how Erickson presumably turned parts of problematic behaviors, cognitions, and/or feelings into assets used by clients in changing their problems. Numerous examples of this "naturalistic," or "utilization approach" can be found in Erickson's writings (Erickson, 1959; Erickson & Rossi, 1979, chapter 3; Rossi, 1989a,b,c,d).

THE UTILIZATION MODEL OF HYPNOTHERAPY

Erickson and Rossi (1979) conceptualized hypnotherapy as a three-stage process: (1) a period of preparation, (2) the activation and utilization of the client's cognitive and affective skills, as well as her/his life experiences, during a period of therapeutic trance, and (3) a recognition, evaluation, and ratification of therapeutic changes that take place. Each of these stages is described and discussed below.

PREPARATION

In this stage the social worker first establishes a therapeutic relationship, or rapport, with the client. The social worker can use any of a number of communication methods to help establish this rapport (see Hepworth & Larson, 1986). For example, the social worker can use the facilitative communication styles (such as active listening and open-ended questions) and avoid use of the so-called nonfacilitative communication styles when interacting with the client (Hepworth & Larson, 1986). Recent research has underscored the importance of this differential use of facilitative and nonfacilitative styles (Nugent, 1992). In Erickson and Rossi's (1979) model, the rapport that social worker and client create together can serve as part of a therapeutic frame of reference within which the client's therapeutic responses develop.

In preintervention interviews with the client the social worker gathers information not only about the client's problems, but also about the client's storehouse of life experiences and learnings that can be used for therapeutic purposes. As much information as possible is obtained about the client's personal history, problems, recreational preferences, field of work, interpersonal skills, mental skills, psychodynamics, temperament, and so forth. In short, as much as possible is learned about the client. The information obtained can suggest to the social worker aspects of the client's life experiences, abilities, and cognitive schema that can be framed (in the social worker's thinking as well as the client's) as resources and strengths that can be used in changing the client's problems. This is an important element in Erickson and Rossi's (1979) model: any part of a client's repertory of life experiences and skills, *including the client's problems,* can be reframed (in both the social worker's and client's minds) into a positive component of problem resolution and may be used as part of problem resolution.

For example, suppose that a client presents with problems with anxiety. The social worker learns during assessment that the client enjoys music and finds listening to music very relaxing. The client's enjoyment of music, and her/his relaxation response while listening to it, could be viewed as important client resources and be utilized by the social worker in at least two ways. First, listening to imagined music could be used as part of a trance induction (see, for example, Erickson & Rossi, 1979, case 5). Second, the relaxation the client experiences while listening to music could be accessed during therapeutic trance and, in a sense, moved out of the context of listening to music and placed into life contexts in which the client experiences anxiety. Similarly, suppose that the client expresses to the social worker the strong belief that he or she is unable to be "hypnotized," that is, unable to experience therapeutic trance. The social worker might use the client's thoughts expressing this doubt as the vehicle for trance induction (see, for example, Erickson, 1959). This aspect of Erickson and Rossi's (1979) model is clearly consistent with the profession of social work's commitment to focus on client strengths.

Another important element of the preparation phase is the creation of a *therapeutic frame of reference.* The social worker purposely frames the client's involvement with the social worker, and the hypnotherapy to be used, into a therapeutic context and attempts to instill in the client an expectancy of change. For example, the social worker might tell the client anecdotes about other clients with similar problems who experienced positive change as a result of hypnotherapeutic intervention. The social worker might also embed indirect suggestions within the anecdotes told to the client during this phase (see below). Schneck (1970, 1975) has described how

Table 15–1
Erickson and Rossi's Five-Stage Model

Stage of Trance Induction Process	Methods Used by Social Worker During Stage
1. Focusing and concentrating attention	Employ client's beliefs, thoughts, and behavior to focus attention inward
2. Disrupting client's habitual mental frames of reference and belief systems	Any process that functions to disrupt client's normal, habitual mental frames of reference, such as shock, doubt, surprise, distraction, confusion, or boredom
3. Initiating unconscious processes	Use of any of the indirect forms of hypnotic suggestion
4. Activating unconscious mental processes	Stimulating client's personal associations and autonomous cognitive and affective processes via procedures in stages (1) through (3)
5. Client's autonomous response— the hypnotic response	Expression of affective, behavioral, and cognitive processes that are experienced by client as occurring autonomously

Based on Figure 1 in Erickson and Rossi (1979), p. 4.

what is said prior to hypnotic trance induction can enhance client response to therapeutic suggestions. Erickson and Rossi (1979) argue that a client's expectations of therapeutic change may lead to a suspension of the client's learned limitations and negative life experiences that contribute to the client's problems. In other words, this creation of an expectancy of change is a part of the therapeutic frame of reference purposely created by the social worker. The suspension of disbelief and the high expectation of positive change has been associated with many spontaneous cures and changes thought to be the result of placebo effects (Erickson & Rossi, 1979, 1981; Coe, 1980). In fact, the purposive cultivation of placebo factors can be considered a part of Erickson and Rossi's (1979) model.

THERAPEUTIC TRANCE

Erickson and Rossi (1979) define therapeutic trance as a:

> . . . period during which the limitations of one's usual frames of reference and beliefs are temporarily altered so one can be receptive to other patterns of association and modes of mental functioning that are conductive to problem-solving. (p. 3)

The trance state is viewed in this model as a state in which the client is receptive to new frames of reference and to creative solutions to problems. Erickson and Rossi (1979) conceptualize the dynamics of trance induction and hypnotic suggestion as a five-stage process, illustrated in Table 15–1.

1. Fixation of Attention

Fixating a client's attention has been the classical approach to initiating trance. Traditionally, the "hypnotist" would have the person fixate her or his gaze on a watch, talisman, spot on the wall, or some other external object that would hold the client's attention. However, an even more effective focus of attention is the client's own body sensations and internal cognitive and affective experience. Encouraging the client to focus on physical sensations (such as comfort), ongoing cognitive experience (such as her/his stream of internal dialogue), or internal imagery (such as consciously created visual images) leads the client's attention inward even more effectively than does a focus on some external object.

Erickson and Rossi (1979) differentiate between "formal" and "informal" trances. In a formal trance the social worker would request the client to focus his or her attention inward to some internal reality, such as the sensations in various parts of the body. A progressive relaxation exercise is one example of a means of having the client focus her or his attention inward to body sensations, in this case the differing sensations of tension and relaxation. This process is labeled a formal induction in that the social worker interrupts ongoing interactions with the client to request that the client focus on inner aspects of the ongoing experience for the purposes of initiating a trance state.

In contrast, an informal trance occurs when the social worker uses an interesting fact, story, or anecdote that serves to fixate the client's attention. Erickson and Rossi (1979), p. 5) note that "anything that fascinates and holds or absorbs a person's attention could be described as hypnotic." Confusion and boredom are also useful trance induction vehicles (Erickson, 1964b; Rossi, 1989a). Erickson and Rossi (1979) refer to the inner absorption experienced by client in response to engaging stories, anecdotes, allegories, confusion, boredom, and so forth as the "common everyday trance." The common everyday trance is defined as those periods during everyday life in which a person becomes so absorbed or preoccupied with some internal experience that the he/she momentarily loses awareness of the external environment. This common everyday trance can be used in the Erickson and Rossi model as effectively as can a formal trance for therapeutic purposes (Erickson & Rossi, 1979).

According to Erickson and Rossi's model, regardless of whether a formal or informal trance is to be induced, the most effective means of focusing and fixating attention is to acknowledge the client's current ongoing experience. Correctly recognizing and acknowledging the client's current experience and reality presumably fixates the client's attention and creates a receptivity to whatever suggestions the social worker may wish to offer to the client. An example of this process is given below in the discussion of *contingent suggestions*. Another example is given by Erickson and Rossi's (1979) discussion of the so-called "yes set." This use of the client's ongoing current behavior and experience as a vehicle for trance induction forms the basis for what Erickson and Rossi (1979) call the "utilization approach to trance induction."

2. Disrupting Habitual Frameworks and Belief Systems

In the Erickson and Rossi (1979) model, the most useful psychological effect of fixating the client's attention is that it tends to disrupt, or depotentiate, the client's habitual mental sets and usual frames of reference for organizing experience. During this brief interruption of normal mental functioning, latent patterns of association and sensory-perceptual functioning have an opportunity to be experienced. These latent patterns of experience may assert themselves in a manner that has been described as hypnotic trance. The depotentiation of client's normal modes of functioning means that learned limitations are suspended and the client becomes more open to new means of experiencing and learning. This openness to new and alternative experiences and solutions to problems is the essence of therapeutic trance (Erickson, Rossi, & Rossi, 1976). According to Erickson and Rossi (1979),

> Psychological problems develop when people do not permit the naturally changing circumstances of life to interrupt their old and no longer useful patterns of association and experience so that new solutions and attitudes may emerge. (p. 7)

The purpose of therapeutic trance, formal or informal, is to enable the clients to find within themselves new frames of reference that allow them to develop solutions to their problems.

3. Initiation of Unconscious Search Processes

In the Erickson and Rossi (1979) model, the fixation of attention and disruption of normal cognitive frames of reference initiates an unconscious search, involving unconscious mental processes, for new frames of reference, experiences, and solutions to problems. The initiation and activation of these unconscious processes constitutes a creative period in which the client can go through a necessary reorganization of his experience. In their model, Erickson and Rossi identify a number of "indirect forms of suggestion" that are presumably facilatators of mental associations and unconscious processes. The social worker using Erickson and Rossi's model would use these forms of verbal and nonverbal communication to initiate unconscious search processes in the client in an effort to stimulate the client to make needed changes and find solutions to her/his problems. The indirect forms of suggestion are discussed later in this chapter.

4. and 5. Activation of Unconscious Processes and Hypnotic Response

The hypnotic response experienced by the client is the natural outcome of the unconscious search processes initiated via fixation of attention, depotentiation of habitual frames of reference, and the use of indirect forms of suggestion. In this model, the hypnotic response appears to happen automatically and autonomously, without the client's conscious, voluntary involvement. When this response occurs, client's may express surprise at what has happened. Erickson and Rossi note that such surprise can be taken as an indication of the genuine, autonomous nature of the response (Erickson & Rossi, 1979).

RATIFICATION OF THERAPEUTIC CHANGE

The third stage of Erickson and Rossi's utilization model of hypnotherapy involves the ratification of therapeutic change. In this stage the social worker will help the clients to recognize and acknowledge changes that they have experienced. Erickson and Rossi (1979) see this stage of the hypnotherapeutic process as being both the most subtle and most important. The social worker will help facilitate client recognition of trance experiences after trance has occurred. This is done so that the client's old negative frames of reference and attitudes do not function to disrupt and prohibit the experience of therapeutic responses resulting from the unconscious search processes that were activated during trance.

Erickson and Rossi (1979) identify several behavioral indicators of trance. These indicators, some of which are listed in 15–2. can be used by the social worker to ver-

Table 15–2
Things to Look for That Indicate Client May Be Experiencing Hypnotic Trance

1. Client has autonomous inner experience of cognitive and affective processes
2. Catalepsy (muscular rigidity, body immobility, lack of awareness of external environment, lack of response to external stimuli)
3. Client reorients to body and/or reports feeling "good" after trance ends
4. Client's voice changes (eg., begins to have a flat voice quality)
5. Client reports sense of comfort and relaxation during and after inner focus
6. Client shows slow, jerky, apparently autonomous muscular movements, such as in hand and arm levitation
7. Client seems to be "hanging on every word" of social worker (i.e., shows a keen response attentiveness)
8. Client's pupils dilate and remain fixed in that state; eyes close; gaze becomes focused and unmoving
9. Client's facial features are smooth and relaxed
10. Client has sense of being dissociated or distanced
12. Client responds to questions in literal manner
13. Client shows loss or retardation of blink, swallow, and/or startle reflexes
14. Client experiences sensory, muscular, and body changes; slowing pulse and respiration
18. Client has spontaneous experience of classical hypnotic phenomena, such as amnesia, anesthesia, analgesia, body illusions, sensory hallucinations, catalepsy, and time distortion
19. Client shows time lag between receipt of suggestions and response to those suggestions

Based on Table 1 in Erickson and Rossi (1979), p. 11.

ify that the client is indeed experiencing trance, and these experiences can be pointed out to the client during trance induction and then again later in the ratification of change phase.

INDIRECT FORMS OF SUGGESTION

A fundamental concept in Erickson and Rossi's (1979) model is *indirect suggestion.* Erickson and Rossi (1989, p. 455) define an indirect suggestion as any suggestion " . . . that initiates an unconscious search and facilitates unconscious processes within subjects so that they are usually somewhat surprised by their own response when they recognize it." Erickson and Rossi (1979, 1989) define and describe numerous forms of indirect suggestion, and the reader is referred to these sources for in-depth coverage. Several forms of indirect suggestion are discussed below.

TRUISMS UTILIZING IDEODYNAMIC PROCESSES

This form of indirect suggestion is a statement of a simple fact about behavior that the client has experienced so often that it is impossible to deny (Erickson & Rossi, 1979, p. 22). For example, a discussion with a client about some psychophysiological or mental process in such a manner that it appears to be nothing more than a discussion about simple facts is an example of truisms utilizing ideodynamic processes. Erickson and Rossi (1979) claim that the verbal descriptions of these processes may function as indirect suggestion by initiating the very ideodynamic processes being talked about from the client's associations and life experiences. For example, the following verbal statement may serve as an indirect suggestion for a client to experience amnesia:

> Everyone has had the experience of forgetting. I have had the experience of getting ready to leave my home knowing that I had something important to do at the office. As I drive into my office I suddenly realize that I have forgotten what the important thing is that I have to do. Others have had the experience of meeting an acquaintance while walking somewhere and not remembering the person's name. You have had many experiences of forgetting.

The next example might serve as an indirect suggestion for the client to solve a problem unconsciously, without conscious awareness:

> A person can have the experience of creatively solving a problem in his unconscious mind. There was this man who had been working very hard on understanding the chemical structure of the benzene molecule. He had been trying unsuccessfully to come up with a structure involving these long chains of molecules. One day, after considerable effort and frustration at solving this problem, he fell asleep and had a dream. In the dream he saw long chains of molecules form into rings as they danced around. He awoke and realized that

a ring structure might be the answer. He was successful in finding a ring structure for the molecule and won a Nobel Prize for this solution. [Note to reader—this is a true story.]

Verbal statements about ideodynamic processes, such as remembering, forgetting, losing awareness of a part of the body, feeling warmth on the skin, and so on, may serve as indirect suggestions and actually initiate a train of associations leading the client to experience the processes being talked about (Erickson & Rossi, 1979).

Not Knowing, Not Doing

As a person relaxes, the parasympathetic nervous system predisposes the person to *not do* as opposed to making active efforts to do something. Unconscious processes occur *without consciousness knowing* how the unconscious processes occur. An attitude of not knowing and not doing can therefore facilitate hypnotic responsiveness, particularly at the start of trance induction (Erickson & Rossi, 1979). Thus, the following verbal statements are examples of *not knowing, not doing* that may facilitate hypnotic responsiveness:

> You can sit there with no need to move and no need to talk. You can relax, without knowing how your muscles let go, and without knowing how relaxed you will become.
> There is no need to listen to me with your conscious mind, you can listen with your unconscious mind without knowing that you are listening.

Interspersal

Words and phrases embedded within a longer verbal statement can be used to give indirect suggestions. These words and phrases can be spoken with a slightly different voice cadence and intonation to help mark them for special attention at the unconscious level, a process that has been called "analogical marking" (Bandler & Grinder, 1975). This process of embedding suggestions in longer verbal statements is called the *interspersal approach* by Erickson and Rossi (1979). This technique can be illustrated as follows. Imagine telling a client a story that starts in the following way. You will note that certain words and phrases are printed in ***bold italics***. These words and phrases are interspersed suggestions that would be spoken with a different voice tone and tempo:

> I once took tennis lessons and learned a lot more than how to play tennis. I was a bit nervous when I first started and I told myself, "The first thing I need to do is ***relax.*** If I do then I can ***just let go*** of some of the fears I have about taking these lessons." My instructor was one who believed in getting me in the thick of things from the beginning. He showed me how to hold the racquet, saying, "Hold it like this, ***comfortably*** wrapping your fingers around the

handle." He showed me how to swing the racquet. He looked like he was able to *feel so very comfortable* while he swung it . . . like he was a natural.

If the bold/italicized words and phrases are pulled out of the context of the story line, they read as follows:

relax . . . just let go . . comfortably . . . feel so very comfortable.

According to Erickson and Rossi (1979), as well as other theoreticians (see, for example, Lankton & Lankton, 1983; Bandler & Grinder, 1975), the client's unconscious mind, because of the slightly different vocal patterns used to mark these interspersed suggestions, may interpret them out of the context of the story and respond to the suggestions. In this case here, the client's unconscious would hear, in addition to the story, the suggestion

relax . . . just let go . . . comfortably . . . feel so very comfortable,

and the client could, presumably, begin to relax and feel comfortable. With suitable additional suggestions the client might respond to the interspersed suggestions by developing a therapeutic trance. A story such as the one started above, with interspersed suggestions, could be the vehicle for an informal trance induction (Erickson & Rossi, 1979; Lankton & Lankton, 1983). Erickson (1966) has described an entire hypnotherapeutic method for pain control that relies primarily on the interspersal approach to giving indirect suggestion. The reader is encouraged to read this source, as it gives a thorough and excellent account of this procedure.

QUESTIONS

As noted above, recent research has suggested that when we are asked a question, our brain continues an exhaustive unconscious search throughout our entire memory system even after we have found an answer that is consciously acceptable (Sternberg, 1975). Questions can be effective indirect forms of suggestion and can be used in a variety of ways. For example, questions can be used as indirect forms of suggestion during trance induction:

How much more comfortable will you become as you continue sitting there, breathing in and out and listening to the sound of my voice?
Will both your hands begin to feel heavier . . . or will one become lighter than the other . . . or will both begin to feel lighter?

Questions can also be used to initiate therapeutic unconscious searches:

What experiences of comfort from your past can your unconscious use for you to remain comfortable when you see a dog in the future?

Will you feel more and more comfortable speaking in front of a group slowly or quickly? . . . Will you notice the change right away, or will you feel comfortable speaking in front of a group several times before you consciously recognize how comfortable you have become?

Erickson and Rossi (1979, chapter 2) show how an entire trance induction can be built upon the use of questions.

IMPLICATION

Implication is an indirect suggestion form in which the message the social worker wishes the client to hear is not spoken directly, but rather is arrived at by the client after an inner search process and an inference. One example of an implication is a suggestion put into an "if————, then ————" form. For example:

If you continue sitting there and take a deep breath, you can begin to speak comfortably about what has been bothering you.

According to Erickson and Rossi's (1979) model, a client who follows this suggestion by continuing to sit and taking a deep breath will, without knowing it, accept the implication that he will talk comfortably about the problems that have been bothering him.

A special form of implication is what Erickson and Rossi (1979) call the *implied directive*. An implied directive has three components:

A. A time-binding introduction;
B. An implied suggestion that takes place within the client; and
C. A behavioral response that signals the social worker when the implied suggestion has been accomplished.

For example, consider the statement:

As soon as your unconscious knows that you will remain awake and alert the next time you receive a hypodermic injection, your right hand can lift off of the chair without conscious effort.

The phrase "as soon as . . . " is the time-binding introduction that frames the requested responses in time. The phrase " . . . your unconscious knows that you will remain awake and alert the next time you receive a hypodermic injection . . . " contains the implied inner response suggested by the social worker. Finally, the phrase " . . . your right hand can lift off the chair without conscious effort" is the behavioral signal that will tell the social worker that the requested inner task has been accomplished.

Contingent Suggestions

A contingent suggestion is a verbal form in which a suggestion is attached to an ongoing, or inevitable, behavioral sequence. As noted earlier, one of the fundamental concepts in Erickson and Rossi's (1979) model is utilization. An important example of utilization is the focusing of the client's attention inward by acknowledging the client's current ongoing experience. Contingent suggestions are one means of doing this. An example of a contingent suggestion is:

> With each breath that you take, you can feel various parts of your body . . . and growing more comfortable.

The ongoing behavior is the client breathing, and the suggestion that is attached with this behavior is " . . . you can feel various parts of your body . . . and growing more comfortable."

Another example of a contingent suggestion is:

> As you continue thinking those thoughts . . . in your mind now . . . your unconscious mind can begin to find a way for you to leave your house and drive by yourself feeling only comfortable feelings.

The ongoing behavior is the thoughts that the client is currently thinking. The contingent suggestion attached to the ongoing behavior is " . . . your unconscious mind can begin to find a way for you to leave your house and drive by yourself feeling only comfortable feelings."

An entire trance induction can be built upon contingent suggestions. The social worker might verbally acknowledge whatever current, ongoing behavior the client is manifesting, attaching to this verbal acknowledgement a series of suggestions for deepening comfort and the activation of unconscious mental processes. An example of such a sequence of contingent suggestions utilizing ongoing client behavior is given below. The reader will note that in this sequence, the portion of the contingent suggestion that acknowledges the client's current ongoing behavior is *italicized,* while the attached suggestion is in **bold.**

> *As you sit there in that chair,* **you can feel certain sensations in your arms and legs.** And *as you feel those sensations that you are currently feeling,* **you may wonder just how much more comfortable you can become.** And as you continue *breathing in . . . and out . . .* **your unconscious can find ways for you to relax more and more, without knowing exactly how it is that you are relaxing, now more and more** *as you breathe in . . and out,* **without any need to consciously pay any attention to me at all, since your unconscious is here and can hear.**

CONSCIOUS-UNCONSCIOUS DOUBLE BIND

According to Erickson and Rossi (1979), the form of indirect suggestion called the conscious-unconscious double bind is based on the fact that while a person cannot voluntarily control unconscious processes, a person can consciously receive messages that can initiate unconscious processes:

> The conscious-unconscious double bind is designed to bypass the limitations of our conscious understanding and abilities so that behavior can be mediated by the hidden potentials that exist on a more autonomous level. (p. 45)

This form of suggestion can be used to downplay the importance of conscious involvement while simultaneously attempting to initiate unconscious involvement. The following example of a conscious-unconscious double bind might be used during a therapeutic trance induction:

> It doesn't matter whether you listen to me consciously, your unconscious is here and can hear and understand everything that I say.

This indirect suggestion implies that it is irrelevant whether or not the client hears consciously what the social worker talks about. It also implies that what is important is the client's unconscious activity. As a second example, suppose that the social worker is working with a client who has a phobia for hypodermic injections, manifested by fainting whenever an injection is given. The following conscious-unconscious double bind might be used during a post-trance ratification of change:

> If your unconscious knows that from now on you will remain awake and alert anytime you receive a hypodermic injection, then it can lift your left hand without your conscious involvement. If it knows that other things remain to be done before you will remain awake and alert anytime you receive a hypodermic injection, then it can lift your right hand without you consciously trying.

This suggestion also implies that conscious involvement is irrelevant and that what is important is the client's unconscious activity. It further focuses the client's attention inward as she wonders how she will respond. Autonomous ideomotor movement of either hand is usually experienced with surprise by the client. This surprise can then be utilized to further develop therapeutic expectancy, regardless of which hand lifts. If the client's left hand lifts in an autonomous manner, then this result can be used to reinforce an expectancy of change. If the right lifts in an autonomous manner, then this result can be used to ratify unconscious involvement, to further develop a therapeutic frame of reference, and as a starting point for a new therapeutic trance, since an autonomous response presumes the development of trance (Erickson & Rossi, 1979).

Other Forms of Indirect Suggestion

Erickson & Rossi (1979, 1989) describe several other forms of indirect suggestion. These communication forms are critically components of the model developed by Erickson and Rossi (1979). The social worker wishing to add hypnotherapeutic interventions to her or his repertoire of intervention skills will need to become comfortable and familiar with these forms.

UTILIZATION

Another important concept in Erickson and Rossi's (1979) model is *utilization*. Utilization refers to the purposive use by the social worker of important behaviors and/or characteristics of the client in ways that are therapeutic. In an important sense, the social worker is using strengths of the client in helping her or him solve problems, or even turning some part of a problem into a part of the solution for the problem. One way that Erickson and Rossi (1979) conceptualize the utilization of client behaviors and characteristics is in the induction of therapeutic trance:

> In this utilization approach the patient's attention is fixed on some important aspect of his own personality and behavior in a manner that leads to the inner focus that we define as therapeutic trance. The patient's habitual sets are more or less depotentiated, and unconscious searches and processes are initiated to facilitate a therapeutic response. (p. 53)

The utilization of client behaviors as a trance induction mechanism can be illustrated from a case the author was involved in a number of years ago. A client was concerned with a problem of flatulence. He was a university student who complained that he had an uncontrollable problem with flatulence that was causing him anxiety in social situations. He had a physical exam and no physical problems were found by the examining physician, so he had been referred to the mental health center in which the author worked. The young man knew that the author worked with hypnosis and had requested that hypnosis be used to help him with his problem. However, he was concerned that he could not go into a trance because of his problem. The decision was made to use his problem as a means of focusing his attention inward. He was asked if he was experiencing his problem right at that point in time in my office, and he replied "yes." He was then asked to focus on the various sensations in his abdomen that were a part of his problem and he was asked a few questions about what he felt. He was then told that the more he became aware of the sensations in his abdomen, the more and more relaxed he could become. The young man continued to focus his attention inward, presumably on his abdominal sensations, and as the author continued to verbally ask him to focus on those sensations and relax, he soon exhibited several behaviors indicative of trance (see Table 15–2). Erickson and Rossi (1979, chapter 3), Erickson (1959), and Rossi (1989a,c) give numerous examples of the utilization of client behavior as a vehicle for trance induction.

Client behaviors, characteristics, and life experiences can also be utilized as components of some problem solution. For example, suppose that a client's presenting problem is a hypodermic needle phobia that is manifested by fainting when an injection occurs. Further suppose that this problem began when the client was eleven years old and that prior to this age the client had experienced no problems with injections. Then, one resource that could be utilized by this client is his experiences with hypodermic injections prior to the age of eleven. The ability to receive an injection without fainting presumably remains within the client's behavioral repertoire. This ability can be accessed and utilized in problem resolution. Erickson and Rossi (1979) give numerous examples of this process (see, for example, case number 1). There are also numerous examples in Rossi (1989,d).

ILLUSTRATIVE CASE EXAMPLE

Erickson and Rossi (1979) provide detailed examples of their three-stage model in clinical application in chapter 6 (see especially case number 5). Below is an illustrative case from some of the author's clinical work and research.

AN INJECTION PHOBIA

This case involved a twenty-three-year-old female college senior who experienced an extreme response to any procedure involving hypodermic needles, such as injections or having blood drawn. Specifically, she would faint as a hypodermic needle entered her arm, regardless of whether she was standing, sitting, or lying down. According to this client, she had fainted like this since she was eleven years old. This response had been consistent, with no exceptions, since she saw her grandfather die in a hospital with "needles sticking into him all over." She also experienced nausea, dizziness, and occasional fainting at the sight of another person being pierced by a hypodermic needle. The client's seventeen-year-old sister confirmed all these details of this client's twelve-year-old problem.

The client was completing her education as a health professional and had been offered a position in a hospital. She was concerned about the blood tests and inoculations required for the position, as well as about coming into contact with others in the hospital who were undergoing procedures involving hypodermic needles. About one month prior to contacting the author she had undergone a physical exam and had fainted while blood was being drawn for a blood test.

INTERVENTION

The intervention for this woman's problem followed Erickson and Rossi's (1979) preparation–therapeutic trance–ratification of change three-stage process. The specifics of each stage are described below.

Preparation.

First there was a pretrance discussion with the client about unconscious processes. In this discussion, *truisms utilizing ideodynamic processes* were used. For example, we discussed the ability of the unconscious mind to solve problems creatively without conscious awareness. Examples were given of this kind of occurrence. One example used was of a person trying to remember someone's name. This person has met someone before, learned his name, but upon meeting that person again walking down the street cannot remember his name. The individual tries hard to remember while speaking with the acquaintance, but cannot remember. The person parts with the acquaintance, continues walking down the street, and begins thinking about something else, having given up trying to remember the acquaintance's name. Then, several minutes later while thinking about something entirely different, the name of the acquaintance comes into conscious awareness unbidden. The person's unconscious continued to search for the acquaintance name while consciousness went on to some other task.

A second example given concerned the experience that people have of "sleeping on a problem." They have a problem and cannot solve it. They then decide to "sleep on the problem," knowing that their unconscious mind will work on the problem while they are sleeping. When they awaken in the morning, they know the solution to their problem. A third example of this process involved the following truism utilizing ideodynamic processes:

A person can have the experience of creatively solving a problem in his unconscious mind. There was this man who had been working very hard on understanding the chemical structure of the benzene molecule. He had been trying unsuccessfully to come up with a structure involving these long chains of molecules. One day, after considerable effort and frustration at solving this problem, he fell asleep and had a dream. In the dream he saw long chains of molecules form into rings as they danced around. He awoke and realized that a ring structure might be the answer. He was successful in finding a ring structure for the benzene molecule and won a Nobel Prize for this solution.

The client was told that hypnosis would be used to help her with her hypodermic needle phobia, and that her unconscious mind would solve this problem, without her conscious awareness of how the problem would be solved. Examples of clients whose problems were solved in this manner were described to her. These examples were used in an effort to create an expectancy of change and further develop a therapeutic frame of reference.

Therapeutic Trance.

At the end of this preparation, a formal trance induction was conducted as follows. The woman was told that the author was going to assist her in developing a hypnotic trance. She was asked to fix her attention on a piece of music that was played. She was asked to imagine in her mind's eye the events described in the music that was played. The client closed her eyes and presumably did as she was instructed. As she did this, she was told that the author could talk to her unconscious mind without her conscious mind needing to pay attention; her conscious mind could focus on the music and images she formed in her mind, while her unconscious listened to what the author said (an example of a *conscious/unconscious double bind*). The author continually talked to her about becoming completely absorbed in the music and the images she formed in her mind in response to the music. In a different tone of voice the author *interspersed* within the suggestions for paying conscious attention to the music suggestions for relaxation and deep comfort. Also *interspersed* were examples of how her unconscious mind could think and solve problems without her conscious awareness.

The client soon began to manifest several behaviors identified by Erickson and Rossi (1979) as indicators of trance experience. Her breathing slowed; her pulse (as seen in her neck) slowed; she showed a lack of startle response to unexpected noises inside, and outside, the room; she lost her swallow and eye blink reflexes; and she showed a complete body immobility. At this point the author gave the client the following therapeutic suggestion (an example of an *implied directive*):

> Now your unconscious mind can do what is necessary, in a manner fully meeting all your needs as a person, to ensure that you remain awake and alert anytime you receive an injection in the future, and as soon as your unconscious knows you will remain comfortably awake and alert when receiving an injection, It can signal by lifting your right hand into the air off the chair.

After giving this suggestion, the author continued to *intersperse* suggestions for comfort and relaxation within suggestions for absorption in the music and inner imagery. Several minutes later the client's right hand quivered and made a spasmodic upward jerk. The author then told the client that he would count backward from 20 to 1, and that she could awaken with the count. The author then counted slowly from 20 to 1, and the client opened her eyes a few seconds after the number 1 was spoken. She reoriented to her body by stretching and rubbing her arms. She commented without being asked that she thought she had been asleep and was unable to remember what had gone on. She also commented that she felt very relaxed and refreshed. The author interpreted these comments as indicators that she had experienced trance: she had reoriented her body after she awoke, felt good after trance, and was apparently experiencing a spontaneous amnesia for trance events (see Table 15–2).

Ratification of Change

The client was asked whether or not she knew that her hypodermic needle phobia had been changed. She responded verbally that she knew nothing of the kind and that as far as she knew she would faint the next time she encountered a procedure involving a needle, just like all the other times. The author responded that, of course, that was what she thought *consciously,* and that she knew something different unconsciously (another example of a conscious/unconscious double bind). She was asked if she wanted to know what her unconscious knew, and she replied affirmatively. She was then given the following instructions:

> I am going to ask your unconscious mind a question that only it knows the answer to. When I ask the question, you will probably have a conscious mind answer as well, but that answer does not necessarily reflect the answer that your unconscious mind has. Your unconscious mind can answer "yes" to the question by lifting your left hand, "no" by lifting your right hand, and "I don't know" or "I don't want to answer" by lifting both hands into the air. After I ask the question, I would like for you consciously to just focus on the sensations in your hands and wait for your unconscious mind to answer the question. The question I am going to ask is this: Will you remain comfortably awake and alert from now on when you undergo any procedure in which you are pierced by a hypodermic needle?

When asked this question, the woman immediately responded that she felt that nothing had changed and that she would faint like she always did. The author responded,

> Yes, that is what you believe consciously, and your conscious mind does not know many things that your unconscious mind knows. Relax, close your eyes, and focus on the sensations in your hands, and let's see how your unconscious mind will respond.

The woman closed her eyes and rested her hands on the arms of the chair in which she was seated. Her breathing slowed, she became immobile, and appeared to relax. Her swallow reflex slowed and stopped altogether in a couple of minutes, and her blink reflex stopped. These were all indicators that the woman was reentering trance. According to Erickson and Rossi (1979), asking a question tends to initiate an unconscious search and reinitiate trance behavior. The author spoke to the woman telling her to just relax and wait for her unconscious answer. After several minutes her left hand quivered and jerked spasmodically off the chair about an inch or so and then immediately fell back onto the arm of the chair. According to Erickson and Rossi's (1979) model, the time lag between asking the woman's unconscious mind the above question and her motor response (hand lifting), as well as the jerky, spasmodic nature of the lift, were consistent with a genuine unconscious response by the client. The woman was told to take a deep breath and open her eyes. After several seconds, she took a deep breath and opened her eyes.

The author asked her if she knew what her unconscious mind had answered. She responded that she had felt her left hand lift, which she "guessed" meant that she wouldn't faint when she got a shot. She told the author that she didn't believe it. The author responded by saying, "That is OK. You can continue to not believe it consciously, while your unconscious knows something different."

At this point our hypnotherapeutic session ended.

OUTCOME

Approximately two months after this single hypnotherapeutic session, which lasted a total of about an hour, the client experienced both hypodermic injections and blood tests as part of a prejob physical. She reported that she remained alert and awake during all of these procedures. She reported to the author that as she prepared to get the injections, she became a little nervous and thought that she would faint, but instead stayed awake. She reported feeling her heart beating a little faster when she felt the needle entering her arm, but otherwise felt no major discomfort and did not faint, much to her surprise. The author was in contact with this client sporadically over the next five years, and during this time she reported undergoing numerous procedures involving a hypodermic needle and each time she remained awake and alert. She also reported being able to see others receiving hypodermic injections without experiencing discomfort.

RESEARCH

There are several types of problems for which research evidence exists suggesting hypnotic interventions can make a positive impact (see Wodden & Atherton, 1982, and Bowers & LeBaron, 1986, for reviews). There is considerable evidence that hypnotic interventions can help control pain associated with numerous medical problems (Hilgard & Hilgard, 1975; Kroger & Fezler, 1976; Kroger, 1977). Hypnosis has been shown to be effective as a pain control intervention with burn patients (Schafer, 1975; Wakeman & Kaplan, 1978). There is evidence that hypnotic procedures can be effective with headaches (Anderson, Basker, & Dalton, 1975). Laboratory studies have suggested that under some circumstances the analgesic effects of hypnotic pain control interventions can exceed the analgesic effects associated with morphine (Sternbach, 1982; Spiegal & Albert, 1983; Bowers & LeBaron, 1986).

There is also evidence that hypnotic interventions can be effective treatments for asthma and psychosomatic problems (Wooden & Atherton, 1982; DePiano & Salzberg, 1979). Deabler, Fidel, Dillenkoffer, and Elder (1973) and Friedman and Taub (1977, 1978) report results of studies suggesting that hypnosis can help in the treatment of hypertension. Hypnosis has been shown to be effective with insomnia (Borkovec & Fowles, 1973; Barabasz, 1976).

The author has conducted some clinical studies on Erickson and Rossi's (1979) model (Nugent, 1989, 1990, 1993). These studies have suggested that Erickson and Rossi's (1979) model may be useful with problems such as agoraphobia (Nugent, 1993); family relationship problems (Nugent, 1990); and performance anxiety, claustrophobia, hypodermic injection phobia, sleep disturbance, and athletic performance problems (Nugent, 1989).

There is some evidence that children may be more amenable than adults to hypnotic procedures (Bowers & LeBaron, 1986). There is also evidence that some people are more "hypnotizable" than others and that this characteristic may be related to who benefits from hypnotic interventions. This evidence has suggested that people who score as highly hypnotizable on measures of hypnotic susceptibility may be more likely to benefit from hypnosis (Wooden & Atherton, 1982; Bowers & LeBaron, 1986). This topic is controversial, however. Erickson and Rossi (1979) maintain that all persons are hypnotizable since therapeutic trance is merely a special case of the common everyday trance, a common phenomenon that every person experiences everyday. The issue in their model is not whether a person is hypnotizable or not. Instead, the issue is how the "hypnotist" approaches the client and utilizes her or his presenting behavior to assist the client in experiencing therapeutic trance.

Research has suggested that hypnosis is *not* effective with certain problems. Evidence suggests that hypnotic interventions are not effective in helping people quit smoking or lose weight, or in treating addictions (Wooden & Atherton, 1982).

Some people have been concerned about the possible harm to clients through the use of hypnosis. Some people express concern that hypnosis could be used to force individuals into engaging in antisocial or criminal behavior (Coe, 1980). Research has suggested that this is *not* true (Erickson, 1939; Orne, 1962; Coe, Kobayashi, & Howard, 1973). Some people also express concern about possible negative aftereffects of hypnosis. Again, the research has suggested that individuals who undergo hypnotic procedures experience no more negative aftereffects than do individuals who are in comparison groups that do not undergo hypnosis (Faw, Sellers, & Wilcox, 1968; Hilgard, 1974; Coe, 1980). There is, in fact, some indication that those who undergo hypnosis may experience more positive aftereffects that those who are in comparison groups that do not experience hypnosis (Coe, 1980).

There is one area in which research has suggested that hypnosis can lead to harm to clients. Research has suggested that hypnosis should *not* be used as an aid in memory retrieval, such as with eyewitnesses. There is evidence that hypnotic procedures can result in inaccurate and even false memories being retrieved (Kihlstrom & Barnhardt, 1993). Such inaccurate and false memory retrieval may lead to negative outcomes with clients (Spiegal, 1980; Smith, 1983; Scheflin & Shapiro, 1989; Yapko, 1990, 1993a,b; Loftus & Ketcham, 1994).

TRAINING AND SUPERVISION

Hypnosis is an intervention procedure that might be used in conjunction with numerous other practice models. However, its appropriate and skilled use takes considerable training and practice. Some have argued that hypnosis is best thought of as an "advanced" psychosocial intervention approach (David Patterson, personal communication, January 1996). While hypnosis can be an effective intervention procedure when used by itself, or in combination with other treatment methods, the author recommends that the social worker interested in using this treatment method do so only after appropriate training. Those interested in learning to use methods developed by Erickson, such as the model described in this chapter, are encouraged to contact the Milton H. Erickson Foundation, 1935 East Aurelius Avenue, Phoenix, Arizona 85020. The Erickson Foundation will be able to help the interested social worker find a qualified trainer in his/her area. Other organizations that the interested social worker might contact for training information are the American Society of Clinical Hypnosis, 800 Washington Avenue S.E., Minneapolis, Minnesota 55414; and the Society for Clinical and Experimental Hypnosis, 140 West End Avenue, New York, New York 10023.

The author also recommends that the social worker make use of appropriate supervision, especially when he or she is first beginning to use hypnotherapeutic interventions in practice.

THE FUTURE OF HYPNOSIS IN SOCIAL WORK PRACTICE

It is difficult to speculate on the future of hypnosis in social work practice. Hypnosis has had a history replete with episodic swings from an accepted procedure, to a method viewed as bogus and practiced only by charlatans, and back again. At least for the near future it seems that hypnosis will be viewed as a potentially useful and effective intervention method, due at least in part to the recent pronouncement by the National Institutes of Health panel, referred to earlier. It is the author's opinion that the future acceptability of hypnosis, and its use in social work practice, will be intimately tied to how much research is conducted on its effectiveness with specific problems. The development of a sound research base on the effectiveness of hypnosis, one that provides clear guidelines as to what types of clients are most likely to benefit from its use, will go a long ways toward establishing hypnosis as an accepted and common intervention procedure in social work practice.

REFERENCES

Alexander, F., & Selisnick, S. (1966). *The history of psychiatry: An evaluation of psychiatric thought from prehistoric times to the present.* New York: Harper & Row.

Anderson, J., Basker, M., & Dalton, R. (1975). Migraine and hypnotherapy. *International Journal of Clinical and Experimental Hypnosis, 23,* 48–58.

Bandler, R., & Grinder, J. (1975). *Patterns of the hypnotic techniques of Milton H. Erickson, M.D.* (Vol. 1). Cupertino, CA: Meta Publications.

Bandura, A. (1969). *Principles of behavior modification.* New York: Holt, Rinehart, and Winston.

Barabasz, A. (1976). Treatment of insomnia in depressed patients by hypnosis and cerebral electrotherapy. *American Journal of Clinical Hypnosis, 19,* 120–122.

Barlow, D. (1988). *Anxiety and its disorders: The nature and treatment of anxiety and panic.* New York: Guilford Press.

Borkovec, T., & Fowles, D. (1973). Controlled investigation of the effects of progressive and hypnotic relaxation on insomnia. *Journal of Abnormal Psychology, 82,* 153–158.

Bowers, K., & LeBaron, S. (1986). Hypnosis and hypnotizability: Implications for clinical intervention. *Hospital & Community Psychiatry, 37,* 457–467.

Braid, J. (1843). *Neurypnology or, the rationale of nervous sleep considered in relation with animal magnetism.* London: John Churchill. Reprinted New York: Arno Press, 1976.

Braid, J. (1847). Facts and observations as to the relative value of mesmeric and hypnotic coma, and ethereal narcotism, for the mitigation or entire prevention of pain during surgical operations. *Medical Times, 15,* 381–382.

Bramwell, J. (1956). *Hypnotism: Its history, practice, and theory.* New York: Julian Press.

Coe, W. (1980). Expectations, hypnosis, and suggestion in behavior change. In F. Kanfer & A. Goldstein (Eds.), *Helping people change: A textbook of methods* (pp. 423–4690). New York: Pergamon Press.

Coe, W., Kobayashi, K., & Howard, M. (1973). Experimental and ethical problems in evaluating the influence of hypnosis in antisocial conduct. *Journal of Abnormal Psychology, 82,* 476–482.

Cournoyer, B. (1996). Should social workers support the use of "hypnosis?" No. In B. Thyer (Ed.), *Controversial issues in social work practice.* Boston: Allyn & Bacon.

Deabler, H., Fidel, E., Dillenkoffer, R., & Elder, S. (1973). The use of relaxation and hypnosis in lowering high blood pressure. *American Journal of Clinical Hypnosis, 16,* 75–83.

Derryberry, D., & Rothbart, M. (1984). Emotion, attention, and temperament. In C.E. Izard, J. Kagan, & R. Zajonc (Eds.), *Emotions, cognition, and behavior.* New York: Cambridge University Press.

DiPiano, F., & Salzberg, H. (1979). Clinical applications of hypnosis to three psychosomatic conditions. *Psychological Bulletin, 86,* 1223–1235.

Edmonston, Jr. (1981). *Hypnosis and relaxation: Modern verification of an old equation.* New York: John Wiley & Sons.

Erickson, M. (1939). An experimental investigation of the possible antisocial use of hypnosis. *Psychiatry, 2,* 391–414.

Erickson, M. (1950). Naturalistic techniques of hypnosis. *American Journal of Clinical Hypnosis, 1,* 3–8.

Erickson, M. (1959). Further clinical techniques of hypnosis: Utilization techniques. *American Journal of Clinical Hypnosis, 2,* 3–21.

Erickson, M. (1964a). Initial experiments investigating the nature of hypnosis. *American Journal of Clinical Hypnosis, 7,* 152–162.

Erickson, M. (1964b). The confusion technique in hypnosis. *American Journal of Clinical Hypnosis, 6,* 183–207.

Erickson, M. (1966). The interspersal hypnotic technique for symptom correction and pain control. *American Journal of Clinical Hypnosis, 8,* 198–209.

Erickson, M. (1967). Further experimental investigation of hypnosis: Hypnotic and nonhypnotic realities. *American Journal of Clinical Hypnosis, 10,* 87–135.

Erickson, M., & Rossi, E. (1979). *Hypnotherapy: An exploratory casebook.* New York: Irvington.

Erickson, M., & Rossi, E. (1981). *Experiencing hypnosis: Therapeutic approaches to altered states.* New York: Irvington.

Erickson, M., & Rossi, E. (1989). The indirect forms of suggestion. In E. Rossi (Ed.), *The nature of hypnosis and suggestion: The collected papers of Milton H. Erickson on hypnosis* (Vol. 1) (pp. 452–477). New York: Irvington.

Erickson, M., Rossi, E., & Rossi, S. (1976). *Hypnotic realities.* New York: Irvington.

Faw, V., Sellers, D.J., and Wilcox, W.W. (1968). Psychopathological effects of hypnosis. *International Journal of Clinical and Experimental Hypnosis, 16,* 26–37.

Fischer, J. (1978). *Effective casework practice: An eclectic approach.* New York: McGraw-Hill.

Foa, E., & Kozak, M. (1991). Emotional processing: Theory, research, and clinical implications for anxiety disorders. In J. Safran & L. Greenberg (Eds.), *Emotion, psychotherapy, and change* (pp. 21–49). New York: Guilford Press.

Freud, S. (1925). *An autobiographical study.* Authorized translation for the 2nd edition by J. Strachey, 1946, New York: W.W. Norton, 1952.

Friedman, H., & Taub, H. (1977). The use of hypnosis and biofeedback procedures for essential hypertension. *International Journal of Clinical and Experimental Hypnosis, 25,* 335–347.

Friedman, H., & Taub, H. (1978). A six-month follow-up of the use of hypnosis and biofeedback procedures in essential hypertension. *American Journal of Clinical Hypnosis, 20,* 184–188.

Fromm, E. (1979). The nature of hypnosis and other altered states of consciousness: An ego-psychological theory. In E. Fromm & R. Shor (Eds.), *Hypnosis: Developments in research and new perspectives* (2nd ed.) (pp. 81–104). New York: Aldine.

Hepworth, D., & Larsen, J. (1986). *Direct social work practice: Theory and skills* (2nd ed.). Chicago: Dorsey.

Hilgard, E. (1965). *Hypnotic susceptibility.* New York: Harcourt, Brace, and World.

Hilgard, E. (1979). Divided consciousness in hypnosis: The implications of the hidden observer. In E. Fromm & R. Shor (Eds.) *Hypnosis: Developments in research and new perspectives* (2nd ed.) (pp. 45–80). New York: Aldine.

Hilgard, E., & Hilgard, J. (1975). *Hypnosis in the relief of pain.* Los Altos, CA: Kaufmann.

Hilgard, J. (1974). Sequelae to hypnosis. *International Journal of Clinical and Experimental Hypnosis, 22,* 281–298.

Horton, D., & Kjeldergaard, P. (1961). An experimental analysis of associative factors in mediated generalizations. *Psychological Monographs, 75,* 515.

Kanfer, F., & Goldstein, A. (Eds.) (1980). *Helping people change.* New York: Pergamon Press.

Kihlstrom, J., & Barnhardt, T. (1993). The self-regulation of memory: For better and for worse, with and without hypnosis. In D. Wegner and & J. Pennebaker (Eds.), *Handbook of mental control* (pp. 88–125). Englewood Cliffs, NJ: Prentice-Hall.

Kroger, W. (1977). *Clinical and experimental hypnosis* (2nd ed.). Philadelphia: J.B. Lippincott.

Kroger, W., & Fezler, W. (1976). *Hypnosis and behavior modification: Imagery conditioning.* Philadelphia: J.B. Lippincott.

Lankton, S., & Lankton, C. (1983). *The answer within: A clinical framework of Ericksonian hypnotherapy.* New York: Brunner/Mazel.

Liebeault, A. (1866). *Du sommeil et des états analogues considérés surtout au point de vue de l'action moral sur le physique (Of sleep and related states, conceived of from the viewpoint of the action of the psyche upon the soma).* Paris: V. Masson.

Loftus, E., & Ketcham, K. (1994). *The myth of repressed memory.* New York: St. Martin's Press.

MacLeod, C., Mathews, A., & Tata, P. (1986). Attentional bias in emotional disorders. *Journal of Abnormal Psychology, 95,* 15–20.

Mandler, G., Nakamura, Y., & Van Zandt, B. (1987). Nonspecific effects of exposure on stimuli that cannot be recognized. *Journal of Experimental Psychology: Learning, Memory, and Cognition, 13,* 646–648.

Mandler, G., & Shebo, B. (1983). Knowing and liking. *Motivation and Emotion, 7,* 125–144.

Nay, W. (1976). *Behavioral intervention: Contemporary strategies.* New York: Gardner Press.

Nisbett, R., & Wilson, T. (1977). Telling more than we know: Verbal reports on mental processes. *Psychological Review, 84,* 231–279.

Nugent, W. (1989). Evidence concerning the causal effect of an Ericksonian hypnotic intervention. *Ericksonian Monographs, 5,* 35–53.

Nugent, W. (1990). An experimental and qualitative evaluation of an Ericksonian hypnotic intervention for family relationship problems. *Ericksonian Monographs, 7,* 51–68.

Nugent, W. (1992). The affective impact of a clinical social worker's interviewing style: A series of single-case experiments. *Research on Social Work Practice, 2,* 6–27.

Nugent, W. (1993). A series of single case design clinical evaluations of an Ericksonian hypnotic intervention used with clinical anxiety. *Journal of Social Service Research, 17,* 41–69.

Nugent, W. (1996). Should social workers support the use of "hypnosis?" Yes. In B. Thyer (Ed.), *Controversial issues in social work practice.* Boston: Allyn & Bacon.

Orne, M. (1959). The nature of hypnosis: Artifact and essence. *Journal of Abnormal and Social Psychology, 58,* 277–299.

Orne, M.T. (1962). Anti-social behavior and hypnosis. In G.H. Estabrooks (Ed.), *Hypnosis: Current problems.* New York: Harper & Row.

Rossi, E. (Ed.) (1989a). *The nature of hypnosis and suggestion: The collected papers of Milton H. Erickson on hypnosis* (Vol. 1). New York: Irvington.

Rossi, E. (Ed.) (1989b). *Hypnotic alteration of sensory, perceptual, and psychophysiological processes: The collected papers of Milton H. Erickson on hypnosis* (Vol. 2). New York: Irvington.

Rossi, E. (Ed.) (1989c). *Hypnotic investigation of psychodynamic processes: The collected papers of Milton H. Erickson on hypnosis* (Vol. 3). New York: Irvington.

Rossi, E. (Ed.) (1989d). *Innovative hypnotherapy: The collected papers of Milton H. Erickson on hypnosis* (Vol. 4). New York: Irvington.

Sarbin, T., & Coe, W. (1972). *Hypnosis: A social psychological analysis of influence.* New York: Holt, Rinehart, and Winston.

Schafer, D. (1975). Hypnosis use on a burn unit. *International Journal of Clinical and Experimental Hypnosis, 23,* 1–14.

Scheflin, A., & Shapiro, J. (1989). *Trance on trial.* New York: Guilford Press.

Schneck, J. (1970). Prehypnotic suggestions. *Perceptual and Motor Skills, 30,* 826.

Schneck, J. (1975). Prehypnotic suggestions in psychotherapy. *American Journal of Clinical Hypnosis, 17,* 158–159.

Shor, R. (1979). The fundamental problem in hypnosis research as viewed from historic perspectives. In E. Fromm & R. Shor (Eds.) *Hypnosis: Developments in research and new perspectives* (2nd ed.) (pp. 15–41). New York: Aldine.

Smith, M. (1983). Hypnotic memory enhancement of witnesses: Does it work? *Psychological Bulletin, 94,* 387–407.

Spiegal, H. (1980). Hypnosis and evidence: Help or hindrance? *Annals of the New York Academy of Science, 347,* 73–85.

Spiegal, D., & Albert, L. (1983). Naloxone fails to reverse hypnotic alleviation of chronic pain. *Psychopharmacology, 81,* 140–143.

Sternbach, R. (1982). On strategies for identifying neurochemical correlates of hypnotic analgesia. *International Journal of Clinical and Experimental Hypnosis, 30,* 251–256.

Sternberg, S. (1975). Memory scanning: New findings and current controversies. *Quarterly Journal of Experimental Psychology, 22,* 1–32.

Wakeman, R., & Kaplan, J. (1978). An experimental study of hypnosis in painful burns. *American Journal of Clinical Hypnosis, 21,* 3–11.

Wooden, T., & Atherton, C. (1982). The clinical use of hypnosis. *Psychological Bulletin, 91,* 215–243.

Yapko, M. (1990). *Trancework: An introduction to the practice of clinical hypnosis* (2nd ed.). New York: Brunner/Mazel.

Yapko, M. (1993a). The seductions of memory. *Family Therapy Networker, 17,* 30–37.

Yapko, M. (1993b). Are we uncovering traumas or creating them? Hypnosis, regression, and suggestions of abuse. In L. Vandecreek, S. Knapp, & T. Jackson (Eds.), *Innovations in clinical practice* (Vol. 12) (pp. 519–527). Sarasota, FL: Professional Resource Press.

Zeig, J. (ed.) (1982). *Ericksonian approaches to hypnosis and psychotherapy.* New York: Brunner/Mazel.

CHAPTER 16

LIFE MODEL THEORY AND SOCIAL WORK TREATMENT

ALEX GITTERMAN

Twenty years have passed since the first presentation of the Life Model (Gitterman & Germain, 1976). During this relatively brief period, dramatic changes have taken place in our society and profession. Social workers today deal with profoundly vulnerable populations, overwhelmed by their continual struggles to survive economic and psychological consequences of poverty and discrimination. Practitioners confront the devastating impact of AIDS, homelessness, substance abuse, chronic mental disorders, child abuse, and family and community violence. Clearly, the miseries and suffering in the 1990s are different in degree and substance from those encountered from the forties through the eighties. With the current attack on "safety net" resources, for many survival is at stake.

Facing these bitter realities, social workers are expected to do more in less time with decreasing resources. Courage, vision, perseverance, creativity, and a widening repertoire of professional methods and skills are essential elements of contemporary practice. A revised and more fully expanded Life Model[1] attempts to respond to these pervasive social changes through four major elaborations (Germain & Gitterman, 1996). First, to be responsive to oppression, social workers must develop competence in community, organizational, and legislative influence and change as well as in direct practice. The second edition of the Life Model specifies methods and skills to move back and forth from helping individuals, families, and groups, to influencing communities, organizations, and legislative bodies. Second, to effectively respond to people's varied needs, social workers must practice at whatever level a particular situation begins and wherever it may lead. The expanded Life Model conceptualizes and illustrates methods and skills distinct to various modalities as well as continuing to describe and specify the common base of social work practice.

Third, people cope with oppression and scapegoating in many different ways. Practitioners must be careful about blaming oppressed people for their troubles. People's coping styles, strengths, and resilience must be understood and supported. In our early writing, the concept of "problems in living" organized ideas about professional assessment and interventions. Unwittingly, this formulation may have implied a deficit in the individual and collectivity. In our current writing, a more neutral stressor–stress-coping paradigm is substituted.

Finally, social workers must be sensitive to people's diverse backgrounds. Stage models of human development assume that social and emotional development follow in fixed, sequential, and universal stages. In our current presentation, a "life course" conception of human development replaces the traditional "life cycle" models.

HUMAN ECOLOGY

In the revised Life Model, the ecological metaphor continues to provide the lens for viewing the exchanges between people and their environments. Ecology, a biological science, examines the relationship between living organisms and all the elements of the social and physical environments. How and why organisms achieve or fail to achieve an adaptive balance with their environments are the major questions of ecological inquiry. Ecological theory, with its revolutionary, adaptive view, provides the theoretical foundation for life-modeled practice (Germain, 1981; Germain & Gitterman, 1986, 1987, 1995, 1996).[2]

PERSON-ENVIRONMENT FIT

Over the life course people strive to improve the *level of fit* with their environments. When we feel positive about our own capacities and hopeful about having our needs and aspirations fulfilled, and when we view our environmental resources as responsive, we and our immediate environments are likely to achieve a reciprocally sustaining condition of *adaptedness*. Adaptive person: environment exchanges reciprocally support and release human and environmental potentials.

However, when perceived environmental and personal limitations are fueled and sustained by oppressive social and physical environments (e.g., racism, sexism, homophobism, ageism, unemployment, pollution), consequences range from heroic adaptation, to impaired functioning, to parasitic exploitation, to individual and collective disintegration. In coping with toxic environments, some people mobilize inner strengths and resiliency to steel themselves against unnurturing environments—to be survivors rather than victims. Others internalize the oppression and turn it against themselves through such self-destructive behaviors as substance abuse and unprotected sex. Still others externalize the oppression, strike back, and vent their rage on others less powerful than they through such behaviors as violence, crime, and property destruction. Readily accessible targets often include family members, neighbors, and community residents. *Dysfunctional* person:environment exchanges reciprocally frustrate and damage both human and environmental potentials.

In dealing with environmental demands, people appraise the adequacy of their environmental and personal resources. *Stress* is the outcome of a perceived imbalance between environmental demands and capability to manage them with available internal and external resources. To relieve the stressful situation, the level of person-environment fit must be improved. This is accomplished by an active change either in people's perceptions and behaviors, or in environmental responses, or in the quality of their exchanges.[3]

THE ENVIRONMENT

Person:environmental exchanges are dynamic rather than fixed processes. Ecological theory emphasizes the reciprocity of person:environmental transactions through which each influences and shapes the other over time. People need to receive from their environment the resources essential for development and survival. Reciprocally, the environment needs to receive the care necessary for its evolution.

The environment consists of *social* and *physical* layers (Germain, 1983). The former consists of the social world of other human beings, ranging from intimate social networks to bureaucratic institutions. The physical layer consists of the *natural* world inherited by human beings and the constructed *built* world of human structures, the *space* which supports, contains, or arranges the structures, and the *temporal rhythms,* fluctuations, and periodicities of environments and of human biology (Germain, 1976, 1978).

Complex *bureaucratic organizations,* a salient feature of the social environment, are prevalent forces in contemporary life. Health, education, and social service organizations profoundly affect most people's lives. In order to carry out its social assignment, an organization develops a mission and evolves structures (e.g., division of labor, chain of command, policies and procedures) to carry out its operations. While organizational mission and structures are essential to service delivery, they simultaneously create tensions and conflicts for professionals and service recipients (Banner & Gagne, 1994; Hasenfeld, 1992; Schmidt, 1992; Weissman, Epstein, & Savage, 1983). For example, an organization's division of labor integrates roles, minimizes duplication, maintains accountability. At the same time, these differential role assignments create vested interest in protecting one's own turf and other mischief. Organizational and client needs are held hostage to turf interest.

Organizational mission and structures are affected by political, economic, and cultural forces (Orfield, 1991). Economic, social, and bureaucratic forces conspire to block access and quality services for vulnerable and oppressed people. Politicians redefine the failures of the economy as behavioral and personality defects of public assistance recipients. Funding sources expect mental health agencies to diagnose and pathologize community residents rather than to view and assist them as residents experiencing life stressors.

Social networks, also a salient feature of the social environment, consist of kin, friends, neighbors, work mates, and acquaintances. Supportive linkages provide essential instrumental (goods and services), expressive (empathy, encouragement), and informational (advice, feedback) resources (Gottlieb, 1988; Thoits, 1986). They serve as essential buffers against life stressors and the stress they generate.

Not all people are able or willing to use available social supports. Some minimize, negate, or deny their difficulties or their need for assistance. Others, while aware of their life stressor(s), are unable to ask for assistance. Self-esteem issues and shame from negative social comparisons may account for their reluctance. Still others are inhibited by their need for privacy.

Not all networks are able or willing to provide available social supports. Loosely knit networks may be unaware of members' difficulties. If sufficient contact is lacking, a member's difficulties remain invisible. Some networks have insufficient resources to meet their members' varied needs. Their resources are to stretched out to incur additional instrumental burdens. Still others withhold available resources for such reasons as selfishness and punishment.

Some networks provide resources, but have a negative impact on recipients (Coyne, Wortman, & Lehman, 1988; Schilling, 1987; Veiel, 1993). Some reinforce deviance, such as drug and gang networks, by supporting dysfunctional behaviors and sabotaging more functional coping behaviors (Duncan-Ricks, 1992; Hawkins & Fraser, 1985). Networks may also scapegoat and reinforce negative self-esteem. Exploitative and parasitic behaviors undermine a member's sense of well-being.

Life events such as sickness and death, job mobility and loss, marital separation and divorce dissolve linkages to significant others. Social and emotional isolation are devastating experiences (Camasso & Camasso, 1986). Without viable networks, people are deprived of life-sustaining instrumental and expressive supports. Widowers who lose social ties maintained by their wives and people suffering from chronic mental illness suffer from impoverished networks (Hamilton, Ponzoha, Cutler, & Weigel, 1989).

The ecological concepts of habitat and niche are particularly relevant for understanding the environment's impact on us (Germain & Gitterman, 1995). *Habitat* refers to places where organisms are found, such as territories and nesting places. People's spatial behaviors are mediated by the texture of space, and by their age, gender, sexual orientation, culture, socioeconomic status, and experiences. The exchanges between people and their habitat takes place within the context of personal space, semifixed space, and fixed space.

Personal space refers to an invisible spatial boundary that we maintain as a buffer against unwanted physical and social contact and to protect our privacy. Since the boundary is invisible, two or more people must negotiate a mutually comfortable distance. When less distance is transacted then desired, we experience crowding and intrusion and react either with physical gestures, or with pronounced withdrawal, or with aggression. When more distance is transacted than desired, we fell the unpleasant state of disengagement and either withdraw or pursue greater intimacy. Since the amount of desired space is influenced by many individual and social factors, it carries the potential for misperception, misunderstanding, and stress.

Semifixed space refers to movable objects and their arrangement in space. Furniture, floors, curtains, paint, decorative figurines, paintings, and lighting provide spatial meanings and boundaries. People rely on environmental props (doors, locks, gates, fences, signs) to regulate interactions with others and to protect their territory within the living dwelling and with the outside world. In families, for example, whose members share limited space, the degree of interpersonal coordination required and the structural limits to privacy create stress. The close proximity, social overload, and spatial constraints are potential sources for interpersonal conflict.

The design of immovable objects and their arrangement in space, *fixed space,* have a profound impact on the quality of life. The high density (i.e., limited space with a large number of people using it) structure and design of high-rise, low-income housing, for example, creates unpredictable and indefensible spaces. With limited control over such public areas as elevators, hallways, and lobbies these spaces represent dangerous threats to survival and are associated with feelings of withdrawal, alienation, and dissatisfaction.

Habitat also consists of the *natural world* of climate and landscape, water sources, quality of air, and animals and plants. The natural world provides the resources essential to the survival of all species. However, lack of attention to preservation of the natural world and careless, destructive abuse of our natural resources endanger us. Exploitative power by dominant groups creates technological pollution by corporations and government agencies of our air, water, soil, and food. Toxic materials are tolerated in disadvantaged neighborhoods, workplaces, and schools.

Beyond supplying resources essential to survival, the natural world also lends special meaning to everyday life. Dubos (1972), a biologist, describes the need of human beings for a sense of kinship with nature, arising out of our evolutionary heritage. The kinship is expressed in our joy of pets and plants, our pleasure from walks in the park and swims in the ocean. Pets, for example, serve numerous functions, such as companionship and protection.

In ecology, *niche* refers to the status occupied in a community's social structure by its individuals and groups. Because dominant groups discriminate on the basis of personal and collective characteristics such as color, gender, sexual orientation, socioeconomic status, physical or mental condition, many people are forced to occupy niches that limit their opportunities, rights, and aspirations. Dominant groups coercively use power to oppress and disempower vulnerable populations, creating and maintaining such social pollutions as poverty, chronic unemployment, lack of affordable housing, inadequate health care and schools, institutionalized racism and sexism, homophobia, and barriers to community participation by those with physical or mental disabilities. Communities of people are placed in marginalized, stigmatized, and destructive niches such as "welfare mother," "ex-addict," "ex-con," "the underclass," "homeless," "borderline," and so on.

INDIVIDUALS, FAMILIES, AND GROUPS

Over the *life course,* individuals, families, and groups experience unique developmental pathways.[4] Diverse human experiences create distinctive transactional processes which occur and recur at any point in the life course. These developmental processes take place within the context of historical, social, and individual time. People born at the same period of time, birth cohorts, experience common formative influences which have a profound affect on their opportunities and expectations.

Because birth cohorts live through a different *historical time* and social forces, they undergo developmental processes of growing up and growing old differently from other birth cohorts (Riley, 1985). For example, the depression of the 1930s, the civil rights movement and war on poverty of the 1960s, the Vietnam War of the 1970s, the dramatic economic changes of the 1980s and 1990s differently shaped the experiences and expectations of adolescents and young adults of the respective birth cohorts. Each birth cohort was affected by its generational events.

Individual biopsychosocial development is also influenced by the timing of collective life issues in a family, group, or community, that is, *social time.* For example, in contemporary society less predictable timetables exist for beginning and completing school, leaving home, remaining single or marrying, having a child, beginning a new career, retiring, and so forth. Similarly, family cultures may have different timetables for male and female developmental expectations. These collective experiences also affect people's experiences over the life course.

Within the context of historical and social time, people construct their respective meaning from life experiences. Personal constructions or narratives, *individual time,* also profoundly influence human development. Essentially, a life course view emphasizes understanding the impact of historical, social, and individual perspectives and sensitivity to the differences in human development.

Over the life course, individuals, families, and groups deal with external *life stressors* and their associated demands (Lazurus & Folkman, 1984). A life stressor (e.g., job change or loss, separation and divorce, death and dying, chronic and acute illness, interpersonal conflict, etc.) creates demands for the individual as well as the collectivity. When we appraise that a stressor exceeds our external and/or internal resources to deal with it, we experience *stress* (manifested physiologically and/or emotionally). Stressful reactions and feelings range from unpleasant, to disquieting, to immobilizing. Intensity is determined by dimensions of the actual stressors, their meaning to the individual and collectivity, and the availability of environmental supports.

When we confront a life stressor, a process of conscious or unconscious *primary appraisal* takes place by which we ask ourselves, "What's going on here?" "Can I deal with it?" "Is this a challenge I can manage or is it a current or future threat of serious harm or loss?" (Lazarus, 1980). We appraise a life stressor as a challenge rather than a threat when we believe we have sufficient personal and environmental resources to master it. Although a perceived challenge might be stressful, feelings of excitement make adrenaline flow and anticipated mastery prevails. In contrast, an appraised threat of harm and loss creates feelings of vulnerability and risk. One person's threat is another person's challenge. The interplay of cultural, environmental, and personal factors as well as past experiences affects primary appraisal processes.

When a life stressor is perceived as a threat, a process of *secondary appraisal* takes place by which we ask ourselves, "What can I do about this situation?" At this moment, we launch our efforts to cope with the stressor. Coping measures primarily consist of efforts to manage our feelings and/or to use personal and environmental resources to manage the stressors. Personal resources include problem-solving skills, flexibility, motivation, belief systems, resilience, optimism, and self-esteem. Environment resources include informal social supports such as family, friends, neighbors; public and private social agencies and various institutions; and the shape and natural dimensions of the physical environment.[5]

When our coping efforts are effective, we experience a sense of relief. When coping efforts fail, physiological and emotional strains are intensified, which can lead to augmented coping efforts, immobilization, or dysfunctional physical, emotional, and social responses. Dysfunctional responses generate more stressors in a downward spiral toward deterioration and disintegration. For example, a terminated romance may trigger a reactive depression. To cope with feelings of abandonment and hopelessness, a person may turn to alcohol to numb the pain. The dependence on alcohol may then create additional stressors at the workplace and with other relationships.

THE LIFE MODEL

PROFESSIONAL FUNCTION

Direct practice level.

The professional function as defined by the Life Model is to *improve the level of fit* between people's (individual, family, group, community) perceived needs, capacities, and aspirations and their environmental supports and resources. Through processes of mutual assessment, worker and service recipient(s) determine practice focus, choosing to:

1. improve a person's (collectivity's) ability to manage stressor(s) through more effective personal and situational appraisals and behavioral skills;
2. influence the social and physical environments to be more responsive to a person's (collectivity's) needs; and
3. improve the quality of person:environment exchanges.

By helping to change their perceptions, cognitions, feelings, or behaviors, their ability to manage a stressor is improved, or its adverse impact may be reduced. By effectively influencing environmental responsiveness, people gain access to desired support and resources and, in turn, develop greater control over their lives. Finally, by improving the exchanges between people and their environments, both actively adapt to the needs and demands of the other. The latter provides greatest opportunities for lasting improvement of level of person:environment fit.

Community, organizational and political levels.

Social workers in practice today deal with profoundly vulnerable populations, overwhelmed by circumstances and events they feel powerless to control. On a daily basis, social workers are constantly reminded of the devastating assault on our clients and the dismantling of entitlements and services. The poor (particularly of color), the sick, the children, the immigrants are blamed for their plight and held to pay for the excesses of the affluent in our society. The anger, the alarm, and the despair intensify as we anticipate the suffering that lies ahead and the inhumanity that permits such injustices.

Corporate and other special interest lobbies assure a widening gap between the poor and the wealthy, as the poor become poorer; the wealthy become wealthier. The gun lobby and polluters reign supreme. While influential voting blocks receive government subsidies, the "safety net" established to mitigate and cushion economic forces is being brutally reduced. Martin Luther King, Jr. mordantly observed that our society preaches socialism for the rich and rugged individualism for the poor.

When community and family supports are weakened, social deterioration increases the risk of personal deterioration. The task of providing direct services to vulnerable and oppressed populations becomes progressively more difficult to accomplish. Within this social context, our professional function must include involvement at the community, organizational, and political levels. In life-modeled practice, professional function includes: *mobilizing community resources* to improve community life; *influencing organizations* to develop responsive policies and services; and *politically influencing* local, state, and federal legislation and regulations.

In this way, the historic polarity of cause *versus* function (Lee, 1929) is replaced with a contemporary melding of cause and function as an essential part of life-modeled practice (Schwartz, 1969). Historically, the profession experienced interpersonal and ideological conflicts between those who emphasized bringing about social change in behalf of social justice, the "cause," as the primary characteristic of social work and those who emphasized "function" as the primary characteristic of social work practice, that is, the technologies used by practitioners to bring about individual change. In reality, however, a cause won requires a function (technology, services, and programs for individuals, families, and groups) to carry it out. A further and specific technology (organization and political advocacy) is required for successfully winning a cause. Clearly, both cause and function must be hallmarks of practice and education for practice if social work is to be ready itself for the new century.

PROBLEM DEFINITION (PERSON:ENVIRONMENT EXCHANGES)

How a problem is defined largely governs what will be done about it. If, for example, the source of a painful life issue is believed to be internal and is defined as psychological, social work interventions will be psychologically guided by a disease model. Goals will refer to internal change through gaining psychological insight.

For example, Billy does not pay attention in school, and the school threatens to transfer him to a special school. Organic disability has been ruled out and the life issue is defined as an emotional disturbance. This emphasis on psychopathology leads to a linear, dichotomized view of the child and his environment. He has an internal disorder that requires psychological "excision." He and his mother might be viewed as having symbiotic difficulties in separating, so mother is added to the treatment program. They might be treated by different therapists. Help focuses exclusively on psychological processes. Little of no attention is given to school, social networks, and neighborhood conditions that might contribute to the life stressor.

If life issues are defined as rooted in social pathology, then intervention is likely to be conceived in social-institutional terms, on a social action (or on a conflict model [Gould, 1987]). Goals will refer to external change and the practice method will be primarily case or class advocacy. In applying the conflict model, Billy's right to stay in school may be won. He can stay in school, but the life issues that had kept him from learning in school may still remain. However, in life-modeled practice the social pathological definition does not preclude individual attention to Billy and his mother as well as to advocacy.

If life stressors are defined as disharmonious *person:environment exchanges,* then interventions are likely to be conceived as improving the *level of fit* between individual and collective need and collective and environmental resources. Goals will prefer to reducing or eliminating the life stressor if possible and strengthening coping skills and environmental resources.

Psychologically oriented skills will be directed to progressive forces in the personality or their development. These include sensory-perceptual capacities, positive emotions, and thinking and problem-solving abilities. Supports in the organizational and network fields and physical settings will be mobilized and used. If needed, the work will include increasing the responsiveness of the organization affecting the client, including the worker's own agency.

In Billy's situation, depending on the source(s) of the stressor(s), several separate or joint entry points into the person:environment field might be possible for effective help:

1. If the stressor arose from Billy's difficulty with the life transition of adapting to a nourishing school environment, help is directed to improving his coping skills through individual or group (other boys in a similar situation as Billy) modality.
2. If the stressor arose from the family's dysfunctional patterns, help is directed to modifying those patterns with the family or a few families experiencing a similar stressor.
3. If the stressor arose from dysfunctional exchanges between Billy and family and school, help is directed on an individual, family, or group basis toward removing barriers in their communication and stimulating mutual problem-solving.
4. If the stressor emerged from the social structure and climate of Billy's classroom, social worker and teacher could undertake classroom meetings. Such meetings are designed to help the children (and teacher) learn to express their feelings and ideas about their shared experiences. Such an approach would not only help Billy, but on a preventive level, it could be helpful to all the children and to the teacher by reducing scapegoating by the children, biased responses and expectations held by the teacher, or other dysfunctional exchanges.
5. If the stressor came from a lack of after-school resources, the worker could try to help the school obtain a grant and develop a program.

6. If the stressor converged from Billy's concerns about overcrowded classrooms, unsafe school bathrooms, or fears of walking past the neighborhood drug users and dealers or assaultive teenagers on his way to school, his parent(s) could be helped to join with other concerned neighborhood or community parents in approaching the school, police, and local legislatures in order to improve school conditions and gain safe school routes.

This analysis is purposively oversimplified to highlight the varied practice options emerging from a broad focus on person:environment exchanges. In reality, Billy's stress most likely arose from multiple sources. Sometimes effective work on one stressor supports coping with others. Other times, work is directed to two or more stressors (guidelines for appropriate focus are discussed later).

The major point is: a social worker using an ecological conceptual lens is more likely to "see" diverse points of entry into a complex situation and less likely to fit a client into a narrow theoretical construction. Our practice theories and models must be responsive to people and their situations rather than fitting their life issues into our own theoretical and practice preoccupations and biases. Similarly, a worker's specialization in individual, family, group, or community practice should not determine what service is provided, but rather the received service should be based on applicant/client needs and preferences.

LIFE STRESSORS SCHEMA

Over the life course, people must cope with three interrelated life issues: difficult life transitions and traumatic life events; environmental pressures; and dysfunctional interpersonal processes. Although these three life stressors are interrelated, each takes on its own force and magnitude and provides focus to practice with individuals, families, groups, communities, organizations, and politics.

1. Difficult life transitions and traumatic life events.
Life transitions include *biological* as well as *social* changes. The physical and biological changes of infancy, childhood, puberty, adolescence, adulthood, and advanced age are universal, but social expectations and patterns associated with the changes vary across cultures. For example, puberty is a biological condition; adolescence is a social status.[6] Biological factors associated with pubertal changes elicit changing responses and demands from the environment of family, school personnel, and peers.

People also experience stress from *entering* new experiences and relationships and *leaving* familiar ones. Beginnings (entrances) generate stress. Entering a new neighborhood, school, relationship(s), job, having a baby, acquiring a new diagnostic label are filled with ambiguity, new role expectations, and challenges. Leavings (endings) are usually more stressful than beginnings. Ending an intimate relationship through separation or death, losing a job, leaving a school, separation from a child or parent are characterized by painful loss and change. Unexpected life transitions are more stressful than expected ones. Similarly, when life entrances and exits come too early or to late in the life course, they are likely to be stressful. For example, a young adolescent who becomes a parent, and an older grandparent who has primary responsibility for parenting, may find that the timing of the experience creates additional stress.

The abruptness, enormity, and immediacy of traumatic life events cause personal crisis and long-lasting residue of pain. Unexpected death and illness, violence of rape, displacement caused by natural disasters, loss of cherished home or job are overwhelming and immobilizing. Severe physical, psychological, and/or social loss is a primary characteristic of trauma.

2. Environmental pressures.
The social and physical environments provide essential instrumental resources and emotional support to the tasks of daily living. They also create significant troubles and distress. For some individuals and collectivities, organizational and informal network resources are available, but they are unable to access or use them. For others, organizational and network structures and functions are unresponsive to their personal styles and needs. And for still others, important organizational and network resources are unavailable and their basic needs remain unmet. Similarly, the physical environment's natural and built resources may be available, but some people are unable to use them. For others, available physical resources are responsive to their styles and needs. And for others, basic natural and built resources are extremely minimal.

3. Dysfunctional interpersonal processes[7].
In responding to life-transitional and environmental stressors, the family and group serve as a resource and buffer. However, problematic internal family or group relationships and communication patterns exacerbate existing stress and/or become yet another painful stressor in people's lives. Dysfunctional family and group processes are expressed in such behaviors as scapegoating, rigid alliances, withdrawal, and hostility. While dysfunctional for individual members and the collectivity, these behaviors may maintain an illusion of functioning and the collectivity's continued existence. For example, scapegoating may stave off disorganization in the family or group at the expense of the individual member. These behaviors become fixed and obstruct potential for mutual support.

Similar dysfunctional processes arise between social workers and clients in the form of discrepant expectations, misunderstandings and misperceptions, value conflicts, and differences in backgrounds (Gitterman & Schaeffer, 1972; Gitterman, 1983, 1989b, 1992a). These processes interfere with the helping process and create additional stress for clients.

A life stressor often generates associated stressors. When it or they are not successfully managed or resolved, additional stressors erupt (the "spread phenomenon"). The following case is an example.

Marcia, a twenty-three-year-old African-American single mother of a two-month-old daughter, Denise, was referred to family services by Ms. Northern, the manager of a single-mothers' residence. Marcia had been living in the residence for the last six months; remaining there was made conditional on her accepting the referral to the agency. In the first session, she expressed anger at Ms. Northern for forcing her to come to the agency and blaming her for all the arguments and fights in the residence. At the same time, Marcia wanted help with the stress in her life—particularly being a single parent and her new role as a mother. She said that at times she is overwhelmed and even angry at Denise "for being so needy." We mutually agreed to focus on two interrelated stressors: (1) her transition to being a single parent, and (2) her environmental transactions with the residence manager and the other residents as well as securing permanent housing. A third stressor evolved from our work, namely her distrust and testing of me (and my reactions).

The *life-transitional* stressor centers on Marica's entry into motherhood and becoming the sole caretaker and responder to the unrelenting demands of a young infant. Marcia's history feeds an ambivalence about her single-mother status and its associated roles. She was placed in foster care at age seven, moved from home to home, and lost contact with her mother at the age of thirteen. While she feels rage at her mother for not wanting her ("I'll probably forgive my mother someday, but right now I'd like to kill her even though she's already dead"), she is trying to forgive her because she recognizes that her mother was a "victim of the system." Soon after giving birth, Marcia looked for a job and child care with minimal success. She states, "I feel stuck, isolated, like I have no life of my own. . . . I can't get off welfare without a job; I can't get a job without child care; and I can't afford child care while on welfare." Marcia feels caught in a "vicious circle" that makes her want to "throw off all responsibility."

Marcia's ambivalence is evident in her vacillation between poignantly questioning whether Denise's needs exceed her ability to give and vehemently asserting that she will sell her body, if she must, to keep Denise happy, safe, well fed, and with her. When Marcia perceives herself to be a capable mother, she is responsive to Denise. However, when the urgency of Denise's needs conflicts with Marcia's needs, she becomes overwhelmed with the depth of her own unmet needs. Marcia's pain becomes more intense and intolerable. At these moments, she impulsively responds to Denise with anger and impatience. Incidents the worker observed during a couple of session illustrate life transitional stress:

1/11: Denise started to fret a little bit. Marcia responded by talking to her in a non-stop, repetitive manner. Denise tried to follow her mother's erratic cues, but looked helpless and confused. She began to cry and Marcia jammed a bottle in her mouth, which began to leak all over. Marcia swore and her anger became overt. Denise began to choke on the milk, and Marcia, trying to control her anger, set Denise on her lap, vigorously patting her back. When Denise regurgitated, Marcia scolded her. She seemed really furious and made a few half-hearted attempts to smooth her rage away by calling Denise by various pet names and telling her that she was loved.

1/25: At the end of the session, Marcia yelled at Denise, "What the fuck?! . . . What did you do now? . . . I can't believe this! . . . Guess what, smarty pants, I brought another set of clothes—na! na!" Marcia continued to swear and became increasingly agitated, bordering on rage, because Denise had soiled her diaper. She was again talking to Denise nonstop, finally yelling, "And that fucking bastard of a father you have is good for shit." She continued talking to Denise as she angrily unsnapped her clothes, saying "stinky, stinky, stinky. . . ."

Marcia feels that Denise, like the rest of the world, is unfair and taking advantage of her. With unresolved feelings of being abandoned by her family and by Denise's father, pressures of being a single parent ("I'm tired . . . I'm hungry . . . I hardly got to wash my face today"), and insufficient environmental supports and resources, Marcia is unable to be predictable and consistent with Denise. With so many of her own needs unmet, Marcia's has difficulty viewing Denise as a separate human being with separate needs.

Marcia's difficult life transitions are exacerbated by severe *environmental pressures*. Marcia lives well below the poverty line, receiving AFDC, Medicaid, and food stamps benefits. She considers herself homeless—having a maximum of six months left at the residence before she must leave. She further states that Ms. Northern "keeps holding it over me that she can kick me out." She adds with bravado, "I am a survivor—I am not going to take shit from anybody," least of all Ms. Northern and the other "girls" in the residence. With neither sufficient income nor the necessary child care to support herself and Denise, Marcia is feeling increasingly hopeless about getting off welfare. Her relationship to her last foster parents represents the single most enduring relationship in Marica's life. She describes them as "my friends when I need them." Outside of her ties to her foster family, her social network is negligible. She complains that she has no friends, that she pushes people away without realizing it. Finally, she has severed all ties with the remainder of her biological family, many of whom live nearby, because "I can't forgive them for refusing to take me and my sister and brothers in when my mom caved in."

Marcia's environment is fraught with severe limitations: chronic racial prejudice and discrimination; lack of affordable housing; limited employment opportunities; unavailability of child care services; Denise's father's heroin addiction; cohabitation with several other young women and their babies; demand for conformity to house rules; a limited social network; and finally, the unceasing and ever-present responsibility for being the sole caretaker of an infant. These environmental stressors combine together, and act independently, to lessen significantly Marcia's ability to tolerate the demands of new motherhood, which has radically changed her life. The social environment only serves to exacerbate Marica's emotional and social neglect and profound sense of despair and worthlessness with which she probably has struggled since childhood.

In working together, *interpersonal stress* also developed between Marcia and the worker. Marcia vacillated between viewing the worker as supportive listener and advisor and as an authority figure not dissimilar from Ms. Northern, who "sits in judgment" of her. In the second session, she commented, "I've got to do the political thing, and that's why I'm here—I've got the picture." Beyond the obstacle posed by a mandated service, Marcia's and the worker's differences in race, social class, and level of education contributed tension to their communication.

ASSESSMENT

Throughout the helping process, social workers make decisions about such issues as: points of entry in person:environment field; goals and tasks; practice modality, methods, time arrangements; and life stressor(s) focus. Professional judgments are made *at any moment in time* about which messages to explore (probe, chase) or when to respond with information and advice or when to point out contradictions between verbal and nonverbal communication. Similarly, *during and after each session* social workers make decisions about focus and next steps. These professional judgments must be based on disciplined reasoning and inferences within the context of sensitivity to differences related to values, beliefs, and perceptions derived from one's social class, race, ethnicity, religion, gender, sexual orientation, age, and mental and physical state.

Valid and reliable decisions rest on three assessment tasks: collecting, organizing, and interpreting data. First and foremost, professional judgments are based on *collected data.* To help an individual, family, or group with life stressors, worker and applicant(s)/client(s) examine available salient information. Salient data include: the nature of the life stressors and their severity; the person(s)'s perceptions of and efforts to deal with the stressors; the person(s)'s perceptions of the role of family, networks, organizations, and features of the physical environment in cushioning and exacerbating the stressors; and expectations, if any, of the agency and social worker. *Mutuality* in stressor definition and collection of other relevant data actively engages applicants/clients in developing with the worker common focus and direction. These data are collected from the person(s)'s verbal accounts, the worker's observations of nonverbal responses, significant others' verbal and nonverbal responses (obtained only with applicant's/client's informed consent), and written reports (also obtained only with the person(s)'s informed consent).

Many applicants/clients are affected by overwhelming life stressors. Practitioners understandably become overwhelmed by harsh environmental realities, multiple stressors, and the associated pain. A schema helps a practitioner to *organize data.* The life stressor formulation (i.e., difficult life transitions and traumatic life events, environmental pressures, and dysfunctional interpersonal processes) provides a tool for grouping and organizing data (see above case situation of Marcia).

The life stressor schema also provides moment-to-moment assessment guidelines for professional interventions. For example, at an early moment in the third session, Marcia complains about her loneliness. At this moment, the social worker must assess whether Marcia is asking for help in exploring her grief associated with developmental transition and losses, or whether she is focusing on the lack of social connections in her life and asking for help with reaching out to organizations and social networks. Or whether at this particular moment she is indirectly voicing some degree of dissatisfaction with the worker's pace or style of helping. At each moment the worker has to assess with Marcia whether she is asking for help with life transitional, environmental, and/or interpersonal stressor(s). From moment to moment, Marcia may change her focus and the social worker must skillfully follow her cues.

The final professional assessment task is to *interpret* the collected and organized data. To be valid, professional inferences must be rooted in disciplined inductive and deductive reasoning rather than in personal values and biases. Using inductive reasoning, social workers engage applicants/clients to pattern and to develop hypotheses about their person:environment exchanges, particularly the *level of fit* between personal strengths and limitations and environmental supports and obstacles. Deductive reasoning is more of a professional and less of a mutual process. The social worker applies relevant theory and research findings to person(s)'s life situation(s). For example, knowledge about post-traumatic stress disorder may help a social worker better understand a person's reactions to an unexpected life stressor.

The assessment tasks of collecting relevant information, its systematic organization, and the analysis of data are common to most practice approaches. However, several beliefs are distinctive to the Life Model.

1. Engaging participation of applicant/client in the assessment process and developing *mutual* understanding.
2. Understanding the nature of person:environment exchanges and the *level of fit* between human needs and environmental resources is the core assessment task.
3. Using the life *stressor schema* to organize and assess data.
4. Emphasizing *moment-to-moment* assessment.

Intervention (Modalities, Methods, and Skills)

In helping people with their life stressors, the social worker may be called on to intervene at the individual, family, group, community, social network, organization, physical environment, or political level(s). Social workers must competently work within all modalities, moving from one to another as situations require. In life-modeled practice, mutual assessment of life stressors and level of person:environment fit determines selection of modality rather than professional specializations and preferences.

Based on a belief that many professional methods and skills are common to most modalities, the Life Model emphasizes and *integrated perspective on practice*. A few formulations are particularly helpful in presenting common practice methods and skills. Life-modeled practice is, like life itself, *phasic*. Its processes constitute three phases: the initial, ongoing, and ending. These phases provide a structure for conceptualizing and illustrating common professional methods and skills. However, in actual practice, these phases are not always distinct; they often appear, recede, and overlap. For example, in brief and episodic work, the temporal limits collapse the phases. Similarly, all beginnings are affected by past endings.

In the initial phase, the auspice of the service rather than the modality differentiates common professional methods and skills. Thus, a person's *degree of choice* (whether the service is sought, offered, or mandated) integrates practice modalities. For example, when a service is offered, the social worker begins by identifying her/his organizational auspice and role and presenting a clear offer of service, which takes into account people's perceptions and definition of their needs. The skills of offering a service are common to working with all modalities. Similarly, the life stressors schema supports an integrated practice related to assessment of, and interventions in, life transitional, environmental, and interpersonal issues.

While emphasizing the common base of social work assessment and interventions, the Life Model also examines the methods and skills specific to each practice modality. For example, in offering a group service the practitioner must have distinctive knowledge and skill in group formation. Forming a group requires achieving compositional balance; developing appropriate time arrangements related to number, frequency, and duration of sessions; deciding on group size; and developing organizational sanctions and supports. Distinctive knowledge and skill is identified for each respective modality.

While the Life Model presents practice principles, methods, and skills for integrative practice as well as for specific modalities, they are not prescriptive. This is so because practitioner style and creativity are indispensable. A mechanical "professionalism" expressed by projecting an impression of neutrality and impersonality is not helpful. Professional skills must be integrated with a humanness, compassion, and spontaneity. The social worker's genuine empathy, commitment, and willingness to become involved speak louder than assuming the "correct" body posture, saying the "right" words, or making the "appropriate" nonverbal gestures. Effective practitioners are "dependably real" rather than "rigidly consistent" (Rogers, 1961, p. 50).

When Professor Turner invited Professor Germain and me to contribute to *Social Work Treatment, Fourth Edition,* we were completing the second edition of the Life Model. Professor Germain had undertaken a new writing project and due to ill health she declined the invitation. In August 1995, she passed away. This chapter is dedicated to her. She had a profound impact on my intellectual development as well as that of many others. A creative and intellectual explorer and discoverer, she roamed the globe of ideas and discovered their relevance for a profession she deeply loved. Never satisfied with the intellectual status quo, she leaped forward into uncharted theoretical territory, found new concepts from ecology, psychology, anthropology, and sociology and made them available to us. Her ideas and words resonate throughout the chapter.

NOTES

1. The term "Life Model" was initially inspired by Bandler, who suggested that practice should be modeled on life itself (Bandler, 1936).
2. Ecological ideas also provide the framework for social work practice in *fields* such as: families and children (Hartman, 1979; Hess & Howard, 1981; Howard & Johnson, 1985; Laird, 1979; Videka-Sherman, 1991); gerontology (Berman-Rossi, 1991; Berman-Rossi & Gitterman, 1992; Freeman, 1984; Germain, 1984b; Tonti & Kossberg, 1983); health

(Black & Weiss, 1991; Coulton, 1981; Germain, 1984a; Getzel, 1991); mental health (Goldstein, 1983, Libassi & Maluccio, 1982; Wetzel, 1978); schools (Clancy, 1995; Germain, 1988; Winters & Easton, 1983); substance abuse (Hanson, 1991); for practice with various *social problems* such as domestic violence (Carlson, 1984, 1991); vulnerable populations (Gitterman, 1991); and for *discrete practice interventions* (Germain, 1982, 1985; Gitterman, 1982, 1983, 1988a,b, 1989a,b, 1992a,b, 1994; Gitterman & Germain, 1981; Gitterman & Miller, 1989; Gitterman & Schaeffer, 1972; Gitterman & Shulman, 1994; Kelley, McKay, & Nelson, 1985).

3. Ecological theory perceives "adaptedness" and adaptation as action-oriented and change-oriented processes. Neither concept avoids issues of power, exploitation, and conflict that exist in the world of nature as well as in the social world of human beings. Adaptedness and adaptation are not to be confused with a passive "adjustment" to the status quo. See Germain and Gitterman 1987b, and Gould, 1987.

4. In the Life Model, "life course" replaces the traditional "life cycle" stage models of human development. Human beings do not experience universally fixed, sequential stages of development. Race, ethnicity, culture, religion, gender, sexual orientation, social class, and historical context have profound influence on individual and collective development.

5. The two interrelated coping functions, *problem solving and management of feelings,* have an interesting reciprocal relation to each other. In many coping responses to stressful person:environment encounters, the two functions may proceed together. However, in the early, acute phase of very severe stressors in particular, it may be difficult to proceed with problem solving until intense negative feelings are brought under some degree of control. Otherwise the feelings are apt to immobilize problem-solving efforts. But such feelings may be difficult to control until the person has experienced some degree of progress in the beginning steps of problem solving. A saving grace in this seeming paradox is an ability to cope with the life stressor by unconsciously blocking out negative feelings temporarily in order that some problem solving can begin. This is frequently seen in the unconscious denial (defense) of people who have suffered a grievous loss or harm.

6. Among some groups or classes in our society, a fully independent adulthood may not be recognized until the twenties. Further, adolescence is not recognized in all societies. In some cultures, puberty alone marks the entry into the rights and responsibilities of adulthood, with no intervening state.

7. For conceptual clarity and consistency, interpersonal processes apply only to when the social worker is involved with a family/group system or subsystem. If a social worker, for example, is working with an abused woman, but not with the partner, the focus is on life-transitional concerns (e.g., separation, grief) and/or environmental concerns (e.g., linkage with community resources, negotiating with her partner, securing a court order of protection). By contrast, a focus on dysfunctional interpersonal processes requires conjoint work with both partners and/or the children.

REFERENCES

Bandler, B. (1963). The concept of ego-supportive psychotherapy. In H. Parad & R. Miller (Eds.), *Ego-oriented casework: Problems and perspectives* (pp. 27–44). New York: Family Service Association of America.

Banner, D., & Gagne, E. (1994). *Designing effective organizations.* Newbury Park, CA: Sage Publications.

Berman-Rossi, T. (1991). Elderly in need of long-term care. In A. Gitterman (Ed.), *Handbook of social work practice with vulnerable populations* (pp. 503–548). New York: Columbia University Press.

Berman-Rossi, T. & Gitterman, A. (1992). A group for relatives and friends of institutionalized aged. In C. LeCroy (Ed.), *Case studies in social work practice* (pp. 186–197). Belmont, CA: Wadsworth.

Black, R., & Weiss, J. (1991). Chronic physical illness and disability. In A. Gitterman (Ed.), *Handbook of social work practice with vulnerable populations* (pp. 137–164). New York: Columbia University Press.

Camasso, M.J., & Camasso, A. (1986). Social supports, undesirable life events, and psychological distress in a disadvantaged population. *Social Service Review, 60,* 381–394.

Carlson, B.E. (1984). Causes and maintenance of domestic violence: An ecological analysis. *Social Service Review, 58* (December), 569–587.

Carlson, B.E. (1991). Domestic Violence. In A. Gitterman (ed.), *Handbook of social work practice with vulnerable populations* (pp. 471–502) New York: Columbia University Press.

Clancy, J. (1995). Ecological school social work: The reality and the vision. *Social Work in Education, 17*(1), 49–47.

Cohen, C., Teresi, J., & Holmes, D. (1986). Assessment of stress-buffering effects of social networks in psychological symptoms in an inner-city elderly population. *American Journal of Community Psychology, 14,* 75–92.

Coulton, C.J. (1981). Person-environment fit as the focus in health care. *Social Work, 26* (January), 26–35.

Coyne, J., Wortman, C., & Lehman, D. (1988). The other side of support: Emotional over involvement and miscarried helping. In B. Gottlieb (Ed.), *Marshaling social support* (pp. 305–330). Newbury Park, Ca.: Sage Publications.

Dubos, R. (1972). *A God within.* New York: Scribners.

Duncan-Ricks, E.N. (1992). Adolescent sexuality and peer pressure. *Child and Adolescent Social Work Journal, 9*(4), 319–327.

Freeman, E. (1984). Multiple losses in the elderly: An ecological approach. *Social Casework, 65*(5), 287–296.

Germain, C.B. (1976). Time: An ecological variable in social work practice. *Social Casework, 57* (July), 419–426.

Germain, C.B. (1978). Space, an ecological variable in social work practice. *Social Casework, 59* (November), 15–22.

Germain, C.B. (1981). The ecological approach to people:environment transactions. *Social Casework, 62* (June), 323–331.

Germain, C.B. (1982). Teaching primary prevention in social work: An ecological perspective. *Journal of Education for Social Work, 18* (Winter), 20–28.

Germain, C.B. (1983). Using social and physical environments. In A. Rosenblatt & D. Waldfogel (Eds.), *Handbook of clinical social work* (pp. 110–134). San Francisco: Jossey-Bass.

Germain, C.B. (1984a). Social work practice in health care. New York: Free Press.

Germain, C.B. (1984b). The elderly and the ecology of death: Issues of time and space. In M. Tallmer et al. (Eds.), *The life-threatened elderly* (pp. 195–207). New York: Columbia University Press.

Germain, C.B. (1985). The place of community within an ecological approach to social work. In S. Taylor & R. Roberts (Eds.), *Theories and practice of community social work* (pp. 30–55). New York: Columbia University Press.

Germain, C.B. (1988). School as a living environment within the community. *Social Work in Education, 10*(4), 260–276.

Germain, C.B. & Gitterman, A. (1986). Ecological social work research in the United States. In *Brennpunkta Sozalier Arbeit* (pp. 60–76). Frankfurt: Diesterweg.

Germain, C.B., & Gitterman, A. (1987a). Ecological perspective. In *Encyclopedia of Social Work* (18th ed.) (pp. 488–499). Silver Spring, MD: National Association of Social Workers Press.

Germain, C.B., & Gitterman, A. (1987b). Life Model versus conflict model. *Social Work, 32* (Nov.–Dec.), 552–553 (Letter to Editor).

Germain, C.B., & Gitterman, A. (1995). Ecological perspective. In *Encyclopedia of Social Work* (19th ed.) (pp. 816–824). Silver Spring, MD: National Association of Social Workers Press.

Germain, C.B., & Gitterman, A. (1996). *The Life Model of social work practice: Advances in theory and practice.* New York: Columbia University Press.

Getzel, G. (1991). AIDS. In A. Gitterman (Ed.), *Handbook of social work practice with vulnerable populations* (pp. 3564). New York: Columbia University Press.

Gitterman, A. (1982). The uses of groups in health settings. In A. Lurie, G. Rosenberg, & S. Pinskey (Eds.), *Social work with groups in health settings* (pp. 6–21). New York: Prodist.

Gitterman, A. (1983). Uses of Resistance: A transactional view. *Social Work, 28* (March/April) 127–131.

Gitterman, A. (1988a). The social worker as educator. In *Health care practice today: The social worker as educator* (pp. 13–22). New York: Columbia University School of Social Work.

Gitterman, A. (1988b). Teaching students to connect theory and practice. *Social Work with Groups, 11*(1/2), 33–42.

Gitterman, A. (1989a). Building mutual support in groups. *Social Work in Groups, 12*(2), 5–22.

Gitterman, A. (1989b). Testing professional authority and boundaries. *Social Casework, 70* (March), 165–171.

Gitterman, A. (1991). Introduction to social work practice with vulnerable populations. In A. Gitterman (Ed.), *Handbook of social work practice with vulnerable populations* (pp. 1–34) New York: Columbia University Press.

Gitterman, A. (1992a). Creative connections between theory and practice. In M. Weil, K. Chau, & D. Southerland (Eds.), *Theory, practice and education* (pp. 13–27). New York: Haworth Press.

Gitterman, A. (1992b). Working with Differences: White teacher and African-American students. *Journal of Teaching Social Work, 5*(2), 65–80.

Gitterman, A. (1994). Developing a new group service. In A. Gitterman & L. Shulman (Eds.), *Mutual aid groups, vulnerable populations and the life cycle* (pp. 59–77). New York: Columbia University Press.

Gitterman, A., & Germain, C.B. (1976). Social work practice: A Life Model. *Social Service Review, 50* (December), 601–610.

Gitterman, A., & Germain, C.B. (1981). Teaching about the environment and social work practice. *Journal of Social Work Education, 17* (Fall), 44–51.

Gitterman, A., & Miller, I. (1989). The influence of the organization on clinical practice. *Clinical Social Work Journal, 17* (Summer), 151–164.

Gitterman, A., & Schaeffer, A. (1972). The white worker and the black client. *Social Casework, 53* (May), 280–291.

Gitterman, A., & Shulman, L. (Eds.) (1994). *Mutual aid groups, vulnerable populations, and the life cycle.* New York: Columbia University Press.

Goldstein, E.G. (1983). Clinical and ecological approaches to the borderline client. *Social Casework, 64* (June) 353–362.

Gottlieb, B. (1988). Marshalling social supports: The state of the art in research and practice. In B. Gottlieb, (Ed.), *Marshalling social support: Formats, processes, and effects.* Newbury Park, CA: Sage Publications.

Gould, K. (1987). Life Model vs. conflict model: A feminist perspective. *Social Work, 32* (July-August), 345–352.

Hamilton, N., Ponzoha, C., Cutler, D., & Weigel, R. (1989). Social networks and negative versus positive symptoms of schizophrenia. *Schizophrenia Bulletin, 15*(4), 625–633.

Hanson, M. (1991). Alcoholism and other drug addictions. In A. Gitterman (Ed.), *Handbook of social work practice with vulnerable populations* (pp. 65–100) New York: Columbia University Press.

Hartman, A. (1979). *Finding families: An ecological approach to family assessment in adoption.* Beverly Hills, CA: Sage Publications.

Hasenfeld, Y. (1992). *Human services as complex organizations.* Newbury Park, CA: Sage Publications.

Hawkins, J., & Fraser, M. (1985). The social networks of street drug users. *Social Work Research and Abstracts, 21*(1), 3–12.

Hess, P., & Howard, T. (1981). An ecological model for assessing psychosocial difficulties in children. *Child Welfare, 60*(8), 499–518.

Howard, T., & Johnson, F.C. (1985) An ecological approach to practice with single-parent families. *Social Casework, 66* (October) 482–489.

Kelley, M.L., McKay, S. & Nelson, C.H. (1985). Indian agency development: An ecological approach. *Social Casework, 66* (December), 594–602.

Laird, J. (1979). An ecological approach to child welfare: Issues of family identity and continuity. In C. Germain (Ed.), *Social work practice: People and environments* (pp. 174–212). New York: Columbia University Press.

Lazarus, R. (1980). The stress and coping paradigm. In L. bond & J. Rosen (Eds.), *Competence and coping during adulthood* (pp. 28–74). Hanover, NH: University Press of New England.

Lazurus, R., & Folkman, S. (1984). *Stress, appraisal and coping,* New York: Springer.

Lee, P. (1929). Social work: Cause and function. *Proceedings, National Conference of Social Work* (pp. 3–20). New York: Columbia University Press.

Libassi, M.F., & Maluccio, A.N. (1982). Teaching the use of ecological perspective in community mental health. *Journal of Education for Social Work, 18* (Fall), 94–100.

Orfield, G. (1991). Cutback policies, declining opportunities, and the role of social service providers. *Social Service Review, 65*(4), 516–530.

Riley, M. W. (1985). Women, men, and the lengthening of the life course. In A. S. Rossi (Ed.), *Aging and the life course* (pp. 333–347) New York: Aldine.

Rogers, C. (1961). The characteristics of a helping relationship. In C. Rogers (Ed.), *On becoming a person* (pp. 33–58). Boston: Houghton Mifflin.

Schilling, R. (1987). Limitations of social support. *Social Service Review, 61* (March), 19–31.

Schmidt, H. (1992). Relationships between decentralized authority and other structural properties in human service organizations: Implications for service effectiveness. *Administration in Social Work, 16*(1), 25–39.

Schwartz, W. (1969). Private troubles and public issues: One job or two? In *Social welfare forum, proceedings of the national conference on social work* (pp. 22–43). New York: Columbia University Press.

Thoits, V. (1986). Social support as coping assistance. *Journal of Consulting and Clinical Psychology, 54*(4), 416–423.

Tonti, M., & Kossberg, J. (1983). A transactional model for work with the frail elderly. In M. Dinerman (Ed.), *Social work in a turbulent world* (pp. 156–166). Silver Spring, MD: National Association of Social Workers Press.

Veiel, H.O.F. (1993). Detrimental effects of kin support networks on the course of depression. *Journal of Abnormal Psychology, 102* (August), 419–429.

Videka-Sherman, L. (1991). Child abuse and neglect. In A. Gitterman (Ed.), *Handbook of social work practice with vulnerable populations* (pp. 345–381). New York: Columbia University Press.

Von Bulow, B. (1991). Eating problems. In A. Gitterman (Ed.), *Handbook of social work practice with vulnerable populations* (pp. 205–233). New York: Columbia University Press.

Weissman, H., Epstein, I., & Savage, A. (1983). *Agency-based social work.* Philadelphia: Temple University Press.

Wetzel, J. (1978). Depression and dependence upon sustaining environments. *Clinical Social Work Journal, 6,* 75–89.

Winters, W., & Easton, F. (1983). *The practice of social work in the schools: An ecological perspective.* New York: Free Press.

CHAPTER 17

A MATERIALIST FRAMEWORK FOR SOCIAL WORK THEORY AND PRACTICE

STEVE BURGHARDT

In 1934, Joan Price, a recent college graduate in education, took a job in a new public relief office located in an old warehouse on the Lower East Side of New York City. Her first desk was a crate she shared with two other workers. Her investigation time in the nearby community took twenty hours a week; paperwork took fourteen. She did not have an M.S.W., and her working conditions made recent unionization appeals by the insurgent Rank and File clubs sound exciting. Her salary was $1,300 a year, about one-third less than her professional supervisor. And the federal government was spending the unheard of amount of $4 billion a year for relief.

In 1984, Joan Price's granddaughter, a recent M.S.W., held a job in a social service department of a major voluntary hospital and worked primarily on discharge planning. She had her own office, but secretarial help had been lost in a recent budget crunch. Her functional responsibilities left her little time to visit the ward, let alone any community; besides, her clients were located throughout the city. Not only were all her forms in triplicate; her productivity was measured in monthly printouts that forced her and co-workers to maintain an active pace. Unionization had been mentioned, but she wondered if that ran counter to professional values. Her salary was $17,300 a year, but had been frozen for two years. The freeze hurt because her expenses for advanced clinical training had just gone up. And welfare state costs were running about $468 billion a year, a 120 percent increase in eight years.

These two vignettes, drawn from actual social work experience, describe how social work in North America has changed over the years. But why has so much changed? How could it be that the welfare state would be so much larger than in the

409

past and yet a social worker's distance from clients so much greater? Why was "private practice" unheard of in social work circles in the 1930s but is the common echo in every social work school's corridors? How could it evolve that Joan Price's granddaughter can have her professional M.S.W. degree and her own office and yet have less job autonomy than her unlicensed predecessor?

The answers to these questions, as contradictory and puzzling as they seem, remain in a jumble without a clear analytical framework that roots the conditions of social work in some clear fashion while exploring the twists and turns of daily practice experience. Without seeing how changes in the size and direction of the welfare state affect how a social worker practices, a practitioner is too often left with the fear that "I'm not doing enough" when particular individual problems continue. Likewise, without being able to see how one's practice experience does affect larger social forces, social workers come to believe that "social change" occurs only through community organization.

I believe that Marxist theory most lucidly places the changing conditions of social work in a framework that holds out continuous possibility for ongoing politicized activity for social workers from every method—case, group, and community work. Of course, to write about the influence of Marxist theory on social work is more than a little intimidating. After all, there is more to Marxism than just Marx. Indeed, there have been so many different kinds of Marxists that Marx himself once declared that he probably wasn't one![1]

Anyone wishing to read about (or, alas, write about!) a synthesis of Marxist theory faces the daunting reality of how profound and widespread the influence of Marxism is throughout the world.[2] No other singular system of thought has so influenced the direction of so much activity and so much discourse; certainly no other work other than the Bible has generated so much debate and so much enlightenment as Marx's *Capital*. As Robert Heilbroner noted, that its insights continue to cause so much controversy and seem so germane to modern life in ways that Adam Smith's *A Wealth of Nations* does not, can be traced to the magnitude of its objectives: not simply an understanding of capitalism itself, but a systematic inquiry into the very processes of our social existence that lurk beneath the trappings of everyday life.[3]

To my mind, these very concerns lie at the heart of social work, although the vehicles for exploring them have often been quite, quite different.

That noted, a work of this kind must place tremendous restrictions on what it can and cannot do. It cannot elucidate all the variations on Marxist theory that exist on even one subject, be it political economy, alienation and class consciousness, the nature and direction of class struggle, or what have you. At the same time, it cannot be a singular presentation of my own Marxist beliefs, although undoubtedly whatever synthesis I attempt will have its particular biases. What I can do is make my approach, assumptions, and objectives clear from the outset. First, I assume that most readers of this anthology will be unfamiliar with and perhaps a little nervous about Marxist theory. That means I must begin with an explanation of what are generally agreed to be the basic outlines of Marxist thought, clarifying the most popular misunderstandings. Second, I believe there is a frightening ignorance of the Old Master's actual writings by both the left and the right, especially in the United States. I will therefore seek to clarify what Marx and Engels actually said on subjects germane to either our understanding of Marxism or its impact on social work itself, differentiating their work from others.* Third, while Marx was a genius and Engels certainly brilliant, neither deserve (nor sought) to be perceived as transcendent gods writing untarnished parables of truth. They were European men of the nineteenth century, and a lot has happened over the last one hundred years or so to reveal their limitations as well as their strengths. In that time, other Marxists, as well as feminists, black nationalists, and (yes!) Freudians have made significant contributions and revisions in their original works. This is especially true in areas related to the growth of the welfare state and the tremendous insights of Freud and other clinical theorists, including the work of many feminists.[4] I plan to address these shortcomings in the work. Finally, my primary objective here is not to turn readers into Marxists right away, as nice and as grandiose as I might think that to be. It is to show that Marxism, as a method of thought and action, is an invaluable tool in the development of one's social work practice that simultaneously liberates social workers from their often self-perceived roles as cooptive agents of social control while making them, in action with their clients, more effective activists in the struggle for major social change.

I plan to return to the case vignettes presented at the start of this chapter to help explain concretely what Marxism means for the individual social worker. As you read through the more theoretical sections of this work, you can know that eventually the practice implications will be made through the prism of these vignettes. By the end, for example, one hopefully can see that the push toward private practice is connected to the pull toward a more centralized, less flexible welfare state that is now required under the crisis-ridden economic conditions of late-twentieth-century capitalism. Through such awareness, of course, comes the increased ability to act in a clearer, more politically conscious way.

A BRIEF OUTLINE OF MARXIST THEORY

This ongoing attempt to see theoretical insight as immediately connected to potential political change quickly distinguishes Marxist theory from other systems of thought. Most modern North American social science creates dichotomies between "thought" and "action." However, Marx, in his earliest writings, always believed there was a necessary unity between thought and action. This connection between apparent opposites is the first of four distinctive elements to Marxist theory: *the use of a dialectical approach to knowledge and practice.*†

---

*In this task I have been aided tremendously by the works of Hal Draper and Robert Heilbroner, whose respective work as Marxologists has been invaluable to me and others seeking demystification. Their most important works regarding this task of demystification are part of the reference material.

†I again wish to acknowledge my debt to Heilbroner here, whose more general framework greatly expedited the more specific focus of this work.

As soon as most people hear the word *dialectics* they either go blank or turn numb, or both. I know I certainly did, seeing dialectics in foreboding, Germanic tones of abstruse reasoning designed to scare activists from understanding. But Marx, from his earliest writings of Feurebach, was always in search of the essence of things that lay beneath the surface appearance, an essence he identified as dynamic and conflictual, one that necessarily has contradictory elements that over time must foster change. I will explore this concept later in greater detail, especially when I look at social work practice.

The second unifying element of Marxism is its materialist approach to history. This approach emphasizes (but does not make all-inclusive) the central role played in history by the productive (economic) forces in a particular epoch. As will be seen later, a materialist approach therefore focuses on the class and social struggles over how and what those productive forces make (be it feudal grains or capitalism's cars, but especially the level of surplus value),* seeing such struggle as the primary motor for change in society. As will be seen, the rise of social work as a profession is tied to this materialistic analysis.

A third common element is a critique of capitalism. This is perhaps the most well-understood element of Marxist thought. Almost everyone notes Marx's analysis and condemnation of what capitalism "is," and all Marxists use his original conceptions as a basis for their own work in exploring capitalism. At the same time, recent Marxist writings help explain how dynamic and changing are the functions of the welfare state under capitalism—functions not as irrelevant to progressive social change as was once argued by the left.

Finally, of course, is the Marxist commitment to socialism. While perhaps most people would readily identify this part of Marxist thought, the discussion on both how one arrives at and what socialism is have meant very different things to very different people. For example, many Socialists are not Marxists; many Marxists deplore the Soviet-Union and/or the Chinese brand of communism; and many Western European Communists are viewed as "reformists" by other Marxists. While this topic will not be focused on in as much detail here as are the other elements of Marxist thought, the examples in this paragraph are meant to suggest that its complexity and importance are equal to the others.

MARXISM'S MATERIALIST APPROACH TO HISTORY: IMPLICATIONS FOR PROFESSIONALISM

In the social production of their existence, people inevitably enter into definite relations, which are independent of them, namely, relations of production

---

*Briefly, surplus value's source lies in the capitalist labor process. Here the worker exchanges his labor with capital to produce a value greater than the value of his labor power. This difference (usually seen in the difference between wages and capital expenses) has such great productive potential that it allows for the self-expansion of surplus value, as profits are reinvested in new and better firms, technology, all of which increase productivity and, over time, profitability.

appropriate to a given stage in the development of their material forces of production. The totality of these relations of production constitutes the economic structure of society, the real foundation, on which arises a legal and political superstructure and to which correspond definite forms of social consciousness. The mode of production of material life conditions the general process of social, political, and intellectual life. It is not the consciousness of people that determines their existence, but their social existence that determines consciousness.[5]

This famous passage from Marx has served as the guiding principle for countless other Marxists in their approach to the study of history. For us, the key elements here are the "forces of production," the social "relations of production," and the "superstructure." Briefly put, people in a society, at any given time in history, have a certain level of productive ability—for example, there is more productive ability under capitalism than under feudalism. The productive forces are people's knowledge and skills, then technology, and the geographic environment. Over time, in the process of developing their productive forces, people develop new economic capabilities *and* new personal desires to change their world even more. This purposive activity, as Gurley emphasized,[6] led to new changes and developments in economic life *and* social life.

For example, under feudalism, people's ideas, values, and aspirations were quite different from those held by people under capitalism, with its higher mode of production. Lords of the manor cared about military conquest and spiritual salvation; they were skilled fighters and often barely literate. Capitalists cared about the profitability of their firms and commerce; literacy and business acumen, not military strategy, were of greater importance. Such changes occurred not simply because technology improved. They occurred because people changed their own values, skills, and objectives in the process of developing that new technology.

So a materialist analysis begins with the perception that the forces of production create the social relations of production, which are the institutions and practices associated with *the way* goals and services are produced, exchanged, and delivered; that is, property relations, the recruitment and development of labor, the methods utilized for extracting and dispensing the surplus product, most often profit, but also benefits and other community needs.[7] In other words, the social relations of production are the class relations revealed through the work process.

As productive forces are always changing, eventually their new forms come into conflict with the prevailing class relations. This growing incompatibility makes conflict between old and new dominant social groupings (baron and capitalist) and between those who work within the emerging productive forms (capitalist and industrial worker) one of inevitable conflict and struggle, as each group fights to hold on to or to enhance its claim over the forces of production. Although only occasionally breaking out into social revolution, this struggle will always be part of economic and social life.

The struggle between class forces that occurs in the ongoing development of the mode of production is a fixture in the materialist conception of history; Marx considered it his most original insight.[8] It sees people as active agents in the making of social change, while rooting their efforts within the particular circumstances afforded by the forces of production at that time. Likewise, Marxists see the superstructure of a society as greatly determined by those forces. The superstructure is made up of a society's institutions (schools, churches, courts), which are seen as a reflection of the prevailing class relations. If the economic mode is transformed, so will be the institutions that support them. For example, the church is much less powerful under capitalism than under feudalism, while schools are more important under capitalism. This reflects the tremendous changes in both classes and ideas; under feudalism, such close church-state relations reinforced fealty to a land-based aristocracy; under capitalism, schools are expected to produce an adequately large labor supply with varying skills for its far more productive, larger workplaces.

THE PRIMACY OF ECONOMIC FORCES IN THE PROCESS OF SOCIAL CHANGE

For a Marxist, then, history is not the study of either great ideas or great men, but primarily of the development of productive economic forces. The formation of ideas can be explained greatly by those material changes. It is here that Marxism has much to contribute to social work's own understanding of itself, especially as a profession, for professionalization assumes a distinctive set of ideas, behaviors, and values that distinguish one craft from another.[9] I will return in later sections to the issue of craft, but here wish to concentrate on the *idea* of social work "from charitable impulse to professional clinician." Most histories of social work begin by tracing society's Poor Laws from the early 1600s up to the present day. This approach is the essence of what Marxism calls *idealism*, the presentation of people's actions as flowing primarily from subjectivity. Sometimes note is made of how communities in the North American Colonial period "cared" for their own poor, implying how ironic it was that such genuine concern was in the economically more barren past while today's richer society shows so much indifference. Regardless of twists and turns in the historical presentation, however, the progression is almost exclusively on the basis of increasing initiatives by the community, not on transformations in the mode of production and the ensuing shifts between class forces that necessitated entirely new methods of community (and, eventually, state) intervention.

A return to Joan Price in the 1930s can make this a little clearer. Her job began after the tremendous crisis of capitalism known as the Great Depression remained unresolved without state intervention. The crisis in the mode of production that left rates of profit falling and huge numbers of workers unemployed caused a shift in class relations between ruling and working classes unlike any before it. Class antagonism, apparently so muted in the 1920s, increased as militant working-class trade union and community organizing occurred across North America. The state intervention that ensued (signaling alterations needed in the superstructure) created public sector social work jobs that had never existed before. The huge numbers of previously unemployed college graduates swelled the ranks of social work, thus increasing pressure on defining how social work was to function. Joan Price and her colleagues, working under conditions quite distinct from those in far more comfortable private agencies, thus found the idea of unionization appealing in ways previous social workers had not.

The value in this example is on the perspective on what is fundamental in the process of change and what is, while not trivial, secondary. Likewise, this places the advance of social work as a profession in a different light. Social work could only develop under the conditions bred by the development of advanced capitalism. It was no more possible to have had "social work" as we know it today before the mid-twentieth century, when the newly advanced mode of industrial capitalism uprooted tens of thousands of workers for its manufacturing requirements and which now had the social surplus to perform certain community-wide charitable functions, than it is today possible to return to agrarian values common to feudal life. The social work field is a product of these conditions, rather than standing outside of them on its own.

Social Work as a Part of Capitalism: Implications for Professionalism

The perspective initially may appear disconcerting: Does this mean social work is capitalist? A tool of capitalism? What about the countless books and articles on ethics, values, and professions that suggest something quite different? Are they seen by Marxists as simply misguided? The answers to all these questions is an unequivocal "yes" as well as "no," though not in the ambivalent sense of hedging answers, but in the materialist, dialectical reality of simultaneous contradictions existing together and changing over time. "Yes," social work, as it is rooted on top of the mode of capitalism, is part of capitalism and cannot stand outside of its epoch. Joan Price could not have found a social work job if that crisis had not occurred under the condition of mid-twentieth-century capitalism. Social work is thus expected to perform tasks of social control. "No," in that social workers, while not independent of larger class forces, are capable of choosing to work in a manner and form that can allow for self-respect, self-determination, and helpful services. Price still had enough job autonomy to work in the field twenty hours a week, using her discretionary skill as she saw fit.

Individuals still choose, but the limits on the field are decided by larger productive forces. For the professional social worker, this frees one to be as actively engaged as possible. People don't have to feel guilty for not accomplishing work that no other grouping in society is attaining at that time. For the Marxist, it is no more possible for the individual social worker to end poverty than for the lone steelworker to stop plant closings. This placement of the social worker's class position on a material rather than an ethical basis ironically gives the individual more freedom to act in a principled fashion than if one were weighed down with the ethical dilemmas that come with primary responsibility for ending homelessness, child abuse, or hunger. It is not a social worker's fault that shelters are no answer to housing for the poor, but that doesn't free one to be indifferent to the quality of care she is able to provide.[10]

Marxism's materialist approach provides a social worker with less guilt but more responsibility—an irony borne by the class position in which the worker is placed and through the choices provided within that position.[11]

We will go into craft issues later on, the point here is that social workers are seen as particular intellectual workers who have their own material interests concerning wage advances and better working conditions. Like other workers, these class interests necessitate organized, collective activity if they are to be met. This class analysis (endemic to materialism) also means that different social workers within the welfare state have different class interests; the line professional in a large H.R.A., working under increased productivity demands and with a declining real income, is in a far different class relationship than is the top-line M.S.W. administrator in charge of increasing that productivity. This differentiation leads Marxists to find similarities in class alignment between many social work clients (especially the working class and working poor) and the line social workers themselves.

Historical materialism explains why there is no reason for guilt in social workers seeking to improve working conditions or wages. It helps clarify why so many social workers seek private practice; not simply as an ethical cop-out, but as an individualized yet powerful vehicle to achieve some sense of control over working conditions and standards of living. (Private practice will be discussed in more detail later.) At the same time, a materialist analysis, in its emphasis on economics, necessarily views professionalization as a reified form of bourgeois class relations, not as an autonomous class grouping capable of sustaining its distinctiveness through its ethical values and skill base alone. If they were, then such behaviors and judgments should be demonstrated consistently across interorganizational lines, just as one can demonstrate that steelworkers (or steel owners) perform highly similar tasks wherever steel plants are found. In fact, as Kayla Conrad and Irwin Epstein found in a thorough examination of the literature, no such consistency on any measure of performance has been maintained.[12]

Instead, consistent with the process of reification—a process that falsely elevates superstructural elements to a position equal in power to economic forces—they found a series of rituals and formalized professional group actions that take on the appearance of real autonomy (holding conferences, licensing, professional group sanctions, etc.). This reified appearance masks the actual class distinctions within the profession itself—that is, while the field is overwhelmingly nonexecutive and female, the professional leadership is overwhelmingly executive and male.[13]

Those using a historical materialist analysis tend to increase their attention to the needs of social workers as workers while downplaying the interests of the profession. At the same time, too much emphasis on economics and a strict interpretation of class relations alone, as tended to occur within the 1930s Rank and File club movement in the United States, would ignore the very real power that professional ideas, craft concerns with clinical intervention, etc., have on individual workers.[14] Too many Marxists have denied the value in discussing ideas, concerns of status, and career advancement that exist within the field and have the power to activate people throughout social work.

They would ignore both Joan Price's and her granddaughter's interest in self-actualization through the work experience: "subjective conditions" with real power. The push toward private practice is an outgrowth of the desire to do meaningful work while facing productivity requirements that lessen job autonomy and trivialize skill in ways Jean Price never faced. The reification of professionalization, which implicitly suggests a profession that is powerful enough as a craft to withstand outside pressures from the larger political economy, unfortunately disguises this interest in job autonomy and creativity as simply "new interventions in practice." The dynamic found in the exploration between altered working conditions, which would be a threat to a significant layer of professional leaders, and the ongoing needs of social workers as skilled workers is too often ignored by the left. Instead, private practice is dismissed as "selling out," which immediately and personally threatens practitioners who otherwise might be open to a more progressive analysis of changing working conditions within the field. This entire topic needs greater exploration, of course, and would necessarily include such issues as ideological hegemony, social reproduction, and legitimation (briefly touched on later). But it must be acknowledged that Marxists and other radical critics of social work have ignored such topics in the past as so much "reformist diversion." Hopefully, the future will find social workers of many ideological stripes arguing over these issues so that human services can and do improve.

MARXISM AND THE CRITIQUE OF CAPITALISM

Everyone knows that Marx was a profoundly astute critic of capitalism. Fewer may realize that his condemnation grew out of a powerful *psychological* insight into the social relations between people that had been created under capitalism. Writing in the first (and most difficult) section of *Capital* (Vol. 1), Marx explored the development of what capitalism produces in such great abundance: the commodity. He explored the commodity's development in order to get beneath its surface appearance as "a thing" and reveal the relationship between people imbedded within it. That relationship, which he called the *fetishism of commodities*, became under capitalism the [definite social relation between men themselves (which) assumes . . . the fantastic form of a relationship between things.][15] As Heilbroner wrote:

> There are few insights in all of Marx's writings as striking as the "fetishism of commodities"—indeed, few in all of social science. The perception that commodities possess the property of exchange value because they are the repository of an abstract form of labor; that this abstract labor testifies to the social and technical relationships of a specific mode of production; *and that a commodity is therefore the carrier and encapsulator of the social history of Capitalism*—all this comes as a stunning realization. [Emphasis added.][16]

There are enough issues here to devote a few lifetimes of work (some have), but any person who has tried to end a depressing workweek through the purchase of a new hat or a pair of gloves can begin to get a glimmer of what Marx was driving at. Under feudalism, people rarely got depressed in their direct relations between work, themselves, family, and kin. They lived at a level of subsistence so meager that new hats and gloves weren't available, let alone purchased. If hats were needed, rudimentary ones were made and worn, not bought: their use value and exchange value, like the labor used to make it, were the same. Social relations and economic relations were very closely integrated yet unproductive: the relationship between producer, the labor process, and the commodity was clear-cut.

Under capitalism the difference between surface level and deeper level social relations grows wider and harder to fathom. So many more commodities are produced, not for immediate use but for market exchange. The social relations necessary for such large-scale production are so much more disparate and nonfamily based that social relations (between people) are turned into material ones and material relations between things are turned into social relations. People no longer interact except when they exchange their commodities, including the commodity of their own labor. Individuals exist for one another only insofar as their commodities exist.[17]

Perhaps most important, human labor, because it is creative and imaginative, has the flexibility to do what no other labor power can: be abstracted, quantified, and refined in ways that produce more and more. In its abstraction, labor itself becomes a commodity that is exchanged for subsistence wages within the mode of capitalist production. In essence, labor power (the actual expenditure of physical and mental energy to produce commodities) is transformed into a particular exchange value (wages) by capital, which is represented not as a "thing" but in the personification of the capitalist. The human relationship of work and production is now abstracted into a battle over wages, prices, and profit.

This struggle, however, lies beneath the apparent equanimity in the capitalist's right, based on his ownership of both private property and technology, to demand a certain rate of return on his "investment" by keeping labor costs as low as possible. The reification of capitalists' rights obscures the telling Marxian observation that capital—technology, instruments, etc.—is not prima facie the capitalist's but is *"dead labor"*—instruments of production made by the labor power of past workers.[18] In turn, these past workers had been paid at an exchange value low enough to allow for greater surplus value, investment in and maintenance of capital, and the purchasing of more property. Such rights assured even more explosive productive capacity as well as further uprooting of older forms of social relationships in community after community.[19]

Without question this process enhanced the material life of capitalist and wage earner alike, although in hardly an equivalent fashion. If that were all there was to this economic scenario, Marx's critique would have been little more than phenomenal carping about too much of a good thing, and social work would have been superfluous before it started. But mystification, if it keeps one from full awareness of the actual relationship one is experiencing, breeds alienation. Likewise, the further extraction of labor power—called "exploitation"[20]—breeds physical and mental exhaustion, family uprooting, and other problems (e.g., pollution) that create greater and greater disharmony. The growth in our material life, Marx observed, correspondingly decreases spiritual life.

THE DYNAMICS OF CAPITALISM AND THE RISE OF THE WELFARE STATE

This unending antagonism between a decline in human relationships in the midst of increasing economic wealth is the yeast to all class struggle, and is what has made the growth of the welfare state inevitable. For as Marx predicted, capitalism, in order to expand its wealth, would become more and more concentrated and centralized, thus uprooting more and more workers, making their social plight even worse.[21] This is what happened during Joan Price's lifetime. At times, this meant that class struggle would grow from individual, atomized sparks of daily resistance to outright rebellion and, eventually, social revolution. Under capitalism, this meant that workers' struggles would be more protracted, wider ranging, and more threatening than they were under feudalism.[22] Likewise, the now-reified needs of capital for mobility and expanded market exchange would require some protection as well.

Marx, not unlike a good social worker, was always aware of the psychological and social dynamics imbedded in economic relations. Writing at a time of both great revolutionary fervor (1848 and 1871) and tremendous economic expansion, Marx's chosen emphasis was on the economic sphere he viewed as primary. His observations about the commodity help us understand the economic and social reasons why the modern state and, within it, the welfare state had to evolve. Since then, however, there have been innumerable arguments about the role of the state, primarily centering on the degree of autonomy held by the state from the ruling class.[23] I agree with Jan Gough, who wrote:

> What distinguishes Marxist theory is not the view that a particular class dominates the institutions of the state (though that is a normal enough state of affairs), but that *whoever occupies those positions is constrained by the imperative of the capital accumulation process.* But at the same time the separation and relative autonomy of the state permits numerous reforms to be won, and in no way acts as the passive tool of one class. We reject here both the pluralist view of the state, that it is a neutral arbiter between competing groups in society, and the crude econometric view, that it is but the instrument of the dominant class in society. [Emphasis added.][24]

This perspective, quite distinct from the 1960s radicals who saw the state as an agent of social control, has important implications for how the welfare state actually functions. Furthermore, it deepens our understanding of the roles social workers can play within the welfare state.[25] Drawing on the work of James O'Connor and Gough, the welfare state is neither the pluralist repository of good intentions and good works nor the economist view of a cabal-like setting filled with agents of social control. They instead argue that, given the ongoing dynamics of capital mobility and accumulation, labor exploitation, and class struggle, the state must perform a set of two contradictory functions, accumulation and legitimation, both of which aid the process of greater capital formation and, under appropriate conditions, reflect significant gains for workers' benefits, subsistence wages, and community services (hereafter called "social wages").

As O'Connor writes, "The state must try to create or maintain the conditions in which profitable capital accumulation is possible. However, the state must also try to create or maintain the conditions for social harmony."[26] All state functions, including those of the welfare state, will have elements of both functions. However, such functions create either social capital (either by increasing the productivity of labor or by lowering the reproduction costs of labor power) or social expenses (which maintain social harmony). Social capital expenditures are indirectly productive for capital; other things being equal, they augment the rate of profit and accumulation in society.[27] Social expenses, on the other hand, are not even indirectly productive for capital. They are a necessary but unproductive expense. Most areas of social welfare state activity, as O'Connor and Gough point out, will contain elements of both legitimation and accumulation (or, if you wish, social capital and social expenses).

For example, some educational spending increases social investment by raising skill levels that improve productivity; some of it serves the reproductive/consumption processes by socializing and integrating the young; some of it serves the legitimation functions by keeping otherwise hostile young people off the streets. *The conflicts in social policy over which element is given greater emphasis (production, consumption, or harmony) is greatly a reflection of the strength and direction of class struggle in society.* While there will be inevitable limits because of capital's preeminent need for greater and greater accumulation, there can be no static definition imposed on social wages wrought by workers and their allies through that class struggle. *Therefore, to struggle for reforms in the welfare state, in terms of policy and practice, as long as they are placed within a broader program for change that clearly addresses the limits of state intervention under capitalism, is to engage in highly progressive work of great meaning to social service workers.*

Marxism helps social workers understand that social welfare (and the social welfare state itself), rather than standing outside of existing class and social forces, is an active part of them. Workers have the potential to function not as simple agents of social control but as individuals utilizing the contradictory functions of the state to open up avenues of potential gain for workers and their families.

It needs reiteration here, however, that until the influence of O'Connor and Gough, many Marxist and radical social workers continued to view the welfare state as solely a repressive apparatus operating at the whim of capitalists. Certain perspectives on the state continue to take that view, although for new, sophisticated reasons.[28] Social workers, however, can find much theoretical insight and practice flexibility in understanding the dual, contradictory functions analyzed by O'Connor and Gough.

DIALECTICS AND THE DEVELOPMENT OF CRITICALLY CONSCIOUS PRACTICE

Historical materialism helps root the actual class relations of social workers as workers. The Marxian analysis of capitalism reveals both the economic exploitation and psychological alienation endemic to the shifting relations of massive commodity production. It helps explain how the ensuing development of the modern welfare state contains both inevitable limits on change and very real opportunity. The use of Marxian dialectics, which has been implicitly integrated in the previous sections, will reveal how the use of contradiction can more fully engage practitioners in their work.

First, dialectics has nothing to do with such static formulations as "thesis-antithesis-synthesis," a concept of dialectics far too linear to make sense.[29] Left in such abstract forms, it is stripped of its material core that is fundamental to Marxism. What Marxian dialectics is concerned with, as Marx reiterated in his afterword to *Capital*, arc the underlying, social relations between different forms of development, analyzing these relations as they changed over time. Thus, Marx studied the commodity in terms of the relationship between the mode of production and the relations of production, noting how changes in a particular form of commodity production (feudalism to capitalism) necessarily created changes in social relations (serf-lord, working class-capitalist). In turn, changes wrought over time between these classes influenced the manner, pace, and direction of future capitalist development.[30] For Marxists, contradiction is not simply "negation of a negation," but a tool for understanding the workings of social organisms as they change over time. By searching for the opposing elements linked to fundamental processes, the "diagnosis" one brings to society is richer and clearer. O'Connor's examination of the legitimation and accumulation functions of the state is a modern political economic example.

Of course, there are many who have called themselves Marxists who use the term "contradiction" with the turgid repetition of an obscure mantra. (I myself have been reduced to a stupor in various coalitions where everything seemed to be a contradiction!) This unfortunate tendency comes about not only from a confusion about the dialectical method. It also flows out of many speakers' desires to see those "contradictions" resolved by the emergence of a higher form of class struggle, preferably with the workers and other oppressed peoples winning. Marx and Engels fervently wanted workers to emancipate themselves, but their dialectical method has nothing to do with prescribing actual future events. They did predict a furthering and intensifying of crisis under capitalism because of the contradictions between the drive for profit and the drive of workers for higher subsistence wages, but such a prediction has not been proven incorrect empirically. What has been incorrect is the pacing and political expectation of events, not the dynamics.

DIALECTICS AND IMPLICATIONS FOR PRACTICE: COMMUNITY ORGANIZATION

In social work, community organizers have perhaps most often used a dialectical method in their approach to their work.[31] Given Marx's emphasis on broad economic and social issues and the fact that the social/historical forces he was writing about were analyzed most often on classwide or national terms, it was inevitable that applications were most often on an equivalent scale. The political organizations that utilized much of his method were only interested in broad-scale organizing, not clinical issues. This is still true today.

For example, the dialectical method helps strategists see the limitations in Ronald Reagan's cuts in housing subsidies by noting the rise in homelessness and the inadequacy of shelters as providing a strategic cutting edge for future mobilization. As one recent Marxist analysis of homelessness analyzed these dynamics, Reagan's support for greater accumulation undercuts the state's legitimate functions drastically, as the funds for shelters prove inadequate to the spiraling need.[32] The push for greater profit through a reduction in *private costs* is pulled against the skyrocketing *social costs* created by the lack of inadequate housing and services for the larger and larger pool of homeless, unemployed people. The strategies flowing out of this dialectical analysis work to "heighten the contradictions" by forcing more "pull" in the direction of the poor—a pull that over time would undermine the accumulation "push." Furthermore, such a contradictory analysis exposes the limitations of the more dominant social grouping at that one moment in time, thus educating and preparing activists for long-time work. Without denying the present dominance of the ruling class in present social relations, a dialectical approach to strategy never succumbs to fatalism. By illuminating the innerconnected dynamics within the social problem, opportunities for change remain alive. Dialectical inquiry helps root community-based organizing strategies in even the most conservative of times.

GROUP WORK

Dialectical inquiry has also been explored recently through group work processes. Well-known writers such as William Schwartz have consciously invoked a "dialectic" in their group work formulations, but have rooted their dynamics between "agency" and the "worker" and her group.[33] While capturing the dynamic tension of dialectics through this approach, the work resists a materialist interpretation by substituting the superstructural element of "agency" into a reified, more permanent position than it deserves. It ignores the larger-scale, "plane of production" issues occurring within the political economy that often affect agencies *and* group life.

A more materialist approach to a dialectical group practice has been identified as an *interventionist model of group practice*.[34] Drawing upon the lessons from the women's movement's use of consciousness-raising groups, here one roots the ongoing dynamics of a group's existence within the larger society's history, noting how such conditions alter group membership functioning. To be brief, in times when there are wide-scale progressive social forces, social work groups will often be more collective in task functioning and find support through task-oriented activity. In keeping with a dialectical tension, the social worker's intervention will here necessarily increase his focus on members' personal and emotional needs. In a conservative period, the dynamics of the group and the focus of practice intervention will shift. Here, where people's needs are greater and task-oriented projects less likely to succeed, members will be more individually and personally focused. The practitioner's focus will shift to increase the awareness of the political and social factors embedded within every individual member's personal problems. Such dialectical inquiry keeps the practitioner and clients alive to both the possible change in *any* one period while locating where there are inevitable limits to any practice solution. Such ongoing awareness holds out the promise of consistently engaged activism that neither fosters illusions nor undercuts client self-actualization—goals consistent with a Marxist framework for long-term social change.

CASEWORK: NEW DEVELOPMENTS IN MARXIST INQUIRY

That said, if that were all Marxism had to offer social work in terms of practice, it would not be enough. Most social workers in North America have worked and will continue to work with individuals, often in clinical settings. There is no question that the least developed area of Marxist inquiry relates to the study and treatment of the individual. Some of this is because Marx and Engels emphasized political economy to the near exclusion of personal relations, with the oft-quoted pamphlet by Engels, *The Origins of the Family*, the most notable exception.[35] Some of this problem occurred because many Marxists and Socialists believed that the emergence of socialism would clear up individual problems; this is why North American and Western European psychoanalytic movements are still so poorly received in the U.S.S.R. And some of the problem has existed because many individual Marxist thinkers and activists have been afraid or unwilling to explore clinical issues, either because of their own personal problems or because they mistook individually based clinical intervention as necessarily dichotomized from and antagonistic to struggles occurring within the larger political economy.[36]

Marxist writers such as Herbert Marcuse[37] and the early Wilhelm Reich[38] did creative and original work in exploring the dynamics of capitalism, individual emotional development, and the response of a Marxian psychoanalysis. However, there is little question that the most important breakthroughs in exploring individual psychological and emotional life and social relations came less from Marxists than from feminists.[39] While it is impossible here to give justice to the debate that has ensued between feminists and Marxists, the tremendous vitality to this discussion has led to an emerging synthesis that continues to utilize the Marxian dialectic surrounding the contradictions between productive and social relations while expanding the framework to include a more central role to sex in the generation and reproduction of social relations.

Briefly, what theorists concerned with a "Socialist-feminist" linkage have concentrated on that is of value for social workers is their analysis of the family and personal life. For example, all of these writers, with varying emphases, analyzed the complex, interrelated structures that defined women's condition: sexuality, reproduction (functions primarily in the family); socialization (functions primarily in society); and production (functions primarily economic in nature). By tracing the historical developments from feudalism to capitalism and examining the rise of both a nuclear family removed from economic production and the intensification of sexism, these authors and others began to explain how and why "personal life," with all the attention to individual sexuality, highly defined women's roles, distinctive individual behaviors, and individually focused therapeutic interventions, came to dominate modalities of thought and action in the West.

They have attempted to do this without sacrificing the importance of the economic sphere. At the same time, this work has been developing a deeper appreciation for a theoretical construct of great value to social workers concerned with clinical and group practices: the role of the *process of social reproduction* that is imbedded in all spheres of economic and personal life. As Andre Gorz wrote some years ago:

> Capitalism, as a complex social formation, does not exist in its present form in some massive and static reality, *but is in the constant process of renewing conditions for its continued existence through all aspects of life.* The concept of social reproduction explains that not only do workers have to be fed, sheltered, and kept healthy if they are to return each day to the factory or work place . . . but [they need] their "own" ideas and attitudes, those which ultimately maintain them within the social hierarchy and which keep them subservient to the routines of daily life under the domination of capitalism. [Emphasis added.][40]

In other words, capitalism doesn't simply "tell" workers to be subservient while at work. The institutions under capitalism—the family, schools, religious bodies, *and* service organizations—develop their own particular processes (in terms of values, standards of behavior, sanctions, etc.) that reinforce ideas about "how the world is." This is in part why so many Marxists rejected clinical approaches to treatment. Its individual-to-individual *form* of interaction, when coupled with its necessary emphasis on emotional dynamics, suggested to them strategic conclusions that were equally individualized and thus reformist. Their error was in mistaking the form for the potential essence within that relationship; with the right content and conscious utilization of process, it is quite possible to undermine the dominant processes of social reproduction and to replace them with a far more liberating process.[41]

Some social workers have begun to utilize their awareness of the contradictions between economic and social relations and the processes of social reproduction within those relations to develop a socially charged practice. This has been especially evident in feminist practice perspectives,[42] but the same issues seem legitimate for racial nationalities and other class and social groupings as well.

By reexamining practice in part by being conscious of the power of social reproduction, such authors as Christopher Lasch, Scott Jacoby, and others have reexplored the history of psychoanalysis.[43] Perhaps surprisingly, their neo-Marxist work sees far more compatibility with the early Freud and later work by such Marxist Freudians as Marcuse and, to a lesser degree, the early Reich and the Frankfurt school. They are far more hostile to the less radicalizing, more benign work of the ego psychologists—such as Heinz Hartmann, Erik Erikson, and Erich Fromm—seeing their work as vitiating the radicalizing dynamics between individual and the inevitable repression demanded from the larger society. Jacoby argues that the contradictory dynamics between the striving individual and the repressive society that give rise to unconscious processes has been baldly replaced by the ego-striving, falsely labeled "strengths" of individuals. Such individuals' particular limitations are thus less a problem of society than within one's self—or, at the very most, that the strengths of individuals makes it possible for one in clinical treatment to eventually work out any individual issues. These neo-Freudian/Marxists see this latter ego psychological perspective as robbing the individual of the insight into the limitations imposed by the larger social order that would necessitate more collective approaches to mental health.

Through their analysis, we can see that an ego psychology based primarily on the strengths of the individual socially reproduces ideas about failure and reform that are individually focused and thus less threatening to society. The neo-Freudian/Marxists argue for a more dialectical model that includes within its practice framework the assumption that capitalism will foster repression of some individual drives (especially sexual and social) that will necessarily undercut human growth and development in ways no one individual alone can overcome.* Such an approach continues to use clinical interventions with the individual but undermines dominant assumptions of social reproduction that are fraught with political significance for the client and worker alike.

THE DYNAMICS OF SOCIAL REPRODUCTION AS APPLIED IN CASEWORK

For the client, this neo-Freudian/Marxist dialectic frees him from total responsibility over his own condition. While particular individual dynamics will demand immense personal effort for change, this materialist approach will also ferret out some of the client's problems within the larger society that demand collective, societal change. For example, anorexia and bulimia may be primarily "female" problems that each woman must work on with tremendous emotional effort, but these problems exist in large part because of the particular forms of sexism fostered under late twentieth-century capitalism that reinforce images of women as thin yet consuming, sexually powerful but economically and socially impotent. To focus only on the eating disorder and the client's inherent "ego adaptability" to overcome such a problem vitiates the critical consciousness imbedded in the more dialectical approach that can note individual strength but also societally determined limitations. Women as a *social grouping* will continue to have these problems, both from generation-to-generation and developmentally throughout their lives in some form, if the sexism of our society is not confronted in more collective ways that forces alterations in our institutions and the ideas they socially reproduce. This combination of joining individual concerns with collective ones is very freeing for the client as he learns to own his responsibility for emotional growth and where he must begin placing demands on the larger society for other forms of change. While neo-Freudian and other, materialist approaches need to deepen their own examinations into practice methodology, the effort holds out much promise for the future.

*This dynamic would occur under any society, only would do so in different ways. This is why the Societ Union continues to be hostile to Freudianism. Hopefully, in the future, other less repressive societies would undercut some of the more damaging forms in which this process now occurs.

The practitioner is freed also from total responsibility over a client. A lot of mental health derives from full employment, job satisfaction, and an end to racism, sexism, and ageism as well. By willingly exploring these dynamics with clients, one reinforces within *oneself* a deeper recognition of how powerful and pervasive are the processes of social reproduction—even on practitioners. Your supervisor finds your attention to racism a "distraction"? Your agency only values clinical expertise that ignores or minimizes social issues? Such emphases within agencies and among departmental hierarchies can be expected for, as Antonio Gramsci noted, the (superstructural) institutions of a society are the vehicles by which the ruling class socially reproduces its ideas about "how the world is."[44] A large social welfare institution, dependent on foundation grants and state financing (both complete with oversight responsibilities) is no more likely to stand outside of that social reproduction process than is any other organization. *That is why, if you attempt to foster client self-determination by engaging in exploration of societally induced constraints on human growth and development (as well as individual strengths), you are engaging in a highly political form of practice.*

Thus, for the caseworker who grapples with the contradictory dynamics between production and social reproduction, there is the opportunity to politicize daily practice without succumbing to empty political phrase-making or to emotional subjectivism. Such engagement in one's clinical work undoubtedly carries over into a practitioner's perceptions about her work life as well. As Thomas Keefe describes a more materialist form of empathy, we can see benefits for the social worker as well as the client:

> Empathy (based on identification of economic constraints for client and worker) is a facilitator of growth. When a worker's empathy is effectively communicated to a client, he or she may be helped to give vent to despair and to work for the constructive expression of rage. The capacity to sense the frustrations and the anger of a client is enhanced by an understanding of the economic realities confronted by both client and worker. The worker's roles of broker, mediator, and advocate . . . demand an empathic skill sensitive to clients and the infrastructural sources of their problem.[45]

To examine this on the worker's own productive dimension increases the likelihood that the social worker will see increased productivity demands as part of the larger society's demands for a more proletarianized work experience. Such proletarianization, when understood as occurring throughout the mode of production, opens the social worker to possible collective solutions at the workplace. On the dimension of social reproduction, the worker engaged in clinical practice would know that the loss of his own work autonomy and creativity would lead to a more intensified process of social reproduction designed to further alienate and demoralize clients. For example, short-term treatment plans, if developed as the primary practice model in an agency, would rob the client of the opportunity to explore longer-term, social and personal problems that defy quick treatment. Clients would be expected to "reform" more quickly than many people can; failure to do so would be perceived as their fault. Noting these practice shifts, the social worker knows that the changes in the mode of production that are stratifying the labor force create these practice demands to replicate types of behavior that make the new labor pool more compatible with this intensified stratification—more deference, fatalism, and a "willingness to accept less" would be some of the behaviors developed through the above.

Equally important, it is just these practice forms, when coupled with the increasing productivity demands in agencies, that are increasing the drives toward private practice. Private practice isn't simply a way to "cop out"—Joan Price's granddaughter no longer has the worker autonomy and job satisfaction of her grandmother, who worked in a nearby community on her own twenty hours a week. At the same time, the contradictions imbedded in private practice—more job autonomy but less community involvement, increased job creativity but heightened atomization, better pay but more vulnerability to long-term market forces—are the very issues that threaten the core legitimacy of social work as a craft.[46] For left unchecked, the surge in private practice creates tensions within the major sources of finance for this field—the insurance companies and banks whose profitability depends on high enough rates of return through maintenance of costs, costs that are skyrocketing as more and more people, unable to find clinic services, seek private treatment.

For the caseworker concerned about both these issues and those related to the process of social reproduction, an awareness of the Marxian dialectic can only enrich one's practice. Working against the tide of privatization and diminished worker autonomy in the workplace, politically and personally, works in favor of the social worker's own material self-interest in ways that speak to broader, collective actions. And there is much one can do on the plane of social reproduction through individual clinical work as well. One can note and then resist certain types of behaviors in her practice; these include the above-mentioned deference and self-blame, which intensify attitudes helpful for accepting the lowest paid positions in all workplaces (held disproportionately by racial minorities, women, and older people); assumptions of class prerogative, which include ideas about professional elitism and the need for centralization of power in all decision making; and diminished expectations, where people at various levels of income learn to "accept less" given the desperate conditions faced by those in even worse economic straits. *If social workers practice in ways that consciously undermine such ideas, they are engaging in forms of empowerment and self-determination through a highly politicized form of practice.* While one recognizes that such individual approaches cannot in themselves be enough to affect the larger political economy, one's utilization of dialectics makes it possible to engage in a process that does help people become more able to directly confront the political economy at a later time.

FUTURE IMPLICATIONS FOR SOCIAL WORK PRACTICE

Marx always stated that socialism could occur only after capitalism and its tremendous capacity (as well as more sophisticated social relations) were in place. Otherwise, planning could only be based on rationing, not distribution of adequate surpluses. The first Socialist revolution (in Russia), which served as a model for all others, was launched with the idea of it spreading to more industrialized countries, for example, Germany. Without that, Lenin knew,[47] they would be faced with economic and social problems that would undermine democratic principles.

Second, each Socialist revolution has been met with hostile political and economic forces that necessitated a more militaristic and stringently ordered social response that further eroded political freedom and more productive economic development. (We see these problems confronting Nicaragua today in the mideighties.) In short, neither the economic nor international political conditions have been available to create the elements of socialism as Marx foresaw (and as people in industrialized countries had come to expect). Faced with colonialism and imperialism from the United States and Western Europe, the people of these countries still fought for something they hoped would be better than the misery of the past; in some places with mixed success, in other places with little at all. The political mistakes— ranging from elitist "vanguardism" to racism and sexism—have been magnified by the economic marginality faced by each.

Economic preconditions for socialism do exist in North America: an advanced industrial mode of production; technology that can be utilized throughout any community; high levels of communication and transportation. It is objectively feasible to have planning that is far more orderly and without the degree of economic and political rationing in precapitalist societies.

But political feasibility is another matter. Marx never proposed that socialism *would* emerge out of capitalism; he predicted only an intensification of alienation and exploitation as the contradictions of capitalism remained unresolved. Such intensification would then lead workers, in alliance with other political cadres, to fight for socialism because they *had to,* not because they *wanted to.*[48] Socialism speaks to collective decision making, democratic organization, and planning because individualized solutions alone cannot occur for everyone under capitalism. For the working class, their solutions to housing shortages, underemployment, etc., to Marxists, had to lead in the direction of socialism. The alternatives, as was said in an oft-quoted phrase, were "socialism or barbarism."

Such stark alternatives captured the boldest choices Marx saw confronting workers under the evolving character of capitalism. There is nothing intrinsically wrong with stating political directions so clearly, except for two not-so-minor problems. First, workers in industrial capitalist countries have not maintained long-term, political opposition to capitalism. There are many reasons for this, ranging from state repression of working-class and Socialist groups to racism within the class.[49] They need further exploration than can be given here. But it cannot be ignored that workers in general have maintained sufficient allegiance to capitalism to not align with political activists seeking its eventual overthrow.

The second problem is one less related to the working class than to the various elites who have led the fight for socialism. Robert Michel's *Iron Law of Oligarchy*[50] is unduly pessimistic and ignores elements of state repression toward Socialist groups at the turn of the century, but his description of self-perpetuating elites continues to haunt progressive groups throughout the twentieth century. Regardless of particular commonly held beliefs about mass self-determination, groups ranging from the German Social Democratic Party in the 1900s to today's social workers, the modern welfare state professionals have all sacrificed collective goals in order to maintain their own positions of power.[51]

Marxists don't lack for reasons to explain these problems—usually centering on some inherent *political* inadequacy. They claim that if the political line or program were changed, the elitism would disappear. However, some of this situation—which today relates to such disparate groups as European social democracy, Third World socialism, and North American liberalism—is in part social psychological. The human needs for self-actualization and a less alienated life, when blocked by the limitations found in any society, as social workers know, will be psychologically displaced elsewhere, either personally or organizationally, if they are not understood and responded to in some consistent fashion.

This awareness of the drive to self-actualization and the ways it can be displaced is a fundamental part of social work professionalism as well. However, social work skills in individual and group dynamics, when placed within a Marxian framework that utilizes a dialectical, historical materialism to center one's practice, has much to contribute here. Without denying the contradictions faced by social work under capitalism, social workers' skills take on an even greater importance than in the past. For social work today is at a crossroads: either greater privatization and individualization (processes congruent with the needs of capitalism today); or, given the increasingly collective, material needs of social workers throughout the welfare state, a more mobilized and socially conscious field of professionals choosing to affect their own history. Either choice, of course, exposes just how political the field of social work really is. Viewing the simultaneous pauperization in communities alongside their own diminished resources at work, social workers may find that choosing between "socialism or barbarism" is perhaps not as unreal as may have once been thought.

NOTES

1. Marx's reply to Ed.Bd.Sachs, *Marx-Engels Works.* Vol. 22 (New York: International Publishers, 1969), p. 69.
2. Robert Heilbroner, in *Marxism: For and Against* (New York: Norton, 1980), discusses this same controversy. He ends with a quotation from Eugene Kamenka that "the only serious way to analyze Marxist or socialist thinking may well be to give up the notion that there is a coherent doctrine called Marxism. . . ." Quoted by Daniel Bell, "The Once and Future Marx," *American Journal of Sociology.* Vol. 9 (July 1977). p. 196. Such a quotation seems unduly harsh, as few would say, for example, that there was a coherent doctrine of behaviorist positivism either.
3   Heilbroner, op. cit., p. 17. See also Hal Draper, *Karl Marx's Theory of Revolution, Vol. I, The State and Bureaucracy: Vol. II, The Politics of Social Classes* (New York: Monthly Review Press, 1977, 1978).
4. On the welfare state, see James J. O'Connor, *The Fiscal Crisis of the State* (New York: St. Martin's Press, 1974); Ian Gough, *The Political Economy of Social Welfare* (London: Macmillan, 1981); on a history of social welfare policy in the United States, see

Frances Fox Piven and Richard Cloward, *Regulating the Poor* (New York: Pantheon, 1971); on feminism, socialism, and issues of clinical and political life, see Nancy Chodorow, *The Reproduction of Mothering: Psychoanalysis and the Sociology of Gender* (Berkeley: University of California Press, 1978); Sheila Rowbotham, *Women's Consciousness, Man's World* (Baltimore: Penguin Books, 1973); Eli Zaretsky, *Capitalism, the Family and Personal Life* (New York: Harper Colophon, 1976).

5. Karl Marx, *Capital, Vol. I,* quoted by John Gurley in *Challengers to Capitalism: Marx, Lenin, and Mao* (San Francisco: San Francisco Book Co.), Chapter 2.

6. See Gurley, "The Materialist Conception of History," in Richard Edwards, Michael Reich, and Thomas Weisskopf (eds.), *The Capitalist System* (Englewood Cliffs, N.J.: Prentice-Hall, 1978), p. 45.

7. See Draper, op. cit., *Vol. II*, for a brilliant discussion of class relations.

8. Robert C. Tucker, *The Marx-Engels Reader* (New York: Hawthorne Press, 1978), p. 220.

9. Ernest Greenwood, "Attributes of a Profession," *Social Work*, Vol. 2, No. 3 (Summer 1957), pp. 45–55; Henry Meyer, "The Profession of Social Work: Contemporary Characteristics," in *Encyclopedia of Social Work* (New York: NASW, 1971), pp. 959–972.

10. *The Urban and Social Change Review*, Vol. 17, No. 1 (Winter 1984), explored these dynamics in great detail regarding the homeless. While all the articles were not Marxist in orientation, they lay out progressive approaches to this work.

11. An important debate within Marxist and social democratic circles is over the possible emergence of a professional-managerial class that under late capitalism may (or may not) have the equivalent social weight of the ruling and working classes. See Pat Walker (ed.), *Between Labor and Capital* (Boston: South Bend Press, 1981) for an overview of this debate.

12. Irwin Epstein and Kayla Conrad, "Limits of Social Work Professionalization," in Rosemary C. Sarri and Zeke Hasenfeld (eds.), *The Management of Human Services* (New York: Columbia University Press, 1977), pp. 163–172.

13. Ruth Brandwein, "Descriptive Attributes of Social Work Agency Management and the Continuation of Sexism," *Social Work*, Vol. 14, No. 3 (June 1981).

14. See Rick Spano, *The Rank and File Movement* (New York: University Press, 1983) for an interesting discussion on the effect of such disinterest on the Rank and File Movement's mobilization efforts. For a thorough examination of the alterations of craft in the twentieth century, see Harry Braverman's *Labor and Monopoly Capital* (New York: Monthly Review Press, 1978).

15. Marx, *Capital, Vol. I.* p. 165.

16. Heilbroner, op. cit., p. 103.

17. Marx, *Vol. I,* p. 167.

18. Ibid., p. 176.

19. The latter sections of *Capital, Vol. I,* graphically describe the shifting nature of productive and class relations in the seventeenth to nineteenth centuries. For a far more modest analysis of these dynamics in a modern form related to community organization, see Steve Burghardt, "The Strategic Crisis of Grass Roots Organizing," in Steve Burghardt, *Against the Current*, Vol. IV, No. 4.

20. Exploitation is an economic term, one loaded with social significance. In its most general sense it means the extraction of labor by one class over another through the productive process. Under capitalism, exploitation occurs after one produces commodities for which she receives no return in wages or benefits. It is *the* economic basis of class struggle under capitalism. As Engels wrote in *Origin of Family, Private Property, and the State*, "Since the exploitation of one class by another is the basis of civilization, its whole development moves in a continual contradiction. Every advance in production is at the same time a retrogression in the condition of the oppressed class, that is, the great majority. What is a boon for one is necessarily a bane for the other," quoted in *Karl Marx and Frederick Engels' Collected Works* (New York: New World Paperbacks, 1968), pp. 591.

21. There are innumerable eloquent examples by Marx on this phenomenon. For example, in a letter criticizing Proudhon, he wrote, "M Proudhon mixes up ideas and things. Men never relinquish what they have won, but this does not mean that they never relinquish the social form in which they have acquired certain productive forces. On the contrary, in order that they may not be deprived of the result attained and forfeit the fruits of civilization, they are obliged from the moment when their mode of carrying on commerce no longer corresponds to the productive forces acquired, to change all their traditional social forms. . . . For example, the privileges, the institutions of the guilds and corporations, the regulatory regime of the Middle Ages, were social relations that alone corresponded to the acquired productive forces and to the social conditions which had previously existed and from which these institutions had arisen. Under the protection of the regime of corporations and regulations, capital was accumulated, overseas trade developed, colonies were founded. But the fruits of these men would have been forfeited if they had tried to retain the forms under whose shelter these fruits had ripened. Hence burst two thunderclaps—the Revolutions of 1640 and 1688. All the old economic forms, the social relations corresponding to them, the political conditions which were the official expression of the old civil society, were destroyed in England. Thus the economic forms in which men produce, consume, and exchange, are *transitory* and *historical*. With the acquisition of new productive facilities, men change their mode of production and with the mode of production all the economic relations which are merely the necessary relations of this particular mode of production." *Karl Marx and Frederick Engels' Collected Works*, op. cit., pp. 670–671. This contradictory dynamic shows the directions of O'Connor's and Gough's works in explaining legitimation and accumulation functions of the state as well.

22. Draper's presentation of Marx's and Engels's ideas on the development of the working class and the reasons for its progression toward increasingly class-conscious levels of militant, collective activity is a brilliant synthesis. See especially Part One of his second volume: "The Proletariat and Proletarian Revolution," in Draper, op. cit., *Vol II*. pp. 17–168.

23. Gough, op cit., p. 186.

24. Ibid., pp. 43–44.

25. I attempt to develop these dynamics within a new dialectic framework for practitioners in *The Other Side of Organizing* (Cambridge, Mass.: Schenkman, 1982).

26. O'Connor, op. cit., p. 7.

27. Gough, op. cit., Chapter 3 examines these dynamics with great thoroughness.

28. See, for example, N. Poulantzas, *Political Power and Social Classes* (London: New Left Books, 1973); R. Milliband, *The State in Capitalist Society* (London: Weidenfeld and Nicholson, 1969). For a recent critique of O'Connor, see Jared Epstein, "The Fiscal Crisis of the State Revisited," in *Against the Current, Vol. 4. No. 2*.

29. As Heilbroner pointed out, we owe this catchy little phrase to Johann Fichte, op. cit., p. 42.

30. See note 21.

31. See Spano, op. cit., on rank and file movement strategy, especially Chapters 2–3; Steve Burghardt, op. cit., especially Chapters 1–2; and my *Organizing for Community Action* (Beverly Hills, Calif.: 1982). At the same time, very influential community organization strategists such as Saul Alinsky were quite anti-Marxist, see his *Rules for Radicals* (Boston: Beacon Press, 1969).

32. Michael Fabricant, "The Industrialization of Social Work Practice," *Social Work*, Vol. 30, No. 5 (1985), pp. 389–395. See Harvey Brenner, *Unemployment and Mental Illness* (Cambridge, Mass.: Harvard University Press, 1976), which explores these dynamics in terms of private costs versus social costs.

33. William Schwartz, "Social Group Work: The Interaction Approach," in *Encyclopedia of Social Work*, Vol. 2 (New York: National Association of Social Welfare, 1971), pp. 1257–1262.

34. Burghardt, *The Other Side of Organizing*, especially Chapters 7 and 8.

35. Engels, *Origin of the Family.*
36. I am not, however, stating that Marxists and other leftists have *more* personal problems than do other groups of people. I believe that the neurotic stances of people on the left tend to be less introspective personally than others, just as I have found clinicians' neurotic styles to be overly introspective. This issue is explored in greater detail in my *The Other Side of Organizing.* Furthermore, some clinical interventions *do* counterpose emotional growth and political activity; some give it short shrift. That dominant clinical methods do so does not mean that individual work *must* be so.
37. Herbert Marcuse, *Eros and Civilization* (Boston: Beacon Press, 1968), is an especially important contribution.
38. See *Sex-Pol, The Writings of Wilhelm Reich*, edited by Bertell Ollman (New York: Dell Books, 1971).
39. There are many important works here. Besides the works referred to in note 4, see Susan Schechter's *Women and Male Violence* (Boston: South End Press, 1982) for both its own analysis of these issues and for a very timely bibliography.
40. Andrew Gorz, *Strategy for Labor* (Boston: Beacon Press, 1967), p. 108. Of course, Marx discussed this in *Capital* one hundred years ago, but with much less emphasis than Marxists, Socialists, and feminists are giving it today. See *Capital, Vol. 1*, p. 577.
41. Paulo Freire, *Pedagogy of the Oppressed* (New York; Seabury Press, 1972), is a brilliant examination of these dynamics in terms of methodology.
42. See especially Chodorow, op. cit.
43. Christopher Lasch, *Haven in a Heartless World* (New York: Praeger, 1981); Scott Jacoby, *Social Amnesia* (New York: Dalton, 1981).
44. Antonio Gramsci develops these and similar ideas around the concept of "ideological hegemony," a brilliant formulation concerning how the ruling class continues to rule through means other than military or economic force. See Antonio Gramsci, *Prison Notebooks* (New York: International Publishers, 1977).
45. Thomas Keefe, "Empathy Skills and Critical Consciousness," *Social Casework*, Vol. 61, No. 7 (September 1980), pp. 307–313; Peter Leonard, "Toward a Paradigm for Radical Practice," in Ray Bailey and Mike Brake (eds.), *Radical Social Work* (New York: Pantheon, 1975), pp. 46–61.
46. Fabricant, "The Industrialization of Social Work Practice," op. cit.
47. Tony Cliff, *Lenin. Vols. I–IV* (London: Pluto Press, 1976, 1977, 1979, 1980); Michel Liebman, *Leninism Under Lenin* (London: Macmillan, 1975).
48. Draper, op. cit., especially Vol. 2.
49. The most thorough example of this in U.S. labor history is Philip Foner's *The History of the Labor Movement in the United States, Vols. I–IV* (New York: International Press, 1947–1980). Equally important in the U.S. is his most recent volume, *The Black Working Class and the U.S. Labor Movement* (Philadelphia: Temple University Press, 1982).
50. Robert Michels, *Political Parties* (New York: Collier Books, 1962).
51. See Piven and Cloward, op. cit., and their *The New Class War* (New York: Pantheon, 1983).

ANNOTATED LISTING OF KEY REFERENCES

Bailey, Ray, and Mike Brake (eds.). *Radical Social Work.* New York: Pantheon, 1975. A collection of articles that examines the contradictions inherent in current social work goals and actual impact.

Burghardt, Steve. "The Strategic Crises of Grass Roots Organizing," in Steve Burghardt, *Against the Current*, Vol. 4, No.4. A contemporary analysis of the dynamics of productive and class relations and their implication for community organization.

Burghardt, Steve. *The Other Side of Organizing*. Cambridge, Mass.: Schenkman, 1982. A helpful presentation of the utility of using a dialectical approach to the analysis of societal events and conditions.

Fabricant, Michael. "The Industrialization of Social Work Practice," *Social Work,* Vol. 30, No. 5 (1985). A discussion of some current trends in practice from a perspective of economic forces.

Karl Marx and Frederick Engels' Collected Works. New York: New World Paperbacks, 1968. A useful and important introduction to the key writings of these two leading thinkers.

Keefe, Thomas. "Empathy Skills and Critical Consciousness," *Social Casework*, Vol. 61, No. 7 (September 1980), pp. 307–313. This article emphasizes the need to understand the client's reality within the economic situation of both client and worker and the need to put our professional efforts on changing both society and clients.

CHAPTER 18

MEDITATION AND SOCIAL WORK TREATMENT

THOMAS KEEFE

Meditation is an ancient discipline wedded to several major psychophilosophical systems arising from diverse cultures. Among others, Native American, Central Asian Sufi, Hindu, Chinese Taoist, widespread Buddhist, and some Christian traditions have cultivated forms of meditation as a source of spiritual enrichment and personal growth. In the last thirty years, meditation began its marriage to the rational-empirical tradition of Western science. In this most recent alliance it is being tested, objectified, stripped of its mystical trappings, and enriched with empirical understanding.

Although testing is underway and final acceptance is some time in the future, the potential of meditation in psychotherapy and social work treatment has already been recognized by some. Meditation is a method that is adjunctive to social work treatment. It is a mechanism for self-regulation and self-exploration. It can help reduce stress and aid coping. Its effectiveness in treating particular problems and persons is becoming clear. It has the potential to be valuable in work with clients from diverse cultures. Yet meditation as a method continues to demand much from, and occasionally challenges, some theories underlying social work treatment for its full description and explanation.

DESCRIPTION AND EXPLANATION: THE MIND AS AN OPEN HAND

Meditation is a set of behaviors. Some of the consequences of meditation are directly observable; others can be indirectly inferred. For the purposes of this chapter, meditation does not refer to the mind's wandering and floating in fantasy or to the mind's laboring along a tight line of logic toward a solution. In contradistinction to these common notions, meditation is the deliberate cultivation of a state of mind exclusive of both fantasy and logic. While there are several varieties of meditation, they all share some common characteristics.

In essence, meditation is the development—or discovery, depending on one's orientation—of consciousness independent of visual and verbal symbolic thought. It is the deliberate cultivation of a mental state conducive to intuition. Meditation usually pairs a relaxed state of the body with either a concentrated or merely attentive focus of the mind. A brief description of this common process in meditation will help orient us to the method.

METHOD

One meditates by focusing attention upon a single thing while physically relaxed. This focus of attention may be a sound (mantra), a design (mandala [Kapleau, 1967]), an object, a part of the body, a mental image, or a prayer. This ostensibly simple task is seldom immediately mastered. Noises, bodily stimuli, internal dialogues, monologues, images, and emotions can constantly interrupt the task to break one's attention. Meditation then becomes a task of, first, continually noticing or being mindful of a distraction; second, recognizing or naming the loss of attention—e.g., "thinking," "feeling," "remembering," and so on; and third, letting go of any resulting chain of associations to return to the meditation focus. This task of releasing attention to a distraction and easily refocusing attention and cultivating an attitude of noninvolvement to the distracting chains of association constitutes meditation for the beginner. I like to use the analogy that *the mind becomes like an open hand. Nothing is clung to; nothing is pushed away.*

Some theorists and practitioners distinguish two prominent forms of meditation. One is a concentrative form in which the meditator's attention is riveted to the meditation object to the exclusion of other stimuli. In contrast, insight or mindfulness meditation described in this chapter stresses the examination of the randomly occurring mental contents often with a naming of each—e.g., memory, fantasy, fear, and so on. There are many variations on these two themes. Interestingly, studies of electroencephalographic changes accompanying representative variations on these two themes indicate changes in brain activity that parallel the form of meditation underway (Anand, Cchhina, & Singh, 1984; Kasamatsu & Hirai, 1984). For advanced meditators, easy attention to the meditation object actually facilitates the examination of randomly occurring internal and external stimuli when they adopt the mental attitude of an "open hand."

EXPERIENCE

Most meditators initially find that their attention is disrupted by a stream of thought. Distractions by the stream of thought seem to present themselves in a hierarchy of personal importance. Those incidents of the recent past evoking the most anxiety or anger seem to intrude first. These are followed by memories or anticipations of decreasing concern. Thoughts, images, and feelings well up, momentarily distract and, if not clung to or elaborated upon, burn themselves out. When paired with the relaxed state of the body and followed by refocusing upon the pleasantness of the meditation object, a *global desensitization* (Goleman, 1976) of cathected thoughts and images occurs. Increasing equanimity and objectivity secure the meditator in an attitude of observation of the thoughts that make up the symbolic self and its constituent concerns.

The meditation behaviors of focusing attention, recognizing when attention is interrupted, sometimes naming the nature of the interruption—e.g., "thinking," "feeling," "remembering," and so on—and deliberately refocusing attention are forms of *discrimination learning* (Hendricks, 1975). Perceptions, thoughts, and feelings are discriminated from the meditation focus. Slowly, the capacity to discriminate thoughts and feelings from any focus of attention is amplified. The meditator discriminates memory and anticipation, fear, and guilt from the immediate focus of attention. He or she cultivates a *present centeredness.* This is operationalized in research as *time competence,* a component of self-actualization (Brown & Robinson, 1993). As this learning to discriminate the ingredients of consciousness or contents of mind becomes easier, an *observer self,* also called watcher self (Deatherage, 1975) or witness (Goleman & Schwartz, 1976), emerges. The observer self is helpful in a variety of areas of functioning.

We must be very clear that the observer self is not an alienated, depersonalized, or neurotic self sustained by dissociative processes or suppression of thought and emotion. It is, instead, a secure subjectivity that, at its most refined level, allows full experience without judgment, defense, or elaboration. In the cultivation of this observer self of meditation, several helpful capacities emerge that are taken up below and further elaborated on as we examine meditation as a technique in personality change.

CAPACITIES LEARNED IN MEDITATION

For those of us involved in social work treatment, examining the learnings transferred from meditation practice into the psychosocial functioning of the meditator may prove valuable. The learnings transferred from meditation can be termed "capacities," and there are several of them.

FOCUS AND INNER DIRECTION

The capacity to focus attention on a single thing or task in present time is enhanced. This is called "one-pointedness of mind" in some traditions. When this is carried over into everyday life, tasks undertaken with this state of mind are completed with less distraction and with the expenditure of less energy. The Buddhists call this state of mind, carried into everyday life, *right mindfulness* (Burt, 1955).

Consider the snow skier: Skiing requires concentration. As speed increases and the slope becomes steeper and the surface more varied, concentration must intensify. If the skier suddenly becomes preoccupied with a distant dropoff, a concern with his or her appearance or relative performance, or an intruding and distracting fear of falling, his or her concentration is broken and the possibility of falling is more likely. The clutched athlete, the self-conscious speaker, the ego-involved attorney, and the overidentified social worker are all momentarily distracted from their intended focus, and this is experienced as loss of inner control. Brown and Robinson (1993), in a study of the relationship between meditation, exercise, and measures of self-actualization, found that meditation alone or in combination with exercise significantly increased subjects' inner directedness over subjects who only exercised and controls.

DISCRIMINATION

The capacity to discriminate along internal stimuli, such as memories, fears, anger, and so forth, provides a measure of enhanced self-awareness that may be useful in empathic relating and communicating one's responses in social situations. Coupled with a present-time focus, the capacity to view these internal processes with a degree of objectivity and nonattached concern allows enhanced performance in complex behaviors.

RECEPTIVE PERCEPTION

Finally, the capacity for an altered mode of perception is cultivated in meditation. The passive-receptive phase of perception, wherein one allows the senses to be stimulated, delaying cognitive structuring and allowing the things perceived to speak for themselves, is enhanced. Psychologists Sidney Jourard (1966) and Abraham Maslow (Goble, 1970) both described this form of perception as necessary to supplement the more active, structured, need-oriented perception. Nyanaponika Thera described the Buddhist view of this perceptual mode generated in meditation as *bare attention.* Thera (1970) elaborated:

It cleans the object of investigation from the impurities of prejudice and passion; it frees it from alien admixtures and from points of view most pertaining to it; it holds it firmly before the eye of wisdom, by slowing down the transition from the receptive to the active phase of the perceptual or cognitive process, thus giving a vastly improved chance of close and dispassionate investigation. (pp. 34–35)

In sum, we see the results of meditation behaviors as including such global experiences and capacities as relaxation, desensitization of potentially charged stimuli, concentration of attention, inner-directedness, intentional present-centeredness, enhanced discrimination, self-awareness, and augmented perceptual modes. Some of these theoretical and subjectively observed capacities have begun to be substantiated by research.

While each of the above capacities has implications for generally enhanced personal and interpersonal functioning, meditation is used to counter specific responses or behaviors seen as symptomatic or problematic for clients. As will be seen later, those supported by research include, most prominently, anxiety and stress, some forms of depression, substance abuse, phobic reactions, and interpersonal difficulties. Generally arising from traditions that are unhampered by notions of health and illness in relation to human behavior, meditation has been used in the personal growth and consciousness development of both the average lay person and the select initiates of particular religious orders. Used as a tool to extend the potential of its practitioners, meditation has been oriented toward the possible rather than the merely adequate or healthy in human functioning. Consequently, there are several ramifications for social work treatment. Meditation has, as shall be seen later, potential for the social work practitioner as well as for the client. It requires no predisposing diagnosis for its use—although there are empirically supported indications for its use and definite contraindicators. It has potential for use with individuals, families, and groups, and in community settings.

ORIGINS AND PATHS INTO SOCIAL WORK TREATMENT

As indicated earlier, meditation comes to us from diverse cultures and traditions. Yet the various forms, whatever their source, express a common origin in humankind's intuitive modes of thought. As an example, the zazen meditation of Zen Buddhism has its origin in the intuitive enlightenment of Siddhartha Gautama, Buddha, in about 544 B.C. (Burt, 1955). Siddhartha was said to have led a life of wealth and indulgence and then a life of asceticism in his quest to find the cause of suffering in the world. After relinquishing these extremes of self-preoccupation, his answer and enlightenment came. His Four Noble Truths, together with his Eightfold Path, served as vehicles for transmission of insight into his wisdom. The Buddha's Eightfold Path includes meditation as one of the routes to freedom from suffering (Beck, 1967). Thus it is a central practice in all branches of Buddhism, although *characteristic* variations have developed in each tradition. Buddhism is thought to have been carried from the northern India of Siddhartha to China in A.D. 520 by Bodhidharma (Kennett, 1972). There the Indian *dhyana* became the Chinese *Ch'an*. Influenced by Taoism in China, meditation was transmitted to medieval Japan, where it is referred to as Zen, which literally means "meditation." Zen found its way to the West by several routes and has been popularized by D. T. Suzuki (1964), Allen Watts (1961), and others.

But Zen is only one form of meditation that has ancient and divergent cultural origins. In fact, meditation has been an important practice in the major world religions: Hinduism, Confucianism, Taoism, Buddhism, Judaism, Islam, and Christianity.

For centuries in India, meditation was taught in the oral traditions of the Hindu Vedas. Then, sometime before 300 B.C., some of these traditions of meditation were written in the *Yoga Sutras* of Patanjali (Wood, 1959). The techniques used in yoga include mantras, visualizations, breath control, and concentration on various postures or parts of the body. The purpose of yoga meditation is to unify the body, mind, and spirit allowing an individual to become whole, integrated, and functioning as Atman, a godlike higher self (Prabhupada, 1972). Ultimately, union with Brahman, or God, is achieved. The Bhagavad-Gita (c. 200 B.C.) suggests meditation as one of the three main ways to achieve freedom from karma (Prabhupada, 1972) or the world of cause and effect.

In China, Confucius recommended meditation as a part of personal cultivation. Later it became the central feature of the Lu Chiu-Yuan school of Neo-Confucianism. Taoists during the same period in China also used meditation to facilitate mystical harmony with the Tao (Welwood, 1977).

Some types of Jewish mysticism incorporate meditation to achieve metaphysical insights. Philo of Alexandria (c. 15 B.C.–A.D. 50) and other Jewish scholars in the Middle Ages used this type of meditation (*Encyclopaedia Britannica*, 1974).

From the twelfth century A.D., Sufism, a popular folk Islam, has encouraged various types of meditation as well as other techniques such as whirling to induce trance. Meditation is considered to be an important remembrance of God. It is also used to facilitate perceptions of inner reality (Al-Ghazzali, 1971).

Christianity, too, is rich in traditions using a variety of meditative techniques, from the early Christian Gnostics to the medieval monasteries to eighteenth-century Greek orthodox teachings. Some original training manuals include *The Philokalis* (Greek Orthodox) and *The Way of Perfection* by St. Theresa of Avila (Jourard, 1966). Recently, the origins of Western forms of meditation have been traced to early Christianity including meditation's decline as a Western tradition in the seventeenth century (Schopen & Freeman, 1992). Driskill (1989) observed that the Christian tradition once recognized the therapeutic as well as the religious value of meditation.

FORM FOLLOWS PHILOSOPHY

Interestingly, the philosophies of the Yogic and Buddhist meditators are reflected in their contrasting meditation behaviors. For example, most Yogic meditators seem to cultivate a habituation effect (Ornstein, 1977) to the object of meditation and experience a loss of perception of the object or a "blending" with it. This subjective experience of habituation corresponds with the brain's productivity of electromagnetic alpha waves that accompany relaxed awareness. These Yogic meditators reduce awareness of outside stimuli and experience a blissful indifference sometimes called *samadhi*. For the Yogi, *samadhi* is a high state of self-transcendent consciousness, a link with the godhead or universal consciousness to be attained through rigor and single-minded devotion.

Advanced Zen meditators undergo that habituation effect and record increased alpha-wave productivity. However, when exposed to outside stimuli while meditating, they respond with sharp, momentary attention as evidenced by corresponding short bursts of beta-wave productivity. These meditators seem to be able to respond repeatedly to external stimuli without habituating to them. Psychologist Robert Ornstein (1977) suggests that they are responding without constructing a visual model or verbal label for the intruding stimulus, perceiving it clearly each time. For the Buddhist, the state of *nirvana*, analogous to *samadhi*, is attained but rejected by the protagonist in favor of an act of *compassion*. This act is to enter the world in a state of wisdom, or *prajna,* there to undertake the work of bringing other sentient beings—or aspects of the larger consciousness—to enlightenment. In interesting ways, then, the internal responses of meditators parallel the doctrines of their traditions. Given these parallels found in other traditions, it seems natural that meditation should become a part of Western therapeutic traditions. The reciprocal influences between meditation and social work should be exciting.

RELEVANCE FOR SOCIAL WORK

While meditation comes to the West by several ancient paths, it has far from penetrated to all parts of our industrial culture. Professional social work, a by-product of the industrial market system, is itself relatively new in humankind's endeavors. Meditation is new to social work. It comes to the profession at a time when variety, diversity, and eclecticism are the norm. As the instability, contradictions, and stresses of socioeconomic change generate a search for relevant modes of treatment, meditation will perhaps be another technique to be taken up in the interest of more effective practice.

This vision of the reasons for the profession's potential interest in meditation rests on a common, contemporary human experience, stress. Basically because of the contradictions and instability of the economic system, we live in an age of *anxiety.* Meditation may fill a symbolic and practical need in our personal and professional psyches. To face the fragmentation and contradictions of our lives, a safe and quiet place of recollect, sort out, and relax is a natural balm. Moreover, if meditation is more than a clinical adjunct technique, but also a facilitator of other social work skills, and a precursor to action as well, it has relevance for the profession as a whole.

Meditation is used or discussed by various psychologists and psychiatrists. Engler notes that techniques from all the major meditative traditions have been incorporated or adopted for use in psychiatric treatment settings (Engler, 1984). Psychologists using biofeedback apparatus are naturally drawn to meditative techniques and their work influences social work colleagues. Psychologists do the lion's share of research on meditation (Shapiro & Walsh, 1984).

Meditation as an aid for psychotherapists themselves (Keefe, 1975) and in the development of empathic skill (Keefe, 1979) has been proposed and examined clinically (Sweet & Johnson, 1990) and by research with mixed results (Pearl & Carlozzi, 1994). Both endeavors have generated interest among clinical social workers and social work educators. Other workers have had experience with meditation, especially Transcendental Meditation (Bloomfield & Kory, 1977), and have incorporated it into their work. While a good fix upon the extent of its use is difficult without a study, one can assume that as more findings are reported in the literature, more interest will be generated in the social work profession.

CROSS-FERTILIZATION AND DIVERSITY

As noted in the historical origins of meditation, the technique has been refined for personal growth and positive behavior change in several cultural traditions (e.g.,

Shapiro, 1994). In each of these traditions, meditation is linked to conceptualizations that can help to explain for practitioners the subjective experiences of meditation and the behavioral and psychosocial outcomes. Each culture has placed meditation within its own context. To use meditation as an adjunct to psychotherapy and social work treatment is to place it within a rational, technological, cultural context. In so doing, we can refine and extend meditation technique and at the same time enrich our own traditions.

Because meditation has its origins in diversity, it has a naturally diverse appeal. In the author's experience, Native American and Asian clients and practitioners have found the contemplative aspects of meditation compatible with their values and self-development. Christians have ranged from very receptive to wary depending on their particular backgrounds. While these observations are from limited clinical and teaching experience, a reasonable generalization is that persons from cultures and subcultures that value contemplation and intuitive modes of thought have good potential to be receptive to meditation as a treatment technique.

MEDITATION, THE PERSONALITY, AND THE CONDITIONED SELF

The experience and outcomes of meditation related to the organization of the personality extend Western psychodynamic conceptualizations. They modify or extend psychodynamically and cognitively oriented social work treatment.

The *ego* or symbolic self in traditional Freudian theory develops out of the necessity to symbolically represent in thought the real objects that meet our needs. Our capacity to symbolize allows for *deferred gratification* in keeping with social reality. Thus, symbol formulation is seen as necessary to creation of meaning and social interaction. Meditation experience does not refute these perspectives, but it does challenge certain assumptions underlying them.

OBSERVING THE SELF

The symbolic self or ego is experienced as a network of verbal and visual symbols linked to emotional or physiological responses. However, as already described, the meditator can develop a capacity to observe the symbolic self as if from a vantage point of equanimity. In meditation, the emotions, internal verbalization, and visualization are recognized, experienced vividly, and sometimes labeled, but they do not become a self-perpetuating stream of thought seen as essential to our fundamental experience and awareness.

As suggested earlier, the advanced meditator generalizes certain capacities learned in meditation to daily functioning. These include the capacities to discriminate memory, fantasy, worry, the accompanying emotional content, and present-time perceptions, and to decide to some degree which cognitive or emotional responses will become stimuli to further responses and which will not. In learning these two faculties, the meditator cultivates the *observer self.* In describing a form of Zen breath meditation useful in psychotherapy, psychologist Gary Deatherage (1975) suggests:

> If a patient is taught over time to note interruptions in breath observation and to label each interruption with neutral terms such as "remembering," "fantasizing," "hearing," "thinking," or "touching," he will quickly discover a rather complicated, but comforting, situation where there is one aspect of his mental "self" which is calm and psychologically strong, and which can watch, label, and see the melodramas of other "selves" which get too involved in painful memories of the past or beautiful and escapist fantasies of the future. By helping the patient to identify for a time with a strong and neutral "watcher self" there begins to develop with him the strength, motivation, and ability to fully participate in, and benefit from, whatever other forms of psychotherapy are being provided to him. (p. 136)

For the meditator, then, the ego or symbolic self is not the basic locus of experience. There is an observer self—or in Deatherage's term, a watcher self—undifferentiated or unconditioned awareness upon which the symbols and felt physiological responses play—like a drama before a mirror.

Until more research is conducted to describe it, this aspect of the meditation process might be described as follows. The process of meditation occupies the focal attention of the rational, linear, verbal function of the personality. Meanwhile a diffuse, nonlinear awareness emerges as the observer self. The meditator experiences the larger linkages of his or her symbolically constructed self with the past, present, and future world. This experience of the "larger self" has again and again been described as ineffable, uncommunicable. This is because our verbal, logical self must focus on single components of what is a panorama of perception and experience undifferentiated in time—past, present, or future—and space—here, elsewhere, and so forth. Because only portions of our more diffuse, intuitive (usually right brain lobe) awareness can be the focus of the narrow beam of our focal attention, only portions of our larger consciousness are immediately accessible to our verbal-logical, verbal-conscious self. This notion of a larger self separate from what we have called our conscious self has provoked much interest.

In "Meditation and the Unconscious: A New Perspective," John Welwood (1977) hypothesized that the "unconscious" of traditional Freudian and Jungian theory limited our understanding of human functioning. In essence, Welwood postulated that the phenomena defined as evidence of an unconscious—forgetting, slips of the tongue, laughter, habit, neurotic symptoms, and dreams—are simply evidence that we function outside of our ordinary focal attention. Rather than postulate an internal, unknowable psychic region inhabited by instincts, Welwood suggested that we might envision a focal attention that defines the *figure* in a universal *ground* of perception and awareness. For Welwood, the ground is not simply an internal structure. Instead, the ground is comprised of felt meanings, patterns of personal meanings, ways the organism is attuned to patterns and currents of the universe, and the immediate present.

Personality Change

While Welwood's particular definition of ground is very different from traditional concepts of the unconscious, the conceptualization is descriptive of the way in which the meditator experiences those aspects of awareness not labeled conscious in traditional psychodynamic terms. In meditation, the ego or symbolic self does not dissolve. The meditator does not become "egoless."

Meditation, instead, facilitates the realization of the socially conditioned nature of the self. That each person has a history of conditioning by the interpersonal context of her world, that she can attend to or be conscious of only a small part of her own social programming at a given time, and that meditation is a means of discovering her potential apart from her social conditioning are realized in meditation. These are the sources of *personality change* in meditation.

In light of meditation, then, the personality is not structured into static conscious-unconscious components. Rather, it is a web of interlacing symbolic meanings, each rooted in the changing social world. The self is like an eddy in a stream. In a sense, it is illusory.

Conscious Control

In cultivating an observer self, the meditator grasps the illusory nature of the symbolically constructed self. Conflicts, anxiety-arousing ideas, and repetition compulsions are the experienced components of this symbolic self. Seen from the vantage of an observer self, their power and control of response are rendered less ominous. This is because the advanced meditator discriminates the sources of problems and decides, with a degree of neutrality, alternative lines of action. As the anxiety or anger related to particular incidents or situations is desensitized in the relaxed state of meditation, their power and control are further diminished as the capacity for intentional decision about behavior and responses is increased. These behaviors can enhance treatment. As Deatherage (1975) puts it: "By becoming aware of the intentional process, one can then intercept and cancel unwanted words or deeds before they are manifested in behavior—something many patients find useful since it places control of their own behavior back at the conscious level" (p. 136). Not surprisingly, meditation is a component in the developing field of inquiry and treatment, behavioral self-control (Shapiro, 1994).

These experiences and outcomes of meditation, therefore, extend and modify traditional psychodynamic and cognitive perspectives, particularly with regard to the nature and function of the unconscious.

The traditional cultural contexts of meditation universally interjected their own myths to explain what exactly comprises the conditioning of the psychosocial self. Communication science, ego psychology, symbolic interactionism, sociology, and other Western sciences fill the void in traditional views of the processes that actually condition the self. However, even Western psychologists and therapists who have taken up the practice and systematic study of meditation fall back to philosophical musings when the parameters of the interpersonal ground are defined. Some use the language of mysticism and speak of the larger self or cosmic consciousness, to which each small ego is linked and of which each person is a small manifestation. This language is very global, and a more precise and critical view of the social realities should not be abandoned for a mystification of social realties. So, without disparaging the potential and wisdom in this view, we need not misuse it to gloss over social conditions. Indeed, those concerned with spiritual development are often the first to acknowledge the inhibiting aspects of social conditions.

Social work, with its particularly broad orientation toward human behavior and the social environment, has a special contribution to make toward an understanding of this larger ground of the self. Social workers are cognizant of the extent to which social conditions interact with the individual psyche and condition its nature, prospects, and levels of a awareness. Briefly extending this orientation, Marx and other materialists postulated that the economic organization or structure of society conditions or shapes the social and ideological life of a society (Marx, 1966). We might caution, then, that the global language of mystical traditions need not supplant critical analysis of the experiences of meditation, for these experiences are behaviors that may carry over into daily functioning with positive benefit to the meditator's personality and social functioning.

PERSONALITY AND SPECIFIC APPLICATIONS

Self-awareness, physical relaxation, stress reduction, desensitization of anxiety-arousing thoughts, self-regulation of problematic behaviors including substance abuse, discrimination of thoughts from other stimuli and self-exploration, and management of mild depression are specific applications of meditation in the treatment of problems.

SELF-AWARENESS

First, learning to be more self-aware—aware of feelings and motivations—can inform one's responses to interpersonal situations. As we shall learn later, the self-awareness of meditation facilitates sensing and then communicating one's responses to others—both behaviors conducive to empathy. Bernard Glueck and Charles Stroebel (1975), in their study of the effects of meditation and biofeedback in the treatment of psychotherapy patients, made detailed observations of the physiological changes occurring during meditation. They found that Transcendental Meditation generated recordable electroencephalographic changes in the brain that parallel relaxation. They think that the repeated sound, mantra, is the vehicle of relaxation that eventually involves both the dominant and nondominant hemispheres of the brain. This response is functional to self-understanding and psychotherapy by allowing "repressed" material to come into consciousness more quickly. This has the potential of permitting more rapid recovery of patients than standard therapeutic treatment would allow.

RELAXATION AND STRESS

Second, learning to relax through meditation is conducive to managing anxiety-related problems. For example, Deane Shapiro (1976) found Zen meditation combined with behavioral self-control techniques effective in reducing anxiety and stress in a client experiencing generalized anxiety and a feeling of being controlled by external forces. Several recent studies have now demonstrated significant results in the use of meditation alone or as a supplement to reduce trait and state anxiety as well as physiological correlates of stress (e.g., Alexander, Swanson, Rainforth, & Carlisle, 1993; DeBerry, Davis, & Reinhard, 1989; Kabat-Zinn, Massion, Kristeller, & Peterson, 1992; Pearl & Carlozzi, 1994; Snaith, Owens, & Kennedy, 1992; Sudsuang, Chentanez, & Veluvan, 1991). In overcoming insomnia in patients, Woolfolk, Car-Kaffashan, McNulty, and Lehrer (1976) found that meditation derived attention-focusing techniques as effective as progressive relaxation exercises in reducing the onset of sleep. Both meditation and relaxation were effective in improving patients beyond controls on six-month follow-up (Woolfolk et al., 1976).

Third, traditional therapy for anxiety-related problems has been broadened in recent years to the domain of ordinary stress. Stress, as a field of inquiry, promises to enrich our ability to prevent more serious symptoms and mental disorder. *Stress is they physical and psychosocial response of a person who perceives external and/or internal demands as exceeding her capacity to adapt or cope* (Fried, 1982). Some stress, of course, challenges or interests. Overstress, however, is a common problem in our industrial society.

Meditation and various forms of relaxation training have been studied for their potential in reducing the physical effects of stress and in helping people self-regulate aspects of their behavior or consciousness related to stress. In the early 1970s, research conducted by Robert Wallace, Herbert Benson, and Archie Wilson (1971) suggested that meditation might produce unique physiological and other changes. Later, other studies suggested that relaxation and various relaxation strategies and hypnosis may have effects similar to meditation (Beary & Benson, 1974; Fenwick, Donaldson, Gillis, Bushman, Fenton, Perry, Tilsley, & Serafinovicz, 1984; Morse, Martin, Furst, & Dubin, 1984; Walrath & Hamilton, 1984). Some studies are clear in indicating that meditation is at least as good as relaxation strategies in helping relieve stress and in lowering autonomic indicators of stress (Goleman & Schwartz, 1984; Marlatt, Pagano, Rose, & Marques, 1984). For example, in their study, Woolfolk, Lehrer, McCann, and Rooney (1982) compared meditation, progressive relaxation, and self-monitoring as treatments for stress. Meditation and progressive relaxation significantly reduce stress symptoms over time. More study is in order in this area. I should note here that in all comparative research, the "halo" effect may make a given technique appear effective or may make "controls" improve as well.

COPING AND SUBSTANCE ABUSE

The advantage of meditation as a strategy in helping clients deal with stress lies in the cognitive domain. What causes a person stress is determined in large part by the perceptions of an event or situation. Events viewed as threats are more stressful than those viewed as challenges in which one will grow. Meditation allows the individual to discover the symbolic meanings, the subtle fears, and other internal stimuli evoked by the event. Strategies, opportunities for coping, calm decisions, and previous successes can be distinguished in the mental contents and consciously enlisted in coping strategies. Moreover, one case study and some theorists support the aforementioned idea that meditation behavior may be transferred to other aspects of life and consciously enlisted to meet stressful events as they occur (Shapiro & Zifferblatt, 1976; Woolfolk, 1984). Maladaptive coping occurs when stress is responded to in ways that cause more problems for the stressed individual than they help. Meditation may help prevent these maladaptive responses, such as substance abuse, which relieve immediate stress but generate long-term physical, psychological, and even interpersonal problems.

Indeed, there is some evidence that meditation can help treat these maladaptive problems once they have developed. Several recent empirical studies indicate significant beneficial effects of meditation or meditation-assisted treatment in recovery and relapse prevention for substance abuse (Denney & Baugh, 1992; Gelderloos, Walton, Orme-Johnson, & Alexander, 1991; Royer, 1994; Taub, Steiner, Weingarten, & Walton, 1994).

A fourth outcome, combining self-awareness and the capacity to relax intentionally, permits an individual to transfer behaviors learned in meditation to other realms of life where there is stress or excessive stimulation that would hamper objective or reasoned functioning. Some studies suggest that meditation may be useful for alcohol and drug abusers to reduce anxiety, discriminate stimuli that evoke the problematic habits, and cultivate an "internal locus of control" (Benson & Wallace, 1984; Ferguson, 1978; Marlatt et al., 1984). One might reason that anxiety-arousing stimuli are less likely to become self-perpetuating in the symbolic system if they are discriminated and desensitized in the meditative process. For example, some individuals have associated worry over coming events with positive outcomes of those events. Worry, intermittently rewarded, is likely to persist, complete with fantasized negative outcomes, anxiety, and preoccupation (Challman, 1975). Meditation enables the individual to discriminate worrisome fantasy and to observe its impact upon the body and overall functioning. Desensitization and a secure observer self enable the individual to recognize worry, minimize its effects, and allow worrisome thoughts to burn themselves out without negative consequences. As the observer self is cultivated, the normal state of consciousness of modern Westerners, complete with split attention, worry, preoccupation, and anxiety, can be sharpened to a mindfulness in which attention is voluntarily riveted to the action at hand. Preoccupation with oneself and how one is performing, worry over consequences, and wandering attention interfere less in the tasks one has decided to do. In a sense, the symbolic self is lost in the activity.

Fifth, observation and discrimination of one's thoughts in meditation enable the meditator to use thoughts and images more as tools to represent reality, to communicate, and to serve as intentional guides to action than as illusory and unintentional substitutes for real circumstances. Symbols and cognitive constructs interfere less with clear present-time perceptions.

DEPRESSION

Finally, meditation as discrimination training may have specific usefulness in helping to manage depression. In her article "Learned Helplessness," social worker Carol Hooker (1976) reviewed literature suggesting that reactive depression is dynamically similar to experimentally induced states of learned helplessness in experimental animals. The work of Martin Seligman (1974, 1975) and others suggests that one may learn, in effect, not to learn when repeatedly subjected to noxious circumstances over which one can find no mastery or control. Under such conditions, one learns that there is no escape, no solutions other than unresponsive withdrawal with little or no mobility, eye contact, or normal need-fulfilling behaviors. Hooker, drawing on the work of Beck (1967), sees this *learned helplessness* as having cognitive components in humans wherein all known avenues of mastery and solution have been tried or rehearsed to no effect. Action and effort have no effect on circumstances. Beliefs about one's effectiveness sustain a depressive reaction. Loss of a loved one to death, for example, is an insoluble trauma. Repetition of guilt-evoking thoughts, self-deprecation, and beliefs that there is no future without the deceased may in some cases sustain depression for extended periods.

Meditation may help the depressed person regain a sense of self separate from the dilemma, partially sustained in the symbol system. Traumatic thoughts associated with the event are desensitized and one learns increasing mastery over the contents of one's depression-sustaining ruminations. Eventually, thoughts that constitute new tasks and new opportunities for mastery and rehearsal of new roles to play can be sustained intentionally and used as guides for action and mastery. A recent empirical study of the effects of a meditation-based stress reduction program found that not only anxiety and panic symptoms were reduced but that depression was reduced and results were maintained at the three-month follow-up (Kabat-Zinn et al., 1992).

Similar processes used with caution and close, informed supervision, elaborated below, may be therapeutic for persons with thought disorders. In other words, observation of thinking, not building upon associations and becoming "lost in thought," is the intent of meditation for enhanced discrimination.

In summary, research indicates meditation is an effective adjunct to treatment of a potentially wide variety of problems. Shapiro (1994) summarized research on meditation in self-regulation and self-exploration observing that the meditation has been stripped of the original cultural and religious contexts to avoid dilemmas and divisiveness. He makes a strong case for reintroducing the context of meditation which fits the social work perspective of valuing cultural diversity and working with the whole person. With this idea in mind we must recognize that some clients and workers will find meditation an alien endeavor, even when it is isolated from its original context. Furthermore, there are certain problems that should not be approached with meditation except with intense supervision by workers skilled in treatment of the problem and in meditation. While definitive studies that show direst contraindications for the use of meditation are few, some guidelines are emerging.

CAUTIONS AND CONTRAINDICATIONS

Some people find meditation more suited to their temperament and culture or beliefs than others. Also, certain severe disorders make the correct practice of meditation difficult or impossible.

ATTITUDE

Anxious but organized persons seem to take to meditation quickly. Relaxation and learning control over focal attention is rewarding and rather immediate. With very anxious, driven people, however, a caution is in order. Meditation of the Zen type, which requires a continued refocusing on the breath or another object of attention, or of those Yogic types that require strict postures and attention, can become a do-or-die endeavor for these persons. Individuals may incorrectly feel compelled to suppress thoughts and emotions. Or they may force their breath in an unnatural way rather than following their natural breathing rhythms. Often this response is not unlike their life-style, in which they constantly push themselves to perform or conform without attention to their own desires and physical needs. The attitude of wakeful awareness is misinterpreted as rigid attention where all interruptions are excluded before their full perception. Sometimes the body is not relaxed, but held rigid and tense. With such persons, the point must be made clear that they are to let go of interrupting thoughts, not push them away or compulsively follow them. The analogy of the mind as an open hand, neither pushing away nor grasping, helps in interpreting the correct mental attitude. In any case, the social worker–therapist must make sure that the client is meditating and not magnifying anxiety, building anxiety-provoking images, or obsessing along an improbable chain of associations about hypothetical, destructive interpersonal events or outcomes.

SEVERE PROBLEMS

Two authors have discussed use of meditation by persons who suffer severe mental problems or who are labeled psychotic or schizophrenic. Deatherage (1975), in discussing limitations on the use of Buddhist mindfulness meditation in psychotherapy, cautions, "While this psychotherapeutic approach is extremely effective when employed with patients suffering from depression, anxiety, and neurotic symptoms, a caution should be issued regarding its use with patients experiencing actively psychotic symptoms such as hallucinations, delusions, thinking disorders, and severe withdrawal" (p. 142). He goes on to note that the particular meditation technique for self-observation requires "an intact and functional rational component of mind, as well as sufficient motivation on the part of the patient to cause him to put forth the effort to do that observation" (p. 142). Arnold Lazarus (1976), discussing psychiatric problems possibly precipitated by Transcendental Meditation, cautions that his clinical observations have led him to hypothesize that T.M. does not seem to be effective with people classified as hysterical reactions or strong depressive reactions. He speculates that "some 'schizophrenic' individuals might experience an increase in 'depersonalization' and self preoccupation" (pp. 601–602).

CULTURE AND IDENTITY FACTORS

As an activity derived from religious traditions, meditation is associated with notions of self-transcendence. This context may be culturally congruent or very alien for a client. Good judgment and sensitivity to the client's culture are very much in order when introducing meditation techniques for this reason alone.

Observation of the conditioned self or ego from a perspective of dispassionate neutrality can be confused with several problematic behaviors. Engler, for example, cautions that borderline personalities and others without a well-developed self may be attracted to meditation. Also, persons in developmental stages struggling with identity may find meditation an unfortunate substitute for dealing with their developmental tasks or discovering "who they are" (Engler, 1984). Persons with very fragile identities, symptoms related to depersonalization, and inadequate ego development are not good candidates for meditation except under close supervision. Following up on research which found a significantly more likely "sensed presence" phenomena in meditators, Persinger cautioned that meditation is contraindicated for subpopulations who may have fragile self-concepts such as borderline, schizotypal, or disassociative personalities (Persinger, 1992). Put very simply, "You have to be somebody before you can be nobody" (Engler, 1984).

SUMMARY AND RESEARCH

In general, therefore, clients or patients with fragile self-concepts or those with severe disorders, whose reality testing, perception, and logical thinking are such that they cannot fully understand meditation instructions or follow through with actual meditation under supervision, are poor candidates for its successful use in treatment. Just as the anxious client may build upon anxiety-arousing associations or the depressed client may ruminate on ineffectiveness and despair instead of actually meditating, clients with severe thought disorders and problems with reality testing may substitute hallucinations, delusions, withdrawal, depersonalization, and catatonic responses for meditation, thereby aggravating their problems.

Glueck and Stroebel (1975), however, found Transcendental Meditation effective as adjunctive treatment with a sample of ninety-six psychiatric patients who would have been expected to have the kind of difficulties outlined here. Preliminary investigation indicated that the higher the level of psychopathology, the greater the difficulty patients had producing alpha waves. Testing Transcendental Meditation against autogenic relaxation and electroencephalogram (EEG) alpha-wave biofeedback training, Glueck and Stroebel found T.M. to be the only one of the three experimental conditions that patients could persistently practice. Consequently, the authors match-paired their meditation sample with a comparison group and found their meditating patients to have higher levels of recovery than both their "twins" and the general patient population. Despite these findings, treatment of the severely depressed and psychotic patients with meditation is experimental and without close supervision and immediate postmeditation checks is contraindicated until further research is done.

PSYCHOSOCIAL HISTORY AND DIAGNOSIS

One phenomenon occurring in most forms of meditation is the intrusion of the memory of events in the meditator's life into the meditative state. Meditators employing Zen and similar concentration techniques usually experience mental images of significant and emotionally intense events replayed before their relaxed mind. Desensitization of these memories has been discussed. But intentional use of meditation to allow significant facts and events of the psychosocial history is possible. Requesting the client to record these memories following meditation, for use in the context of treatment and for rounding out a more complete psychosocial history, may be helpful to workers with psychodynamic and psychoanalytic orientations and those helping clients with family-of-origin work.

The diagnostic value of meditation, implicit in earlier discussions, lies in the nature of the difficulty that the client has in meditating correctly. Elsewhere, the author has discussed optimal psychosocial functioning based on Eastern conceptualizations related to and developed from meditation (Keefe, 1978). Briefly stated, the capacity to attend to activities one is about without interference by irrelevant ideation and worry suggests a positive level of functioning. Meditation evokes memories and worries that intrude upon the meditation task. Repetitive anxiety or guilt-associated thoughts will indicate to the meditator and the worker or therapist those areas of conflict or "unfinished business" that hinder the client's functioning. Repetitive self-destructive images will indicate disturbed role rehearsal or depression. Conflicts from pushing or driving oneself will manifest themselves in forced breath or lack of relaxation in meditation.

THE THERAPEUTIC RELATIONSHIP

There are several behaviors learned in meditation that would theoretically contribute to enhanced empathic functioning on the part of the social worker who meditates. Some preliminary study suggests that this notion should be researched further (Keefe, 1979).

First, learning increased voluntary control over one's attention permits one to shift from attending to the various verbal and nonverbal communications of the client to one's own emotional responses to the client. This ability to sense one's own emotional reactions from moment to moment facilitates sensing and verbalizing feelings that parallel those of the client. Accurate reflection of these feelings to the client, of course, is a major component in therapeutic empathy (Rogers, 1975), a worker skill conducive to positive behavior change for the client.

Second, learning to discriminate internal or cognitive stimuli from perceptual stimuli in meditation and learning to gain a measure of voluntary control over cognitive processes can enhance empathic functioning in another way. The worker can hold complex cognitive elaboration in abeyance and allow himself to perceive the client as she is, without premature diagnosing or other cognitive elaboration coloring his bare attention to the client as she is. This intentional slowing of the perceptual process that allows the client to speak for herself holds the worker in the present time—where emotions are felt, where the worker can by fully with the client, and where behaviors are changed.

Third, the meditating worker is likely to have cultivated a strong centeredness or observer self not easily rattled by the stresses or intense emotional interaction. Therefore, staying with the client in her deepest feelings, as Carl Rogers (1975) described high-level empathy, becomes more likely. And because such a worker has a perspective on his own reactions, countertransference responses may be more accessible.

Supervision would naturally include sharing of meditation experiences to help in refocusing. Dubin (1991) recommends meditative techniques in psychotherapy supervision to help learn theory, case management, and how to deal with countertransference. Meditation can assist the worker sharing about and dealing with countertransference or other issues of problematic attachment.

Meditation as an adjunctive technique to treatment has a virtue common to all profound and shared experiences. It is an experience a worker can teach and then share with the client that may serve as a basis for communication, trust, and mutual discovery when other bases for relationships are less productive. In this sense, meditation can be a common ground of mutual experience that can strengthen a therapeutic relationship.

TEACHING MEDITATION: ONE TECHNIQUE

There are several techniques for meditation useful as adjuncts for treatment. Among the more prominent are Yogic mantra techniques, Benson's relaxation technique (Glueck & Stroebel, 1975, p. 314), Transcendental Meditation (Bloomfield & Kory, 1977), and Zen techniques. The technique to be briefly described here is a form of Zen. The general instructions are readily found in a variety of texts. Expert instruction and a good period of time meditating are recommended for workers considering meditation as an addition to their repertoire of techniques.

The client is instructed to meditate half an hour each day in a quiet place where she is unlikely to be interrupted. The client is asked to briefly record in a log her meditation experiences for later discussion with the worker. The meditation posture as suggested by Kapleau (1967) is as follows:

1. A sitting position with the back straight.
2. Sitting cross-legged on a pillow is ideal for some.

3. If uncomfortable, sit in a straight chair without allowing the back to come to rest against the back of the chair.
4. The hands should be folded in the lap.
5. The eyes may be opened or closed; if open, they are not to focus on any particular thing.
6. The back must be straight for comfort since slumping causes cramping.
7. Loose clothing around the waist is suggested.

The client is instructed to focus on the breath manifest in the rising and falling of the abdomen and to begin the first session by counting each exhalation up to ten and beginning again. Thereafter, the client may simply follow the natural—unforced, uncontrolled—breath for the duration of each session. The attention should be focused on the surface of the center of the body about an inch below the navel.

The client is told that there will be frequent intrusions of thoughts, feelings, sounds, and physical responses during her concentration. The response to these is in every case an easy recognition that attention has wandered and refocusing to the breath is necessary. Relaxing the muscles around the eyes and the tongue and throat is helpful in letting go of visual and verbal thoughts.

Repressed material will usually emerge as insights. These are automatically paired with a relaxed state. The client should be instructed that, if the meditation becomes upsetting or frustrating, she should stop and resume the following day or wait until the next appointment with the therapist. Particular cautions with special clients were enumerated above. Generally, if the experience is not pleasant and rewarding, it may be evidence the client is pushing rather than allowing mental content to flow.

SETTINGS AND LEVELS OF INTERVENTION

Meditation is a worldwide phenomenon. It is practiced in settings as varied as Japanese corporate offices, quiet monasteries in all parts of the world, downtown apartments, and mental health centers. Most physical settings where social workers practice would be conducive to meditation. While each agency has its own major theoretical orientation or admixture of orientations, few would preclude meditation as an appropriate technique if thoughtfully and systematically introduced. While a psychodynamically oriented worker would define and describe meditation behavior and results differently than a behaviorist or an existentialist, the technique is not tied to a single system or culture. Therefore, agency acceptance hinges more upon tolerance for innovation, interest in research, and openness to new ideas. Meditation as a social work technique was thought to be well out of the mainstream and esoteric a few years ago, but it has gained wide acceptance in related disciplines and promises to become a more common technique in work with individuals, families, and groups.

Because meditation tends to be an individual activity, it is naturally thought of as a mode for individual treatment only. However, in addition to its use and ramifications for individual treatment, meditation is useful for certain kinds of groups, including families.

Group meditation can enhance group processes. Beginning and ending a group with a meditation session can enhance group feeling and mellow out intense feelings enough to allow their sharing, analysis, and discussion. A group meditation sets the atmosphere for constructive interaction. Meditation to end a group meeting has similar effects and supports solidarity and identity within the group.

A few years ago receptivity to meditation was largely restricted to young people and the religiously or spiritually oriented. But over the years the various forms—Transcendental Meditation in particular—have crossed many class and age barriers and is widely practiced (Bloomfield & Kory, 1977). Increasingly, meditation can be introduced into group work with a variety of people. The author has used individual meditation to begin and group chants to end treatment groups for college-age youth and for sex-role-consciousness-raising treatment groups for married persons ranging in age from twenty-two to forty-five. Meditation for family treatment may help to reduce conflict and give the family a positive, common experience to share and discuss.

The use of meditation to facilitate family-of-origin history taking suggested above could be a part of an actual family treatment session. Sometimes the level of conflict and individual arousal is such that constructive communication in a treatment session is hampered. Twenty minutes of meditation may allow sufficient calming to enhance communication. Except for young children and the contraindications already discussed, family members may be helped regardless of age. The particular phenomenon of enmeshment, or very dependent adult members without a secure sense of self apart from the family, may be helped through meditation. Just as with individual clients, sensitivity to the receptivity and experiences of each family member would be essential. While not a substitue for other techniques, meditation may be useful as an adjunct to family treatment, and systematic use and assessment may support its utility.

Claims of increased harmony and lower crime rates have been made as resulting from certain percentages of meditation in given communities (Bloomfield & Kory, 1977, pp. 238–284). In the judgment of this author, these findings require some critical assessment. But, obviously, if meditation contributes to personal functioning, certain aspects of community life will be enhanced.

But much research must be done to determine the long-term effects of the various forms of meditation on individuals, groups, families, and communities. Optimal personal and group functioning does not lead directly to more harmonious community life if the social order is fundamentally exploitive and contradictory. As with many forms of treatment techniques, the gaps in our knowledge about meditation, as an adjunct to treatment at whatever level of intervention, are many, and considerable research is still in order.

IMPLICATIONS FOR RESEARCH

Meditation is a widely studied behavior. Nevertheless, our understanding of it is incomplete. As a treatment technique, it has been found valuable in a variety of situations. However, there is growing knowledge of the appropriate forms of meditation, contraindications, the relative value of meditation and other relaxation techniques, and even the effects of meditation on stress and anxiety, substance abuse recovery and prevention, depression, the nervous system, psyche, and social life.

Although there is much clinical evidence and intuitive exploration, the research concerning subset meditation phenomena is sparse. These include the desensitization, discrimination, and observer self mentioned earlier. Clinicians must begin to refine the appropriate use of meditation for particular kinds of clients and particular kinds of problems. Together with researchers, we must deduce where it helps and where it does not. Use of meditation with groups and families needs more study. Researchers also have rich opportunities to follow the differential effects of meditation used with various clinical problems and various personalities.

Being a technique of potentially great value for social work, meditation must continue to be examined empirically. Hopefully, it will not be picked up "whole hog" and incorporated into practice without critical evaluation. This would render it, like some other techniques, a passing fancy, soon discarded in favor of new approaches. Nor should meditation be disregarded as the esoteric product of foreign and bygone cultures. Despite barriers that exclude the wisdom of other cultures and other lands from our consideration, a critical openness and valuing of diversity in the treatment domains is in order. We must try out, test, and incorporate meditation as an adjunct to treatment where it benefits our clients, our practice, and ourselves.

CONCLUSION

Meditation is, of course, more than just an adjunct to social work treatment. Meditation and its potential for better understanding ourselves and our functioning may flourish in our culture independent of the helping professions and their practice. If we in social work and others in related professions find it a powerful adjunct to treatment, we should not attempt to subsume it as ours alone. Indeed, Shapiro (1994) argues a strong case for reintroducing the cultural contexts of meditation where it is used. Such an endeavor would enrich the diversity of the cultural and philosophical basis of the treatment where meditation is used. It may even help us to reach clients from particular cultures with strong meditation traditions. It gives us new perspectives on the development of the self, amplifies our understanding of subjective experience, provides insights into what constitutes optimal psychosocial functioning, and provides an empirically supported tool for dealing with stress anxiety and maladaptive coping such as substance abuse.

Meditation is at once a vehicle of consciousness and a portal to individual potential. It can be used to liberate, to extend individual functioning, and thereby help to create social change in the democratic interest. It could also be used to mystify, to distract people from their social concerns related to their personal problems. How the technique will be used by social work is related to the conscience, wisdom, and position of the profession in the years of profound social change ahead.

This chapter began by identifying meditation as a set of behaviors. Meditation is, of course, the embodiment of a larger theory of self, coping, and change. For this reason it has begun to take interesting routes in the social work profession. It is a part of the field of stress management and finds frequent mention in that literature (e.g., Nucho, 1988). But it is also naturally linked to mainstream social work literature (Smith, 1995; Carroll, 1993; Cowley, 1993). As social workers openly discuss addressing the "whole person" or the spiritual aspects of a client's experience, the understandings of that experience can be enhanced by familiarity with meditation-related phenomena such as global desensitization and an observer self. This perspective does not require adoption of the theological stance nor the introduction of religion as a component of treatment. It does have the potential to help us understand our clients more fully. As long as social work is concerned with helping people secure themselves and make good choices, meditation and its body of related theory should have a role to play. Finally, deep in the heart of meditation lies the insight that is the root of both compassion and social action: to help others is to help ourselves. Whether he is a clinician, a social activist, or both, this is a message every social worker can hear.

A BRIEF CASE EXAMPLE: THE USE OF MEDITATION IN THE TREATMENT OF FUNCTIONAL BOWEL DISEASE

A thirty-six-year-old woman, married and the mother of three children—aged three, seven, and twelve—living in California, was referred by her physician. She was suffering abdominal pain. Extensive physical examinations and tests had all been negative, although she had recently had an increase in pain when she was under stress. She wanted to understand why she was having these troubles and how she could control them.

She had been experiencing an increase in pain over the past year. She had gone on special diets, consulted several health care professionals, and taken many different medications, but there was no change in her distress, which was becoming overwhelming. She said she was becoming increasingly depressed, anxious, and overly self-critical as her symptoms continued and there seemed no hope for any change in them. Psychological tests completed at the time of the initial evaluation confirmed that she was indeed severely depressed, with little energy. There seemed to be emotional overlay to her pains.

The client was quick to agree to short-term outpatient treatment of eight weekly sessions. The goals would include developing some understanding of her emotions, the stresses in her life, and her coping skills and difficulties, and learning various types of relaxation techniques. It was also agreed that the results of the psychological tests would be fully reviewed with her in the third session. In addition, she was helped to work through some unresolved feelings from earlier years that were related to her parents' divorce and the death of her first husband. She explored how she could utilize some of her past coping skills with some of her present difficulties.

The client was experiencing many stressful and unstable living conditions at the present time while her husband was building their new home. This necessitated their living in a series of different friends' homes. Her husband had been so involved in building their dream home that he had not involved her in the process. He was included in one of the outpatient sessions in order to increase communication between them and to help them to reinstitute their previous level of positive interactions, which had been present in the year previous to all of these changes.

In the second treatment session the client was taught a passive, modified hypnotic relaxation technique that was tape-recorded for her daily use at home. She was quite pleased with her ability to immediately relax and experienced a definite decrease in her abdominal pains. She was instructed to listen to the tape recording of the relaxation four times a day and to record her responses each time in a "Relaxation Log" that she was to bring with her to each session.

The following week the patient had several days without any pain until she would forget to use the technique because she felt "so good." The patient continued with the passive, therapist-directed relaxation techniques by listening to the tape recording daily. The worker was very directive with this technique. The client was slowly encouraged to try the relaxation technique on her own, without using the tape. She quickly became able to do this.

After the fourth treatment session, the client was introduced to a new technique designed to help her relax on her own, to become more comfortable with her own body, and to learn how she could help herself on an ongoing basis. It was presented to her as a new coping skill that she could continue to utilize after the termination of treatment. Since the client was now feeling much better, she was eager to increase her skills in this area. She was therefore given oral and written instructions for meditation. She was asked to take the instructions home, read them, and try to implement them in her daily routine. Initially she had some difficulty in being totally comfortable with the technique, so she continued listening, once a day, to the relaxation tape. However, she found less need to rely on the tape recording as she increased her ability to relax with the meditation. After one week, the client found that she was able to relax just as fully as she had with the tape recording. Further, she felt quite proud of her ability to do it on her own. By the last session she was able to relax without any reliance on the tape. She found that if she meditated once a day, she had no pain and could reduce any stresses that arose by short relaxation techniques, which she would go over in her mind. At that point she had been totally pain-free for three weeks. Follow-up contacts with the patient one month after formal termination of treatment showed that she continued to do her daily meditation, was pain-free, felt much more confident in her abilities in her abilities and coping skills, and felt that all aspects of psychotherapy, relaxation, and finally meditation had been quite beneficial to her. She recognized the benefits of continuing to practice what she had learned, and her family was quite supportive.

REFERENCES

Alexander, C.N., Swanson, G., Rainforth, M., Carlisle, T., et al. (1993). Effects of the transcendental meditation program on stress reduction, health, and employee development: A prospective study in two occupational settings. *Anxiety, Stress and Coping: An International Journal, 6*(3), 245–262.

Al-Ghazzali (B. Behari, Trans.) (1971). *The revival of religious sciences.* Farnham, Surrey, Eng.: Sufi.

Anand, B.K., Cchhina, G.S., & Singh, B. (1984). Some aspects of electroencephalographic studies in yogis. In D.H. Shapiro & R.N. Walsh (Eds.), *Meditation: Classic and contemporary perspectives* (pp. 475–479). New York: Aldine.

Beary, J.F., & Benson, H. (1974). A simple psychophysiologic technique which elicits the hypometabolic changes of the relaxation response. *Psychosomatic Medicine, 36,* 115–120.

Beck, A.T. (1967). *Depression: Clinical experimental and theoretical aspects.* New York: Harper & Row.

Benson, H., & Wallace, K., with technical assistance of E.C. Dahl and D.F. Cooke. (1984). Decreased drug abuse with transcendental meditation—A study of 1,862 subjects. In D.H. Shapiro & R.N. Walsh (Eds.), *Meditation: Classic and contemporary perspectives* (pp. 97–104). New York: Aldine.

Bloomfield, H.H., & Kory, R.B. (1977). *Happiness.* New York: Pocket Books.

Brown, L., & Robinson, S. (1993). The relationship between meditation and/or exercise and three measures of self-actualization. *Journal of Mental Health Counseling, 15*(1), 85–93.

Burt, E.A. (Ed.). (1955). *The teachings of the compassionate Buddha.* New York: New American Library.

Carroll, M. (1993). Spiritual growth of recovering alcoholic adult children of alcoholics. Unpublished doctoral dissertation, University of Maryland, College Park.

Challman, A. (1975). The self-inflicted suffering of worry, cited in "Newsline." *Psychology Today, 8*(8), 94.

Chang, J. (1991). Using relaxation strategies in child and youth care practice. *Child and Youth Care Forum, 20*(3), 155–169.

Cowley, A.D. (1993). Transpersonal social work: A theory for the 1990's. *Social Work, 38*(5), 527–534.

Deatherage, G. (1975). The clinical use of "mindfulness" meditation techniques in short-term psychotherapy. *Journal of Transpersonal Psychology, 7*(2), 133–143.

DeBerry, S., Davis, S., & Reinhard, K. (1989). A comparison of meditation-relaxation and cognitive/behavioral techniques for reducing anxiety and depression in a geriatric population. *Journal of Geriatric Psychiatry, 22*(2), 231–247.

Denney, M., & Baugh, J. (1992). Symptom reduction and sobriety in the male alcoholic. *International Journal of the Addictions, 27*(11), 1293–1300.

Driskill, J.D. (1989). Meditation as a therapeutic technique. *Pastoral Psychology, 38*(2), 83–103.

Dubin, W. (1991). The use of meditative techniques in psychotherapy supervision. *Journal of Transpersonal Psychology, 23*(1), 65–80.

Encyclopaedia Britannica (1974), Macropoedia (Vol. 10) (p. 183). London: Benton.

Engler, J. (1984). Therapeutic aims in psychotherapy and meditation: Developmental stages in the representation of self. *Journal of Transpersonal Psychology, 16*(1), 25–61.

Fenwick, P.B.C., Donaldson, S., Gillis, L., Bushman, J., Fenton, G.W., Perry, I., Tilsley, C., & Serafinovicz, H. (1984). Metabolic and EEG changes during transcendental meditation: An explanation. In D.H. Shapiro and R.N. Walsh (Eds.), *Meditation: Classic and contemporary perspectives* (pp. 447–464). New York: Aldine.

Ferguson, M. (Ed.). (1978, February 20). Valuable adjuncts to therapy: Meditation, relaxation help alcoholics cope. *Brain-Minded Bulletin, 7*, 2.

Fried, M. (1982). Endemic stress: The psychology of resignation and the politics of scarcity. *American Journal of Orthopsychiatry, 52,* 4–16.

Fromm, E., Suzuki, D.T., & DeMartino, R. (1970). *Zen Buddhism and psychoanalysis.* New York: Harper & Row.

Gelderloos, P., Walton, K., Orme-Johnson, D., & Alexander, C. (1991). Effectiveness of the transcendental meditation program in preventing and treating substance misuse: A review. *International Journal of the Addictions, 26*(3), 293–325.

Glueck, B.C., & Stroebel, C.F. (1975). Biofeedback and meditation in the treatment of psychiatric illness. *Comprehensive Psychiatry, 16*(4), 303–321.

Goble, F. (1970). *The third force.* New York: Pocket Books

Goleman, D. (1975). Mental health in classical Buddhist psychology. *Journal of Transpersonal Psychology, 7*(2), 176–183.

Goleman, D. (1976). Meditation and consciousness: An Asian approach to mental health. *American Journal of Psychotherapy, 30*(1), 41–54.

Goleman, D., & Schwartz, G.E. (1984). Meditation as an intervention in stress reactivity. In D.H. Shapiro and R.N. Walsh (Eds.), *Meditation: Classic and contemporary perspectives* (pp. 77–88). New York: Aldine.

Hendricks, C.G. (1975). Meditation as discrimination training: A theoretical note. *Journal of Transpersonal Psychology, 7*(2), 144–146.

Hooker, C.E. (1976). Learned helplessness. *Social Work, 21*(3), 194–198.

Jourard, S. (1966). Psychology of transcendent perception. In H. Otto (Ed.), *Exploration in human potential.* Springfield, IL: Charles C Thomas.

Kabat-Zinn, J., Massion, A., Kristeller, J., Peterson, L., et al. (1992). Effectiveness of meditation-based stress reduction program in the treatment of anxiety disorders. *American Journal of Psychiatry, 149*(7), 936–943.

Kapleau, P. (1967). *Three pillars of Zen.* Boston: Beacon Press.

Kasamatsu, A., & Hirai, T. (1984). An electroencephalographic study of the Zen meditation (Zagen). In D.H. Shapiro & R.N. Walsh (Eds.), *Meditation: Classic and contemporary perspectives* (pp. 480–492). New York: Aldine.

Keefe, T.W. (1975, March). A Zen perspective on social casework. *Social Casework, 56*(3), 140–144.

Keefe, T.W. (1975, April). Meditation and the psychotherapist. *American Journal of Orthopsychiatry, 45*(3), 484–489.

Keefe, T.W. (1976). Empathy: The critical skill. *Social Work, 21*(1), 10–15.

Keefe, T.W. (1978). Optimal functioning: The Eastern ideal in psychotherapy. *Journal of Contemporary Psychotherapy, 10*(1), 16–24.

Keefe, T.W. (1979). The development of empathic skill: A study. *Journal of Education for Social Work, 15*(2), 30–37.

Kennett, J. (1972). *Selling water by the river: A manual of Zen training* (p. 302). New York: Vintage Books.

Kohr, R.L. (1977). Dimensionality in meditative experience: A replication. *Journal of Transpersonal Psychology, 9,* 193–203.

Lazarus, A.A. (1976). Psychiatric problems precipitated by transcendental meditation. *Psychological Reports, 39,* 601–602.

LeShan, L. (1975, February 22). The case of meditation. *Saturday Review, 2*(11), 25–27.

Linden, W. (1973). Practicing of meditation by school children and their levels of field dependence-independence, test anxiety, and reading achievement. *Journal of Consulting and Clinical Psychology, 41*(1), 139–143.

Linden, W. (1984). Practicing of meditation by school children and their levels of field dependence-independence, test anxiety, and reading achievement. In D.H. Shapiro and R.N. Walsh

(Eds.), *Meditation: Classic and contemporary perspectives* (pp. 89–93). New York: Aldine.

Marlatt, A.C., Pagano, R.R., Rose, R., & Marques, J.K. (1984). Effects of meditation and relaxation training upon alcohol use in male social drinkers. In D.H. Shapiro and R.N. Walsh (Eds.), *Meditation: Classic and contemporary perspectives* (pp. 105–120). New York: Aldine.

Marx, K. (1966). Preface to Contribution to the critique of political economy. In E. Allen (Ed.), *From Plato to Nietzsche* (p. 159). New York: Fawcett.

Miller, W.R., & Seligman, M.E. (1973). Depression and the perception of reinforcement. *Journal of Abnormal Psychology, 82,* 62–73.

Morse, D.R., Martin, J.S., Furst, M.I., & Dublin, L.L. (1984). A physiological and subjective evaluation of meditation, hypnosis and relaxation. In D.H. Shaprio & R.N. Walsh (Eds.), *Meditation: Classic and contemporary perspectives* (pp. 645–665). New York: Aldine.

Nucho, A. (1988). *Stress management* (chapter 8). Springfield, IL: Charles C Thomas.

Ornstein, R.E. (1977). *The psychology of consciousness* (2nd ed.). New York: Harcourt, Brace Jovanovich.

Pearl, J.H., & Carlozzi, A. (1994). Effect of meditation on empathy and anxiety. *Perceptual and Motor Skills, 78*(1), 297–298.

Persinger, M.A. (1992). Enhanced incidence of "the sensed presence" in people who have learned to meditate: Support for the right hemispheric intrusion hypothesis. *Perceptual and Motor Skills, 75*(3, pt. 2), 1308–1310.

Prabhupada, Swami A.C.B. (1972). *Bhagavad Gita as it is.* New York: Bhaktivedanta Book Trust.

Rogers, C.R. (1975). The necessary and sufficient conditions for therapeutic personality change. *Journal of Consulting Psychology, 21*(2), 95–103.

Royer, A. (1994). The role of the transcendental meditation technique in promoting smoking cessation: A longitudinal study. *Alcoholism Treatment Quarterly, 11*(1–2), 221–239.

Schopen, A., & Freeman, B. (1992). Meditation: The forgotten Western tradition. *Counseling and Values, 36*(2), 123–134.

Seligman, M.E.P. (1974). Depression and learned helplessness. In R.J. Friedman & M.M. Katz (Eds.), *The psychology of depression: Contemporary theory and research* (pp. 83–107). New York: Halstead Press.

Seligman, M.E.P. (1975). *Helplessness: On depression, development and death.* San Francisco: Freeman.

Shapiro, D.H. (1976). Zen meditation and behavioral self-control strategies applied to a case of generalized anxiety. *Psychologia: An International Journal of Psychology in the Orient, 19*(3), 134–138.

Shapiro, D.H. (1994). Examining the content and context of meditation: A challenge for psychology in the areas of stress management, psychotherapy, and religion/values. *Journal of Humanistic Psychology, 34*(4), 101–135.

Shapiro, D.H., & Walsh, R.N. (Eds.). (1984). *Meditation: Classic and contemporary perspectives.* New York: Aldine.

Shapiro, D.H., & Zifferblatt, S.M. (1976). Zen meditation and behavioral self control: Similarities, differences, and clinical applications. *American Psychologist, 31*(7), 519–532.

Smith, E.D. (1995). Addressing the psycho-spiritual distress of death as reality: A transpersonal approach. *Social Work, 40*(3), 402–413.

Snaith, P.R., Owens, D., & Kennedy, E. (1992). An outcome study of a brief anxiety management programme: Anxiety control training. *Irish Journal of Psychological Medicine, 9*(2), 111–114.

Sudsuang, R., Chentanez, V., & Veluvan, K. (1991). Effect of Buddhist meditation on serum cortisol and total protein levels, blood pressure, pulse rate, lung volume and reaction time. *Physiology and Behavior, 50*(3), 543–548.

Suzuki, D.T. (1964). *An introduction to Zen Buddhism.* New York: Grove Press.

Sweet, M., & Johnson, C. (1990). Enhancing empathy: The interpersonal implications of a Buddhist meditation technique. *Psychotherapy, 27*(1), 19–29.

Taub, E., Steiner, S., Weingarten, E., & Walton, K. (1994). Effectiveness of broad spectrum approaches to relapse prevention in severe alcoholism: A long term, randomized, controlled trial of transcendental meditation, EMG biofeedback and electronic neurotherapy. *Alcoholism Treatment Quarterly, 11*(1–2), 187–220.

Thera, N. (1970). *The heart of Buddhist meditation.* New York: Weiser.

Wallace, R.K., Benson, H., & Wilson, A.F. (1971). A wakeful hypometabolic state. *American Journal of Physiology, 221*(3), 795–799.

Walrath, L.C., & Hamilton, D.W. (1984). Autonomic correlates of meditation and hypnosis. In D.H. Shapiro & R.N. Walsh (Eds.), *Meditation: Classic and contemporary perspectives* (pp. 645–665). New York: Aldine.

Walsh, R. (1977). Initial meditative experiences: Part I. *Journal of Transpersonal Psychology, 9*(2), 161.

Watts, A. (1961). *Psychotherapy East and West.* New York: Ballantine.

Welwood, J. (1977). Meditation and the unconscious: A new perspective. *Journal of Tranpersonal Psychology, 9*(1), 1–26.

Wood, E. (1959). *Yoga.* Baltimore: Penguin.

Woolfolk, R.L. (1984). Self-control meditation and the treatment of chronic anger. In D.H. Shapiro & R.N. Walsh (Eds.), *Meditation: Classic and contemporary perspectives* (pp. 550–554). New York: Aldine.

Woolfolk, R.L., Car-Kaffashan, L, McNulty, T., & Lehrer, P. (1976). Meditation as a training for insomnia. *Behavior Therapy, 7*(3), 359–365.

Woolfolk, R.L., Lehrer, P.M., McCann, B.S., & Rooney, A.J. (1982). Effects of progressive relaxation and meditation on cognitive and somatic manifestations of daily stress. *Behavior Research and Therapy, 20*(5), 461–467.

Yu, L.K. (1972). *The secrets of Chinese meditation* (Charles Luk, Trans.). New York: Weiser.

CHAPTER 19

NARRATIVE THEORY AND SOCIAL WORK TREATMENT

PATRICIA KELLEY

Narrative therapy is a major trend of the nineties. It has even reached the popular press, as *Newsweek* (Cowley & Springen, 1995) had a feature story on it. It has had prominence in the professional literature also, especially in social work and marriage and family therapy journals. What is narrative therapy? What is its theoretical base? How does it fit into the existing practice theory of social work? How does it fit into the social work value frame? These questions will be addressed in this chapter, and, in addition, how narrative therapy connects to other approaches will be assessed.

OVERVIEW

The narrative approach described and discussed in this chapter will draw mainly on the works of White and Epston (1990), family therapists from Australia and New Zealand, respectively (White's original training is in social work). They developed this approach in the 1980s, but it became popularized in North America after their book, *Narrative Means to Therapeutic Ends,* was published on this continent in 1990. While some elements of their approach were fairly unique at that time, their work emerged and codeveloped in relation to theoretical and practice developments occurring in North America and Europe. Their approach falls under the general rubric of "constructivist therapy" several models of which emerged at about the same time and which all developed in relationship to the postmodern culture which crossed many academic disciplines (see Carpenter, chapter 7, for further discussion of constructivism). In the 1980s, also, Anderson and Goolishian (1988) in Texas; Boscolo and Checchin of Milan, Italy; Penn and Hoffman of the United States, who worked with the Milan group (Boscolo, Checchin, Hoffman, & Penn, 1987); and Tomm (1987) of Alberta, Canada, who had studied with the Milan group, all wrote about these newer constructivist approaches.

Clearly, something new was brewing in the therapy world, especially in family therapy. Hoffman, a social worker who is a prominent family therapist, has described the earlier swing of family therapists away from the emphasis on intrapsychic focus to systems views with emphasis on interpersonal processes and behavior, as now swinging back to more emphasis on ideas, beliefs, feelings, and myths (Hoffman, 1985). While systems approaches are based on cybernetic theory, a mechanistic theory of control which Hoffman (1985) declared has lost its usefulness, constructivist therapies are based on second-order cybernetics, which renders observations as dependent upon the observer. The systems theories, like the behavioral and cognitive approaches emerging in the same time period, were based on the modernist view of objectivity, rationality, and knowing through observation. The postmodern view, which has been embraced by scholars across many disciplines from art and literature to social sciences, on the other hand, recognizes the many realities and truths that coexist and sees reality as being socially constructed rather than given (Neimeyer, 1993).

RELATIONSHIPS TO OTHER THEORIES

Postmodern theory is a form of critique for some, while it is a contemporary experience for others (Lowe, 1991). The narrative approaches borrow from the constructivists in the field of literary criticism, where narratives are taken apart and analyzed for meaning, and from the social constructionists in the field of social psychology, where reality is viewed as coconstructed in the minds of individuals in interaction with other people and societal beliefs. Neimeyer characterizes constructivism as a "metatheory that emphasizes the self organizing and proactive features of human knowing" (1993, p. 221) and as a view of humans as "meaning making agents" (p. 222). The roots of constructivist therapies can be traced to many sources, especially George Kelly's Personal Construct Theory, first articulated in the 1950s (Kelly, 1955). Kelly himself cited semanticist Korzybski (1933), who was also drawn upon by cognitive (Ellis, 1962) and systems (Watzlawick, Weakland, & Jackson, 1967) therapists, and by Moreno (1937), who developed psychodrama. Constructivist therapy has been compared to cognitive therapy (Neimeyer, 1993) and to the systems approaches (Kelley, 1994, 1995), and its emphasis on meaning connects it to the existential approaches (see Krill, chapter 11). White and Epston (1990) state that they drew on the works of French philosopher and historian Michel Foucault (1980), as well as Jerome Bruner (1986) and Gregory Bateson (1972), in the development of their narrative therapy. It is interesting to note that the systems thinkers also drew heavily on Bateson. Narrative therapy, it seems, is a new paradigm for viewing human change in some respects, but in other ways it can be seen as evolving out of existing practice theories.

The narrative, postmodern approaches to practice can be useful for social workers, who, as noted by Scott (1989), search for the meanings of events and behaviors as preconditions for action. The emphasis on understanding and meaning is useful as we work with the diverse clients of today's practice. The implications of postmodernism for social work practice have been discussed by several social work scholars

(Gorman, 1993; Pardeck, Murphy, & Choi, 1994; Pozatek, 1994; Saleebey, 1994; Sands & Nuccio, 1992), and these approaches have been found useful for multicultural practice (Holland & Kilpatrick, 1993; Kelley, 1994; Waldegrave, 1990), persons facing adversity (Borden, 1992), family violence offenders (Jenkins, 1991), and multi-need families (Kelley, 1993). Wynne, Shields, and Sirkin (1992), although not social workers, have discussed the usefulness of these approaches in health care settings, an idea applied to social work in health care settings by Kelley and Clifford (1995).

BASIC ASSUMPTIONS

Knowledge is power, and self-knowledge can empower people. White and Epston (1990) believe that we all "story" our lives to make sense out of them. We cannot remember all of our lived experience; there is too much material and too many experiences unrelated to each other to retain it all, so our narrative structuring experience is a selective process. We arrange our lives into sequences and into dominant story lines to develop a sense of coherence and to ascribe meaning to our lives. As we develop our dominant story line, we remember events that support it and forget (White and Epston say "subjugate") other life experiences that do not fit into the dominant story line. Certain events may be imagined or exaggerated to fill in the gaps of a story. White and Epston's concept of subjugated knowledge is similar to the psychodynamic concept of unconscious, in that both refer to forgotten material. They are different, however, in that "subjugated knowledge" refers to life experiences that are not remembered because they do not fit into the dominant story, whereas the psychodynamic idea of unconscious refers to memories that are repressed because they are painful.

Narrative therapy is similar to postmodern literary criticism, where the story line is deconstructed as the plot, characters, and time line are reassessed for meaning. Many times, presenting problems of clients fall within the dominant story line, and often clients have authored problem-saturated stories of their lives. These stories limit the clients' views of themselves and others and can immobilize them from action. Their problem-saturated stories have been co-constructed with others around them, often family members, employers, social service workers, and other helpers. For example, social service agencies working to help multi-need families can do too much for them (Imber-Black, 1988), giving the message that they are incompetent, and their dominant narrative becomes that of a "multi-problem" or "dysfunctional" family. Similarly, Wynne, Shields, and Sirkin (1992) discuss how, for chronically ill people, the illness may become the dominant story line, as the family and professional helpers gradually become more involved with the patient, and the coconstructed reality is that the patient *is* the illness, as opposed to being afflicted with it. A goal of narrative therapy is to help the client see more realities, which offers more alternatives for them. As Neimeyer has noted (1993), such therapy is more creative than corrective and is more reflective and elaborative than persuasive or instructive.

ROLE OF SOCIAL WORKER/THERAPIST

As narrative therapy helps clients reauthor their lives through seeing other truths and other possible interpretations of events, the role of the therapist is to listen, wonder, and ask reflective questions. Clients are invited to assess other realities, which are not necessarily more true, but are also true. For most narrative therapists, the harsh realities of many clients' lives, such as poverty, racism, or violence, are not denied as just constructs of the mind, but the power given to these adverse events and the control they have over clients' lives are challenged. Questions are introduced which help the client assess other ways to view a situation, analyze for alternative meanings, and find other aspects of their lives, often involving strengths and coping, which may have been lost in the overfocus on problems. In this postmodern view, the therapist is not an outside objective observer, but is part of the change system and there is reciprocal influence between client and clinician. Thus, the therapist does not just hear the client's story, but co-creates it with the client, hopefully with the client creating some new stories. History is not a collection of facts to be remembered, but is created in the telling. The therapist's role is nonhierarchical, especially compared to either psychodynamic or systemic therapists. The therapist is not the expert on the problem or the client's life, the client is. The therapist takes a "not knowing" position (Anderson & Goolishian, 1988), which invites the client to do more exploring.

CULTURAL SENSITIVITY

Narrative therapy is culturally sensitive because it does not presume a way of being, but aims to understand the client's reality. the therapist listens for ways in which gender, culture, and social and economic context may shape the client's world view. The "not knowing" position (Anderson & Goolishian, 1988) is useful in this respect, too, as the therapist learns from the client. Waldegrave (1990), especially, has discussed ethnic-sensitive constructivist therapy, for as noted by Lowe (1991), these therapeutic discourses can encourage discussion of social justice, poverty, gender, and power. At the Family Centre in New Zealand, Waldegrave and colleagues have developed "just therapy" (meaning socially just), where therapists and clients together "weave webs of meaning" (Waldegrave, 1990, p. 10), where political as well as clinical responses are required, and where cross-cultural consultants are used on the therapy teams.

VIEW OF HUMAN NATURE

The view of humanity underlying this approach is that humans are complex and multifaceted. Underlying pathology is not presumed. Rather than listening for underlying "root causes," the social worker listens for underlying strengths which can be mobilized, for signs or signals of "exceptions" to the problems (de Shazer, 1991) which have often been ignored, or "unique outcomes" (White & Epston, 1990) which cannot be explained by the client's story, and for times when things have gone well. Here, similarities to solution-focused therapy of social workers Insoo Berg and Steve de Shazer (de Shazer, 1991) can be seen. Borden (1992) discusses the importance of helping the clients assess the past, experience the present, and anticipate the future as specific life experiences are incorporated into the ongoing life story. While attention is paid to the past, the focus is on helping the client not to be stuck in the past but to develop a progressive, forward-looking narrative.

Narrative therapists see the clients in context, that is, part of a cultural whole, where views of self and the world are co-constructed in interaction with cultural and societal norms. Clients are invited to assess the truths they have assumed, and to challenge views which have not been useful. In this way, they may empower themselves to work on their own behalf or for social change. Further, as needs are assessed with client and clinician working together, the client may be made aware of resources available and the clinician may suggest a referral. Making lists of referrals to solve problems, however, is not part of this approach.

In a sense, then, the clients become their own case managers, assessing their own needs and monitoring the services they receive. In this view, biological bases of some conditions are not denied, nor is the potential usefulness of psychotropic medications for some people. The diagnosis and treatment of medical conditions are not in the realm of social work treatment, however, and clients are encouraged to discuss such concerns with physicians. Clients on psychotropic medications are encouraged to develop a partnership relationship with the prescribing physicians, working together to fight the effects of the illness, rather than becoming passive recipients of treatment.

SOCIAL WORK TREATMENT

The goal of narrative treatment approaches in social work practice is for clients first to understand, and then to broaden and change, the stories around which they have organized their lives. This work may involve helping the client to challenge the problem-saturated dominant story as the only truth, and to find other aspects of his or her life which may also be true. The discovery of more realities and more truths can free clients to see more alternatives and ways out of an impasse. It can also help clients recognize and mobilize the strengths they already possess and are using, but may have ignored in the focus on problems.

Through dialogue between social worker and client, these problem-saturated stories are gradually deconstructed as the worker introduces questions that challenge the client's narrow view of reality or draw out facets of the client's life that have previously been ignored. Some constructivist and constructionist approaches offer little guidance to the worker or client and little structure to the process. The "down under" therapists from New Zealand and Australia (Jenkins, 1991; Waldegrave, 1990; White & Epston, 1990) offer a bit more structure, and they challenge not-useful stories more than many of their North American counterparts. All stories are not seen as equally useful.

The narrative model offered by White and Epston (1990) is helpful for teaching and for practice because it names specific practices and outlines stages of the process without being too prescriptive or technique driven. Constructivist therapists in general do not distinguish between the "assessment" and "treatment" stages of practice, for they view assessment as an ongoing and ever-changing process, in the hope that all sessions are therapeutic. All clinicians know, however, that there are some elements of the helping process which are more appropriate in earlier stages and some things more useful later in the process. For this reason, White and Epston's (1990) discussion of the stages of their narrative approach as "deconstruction" and "reconstruction" is useful.

DECONSTRUCTION STAGE

In the deconstruction stage, the clients' existing stories are heard and then deconstructed. Even here there are stages; it is important not to deconstruct the client's story too soon. Most people need to have their problem story heard before they can move to other areas. First, the clinician carefully listens to the client's story: What does he or she define as the presenting problem? How does the client experience it? What meaning is ascribed to it, and how is it viewed in light of historical events? This process is similar to the joining or relationship-building process of any good therapeutic endeavor. Asking questions to elicit the full meaning here is important. Who else is involved in this problem? What events in the past have contributed to its development? How did this problem evolve over time? What has been tried to fight the effects of the problem? How has this problem affected other aspects of the client's life? As in any good therapeutic encounter, the development of an empathic relationship is important. This empathy is important for developing trust, but is also important in helping the clinician understand the client's reality more fully. While the careful listening and reflecting is similar to most therapeutic approaches, the way the questions are worded is specific to the narrative approach.

Externalizing the problem, a key idea in this narrative therapy, begins in the joining stage and continues throughout the treatment process. The purpose of this externalization is to separate the person from the problem, to view it as not intrinsic to the person but as something that has interfered with the person's life and needs to be challenged. Thus, at the early stages, where the client's story is being heard and understood, the nature of the reflective questions gradually shifts the view as to where the problem resides. "When did you first notice that this depression began to interfere with your work?" "How did it happen that Andy's temper took over so much of his life? Who first noticed it? Who has been affected most by it?" It is important to distinguish between taking responsibility and viewing a problem as not intrinsic to the person. Clients are encouraged to take responsibility for fighting the effects of the problem and for their own behaviors.

Even the effects of physical illness can be externalized through questions about the effects of the illness on the person's life, and about the process by which it took on so much power over the person's life, and about how it has interfered with other aspects of the person's life, including relationships. As the client is able to separate from the problem, it becomes more manageable, and the problem, not the person, becomes the target for change. The client and therapist join together to fight the effects of the problem. At this early stage, even before deconstruction, the clinician listens carefully to the client's definition of the problem and begins to objectify the problem through the use of metaphors, through summary, and through the nature of the reflective questions.

The importance of language in shaping meaning has been discussed by many theorists and therapists over the years (Anderson & Goolishian, 1988; Bateson, 1972; Ellis, 1962; Grinder & Bandler, 1976; Watzlawick, Weakland, & Jackson, 1967), including narrative proponents. The way questions are worded is an important aspect of this work. White (1989) has described the way in which he helped a family with a twelve-year-old son with behavior problems to "escape from trouble." He asked family members to describe the ways in which John's problems had "plagued" his life and "influenced" their lives. White also asked the parents how they had coped with John's troubles and how they had become involved with them.

Narrative therapists, unlike those from several other schools, do not assume that the clients themselves "need" the problem or that it symbolizes a deeper problem, as do some psychodynamic therapists, nor do they believe that it "serves a function" for the family unit, as believed by some systemic proponents. It is assumed that clients want the problem solved or remediated, but that they have gotten stuck in finding ways to do so. Thus, words like "unmotivated" or "resistant" are not considered useful. This belief in the clients and what they say is very respectful, and thus consistent with social work values. While it is not presumed that clients need problems, it is recognized that they and family members and friends may have helped to maintain the problems, possibly through their efforts to solve them. Thus the influence questions are useful in bringing about discussion on that matter. For example, family members may be asked how they were recruited into and influenced by the client's problem.

After the first part of the deconstruction stage, where the clients' views are heard, understood, and acknowledged, the therapist gradually begins to help the client deconstruct the dominant story through continued summarizing and questioning. It is important to note here that the story is not disputed or seen as not true, for that would not be respectful and the client would not feel validated. Instead, the story is fully discussed and analyzed for meaning, and other interpretations and other meanings can be assessed, bringing about alternative truths which are also valid. At this point, the "relative influence" of the problem's effects on the individual or family is mapped across time and across spheres. How has this problem affected the client in the past, present, and anticipated future across intellectual, personal, interpersonal, and social spheres?

For example, in the White case of helping the family "escape from trouble" mentioned above, it became clear through discussion that John's "trouble" had interfered with his life at school, academically and with classmates, and at home in his relationship with his parents. In addition, the problems had "crept into" his parents' lives and affected their relationship with each other as well as their own work productivity. Ways in which the "trouble" had caused guilt in John and feelings of helplessness in his parents were discussed. Questions were introduced to John regarding what would happen if he were to further "succumb" to trouble, and to his parents about what might be the possible effects of their continued participation in the problem. Should they accept John's invitation to join him in participating in trouble or should they renounce it and escape from it? This very careful dissection of the effects of the problem across all spheres of life and the assessment of what might happen in the future if it is allowed to dominate challenge the family to find new ways to handle the problem. The clients can now work with the clinician to explore ways to defend themselves against the effects of the problem and to fight it when necessary. Since the problem is externalized, the client does not need to defend himself or herself to the clinician, but can join with the clinician to find ways to defend against this problem which is interfering with his or her life.

As the problem stories are gradually deconstructed through a dialogue between client and clinician, the clinician obtains a full history of the problem. The clients discuss events that they believe led up to the problem's formation. Not only the events, but the thoughts, beliefs, and social interactions around the events, are assessed for influence in the past, present, and possible future. Clients might be asked to ponder how the same events may have been viewed by others, or even how they might view it themselves if they were not involved. For example, a victim of childhood abuse may have blamed herself or himself, but may now begin to see that being a child and in a helpless position may have had some bearing on the situation. Alternative futures are also discussed: How would it be if things were different and who would do what? Who would first notice the difference? What would a better future look like? Here, again, similarities to de Shazer's (1991) solution-focused therapy may be noted. This "visioning" of a desired future helps clients begin to think about ways in which they might get there.

RECONSTRUCTION STAGE

In the second stage, the reconstruction stage, other truths are found which are also true but may have been subjugated because they did not fit into the dominant theme. It is a knowledge-expanding, more than knowledge-changing, experience. This subjugated knowledge is brought out through careful listening for "unique outcomes" (White & Epston, 1990) as clients tell their stories. These are events or outcomes that cannot be explained by the dominant story. For example, a man has described his problem as being a bully, stating that he has always been mean and has had a temper problem most of his life. How it has interfered with his relationships with peers and colleagues as a child and as an adult and how it has caused a breakup of his marriage (the precipitating problem) and interfered with his relationship with his children are discussed. How it has also hurt himself, causing feelings of guilt and lowered self-esteem, is also examined. Looking to the future, he sees a lonely existence if this problem continues to dominate his life. It is important to obtain his view of this situation, not to assume that this is bad behavior (even if it is) which he wants to stop (he may not). The purpose of helping him to separate from the problem is not to alleviate him from responsibility for his actions, but to help him assess its effects on self and others, make a decision as to what he wants to do about it, and then develop ways to manage and control it (the problem). In fact, responsibility was implied here as the client was asked about how this temper had taken over his life, and how he had let this happen.

Here the unique outcomes were not easy to find at first, but careful listening helped to uncover some. If he is such a "tough guy," where did he find the gentleness to visit his grandmother in a nursing home? How was he able to muster enough caring to take care of his dog so well? Again, the similarities to de Shazer's (1991) solution-focused therapy can be seen, but instead of asking for "exceptions," which the client may not see, the therapist carefully sorts through the conversation in a detectivelike manner, to find the evidence. Just as the dominant story has been deconstructed to find who was involved in the construction of the tough guy identity, now the client is asked to think about who may have helped him develop this gentler side. Gradually, a discussion of a relationship with a caring grandfather is brought out, and a gentle but manly teacher is also remembered. In addition, the cultural message in the media of needing to be tough to be a man is also compared to the conflicting social message about the honorable gentleman treating women and children well. Knowing there is another side to him helps the client find ways to fight the effects (i.e., his problem-causing behavior) of the tough side, but allows him to keep aspects of that side, while exploring and developing other aspects of himself, such as the gentle side.

In another situation, a family that was viewed by others in the community as well as themselves as being a poor and "out of control" family, with "violent" adolescent boys, was challenged in this narrow definition of itself. They began to see they are also a resourceful family that has coped with poverty and has found a way for mother to be home with the young children by day and earn some money holding an evening job by having the adolescent boys baby-sit after school. This discussion also challenged the "violent boys" idea, although the fact that they acted violently in school sometimes was not ignored. Seeing other aspects of themselves did help them to see that they had alternatives as to which side of themselves they wanted to develop and in which situations. Here, the social worker did not tell the boys what they must do, but helped them see the options. Both the family and the school reported a marked decrease in violent behavior over the school year.

In another example, a social worker in a coping skills group for chronic pain patients helped the patients find ways in which they were already coping with the illness and see that there were times when they could fight the effects of the illness and when the pain was not as bad. At first most of the patients believed the pain was always there and there was nothing they could ever do. Through careful listening by the worker and each other, they found that there were times when things were better and they all found ways in which they were already coping (Kelley & Clifford, 1995). The illness was externalized by the social worker asking them, "if this illness were a member of the family, how would you treat it?" The group members began to discuss this question with great interest. Some found ways they would fight the illness and reject it, while others said that since it was there to stay they would look for ways to accommodate it and learn to live with it. The social worker did not teach them how to cope, but instead, through careful listening, times when the patients were already coping were identified, challenging the view that they were totally help-less.

At this reconstruction stage, then, the clients are helped to reconstruct their views of reality by making it broader, not different. A depressed woman, who remembers her childhood as one deprived of maternal touching because her mother was criti-cally ill when she was a child and died when the client was eleven, was asked if she remembered any times that her mother had the time and energy to touch her. The client remembered her mother combing her hair every day and how good it felt. The tragedy of her mother being so sick that she only did tasks required to be the mini-mum "good mother" was never minimized, but the client was also helped to remem-ber other aspects of her childhood. She reports that she finds it comforting, when depressed now, to think about how good it felt when her mother combed her hair. Dolan (1991), in her work with sexual abuse survivors, has noted that having these clients tell their stories over and over can revictimize them if corrective experiences are not infused into the process. Helping clients broaden their life stories, rather than "polishing" their problem-saturated stories, is a corrective experience.

Length of Treatment

Because of the philosophical nature of constructivist approaches to treatment, it is of-ten assumed that the process is a long-term one, and questions have been raised about how such a long process can be applicable in today's social work practice arena. An interesting aspect of the narrative approach of White and Epston (1990) is that they use relatively few sessions, often as few as six or seven, although there is no set idea as to number. Clients are usually asked at the end of each session if they would like to return, and if so, how soon. Unlike some constructivist therapists, narrative thera-pists may ask the clients to do some activities between sessions. For example, in helping the family and boy "escape from trouble," already discussed, White (1989) encouraged the family to plan escape meetings where all the family members re-viewed the progress of their flight from escape. The meetings were formal in struc-ture and even had minutes taken.

While the number of sessions are usually few, they are usually spread out over a longer time period than every week, to give the family time to think about and try new things. With families, especially, playful ideas and metaphors are used in asking them to try new things. In addition to asking members to try something different be-tween sessions, White uses many forms of writing to expand the impact of each ses-sion. He often uses "therapeutic letters" to clients from the therapist between sessions which summarize his notes as to how he heard the client describe the prob-lem and also record any solution knowledge obtained in the session. The therapist re-quests client corrections, deletions, and additions to make the statements more accurate. Clients report that each letter is worth about four sessions (White, 1992). While some might question the time involved in this process, these letters can also be used as case notes. White also finds taking notes in session helpful, not distracting, and he uses these notes to read statements back to clients to check for accuracy. Other forms of writing may also add to the value of sessions, too, such as client writing to self or therapist, art or poetry, or charts and checklists (Kelley, 1990). White and Epston use certificates and documents, such as an "Escape from Guilt Certificate" (1990, p. 199), or a "Diploma of Special Knowledge" (p. 201), which are especially useful with children.

White (1992) also reports other strategies he used to reduce the number of sessions but expand their power. In addition to the letters and documents, he may have "ceremonies of redefinition" (e.g., parties for children) where the victory over the problem is celebrated, or he may encourage the family to use "consultants," who are people in the clients' lives whom they can talk to for enlightenment about a problem or solution. He also reports that his use of "reflecting teams," discussed in the training section of this chapter, extends the impact of each session.

PRINCIPAL APPLICATIONS IN SOCIAL WORK PRACTICE

As can be seen from the above discussion, a primary application of narrative work has been in family therapy and social work with families. As with the systems approaches, the focus on interaction between people makes narrative approaches especially useful with couples and families. However, it is also beneficial in work with individuals and its usefulness in group work has been explored (Kelley & Clifford, 1995). While rarely addressed in the literature, the use of narrative approaches in community work seems plausible. In fact, at the Family Therapy Centre in Auckland, New Zealand, community work and social action go hand in hand with the family therapy in Waldegrave's "just therapy" (1990). Waldegrave is not a social worker, but his emphasis on social justice is very much in the tradition of social work.

POTENTIAL PROBLEMS AND COUNTERINDICATIONS

While there is a wide range of applications of narrative-type approaches in social work, some questions have been raised regarding their use with specific populations. Some might fear that the deemphasis on "reality" and the focus away from the problem story together could minimize the clients' problems, especially in cases of sexual abuse or family violence. This is a real problem if the social worker deconstructs the story too quickly or denies the client's reality, but should not be problematic if the client is carefully listened to and attended. In a related concern, some might see this approach as superficial because it does not get at "root" causes or underlying pathology in deeply disturbed individuals. Since these ideas do not fall within the constructs of postmodern theory, narrative therapists would not see such concerns as relevant. Some social workers might fear that the process of externalization could reduce a perpetrator's responsibility for violence or other crimes. White and Epston (1990, p. 65) speak directly to this matter and note that helping people separate from the problem and assessing it objectively can help them assume more responsibility for it. Social workers and other professionals express the idea that talking is not enough for some clients, that concrete services and possibly even medication may be required for the amelioration of some problems facing clients. Narrative therapists agree and believe that their approach can facilitate complementary services. Finally, there is a practical concern that without the use of labels, cross-disciplinary discussion may be impeded and that reimbursement for services may be denied. These are concerns to ponder and are not completely solvable. It should also be noted that labels may not have to be discarded in some situations, but the power given the labels can be challenged.

Because the narrative approaches are relatively new and there is so little research, it is difficult to say at this time which populations may or may not be well served by this approach. While narrative therapists report case studies with successful outcomes with a range of clients, future work needs to be aimed at isolating those clients best served by such approaches. The questions raised about their usefulness with some perpetrators of violence and with substance abusers need to be more fully addressed. In addition, care needs to be taken in externalizing problems with persons experiencing serious emotional problems, who may already have trouble differentiating between themselves and outside forces.

ADMINISTRATIVE AND TRAINING FACTORS

Narrative therapy is used mainly by clinical social workers, family therapists, and psychologists all of whom have graduate degrees. It involves more than story telling; it involves story changing through intensive listening and questioning in a specific manner, which is usually learned in special post-degree training. The "conscious use of self" and transference/countertransference issues discussed by psychodynamic social workers is also considered important by narrative social workers, although they many not use those terms. Narrative social workers need to be very clear about their own issues, views, and experiences, to separate them from those of the clients. Since the client's history and reality are coconstructed through dialogue, the social worker can not be an outside observer but is part of the change system through reciprocity. Great care must be taken to hear and understand the client's reality, and to individualize each client. Thus, there is no set of techniques or prescriptions; each client is viewed differently and treatment involves whatever fits his or her particular situation. A great deal of self-awareness and willingness to set aside one's own world view is required to work in such a manner.

Although narrative approaches are beginning to be infused into the academic social work curriculum (Kelley, 1995), most training has been conducted at family therapy training centers or at select social service agencies. Training and supervision in this approach are usually carried out through the use of the reflecting teams, which are also part of the therapeutic process for clients. This reflecting-team idea was first developed by Andersen in Norway (1987) and involves team members behind a one-way mirror "trading places" with the family at some point in the interview and reflecting back their ideas through discussion about what they thought they heard the family say. This reflection by outside persons encourages deeper discussion by the family members. Through serving on the reflecting teams, trainees learn to focus their listening, and they learn to discover unique outcomes. If the trainees do not hear the clients accurately, it is the clients themselves who point that out to them. After the family listens to the reflecting team's discussion, they trade places again and they discuss their ideas as to what they heard the team members say. Trainees can learn by being on either side of the mirror, and the teacher can teach from either side, and through subsequent discussions after the sessions. White reports (1992) that most of his clients say that these teams also reduce the number of sessions needed, by increasing the impact of each session. The family members must, of course, give permission for the team to observe them and they may request to meet them first. Even though these teams reduce the number of sessions needed by a client, the number of therapists required usually means this can only be practiced where there are trainees to serve this function. Thus, the case vignette that follows is written by team members of a family therapy training unit in a community mental health center, where reflecting teams are used. The author's own cases are noted throughout this chapter, but the following case example is used to demonstrate the reflecting team as an integral part of treatment and training.

CASE VIGNETTE: THE SMITH FAMILY

Case presented by Patricia Hayek, MSW, LSW, and Stephen Trefz, MSW, LSW, Mid-Eastern Iowa Community Mental Health Center, Iowa City, Iowa.

Ms. Smith called the Community Mental Health Center wanting help to reunify her family. She had two daughters, Rachel, twelve years of age, and Betty, ten years of age. Rachel was currently in foster care. Ms. Smith, who is divorced from the girls' abusive father, reported that Rachel had been removed from the home due to violent outbursts against Betty and Ms. Smith. Ms. Smith stated that both she and Betty are afraid of Rachel, who has a long history of therapy and seven out-of-home placements to treat her symptoms of aggression and depression. The initial goal of therapy, therefore, was to learn more about what was keeping this family in an "uproar" and to discern what close ties do exist.

The family was offered the opportunity to work with the Center's Family Therapy Team. The process of working with a team of therapists using a one-way mirror and the idea of a reflecting team were explained. The family accepted the offer to work in this manner. At the intake appointment, the family was introduced to the team and had an opportunity to inspect the observation room. The team consisted of five therapists: two primary therapists (PT) working with the family, and three trainees who were members of the reflecting team (RT) behind the mirror. The family talked about their concerns for forty to fifty minutes before taking a break to listen to the reflections. At this point, the reflecting team came into the room and discussed the situation with each other while the family and primary therapists sat in the room and listened. Then, the team went behind the mirror again while the family and therapists discussed the reflections for another fifteen minutes.

The first two sessions with the family consisted of refereeing intense, aggressive physical and verbal arguments between the siblings and their mother. Containing the two girls' aggressive behavior became paramount. Stories of abuse and violence began to emerge including: domestic violence, verbal abuse, physical fights between siblings, out-of-control children, and an overwhelmed mother who had recently begun to reclaim her life after divorcing her abusive husband. Other themes that began to develop were ideas about good and bad children, comparing Rachel to the abusive father, and Rachel in turn defending her father. The primary therapists working with the family began asking questions to understand how the family experienced these problems and what meaning they ascribed to them. They also asked questions to reveal and clarify the many realities constructed by this family. The dominant story included fear, violence, abuse, lack of respect, criticism, hopelessness, and resignation to out-of-control lives. Questions were also asked to determine:

1. Who else was involved in the construction of the story? Example: How did Dad fit into all of this? Who would agree/disagree? Who else needs to be included when we talk about your family?
2. What events contributed to its development? Example: Martha (Ms. Smith), how did your divorce affect the story of your family?
3. How did this story developed over time? Example: What was it like before? Has there always been fighting in your family? When wasn't there fighting? What has occurred in your family since you made the appointment?
4. What had been tried to counter the effects of this story on themselves and the family?

EXAMPLE

How have you stood up to violence in your family? How have you been able to resist violence's invitation to hurt one another? (Note the externalization of violence.) These questions were asked to explore alternatives meanings and to create space for nondominant themes and stories to emerge. After the second chaotic session, the reflecting team made the following comments:

RTMember #1: I'm wondering what the girl's behavior means.
RTM#2: I was wondering that also. I was wondering what they are trying to say. Are they trying to say things that can't be said in this family? I'm wondering what can and can't be talked about.
RTM#3: What could be so hard to express that they could find no words for it? I wonder who might be the first to make some attempts at using some words instead of hurtful behavior.

RTM#2: How would it be for this family not to fight and spar? Would it be boring? Is fighting better than not talking?

RTM#1: I saw Rachel show lots of different emotions and one of them seemed to be sadness. What do you think that sadness was about?

RTM#3: I heard a lot about Rachel's father from Martha and her description sounded pretty brutal. I was wondering how that was for Rachel to hear. I would be interested in hearing other perspectives on Dad and what would need to happen for those alternative descriptions to be heard.

RTM#2: Yeah, I was thinking about the comparison that Martha makes about Rachel and Dad. Are there other ways they're similar other than the swearing and fighting?

RTM#1: Do you mean, "Did Rachel get some of those 'good' qualities from her dad like loyalty and defending the family against outsiders?"

RTM#2: Yes, exactly.

The post-reflection discussion by the family revealed that Rachel's father, although an alcoholic who was abusive to Ms. Smith, was also a good provider to the family and a caring father in some ways. Ms. Smith was encouraged to pay attention between sessions to positive qualities that Rachel displayed that could be attributed to her father. The family was also encouraged to pay attention to the times when they stood up to abuse and did not let it overpower their interactions.

In looking for differences and times when the family was not chaotic, the family reported that they were calmer and more respectful of each other when the maternal grandfather was present. The mother reported that she felt more confident and competent and that her daughters behaved themselves in his presence. The team was intrigued by this difference and wanted to learn more about the grandfather's effect on the family. To experience it themselves, they asked the family members if they would be willing to invite him to the next session. They agreed.

The following session was markedly different when the grandfather accompanied his daughter and granddaughters. Ms. Smith and her daughters were dressed and groomed better than before. There was less verbal sparring, and conversation was not interrupted by verbal or physical outbursts. During this session more information was gathered about the now-deceased maternal grandmother, and about how Ms. Smith was raised. The grandfather was given an opportunity to describe his granddaughters and to describe his daughter when she young. The girls spoke about their memories of their grandmother and Ms. Smith remembered her childhood fights with her brothers. No effort had to be exerted in controlling Rachel and Betty from destructive behavior.

REFLECTIONS #2

RTM#1:   I felt I was at a family reunion hearing this family talking about the old days. I heard the grandfather and Martha talk about how she and her brothers fought when they were young and I wondered how those fights were resolved.

RTM#2:   I wondered how Martha and the girls felt today. They interacted differently when the grandfather was present. I wonder if Pat and Stephen [primary therapists] felt the difference?

RTM#3:   It seemed as though the grandfather was so flexible today. He always had something good to say about someone. What effect do you think his comments had on today's conversations?

RTM#1:   Everyone seemed to enjoy themselves today as they reminisced about past events. I felt today's meeting was much different from last time. I wonder if it was different for the family.

RTM#3:   Rachel got so animated talking about her grandmother.

RTM#2:   Rachel also began to cry when they were talking about Grandma.

RTM#3:   Rachel showed a soft spot when others discussed sad events. Do you think others noticed this softness? What do you think would help increase softness in this family? Is it okay to be soft?

POST-REFLECTION DISCUSSION

The family agreed that the session was much calmer and enjoyable. They also were perplexed about why that occurred. A variety of hunches were offered by the family and the therapists. A consensus began to form that it had to do with the respect and validation that was exhibited by the grandfather. Martha and her daughters agreed that they would look for ways to show the same respect to one another at home as they did during the session in the grandfather's presence.

FOLLOW-UP

The family has been seen five more times over the next six months. While Rachel is still in placement, there is work toward reunification (requiring close work with other social agencies). There is less fighting and more open discussion in this family now. In these discussions, some good traits of the father have been acknowledged, but the reasons why the mother could not stay in that relationship have also been discussed more fully.

EMPIRICAL BASE

Very little empirical research has been conducted testing narrative approaches. Postmodernism, by definition, denies the possibility of objectivity, which is at the core of empiricism. For this reason, postmodern approaches have been criticized for keeping social work out of the scientific field where it should be placed (Epstein, 1995). While constructivists are uncomfortable with the assumption of linear relationships among variables needed for most statistical procedures, Neimeyer (1993), a psychologist, has pointed out that there are several research methods that are appropriate to assess outcomes in constructivist psychotherapy. He notes several examples, including the use of repertory grids, transcript analysis of developmental levels, task analysis of change events, stochastic modeling, and time series studies. He also notes, as have others, that more conversational ways of inquiry and of understanding personal meanings need to be explored, too. He stresses the need for diverse approaches to research for fuller understanding. Ethnographic qualitative research approaches and transcript analysis have been found useful in studying constructivist approaches (Kelley & Clifford, 1995; Rigazio-DiGilio & Ivey, 1991), and White and Epston (1990) and others use the case study method in assessing outcome, noting symptom relief in clients. Finding new ways of measuring outcomes in narrative therapy and then conducting more research on these newer approaches are important directions for the future.

PROSPECTUS

The postmodern approaches to social treatment which have become so prominent in the family therapy movement are relevant for and are becoming utilized by social workers. Because this theory is part of a cross-disciplinary trend, and because the approaches are useful with a wide variety of clients, this trend is likely to grow. More research will need to be conducted and new ways of conducting research will need to be found, however, before these approaches are fully accepted in the profession. Social worker and family therapists Hoffman (1990) has expressed the hope that this movement will facilitate a return of therapy as an art of conversation as opposed to a pseudo-scientific activity. She also expressed beliefs that the aesthetic metaphors are "closer to home" than the biological or machine metaphors, as we work with our clients, and she expressed the hope that these metaphors will also create an "emancipatory dialogue" (p. 11) that is socially and politically sensitive to our clients' needs. Indeed, the aim of narrative approaches of understanding and individualizing each client in his or her social context, and the emphasis on mobilizing strengths, is in the best tradition of the social work profession.

REFERENCES

Andersen, T.C. (1987). The reflecting team: Dialogue and metadialogue in clinical work. *Family Process, 26,* 415–428.

Anderson, H., & Goolishian, H.A. (1988). Human systems as linguistic systems: Preliminary and evolving ideas about the implications for clinical theory. *Family Process, 27,* 371–393.

Bateson, G. (1972). *Steps to an ecology of mind.* New York: Ballantine.

Borden, W. (1992). Narrative perspectives in psychological intervention following adverse life events. *Social Work, 37*(2), 135–141.

Boscolo, L., Cecchin, G., Hoffman, L., & Penn, P. (1987). *Milan systemic family therapy.* New York: Basic Books.

Bruner, J. (1986). *Actual minds, possible worlds.* Cambridge, MA: Harvard University Press.

Cowley, G., & Springen, K. (1995, April 17). Rewriting life stories. *Newsweek,* 70–74.

de Shazer, S. (1991). *Putting difference to work.* New York: W.W. Norton.

Dolan, Y.M. (1991). *Resolving sexual abuse: Solution focused therapy and Ericksonian hypnosis for adult survivors.* New York: W.W. Norton.

Ellis, A. (1962). *Reason and emotion in psychotherapy.* New York: Stuart Press.

Epstein, W.M. (1995). Social work in the university. *Journal of Social Work Education, 31*(2) 281–293.

Foucault, M. (1980). *Power/knowledge: Selected interviews and other writings.* New York: Pantheon Books.

Gorman, J. (1993). Postmodernism and the conduct of inquiry in social work. *Affilia, 8*(3), 247–264.

Grinder, J., & Bandler, R. (1976). *The structure of magic II.* Palo Alto, CA: Science and Behavior Books.

Hoffman, L. (1985). Beyond power and control: Toward a "second-order" family systems therapy. *Family Systems Medicine, 3,* 381–396.

Hoffman, L. (1990). Constructing realities: An art of lenses. *Family Process, 29,* 1–12.

Holland, T., & Kilpatrick, A. (1993). Using narrative techniques to enhance multicultural practice. *Journal of Social Work Education, 29*(3), 302–308.

Imber-Black, I. (1988). *Families and larger systems.* New York: Guilford Press.

Jenkins, A. (1991). *Invitation to responsibility: The therapeutic engagement of men who are violent and abusive.* Adelaide, S.A.: Dulwich Centre Publishing.

Kelley, P. (Ed.) (1990). *Uses of writing in psychotherapy.* New York: Haworth Press.

Kelley, P. (1993). Constructivist therapy: Getting beyond the victim stance. In *Empowering families* (juried papers from 6th Annual Conference) (pp. 173–180). Cedar Rapids IA: National Association for Family Based Services.

Kelley, P. (1994). Integrating systemic and post systemic approaches in social work with refugee families. *Families in Society, 75*(9), 541–549.

Kelley, P. (1995). Integrating narrative approaches into clinical curriculum: Addressing diversity through understanding. *Journal of Social Work Education, 31,* 3.

Kelley, P., & Clifford, P. (1995). Coping with chronic pain: Assessing narrative approaches. Paper delivered at The First International Conference on Social Work in Health and Mental Health, Hebrew University, Jerusalem, Israel, Jan. 25, 1995.

Kelly, G. A. (1955). *The psychology of personal constructs* (Vols. 1&2). New York: W.W. Norton.

Korzybski, A. (1933). *Science and sanity* (4th ed.). Lakeville, CT: The International Non-Aristotelian Library Publishing Company.

Lowe, R. (1991). Postmodern themes and therapeutic practices. *Dulwich Centre Newsletter, 3,* 41–52. Adelaide, S.A.: Dulwich Centre Publishing.

Moreno, J.L. (1937). Inter-personal therapy and the psychopathology of interpersonal relationships. *Sociometry, 1,* 9–76.

Neimeyer, R.A. (1993). An appraisal of constructivist psychotherapies. *Journal of Consulting and Clinical Psychology, 61*(2), 221–234.

Pardeck, J.T., Murphy, J.W., & Choi, J.M. (1994). Some implications of postmodernism for social work practice. *Social Work, 39*(4), 343–346.

Pozatek, E. (1994). The problem of certainty: Clinical social work in the postmodern era. *Social Work, 39*(4), 396–401.

Rigazio-DiGilio, S.A., & Ivey, A.E. (1991). Developmental counseling and therapy: A framework for individual and family treatment. *Counseling and Human Development, 24,* 1–20.

Saleebey, D. (1994). Culture, theory, and narrative: The intersection of meanings in practice. *Social Work, 39*(4), 351–359.

Sands, R. & Nuccio, K. (1992). Postmodern feminist theory and social work. *Social Work, 37*(6), 489–494.

Scott, D. (1989). Meaning construction and social work practice. *Social Service Review, 63,* 39–51.

Tomm, K. (1987). Interventive interviewing: Part II, Reflective question as a means to enable self healing. *Family Process, 26,* 167–184.

Waldegrave, C. (1990). Social justice and family therapy. *Dulwich Centre Newsletter, 1,* 6–46. Adelaide, S.A.: Dulwich Centre Publishing.

Watzlawick, P., Weakland, J.H., & Jackson, D.D. (1967). *Pragmatics of human communication.* New York: W.W. Norton.

White, M. (1989). Family escape from trouble. *Selected Papers, 1*(1), 59–63. Adelaide, S.A.: Dulwich Centre Publishing.

White, M. (1992). The re-authoring of lives and relationships. A workshop presentation, Iowa City, IA, Oct. 5–6, 1992.

White, M., & Epston, D. (1990). *Narrative means to therapeutic ends.* New York: W.W. Norton.

Wynne, L.C., Shields, C.G., & Sirkin, M.I. (1992). Illness, family theory, and family therapy: Conceptual issues. *Family Process, 31*(1), 3–18.

CHAPTER 20

NEUROLINGUISTIC PROGRAMMING THEORY AND SOCIAL WORK TREATMENT

G. BRENT ANGELL

OVERVIEW

OVERVIEW OF THEORY

Neurolinguistic programming (NLP) is a modern theory of counseling and psychotherapy that uses communication to understand and change human behavior. For social workers, NLP provides a unique, sense-making way of understanding the helping process that is useful in conducting assessments, building rapport, and facilitating client development. Focusing on the individual's subjective experience, NLP frames human behavior in terms of how the client receives, interprets, and transmits sensory stimuli. Often described as a model rather than a theory of practice, NLP is concerned with the patterns of verbal and nonverbal communication of feelings and behaviors.

NLP is an approach geared to the practice of therapy and not to the theory of practice. This differs dramatically from the practice theories that are interested in trying to understand the reasoning behind human feelings and behavior. The dynamism of NLP lies in the fact that it can be used as a stand-alone practice approach or incorporated with other theories of practice used by social workers (Field, 1990; House, 1994; Ignoffo, 1994; Mercier & Johnson, 1984). In essence, NLP is the epitome of what an interlocking theoretical perspective should be.

HISTORICAL ORIGINS

NLP has undergone a transformation since its conception by Bandler and Grinder and others in the early 1970s (Dilts, 1976; Lankton, 1980). Originally hailed as a

480

model of practice that could be used on its own or in conjunction with other practice approaches, NLP seemed to have fallen out of vogue by the late 1980s. Internal difficulties within the NLP camp, skeptical conservatism on the part of the established psychotherapeutic elite, and the expense and rigor of training did little to promote the approach as an acceptable mainstream practice model (Clancy & Yorkshire, 1989). However, the "quick fix" promises made by the model's proponents kept the embers of NLP glowing in the psychotherapeutic hearth. In fact, practitioners from a variety of fields continue to advocate the use of NLP due to its unique framework for understanding human behavior and effective intervention techniques. Experience has shown that NLP is helpful in dealing with a wide range of intrapsychic and interpersonal problems encountered in clinical treatment (Andreas, 1992; Field, 1990; House, 1994). Many of the concepts and techniques of NLP have been merged with other approaches whose devotees are committed to time-limited, cost-effective, efficient, client-empowering, technique-driven approaches (Ignoffo, 1994).

NLP focuses on awareness and change in the here and now. Steeped in psychology, philosophy, transformational grammar, and cybernetics, NLP has had a broad influence on the helping professions, education, and business. The originators of NLP minutely examined the patterns of communication of prominent psychotherapists, focusing on what they did that worked rather than on the theories themselves.

Bandler and Grinder were initially influenced in the development of NLP by their studies of Chomsky's (1957) transformational grammar explanation of language formation (Bradley & Biedermann, 1985). In addition, Edmund Husserl's phenomenological conceptualization of real versus perceived human experience and its parallels in psychologist Wilhelm Wundt's notion of the conscious "outworks of the mind" vis-à-vis the deeper, hidden unconscious levels aroused Bandler and Grinder's interest in the importance of subjective experience as it is perceived and transformed into communication by the individual.

With this as a backdrop, Bandler and Grinder systematically went about analyzing the work of such famous practitioners as experiential family therapist Virginia Satir; Gestalt's Fritz Perls; metaphor-based hypnotherapist Milton Erikson; and cybernetic anthropologist Gregory Bateson. The fruits of these endeavors led Bandler and Grinder and their contemporaries to a new understanding of the intricacies of human communication as played out in psychotherapy. In turn, they synthesized this knowledge into a technologically based approach to practice that brought about quick and profound behavioral change through communication modification.

PATH INTO SOCIAL WORK

NLP is a blend of therapy, hypnosis, linguistics, and positive thinking that has been used across disciplines by practitioners seeking new ways of understanding and providing treatment. NLP is attractive to social workers because its principles are closely aligned with the values of the profession, including the transmission of knowledge and skills, appreciation of difference, and client empowerment. The model's allure also lies in its brief solution-focused approach. Today's reduced client-contact time frame fits with what NLP has to offer to both service consumers and providers. In addition, NLP's focus on communication rather than pathology has applicability to all interpersonal practice situations.

From a social work perspective, the association of Bandler and Grinder and their cohorts with some of the key players in modern psychotherapy entices many to the approach. In particular, NLP's liaison with Virginia Satir, a social worker and family therapist, brough significant attention to the model. However, the enduring aspect of NLP appears to be its compatibility with many existing theories of practice representing diverse specialties and disciplines.

MacLean (1986), Zastrow (1995), Zastrow, Dotson, and Koch (1987), and Zastrow and Kirst (1994) devote particular attention to the application of NLP to social work practice by providing essential information on the model and its strategies. More relevant, perhaps, is the growing trend to provide "skills lab" training to social work interns prior to or in conjunction with their field practicum. Ivey's (1994) work on intentional interviewing and counseling, for example, draws extensively on NLP for its intervention framework and is used across disciplines (including social work) as a basic skills and methods training text. Ivey's fundamental premise is to examine "what works" in the therapeutic process in a systematic way that facilitates the development of competencies in assessment, intervention, and outcome. It is obvious that Ivey has been significantly influenced by NLP and the approach's utility in skills building from a multicultural perspective. In a similar vein, Cournoyer (1996), a social work educator, has developed a widely used skills training manual that draws upon the works of Ivey and Bandler and Grinder (1979, 1982) in the development of a conceptual framework. This text provides social workers with a solid base for beginning practice that employs many of the fundamental skill-building concepts inherent in NLP. This emphasis on skill building, founded on concepts and methods borrowed from NLP, ensures that beginning social workers will invariably be exposed to some of the main tenets of this model.

In summary, it is NLP's flexibility that attracts social workers. The model's inclusion of and compatibility with other treatment approaches is what holds their fascination.

BASIC ASSUMPTIONS

PRESUPPOSITIONS OF NEUROLINGUISTIC PROGRAMMING

NLP is founded on comprehending the three-stage process by which human beings receive and send information, that is, communicate. First, by way of sights, sounds, feelings, tastes, and smells, experience is received from the environment and subsequently processed by the individual (neuro). Second, sensory information is interpreted, sorted, and transformed into a meaningful and communicable format (linguistic). Finally, prior to transmission, verbal and nonverbal communication is organized by the individual to ensure the greatest probability of success in securing preferred ends (programming) (Zastrow, 1995).

INTERNAL RESOURCES

Embodying the practice axiom of "starting where the client is," NLP conceptualizes the therapeutic relationship from the perspective of the client's worldview. The model holds the individual's perspective on experience to be paramount over that of others, including the attending social worker. Using a strengths perspective, NLP assumes that the client has or can create the internal resources necessary to get his or her needs met (Yapko, 1984). What may be problematic, from the client's perspective, is that certain behaviors or strategies that have adequately met needs in the past may prove insufficient in meeting the challenges of the present. In these instances, particular difficulties are framed in terms of the individual's having a limited repertoire of choices available to meet his or her goals rather than by "blaming the victim" and citing personal deficiency. The objective of social workers employing NLP, therefore, is to assist the client in identifying or generating internal resources that would permit him or her to author a greater range of options and thereby increase his or her likelihood of achieving desired behavioral outcomes (Ivey, 1994; MacLean, 1986; Pesut, 1991).

SENSITIVITY TO DIFFERENCE

By nature, the approach's subjective focus on personal communication is sensitive to individual and, consequently, cultural difference. Linguistic variation, which is central to an individual's personal and cultural distinctiveness, is accounted for in NLP by focusing on the client's unique interpretation and communication of experience. Eye contact, voice tone, body language, and accent are just a few examples of how people differ between and within cultural groups. By approaching understanding in this way, social workers can attend to variations at an individual and cultural level. In so doing, they journey with the client in seeking out, in a culturally intentional fashion, an array of possible alternatives, options, and choices instead of looking for the mythical "right" response (Ivey, 1994; Ivey, et al., 1993; Sandhu et al., 1993).

DEEP AND SURFACE STRUCTURE

NLP views personality as a linguistic transformation achieved through a synthesis of the individual's language, acts, and mannerisms originating from a blending of subjective experience, imagination, and memory. Each person naturally gleans from experience a complete range of sensory-based data and carries within, at an unconscious level, the "deep structure" of his or her experience. What is made available to the conscious self or "surface structure," however, is a distillation of this sensory information. Context and need result in the individual's editing his or her rendition of experience into patterned responses by distorting, deleting, and generalizing deep structure information to make it fit his or her surface structure needs (Bandler & Grinder, 1975).

NLP defines distortions as representations of reality wherein the original meaning has been altered from the deep structure to fit desired surface structure needs. Deletions are defined as the removal of segments of the deep structure, making them unavailable to the surface structure. In generalizations, one specific deep structure event can be made to represent an entire class of phenomena on the surface. Distortions, deletions, and generalizations are viewed as normal and necessary in the assignment of meaning to experience. It is the "right and duty" of the individual's unconscious deep structure to keep unpleasantness from the conscious surface structure. It is these same repressed deep structure remnants of experience that can both fetter and facilitate change. Like a mine, the deep structure holds stored experiences and coping strategies that are the internal resources needed by the surface structure to forge meaning and create patterns of communication and behavior. Some patterns effectively meet client's needs, while others are experienced as limited and limiting.

TREATMENT

PRINCIPAL THERAPEUTIC GOAL

NLP focuses on the intricacies of how communication takes place in the here and now. It is concrete, not abstract. The central therapeutic goal of the model is to bring about change in the meaning that the individual gives to experience as relayed in communicable verbal and nonverbal patterns and strategies. Social workers using NLP accept the following assumptions as fundamental to successful change occurring in the treatment process:

- Clients are motivated to change. Whether voluntarily or involuntarily, clients hope to get help. Even court-ordered clients have chosen to enter treatment rather than be incarcerated.
- Clients have the internal resources necessary to make changes. The challenge is accessing internal resources to get needs met.
- Clients accept the social worker as the synergist of change. Through modeling and direction, the social worker guides clients in discovering new choices that are goal specific.

TREATMENT CONCEPTS AND STRATEGIES

Preferred Representational Systems

Surface and deep structure representations of experiences are crafted from data arriving by way of "representational systems" consisting of sight (visual), sound (auditory), touch (kinesthetic), smell (olfactory), and taste (gustatory). These sensory-based representational systems frame how human beings experience and respond to the world. Each person gathers and encodes information from experience in a unique, idiosyncratic way. Rapport, leading to effective assessment and intervention with a client, is based on being able to accurately identify the representational system favored by the individual. By identifying the predicates (adverbs, adjectives, and verbs) used by the client, the social worker can match his or her communication style to the client's preferred representational system.

The most frequently used predicates relate to visual, auditory, and kinesthetic representational systems. Table 19–1 lists some commonly used visual, auditory, and kinesthetic predicates. Social workers choosing to use NLP need to become adept at deciphering and using preferred representational system predicates, as they are pivotal to rapport building and treatment intervention.

There is no supercultural yardstick by which to measure the preferred representational system and corresponding predicates used by clients. Practitioners employing these concepts and techniques must keep in mind that there will in all likelihood be variance between and within cultures. Therapy is an intentional process that begins as the social worker assumes an active role in determining and utilizing the unique sensory representational system presented by the client.

To give the reader a sense of how predicate matching takes place, a series of sample client/worker exchanges follows. The first example of visual predicate matching:

CLIENT: I can't *picture* myself doing it any differently. I'm *in the dark* as to what to do.
WORKER: It *appears* to me you *foresee* having a hard time *imagining* what course of action to take. Let's *see* if I can't help you *look* at this another way so that you can gain a *clearer perspective*.

The following is an example of auditory predicate matching:

CLIENT: It seems like every time I *say* something, I get *yelled* at for *stating* my opinion.
WORKER: When I *listen* to you *speak* I *hear* your *pronounced* unhappiness. *Sounds* to me like you wish others were more *in tune* with you. You want to be *heard*.

Table 19–1
Representational Systems Predicates

Visual	Auditory	Kinesthetic
appear	deafening	caress
bright	ear-splitting	feel
clear	harmony	handle
clouded	hear	hard
look	in tune	hit
picture	lend an ear	hold
observe	listen	mushy
show	loud	pat
vague	noisy	sharp
view	pronounced	soft
visible	rings a bell	stroke
visualize	sounds	touch

And the following exchange illustrates kinesthetic predicate matching:

> CLIENT: I can't *handle* this anymore. *He rubs me the wrong way.* I've *racked my brain* trying to get *in touch* with why he *feels* the way he does but every time I *catch* myself getting close I get this *cold feeling* all over and I *break down.*
>
> WORKER: I'm *in touch* with you. I have a *feeling* that you are *backing down* from him because of how he acts towards you. I'd like you *to toss around* the idea of *digging in* and working this thing out instead of *feeling* like you are *up against the wall.* Do you feel that you can *take a firm stand* and *grasp hold* of the situation?

In instances where the social worker cannot identify the client's preferred representational system, an overlapping approach may be warranted. Overlapping ensures that the worker covers the range of possible predicates used by the client and also models for the individual alternative patterns of communication (Ivey, 1994; Lankton, 1980). An example of overlapping predicates is indicated in the following client/worker dialogue:

> CLIENT: I don't like *feeling* this way. You *heard* what she said. I can *see* that I've got to make a decision but I *feel stuck.*
>
> WORKER: I sense you're having a *hard* time *hearing* what she has to *say.* It takes work to *look* at things from someone else's *viewpoint.* As you *get in touch* with your *feelings* allow yourself the opportunity to *toss around* some different options.

Eye-Accessing Cues

A shortcut for identifying a client's representational system is to attend to the client's eye movements as displayed in Figure 19–1. By observing where the client looks when asked sensory-nonspecific questions, the social worker can access cues to the individual's preferred representational system. Phrases that contain sensory-unspecified words allow the client to randomly access his or her preferred representation system. Examples of sensory-neutral word groups that allow the social worker to quickly identify the client's preferred representational system include the following:

Think about what you would do differently.

Consider what it is that you like to *remember* about that experience.

Be aware of your most intimate experience.

A client whose gaze is cast up and to the left or right is said to have a preferred representational system that is visual. Looking left, right, or downward to the left indicates a preferred representational system that is auditory. The client who glances down and to the right is kinesthetic in his or her preferred representational system.

FIGURE 19-1 VISUAL ACCESSING CUES FOR A NORMALLY ORGANIZED RIGHT-HANDED PERSON

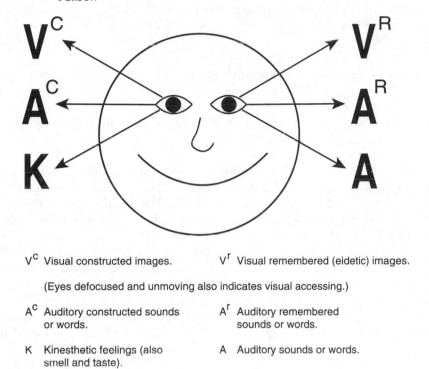

V^c Visual constructed images.　　　V^r Visual remembered (eidetic) images.

(Eyes defocused and unmoving also indicates visual accessing.)

A^c Auditory constructed sounds　　A^r Auditory remembered
or words.　　　　　　　　　　　　sounds or words.

K　Kinesthetic feelings (also　　　A　Auditory sounds or words.
smell and taste).

From *Frogs into Princes* by Richard Bandler and John Grinder. © 1979 Real People Press.

Eyes that are defocused and centered indicate a client who is visual. The exception to this guide is the case of left-handed clients in whom the downward kinesthetic and auditory looks are reversed.

The Four-Tuple
The four-tuple is a way of representing the client's repertoire of representational systems from most to least preferred. As such, this construct provides the social worker with a useful way of recording how the client frames experience according to the senses and their locus. The visual (V), auditory (A), kinesthetic (K), and olfactory/gustatory (O) senses are assigned a locus that is either internal[(i)] or external[(e)], depending on how they are generated. Internal refers to remembered images and external pertains to experiences of the present. For example, an individual with an internal-only four-tuple locus would be so inwardly focused that he or she would be oblivious to what was happening in the outside world. His or her four-tuple would be depicted as V^i, A^i, K^i, O^i. An individual showing only an external locus would affectively seem disconnected from his or her inward feelings, preferring to be sensorially

tuned in to what was going on in his or her milieu. This individual's four-tuple would be represented as V^e, A^e, K^e, O^e. In fact, most would show a mixture of past remembering and present experiencing, and their four-tuple sequence of accessing cues might appear as A^e, K^e, V^e, O^e.

Metaphors

Metaphors are used extensively in NLP to convey to the client desirable communication and behavioral changes in a manner that effectively reduces resistance associated with the model's direct problem-solving approach. By using a metaphorical story that parallels the identified problem, the practitioner can illustrate how things have come to be the way they are and how, by creating alternatives based on the client's own resources, things could be different.

Frequently based on the client's own experience, the narratives that unfold serve as catalysts for change by redirecting the client to seek new ways of knowing and doing. The social worker's skill in crafting solution-focused analogies attends to the need of the client (who, for whatever reason, is reluctant to accept directive counsel) for alternative patterns of communication and behavior.

For example, a colleague, James Cavanaugh, shared with me the metaphor that he used during a discharge interview from a substance abuse treatment center: the story of his first ride on a roller coaster and subsequent commitment to staying off that ride. This commitment was broken within ten minutes when one of his friends, looking for someone to ride with, offered a free ticket. His account of the misery of being cranked up that hill once again, only this time screaming, "Let me off this ride," was definitely not about relapse prevention, at least at a surface structure level.

Anchoring

Sights, sounds, feelings, smells, and tastes constantly bombard the sensory organs. In order to process this information, the individual deciphers and encodes the new stimuli by assigning them value based on past experience. Described as anchoring, this process creates a series of templates, both positive and negative, that are used by the individual to understand and give meaning to new experience. When positive anchors are reinforced, the individual feels validated and empowered. Conversely, when negative anchors are reinforced, the individual experiences disapproval and feels powerless. A social work may often find that the client's association between current subjective experience and previously formed anchors is incongruent. In these situations, the individual may find him or herself affectively off track when attempting to send or interpret communication and behavior. With time and repeated exposure, negative anchors can become reinforced to such an extent that the individual's alternative responses to a given situation become severely limited. Anchoring, therefore, is a process through which other, more satisfying behaviors, distilled from a client's past positive experiences, can be generalized to the presently sensed limitation. These can then be edited for change in the present context by collapsing together similar experiences with new meaning that lead to positive alternative surface structure choices and strategies.

Anchors, which are frequently associated with physical contact such as a touch on the arm or shoulder, provide the social worker with the opportunity to moor both experience and change. Anchors may cover each of the representational systems, and are often related to certain discernible contexts wherein the particular sense was stimulated.

Besides touch (kinesthetic), inflecting and directing the voice (auditory) or looking at and away from the client (visual) can be used to anchor. Smells and tastes are not as much a part of the therapeutic process as they could be. The meaning associated with or assigned to the anchor can have differing connotations depending upon the person and the circumstances. For example, the social worker's office, as the place where problematic feelings and behaviors are expressed and solutions found, can become a context anchor with either a negative or a positive connotation.

As the client recounts a feeling or behavior, certain sensory anchors are also stimulated and conveyed. By acknowledging and re-anchoring these memories in the here and now, the social worker gives them meaning in the present. In the following brief client/worker exchange, visual, auditory, and kinesthetic anchors are used to change the affective content of the individual's experience. The first illustrates a negative anchor:

WORKER: So, what brings you to see me today?
CLIENT (looking down and to the right): I'm feeling so upset because my grandmother died.
WORKER (in a concerned voice, looking at the client and firmly touching his or her shoulder): I'm so sorry for your loss. (Softly, loosening and removing hand, looking away): Things will get better.
CLIENT continues to look down, shaking head from side to side, and begins to cry.

The following, slightly different exchange, illustrates a positive anchor:

WORKER: So, what brings you to see me today?
CLIENT (looking down and to the right): I'm feeling so upset because my grandmother died.
WORKER (speaking in a soft monotone, looking down and away from the client): I'm so sorry for your loss. (Looking at the client, touching his or her shoulder with intensifying firmness, and speaking in a convincing, reassuring voice): Things will get better.
CLIENT nods head and smiles.

Change Personal History
Life is like leaving home on a never-ending journey. One of the first things you do in preparation for travel is to pack your bags. Invariably a host of others, including family and friends, "help" you get ready by giving you things to take with you. As you travel you invariably discover that some of the things packed are very useful and you

rely on them much more than others; others become indubitably burdensome. So you try to repack your bags along life's highway, only to find that what you need has become mixed in with what you do not want. Your nice neat luggage is bursting at the seams and does not look orderly at all. You begin to wish that you could just change the whole thing and start over again instead of feeling stuck with all this extra baggage for the duration of your journey.

Our personal experience as human beings is much the same. Each of us carries baggage from our past experiences on our journey through life. Some of what we carry we use frequently in our internal dealings with self and external dealings with others. However, other "bags" we carry seem to serve no purpose at all save to weigh us down, thus interfering with our journey. What would it be like if you could repack your bags while in transit? This would allow you to reconstruct personal limitations into new behavioral possibilities. What an exciting thought! NLP's Change Personal History allows you to do just that—change the past.

The Change Personal History is a therapeutic technique used to amend the past, in the present, for the future. By imagining again the past, the individual takes his or her personal history and modifies and improves it. The approach involves taking limiting psychosocial ways of behaving, founded in past responses to stimulus overload, and transforming them into adaptive ways of behaving by changing the historical context. Central to the technique are the concepts of visualization, suggestion, and anchoring. The Change Personal History process requires the social worker to do the following.

1. Ask the client to identify and relate an unpleasant feeling or behavior pattern that he or she has experienced. Have the client sensorially imagine the feelings, sights, sounds, smells, and tastes associated with the experience. Look for a behavioral cue (e.g., head nod, body posture, muscle tone, breathing pattern, eye flutter, etc.) signifying that the client is in touch with the experience. Anchor the unpleasant pattern kinesthetically with a touch on the arm or shoulder. Release the anchor and reorient the client to the present.

2. Using the anchored unpleasant pattern as a conveyance, ask the client to go back through time and locate other instances in which he or she felt this way and identify the particular patterns in turn. Again, have the client sensorially recreate the feelings connected with each experience. For each pattern, identify a behavioral cue, anchor the pattern, release the anchor, and reorient the client. Three to four such experiences should suffice.

3. Ask the client how he or she dealt with the past experiences one by one and reframe the way in which he or she coped with each situation in terms of positive behavioral resources. As each coping resource is presented, have the client sensorially revisit the experience and look for a behavioral response that implies that the resource did in fact aid the client in dealing with the pattern. Once this is achieved, anchor, release, and reorient the client. If a resource cannot be found, assist the client in creating the necessary resources to help him or her deal with the unpleasant pattern. Remember to validate the resource by looking

for a behavioral response and to follow up with anchoring, releasing, and reorienting the client.

4. Combining the response anchors, have the client go to each of the identified past experiences and change the personal history of each by using the added resources. Anchor each change and have the client acknowledge that he or she is satisfied with the change before proceeding to the next pattern.

5. To ensure that the desired changes have taken place, have the client recall each experience before the anchors were put in place, while at the same time observing the client's behavioral response. If he or she appears to be still troubled by the necessary pattern, create additional resources and repeat the preceding step.

6. Finally, have the client imagine the next time a situation similar to the past ones is likely to occur. Suggest that the client take the needed resource along. Using no anchors, observe the client's behavioral response. If the desired change has occurred, it will be noticeable and communicated. If this test of whether or not changes have been generalized fails, repeat steps 4, 5, and 6 (Bandler & Grinder, 1979).

The Change Personal History is an effective way to help clients work through painful personal histories. Importantly, it does not require the client to verbalize his or her unpleasant experiences but merely to re-experience them through mental imagery. Again, the resources of the deep structure are used to create an alternative surface structure narrative that is more desirable to the individual. This not only expedites recovery but reduces intrusiveness, protects client privacy, and provides a heightened sense of personal control over the therapeutic process.

Reframing

The significance of any event depends upon the meaning assigned to it—or how it is framed. When the frame of reference is changed, meaning and significance are altered. In NLP, the therapeutic technique of transforming undesirable thoughts, feelings, and behaviors into desirable resources aimed at meeting the client's needs is called reframing.

NLP assumes that all behavior, whether problematic or not, is founded upon positive intention. The fact that a behavior is not rewarding to the individual suggests that links between intention and outcome are flawed. Through reframing, alternative outcomes are generated linking the client's positive intention to positive outcome using existing or constructed resources.

The purpose of this technique, therefore, is to change, by the modification of meaning, both response and resulting behavior, facilitating resolution between conflicting parts of the self. In so doing, the client's negative behavior is transformed to coincide with his or her positive intention. The power of this technique is that resources can be created through the use of metaphorical, anecdotal, humorous, and narrative imagery.

Reframing unwanted patterns of feelings, thoughts, and behaviors into functional resources allows the client to link deep structure intention with surface structure outcomes. In NLP, there are a number of ways in which to conduct a reframe (Bandler & Grinder, 1982).

Reframing is used during the natural flow of the therapeutic interview to aid the client in separating positive intentions from negative behaviors. Once this is achieved, the social worker can assist the client in combining positive intentions with more congruent positive behaviors. In all reframes, a distinction is made between how the individual's internal aid external congruency issues are handled.

Issues related to internal incongruity, for example, are dealt with by reframing the content of the client's communication and behavioral presentation. This type of reframe allows the social worker to attend to discord between what the client intends and what he or she exhibits. External congruity, on the other hand, is labeled as context related. By reframing the context, the social worker can address variance between what the client intends and the way the others see him or her communicating or behaving.

One systematic way of assisting clients in making desired content and context changes involves the six-step reframe pattern. The following is a summary of the basic steps involved in conducting a reframe intervention.

1. Have the client locate a pattern of communication or behavior that he or she wants to change. Desensitize the pattern by having the client assign it a "code name" number, letter, or color (for the purposes of this example, the pattern will be referred to as "Z").

2. Establish a communication link with the "part" of the client responsible for pattern Z. Giving the client the option to close his or her eyes may help expedite the process. Then proceed by having the client ask his or her unconscious mind, "Will the part that is responsible for Z communicate with me in consciousness?" Look for a verbal or nonverbal response to the question asked. Establish a yes/no signal based on the client's response. To assist the client, suggest that an increase in the pattern's sensory-based brightness, volume, or intensity means yes and a decrease represents no.

3. Distinguish between the pattern and the outcome. Separate the client's behavior, pattern Z, from the positive intention of the part that is responsible for Z. Keep in mind the unwanted behavior has been created as a way to achieve some positive outcome. Unfortunately, instead of aiding the client, Z is problematic. Have the client ask the part that controls Z, "Would you be willing to let me know in consciousness what you are trying to do for me by providing me with pattern Z?" If you get a yes response, ask the part to go ahead and communicate its intention. If you get a no response, proceed with unconscious reframing, presupposing positive intention. Have the client affirm the positive intention of the part that runs Z. Ask the client to ask the part that runs Z, "If there were ways to accomplish your positive function that would work as well as or better than Z, would you be interested in trying them out?"

4. In conjunction with the client, create alternative ways of achieving an outcome. Access a creative part, and generate new behaviors to accomplish the positive

function. Aid the client in accessing experiences of creativity and anchor them, or ask the client, "Are you aware of a creative part of yourself?" Have the part of the client that runs Z communicate its positive function to the creative part. Allow the creative part to generate more choices to accomplish that function, and have the part that runs Z select three choices that are at least as good or better than Z. Have it give a yes signal each time it selects such an alternative.

5.   With the client, ask the part, "Are you willing to take responsibility for using the three new alternatives and are you willing to do so in the appropriate context?" This provides a future-based pact with the part. In addition, you can ask the part at the unconscious level to identify the sensory cues that will trigger the new choices, and to experience fully what it's like to have those sensory cues automatically bring on one of the new choices.

6.   Ecological check. Ask the part to remain calm, blank, or quiet. Now ask the following question and report any changes: "Is there any part of you that objects to any of the three new alternatives?" If there is a yes response, recycle to step 2 above. If not, thank the part, and again, ask the part to remain calm, blank, or quiet (Bandler & Grinder, 1982).

Reframing is not a new concept; separating and integrating "parts" is an important tool in other therapies (e.g., Gestalt and experiential family therapy), but the efficient way in which NLP presents it is new. Using this technique systematically allows the social worker to assist clients in redefining experience through the creation of alternative responses.

THERAPEUTIC APPLICATIONS

Intervention with Dyads and Families

Although most frequently associated with individual treatment, NLP has long been used in working with a full range of client systems. In particular, from its earliest beginnings, NLP has been associated with dyadic and family therapy (Davis & Davis, 1983; Grinder & Bandler, 1976). As an individual treatment, the model's concepts and techniques can form the basis for one's practice or be used in conjunction with other treatment theories. The experiential therapy approach originated by Virginia Satir, for example, is dialectically connected with NLP and shares many of the model's concepts and techniques (Andreas, 1991; Bandler et al., 1976; Nichols & Schwartz, 1995). The concepts and therapeutic techniques of NLP enhance the social worker's bid to establish an atmosphere conducive to positive change starting where the client is. Enabled by the strategies, the social worker can readily identify and bridge inner and interpersonal incongruence that skews communication and hampers growth. In particular, the dyad or family member's establish personal congruence between their inner subjective experience feelings of discomfort, frustration, and physical distance associated with having positive intentions misunderstood because of mismatched communication can be effectively addressed through NLP.

The goal of therapy with dyads and families is change, not homeostasis. Change involves helping system members establish personal congruence between their inner subjective experience and the patterns of communication and behavior presented to the outside world. Recognizing and accepting personal difference as normal permits dyads and families to draw upon the uniqueness of the individual members in support of personal and systemic goals. The objective, therefore, is to help members realize that personal change leads to system change. In order to reach this end, dyad and family members need to understand that the patterns of feelings and behaviors that drain individuals also deplete the system as a whole. Likewise, resources that empower individuals also serve to nourish and enrich the entire system.

The use of NLP in working with dyads and families requires the social worker to initiate change by modeling desired behaviors and patterns of communication. Focusing on the here and now instead of on what was or should be, the social worker uses the system member's resources to create new patterns of interaction and communication aimed at bringing about desirable personal and mutual outcomes.

The point of entry for the social worker working the dyads and families is to identify how system members see themselves personally and present themselves publicly. In NLP, this process of self-discovery is founded on determining each individual's preferred representational system and communication category. Preferred representational systems, as already discussed, are the verbal and nonverbal sensory-based pathways used by the individual to take in, give meaning to, and send information gathered from experience. Communication categories, on the other hand, are the linguistically linked behavior role extremes that individuals assume when under stress.

In NLP, communication categories are made up of four basic character roles that relate to how the individual presents and is perceived. The first is the placater. This individual's personification is one of servitude at any cost. Neglecting the needs of the self, he or she is always trying to do the right thing by pleasing and appeasing others. The blamer is the second communication category. This person is preoccupied with gaining and maintaining power at other's expense. Neglecting the needs of the other, obstreperous and autocratic, the blamer's self-focus leads him or her to see others as inept and at fault. The computer is the third characterization. Presenting a super-reasonable front, the computer is an individual who is seemingly devoid of affect for self or others, relying instead on the context and what intellectual correctness demands. The distracter is the final communication category. The image the distracter projects is the heedless anarchist unconcerned for self, others, or situation. The distracter is fueled by wayward spontaneity in pursuit of the irreverent and irrelevant. (Bandler et al., 1976; Grinder & Bandler, 1976).

Understanding the system member's preferred representational system and communication category allows the social worker to begin to understand the distortions, deletions, and generalizations that the individual uses to frame and constrain his or her subjective experience and that of other dyad and family members. Quite literally, system members under personal or collective stress have trouble switching from one representational system to another and become typecast into one or the other communication category. This reliance on a single preferred representational system limits the individual's ability to establish and maintain rapport with others whose communication base differs from his or her own. The system members, in effect, are speaking different languages.

Since message congruity is so fundamental to positive interpersonal relationships, NLP focuses concerted attention on understanding and changing the internal meaning and external intent of verbal and nonverbal communication. To do so, the social worker determines the experience-based resources and associated anchors used by the individual to produce undesirable patterns. This comprehension aids the social worker in reframing the meaning and intent by way of modeling and intervention to set in place desirable patterns and allied positive anchors.

Achieving change in dyads and families through reframing is accelerated by determining the base upon which the problematic response is founded. In NLP, issues to be reframed are categorized according to whether they are content- or context-related.

Content reframing refers to the social worker's working with the client to attach a positive intent to an external behavior. In a dyadic session, an unhappy wife who bursts into tears because of her husband's constant fault finding may have this communication pattern reframed in terms of his extreme concern for her. By reframing the husband's negative actions into positive intentions, the social worker sets the stage for the wife to have her negative feelings reframed into positive responses.

Context reframing deals with changing the client's negative internal response to another member's external behavior. In a family scenario, consider the father who is frustrated trying to curb his son's behavioral noncompliance. In this case, the father might be commended for training his son to be insubordinate, as this behavior will help him be independent when he needs to be. This context reframe compels the father to consider alternative explanations for his son's conduct while at the same time validating the son's behavior, thereby causing the two to redefine their relationship and explore new ways of communicating intent.

Similar to the way in which the social worker would use NLP in individual treatment, the systems focus in dyad and family treatment requires the practitioner to deploy his or her skills concurrently with multiple members who express diverse needs. Of course, the ramifications of successful intervention exponentially increase the potential for new learning. As can be imagined, NLP is a powerful model of practice with dyads and families that sees the social worker directing family members in taking responsibility for change.

Intervention with Groups and Communities

Group and community workers can benefit from integrating the concepts and strategies of NLP into their practice. Specifically, pathways to effective communication can be opened using the rapport-building skills inherent in NLP's understanding of representational systems, predicate matching, anchoring, and reframing.

In group work, for instance, NLP has been found to be a useful adjunct to other practice approaches by enhancing between-member rapport and transcending the various stages of group maturation (Chiders & Saltmarsh, 1986). As well, specific group work interventions with clients suffering from anxiety and phobic disorders have been conducted with marked success (Shelden & Shelden, 1989).

Group and community workers searching for a model of practice that will enhance their leadership abilities and reinforce their capacity to influence the change process will find NLP a definite asset to their professional practice. From preliminary indications, NLP appears to be an effective group and community work approach; however, the full extent of the model's applicability to these practice situations is yet to be known.

PRINCIPAL APPLICATIONS IN SOCIAL WORK PRACTICE

NLP, while directive in its approach to client development, safeguards the individual's right to self-determination. Certainly, NLP is a model that empowers clients and is sensitive to individual and group difference. Starting where the client is makes NLP an important model for social workers. The uses of NLP in practice are varied and support the model as a potent interlocking treatment (Dilts, 1983).

In the treatment of substance abuse, NLP has been found to be of particular benefit. Several authors have indicated the positive impact that NLP has on understanding and working with substance abusers and their families (Davis, 1990; Doorn, 1990; Hennman & Hennman, 1990; Isaacson, 1990; Sterman, 1990a, b, c, d, e; Tierney, 1990).

In particular, NLP is an effective family treatment approach to working with alcoholics and their codependent significant others (Davis, 1990). The model's communication base provides an important means by which family members can begin to deal with incongruent communication patterns. In the pre-abstinence phase, NLP helps family members detach from the addict, thereby allowing each to develop his or her own communication skills. In the post-abstinence phase, NLP aids in reducing past patterns of communication and behavior by drawing upon the positive intent of codependent family members to create more enriching pathways of interaction.

Persons suffering from post-traumatic stress disorder have also been effectively assisted by the use of NLP strategies (Gregory, 1984). By combining several of the model's treatment strategies, the worker can effectively desensitize clients and achieve symptom remission. The particular techniques employed in working with post-traumatic stress disorder sufferers include visual kinesthetic disassociation, change personal history, reframing, and anchoring.

Working with the client's preferred representational system to establish rapport and construct an imaginary scrapbook of the client's positive life events has been found to be effective in lowering anxiety and depression levels (Hossach & Standidge, 1983). In addition, NLP has demonstrated effectiveness in treating a number of presenting problems—anticipation of loss, phobia, and fear of authority figures (Bandler, 1984; Einspruch & Forman, 1988).

NLP has also been applied in the assessment and treatment of adults who were sexually abused as children (Shelden & Shelden, 1989). Specifically, the rapport-building aspects of the model are useful in facilitating client disclosure of early abuse trauma as it relates to adult psychosocial difficulties.

Like any model of practice, NLP does have limitations. In particular, the model's emphasis on cognitive and sensory communication pathways results in its having limited effect with clients who are taking psychotropic medications or are substance abusers. As well, individuals seeking to achieve a past-oriented understanding of why they feel and behave the way they do, and practitioners uncomfortable with using a directive client-influencing approach, will be dissatisfied with NLP's techniques. However, both clients and social workers will find merit in NLP's conceptual framework in helping them grasp personal and interpersonal patterns of communication and behavior.

ADMINISTRATIVE AND TRAINING FACTORS

NLP has been shown effective in a wide array of applications. Although many of the principles of NLP are easily learned sense-making practice principles, the more advanced techniques do require specialized training. Normally, training in NLP is gained through regionally offered workshops or via co-workers who have been instructed in the intricacies of the model. Training in NLP is very much experientially based and the learning curve for beginners is dramatic. Once trained, the practitioner requires little direct supervision whether he or she uses NLP as his or her primary model of practice or in conjunction with another treatment theory. However, experience has shown that ongoing peer or group consultation is helpful in fine-tuning the approach's conceptual and technical aspects. Social workers need to keep in mind that NLP evolved out of the interview room, not the classroom.

CASE VIGNETTES

INDIVIDUAL TREATMENT

A thirty-two-year-old woman, recently diagnosed with multiple sclerosis, entered therapy to find help in dealing with her fears related to the disease's incapacitating effects. Currently in remission, she was depressed over the sensory and motor disturbances she had experienced and was anxious about her heightened risk of cognitive and behavioral debilitation. As there is no known cure for multiple sclerosis, the woman was hoping that psychotherapy could at least help her calm down enough to face the challenges of living with the disease.

What is known about multiple sclerosis is that there appears to be a correlation between the degree of stress and anxiety experienced by the sufferer and his or her potential for relapse. What the exact connection between the psyche and soma is, however, remains unknown. It was the goal of treatment, therefore, to decrease the client's potential for symptom recurrence by lowering her stress and anxiety levels.

Rapport was established using the client's preferred representational system and associated predicates to mirror her mannerisms and map her communication. Discussing in depth the etiology of her disease, the worker used a series of verbal and visual anchors to separate the client's positive wishes for herself from her negative behavioral presentation associated with her multiple sclerosis symptoms.

It was then decided that a Change Personal History pattern would be used to create alternative possibilities for the client than those afforded by her ailment. At the conclusion of the intervention, the client was evaluated to determine whether or not the desired change had been sufficiently seated for her future use. It was ascertained that the client was having difficulty envisioning herself using the needed resources to handle prospective like situations differently.

In such instances, there is an indication that the client is receiving some secondary gain from the intent/outcome incongruity. This was confirmed by the client when questioned about how others were perceiving her illness. She exclaimed that she was receiving an inordinate amount of attention from her family and friends and quite liked their mindfulness of her well-being. The social worker moved to using the six-step reframe.

The client was asked to determine whether she was willing to lose the secondary gains associated with her having multiple sclerosis. After the client provided repeated reassurances (all of which were anchored), the six-step reframe technique was undertaken and an ecological check administered. The client's self-report over a one-year period indicated that she no longer felt depressed or anxious and had remained symptom-free. She attributed her success to her new-found ways of managing stress.

DYAD TREATMENT

A husband and wife came to counseling to seek help for their faltering relationship. They attributed their marital problems to "not being able to communicate." The fact was, they did communicate very well, just not in a manner that either could recognize.

The husband was frustrated with his wife's "refusal" to attend to his sexual needs. In response, he stated, he had started binge drinking to get away from her but found himself seeking her out when intoxicated, hoping that she might change her mind and warm up to him. The wife had "tuned out" her husband completely. She felt she could not be intimate with someone who was unable or unwilling to carry on a conversation with her. The fact that he was always making sexual advances toward her when he was drinking only further turned her off, and his garbled drunkard's speech only made things worse. She had nothing more to say on the matter.

This couple's difficulties were related to their negative internal responses to similarly negative external behaviors. Both were distorting, deleting, and generalizing their shared experience to such an extent that they were totally misreading each other's communication. The stress they were under had resulted in each of them reverting to using only one representational system. Yet each espoused the same intent, to communicate more effectively. The trouble was they did not know how to reinitiate the process.

The couple's common intention was presented and intervention began with the social worker modeling for the husband and wife how to recognize and communicate using the other's preferred representational system. In addition, a context reframe was conducted to change the couple's negative internal responses to each other's external behavior. Using their shared intention as a conduit to effective communication, the social worker reframed the husband's and wife's animated responses to one another as resources indicative of positive concern for one another. The social worker anchored this positive change in perception for the couple, and for "homework" suggested they find three new ways of conveying caring using the partner's preferred representational system. Each was asked to consider what he or she would do differently in the future and the projected changes were anchored. At the clients' initiative, a second session was conducted to evaluate the treatment intervention. The wife indicated that things were much better and that, because her husband's drinking seemed under control, she felt much more responsive to his amorous advances. The husband commented that as far as he could tell, communication between him and his wife had increased dramatically.

EMPIRICAL BASE

NLP lends itself well to empirical research due to its clear and concise concepts and patterns of intervention. However, theoreticians and practitioners of NLP view scientific inquiry to be the antithesis of the subjective systematic client-centered view of their approach. Be that as it may, a significant amount of research has been conducted on the efficacy of NLP. The findings on the validity of NLP are mixed and inconclusive, though, and long-term studies on the treatment effects of NLP have not been conducted.

Much of the research that does exist has been conducted on the approach's basic assumptions regarding preferred representational systems, predicate matching, and eye accessing cues. NLP's detractors point to the likelihood that the techniques associated with the model's basic theoretical concepts lack support (Elich et al., 1985; Fromme & Daniell, 1984; Gumm et al., 1982; Krugman et al., 1985; Sharpley, 1984, 1987). Others have concluded the exact opposite, finding the concepts and strategies of NLP to be highly effective in understanding and treating a broad range of client issues (Davis, 1990; Dilts, 1983; Einspruch & Forman, 1988; Graunke & Roberts, 1985; Gregory, 1984; Hossach & Standidge, 1983; Shelden & Shelden, 1989). However, many of the tenets of NLP have yet to be tested (Zastrow, 1995).

In particular, criticism has been leveled at NLP's claim that therapeutic change is founded on starting where the client is and guiding him or her toward psychotherapeutic change. Zastrow (1995), for example, suggests that keying in on rapport building and guidance focused on what is observable neglects patterns of thought that are pivotally linked to emotional and behavioral disorders. However, research on the helping process would suggest that establishing a relationship and guiding the client are the most essential qualities in effective treatment (*Consumer Reports,* 1995; Goldstein, 1990; Meredith, 1986; Turner, 1986).

In summary, NLP offers social workers an intentional treatment model geared toward discernible rather than chance outcomes. Lacking scientific validation, proponents of NLP stress that since the model is not a science it cannot be adequately tested. Their attitude is "If it works, it works."

PROSPECTUS

NLP is a user-friendly approach to understanding and conducting treatment, even though many writers, trainers, and practitioners have expended a great deal of effort in trying to mystify and complicate the approach's concepts and techniques. This seems to fly in the face of the original intention of the model's founders to synthesize and simplify what works in the therapeutic process. Be that as it may, NLP does have an important contribution to make to social workers in terms of how they understand and work with people.

NLP's framework draws upon a diverse theory and practice base and is connected to a variety of allied professions including psychiatry, psychology, nursing, education, and various fields of counseling. It is because of this broad conceptual and pragmatic at base that NLP continues to be a popular primary model of practice and a supplement to other theoretical perspectives.

REFERENCES

Andreas, S. (1991). *Virginia Satir: The Patterns of Her Magic.* Palo Alto, CA: Science and Behavior Books.

Andreas, S. (1992). *Neuro-linguistic Programming.* New York: Guilford Press.

Bandler, R. (1984). *Magic in Action.* Cupertino, CA: Meta Publications.

Bandler, R., & Grinder, J. (1975). *The Structure of Magic.* Vol. 1. Palo Alto, CA: Science & Behavior Books.

Bandler, R., & Grinder, J. (1979). *Frogs into Princes: Neurolinguistic Programming.* Moab, UT: Real People Press.

Bandler, R., & Grinder, J. (1982). *Reframing: Neuro-linguistic Programming and the Transformation of Meaning.* Moab, UT: Real People Press.

Bandler, R., Grinder, J., & Satir, V. (1976). *Changing with Families.* Santa Clara, CA: Science and Behavior Books.

Bradley, E.J., & Biedermann, H.J. (1985). Bandler and Grinder's NLP: Its historical context and contribution. *Psychotherapy 22*(1), 59–62.

Chiders, J.H., & Saltmarsh, R.E. (1986). Neurolinguistic programming in the context of group counseling. *Journal for Specialists in Group Work 11*(4), 221–227.

Chomsky, N. (1957). *Syntactic Structures.* The Hague-Paris: Mouton.

Clancy, F., & Yorkshire, H. (1989). The Bandler method. *Mother Jones,* February/March, 23–64.

Does therapy help? (1995). *Consumer Reports,* November, 784–789.

Cournoyer, B. (1996). *The Social Work Skills Workbook* (2nd ed.). Pacific Grove, CA: Brooks/Cole.

Davis, D.I. (1990). Neuro-linguistic programming and the family in alcoholism treatment. In C.M. Sterman (ed.), *Neuro-linguistic Programming in Alcoholism Treatment* (pp. 63–77). Binghamton, NY: Hawthorn Press.

Davis, S.L.R., & Davis, D.I. (1983). Neuro-linguistic programming and family therapy. *Journal of Marital and Family Therapy 9*(3), 283–291.

Dilts, R. (1976). *Roots of Neurolinguistic Programming.* Cupertino, CA: Meta Publications.

Dilts, R. (1983). *Applications of Neurolinguistic Programming.* Cupertino, CA: Meta Publications.

Doorn, J.M. (1990). An application of hypnotic communication to the treatment of addictions. In C.M. Sterman (ed.), *Neuro-linguistic Programming in Alcoholism Treatment* (pp. 79–89). Binghamton, NY: Hawthorn Press.

Einspruch, E.L., & Forman, B.D. (1988). Neuro-linguistic programming in the treatment of phobias. *Psychotherapy in Private Practice 6*(1), 91–100.

Elich, M., Thompson, W., & Miller, L. (1985). Mental imagery as revealed by eye movements and spoken predicates: A test of neurolinguistic programming. *Journal of Counseling Psychology 32*(4), 622–625.

Field, E.S. (1990). Neurolinguistic programming as an adjunct to other psychotherapeutic/hypnotherapeutic interventions. *American Journal of Clinical Hypnosis 32* (3), 174–182.

Fromme, D.K., & Daniell, J. (1984). Neurolinguistic programming examined: Imagery, sensory mode, and communication. *Journal of Counseling Psychology 31*(3), 387–390.

Goldstein, H. (1990). The knowledge base of social work practice: Theory, wisdom, analogue, or art? *Families in Society: The Journal of Contemporary Human Services 71*(1), 32–43.

Graunke, B., & Roberts, T.K. (1985). Neurolinguistic programming: The impact of imagery tasks on sensory predicate usage. *Journal of Counseling Psychology 32*(4), 525–530.

Gregory, P.B. (1984). Treating symptoms of post-traumatic stress disorder with neuro-linguistic programming. In R. Bandler, *Magic in Action.* Cupertino, CA: Meta Publications.

Grinder, J., & Bandler, R., (1976). *The Structure of Magic.* Vol. 2. Palo Alto, CA: Science & Behavior Books.

Gumm, W.B., Walker, M.K., & Day, H.D. (1982). Neurolinguistics programming: Method or myth? *Journal of Counseling Psychology 29*(3) 327–330.

Hennman, J.O., & Hennman, S.M. (1990). Cognitive-perceptual reconstruction in the treatment of alcoholism. In C.M. Sterman (ed.), *Neuro-linguistic Programming in Alcoholism Treatment* (pp. 105–123). Binghamton, NY: Hawthorn Press.

Hossach, A., & Standidge, K. (1983). Using an imaginary scrapbook for neurolinguistic programming in the aftermath of a clinical depression: A case history. *The Gerontologist 33*(2), 265–268.

House, S. (1994). Blending neurolinguistic programming representational systems with the RT counseling environment. *Journal of Reality Therapy 14*(1), 61–65.

Ignoffo, M. (1994). Two compatible methods of empowerment: Neurolinguistic hypnosis and reality therapy. *Journal of Reality Therapy 13*(2), 20–25.

Isaacson, E.B. (1990). Neuro-linguistic programming: A model for behavioral change in alcohol and other drug addiction. In C.M. Sterman (ed.), *Neuro-linguistic Programming in Alcoholism Treatment* (pp. 22–47). Binghamton, NY: Hawthorn Press.

Ivey, A.E. (1994). *Intentional Interviewing and Counseling: Facilitating Client Development in a Multicultural Society* (3rd ed.). Pacific Grove, CA: Brooks/Cole.

Ivey, A.E., Ivey, M.B., & Simek-Morgan, L. (1993). *Counseling and Psychotherapy: A Multicultural Perspective* (3rd ed.) Needham Heights, MA: Allyn & Bacon.

Krugman, M., Kirsch, I., Wichless, C., Milling, L., Golicz, H., & Toth, A. (1985). Neurolinguistic programming treatment for anxiety: Magic or myth? *Journal of Counseling Psychology 53*(4), 526–530.

Lankton, S. (1980). *Practical Magic: A Translation of Basic Neuro-linguistic Programming into Clinical Psychothearpy.* Cupertino, CA: Meta Publications.

MacLean, M. (1986). The neurolinguistic programming model. In F.J. Turner (ed.), *Social Work Treatment.* New York: Free Press

Mercier, M.A., & Johnson, M. (1984). "Representational system predicate use and convergence in counseling: Gloria revisited." *Journal of Counseling Psychology, 31*(2), 161–169.

Meredith, N. (1986). Testing the talking cure. *Science 7*(5), 30–37.

Nichols, M.P., & Schwartz, R.C. (1995). *Family Therapy: Concepts and Methods* (3rd ed.). Boston: Allyn & Bacon.

Pesut, D.J. (1991). The art, science, and techniques of reframing in psychiatric mental health nursing. *Issues in Mental Health Nursing 12*(1), 9–18.

Sandhu, D.S., Reeves, T.G., & Portes, P.R. (1993). Cross-cultural counseling and neurolinguistic mirroring with Native American adolescents. *Journal of Multicultural Counseling and Development 21*(2), 106–118.

Sharpley, C.F. (1984). Predicate matching in neurolinguistic programming: A review of research on the preferred representational system. *Journal of Counseling Psychology 31*(2), 338–348.

Sharpley, C.F. (1987). Research findings on neurolinguistic programming: Nonsupportive data or an untestable theory? *Journal of Counseling Psychology 34*(2), 103–107.

Shelden, V.E., & Shelden, R.G. (1989). Sexual abuse of males by females: The problem, treatment modality, and case example. *Family Therapy 16*(3), 249–258.

Sterman, D.M. (1990a). A specific neuro-linguistic programming technique effective in the treatment of alcoholism. In C.M. Sterman (ed.), *Neuro-linguistic Programming in Alcoholism Treatment* (pp. 91–103). Binghamton, NY: Hawthorn Press.

Sterman, C.M. (1990b). Are you the product of my misunderstanding? or The role of sorting mechanisms and basic human programs in the treatment of alcoholism. In C.M. Sterman (ed.), *Neuro-linguistic Programming in Alcoholism Treatment* (pp. 125–140). Binghamton, NY: Hawthorn Press.

Sterman, C.M. (1990c). Neuro-linguistic programming as a conceptual base for the treatment of alcoholism. In C.M. Sterman (ed.), *Neuro-linguistic Programming in Alcoholism Treatment* (pp. 11–25). Binghamton, NY: Hawthorn Press.

Sterman, C.M. (1990d). Neuro-linguistic programming rapport skills and alcoholism treatment. In C.M. Sterman (ed.), *Neuro-linguistic Programming in Alcoholism Treatment* (pp. 49–61). Binghamton, NY: Hawthorn Press.

Sterman, C.M. (1990e). Neuro-linguistic programming as psychotherapeutic treatment in working with alcohol and other drug addicted families. *Journal of Chemical Dependency 4*(1), 73–85.

Tierney, M.J. (1990). Neuro-linguistics as a treatment modality for alcoholism and substance abuse. In C.M. Sterman (ed.), *Neuro-linguistic Programming in Alcoholism Treatment* (pp. 141–154). Binghamton, NY: Hawthorn Press.

Turner, P. (1986). The shrinking of George. *Science 7*(5), 38–44.

Yapko, M.D. (1984). Implications of the Ericksonian and neurolinguistic programming approaches for responsibility of therapeutic outcomes. *American Journal of Clinical Hypnosis 27*(2), 137–143.

Zastrow, C. (1995). *The Practice of Social Work* (5th ed.). Pacific Grove, CA: Brooks/Cole.

Zastrow, C., Dotson, V., & Koch, M., (1987). The neuro-linguistic programming treatment Approach. *Journal of Independent Social Work 1*(1), 29–38.

Zastrow, C., & Kirst, K.K. (1994). *Understanding Human Behavior and the Social Environment* (3rd ed.). Chicago: Nelson Hall Publishers.

CHAPTER 21

PROBLEM-SOLVING THEORY AND SOCIAL WORK TREATMENT

JOANNE TURNER AND ROSE MARIE JACO

OVERVIEW

P roblem-solving theory stands as one of the important contemporary theories of
social work practice. Its importance is twofold: First, it is a theory developed by
a social worker. It is indeed a theory we can call our own. As well, it is a theory that
has influenced the development of other theories and the practice of many social
workers who might not recognize its impact on their practice. It originated and was
developed in the work of Helen Harris Perlman of the University of Chicago in the
1950s, and was later enhanced by the work of many others, as will be discussed below. As Perlman herself said so often, like all theories it is one that has been built on
the foundation stones of many other thinkers, but nevertheless is sufficiently unique
to stand in its own identity. Her major work, *Social Casework: A Problem Solving
Process,* was published in 1957 and has made a significant contribution to the continuing evolution of the theoretical base of social work.

The theory first emerged as an effort to make practice more pragmatic and here
and now, as opposed to the mistakenly perceived rigidity of the diagnostic school's
position that the therapeutic process should be built on a formal diagnosis and treatment plan. In its original formulation, it was seen as a theory of "casework," but it is
now viewed as having applications to all modalities of practice.

CONCEPT OF PROBLEM SOLVING

Problem solving can be defined as a "cognitive activity aimed at changing a problem
from the given to the goal state" (Mayer, 1994, p. 600) or, more definitively, as "a
systematic, step-by-step thinking and acting process that involves moving from an
undesired to a desired state" (Gelfand, 1988, p. 1). For human beings, problem solving is as normal and fundamental as breathing. It expresses people's natural capacity
to use their cognitive powers of reason and logic to attain the goals they value, an

ability that develops in increasingly complex ways from infancy to adulthood. This capacity enables people to obtain information from their environment and use that information to design ways of meeting their biological, psychological, cultural, and social needs (Flavell et al., 1993).

The ability to problem solve is so essential to human existence that it emerges at a very early stage of life and continues to develop and to be used throughout the balance of the life span. Why should this be so? It appears that the very fact of being alive challenges people to continually apply their problem-solving powers in order to resolve the large and small dilemmas that living presents to them. Perlman saw living as a problem-solving process, and she described life as "a continuous change and movement in which the human being works on so adapting himself to external objects, or them to himself as to achieve maximum satisfactions. This is the work in which every human being engages from the moment of birth to that of death" (Perlman, 1957, p. 53).

PROBLEM SOLVING AND SOCIAL WORK

Problem-solving theory has a central place in the social work field because many aspects of the profession correspond closely to this dominant feature of human nature. However, we must make this comparison with caution, because, as Woehle warns, even though within an ecosystems perspective rational problem solving is a sound analogy for the social work process, "rationally it is like the social work process, not the underlying 'truth' of the process" (1994, p. 76). Just as we might say that the human mind operates like a computer, although we know that it is not a computer.

Having acknowledged the limitations of the comparison, we can first look at the purpose of social work itself. Like all other professions, social work was established by society to undertake a problem-solving function in a particular area of human and societal concern. For social work, that concern has two aspects: to enable people to meet their psychological and social needs in interaction with society, and to create a society that supports people's efforts to become self-fulfilled (Boehm, 1959).

Secondly, as a direct practice theory for working with individuals, couples, families, and groups, problem solving draws a conceptual map to guide both worker and client through the stages and steps involved in a change process designed to move people from problem to solution (Compton & Galaway, 1994). Finally, for social workers and other professionals engaged in social planning and policy formation, problem solving offers a logical process for assessing a social problem, reviewing options for addressing it, and working out a plan designed for its amelioration. So convergent are the processes of problem solving and social work that problem solving is referred to by some theorists as the basis for generalist practice (Compton & Galaway, 1994, p. 49; see also Kirst-Ashman & Hull, 1993, p. 25), and by McMahon as "the general method of social work practice" (1990, pp. 20–22). McMahon's holistic conceptualization of practice embeds the skills of problem solving in an ecological framework that also encompasses the value system and knowledge base of the profession, used in concert with interpersonal helping approaches (1990, pp. 20–22).

HISTORICAL ORIGINS

Problem solving appeals to social work practitioners because it taps into the basic urge people have to meet their needs through using their power to think and plan. Accessing the energy contained in clients' drive to reach their goals is an essential part of the helping process at every level of intervention. For Perlman, who introduced the profession to the concepts of problem solving through her theorizing about casework, this approach includes the client's "perceptions of inner wants and needs and the outer realities, of mediation between them, of consideration of choices and alternatives, of anticipation of outcomes and their costs and rewards." She hypothesized that these cognitive processes do not remain entirely in the realm of thought, but are infused with feelings (1986, p. 247).

Perlman constructed the path upon which problem solving moved into the realm of social work thought when she shared her realization that strong parallels exist between the natural efforts clients make to satisfy their needs and a professional helping process that focuses on strengthening clients' ego functioning skills. "Thus problem solving as a process of the exercise of coping powers became a casework process" (Perlman, 1970, p. 134). For her, problem solving combined the insights of cognitive theory and the affective emphasis of psychoanalytic thought in an active helping method closely allied to the innate strivings of human nature. She summarized this concept thus:

> A *person* beset by a *problem* seeks help with that problem from a *place* . . . and is offered such help by a professional social worker who uses a *process* which simultaneously engages and enhances the person's own problem solving functions, and supplements the person's own problem solving resources (1970, p. 136).

Perlman was to later add to these components two other elements: the *professional person* who works through the process with the client, and the term "provisions," which refers to material goods, opportunities, relationships, and social support (1986, p. 254).

In describing how she arrived at the model, Perlman notes that she was in rebellion over the deterministic focus that viewed clients largely as malfunctioning people weighted down by a past that they had to process thoroughly before they could begin to cope with their problems. She wished to find a means of accessing people's inner strengths so they could grapple effectively with their current issues, without the lengthy process of introspection and working through then in vogue in social work helping (1986, p. 248).

Perlman blended this sequence with insights gained from Erikson's work on social roles and life-phase tasks, and from White's thinking about the conscious efforts humans make toward achieving mastery in their world (Perlman, 1986, p. 253). Incorporated in her approach were formulations from the functional school of social work practice, including a focus on present time, the use of the professional relationship to motivate clients, the beginning-middle-end pattern inherent in all helping encounters, and the need to partialize the problem by selecting that aspect most amenable to change (1986, pp. 249–251).

SOCIAL WORK LITERATURE

Although Perlman had begun to try out some of her ideas in earlier journal articles, the first general introduction of problem-solving theory to the profession took place with the publication of Perlman's famous "green book," *Social Casework: A Problem-Solving Process,* published in 1957. This book, which went through many subsequent printings, stood as the principal casework text for many classes of students in many schools of social work in many countries, and is one of the best-known methods texts in the profession. Subsequent to it, Perlman wrote other articles describing the theory, the most recent included in the last edition of this volume. One frequently overlooked publication of this writer is *Persona: Social Role and Personality.* This book, although principally on role theory, in fact presents further thinking on her ideas about problem solving.

Following these initial publications, Perlman's thinking was taken up quickly by others such as David Hollowitz, who expanded the concepts into work with families, as did Jay Haley, Spitzer, and Welsh, who also further developed the general applicability of the theory in a 1976 book, *The Problem Solving Approach to Adjustment: A Guide to Research and Intervention.*

Goldstein notes that Perlman's efforts to build a model that would bridge the gulf between the diagnostic approach, based on psychoanalytic theory, and the functional school, rooted in the behavioral sciences, were not a total success, as the strong adherents to each position judged their beliefs to have been minimized to an unacceptable degree in her explication of problem solving (Goldstein, 1984, pp. 31–32). For example, in Bartlett's 1970 analysis of the common values, knowledge, and interventive techniques used by social workers, the term "problem solving" does not appear, although Perlman's work had been available for more than a decade. Bartlett's examination of the interventions common to social work practice in that era is marked by a lack of specificity that could well have been counteracted by the introduction of problem-solving concepts. In the same vein, it is of interest to note that as influential as Perlman's work has been, problem solving is not presented as a distinct practice theory in either of the last two editions of the *Encyclopedia of Social Work.*

However, it was only a few years after Bartlett's work, in 1975, that Siporin referred to "the currently predominant conception of practice as a goal-directed *problem-solving process"* (1975, p. 51). He went on to note that this approach applied to all of the practice methods, as well as to administration and policy planning. Siporin urged practitioners to be pluralistic and eclectic in their choice of theories, and presented problem solving as one of the six models from which they might choose their range of interventions (1975, pp. 155–156). Pincus and Minihan, in 1973, had already incorporated problem solving into their ecological systems approach to practice, as had Brill in that same year, in her comprehensive analysis of the social work helping process. Over a period of twenty years, Reid and his collaborators wrote a series of books on task-centered practice in social work that had their origins in research on brief treatment carried out in the 1960s, but which also owed much to the logic of the problem-solving approach as developed by Perlman (Reid, 1992, p. 12).

CURRENT EVOLVING PERSPECTIVES

As noted above, some authors, particularly in undergraduate writing for generalist social work practice, focus on problem solving as the framework within which all helping activities with the client and their collaterals take place (McMahon, 1990). Bloom sets out an energetic interpretation of generic problem solving in which he includes the headings "get ready," "get set," and "go" (McMahon, 1990, pp. 104–109). In the "get ready" stage, the worker prepares to be helpful by recalling knowledge related to the presenting problem, community resources, and interventions likely to be useful. In the "get set" stage, the worker prepares the self psychologically to be receptive to the client and summons to awareness the values that will be used to inform the helping process. Finally, in the "go" stage, the worker applies the steps of problem solving in conjunction with interpersonal helping skills and sensitivity to cultural and gender issues. Problem-solving theory has naturally evolved by incorporating new perspectives, and the original problem-solving process has been adapted to include additional insights, such as in its transformation into an intentional client-empowering operation by Dubois and Miley (Dubois & Miley, 1996, pp. 214–215; Johnson, 1995, pp. 65–79).

In social work literature, the process of problem solving has been so integrated into the cognitive basis of social work that it echoes as an underlying structure in many interventive approaches, even when the focus is principally psychodynamic in nature. Problem solving, however, is clearly the central concept around which the problem-solving method of practice itself is organized, and is an explicit, if partial, foundation for task-centered social work, crisis intervention, planned short-term treatment, and the life model approach. The incorporation of problem-solving principles into many aspects of social work practice is eased by the fact that they do not violate the value system of the profession but support it, particularly in empowering the client to effectively manage problems in living (Germain & Gitterman, 1980, p. 101). The method can be used effectively in the context of cultural and gender-sensitive practice, as it is inherently neutral in the manner in which these issues distinguish people. Instead, it lends itself well to the concept of theoretical diversity, advocated by Turner (1986), in that, while it provides a structured framework for worker and client to follow, it is not in itself a method of intervention. This leaves worker and client free to match the means of creating change with the nature of the problem and the resources available, and to incorporate new treatment perspectives as they emerge.

CURRENT THEORETICAL STATUS

The roots of problem solving have been reviewed in the historical account of its development, and will now be examined from a different perspective. Although he included it in the last edition of *Social Work Treatment,* Turner indicated then that he did not see Perlman's conceptualization as a completed theory but rather as a "system of propositions from which hypotheses could be developed and a theory built" (Turner, 1986, p. 7). Compton and Galaway also refer to problem solving as a process or model rather than a theory, and they describe it as "a series of interactions between the client system and the practitioner, involving integration of feeling, thinking and doing, guided by a purpose and directed toward achieving an agreed-upon goal" (1994, p. 43). It is our view that, based on Turner's definition of a practice theory in Chapter 1 of this book, it is now clearly to be viewed as a social work theory. If we accept this, what can we look to as its conceptual foundations?

PRINCIPAL CONCEPTS

Problem solving is the rational process human beings use to negotiate a world of reality that is extremely complicated and, at times, both unknowable and unpredictable. Therefore, it is not always possible for people to follow the obvious guideline the model sets forth, that one must choose the path that leads most directly to a desired goal. In reviewing this complex picture, DeRoos notes that the

> rational decisions one makes for problem solving represent a subjective orientation to an incomplete picture of the objective world. This incomplete picture is our representation of objective reality, a simplified model of objective reality. Our actions are then in accordance with the model, not with objective reality (1990, p. 278).

Common wisdom and experience seem to indicate to people that they can never know all that they need to know in order to make a "perfect" decision, so they tend to reach for those that are "good enough." Nevertheless, in order to achieve even a modest level of success, information must be assembled and processed, and for this, people use a mental model called a "heuristic." In logic, a heuristic device is a piece of knowledge or "rule of thumb learned by trial and error" (McPeck, 1981, p. 17). Heuristics serve the problem solver as a template for decision making when algorithms would cost too much in the amount of information, processing power, or time needed (DeRoos, 1990, p. 278). Algorithms are procedures that are guaranteed to solve all classes of problems (Gilhooly, 1988, p. 22) and are clearly of much more use in the world of mathematics and science than in the world of human affairs.

Wimsatt notes that heuristics have certain characteristics that limit their usefulness as tools. They do not guarantee a correct solution although they cost substantially less in time, money, and effort than an algorithm (assuming that one is available for the specific human situation), and they produce systematic patterns of failure and error (DeRoos, 1990, p. 278). Despite these limitations, human beings are not as constrained as they might be in their problem solving because, "through the convergent application of multiple heuristics, one increases the likelihood of attaining a desirable outcome" (DeRoos, p. 280); although heuristic correspondence with the real world may be imperfect, it is sufficiently congruent with reality to allow people to function adequately (p. 281).

It appears that "heuristic problem solving focuses on the most solution-relevant variables (from the perspective of the problem solver) in a particular situation and ignores other variables. In that manner a very complex process can be coped with" (Osmo & Rosen, 1994, p. 123). In addition to using heuristic devices, human beings need to have knowledge of the world and their specific problematic issue, and the ability to apply this knowledge in a problem-solving process (DeRoos, 1990, p. 278).

BASIC ASSUMPTIONS

It remained for Compton and Galaway, in 1975, to elaborate upon and expand the basic model that Perlman had first conceptualized nearly twenty years before, and to make their thoughts available to social work students in textbook form. The authors note that their expansion and deepening of the Perlman model resulted in "extending the problem solving process to groups, organizations, and communities and in broadening our model to include more emphasis than one finds in Perlman's work on transactions with and change in other social systems" (1994, p. 49).

As Compton and Galaway have theorized extensively about how problem solving works, much of the following material will be drawn from their deliberations (1994). The authors note that all of their assumptions are based on five theories drawn from those related to human development and the transactions people undertake with the social environment. These theories include systems theory, communications theory, role theory, ego psychology, and concepts of human diversity (1994, p. 57). Among the many assumptions they make, one is that problems in living do not represent weakness and failure on the part of a client, but rather are the outcome of a natural process of human growth and change (1994, p. 44). If problems are an inevitable part of life, the capacity to solve them is also accessible to people. The process may be blocked for clients because they lack knowledge, have inadequate resources, or experience emotional responses that impair their ability to problem solve. However, as part of the problem-solving method, the social worker consciously works at creating a collaborative relationship that can be used to motivate and support clients to do the hard work of thinking and feeling through their problematic situation.

The relationship between client and worker in all modalities of practice is a source of encouragement and creative thinking in the problem-solving process. Of this Compton and Galaway say:

Relationship is the medium of emotions and attitudes that acts to sustain the problem solving process as practitioner and client work together toward some purpose. Thus . . . the problem solving process can be thought of as operating through a partnership resting on the ability of each partner to relate and communicate with the other (1994, p. 43).

Clearly, the assumption is that client and worker will be able to communicate about problems, goals, resources, planning, and implementation. However, the authors are firm that the "burden of rational headwork lies with the practitioner, not the client," so although clients could benefit from learning the problem-solving process, there is no expectation that they must bring that knowledge with them to the helping interaction. In fact, the position is taken by some problem-solving theorists that clients experience some of their problems in living because they lack well-developed problem-solving skills. For example, Hepworth and Larsen devote a chapter of their text to outlining a method for teaching problem-solving skills to clients who lack this experience so that they can apply it in daily interactions (Hepworth & Larsen, 1990, pp. 415–424).

Hepworth and Larsen outline the assumptions they make about teaching problem solving as follows:

> (1) people want to control their own lives and to feel competent to master the tasks they see as important; (2) motivation for change rests on some integration between a system's goal and its hope-comfort imbalance; (3) the social worker is always engaged in attempting to have some interactions or transactions with or among systems; (4) systems are open, and input across their boundaries is critical for their growth and change; (5) while a system must have a steady state for its functioning, it is constantly in flux; and (6) all human systems are purposive and goal seeking (1990, p. 57).

USING PROBLEM SOLVING TO ACHIEVE CHANGE

Compton and Galaway make the point that while the written description of problem solving is linear in nature, the application of the model in real life situations is circular. In any of the stages, the worker or client could loop back to an earlier stage or forward to a step that lies in the future, if the circumstances require it. The process is flexible in nature, allowing considerable latitude in its application. A modified summary of Compton and Galaway's short form outline of the problem-solving model follows. The longer form maintains the basic sequence, but elaborates on each step (Compton & Galaway, 1994, pp. 59–61).

PROBLEM-SOLVING MODEL

I. *Contact Phase*
    A. **Problem identification**—as seen by client, others, and worker. Problem for work is defined.
    B. **Goal identification**—short- and long-term goals stated. What does client wish for or need? What resources are available?

    C. **Contract**—preliminary in nature as it consists of clarifying the agency's resources and committing to further study of the problem.

    D. **Exploration**—of the client's motivation, opportunities, and capacities.

II. *Contract Phase*

    A. **Assessment and evaluation**

        How are problems related to needs of client system?

        What factors contribute to the creating and maintaining of the problem?

        What resources and strengths does client have?

        What knowledge and principles could be applied from social work practice?

        How can the facts best be organized within a theoretical framework in order to resolve the problem?

    B. **Formulation of a plan of action**

        Set reachable goals

        Examine alternatives and their likely outcomes

        Determine appropriate method of service

        Identify focus of change efforts

        Clarify roles of work and client

    C. **Prognosis**—what is worker's hope for success?

III. *Action Phase*

    A. **Carrying out the plan**

        Specify point of intervention and assign tasks

        Identify resources and services to be used

        Indicate who is to do what and when

    B. **Termination**

        Evaluate with client system accomplishments and their meaning

        Learn with client about reasons for lack of success

        Talk about ways to maintain gains

        Cope with ending of relationship

        Review supports in natural network

    C. **Evaluation**

        A continual process throughout contact

        Were purposes accomplished?

        Were appropriate methods chosen to induce change?

        What has client learned that can be used in ongoing problem solving?

        What can worker learn to help with similar cases?

PROBLEMS WITH APPLYING THE MODEL

One of the difficulties in applying problem solving to real-life situations is that it is too challenging to process all of the information called for in the various stages (Osmo & Rosen, 1994, p. 123) and as a consequence, people choose the solution that best satisfies, although it may be far from optimal. In a more specific analysis, Johnson and Johnson identify the blocks that exist to using problem solving effectively in groups. However, with some accommodation, the issues they raise relate to problem solving in all human contexts (1975, pp. 269–270). Their list follows:

1. *Lack of clarity in stating the problem:* this step requires time, as the process is bound to fail if people attempt to solve the wrong problem, or one that is only partially defined.
2. *Not getting the needed information:* minimal information results in poor problem definition, fewer alternative strategies, with consequences inaccurately predicted.
3. *Poor communication among those involved in the process:* communication is central to the entire method from definition to task allocation, so clarity and comprehensiveness must remain goals of the interchange.
4. *Premature choice or testing of alternative strategies:* when the process discourages creative thinking and free expression, a direction which has not been thoroughly discussed might be chosen.
5. *Climate in which decisions are made is critical or demands conformity:* such a situation violates the self-determination value of social work and impoverishes the process.
6. *Lack of skills in problem solving:* people can be trained to use the method in the context of their current problem.
7. *Motivation is lacking:* people who problem solve must have some need to change their situation and hope that it can be changed. Pressure to change may come from many sources, but the experience of engaging in the process itself can generate hope.

TREATMENT: PRINCIPAL THERAPEUTIC CONCEPTS

In the early conceptualization of this approach, Perlman conceived of problem solving as her contribution to what social casework should be. In that conceptualization, it was clearly seen as a process rather than a goal and much effort was put into thinking about how to make the process happen. For her, the process involved an active engagement of the client in recognition and ownership of the problem. She was strongly influenced by the work of John Dewey and his conviction that learning was problem solving (Perlman, 1957, p. 247). This notion fits very well with Perlman's own conviction that social work practice had to move away from an overemphasis on pathology to an increased recognition of the health or the strengths the client possessed to deal with the problem. This was also a good fit with Perlman's original position, in which she did not see the problem as intrapsychic or within the client, but primarily as a problem or problems in daily living that impeded the level of satisfaction the client experienced in daily activities. Thus, the problem-solving process is a tool for resolving problems that arise in the course of everyday life (Bunston, 1985) and impede the level of satisfaction persons experience in their daily activities.

As mentioned earlier, several of the initial therapeutic concepts developed in the problem-solving process were drawn from the functional school, particularly the work of Jessie Taft and Virginia Robinson. The belief that clients come for help only when they feel that a crisis exists emphasizes the here and now and Perlman's conviction that the potential for change is strongest when the client is motivated to seek help (Perlman 1986, p. 249). She stresses, as did theorists such as Hollis (1964) in her psychosocial model, that one must begin where the client is, but she saw herself parting from the psychosocial school, which she believed required study and diagnosis as a precedent to treatment. For Perlman, the person is always in the process of being and becoming, which suggests more emphasis on the person in the present and much less emphasis on the influence of past life events.

The concepts of the importance of the *place,* that is, of the agency itself, was explored in the early formulations of problem solving, in particular, the importance of the client's preconceptions of the agency's expectations and the client's expectations of the agency. Perlman argued that the client's perceptions and expectations of the agency needed to fit within the service mandate of the agency, which often dictated the nature of the intervention for the client. Since the early theoretical constructs around the importance of the agency, a much more formal type of contracting between worker and client in a variety of different agency settings has evolved.

The importance of *time* is a well-recognized therapeutic concept associated with the problem-solving process. The realization that each intervention has a beginning, middle, and end was discussed by Perlman as an important and often overlooked concept. This same idea is also found in the writing of Florence Hollis, Mary Woods, and Francis Turner. In the developing phases, a good deal of attention was given to the beginning and end of the helping process. There was a general acknowledgment that the middle phase was perhaps least well understood, although more recently it has been recognized as the crucial part of the interventive time span in which often the most meaningful work is done by the client and the therapist. However, originally the end of the process was seen as a time to review what had happened, to take stock and decide whether treatment would terminate or continue on into some other area identified as problematic by the client. The concept that a definite time period was beneficial to the tasks accomplished has proven useful for social work therapists. In fact, it was developed in much more detail by William Reid in his planned short-term treatment and still further expanded in collaboration with Laura Epstein in their work on task-centered practice (Reid & Epstein, 1977).

Partialization is another work contribution of problem-solving theory. This concept emerged from casework but later moved into other interventive methods; it involved taking a complex, or set, of problems and breaking them into smaller and more manageable pieces for focus and work within the therapeutic context. Social workers have found this approach particularly useful in work with multiple-problem families or crisis-oriented clients. It reduces anxiety and mobilizes energy on the part of the client to work on a piece of the overall problem. A further advance came when it was recognized that a small success in one area of a larger problem cluster often provided motivation for the client to transfer this initial ability to problem solve to other larger and more complex areas of difficulty.

Perlman viewed problem solving as a method of *intervention.* Other practice models incorporated the problem-solving process into their theoretical approach "by relating it to the knowledge, values and skills necessary to engage in effective practice" (Bunston, 1985, p. 225). The original focus of intervention was the person's inability to cope with a problem due to some lack of motivation or opportunity. Underlying this approach was the basic assumption that all of human living involves problem solving on a daily basis and that persons must solve problems to gain pleasure and satisfaction rather than frustration and punishment. Perlman sees a strong relationship between education and therapy, as did her teacher Gordon Hamilton in earlier years. This is particularly so in that both promote a person's confidence and gratification in his or her ability to employ problem-solving strategies in a helpful manner. It was acknowledged that education is chiefly addressed to intellectual abilities and therapy to motivational drives and directions; therefore, casework was seen as being halfway between education and therapy (Perlman, 1957).

Problem-solving therapy is a present-centered, reality-based model of practice that focuses on where the client is at the crucial time of needing and seeking out help. It expects that persons have an ability to work toward both solving their problems and using their powers to bring about new experiences both rewarding and fulfilling in terms of an increased competence to handle the problems of everyday life. It also acknowledges that such a drive may be waiting to be channeled and engaged in a more effective form of coping with a present dilemma. In short, it explains the presence of a drive for the expansion of the sense and use of self. This concept was later expanded by Germain and Gitterman in the development of the life model, which emphasizes the ongoing transactions between persons and their environment (1980).

A major component of the helping relationship was its focus on the present, as well as its acknowledgment of the power of the therapeutic relationship to motivate and engage the client in working on the identified problem. Problem solving shares with psychodynamic theory a belief in the necessity for an empathetic, caring, supporting, enhancing type of relationship and acknowledges that such an approach works particularly well with clients who are trusting, responsive to warmth, and able to reach out for help when needed. The problem-solving approach, however, also is able to respond to and engage the resistant and nonvoluntary client and the natural ambivalence that occurs when negative feelings arise or when expectations are not fully met. In the relationship-building process, Perlman often described as the first problem to be solved the need to draw out negative attitudes and feelings from the client to demonstrate the worker's ability as therapist to accept and deal with projected anger or suspicion (1957, pp. 154–155).

The nature of the helping relationship centered on the present minimizes the significance of transference and the impact of the unconscious. Like the existentialist approach, this theory emphasizes the authenticity between the worker and the client rather than recreating an earlier relationship, as might be seen from a transference perspective.

For Perlman, the concept of assessment or diagnosis represented a significant departure from the diagnostic school. Originally she called this process diagnosis, but later preferred the term "diagnostic assessment." Instead of viewing this process as a prelude to treatment, as she interpreted the position of the psychosocial school, the process was viewed as one that was ongoing throughout the life of the case. Its principal focus was on assessing the client's motivation and how to best engage it in the process. The motivation was to be connected as quickly as possible with available opportunities. This process was given the designation M-C-O, where M stood for motivation, C for capacity, and O for opportunity. This formulation was later used by Lillian Ripple and her associates in their research. Ripple, as cited by Perlman, described it as follows: "the client's use of casework service as determined by his motivation, his capacity, and the opportunities afforded him by his environment and by the social agency from which he seeks help" (1986, p. 252).

While the term "diagnostic assessment" is retained, it is seen as a much more present and ongoing process in which the person's ability to work on the identified problems with whatever coping capacities are available is assessed. Diagnosis then, in this theory, focuses on clarifying the nature of the problem, the outcome desired by the client, and the ability of the client to work toward that outcome.

The concept of *social history* in problem-solving theory mainly concerns who the client is. It is a process that is ongoing and is used to help the client understand his or her situation. Perlman suggests that it is only necessary to look at past events when such events directly affect the present situation, as in problems related to intergenerational illness such as depression or alcoholism.

Since its earliest days, problem-solving theory has focused primarily on the beginning phase of treatment. There are several reasons for this emphasis. Primarily it is because of the awareness of the importance of engaging new clients in a process in which they move from the role of applicant to one in which they participate in the services offered with the assistance of a supportive, clarifying helping person. Secondly, this theory stresses the necessity to partialize the problem to be treated in order to permit examination in depth of its parts. This was based on a more fundamental concept that held that the most crucial elements of the interventive process, particularly regarding the client's participation, are found and experienced within the first few hours shared by the therapist and client. Further, this theory holds that it is clients with motivation and capacity who are best able to use the help offered by a problem-solving approach. Thus, with other types of clients, the progress may be much slower and some steps may need to be retraced several times. But Perlman insists that the essential process is the same:

> a responsiveness to feeling; its acceptance, along with the expectation that it may need to change; the stimulation of consideration and reflection on behaviours as they affect the problem; the examination of possible alternatives and the anticipation of their "pay-off"; and the making of some decision or choice, minuscule though it may be about who is to do what, and how (1986, p. 259).

PRINCIPAL APPLICATIONS IN SOCIAL WORK PRACTICE

As discussed earlier in this chapter, problem solving is an approach that allows worker and client the freedom to match appropriate means of introducing change into the client's system in congruence with the nature of the problem and the available resources. As human beings, when we problem solve, we make a subjective decision or interpretation based on our orientation or our model of objective reality. The fact that the solutions we use are successful demonstrates over time that they are based upon reality, which, although subjective, correlates with the objective reality of the actual world. In social work practice, the basis of much of our professional interventations is frequently described as "practice wisdom," which is described as a marriage of our knowledge base, our accumulated experience, and our professional judgment blended into every interventive process that we undertake.

In her study, DeRoos (1990, p. 282), analyzing the concept of practice wisdom, describes two related concepts from the writings of Donald Schon (1983). "Knowing-in-action" describes the practice of a skillful social worker; it reflects spontaneous behaviors that do not stem from prior intellectual cognition. DeRoos cites Schon as follows:

> Common sense admits to the category of know-how, and it does not stretch common sense very much to say that the know-how is in the action. . . . Although we sometimes think before acting, it is also true that in much of the spontaneous behaviour of skillful practice, we reveal a kind of knowledge which does not stem from a prior intellectual operation (1990, pp. 50–61).

For example, in an initial meeting with a disturbed client, an experienced social worker may make the judgment within the first few minutes that the person is a danger to himself or to someone else and may move immediately to take the appropriate action. This, even though the social worker has never before seen this particular client. Schon's second problem-solving concept is "reflecting-in-action" (pp. 54–59). Reflecting-in-action involves a conscious evaluation undertaken in the course of the action itself. It is different from knowing-in-action, which refers to the various cognitive and behavioral problem-solving habits that we may have developed and internalized. Reflecting-in-action is turning "thought back on action and on the knowing which is implicit in action" (Schon cited in DeRoos, 1990, p. 283). As we know, the skilled social worker effectively reflects in action and achieves desired results because the evaluation of action and trial and error action may work interactively. However, in some instances, this, the level of performance, is not sufficient to achieve satisfactory results and a competent practitioner is required to reflect in action. At this level of knowing, the social worker continually evaluates unexpected outcomes, which promotes effective functioning, even as one model is revealed as imperfect or incomplete (DeRoos, 1990, pp. 283–284). Reflecting-in-action allows one to modify or extend the practice model to more effectively adapt to the conditions of the practice as it is occurring. Over the years, subsequent classes of students and practitioners have longed for a practice model that is essentially stable but also flexible enough to be adapted to particular situations. Many are disillusioned to learn that practice knowledge cannot be explained in such simplistic terms. Only later do they come to realize that the validity of a particular model, and of their own practice wisdom, is shown by the results of their application in practice. If practice intervention is successful over a period of time, then for practical purposes, as DeRoos points out (1990, p. 281), the model is valid. The importance of practice wisdom is realized when social workers operating on the basis of a practice model are able to uncover what is common and unique in a practice situation, and to find adequate solutions to problems for which there are no preexisting solutions. Finally, practice wisdom is seen as a process more basic than the formalized methods of learning and problem solving with which students and practitioners alike struggle on a daily basis. It is, as DeRoos points out, "a process of discovery, in action related to one's living effectively in the world. It is the extension of that process to the social work practice arena which allows one to become an effective practitioner and to gain what social workers have come to call practice wisdom" (1990, p. 285). The nature of the relationship between practice wisdom and a problem-solving practice model has important implications for every type of client system.

Over time, problem solving expanded to included applications to the small group and the family. In discussing the importance of problem solving in the many types of groups with which social workers are involved, Johnson and Johnson note that "the adequacy of group problem solving is the primary focus of group skills," and they go on to describe the special challenges of implementing the steps of problem solving when many minds are brought to bear on the task of choosing the most suitable solution to an issue with a variety of interpretations (1975, p. 257). Approaches to finding a common ground among the varied perspectives that are inevitable in a group are examined by Sheafor, Horejsi, and Horejsi (1988, pp. 472–482).

In the context of the family, systems theory combines with problem solving to produce a process that is sensitive to the multiple needs of the individuals who make up the family, but is also alert to the necessity of the family system as a whole to survive and thrive. Haley wrote a pioneering work blending these themes of meeting individual and family needs through a problem-solving experience (1976). This approach has been outlined as well by Epstein and Bishop, who describe their intervention as one in which family members "develop effective problem-solving methods which can be generalized for use in resolving future difficulties" through participation in a seven-stage problem-solving process that includes clarifying communication techniques and effective role performance (1981, pp. 444–482).

EMPIRICAL BASE

Problem solving provides social work with the foundation necessary to scientifically analyze a particular interventive approach with a client system. Bloom and Fischer outline in detail how the single-subject design method is used to evaluate whether change is a result of social work intervention, chance, or other factors (1982). They advocate that all practitioners adopt a systematic approach to monitor the course and outcomes of their work with clients in order to respond to societal and professional pressures to demonstrate accountability and effectiveness. Similar pleas for evaluating practice are expressed by McMahon (1990, pp. 245–293) and Kirst-Ashman and Hull (pp. 268–291), who correlate the measurement of progress or regression in a particular case with the worker's having followed a problem-solving sequence that specifies the goals to be attained, so that the question of whether or not a problem has been resolved can be determined.

Research questions related to the problem-solving method itself abound. In their analysis of how social workers use knowledge, Ashford and LeCroy indicate that there are three basic models of knowledge utilization: the research and development model, in which basic research leads to practical application; the problem-solving model, in which the identification of a problem leads to research directed toward resolving it; and the interactive model, in which researchers and practitioners work together interactively and continuously (1991, p. 307). The authors identify one of the major gaps in the literature on the problem-solving approach as research on how social workers use information in day-to-day problem solving (p. 309), and how they state the problem they wish to solve, which is the first step in knowledge seeking (p. 315).

Maluccio proposes that more focus be placed on the study of natural problem solving (1983). This question of how people actually solve problems when faced with normal life circumstances is underlined by Osmo and Rosen's research, which indicates that, "in attempting to solve interpersonal problems of daily life, people do not follow a uniform strategy, and that differences in strategy are attributable in part to the specificity of the problem situation" (1994, p. 135). They suggest that more research be done on "assessing a client's flexibility-rigidity for coping with a variety of problems" and on "the extent to which workers should adhere to normative standards in their problem solving efforts" in view of the differences in emphasis clients need, based on whether they have specific or nonspecific information about the problem (1994, p. 136). Finally, Heppner raises the research question of how effective it is to teach problem solving to clients, an approach that is almost an article of faith but about which proof of effectiveness is essential (1978, p. 372). He goes on to state that other problem-solving research might focus on making objective and subjective realities more congruent, on aspects of training that would encourage the transferability of skills, and on the clues an individual attends to when making a decision (1978, p. 372).

LIMITATIONS

Although it is evident that much of contemporary social work clinical practice in North America does deal with reasonably intact persons struggling with the day-to-day problems of our complex lives, these are not the only situations met with in practice. Thus, like all theories, there are limitations to the applicability of problem solving. The first limitation would appear when we are dealing with highly disturbed people and different kinds of interventive skills and different goals for clients are needed. Certainly there are disturbed persons for whom a problem-solving approach could be utilized; however, there are other situations in which the focus of treatment will be of a different nature; for example, when dealing with a suicidal client, the stress will be on engaging with the person in a facilitating manner.

There is also the question of whether this theory is applicable to all ethnic and cultural groups. Since it has a very cognitive and action-oriented basic value, this may not fit the worldview of clients whose expectation of the helping process might be much different from dealing with immediate problems in daily living. Neither does it seem appropriate for persons who come to us from a position of strength and whose goal is to deal with some unfinished business from the past; for these people, much long-term uncovering work will be required. The same holds true for persons in highly transitional situations such as marriage, separation, or death; here again, the therapeutic task will frequently be of a much different nature than that of problem solving. Of course, one could extend the definition of *problem* to include any wish that a person has for change. However, this does not appear to be what Perlman and those who have further developed her theory have in mind.

PERSPECTIVES

Problem-solving theory is not generally viewed as "the currently predominant conception of practice," as Siporin referred to it in 1975 (p. 51). Rather, it seems to have been so completely absorbed into much of social work thought and process that it has essentially become the basic method that underlies much of practice in addition to the generalist approach. Its incorporation into social work practice has been gradual, and greatly unacknowledged. Nevertheless, the logical sequence of moving from problem to solution through a series of stages is evident in many practice theories, whatever their notions of human behavior or planned change.

Perhaps problem solving meets the concerns Hearn expressed in 1979 when he noted that the profession needed "ways of thinking about social work as a whole" because theories about specific methods did not address the basic purpose and procedures of the field. "The serious consequences of this deficiency in the theory of social work is that it has led us to practice as specialists more than as generalists, and without a generalist base to anchor our specialties" (p. 350). Much research needs to be done on ways for social workers to make more effective use of problem-solving theory in a more precise manner, since its correspondence to the logical processes of the human mind makes the method both practical and intuitively appealing.

BIBLIOGRAPHY

Armstrong, M.C. (1981). Toward a marital contract: A model for marital counseling. *Journal of Contemporary Social Work 62*(9), 520–528.

Ashford, J.B., & LeCroy, C.W. (1991). Problem solving in social work practice: Implications for knowledge utilization. *Research on Social Work Practice.* Vol. 1. 301–319. Beverly Hills, CA: Sage, 306–309.

Bartlett, H.M. (1970). *The Common Base of Social Work.* Washington, DC: National Association of Social Workers.

Bently, K.J., Rosenson, M.K., & Zito, J.M. (1990). *Promoting Medication Compliance: Strategies for Working With Families of Mentally Ill People.* Washington, DC: National Association of Social Workers, 274–277.

Bloom, M. (1990). *Introduction to the Drama of Social Work,* Itasca, IL: Peacock Press.

Bloom, M., & Fischer, J. (1982). *Evaluating Practice: Guidelines for the Accountable Professional.* Englewood Cliffs, NJ: Prentice-Hall.

Boehm, W. (1959). *Objectives of the Social Work Curriculum of the Future.* Vol. 1. New York: Council on Social Work Education.

Brill, N. (1985). *Working With People: The Helping Process,* 2nd ed. Philadelphia: Lippincott. 1st edition 1973.

Bruckner, D.F., & Johnson, P.E. (1987). Treatment for adult male victims of childhood sexual abuse. *Journal of Contemporary Social Work, 68*(2), 81–87.

Bunston, T. (1985). Mapping practice: Problem solving in clinical social work. *Journal of Contemporary Social Work* (April).

Compton, B., & Galaway, B. (eds.) (1994). *Social Work Processes* (5th ed.). Pacific Grove, CA: Brooks/Cole.

Davis, S. (1988). *"Soft" Versus "Hard" Social Work.* Washington, DC: National Association of Social Workers, 373–374.

DeRoos, Y.S. (1990). The development of practice wisdom through human problem-solving processes. *Social Service Review* (June), 277–287.

Dewey, J. (1933). *How We Think* (rev. ed.). New York: Heath.

Dubois, B., & Miley, K.K. (1996). *Social Work: An Empowering Profession* (2nd ed.). Boston: Allyn & Bacon.

D'Zurilla, T.J., & Goldfried, M.R. (1971). Problem solving and behavior modification. *Journal of Abnormal Psychology 78,* 107–126.

Epstein, N.B., & Bishop, D.B. (1981). Problem-centred systems therapy of the family. In A.S. Gurman and D.P. Kniskern (eds.), *Handbook of Family Therapy.* New York: Brunner/Mazel.

Erikson, E. (1959). *Identity and the life cycle.* New York: W.W. Norton.

Flavell, J.H., Miller, P.H., & Miller, S.A. (1993). *Cognitive Development* (3rd ed.). Englewood Cliffs, NJ: Prentice-Hall.

Gammon, E.A., & Rose, S.D. (1991). The coping skills training program for parents of children with developmental disabilities: An experimental evaluation. *Research on Social Work Practice, 1*(3), 244–256.

Gelfand, B. (1988). *The Creative Practitioner: Creative Theory and Method for the Helping Services.* New York: Haworth Press.

Germain, C., & Gitterman, A. (1980). *The Life Model of Social Work Practice.* New York: Columbia University Press.

Gilhooly, K.J. (1988). *Thinking, Directed, Undirected and Creative.* London: Academic Press.

Goldberg, D., & Szyndler, J. (1994). Debating solutions: A model for teaching about psychosocial issues. *Journal of Family Therapy 16,* 209–217.

Goldstein, E.G. (1984). *Ego Psychology and Social Work Practice.* New York: Free Press.

Gurman, A.S., & Kniskern, D.P. (eds.). (1981). *Handbook of Family Therapy.* New York: Brunner/Mazel.

Haley, J. (1976). *Problem-Solving Therapy.* San Francisco: Jossey-Bass.

Hartman, A. (1978). Diagrammatic assessment of family relationships. *Social Casework 59*(8), 375–387.

Hearn, G. (1979). General systems theory and social work. In F.J. Turner (ed.), *Social Work Treatment: Interlocking Theoretical Approaches.* New York: Free Press.

Heppner, P.P. (1978). A review of the problem-solving literature and its relationship to the counseling process. *Journal of Counseling Psychology 25*(5).

Hepworth, D.H., & Larsen, J.A. (1990). *Direct Social Work Practice: Theory and Skills.* Belmont, CA: Wadsworth.

Hollis, F. (1964). *Casework: A Psychosocial Therapy.* New York: Random House.

Johnson, D.W., & Johnson, F.P. (1975). *Joining Together: Group Theory and Group Skills.* Englewood Cliffs, NJ: Prentice-Hall.

Johnson, L.C. (1995). *Social Work Practice: A Generalist Approach* (5th ed.). Boston: Allyn & Bacon.

Kirst-Ashman, K.K., & Hull, Jr., G. H. *Understanding Generalist Practice.* Chicago: Nelson Hall Publishers, 1993.

Mackey, R.A., Burek, M., & Charkoudian, S. (1987). The relationship of theory to clinical practice. *Clinical Social Work Journal 15*(4).

Maluccio, A.N. (1983). Planned use of life experiences. In A. Rosenblatt and D. Waldfogel (eds.), *Handbook of Clinical Social Work.* San Francisco: Jossey-Bass, 134–154.

Martella, R., Marchand-Martella, N.E., & Agran, M. (1993). Using a problem-solving strategy to teach adaptability skills to individuals with mental retardation. *Journal of Rehabilitation* (July, August, September), 55–60.

Mayer, R.E., (1994). Problem Solving. *Encyclopedia of Human Behavior.* Vol. 3. San Diego: Academic Press, 599–602.

McGoldrick, M. (1982). Ethnicity and family therapy: An overview. In M. McGoldrick, J.J. Pearce, and J. Giordano (eds.), *Ethnicity and Family Therapy.* New York: Guilford Press, 3–29.

McMahon, M.O. (1990). *The General Method of Social Work Practice: A Problem-Solving Approach* (2nd ed.). Englewood Cliffs, NJ: Prentice-Hall.

McPeck, J. (1981). *Critical Thinking and Education.* Oxford: Martin Robertson.

Osmo, R., & Rosen, A. (1994). Problem specificity and use of problem-solving strategies. *Journal of Social Service Research 20*(1/2).

Perlman, H. (1957). *Social Casework: A Problem-solving Process.* Chicago: University of Chicago Press.

Perlman, H. (1968). *Persona: (Social Role and Personality).* Chicago: University of Chicago Press.

Perlman, H. (1970). The problem-solving model in social case work. In R. Roberts and R. Nee (eds.), *Theories of Social Casework.* Chicago: University of Chicago Press.

Perlman, H. (1986). The problem-solving model. In F.J. Turner (ed.), *Social Work Treatment* (3rd ed.). New York: Free Press.

Pincus, A., & Minihan, A. (1973). *Social Work Practice: Model and Method.* Itasca, IL: Peacock Press.

Reid, W.J. (1992). *Task Strategies: An Empirical Approach to Clinical Social Work.* New York: Columbia University Press.

Reid, W.J. (1985). *Family Problem Solving.* New York: Columbia University Press.

Reid, W.J., & Epstein, L. (1977). *Task Centered Practice.* New York: Columbia University Press.

Roberts, R.W, & Nee, R.H. (1970). The problem-solving model in social casework. In R.W. Roberts & R.H. Nee (eds.), *Theories of Social Casework.* Chicago: University of Chicago Press.

Schon, D. (1983). *Reflective Practitioner: How Professionals Think in Action.* New York: Basic Books.

Segalman, R. (1970). A problem-solving model for professional practice: A social worker's view. *Professional Psychology 1*(5), 453–454.

Sheafor, B.W., Horejsi, C.R., & Horejsi, G.A. (1988). *Techniques and Guidelines for Social Work Practice.* Boston: Allyn & Bacon.

Siporin, M. (1975). *Introduction to Social Work Practice.* New York: Macmillan.

Smiley, C.W. (1982). Managing agreement: The Abilene paradox. *Community Development Journal 17*(1), 54–59.

Spivack, G., Platt, J., & Shire, M. (1976). *The Problem-Solving Approach to Adjustment: A Guide to Research and Intervention.* San Francisco: Jossey-Bass.

Stanton, D.M. (1981). An integrated structural strategic approach to family therapy. *Journal of Marital and Family Therapy 7*, 427–439.

Taylor, J.W. (1984). Structured conjoint therapy for spouse abuse cases. *Journal of Contemporary Social Work 65*(1), 11–18.

Turner, F.J. (1986). The problem-solving model. In F.J. Turner (ed.), *Social Work Treatment: Interlocking Theoretical Approaches.* New York: Free Press, 247–266.

Weingarten, H., & Leas, S. (1987). Levels of marital conflict model: A guide to assessment and intervention in troubled marriages. *American Journal of Orthopsychiatry 5*(3), 407–417.

White, R.W. (1959). Motivation reconsidered: The concept of competence. *Psychological Review 66*.

Wimsatt, W.G. (1981). Robustness, reliability, and overdetermination. In M.B. Brewer and B.E. Collins (eds.), *Scientific Inquiry and the Social Sciences.* San Francisco: Jossey-Bass.

Woehle, R. (1994). Variations on a theme: Implications for the problem-solving model. In B. Compton and B. Galaway (eds.), *Social Work Processes* (5th ed.). Pacific Grove, CA: Brooks/Cole.

CHAPTER 22

PSYCHOANALYTIC THEORY AND SOCIAL WORK TREATMENT

HERBERT S. STREAN

P sychoanalysis as a theory of personality, a form of psychotherapy, and a research tool has undergone several modifications in the last two decades. Although Freud's notions still undergird much of psychoanalytic theory and practice, additions and modifications have come from ego psychology, the object relations school, self psychology, as well as other orientations.

In this chapter we will review some of the major concepts and constructs of mainstream Freudian analysis and also discuss some of the key contributions that have emerged from other perspectives. Our major focus in this chapter is to demonstrate how psychoanalysis' orientation to the human personality, its therapeutic approach, and its research focus can be of profound assistance to those social workers who wish to help individuals, dyads, families, and groups modify and enhance their psychosocial functioning.

PSYCHOANALYSIS: A THEORY OF PERSONALITY

One of the main postulates of psychoanalytic theory is the principle of *psychic determinism*. This principle holds that in mental functioning, nothing happens by chance. Everything a person feels, thinks, fantasizes, dreams, and does has a psychological motive. How individuals earn a living, whom they choose to marry, what kind of love they give and receive, how they interact with their children, and how much pleasure they extract from work and love are all motivated by inner *unconscious* forces (Fine, 1979; Freud, 1939).

While external factors are always impinging on the human being, the notions of psychic determinism and the unconscious help the social worker recognize that the behaviors of individuals, dyads, groups, and organizations are not only reactions to situational variables such as family, friends, and neighborhood, but are also shaped by unconscious wishes, unconscious fantasies, unconscious defenses, and unconscious ethical imperatives.

The notion of the unconscious is of enormous aid to social workers in helping them better understand the client's presenting problem. Psychoanalytic practitioners and theorists have been able to demonstrate, for example, that every chronic marital complaint is an unconscious wish of the complainer. The husband who constantly complains that his wife is cold and unresponsive unconsciously wants such a wife— a warm and responsive wife would scare him—and that is why he stays married to the woman about whom he constantly complains. Similarly, parents who consistently complain that their children are too aggressive, or oversexed, or too tomboyish or too effeminate unconsciously provoke and sustain such behavior in their children. Close examination of parent-child interaction inevitably demonstrates that parents subtly reward their children for the very behavior they consciously repudiate (Hamilton, 1958; Strean, 1994).

As social workers utilize the notion of the unconscious in their assessments and treatment plans, they begin to consider with the client who constantly feels rejected by her employer just why this client unconsciously wants to be demeaned by her employer and humiliated by one she experiences as a parental figure. They see the value of exploring with the student who constantly fails the possible gratifications and protections the student derives from failing. They eventually realize that clients who are very depressed about their single or marital status may unconsciously desire that status. And to help a sexually impotent man they may ask themselves, "What unconscious protection and unconscious gratification does this client get from having a flaccid penis?"

When social workers utilize the concept of the unconscious in their work, they begin to recognize that the tempestuous battles of a married couple, the alienation and divisiveness in a family or group, and the dissension in an organization or. community all have unconscious meaning that must be understood before therapeutic assistance can be given.

Freud saw the human personality from several distinct but intermeshing points of view: structural, topographic, genetic, dynamic, economic, interpersonal, and cultural. These points of view, when combined, are called the metapsychological approach, and all of them are needed to fully comprehend the functioning of the human personality.

The metapsychological approach utilized by psychoanalysis is the most complete system of psychology available. It considers both the inner experiences and the outer behavior of individuals, both their presents and their pasts, their individual situations and their social circumstances. The completeness of the psychoanalytic approach is often obscured by a variety of misrepresentations that are to be found in both professional and popular literature (Fine, 1973, 1979).

Many writers agree that psychoanalysis represents, in the social sciences, the greatest revolution of the twentieth century. It has given mankind a new research tool through the concept of the unconscious and allied factors; it has clarified the possibilities of happiness that exist in philosophies that have been prevalent in previous centuries; and it has provided a solid basis for the investigation of human beings in all of their psychological and social functioning (Allan, 1974; Auden, 1947; Hale, 1971; Jones, 1953; Parsons, 1951).

THE STRUCTURAL POINT OF VIEW

One of the most helpful orientations that psychoanalytic theory can provide for the social worker is the structural point of view. This perspective points out that there are many aspects of the human psyche that interact and are interdependent. The id, the most primitive part of the mind and totally unconscious, is the repository of the person's drives and is concerned with gratification. The ego, which develops out of experience and reason, is the executive of the personality; it mediates between the inner world of id drives and of superego commands and the demands of the external world. Some of the functions of the ego are judgment, reality testing, frustration tolerance, and relating to others; the ego also erects defenses against anxiety. By assessing a client's ego strengths and weaknesses, the social worker can determine how well she is adapting, because the more severe the client's disturbances, the less operative are the ego functions and vice versa.

The superego is the judge or censor of the mind and is essentially the product of interpersonal experiences. It is divided into two parts, the conscience and the ego ideal. The conscience is that part of the superego which forbids and admonishes— "Thou shalt not!"—while the ego ideal is the storehouse of values, ethical imperatives, and morals. It commands the person in the form of "Thou shalt."

Social workers sometimes overlook the fact that a client with a punitive and exacting superego usually has strong id wishes, usually of a murderous nature, that cause great anxiety. Rather than constantly live with unbearable anxiety, the individual with unacceptable id wishes arranges for the superego to constantly admonish— for example, "Thou shalt not enjoy pleasure!" By staying away from potentially pleasureful situations, the individual does not have to face the murderous and sadistic fantasies that are in conflict with the superego's commands. To appreciate a human phenomenon, the social work clinician must note how the mind and body are transacting and become aware of what drives, what defenses, and what ethical imperatives are opposing each other and which are working together. This interaction of id, ego, and superego is particularly helpful in understanding and assisting clients with what is still a neglected area in social work practice, namely, our clients' sexual lives and their sexual fantasies.

This can be so stated because in social work practice there is hardly a social work text that carefully examines the sexual dimension of our clients' lives and includes a discussion of the inevitable sexual transference and sexual countertransference issues in client-clinician interaction. To this day, it appears to be much easier for the model social worker to say to the client, "You seem to feel angry at me" than it is to say "You seem to want to have sex with me."

The structural point of view leads to the fact that what is at the root of our clients' sexual inhibitions and sexual conflicts is the anxiety that emanates from their unacceptable childish id wishes. If the worker can allow herself to be a benign superego in the treatment situation and encourage the client to explore and verbalize id wishes to devour, to soil, to oedipally compete or homosexually seduce, anxiety is reduced and the ego becomes stronger—strong enough to enjoy a more mature sexual relationship with someone of the opposite sex.

The structural point of view that regards the human being as a complex organism is, of course, not the perspective that most sex therapists utilize. Many of them erroneously contend that sex is essentially a bodily experience and forget that to make love successfully and enjoyably hate must be reduced, infantile wishes must be mastered, the superego must become less oppressive, and self-esteem must become reasonably sufficient.

Anybody working with human beings on a therapeutic basis should understand how id, ego, and superego function. For example, the person seeking help who consistently fails at work or in love relationships usually has unresolved infantile id wishes for which he has been busily punishing himself. These id wishes have to be discussed in treatment so that clients can see for themselves, in the company of a nonpunitive helper, just how and why they are arranging to fail. Problems that individuals bring to social work clinicians—such as parent-child conflicts, marital disturbances, family pathology, crime, drug addiction, and even poverty—should be appraised in terms of their unique id wishes, superego mandates, and ego functions in addition to the significant environmental factors.

THE EGO AND DEFENSES

As psychoanalytically oriented clinicians observed their clients with greater precision, they began to conceptualize the ego not only as a mediator but as a psychic structure that has autonomy and power of its own (Erikson, 1950; A. Freud, 1946; Hartmann, 1951, 1964). Further psychoanalytic research has revealed that the ego's power arises primarily from the development of "secondary processes": locomotion, cognition, memory, perception, and rational thought and action.

Once the ego was considered to be more than a mediator, psychoanalytically oriented clinicians became much more interested in their clients' strengths as well as in their neurotic difficulties. In their diagnostic assessments, they now try to determine what gives the client mature pleasure, what parts of the psyche are *not* involved in conflict, and which dimensions of the personality do *not* need to be modified. The psychoanalytically oriented social worker asks, for example, "Have the ego's defenses been overdeveloped?" "Is the client's social situation such that these defenses are necessary adaptations to the environment—for example, a decrepit ghetto?" (Stream, 1994).

One of the most important ego functions to which the analytically oriented clinician gives much attention is how the client defends against anxiety. When an impulse such as a sexual wish or an aggressive desire is activated, and the person feels that further acknowledgment of the impulse will conflict with ethical mandates or other superego commands, he erects defenses against experiencing the impulses.

Whenever the ego senses that acting on an impulse or even just feeling it will create danger, the ego produces anxiety. The anxiety serves as a *signal* of the impending danger and offers opposition to the emergence of unacceptable impulses. Such opposition is referred to as *defense* (A. Freud, 1946).

Some of the defenses utilized by the ego are *repression, reaction formation, isolation, protection, turning against the self, regression,* and *undoing* (A. Freud, 1946). Repression bars from consciousness the id impulse that creates anxiety so that in the individual's conscious life the forbidden wish does not exist. Reaction formation is a mechanism whereby one of a pair of ambivalent attitudes is rendered unconscious by overemphasis on the other—e.g., an individual may find himself feeling uncomfortable with certain hateful feelings; therefore, he overemphasizes his love. Isolation is a defense used to protect the individual against the danger he would feel if he experienced certain emotions in association with certain thoughts—e.g., in order not to feel the full impact of anger, a person might experience the angry thoughts consciously but not permit herself to feel the intensity of her rage, or she might feel the physiological accompaniments of rage, such as rapid heartbeat, but not have any angry ideas at her conscious disposal.

In projection, the individual attributes unacceptable wishes to some other person—e.g., "You have homosexual fantasies toward me, not I toward you." When the individual feels certain emotions toward another person but finds these emotions taboo, he may use the defense mechanism of turning against the self. For example, rather than feeling rage toward another person, particularly one who is valued, loved, or feared, the individual abuses and demeans himself instead.

If adaptation is difficult or reality presents a danger, one may use the defense mechanism of regression—i.e., the return to a less mature form of psychological functioning. For example, a child of three or four who has difficulty coping with anger about the arrival of a baby sister may regress by soiling and urinating in bed, even though he has been toilet-trained for some time. Undoing is an action whose purpose is to disprove the harm the individual unconsciously imagines may be caused if he were consciously to feel certain sexual or aggressive wishes.

In all defense mechanisms there is always an attempt to repudiate an impulse. To the id's "yes" the ego defends itself by saying "no," thus avoiding the danger of the forbidden impulse coming to consciousness. The ego can and does use as a defense anything available to it that will lessen the danger arising from the demands of an unwanted instinctual drive (Brenner, 1955).

Every good psychosocial assessment should involve a description of the client's major defense mechanisms, other ego functions and dysfunctions, major superego mandates, and frightening id wishes; it is particularly important that it be noted how these various parts of the psychic apparatus interact.

EGO PSYCHOLOGY

What has been evolving as a branch of psychoanalysis and with its own unique concepts is ego psychology. It covers the areas of study, research, theory building, and clinical application that place emphasis on, and are presented from the vantage point of, the ego as personality. In contrast to early psychoanalysis, which focused mainly on id (or drive) psychology with limited attention paid to the ego as personality, self, or defense, ego psychology has helped clinicians more fully appreciate the total person. In many ways ego psychology may be considered the combined work of Anna Freud (1946) on defenses, Hartmann's (1951) elaboration of ego adaptation, and Erikson's (1950) views of psychosocial tasks which integrate the inner and outer worlds of the human being. All of these perspectives have been enthusiastically embraced by many clinical social workers in varied settings and with different specializations.

What ego psychology has been able to provide psychoanalysis is the claim that psychoanalysis is not only a study of neuroses and psychoses, but is a general psychology of the mind, "normal" and "abnormal."

SELF PSYCHOLOGY

One of the most popular modifications of psychoanalytic theory has come from Heinz Kohut, who founded self psychology in the 1970s. Self psychology recognizes as the most fundamental essence of human psychology the individual's need to organize his or her psyche into a cohesive configuration, the self, and to establish self-sustaining relationships between this self and its surroundings. The self strives to maintain coherence, vigor, and balanced harmony among its parts (Kohut, 1971).

One of self psychology's major concepts is the notion of "the self object." The self object is one's subjective experience of another person who provides a sustaining function to the self within a relationship, evoking and maintaining the self by his or her presence or activity, such as a loving mother (Kohut, 1971, 1978). Although the term is applied to the participating persons in the individual's social orbit, it is used mainly to describe the intrapsychic experiences of various types of relationship between the self and others.

Self psychology has also popularized various forms of transference states. Among them are the self object transference, which refers to the displacement onto the therapist of the patient's need for a responsive self object matrix; the mirror transference refers to the recapitulation within the treatment situation of a wish for acceptance, approval, and confirmation of the self by the self object matrix to strengthen the damaged pole of ambitions; the idealizing transference exists when the wish for idealization or merger with a strong and wise self object is reestablished in order to strengthen the damaged pole of ideas (Kohut, 1971, 1978).

Reppen (1985) in *Beyond Freud* has suggested that Kohut's emphasis on empathy is viewed as his major contribution to psychoanalytic theory and practice.

OBJECT RELATIONS THEORY

Although object relations theory has been considered a post-Freudian development, Freud (1938, 1939) used the term in a variety of ways. An object, according to Freud, can be a real, tangible, physical person or thing, as distinguished from a subject. It can also be the mental image of some other person or thing. Finally, the object can refer to a theoretical construct, different from both a real person or thing but implying some lasting organizational structure (Moore & Fine, 1990).

The terms "object relations" and "object relationships" are often used interchangeably to designate the attitudes and behavior of someone toward his or her object. In order to preserve the distinction between what is external and what is intrapsychic, psychoanalysts use the term "object relationship" to describe the interaction between a subject and another actual person and reserve the term "object relations" for the psychological phenomena relating to objects' representations within the mind.

Object relations theory is a system of psychological explanations based on the premise that the mind is comprised of elements taken in from the outside, primarily aspects of the functioning of other persons. This occurs through the process of internalization (Moore & Fine, 1990).

Object relations theory deals with the motivations for relationships, the development of interpersonal relationships from infancy to more complex relatedness in adult life, and the structured aspects of enduring and distinctive patterns of relationships that characterize individuals.

Although there are many prominent object relations theorists, two of the outstanding ones whose work we will briefly consider are Melanie Klein and Donald Winnicott.

From her work with children, Melanie Klein became convinced that the superego begins in early infancy, in contrast to Freud's notion that it is the "heir to the Oedipus complex" and manifests itself at about age three. Klein contended that the young toddler experiences the superego as a variety of figures that actually function within the toddler's body. The internal figures were once external objects that are later introjected.

In studying the superego, Klein discovered the vital part that reparation plays in mental life and believed that reparation includes the variety of processes by which the ego undoes harm done in fantasy and restores, preserves, and revives objects (Klein & Riviere, 1937; Lindon, 1966).

In her analysis of children, Klein saw introspection and projection constantly at work. She asserted that introjection and projection function from the beginning of postnatal life. Introjection implies that the outer world is experienced as taken into the self and becomes part of the infant's inner life. Projection is a process whereby the infant attributes to other people feelings that operate within. These two processes continue throughout life (Klein & Riviere, 1937; Lindon, 1966; Segal, 1964).

According to Klein, another of the activities of the infantile mind is "splitting," which is the tendency to separate impulses and objects into various aspects, good and bad, damaged and undamaged. This process also continues throughout life.

Allied with splitting is projective identification. This involves the splitting off of those qualities of one's own mind that are experienced as dangerous and projecting them onto some other person, and then identifying with the person (Segal, 1964).

Another object relations theorist, Donald Winnicott, has contributed a number of concepts to psychoanalysis which have been used by many clinicians, particularly by social workers. "A good-enough mother" (which every child needs in order to mature) offers "a holding environment" that provides an optimal amount of constancy and comfort for the infant who is wholly dependent on her (Winnicott, 1971).

"Holding" is a maternal provision that organizes a facilitative environment which the dependent infant needs. Holding refers to the natural skill and constancy of the good-enough mother (Winnicott, 1971). Many social workers conceptualize their work so as to be a good-enough mother who provides a "holding environment" in the treatment situation.

The "true self" (Winnicott, 1965) is the inherited potential that constitutes the "kernel" of the child. Its continuing development and establishment are facilitated by a good-enough mother who provides a healthy environment and a meaningful responsiveness to the very young infant's sensorimotor and postural self.

A "false self" (Winnicott, 1965) indicates the absence of a true self, usually in a schizoid individual. If the mother is unable to care for "the id self" of the infant and imposes herself and her own needs on the youngster, a false self emerges.

THE TOPOGRAPHICAL POINT OF VIEW

The topographical approach refers to the *conscious, preconscious,* and *unconscious* states of mind. The conscious is that part of our mental activities of which we are fully aware at any time; the preconscious refers to thoughts and feelings that can be brought into consciousness quite easily; the unconscious refers to thoughts, feelings, and desires of which we are not aware but which powerfully influence all of our behavior. The unconscious not only consists of drives, defenses, and superego mandates, but it also contains memories of events and attitudes that have been repressed. It is only when unconscious wishes are discharged in fantasies, dreams, or neurotic symptoms that the unconscious becomes known. Otherwise it acts silently and completely beyond the awareness of the observer (Freud, 1938, 1939).

One of the chief characteristics of the unconscious is the *primary process,* a tape of mental functioning radically different from rational thinking. The primary process is best observed in dreams, which are frequently illogical or primitive, and do not adhere to the laws of reality. Contrasted to the primary process is the *secondary process,* which governs conscious thinking. It is rational, logical, and obeys all the rules of reality.

As indicated earlier in this chapter, one of the basic tenets of psychoanalysis is that the unconscious is always operative in all behavior, adaptive and maladaptive. It accounts for how hostile or loving a person is. Unconscious wishes, unconscious defenses, and unconscious superego mandates play a major role in sexual choices, sexual inhibitions or sexual abstinence. They determine, in many ways, how fulfilled or unfulfilled the person is on the job. The topographic point of view states that to understand and help a client, whether it be an individual or a group, the unconscious meaning of the client's behavior should be well understood. The psychoanalytically oriented practitioner always wants to know the unconscious purpose of painful symptomatology. For example, the practitioner asks himself questions like: What unconscious protection and unconscious gratification does this client get from his ulcers or migraine headaches? What unconscious protection and gratification does this spouse derive from her mate's constant criticisms?

Because unconscious wishes, defenses, and memories strongly influence interpersonal behavior as well as the individual client's self-image and self-esteem, the unconscious appears to be an indispensable concept in diagnosis and treatment.

The Genetic Point of View

Another perspective from psychoanalytic theory that can be useful to the clinician is the genetic or developmental point of view. According to this perspective, all human beings are recapitulating their pasts in the present. The man who hates his boss is frequently fighting an old battle with his father. The woman who is uncomfortable with her husband may be seeking revenge on one or both of her parents. Parents who cannot cope with their children's dependency, sexuality, or aggressiveness have probably not come to terms with their own childish wishes.

In assessing maladaptive behavior, an understanding of the client's psychosexual development seems crucial for treatment planning. For example, Mr. Jones' alcoholism may be a manifestation of acute problems on the trust-mistrust or oral level and he may prefer to suck on a whiskey bottle than depend on the love of another person whom he despises and distrusts. On the other hand, alcoholic Mr. Smith may have all kinds of sexual anxieties and therefore his alcoholism may be interpreted as a type of behavior that is safer for him than is sex. Treatment for the two men will have to be different. In Mr. Jones' case, he will probably need a therapeutic experience that will enable him to express his oral sadism and mistrust of maternal figures, including the therapist. However, if Mr. Smith's alcoholism is a regression that serves to protect him against sexual anxiety at an oedipal level, the therapeutic task, in all probability, will be to help him feel more comfortable with his unacceptable incestuous wishes and frightening phallic sadism.

During the first five or six years of life, a child experiences a series of dynamically differentiated stages that are of extreme importance for the formation of personality. In the oral stage (from birth to about age eighteen months) the mouth is the principal focus of dynamic activity; in the anal phase (from approximately eighteen months to three years) the child turns her interests to elimination functions; in the phallic stage (age three to six) she forms the rudiments of sexual identity; in latency (ages seven to eleven) erotic and libidinal interests are quiescent; and at puberty there is a recrudescence of biological drives, particularly of the oedipal interests that emerged during the phallic phase. Ambivalence toward parents and other authority figures is also characteristic of puberty and adolescence (A. Freud, 1946).

According to Freudian theory, children are *polymorphously perverse*; that is, they can derive pleasure from bodily activity. From the ages of three to five, the child engages in extensive sexual exploration and tries to find out where babies come from. Frequently she believes that babies are conceived by eating and are born through the rectum; often, a child regards sexual intercourse as an act of sadism. Sex never remains a subject of indifference for any child, and even if she is uninformed about sexual matters, there will be fantasies about them.

A phase of development that is a central complex in psychoanalytic theory and occurs in the phallic period is the Oedipal complex. The familial arrangements that a child experiences in most societies create in him a wish to replace the parent of the same sex and to have bodily contact with the parent of the opposite sex. One of the consequences of the oedipal conflict is castration anxiety in the male and penis envy in the female. The boy anticipates castration as a retaliation for his murderous thoughts about his father and the girl envies the penis because it appears to be a valuable piece of property. The penis is valuable to the girl because it is a part of the father whom she treasures and also because all children want to own everything they see that is not theirs (Freud, 1938).

Although Freud contended that penis envy is a biological fact of life, most contemporary authors believe that it is a cultural phenomenon in that girls are frequently educated to idealize boys and men. The abundance of clinical data from the play of girls in play-therapy and the associations from the dreams and fantasies of women in intensive psychotherapy strongly suggest that penis envy derives from interpersonal experiences with family members.

Responding to the strong denial that many individuals demonstrate regarding penis envy, Reuben Fine has stated: "It should be emphasized that penis envy is essentially a clinical observation about what women feel, not a derogation of women. Psychoanalysis believes very strongly in the liberation of women, and should be looked upon as one of the major movements in that direction" (Fine, 1973, p. 13).

What is sometimes overlooked in the history of the psychoanalytic movement is that Freud worked very hard to bring women into the profession. Many of his outstanding colleagues, such as Helene Deutsch, Marie Bonaparte, Lou Andreas-Salome, Hilda Doolittle, Ruth Mack Brunswick, and Joan Riviere, have described how psychoanalysis, more than many other professions, helped women achieve and fulfill themselves professionally (Freeman and Strean, 1981).

As mentioned earlier, Erik Erikson greatly expanded Freud's theory of genetic stages of instinctual development by placing development into a social and cultural matrix (Erikson, 1950). He emphasized the tasks of ego mastery presented by each stage of maturation. His eight nuclear conflicts or developmental crises—trust vs. mistrust, autonomy vs. shame and doubt, initiative vs. guilt, industry vs. inferiority, identity vs. role diffusion, intimacy vs. isolation, generativity vs. stagnation, and integrity vs. despair—correspond to Freud's stages of orality, anality, genitality; latency, puberty, etc.

According to Erikson, the human being not only unfolds according to predetermined biological phases, but human maturation cannot be viewed apart from the social context in which it transpires. For example, an infant's functioning during the oral phase cannot be assessed without taking into consideration transactions with the mother. If the infant and mother mutually gratify each other in many basic ways—

e.g., during feeding, playing, etc.—the child will learn to "trust" rather than "distrust" his environment. Similarly, if the child is helped to forgo certain pleasures and take on some frustration during toilet training (anal phase), he will develop a sense of "autonomy" rather than feel "shame and doubt." If parents help their child feel comfortable with his sexual interests and impulses, the child will be more apt to participate creatively and constructively in interpersonal relationships, and be "industrious" rather than feel "inferior."

Another important concept in Freudian theory is fixation. The term "fixation" is used to describe certain individuals who have never matured beyond a certain point of psychosocial development and are unable, in many ways, to mature further. Individuals may be fixated at any level of development—oral, anal, phallic-oedipal, etc. As part of the diagnostic assessment, the therapist has to determine where the client is fixated. Has she ever learned to trust? Or has she ever established sufficient autonomy? Or, perhaps she has never mastered the maturational task of learning how to relate intimately with another human being.

It is not always easy to determine whether a particular symptom or interpersonal difficulty is a manifestation of regression or fixation. In order to be sure, the therapist has to take into consideration the many dimensions of the client's current functioning, history, and transference reactions to the therapist.

The therapist is not only eager to establish what stage of development the client's conflict is at, but perhaps of more importance, he wants to know how significant others have responded to the patient's needs at a particular stage of development. A client suffering from alcoholism and one suffering from drug addiction may both be trying to cope with anxieties emanating from the oral period. However, in one case the client may have been underfed and in the other instance, she may have been overfed and indulged. If the client has been overfed, she will need an experience in therapy where she can learn to take on some frustration, develop controls, and defer gratification—that is, be weaned. If, on the other hand, she was insufficiently nourished, the therapist will attempt to create an atmosphere in which aggressive desires and oral hunger can be expressed and eventually be considered more acceptable to the patient.

As has already been implied, knowledge of the patient's maturational deficits not only helps the clinician understand the client's maladaptive behavior with more certainty, but appreciation of the client's maturational conflicts provide guides for treatment. Is the homosexual patient defending against an oedipal conflict? Or, is he identifying with an oral mother so that by feeding his sexual partner, he is vicariously ministering to his own oral hunger? Is the gambler storing up "gold" in his fantasies, which would signify an anal problem, or is he omnipotently striving to be an emperor, a conflict that evolves from the early oral phase when the baby wants to be a narcissistic king? Is the addict pricking herself in a phallic manner or is she feeding herself in an oral manner? These are crucial questions that the psychoanalytically oriented clinician will ask because he is very dedicated to the notion that each client's past participates and shapes current functioning.

THE DYNAMIC POINT OF VIEW

The dynamic point of view refers to Freud's instinct theory, which is concerned with libidinal and aggressive drives. Recognizing the interaction of nature and nurture in the development of the human being, the drives or instincts represent the "nature" factor (Rapaport, 1951). An instinct has four characteristics: source, aim, object, and impetus. The source is a bodily condition or need—e.g., hunger, sex, or aggression. The aim is always to achieve gratification. The object includes both that on which the need is focused—e.g., food—and all the activities necessary to secure it—going to the refrigerator, ingesting, masticating, etc. The impetus of an instinct is its strength, which is determined by the forces or intensity of the underlying need—e.g., hunger, sexual need, aggressive wish—and these needs vary in quantity in different individuals or in the same individual at different times.

In making a diagnostic evaluation, the clinician first wants to ascertain if his client's instincts are being gratified. Is he getting enough food and enjoying it? If not, why not? Is he realistically being deprived and/or is he arranging to feel deprived? Does gratifying the hunger instinct create anxiety for the client and is that why he does not want to eat too much? Similar questions may be asked of the client regarding his sexual life and elimination habits. The answers to these questions help the therapist pinpoint conflict, plan intervention, gauge the patient's motivation, and determine his capacity for a working relationship with the therapist.

THE ECONOMIC POINT OF VIEW

The economic point of view stresses the quantitative factor in mental functioning. According to this principle, all behavior is regulated by the need to dispose of psychological energy. Energy is discharged by forming "cathexes," that is, investing a person or an object with psychological energy. Something or somebody is cathected if the object or person is emotionally significant to the person.

Freud felt that energy is needed to fuel the psychic structure and he saw this energy coming from the sexual drives. Later, Heinz Hartmann (1964) concluded that the ego works with "deaggressivized" and "desexualized" energy, which he called "neutral" energy. It should be stated that the energy concept is among the most controversial in the field and many theoreticians contend that it can be dispensed with entirely (Fine, 1973).

INTERPERSONAL RELATIONSHIPS, CULTURE, AND VALUES

According to psychoanalytic theory, how an individual relates to others is essentially based on how she experienced herself vis-à-vis family members. The vicissitudes of interpersonal relationships depend very heavily on transferences from the individual's family structure. Although the concept of transference is largely used in connection with psychotherapy, it is a universal characteristic of human beings. The kinds of experiences that offer gratification in the family tend to be pursued, while those that frustrate the individual tend to be avoided. Most relationships in adult life reflect the kinds of gratifications and frustrations that the person experienced in her own nuclear family.

Freud suggested that the child proceeds from a narcissistic stage, in which she is concerned only with herself, to an anaclitic stage, in which she is dependent upon somebody else, and eventually to a stage of object love (Freud, 1933). In object love, there is a mutuality between the person and another human being and this love involves a synthesis of tender and erotic feelings toward the opposite sex. Hartmann (1964) has proposed a movement in relationships from those that are "need-gratifying" to those where there is mutuality and "constancy." Fine (1975) has suggested that relationships start off as "attachment" in infancy and move to "admiration" (of the parents), "sexuality," then to "intimacy," and finally to "devotion." All love relationships, according to Fine, have these phases of interpersonal maturation as components.

In his early work, especially in *Totem and Taboo* (1913), Freud claimed that the same psychological mechanisms were to be found in all cultures. While the same libidinal and aggressive drives exist in all human beings and all cultures, they are molded in different ways by different societies.

One of the most notable attempts to unify psychoanalysis and the study of culture was made by Kardiner (1945). He coined the term "basic personality structure" to designate a group of character traits in the modal individual of a particular culture. This concept was a refinement of the older term "national character." An example of an American character trait is "ambitiousness."

The question of whether there are any values inherent in psychoanalysis has been much debated. Freud did not speak of values too much but did take the position that the mature person is one who can love and work. Fine (1981) has attempted to extend Freud's image of love and work and has argued that psychotherapy is the first scientific attempt to make people happy. His "analytic ideal" involves the pursuit of pleasure, the release of positive emotions, elimination of hatred and other negative emotions, enjoying sex, acquiring a meaningful role in the family and a sense of identity in a larger society, engaging in some satisfying form of work, pursuing some form of creative activity, and being able to communicate with other people.

A PSYCHOANALYTIC VIEW OF PSYCHOPATHOLOGY

According to psychoanalytic theory, whenever an individual is suffering from a neurotic symptom, such as an obsession, phobia, or psychosomatic disease, psychic conflict is always present. The individual's defenses—e.g., projection, denial—which have been used to protect him against ideas, thoughts, or memories that are unbearable and cause anxiety, have broken down. As mentioned earlier, anxiety is a warning to the person that some unacceptable thought or action will reach consciousness (Freud, 1923). If the drive is too strong or the defense too weak, anxiety erupts and the person forms a neurotic symptom. The symptom expresses concomitantly the individual's impulse and his dread of the impulse. In a phobia—e.g., fear of going out on the streets—two variables are at work: the very situation that the individual fears—the street—and also the fact that the street excites him. The stimulation that is induced causes anxiety because the excitement emanates from sexual fantasies that are unacceptable. A symptom is often referred to as a "compromise formation" because it is a composite expression of the patient's wishes, anxiety, defenses, and fears.

Bob, an eighteen-year-old college freshman, reported to his social worker that he was plagued by obsessive thoughts and compulsions. The obsessive thoughts took the form of constantly wanting to blurt out in class, "Drop dead, drop dead!" The thoughts created anxiety and interfered with his concentration. In addition, when Bob left his dormitory room he was compelled to make sure that the door was locked. Even after he checked it several times, he had to go back to make sure it was closed.

As the social worker and Bob reviewed the client's history it became quite clear that Bob was very angry about being away from home for the first time in his life. At home and in his community, Bob was loved by all and felt very important; at college, he was one of many and not particularly well known. This situation punctured his narcissism and activated a great deal of anger toward his college peers and toward college authorities. However, the anger that Bob felt about missing home and being in college was unacceptable to him. He repudiated his dependency feelings (denial) and repressed his anger. Nonetheless, his drives were intense and his defenses were not strong enough to negate them. Consequently, his anger erupted in the obsession, "Drop dead, drop dead!"

Unconsciously, Bob wished that his parents and friends would perhaps surprise him by visiting him on campus. Unconsciously, he wished to leave his door open so they could walk in and be there when he returned from classes.

As Bob was able to share with his social worker his fantasies of kissing and hugging his parents and being a young boy again, his symptoms diminished. As he could acknowledge his anger and his dependency and particularly his wishes to be bathed and fed by mother and cuddled by father, he did not need to use as much energy to defend himself and his functioning improved.

Freud never abandoned the idea that the roots of a psychoneurosis lie in disturbance of the libidinal life of childhood. However, he soon recognized that the stories his patients told him of having been sexually seduced in childhood were, in fact, fantasies rather than real memories, even though the patients themselves believed them to be true. Although this discovery was at first a blow to Freud, he made a step forward by recognizing that, far from being limited to childhood, such exceptional, traumatic events as seductions, sexual interests, and activities are a normal part of human psychic life from earliest infancy on (Brenner, 1955).

The conclusion of Freud's that many patients fantasize being seduced but were not really sexually seduced has been challenged. In his book *The Assault on Truth:*

Suppression of the Seduction Theory Masson (1984) contends that Freud found the idea of children being sexually seduced so intolerable that he altered the truth. According to Masson, many of Freud's patients were sexually abused, but Freud refused to acknowledge it in writing. It would appear from a careful review of Freud's writings that although he may have "covered up" some of the truth, he did point to parents actually being openly seductive, such as in his own case of "Little Hans."

In his research on the psychoneurotic symptom, Freud compared a symptom to a dream in that both are compromise formations between one or more repressed impulses and those forces of the personality that oppose the entrance of forbidden impulses into conscious thoughts and behavior. Freud was able to demonstrate that neurotic symptoms, like the elements of a dream, had meaning. Symptoms, like dreams, can be shown to be the disguised and distorted expressions of unconscious fantasies.

By permitting a partial and disguised emergence of an id wish via the psychoneurotic symptom—e.g., Bob's obsession, "Drop dead!"—the ego is able to avoid some of the anxiety it would otherwise develop. By permitting an impulse, a fantasized gratification (like in a dream) that is disguised and distorted, the ego can avoid the displeasure of experiencing extreme anxiety. By coping with his unacceptable thoughts through an obsession, Bob was able to ward off his murderous wishes, his anxiety, and his guilt. This is what is known as the *primary gain* of a neurosis, that is, warding off a dangerous impulse from consciousness and diminishing anxiety and guilt.

Secondary gain refers to the efforts of the ego to exploit the gratifying possibilities of a neurotic symptom. For example, a child may enjoy the overprotection and solicitude he receives when he brings to his parents' attention his school phobia. Similarly, an adult with a psychosomatic problem such as an ulcer may be able to get tender love and care when he complains of acute stomachaches.

It is important to recognize that the difference between the functioning of a "normal" individual and that of a neurotic is one of degree. All individuals have id impulses and most people experience in themselves sadistic, masochistic, incestuous, or murderous wishes that are not acceptable to them. When defenses, which all individuals use, are not strong enough to cope with id wishes, anxiety erupts and symptoms appear.

Fine (1973) has stated:

From the beginning, therapy and theory in psychoanalysis have developed together. The significance of this simultaneous development is that the hypotheses of psychoanalysis have been subject to empirical tests at every step of the way. At an early point in the history of the science, it became apparent that the difference between the "patient" and the "nonpatient" or the difference between the "neurotic" and the "normal" is only one of degree. Furthermore, the method that psychoanalysis developed was one which relies very intensively on a deep and profound study of each individual. As a result, the kind of therapy that was practiced and is practiced now is also a type of research. (pp. 6–7)

PSYCHOANALYSIS: A FORM OF THERAPY

The psychoanalytic theory of therapeutic intervention parallels its metapsychological orientation to personality functioning. Just as the psychoanalytic theory of human behavior contends that the individual's adaptation to life cannot be fully understood unless the meaning of id wishes, ego defenses, superego admonitions, and history are exposed, a similar perspective is needed in therapy. Clients cannot be substantially helped, psychoanalysis alleges, unless they become aware of certain id wishes, face persistent superego admonitions, and recognize how they are distorting the present and perceiving it as if it were part of their childhood. If neurotic and other dysfunctional behaviors are to be significantly altered, clients must become sensitized to how they are unconsciously arranging a good part of their own misery.

FREE ASSOCIATION AND THE FUNDAMENTAL RULE

To help clients become aware of how they are unconsciously arranging to distort their love and work relationships and not achieving the happiness they consciously desire, they are asked by the therapist to observe "the fundamental rule" (Freud, 1904). This rule prescribes that the client should say *everything* that comes to mind—feelings, thoughts, memories, dreams, and fantasies. While clients in psychoanalysis usually "free associate" on a couch and are seen several times a week, the "free association" rule has much pertinence to social work practice. Many social work clinicians fail to appreciate that one of the most helpful experiences they can offer their clients is to quietly listen to them without interrupting with questions, supportive remarks, or interpretations. Social workers frequently feel that "to earn their keep" they must talk. Often, their talking is to quell their own anxiety and does not really help their clients grow.

As the client tells an unintrusive and empathetic listener what she feels and thinks, the client begins to see for herself how she is writing her own script and arranging for her own successes and failures. If she talks uninterruptedly, she will hear herself verbalize fantasies to battle, wishes to provoke, desires to seduce, fears of interacting, and urges to be mistreated.

If the social worker assumes a neutral position and does not side with or oppose the client as he talks about his conflicted marriage or upsetting relationship with employer or family members, the client's self-esteem usually rises. The client begins to feel very much like a child who has confessed a misdeed to an understanding and empathetic parent who does not censure him for what he has reported. Usually, this experience reduces anxiety and heightens self-confidence inasmuch as the therapist is experienced as a benign superego.

As the client is helped to talk without being questioned, advised, or supported, he begins to recall memories that influence his functioning in the present. He begins to see how his battle with a colleague is part of an unresolved problem with a sibling or that his oversensitivity to his wife's demands may be due to his wish to keep her as the punitive mother of his past.

As the client is not judged, censured, or criticized for her productions, she becomes less hateful and more loving. Rather than demean others when they do not agree with her, she tries to recapitulate what her therapist has done with her—understand and empathize. As she is less judgmental with relatives, friends, and colleagues, they appreciate her more.

RESISTANCE

Although most clients welcome the idea of saying everything that is on their minds and usually feel better during the early stages of the therapeutic encounter, eventually the therapy becomes painful and creates anxiety. As clients discover parts of themselves that have been repressed, confront sexual and aggressive impulses, and recover embarrassing memories, they begin to feel guilt and shame. Then they may become silent, evasive, or want to quit the therapy altogether. Or, clients may discuss certain incidents from their pasts or current circumstances and then become angry at the therapist for not reassuring, praising, or admonishing them.

When clients stop producing material and cease to examine themselves, we refer to this kind of behavior as *resistance*. Resistance is any action or attitude of the client's that impedes the course of therapeutic work. Inasmuch as every client, to some extent, wants unconsciously to preserve the status quo, all therapy must be carried out in the face of some resistance (Strean, 1983).

What is referred to as a defense in the client's daily life—e.g., projection, denial, repression, etc.—are resistances in the therapy. If, for example, a client has a tendency to project his anger onto his spouse and other individuals, in the therapy he will try to avoid examining his own angry thoughts and feelings and will instead report how his wife, friends, and relatives are hostile to him. From time to time he will also accuse the therapist of being contemptuous toward him.

Resistance is not created by the therapy. The therapeutic situation activates anxiety and the client then uses habitual mechanisms to oppose the therapist and the therapy (Greenson, 1967). To a greater or lesser degree, resistances are present from the beginning to the end of treatment (Freud, 1912).

Psychoanalytic therapy is characterized by a thorough and systematic examination of resistances. The therapist attempts to uncover how the client resists, what she is resisting, and why she is doing so. Usually the purpose of resistance is to avoid such painful emotions as guilt or shame, and frequently the guilt or shame has been aroused by an unacceptable id impulse (A. Freud, 1946).

In contrast to other forms of therapy that evade resistance or attempt to overcome them by suggestion, praise, punishment, drugs, shock, or persuasion, a psychoanalytically oriented therapy seeks to uncover the cause, purpose, mode, and history of the resistances (Knight, 1952).

Resistance takes many forms. To ward off anxiety, a client can resist treatment by coming late to sessions, absenting himself altogether, becoming very silent, refusing to pay fees, or a variety of other direct and indirect ways. The psychoanalytically oriented therapist takes the position that behavior in and of itself does not tell us very much. A resistance like lateness to appointments can have different meanings for different clients. For one client, it is a way of warding off the anxiety that is connected with feelings of intimacy. For another client, it can be a way of expressing contempt toward the therapist, and for still another client, it may be a way of trying to see if the therapist is sufficiently concerned about him, and if the therapist will ask questions about the lateness.

It is extremely important to hear the client's associations about his resistive behavior. Frequently, it takes a good deal of time before the therapist can be absolutely certain just what the resistive behavior is all about. Furthermore, as Langs (1976) has pointed out, one must always consider the therapist's possible contribution to the formation of the client's resistive behavior. Is the therapist behaving in such a way that the client wants to come late, not cooperate, or quit the treatment?

A resistance that is often overlooked in social work practice is when the client utilizes his situation as a resistance. People often seek out a social worker because they have some situational problem—a poor marriage, a conflicted parent-child relationship, an unsatisfactory job, etc. While a client's spouse, parent, employer, or teacher may not always be mature individuals responsive to the client's needs, it is very important to recognize that when clients continually focus on the problems that significant others impose on them, this is usually a sign of resistance. Most individuals would rather believe that their unhappy marriages, unsatisfactory jobs, or unstimulating interpersonal relationships are caused by forces outside themselves. Frequently, clients hope, and sometimes demand, that the social worker manipulate their environments and change the spouse, boss, or teacher. However, what is of most help to these individuals is to see the many ways they are determining their own fates and writing their own scripts. Usually, when the social worker ascribes all of the client's difficulties to the latter's situation, he is overidentified with the client and does not want to see the client's contributions to the situational difficulties.

In sum, when an individual enters into a therapeutic relationship, part of the person unconsciously works against progress. All clients, no matter how much they consciously want their lives to be different and no matter how much they are suffering, still fear change. Resistances are facts of therapeutic life, and the unconscious reasons for their unique expression must be understood by both client and therapist. Clients resist therapy for many reasons. They worry that they will be punished for their aggression, entrapped for their sexual wishes, demeaned for their dependency, and scoffed at for their childishness. It takes much patient work on the client's and therapist's part to resolve resistances

TRANSFERENCE

Perhaps the most valuable contribution of psychoanalytic theory is the concept of "transference." Anyone who is engaged in helping others make changes in their lives recognizes that in the face of all logic and reason, the client may often behave in an obstinate manner. Therapeutic progress is always hindered by the client's major resistance, the transference—feelings, wishes, fears, and defenses that influence the client's perceptions of the therapist. Transferential reactions are unconscious attempts by the client to recapitulate with the therapist types of interpersonal interactions similar to those she experienced with significant persons in the past. Every client experiences the therapist not only in terms of how she objectively is, but in terms of how she wishes the therapist to be and fears the therapist might be (Freud, 1912).

If therapists do not understand how they are being experienced by their clients, they cannot be very helpful to them. Each client responds to questions, clarifications, interpretations, directions, or environmental manipulation in terms of her transference to the therapist. If Ms. Brown loves her therapist, she will be inclined to accept and constructively utilize his therapeutic interventions; if she hates the therapist, even the most neutral question, "How do you feel?" for example, will be suspect. Finally, if she has mixed feelings toward the therapist, she will respond to virtually all interventions with ambivalence

One of the major tasks of the analytically oriented clinician is to help the client see how and why she experiences the therapist as she does. Why does the client act like a compliant child and accept everything the therapist says? Or, why does she argue with the therapist every time the latter says something? Why is the therapist's silence experienced by one client as rejection and by another as love?

Helping clients experience and understand their transference reactions is far from just a didactic exercise. As clients see that their perceptions of and responses to the therapist are similar to their perceptions and responses to significant others, they begin to get some conviction and some understanding of their own role and their own contribution to their interpersonal difficulties.

While transference reactions are always traceable to childhood, there is not a simple one-to-one correspondence between the past and the present, although sometimes there is a direct repetition, such as when the client is quite convinced that the therapist is almost identical to his father, mother, or siblings. On other occasions, there can be a compensatory fantasy to make up for what was lacking in childhood (Fine, 1982).

When the therapist recognizes that transference exists every time a client meets with a clinician, the therapist can look at her therapeutic results more objectively. If the client wants her to be an omnipotent parent to whom he can cling, then he will fight interventions aimed to help him become more autonomous. If the client wants the therapist to be a sibling rival, then he will use the therapist's interventions to continue his sibling fight. Because the client views all of the therapist's interventions through the lens of his transference, the therapist should explore with the client why he wants to perceive the therapist the way he does.

Transference exists in all human relationships. We transfer onto others parental and sibling introjects, unacceptable id wishes, superego mandates, ego-ideals, and many other unconscious elements. There is no such thing as a client who has "no transference" or in whom transference fails to develop. As clinician and client accept transference as another fact of therapeutic life and constantly study the client's transference responses, they gain an appreciation of the nature of the client's conflicts and aspects of his history that are contributing to his dysfunctional behavior (Menninger, 1958).

COUNTERTRANSFERENCE

Countertransference is the same dynamic phenomenon as transference, except that it refers to those unconscious wishes and defenses of the therapist which are always part of his perception and treatment of the client. Frequently, the client represents for the therapist an object of the past on whom past feelings and wishes are projected.

One of the major advances in psychoanalytic theory and practice during the last two decades has been the broadening of our understanding and use of the concept of countertransference. From Freud's (1912) original position that countertransference arises as a result of the patient's influence on the analyst's unconscious feelings and should be overcome quickly, current practitioners tend to view countertransference as including "all of the emotional reactions at work" (Abend, 1989, p. 374). Rather than an obstacle to be overcome, countertransference is now regarded by most dynamically oriented clinicians as "all those reactions of the analyst to the patient that may help or hinder treatment" (Skalter, 1987, p. 3).

The increased examination and discussion of countertransference has helped most therapists to recognize that the therapeutic process is always an interactive one. Boesky (1990), a contemporary psychoanalyst, has said, "I consider the 'purity' of a theoretic analytic treatment in which all of the resistances are created only by the patient, to be a fiction. If the analyst does not get emotionally involved sooner or later in a manner that he had not intended, the analysis will not proceed to a successful conclusion" (p. 573).

Another illuminating insight that has evolved from the study of countertransference in greater breadth and depth is the current view that it is a central component in the therapist's use of treatment procedures. How and when the therapist is silent, poses questions, confronts, clarifies, or interprets is based on his or her countertransference at the time of the intervention (Jacobs, 1986). Usually the awareness of countertransference is retrospective, preceded by countertransference enactment (Renik, 1993).

Insufficient attention is still paid to countertransference reactions in social work schools and social agencies; yet it is probably one of the most important variables in client dropout. If, for example, the social worker has unresolved problems connected with his own aggression, he may need to placate or be ingratiating with his client. The client, therefore, cannot improve because it is not safe to express aggression toward the therapist and she may have to act out unverbalized hatred by quitting treatment. Similarly, if a therapist is threatened by his own unconscious homosexual feelings, he may be unable to detect homosexual implications in a client's material or may perceive them where they do not exist. Not feeling understood, the client may leave the treatment situation in frustration.

Therapy usually proceeds well when the clinician likes the client. If the clinician does not really care for the person she treats, this will be reflected in her interventions and the client will sense it. While a positive countertransference is a desirable attitude, like a positive transference, it must be studied carefully (Fine, 1982).

A temptation for many social workers is to love their clients too much. When this occurs, the client is not perceived accurately or treated objectively. In their overidentification, social workers often support clients against their real or fantasized opponents rather than helping them understand their own interpersonal conflicts. Overidentification frequently takes place in working on parent-child and marital conflicts where the social worker forms a love and beloved relationship with one spouse or member of a parent-child dyad and covertly or overtly supports the client in his attacks on other family members.

Therapists are human beings and are more like their clients than unlike them (Sullivan, 1953). Because therapists have wishes, defenses, and anxieties, it is inevitable that their vulnerabilities will be activated in the therapeutic situation and that they will feel hostility toward some of those whom they want to help. It is often difficult for social workers to acknowledge their hostility toward their clients because in our profession angry feelings are considered a liability. Frequently, hostile feelings are denied and repressed, and so they manifest themselves in disguised and subtle forms. Two common expressions of disguised hostility are the use of diagnostic labels and alterations of therapeutic plans (Fine, 1982).

When clients are distrustful, isolate themselves from the clinician, miss appointments, and are unrevealing, it is quite understandable that the therapist gets discouraged, questions her own skills, and feels quite angry at the client, who does not show any progress. In anger, the therapist can give the client a diagnostic label that usually implies deep pathology and poor prognosis. For example, it is infrequent that the label "borderline" is used benignly. Rarely are social work categories such as psychopath, sociopath, hard-to-reach, poorly motivated, ambulatory schizophrenic, pseudoneurotic schizophrenia, acting-out character disorder, or narcissistic character disorder used empathetically and with warmth and concern. In the days of Mary Richmond, the social worker would honestly and simply say, "Client uncooperative, case closed!" Today, a closing summary might read: "The client's motivation was poor, the quality of his object relations was shallow, his ego was fragmented, his superego had many lacunae, and his transference was negative. Repeated attempts to help him mature were highly resisted. Case closed."

Not only do pejorative diagnostic labels usually denote a negative countertransference, but the constant changing of therapeutic modalities can also be an expression of hostility toward the client. Many a client has been placed in a group so that the therapist could subtly encourage the group members to attack the client. Family therapy has been abused in this manner, too. Occasionally, short-term treatment can be prescribed in order to reject the client. Often drugs, shock therapy, and backward isolation are utilized in the service of an unrecognized negative countertransference. Like transference, positive and negative countertransference are ubiquitous and should always be understood.

Technical Procedures in Psychoanalytic Psychotherapy

As the client talks about what is on his mind, he will run into resistances and transference reactions that evolve from his own unique psychodynamics. Much of the analytically oriented therapist's efforts are devoted to helping the client understand his unique transference reactions and his unique resistances. What are the specific activities of the therapist that will help the client resolve his conflicts?

One of the major tasks of the analytically oriented therapist is to *listen*. As the client produces material, themes emerge and the therapist *asks questions* so that persistent themes receive further elaboration. As certain resistances and other maladaptive behavior become clear to the therapist, she *confronts* the client with it; that is, she draws the client's attention to a particular phenomenon—e.g., persistent lateness to appointments—and tries to help him recognize what he has been avoiding and will have to be further understood. *Clarification,* which involves bringing the psychological phenomena with which the client has been confronted (and which he is now more willing to consider) into sharp focus, usually follows confrontation. It involves the "digging out" of significant details from the past that contribute toward the etiology of the phenomenon. *Interpretation* of the psychodynamic meaning of the patient's thoughts, feelings, and fantasies, especially in terms of their psychogenetic origin, is the hallmark of psychoanalytic therapy. Its goal is *insight:* that is, the client achieves more self-understanding. *Working-through* is the integration of understanding by repeating, deepening, and extending the understanding of resistances and transference. Finally, the client *synthesizes* the insights by working out an adequate way of living in which anxieties are kept to a minimum and pleasure is derived from living (Fine, 1982; Greenson, 1967).

As we have already suggested, effective *listening* by the clinician inevitably reduces anxiety and guilt, raises self-esteem, and unleashes energy for more constructive problem solving. An attentive listener must demonstrate that he has grasped the essential points of his client's story. This is frequently done by asking pertinent questions that truly engage the client, clarify ambiguities, and complete a picture of the client's external pressures and internal stresses (Kadushin, 1972).

In order to help the client become aware of the unconscious forces that are contributing to his problems, the therapist has to *confront* him with certain behavior of which he is unaware, such as absences from interviews after expressing warm feelings toward the therapist. It is extremely important, when confronting a client, that the therapist has enough evidence available to support the confrontation and some assurance that the confrontation will be meaningful to the client. Usually a confrontation is most meaningful to the client when the latter has some conviction, himself, about the issues being presented by the therapist.

It is not enough for the client to become aware of an impulse, wish, or idea that has been unconscious; it is equally important that he understand why he is seeking the gratification of the impulse or wish, and what effect it has on his life.

After Mr. Sidney recognized that he was late for interviews with the therapist because he felt hostile toward him, he needed help in clarifying some of the dynamics of his hostility. By studying his transference reactions to the therapist he slowly realized that he was afraid of "falling in love with older men." After Mr. Sidney spoke of several memories of his father and how he yearned for him as a boy, the therapist could clarify for Mr. Sidney that he was avoiding looking at how much he missed a father, and how much he secretly craved to hug, kiss, and fondle his father.

Currently, the term "interpretation" is being used in the psychoanalytic nature to mean a variety of activities (Sandler, 1973):

1. The therapist's inferences and conclusions regarding the unconscious meaning and significance of the client's communications and behavior.
2. The communication by the therapist of his inferences and conclusions to the client.
3. All comments made by the therapist—confrontations, clarifications, questions, etc.
4. Verbal interventions specifically aimed at bringing about dynamic change through the medium of insight.

In order to differentiate interpretation from other therapeutic activities such as confrontation and clarification, interpretation may be considered that activity which makes conscious the unconscious meaning, source, history, mode, or cause of a given psychic event. Interpretations are of three main types: *uncovering, connective,* and *integrative* (Fine, 1982). The uncovering interpretation is one in which some concealed wish is brought to consciousness. Sometimes the wish is expressed in the client's associations and sometimes it is inferred from the material. The inference cannot be too removed from the client's associations, otherwise it will have little significance to the client.

In the connective interpretation, the present is tied up with the past so that the client can see how he is distorting the present by waging old battles and is still seeking childish gratifications.

The integrative interpretation involves pulling together material from a variety of different sources. It is offered so that the client's problems and life situation are seen in a more adequate perspective than the way he is looking at them. Like all interpretations, integrative interpretations have to be repeated a number of times until the client is able to formulate a perspective in his own terms. With the therapist's help, as the client associates to his past and present, examines fantasies, dreams, defenses, and interpersonal relationships, the client achieves *insight*.

Insight is a dimension of psychotherapy that has been very much misunderstood. Many books, movies, and plays seem to imply that one insight will heal a neurosis. This *never* takes place. An insight has to be "worked through"—that is, elaborated, reviewed, and reconsidered—before it can have a real effect on the client's functioning.

To be effective and alter functioning, insight requires the lifting of repressions, the recovery of lost memories, the feeling of affects that were suppressed, and involves a new grasp of the significance and interrelations of events. Recollections take on a meaning that the client had not realized heretofore. It is in the latter connection that he will say, as Freud pointed out, "As a matter of fact I've always known it; only I never thought of it" (Freud, 1939).

Insight, to be effective, *always* must be accompanied with genuine affects and a real sense in the client of how she has distorted her perceptions. Usually a client verbalizes insights and there is no change in her functioning; she is defending against the recall of a memory, repressing a fantasy or an idea, or refusing to experience certain feelings.

Once the client comes to an insight—e.g., understands that her job failure is part of her battle with her father—the same interpretation usually has to be reviewed several times by patient and therapist before the conflict ceases to be a problem. This is what is meant by "working through." Greenson (1967) has described working through as "referring in the main to the repetitive, progressive, and elaborate explorations of the resistances which prevent insight from leading to change . . . a variety of circular processes are set in motion by working through in which insight, memory, and behavior change influence each other" (p. 42).

If insights are worked through, then there will be sustained change. Symptoms and maladaptive defenses will be given up. However, "working through" is like any learning process; it takes time to integrate new ways of looking at attitudes, thoughts, and interpersonal behavior. The client characteristically moves ahead two steps and falls back one. The same issues, fears, decisions must often be "worked through" over and over before the patient can assimilate them and make them her own. When the client has worked out an adequate way of living in which anxieties can be kept to a minimum and pleasure from realistic ventures is at a maximum, *psychosynthesis* has taken place and the client is ready to enjoy work and love.

PSYCHOANALYTIC APPLICATIONS TO FAMILIES AND GROUPS

As the unit of diagnostic and therapeutic focus in social work practice and theory became modified and moved from the individual to the dyad and then to the family and small group, clinicians relied less on psychoanalysis and more on role theory, system theory, and other perspectives. Inasmuch as psychoanalytic theory has concentrated mainly on the individual, this was a natural and inevitable development.

Despite psychoanalysis' heavy concentration on the individual, social workers have borrowed several concepts and practice principles from psychoanalysis in its work with larger units of attention. In its work with marital couples, social workers have been able to utilize several of Freud's (1914) notions regarding the irrational components of falling in love and how the child in the adult is always being asserted in marital conflict. Most social workers recognize how the unconscious is always at play in marital conflict (Fine, 1982) and that a chronic marital conflict is almost always an expression of an unconscious wish (Strean, 1985). Several psychoanalytic writers have helped social workers appreciate the unconscious collusion in marital interaction, that is, when marital partners sustain and reinforce their individual neuroses (Dickes, 1967; Eisenstein, 1956). Lloyd and Paulson (1972) pointed out that in a conflicted marriage each partner "maintains an internal world that the other supports. By confirming one another's projections, they help each other to maintain a closed internal system, protected from modification by reality" (p. 410).

One of the major contributions that psychoanalysis has made to marital counseling in social work is the recognition that marital conflicts are symptomatic of the couple's unresolved developmental problems. Spouses turn each other into their punitive superegos, unfulfilled ego ideals, disparaged self-images, and more (Meissner, 1978).

In helping couples resolve their conflicts, notions of transference and resistance are utilized. However, the psychoanalytically oriented practitioner is mainly interested in determining how husband and wife transfer introjects onto each other and how they resist treatment as a couple.

With the aid of psychoanalytic theory, child guidance workers by the 1940s began to realize that a child had unconscious meaning to parents whose own anxieties and fantasies influenced the growth and development of the child. Professionals learned that a childhood behavior disorder or neurosis was often, if not always, unconsciously induced and sustained by the parents and that therapeutic modifications in the child's behavior, no matter how positive, adversely affected the parents' equilibrium (Strean, 1994).

The psychoanalytically oriented therapist recognizes that as a parent describes a child, the parent's unconscious wishes, anxieties, and defenses frequently distort the presentation of the child's problems. Further, a psychoanalytic perspective on child pathology alleges that if a child is emotionally disturbed, one and probably both of the parents have unresolved maturational conflicts of their own which the child reactivates (Feldman, 1958; A. Freud, 1965).

By the late 1950s, as the entire family became the major unit of attention in social work, some of the insights from psychoanalysis were utilized in family treatment. Ackerman (1958) pointed out that all family members are engaged in unconscious communication, collude to ignore certain realities (for example, the alcoholism of a parent), and act out their joint pathology by choosing one member to be a scapegoat.

Psychoanalysts pointed out that because all members of a family are unconsciously engaged with each other, when one or more members seek out a social agency, this event has meaning for everybody and they all are unconsciously partici-pating in it. Psychoanalyst Peter Neubauer stated as early as 1953:

> A step forward of one family member may disturb several of the others and could, therefore, create additional disturbances. . . . In making recommenda-tions, the agency that is family oriented must be aware of the effect of any treatment on the total family. It might at times exclude a procedure which may be helpful to one member of the family, if it would be unadvisable for the family as a whole. (p. 115)

Although most people correctly regard psychoanalysis as a theory that is con-cerned with the individual, it has never ignored the individual's interpersonal rela-tionships. In 1922 Freud stated:

> In the individual's mental life someone else is invariably involved, as a model, as an object, as a helper, as an opponent, and so from the very first, In-dividual Psychology is at the same time Social Psychology as well—in this extended but entirely justifiable sense of the words. (pp. 1–2)

In the same work from which this statement came, *Group Psychology and the Analysis of the Ego,* Freud addressed a number of group phenomena. He pointed out that the relationship of an individual "to his parents and to his brothers and sisters, to the object of his love and to his physician, in fact all the relations which have hitherto been the chief subject of psychoanalytic research" recapitulate themselves in the in-dividual's group behavior. Freud noted that in a group one observes "the character of a regression." Emotions are usually intensified and intellect is inhibited. The group, Freud pointed out, is held together by the members' erotic feelings toward one an-other, and when an individual gives up his distinctiveness in a group and lets its mem-bers influence him, "he does it because he feels the need of being in harmony with them rather than in opposition to them" (Freud, 1922, p. 40).

Freud viewed the role of the leader of the group as crucial because he is experi-enced as a father figure who induces the members to give up much of their narcis-sism. Group members make the leader their ego ideal and identify with him, and it is because of the emotional tie with the leader who cares about the group members that the individuals in the group can identify with each other. A group was defined by Freud as "a number of individuals who have put one and the same object in the place of their ego ideal and have consequently identified themselves with one another in the ego" (1922, p. 61).

Therapeutic experience has expanded the psychoanalytic view of group processes. S. R. Slavson (1964), the founder of psychoanalytic group therapy, pointed out: "It has been shown that the group serves *in loco maternis*. The leader usually represents symbolically the father figure while the group represents the com-plementarity of the mother" (p. 27). Scheidlinger (1976) in "On the Concept of the 'Mother Group'" concluded that one of the major dynamics in a group is the members' unconscious wish to restore an earlier state of unconflicted union with the mother. There is in each member, according to Scheidlinger, a regressive pull to move toward a need-gratifying relationship with the mother.

As psychoanalytically oriented group therapists have studied group phenomena, they have been able to pinpoint those variables that endanger group cohesion, such as the uninhibited expression of sexual and/or aggressive drives, marked egocentricity in individual members, extreme competitiveness and jealousy, excessive negative transference reactions, and excessive frustration originating from the leader or group code (Rosenthal, 1977).

Transferences emerge in a group as they do in individual therapy and in all therapies. In a group they are multiple: an individual can be experienced as a mother by one member, as a father by another, and as a sibling by still another. Similarly, that individual often "finds" parents and siblings in the group. Usually the leader is experienced as a parent. As group members see how they distort perceptions in the group, they can begin to appreciate how they misconstrue other interpersonal relationships.

From a psychoanalytic perspective, the use of groups in social work practice seems to be best indicated for clients whose difficulties lie in their social and interpersonal relationships. In a group they can examine their interactions with peers and locate which forms of interaction lead to conflictual relationships. With his or her knowledge of the members' histories, fantasies, and psychic structures, the group leader can help to stimulate the kind of interaction that will enable the members to unravel neurotic distortions and unresolved transferences.

PSYCHOANALYSIS AND RESEARCH

Psychoanalytically oriented psychotherapy has been subjected to evaluation on numerous occasions. The classic studies in the literature report that between fifty and seventy percent of the clients studied terminated treatment as markedly improved. The first study was published by Fenichel (1930), who reviewed the work of the Berlin Psychoanalytic Institute from 1920 to 1930. In 1936, Jones reported on work done at the London Psychoanalytic Institute and, similar to Fenichel's conclusions, found that of the hundreds of patients who were involved in psychoanalytically oriented therapy, about sixty percent gave up their symptoms permanently and improved their ego functioning and interpersonal relationships substantially.

In 1937, Alexander reviewed the work of the Chicago Institute for Psychoanalysis from 1932 and 1937; he found that about sixty-five percent of patients treated psychoanalytically improved in their functioning and gave up maladaptive character traits and neurotic symptomatology.

Since the 1940s, studies by Knight (1952) Ferenczi (1955), Feldman (1968), and Strupp (1972) have demonstrated that a psychoanalytically oriented therapy can enhance functioning, diminish anxiety, increase self-esteem, and improve interpersonal functioning.

It has been an old claim that psychoanalysis is untestable scientifically, but those who make the claim ignore the evidence. In their book *The Scientific Credibility of*

Freud's Theories and Therapy, Fisher and Greenberg (1977) tried to describe every reported experiment relevant to psychoanalysis. They concluded that it is "clearly verified" that Freud's ideas can be reduced to testable ideas and not only are the ideas testable, but they have been tested. They show that the quantity of experimental research data on psychoanalytic ideas "greatly exceeds" that available for most other personality theories. Fisher and Greenberg reported that the existence of unconscious motivation is supported by so much scientific research that little doubt remains. In general, they were impressed with how often the results have borne out Freud's expectations.

In a recent book, *Psychoanalysis as a Science,* Leopold Bellak (1993) demonstrates the fact that many psychoanalytic hypotheses are experimentally verifiable, publicly demonstrable, and repeatable. He shows how experimentally controlled research can demonstrate the validity of a concept such as projection, or how treatment progress can be measured in psychoanalytic therapy. Bellak's major contribution is to operationalize personality and treatment concepts in order to measure them empirically.

The difficulty with much research on human beings is that it must take full account of introspective data. If one human being asks another a question, the answer is a variable one. It depends on the question and the relationship between the questioner and the questionee. Few theories, with the exception of psychoanalytic theory, allow for internal motives in doing research on human beings. Few recognize that what a subject tells the experimenter depends on many transference and countertransference factors, resistances and counterresistances, and a host of other unconscious variables.

While psychoanalysis, like all theories of personality and theories of treatment, is not perfect, and some studies have demonstrated positive outcomes, it is already clear that, psychoanalytically, psychotherapy is effective in many situations. Despite the fact that most people come to a therapist only when they have become desperate, there is evidence that individuals who undergo psychoanalytic therapy move toward what Fine (1981) has called the "analytic ideal": they can love more genuinely; seek pleasure; have sexual gratification; have a feeling for life, yet one that is guided by reason; have a role in the family; have a sense of identity; be creative; work; have a role in the social order; be able to communicate; and be free of symptoms.

PROSPECTUS

Psychoanalysis as a theory of personality and psychopathology, a method of therapy, and a means of research has been adored and abhorred, demeaned and acclaimed by both mental health professionals and the public at large. Social work's relationship with psychoanalysis reflects this ambivalence. Until the 1950s, much of social work theory and practice relied on psychoanalytic concepts and practice principles. With the advent of other social science and psychological perspectives, this is no longer the case. Just as psychoanalysis' status in society has receded, the same is true in social work.

Although Freud has been called the "Darwin of the mind," who fathered modern psychiatry, psychology, social work, child rearing, education, and sexuality, he has been labeled as "doctrinaire," "phallocentric," and a "betrayer of women." In social work, psychoanalytic concepts have been idealized and derided. What seems to be lacking in current social work dialogues is a frank, objective appraisal of what psychoanalysis can and cannot offer social work treatment.

From this writer's perspective, psychoanalysis can help social workers better understand the unconscious meaning of the client's problems and behavior, be sensitive to how the client's history is recapitulated in the present, note how the client copes with anxiety, and how he or she defends himself or herself from inner and outer danger. Further, social work practitioners should be aware of how the client unconsciously experiences the therapist (transference) and how the therapist subjectively experiences the client (countertransference). All social workers should have some understanding of how and why all clients resist help and how resistances can be resolved.

Because psychoanalysis activates so much emotion, its basic tenets have not been well examined in social work settings in recent decades. In many instances, psychoanalysis is ignored. As the client's treatment needs are given priority, as texts such as this one become more an integral part of the social workers' knowledge base, psychoanalysis will be more and better utilized in social work treatment in the years ahead. It will be acknowledged that all clients have an unconscious which affects their day-to-day behavior and interactions. It will be accepted that the client's history is being recapitulated constantly. Transference, countertransference, resistance, and counterresistance will be utilized in the social worker's treatment interventions as powerful aids, and Freud will be considered "more human than otherwise" (Sullivan, 1953).

REFERENCES

Abend, S. (1989). Countertransference and Psychoanalytic Technique. *Psychoanalytic Quarterly, 30.*

Ackerman, N. (1958). *The psychodynamics of family life.* New York: Basic Books.

Alexander, F. (1937). *Five-year report of the Chicago Institute for Psychoanalysis.* Chicago: Chicago Institute for Psychoanalysis.

Allan, E. (1974). Psychoanalytic theory. In F. J. Turner (Ed.), *Social work treatment.* New York: Free Press.

Auden, W. (1947). *The age of anxiety.* New York: Random House.

Bellak, L. (1993). *Psychoanalysis as a science.* Boston: Allyn & Bacon.

Boesky, D. (1990). The psychoanalytic process and its components. *Psychoanalytic Quarterly, 54.*

Brenner, C. (1955). *An elementary textbook of psychoanalysis.* New York: International Universities Press.

Dickes, H. (1967). *Marital tensions.* New York: Basic Books.

Eisenstein, V. (1956). *Neurotic interaction in marriage.* New York: Basic Books.

Erikson, E. (1950). *Childhood and society.* New York: W.W. Norton.

Feldman, F. (1968). Results of psychoanalysis in clinic case assignments. *Journal of the American Psychoanalytic Association, 16.*

Feldman, Y. (1958). A casework approach toward understanding parents of emotionally disturbed children. *Social Work, 3,* 23–29.

Fenichel, O. (1930). *Zehn Jahre Berliner Psychoanalytisches Institute.* Berlin: Berlin Psychoanalytic Institute.

Ferenczi, S. (1955). The problem of the termination of the analysis. In *Final contributions to the problems and methods of psychoanalysis.* New York: Basic Books.

Fine, R. (1973). Psychoanalysis. In R. Corsini (Ed.), *Current psychotherapies.* Itasca, IL: F. E. Peacock Publishers.

Fine, R. (1975). *Psychoanalytic psychology.* New York: Jason Aronson.

Fine, R. (1979). *The history of psychoanalysis.* New York: Columbia University Press.

Fine, R. (1981). *The psychoanalytic vision.* New York: Free Press.

Fine, R. (1982). *Healing of the mind* (2nd ed.). New York: Free Press.

Fisher, S., and Greenberg, R. (1977). *The scientific credibility of Freud's theories and therapy.* New York: Basic Books.

Freeman, L., & Strean, H. (1981). *Freud and women.* New York: Ungar.

Freud, A. (1946). *The ego and the mechanisms of defense.* New York: International Universities Press.

Freud, A. (1951). Observations of child development. In *The psychoanalytic study of the child* (Vol. 6). New York: International Universities Press.

Freud, A. (1965). *Normality and pathology in childhood.* New York: International Universities Press.

Freud, S. (1904). *Freud's psychoanalytic procedure,* Vol. 7, *Standard edition.* London: Hogarth Press.

Freud, S. (1912). *The dynamics of transference,* Vol. 12, *Standard edition.* London: Hogarth Press.

Freud, S. (1913). *Totem and taboo,* Vol. 12, *Standard edition.* London: Hogarth Press.

Freud, S. (1914). *Introduction to narcissism,* Vol. 12, *Standard edition.* London: Hogarth Press.

Freud, S. (1922). *Group psychology and the analysis of the ego.* Vol. 19, *Standard edition.* London: Hogarth Press.

Freud, S. (1923). *The ego and the id,* Vol. 19, *Standard edition.* London: Hogarth Press.

Freud, S. (1933). *New introductory lectures on psychoanalysis,* Vol. 22, *Standard edition.* London: Hogarth Press.

Freud, S. (1938). *The basic writings of Sigmund Freud.* New York: Random House (Modern Library).

Freud, S. (1939). *An outline of psychoanalysis,* Vol. 23, *Standard edition.* London: Hogarth Press.

Greenson, R. (1967). *The technique and practice of psychoanalysis.* New York: International Universities Press.

Hale, N. (1971). *Freud and the Americans.* New York: Oxford University Press.

Hamilton, G. (1958). A theory of personality. Freud's contribution to social work. In H. J. Parad (Ed.), *Ego psychology and dynamic casework.* New York: Family Service Association of America.

Hartmann, H. (1951). *Ego psychology and the problem of adaptation.* New York: International Universities Press.

Hartmann, H. (1964). *Essays on ego psychology.* New York: International Universities Press.

Jacobs, T. (1986). On countertransference enactment. *Journal of the American Psychoanalytic Association, 43.*

Jones, E. (1936). *Decennial report of the London Clinic of Psychoanalysis.* London: London Clinic of Psychoanalysis.

Jones, E. (1953). *The life and work of Sigmund Freud* (Vol. 1). New York: Basic Books.

Kadushin, A. (1972). *The social work interview.* New York: Columbia University Press.

Kardiner, A. (1939). *The individual and his society.* New York: Columbia University Press.

Kardiner, A. (1945). *The psychological frontiers of society.* New York: Columbia University Press.

Klein, M., & Riviere, J. (1937). *Love, hate and reparation.* London: Woolf and Hogarth Press.

Knight, R. (1949). A critique of the present status of the psychotherapies. *Bulletin of the New York Academy of Medicine, 25,* 100–114.

Knight, R. (1952). An evaluation of psychotherapeutic techniques. In R. Knight & C. Friedman (Eds.), *Psychoanalytic psychiatry and psychology.* New York: International Universities Press.

Kohut, H. (1971). *The analysis of self.* New York: International Universities Press.

Kohut, H. (1977). *The restoration of the self.* New York: International Universities Press.

Kohut, H. (1978). *The search for the self.* New York: International Universities Press.

Langs, R. (1976). *The bipersonal field.* New York: Jason Aronson.

Langs, R. (1981). *Resistances and interventions.* New York: Jason Aronson.

Lindon, J. (1966). "Melanie Klein—Her view of the unconscious. In F. Alexander, S. Eisenstein, & M. Grotjahn (Eds.), *Psychoanalytic pioneers.* New York: Basic Books.

Lloyd, R., & Paulson, I. (1972). Projective identification in the marital relationship as a resistance in psychotherapy. *Archives of General Psychiatry, 27,* 410–413.

Masson, J. (1984). *The assault on truth: Suppression of the seduction theory.* New York: Farrar, Straus & Giroux.

Meltzoff, J., & Kornreich, M. (1970). *Research in psychotherapy.* New York: Atherton Press.

Menninger, K. (1958). *Theory of psychoanalytic technique.* New York: Basic Books.

Meissner, William (1978). "The Conceptualization of Marriage and Family Dynamics from a Psychoanalytic Perspective." In T. Paolino and B. McCrady (Eds.), *Marriage and marital theory.* New York: Brunner/Mazel.

Moore, B., & Fine, B. (1990). *Psychoanalytic terms and concepts.* New Haven: Yale University Press.

Parsons, T. (1951). *The social system.* Glencoe, IL: Free Press.

Rapaport, D. (1951). *The organization and pathology of thought.* New York: Columbia University Press.

Neubauer, Peter. (1953). "The Psychoanalyst's Contribution to the Family Agency." In M. Heiman (Ed.), *Psychoanalysis and social work.* New York: International Universities Press.

Renik, O. (1993). Analytic interaction. Conceptualizing technique in light of the analyst's irreducible subjectivity. *Psychoanalytic Quarterly, 62.*

Reppen, J. (1985). *Beyond Freud: A study of modern psychoanalytic theorists.* Hillsdale, NJ: Analytic Press.

Rosenthal, Leslie. (1977). "Qualifications and Tasks of the Therapist in Group Therapy with Children," in *Clinical Social Work. 5 (3).*

Sandler, J. (1973). *The patient and the analyst.* New York: International Universities Press.

Schafer, R. (1977). The interpretations of transference and the conditions for loving. *Journal of the American Psychoanalytic Association, 25.*

Scheidlinger, S. (1976). "On the Concept of the Mother Group." In M. Kissen (Ed.), *From Group Dynamics to Group Psychoanalysis.* New York: Halsted Press.

Segal, H. (1964). *Introduction to the work of Melanie Klein.* New York: Basic Books.

Skalter, E. (1987). *Countertransference.* Northvale, NJ: Jason Aronson.

Slavson, Samuel. (1964). *A textbook in analytic group psychotherapy.* New York: International Universities Press.

Strean, H. (1979). *Psychoanalytic theory and social work practice.* New York: Free Press.

Strean, H. (1983a). *Resolving resistances in psychotherapy.* New York: Wiley.

Strean, H. (1983b). *The sexual dimension.* New York: Free Press.

Strean, H. (1985). *Resolving marital conflicts.* New York: Wiley.

Strean, H. (1994). *Essentials of psychoanalysis.* New York: Brunner/Mazel.

Strupp, H. (1972). Ferment in Psychoanalysis and Psychotherapy. In B. Wolman (Ed.), *Success and failure in psychoanalysis and psychotherapy*. New York: Macmillan.

Sullivan, H. (1953). *The interpersonal theory of psychiatry*. New York: W. W. Norton.

Winnicott, D. (1965). *The maturational processes and the facilitating environment*. New York: International Universities Press.

Winnicott, D. (1971). *Therapeutic consultations in child psychiatry*. New York: Basic Books.

ANNOTATED LISTING OF KEY REFERENCES

Fine, R. (1982). *The healing of the mind* (2nd ed.). New York: Free Press. A clear, concise description of the psychoanalytic treatment process. With many case examples, describes the honeymoon phase of treatment, the first treatment crisis, resolving resistances and transference problems, and termination.

Freud, A. (1946). *The ego and the mechanisms of defense*. New York: International Universities Press. An important basic work in understanding how individuals protect themselves from anxiety. An excellent and clear description of the major defenses and their functions.

Freud, S. (1950). *Collected papers*. London: Hogarth Press. These twenty-four volumes, edited by James Strachey, bring all of Freud's notions together. Expositions include papers on psychosexual development, transference, countertransference, resistance, group psychology, the unconscious, and much more. Many readable case illustrations.

Strean, H. S. (1994). *Essentials of psychoanalysis*. New York: Brunner/Mazel. Presents a thorough review of Freud's major concepts, a separate chapter on all of the important psychoanalytic modifiers and their contributions, a description of the psychoanalytic treatment process, and a review of research in psychoanalysis.

CHAPTER 23

PSYCHOSOCIAL THEORY AND SOCIAL WORK TREATMENT

MARY E. WOODS AND HOWARD ROBINSON

INTRODUCTION AND OVERVIEW

In many respects, all social work practice—historically and currently—has relied on psychosocial concepts. Whether the focus of attention is on the individual and family, on large communities and organizations, on various kinds of societal dysfunction, or on theories about social change, social work is and—since the early years of the twentieth century—always has been dedicated to the alleviation of suffering and to the enhancement of human life.

More particularly, what has become known as the psychosocial approach to social work grew out of efforts (especially, but not exclusively, by caseworkers) to support the well-being of individuals and families and to respond to people's need to restore social functioning and to better their interpersonal relationships and life situations—especially in the face of social deprivation and catastrophe. In spite of shifting emphases over the years, the psychosocial perspective has *consistently* recognized the influences of biological factors, internal psychological and emotional processes, external social and physical conditions, and the interplay among these. Psychosocial caseworkers (now sometimes referred to as clinical social workers) seek to help clients—individuals, families, and larger groups—to reduce problems arising from some kind of disequilibrium between them and their environments. A fundamental step in the psychosocial method is the study of individuals and families, their impinging environments, and the "person-in-situation gestalt" so that meaningful assessments or diagnoses of these can be formulated. The context of the client is inevitably made up of many interacting systems, several of which may need to be studied in order for the social worker and client to decide how to proceed.

Based on the worker's and client's *mutual* understanding—of the problems and their origins, of the clients' goals and motivations, and of the balance of forces—interventions can be planned. It is important to emphasize that psychosocial treatment often is *not* aimed at the so-called "pathological" or "dysfunctional" aspects of the gestalt; rather, interventions are tailored to address those aspects that are most accessible and most capable of change. Treatment strategies, therefore, depend on a very careful analysis of the relevant forces or systems to determine which are actually amenable to modification. Ameliorization of the client's environment may result in enduring changes in the personality or family system; by the same token, new initiatives or creative adaptations that people make in the face of external assaults can be key to modifying their life situations and—in some cases—even their larger environments. Sometimes a small shift in the balance of forces can create remarkable differences; for example, one person finally refusing to tolerate harassment on the job may trigger similar protests from others, thereby forcing long overdue changes in the workplace.

The goals of psychosocial workers are to work collaboratively with clients to recover, to reinforce, and to mobilize strengths and coping abilities, to locate resources, and to find optimal "fits" between people and their social or physical surroundings. Change in one part of a personality, family, or larger social system necessarily brings changes in other systems. Just as a person with a weak or injured knee may be helped by strengthening muscles in the lower leg and thigh, so can the clients of social workers buttress one aspect of the interacting system to assist another or others. A symptomatic child may enjoy rapid relief when the parents' marital system is improved; when a person modifies his or her harsh superego, or gains in self-esteem, a heretofore stymied personality system may be freed up enough to find creative ways to address current crises, challenges, or hardships; a distant father who takes more leadership in a family may reduce tensions among other family members, even without these being directly confronted; and however unfair it may be, it is usually more immediately effective for a laidoff industrial worker to retrain or consider new job options than to wait for changes in the larger economic or political system.

Research and "practice wisdom" confirm that the worker-client relationship is crucial to the success of psychosocial treatment and one of its most powerful tools. The worker's effort is to demonstrate nonpossessive warmth and concern, nonjudgmental acceptance, genuineness, accurate empathy, a profound respect for the importance of self-direction, and realistic optimism about change. To do this, the worker consistently strives to be objective, "other-centered," and disciplined in the "use of self." Of course, the manner in which attitudes are conveyed must be fashioned to the particular client's needs and goals. The science and art of psychosocial treatment usually involves the use of a blend of treatment procedures and worker-client communications and, often, "concrete" services. Generally speaking, the greater the client's trust and *active* involvement in the treatment process and in fostering desired changes, the greater and more enduring does the capacity for mastery and autonomy become.

As we shall discuss later in the chapter, the psychosocial approach is an open, flexible system of thought that draws on many sources. As new information and ideas emerge from social work experience and from related fields, additional light is shed on our understanding of personality, social forces, and the interplay between them. In recent decades, systems and ecological concepts have been extremely helpful in refining our understanding of the person-situation gestalt.

Over the centuries, societies have been rife with economic and political injustices, poverty, discrimination, and intolerable conditions of one sort or another. While these vary somewhat according to time and place, from social work's beginnings, noxious social forces have profoundly affected the lives of many, many people. Currently, as before, psychosocial workers are committed to doing all they can to fight on every conceivable level against all forms of social abuse and oppression. Deprivation, inequity, and hatred or alienation on the basis of race or ethnicity, class, gender, sexual orientation, age, or disability are unacceptable to the advocates of the psychosocial approach. While social workers who share this point of view may have to put major emphasis on helping people individually or as families, at *all* times broader social concerns remain in the forefront of their minds and efforts.

HISTORICAL ORIGINS AND DEVELOPMENT: THE EARLY YEARS

Given our thesis that people and their surroundings are intertwined, it should come as no surprise that social work has always been profoundly influenced by the condition and demands of the day. During some periods, socioeconomic forces received the greatest attention; at other times, there was keener interest in understanding personality development and functioning. Yet it is important to note that in spite of some rather radical shifts in emphasis during the twentieth century, social workers—including caseworkers—never totally ignored the importance of the social environment or of psychological factors as these affected people and their dilemmas. And, as our theory and knowledge base matured, the tendency to neglect either component diminished significantly.

Over the years, in response to pressing problems and concerns, some very gifted social work pioneers emerged. Their dedication to social change and to the alleviation of individual suffering profoundly impacted the evolution of psychosocial casework.

MARY RICHMOND REMEMBERED

Although American social work has roots in the nineteenth-century charity organization society movements of North America and Great Britain (Woodroofe, 1962), it was the perceptive and hardworking Mary Richmond, through her teachings and writings, who actually set the stage for the development of modern casework theory and practice. With her first book, *Friendly Visiting Among the Poor: A Handbook for Charity Workers*, published in 1899, she began a long and painstaking process of formulating and evaluating practice concepts and techniques. For more than a quarter-century thereafter, as her subsequent writings reveal (1917, 1922, 1930), she and her associates constantly examined their theories about practice, modifying and elaborating them as new evidence appeared, always trying to respond to concerns and questions raised by the growing number of social workers. A brief review of some of her major ideas and findings will demonstrate how today's psychosocial casework is still guided by principles originally articulated by Richmond.

First, it became increasingly apparent that "good deeds," "good intentions," and "friendly visiting" were simply not good enough, in contrast to earlier views, "character defects" or "weak wills" did not explain widespread poverty or other terrible circumstances facing clients. *Focus on the individual alone did not always help.* Social relations and the environment—past and present—were major forces shaping personality. Reflecting on her own experience, as well as developments in the sociology of the time, Richmond became convinced that external influences had to be addressed in order to promote a better adjustment between individuals and their surroundings. Following this line of thinking, Richmond presaged the family therapy movement that burgeoned several decades later by suggesting that, when possible, the individual should be seen in the context of the family, in the home environment. We still agree with the wise Miss Richmond, who wrote that the father should be seen, and that keeping the family in mind should extend "beyond the period of diagnosis, of course." Without a family view, "we would find the good results of individual treatment crumble away" (1917, pp. 134–159). Furthermore, "mass betterment and individual betterment are interdependent," with "social reform and social case work of necessity progressing together" (p. 25). Only then could pressures be reduced, opportunities increased, and social relationships improved. Thus, *Richmond's dual focus on people and their environments marked the beginning of the person-in-situation orientation of psychosocial practice today.*

Second, and of equal importance, Richmond promoted the idea that caseworkers' actual experiences should be subjected to critical analysis, that their efforts must be measured by the best standards available. After a detailed and systematic examination of case materials from a broad range of settings, she—along with others who worked with or were taught by her—endeavored to describe and codify concepts that could then be transmitted from one generation to the next. In *Social Diagnosis* (1917) and in later works, she outlined specific approaches to the collection of "social evidence" from which inferences were to be drawn, thereby leading up to *social study, diagnosis, and treatment planning,* processes still basic to the efforts of psychosocial workers. *With Richmond at the helm, a real profession—based on and guided by data collected from practice experience—was launched.* The scientific side of social work was introduced. Casework was no longer represented by friendly, charitable, well-to-do volunteers who visited and taught self-control to the "unfortunate." Instead, *agencies were staffed by trained, supervised, paid, accountable workers.*

Third, Richmond learned from the study of case histories that an analysis of social evidence necessarily leads to *differential diagnosis and differential treatment.* In other words, *treatment must be individualized.* In her own language, she cautioned against generalizing and stereotyping. Young couples who seek material relief, for example, can be very different from one another and should be evaluated "one by one." She pointed out that there are many differences among "deserters" and among "inebriates." It is "more important to understand the main drift of their lives than the one incident which brings them to our attention" (1917, p. 146). Like many other "social disabilities," these "are not so much separate entities as outcroppings of more intimate aspects of the individual's personal and social life." She urged that we push "beyond such 'presenting symptoms' to the complex of causes farther back" (p. 158). A particular problem cannot be solved by identifying one factor, but must be understood as part of a whole. To this day, we know how tempting it can be on the one hand, yet disastrous on the other, to make assumptions about clients on the basis of their backgrounds (ethnicity, sexual orientation, etc.), the specific problems they bring to social workers (addiction, childhood abuse, etc.), or their clinical diagnoses ("borderline," "passive aggressive," etc.). We have Mary Richmond to remind us that each person and each family is unique and must be studied and listened to separately, with *all* germane particulars taken into account.

Finally, relying on a broad empirical base of many cases, Richmond would identify and evaluate treatment strategies. She cautioned her readers: "Case records often show a well-made investigation and a plan formulated and carried out, but with no discoverable connection between them" (1917, p. 348). She urged a methodical review of the findings to reveal contradictions or gaps before rushing into a plan of action—advice that, as we all well know, still holds up! Through an approach since known as *indirect treatment,* Richmond sought to define procedures for intervening in the client's environment, for locating resources, and for cooperating with all possible sources of assistance and influence. The second major approach developed by Richmond—the influence of "mind upon mind," thereafter referred to as *direct treatment*—stressed the importance of a *trusting worker-client relationship* in which suggestions and gentle persuasion would best be received; to some extent, the importance of the client's point of view and of mutual decision making were discussed, although these aspects were not yet fully developed. In short, Mary Richmond was a pioneer in the process of standardizing and defining casework procedures, even though, as we shall see, these would require significant refinements in future years (Richmond, 1922, 1930).

Psychosocial workers are profoundly indebted to Richmond for her originality and insights; she had a prophetic influence on practice. We underscore her contributions here because it strikes us that recurrent swings of the pendulum sometimes have been unnecessarily extreme, simply because the fundamentals of previous knowledge were overlooked or misunderstood. For the sake of continuity, therefore, we take this opportunity to urge that Richmond's place in history be preserved. She provided a solid foundation from which practice theories continually evolve.

PSYCHOLOGY AND PSYCHIATRY BURST UPON THE SOCIAL WORK SCENE

While the contributions of Mary Richmond and social workers of her era may not be well enough remembered, the dramatic impression made by new theories of psychology and psychiatry is well known. After World War I and through the 1920s, the sociological basis of casework was partially obscured by the deluge of new ideas about personality development and the importance of the emotional life, including the far-reaching influences of childhood experience. Many new psychological theories commanded attention. Undoubtedly, out of zeal to help clients by understanding the intricacies of personality more deeply than Richmond had, there was a frenzied period when bits of knowledge were grabbed up, often in a haphazard manner. As a result, there were some reckless uses and abuses, with little systematic understanding of how the new—sometimes conflicting—ideas could illuminate casework practice.

Soon, Freudian ideas in particular were strongly influencing social work thinking and practice, although Adler, Rank, and Jung also gained followers. As social workers incorporated psychoanalytical theory, they used their knowledge to gain a better grasp of the inner lives of their clients: the underlying—often unconscious—motives, forces, and conflicts that might account for their behaviors, emotional attitudes, and personality development. In some social work circles, the psychiatric specialty was considered the most prestigious. Often trained and guided by psychiatrists, social workers were treating clients above the poverty line, trying to help them grapple with internal forces. At times, the impact of current family or socioeconomic influences was downplayed. Reflecting individualistic philosophies of the time, inner "weakness" was again too often blamed—albeit in a different way than earlier—for miseries or crises that were primarily social in origin. Sad to say, psychological inadequacy was quite commonly seen as responsible for poverty and dependency, even into the early years of the Great Depression. It has been suggested by some students of social work history that if Richmond's foundation of knowledge and thinking had been more fully grasped by social workers, the integration of psychoanalytic concepts would have been more gradual, more orderly, and less likely to have overshadowed the social emphases and other basic principles laid out in *Social Diagnosis*.

A major, sometimes bitter, but always intense dispute developed among social caseworkers in the 1930s. Under the leadership of Jessie Taft and Virginia Robinson, the newly formed "functional," Pennsylvania School, or Rankian approach (Robinson, 1930; Taft, 1937) challenged the ideas of the "diagnostic," "differential" or Freudian school. Based in part on Rank's *Will Therapy* (1936), the functionalists deemphasized history taking and diagnostic inquiry. Rather, treatment was determined by agency function, including limitations of time and procedures. The client's will—positive and negative—was believed to be stimulated thereby, as the client decided whether or how to use the services. The client's capacity to find solutions and to plan actions—in the present and in the future—was thought to be fostered in this way. The diagnostic school, on the other hand, was committed to careful history taking and individual diagnosis as guides to treatment planning. Gordon Hamilton, a leading exponent of the diagnostic approach, used the term *"psychosocial"* in her influential text *Theory and Practice of Social Casework* (1940), although the expression was apparently first coined by Hankins (1930). A few of many other proponents of the diagnostic, psychosocial approach were Florence Hollis, Annette Garrett, Florence Day, Lucille Austin, and Bertha Reynolds.

As divided as social work thinkers were—until the 1950s—by these divergent viewpoints, there is no doubt that the psychosocial or diagnostic approach, which ultimately prevailed, assimilated some of the ideas of the functionalists, as these conformed with experience. Specifically, social history taking became less extensive, information was gathered more selectively, and, as time went on, there was greater recognition of the fact that treatment begins immediately—not after all of the evidence is in. Furthermore, as the general social climate became less authoritarian and as ideas about self-determination were popularized, persuasive and directive techniques gave way to efforts to help clients think more for themselves, define their own goals, use their own judgment, and arrive at their own solutions. With many of Richmond's concepts still applicable, modifications and additions—including the incorporation of some of Freud's thinking—enriched the psychosocial framework. During the 1940s, social workers challenged themselves to define how psychoanalytic concepts could best be used by caseworkers, and how casework and psychoanalysts differed. It is safe to say, however, that—in spite of the clarity achieved—social workers probably deferred to psychiatrists more often than was necessary, sometimes downplaying their own unique body of knowledge and expertise. Indeed, instances of that tendency can be witnessed to this day.

EGO PSYCHOLOGY EXPANDS OUR HORIZONS

The introduction of theories of ego psychology, especially in the 1950s, had profound implications for psychosocial casework. Still based on psychoanalytic theory, ego psychology was nevertheless a departure from Freud's earlier thinking in certain important aspects. Functions of the ego were seen as autonomous, and thus not at the mercy of unconscious libidinous sexual and aggressive drives (the id). Various features of the ego could be worked with directly—to defend against overwhelming demands of the id even under stress, to assuage or shore up expectations of the conscience or superego, to creatively adapt or respond to external realities. Treatment therefore could be focused upon the ego rather than on unconscious forces interpreted (and sometimes misinterpreted!) by the worker. Important intrapsychic work was possible without the direct analysis of unconscious material. The individual was not passively shaped by past events, repressed conflicts, or environmental assaults; the ego was recognized as an active and powerful resource for change. More specifically, *ego-supportive treatment*—sometimes misunderstood as simple warmth or reassurance—aimed to bolster, conserve, and/or restore ego functions. Necessary defenses, mastery and competence, intellectual processes, reality testing and judgment, impulse regulation and initiative, among other qualities, were nurtured. Relative autonomy from the id *and* less reactivity to external demands allowed the individual to develop self-understanding and strategies for creatively coping with life circumstances, rather than being totally ruled by them.

Anna Freud's explication of ego defenses (1946), Hartmann's identification of autonomous ego functions (1939), White's theory of a drive for efficacy and competence (1959), and Erikson's psychosocial developmental stages (1950, 1959) were among the many ideas that were of great interest to psychosocial workers. Rather than embracing them indiscriminately, however, social work writers sought to accomodate the new thinking in measured ways that could illuminate practice (Parad, 1958; Parad & Miller, 1963). Perlman's enduring classic, *Social Casework: A Problem-solving Process* (1957), not only attempted to bridge the diagnostic and functional schools, but also addressed the importance of supporting clients' capacity to think through problems, to take charge of their lives in ways that now might be thought of as "proactive." Brief, task-centered, and crisis-oriented therapies, and—a few decades later—cognitive therapy, among so many others, are therapeutic consequences of social work's appreciation of the ego's role and its potential strengths as people are helped to grapple with inevitable life dilemmas as they strive for resolution and fulfillment. Features of the interpersonal theories of Horney and Sullivan, and Rogers's client-centered approach to treatment, were all more systematically considered once the importance of ego functions had been incorporated.

KNOWLEDGE FROM THE SOCIAL SCIENCES

By the time Florence Hollis published the first edition of *Casework: A Psychosocial Therapy* in 1964, there was already an impressive accumulation of knowledge from the social sciences that was being incorporated—selectively, as it proved helpful—by the psychosocial framework. We can only touch on a few examples here. In the 1930s, anthropologists Ruth Benedict and Margaret Mead captured the attention of social workers, as well as the general public, by describing vast differences among cultures in customs relating to childrearing, marriage, sexual behavior and roles, treatment of the elderly, and so on (Benedict, 1934; Mead, 1935). Abram Kardiner's studies on culture and behavior drew attention (1939). Caseworkers became much more attuned to the influence of culture on the personalities and attitudes of their clients. Studies of the often devastating effects on individuals and families of the economic hardships experienced during the Great Depression (Angell, 1936; Cavan & Ranck, 1938; Komarovsky, 1940) were widely read by social workers.

During the 1940s and the 1950s, in spite of the conservative climate following World War II and social work's tendency to be preoccupied with psychological matters, informative sociological research on marriage and the family burgeoned. Ackerman, among others influenced by the social sciences, launched the modern family therapy movement. Along other lines, persuasive evidence was uncovered that mental health professionals brought a negative bias to the diagnosis and treatment of poor and minority patients. Even caseworkers—always advocates of equal rights—learned that their own clinical judgments could be skewed by socioeconomic factors. During this period, the influence of cultural differences between worker and client came to be better understood; in treatment, open and mutual discussion of these matters was recommended. Studies on the relationship between closed opportunity structures and social deviance (Cloward, 1959), and new information on the political powerlessness and disenfranchisement of large portions of the population, were of enormous importance to social workers' understanding of the times. New knowledge about role behavior and communication foreshadowed further developments in these areas.

In the 1960s, a decade when important and diverse social protests were initiated, knowledge on all fronts was snowballing and many new treatment emphases were emerging. It was fortunate that, in *Casework* (1964), Hollis had so clearly spelled out the basic principles and theoretical framework upon which psychosocial casework rested; henceforth, new ideas could be evaluated and, if they seemed potentially sound and useful, incorporated without threatening the fundamental integrity of the psychosocial approach itself. Due to Hollis's clarity about the inseparability of the psychodynamic and social components in individual and family functioning, radical swings of the pendulum in one direction or another were averted. Some other social work approaches, not as well grounded in their points of view, have had to struggle harder to find the balance between the individual and the social perspective, between a focus on the person and the milieu. Future editions of *Casework*, including the most recent one (1990), have demonstrated how the framework can be expanded to integrate many new ideas and methods consonant with psychosocial theory without automatically discarding old ones that have held up over time. Along similar lines, because of the well developed foundation provided by Hollis and those who followed her, psychosocial workers are less likely to be diverted when familiar, reliable concepts are reintroduced, dressed up with new labels and language.

PRINCIPLES AND ASSUMPTIONS UNDERLYING PSYCHOSOCIAL TREATMENT

Psychosocial workers believe that people *of all ages* have the capacity to grow, learn, adapt, and—at least to some degree—modify their social and physical environments. Indeed, when people are engaged in empathic human relationships—with their loved ones and with social workers—untapped wellsprings of strength, creativity, and resilience are often released. Our appreciation of this human drive for growth-oriented relationships is supported by object relations theories (Mahler, 1968; Mahler et al., 1975; Winnicott, 1965) and studies demonstrating the profound implications of attachment, separation, and loss (Ainsworth, 1973; Bowlby, 1969, 1973). As we shall discuss further, the experience of a worker's positive, nonpossessive, empathic regard may trigger changes within the personality system that continue long after client and worker have separated. As clients discover new ways of responding to life's challenges, serious problems of adjustment in the future may be *prevented*.

Ego psychology, as we have indicated, modified some of the deterministic elements of Freud's theories and promoted, thereby, a proactive orientation to change throughout the life course, a position fully supported by the psychosocial approach. Nevertheless, Freud's theories about the structure and development of personality systems continue to inform our understanding of individual functioning. Specifically, we assume that:

1. Significant feelings and thoughts lie outside of awareness.
2. Personality is a fluid and dynamic system of forces that influences behavior; even small internal modifications reverberate within the personality as a whole, often serving to alter thinking, feeling, and behavior over time.
3. Defenses are constructed that serve both positive and negative ends.
4. Symptoms are adaptive attempts to uncover and resolve internal conflicts.
5. "Neurosis" is actually social in origin, rooted in an individual's experience in relationships, not a manifestation of constitutional weakness as some pre-Freudian theorists postulated.

Psychological systems, however, do not stand alone, but constantly interact with biological and social systems. The process of aging or changes in health, for example, affect the personality; conversely, the stability or instability of the personality influences the health or the course that the aging process takes. Biologically based disorders, such as schizophrenia, endemic depression, attention deficit/hyperactivity disorder, and pervasive developmental delay, are all in constant interaction with the emotional system. At a broader level, we know that situational conditions influence the expression of biologically based disorders and that environmental forces, from poor nutrition in childhood to toxic chemicals in the workplace, impact the biology of us all. When people are disabled by disease, stress is placed, in turn, on the family members and others who support and sustain them. Those in attendance can feel they are doing a thankless job, and often require attention and support to recognize the value of their efforts. Psychosocial workers, therefore, address all relevant systems— biological, social, and psychological—that influence a person's situation.

The psychosocial approach is solidly grounded in the idea that people's behaviors develop within the context of many open systems interacting in mutually causative ways. Human adaptation is based upon a dynamic interplay between person and situation in which new and shifting equilibriums are continually established to make a better fit between individual needs and environmental resources. Change in any one system inevitably creates change in others. When a parent is laid off from work, stress is placed on the whole family, a stress that a child may act out by misbehaving in school. The recovery of a spouse from alcohol addiction will shift the marital system, usually requiring a new definition of the relationship. Thus, psychosocial practice is based upon the *systemic* understanding of adaptation and change. This understanding is crucial to *prevention*: intervention is not reserved for the treatment of dysfunction.

In many cases, family systems provide the *most* significant context for personality growth and development. Often problems of fit among family members—parents with children, husbands with wives, siblings with siblings—are mutual, "no-fault" interactions that can be mollified, at least to some degree. Over and over again, we have seen how one shift—sometimes a relatively small one—in support patterns *within the family system* can result in a "corrective" experience for its members. Positive effects then go beyond those derived specifically from the worker-client alliance. By directly facilitating nurturing family relations, we frequently provide the best and most *lasting* therapy of all!

As we know, families are also subject to stresses—sometimes overwhelming stresses—that come from larger systems, including poverty, racism, and dehumanizing bureaucracies. The daily lives of many of our clients are pervaded by these forces. Ideally, the community and social resources provide a "holding environment" for families, analogous to the support that families—at their best—offer individual members. When one system does not bolster the healthy functioning of another, the consequences resonate at all levels. Too often, communities offer few day-care services and sparse employment opportunities, continuing to alienate people who have been ignored or oppressed for generations. Disabling tensions within a family can result, profoundly affecting relationships and the development of the children who try to grow there. If the larger social systems are not immediately amenable to change, it may fall upon the family to search for creative solutions to their dilemmas. When family functioning is enhanced, members may then work together to promote a healing home environment, thereby buttressing their capacity to struggle against external assaults as well. Psychosocial workers know that they cannot always make an immediate impact on the dehumanizing experiences that large numbers of clients face; they *do* know, however, that the help they offer on various levels can make a very significant difference to many families and individuals.

Psychosocial workers are keenly aware that people ascribe individual and collective meanings to events and situations. Based on a lifetime of family and social experience, each person represents a subjective universe of perception. How people view and interpret their lives, find a sense of self and define their purposes is, in part, culturally influenced (McGoldrick et al., 1982). As essential as it is, ethnic sensitivity on the part of a worker is not enough; in fact, care must be taken to avoid misusing generalizations, applying them where they do not belong. Ultimately, only the individuals involved—often, of course, with the help of a trained listener—can construct a perspective on and evaluation of their own lives and visions.

The psychosocial framework, eclectic yet selective, continues to be built upon many bodies of knowledge—including psychiatry, psychology, sociology, and anthropology, as well as the discipline of social work. Psychosocial workers, for example, may use theories as diverse as those of Kohut (1971, 1977) and Kernberg (1975, 1984), interpersonal concepts of social role (Biddle & Thomas, 1966; Davis, 1986), studies on family communication (Nelsen, 1980; Satir, 1967), and macro perspectives (Bertalanffy, 1968; Bronfenbrenner, 1989), to fully understand the intrapsychic, interpersonal, and environmental aspects of a client's situation. Experience has taught us that effective intervention on the individual, interpersonal, and organizational levels requires a multiplicity of concepts; *no single idea or practice technique can address the broad range of concerns and dilemmas clients bring to social workers.*

THE VALUE BASE

Basic values guide every aspect of psychosocial theory and practice. By definition, ideas or treatment methods that are not compatible with these values cannot be embraced by the framework. It is understood by proponents of this approach that there is no expediency compelling enough to compromise the standards.

An essential and enduring value is the abiding respect for the *innate worth* of every individual. From this follows a profound concern for and commitment to the *well-being* of individuals. It has long been believed by social workers in general that each person has the right to choose his or her style of life, however unique or unappealing it may be to someone else, as long as that person does not unduly infringe upon the rights of others. Political or institutional constraints or pressure groups cannot deter us from doing all we can to help people overcome barriers to self-fulfillment and gain access to opportunities that promote their potential and aspirations. For example, antiunion board members of our agency should not discourage us from facilitating the efforts of clients who want to organize employees at their workplace. Members of religious groups that rail against homosexuality or abortion have every right to conduct their lives as they see fit, but they cannot suppress our efforts to help people who make different choices on these matters. Obviously, it is not in anyone's interest for us to wage battle vindictively against people who try to impose their views on others. Rather, when possible, our training and experience direct us to find ways to mediate and educate, in hopes of promoting a climate in which differences do not have to lead to coercion or scare tactics—from either side. Our own opinions on controversial issues are not what count; our abiding belief in the rights of people to determine what course they themselves want to follow is the fundamental value that influences how we work.

Two essential characteristics of the psychosocial worker's attitudes toward people coming for help flow from these values: First, *acceptance*, and second, respect for the client's right to be *self-directive*, that is, to make his or her own decisions; this concept is sometimes referred to as *self-determination*.

By *acceptance* we mean that we sustain an attitude of warmth and goodwill, whether or not the client's manner and behavior are personally appealing to us. To be helpful, acceptance must go beyond objectivity, tolerance, or intellectual understanding of a person's behavior or plight. *Empathy*, the capacity to enter into and grasp the inner feelings or subjective state of another, is a critical component of acceptance. For the most part, it is only when the worker can be genuinely empathic that the client—who initially, for whatever reasons, may be distrustful or ashamed—can begin to feel understood and not judged. The more we are able to "feel with" the many painful situations and dilemmas of our clients—becoming attuned to the desperation, anger, and hopelessness that can accrue from disappointment, deprivation, bigotry, abuse, violence, and rejection—the more likely we will be able to engage them in a constructive partnership.

The right of individuals to *self-direction*, as already indicated, is central to the psychosocial perspective. The more clients make their own decisions and conduct their own lives, the better; the less the caseworker tries to assume clients' responsibilities or direct their actions or choices, the better. Certainly, many clients are physically or emotionally handicapped, or so limited by socioeconomic circumstances, that their options seem few. Nevertheless, we do all we can, first, to intervene in the environment to maximize opportunities, and second, to support people who—for various reasons—have been unwilling or unable to make decisions or take the steps on their own behalf that *are* within the realm of possibility. We know from repeated experience that even small opportunities for autonomous action (such as allowing nursing home patients to select from a menu or plan furniture arrangements in their rooms) can help people feel less hopeless and more competent and independent. Along similar lines, respect for the individual is demonstrated by our humility, by listening to our clients, by conveying to them that *they* are *the* experts on their lives, and that their unique attributes and worldviews are important and understood.

The client's right to *confidentiality* conforms with the values already mentioned. Without exception—other than in situations that are life-threatening or nearly so, or sometimes when a minor is involved—clients have the right to give or withhold permission before any information about them is shared. Often, when clients are given straightforward explanations of why conversations with others or conjoint interviews might enhance their goals, consent is easily given. But, in these days of mandated reporting and bureaucratic intrusions on worker-client relationships, meticulous attention to the client's right to privacy is more necessary than ever.

THE WORKER-CLIENT RELATIONSHIP

Years of experience and research have demonstrated that successful casework depends heavily on the quality of the relationship between client and worker. Beck and Jones (1973) found that in family agencies, good worker-client relationships—more than any other client or service characteristic analyzed—were significantly associated with positive treatment outcomes.

Positive therapeutic relationships stem from the worker's demonstration of nonpossessive warmth and concern, genuineness, accurate empathy, and nonjudgmental acceptance, along with the worker's capacity to communicate optimism and professional competence. Of course, clients must mobilize some measure of courage, hope, and motivation to join with the worker, to trust in the worker's ability to help. Thus, worker and client both contribute essential ingredients to the mutual alliance.

Needless to say, numerous obstacles can stand in the way of effective worker-client collaboration. People seeking help characteristically feel anxious, sometimes attaching feelings of shame or failure to their unresolved difficulties. Fear of dependence on another may create apprehension. Perceived differences in age, sex, race, ethnic background, or class can reinforce anticipatory fears that the worker cannot truly understand their circumstances or needs. When clients have been victims of racism and social oppression, as many of our clients have been, the perception of power differentials can fuel client distrust and caution (Pinderhughes, 1989). The relationship is often affected by the circumstances surrounding referral: many clients are urged into treatment by spouses; teenagers and children are sometimes forced by parents or school systems; others are mandated by courts. External authority systems may direct a client into treatment, but that person's willingness to engage in the work may be impeded thereby. Often enough, involuntary clients harbor suspicions about the allegiance of the worker, questioning the worker's commitment to their concerns and needs. Through training, experience, and self-discipline, however, psychosocial workers become attuned to realistic and unrealistic negative client reactions, appreciating the kinds of life histories that have given rise to defensive attitudes (Woods & Hollis, 1990). The worker learns to *respond* to underlying needs and feelings rather than *react* to seemingly hostile or rejecting behaviors. It is the worker's responsibility, of course, to try to bring out into the open the differences or negative reactions that emerge; in this way, obstacles can be converted into opportunities for greater trust, mutual understanding, and collaboration.

To be effective, social workers must be well acquainted with *their own* patterns of response and the emotional triggers that can render them reactive, and therefore, countertherapeutic. Academic and experiential grounding in the dynamics of countertransference and—we believe—personal therapy are needed to prevent workers from corrupting the treatment relationship with unprocessed emotional reactions deriving from their own past experiences or current concerns. When workers know and trust their subjective feelings, they not only avoid many countertransference pitfalls, but can use these responses as signals to personality issues and as guides to intervention (Scheunemann & French, 1974). Self-awareness is also essential in helping workers determine which of their personal feelings are expressed and which are not; from the psychosocial point of view, self-disclosure is vigilantly guarded against unless it is truly the client's interest (Goldstein, 1994; Woods & Hollis, 1990).

The worker-client relationship may serve as a *corrective emotional experience*, different from patterns of interaction with original caretakers. When, for example, a worker encourages independence and self-direction in a client who historically had controlling caretakers, the new interpersonal experience can promote client growth. Other clients, in contrast, who were neglected or received too little guidance, may need a worker to provide firm, caring limits that help to contain anxiety or acting out; self-esteem can be nurtured thereby. Still others may need repeated demonstrations of reliability and empathy by a worker who is neither judgmental nor punitive. These new interpersonal experiences can help clients to consolidate developmental tasks by repairing some of the past gaps, delays, or traumas that hindered healthy maturation; ideally, the more benign relationship model is internalized.

APPROACHES TO INTERVENTION

PSYCHOSOCIAL STUDY

Gathering Facts Versus Interpreting Facts

In psychosocial casework, primary emphasis is placed on trying to understand clients' dilemmas and what has contributed to them. This understanding, which we refer to as the psychosocial study, requires observation and the gathering of accurate facts that are then arranged in an orderly manner. Often, but certainly not always, the bulk of the data is obtained in early interviews; however, selective collection of facts usually continues as long as the contact lasts, as new understandings and treatment emphases emerge. Although they may proceed simultaneously, the psychosocial study is separate from the diagnostic understanding, which represents *the thinking of the worker about the facts*. Keeping facts and their interpretation as distinct as possible helps steer the worker away from skewing facts to fit theory.

Initial Interviews

Fact gathering commences as the worker elicits from clients their perception of the problem, what they think led up to it, how they have attempted to remedy it, what they believe might help now, and what other people, agencies, or systems are involved. The worker's inquiries not only help clients feel understood, but the importance of their participation in thinking through the current difficulties is underscored. Furthermore, the very act of recounting their impressions may enable them to view their difficulties in a new light. Meanwhile, of course, the worker searches for what, *in systemic terms,* may contribute to the problem. In the words of Florence Hollis (1970), the "person-in-interaction-with situation" is the "minimum unit of attention" (pp. 46–47), for a *set* of interacting forces is always at play, be it the individual personality system, a parent-child system, a marital or family system, or health, school, or work systems. A person's report of fatigue, disinterest in life, and sense of hopelessness, for example, may involve multiple system influences such as genetic predisposition to depression, unresolved tension at home with a teenager, a rift in the marital relationship, coronary heart disease, anticipated loss of employment, chronic shortage of money, and/or brutalizing bigotry. The biopsychosocial study spells out the systemic and transactional context of the person's difficulty, thereby enabling client and worker to discern the set of interlocking factors that contribute to it; by recognizing these, together they will be able to identify points of access for intervention.

Additional Sources of Information

While the client's own statements and reflections provide the most essential base for psychosocial study, other sources of information, including observations of the client's nonverbal behaviors and demeanor and the dynamic of the client-worker relationship, usually prove useful. Here again, fact gathering rather than interpretation is the initial goal. Body posture, eye contact, and gestures all may provide clues to client feeling states or attitudes toward the worker, but accurate *decoding* of these requires sensitivity to cultural patterns and to individual meanings assigned by the client. In the end, of course, the client is the best source of information about what nonverbal messages actually signify. Also, if permission is given and the reasons for it are clearly understood by the client, contact with collaterals reveal facts of which the client is either unaware or for some reason is ignoring.

Conjoint interviews provide the worker with *in vivo* information about interpersonal transactions otherwise difficult to capture from client report alone. A husband may complain that his wife is distant and unfeeling, but, upon seeing the couple in action together, the worker may discern that the husband is also pushing the wife away, preventing opportunities for closeness. Dynamics between parents and children become apparent in conjoint sessions where communication styles, relationship patterns, emotional responses, and distortions and discrepancies in perception are open to view and discussion. During an exploratory family session, a father may become anxious and angry when his wife cries; the son, feeling blamed, withdraws. Mutual investigation of these interactions reveals that the father interprets his wife's crying as a demand he cannot meet; the wife perceives her husband's anger as indifference to her pain; the son assumes he is to blame for the upset of both parents. Clearly, this information would be much more difficult to obtain in an individual meeting with any one family member. Of course, once the worker explains the reasons for suggesting conjoint meetings, the decision to invite others into treatment must ultimately rest with the client.

Psychosocial study of children often requires collateral interviews with parents, teachers, and helping professionals; influential participants in the child's world often become primary sources of significant psychosocial information. Since children tend to be especially sensitive to milieu, direct observation of the parent-child or child-family relationships (sometimes in the home) can throw important light on dynamics among family members that may be relevant to the child's situation. Observations at school can provide a picture of the child in interaction with other children and with school personnel.

Early Life History and Exploration of Life-stage Factors

How extensively or deeply early life history is explored depends on concerns presented by the client. Since psychosocial casework focuses on conscious and preconscious material—in contrast to psychoanalysis—the uncovering of repressed early feelings or memories is *not* the aim of the study. However, family-of-origin issues and early developmental information that seem *directly pertinent* to either client or worker are often pursued or clarified. Such explorations may naturally follow a theme that is unfolding in the course of discussions about the origins of the difficulty. Clients themselves often wonder or notice how current behavior patterns relate to childhood relationships or early developmental phases. A woman may declare: "Everything changed when I was twelve and my father left home, just as I was going into adolescence; from an outgoing, confident child I turned into a withdrawn teenager who was deathly afraid of the opposite sex." As we shall see in our discussion of treatment, such information can become the basis for reflection on the dynamics of response patterns and developmental events that influence present concerns.

Many problems in living emerge during the developmental phases of the individual and family life cycle, requiring shifts in personal adjustment and in the family equilibrium. A child's maturation into adolescence, for example, brings with it tasks, challenges, and anxieties for the teenager, the family, and the community. Attention to expected stages and transitions of family life—referred to by Scherz as "normative crises" (1971) —broadens the focus of study while normalizing situations that clients may label as unusual or pathological. Anxiety often accompanies shifts in parental roles and tasks. For example, limit setting with toddlers challenges mothers in ways that nursing an infant does not; learning to respond to rebellious teenagers calls for negotiating skills that are usually different from those needed to communicate with younger children; becoming a caretaker to frail elderly parents sometimes means that roles are radically reversed from just a few years ago. Clients often feel relief when they realize that their confusion or frustration is experienced by many others in the same situation. A simple comment by the worker, such as, "Of course you are feeling pressured by these changes, just about anyone would," can quickly free the client to redefine the problem and seek new solutions.

The effects of life-stage transitions—marriage, parenthood, divorce, retirement—may require careful scrutiny (Carter & McGoldrick, 1989; Golan 1981). Without doubt, the death of a parent has a very different impact when experienced at five rather than at fifty-five. Expectations people carry into new life phases influence the capacity to cope and make adjustments. For example, when elderly grandparents suddenly become guardians of three grandchildren orphaned by AIDS, we need to understand what the role shift means to them. Have their dreams of leisure—at long last—been shattered? Do the burdens of their new roles feel overwhelming? Is taking on the responsibility consonant with cultural expectations and viewed stoically as rightful duty? Or, does having children in the home invigorate the grandparents, bringing a new sense of purpose to their lives? Psychosocial study is enhanced when we *listen carefully* to clients for the meanings that only *they* can specify. This point was made crystal clear to one of the writers in an initial interview with a client whose husband had died in a tragic accident a few years before. To the worker's expression of sorrow the wife responded, "Yes, it was terrible. But imagine how much worse it would have been if I had been in love with him!"

PSYCHOSOCIAL ASSESSMENT AND INTERVENTION

Assessing Person-in-Situation

Psychosocial assessment begins by thinking *critically* about the facts gathered in the psychosocial study. Now, the worker's task is to conceptualize *how* the multiple systems at play within the person-situation configuration are *mutually interacting.* In most cases, even in brief contacts, the worker analyzes how situational stresses, life events, personality functioning, family context, and other relevant forces are working together to create the particular dilemma facing the client.

More specifically, assessment simultaneously addresses and formulates hypotheses about two major matters: 1) *How* and *why* a problem exists, and 2) *Who* and *what* within the person-situation gestalt is accessible to change. Only after determining *where we can enter* the constellation of multiple systems, and *which system or systems are probably most amenable to change,* can effective treatment strategies be designed. Assessment, therefore, must identify *points of access* and evaluate the *capacity, motivation, and opportunity* (Ripple et al., 1964) for change—of individuals, the family, social networks, and communities. There are common questions the worker considers: What individual strengths can be tapped? What family members are most accessible or most motivated? What community systems and resources can be located or mobilized? If, for example, a husband seeks marital counseling to save his marriage, but his wife is absolutely determined to pursue divorce, no amount of intervention will reunite the couple. However, the divorcing couple may then contract for help in working as a team to support their young son, rather than allowing him to be caught in the crossfire of anger between them. The worker's knowledge of a support group for children of parents who are separating may provide the youngster with an opportunity to feel less alone in his plight. In another case, housing may not be available for a family made homeless by fire, but extended family and/or community networks might be mobilized to provide emergency relief. Even in the face of terminal illness—when it might seem that little can be done—hospice care can be located, family caretakers supported, and the ill person's participation in decision making or in sharing feelings with loved ones may be facilitated.

As should be clear by now, from the psychosocial perspective, individual personality functioning is *part* of assessment, not the *whole*. Certainly, strengths and limitations of a client's ego functioning are important to evaluate, but "individual" performance is *always* mediated by situational factors: as we all know, the same person can feel and behave very differently in different contexts. For example, at work, where she is valued and successful, a woman may feel comfortable, cheerful, and competent. On the other hand, at home as a single mother living with a belligerent teenage son, she may feel hopeless, depressed, and like a failure.

Psychosocial workers believe that the descriptive categories of psychiatry refer to *conditions,* not to people themselves. Thus, people with characteristics of borderline personality disorder are not "borderlines." *We are concerned with how conditions— psychiatric or otherwise—may affect the achievement of goals desired by a client.* Of most relevance is the assessment of how the individual's capacities, support systems, and social resources can be mobilized to surmount obstacles.

Case Vignette

Joseph, a 16-year-old Irish-Italian boy from a blue-collar, lower-middle-class family, was initially referred by his mother for *individual* treatment. She complained of his "angry outbursts at home," frequent and violent fights with peers, and verbal abuse of his younger brother. Psychosocial study revealed, however, that the *entire family system* was in crisis. The father, years ago diagnosed with multiple sclerosis, was becoming increasingly disabled and fearful of losing his job and health benefits; he was depressed, argumentative, and frequently critical of Joseph. The mother, overloaded with worry and responsibility yet trying to pacify the father, was making rigid demands on her son. She reported that she was frightened of the future and admitted that she tried to "overcontrol everything" in the family. Conflicts between Joseph and his parents were heightened by the boy's need to individuate and emancipate himself from the family. Yet, the parents' cultural ethic that the children must "love and obey" them placed Joseph in a bind; he felt restrained from taking the next developmental step—that is, making age-appropriate decisions and pursuing his own interests. "They never allow me out of their sight," he complained. Furthermore, the boy—who, the worker surmised, longed for a strong male in his life—could not seem to muster respect for his physically weak, albeit forceful and judgmental, father.

As it turned out, after the first family meeting, Joseph announced to the worker that he would not return; he had explained how his parents were treating him, he said, and it was up to *them* to change. With a little support from the worker, the mother—who seemed to be the most self-aware and engageable family member—decided to continue treatment; she saw the need to make changes in her own behavior. Spontaneously, she connected her current fear of loss to a history of loss in her family of origin. Soon, she was able to encourage her reluctant husband to join in sessions with her; for the first time, they spoke openly with each other about the future and the impact of the father's illness on all of them. It was revealed that the younger son previously described as the "easy" one was becoming increasingly withdrawn; with the worker's help, the parents worked together to prepare for an upcoming conference with the child's teacher. Both were able to see how Joseph had been scapegoated by the family process that was so weighed down by sorrow and fear. Above all, the parents themselves were no longer arguing, with each other or with their children. With more mutual support, each was less alone in the crisis. The worker introduced the parents to the local MS organization, which offered a group for spouses. That organization also steered the father to a consultant on medical insurance and benefits, as well as to a physical therapy program. Before termination, at the urging of the parents, the boys agreed to a family meeting. Tensions in the household had diminished considerably. The parents' new ability to talk openly about difficult issues, and to listen to each other, allowed the boys to feel less burdened by the gloomy, angry, and anxious family climate. Now that the illness could be discussed, and Joseph no longer felt so criticized and controlled by his parents, he was able to share sadness with his father—about the illness and about some of his own previous behavior.

In this illustration, assessment of the various components contributing to the family's crisis, and of the accessibility of the mother in particular, was instrumental in treatment that *tipped the balance of forces* within the family, bringing greater relief for each member. Had the worker tried to pressure the unwilling Joseph to get help, or had she insisted on individual sessions for the ill father, surely the treatment would have failed. The mother's interest in making changes in her own emotional reactions and behavior ultimately resulted in a shift in the equilibrium of the entire system.

Psychosocial Interventions

As the case example demonstrates, psychosocial treatment often uses a blend of individual, couple, family, and environmental modalities. When indicated by the assessment, collateral meetings with significant others and group work expand the range of direct practice. In work with symptomatic children, family members are often the *most* important resource for change. Selma Fraiberg and colleagues (1975) discovered how intervention with parents directly affected the future health and development of children "at risk." Chethik (1989) calls for a variety of collateral procedures to shift dysfunctional family interactions that impede healthy family development. Van Fleet (1994), in a treatment called "filial therapy," coaches parents to improve the "goodness of fit" between them. Treating children and adolescents in the context of the family is an established part of psychosocial work and can help young *and* old enhance family relationships (Arnold, 1978; Combrinck-Graham, 1989; Minuchin, 1974; Satir, 1967; Wachtel, 1994). Multifamily group meetings and family psychoeducation are utilized to help psychiatrically hospitalized teens and young adults reenter their communities; family members taking care of loved ones with schizophrenia are supported by such interventions (McFarlane, 1983).

Whether arranging for a home health attendant to assist an ill parent, or advocating for a client's right to receive a housing allowance, when the *joint assessment* of worker and client so indicates, psychosocial workers intervene directly within a client's social and community milieu. *Environmental procedures* categorized by Hollis (Woods & Hollis, 1990) include worker roles as *provider* and *locator* of resources, *interpreter* and *mediator* with collaterals, and *aggressive intervener* (or client advocate), all of which are integral to the dual focus of person and situation that defines psychosocial practice. Turner adds the role of *broker,* when the social worker functions as "coordinator and manager of various services and resources in which the client is involved" (1986, p. 496). As Turner points out, social workers as "service managers" are needed in our increasingly "multiservice" environment.

Psychosocial workers frequently work collaboratively with other helping professionals on treatment teams or community task forces. Assessment of young children at risk almost always requires expertise that only a team approach provides. Along the same lines, social workers often spearhead meetings with other providers to develop coordinated treatment plans for families utilizing multiple services; without such collaboration, families and individuals can fall through the cracks and may end up with inadequate service or no service at all.

Typology of Worker-Client Communications

Based on systematic research of hundreds of case records, Florence Hollis and colleagues categorized worker-client communications that have become fundamental to *all* modalities of direct psychosocial practice (Hollis, 1968; Woods & Hollis, 1990). The six major categories of treatment procedures are used differentially by the worker—in different ways at different times, in the service of *mutually determined* goals: to build rapport; to offer suggestions; to help clients discharge pent-up feelings; to gather information; and to encourage reflective consideration of clients' present circumstances, of their own patterns of behavior, and of the influence of early life experiences on their present attitudes and actions. Sometimes the worker takes a great deal of initiative in these communications; in other instances, the client leads the explorations and reflections. A brief summary of these procedures follows.

1. *Sustainment* refers to those verbal and nonverbal communications that demonstrate interest, acceptance, empathic understanding, reassurance, and encouragement. An understanding nod or smile, statements such as "Those feelings are natural" or "Say more" help reduce clients' anxieties and encourage them to trust the worker enough to share their concerns.

2. *Direct influence* consists of various degrees of carefully considered suggestion or advice: "Would it help to____?" "It might be better to____," or "I think you ought to____." *Parent guidance* and *crisis intervention* can require direct influence, with workers sometimes expressing strong opinions, even urging the client to follow a particular course of action. Preferably, of course, clients arrive at decisions by way of their own thinking, but there are times when some degree of direction is clearly indicated.

3. *Exploration, description, and ventilation* describe communications between client and worker that elicit knowledge of the facts of the client's situation and bring out feelings about it. A worker might say, for example: "Please tell me a little more about the problem at work," or "Just what is it that happens when you and your family get together?" When the feelings are ventilated, clients often experience immediate emotional relief.

4. *Reflection of person-situation configuration* helps clients become more aware of perceptions, thoughts, and feelings concerning their *current* circumstances and interactions with others. A father, angered and confused by his daughter's disobedience, might be asked: "Can you think of anything upsetting your daughter right now that could make her so defiant?" and "What is it that makes her behavior so difficult *for you*?" Invitations to explore the client-worker relationship are also part of person-situation reflection: "I was wondering if you thought I was judgmental (or indifferent or angry)."

5. *Pattern dynamic reflection* helps to identify behavioral tendencies of clients, or patterns of thinking and feeling that lead them to particular actions or ways of thinking about events. Patterns of behavior can be clarified: "Do you think you tend to seek closeness with people who are not available?" or "Does it seem to you that you sometimes argue with people who are not available?" or "Does it seem to you that you sometimes argue with your son when you are really annoyed with your husband?" These procedures also encourage clients to explore their intrapsychic functioning: "Have you noticed how you criticize yourself and devalue your own ideas?" or "I wonder if you wish others would take care of *you* the way you devote yourself to them."

6. *Developmental reflection* moves clients to consider family of origin or early life experiences that contribute to current personality and functioning. Asking, "Have you had feelings like this before?" can help people connect feelings of the present with situations in the past; sometimes just one such question prompts the client to recognize relationships between specific early experiences and current actions or attitudes. Parents of teenagers can be helped to reflect on their own earlier stages: "What was adolescence like for *you*?" Sensitively phrased inquiries may promote developmental insight: "Do you think you withdraw

from your boss, expecting him to be critical the way your father was?" Questions rather than interpretations are usually preferable; then the client can feel free to disagree, or correct the worker's opinion.

Illustration

A client complains about a stormy relationship with his wife (ventilation), carefully watching the worker for signs of disapproval. The worker nods his head as if to say, "I understand" (sustainment), and encourages the client: "Tell me more so I can really understand what your marriage is like for you." The worker's nonjudgmental, concerned attitude aids the client in further probing the situation (sustainment and exploration). As the client gives more details, he expresses feelings of inadequacy and self-doubt (ventilation), but is reassured by the worker's comment that "close relationships are often confusing and filled with intense feelings" (sustainment). This reassurance leads the client to describe frequent and "verbally abusive" fights. He shares feelings of shame and remorse (ventilation). While acknowledging the client's feelings, the worker encourages him to discuss exactly what transpires (sustainment and exploration). As the client continues, the worker gently asks, "How does it feel to you when you find yourself calling your wife those names?" With the aid of the worker, the client speaks of his anger when his wife pushes him away (person-situation reflection). When the worker asks what being pushed away means to him, the client responds, "I always feel like it don't matter when someone turns away from me" (pattern-dynamic reflection). In future sessions, the client initiates comments about his childhood—his father's frequent absence and his mother's preoccupation with a chronically ill sister. With little help from the worker at this point, he sees the link between his strong reaction to his wife and the feelings he had so many years ago (developmental reflection).

TECHNICAL AIDS TO ASSESSMENT AND INTERVENTION

Organizing psychosocial information into *visual diagrams* often facilitates understanding of the person-situation gestalt (Meyer, 1993, ch. 6). These technical aids may become a form of intervention, with worker and client working *collaboratively* to arrange information that then throws light on the client's current and past contexts. The *ecomap* (Hartman, 1978) helps to identify social resources, supportive networks, and areas of stress within the individual's or family's ecosystem. The *genogram* (Bowen, 1978; Guerin & Pendagast, 1976; McGoldrick & Gerson, 1985) graphically displays a gold mine of family information, patterns and relationships over generations, from which hypotheses emerge about how current concerns may relate to family history. The *developmental assessment wheel*, developed by Vigilante & Mailick (1988), visually captures the breadth of psychosocial assessment, reminding us to include cultural, social, material, developmental, spiritual, and historical factors as we evaluate people's problems in living.

SETTINGS FOR PSYCHOSOCIAL PRACTICE

The many practice modalities used by psychosocial workers—including individual, marital, family, and group treatments and work with collaterals and the environment—take place in a variety of locations. By the same token, long-term and brief therapies, crisis intervention, preventive treatment, aggressive outreach, and trauma treatment are conducted in a vast range of settings. Among others, these include schools, community-based agencies, storefronts, work sites, hospitals, railroad stations, client homes, private offices, and scenes of disaster. In some areas, family preservation programs provide intensive, twenty-four-hour service in clients' homes. Needless to say, the ability to provide services where they are most needed can depend on the whims of people of influence in the public and private sectors. Financial cuts, negative attitudes about some client groups, and bureaucratic interference or indifference can result in drastic—often inhumane—decisions about how and where services are rendered.

INTEGRATION OF NEW PERSPECTIVES WITH ESTABLISHED PRINCIPLES

Historically, psychosocial workers have evaluated their practice through empirical case study research (Woods & Hollis, 1990). Qualitative research methods, such as participant-observer research, naturalistic inquiry, ethnographic study, and narrative and constructivist approaches are consonant with the case study traditions of psychosocial practice and with the humanistic values that underlie the approach. As positivist science continues to come under attack (Heineman, 1981; Pieper, 1989), and as social work articulates more clearly concepts of "tacit understanding" and "practice wisdom" (Imre, 1984, 1985), we may enjoy a growing partnership with qualitative research that addresses what is important to psychosocial practice; indeed, quantitative methods may not adequately measure all we need to know. The connection between qualitative research and psychosocial practice was noted by Sherman and Reid: "We could justifiably say the case study method described by Mary Richmond (1917) in *Social Diagnosis* is a legitimate form of qualitative research" (1994, p.1). Whether qualitative or quantitative methods are chosen, however, we advocate systematic evaluation of our practices and procedures relevant to the relationship-oriented work that we do, and consonant with the client-centered values we hold.

More than ever, psychosocial practitioners need to make holistic assessments and plan multiple interventions. The complex practice issues that surround HIV disease, homelessness, unemployment, and institutional racism, among many other social concerns, involve *no less* than individuals, families, communities, and the body politic as a whole. Service provision at *all levels* of human systems is critical to our work, as Taylor-Brown (1995) has thoroughly illustrated in her review of direct practice with HIV/AIDS populations.

We have come a long way since Mary Richmond first published *Social Diagnosis*, the landmark text of 1917 that established core *principles* of psychosocial practice. What enables the psychosocial approach to remain vital and balanced is the ability of its practitioners to discriminate trends from principles. As an open system of thought, the framework admits new theory and knowledge only when these conform to established concepts. In this way, psychosocial treatment can expand without diffusing its unique identity. New treatment ideas and models that do not adhere to the underlying values cannot be accepted. Accurate study, assessment and differential treatment planning are essential to practice, even when time limits are set. Values of mutuality, client self-direction, and confidentiality can never be compromised, regardless of time factors, modality of treatment, the client's choice of goals, or impinging social and political pressures. Guided by a rich history of dedication and experience, psychosocial practitioners will continue to expand their horizons in response to current needs and new challenges.

REFERENCES

Ainsworth, M. (1973). The development of mother-infant attachment. In B. Caldwell & H. Ricciuti (eds.), *Review of Child Development Research* 3:1–94. Chicago: University of Chicago Press.

Angell, R. (1936). *The Family Encounters the Depression.* New York: Scribner.

Arnold, L. (1978). *Helping Parents Help Their Children.* New York: Brunner/Mazel.

Beck, D., & Jones, M. (1973). *Progress in Family Problems.* New York: Family Service Association of America.

Benedict, R. (1934). *Patterns of Culture.* New York: Houghton Mifflin.

Bertalanffy, L. (1968). *General Systems Theory: Foundations, Development Application.* New York: Braziller.

Biddle, J., & Thomas, E. (eds.). (1966). *Role Theory: Concepts and Research.* New York: Wiley.

Bowen, M. (1978). *Family Therapy in Clinical Practice.* New York: Jason Aronson.

Bowlby, J. (1969). *Attachment and Loss.* Vol. I: *Attachment.* New York: Basic Books.

——— (1973). *Attachment and Loss.* Vol. II: *Separation Anxiety and Anger.* New York: Basic Books.

Bronfenbrenner, U. (1989). Ecological systems theory. *Annals of Child Development,* 6: 187–249.

Carter, B., & McGoldrick, M. (eds.). (1989). *The Changing Family Life-Cycle: A Framework for Family Therapy* (2nd ed.). Boston: Allyn & Bacon.

Cavan, R., & Ranck, K. (1938). *The Family and the Depression.* Chicago: University of Chicago Press.

Chethik, M. (1989). *Techniques of Child Therapy: Psychodynamic Strategies.* New York: Guilford Press.

Cloward, R. (1959). Illegitimate means, anomie and deviant behavior. *American Sociological Review,* 24:164–176.

Combrinck-Graham, L. (ed.). (1989). *Children in Family Contexts: Perspectives on Treatment.* New York: Guilford Press.

Davis, L. (1986). Role theory. In Francis J. Turner (ed.), *Social Work Treatment: Interlocking Theoretical Approaches* (3rd ed.) (pp.541–563). New York: Free Press.

Erikson, E. (1950). *Childhood and Society*. New York: W.W. Norton.

———. (1959). *Identity and the Life Cycle*. New York: International Universities Press.

Fraiberg, S., Adelson, E., & Shapiro, V. (1975). Ghosts in the nursery. A psychoanalytic approach to the problems of impaired infant-mother relationships. *Journal of the American Academy of Child Psychiatry 14*(3), 387–421.

Freud, A. (1946). *The Ego and the Mechanisms of Defense*. New York: International Universities Press.

Golan, N. (1981). *Passing Through Transitions: A Guide for Practitioners*. New York: Free Press.

Goldstein, E. (1994). Self-disclosure in treatment: What therapists do and don't talk about. *Clinical Social Work Journal 22*(4), 417–433.

Guerin Jr., P., & Pendagast, E. (1976). Evaluation of family system and genogram. In Philip Guerin, Jr. (ed.), *Family Therapy* (pp. 450–464). New York: Gardner Press.

Hamilton, G. (1940). *Theory and Practice of Casework*. New York: Columbia University Press.

Hankins, F. (1930). Contributions of sociology to social work. *Proceedings of the National Conference of Social Work*. Chicago: University of Chicago Press.

Hartman, A. (1978). Diagrammatic assessment of family relationships. *Social Casework*, 59:465–476.

Hartmann, H. (1939). *Ego Psychology and the Problem of Adaptation*. New York: International Universities Press.

Heineman [Pieper], M. (1981). The obsolete scientific imperative in social work research. *Social Service Review*, 55 (September): 371–97.

Hollis, F. (1964). *Casework: A Psychosocial Therapy* (1st ed.). New York: Random House.

———. (1968). *A Typology of Casework Treatment*. New York: Family Service Association of America.

———. (1970). The psychosocial approach to the practice of casework. In R. Roberts & R. Nee (eds.), *Theories of Social Casework* (pp. 33–75). Chicago: University of Chicago Press.

Imre, R. (1984). The nature of knowledge in social work. *Social Work 29*(1), 41–45.

———. (1985). Tacit knowledge in social work research and practice. *Smith College Studies in Social Work 55*(2), 137–149.

Kardiner, A. (1939). *The Individual and His Society*. New York: Columbia University Press.

Kernberg, O. (1975). *Borderline Conditions and Pathological Narcissism*. New York: Jason Aronson.

———. (1984). *Severe Personality Disorders*. New Haven: Yale University Press.

Kohut, H. (1971). *The Analysis of the Self*. New York: International Universities Press.

———. (1977). *The Restoration of the Self*. New York: International Universities Press.

Komarovsky, M. (1940). *The Unemployed Man and His Family*. New York: Dryden Press.

Mahler, M. (1968). *On Human Symbiosis and the Vicissitudes of Individuation*. New York: International Universities Press.

———, Pine, F., & Bergman, A. (1975). *The Psychological Birth of the Human Infant*. New York: Basic Books.

McFarlane, W. (ed.). (1983). *Family Therapy in Schizophrenia*. New York: Guilford Press.

McGoldrick, M., & Gerson, R. (1985). *Genograms in Family Assessment*. New York: W.W. Norton.

McGoldrick, M., Pearce, J. K., & Giordano, J. (eds.). (1982). *Ethnicity and Family Therapy*. New York: Guilford Press.

Mead, M. (1935). *Sex and Temperament in Three Primitive Societies*. New York: William Morrow.

Meyer, C. (1993). *Assessment in Social Work Practice*. New York: Columbia University Press.

Minuchin, S. (1974). *Families and Family Therapy*. Cambridge: Harvard University Press.

Nelsen, J. (1980). *Communication Theory and Social Work Practice*. Chicago: University of Chicago Press.

Parad, H. (ed.). (1958). *Ego Psychology and Dynamic Casework*. New York: Family Service Association of America.

Parad, H., & Miller, R. (eds.). (1963). *Ego-oriented Casework: Problems and Perspectives.* New York: Family Service Association of America.

Perlman, H. (1957). *Social Casework: A Problem-solving Process.* Chicago: University of Chicago Press.

Pieper, M. (1989). The heuristic paradigm: A unifying and comprehensive approach to social work research. *Smith College Studies in Social Work,* 60:8–34.

Pinderhughes, E. (1989). *Understanding Race, Ethnicity, and Power: The Key to Efficacy in Clinical Practice.* New York: Free Press.

Rank, O. (1936). *Will Therapy.* New York: Knopf.

Richmond, M. (1899). *Friendly Visiting Among The poor: A Handbook for Charity Workers.* New York: Macmillan.

———. (1917). *Social Diagnosis.* New York: Russell Sage Foundation.

———. (1922). *What Is Social Casework?* New York: Russell Sage Foundation.

———. (1930). *The Long View.* New York: Russell Sage Foundation.

Ripple, L., Alexander, E., & Polemis, B. (1964). *Motivation, Capacity and Opportunity.* Chicago: University of Chicago Press.

Robinson, V. (1930). *A Changing Psychology in Social Case Work.* Chapel Hill: University of North Carolina Press.

Satir, V. (1967). *Conjoint Family Therapy.* Palo Alto, CA: Science and Behavior Books.

Scherz, F. (1971). Maturational crises and parent-child interaction. *Social Casework* 52: 301–311.

Scheunemann, S., & French, B. (1974). Diagnosis as the foundation of professional service. *Social Casework,* 55 (March), 135–141.

Sherman, E., & Reid, W. (eds.). (1994). *Qualitative Research in Social Work.* New York: Columbia University Press.

Taft, J. (1937). The relation of function to process in social casework. *Journal of Social Work Process,* 1:1–18.

Taylor-Brown, S. (1995). HIV/AIDS: Direct practice. In *Encyclopedia of Social Work* (19th ed.). Vol. 2 (pp. 1291–1305). Washington, DC: NASW Press.

Turner, F. J. (1978). *Psychosocial Therapy: A Social Work Perspective.* New York: Free Press.

———. (1986). Psychosocial theory. In F.J. Turner (ed.), *Social Work Treatment: Interlocking Theoretical Approaches* (3rd ed.) (pp. 484–513). New York: Free Press.

Van Fleet, R. (1994). *Filial Therapy: Strengthening Parent-Child Relationships Through Play.* Sarasota, FL: Professional Resource Press.

Vigilante, F., & Mailick, M. (1988). Needs-resource evaluation in the assessment process. *Social Work,* 33:101–104.

Wachtel, E. (1994). *Treating Troubled Children and Their Families.* New York: Guilford Press.

White, R. (1959). Motivation reconsidered: The concept of competence. *Psychological Review,* 66:297–333.

Winnicott, D.W. (1965). *Maturational Processes and the Facilitating Environment.* New York: International Universities Press.

Woodroofe, K. (1962). *From Charity to Social Work in England and in the United States.* Toronto: University of Toronto Press.

Woods, M., & Hollis, F. (1990). *Casework: A Psychosocial Therapy* (4th ed.). New York: McGraw-Hill.

CHAPTER 24

ROLE THEORY
AND SOCIAL WORK TREATMENT

LIANE VIDA DAVIS

INTRODUCTION

In what may be the most widely referenced book on role theory within social work, Bruce Biddle and Edwin Thomas observed almost twenty years ago that "Role theory is a new field of inquiry. . . . Indeed, with the exception of fragmented commentary, the scholars of role have not identified, articulated, and analyzed the component aspects of role theory: namely its domain of study, perspective, language, body of knowledge, theory, and method of inquiry" (6, p. 3).

Close to fifteen years later Biddle observed that the failure of the scholars of role theory to generate an integrative theoretical statement had resulted in considerable ambiguity about its central assumptions and domain of study (5). Perhaps role theory has failed to generate an integrative theoretical statement because, as Marvin Shaw and Phillip Costanzo have suggested, it is not a theory. For them "(r)ole theory is a body of knowledge and principles that at one and the same time constitutes an orientation, a group of theories, loosely linked networks of hypotheses, isolated constructs about human functioning in a social context, and a language system which pervades nearly every social scientist's vocabulary" (51, p. 295).

Despite this confusion as to its domain, there is little doubt that "the constructs of role theory are exceptionally rich in their empirical referents and provide an approach to the analysis of social behavior which is missing from many other theories" (14, p. 244). Furthermore, because role theory seeks to explain the ways in which the behavior of the individual is directly and indirectly influenced by the social environment, it is a system that is both congruent with and can provide theoretical and empirical support for social work's historical emphasis on person-environment transactions. As Herbert Strean observed in the earlier editions of this book, "role carries a considerable freightage of meaning in social work because it implies a means of individual expression as well as dimension of social behavior" (54, p. 387).

HISTORICAL ORIGINS

Role theory has roots within both academic and nonacademic institutions. The concept of role itself is drawn from the theater and has been passed down through the centuries to characterize the observable behaviors that persons enact in their patterned interactions with others (46). It captures the central view of role theory that we play many parts in our lives whose basic scripts are provided by others yet whose enactment is uniquely our own.

Other role theory constructs are rooted within the many disciplines of formal social science. This interdisciplinary perspective on human conduct is, for many, its major strength (2, 5, 44, 46). There is only space to mention a few of the historic luminaries whose contributions on role have had a significant influence on the ways in which we as social workers practice. George Herbert Mead, the sociologist, introduced the concept of *role taking* and focused on its significance in the development of an individual's self-concept (33). We lay the foundation for a sense of who we are by identifying with significant others, internalizing their attitudes as our own, and seeing ourselves as others see us. Joseph L. Moreno introduced the use of *role playing* as a therapeutic technique to be used for both the learning of new behaviors and to facilitate clients' ability to understand another's perspective (38). Ralph Linton, the anthropologist, and Robert K. Merton, the sociologist, were more concerned about the relationship between the social structure itself and the ways in which persons fulfilled their socially designated obligations (27, 36). Linton distinguished between the static aspects of role behavior—that is, the positions or statuses designated by social systems—and their dynamic aspects—that is, the patterned behaviors, or roles, expected of and enacted by those who occupied them. Linton conceived of persons as enacting one role for each of the many statuses they occupied. Merton observed that there were actually a set of different roles—that is, a role-set—potentially associated with each status. Together, their contributions make us aware of the myriad ways in which the behaviors we enact in interaction with others are influenced by the positions we occupy in society and vary as we interact with different persons.

ROLE THEORY: WHAT IS IT?

My failure to define the subject matter of role theory thus far has not been an oversight. In part it has been to demonstrate that many of its concepts are accessible to persons with little formal education in the theory itself. This has been both a strength and a weakness for its theoretical development and utilization. It has resulted, on the one hand, in the widespread application of its central concepts across a broad array of situations by both lay persons and professionals. On the other hand, this utilization has occurred with a rather broad disregard for the carefully operationalized definitions of central constructs offered by the theorists. This rather liberal, if inexact, incorporation of role theoretic constructs into common usage has been aided by the wide diversity of definitions and usages offered by the theorists themselves.

One of the major reasons the domain of role theory is so difficult to define is that it takes on different identities depending in large part on the discipline of the writer. It is, for example, somewhat different for psychologists than it is for sociologists. Social psychologists are primarily concerned with the ways in which socially prescribed roles influence the behavior of persons. They focus their attention on such issues as:

the processes by which individuals are socialized into role behavior; the stresses placed on the individual by the necessity to perform multiple roles; the impact on the individual of the sanctions imposed for violation of normative role behavior; the ways in which the interaction between persons is structured by their role expectations of one another and of themselves in their complementary positions; the ways in which an individual's sense of self is influenced by the various positions she occupies and the effectiveness with which she plays her roles. Most recently, concern for role within social psychology has been focused on the myriad ways in which persons' public selves—that is, their public role behavior—and their private selves diverge from one another, as well as the reasons for and the consequences of such discrepancies (51).

Sociologists are more concerned with the macro issue of how the system of role behaviors helps maintain the social structure itself. Since the stability of the social structure depends in part on the extent to which individuals enact normative role behaviors, concern is focused on such issues as: the mechanisms used to assure conformity to socially normative behaviors; the impact of engaging in deviant behaviors; the relationship between those in positions of social control and those in positions to have their behavior controlled; as well as the myriad ways in which the behavior of individuals in their daily interactions reflects social rather than psychological forces.

CENTRAL TERMS

As indicated earlier, one of the major sources of confusion for the student of role theory has been the myriad ways in which central terms have been defined. In selecting the central terms I have chosen to provide the most commonsensical definitions, high-lighting those instances in which the differences appear to be qualitatively significant.

Social position and *social status* are often used interchangeably in the literature to refer to a "socially recognized category of actors" (56, p. 439). While *status* seems to be more frequently used than *position,* I prefer to use *position* because it is less value-laden. Positions are classifications of persons (6). Among common positions are teachers, social workers, women, children, fathers. The major confusion in the literature is whether position refers solely to the identity or carries other meaning. Some include the associated behavioral expectations within the definition of position (46), others include the placement of the position within the social structure itself (50).

Ascribed positions are those that are independent of the qualities of the individual and depend instead on accidents of birth, social experience, or maturity. Common ascribed positions are woman, man, child, adult, black, handicapped person. Kingsley Davis has observed that ascribed positions have primacy over those achieved since they are often based on characteristics present at birth and, as a result, lay the foundation for subsequent socialization (13).

Achieved positions are those that are attained through skill or effort. Common achieved positions are social worker, musician, politician. It has been observed by many that the distinction between ascribed and achieved positions is not as clear in reality as it is in theory (5, 13). One enters most positions through a combination of ascription and achievement. Hard work and intelligence are certainly requisites for becoming a college professor. There is little doubt, however, that entry into the position of college professor is facilitated by having been born a white male in a family that has both an adequate income and a set of values that places a high priority on education. Knowing that there is a mechanism to change one's position serves to motivate persons toward social ends (13).

Status refers to the value of the position (5). Among the most common criteria used to determine status are: prestige, wealth, and authority. A position has a higher status if its occupants have more prestige, are wealthier, and are able to wield authority.

The relationship between status and position is well illustrated with reference to the differential status of the ascribed positions of men and women. Almost twenty years ago, Kingsley Davis commented on the fact that in every society sex difference is used as a way of assigning and giving a monopoly to different statuses which in turn results in one sex receiving more status than another, causing tension between such ascriptions.

Role refers to the characteristic behaviors enacted by persons occupying social positions. A role is "a patterned sequence of learned *actions* or deeds performed by a person *in an interaction situation* [emphasis added]" (46, p. 225). The concept of role serves as a metaphor to denote that "conduct adheres to certain 'parts' or statuses rather than to players who recite or read their 'parts'" (45, p. 101). Roles are classifications of behaviors (6). They do not exist in isolation but are designed to "fit in with the reciprocal functions of a partner in a relationship" (30, p. 9).

The concept of *role partner* has been introduced to capture this socially interactive, reciprocal, nature of role behavior (51). The role of mother is enacted vis-à-vis the role of child or the role of father; the role of social worker is enacted vis-à-vis the role of client or the role of psychologist.

Role-set refers to the varied roles potentially associated with any single position. Social workers, for example, enact one set of behaviors for clients, another set of behaviors for supervisors, another set of behaviors for the agency administrator, and yet another set of behaviors for their peers.

Role expectations are the set of expectations for the behaviors of a person or a position held by a particular person or by a generalized other. Since roles are enacted in interaction with another, there are both role expectations held by the actor (also referred to as ego) and reciprocal role expectations of the other (also referred to as alter). Expectations include both *rights* and *obligations* (36, 46). In common parlance many of the "oughts" and the "shoulds" to which persons are subjected derive from role expectations.

Role expectations vary in the generality with which they are held by others. Some are held by society in general, others are group specific, still others are more idiosyncratic. Society, for example, holds certain expectations of mothers; however these differ as a function of ethnicity or socioeconomic class. A specific child may, furthermore, have his own expectations of how his mother should behave.

Role complementarity exists when the role behavior and role expectations of persons in an interpersonal system are harmonious. "The *principle of role complemen-*

tarity . . . states that role definitions, expectations, and enactive behaviors of people should fit together and mutually complete each other's needs" (52, p. 106). Lack of complementarity may result from: lack of knowledge of the role system; discrepant goals on the part of the role partners; disagreement as to the right of one of the partners to occupy the role; and absence of appropriate resources to facilitate role performance (30). Role complementarity results in satisfactory role relationships; lack of complementarity results in dissatisfactory relationships as well as individual and interpersonal stress.

Norms are role expectations that serve to prescribe behaviors that *ought* to be performed by the person holding a given position. "[I]t is largely through . . . (norms) . . . that . . . (a person's) . . . conduct is regulated and integrated with the conduct of his fellows" (12, p. 110).

While norms and expectations have frequently been used interchangeably in the literature, Shaw and Costanzo suggest that it is more useful to reserve the term "norm" for role expectations that are socially prescribed (51). Other expectations, more idiosyncratic in nature, assist us in anticipating the behavior of specific others enacting their roles. While not necessary for society in general, these expectations facilitate interpersonal behavior as they enable persons to predict the behavior of those with whom they regularly interact.

It is a norm for fathers to financially support their families. While it is not normative as yet, there are an increasing number of fathers who are also engaging in extensive child care behaviors vis-à-vis their children. Thus, a specific mother may expect a specific father to bathe, feed, clothe, and engage in other care taking activities for his own child.

Social identity is the sense of ourselves that we derive from the positions we occupy and the adequacy with which we and significant others judge our role performance. It is through the reciprocal interactions one has with others, the repeated experience of describing who we are, that we develop and internalize our social identity (45). At one and the same time we may be mothers in relation to children, children in relation to mothers, students in relation to teachers, and teachers in relation to students. Our social identity reflects the complexity of these myriad role relationships. The concept of social identity implies, furthermore, that a part of our self-identity changes along with the changes in the roles we enact.

CONCEPTS THAT DESCRIBE ROLE-RELATED DIFFICULTIES

There are a number of constructs in the role literature that describe role situations that are likely to result in the experiencing of intrapersonal stress and/or interpersonal difficulties. These constructs are especially useful for the social worker interested in accurately utilizing role theory terminology for understanding impediments to, and intervening to facilitate, effective role performance.

Role conflict is generically used by some theorists to refer to difficulties that persons experience in the performance of their roles. More exactly, role conflict occurs when a person experiences incompatible demands in the performance of his designated roles. Role conflict may be experienced only internally or may be expressed inter-personally (52). Two subtypes of role conflict have been identified in the literature:

Interrole or interposition conflict occurs when the role expectations associated with various positions held by an individual are incompatible with one another (51, 57). For example, many women in contemporary society experience interrole conflict in attempting to adequately fulfill their roles as worker, wife, and mother.

Intrarole or intraposition conflict occurs when the expectations associated with a single position are incompatible with one another (51, 57). This is likely to occur when there is lack of consensus about role expectations. For example, a woman may experience intrarole conflict when the expectations of the role of mother held by her own mother, her husband, and herself are incongruent with one another.

Role ambiguity occurs when the expectations for adequate role performance for a given position are unclear or incomplete (5, 57). It has also been used to refer to roles for "which no place has been made in the social system" (42, p. 151). There are many persons who, upon entering positions, need to learn appropriate role expecta-tions; that is, be socialized. This is not in itself role ambiguity, it is only such if the role expectations themselves are unclearly defined. Role ambiguity will be expected when new roles are developing or old roles are in the process of being redefined. For example, one would expect a substantial amount of role ambiguity to exist for those persons trying nontraditional couple relationships, such as egalitarian marriages and lesbian and gay couples.

Role overload occurs when a person is faced with a set of roles that are too com-plex. There is no simple relationship between the number of roles that a person can handle and the amount of role overload experienced. Some persons thrive on multi-ple roles, others are stressed by only a few (5). Some women, for example, thrive in balancing family and work obligations, others experience considerable stress.

Role discontinuity refers to the lack of similarity between the roles an individual is expected to perform at various stages of the life cycle or at sequential points in time. This term, first introduced by Ruth Benedict, is usefully applied to understand-ing the stresses that a person experiences and the supports that are required to facili-tate the transition from a familiar role to a dissimilar one (5). Common instances of role discontinuity occur in the transition from worker to retired person, from married person to single person, from alcoholic to recovering alcoholic.

DEVIANT AND VARIANT ROLES

Society creates norms largely to regulate and integrate the behavior of persons, thereby ensuring a stable social structure. While there is considerable disagreement about the causes of deviant behavior, the development of deviant identities, and the subsequent enactment of deviant roles, there is substantial agreement about those roles that are considered to be deviant (20, 47, 48). Among the more commonly dis-cussed roles are those of mental patient, alcoholic, prisoner, delinquent, gay, and lesbian. Furthermore, there is agreement that society systematically "punishes" those who engage in deviant behaviors in order to force their conformity and/or to assure the continued conformity of others.

Persons may learn to enact deviant roles through modeling, as in the case of the alcoholic; they may enact them because they have been denied access to normative roles, as in the case of the delinquent (11, 45); or they may enact them because society is intolerant of behavior that is different, as in the case of the gay or lesbian. Regardless, deviant roles are stigmatized by society, and, as a result, persons who enact them may internalize a degraded social identity (45).

ROLE THEORY AND ITS RELATIONSHIP TO OTHER THEORIES

Because of its interdisciplinary nature and the generality with which social scientists have used the language of role, role theory at times seems to both incorporate and to be incorporated into many other theoretical perspectives. There are few theories with which it comes into critical conflict. The major issues are those of differential emphasis.

Role theory does differ substantially from psychoanalytic theory, for example, by emphasizing the social determinants of behavior, by focusing on contemporaneous conflicting role expectations and role performance as major sources of psychological distress, and by emphasizing the primarily conscious facets of social relationships.

Because role behavior is learned through such processes a modeling, identification, and reinforcement, it draws directly on, and is therefore congruent with, a social learning approach to both understanding human behavior and social work intervention. However, it differs from a social learning theory perspective in the holistic quality of what is learned. Role theory is less concerned with how persons learn the specific behaviors they enact in their myriad roles and more concerned with how they learn and enact "the generic quality of the behavior and the goals and motives of that behavior" (51, p. 300).

In this sense it is similar to theories of behavior that focus on the organizing influence of cognitions on behavior and feelings (22, 29, 34, 35). It is also congruent with a symbolic interactionist perspective within sociology that focuses attention on the ways in which behavior and thoughts are created in the process of interacting with others (4).

ROLE THEORY'S ENTRY INTO SOCIAL WORK

Because of social work's historical emphasis on the person-environment configuration, role concepts have found a comfortable home within social work. Florence Hollis, in her psychosocial approach to casework, emphasized the utility for diagnosis of understanding the ways in which normative expectations are dependent on gender, age, and class as well as the ways in which they can help locate "the spots at which external pressures are strong and the ways in which the individual is reacting in an unhealthy fashion" (25, p. 187). As with many subsequent social work theoreticians, she also used role theory to conceptualize the client-worker relationship and the ways in which the client's initial expectations regarding the role of the social worker influence the subsequent course of treatment.

There is perhaps no book in the social work practice literature that better captures the broad perspective that role theory has to offer than Helen Harris Perlman's *Persona: Social Role and Personality.* "Persona," the Latin word for the masks used in Greek dramas, is used to capture the notion that we know others through the varied masks we don in our interactions with others. Perlman's major thesis throughout this book is that the transactions between individuals and their environments are, for the most part, "contained and aligned by socially defined position and their functions— by roles" (42, p. 3).

She emphasizes the fact that society merely provides the basic script for behavior. It is within the ongoing transactions between persons that the scripts are acted out, the role behaviors finely tuned.

The importance of role theory for Perlman is best expressed in her belief that change in adulthood occurs through the roles we play.

> Personal change in adulthood, then, in large or small degree, of one or more dimensions, may be given thrust, undergirding, direction, and shaping by the person's experience of action, of making things happen, in the adult roles he undertakes to carry. The tensions generated within transactions between persons bound in role relationships, the emotional involvement of mutuality or conflict, the investment of self—of anxieties, hopes, fears, wishes—in the struggle for gratification and rewarding outcomes, the discharge of tension in the "doing" of a role, the feedback from other persons or from circumstances that give evidence of competence and "payoff"—all these moving forces are involved in active performance of vital roles (42, p. 36)

Perlman also understands the value of role prescriptions for facilitating the daily interactions between persons, freeing up energies for the more important decisions of life. And she, too, focuses attention on the use of role theoretic concepts for understanding early client-worker relationships (42, p. 166).

CONTEMPORARY APPLICATIONS OF ROLE THEORY WITHIN SOCIAL WORK

Contemporary social work texts are replete with references to role theory. The concepts of role provide a language congruent with social work's historical focus on transactions between persons and their environment. It can be used to talk about the distress that persons experience when they and their environments are ill-matched; it also can facilitate talking about many of the interventions that social workers use to restore a balance between persons and their environments.

The application to social work practice can best be divided into three major areas: intake; assessment and diagnosis; and intervention strategies and techniques for various units of practice.

THE USE OF ROLE THEORY CONCEPTS AT INTAKE

There is ample evidence that clients and workers differ in their expectations of what both "good" clients and "good" social workers do (30, 32, 40). This lack of clarity about client and worker role behavior is understandable given that many persons seeking social work intervention have had little prior direct experience with social workers and have derived their knowledge from the too-frequently inaccurate stereotypes perpetuated by the media or from secondhand knowledge of the behaviors of many persons who, while carrying the label social worker, are often not professionally educated.

The misunderstanding of appropriate client and social worker roles has a number of implications for the social work treatment process. There is, for example, evidence that lack of congruence between client and social worker as to their respective roles is a significant factor in premature termination from treatment (9, 30, 40). Furthermore, there is ample evidence that "continuance can be increased, and/or positive outcomes enhanced, when the initial contacts with the client are devoted to structuring the mutual expectations of client and practitioner" (15, p. 140). From this perspective, therefore, effective social work practice can be enhanced by educating clients as to "helpful client behaviors" (17, p. 73).

As noted earlier, social workers have historically recognized the importance of clarifying role expectations during the initial stages of the treatment process (19, 33). Recent practice literature has focused on identifying a set of practice skills, referred to as *role induction procedures,* that can effectively accomplish what is primarily an educative function.

Role induction begins by "starting where the client is" and exploring the expectations that the client holds when he enters the social work agency. As Dean Hepworth and JoAnn Larsen note, sometimes clients convey these expectations with little prompting from the social worker: "A woman dragging her reluctant husband to a family service agency for marital therapy began the initial interview by telling me: 'I'm frustrated because he won't listen to me. I was hoping that you could tell him how to behave and that, if he heard it from somebody other than me, he would listen and change'" (24, p. 272).

Only after the clients have been helped in verbalizing the expectations they hold both of the role of social worker and of the role of client, should the social worker *educate* the client as to more appropriate role behaviors that will better achieve the client's goals and also respect basic social work values. Establishing formal contracts with clients has been suggested as one way to ensure that both client and worker are in agreement as to their respective roles (15, 24, 31, 49).

Regardless of the direction of change that is in the client or the worker, there is little doubt that clarification of social worker and client roles early in the treatment process can enhance the likelihood that treatment will be effective as well as resulting in increased congruence between worker and client as to their satisfaction with the treatment outcome.

ASSESSMENT

During assessment, role theory is valuable in focusing our attention on: (1) the ways in which clients' problems are created out of their incomplete and inadequate social- ization into the myriad roles they are expected to enact in their daily lives; (2) the ways in which their difficulties stem from insufficient contemporary support for the roles that are expected of them; as well as (3) the inherently interactive nature of many of the problems that individuals think are their own. Because it emphasizes the social determinants of human behavior and human interaction, it serves to embed the assessment of persons and the problems they are experiencing within an ongoing in- terpersonal and societal context.

Carel Germain and Alex Gitterman's ecological systems* theory approach to practice easily incorporates the language of role to identify ways in which status and role influence both the practice of social work and the problems that social work clients experience (19).

Concepts of role also help focus our attention on the relationship between posi- tions, status, and access to resources and power. At this time in our profession, when there seems to be considerable emphasis on treating the person (or persons), it is all too easy to forget the extent to which the problems of social work clients are due to the positions they have been born into, or otherwise achieved through no choice of their own, that have denied them access to the resources others more fortunate have in abundance. The use of role theory directs us away from excessive concern with in- dividual psychopathology and toward an understanding of the social determinants of such behavior. The following case vignette provides a good example of a situation where role concepts such as role overload, role conflict, and role ambiguity are im- portant to gain a full picture of the presenting situation.

> Beth, a thirty-four-year-old single parent, sought services at a family services agency. She talked almost obsessively about her ex-husband, his wealthy girl- friend, and how she was struggling financially while they led an easy life. During the initial interview she kept secret the fact that she had recently been convicted of embezzling funds from her former employer and was facing court sentencing in a few weeks. She did talk of her lengthy history as an abused wife, of having been placed in a mental hospital by her ex-husband early in their marriage. She cried easily, seemed to see herself as totally unable to care for herself or her two chil- dren, talked freely of the need for a man to help her.
>
> It would have been easy, early in the assessment, to focus on her "dependent personality," on her "learned helplessness," yet that would have missed an es- sential component of the problem. She was a newly singled parent. She was cut

*See Chapter 23.

off abruptly from financial resources that she and her children needed to live adequately. Because of her job, low-paying as it was, she was denied access to many of the services that she might have received had she been unemployed. And, furthermore, the system could not protect her from a husband who only erratically chose to provide his court-mandated support payments. Thus, she had few supports for the multiple roles she was playing.

Role theory helps us identify the status-role demands that are likely to be significant sources of stress for people. This is especially important today given the many changes that are currently occurring in society that influence role behaviors. For this reason, role theory provides an especially useful perspective for understanding many of the stresses that individuals, couples, and families are experiencing today that bring them to seek social work assistance.

Individual Assessment

At the individual level, there has been a noticeable increase in the numbers of persons who are experiencing distress from role changes engendered by marital dissolution. Wives become single persons and single parents; they lose the high status that had previously accrued to them through their role as wife to a successful husband and, as a result, feel a devalued self-identity. Husbands become single persons, part-time fathers, or, sometimes, nonparents.

An increasing number of persons are choosing to adopt openly what are considered, by many, to be deviant, generally stigmatized, roles. For example, as men and women are more openly enacting gay and lesbian roles they may present themselves at a family service agency for help in coping with family pressures to adopt more conforming roles.

Policy decisions have brought others in deviant roles into greater contact with the larger society. The various deinstitutionalization policies of the last two decades have increased the visibility of the mentally ill, the mentally retarded, and the physically handicapped, while not simultaneously significantly influencing social attitudes regarding their deviant identities. They, too, may require social work intervention to moderate the impact of the social stigmatization.

Couple Assessment

At the couple level, social workers are increasingly confronted with persons who, while intellectually committed to enacting their couple roles in nontraditional ways, often discover a lack of support for their behaviors and, as a result, experience psychological conflict in their enactment (43). While especially true among young couples, there are also an increasing number of older persons who may seek counseling to assist in the renegotiation of their roles vis-à-vis their marital partner when the woman decides to reenter the labor market. While still a relatively small group, gay and lesbian couples are also beginning to see social workers for their relationship difficulties, which often center around the absence of role models and the need to invent new roles for themselves.

Family Assessment

At the family level, social changes are reflected in the large number and varieties of nontraditional families. By the standards of the 1950s or 1960s, there are presently more deviant family types than there are normative family types. There are both dual-work and dual-career families; there are single-parent families; there are blended, re-constituted, stepparent families; there are gay and lesbian families. Each of these family forms requires that new role behaviors be learned, new role expectations internalized, new social supports provided. Not surprisingly, social workers are often turned to for assistance in this process.

Role theory offers a non-pathology-oriented perspective from which to assess clients and the problems they present. During the assessment process it directs us to consider: first, conditions that are facilitating or inhibiting the learning or perfor-mance of desired role behavior; and second, the contributions of role conflict, in the broadest sense, to intrapersonal and interpersonal stress. For example, in assessing a single parent who has been referred to the Child Abuse Hotline, a social worker us-ing role theory would be concerned about (1) the availability and accessibility of so-cial supports for effective parenting behavior (daycare, supportive adults, financial resources); (2) opportunities for the single parent to have learned parenting behavior (that is, who were the role models and how effective were they in their parenting be-havior?); and (3) present-day conflicts that may exist in carrying out parental, occu-pational, and social roles. Even when assessing personal capacities in this case, a role theory perspective would look at them in terms of their impact on the learning and/or performance of role behaviors. In what ways, for example, does having a specific handicapping condition influence the learning and/or performance of parenting be-haviors? How does this person's difficulty establishing intimacy interfere with her ability to parent effectively?

The message that is communicated throughout the assessment process is that the problem does not reside within the individual, but is instead located in the transaction between the individual and society. In some instances the individual may, for a vari-ety of reasons, be failing to perform adequately socially expected roles; in other in-stances, the individual may be choosing to enact socially deviant roles. Interventions may include providing appropriate role models for the learning of new behaviors, ad-vocating for services to support the performance of role behavior, facilitating a sup-port group for persons choosing to openly enact deviant role behaviors, and lobbying for antidiscriminatory legislation for socially stigmatized persons.

IMPLICATIONS FOR SOCIAL WORK TREATMENT

INDIVIDUAL TREATMENT

Role theory's application to individual treatment follows directly from the previous discussion. Many persons who are seen by social workers come or are referred be-cause they are having difficulty adequately fulfilling the various roles that they are "supposed" to be playing. Young persons may have difficulty performing such socially expected roles as student, boyfriend or girlfriend, or even parent. Older persons may have difficulties enacting their roles as worker, parent, spouse, child. As has been suggested, many of the interventions are aimed at providing an environment that is facilitative of adequate role performance. That may mean advocating within a school setting for a teenager; it may mean advocating at the local social services department for a teenage mother. Sometimes, however, the inability to perform adequately in expected roles is due to lack of knowledge of role expectations and lack of skills in the performance of role behaviors. When this is the case, social work interventions can be directed toward teaching the appropriate role behaviors either in individual or in group treatment.

While there are many ways for learning appropriate role behavior, perhaps the most promising contemporary one involves a variety of cognitive behavioral techniques. Cognitive behavioral theory has taught us the importance of breaking down what is taught into teachable components. There have been, for example, a plethora of training models for the teaching of assertion skills held to be important for the performance of a wide variety of roles. Recently, Richard Barth and Steven Schinke have extended this perspective to showing adolescent parents a set of skills to facilitate their utilization of social supports by teaching them to reach out to others, to request help from others, and to seek help appropriately (3, p. 531). Their training program, an exemplar of the many that have come into widespread use in recent years, teaches a variety of interpersonal and cognitive skills by describing them, providing examples, demonstrating their use in role plays, practicing their use through role play, and providing feedback. While the training program itself may seem highly specific, their overall approach recognizes the importance of skills to the wide variety of roles that persons play in their lives.

Individual treatment can go beyond the educative function in assisting persons with role difficulties. Many persons seek counseling because of the guilt (or other negative emotions) they experience when they feel they are not carrying out their socially expected roles in an acceptable manner. Certainly an appropriate social work intervention is to explore clients' feelings about their inadequate role performance as well as to help them more realistically appraise their role performance.

> Beth, whom we met before, felt a failure as a mother. Unable to provide her children with the tangible comforts that her ex-husband lavished on them during their infrequent visits, she seriously questioned whether she should relinquish her children to him. She felt inadequate as a mother, as a provider for her children's needs. Counseling focused on helping her define for herself what good mothering was (something that she herself had lacked in her own childhood) and in reevaluating her own competencies as a mother.

There has recently been a wealth of literature on the predictable changes that persons go through in adulthood as they evaluate and reevaluate their performance in the central roles in their lives (26, 59). While many persons go through these changes with minimal stress, others turn to social workers when they experience extreme dissatisfaction with the ways in which their lives have developed, yet are unable to envisage the possibility of change. By the time they come for counseling they may have had their self-esteem seriously undermined and present with symptoms of clinical depression as in the following case.

> Paul, a civil servant, came in for counseling six months before his fiftieth birthday presenting as major problems the tremendous unhappiness he felt in his job, his sense of worthlessness at having failed to fulfill his parents' (and his own) expectations, and a strong desire to do something more meaningful with his life yet with a total inability to see any feasible alternatives. While assessment suggested the presence of some personality traits that had probably served to impede his job advancement, Paul was an exceptionally bright and able man whose abilities had not been utilized by an occupational system that oftentimes failed to reward accomplishment. Treatment was multipronged: (1) he was referred for career counseling to explore alternative options; (2) the salience of other roles, from which he obtained far more positive feedback and in which he felt successful, were heightened so that they became more significant contributors to his social identity and his sense of self-worth; (3) he learned to invest less energy and less of his self-esteem in his work role; and (4) his wife's assistance was enlisted to provide additional support in decreasing the value of his work role and increasing the value of his spousal role to his sense of worth.

Many of the roles we take on in life are those we are taught we must play. Persons often come into counseling because they are caught in conflicts between the oughts and the wants. Often, prior socialization is so strong that the clients do not see the possibility of alternative roles or are fearful of admitting the possibility they do see to themselves or to significant others. Individual counseling can provide them with a safe and supportive environment in which to evaluate major life decisions.

> Donald, doing poorly in college, used social work counseling to explore joining the army. Because he was facing this decision in the post-Vietnam era, he had little social support for his decision to give up a highly valued position, that of college student and eventually of professional, to take on a recently devalued position, that of soldier. The supportive, nonjudgmental atmosphere of the therapeutic relationship allowed him to decide to quit school and pursue an army career.

GROUP TREATMENT

Oftentimes the role problems people experience can best be treated within a group setting. This is especially appropriate when the difficulties that are experienced are due to lack of social support for role behavior. The popularity and diversity of self-help groups organized around themes of role attests to the importance of group support for coping with a variety of role difficulties. Some revolve around themes of role transition: Children of Separated and Divorced Parents; Post-Stroke Association; Sharing and Caring for Post-Cardiac Patients; Stepfamilies; Equal Rights for Fathers; Parents Without Partners. Others offer support to persons with socially deviant identities: Alcoholics Anonymous; Gamblers Anonymous; Parents Without Partners; Adult Children of Alcoholics; Recovery for Persons with Nervous Symptoms.

Social workers have long recognized the value of professionally led support groups for persons experiencing role transitions. It is not uncommon for family service agencies to run ongoing groups for separated and divorced persons, for retiring persons, for single parents. Although less common, because less socially sanctioned, there are also professionally led support groups for persons experiencing the social strain of having chosen to enact a deviant or variant life-style.

Social group work is especially useful for resocializing persons into normative role behavior. Charles Garvin has noted that social group work can be used both to bring about the resocialization of persons "who have not yet determined that they wish to fulfill a nondeviant, socially acceptable role" as well as for persons who voluntarily elect to attain new role behaviors. In this way, social group work performs both a social control and an educative function for society (18, p. 49).

One of the primary group techniques for teaching new role behaviors is that of role playing. Ronald Toseland and Robert Rivas have identified nine structured and unstructured role playing procedures (58). They include.

Own role: In this, the member plays the protagonist out of his own experience, while other group members enact reciprocal roles. This is useful for both assessing a person's interpersonal skills and for learning new behaviors.

Role reversal: In this, the member takes on the role of another person. This enables her to see the situation from another's perspective, thus enhancing empathy.

Autodrama, monodrama, and *chairing:* In this, the member, while moving from chair to chair, plays the multiple roles that represent the different ways he sees himself. This is especially useful for helping a person become aware of the interrelationships among the myriad roles enacted in his life.

Sculpting and *choreography:* In this, the member uses the group to choreograph a dramatic reenactment of a real or symbolic situation in her life. The emotional involvement of the participants in the process makes it useful both for assessing and for gaining new perspectives on conflictual experiences.

Toseland and Rivas identify five additional procedures that can be used as adjuncts to supplement the impact of those discussed above. They include "on-the-spot interview," "soliloquy," "doubling," "mirror," and "sharing."

Family Treatment

Because of its focus on the transactional nature of human dysfunction, family treatment easily incorporates role terminology, albeit on its own terms. Family therapists have, for example, been far less concerned with the socially prescribed roles that persons generally enact in their families—that is, mother, father, daughter, son—and far more concerned with what have been referred to as "irrational role assignments" by which family members explicitly or implicitly are assigned roles that are reflections of unconscious attempts to act out conflicts originating in early family experiences (16, p. 274).

Among the classic roles of concern to family therapists has been that of the "scapegoat" (the "crazy person," the "sick one") who acts as the safety valve to defuse potentially destructive family disharmony (1, 21). A more elaborate view of the family system as it enacts roles is the "drama triangle," in which the roles of Persecutor, Victim, and Rescuer are alternately enacted by different family members.

Family therapists agree on the necessity to disrupt the nature of the family role relationships in dysfunctional family systems whose stability is achieved at the expense of its individual members through a range of strategies.

COMMUNITY PRACTICE

One of the central aims of community practice is to enhance the effectiveness with which persons receive services from social welfare institutions. While a caseworker advocates for the individual client, the community worker's concern is with effecting change in the institutions themselves or in the transactions between the institutions and the service recipients. It has been suggested that role concepts are, therefore, especially relevant to help the community worker understand and assess the relationship between the individual and the social structure. They focus the worker's attention on "the role relationships of the actors in agency and institutional systems—the clients, agency personnel, policymakers, and community reference groups" (7, p. 30).

Role concepts are also useful for understanding the ways in which the community worker functions to effect such changes. Social planner, grassroots organizer, interagency policymaker, administrator, program director, social reformer, social engineer, as well as the more generic community organizer, have all been identified as relevant community worker roles (7, 52). The social planner may formulate social policy or develop and improve existing services and the manner in which they are delivered to the clients. The community organizer may establish linkages between community members and groups in order to foster social integration and facilitate the identification and development of necessary services within the community.

The social worker often functions in these roles because there is an absence of other persons within the community to carry them out. Sometimes it is necessary for the social worker to enact the role in order that a task may be accomplished; at other times it may be more appropriate for the social worker to teach community persons to fulfill the needed roles. George Brager and Harry Specht have suggested that the unique contribution of the social worker within the community is his "knowledge of the requisite roles to be filled and his skill in helping constituencies to fill them" (7, p. 85).

RESEARCH IMPLICATIONS FOR SOCIAL WORK

As this article suggests, the perspective of role theory offers a number of opportunities for social work researchers. Despite this, there is little new literature that draws upon its perspective. A few suggestions as to ways to apply role theory to social work research are presented below.

Many of the clients that social workers see are involved in role transitions. It would certainly be beneficial to clients and practitioners to examine the impact of different treatment modalities on the stress experienced from such role transitions. Under what conditions is group treatment more effective at facilitating role transitions than is individual treatment? For what types of clients and what kinds of role transitions? Since many of the role transitions occur within families, when should family treatment be the preferred model of intervention?

Clients of social workers are often enacting deviant and/or stigmatized roles. While there has been research on treatment models for resocializing abusive parents (8), there is a need for similar research on intervention models to prevent socialization into dysfunctional parental role behavior.

Social workers have had a historic concern with delinquency prevention. One of the more recent trends in delinquency programs has been the widespread development of diversionary programs designed to prevent predelinquents from the further learning of delinquent behaviors and the subsequent stabilization of a delinquent self-identity. There has been criticism of both the effectiveness with which diversionary programs can prevent adolescents from being stigmatized (10) and of the weak relationship between casual theories of delinquency and intervention strategies used in such programs (23). Social work researchers can certainly utilize a role theoretic perspective to facilitate the development and evaluation of such programs.

CONCLUSION

Despite the many references to role constructs within social work literature, it has been only peripheral in the development of our knowledge base. This is ironic given the congruence of its central tenets with social work's emphasis on the person as she transacts with her environment.

Role theory offers one perspective to help free social workers from excessive concern with the "inner space" of the client and direct their attention to the myriad ways in which the behavior of clients is influenced by their contemporary interpersonal relationships as well as the society that both defines and enforces conformity to appropriate role behavior.

As social workers we also must be continuously aware that it is the majority society, to which most of us belong and whose values we have internalized, that defines normative role behavior. Helen Harris Perlman reflects this sensitivity to cultural differences when she writes:

Nowhere within the thought-action perspectives that social role provides is there prescription for imposing the helper's norms upon the helped, nor for imprisoning the helped person in the mores and standards, middle class or other, of the helper. Nothing in the role concept bespeaks rigidity or authoritarianism. . . . The *client's* role affects and ideas are brought to the forefront,

not the helper's; the demands and requirements lie in his reality, in his transactions with people and tasks, not in some prestructured imposition by his
helper (42, pp. 223–224).

Thus, social work from a role theory perspective understands the influence of the
social structure but protects the individual's right to self-determination.

REFERENCES

1. Ackerman, Nathan. "Prejudicial Scapegoating and Neutralizing Forces in the Family
    Group, with Special Reference to the Role of 'Family Healer,'" in J. Howells (ed.),
    Theory and Practice of Family Psychiatry. New York: Brunner/Mazel, 1968.
2. ———. *The Psychodynamics of Family Life.* New York: Basic Books, 1954.
3. Barth, Richard P., and Steven P. Schinke. "Enhancing the Social Supports of Teenage
    Mothers," *Social Casework,* Vol. 65 (1984), pp. 523–531.
4. Berger, Peter L., and Thomas Luckmann. *The Social Construction of Reality.* New
    York: Anchor Doubleday, 1967.
5. Biddle, Bruce J. *Role Theory: Expectations, Identities, and Behaviors.* New York: Aca-
    demic Press, 1979.
6. ———, and Edwin Thomas (eds.). *Role Theory: Concepts and Research.* New York:
    Wiley, 1966.
7. Brager, George, and Harry Specht. *Community Organizing.* New York: Columbia Uni-
    versity Press, 1973.
8. Breton, Margot. "Resocialization of Abusive Parents," *Social Work,* Vol. 26 (1981), pp.
    119–122.
9. Briar, Scott. "Family Services," in H.S. Maas (ed.), *Five Fields of Social Service: Re-
    views of Research.* New York: National Association of Social Workers, 1966.
10. Bullington, Bruce, James Sprowls, Daniel Katkin, and Mark Phillips. "A Critique of
    Diversionary Juvenile Justice," *Crime and Delinquency,* Vol. 24 (1978), pp. 59–71.
11. Cloward, Richard, and Lloyd Ohlin. *Delinquency and Opportunity: A Theory of Delin-
    quent Gangs.* New York: Free Press, 1960.
12. Davis, Kingsley. "Social Norms," in Bruce J. Biddle and Edwin Thomas (eds.), *Role
    Theory: Concepts and Research.* New York: Wiley, 1966.
13. ———. "Status and Related Concepts," in Bruce J. Biddle and Edwin Thomas (eds.),
    Role Theory: Concepts and Research. New York: Wiley, 1966.
14. Deutsch, Morton, and Robert H. Krauss. *Theories in Social Psychology.* New York: Ba-
    sic Books, 1965.
15. Fischer, Joel. *Effective Casework Practice: An Eclectic Approach.* New York: McGraw-
    Hill, 1978.
16. Framo, James L. "Symptoms from a Family Transactional Viewpoint," in C.J. Sager
    and H.S. Kaplan (eds.), *Progress in Group and Family Therapy.* New York: Brun-
    ner/Mazel, 1972.
17. Gambrill, Eileen. *Casework: A Competency-Based Approach.* Englewood Cliffs, N.J.:
    Prentice-Hall, 1983.
18. Garvin, Charles. *Contemporary Group Work.* Englewood Cliffs, N.J.: Prentice-Hall,
    1981.
19. Germain, Carel B., and Alex Gitterman. *The Life Model of Social Work Practice.* New
    York: Columbia University Press, 1980.
20. Gove, Walter R. *The Labeling of Deviance: Evaluating a Perspective.* New York: Wiley,
    1975.
21. Haley, Jay. *Strategies of Psychotherapy.* New York: Grune and Stratton, 1963.

22. Harris, Ben, and John Harvey. "Attribution Theory: From Phenomenological Causality to the Intuitive Social Scientist and Beyond," in Charles Antaki (ed.), *The Psychology of Ordinary Explanations of Social Behaviour.* London: Academic Press, 1981.

23. Hawkins, J. David, and Mark W. Fraser, "Theory and Practice in Delinquency Prevention," *Social Work Research and Abstracts,* vol. 7 (1981), pp. 3–13.

24. Hepworth, Dean H., and JoAnn Larsen. *Direct Social Work Practice.* Homewood, Ill.: Dorsey Press, 1982.

25. Hollis, Florence. *Casework: A Psychosocial Therapy.* New York: Random House, 1964.

26. Levinson, Daniel J. *The Seasons of a Man's Life.* New York: Ballantine, 1979.

27. Linton, Ralph. *The Study of Man.* New York: Appleton-Century, 1936.

28. Loewenstein, Sophie Freud. "Inner and Outer Space in Social Casework," *Social Casework,* Vol. 59 (1979), pp. 19–28.

29. Mahoney, Michael J. *Cognition and Behavior Modification.* Cambridge, Mass.: Ballinger, 1974.

30. Maluccio, Anthony N. *Learning from Clients.* New York: Free Press, 1979.

31. ———, and Wilma D. Marlow. "The Case for the Contract," *Social Casework,* Vol. 19 (1974), pp. 28–36.

32. Mayer, John E., and Noel Timm. *The Client Speaks: Working Class Impressions of Casework.* London: Routledge, 1969.

33. Mead, George Herbert. *Mind, Self and Society.* Edited by Charles W. Morris. Chicago: University of Chicago Press, 1934.

34. Meichenbaum, Donald. *Cognitive-Behavior Modification.* New York: Plenum Press, 1977.

35. Merluzzi, Thomas V., Thomas E. Rudy, and Carol R. Glass. "The Information-Processing Paradigm: Implications for Clinical Science," in Thomas V. Merluzzi, Carol R. Glass, and M. Genest (eds.), *Cognitive Assessment.* New York: Guilford Press, 1981.

36. Merton, Robert K. *Social Theory and Social Structure.* Glencoe, Ill.: Free Press, 1957.

37. Minuchin, Salvador. *Families and Family Therapy.* Cambridge, Mass.: Harvard University Press, 1974.

38. Moreno, Joseph L. *Who Shall Survive?* Washington, D.C.: Nervous and Mental Diseases Publishing Co., 1934.

39. Nisbett, Richard, and Lee Ross. *Human Inference: Strategies and Shortcomings of Social Judgment.* Englewood Cliffs, N.J.: Prentice-Hall, 1980.

40. Overall, Betty, and Harriet Aronson. "Expectations of Psychotherapy in Patients of Lower Socioeconomic Class," *American Journal of Orthopsychiatry,* Vol. 31 (1963), pp. 421–430.

41. Parsons, Talcott. *The Social System.* New York: Free Press, 1951.

42. Perlman, Helen Harris. *Persona: Social Role and Personality.* Chicago: University of Chicago Press, 1968.

43. Rice, David G. *Dual-Career Marriage: Conflict and Treatment.* New York: Free Press, 1979.

44. Rommetveit, R. *Social Norms and Roles.* Minneapolis: University of Minnesota Press, 1954.

45. Sarbin, Theodore R. "Notes on the Transformation of Social Identity," in L.M. Roberts, N.S. Greenfield, and M.H. Miller (eds.), *Comprehensive Mental Health: The Challenge of Evaluation.* Madison: University of Wisconsin Press, 1968.

46. ———. "Role Theory," in G. Lindzey (ed.), *Handbook of Social Psychology, Vol. 1,* Cambridge, Mass.: Addison-Wesley, 1954, pp. 223–258.

47. Schur, Edwin M. *Interpreting Deviance.* New York: Harper and Row, 1979.

48. ———. *Labeling Deviant Behavior.* New York: Harper and Row, 1971.

49. Seabury, Brett A. "The Contract: Uses, Abuses, and Limitations," *Social Work,* Vol. 21 (1976), pp. 16–23.

50. Secord, Paul, and Carl Backman. "Personality Theory and the Problem of Stability and Change in Individual Behavior," *Psychological Review,* Vol. 68 (1961), pp. 21–32.
51. Shaw, Marvin R., and Phillip R. Costanzo. *Theories of Social Psychology,* 2nd edition. New York: McGraw-Hill, 1982.
52. Siporin, Max. *Introduction to Social Work Practice.* New York: Macmillan, 1975.
53. Stierlin, Helm. *Psychoanalysis and Family Therapy.* New York: Aronson, 1977.
54. Strean, Herbert S. "Role Theory," in Francis J. Turner (ed.), *Social Work Treatment,* 2nd edition. New York: Free Press, 1979.
55. ———. "The Application of Role Theory to Social Casework," in Herbert Strean (ed.), *Social Casework: Theories in Action.* Metuchen, N.J.: Scarecrow Press, 1971.
56. Stryker, Sheldon. "Symbolic Interaction as an Approach to Family Research," in J.G. Manis and B.N. Meltzer (eds.), *Symbolic Interaction: A Reader in Social Psychology,* 2nd edition. Boston: Allyn and Bacon, 1972.
57. Thomas, Edwin J., Ronald A. Feldman, with Jane Kamm. "Concepts of Role Theory," in Edwin J. Thomas (ed.), *Behavioral Science for Social Workers.* New York: Free Press, 1967.
58. Toseland, Ronald W., and Robert F. Rivas. *An Introduction to Group Work Practice.* New York: Macmillan, 1984.
59. Vaillant, George. *Adaptation to Life.* Boston: Little Brown, 1977.
60. Watzlawick, Paul, John Weakland, and Richard Fisch. *Change: Principles of Problem Formation and Problem Resolution.* New York: Norton, 1974.
61. Weeks, Gerald R., and Luciano L'Abate. *Paradoxical Psychotherapy: Theory and Practice with Individuals, Couples, and Families.* New York: Brunner/Mazel, 1982.

ANNOTATED LISTING OF KEY REFERENCES

Biddle, Bruce J. *Role Theory: Expectations, Identities, and Behaviors.* New York: Academic Press, 1979. In this book, Biddle presents an integrated theoretical approach to role theory. It will be most useful to the social work researcher seeking clarity about ways to operationalize central role terminology.

Biddle, Bruce J., and Edwin Thomas (eds.). *Role Theory: Concepts and Research.* New York: Wiley, 1966. This book remains the most comprehensive book on role theory for a social work audience as it provides numerous brief chapters in which roles concepts are applied to issues of concern to social workers.

Perlman, Helen Harris. *Persona: Social Role and Personality.* Chicago: University of Chicago Press, 1968. This book still provides an excellent example of the varied ways in which role theory can be fruitfully applied to understanding a variety of individual and family problems confronting social work clients.

Rice, David. *Dual-Career Marriage: Conflict and Treatment.* New York: Free Press, 1979. This is but one of the recent books that focuses attention on the role conflicts engendered by changing social norms vis-à-vis the roles of men and women in marriages. It is unique in that Rice relates the role conflicts to issues in marital counseling.

CHAPTER 25

SYSTEMS THEORY
AND SOCIAL WORK TREATMENT

DAN ANDREAE

The purpose of this chapter is to illustrate the relevance, applicability, and contributions of general systems theory to social work practice whether working with individuals, marital couples or other paired relationships, families, groups, organizations, or communities. By understanding the elements comprising general systems theory, as well as its history, philosophy, principles, and techniques, social workers will be in a position to utilize this approach in a variety of settings and circumstances. The first section of this chapter will outline the concepts associated with general systems theory and the second part of the chapter will apply it specifically to family systems and interpersonal dynamics.

Social workers have a variety of treatment modalities at their disposal in order to affect change and promote optimum functioning. These could include such approaches as psychoanalytically oriented interventions, behavioral treatment models, client-centered therapy techniques, or brief therapy procedures, to name but a few possibilities. Regardless of the particular methodology or combination of approaches employed, social workers possess an in-depth understanding of the relationship of the individual to various environments and the synergistic relationship that each entity has to the other. It is this contextual understanding of the holistic nature of human functioning that is unique to social work practice as opposed to most other helping professions, which tend to adopt a more individual-centered perspective to treatment. Social workers are taught to recognize that all parts of any system are interrelated, interconnected, and interdependent and therefore it is imperative to take into account the influence of various systems and subsystems on client functioning.

DEFINITION

Of all the theoretical paradigms utilized by social workers, general systems theory perhaps most clearly articulates this reality. According to Gordon Hearn in *Social Work Treatment: Interlocking Theoretical Approaches*, edited by Dr. Francis Turner,

601

general systems theory is defined as "a series of related definitions, assumptions and postulates about all levels of systems from atomic particles through atoms, molecules, crystals, viruses, cells, organs, individuals, small groups, societies, plants, solar systems and galaxies. General Systems Behaviour Theory is a sub-category of such theory dealing with living systems extending from viruses through societies. Perhaps the most significant fact about living systems is that they are open systems with important inputs and outputs. Laws which apply to them differ from those applying to relatively closed systems."[1]

General systems theory is intended to elaborate properties, principles, and laws that are characteristic of "systems" in general, irrespective of their particular kind, the nature of their elements, and relations or "forces" between them. A "system" may also be defined as a complex of elements with interactions, these interactions being of an ordered (nonrandom) nature. Being concerned with formal characteristics or entities called systems, general systems theory is interdisciplinary; that is, it can be employed for phenomena investigated in different traditional branches of scientific research. It is not limited to material systems but applies to any "whole" consisting of interrelating components. General systems theory can be developed in various mathematical languages, vernacular language, or can be computerized.[2] According to systems theory, the difference between a "collection" and a "system" is that in a collection, the parts remain individually unchanged, whether they be isolated or together; that is to say, they are simply a sum, whereas in a system, the parts necessarily become more than the sum of parts. Systems are not static but dynamic, and in a constant state of flux. Not only are systems in constant movement but also the interfaces between systems are constantly in the process of change.[3]

HISTORICAL CONTEXT OF GENERAL SYSTEMS THEORY

General systems theory represents a methodological approach to understanding the world. Since its earliest use in classical astronomy to its subsequent formalization in the metaphysics of Kant and Hegel, the utility of systems theory has been demonstrated in the conceptual breakthroughs of Darwin, Freud, Weber, and particularly Einstein. The wide usage of the systems approach since the late nineteenth century by the physical sciences was fostered by the necessity to overcome the overpowering skepticism that was occurring with sciences whose principles were based on the naïve conception of simple one-way cause-and-effect ideas. Early in the Enlightenment period, the philosopher David Hume demonstrated that to assume "A" causes "B" simply because "A" and "B" were in close proximity to each other in time and space was erroneous. He argued that there were no logical or empirical ways to prove that the supposed relationship between variable factors was not spurious (an artifact of our limited reasoning capabilities).[4]

Certainly, prior to systems theory the world was fundamentally mechanistic and reductionist. Complex phenomena were explained by breaking down and analyzing the separate, simpler parts. These increasingly smaller units were investigated in order to understand the cause of larger events. In this simple, mechanistic view of the physical universe it made sense to think of linear causality; A causes B, which acts upon C, causing D to occur. Gregory Bateson, a cultural anthropologist by training but with a profound interest in cybernetics (the study of methods of feedback control within a system), provided many of the theoretical underpinnings for the application of systems theory to human relationships. He labeled this stimulus-response paradigm as the Billiard Ball Model: a model that describes a force moving in only one direction and affecting objects in its path, and called instead for a focus on the ongoing process and development of a new descriptive language that emphasizes the relationship between parts and their effects on one another. Therefore, according to Bateson, A may evoke B but it is also true that B evokes A. Shifting to a perspective that emphasizes circular causality helps to conceptualize, for example, a family's behavior in current transactional terms, as a network of circular loops in which every member's behavior impacts on everyone else. People mutually affect one another and there is no specific behavioral event.[5]

Indeed, an essential way in which a system, such as a family, maintains itself as a self-regulating system is through the constant exchange of information fed back into the system. This information automatically triggers necessary changes to keep the system fluid and functional. In systems theory, feedback loops (circles of response from which there is a return flow of information into the system) are operating, and information is being processed through the system. The concept of feedback loops was developed by Norbert Weiner, a mathematician and pioneer in the field of cybernetics, who defined feedback as a method of controlling systems by reinserting into it the results of past performance. Stated another way, information about how a system is functioning is looped back (feedback) from the output to the input, thus modifying subsequent input signals. Feedback loops are the circular mechanisms whose purpose is to introduce information about a system's output back to its input in order to alter, correct, or ultimately govern the system's functioning.[6] The social work practitioner therefore needs to analyze the various repetitive links that keep the loop locked in place regardless of the system under study (and thus maintain the mutually defeating interaction patterns) which prevent individuals or units who make up the particular system from moving on to more productive and fulfilling activities.

The importance of systems theory was originally grasped by Ludwig Von Bertalanffy (1901–1972), who, as the putative founder of systems theory, understood the organismic connection early in his career. He recognized that a system, whether it be an atom, a cell, a Gestalt pattern, or an integrated universe of symbols, has holistic properties that are not found separately within the parts. Rather these properties arise from the relations taken on by the parts forming the whole. In the late 1920s, he emphasized under the title of "organismic biology" the necessity of regarding the living organism as an "organized system" and defined the fundamental task of biology as the "discovery of the laws of biological systems at all levels of organization." This led Von Bertalanffy in the 1930s and 1940s to develop the concept of general systems theory, which to him represented a complex of component parts or interacting elements that may together form an entity. This new synthetic approach to understanding nature can be defined as "an interdisciplinary doctrine elaborating principles and models that apply to systems in general irrespective of their particular kind, elements and forces involved." Therefore, Von Bertalanffy's goal was to achieve a general perspective, a coherent view of the "world as great organization," a framework in which all disciplines could be understood in their place. However, he recognized that such a worldview would not be completed if it did not provide a way of understanding and placing into context the most complex human system of all, the human being.[7]

Historically, the major focus in the behavioral sciences prior to general systems theory had been on individual functioning as reflected in such approaches as psychoanalytic theory, classical behaviorism, and neo-behaviorism as well as learning theories. Although each of these psychological paradigms is essentially different, they do share certain commonalities, one being the assumption that the psychological organism is essentially reactive; that is, behavior is to be considered as a response, innate or learned, to a stimulus. From this perspective all current behavior was seen as a result of a series of outside forces that built upon one another in sequence, ultimately producing the behavior in question.[8]

For the psychoanalyst, such forces are likely to result from early childhood experiences. For the behaviorally oriented, the causes are more likely to be found in the past and present learning experiences and schedules of reinforcement. From the biological perspective, behavior is seen as determined by genetic inheritance. By attending exclusively to the individual, however, these viewpoints failed to examine the contexts in which, as well as the process by which, the current behavior occurs. They fail to understand fully the complexity of what transpires within a system in which the individual is involved. The systems view, by comparison, is more holistic and better attuned to targeted interpersonal relationships and stresses the reciprocity of behaviors between people. Circular causality emphasizes that forces do not simply move in one direction, each caused by the previous event, but rather become part of a causal chain, each event influenced by the other.[9]

Also, the mechanistic view of linear causality was fundamental to the consideration of the goal of psychobiological behavioral phenomena as reestablishment of a disturbed equilibrium (homeostasis), a reduction to tensions arising from unsatisfied drives as postulated by Freud, the gratification of needs as described by the psychologist Hull, or to operant conditioning as hypothesized by B. F. Skinner. The needs, drives, and tensions in question were essentially biological while the seemingly higher processes in humans were considered secondary and eventually reducible to primary biological factors such as hunger, sex, and survival. For a variety of reasons, this view of humans as automatons proved unsatisfactory to many theorists and practitioners. In the early twentieth century an alternative view of human problems and their alleviation began to emerge. There was a growing dissatisfaction with the mechanistic or analytical explanation in various branches of science and mathematics that had a significant impact on psychology and social work. The departure from this paradigm of linear causality in the behavioral sciences is represented in the concepts of developmental psychology as reflected in Piaget's genetic epistemology as well as with neo-Freudian developments such as Carl Rogers' client-centered therapy, Abraham Maslow's self-actualization psychology, the personality theories of Murray Allport as well as phenomenological and existential approaches. The common features to all of these emerging alternatives is that they did not treat human beings as reactive robots, but rather as active personality systems, and they recognized that systems are capable of dynamic change and growth as opposed to the homeostatic models of earlier times.[10]

Social workers today, as helping professionals, incorporate several of these progressive modalities into their repertoire of intervention strategies and techniques. These new approaches proved compatible with social work practice, as social workers recognize the necessity of understanding the nature of the person-environment interrelatedness and person-situation transactions. General systems theory provides social work practitioners with a conceptual framework that shifts attention from the cause-and-effect relationship between paired variables (does the environment cause the person to behave in a certain way, or does the person affect the environment in a certain way?) to a person/situation as an interrelated whole. The person is observed as part of his or her total life situation; personal situations are a whole in which each part is interrelated to all other parts in an intricate way through a complex process in which each element is both cause and effect. These dynamic interactions, transactions, and organizational patterns that are critical to the functioning of both the individual and situations are only observable when the entire system is studied. In attempting to understand a problem in social functioning, a social worker cannot achieve understanding simply by adding together as separate entities the assessment of the individual and the assessment of the environment. Rather, the social work practitioner must strive for a full understanding of the complex interactions between the client and all levels of the social and physical system as well as the meaning that the client assigns to each of these interactions.[11]

THE FAMILY SYSTEM

One of the major contributions of social work to furthering general systems theory has been in the field of family systems and dynamics. A family traditionally has been defined as two or more people related by blood, marriage, or adoption and who reside together (Nye & Bernardo, 1973).[12] However, in a 1990 survey by Seligman (1992) that randomly selected 1,200 adults who were asked to define the word *family*, only twenty-two percent selected this conventional definition. Almost three-quarters of the people surveyed chose a more expansive definition that defined family as "a group of people who love and care for each other."[13] Social workers treat individuals, many of whom function in dyads and often within family units. Every client, even if living alone, originally grew up in a complex family structure and was profoundly affected by his or her involvement.

The composition of the family has undergone significant change in recent decades and now encompasses many different constellations. These include the nuclear family, a family that encompasses only parents and unmarried children; single-parent families, a family consisting of one parent and one or more children; a common-law union, that is, a family including a man and a woman who are not legally married with or without children; a reconstituted family, consisting of a husband and wife with children from a previous marriage/union of one of the spouses; a blended family, consisting of a husband and wife who are not necessarily married that includes children from one or more marriages/unions; an extended family, which includes more than parents and unmarried children, e.g., grandparents, married children, or other relatives living in the same residence; consanguine family, consisting of a family organization in which the primary emphasis is on the blood relationship of parents and children or brothers and sisters rather than on the marital relationships of husband and wife; a conjugal family, in which the primary emphasis is placed on the husband/wife relationship rather than blood relationships; same-sex couples consisting of two individuals of the same sex with or without children.[14]

Regardless of the form taken by the family unit, it serves certain instrumental and expressive functions for family members, including providing for socialization, safety, certain resources, care, and protection, and, in most cases, as a source for procreation. The family system represents a subsystem of the larger community of which the following assumptions may be made:

1. The whole is greater than the sum of its parts.
2. Changing one part of the system will lead to changes in other parts of the system.
3. Families become organized and developed over time. Families are always changing and, over the life span, family members assume different roles.
4. Families are generally open systems in that they receive information and exchange it with each other and with people outside the family. Families vary in their degree of openness and closedness, which can vary over time and according to circumstances.
5. Individual dysfunction is often reflective of an active emotional system. A symptom in one family member is often a way of deflecting tension away from another part of the system and hence represents a relationship problem.[15]

Andolfi (1979)[16] notes that family members are studied in terms of their interactions and not merely on their intrinsic personal characteristics. More than a sum of what each family member adds to the whole, it is the ongoing relationship between and among family members, their mutual impact, that requires the attention of a social work practitioner. From a systems perspective, every event within a family is multiply determined by all the various forces operating within that system. This global view, in which the fundamental unit of study is not the individual but rather the system itself, calls for examination of the family's established behavioral sequences and patterns. Families form representative patterns over time and it is this patterning over time that is the essence of the family system (Segel & Ben, 1983).[17] As Constantine (1988) points out, the family is a good example of the complexity for the study of which systems theory is most appropriate.[18]

The family system consists of four major subsystems, including (1) spousal in the broadest sense; (2) parent-child; (3) sibling; and (4) the smallest subsystem, the individual.[19]

ENVIRONMENTAL INFLUENCES

The individual as well as all members of the family unit must coexist within different environments including work, school, church, government institutions, etc. For the purpose of social work practice, "environment" may be defined as "a continuation of people and their interactions and transactions in a particular geographic, socially-defined and constructed space over a particular period of time, both in the individual's and the family's life and in the life of the social and cultural systems" (Germain,[20] Pincus & Minihan,[21] Siporin,[22]). The environment, therefore, is us and we are the environment. From the moment of birth, it becomes an intimate part of each individual and presents each person with the material from which people construct their lives through the choices that are made and the social transactions that occur in response to the opportunities and deprivations presented to each person. This recognizes that in a stratified society, some people will be afforded better life chances than others due to such factors as a family's social status, level of income, education, geographical location, and access to resources.

The social environment deals with several layers, including that of the individual, group, family, community, institutions, class, and culture. In addition to the social environment with its various range of systems, the environment also includes large divisions such as the physical—this is divided further into the natural physical environment (i.e., climate) and the constructed environment such as shelter to protect people from various natural phenomena of the environment and various unforeseen climatic events of nature. The environment is temporal, consisting of time and space. Because human life is finite and is lived in certain defined spaces, time and space are critical environmental dimensions. The individual's space can be divided into two subclasses: general and personal. Most human beings construct shelters to protect themselves from the environment but, in doing so, also construct personal and/or family space that gives them a certain privacy from the group. While this construction of shelter and marking of private space may be different from culture to culture, such effort in generally found in all cultures. Most Canadians see their shelter in relation to time and space. The shelter needs to be readily accessible to one's place of employment or education. Being the private world, it also needs to meet certain other criteria, such as having certain electrical appliances, heat, and perhaps air conditioning, as well as a certain level of attractiveness depending on individual preference. In evaluation of our private space, we are able to create a demand (through money or other resources) which then intersects with feelings that an individual might have about himself or herself.[23]

There are four key domains of environmental interactions for individuals and families, including the situation, micro, meso, and macro levels. The "situation" is that part of the environment that is accessible to the individual's perception at any given moment. Situations play an important part because "it is in actual situations that we encounter and form our conceptions about the world and develop specific kinds of behaviours for dealing with it." Situations present the information that individuals process and they offer the feedback necessary for building valid conceptions of the outer world. Knowledge about actual situations that an individual has encountered dealing with the accompanying physical, social, and cultural macro environments, will help the social worker to understand behavior at different stages of development.[24]

The micro level is defined by Magnusson and Allen as "that part of the total physical and social environment that an individual is in contact with and can interact with directly in daily life during a certain period of time."[25] This level of the environment includes the individual's experience in his or her family, experiences at school, at work, in other social situations, or during leisure time, so that no other person experiences this environment in a similar way. The micro environment is very important in the development of the individual and it determines the type of situations that an individual will encounter.

The meso level is "that part of the environment that in some way or other influences and determines the character and functioning of the micro-environment" (Magnusson & Allen, 1983).[26] It includes relationships between major groups, organizations, and institutions that touch the daily life of the individual such as school, work, church, recreation, and community resources.

The macro level is common to most members of groups living in it and involves the physical, social, cultural, economic, and political structures of the larger society in which individuals grow up, including technology, language, housing, laws, customs, and regulations. All of these levels impinge upon each other in a synergistic manner, the whole being reflected or contained in each of the parts and all parts being complementary aspects of the whole. The whole is thus indivisible without sacrificing its essence and context, no more than the human body is divisible into different organ systems without losing its unique essence.

For example, language is an element of the larger macro system but is also a critical part of each individual. Some of the macro-level environment is part of each individual system. It is often easy for the social worker to overlook the meaning and influence of the macro system to the smaller system. Some factors in the environment operate at all levels. Most important is the extent to which the environment sets limits on the behavior of individuals and offers opportunities for their development. The actual environment does have an impact on behavior and development, but it is the individual's perception of and interaction with that environment that has the most influence. The three environments that a social work practitioner should be aware of are (1) the actual environment; (2) the environment as perceived by the client; and (3) the environment as perceived by the practitioner.[27]

RULES AND ROLES OF THE FAMILY

It is important for a social work practitioner to realize that family systems are also governed by rules, for the most part unstated, which have typically been developed and modified through trial and error over a period of time. Such rules (e.g., who has the right to say what to whom, what is expected of males and females, the role of adults versus children) determine what is permitted and what is forbidden within the family and this in turn serves the necessary function of regulating each member's behavior toward the others. The origin of such rules is embedded in years of explicit and implicit negotiation among family members. The rules themselves become so fine-tuned in most cases that they are taken for granted by all individuals and only draw attention when an effort is made by a member (an early adolescent in many cases) to change the long-standing regulations.[28]

Each family member also engages in different roles within a family system that can change depending on the family dynamics, requirements at the time, and external circumstances. Roles are defined as "actual patterns of interaction with others."[29] Key concepts associated with roles of which a social worker should be aware include:

1. role contiguity, whether person A's expectations of A's behavior is the same as person B's expectations of A's behavior;
2. role competency, whether or not a person has the skill and knowledge to meet the expectations that he/she or others have of that role (e.g., becoming a parent);
3. role ambiguity, whether or not role expectations are explicit—do people have a clear understanding of what is expected of them (e.g., the role of a new stepparent)?; and
4. role conflict—a person is in one role with certain expectations but that same person may also be in another role where there are different expectations. Sometimes, the expectations of these roles are in conflict with each other (e.g., being a mother as well as a full-time student).[30]

OPEN AND CLOSED SYSTEMS

Family systems are open or closed depending on the degree to which they are organized and interact with the outside environment. An open system receives input such as matter, energy, and information from its surroundings and discharges output into the environment.[31] Theoretically, closed systems are rarely, if ever, completely isolated or closed off from the outside. For a family to be truly operating in a closed system, all outside transactions and communications would have to cease to exist, which is highly improbable.[32] As mentioned earlier, systems of all levels seem to vary from time to time in terms of their openness and closedness. Family systems with which social workers work often seem to be too open or too closed for their own good or the welfare of others. Family systems go through cycles of opening and closing according to their perceptions of the potential security or threat in the impinging environment. Much of social work practice is dedicated to helping the client achieve an optimal degree of openness for the conditions of the moment and the capacity to change this state as conditions alter.

The operation of a closed system is as described by Newton's Second Law of Thermodynamics, which holds that a certain quantity called entropy or degree of disorganization within the system tends to increase to a maximum until the process ends in a state of stable equilibrium. Entropy is present in all systems, but in open systems, the opposite process, which general systems theorists have called negentropy, is also present. This occurs because open systems have access to free energy upon which they can organize and build. That systems are open means not simply that they engage in interchanges with the environment, but the fact that they exchange is an essential factor underlying the system's viability, reproductive capacity, or continuity and its ability to change. The typical response of natural closed systems to an intrusion of environmental events is a loss of organization, or a change in the direction of dissolution of the system (although, depending on the nature and strength of the intrusion, the system may sometimes move to a new level of equilibrium). On the other hand, the typical response of open systems to environmental intrusion is elaboration or change of their structure to a higher or more complex plane. Both open and closed systems attain stationary states. In closed systems, it is a state of equilibrium or rest; in open systems, it is a dynamic interplay of forces giving the appearance of rest but in actual reality, a steady state or a quasi-stationary equilibrium according to psychologist Kurt Lewin's concepts.[33]

Some families with whom social workers interact, such as recent immigrants, are members of insular ethnic groups existing in relative isolation, communicating only among themselves, suspicious of outsiders and thus fostering dependence on the family. Children may be instructed to trust only family members and no one else. Certain cultural groups engage in varying degrees of what is termed institutional completeness, whereby most, if not all, of their instrumental and expressive needs are met within their own peer group systems. As characterized by Constantine (1986),[34] regulated predominantly by deviation of attenuating (negative) feedback loops, such families need to hold onto the traditions and conventions of the past and thus avoid change. Sauber (1983)[35] describes such families as maintaining strict taboos regarding who and what should be admitted into the household, restricting the introduction of news and certain kinds of music, and screening visitors. New information and new outlooks are seen as threatening to the status quo in closed systems. As Kantor and Lehr (1975)[36] describe them, closed family systems enforce strict rules and a hierarchical and often patriarchal structure that causes individual members to subordinate their needs to the welfare of the group. Family loyalty is paramount; rules are absolute; traditions must be observed. One's deviation in behavior can only lead to chaos from this perspective. As White (1978) describes closed family systems, parents see to it that doors are kept locked, family reading material and television programs are screened, children are expected to report their comings and goings scrupulously, and rigid daily schedules are adhered to as closely as possible. Stability of such arrangements is achieved through the maintenance of traditions.[37]

Open systems use both negative (attenuating) and positive (amplifying) feedback loops. They are considered to be operating on the systems principle of equifinality, meaning that the same end state may be reached from a variety of different starting points. Closed systems, in contrast, do not have the property of equifinality and their final state is mainly determined by their initial conditions. Within open systems, not only may the same results be accomplished from different initial conditions, but the same initial state may produce different results. The major point here is that to appreciate family functioning, the social worker must study the organization of the family system, the group's interactive process, rather than the search for the origins or outcomes of these interactions. In open systems, when a variety of inputs is possible, the family feedback process is an overriding determinant of how it functions. Since a number of pathways lead to the same destination, there is no simple or correct way for families to raise children or to ensure a successful relationship. Uncertain beginnings do not necessarily mean that a relationship will fail; an unstable start may be compensated for by the introduction of corrective feedback as the relationship evolves. By the same token, a relationship that gets off to a positive start may later decline for a variety of reasons. The concept discussed earlier of causality, a linear description in which A inevitably leads to B, overlooks the central role played by the family's interactive process. The concept of equifinality means that the social work practitioner may intervene with a family at any of several points utilizing any of several therapeutic techniques to attain the same desired results.

In open systems, members are free to move in and out of interactions with one another, with extended family members (such as grandparents, aunts, uncles, or cousins), or with extrafamilial systems such as school, church, neighbors, or teachers. In contrast to the relatively closed family system, to which conformity and tradition are closely adhered, open family systems tend to stress adaptability to unfamiliar situations, particularly if that serves a purpose or a goal that the family considers worthwhile. Because an open and honest dialogue both within and outside the family is encouraged most of the time, disagreement or dissent may be common and not viewed as a threat to the ongoing viability of the family unit. Negotiation, communication, flexibility in shifting roles, interdependence, and authenticity are hallmarks of an open system.[38] As previously noted, in systems theory, open systems are said to have negentropy in that they are organized to be adaptable, open to new experiences, and able to alter patterns that are inappropriate to the current situation. Through exchanges outside of their own boundaries, open systems increase the chance of becoming more highly organized and developing resources to repair minor or temporary breakdowns in efficiency (Nichols & Everett, 1986).[39]

The lack of social exchanges in closed systems decreases their ability to deal with stress. Limited or perhaps nonexistent contact with others outside the family may lead to fearful, confused, and ineffective responses. In extreme cases of rigid systems and/or persistent stress, chaos and anarchy may follow within the family.[40]

BOUNDARIES

Each family system has boundaries, which can be defined as invisible lines of demarcation that separate the family from the outside, nonfamily environment.[41] Boundaries are useful, if arbitrary, metaphors for defining the overall system as a functioning unit or entity. They exist around the family as a whole, around its subsystems, and around individual family members. Without boundaries, there would be no progressive differentiation of functions in individuals or in separate subsystems, and hence, as Umbarger (1983)[42] contends, no system complexity. Without such complexity, a family's ability to create and maintain an adaptive stance in society is undermined. Adaptability is essential if the system is to avoid the forces of entropy and ultimate decay. All members of a family participate in several subsystems simultaneously and each subsystem stands in dynamic relationship with the others, both influencing and being influenced by others. Each subsystem with its own dynamic boundaries is organized to perform the functions necessary for the family as a whole to go about its tasks smoothly and effectively.

Boundaries circumscribe and protect the integrity of the system and thus determine who is regulated as inside and who remains outside the system. Within the family itself, boundaries differentiate subsystems and help to achieve and define the separate subunits of the total system. As Salvador Minuchin (1974)[43] notes, they must be sufficiently well defined to allow subsystem members to carry out their functions without undue interference. At the same time, they must be open enough to permit contact between the members of a subsystem and others. The clarity of a subsystem's boundaries is more important than who performs what functions.[44]

Boundaries may also be comprised of boundaries and nonphysical dividers that separate one system from another (family from family) or one part of a system from another part (one member of a family from another). They can represent physical boundaries such as walls separating one dwelling from another, or one room from another. Walls around a house may delineate territory, reality, space, and privacy.[45]

Of course, boundaries may also be emotional and psychological. Deviation from appropriate subsystem boundaries may occur in one of two ways, through either enmeshment or disengagement. In enmeshment, the boundary is too permeable and thus family members become overly involved and intertwined with each other's lives. In disengagement, there are overly rigid boundaries, with family members sharing a house but operating as separate units, with little interaction or exchange of feelings or sense of connection with one another. Little support or concern for family loyalty is evident in disengaged families. At their extremes, enmeshed families run the risk of prohibiting separations by viewing them as acts of betrayal, thus making autonomy virtually impossible. As a result, disengaged families, whose members remain oblivious to the effects of their actions on one another, may thus preclude their members from ever developing caring relationships with one another (Goldenberg & Goldenberg, p.52).[46] According to eminent Toronto social worker and theorist Dr. Eva Philipp, "Families may be both enmeshed and disengaged to varying degrees at the same time. For example, a parent may be symbiotically involved with a child and yet be rejecting and oblivious to the child's needs. It is therefore not a question of mutual exclusivity. It is possible for both to coexist within the same family unit."[47]

STABILITY AND CHANGE

Dynamic systems, whether family or otherwise, must maintain their continuity while tolerating change. Evolution is a normal and necessary part of every system's experience including the family system as it progresses through the life cycle. However, as Nichols and Everett (1981)[48] observe, a crucial question facing any system is how much change it can tolerate and still survive. Systems theorists have employed the terms "morphostasis" and "morphogenesis" to describe a system's ability to remain stable within the context of change, and conversely, to change within the context of stability. In order to maintain a healthy balance, both processes are necessary. With any system, tensions inevitably exist between forces seeking constancy and the maintenance of the status quo, on the one hand, and opposing forces demanding change, on the other. Morphostasis calls for a system to emphasize interactions involving negative or deviation attenuating feedback. It refers to the systems tendency toward stability or a state of dynamic equilibrium. Morphogenesis, on the other hand, demands positive or deviation amplifying feedback in order to encourage growth, innovation, and change.[49]

Systems theorists such as Maruyana (1968) and Hoffman (1981)[50] pointed out that the survival of any system depends on the interaction of these two key processes. Unlike homeostasis, which is the maintenance of behavioral constancy in a system, morphostatic mechanisms operate to maintain the system's structural constancy. Morphogenetic mechanisms, however, seek to push the system toward new levels of functioning allowing it to adapt to changing conditions.

This view is reinforced by Umbarger (1983),[51] who stresses that both stability and change are necessary for effective family functioning; that is, stability and change are necessary for the continuity of any family or system. Paradoxically, family stability is rooted in change. A family must maintain enough regularity and balance to maintain adaptability and preserve a sense of order and sameness. At the same time, it must subtly promote change and growth within members and the system as a whole.

Salvador Minuchin (1974)[52], focusing on the family's structural components, notes that responding to these pressures calls for "a constant transformation of the position of the family members in relation to one another so they can grow while the family system maintains continuity." Minuchin argues that family dysfunction results from rigidity of its transactional patterns and boundaries when faced with stress and the corresponding resistance of exploring alternate solutions. Minuchin contends that families that function effectively adapt to life's inevitable stresses in ways that preserve continuity while facilitating family restructuring as required. It must be recognized that no family functions optimally in all circumstances over periods of time. There are great fluctuations in families' abilities to cope, and indeed families are both functional and at the same time dysfunctional depending on the area under question.

SUMMARY

In conclusion, general systems theory offers social work practitioners a unique and profound perspective on the complex functioning of individuals, groups, families, organizations, and communities in Canadian society. This paradigm contributes to understanding the dynamic web and interconnectedness of various relationships and offers hope that changes can occur at any level of any system by understanding the interconnectedness and interrelatedness of its parts. It is recognized that when individual clients are being treated, direct access to other family members or systems may not be possible. Yet being aware of the existence of important systems and subsystems to a client can provide for a more comprehensive and effective assessment and treatment plan. Indeed further research is required to test, and expand upon, existing systems concepts which will undoubtedly further enrich this approach in the future. Utilized by itself or in combination with other methodological orientations, general systems theory has enormously enhanced the repertoire of social workers in all areas of practice who wish to bring about better human and social conditions on several interlocking levels.

NOTES

1. Turner, F.J. (1974). *Social work treatment: Interlocking theoretical approaches.* New York: Free Press, p. 343.
2. Von Bertalanffy, L. (1981). *A systems view of men.* P.A. La Violette, Ed. Boulder, CO: Westview Press, p. 109.
3. Ibid., p. ix.
4. Jenson, A.F., with Metcalfe, H.C. (1971). *Sociology: Concepts and concerns.* Chicago: Rand McNally, p. 132.
5. Goldenberg, H., & Goldenberg I. (1994). *Counselling today's families* (2nd Ed.). Pacific Grove, CA: Brooks/Cole Publishing Company, p. 40.
6. Ibid., p. 41.
7. Von Bertalanffy, L. *A systems view of men,* p. xv.
8. Ibid., p. 110.
9. Ibid., p. 109.
10. Ibid., p. 110.
11. Compton B.R., & Galway, B. (1989). *Social work processes.* Belmont, CA: Westworth Publishing Company, p. 123.
12. Nye & Bernardo (1993) in *Basic sociology. A Canadian introduction* (4th Ed.). J.J. Teevan, Ed. Scarborough, Ontario: Prentice-Hall Canada, p. 259.
13. Seligman, J. (1993) in *Social problems in Canada. Issues and challenges.* E.P. Nelson, & A. Fleuras, Eds. Scarborough, Ontario: Prentice-Hall Canada, p. 289.
14. Teevan, J.J., Ed. *Basic sociology. A Canadian introduction* (4th Ed.). Scarborough, Ontario: Prentice-Hall Canada, p. 259.
15. Notes from Social Work lectures at McMaster University transcribed by Jennifer Krawczyk, February 1995.
16. Andolfi, M. (1994) in Goldenberg & Goldenberg, p. 39.
17. Segel & Ben (1994) in Goldenberg & Goldenberg, p. 39.
18. Constantine (1994) in Goldenberg & Goldenberg, p. 39.
19. Notes from Social Work lectures at McMaster University transcribed by Jennifer Krawczyk, February 1995.
20. Germain (1989) in Compton & Galway, p. 201.
21. Pincus & Minihan (1989) in Compton & Galway, p. 201.
22. Siporin (1989) in Compton & Galway, p. 201.
23. Ibid., p. 101.
24. Ibid., p. 103.
25. Magnusson & Allen (1989) in Compton & Galway, p. 104.
26. Ibid., p. 104.
27. Ibid.
28. Goldenberg & Goldenberg, p. 51.

29. Tepperman, L., & Rosenberg, M. (1995). *Macro/micro. A brief introduction to sociology* (2nd Ed.). Scarborough, Ontario: Prentice-Hall Canada, p. 15.
30. Notes for Social Work lectures at McMaster University transcribed by Jennifer Krawczyk, February 1995.
31. Goldenberg & Goldenberg, p. 43.
32. Ibid., p. 44.
33. Turner, p. 347.
34. Constantine (1994) in Goldenberg & Goldenberg, p. 44.
35. Sarber (1994) in Goldenberg & Goldenberg, p. 44.
36. Kantor & Lehr (1994) in Goldenberg & Goldenberg, p. 44.
37. White (1994) in Goldenberg & Goldenberg, p. 44.
38. Goldenberg & Goldenberg, p. 44.
39. Nichols and Everett (1994) in Goldenberg & Goldenberg, p. 46.
40. Ibid., p. 46.
41. Ibid., p. 50.
42. Umberger (1994) in Goldenberg & Goldenberg, p. 51.
43. Minuchin (1994) in Goldenberg & Goldenberg, p. 51.
44. Ibid.
45. Notes from social work lectures at McMaster University transcribed by Jennifer Krawczyk, February 1996.
46. Goldenberg & Goldenberg, p. 52.
47. Interview with Toronto social work psychotherapist Dr. Eva Philipp, April 1996.
48. Nichols and Everett (1994) in Goldenberg & Goldenberg, p. 51.
49. Ibid., p. 52.
50. Maruyana and Hoffman (1994) in Goldenberg & Goldenberg, p. 53.
51. Umberger (1994) in Goldenberg & Goldenberg, p. 53.
52. Minuchin (1994) in Goldenberg & Goldenberg, p. 53.

BIBLIOGRAPHY

Andolfi, M. (1994) in *Counselling today's families* (2nd Ed.). H. Goldenberg, and I. Goldenberg, Eds. Pacific Grove, CA: Brooks/Cole Publishing.

Bernardo, F.M. (1993) in *Basic sociology: A Canadian introduction* (4th Ed.). J.J. Teevan, Ed. Scarbourough, Ont. Prentice-Hall Canada.

Compton, B.R., & Galaway, B. (1989). *Social work processes.* Belmont, CA: Westworth Publishing Company.

Constantine, L.L. (1994) in *Counselling today's families* (2nd Ed.). H. Goldenberg, and I. Goldenberg, Eds. Pacific Grove, CA: Brooks/Cole Publishing.

Germain, C. (1994) in *Counselling today's families* (2nd Ed.). H. Goldenberg, and I. Goldenberg, Eds. Pacific Grove, CA: Brooks/Cole Publishing.

Goldenberg, H., & Goldenberg, I. (1994). *Counselling today's families* (2nd Ed.). Pacific Grove, CA: Brooks/Cole Publishing Company.

Hagendorn, R., Ed. (1981). *Essentials of sociology.* Toronto, Ont.: Holt, Rinehart and Winston of Canada.

Jenson, A.F., with Metcalf, H.C. (1971). *Sociology: Concepts and concerns.* Chicago: Rand McNally.

Interview with Toronto social work psychotherapist Eva Philipp, April 1996.

Kantor, D. & W. Lehr. (1994) in *Counselling today's families* (2nd Ed.) H. Goldenberg, and I. Goldenberg, Eds. Pacific Grove, CA: Brooks/Cole Publishing.

Kuhn, A. (1974). *The logic of social systems.* San Francisco: Jossey-Bass.

Loomis, C.P. (1960). *Social systems. The Van Nostrand Series in Sociology.* Toronto, Ont.: D. Van Nostrand Company (Canada).

Magnusson, D. & V.L. Allen. (1989) in *Social work processes.* B. Compton and B. Galaway, Eds. Belmont CA: Westworth Publishing.

Maruyama, M. & L. Hoffman. (1994) in *Counselling today's families* (2nd Ed.). H. Goldenberg, and I. Goldenberg, Eds. Pacific Grove, CA: Brooks/Cole Publishing.

Minuchin, S., (1994) in *Counselling today's families* (2nd Ed.). H. Goldenberg, and I. Goldenberg, Eds. Pacific Grove, CA: Brooks/Cole Publishing.

Nelson, E.D., & Fleuras, A. (1993). *Social problems in Canada. Issues and challenges.* Scarborough, Ont.: Prentice-Hall Canada.

Nichols, W.C. & C.A. Everett. (1994) in *Counselling today's families,* (2nd Ed.). H. Goldenberg and I. Goldenberg, Eds. Pacific Grove, CA: Brooks/Cole Publishing.

Notes from social work lectures at McMaster University transcribed by Jennifer Krawczyk, February 1995.

Pincus, A. & A. Minahan (1989) in *Social work processes.* B. Compton, and B. Galaway, Eds. Belmont CA: Westworth Publishing.

Sauber, S.R. (1994) in *Counselling today's families* (2nd ed.) H. Goldenberg, and I. Goldenberg, Eds. Pacific Grove, CA: Brooks/Cole Publishing.

Segel, L., & J.B. Bavelas (1994) in *Counselling today's families* (2nd Ed.). H. Goldenberg, and I. Goldenberg, Eds. Pacific Grove, CA: Brooks/Cole Publishing.

Seligman, J. (1993) in *Social problems in Canada. Issues and challenges.* E.P. Nelson, A. Fleuras, Eds. Scarborough, Ont.: Prentice-Hall Canada.

Siporin, M. (1989) in *Social work processes,* B. Compton, and B. Galaway, Eds. Belmont, CA: Westworth Publishing.

Teevan, J.J., Ed. (1993). *Basic sociology. A Canadian introduction* (4th Ed.). Scarborough, Ont.: Prentice-Hall Canada.

Tepperman, L., & Rosenberg, M. (1995). *Macro/micro. A brief introduction to sociology* (2nd Ed.). Scarborough, Ont.: Prentice-Hall Canada.

Turner, F.J. (1974). *Social work treatment: Interlocking theoretical approaches.* New York: Free Press.

Umbarger, C.C. in *Counselling today's families* (2nd Ed.). H. Goldenberg, and I. Goldenberg, Eds. Pacific Grove, CA: Brooks/Cole Publishing.

Von Bertalanffy, L. (1981). *A systems view of men.* P.A. La Violette, Ed. Boulder, CO: Westview Press.

White, (1994) in *Counselling today's families* (2nd Ed.) H. Goldenberg, and I. Goldenberg, Eds. Pacific Grove, CA: Brooks/Cole Publishing.

CHAPTER 26

TASK-CENTERED SOCIAL WORK

WILLIAM J. REID

OVERVIEW

Task-centered social work evolved from a model of casework tested in the mid-1960s (Reid & Shyne, 1969). The results suggested that brief psychosocial casework might provide a more efficient means of helping individuals and families with problems in family relations than conventional, long-term forms of psychosocial practice. Using that brief service approach as a starting point, the author, in collaboration with Laura Epstein, attempted to develop a more comprehensive, systematic, and effective model of short-term treatment (Reid & Epstein, 1972). In its initial conception the task-centered approach utilized the time-limited structure and techniques of short-term psychosocial casework as a means of helping clients devise and carry out actions or tasks to alleviate their problems. Perlman's (1957) view of casework as a problem-solving process and Studt's (1968) notion of the client's task as a focus of service were particularly influential in this beginning formulation.

Since its inception, the task-centered system has continued to grow and change. In fact, our intent was to create an approach to practice that would continue to evolve in response to continuing research and to developments in knowledge and technology consonant with its basic principles. The model was designed to be an open, pluralistic practice system that would be able to integrate theoretical and technical contributions from diverse sources. In keeping with this design feature, the model is not wedded to any particular theory of human functioning or to any fixed set of intervention methods. Rather, it provides a core of value premises, theory, and methods that can be augmented by compatible approaches.

This core incorporates a number of basic principles that continue to evolve. A current summary is provided below.

TASK-CENTERED MODEL: BASIC CHARACTERISTICS AND PRINCIPLES

EMPIRICAL ORIENTATION

Preference is given to methods and theories tested and supported by empirical research; hypotheses and concepts about the client system need to be grounded in case data; speculative theorizing about the client's problems and behavior is avoided; assessment, process, and outcome data are systematically collected in each case; a sustained program of developmental research is used to improve the model.

INTEGRATIVE STANCE

The model draws selectively on empirically based theories and methods from compatible approaches—e.g., problem-solving, cognitive-behavioral, cognitive, and family structural.

FOCUS ON CLIENT ACKNOWLEDGED PROBLEMS

Focus of service is on specific problems clients explicitly acknowledge as being of concern to them.

SYSTEMS AND CONTEXTS

Problems occur in a context of multiple systems; contextual change may be needed for problem resolution or to prevent problem recurrence; conversely, resolution of a problem may have beneficial effects on its context.

PLANNED BREVITY

Service is generally planned short-term by design (six to twelve weekly sessions within a four-month period).

COLLABORATIVE RELATIONSHIP

Relationships with clients emphasize a caring but collaborative effort; the practitioner shares assessment information, avoids hidden goals and agendas; extensive use is made of client's input in developing treatment strategies not only to devise more effective interventions, but to develop the client's problem-solving abilities.

STRUCTURE

The intervention program, including treatment sessions, is structured into well-defined sequences of activities.

PROBLEM-SOLVING ACTIONS (TASKS)

Change is brought about primarily through problem-solving actions (tasks) undertaken by clients within and outside of the session. Particular emphasis is placed on mobilizing clients' actions in their own environments. The primary function of the treatment session is to lay the groundwork for such actions. In addition, practitioner tasks provide a means of effecting environmental change in the client's interest.

During the past two decades the evolution of the model has been characterized by developments in theory and method as well as by the generation of various adaptations for particular settings and populations. Among major sources for development of the model as a whole have been theories of learning and cognition as well as problem-solving, behavioral, cognitive-behavioral, and structural family therapy approaches. Variations of the model have been devised for work with groups (Beilenberg, 1991; Fortune, 1985; Garvin, 1974, 1985; Kilgore, 1995; Pomeroy, Rubin, & Walker, 1995; Raushi, 1994; Rooney, 1977), family units (Reid, 1985, 1987; Reid & Donovan, 1990), as a method of case management (Bailey-Dempsey, 1993), as a system of agency management (Parihar, 1983, 1994), as a model for clinical supervision (Caspi, 1995), and as an approach to community work (Ramakrishnan, Balgopal, & Pettys, 1994). In the course of this evolution the model has maintained a social work focus, with attention to the distinctive functions and needs of that profession.

Specific adaptations have been developed for most settings in which social workers practice, including child welfare (Rooney, 1981; Rzepnicki, 1985; Salmon, 1977), public social services (Rooney, 1988; Rooney & Wanless, 1985), school social work (Bailey-Dempsey, 1993; Epstein, 1977; Reid & Bailey-Dempsey, 1995; Reid, Epstein, Brown, Tolson, & Rooney, 1980); corrections (Bass, 1977; Hofstad, 1977, Larsen & Mitchell, 1980), medical (Wexler, 1977; Abramson, 1992), industrial (Taylor, 1977; Weissman, 1977), geriatric (Cormican, 1977; Dierking, Brown, & Fortune, 1980; Naleppa, 1995; Rathbone-McCuan 1985), family service (Benbenishty, 1988; Hari, 1977; Wise, 1977), and mental health (Brown, 1980; Ewalt, 1977; Newcome, 1985). The basic principles and methods of the model can be found in a series of volumes that have appeared since the early 1970s (Doel & Marsh, 1993; Epstein, 1980, 1988, 1992; Fortune, 1985; Goldberg, Gibbons, & Sinclair, 1985; Parihar, 1983; Rooney, 1992; Reid, 1978, 1985, 1992; Reid & Epstein, 1972, 1977; Tolson, Reid, & Garvin, 1994).

In this chapter a review of the task-centered system of clinical practice will be presented, that is, the use of the task-centered approach in work with individuals, families, and groups. The review will encompass the major theoretical formulations that underlie the practice model; the model itself, that is, the strategy and methods that guide work with clients; its range of application; and research evidence relating to the efficacy of the model. The chapter will conclude with an illustrative case.

BASIC ASSUMPTIONS

Both our initial and subsequent theoretical work have been based on the premise that the essential function of task-centered practice is to help clients move forward with solutions to psychosocial problems that they define and hope to solve. The primary agent of change is not the social worker but the client. The worker's role is to help the client bring about changes the client wishes and is willing to work for.

The theoretical base of the model consists largely of formulations concerning the nature, origins, and dynamics of psychosocial problems. A problem classification defines the types and range of difficulties considered to be targets of the model. Included are problems in family and interpersonal relations, in carrying out social roles, in decision making, in securing resources, and emotional distress reactive to situational factors. At the same time, target problems are part of a larger context that must always be taken into account. The context of a problem can be seen generally as a configuration of factors that may interact with the problem. The context includes obstacles to solving the problem and resources that can be applied to work on it. These obstacles and resources in turn can reflect almost any aspect of the multiple systems of which the client is a part.

It is assumed that problems generally reflect temporary breakdowns in problem coping that set in motion forces for change. These forces, which include the client's own motivation to alleviate distress and resources in the client's environment, operate rapidly in most cases to reduce the problem to a tolerance level, at which point the possibility of further change lessens. If so, then clients might be expected to benefit as much from short-term treatment as from more extended periods of service. Placing time limits on service might be expected to enhance effectiveness by mobilizing efforts of both practitioner and client. Effectiveness would be further augmented by concentrated attention on delimited problems in which practitioners would help clients formulate and carry out problem-solving actions.

The planned brevity of the model is then based on the proposition that effectiveness of interpersonal treatment is relatively short-lived—that is, that the most benefit clients will derive from such treatment will be derived within a relatively few sessions and a relatively brief period of time. The proposition has been supported by a large amount of research evidence which suggests the following: (1) recipients of brief, time-limited treatment show at least as much durable improvement as recipients of long-term, open-ended treatment (Gurman & Kniskern, 1981; Johnson & Gelso, 1982; Luborsky, Singer, & Luborsky, 1975; Reid & Shyne, 1969; Koss & Butcher, 1986); (2) most of the improvement associated with long-term treatment occurs relatively soon after treatment has begun (Meltzoff & Kornreich, 1970; Strupp, Fox, & Lessler, 1969; Orlinsky & Howard, 1986); (3) regardless of their intended length most courses of voluntary treatment turn out to be relatively brief—the great majority of such treatment courses probably last no longer than a dozen sessions or a three-month time span—a generalization which suggests that most people may exhaust the benefits of treatment rather quickly (Beck, Fahs, & Jones, 1973; Garfield, 1994).

The psychosocial problems that make up targets of intervention are always the expression of something that clients want which they do not have; problems are ultimately defined by the self-perceived motivations of the client rather than by constructs in the mind of the practitioner. The usual and most effective way to obtain what one wants is to take action to get it. Since clients are human beings, their actions are guided by sophisticated sets of beliefs about themselves and their worlds, beliefs that help them form and implement plans about what they should do and how they should do it. Since their problems are psychosocial, their plans and actions usually will involve others—the individuals, groups, and organizations that make up their social systems. These actions will be shaped in turn by their evaluation of the responses of these systems. This theory does not attempt to deal with remote or historical origins of a problem, but rather with current obstacles that may be blocking the resolution or with resources that may facilitate it.

These formulations, more than some others that guide social work practice, stress people's autonomous problem-solving capacities—their ability to initiate and carry through intelligent action to obtain what they want (Goldman, 1970). In this conception, the person is seen less a prisoner of unconscious drives than in the theories of the psychoanalyst and less a prisoner of environmental contingencies than in the views of the behaviorist. Rather, people are viewed as having minds and wills of their own that are reactive but not subordinate to internal and external influences. We think those human problem-solving capacities—complex, ingenious, and, in the main, quite effective—deserve more prominence than they have received in theories of helping. We have tried to build our theory accordingly.

TREATMENT

The basic strategy and selected methods of the task-centered model will be presented as they are used in work with individual clients. Variations for practice with families and groups and in case management contexts will then be taken up.

STRATEGY

Guided by the foregoing theory, the practitioner helps the client identify specific problems that arise from unrealized wants and that are defined in terms of specific conditions to be changed. Work proceeds within the structure of contracts in which the client's problems and goals and the nature and duration of service are explicitly stated and agreed on by both practitioner and client. Analysis of a problem leads to consideration of the kinds of actions needed to solve it, what might facilitate those actions, and obstacles standing in the way of their implementation. Change is effected primarily through problem-solving actions or tasks that clients and practitioners undertake outside the interview. Practitioners help clients select tasks. They facilitate task work through assisting clients in planning task implementation and establishing their motivation for carrying out the plan. They help clients rehearse and practice tasks and analyze obstacles to their achievement. Reviews of the client's accomplishments on each task allow the practitioner to provide corrective feedback on the client's actions and serve as the basis for developing new tasks.

To supplement the client's problem-solving efforts, the practitioner may carry out tasks within the client's social system. These tasks are usually designed to assist others in facilitating the client's tasks or to secure resources from the system that clients cannot readily obtain on their own. Although clients' problems may be resolved exclusively through practitioner tasks, the theory and methodology of the system are obviously oriented toward problems in which at least some client initiative is indicated and will be of the most value when such problems are at issue.

The central and distinctive strategy of the present system is found in its reliance on tasks as a means of problem resolution. The client's and practitioner's efforts are devoted primarily to the construction, implementation, and review of tasks. The success of these tasks largely determines whatever benefit results from the application of the model.

The stress on tasks is an attempt to build upon the considerable capacity of human beings to take constructive action in response to difficulty. In effect, we have modeled our intervention strategy after the way most people resolve most of their problems—by doing something about them.

To be sure, the problems brought to the attention of social workers have usually not yielded to the client's problem-solving initiatives. Nevertheless, we assume that a capacity for problem-solving action is present. It is the social worker's responsibility to help the client put this capacity to work.

The strategy we advocate leads to a parsimonious form of intervention that respects clients' rights to manage their own affairs. If clients are clear about what is troubling them and have a reasonable plan for resolving the difficulty, the practitioner's role may be limited largely to providing encouragement and structure for their problem-solving efforts. If more is needed, more is supplied, to the extent necessary to help clients resolve their difficulties. Even when the practitioner's involvement is great, its purpose is to develop and augment the client's own actions. Thus practitioners may need to help clients determine what they want and in the process may need to challenge wants that are unrealizable. Practitioners may need to help clients identify and modify action and interaction sequences contributing to the difficulty, to provide corrective feedback on their actions, to teach them necessary skills, to work with them to alter beliefs that are interfering with problem solving, to bring about changes in the social system and to secure resources from it, and even to suggest specific tasks for them to carry out. But whatever is done is done collaboratively and leads to actions that must be agreed to by the client. The decisive actions in most cases are those that clients themselves perform in their own way and on their own behalf.

Enabling clients to take constructive and responsible action in their own interests has an important corollary: the action so taken is likely to be incorporated as part of their strategies for continued coping with their problems. Since the client has participated in its planning, has an understanding of its rationale, agreed to carry it out, actually implemented it, and reviewed its results, one can assume that the action is more a part of him or her and, if successful, is more likely to be used again with appropriate variations, than if he or she were simply following the practitioner's instructions or unwittingly responding to contingencies arranged by others.

Practitioner-Client Relationship

In the task-centered approach, the relationship between the practitioner and client provides a means of stimulating and promoting problem-solving action. Their sessions together do not provide the essential ingredients of change; rather they serve to set in motion and guide subsequent actions through which change will be effected. It is assumed, nevertheless, that this purpose will be facilitated through a relationship in which the client feels accepted, respected, liked, and understood. This kind of relationship is considered fundamental in task-centered as well as in most forms of interpersonal practice, although it has been difficult to define and measure the various qualities it is supposed to contain.

In one attempt at a definition, Perlman (1957) described a good treatment relationship as containing both support and expectancy. Its supportive elements have perhaps been given the greater weight in social work practice theory. Within the task-centered system, the expectations the practitioner conveys to the client are viewed as a therapeutic force of at least equal importance. The practitioner expects the client to work on agreed-upon problems and tasks and communicates these expectations to the client both explicitly and implicitly. While the client's decision to reject help is respected, the client is held accountable for following through once a contract has been established. These positions are not inconsistent: they reflect an acceptance of the client as a person who can make responsible decisions. Expectations, if clearly communicated, serve to influence the client's reactions, since the client is likely to regard the practitioner as an authority who can be trusted to advance his or her interest and whose approval is important. The practitioner's reaction, which is likely to be more approving if clients make an effort to resolve their problems than if they do not, serves to strengthen the force of these expectations. This is as it should be if the practitioner's relationship is to be used to full advantage on the client's behalf. But if clients are to be helped to resolve problems, qualities of the relationship must be fused with specific problem-solving methods. The relationship provides the raw material but not the finished product.

Contextual Change

The immediate purpose of the model is to help clients resolve problems through enabling them to plan and execute necessary problem-solving actions. An effort is made, however, to help clients alleviate target problems in ways that will exert a positive influence on the context of the problem. Whereas significant contextual change is not a fixed objective in all cases, it is generally sought after as a means of facilitating solutions, of preventing recurrences and side effects, and of strengthening the client's problem-solving abilities. Contextual change is essentially defined and limited by the nature of the target problem. It is not just any change that would help the client. Practitioners move from the target outward by degrees, giving priority to contextual change most directly relevant to the problem at hand. Two major ways of achieving such change have been identified.

First, contextual change can occur as a direct consequence of alleviation of a target problem. Changes in target problems can produce "ripple effects." Improvement in Kevin's grades may lead to a positive change in his teachers' attitudes toward him, which, in turn, may result in more cooperative behavior on his part.

Second, contextual change may occur in the process of working through obstacles preventing resolution of target problems. For example, in order to help a withdrawn adolescent make friends, the practitioner may need to deal with the youngster's depreciated self-image. Unlike some approaches, the manifest problem is not seen as a point of entry to the "real difficulties" underneath. Although the problem remains the focus of attention, its resolution may require considerable change in its context.

The treatment strategy is guided by principles that maximize the clients own problem-solving activities and potentials. It is assumed that, in general, clients can be best helped if they are provided with an orderly, facilitative structure in which to work out immediate problems and to develop problem-solving skills, with the practitioner in the roles of guide and consultant.

Although clients' limitations are realistically appraised, emphasis is placed on identification of their strengths, competencies, and resources. Accordingly, clients are helped to devise their own solutions with the practitioner's assistance. Should these efforts be blocked by obstacles, increased attention is paid to contextual factors that may be responsible for the obstacles. The practitioner assumes more of a leadership role and pushes for greater contextual change as is necessary in order to help the client work through obstacles preventing problem resolution. These principles serve to organize contributions from a broad range of treatment approaches.

PRACTITIONER-CLIENT ACTIVITIES

The central strategy of the model is effected through a series of activities carried out in a collaborative manner by the practitioner and client. Although specific practitioner techniques, such as encouragement, advice giving, role playing, and exploration, are important in this process, stress is placed on the practitioner's and client's joint problem-solving efforts. The major activities are outlined briefly below.

Problem Exploration and Specification; Assessment
Problems are explored and clarified by the social worker and the client in the initial interview. As suggested, the focus is on what the client wants and not on what the practitioner thinks the client may need. The practitioner may point out, however, potential difficulties the client has not acknowledged or the consequences that may result if these difficulties are allowed to go unattended. In other words, the target problem is not necessarily defined by what clients say they want initially, but rather by what they want after a process of deliberation to which practitioners contribute their own knowledge and point of view. As a result, clients may alter their perception of their problems or, in the case of "involuntary clients," may realize they have difficulties they may wish to work on. But at the end of this process, normally at the close of the first or second interview, the practitioner and client must come to an ex-

plicit agreement on the problems to be dealt with. These problems are defined as discrete, numerable entities and are specified in terms of specific conditions to be changed. The problem is generally summarized in a single sentence (the problem statement) and then specified.

For example, the case of Mrs. N., who was seen concerning difficulties in caring for her two-year-old daughter, Ann, produced the following problem statement and specification:

PROBLEM 1

Mrs. N. constantly loses her temper with Ann, frequently shouting at her and slapping or shaking her. Mrs. N. becomes quickly irritated whenever Ann won't obey. Mrs. N. generally starts shouting at her when these things happen. If Ann then persists in the behavior or starts to cry, Mrs. N. usually will scream at her and then slap her or shake her. During the past week, Mrs. N. lost her temper with Ann on the average of about five times a day and slapped or shook her at least once a day.

As the example above illustrates, problems are spelled out in concrete terms and in language the client can understand. Estimated frequencies of problem occurrence over a specified period add additional precision to the problem description and provide a baseline against which change in the problem can be measured. The problem of most concern to the client normally becomes the primary focus in treatment, although usually more than one problem is defined and worked on.

Exploration of the context of the problem is concentrated upon identifying the manipulable causes that are contributing to it or resources that can help solve it. What are the immediate causative factors in the client's beliefs, actions, or environment that the practitioner or the client can do something about? We are interested in causal analysis only as a means of arriving at possible solutions. Exploration may also include pertinent history and general contextual factors involving health, family, work, school, and other relevant aspects of the client's situation.

Problem exploration is the data-gathering tool for assessment activities, which involve efforts to understand the dynamics of the problem and its contextual features as well as to delineate the frequency and severity of its occurrence. A largely cognitive process, assessment is led by the practitioner but should also involve the client as collaborator. While the practitioner can contribute professional knowledge, the client has unique personal knowledge of the problem and its context. Assessment is essentially problem-focused. It starts with the problems to be dealt with and incorporates whatever information about the client's situation, such as history, personality, that might be relevant to those problems.

In exploring and assessing problems, practitioners may make use of a variety of diagnostic theories, depending on what best fits the problem at hand. In the task-centered model, problems are derived empirically from clients' views of their difficulties as these are clarified in dialogues with practitioners. Practitioners do not use theory to formulate problems but rather start with a description of the problem ("Mrs. N. loses her temper with her child") and then scan relevant knowledge, including theories, to locate possible explanations.

Certain guidelines are offered for this eclectic use of theory: (1) Whatever hypotheses are selected to explain the problem should be evaluated through case data. This involves analyzing evidence to determine the likelihood of the hypothesis holding in the particular case. (2) Preference is given to theories that have been supported by empirical research. (3) The practitioner does not fix on a single explanation but rather considers alternative explanations in a search for the theory that provides the best fit with the problem and case at hand.

Contracting

The practitioner and client develop an oral or written contract in which the client agrees to work with the practitioner on one or more explicitly stated, acknowledged problems. The contract may also include a statement of the client's goals in relation to the problem—that is, what kind of solution of the problem does he or she want to achieve? Clients need not even be highly motivated to solve their problems but must at least agree to work on them. Once the contract is formed, we try to hold to its terms. We try to avoid the kind of practice in which clients have agreed to see social workers for one kind of problem but the social workers attempt covertly to treat them for another.

The contract then states at least one problem that the practitioner and client will begin to work on. The contract also includes an estimation of the limits of treatment, usually expressed in terms of an approximate number of sessions and length of time. We normally limit treatment to eight to twelve interviews, weekly or twice weekly, within a one-to-three-month time span. The contract is open to renegotiation at any point, to include new problems or longer periods of service.

Task Planning

Once agreement has been reached on the targets and duration of treatment, tasks are formulated and selected in collaboration with the client and their implementation is planned. A task defines what the client is to do to alleviate his or her problem. The task may be cast in relatively general terms, giving the client a direction for action but no specific program of behavior to follow. We call these general tasks. For example, Mr. and Mrs. C. are to develop a plan for the care of their mentally retarded daughter. Or a task may be very specific or what we term "operational." Operational tasks call for specific action the client is to undertake. Mr. A. is to apply for a job at X employment agency within the next week, or Johnny is to volunteer to recite in class on Monday. The push in the model is toward task specificity. Thus an effort is made to spell out broadly defined tasks in terms of specific operational tasks. In order for a proposed course of action to be considered a task, the client must agree that he or she will try to carry it out. The client's express commitment to try to achieve the task is crucial.

In some cases the nature of the problem and the client's circumstances may point to a particular course of action, which can then be developed. In others, alternative actions need to be considered and appraised. The process works best if both the practitioner and the client can freely suggest alternatives as they come to mind, without too much consideration initially as to their appropriateness. Research on problem solving indicates that this kind of "brainstorming" is an effective means of devising solutions, perhaps because it stimulates imaginative thinking about a wide range of approaches to a difficulty (Osborn, 1963). The best alternatives can then be selected for more serious consideration. In addition to suggesting alternatives, practitioners try to encourage clients to generate their own. At this stage, practitioner criticism of particular client proposals is kept to a minimum.

Often the practitioner is the primary generator of alternatives. Clients may not be able to produce much on their own. Moreover, the practitioner may have special knowledge about kinds of tasks that generally work well for particular problems. Our research, to date, does not indicate a relationship between who originated the idea for the task and task accomplishment. Tasks initially proposed by practitioners tend to show about the same amount of progress as those suggested by clients. It should be kept in mind, however, that the practitioner proposes *ideas* for tasks, which are then discussed with the client. The client's contributions normally become a part of the task plan. The practitioner does not "assign" the task to the client.

An agreement between practitioner and client on the client's task—that is, on what he or she is to do—may occur after alternatives have been sorted out and the best selected. Generally an agreement at this point concerns the global nature of the client's proposed action, and not the detail, which is developed subsequently. In some cases the practitioner may prefer to explore in some depth the strategies and tactics of carrying out a possible task before reaching agreement on it with the client. This option may be used when extensive planning of a possible task may be necessary before a judgment can be made about its usefulness. In any event, a final agreement on the task is made at the end of the planning process, after it is determined what the execution of the task will involve.

Whatever the level of client action under consideration, the process proceeds until a plan is developed that the client *can begin to execute prior to his or her next visit with the social worker.* The plan may consist chiefly of a general task (to look for an apartment) together with one or more operational tasks that he can carry out in the interim (to contact a rental agency). Or it may be built around one or more operational tasks. The plan always contains at least one operational task. In addition, it generally includes some guidelines for the execution of the operational task(s).

For the plan to work, it is essential that the client emerge with a clear notion of what he or she is to do. To this end, the practitioner and client go over the plan in summary fashion, normally at the end of the interview. This final wrap-up may be preceded by summarizations of parts of the plan during the process of its formulation. Summarizing the plan gives the practitioner the opportunity to convey to the client the expectation that it will be carried out and that his or her efforts will be reviewed. "So you will try to do————. We'll see how it worked out next time we meet."

The same principles are applied to planning of practitioner tasks or actions the practitioner will take outside the session in an attempt to bring about desired changes in the client's social system. Although such actions may not be planned in detail with the client, their consideration as tasks not only enables the client to understand and perhaps help shape the worker's environmental interventions, but makes the worker accountable, as is the client, for task performance.

Establishing Incentives and Rationale
The social worker and client develop a rationale or purpose for carrying out the task if it is not already clear. Either the practitioner or the client might first consider the potential benefit to be gained from completing the task. What good will come of it? The practitioner reinforces the client's perception of realistic benefits or points out positive consequences that the client may not have perceived.

Anticipating Obstacles
An important practitioner function in task planning is to help the client identify potential obstacles to the task and to shape plans so as to avoid or minimize these obstacles. This function is implicitly addressed when the practitioner presses for specificity in the task plan. As details of how the tasks are to be done are brought out, possible obstacles can be identified and dealt with. A more explicit approach is to ask clients to think of ways that a task might fail (Birchler & Spinks, 1981). If substantial obstacles appear, techniques of contextual analysis (below) can be used. Alternatively, the task can be modified or another developed.

Simulation and Guided Practice
The practitioner may model possible task behavior or ask clients to rehearse what they are going to say or do. Modeling and rehearsal may be carried out through role play, where appropriate. For example, if the client's task was to speak up in a group, the practitioner might take the role of the leader of the group and the client could rehearse what he or she might say if called on. Or the roles could be reversed, with the worker modeling what the client might say. Guided practice is the performance of the actual (as opposed to simulated) task behavior by the client during the interview; thus, a child may practice reading or a marital pair more constructive forms of communication, with the worker taking a coaching or teaching role. Guided practice can also be extended to real-life situations. For example, a practitioner might accompany a client (with a fear of going to doctors) to a medical clinic.

Problem and Task Review
The client's progress on problems and tasks is routinely reviewed at the beginning of each session. The review covers developments in the problem, and what the client has and has not accomplished in tasks to resolve it. Practitioner tasks are reviewed in a similar manner. What the practitioner does next depends on the results of the review. If the tasks have been substantially accomplished or completed, the practitioner may formulate another task with the client on the same problem or a different prob-

lem. If the task has not been carried out or only partially achieved, the practitioner and client may discuss obstacles, devise a different plan for carrying out the task, or apply other task implementation activities. The task may be revised or replaced by another or the problem itself may be reformulated.

Contextual Analysis

During the course of the review of tasks and problems, obstacles to task achievement and problem change are usually encountered. The essential difference between a target problem and an obstacle is that the former is a difficulty that the client and practitioner have contracted to change, and the latter is a difficulty standing in the way of progress toward resolution of a target problem.

Whereas obstacles block progress, resources facilitate it. Resources are usually found in strengths and competencies of individual clients, in the ties of loyalty and affection that hold families together, and in the intangible and tangible supports provided by external systems. However, a given characteristic may serve as either an obstacle or resource depending on its function in relation to the problem.

In *contextual analysis* the practitioner helps clients to identify and resolve obstacles as well as to locate and utilize resources. The discussion is led by the practitioner, who relies on focused exploration, explanations, and other methods designed to increase the client's understanding. The process may overlap with the problem and task reviews, when obstacles and resources may emerge and be explored. The practitioner may help clients modify distorted perceptions or unrealistic expectations. Dysfunctional patterns of behavior or interactions may be pointed out. Obstacles involving the external system, such as interactions between a child and school personnel or the workings of a recalcitrant welfare bureaucracy, may be clarified or resources within these systems may be searched for.

Terminating

The process of terminating is begun in the initial phase when the duration of treatment is set. In the last review, the practitioner and client review progress on his or her problems. Clients are helped to plan how they will continue work on their tasks or to develop new ones they might undertake on their own. What the client has achieved is given particular stress. Extensions beyond agreed-upon limits are normally made if the client requests additional service. Extensions, which usually involve a small number of additional sessions, occur in only a minority of cases in most settings.

Work with Families and Formed Groups

The strategy that has been outlined for treatment of the individual client is applied, with certain modifications, to work with clients in groups. Specific adaptations have been developed for two types of groups: families (or individuals who live together) and groups assembled expressly for the purpose of helping members work on individual problems.

From its beginning the task-centered approach has been used as a method of helping families. Early efforts emphasized work with family dyads, marital and parent-child pairs. Recently attention has been given to treatment of larger family units (Fortune, 1985; Reid, 1985, 1987, Tolson, Reid, & Garvin, 1994).

Families

Treatment of a family unit, like treatment of the individual client, focuses on resolution of specific client-acknowledged problems and associated contextual change. Problems are seen as occurring in a multisystems context in which the family is a major, though not always the most critical, system. To understand problems and their contexts, use is made of research and theory on family interaction as well as specific contributions from behavioral, structural, strategic, and communications schools of family therapy.

In most cases family members are seen together, and to the extent possible, problems are defined in interactional terms. In addition to tasks carried out by individual family members and the practitioner, as in the general model, use is made of tasks undertaken jointly by family members, either in the session or at home. Tasks within the session (session tasks) generally involve family members in face-to-face problem-solving efforts, structured and facilitated by the practitioner, who may in addition help family members improve skills in problem-solving communication. Additional kinds of session tasks involve use of role play and live enactments of family interactions. Possible solutions devised by family members in their problem-solving work in the session are used as a basis for tasks to be carried out at home.

The theme of collaborative effort is continued in these home tasks. Shared tasks, which family members do together, provide a means for continuing at home problem-solving and communication tasks worked on in the session, for enabling family members to work together on practical projects, such as home improvements, and for affecting relationships between family members.

Reciprocal tasks make use of the principle of reciprocity in arranging for exchanges between family members. Exchanges may involve comparable behaviors and rewards (or noncompliance for penalties)—the form reciprocal tasks usually take between unequals, such as parents and children.

Whatever their form, reciprocal tasks require that participants express a willingness to cooperate and regard the exchange as equitable. Although it is important to work out the details of the exchange in the session, a "collaborative set" (Jacobson & Margolin, 1979) is essential to ensure that participants are prepared to accept reasonable approximations or equivalents of expected behavior rather than letter-of-the-law performance and are willing to adjust expectations in the light of unanticipated circumstances. All of this suggests that work in the session toward clarifying and negotiating conflicts around particular issues precedes the setting up of reciprocal tasks to deal with the issues at home. If reciprocal tasks are "tacked on" at the end of session without sufficient preparatory work, they are likely to fail.

Session and home tasks are used to bring about contextual change. Frequently such change is necessary to resolve obstacles in family interaction that may be blocking solutions to problems. For example, a coalition between mother and son may be undermining the father's attempts at discipline. Session and home tasks may be designed to weaken the mother-son coalition and to strengthen the parental alliance. In this way, as well as in others, the model draws on the strategies of systems-based, especially structural, family therapy.

A fundamental principle, however, is to concentrate on alleviating target problems through relatively simple, straightforward tasks. These tasks may be designed to effect contextual change in passing, but the target problems should be the first priority. Structural dysfunctions, underlying pathologies, and so on are left alone unless they intrude as obstacles. To the extent they do, practitioners can then shift toward tasks more directed at contextual change—tasks, including paradoxical varieties, that may be aimed at structural modifications. This progression from the simple to the not-so-simple fits the needs of social workers who deal with a wide range of family types, from normal to highly disturbed, across a wide variety of problems and settings, and who may not be expert in family therapy. Many families do not want a change in structure; many problems do not require it; and many practitioners lack the skill to effect it.

The family treatment variation is viewed as part of a more comprehensive system of task-centered practice. Although work with the family as a unit is generally seen as the treatment of choice when target problems consist of difficulties in family relationships, this method must be evaluated against other options when the target problem involves the behavior of a member outside the family context, such as a child's difficulty at school. Although family treatment may be indicated if problems are reactive to family processes or if families can be used as a resource for solving them, work focused on the individual and the setting in which his or her difficulty occurs may prove to be a more effective alternative. By incorporating within a single framework methods for work with individuals, family units, and the environment, the model facilitates flexible, combined approaches to helping client systems resolve problems.

Groups

The principles of conjoint treatment that have been presented can be applied to any situation in which target problems involve interaction of members of natural groups—that is, groups that have a life apart from the treatment session. Somewhat different principles apply when clients are treated for individual problems within the context of a formed group—that is, a group created to help individuals with their own concerns. The ultimate change target against which success is measured is not interaction of group members outside the session but rather resolution of the separate problems of each. Within the task-centered framework, the term "group treatment" is used to describe this form of intervention. The strategies and methods of task-centered group treatment have been presented elsewhere in detail (Fortune, 1985; Garvin, 1985; Kilgore, 1995; Raushi, 1995; Rooney, 1977; Tolson, Reid, & Garvin, 1994).

In task-centered group treatment, the group process is used to further the basic activities of the model. Group members, guided by the leader, help one another to specify problems, plan tasks, rehearse and practice behavior, analyze obstacles to task achievement, review task progress, and so on. The leader's role is to make effective use of this process through orchestrating his or her own interventions with the contributions of group members.

In order that the contribution of members can be used to best advantage, groups are made relatively homogeneous in respect to target problems. Thus, a group may be formed around problems of academic achievement or posthospitalization adjustment. As a result, group members have firsthand knowledge of the kind of problems others are experiencing and are thus in a good position to provide support and guidance. Moreover, members can more readily apply lessons learned from the task work of others to their own situations.

While it does not permit the kind of sustained, focused attention on individual problems and tasks possible in one-to-one treatment, the group mode has certain distinct advantages. Group members in the aggregate may possess more detailed knowledge than the leader about intricacies of the target problems. Given this experiential knowledge base, the group can often suggest task possibilities that may not have occurred to either the leader or the member being helped at the moment. Gaining recognition from a group provides an incentive for task accomplishment not available in individual treatment; in particular, a member who carries out a task successfully can serve as a model to others. These advantages are not always realized, however. Groups may become unfocused and discordant. Members may become competitive and overly critical. Certain participants may become objects of group hostility—the well-known scapegoating phenomenon. In order to exploit the potentials of this medium and to avoid its pitfalls, the group leader needs to exert a constructive influence on the dynamics of the group. The purpose of the group generally—to help individual members with their target problems—needs to be clarified and kept in view. The communications of the participants must be channeled in relation to the purpose.

Beliefs that members have about one another and about appropriate behavior in the group influence the sociometric and normative structures of the group. The practitioner attempts to encourage beliefs that are functional for the group's purpose: for example, that all participants are worthwhile persons who deserve help in working out their problems; that each has to find a solution that is right for him or her; that each has a right to a fair share of attention and assistance from the leader and the groups. Shared beliefs about how the group should conduct itself become the basis for group control of the behavior of its members. The practitioner attempts to foster group-control efforts that will maintain focus on problems and tasks; that will facilitate sharing of relevant information (but discourage prying into aspects of the members' lives not germane to work on their problems); and that will stress positive reactions to task accomplishment over negative responses to task failure.

Leadership within the group is an additional facet that needs to be attended to and used constructively. Although the practitioner normally assumes the primary leadership role in task-centered groups, he or she may use members as co-leaders for particular purposes—one member may be particularly adept at reducing tension in the group; another at keeping the group focused on the business at hand.

While procedures for forming and conducting groups vary, the following format is typical. Preliminary individual interviews are held with prospective group members to determine primarily if the applicant has at least one problem that would fall within the prospective focus of the group, and to orient him or her to the general structure and purpose of the group treatment model. In the initial group meeting, clients are asked to state the problems they wish to work on and to assist one another in problem exploration and specification. A contractual agreement is reached on the purpose of the group and its duration (which is planned short-term as in individual treatment). In subsequent sessions each member, in turn, formulates, plans, practices, and reviews tasks with the help of the practitioner and other group members. In addition, the practitioner may undertake tasks outside the session on behalf of a single client or the group as a whole, or group members may perform extrasession tasks to help one another with their problems.

Case Management

Problems of coordination are inevitable when a case involves multiple service providers. Often the social worker is one of a half dozen or more practitioners serving the same client. For example, work with a troubled child and his or her family may involve a school social worker, one or more teachers, a school psychologist, a school nurse, a probation officer, and a case worker from a county child protection unit. In a mental health setting the "cast of characters" in a given case might include a social worker, a psychiatrist, a clinical psychologist, a mental health aide, a sheltered workshop supervisor, an occupational therapist, and the director of a group home.

In such "multiple-provider" cases, a task-centered case management structure provides a useful device for monitoring and facilitating coordination among different actors (Bailey-Dempsey, 1993; Reid & Bailey-Dempsey, 1994). In task-centered case management, the social worker functions as a case manager or coordinator. Usually a case management team meeting is used to bring participants together, with the client also present as a participant. In these sessions aspects of the client's problems that involve coordination among participants are discussed and tasks for relevant participants, including the client, are developed. In addition to helping develop tasks, the social worker records the tasks on a sheet. If possible, copies of the sheet are made and distributed to all participants. The social worker may take responsibility for monitoring and recording task progress and for serving as a facilitator and coordinator— e.g., giving reminders. He or she may also conduct a task review at a subsequent meeting of the participants. In addition to carrying a case management role, the practitioner usually works directly with the client system, using individual- or family-oriented task-centered methods, as appropriate.

RANGE OF APPLICATION

A question inevitably asked of any treatment system, in one form or another, is "For what kind of case is, and is not, the system applicable?" In answering this question, it is important to distinguish between use of the system as a whole and use of activities for task planning, implementation, and review. The latter have, of course, a much wider range of application than the former. In fact, sequences of task-centered activities can be used in almost any form of treatment to enable clients to define and carry through particular courses of action. Thus, a practitioner might use task-centered methods during the course of long-term psychosocial treatment to help the client translate into action some aspect of insight into his or her problems.

When the task-centered system is used in full as the sole or primary method of treatment, its range of application, while narrower, is still broad enough to serve as a basic approach for the majority of clients seen by clinical social workers. But the majority is not all. It is possible to identify certain types of clients for whom the model in full may not provide the optimal mode of practice. Such types would include the following: (1) clients who are not interested in taking action to solve specific problems in their life situations, but who rather want help in exploring existential issues, such as concerns about life goals or identity or who wish to talk about stressful experiences, such as loss of a loved one, with an accepting, empathic person; (2) clients who are unwilling or unable to utilize the structure of the model—for example, clients who prefer a more casual, informal mode of helping or clients faced with highly turbulent situations in which it is not possible to isolate and follow through on specific problems; (3) clients who wish to alter conditions, such as certain psychogenic and motor difficulties, for which it is not possible to identify problem-solving tasks that the client is able to carry out; (4) clients who wish no help but may need to be seen for "protective reasons."

Although all these categories merit elaboration, the last in particular requires additional comment because of frequent misunderstandings concerning the use of the model with involuntary clients. The task-centered approach can be used with many persons who may not have sought the social worker's help or who may be initially reluctant to accept it since the social worker, as noted, does have the opportunity to influence the clients' conceptions of their problems. Many of these cases involve "mandated" problems, which are essentially problems that are defined not by the client but by the community and its representatives, including the practitioner. Essentially, the social worker needs to reveal to the client at the onset the general shape of these mandated problems (Rooney, 1992). As Rooney (1992) and Rzepnicki (1985) have suggested, a reasonable next step is work with the client and relevant community agencies in an effort to negotiate problem definitions that are acceptable to those involved. In our experience, such problem definitions can usually be found. In some cases the most honest and viable formulation is that the problem is the practitioner's and agency-imposed presence in the client's life; the client and practitioner can then work collaboratively to accomplish what is needed to eliminate this intrusion.

EFFECTIVENESS OF THE TASK-CENTERED APPROACH

The effectiveness of individual, family, and group forms of the task-centered model in alleviating specific problems of living has been demonstrated in a number of controlled group experiments (Gibbons et al., 1978; Larsen & Mitchell, 1980; New-come, 1985; Reid, 1975, 1978; Reid et al., 1980; Reid & Bailey-Dempsey, 1995). Results from these studies have been supported by the findings of a variety of controlled single-case experiments (Kilgore, 1995; Rzepnicki, 1985; Thibault, 1984; Tolson, 1977; Wodarski, Saffir, & Fraser, 1982). Populations in these studies have included psychiatric patients, distressed marital couples, sick elderly patients, families seeking to regain their children from foster care, schoolchildren with academic and behavioral problems, sexual offenders, and delinquents in a residential center. Other studies in which controls were not used have provided further evidence of the effectiveness of the model with clients from these and other populations. (See, for example, Fortune, 1985; Goldberg, Gibbons, & Sinclair, 1984; Naleppa, 1995; Rauschi, 1994; Reid & Epstein, 1977; Reid, 1994.) In fact, to my knowledge, there has been no study, controlled or otherwise, of the outcomes of the task-centered model that has yielded negative findings.

However, it is important to underscore that problem alleviation is not problem resolution. Frequently the effects of the model may be confined to some reduction in the client's difficulties or to enabling him or her to better cope with them. Moreover, there are still many unanswered questions about the effectiveness of the model. Knowledge of the impact of the model beyond immediate target problems is still quite limited. Finally, studies of the durability of the approach have produced mixed results. For example, long-term effects were documented by Gibbons et al. (1978) in their study of self-poisoning clients, but Reid and Bailey-Dempsey (1995) found that gains achieved in the use of the task-centered case management model with middle-school girls at risk of failure did not carry over to the following year. Quite possibly the durability of effects of the model varies with the kind of population or problem to which it is applied. This issue is among the many to be addressed in future research.

CASE ILLUSTRATION

The following case illustrates basic features of the model as well as application to work with families:

> Mrs. Johnson contacted a family agency because of problems concerning her sixteen-year-old daughter, Nancy, and the resulting fighting in her family. In an initial interview with the parents, Nancy and her fourteen-year-old brother, Mark, the family members presented their views of their problems. Mr. J. began the session with a stream of complaints about Nancy. Her "attitude" toward him and his wife was "hostile." She did not accept his beliefs or standards. Any attempt to communicate with her was futile. He then turned to the problem that precipitated their contact with the agency: Nancy's insistence that her boyfriend, Mike (age nineteen), be allowed to visit in their home over the weekend.
>
> Mr. J. had objected to Nancy's relationship with Mike ever since Nancy's pregnancy and abortion about six months previously, but had accepted it because Nancy was determined to see Mike anyway. Mr. J. even tolerated Mike's coming

to their home but did not want him there all weekend (Mike would stay over Friday and Saturday night, using a spare room). Mr. J. saw Mike as an unwelcome intruder whose presence deprived Mr. J. of his privacy.

Joining in, Mrs. J. complained of Nancy's nagging her to get permission to do things her father might not allow. If Mrs. J. refused, Nancy would become belligerent and insulting. On top of this, Mrs. J. would usually be the one to patch things up between Nancy and her father. Nancy said little but expressed bitterness that her parents were trying to disrupt her relationship with Mike. When asked about his views of the problem by the practitioner, Mark commented in a somewhat detached way that the fighting between his mother and Nancy was the main difficulty.

From the family's presentation of the problems and their interactions in the session, the practitioner was impressed with the father's lack of real control and Nancy's efforts to get what she wanted through her mother, who was put in the middle. Further exploration made clearer the mother's "peacekeeping" role and her discontent with it. The practitioner presented this picture as an additional problem to be considered.

In ranking the problems that had been brought up, the family agreed that the issue of greatest priority concerned the conflict over Mike's visiting. They accepted the practitioner's formulation of "mother's being in the middle" as a second problem.

The family was seen for seven additional sessions. The main interventions were structured around problem-solving tasks in the session and at home. These tasks were designed to achieve a compromise around Mike's visiting and, in the process, to work on the dysfunctional interaction patterns that had been identified. Initially, these tasks were designed to bring about more direct communication between Nancy and her father as well as more cooperation between the parents. It became apparent, however, that the interaction pattern was more complex than originally thought. Mrs. J. was not the only peacemaker. Mr. J. frequently assumed this role with Nancy and her mother. The parents were then coming to each other's rescue without taking responsibility either individually or jointly for dealing with Nancy's behavior. In subsequent family problem-solving tasks, each parent agreed to take responsibility for settling his or her differences with Nancy without trying to rescue the other. At the same time, an effort was made to encourage the parents jointly to develop rules that each could apply consistently in dealing with Nancy.

Midway in treatment, a compromise was reached on Nancy's relationship with Mike. Mike could spend one night a week at the J.'s home but would not be there on the weekend. Interestingly enough, the solution was suggested by Mark who had remained somewhat on the sidelines in the family discussions. The plan was implemented and, perhaps to everyone's surprise, held up.

The case ended on a positive note. The immediate problem had been worked through and the family members, in their evaluation of treatment, indicated that their situation as a whole was better. In her consumer questionnaire, Mrs. J. commented that the experience had been a "good lesson in problem working."

The case illustrates several features of the model. Focus was on the specific problem the family wanted most to solve. The major intervention strategy was based on tasks in which family members struggled toward a solution in their own way. At the same time, dysfunctional patterns of intervention that might underlie this and other problems were explicitly identified with the family or worked on as a part of the problem-solving tasks. Not all cases present such opportunities to achieve contextual change within the context of family problem solving. In this case, they were present and were well utilized by the family and practitioner.

SUMMARY

Task-centered treatment is a system of brief, time-limited practice that emphasizes helping clients with specific problems of their own choosing through discrete client and practitioner actions or tasks. Service interviews are devoted largely to the specification of problems, and to the identification and planning of appropriate tasks, which are then carried out between sessions. Although there are limits on its range of application, it is offered as a basic service for the majority of clients dealt with by clinical social workers. The core methods of the approach, notably activities designed to help clients plan and implement problem-solving tasks, can be used within most practice frameworks.

REFERENCES

Abramson, J. (1992). Health-related problems. In W.J. Reid (Ed.), *Task strategies: An empirical approach to social work practice.* New York: Columbia University Press. 1992 (225–249)

Bailey-Dempsey, C. (1993). A test of a task-centered case management approach to resolve school failure. Doctoral dissertation, University of New York at Albany, 1993.

Bass, M. (1977). Toward a model of treatment for runaway girls in detention. In W.J. Reid & L. Epstein (Eds.), *Task-centered practice.* New York: Columbia University Press.

Beck, D.F., & Jones, M.A. (1973). *Progress on family problems: A nationwide study of clients' and counselors' views on family agency services.* New York: Family Service Agency of America.

Beilenberg, L.T. (1991). A task-centered preventive group approach to create cohesion in the new stepfamily. *Research on Social Work Practice, 1,* 416–433.

Benbenishty, R. (1988). Assessment of task-centered interventions with families in Israel. *Journal of Social Service Research, 11,* 19–43.

Birchler, G.R., & Spinks, S.H. (1981). Behavioral-systems marital and family therapy: Integration and clinical application. *American Journal of Family Therapy, 8,* 6–28.

Brown, L.B. (1980). Client problem solving learning in task-centered social treatment. Dissertation, University of Chicago.

Caspi, J. (1995). Task-centered model for social work field instruction. Doctoral dissertation proposal, University of New York at Albany, 1995.

Cormican, E.J. (1977). Task-centered model for work with the aged. *Social Casework, 58,* 490–494.

Dierking, B., Brown, M., & Fortune, A.E. (1980). Task-centered treatment in a residential facility for the elderly: A clinical trial. *Journal of Gerontological Social Work, 2,* 225–240.

Doel, M., & Marsh, P. (1993). *Task-centered social work.* London: Wildwood House.

Epstein, L. (1977). A project in school social work. In W.J. Reid & L. Epstein (Eds.), *Task-centered practice.* New York: Columbia University Press.

Epstein, L. (1980). *Helping people: The task-centered approach.* St. Louis: C. V. Mosby Co.

Epstein, L. (1988). *Helping people: The task centered approach.* Columbus, OH: Merrill Publishing Company.

Epstein, L. (1992). *Brief treatment and a new look at the task-centered approach* (3rd ed.). New York: Macmillan.

Ewalt, P.L. (1977). A psychoanalytically oriented child guidance setting. In W.J. Reid & L. Epstein (Eds.), *Task-centered practice.* New York: Columbia University Press.

Fortune, A.E. (1985). *Task-centered practice with families and groups.* New York: Springer.

Garfield, S.L. (1994). Research on client variables in psychotherapy. In A.E. Bergin & S.L. Garfield (Eds.), *Handbook of psychotherapy and behavior change* (4th ed.) (pp. 190–228). New York: Wiley.

Garvin, C.D. (1974). Task-centered group work. *Social Service Review, 48,* 494–507.

Garvin, C.D. (1985). Practice with task-centered groups. In A.E. Fortune (Ed.), *Task-centered practice with families and groups.* New York: Springer.

Gibbons, J.S., Butler, J., Urwin, P., & Gibbons, J.L. (1978). Evaluation of a social work service for self-poisoning parents. *British Journal of Psychiatry, 133,* 111–118.

Goldberg, E.M., Gibbons, J., & Sinclair, I. (1984). *Problems, tasks and outcomes.* Winchester, MA: Allen and Unwin.

Goldman, A.I. (1970). *A theory of human action.* Englewood Cliffs, NJ: Prentice-Hall.

Gurman, A.S., & Kniskern, D. (1981). Family therapy outcome research: Knowns and unknowns. In A.S. Gurman & D.P. Kniskern (Eds.), *Handbook of family therapy.* New York: Brunner/Mazel.

Hari, V. (1977). Instituting short-term casework in a "long-term" agency. In W.J. Reid & L. Epstein (Eds.), *Task-centered practice.* New York: Columbia University Press.

Hofstad, M.O. (1977). Treatment in a juvenile court setting. In W.J. Reid & L. Epstein (Eds.), *Task-centered practice.* New York: Columbia University Press.

Jacobson, N.S., & Margolin, G. (1979). *Marital therapy: Strategies based on social learning and behavior exchange principles.* New York: Brunner/Mazel.

Johnson, D.H., & Gelso, C.J. (1982). The effectiveness of time limits in counseling and psychotherapy: A critical review. *Counseling Psychologist, 9,* 70–83.

Kilgore, D. K. (1995). Task-centered group treatment of sex offenders. Doctoral dissertation, University of New York at Albany.

Koss, M., Butcher, J.N. (1986). Research on brief psychotherapy. In S.L. Garfield and A.E. Bergin (Eds.), *Handbook of psychotherapy and behavior change.* New York: John Wiley & Sons.

Larsen, J., & Mitchell, C. (1980). Task-centered strength oriented group work with delinquents. *Social Casework, 61,* 154–163.

Luborsky, L., Singer, S., & Luborsky, L. (1975). Comparative studies of psychotherapy. *Archives of General Psychiatry, 32,* 995–1008.

Meltzoff, J., & Kornreich, M. (1970). *Research in psychotherapy.* New York: Atherton Press.

Mitchell, K.M., Bozarth, J.D., & Krauft, C.C. (1977). A reappraisal of the therapeutic effectiveness of accurate empathy, nonpossessive warmth and genuineness. In A.S. Gurman & A.M. Razin (Eds.), *Effective psychotherapy: A handbook of research.* New York: Pergamon Press.

Naleppa, M. (1995). Task-centered case management for community living elderly. Doctoral dissertation proposal, University of New York at Albany.

Newcome, K. (1985). Task-centered group work with the chronic mentally ill in day treatment. In A.E. Fortune (Ed.), *Task-centered practice with families and groups.* New York: Springer.

Orlinsky, D.E., & Howard, K.I. (1986). Process outcome in psychotherapy. In S.L. Garfield & A.E. Bergin (Eds.), *Handbook of psychotherapy and behavior change.* New York: John Wiley and Sons.

Osborn, A.F. (1963). *Applied imagination: Principles and procedures of creative problem solving* (3rd ed.). New York: Scribner's.

Parihar, B. (1983). *Task-centered management in human services.* Springfield, IL: Charles C Thomas.

Parihar, B. (1994). Task-centered work in human service organizations. In E.R. Tolson, W.J. Reid, & C.D. Garvin (Eds.), *Generalist practice: A task-centered approach.* New York: Columbia University Press.

Perlman, H.H. (1957). *Social casework: A problem-solving process.* Chicago: University of Chicago Press.

Pomeroy, E., Rubin, A., & R. Walker (1995). Effectiveness of a psychoeducational and task-centered group intervention for family members of people with AIDS. *Social Work Research, 19,* 142–152.

Ramakrishnan, K.R., Balgopal, P.R., & Pettys, G.L. (1994). Task-centered work with communities. In E.R. Tolson, W.J. Reid, & C.D. Garvin (Eds.), *Generalist practice: A task-centered approach.* New York: Columbia University Press.

Rathbone-McCuan, E. (1985). Intergenerational family practice with older families. In A.E. Fortune (Ed.), *Task-centered practice with families and groups.* New York: Springer.

Raushi, T.M. (1994). Task-centered model for group work with single mothers in the college setting. Doctoral dissertation, University of New York at Albany.

Reid, W.J. (1975). A test of a task-centered approach. *Social Work, 20,* 3–9.

Reid, W.J. (1978). *The task-centered system.* New York: Columbia University Press.

Reid, W.J. (1985). *Family problem solving.* New York: Columbia University Press.

Reid, W.J. (1987). The family problem solving sequence. *American Journal of Family Therapy, 14,* 135–146.

Reid, W.J. (1992). *Task strategies: An empirical approach to social work practice.* New York: Columbia University Press.

Reid, W.J. (1994). Field testing and evaluating innovative practice interventions: The development process. In J. Rothman & E.J. Thomas (Eds.), *Integrative perspective on intervention research.* New York: Haworth Press.

Reid, W.J., & Bailey-Dempsey, C. (1994). Content analysis in developmental research. *Journal of Research on Social Work Practice, 4,* 101–112.

Reid, W.J., & Donovan, T. (1990). Treating sibling violence. *Family Therapy, 71,* 49–59.

Reid, W.J. & Epstein, L. (1972). *Task-centered casework.* New York: Columbia University Press.

Reid, W.JH., & Epstein, L. (Eds.) (1977). *Task-centered practice.* New York: Columbia University Press.

Reid, W.J., Epstein, L., Brown, L.B., Tolson, E., & Rooney, R.H. (1980). Task-centered school social work. *Social Work in Education, 2,* 7–24.

Reid, W.J., & Shyne, A. (1969). *Brief and extended casework.* New York: Columbia University Press.

Rooney, R.H. (1977). Adolescent groups in public schools. In W.J. Reid & L. Epstein (Eds.), *Task-centered practice.* New York: Columbia University Press.

Rooney, R.H. (1981). Task centered reunification model for foster care. In A.A. Malluccio & P. Sinanoglue (Eds.), *Working with biological parents of children in foster care.* New York: Child Welfare League of America.

Rooney, R.H. (1988). Measuring task-centered training effects on practice: Results of an audiotape study in a public agency. *Journal of Continuing Social Work Education, 4,* 2–7.

Rooney, R.H. (1992). *Strategies for Work with Involuntary Clients.* New York: Columbia University Press.

Rooney, R.H., & Wanless, M. (1985). A model for caseload management based on task-centered casework. In A E. Fortune (Ed.), *Task-centered practice with families and groups.* New York: Springer.

Rzepnicki, T.L. (1985). Centered intervention in foster care services: Working with families who have children in placement. In A.E. Fortune (Ed.), *Task-centered practice with families and groups.* New York: Springer.

Salmon, W. (1977). A service program in a state public welfare agency. In W.J. Reid & L. Epstein (Eds.), *Task-centered practice.* New York: Columbia University Press.

Strupp, H.H., Fox, R.E., & Lessler, K. (1969). *Patients view their psychotherapy.* Baltimore: Johns Hopkins Press.

Studt, E. (1968). Social work theory and implication for the practice of methods, *Social Work Education Reporter, 16,* 22–46.

Taylor, C. (1977). Counseling in a service industry. In W.J. Reid & L. Epstein (Eds.), *Task-centered practice.* New York: Columbia University Press.

Thibault, J.M. (1984). The analysis and treatment of indirect self-destructive behaviors of elderly patients. Dissertation, University of Chicago.

Tolson, E. (1977). Alleviating marital communication problems. In W.J. Reid & L. Epstein (Eds.), *Task-centered practice.* New York: Columbia University Press.

Tolson, E.R., Reid, W.J., & Garvin, C.D. (1994). *Generalist practice: A task-centered approach.* New York: Columbia University Press.

Weissman, A. (1977). In the steel industry. In W.J. Reid & L. Epstein (Eds.), *Task-centered practice.* New York: Columbia University Press.

Wexler, P. (1977). A case from a medical setting. In W.J. Reid & L. Epstein (Eds.), *Task-centered practice.* New York: Columbia University Press.

Wise, F. (1977). Conjoint marital treatment. In W.J. Reid & L. Epstein (Eds.), *Task-centered practice.* New York: Columbia University Press.

Wodarski, J.S., Saffir, M., & Frazer, M. (1982). Using research to evaluate the effectiveness of task-centered casework. *Journal of Applied Social Sciences, 7,* 70–82.

CHAPTER 27

TRANSACTIONAL ANALYSIS THEORY AND SOCIAL WORK TREATMENT

MARLENE COOPER AND SANDRA TURNER

Based on the belief that people can and should take responsibility for their own destinies, and that given the proper support, encouragement, and guidance, they can lead full and productive lives, Transactional Analysis is an optimistic treatment approach that is ideally suited to the social work profession. It is also a theory of personality development that provides a unique perspective for exploring interpersonal interaction. Because of its flexibility, Transactional Analysis has been utilized in a multitude of settings, including hospitals, prisons, schools, institutions, and workplaces. As a theory of personality and a treatment approach, it can be employed in understanding and describing psychodynamic systems as well as interpersonal dynamics. It is effectively applied in individual, conjoint, family, and group interventions.

Transitional Analysis was founded by Eric Berne, M.D., in the 1950s. Berne lived from 1910 to 1970, and was trained as a physician in the early 1950s when psychoanalysis was the primary method of treating emotional problems. His teachers, who influenced much of his early work, were Eugene Kahn and Paul Federn, students of Sigmund Freud. Berne was also greatly influenced by Carl Jung, Wilhelm Reich, Charles Darwin, and Erik Erikson. Transactional Analysis has been linked with Adlerian therapy.

Early in his medical training, Berne became interested in the relationship between the mind and the body, and particularly in human intuition. He turned to psychoanalysis, and Erik Erikson, who had a profound effect on his work, was his analyst. Berne departed from Freud in his conceptualization of the structure of personality. In Freudian theory, the ego, id, and superego are hypothetical constructs, whereas Berne's comparable ego states (parent, adult, and child) are observable phenomena

[Berne, 1961]). Berne did not discount the power of the unconscious, but he was more interested in actual happenings in his clients' lives—events that could be recalled—than in unconscious processes. He conceived of the unconscious as memories of feelings and experiences that were accessible to conscious thought (Dusay, 1972). This was his second major departure from Freudian theory.

In 1958 Berne started the San Francisco Social Psychiatry Seminars, a nonprofit educational corporation. Initially, it was comprised of a small group of mental health professionals and students who discussed various approaches to psychotherapy, including Berne's theory of Transactional Analysis, which he was developing at that time. These seminars grew in size and scope, were granted a charter, and eventually their name was changed to the Eric Berne Seminars of San Francisco in honor of their founder. Since its inception, Transactional Analysis has been multicultural, and the International Transactional Analysis Association was founded in 1965. This organization has an international standing with more than six thousand members, a third of whom are social workers. Transactional Analysis is very popular in Eastern Europe and Southeast Asia. It is the official national therapy of India, and it is also very highly regarded in Japan.

There is a formal system of training and certification and it is recommended that those who wish to practice Transactional Analysis become certified. To be certified, a candidate must participate in a two-year program, facilitate a Transactional Analysis group for one year, pass a written examination, and present three hours of clinical work to an oral review board.

THEORETICAL FOUNDATION

Transactional Analysis, as conceived of by Berne, is a personality theory which later was expanded into a system of social intervention or psychotherapy. The basic assumption of Transactional Analysis is that the personality is made up of three ego states: parent, adult, and child. Berne conceptualized the ego as divided in this way after observing that his patients had a part of them that was childlike as well as adult. He believed that he could actually speak directly to the different parts of the ego, and that patients could reexperience the feelings that they had as children in the present as well as recall the events that triggered those feelings.

Another theoretical aspect of Transactional Analysis is what Berne called social intercourse. This occurs between people, usually in the form of "strokes." Strokes can be in the form of physical or verbal contacts and imply recognition of another's presence. An exchange of strokes constitutes a transaction, which is the unit of social intercourse.

According to Berne, social intercourse is laden with games. Games are so significant that Berne, in 1964, devoted a whole book to them: his best-selling *Games People Play*. Some games are positive and some negative. But even with all of the difficulties that games present, any kind of social intercourse is better than none. Studies done on rats showed that both gentle touching and painful electric shocks were equally effective in promoting health (Levine, 1957). More will be said about strokes and games later.

THE THREE BASIC ASSUMPTIONS

There are three overarching assumptions in Transactional Analysis:

1. "I'm OK, you're OK." The basic premise of Transactional Analysis is that people are born OK, or in a state of health. It is the parental environment that either fosters health and growth, or interferes with development.
2. People are capable of being active participants in the problem-solving process and therapists should enlist their clients as active partners in the work.
3. Transactional Analysis assumes that people are basically good and capable of leading healthy and satisfying lives that do not intrude upon the lives of others. The goal of the therapy is to produce a "cure." When problems seem incurable, it is attributed to a lack of knowledge or inability to find a solution.

In sum, Transactional Analysis assumes that people can and should take responsibility for their own destinies (life scripts), and that given the proper support and guidance (positive strokes), they can lead full and productive lives (change negative life scripts into positive life scripts).

THE FOUR LIFE POSITIONS

Transactional Analysis holds that there are four possible life positions that one takes about oneself and others. These are thoroughly described by Harris (1967) in his seminal work on the subject: *I'm OK—You're OK.* These positions are:

a. I'M NOT OK—YOU'RE OK
b. I'M NOT OK—YOU'RE NOT OK
c. I'M OK—YOU'RE NOT OK
d. I'M OK—YOU'RE OK.

The first three of these positions are unconscious decisions that were made early in life. I'M NOT OK—YOU'RE OK is the first decision that is made. The growing child is at the mercy of his caregivers. When children are nurtured, or "stroked," they develop a healthy sense of self-esteem and feelings of well-being. If stroking does not occur, or occurs inconsistently, feelings of NOT OK accumulate.

In adulthood, NOT OK persons evidence difficulties in interpersonal relationships. These manifestations of not being OK occur at both ends of the mental health continuum At one end, one sees adults who still feel hopeful that strokes might be forthcoming, even if they are not constant. However, they may be constantly seeking approval in order to gain these strokes. And ultimately, they may conclude that no matter what they do, they are still NOT OK. They may live out this position through a "life script" that confirms that they are NOT OK by withdrawing from intimacy, as contact with others is painful, or by seeking strokes through fantasy, which becomes more pleasurable than reality. Another person's "script" may be to seek "negative stroking" through provocative behavior. The ultimate resolution of this NOT OK position is to give up entirely. One sees this at the end of the mental health continuum that veers toward psychopathology, in the extreme regression found in severe mental illness or in the desperate act of the suicidal patient.

In the second position, I'M NOT OK—YOU'RE NOT OK, the person decides that if I AM NOT OK, then NEITHER ARE YOU. If strokes do not come, difficulties with interpersonal relationships develop. The conclusion is that not only is there something wrong with the person, the me, but there is also something wrong with the other, or you. These adults have problems with intimacy, with accepting and giving love, sharing, and ultimately, with feeling joy. A hopeless view of life prevails, or severe mental disturbances emerge where one behaves in regressive ways in order to receive the strokes that were lacking in childhood.

I'M OK—YOU'RE NOT OK

These adults were victims of childhood abuse. They have survived the brutality of parents by self-stroking: they learned to give comfort to themselves. As adults, these OK selves may be unable to take responsibility for their own actions. They may believe that others are always be at fault. One sees adults in this position who project blame onto others, seemingly incapable of self-awareness. Or, criminal behavior results from antisocial personalities who have no conscience. The ultimate expression of the I'M OK—YOU'RE NOT OK position is homicide.

I'M OK—YOU'RE OK

This is the fourth position. It is a conscious and verbal decision, based on thought, reflection, and action, and not on feelings. People become OK by exposing the childhood feelings underlying the first three positions, by examining the behavior that perpetuates the positions, and by making conscious decisions to change.

KEY CONCEPTS

The following key concepts form the basis of Transactional Analysis theory.

EGO STATES

Berne conceived of an ego state as a "system of feelings accompanied by a related set of behavior patterns" (Berne, 1968, p. 23). The personality is made up of three ego states—the parent, the adult, and the child. The parent ego state is similar to the superego in analytic theory. It is a strict code of rules and prescriptions about how one should live. These prescriptions are mostly critical and do in fact come from parents or parental figures. Messages such as "you're not working hard enough," "you're not doing your best," "try harder to please others," and the like are examples of critical messages that become incorporated into the parental ego state (Berne, 1964).

The adult ego state is most similar to the Freudian ego in psychoanalytic terms and is that part of the personality that is oriented to reality. It is logical, rational, and has been linked to a computer in that it takes in, stores, and processes information about oneself and the environment. Practitioners of Transactional Analysis work with the adult ego state in patients more often than with the child or parent ego state. Berne (1968) believed that everyone has an adult ego state that is more or less accessible, but sometimes needs help in activating it.

The child ego state resembles the id, in psychoanalytic terms, and a person acting from this ego state actually behaves and sounds like a child, regardless of how old the person may be. This state contains natural feelings, behaviors, sensations, and desires which may have been present since birth. It includes the physical anatomy as well. The child ego state is in many ways the most valuable and desirable part of the personality. It is the source of pleasure, freedom, and creativity. It has been described as the center of social being (Coburn, 1986). The child either functions naturally and freely or is ruled by negative parental directives. These directives interfere with the "pure" child ego state and can cause confusion and bad feelings about oneself (Coburn, 1987).

The optimal way of functioning is to be able to access the appropriate ego state at any time. For example, if the situation calls for spontaneity and fun, then the child ego state would be the most appropriate, but if important decisions need to be made and acted upon, then the adult ego state would be the most effective one to access. The three ego states are symbolized by three distinct circles, which represent the parent, adult, and child (see Figure 27–1). One can determine which ego state is currently activated by observing behavior and reactions elicited by the behavior. For example, a woman who always raises her hand to speak is in a child ego state; a man who uses expressions that his mother always used (particularly if they are negative) is most likely in a parent ego state (Berne, 1968).

INTERPERSONAL TRANSACTIONS

According to Berne (1961), transaction is a social intercourse that occurs between two persons' ego states. Transactions occur both on a social level, which is overt, and on a psychological level, which is covert. There are actually transactions taking place on six different levels at any given time because each person has three different ego states that may interact with the three ego states of another. A parent ego state may be relating to another parent state or to a child or adult state at any given time. An example

FIGURE 27–1. EGO STATES

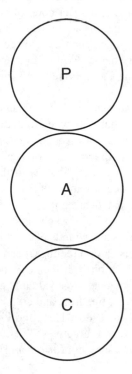

of an adult-to-adult ego state communication is two people solving a problem together; parent-to-child communication is one person "scolding" another.

STROKES

This is a core concept in Transactional Analysis. Human beings have an ongoing need for social approval or "strokes." A stroke is a general term describing intimate physical contact and in social and Transactional Analysis terms it implies the act of recognizing another's presence (Berne, 1968). Telling someone that he or she is a special person and is valued (basically that he or she is "OK") is an example of a positive stroke which people need throughout their lives. Transactional Analysis therapists are trained to give positive strokes right from the very beginning when a client calls for help by supporting their decision to come in. Other nonverbal strokes convey an attitude and atmosphere of acceptance, warmth and, optimism about change (Coburn, 1986).

Scripts

A script is a life plan or existential "road map" that one makes early in life. Generally, by the age of five, children have made up their scripts which say that they are either basically OK and in the mainstream or not OK and on the fringes of social and emotional life (Finnegan, 1990). Transactional Analysis practitioners believe that negative scripts can be converted to positive ones, since everyone is capable of being or becoming OK.

Rackets

These are chronic bad feelings that are left over from childhood. Like games, they are removed from our awareness. Rackets provided a way to gain recognition when the expression of real feelings was unacceptable. Examples of rackets include anger, depression, anxiety, and confusion. Rackets support scripts and have three components: script beliefs and feelings, racket displays, and reinforcing memories. An intervention that stops the script and leads to new alternatives for thinking and feeling will stop the functioning of the racket system. For example, a shy, retiring woman with a Don't Be Important script keeps the script active by her nonassertive behavior. Confronting the behavior and analyzing her intent and its outcome can lead to change. She may try friendly, outgoing behavior that brings positive strokes from others and allows her to let go of the script. Analyzing games, rackets, and scripts can lead to awareness of bad feelings (Coburn, 1986).

Games

Berne defines a game as:

> . . . an ongoing series of complementary ulterior transactions progressing to a well-defined, predictable outcome. Descriptively it is a recurring set of transactions often repetitive, superficially plausible, with a concealed motivation, or more colloquially, a series of moves with a snare, or gimmick. (1964, p. 48)

Harris (1967) believes that games originate in the childhood game of "mine is better than yours." This game is played to bring relief from the position that the child feels, being small and helpless and viewing the parent as large and powerful, that I'M NOT OK—YOU'RE OK. The aim is to bring relief to this unjust situation by countermeasures such as beating up little brother, kicking the cat, finding someone who has more toys. Grown-ups indulge in adult versions of his game by accumulating possessions or getting "one-up" on their neighbors.

Berne has given some amusing names to his games. "Kick me," "now I've got you, you S.O.B.," "try and catch me," and "so's your old man" are some of them. All games ultimately produce misery, but they are preferable to having no relationship at all. At least in misery, the relationship is preserved. Harris (1967, pp. 148–149) illustrates the nature of games through the following vignette with Jane, a young career woman, and her friend, as players of the game called "why don't you, yes but."

JANE: I am so plain and dull that I never have any dates.
FRIEND: Why don't you go to a good beauty salon and get a different hairdo?
JANE: Yes, but that costs too much money.
FRIEND: Well, how about buying a magazine with some suggestions for different ways of setting it yourself?
JANE: Yes, but I tried that—and my hair is too fine. It doesn't hold a set. If I wear it in a bun, it at least looks neat.
FRIEND: How about using makeup to dramatize your features, then?
JANE: Yes, but my skin is allergic to makeup. I tried it once and my skin got rough and broke out.
FRIEND: They have lots of good new nonallergenic makeups now. Why don't you go see a dermatologist?
JANE: Yes, but I know what he'll say. He'll say that I don't eat right. I know I eat too much junk and don't have well-balanced meals. That's the way it is when you live by yourself. Oh, well, beauty is only skin deep.
FRIEND: Well, that's true. Maybe it would help if you took some adult education courses, like in art or current events. It helps make you a good conversationalist, you know.
JANE: Yes, but they're all at night. And after work I'm so exhausted.
FRIEND: Well, take some correspondence courses, then.
JANE: Yes, but I don't even have time to write letters to my folks. How could I ever find time for correspondence courses?
FRIEND: You could find time if it were important enough.
JANE: Yes, but that's easy for you to say. You have so much energy, I'm always dead.
FRIEND. Why don't you go to bed at night? No wonder you're tired when you sit up and watch TV every night.
JANE: Yes, but I've got to do something fun. That's all there is to do when you're like me.

Jane's efforts to defeat her friend underline her NOT OK position and prove that there indeed is no hope for her. The benefit to Jane is that if she continues to play the game, she does not have to change, because nothing can be done. Harris points out that a variant of this game is often played between clients and helping professionals. By frustrating the therapist, the client maintains the status quo.

The concept of games is best understood in terms of the graphic symbols that Berne and others developed to represent some of the basic Transactional Analysis views (circles represent the ego states, and arrows show the communication between them). Since transactions between two persons' ego states take place on an overt level (social) and a covert level (psychological), a game occurs when there is communication on both of these levels at the same time. Generally, these ulterior interactions, which can be considered games, are negative and the people involved have bad feelings about the communication. (See Figure 27–2.)

EGOGRAMS

An egogram is a bar graph that represents the amount of energy placed in each ego state. The difference between this and the three circles, which show which of the three ego states are involved, is that the egogram demonstrates how much energy is invested in the different ego states at any given time. The higher the column on the egogram, the greater the amount of energy that is expended in an ego state. The ego states are related to each other so that when more energy is going into one state, another ego state will lose energy.

Dusay (1972), who developed the egogram, conceptualized five functional ego states. The P (parent) is divided into the CP (critical parent) and NP (nurturing parent). The (A) adult is not divided; and the C (child) is divided into the FC (free child) and the AC (adapted child). A person who is feeling depressed or suicidal will have an egogram that is very high in the columns of critical parent (CP), adult (A), and adapted child (AC), and low in nurturing parent (NP) and free child (FC) columns Because each person's personality is unique, these five psychological forces are aligned differently in each individual.

FIGURE 27–2. ULTERIOR TRANSACTIONS

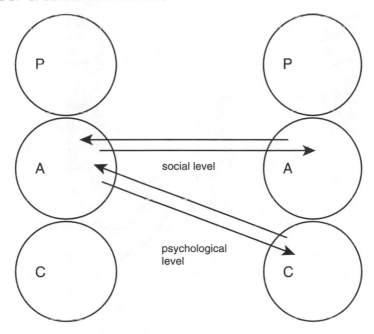

FIGURE 27–3. EGOGRAMS

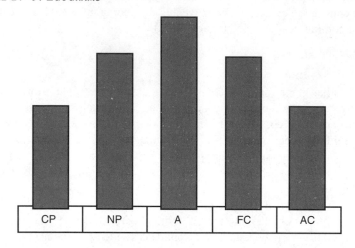

"Bell-Shaped" Egogram

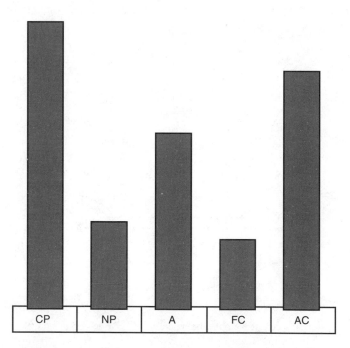

"Depressed or suicidal" egogram (DUSAY AND DUSAY, 1989, p. 410)

ANALYZING A TRANSACTION

A transaction is made up of a stimulus and a response. The stimulus is sent from one person's ego state to that of another. If the response to the stimulus comes from the expected ego state, it is called a *complementary transaction.* A *crossed transaction* occurs when the response comes from an unexpected ego state. Then the communication stops and can only be resumed if one or both persons makes a change in ego states. An *ulterior transaction* is when messages are sent at both a psychological and social level. The psychological level is hidden, and the communication rule is that the response given will be to the underlying psychological message (Berne, 1972).

Harris (1967) presents the following examples of these three different levels of transactions. A complimentary transaction between a Parent and Child might take the following form: The husband (Child) is sick with a fever and wants his wife's attention. The wife (Parent) knows he is ill and is willing to take care of him. This can be satisfactory indefinitely as long as she is willing to mother him. Many happy marriages occur between Parent and Child as long as neither party wishes to change roles. If the roles are disturbed, the parallel relationship is shaken, and trouble begins (p. 102).

Berne's classic example of a crossed transaction, cited by Harris (p. 106), occurs between husband and wife. The husband asks: "Dear, where are my cuff links?" (An adult stimulus, seeking information.) A complementary response by the wife would be, "In your top left dresser drawer," or "I don't know but I'll help you find them." However, if Dear has had a rough day and has saved up a quantity of "hurts" and "mads" and she screams, "Where you left them," the result is a crossed transaction. The stimulus was Adult but the wife turned the response over to the Parent. Now the communication has stopped, husband and wife can't talk about cuff links anymore; they first have to discuss why he never puts his things away.

The purpose of Transactional Analysis is to discover which part of each person—Parent, Adult, or Child—is originating each stimulus and response. Clues can be found in verbal expressions and body language. Harris discusses the clues that help patients analyze these transactions. Some Parent clues that are physical include typical Parent gestures such as a furrowed brow or pursed lip. Verbal examples are "I'll never let you do such and such again" or "I always have to remind you." Evaluative words help to identify the Parent, as well as shoulds and oughts.

Child clues in the physical sphere include pouting, rolling eyes, shrugging shoulders, and nail biting. Verbal child clues include such phrases as "I don't know," "I wish," "I want."

Adult clues are straightforward; adult words consist of why, what, when, where, how, and how much. "I think," "I see," "It is my opinion" indicate that the Adult is processing the data.

Social situations provide examples of each type of transaction. The role of the Transactional Analysis trainer is to build the strength of the Adult by helping the patient become aware of the Parent and Child signals and transactions. Aroused feelings are a clue that the Child has been "hooked." With self-awareness, the patient is freed from externalizing the feelings of the "NOT OK CHILD" into actions. Knowledge of the Parent and Child helps the patient to separate these parts of the self from the Adult. One way to do this is by monitoring the internal dialogue. When one feels sad or gloomy, one can ask: "Why is my Parent beating on my Child?" When one can recognize "that is my Parent," or "that is my Child," the act of questioning has shifted to the Adult state.

Transactional Analysis encourages sensitivity to one's own Child, which enables the client to become sensitive to the Child in others. The building blocks that Harris identifies, which enable one to become a strong adult, are: learning to recognize the vulnerable, fearful Child and expressing these feelings; learning to recognize the Parent with its injunctions, fixed positions, and modes of expressing; becoming sensitive to the Child in others—stroking it, protecting it; counting to ten, if necessary, in order to give the Adult time to process the data coming from the computer, and to sort out Parent and Child from reality; and working out a system of values so that decisions can be made within an ethical framework. Finally, Harris tells patients: "When in doubt, leave it out. You can't be attacked for what you didn't say" (Harris, 1967, p. 122).

TIME STRUCTURING

In Transactional Analysis, there are six types of experiences which are inclusive of all transactions. They are withdrawal, rituals, activities, pastimes, games, and intimacy. Withdrawals, although not a transaction with others, can take place within a social setting. One can withdraw into fantasy during a boring conversation. Rituals are socially programmed uses of time where everyone agrees to do the same thing. Rituals provide safety and predictability. There are religious rituals as well as cocktail party rituals. As with withdrawal, rituals can separate people, as they keep others at a social distance.

Activities, as defined by Berne, are a "common, convenient, comfortable, and utilitarian method of structuring time by a project designed to deal with the material of external reality" (1961, p. 85). Common activities are reading, housekeeping, work. These activities can be satisfying in and of themselves, or lead to satisfaction in the nature of strokes received for a job well done. Pastimes are defined as "an engagement in which the transactions are straightforward" . . . "they may be indulged in for their own sake, and bring enjoyment" (p. 98). With neurotics, they may be a way of "passing" or structuring time. Waiting until one gets to know people better, waiting until vacation comes, and waiting until there is a cure are considered neurotic pastimes. Some amusing names that Berne has given to pastimes include: "small talk," "general motors" (comparing cars), "Do you know (so and so)?" "How much (does it cost)?" "What became of (good old Joe)?" and "martini?" (I know a better way). Pastimes produce strokes, but help us to avoid intimacy.

Games help us to structure time with some strokes, but, like pastimes, also avoid intimacy. Those whose NOT OK position makes relatedness impossible derive something out of games, which is better than the isolation that comes with no contact at all.

Intimacy between two people exists independent of the first five ways of time structuring. It is based on mutual acceptance in each party of the I'M OK—YOU'RE OK position. It is predicated on giving and sharing in a relationship in which the Adult in both persons is in control and allows for spontaneity of the natural Child. Intimacy provides warmth, security, and unconditional strokes.

BUILDING THE THERAPEUTIC RELATIONSHIP

The work of Transactional Analysis is to develop autonomous functioning in clients. The treatment model is short-term, and dependence on the therapist is not encouraged.

The concepts of Transactional Analysis are explained to the client, presented in pictures of circles, bar graphs, and arrows. This is done to further an understanding of the therapist's point of view and method of working. It serves to demystify the therapy and to build a partnership or collaboration between the client and worker.

Transactional Analysis focuses on accomplishing change which is defined by the treatment contract. The contract should be an Adult-to-Adult interaction and an agreement between the client and the therapist about the goals and methods of treatment. Contracts contain explicit goals for new behavior such as "I'm going to spend more time with my daughter," "I'm going to run three miles a week," "I'm going to send out a résumé for a new job." The contract should be flexible and able to be renegotiated at any time.

Transactional Analysis believes in a partnership between patient and therapist. This assumption is akin to the social work principle of working with the client rather than working on the client, and "starting where the client is" (Shulman, 1992). The collaborative nature of the therapeutic relationship makes the process of change an empowering one, wherein clients pull from their own inner resources to activate their potential for leading better lives.

The Transactional Analysis therapist helps to create an atmosphere that is nurturing of the client's Child ego state by helping the client to be as comfortable as possible: the setting is informal.

A TREATMENT APPROACH FOR A VARIETY OF POPULATIONS

Transactional Analysis, with its ability to raise self-esteem and improve interpersonal communication, achievement, and mental health in general, is applicable to a wide range of populations and helpful to clients at all stages of the life cycle. While we don't have data on the universality of this treatment approach, one could speculate that, because of its very humanistic base, the application of Transactional Analysis cuts across cultures and ethnicities. Following are some examples of Transactional Analysis with different populations.

Children

Children have been helped to improve coping behaviors and increase self-awareness (Pardeck & Pardeck, 1981).

The Elderly

Using Transactional Analysis techniques in short-term cognitive group therapy, Mills (1986) helped elderly patients to gain more life satisfaction and to *decrease anxiety and depression levels.*

The Medically Ill

Transactional Analysis has been used effectively with the medically ill persons who have been discounted as children and consequently have given up childlike qualities of curiosity and creativity. They benefit greatly from permission to be, to think, and to feel. These capacities are then practiced within the therapeutic context (Coburn, 1986). In the treatment of asthma, Transactional Analysis techniques have helped to diminish developmental factors that originally triggered or reinforced the asthmatic symptoms during childhood (Lammers, 1990). Transactional Analysis therapists use warmth, humor, and the offering of positive strokes during the change process. These stroking transactions reinforce client autonomy initially by providing praise for the client's coming for help while acknowledging the difficulties inherent in becoming a client. Smiles, attentive listening, acceptance, understanding, supportive touching are all positive strokes conveyed by the therapist who is always optimistic about the client's ability to change and expresses the caring and nurturing that helps to facilitate the change process (Coburn, 1986).

In building a therapeutic partnership, those who work within a Transactional Analysis framework will minimize transference reactions. The therapist also provides rules to help the client feel secure and protected. Clients are expected to come to sessions mentally alert (free of substances), so that they are ready to think about the work that is taking place. Respect for confidentiality is essential. There is no physical or sexual acting out, and no self-destructive or other-destructive behavior. By his or her own ethical and mature behavior, the therapist provides a model for the client to follow.

Transactional Analysis therapists must be aware not only of the client's script issues, but of their own, just as the clinical practitioner needs to be in touch with issues of transference and countertransference. The therapist assesses the developmental level of the patient's Child ego state as the patient attempts to set up the therapist to conform to his or her script.

Resistance in Transactional Analysis is viewed as an obstacle to progress, and the client is helped to discover what is in the way right from the start. Berne was optimistic that problems could be solved by working together, and that finding the solution was a discovery that should be approached with enthusiasm.

VALUE BASE

Because Transactional Analysis fosters optimism, good feeling, self-determination, and autonomy, it is harmonious with the ethics and values of the social work profession. The caring position taken by the therapist in establishing the treatment relationship is supported in practice. The notion that people deserve to feel better and have the right to make their own decisions about the direction of their lives is what makes Transactional Analysis inherently empowering. The emphasis on resilience and what is "right" about a person was a radical departure from the psychoanalytic model that was dominant in the 1950s, which focused on pathology. The strength perspective inherent in Transactional Analysis is at the very heart of social work practice.

REDECISION THERAPY

Goulding (1989, 1990) used the basic tenets of Transactional Analysis to develop his concept of redecision therapy. This method is a refinement of Berne's original concept of making a cognitive decision to change one's life script. Berne believed that the life scripts that were written in childhood could be changed in adult life. Goulding's redecision work is a brief therapy that concentrates on the Child ego state as well as the Adult ego state. People are helped by the therapist to regress to the original decisions that they made as children. They are then encouraged to make redecisions about their life scripts in their Adult states. Redecision therapy places responsibility on individuals for accepting or rejecting the directives of their parents or parental figures. In redecision therapy, familiar bad feelings, behavior, and attitudes such as guilt, anger, discounting, cruelty, and dependency are bought to awareness by the combined use of Transactional Analysis, Gestalt, and behavioral techniques, discussion, and/or group interaction.

A dramatic example of redecision therapy with a suicidal patient is given by Goulding (1982). The patient, a psychiatrist, who will be called Dr. X., attended a one-month training workshop where he spoke of his suicidal ideation. Goulding asked him if he would refrain from killing himself while in the workshop. The patient then promised the therapist that he would not kill himself that month. The therapist replied that he wasn't interested in promises. "This is not for me; it's for you," he said. Dr. X. replied: "I understand. I will not kill myself this month," a statement that assured the therapist that he was willing to comply.

Goulding asked Dr. X. to fantasize that his mother was sitting in the chair across from him, and to say to her, "I will not kill myself." Dr. X. replied that he had attempted this exercise several times before, but still didn't feel any different. He was still frightened that if things got too bad, he would try again to kill himself, and possibly succeed. Goulding responded: "Will you be that part of you that has not allowed you to kill yourself in the past—the part of you that didn't take quite enough pills, that allowed yourself to be found, that survived after your heart had stopped beating. Will you put the rest of you in the other chair and talk to the rest of you?" Dr. X., in a loud, convincing voice, said: "I will not let you kill me. I want to be alive and stay alive. I will not let you kill me." Goulding asked if he would take the other part. Dr. X. stated: "I hear you and you really want to live, don't you?" Then, crying loudly, he said, from the second chair: "I won't kill you. I won't kill myself." He then sat down in the first chair and said spontaneously, "I am the most powerful part of me, and I will not let anything happen to me that ends in my death." Ten years later, according to Goulding, the man was still alive, and no longer depressed (Goulding, 1982, p. 333).

This vignette illustrates the techniques and premises of redecision therapy. Goulding believes that it is not enough to make a decision from the Adult ego state. It has to be made from the free Child in order for it to be permanent.

PRACTICE APPLICATIONS

Transactional Analysis can be used by social workers in direct practice, education, and administration. In general, all persons concerned with improving communication and social and interpersonal change can profit from its teachings. Settings where Transactional Analysis has been employed include hospitals, prisons, schools, institutions, and workplaces. As a theory of personality and a treatment approach, Transactional Analysis can be helpful in understanding and describing interpersonal dynamics and psychodynamic systems.

Because of its versatility, Transactional Analysis is suited for work with groups, individuals, couples, and families. The following are some examples.

WITH GROUPS

In group, individuals often work on changing certain behaviors in order to obtain what they want. Members contract for specific issues to work on, and often approach the therapist one-on-one within the group setting, while other group members work on scripts and redecisions. Observing others working with the therapist on scripts and redecisions often helps group members to see a similar ability to change.

WITH INDIVIDUALS

In individual therapy, Transactional Analysis helps clients to unleash the spontaneity that may have been stymied by parents in childhood and reclaim personal control and choice. Concepts such as "script analysis" provide a simple method for reframing past experiences (Coburn, 1987). Clients who have been discounted as children receive the positive strokes that they were denied. The treatment relationship promotes client growth by providing a safe, nurturing, supportive experience.

WITH COUPLES

In conjoint therapy, couples experiencing poor communication or destructive behaviors can change the dynamics of their ego states to achieve more personal autonomy and independence. For example, a husband might be acting dependent and childish and the wife taking on the role of a parent. The positions might shift, setting up a cycle of competition for the Child position in the pair. Confrontation of this symbiosis helps to break the deadlock and furthers change in the ego states.

With Families

Within a family context, parents and children trained in Transactional Analysis learn to become aware of and take responsibility for their own feelings, work out decisions, and change current patterns of dysfunction, again with the goal of promoting more autonomy and improving communication. Intimacy is furthered, as well as pleasure.

The Developmentally Disabled

Transactional Analysis has been used with the developmentally disabled to teach problem-solving skills and adult role behavior (Laterza, 1979). Studies have shown that Transactional Analysis instruction enhances self-esteem in learning-disabled students (Golub & Guerriero, 1981).

Employees

Transactional Analysis is well suited to the workplace as it teaches communication skills that can improve the quality of one's work life (Nykodym, Longenecker, Clinton, & Ruud, 1991). It has been widely represented in academic settings, helping students learn to trust themselves, think for themselves, and make their own decisions, as well as improve the interaction between teachers and students (Champney & Schultz, 1983; Burton & Dimbleby, 1988).

Minorities and Other Oppressed People

Transactional Analysis can be an effective change agent to use with people of color and other oppressed populations. It can heighten social consciousness and promote personal freedom, as well as increase self-esteem. Moderate support for improving the self-concept of Afro-American adolescents is demonstrated in the literature by Hlongwane and Basson (1990). Mohawk (1985) describes the benefits of ego state analysis with Native Americans who have been dehumanized by being made to feel like children confronted by a critical parent. Transactional Analysis is applicable to work with women survivors of childhood sexual abuse (Apolinsky & Wilcoxan, 1991) and as a model in treatment of spouse abuse (Steinfeld, 1989).

SIMILARITIES TO OTHER TREATMENT MODELS

COGNITIVE THERAPY

Cognitive therapy, as developed by Beck (1972), incorporates many of the principles of Transactional Analysis. Both therapies emphasize the importance of changing one's self-image. However, cognitive therapy does not use the same colloquial terms or symbolic representations as does Transactional Analysis. Cognitive therapy and Transactional Analysis both have as treatment goals the changing of consciousness so that the client's perceptions and thoughts are more realistic, and best further his or her desires. In Transactional Analysis, a discount is a denial of reality. Games begin with a "discount" of self, others, or a situation. An awareness of this system of unreality helps the patient to move forward in life and obtain desired goals. Awareness of childish fears that interfere with logical thinking is encouraged. While cognitive therapy places more emphasis on helping people get in touch with how they think, and the beliefs and assumptions that underlie their thought processes, Transactional Analysis concentrates more *on* social intercourse.

Both cognitive therapy and Transactional Analysis have as their basis a collaborative mode, with mutual agreement on the goals to be obtained in the change process. One major difference between the therapies is that cognitive therapy is not recommended for use with patients who are thought disordered or delusional. Transactional Analysis is used with all diagnostic categories. Harris (1967) describes using Transactional Analysis in groups comprised of psychotic persons as well as those with stronger reality testing. His groups have witnessed actively hallucinating patients describe the Parent-Child dialogue that the patient perceived as originating outside of herself. Harris claims that the freed-up adults in the group are not disturbed by these overt manifestations of what he calls "transitory mental disturbances," and that they tend to be supportive and stroking.

GESTALT THERAPY

Gestalt therapy (Perls, 1969) is also similar to Transactional Analysis, but Gestalt therapy places less emphasis on cognition and more on experiencing change via the emotions. These emotions are often acted out by using techniques such as the empty chair. With this exercise, the client imagines that a significant person, such as a parent, is seated in the chair, and speaks to the person in the chair as if he or she were actually present. Both treatments include the use of groups and encourage the expression of feelings.

ENCOUNTER GROUPS

Encounter groups have much in common with Transactional Analysis, and both movements originated at about the same time. Both therapies primarily utilize the group model. Marathon workshops are also included in the treatment. Transactional Analysis therapists tend to be more selective in their use of techniques, matching technique to ego state; for example, a technique such as pounding a pillow, frequently used in Gestalt therapy, would not be considered for all ego states in Transactional Analysis.

TREATMENT OF SUBSTANCE ABUSE

The current Recovery Movement owes a huge debt to Transactional Analysis. Much of the "inner child" work (see, for example, Bradshaw, 1988) is based on the notion of freeing the spontaneous child from the restraints of the internalized restrictive parent. In fact, so close to Transactional Analysis is the "inner child" work that a recent popular novel by Wendy Kaminer (1992) debunking the recovery movement satirized Berne by its title: *I'm Dysfunctional, You're Dysfunctional.* In working with all types of clients recovering from addictions, analysis of games people play can bring to awareness the subtleties of their explicit and implicit communication patterns with significant others. By using this method, the worker can help alcoholics and significant others understand their dysfunctional transactional ego states and ulterior games (Gitterman, 1991).

LIMITATIONS OF THE APPROACH

The limitations of Transactional Analysis have not been thoroughly studied. Although Coburn (1986) felt that because of the cognitive aspects of this treatment, patients who are mentally confused, delusional, or who do not have a firm grasp on reality would not benefit, Goulding (1982) believed differently.

The success of the approach in clinical settings seems to hinge on the positive optimistic quality of the client/therapist relationship, which may bring some limitation for certain clients. However, there is no clear evidence yet to support this assumption (Coburn, 1986).

RESEARCH ON TRANSACTIONAL ANALYSIS: OUTCOME STUDIES

Miller and Capuzzi (1984) have reviewed the effectiveness of Transactional Analysis as a method for improving interpersonal communication skills and promoting mental health. Their paper reports that crisis intervention volunteers noted increased service delivery and increased staff involvement after Transactional Analysis training (Brown, 1974). Greater improvements in the attitudes of juvenile delinquents were noted by Jesness (1975). In comparing the effects of encounter group experiences, Transactional Analysis has been beneficial in some cases, but positive effects seem to be related to therapist and client characteristics, rather than to the treatment approach (Lieberman et al., 1973). This is generally true for most models of treatment.

It is in the realm of education that Transactional Analysis studies have demonstrated significant benefits. Amundson (1975), with Sawatsky (1976), found that after instruction of elementary school children in Transactional Analysis, self-esteem increased as did a greater acceptance of others. Transactional Analysis training has been associated with improved achievement, increased school attendance, and behavioral improvement in a group of socially maladjusted high-school students (Erskine & Maisenbacherf, 1975). Both elementary and college students have been found to exhibit an increased internal locus of control after training (the ability to attribute events to one's own effort and ability rather than to outside forces) (Amundson, 1975; Peyton, Morris, & Beale, 1979). Middle-school students showed improved conduct after Transactional Analysis training (Sansaver, 1975). Attendance rates have improved with high-school students, and the frequency of unacceptable behavior has been reduced (Smith, 1981).[1]

Social work clients have said that they were personally satisfied with Transactional Analysis, pointing to gains such as increased self-awareness, improved communication skills, and, in general, overall improvement in well-being. Future research studies could utilize case study research, with single-subject design methodology to better determine the efficacy of Transactional Analysis as a treatment model and to ensure accountability in social work practice.

THE FUTURE OF TRANSACTIONAL ANALYSIS AND SOCIAL WORK PRACTICE

As we move into an era where cost containment dictates our national health policies, it is anticipated that social workers will rely more heavily than ever before on brief treatment models of intervention. Transactional Analysis, with its emphasis on problem-solving strategies, is ideally suited to short-term work. The flexibility of the treatment approach allows for its application to a wide range of client problems and populations, and it can easily be adapted to a variety of social work settings. For these reasons, we foresee a role for Transactional Analysis in social work practice in the future. Currently, the number of transactional analysts who are social workers appears to be relatively small. As interest in different practice areas is often generated in the classroom, we encourage social work schools to include content on Transactional Analysis in their curriculum so that students may learn of its value and applicability in the managed-care atmosphere of the current decade.

REFERENCES

Amundson, N. (1975). Transactional Analysis with elementary school children: A pilot study. *Transactional Analysis Journal, 5,* 250–251.

Amundson, N.L., & Sawatsky, D. (1976). An educational program and Transactional Analysis. *Transactional Analysis Journal 6,* 217–220.

Apolinsky, S., & Wilcoxon, S. (1991). Adult survivors of childhood sexual victimization: A group procedure for women. *Family Therapy, 18*(1), 37–45.

Beck, A. (1972). *Depression: Causes and treatment.* Philadelphia, PA: University of Pennsylvania Press.

[1](For a complete report of outcome studies in transactional analysis, see Cooper & Turner, *Encyclopedia of Social Work,* 1995.)

Berne, E. (1961). *Transactional analysis in psychotherapy.* New York: Grove Press.
Berne, E. (1968). *Games people play.* London, England: Penguin.
Berne, E. (1972). *What do you say after you say hello?* New York: Grove Press.
Bradshaw, J. (1988). *Bradshaw on: The family.* Deerfield Beach, FL: Health Communications.
Brown, M. (1974). Transactional Analysis and community consultation. *Transactional Analysis Journal, 4,* 20–21.
Burton, G., & Dimbleby, R. (1988). *Between ourselves: An introduction to interpersonal communication.* London, England: Edward Arnold, Publisher.
Champney, T.F., & Schultz, F.M. (1983). A reassessment of the efficacy of psychotherapy. Paper presented at the fifty-fifth annual meeting of Midwestern Psychological Association, Chicago, IL, May 5–7.
Coburn, D.C. (1986). Transactional analysis: A social work treatment model. In F.J. Turner (Ed.). *Social work treatment: Interlocking theoretical approaches* (pp. 454–481). New York: Free Press.
Coburn, D.C. (1987). Transactional Analysis. In *Encyclopedia of social work* (18th ed.) (pp. 770–777). Silver Spring, MD: National Association of Social Work.
Cooper, M., & Turner, S. (1995). Transactional Analysis. In *Encyclopedia of social work* (19th ed.). Silver Spring, MD: National Association of Social Work.
Dusay, J. (1972). Egograms and the constancy hypotheses *Transactional Analysis Journal, 2*(3), 37–41.
Dusay, J., & Dusay, K.M. (1989). Transactional Analysis. In R.J. Corsini (Ed.), *Current psychotherapies.* Itasca, IL: Peacock Publishers.
Erskine, R.L., & Maisenbacherf, J. (1975). The effects of a Transactional Analysis class on socially maladjusted high school students. *Transactional Analysis Journal, 5,* 252–254.
Finnegan, W. (1990). Drug dealing in New Haven, part I. *New Yorker,* September, 60–90.
Gitterman, A. (1991). *Handbook of social work practice with vulnerable populations.* New York: Columbia University Press.
Golub, S., & Guerriero, I. (1981). The effects of a Transactional Analysis training program on self-esteem in learning disabled boys. *Transactional Analysis Journal, 2,*(13), 1.
Goulding, M.M. (1990). Getting the important work done fast: Contract plus redecision. In J.K. Zeig & S.G. Gilligan (Eds.), *Brief therapy: Myths, methods and metaphors.* New York: Brunner/Mazel. (pp. 303–317).
Goulding, R.L. (1982). Transactional Analysis/Gestalt, redecision therapy. In G.M. Gazda (Ed.), *Basic approaches to group psychotherapy and group counseling* (pp. 319–351). Springfield, IL: Charles C Thomas.
Goulding, R. (1989). Teaching transactional and redecision therapy. *Journal of Independent Social Work, 3*(4), 71–86.
Harris, T. (1967). *I'm OK—You're OK.* New York: Avon.
Hlongwane, M.M., & Basson, C.J. (1990). Self-concept enhancement of black adolescents using Transactional Analysis in a group context. *School Psychology International, 11*(2), 99–108.
Jesness, C. (1975). Comparative effectiveness of behavior modification and Transactional Analysis program for delinquents. *Journal of Consulting and Clinical Psychology, 43,* 59–79.
Kaminer, W. (1992). *I'm dysfunctional, you're dysfunctional.* New York: Addison-Wesley.
Lammers, W. (1990). From cure to care: Transactional Analysis treatment of adult asthma. *Transactional Analysis Journal, 20*(4), 245–252.
Laterza, P. (1979). An eclectic approach to group work with the mentally retarded. *Social Work with Groups, 2*(3), 235–245.
Lieberman, M., Yalom, I., & Miles, M. (1973). *Encounter groups: First facts.* New York: Basic Books.
Levine, S. (1957). Infantile experience and resistance to physiological stress. *Science, 126,* 405.

Miller, C.A., & Capuzzi, D. (1984). A review of Transactional Analysis outcome studies. *American Mental Health Counselors Association Journal, 6*(1), 30–41.

Mills, R. (1986). *Short term cognitive group therapy with elderly clients: Training manual for mental health professionals* (Vol. 1692) (pp. 132–136). Denver University, Colorado Seminary. Washington, DC: Department of Health and Human Services.

Mohawk, J. (1985). In search of humanistic anthropology. *Dialectical Anthropology, 9*(1–4), 165–169.

National Association of Social Work (1987). *Encyclopedia of social work* (18th ed.) Silver Spring, MD: National Association of Social Work.

Nykodym, W., Longenecker, C., Clinton, O., & Ruud, W.N. (1991). Improving quality of work life with Transactional Analysis as an intervention change strategy. *Applied Psychology: An International Review, 40*(4), 395–404.

Pardeck, J.A., & Pardeck, J.T. (1981). Transactional Analysis as an approach to increased rational behavior and self-awareness in children. *Family Therapy, 8*(2), 113–120.

Perls, F. (1969). *Gestalt therapy verbatim.* New York: Bantam.

Peyton, O., Morris, R., & Beale, A. (1979). Effects of Transactional Analysis on empathy, self-esteem, and locus of control *Transactional Analysis Journal, 9,* 200–203.

Sansaver, H. (1975). Behavior modification paired with Transactional Analysis. *Transactional Analysis Journal, 5,* 137–138.

Shulman, L. (1992). *The skills of helping.* Itasca, IL: Peacock Publishers.

Smith, R. (1981). GEM: A goal setting, experiential, motivational program for high school students. *Transactional Analysis Journal, 11,* 256–259.

Steinfeld, G. (1989). Spouse abuse: An integrative interactional model. *Journal of Family Violence, 4*(1), 1–23.

Turner, F.J. (Ed.) (1986). *Social work treatment: Interlocking theoretical approaches.* New York: Free Press.

CHAPTER 28

TRANSPERSONAL SOCIAL WORK

AU-DEANE S. COWLEY

OVERVIEW

As clinical social work developed out of philanthropy, settlement movements, community service organizations, and charity work, its person-in-environment approach during the early 1900s was influenced by the medical model and psychoanalytic theory. By 1929 social work had started to carve out its special place in the helping professions, and the Milford Conference affirmed that there was a distinctive approach that could be called "generic social casework." In the early 1930s the thrust of social work interventions shifted toward a psychosocial approach with an emphasis on internal as well as environmental factors (Dorfman, 1988). Even as the profession expanded its scope of practice, a split between the diagnostic (clinical) and functional (environmental) approaches developed that lasted for about 25 years. In the late 1950s Perlman's *Social Casework* attempted to heal the rift by positing a problem-solving approach (Dorfman, 1988). Task-centered, client-centered, and other psychological perspectives, in turn, influenced social work practice as it continued to evolve. Currently, a philosophical rift has developed in the profession regarding the role of clinical social work practice. There are those who would restrict social work's rightful domain to working for social justice and serving the disadvantaged (Specht, 1994). Others would expand social work's area of concern to also include people able to pay for the services of a private practitioner. Transpersonal practice would support the latter view.

In the nineties the state of clinical practice can be described as pluralistic. Direct social work practice calls for a broad assessment across multiple systems (Hepworth & Larsen, 1993). However, even as social work practice has become more comprehensive and has moved toward a multidimensional assessment of intrapersonal and environmental systems, one aspect of the client system has too often been ignored and omitted. The neglected aspect is the spiritual dimension. As early as 1967 an article in *Social Casework* by Solomon observed that what was needed by social work

663

practitioners was an increased understanding of the moral and spiritual aspects of our clients. Over the years, the social work literature has included other pleas for an integration of the spiritual dimension into clinical social work practice (Spencer, 1957; Stroup, 1962; Cox, 1985; Vincentia, 1987; Canda, 1988a,b, 1989; Denton, 1990). However, issues related to religion and spirituality have yet to be adequately addressed by the profession. Even though practitioners are being pushed by many of the people they serve to take value conflicts and spiritual concerns into account, few social workers have incorporated the theory that specifically addresses the spiritual dimension—transpersonal theory—into their practice. Therefore, social work practitioners may be ill-prepared to deal with spiritual emergencies (Grof & Grof, 1989), satanism (Wheeler et al., 1989), or other challenges that are primarily spiritual in nature.

HISTORICAL CONTEXT OF TRANSPERSONAL THEORY

Since much of social work's clinical theory has been influenced by the historical development of various psychological theories, it may be helpful to place transpersonal theory into an historical context. Throughout the evolution of psychotherapy, theories and models have acted as social indices by responding to the social ills of the day (London, 1974, 1986). As each successive theory emerged out of its own unique place in history, it added important insights to expand the understanding of human growth and development, as well as provide models and interventions for clinical practice. Even though, in his initial article describing therapy as a reactive trade, London described only three "phases" or "stages" of psychotherapy, the views he expressed then are applicable to the evolution of what is now referred to as the Four Forces of psychology.

THE FIRST FORCE

Around the turn of the century Freud's psychoanalytic theory grew out of an Age of Repression as experienced by the guilt-ridden, inner-directed man (London, 1974). From the beginning psychoanalysis was essentially a theory of intrapsychic functioning (Pine, 1985, p. 11). First Force (dynamic theory) took human behavior out of the realm of mystery by providing explanations based on the deterministic science of the Newtonian/Cartesian World view. It also made it distressingly clear that unconscious drives and impulses, left undiscovered, could sabotage conscious desires. Even though Freud wrote about "soul making" (Bettelheim, 1983), his work clearly focused on the basement of human nature. For example, the index to Freud's complete works contains over 400 references to neurosis and none to health (Walsh & Shapiro, 1983, p. 5).

> Freud's model of man as an organism seeking relief from tension, forced to negotiate a compromise between instinct, reason, and society, leaves even the most successful negotiator in a position of impoverishment as pathological,

in its own way, as any illness listed in the diagnostic manual. (Walsh & Shapiro, 1983, p. 38)

Because First Force theory historically focused primarily on pathology, its view of therapy as a process whereby the patient replaces neurotic conflict by learning to live with everyday unhappiness was essentially pessimistic (Brown, 1988).

According to Pine (1985), First Force theories evolved across three great waves. Freud's drive psychology was the first wave. Ego psychology with a view that focused on the ego, its development, and its functions was the second. The third wave, object relations, added key understandings about the importance of early object relationships, developmental deficits of early childhood, and the role of defense mechanisms. Object relation's focus on child observation and the progressive differentiation of self from other gave birth to a body of literature on self-esteem and self-psychology.

Generally speaking, all of the models of dynamic theory did a better job of exposing pathology and offering developmental explanations about how it came to be than they did in providing guidelines for specific clinical interventions. Having uncovered repressed psychological data, many practitioners were left unclear as to what to do with it. How could such mysterious, unconscious forces ever be tamed? Additionally, another problem limited the use of this approach as time went on: Its concepts were not amenable to research.

THE SECOND FORCE

Over time, the criticisms about Freud's theory as being too reductionistic and deterministic led to a search for more practical and precise conceptualizations. Psychoanalytic premises related to repression weren't a good fit for symptoms of the day in a time of free love, sexual revolution, and value deficits (Schnall, 1981). To treat the stress and strain experienced by the other-directed man in an Age of Anxiety (London, 1974), Second Force behavioral theory came to the fore. The behavioral approach sought to create order out of chaos by focusing on the importance of social learning and the process of socialization. It demonstrated that much of human behavior could be objectified, operationalized, tested, and shaped with proper reinforcers. Specificity and concreteness in understanding human behavior provided not only documentable relief for behavioral symptoms, but concepts and interventions that could be quantified. Structural, strategic, and cognitive therapies delivered observable results and demonstratable success. This more empirical focus brought confidence to the scientific-minded researcher/practitioner in an age of accountability.

THE THIRD FORCE

In the mid- to late 1940s, again reflecting changes in the social context, discontent with the mechanistic methods of behaviorism accumulated. The longing for more heart and personal connection between the healer and the client to be healed called forth a new approach. Virginia Satir described it as follows:

At the end of World War II, we all heaved a sigh of relief and had hope of building a more just world. The United Nations was a manifestation of that dream. These hopes were also translated into a new psychological construct—the human potential movement. In 1946 we heard the voices of Abraham Maslow, Rollo May, Carl Rogers and others who believed that human beings are and can be more than what their behavior led us to believe. We set on a journey to find out what else there was in the human being that had not yet been discovered and assessed. (Satir, 1987, p. 60)

That journey of discovery emerged out of an Age of Ennui to serve psychological man in the search for self-fulfillment (London, 1974). It resulted in the development of three Third Force theories: (1) humanistic theory, to help individuals move toward being more fully human and self-actualized; (2) experiential theory, to bring back sensation, feeling, and the phenomenological awareness; (3) existential theory, to deal with crises that occur when life loses its meaning and purpose. The human growth and potential movement dared to suggest that a person didn't need to be sick in order to get better. This idea of undergoing a therapeutic process for the purpose of growth rather than cure represented a dramatic change in focus.

Until now, psychotherapy has been mainly reactive to feeling bad, that is to having symptoms. Now it is reacting to not feeling good—that is, to a faulty life-style. . . . Men want to be healthy, wealthy and wise in that order. As each is gained, the next gets wanted more. (London, 1974, p. 68)

And so it was, as individuals in an affluent society became more healthy, many of their contemporary ailments began to express symptoms related to the existential vacuum, and to require remedies that were experiential and philosophical in nature.

Third Force psychology reflected a beginning, culture-wide shift away from the Newtonian-Cartesian world view. Some seekers moved out of the mainstream of traditional Western psychology and began exploring the contemplative practices and psychological traditions of the East. When some theorists began to include traditions that were transrational and included extrasensory data, reactions from others ranged from horrified to celebratory. However, neither reaction altered the determination of Third Force pioneers to expand psychology to transcend the limits of the observable and the measurable (Grof, 1985).

Ultimately, it took the courage of an intellectual loner like Abraham Maslow to challenge mainstream psychological research to search for the farther reaches of human nature (Maslow, 1971).

Abraham Maslow was convinced that the value-life of human beings is biologically rooted. There seemed to him to be a species-wide need (comparable to the need for basic food elements and vitamins) for what he called "B" (for being) values, e.g., truth, goodness, beauty, wholeness, justice, playfulness, meaningfulness, etc. These values are biological necessities for avoiding illness and for achieving one's full potential. The epidemic of spiritual illnesses ("metapathologies") resulting from deprivation of these values include anomie, alienation, meaninglessness, loss of zest for life, hopelessness, boredom, and axiological depression. (Clinebell, 1995, p. 92)

Maslow's early work radically revised our picture of the human species and created a vastly expanded map of human possibilities (Leonard, 1983).

In his later work, Maslow's view of human potential continued to expand, and his explorations of human potential delineated three groups of optimally healthy people: self-actualizers, transcenders, and transcending self-actualizers. Eventually, Maslow came to believe that even his definition of self-actualized transcenders was not expansive enough to encompass the highest levels of human potential:

> Maslow has found that the self that was actualized could still be isolated in an alien world. Building on the theory of Erich Fromm (and resonating with Carl Jung and William James before him), Maslow postulated that we long to transcend our aloneness and belong to the cosmos. Even when we have fulfilled every secular need, the hunger for transcendence is not satisfied. So it was a short step, from actualization to transcendence and from plateau experiences to the "cosmic connection." (Bradshaw, 1988, p. 228)

Maslow, who read extensively in Eastern literature, is considered the philosophical father of both humanistic and transpersonal theories. Near the end of his life, Maslow was still seeking more. He made another call for yet a fourth psychology that would be:

> . . . transpersonal, trans-human, centered in the cosmos rather than in human needs and interests, going beyond humanness, identity, self-actualization, and the like. (Wittine, 1987, 53)

By 1969 this Fourth Force of psychology had established some common parameters as well as a professional journal.

THE FOURTH FORCE

The transpersonal approach has evolved out of a cultural context exacerbated by not only an existential vacuum, but a spiritual one as well. It serves the dispirited man/woman in an age characterized by a lack of traditional values (Schnall, 1981). Building on the work of Jung, Assagioli, Maslow, Rogers, Wilber, Grof, Boorstein, Tart, Walsh, Vaughn, Welwood, Washburn, and many others, Fourth Force Transpersonal Theory is particularly suited to treat postmodern maladies in a drugged and violent society. A common symptom of the day (often misinterpreted as clinical depression) is a sense of demoralization or dispiritation (Bugental & Bugental, 1984). When Bradshaw (1988) described the "hole in the soul," his words hit home for a lot of people. This modern-day malaise of the soul has also been described by Goldberg as follows:

> In a word, we live in an era in which men find it onerous to accept responsibility for their own actions and for the embittered and hollow course their existence has taken. . . . Much of our agony is in the soul. (Goldberg, 1980, p. 1)

It seems to follow that if much of our agony is in the soul, practitioners who seek to relieve it must, like Freud, get involved in the process of soul making (Bettelheim, 1983). However, it seems that concepts like "soul making" seem to have lost favor as modern science and issues related to accountability have increasingly pushed social workers to abandon the moral and religious roots of their profession (Reid & Popple, 1992).

In the "new age" questions have been raised about how to resacralize a professional context that has become increasingly secular. The respiritation of the larger social context has become one of the tasks of Fourth Force Theory. Reactive to the spiritual void within a troubled society, transpersonal literature began to accumulate. Some writers, like Wilber (1977, 1981, 1983a,b), Fowler (1981), Metzner (1986), and Washburn (1988), wrote about human evolution and developed human growth and behavior models that took the spiritual dimension and transpersonal levels of development into consideration. Others wrote more broadly about exceptional states of well-being, the unconscious search for God, and transpersonal issues: Frankl (1975); Keyes (1975); Walsh and Vaughn (1980 a,b); Boorstein (1980); May (1982); Walsh and Shapiro (1983); Bettelheim (1983); Walsh (1984); Tart (1986); Wiedemann (1986); London (1986); Anthony, Ecker, and Wilber (1987); Houston (1987, 1988); Grof (1988); Zukav (1989); Cowley (1993); Cowley and Derezotes (1994); among others.

Of special interest to clinical practitioners are those who have written about how to utilize transpersonal theory for practice with issues involving the spiritual dimension, like death and dying, addictions, and the longing for spiritual growth. This group includes Assagioli (1965); Tart (1975); Small (1982); Khan (1982); Ferrucci (1982); Hendricks and Weinhold (1982); Lovinger (1984); Welwood (1986); Boorstein (1986); Wilber, Engler and Brown, 1986; Grof and Grof (1987, 1989); Brown (1988); May (1988); Houston (1988); Weinhold (1989); Vaughn (1991); Whitmore (1991); Nelson (1994); Smith (1995); Derezotes (1995); and others. These transpersonal theorists challenge clinical minds that are steeped in the first three forces to expand their thinking beyond traditional boundaries to include the phenomenological, the intuitive, and the transrational.

Since empiricism has been given emphasis in our culture and in academe, it is little wonder that a psychology focused on spiritual development and expanding psychological understanding to include nonordinary states of consciousness was basically ignored by mainstream social work literature until the early nineties. When the Council on Social Work Education included religion in its guidelines for diversity, educators and practitioners were pushed into the void they had been avoiding.

The transpersonal approach is not to be confused with New Age practices that are "flaky" (Bodian, 1988) or spiritual charlatans who seek to induce dependence on an external cultlike authority. Just as any theory can be used, or abused, spiritual practices, concepts, and theories can be applied in both adaptive and unhealthy ways (Keen, 1983). In a world where many of our clients shop in "psychospiritual supermarkets," social workers need to be knowledgeable about what constitutes an authentic path to inner transformation, as opposed to shallow pseudomystical psychopathology masquerading under the guise of higher development (Anthony, Ecker, & Wilber, 1987).

Spiritual quackery can be ludicrous as well as dangerous. Some advertisements even offer seminars or various types of tapes and spiritual technologies which claim to elevate the consumer "instantly" to the same levels of higher consciousness that are occasionally achieved only after many years of dedicated spiritual practice. Such bogus offers prey on the vulnerable and can induce "spiritual emergencies" (Grof & Grof, 1989). Experimenting with altered states of consciousness may damage weak ego structures. Spontaneous rising of kundalini energy, egoitis, ego inflation, and simply going about in a "psychic smog" (Ferrucci, 1982) are just a few of the possible negative outcomes mentioned in the literature that may await unsuspecting or unprepared spiritual seekers. People who expose themselves to various kinds of "spiritual practice" without first developing the ego strength to balance them have experienced regressive states, sometimes to the point of open psychosis requiring hospitalization (Crittenden, 1980; Aurobindo, 1971). Table 28–1 offers a summary of thematic dimensions of each of the four forces of psychology.

TRANSPERSONAL TERMINOLOGY

The root meaning of the word *psychology* comes from the Greek "psukhe," meaning spirit, soul, life and breath, and from the Greek *logis,* meaning word, speech, reason. Psychology, then, originally meant the word or language of the spirit or soul. *Transpersonal* means "beyond/through," and *persona* means "mask" (Wittine, 1987, p. 52). In psychology, therefore, the transpersonal approach is focused on spirit (the breath of life), and on understanding the language and development of the spiritual or sacred dimensions of being that lie "beyond" the personal or ego level. Houston calls this getting in touch with the "deeps"; Pierre Teilhard de Chardin referred to it as participating in noogenesis or movement to point omega; Sri Aurobindo saw it as a journey toward perfection. This quest to grow beyond ego by transcending the personal has been described variously through time as: enlightenment, salvation, individuation, gnosis, liberation, awakening, One Mind, bhava samadhi, Aurobindo's "supermind," and so on.

Whatever the terminology utilized, the evolutionary process involved is one of dynamic movement to achieve the purposiveness of the patterns of possibility (entelechy) encoded in each of us (Houston, 1988). *Syntropy,* or the innate drive in all living matter to perfect itself by reaching higher and higher levels of organization, harmony, and order (Szent-Gyoergyi, 1974), is another term that applies to the journey

Table 28–1
Summary of Thematic Dimensions of Four Force Theories

Theme	Dynamic	Behavioral	Experiential	Transpersonal
Prime concern	Sexual repression	Anxiety	Alienation	Spiritual dimension
Concept of pathology	Instinctual conflicts; early libidinal drives and wishes that remain out of awareness, i.e., unconscious	Learned habits: excess of deficit behaviors that have been environmentally reinforced	Existential despair: human loss of possibilities, fragmentation of self, lack of congruence with one's experience	Ego attachments: identification with illusions, dis-ease of spiritual dimension, "hole in the soul," disspiritation, morbid preservation
Concept of health	Resolution of underlying conflicts; victory of ego over id, i.e., ego strength	Symptom removal: absence of specific symptom and/or reduction of anxiety	Actualization of potential: self-growth, authenticity, and spontaneity	Self-transcendence: Wholeness, balance, harmony, going (beyond ego), individuation
Mode of change	Depth insight: understanding of the early past, i.e., intellectual-emotional knowledge	Direct learning: behaving in the current present, i.e., action or performance	Immediate experiencing: sensing or feeling in the immediate moment, i.e., spontaneous expression of experience	Self-healing: i.e., disidentification, spiritual practice, holotropic, breathwork, imagery
Time approach and focus	Historical: subjective past	Nonhistorical: objective present	A-historical: phenomenological moment	Transtemporal, nonlocal: unitive consciousness
Type of treatment	Long-term and intense	Short-term and not intense	Short-term and intense	Evolution/transformation over the life span
Therapist's task	To comprehend unconscious mental content and its historical and hidden meanings	To program, reward, inhibit, or shape specific behavioral responses to anxiety-producing stimuli	To interact in a mutually accepting atmosphere for arousal of self-expression (from somatic to spiritual)	To enable seeker to tap inner truth/transrational resources
Primary tools techniques	Interpretation: free association, analysis of transference, resistance, slips, and dreams	Conditioning: systematic densitization, positive and negative reinforcements, shaping	Encounter: shared dialogue, experiential games, dramatization or playing out of feelings	Spiritual/contemplative practices: meditation, imagery, I AM affirmations, yoga
Treatment model	Medical: doctor-patient or parent-infant (authoritarian), i.e., therapeutic alliance	Educational: teacher-student or parent-child (authoritarian), i.e., learning alliance	Existential: human peer-human peer or adult-adult (egalitarian), i.e., human alliance	Transpersonal: soul to soul (not eclectic but a synthesis) of all theories/models
Nature of relationship to cure	Transferential and primary for cure: unreal relationship	Real but secondary for cure: no relationship	Real and primary for cure: real relationship	Real and primary for cure: reciprocal, unconditional love and mutual compassion
Therapist's role and stance	Interpreter-reflector: indirect, dispassionate, or frustrating	Shaper-adviser: direct, problem-solving, or practical	Interactor-acceptor: mutually permissive or gratifying	A servant, guide, evocateur, midwife, and/or cocreator.

First 3 Forces:, Karasu, R.B., & L. Bellak, (Eds.) (1980). *Specialized Techniques in Individual Psychotherapy,* New York: Brunner/Mazel.
4th Force: Cowley, Au-Deane S., (1992). Class Handout for Advanced Practice with Individuals, Graduate School of Social Work, University of Utah.

of all animate life toward increasingly more complex levels of organization and potentiality. The drive within each soul to become all that it can be and then to unite with unitive consciousness (or with something larger than the individual self) is a universal urge toward wholeness and self-transcendence. This dual urge, first toward individuation and then toward cosmic connection, was referred to by Jung as the religious instinct. Wilber posits:

> . . . evolution is best thought of as Spirit-in-action, God-in-the-making, where Spirit unfolds itself at every step of development, thus manifesting more of itself, and realizing more of itself, at every unfolding. (Wilber, 1996, p. 10)

In transpersonal theory, the terms "spirit", "spiritual," and "spiritual dimension" are expressly separated from any reference to theology—not ever to be confused with the term "religious"—spirituality may have nothing to do with church membership or attendance. It is crucial that social work educators and practitioners make certain students and clients understand that talking about spirituality and transpersonal theory (which contains references to Eastern philosophies and contemplative practices) is *not* meant to be interpreted as an attack on their religious belief systems.

> Transcending tradition does not imply devaluing tradition; it does imply recognizing the relative nature of spiritual teachings as they have been handed down across generations in every culture since the beginning of recorded history. Every tradition offers comforting illusions for those who would escape from freedom and roadmaps to liberation for those who choose to follow them. (Vaughn, 1995, p. 49)

According to transpersonal definitions of spirituality, an individual can develop a higher consciousness within any race, gender, religious tradition, or sexual orientation. Indeed, a humanist or an atheist can have a profound spiritual life (Bloomfield, 1980, p. 124).

> The spiritual dimension, which Frankl calls the noos, contains such uniquely human attributes as our will to meaning, our goal orientation, our creativity, our imagination, our intuition, our faith, our vision of what we can become, our capacity to love beyond the physiopsychological, our capacity to listen to our conscience beyond the dictates of the superego, our sense of humor. It also contains our self-detachment or ability to step outside and look at our selves, and our self-transcendence or ability to reach out to people we love and causes in which we believe. In the area of spirit we are not driven; we are the drivers, the decision-makers. (Fabry, 1980, p. 81)

In a recent article Vaughn had this to say about spirituality:

> As an innate capacity that exists in every human being, spirituality cannot be limited to any set of doctrines or practices. From a psychological perspective,

spirituality is a universal experience, not a universal theology. (Vaughn, 1995, p. 52)

In the frontispiece of the first issue of the *Journal of Transpersonal Psychology* Anthony Sutich made history when he introduced and defined transpersonal psychology's domain as:

. . . concerned specifically with ultimate values, unitive consciousness peak experiences, ecstasy, mystical experience, awe, transcendence of the self, spirit, oneness, cosmic awareness, and related concepts, experiences and activities. (Sutich, 1969)

As the transpersonal approach has developed since 1969, a distinguishing feature is its inclusion of the spiritual dimension. Practitioners with a transpersonal perspective seek to help clients expand their consciousness, deal with issues of meaning and purpose in life, and legitimize their transpersonal (transrational) experiences. The transpersonal approach does not attempt to supplant other approaches, but rather to complement and expand them (Vaughn, 1986, p. 148). Transpersonal theory also builds on generally accepted developmental theories as they trace the evolution of consciousness over the life span.

THE PROCESS OF SPIRIT UNFOLDING

By synthesizing and incorporating the wisdom of Eastern contemplative practices with conventional Western psychologies, the transpersonal approach sees the journey of human "unfolding" as an evolutionary as well as hierarchical process. Sometimes referred to as a process of decentration, growth is charted from a beginning position described as "undifferentiated matrix." The first step toward becoming fully human requires achieving order out of chaos by building an ego structure out of unmetabolized affects, images, and prepersonal experiences. Only after one has successfully negotiated stages related to separation and individuation and achieved a beginning sense of personal identity (or strong structuralization of ego) do self-actualization and higher states of consciousness become developmental possibilities.

The process of decentration across the full spectrum of human consciousness requires a biopsychosocial-spiritual journey that takes the individual across a continuum from an egocentric position that believes "I am the universe," toward a position beyond ego where the person can potentially realize a sense of unitive consciousness and an experience of oneness with all that is. As the individual participates in an evolutionary process moving from the simple to the more complex, a series of hierarchical and invariant stages unfold, with each stage having a "higher order" of structure or a more adaptive way of knowing-and-being-in-the-world.

Each newly emerging stage constitutes a transformation from the old way of knowing and provides the individual with a qualitatively different and more adequate way of knowing. An advance in stage offers the person wider perspectives, greater problem-solving effectiveness across a greater range of domains, and liberation from the constraints of the former stage. (Rosen, 1988, p. 318)

This view of human potentiality requires an expansion beyond what Western psychology has traditionally seen as the optimal possibility for human growth and provides a lure toward becoming fully human.

Typically the journey in our culture stops with reaching adulthood. It ends once a strong ego and a strong sense of reality is developed. From this perspective there is no need for a further journey. The transpersonal view is that the ultimate meaning of life is encountered when one moves beyond this preoccupation with self-identity. (Keen, 1983, pp. 7–8)

Transpersonal theory is not a theory that celebrates just the separation of self from ego, but paradoxically also recognizes that each step toward individuation ultimately leads one back to a connection with the whole: Each decentering takes the individual further from an identification with the individual self, and toward identification with the all (Bee, 1986, p. 341).

Although the ego or personal identity level is viewed by transpersonal psychology as a necessary prerequisite to further development up the ladder of being, Wilber cautions about the dangers inherent in making an exclusive identification with any level of being. "Morbid preservation" is a term that has been equated with developmental arrest or Freud's concept of "fixation" to describe the unwillingness of the ego to release one level of growth in order to achieve the next (Wilber et al., 1986, p. 82). Morbid preservation at the personal level is a process wherein the ego becomes a "trap" and thus changes from a structure that at first protects, to one that ultimately incarcerates. The call to go "beyond ego" is not, however, to be translated into an aggression *against* ego:

Trying to induce change by waging an assault on the ego structure is a common mistake that various spiritual and therapeutic approaches make. Sometimes this kind of "therapeutic aggression" is quite blatant . . . and sometimes it takes more subtle forms of persuasion and confrontation which imply that one would be a better person if one were different from the way one is. Unfortunately, such attacks on the personality structure rob people of what it is they have to work with. This can leave them in a state of helplessness and dependency. (Welwood, 1986, p. 132)

Far from encouraging or inducing dependency, the transpersonal approach sees its mind-body-spirit approach as one that seeks to empower people and help them become increasingly more aware. Higher states of consciousness and character result when one integrates the fruits of six common elements of transpersonal practices: (1)

ethical training, (2) concentration, (3) emotional transformation, (4) redirection of motivation, (5) refinement of awareness, and (6) cultivation of wisdom (Walsh & Vaughan, 1993). The journey of seeking one's highest potential is seen as a lifelong process of expanding and refining one's consciousness as it moves toward wholeness.

> Spiritual healing is a process of becoming whole or holy. Most specifically, I would define it as an ongoing process of becoming increasingly conscious. (Peck, 1987, p. 33)

Social work has long been concerned with how to bring about the good person in a good society. Transpersonal theory's focus on developing higher states of individual consciousness that eventuate in a heightened sense of social connectedness and responsibility is a goal that is compatible with the mission and purposes of the profession.

THE NATURE OF CONSCIOUSNESS

Talk of consciousness and consciousness-raising did not begin with the New Age or the Women's Liberation Movement. Robert Ornstein (1972) observed that psychology is and always has been primarily the science of consciousness. Bugental (1978) expanded on Ornstein's definition by calling psychotherapy the art, science, and practice of studying the nature of consciousness and of what may reduce or facilitate it. Whether we have called it making the unconscious conscious (First Force), taking effective control over our lives (Second Force), becoming more fully human (Third Force), or moving beyond ego (Fourth Force), psychological theories have sought to help client systems become more mature and more skilled in the important tasks of loving and working.

In the West, attempts to facilitate the development of consciousness (or increased structuralization of ego) were augmented by Freud's theory. However, according to Bettelheim, key concepts of Freud's work were mistranslated and sometimes even totally misunderstood. Specifically, the terms Freud used when he divided the structure of consciousness into three parts have been mislabeled: Freud wrote about chaotic *it*, not id; the *I*, not ego; and the *above I*, rather than the superego (Bettelheim, 1983).

Jung was one of the first to call attention to the centrality of consciousness in human development. Like Freud, Jung's way of conceptualizing different aspects of consciousness, was also three-tiered and included: shadow, ego, and Self (Campbell, 1971). In a like manner, Roberto Assagioli (1965), an Italian contemporary of Freud, designated three different levels or structures within consciousness that he called lower consciousness, middle consciousness, and superconsciousness. When Freud's, Jung's, and Assagioli's paradigms are compared to three general levels of consciousness suggested by Ken Wilber's transpersonal Full Spectrum Model, similarities are apparent (Wilber et al., 1986). Each of the four views represented in Table 28–2 depicts consciousness as evolving out of an undifferentiated matrix, and moving toward

Table 28–2
Three Levels of Consciousness

Freud	Jung	Assagioli	Wilber
"Above I" (not superego)	self	superconsciousness	transpersonal level
"I" (not ego)	ego	middle consciousness	personal level
"It" (not id)	shadow	lower consciousness	prepersonal level

a kind of personhood or personal identity with a sense of boundaries. In all four views the possibility of developing a level of consciousness that is larger than the individual ego is posited.

Although Freud, Jung, and Assagioli acknowledged levels of consciousness that go beyond ego, only Wilber's transpersonal approach proposes a theory that explicates for the practitioner what higher states of consciousness look like, what pathologies exist at higher levels of consciousness, and further, what interventions work best with various levels of consciousness.

It is important to keep in mind that transpersonal theory is not unidimensional, but is composed of many strands. Like First, Second, and Third Force theories before it, several models of clinical practice are beginning to emerge under the broad umbrella of Fourth Force Transpersonal Theory. Each model offers an opinion about human potentiality and what it means to be fully human, as well as a distinctive view about the developmental tasks or remedies involved in the facilitation of human development up the ladder of being. A sampling of some of these transpersonal models, with particular attention given to a proposed Fourth Force model for transpersonal social work practice, will be presented in the remainder of this chapter.

MODELS OF TRANSPERSONAL THEORY

Some theorists, like Jung, Grof, Washburn, and Levin, envision the transpersonal in the "depths" or "dynamic ground" (Washburn, 1994), while others, like Assagioli, Small, Wilber, and Cowley, refer to transpersonal states as being higher states of consciousness "up" the ladder of being. Therefore, poetic license has been taken in Table 28–3, since this representation of the various levels of each transpersonal model is an attempt to provide a paradigm that will allow general comparisons to be made between models. This beginning effort to identify transpersonal models does not claim to be inclusive of all models available. I have not attempted to include Mindell's process-oriented model (1985) or other models that do not posit hierarchial or developmental levels, and thus do not lend themselves for comparison.

PSYCHOSYNTHESIS

Even though Jung's work is sometimes considered transpersonal in nature because he took into account transrational or psychic level aspects of being, probably the first

Table 28–3
Transpersonal Models

Psychosynthesis	Self-Creation	Holotropic Breathwork	Full-Spectrum Model	Transpersonal Practice
Roberto Assagioli (1965)	Jacquelyn Small (1982)	Stanislav Grof (1985)	Ken Wilber (1986)	Au-Deane Cowley (1996)
	Self-mastery Basic Urge: Unity	Transpersonal domain	TRANSPERSONAL	Spiritual Maturation
			Causal	
Super- consciousness	Intuition/altruism Basic urge: compassion	Level of birth and death	Subtle Psychic	Moral Maturation
	Comprehension/ authenticity		PERSONAL	Psychosocial Maturation
Middle Consciousness	Basic urge: understanding Harmonizing bridge Basic urge: awakening harmonizing	Individual consciousnees	Existential Formal-reflexive Rule/role	Cognitive maturation
	Self-definition Basic urge: identity seeking	Sensory level	PRE-PERSONAL Rep. mind	Affective maturation
Lower Consciousness	Self-gratification Basic urge: passion Self-preservation Basic urge: fear		Pahntasmic-emotional Sensoriphysical	Physical maturation

clinical model that had spiritual development as its main focus was Roberto Assagioli's (1965) model of psychosynthesis. Assagioli began developing his ideas in Italy in 1910. He worked to find the common boundaries of medicine, education, and religion, as well as to provide a corrective view of human psychology to balance Freud's emphasis on pathology. His position was not that psychoanalysis was an incorrect approach, but rather that it was incomplete (Kramer, 1995, p. 22). The process of psychosynthesis is a subjective one of balancing, harmonizing, and integrating the various aspects of human experience.

> In psychosynthesis there is no "chart on the wall" which tells the counselor what a Self-realized human being should be like. There are no ultimate Truths, no recipes to follow, only the incredible wisdom of the unfolding Self and its aspirations for meaning and purpose. (Whitmore, 1991, p. ix)

Assagioli introduced the idea of "subpersonalities" and saw the integration of all of one's parts as a process essential to reaching the goal of psychic wholeness. He introduced disidentification exercises intended to help one to view the self impartially and give up false identifications, distorted attitudes, and unfounded beliefs. Assagioli wanted to help people get in touch with the core (or real) self. Taking the psyche's inherent thrust toward mature self-realization as a basic premise, psychosynthesis recognizes values, meaning, peak experience, and the unquantifiable, ineffable essence of human life as integral elements in the counseling process (Whitmore, 1991). Assagioli was probably one of the first to point out that "not all serious psychological disturbances were to be understood as symptoms of pathology, but rather some are to be understood as crises of spiritual awakening" (Washburn, 1988, p. 2).

SELF-CREATION

Out of her twelve-step work with addictions and recovery, Jacquelyn Small (1982) developed a transpersonal model with seven hierarchial levels. In this transpersonal model, therapists serve as guides in facilitating the processes of inner work and personal evolution. Through breath work, karmic balancing, seed thoughts, imagery, meditation, centering, processing, developing an observer self, transmutation of emotions, disidentification, work-on-oneself, and other techniques and exercises, individuals are helped to redefine the soul through a process of self-creation. Small holds that the work of the transformer (therapist of the future) is to remind us of our essence, the self we were intended to be before we lost our way.

HOLOTROPIC BREATHWORK

In 1985 Stanislav Grof developed a Holotropic Breathwork Model. The term "holotropic" is derived from the Greek *holos* (whole) and *trepein* (aim for or move in the direction of). Holotropic literally means aiming for wholeness or moving in the direction of totality. A basic premise of this approach is that healing results from experiential exercises that help one overcome inner fragmentation and a sense of isolation from the world (Grof & Grof, 1987). In Grof's (1985) cartography of inner space, he posited four distinct levels or realms of the human psyche: (1) the sensory barrier; (2) individual consciousness (or the biographical realm); (3) the level of birth and death (which includes the perinatal realm with four Basic Perinatal Matrices); and (4) the transpersonal domain (which taps sources of information clearly outside of the conventionally defined range of individual consciousness). Stanislav and Christina Grof have also written about spiritual emergencies (Grof & Grof, 1989) and the stormy search for the self (Grof, 1990).

FULL SPECTRUM MODEL

Ken Wilber's Full Spectrum Model (Wilber et al., 1986) is a clinically oriented model that is in complete agreement with Western developmental theories up to the personal level of development. Wilber calls on the Eastern contemplative practices for theory related to the transpersonal or spiritual domain. As a result of this synthesis of East and West, Wilber has developed what he calls a master template of the nine most central and functionally dominant structures of consciousness. According to Wilber's model, consciousness arises out of an undifferentiated matrix into: three prepersonal levels (sensoriphysical, phantasmic-emotional, rep.-mind); three personal levels (rule-role, formal-reflexive, existential); and three transpersonal levels (psychic, subtle, causal).

Wilber's Full Spectrum Model is developmental, structural, hierarchical, and systems oriented. He has concluded that mind can be viewed as a spectrum of states or phase-specific levels of consciousness. These states are not discrete but infinitely shade into one another. A person is not confined to one level, but usually has a dominant mode and spends most of waking life within a very narrow range of the spectrum. Wilber posits that the overall level of self-structuralization (or dominant level of consciousness) is what determines the particular types of needs, motivations, cognitions, object relations, defense mechanisms, and pathologies the individual will exhibit (Wilber et al., 1986).

Wilber's charts representing hierarchial levels of consciousness are not meant to be interpreted as meaning that "higher" or "deeper" levels of consciousness are "better." A well-integrated psyche will be able to access and utilize all levels of consciousness appropriately. A key concept is that the more developed or mature the person is, the more freedom of choice is possible, since the more conscious one is, the more aspects and capacities are available for use at any given moment in time. In other words, the higher levels of consciousness include the lower, embrace them, but also extend beyond them (Wilber et al., 1986). Conversely, a person operating at the first or prepersonal level does not have access to the "higher" states of consciousness. Each level or band of consciousness manifests stage specific challenges and requires differential interventions.

> According to Wilber, the great diversity of psychological and psychotherapeutic schools reflects not so much interpretation of, and opinion about, differences in the same set of problems or differences in methodology, as a real difference in the levels of the spectrum of consciousness to which they have adapted themselves. The major mistake of these discrepant schools is that each tends to generalize its approach and apply it to the entire spectrum, whereas it is appropriate only for a particular level. Each of the major approaches of Western psychotherapy is thus more or less "correct" when addressing its own level and grossly distorting when applied inappropriately to other bands. A truly encompassing and integrated psychology of the future will make use of the complementary insights offered by each school of psychology. (Grof, 1985, p. 132)

Wilber's model offers the clinician a theoretical base for new DSM-IV nomenclatures related to spiritual matters. It also provides guidelines to help the practitioner choose systematically from a wide range of interventions while adhering to a consistent theoretical structure. Unlike Maslow's "metapathologies," Wilber points out that pathologies exist at all levels of consciousness, and that those occurring at the transpersonal level can be "serious" or "profound" (Wilber et al., 1986). His view concurs with object relations theory in stating that the earlier in development that a deficit, lesion, or arrest occurs, the more severe the pathological result.

Since interventions that are appropriate and effective at one level of development may be contraindicated and ineffective for symptoms or problems originating on a different level of structuralization, accurate diagnosis and effective intervention depend on the practitioner's having a complete understanding of the entire spectrum of consciousness. For example, in working with prepersonal psychoses, Wilber proposes interventions that are medication or pacification oriented: for the narcissistic/borderline client, the therapeutic emphasis is on structure building; for psychoneuroses, uncovering techniques are suggested. At the personal or ego level: script pathology is ameliorated with script analysis; identity neuroses with introspection; existential pathology with existential therapy. For pathologies of the transpersonal realm contemplative practices are recommended. Wilber's suggested remedies at the transpersonal level uses terms and processes not easily understood or accessed by most mental health practitioners—for instance, terms like "path of yogis, saints and sages." Even though Wilber believes his structure of consciousness to be genuinely cross-cultural and universal, in the spirit of building on his model, some terminology he utilizes must be translated into more culturally friendly terms. Wilber also suggests the following caveats:

> Needless to say, the standard cautions and qualifications about using such hierarchical models of pathology should be kept in mind; i.e., no pure cases, the influence of cultural differences, genetic predispositions, genetic and traumatic arrest, and blended cases. (Wilber et al., 1986, pp. 107–108)

Wilber's beginning effort to articulate a comprehensive and inclusive, integrative theory in his Full Spectrum of Consciousness Model in 1986 apparently did not reach many front-line social workers. Even a decade later, I believe it would be safe to say that the Full Spectrum Model has not been incorporated into social work education and clinical practice to any extent. Apparently there is still some skepticism and fear of being unprofessional associated with anything described as spiritual. Therefore, some social work practitioners have been ambivalent (or even disdainful) toward any Fourth Force theory that sought to include the spiritual dimension and openly deal with transrational experiences. However, Wilber's inclusive Full Spectrum Model meets many of the criteria called for by Lazarus (1987) when he wrote: "Psychotherapy is in dire need of broader integrative theoretical bases" (1987, p. 166). Lazarus also postulated:

> We need a clinical thesaurus that would cross-reference an objective body of actual operations of patient/therapist interactions across many conditions. We need to operationalize and concretize therapist decision-making processes. . . . Eventually, a super-organizing theory may emerge, a superstructure under whose umbrella present-day differences can be subsumed and reconnected. (Lazarus, 1987, p. 166)

Since Wilber's Full Spectrum Model is not an eclecticism, but a synthesis, it may be that broad umbrella. It does not attempt to supplant other traditional therapeutic approaches, but postulates that each of the Four Force theories is appropriate for problems of living and pathologies that occur at different levels of the spectrum of consciousness. Wilber sees the Four Force theories working together in complementary rather than competitive ways (Ingram, 1987).

TRANSPERSONAL PRACTICE

The model of transpersonal practice proposed by this author builds on Wilber's Full Spectrum of Consciousness Model (Wilber et al., 1986). It has five major premises: (1) All psychological theories arise out of a specific cultural context to treat the social ills of the day. (2) The distinguishing social malaise of our time is spiritual in nature and requires Fourth Force Transpersonal theory for its amelioration since it alone includes the transpersonal dimension. (3) Clinical assessments to be thorough need to be multidimensional. (4) In addition to other knowledge of developmental theory, practitioners need also to understand the developmental line within the dimensions assessed. (5) Transpersonal practice offers a needed comprehensive, inclusive Fourth Force Model to aid social work practitioners in making decisions about which theories, models, and interventions to utilize in individualizing each client system they serve.

Transpersonal practice works with client systems at every level on the Full Spectrum of Consciousness. Environmental concerns, symptom relief, structure building, behavioral change, relationship issues, maltreatment, addiction, personal growth, and so forth are included in its domain. The distinctive additional goal the transpersonal practice model opens up is related to the spiritual quest: to help clients who are experiencing existential and spiritual unrest reach a point of spiritual health, a sense of integration or wholeness, peace of mind, and/or a sense of connection to a larger whole that gives life purpose and meaning.

Central to this approach is the notion that understanding the level of development of a client, in each of the basic dimensions of being, will help the therapist to be more effective in choosing appropriate interventions:

> Psychology, as I see it, is applied developmental psychology. The therapist uses his or her knowledge of normal development to reach some conclusions about the reasons for a patient's malfunctioning and how one may enter the developmental spiral either to foster or to reinstitute a more productive, or at least less destructive, developmental process. (Basch, 1988, p. 29)

Like other Fourth Force models, transpersonal practice is concerned with the development of consciousness, but, in typical social work fashion, it looks not only at the development of intrapsychic structures ("inner forces"), but also takes into account the impact of the larger social context in which the individual is embedded ("outer forces"). Theoretically, transpersonal practice draws on the constructivist-developmental paradigm for the "inner forces" (Kegan, 1982; Rosen, 1988) and the eco-systems paradigm for the "outer forces" (Meyer, 1988). (See Figure 27–1.)

In the Transpersonal Practice Model, human consciousness is seen as many faceted and inclusive of at least six different developmental lines or dimensions of being: physical, affective/emotional, cognitive, psychosocial (social-behavioral-interpersonal), moral, and spiritual.

> Actually ego psychologists no longer think in terms of stages of development in the global sense, but in terms of different "developmental lines" for different psychological functions with the relationship between them constituting the organization of the psyche at any point in time. (Wilber et al., 1986, p. 26)

By pinpointing where the client is within each developmental line of six dimensions assessed, the transpersonal practitioner is able to get a more accurate view of the person-in-situation. In the following 1987 description (although he uses the term "unit" or "system" instead of "dimension"), Wolberg makes a strong case for why a multidimensional approach to clinical intervention is essential;

> A systems approach recognizes that no unit of psychopathology exists in isolation, but rather it is part of an aggregate of interrelated units. These consist of interacting biochemical, neurophysiological, developmental-conditioning, intrapsychic, interpersonal, and spiritual-philosophic systems that determine how a person thinks, feels, and behaves. . . . The most immediate help (to the client-system) will be rendered by diagnosing and targeting initial treatment on the system area most importantly implicated. (Wolberg, 1987, p. 256)

By assessing the developmental strengths and deficits of the client in each dimension of being, the transpersonal practitioner can target interventions to the developmental lines most salient to the client's problems in living. In this way the transpersonal practitioner "respects the autonomy of the growing person, while at the same time offering a vision of 'what ought to be' for optimum functioning" (Rosen, 1988, p. 317). The developmental line for six dimensions of being is charted in   Figure 28–4.

MULTIDIMENSIONAL ASSESSMENT

Human functioning is incredibly complex. So many factors impinge on an individual's functioning at any given moment over a life span: genetic and biochemical factors, faulty learning, deficits in opportunities, risks and trauma of various kinds, sociocultural and environmental factors, and so on. The challenge to find a comprehensive model to guide multidimensional assessments has been succinctly expressed:

> We need a coherent model of human functioning that generates efficient and effective treatment strategies, one that considers the whole person and yet

FIGURE 28–1. AN EGO-SYSTEMS/CONSTRUCTIVIST-DEVELOPMENTAL FRAMEWORK FOR UN-
DERSTANDING HUMAN BEHAVIOR IN THE SOCIAL ENVIRONMENT OVER THE
LIFE CYCLE

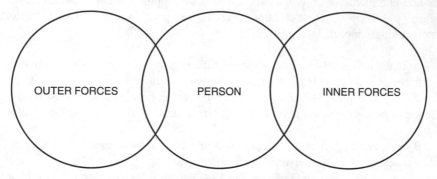

MUTUAL ADAPTATION/RECIPROCITY*

ECO-SYSTEMS (Meyer, 1988)

CONTRUCTIVIST-DEVELOPMENTAL
(Rosen, 1988)

CONTEXTUAL VARIABLES (Person-in-situation):

1. Family/relationships
2. Social institutions
3. Physical environment
4. Racial/cultural factors
5. Gender issues
6. Economic situation
7. Historical factors
8. Macro system factors

MULTIDIMENSIONAL DEVELOPMENT:

1. Physical/biological
2. Emotional/affective
3. Cognitive/mental
4. Social/relational
5. Moral
6. Spiritual

KEY CONCEPTS:

CONNECTEDNESS: Systems/subsystems
are interrelated
        Individual
Boundaries
Habit-patterned behavior
Nonlinear (not cause and effect)
Equifinality (multimodal)
Adaptation (not "cure")

KEY CONCEPTS:

Two currents pull on us from birth to death:
    Conservative = assimilation
    Progressive = accommodation
There is an intrinsic motivation to
    maximize potential.
    Development moves through a series
        of hierarchical and invariant stages.
Psychological or behavioral problems are
    viewed as "developmental lags."
Decentering is the process of differentiation
    and integration that moves from an
    egocentric view toward self-mastery
    and a sense of generativity.

*Both eco-systems and constructivist-developmental paradigms view human growth as occurring through a process of EQUILIBRATION: adaptation or reorganization and a higher form of understanding, i.e., discrepancies induce disequilibrium that ultimately leads to equilibration.

Table 28-4
Multidimensional Development

Krueger (1989)	Basch (1988)	Ivey (1986)	Erikson (1950)	Kohlberg/Woolf (81/84)	Wilbert (1986)
(Physical Dev)	(Affective Dev)	(Cognitive Dev)	(Psychosocial Dev)	(Moral Dev)	(Spiritual Dev)
6. Self-empathy Self-soothing Self-mastery	5. Attunement	6. Deconstruction paradox	8. Ego Integration vs. Despair Accrued strength = wisdom	6. Universal Mind Harmony Congruence	9. Causal Level 8. Subtle Level 7. Psychic Level
		5. Dialectic thesis/ antithesis synthesis			6. Vision-logic
	4. Empathic understanding beyond self-referential		7. Generativity vs. Stagnation/ Self-absorption Accrued strength = Caring	5. Principled "Spirit of the law" Reciprocity	
		4. Formal Identifying patterns (12 yr.–?)	6. Intimacy vs. Isolation Accrued strength = Love		5. Formal-reflexive
		3. Concrete Emphasis on objective reality (7 yr.–12 yr.)	5. Identity vs. Identity Diffusion Accrued strength = Fidelity (12 yr.–Z)	4. Law-Oriented Cares about: self, other, context "Letter of the law"	4. Rule/Role mind
5. Self-as-a-Whole Integration of body/mind (36 mo.–6 yr.)	3. Emotion Feeling states are joined w/experience (24 mo.–?)		4. Industry vs. Inferiority Accrued strength = Competence (6 yr.–12 yr.)	3. Pleaser Cares about: self and other	

Table 28-4 (Continued)
Multidimensional Development

Krueger (1989)	Basch (1988)	Ivey (1986)	Erikson (1950)	Kohlberg/Woolf (81/84)	Wilbert (1986)
(Physical Dev)	(Affective Dev)	(Cognitive Dev)	(Psychosocial Dev)	(Moral Dev)	(Spiritual Dev)
4. Body Mind Mental representation of one's body. (18 mo.–36 mo.)	2. Feeling Sensations are abstracted, objectified (18 mo–24 mo.)	2. Pre-operational Magical, irrational, ineffective thinking (2 yr.–7 yr.)	3. Initiative vs. Guilt Accrued strength = Purpose (3 yr.–6 yr.)		3. Representational mind
3. Body Self Physical boundaries (15 mo.–18 mo.)		1. Sensori-Motor Embedded in own sensory construction of the world (18 mo.–24 mo.)	2. Autonomy vs. Shame & Doubt Accrued strength = Will (1 yr.–3 yr.)	2. Self-Centered Cares about self	2. Phantasmic-emotional (Image mind)
2. Symbiotic (1 mo.–15 mo.)	1. Affect Unconscious Automatic response (0–18 mo.)		1. Trust vs. Mistrust Accrued strength = Hope (0–1 yr.)	1. Premoral Doesn't know how to care	1. Sensori-physical
1. Undifferentiated (0–1 mo.)					

provides precision without sacrificing comprehensiveness. (Gazda, 1989, p. 403)

In making an initial assessment, the transpersonal practitioner is looking for clues that will help to ascertain which dimensions of being are manifesting the most distress. The dimensions are assessed on an ongoing basis as the processes of establishing a relationship and negotiating goals and contracts proceed. Although the various dimensions are delineated separately for purposes of education and assessment, they are recognized as experientially inseparable with the mind-body-spirit as one information system with peptides acting as messengers between the nervous system, the endocrine system, and the immune system (Rossi, 1987). As Capra has reminded us, distinction is not the same as separation (Capra, 1990).

PHYSICAL ASSESSMENT AND MATURATION

The body provides many surface clues easy to assess: appearance, general state of health, use of medications, belief systems related to the body/health, nutrition, exercise, and so forth. Since the physical body is the instrument through which human becoming is experienced, physical sensations are our first sense of existence. Physical symptoms continue across the life span to offer important clues about the organism's relationship with the rest of its parts. Early sensations, or the nine basic affects, are viewed as "the primary innate biological motivating mechanisms" (Tomkins, 1981), and observation of body language usually gives us the most accurate understanding of a client's communication. Too often, social workers neglect a thorough assessment of the physical, and thus miss out on important clues to intrapsychic functioning due to biophysical problems like brain tissue damage, neurological disorders, thyroid or blood sugar imbalance, circulatory disorders associated with aging, ingestion of toxic substances, malnutrition, and other forms of chemical imbalance (Lantz, 1978)

Equally important to assess is where the individual is in terms of Krueger's developmental line since "the formation of a healthy body self is prerequisite to the experience of further expansion and cohesiveness of the total sense of self" (Krueger, 1989, p. 15). Krueger's line of development within the physical dimension includes five levels: (1) a sense of being undifferentiated or symbiotic; (2) an awareness of physical boundaries or having a sense of a body self (the idea of "I"); (3) an ability to form mental images or representations of things/people not physically present; (4) a capacity to make mental representations, but still working on healing the mind body split. Level five represents optimal maturation for the physical dimension. At this level of physical development the person has healed the mind-body split and developed a capacity for self-empathy, self-soothing, and self-mastery.

AFFECTIVE ASSESSMENT AND MATURATION

Affectivity is viewcd as the primary innate biological motivating mechanism (Tomkins, 1981):

> It is affect that gives texture to experience, urgency to drives, satisfaction to relationships, and motivating power to purposes envisioned in the future. The affect system and drive system are distinct, interrelated motivators. They empower and direct both behavior and personality, but the drives must borrow their power from affect. (Kaufman, 1989, p. 61)

Often the prime factors in a case point to disturbances in affective development (Basch, 1988). Emotional distress or dis-ease can manifest in a variety of ways: depression, mania, uncomfortable feelings, inappropriate or erratic affect, being overemotional or underemotional, an inability to connect feelings with situations or experiences, and even as a lack of capacity to understand what self or other is feeling. Therefore, an important part of assessing the affective or emotional dimension is a matter of ascertaining where in the developmental line the individual is operating. Some clients much older than one year seem to be still operating at a primitive level of unconscious and automatic reactivity: "If you feel it, do it," It may be part of the work of the therapist to teach such a client to mature emotionally by: (1) getting in touch with feelings and emotions; (2) giving emotions a name; and (3) learning how to link affects or feelings with the experiences that activate them.

"It is affect that gives meaning or a sense of force to our thoughts and behavior" (Basch, 1988, p. 66). This observation by Basch underscores the importance of knowing where the client is affectively.

> Freud acknowledged the centrality of emotional life for psychotherapy when he said that defense is always directed against affect. That is to say, whatever a patient may be struggling with in therapy, at bottom is always an affective experience that he or she cannot deal with effectively. Freud emphasized, and dynamic psychiatry still operates on that principle today, that a patient's intellectual knowledge of his or her problems is of little use if the affect attached to those problems has not also come into and been worked on in treatment. (Basch, 1988, pp. 65–66)

Helping someone become emotionally mature is often the real challenge of therapy. Optimal maturation (a high E.Q.) would result in a person who was not only in touch with his/her emotions but also a person who has the capacity to be in tune (attuned) to the emotional states of others.

COGNITIVE ASSESSMENT AND MATURATION

Cognition has characteristically been viewed as an important aspect of well-being, hence the term "mental" health. The Buddah said that all suffering comes from wrong beliefs. Cognitive therapists would agree. Delineating what is mentally healthy or intellectually competent requires a consideration of various factors besides I.Q. Attitudes and belief systems play an integral part in an individual's definitions of what constitutes personal and interpersonal pleasure or pain. Another important aspect of cognition that affects quality of life is developmental in nature. Put simply, some people just never learn how to think at mature and complex levels.

The research of Piaget has helped demonstrate that the development of cognitive capabilities occurs across predictable stages: sensorimotor, preoperational, concrete, and formal. Knowing how to identify the cognitive level or thinking style of a particular client is important is the practitioner is to choose interventions that "match" (and therefore can be understood) the client's dominant mode of processing his/her world. In Ivey's "style-shift" *Developmental Therapy* (1986), he not only suggested how the therapist could ask "transformational questions" to help teach someone how to think in more complex and mature ways, he also posited two additional levels or stages of more complex cognition that are relevant to transpersonal theory: dialectic and deconstruction.

Significant clinical progress is unlikely until a client has the capacity to move beyond splintered and chaotic thinking to process experience at the concrete operations level. Substantial change is unlikely until a person has also learned how to process at the formal operations level where one is able to perceive patterns of behavior. It is unlikely that a practitioner can interrupt unproductive or destructive cycles of behavior until the client is able to cognitively grasp the fact that he or she is involved in cocreating vicious cycles or repetitious reactions. The person who is cognitively mature has access to the whole range of cognition including Ivey's more complex levels. Thus, he/she is able to see both thesis and antithesis, as well as handle both paradox and deconstruction without undue stress.

According to Ivey, perturbation of a client system's of mode of thinking through effective confrontation is the core method of advancing developmental transformation (Ivey, 1986, p. 204). Basch also views the process of confrontation or perturbation as an important way to challenge the client to grow:

> Psychotherapy could be defined as the art of effective perturbation—the act of confronting client discrepancies and contradictions wisely and accurately and in a timely fashion. Effective confrontation of client behavior is a major precursor to growth, development, and later integration of new knowledge and skills. (Basch, 1988, pp. 191–192)

Some clients will span the range of levels of cognition, and some will need the clinician's coaching and modeling to move up the line of cognitive development to become more mature or complex thinkers.

Psychosocial Assessment and Maturation

No assessment is complete without looking at the psychosocial dimension to ascertain how clients have balanced various stages of development, as well as how they handle the social, interpersonal, and behavioral aspects of their lives. If a person is stuck at the level of trust versus mistrust, that is where the worker must begin. Without the accrued ego strength of autonomy, it is highly unlikely that the client will be able to take initiative on his or her own behalf without experiencing feelings of inferiority. Until a person develops a firm sense of identity, and the personal boundaries that entails, he or she is not equipped psychologically for committed, intimate relationships. When one is not successful in terms of identity or intimacy, self-absorption and stagnation are logical consequences. Without generativity one falls into despair rather than wisdom in old age. Too often the problems in living with which client systems contend are influenced by developmental transitions that go unidentified. Reframing some of the transitory discomfort of growth along the life span as developmental "passages" (Sheehy, 1976), "transformation" (Gould, 1978), "necessary losses" (Viorst, 1986), or "adaptation to life" (Vaillant, 1977) can not only be very reassuring to the client, but also productive for the overall helping process.

Problems of living and the impact of macro systems are an integral part of transpersonal practice. The eco-systems perspective provides a conceptual stance for assessing environmental and horizontal stressors. Accordingly, the transpersonal practitioner does a kind of "environmental impact" study to identify factors that might influence the client's sense of well-being. Problems may run the gamut from the color of paint in a home or office, to the effect that national or global events can have on the functioning of individuals, groups, couples, families, organizations, and societies.

In terms of psychosocial maturation, ego strengths required for ego integration are accrued as developmental tasks are balanced across the life span. An important part of the psychosocial assessment is pinpointing which developmental crises seem to be unbalanced or "stuck" in a maladaptive modes. This information allows the clinician to function as a developmental partner (Krueger, 1989) by providing specific structure building experiences for the client.

Moral Assessment and Maturation

Kohlberg/Woolf's (Woolf, 1984) view of moral development offers a paradigm for understanding the level of moral development the client has achieved. If moral development has been arrested, guidelines for helping the client to develop more prosocial behaviors and principled relationships are inherent in Kohlberg's theory. Morally, some clients are still operating at the "premoral" or "amoral" level, since they have never learned to care about self, other, or the social context. The next level up, self-centered, is a challenging one to work with because the capacity for including the other or the social context is nonexistent or very limited. At the pleaser level of moral development, an individual knows how to care about the other and the social context, but often "cares" at the expense of selfhood. Law-oriented clients are capable of caring about self, other, and the social context, but may go about it with such a rigid adherence to the "letter of the law" mentality that their lack of flexibility can make life difficult for themselves as well as for others. The person who has reached principled levels of moral development has the capacity to act according to "the spirit of the law," i.e., in compassionate, fair, caring, and sharing ways. Occasionally the morally mature, universal-minded walk among us and demonstrate the moral attributes of a harmonizer/peacemaker.

Spiritual Assessment and Maturation

By distinguishing between moral development and spiritual development, the therapist is able to bring yet another aspect of specificity to the task of choosing appropriate interventions. However, assessing a client's connection to spirit is not always a salient focus. Obviously, until basic needs for food, shelter, belonging, self-esteem, and self-actualization are met, self-transcendence is not an appropriate focus for intervention. Indeed, some may ask if social work should concern itself at all with a theory so clearly geared to working with "the haves" instead of the "have nots." Spiritual assessment and maturation become an area for focus when the client is experiencing spiritual malaise or feels deprived of nonmaterial resources and desires to strengthen spiritual capacities. At that time in the therapeutic process, it is crucial that the worker has a conceptual framework for identifying where the individual is in terms of spiritual development so that the process of spiritual maturation may be supported.

Wilber's Full Spectrum of Consciousness Model makes a beginning attempt to describe three levels of spiritual or transpersonal development where qualities like equanimity, compassion, and unconditional love are actively cultivated. At the psychic level, a person begins to open up the transrational. Consciousness, at subtle and causal levels, begins to transcend the self and to experience unitive states. When assessing these transpersonal levels of the spiritual dimension, the practitioner steps into the ineffable, the unnamable, and the mysterious. No "fact" is available here, nor is there any likelihood of prediction. With indigenous and Eastern practices leading the way, Transpersonal Theory works out of a postmodern view that takes intuition (inner vision) and other nonlinear ways of knowing into account. Optimal spiritual maturation involves ("inner work"), which is expected to evidence in action (or "outer work") to benefit relationships, family systems, organization, local communities, nations, the global family, and the ecological health of the planet.

Ideally, in a global village beautifully alive with diversity, all clinical social workers would be equally versed in all of the Four Forces. When this is not the case, issues related to the spiritual dimension will require transpersonal interventions and referrals to practitioners conversant with that theoretical approach. The Transpersonal Practice Model introduced in this chapter seeks to build on Wilber's Full Spectrum Model. By providing more specificity to developmental lines, its interventions are necessarily unique to each client system. By more accurately determining where structure building needs to occur to reactivate patterns of growth toward optimal potential, the person is intentionally helped to move toward maturation in each dimension of being. This takes Nelson's insightful observation into account: "Only when people engage in treatment specific to their level of consciousness can they resume growth" (Nelson, 1994, p. 375).

Central to the Transpersonal Practice Model is the notion that to be healthy (whole), one must actualize, balance, and mature all of one's aspects or dimensions. Therefore, health in the transpersonal sense is not seen as a process of adjustment to society, because society itself may be sick. Nor is health defined solely in the language of the market place by values of competition, productivity, status, or unmitigated self-interest. The transpersonal approach is concerned with developing the values of the spirit required for full personhood and planetary citizenship, such as: cooperation, receptivity, reciprocity, and altruism. These value-laden goals are pursued while at the same time the unique growth pattern of each individual/system is honored.

THE FOUR FORCES

Like Wilber's Full Spectrum Model, Transpersonal Practice postulates that each of the various Four Force theories may be appropriately utilized when intervening with problems of living and pathologies that occur at different levels of the spectrum of consciousness. After determining in which dimensions developmental deficits have occurred, the transpersonal practitioner is able to design person-specific, multimodal interventions that utilize the theories, models, and skills/techniques of each of the Four Forces selectively and integratively. Since each of the four broad umbrella theories has a different focus, view of pathology, what constitutes health, the curative process, and the nature of the helping relationship, and so on, various models and favored interventions, skills, or techniques utilized by the different theories can be identified. In making the conceptual distinctions about which models "fit" with each theory, and which clinical skills or interventions "match" the models and theories chosen, one is admonished to remember that each theory makes fundamentally different assumptions. Lazarus distinguished clearly the differences between choosing a theory (or theories) to guide the therapeutic process and choosing specific interventions or techniques to accomplish designated goals within that process. Lazarus pointed out that one must be theoretically "pure" while acknowledging that, at the same time, one could be technically "eclectic" (Lazarus, 1987, p. 166).

> . . . By underscoring the virtues of technical eclecticism and the dangers of theoretical eclecticism, I hope to pave the way for a sincere appreciation of the scientific method, the significance of breadth versus depth approaches, and the overriding need for specificity. (Lazarus, 1987, p. 165)

When a practitioner is able to intentionally pick which theory, model, and intervention is the best "match" for intervention in a specific dimension of an unique client system, at a given moment in the therapeutic process, he/she gets closer to answering the classic question asked by Gordon Paul in 1967: "What treatment, by whom is most effective for this individual with that specific problem, under which set of circumstances, and how does it come about?" See Table 28–5 for a beginning effort to operationalize a clinical thesaurus for each of the Four Forces (theories, models, interventions, etc.). It is hoped that such a chart can be a helpful aid for students and beginning practitioners as they attempt to make some sense out of the plethora of theories, models, and skills that are available for their use.

THE IMPORTANCE OF A PREMISE

Maslow's major premise was succinctly expressed in what later became known as "Maslow's Metaphor": Freud supplied to us the sick half of psychology, and we must now fill it out with the healthy half (Wittine, 1987, p. 54). Just how important was Maslow's premise that we must study the farther reaches of human nature? What difference does it make what premises we use to guide our practice? I think the answer to both questions is "extremely important." Whether or not the evolution of consciousness within individuals or societies takes place in the years ahead will depend to a large degree on the belief systems that shape and guide us personally and professionally. Premises held by those in the helping professions about the possible human and the boundaries of exceptional health and well-being will help to determine our future as a species. As Allport sagely observed:

> By their own theories of human nature, psychologists have the power of elevating or degrading that same nature. Debasing assumptions debase human beings; generous assumptions exalt them. (Walsh & Shapiro, 1983, p. 31)

Our premises about human potential shape our perceptions and influence our areas of inquiry and therefore act in self-validating ways (Walsh & Vaughn, 1980a, p. 17).

> If our prevailing cultural and psychological models have underestimated what we are and what we can become then perhaps we have set up a self-fulfilling prophecy. In such a case, the exploration of extreme psychological well-being, and the permeation of that knowledge into psychology and the larger culture, becomes a particularly important undertaking. Indeed, it may even be that shifting our self concept may be one of the most strategic interventions for personal and cultural transformation. What is envisaged as possible may become a compelling vision and attraction. (Walsh & Shapiro, 1983, p. 10)

Traditional Western psychology (the first three forces) has been challenged to deal with spiritual concerns and symptoms, and it has been found lacking. Conventional theories have also failed to inspire the lure to being so desperately needed in a time when "we are in a race between consciousness and catastrophe" (Walsh & Vaughn, 1993, p. 134).

Table 28–5
The Four Forces

Theory	Dynamic	Behavioral	Humanistic Experiential Existential	Transpersonal

Focus	Dynamics/past	Specific behaviors	Awareness
			Human experience
			Self responsibility
				Spiritual
				  dimension
				Transcendence
				Metabolizing
				  COEXs

Level of
  individuation
  focused on
	"IT"
	Prepersonal
		"I"
		Personal
			"I"
			Personal
				Above "I"
				Transpersonal
				"Beyond ego"

View of pathology	Instinctive
	  conflicts
	Chaotic "it"
	Disorganization
	Repetition
	  compulsion
	Deficits of dev.
		Faulty learning
		Dysfunctional
		  behavior
		Patterns of
		  expectations
		State dependent
		  learning
			Reduced potential
			Alienation from
			  feelings
			Meaninglessness
				Ego attachments
				Lack of purpose
				Egoitis
				Dark night of the
				  soul

View of health	Ego over id A personal self Firm boundaries	Remove symptoms Change behaviors Correct faulty learning	Reaching potential Being authentic Purpose in life Open to goodness	Wholeness One mind Nonattached

Curative process	Long term, intense
	Make unconscious
	  conscious
	Structure building
	Restructure
	  personality
		Education
		Learn new
		  behaviors
		Short-term
		  structured
		Self management
		Diagnostic tests
			Eclectic
			Use of relationship
			Here & now focus
			Opening to
			  goodness
			Removing blocks
			  to growth
			Making meaning
				Self healing
				Disidentification
				Integration:
				Balance of
				  unconscious
				  conscious
				  supraconscious
				Healing is wholing

Nature of the
  helping
  relationship
	Vertical
	Medical model
	Objective
		Vertical
		Educative
		Direct teaching
		Measurable goals
			Horizontal
			Person-to-person
			Process oriented
			Pehnomenological
			Remove blocks to
			  growth
			Facilitator
				Reciprocal
				Servant/co-voyage
				Mutuality
				Guide
				Midwife
				Evocateur

Models	Psychoanalysis
	Jungian
	Object relations
	Aderlian
	Eriksonian
	Self psychology
	Ego psychology
	TA
		Behavior mod.
		Cognitive beh.
		  mod.
		RET
		Reality therapy
		Task centered
		  casework
			Humanistic
			Person centered
			Experiential
			Gestalt
			Logotherapy
				All theories/
				  models
				Jungian
				Psychosynthesis
				Therapia
				Holotropic
				Full spectrum
				Process oriented
				Self-creation
				Transpersonal
				  practice

Table 28–5 (Continued)
The Four Forces

Theory	Dynamic	Behavioral	Humanistic Experiential Existential	Transpersonal
Interventions	History taking	Anchoring	Therapeutic love	Dis-identification
(skills/	Free association	Self monitoring	Visualization	Meditation/yoga
techniques)	Sentence stems	Thought stopping	Creative imagery	Visualization
	Dream analysis	Cog. restructuring	Empty chair	Active imagination
	Catharsis	Reinforcement	Top dog/bottom	Eidetic imagery
	Transference	Densisitization	dog	Metaphor
	Resistance	Modeling/imitation	Strength	Paradox
	Slips	Shaping	bombardment	Imagery/healing of
	Interpretations	Positive self talk	Gestalting dreams	memories
	Insight	Substitution	Stream of	I am affirmations
	Working through	Rehearsal/role play	awareness	Dream work
	Exaggeration	Redecision therapy	Positive selftalk	Seeding
	"Spit in soup"	Biofeedback	Fantasy	Listening to sage
	L.S.I.G.	Relaxation training	Experiential/aware-	within
	Early recollections	Stress management	ness exercises	Intuition (inner
	Script analysis	Self-efficacy	De-repressing	vision)
	Ego-gram	training	Re-experiencing	Detached observer
	Ego-state analysis	Skills training	Confrontation	Interpreting up
	Structure-building	Behavioral	Affective work	Interpreting down
	Uncovering	contracts	Being present	Socratic dialogue
	Play therapy	Homework	Choreography	Evocative music
	Character analysis	Action tasks	Psychodrama	Journals/diaries
	Reparenting	Confrontation	Observation	Breathing
		Persuasive arguing	Looking for	techniques
		Internal dialogues	patterns, themes	Shadow work
		Aversion therapy	Dereflexion	Wisdom circles
		Sex therapy	Philosophizing	Community
		Bibliotherapy		building

MAKING A PARADIGM SHIFT

The good news is that there is an ascendant ontology behind the evolution of con-sciousness. The bad news is that to include the theory and models proposed by the transpersonal approach into social work practice will require nothing less than a par-adigm shift for social workers who have been predominantly educated in the first three forces of psychology. Old paradigms die hard, and knowing that existing ther-apies are inadequate (or incomplete) and establishing new ones to take their place are very different issues. Grof reminds us that once a theory has achieved the status of a paradigm, it will not be declared invalid unless a viable alternative is available (Grof, 1985). Now that Fourth Force Theory is available, incorporating it into social work education and practice is the next step. If traditional psychotherapies can be utilized to strengthen the ego "so that it can endure the eventual weaning from unreality that human maturity requires" (Boorstein, 1980, p. 4), then transpersonal theory can provide guidelines for the worker to accompany the person-in-becoming in the quest for optimal states of being, and, in some cases, toward self-transcendence.

HEALING SPLITS

The Transpersonal Practice Model repossesses the spiritual-philosophic values present at social work's inception. It has the potential to heal the profession by "retrieving the soul of social work" (Canda, 1995) and, thus, reconnecting it to its origins in philanthropy, theology, and moralism (Weick, 1992). Since the transpersonal approach takes the spiritual dimension into account, it can also offer hope to a secular society that has been artificially divorced from its Source. According to Ernest Rossi:

> We can view the entire history of psychotherapy as a series of efforts to heal the artificial divisions in man's nature. . . . the basic problem is always a dissociation or split that needs to be healed. (Rossi, 1987, p. 370)

Even though transpersonal theory is still in its infancy as a theoretical approach (Washburn, 1988) and will call for a creative cosmology in terms of research (Peile, 1993), part of its attraction and promise for social work practice lies in its capacity to serve as catalyst for healing splits within individuals, and the "therapeutic wars" within clinical practice (Saltzman & Norcross, 1990). By acknowledging the important contributions of all major psychological theories, and by taking into account and validating the transrational nature of the spiritual dimension, the artificial divisions and omissions in clinical practice can be healed or made whole. Transpersonal theory's promise for practice with groups, couples, and families, administration, and community practice remains to be explored.

Wilber has presented his Full Spectrum of Consciousness Model "to show the strong possibilities rather than the final conclusions" (Wilber et al., 1986). In presenting Transpersonal Practice as a Fourth Force Model, I can only echo Wilber's plea:

> . . . that given the state of knowledge already available to us, it seems ungenerous to the human condition to present any model less comprehensive—by which I mean, models that do not take into account both conventional and contemplative realms of human growth and development. (Wilber et al., 1986, p. 159)

REFERENCES

Anthony, D., Ecker, B., & Wilber, K. (1987). *Spiritual choices: The problem of recognizing authentic paths to inner transformation.* New York: Paragon House.

Assagioli, R. (1965). *Psychosynthesis.* New York: Viking Press.

Aurobindo. S. (1971). *Letters on yoga.* Pondicherry, India: Sri Aurobindo International University Center.

Basch, M. (1988). *Understanding psychotherapy: The science behind the art.* New York: Basic Books.

Bee, N. (1986, Fall). Psychology's journey toward spirituality. *American Theosophist, 74*(9), 338–342.

Bettelheim, B. (1983). *Freud and man's soul.* New York: Alfred A. Knopf.

Bloomfield, II. (1980). Transcendental meditation as an adjunct to therapy. In S. Boorstein (Ed.). *Transpersonal psychology.* (pp 123–140). Palo Alto, CA.: Science and Behavior Books.

Bodian, S. (1988, July/August). Critiquing the New Age with Ken Wilber and David Spangler. *Yoga Journal,* 45–118.

Boorstein, S. (Ed.) (1980). *Transpersonal psychotherapy.* Palo Alto, CA: Science and Behavior Books.

Boorstein, S. (1986). Transpersonal context, interpretation and psycho-therapeutic technique. *Journal of Transpersonal Psychology, 18*(2), 124–129.

Bradshaw, J. (1988). *Bradshaw on: The family.* Deerbeach, FL: Health Communications.

Brown, D. (1988, Spring). The transformation of consciousness in meditation. *Noetic Sciences Review* (6), 14.

Bugental, J. (1978). *Psychotherapy and process.* Reading, MA: Addison-Wesley.

Bugental, J., & Bugental, I. (1984, Winter). Dispiritedness: A new perspective on a familiar state. *Journal of Humanistic Psychology, 24*(1), 49–67.

Campbell, J. (1971). *The portable Jung.* New York: Viking Press.

Canda, E. (1988a). Conceptualizing spirituality for social work: Insights from diverse perspectives. *Social Thought, 13*(1), 30–46.

Canda, E. (1988b). Spirituality, religious diversity, and social work practice. *Social Casework, 69(4), 238–247.*

Canda, E. (1989, Winter). Religious content in social work education: A comparative approach. *Journal of Social Work Education, 25*(2), 36–45.

Canda, E. (1995, Fall). Retrieving the soul of social work. *Society for Spirituality and Social Work Newsletter, 2*(2), 5–8.

Capra, F. (1990, Summer). Life as mental process. *Quest, 3*(2), 7–11.

Clinebell, H. (1995). *Counseling for spiritually empowered wholeness: A hope-centered approach.* New York: Haworth Press.

Cowley, A. (1993, September). Transpersonal social work: A theory for the 1990s. *Social Work, 38*(5), 527–534.

Cowley, A., & Derezotes, D. (In 1994 winter). Transpersonal psychology and social work education. *Journal of Social Work Education.*

Cox, D. (1985). The missing dimension in social work practice. *Australian Social Work, 38*(4), 5–11.

Crittenden, E. (1980). A Jungian view of transpersonal events in psychotherapy. In S. Boorstein (Ed.). *Transpersonal psychotherapy* (pp. 57–78). Palo Alto, CA: Science and Behavior Books.

Denton, R. (1990, Winter). The religiously fundamentalist family: Training for assessment and treatment. *Journal of Social Work Education. 26*(1), 6–14.

Derezotes, D. (1995). Spiritual and religious factors in practice: Empirically-based recommendations for social work education. *Arete, 20*(1), 1–15.

Dorfman, R. (1988). The development of a discipline. In Dorfman R. (Ed.), *Paradigms of clinical social work* (pp. 3–24). New York: Brunner/Mazel.

Erikson, E. (1950). *Childhood and society.* New York: W.W. Norton.

Fabry, J. (1980). Use of the transpersonal in logotherapy. In Seymour Boorstein (Ed.), *Transpersonal psychotherapy.* Palo Alto, CA: Science and Behavior Books.

Ferrucci, P. (1982). *What we may be.* Los Angeles: J.P. Tarcher.

Fowler, J. (1981). *Stages of faith: The psychology of human development and the quest for meaning.* San Francisco: Harper & Row.

Frankl, V. (1975). *The unconscious god.* New York: Simon & Schuster.

Gazda, G. (1989). *Group counseling: A developmental approach.* New York: Simon & Schuster.

Goldberg, D. (1980). *In defense of marcissism.* New York: Gardner Press.

Gould, R. (1978). *Transformation: Growth and change in adult life.* New York: Simon & Schuster.

Grof, C. (1990). *The stormy search for the self.* Los Angeles; J.P. Tarcher.

Grof, S. (1985). *Beyond the brain.* Albany: State University of New York Press.

Grof, S. (Ed.) (1988). *Human survival and consciousness evolution.* Albany: State University of New York Press.

Grof, S., & Grof, C. (1987, March/April). Holotropic therapy: A strategy for achieving inner transformation. *New Realities, 7*(4), 7–12.

Grof, S., & Grof, C. (Eds.). (1989). *Spiritual emergency: When personal transformation becomes a crisis.* Los Angeles: J.P. Tarcher.

Hendricks, G., & Weinhold, B. (1982). *Transpersonal approaches to counseling and psychotherapy.* Denver: Love Publishing Co.

Hepworth, D., & Larsen, J. (1993). *Direct social work practice: Theory and skills.* Pacific Grove, CA: Brooks/Cole Publishing Company.

Houston, J. (1987). *The search for the beloved: Journeys in sacred psychology.* Los Angeles: J.P. Tarcher.

Houston, J. (1988, March/April). Sacred psychology: An introduction to the nature of the quest. *New Realities,* 41–45.

Ingram, C. (1987), September/October). Ken Wilber: The pundit of transpersonal psychology. *Yoga Journal,* 40–49.

Ivey, A. (1986). *Developmental therapy.* San Francisco: Jossey-Bass.

Kaufman, G. (1989). *The psychology of shame: Theory and treatment of shamed-based syndromes.* New York: Springer.

Keen, S. (1983). Uses and abuses of "spiritual technology" in therapy. *Common Boundary. 1*(5), 7–8.

Kegan, R. (1982). *The evolving self: Problem and process in human development.* Cambridge, MA: Harvard University Press.

Keyes, K. (1975). *Handbook to higher consciousness.* Marina del Rey, CA: DeVorss.

Khan, P.V.I. (1982). *Introducing spirituality into counseling and therapy.* Santa Fe, NM: Omega Press.

Kohlberg, L. (1981). *The philosophy of moral development.* San Francisco: Harper & Row.

Kramer, S. (1995). *Transforming the inner and outer family: Humanistic and spiritual approaches to mind-body systems therapy.* New York: Haworth Press.

Krueger, D. (1989). *Body self and psychological self.* New York: Brunner/Mazel.

Lantz, J. (1978). Cognitive theory and social casework. *Social Work, 23,* 361–366.

Lazarus, A. (1987). The need for technical eclecticism: Science, breadth, depth, and specificity. In J. Zeig (Ed.), *The evolution of psychotherapy.* New York: Brunner/Mazel.

Leonard, G. (1983, December). Abraham Maslow and the new self. *Esquire,* p. 326.

Levin, D. (Ed.). (1987). *Pathologies of the modern self: Postmodern studies on narcissism, schizophrenia, and depression.* New York: New York University Press.

London, P. (1974, June). From the long couch for the sick to the push button for the bored. *Psychology Today. 8*(1), 63–68.

London, P. (1986). *The modes and morals of psychotherapy.* New York: Hemisphere Publishing Corporation.

Lovinger, R. (1984). *Working with religious issues in therapy.* New York: Jason Aronson.

Maslow, A. (1971a). *Toward a psychology of being.* Princeton: Van Nostrand.

Maslow, A. (1971b). *The farther reaches of human nature.* New York: Viking/Compass.

May, R. (1982). *Physicians of the soul: The psychologies of the world's great spiritual teachers.* New York: Crossroad.

May, G. (1988). *Addiction and grace: Love and spirituality in the healing of addictions.* San Francisco: Harper.

Meyer, C. (1988). The eco-systems perspective. In R. Dorfman (Ed.), *Paradigms of clinical social work.* New York: Brunner/Mazel.

Metzner, R. (1986). *Opening to inner light: The transformation of human nature and consciousness.* Los Angeles: J.P. Tarcher.

Mindell, A. (1985). *Working with the dreaming body.* New York: Arkana, Viking Penguin.

Nelson, J. (1994). *Healing the split: Integrating spirit into our understanding of the mentally ill.* New York: State University of New York Press.

Ornstein, R. (1972). *The psychology of consciousness.* New York: Penguin Books.

Paul, G. (1967). Strategy of outcome research in psychotherapy. *Journal of Consulting Psychology.* 31, 109–118.

Peck, M.S. (1987, May/June). A new American revolution. *New Age Journal,* 32–37, 50–51.

Peile, C. (1993, March). Determinism versus creativity: Which way for social work? *Social Work, 38*(2), 127–134.

Pine, F. (1985). *Developmental theory and clinical practice.* New Haven, CT: Yale University Press.

Reid, P., & Popple, P. (1992). *The moral purposes of social work: The character and intention of a profession.* Chicago: Nelson-Hall.

Rosen, H. (1988). The constructivist-developmental paradigm. In R. Dorfman (Ed.), *Paradigms of clinical social work.* New York: Brunner/Mazel.

Rossi, E. (1987). Mind/body communication and the new language of human facilitation. In J. Zeig (Ed.), *The evolution of psychotherapy* (pp. 369–387). New York: Brunner/Mazel.

Saltzman, N., & Norcross, J. (Eds.) (1990). *Therapy wars: Contention and convergence in differing clinical approaches.* San Francisco: Jossey-Bass.

Satir, V. (1987). Going beyond the obvious: The psychotherapeutic journey. In J. Zeig (Ed.), *The evolution of psychotherapy.* New York: Brunner/Mazel.

Schnall, M. (1981). *Limits: A search for new values.* New York: Crown.

Sheehy, G. (1976). *Passages: Predictable crises of adult life.* New York: Dutton.

Small, J. (1982). *Transformers: The therapists of the future.* Marina del Rey, CA: De Vores & Co.

Smith, E. (1995, May). Addressing the psychospiritual distress of death as reality: a transpersonal approach. *Social Work, 40*(3), 402–413.

Solomon, E. (1967). Humanistic values and social casework. *Social Casework, 48*(1), 26–32.

Specht, H. (1994). *Unfaithful angels.* New York: Free Press.

Spencer, S. (1957). Religious and spiritual values in social casework practice. *Social Casework, 38*(10), 519–525.

Stroup, H. (1962, March/April). The common predicament of religion and social work. *Social Work. 7*(2), 89–93.

Sutich, A. (1969). Some considerations regarding transpersonal psychology. *Journal of Transpersonal Psychology, 1*(1), 11–20.

Szent-Gyoergyi, A. (1974). Drive in living matter to perfect itself. *Synthesis I, 1*(1), 14–26.

Tart, C. (Ed.) (1975). *Transpersonal psychologies.* London: Routledge & Kegan Paul.

Tart, C. (1986). *Waking up: Overcoming the obstacles to human potential.* Boston: New Science Library/Shambhala.

Tomkins, S. (1981). The quest for primary motives: Biography and autobiography of an idea. *Journal of Personality and Social Psychology, 41,* 306–329.

Vaillant, G. (1977). *Adaptation to life.* Boston: Little, Brown.

Vaughn, F. (1986, Spring). Transforming consciousness in psychotherapy: A transpersonal approach. *American Theosophist,* 147–155.

Vaughn, F. (1991). Spiritual issues in psychotherapy. *Journal of Transpersonal Psychology, 23*(2), 105–120.

Vaughn, F. (1995, Winter). Spiritual freedom. *Quest, 8*(4), 48–55.

Vincentia, J. (1987, Winter). The religious and spiritual aspects of clinical practice: A neglected dimension of social work. *Social Thought*, 12–23.

Viorst, J. (1986). *Necessary losses: The loves, illusions, dependencies and impossible expectation that all of us have to give up in order to grow*. New York: Simon & Schuster.

Walsh, R. (1984). *Staying alive: The psychology of human survival*. Boulder, CO: Shambhala/New Science Library.

Walsh, R., & Shapiro, E. (Eds.). (1983). *Beyond health and normality: Explorations of exceptional psychological well-being*. New York: Van Nostrand Reinhold.

Walsh, R., & Vaughn, F. (Eds.) (1980a). *Beyond ego: Transpersonal dimensions in psychology*. Los Angeles: J.P. Tarcher.

Walsh, R., & Vaughn, F. (1980b). Comparative modes of psychotherapy. In S. Boorstein (Ed.), *Transpersonal psychotherapy*. Palo Alto, CA: Science and Behavior Books.

Walsh, R., & Vaughn, F. (1993). The transpersonal movement: A history and state of the art. *Journal of Transpersonal Psychology, 25*(2), 123–139.

Washburn, M. (1988). *The ego and the dynamic ground: A transpersonal theory of human development*. Albany: State University of New York Press.

Washburn, M. (1994). *Transpersonal psychology in psychoanalytic perspective*. Albany: State University of New York Press.

Weick, A. (1992, Spring/Summer). Publishing and perishing in social work education. *Journal of Social Work Education, 28*(2), 129–130.

Weinhold, B. (1989). Transpersonal theories in family treatment. In D. Fenell & B. Weinhold (Eds.), *Counseling families*. Denver, CO: Love Publishing Co.

Welwood, J. (1986). Personality structure: Path or pathology? *Journal of Transpersonal Psychology. 18*(2) 131–142.

Wheeler, B., Wood. S., & Hatch, S. (1989). Assessment and intervention with adolescents involved in Satanism. *Social Work, 33,* 547–550.

Whitmore, D. (1991). *Psychosynthesis counselling in action*. Newbury Park, CA: Sage Publications.

Wiedemann, F. (1986). *Between two worlds: the riddle of wholeness*. Wheaton, IL: Theosophical Publishing House.

Wilber, K. (1977). *The spectrum of consciousness*. Wheaton, IL: Quest Publications.

Wilber, K. (1981). *Up from Eden: A transpersonal view of human evolution*. New York: Anchor Press/Doubleday.

Wilber, K. (1983a). The evolution of consciousness. In R. Walsh & D. Shapiro (Eds.), *Beyond health and normality: Explorations of exceptional psychological well-being*. New York: Van Nostrand Reinhold.

Wilber, K. (1983b). Where it was, there I shall become: Human potential and the boundaries of the soul. In R. Walsh & D. Shapiro (Eds.), *Beyond health and normality: Explorations of exceptional psychological well-being*. New York: Van Nostrand Reinhold.

Wilber, K. (1996). *A brief history of everything*. Boston: Shambhala.

Wilber, K., Engler, J., & Brown, D. (1986). *Transformations of consciousness*. Boston: New Science Library/Shambhala.

Wittine, B. (1987, September/October). Beyond ego. *Yoga Journal,* 51–57.

Wolberg, L. (1987). The evolution of psychotherapy: Future trends. In J. Zeig (Ed.), *The evolutions of psychotherapy*. New York: Brunner/Mazel.

Woolf, V. (1984). The good life seminars. Lecture series presented in Provo, Utah.

Zukav, G. (1989). *The seat of the soul*. New York: Simon & Schuster.

CHAPTER 29

AN INTERLOCKING
PERSPECTIVE FOR
TREATMENT

FRANCIS J. TURNER

AN OVERVIEW

Once again we have reached the termination of our voyage during which we visited twenty-seven models of social work theory, each of which is important for contemporary practice. And as on three previous occasions, I need to step back and ask, what have we learned from this venture?

Unlike what I had expected when this process first began, some twenty-five years ago, the emergence of new theories of practice has not diminished. Then we had fourteen systems: now we have twenty-seven. Some decry this, but I welcome it! For this expansion of diversity reminds us once again how complex is our field as we practice in a highly diverse and ever-changing multicultural world. This reality also reminds us how naïve we were when we attempted to include the scope of social work into any single theoretical framework. In addition, this development has helped us become more open to new ideas, concepts, strategies, methodologies, techniques, and technologics, all of which have enriched our practice.

Nor has there been any movement toward the emergence of a mega-theory which would begin to tie together this wealth of concepts and practices; although the development of the "Fourth Force" in theory development, as discussed by Dr. Cowley in Chapter 28, speculates on this possibility (Curnock & Hardicker, 1979).

There is now much less faddism about new theories than before, although still a tendency in some to be fashionable. There is, as well, a growing tolerance of differences among theories and theorists. There is more acceptance of the idea that a great unifying panacea is not going to emerge, nor will a major theoretical breakthrough occur that will make everything clear and precise. This awareness has in turn made us more cautious, humble, critical, outward-looking, and curious about both the processes of building theory and the use of theories as they emerge (Caspi, 1992).

As well, there is a growing interest and comfort in comparing notes between theories and examining their conceptual bases—not in an argumentative, self-validating way but in an exploratory manner, seeking a broadening of purview. In doing so, however, there is still a tendency in our profession to prefer the new to the old even though, as the authors of these so called *tradiational theories* demonstrate in their respective chapters, there is still much to be learned from them. The chapters on functional, psychosocial, and problem-solving theories are good examples attesting to this.

Our growing comfort with the need to be multitheoretical continues. This is accompanied by the understanding that systems are helped, not threatened, when they seek and incorporate interconnections with other systems. The "holy wars" of earlier years have all but disappeared as the awareness grows that each system has something to teach us. The belief that a strong theory base enhances practice is evident, but not universal; thus there exists an equally strong awareness of our challenge to demonstrate this.

With this growing comfort in looking over one another's theoretical shoulder in a collegial manner comes an appreciation of the need to look not only at differences among theories but also similarities. Throughout, there is an understanding that within the differences there is a common thread, or indeed common threads, that unify. Each, even if adapted from other sources and other disciplines than social work, is indeed a social work theory in that being adapted to our needs each addresses that "*person in situation*" reality which is the cornerstone of the profession. In this vein all of the chapters in this volume were written by social workers each of whom has examined the tenets of a particular system and demonstrated its relevance and utility to social work practice theory.

WHAT IS NEW?

But much of what has just been said was identified in the third edition of this volume. Have there been observable changes in our addressing theoretical plurality? Certainly the fact that in the ten years since the last edition we have added six new theories marks the march to increasing complexity. Further, as alluded to above, there has been a marked shift to a much greater incorporation of the concept of *interlocking* and interinfluencing. Virtually all of the chapters indicate areas in which there are connections and commonalities with other systems—to a much greater extent than in an earlier day. As part of this, the range of writing about various theories and the place of theory in practice has expanded (Mishne, 1993). This reflects a growing interest in the differential application of theories as well as an expanding commitment to explore the specific applications of each theory through either practice or more formal research.

As noted, one of the advantages, or rather windfalls, of a familiarity and comfort with an interlocking perspective is the contribution that this makes to the expansion of concepts once thought to be precise in definition and reification. The question of the unconscious is a good example. In the last edition it was pointed out that there was a broadening of perception as to the relative importance of the unconscious in practice. This still remains, with a generalized acceptance that there is an unconscious component to all personality structure regardless of theory, the differences between theories being in the importance that it is given. However, we have now moved beyond this to an expanded perception of what is meant by the unconscious and how it manifested. Some of the discussion in the use of meditation and cognitive thinking has contributed to this.

Another example of expanded and enriched perception relates to the "situation" segment of "person in situation." Here we are continuing to progress in our awareness of both the complexity and importance of understanding our clients' social reality. In so doing we are developing approaches that make use of this expanded awareness in a therapeutic manner.

Another concept where there has been considerable broadening and enrichment is in regard to the expanded concept of the helping relationship. This awareness relates to a richer understanding of such things as power, transference, and values as components of the relationshp between client and worker, but as well of the growing appreciation of the diversity of forms that this relationship can take.

Within these chapters a diminution in the focus on pathology as the primary target of intervention can be noted. Instead, we are observing a thrust to build our diagnosis, and plan our treatment on the clients' goals and aspirations within the parameters of their strengths and available resources. In so doing, increased understanding and attention is given to the client's social reality and his/her or their perception of it within the broad base with which it is composed. Pathology is not denied or excluded from the purview of the social worker clinician but is seen in a much more comprehensive way, so that when present it must be viewed in context and as only one part of the client's reality with which we deal.

Diagnostic responsibility remains at the forefront of our practice. What is meant by this term is highly varied. However defined, it relates to our need to take responsibility for what we do, knowing what is appropriate and what is inappropriate. Each author has identified the limitations and counterindications for the application of the theoretical system which she/he addressed. The implication of this is that we need to know these limitations and their implications for each client we meet: the true role of diagnosis.

Although not as predominant a development as expected with the increasing permeability between theoretical systems and their applications, the need for an expanded understanding of the physical and biological components of our clients' reality is emerging. This growing awareness of the effects of our biological reality on our psychosocial functioning increases our responsibility to give these aspects of our clients' more attention. Gestalt and its awareness of the way our body and its functioning can convey messages about our psychological status, meditation's interest in body and mind connections, and neurolinguistics' focus on understanding the neurological base of communication have helped bring into clearer focus the relevance of this material to our practice, as has the chapter on transpersonal social work.

Perhaps the most important new theme that emerges in this collection is the expanded understanding and appreciation of the fact that theories are open, dynamic systems that grow, change, and develop as they both interact with other systems and are variously applied by practitioners. The earlier tendency in the helping professions of seeing various theories as virtually closed systems whose ramparts needed to be protected against contamination and assault from other systems has virtually disappeared. From this perspective much change can be observed in the presentation of the various systems in comparison to the earlier editions of this text. An example of the intensity of earlier isolation between two systems is well described by Dr. Dunlap in discussing the early days of the diagnostic-functional schism.

On the other side, an excellent example of the development of a theory and its incorporation of new material can be observed in the discussion regarding crisis theory by Dr Ell. Here we see the movement from the important but narrow view of crisis to the incorporation of concepts such as critical stress reactions and post-traumatic stress reactions.

Much of this growing comfort with the dynamic growth and development of theories and a move away from cultism and dogmatism has resulted from the expansion of the research base of each system. As more research on various uses and outcomes of such use for each theory is carried out and the predominance of findings continues to support the effectiveness of each system in various situations, there is a lessening of the need to preach and attempt to win converts (Rubin, 1985; Thomlison, 1984). This has been supplanted by a growing comfort with exploration and experimentation resulting in changes and modifications of systems as data emerge. Along with an expanded commitment to research is an enriched purview of the parameters and techniques of research.

Throughout, however, there is an emphasis on the client's current reality: the inherent thrust to growth, health, and strength; to the ability to reason, to take responsibility to change both self and situation, to adjust, to plan reflectively on both our present and future life, and to be accountable within the realities in which we live. This theme is not a naïve one that holds that a client can change all aspects of her/his reality. The crushing impact of poverty, racism, political oppression, and lack of the basic necessities of life is understood and decried. But within there is a theme that is less pessimistic than before of the extent to which change can take place. Undoubtedly there are differences in the weighting of the various components of the client's reality within and among the spectrum of theories. As well, there are differences in perception about the potential for change of individuals and groups, but again there is more consensus than disagreement on the importance of the components of the significant environments and their intermixture. An inherent theme here is to view the client more as an equal, a fellow human being in search for meaning, rather than as an interesting object of study.

WHAT IS STILL TO BE DONE?

As described above, we have indeed come far. However, just as certainly we have far to go in our quest for the optimal method of tapping the richness of this theoretical diversity for the good of our client. As I read and reread the spectrum of contributions

I noted some commonalities of areas where I think we need to continue to work as we move on in our theoretical odyssey.

Clearly we have come far in incorporating a concept of a pluralistic methods approach to practice. All of the theories presented speak about their applications for work with individuals, families, and groups. This is critical as we work to move away from a concept of each practitioner needing to fly a particular methodological flag. However, there is still some unevenness in this, especially in two areas. The first of these relates to work with dyads, which is an important aspect of our practice, whether such dyads be married couples, two siblings, a permanent relationship between a couple, two friends, two persons with a specific commonality, or indeed two strangers. This is an area of practice where underutilization appears to be the common picture; furthermore, it is a topic only sparsely addressed in many of our methods books.

Dyadic work is a type of intervention which when properly used can be a powerful medium of help and when incorrectly used can be highly hurtful. There are implications for this form of intervention in each of the theories presented here and it is hoped that as we continue to progress more attention will be given to this modality of practice in the future. It is particularly important to address this because of the interesting challenge presented by triadic relationships in such matters as power, transference, coalitions, scapegoating, sibling rivalry, and so on.

A further methodological challenge for all theories relates to the macro components of practice. Especially here in North America we are still a long way from putting behind us the long-standing, intrafamilial micro-macro tensions. This author has long hoped that as we became more comfortable with theoretical and methodological plurality, we would move toward a resolution of this division. As mentioned in Chapter 1, for a theory to be relevant to social work, it must speak to the "person in situation" paradigm and how change is brought about in each factor of this paradigm including the "situation." Thus even the most individualistic therapy-based theory, to be truly a social work theory, must understand and address the larger systems that impinge on the lives of our clients. This is relevant for systems and situations in themselves as well as in their potential to impact on individuals, dyads, families, and groups.

Thus each of our theories needs to examine its potential and relevance for community work. Interestingly meditation, a system one would consider initially to be as far away from macro practice as is imaginable, does address the potential impacts of its methods on community life and social change. Existentialism also speaks to this component of practice. It is hoped that was we move forward in the task of boundary opening and crossing more attention will given to the application of all of our theories to large systems practice.

As before all of the articles in the volume were written by North Americans. Each addresses the extent to which it is applicable to a multicultural clientele, much more than in earlier editions. Whether we have fully examined the extent to which each system has worldwide application needs to be left as an open question. As the profession becomes more and more worldwide, with a commonality of values, knowledge, and skills, much work is needed to be done in examining the relative efficacy of each system in relation to the culture in which it is practiced. To date the book has had a rather large international impact. In a future edition it would be hoped that a more international authorship will be sought to begin to reflect more pointedly the general application, or lack thereof, of different theories.

Two areas, identified previously in the third edition, still require both attention and further work. The first relates to the question of the role of technology in treatment. Although it is not as yet a strong theme in the literature, there is some beginning awareness that technology is an emerging societal variable that we need to begin to incorporate into our theoretical perspectives of practice. Clients are being influenced by this aspect of society in a myriad of ways, certainly not all negative. Indeed, technology brings considerable information, satisfaction, community awareness, entertainment, and learning to society. We need to do two things here: first, to develop more interest and sensitivity to the various aspects of these impacts on clients; and second, to examine in greater detail the extent to which technology can be used as adjuncts in intervention.

Another aspect of theoretical differences relates to the possible relationship between the nature of a service setting and the sociopolitical climate in which it finds itself and the influence of these on the theoretical orientation of practitioners. For example, it may be that in times of economic restraint and strongly held negative reactions by large segments of society to social needs that theories which stress client accountability and autonomy will be prevalent. Certainly we in North America are in the midst of a period where "short-term problem solving" is the "administrative fashionable mode" although this may not be what is best for all clients.

It is gratifying to note the extent to which the research base of most of our theories has expanded. All of the bibliographies are much richer than before, not only from the perspective of being updated since the last edition, but also reflecting the amount of research that has been conducted to test our various aspects of a theory or the application of a theory to a particular setting, problem, or client group.

What we still need, of course, is more work that focuses precisely on the differential use of theories in similar situations. That is, can we begin to demonstrate that there are different outcomes when different theories are used in similar situations?

Interesting as such questions are from a conceptual perspective, of perhaps even more importance is the responsibility to continue to expand our knowledge as to when the use of a particular theory is counterindicated. Accompanying the earlier-mentioned growing comfort with openness to change in theories is an expanded readiness to accept that all theories are not useful for all clients all of the time. The authors of the various chapters have addressed this question well. Often the comments about counterindications are speculative, stemming from a rich experience with the particular theory's use. What we need to do now is to expand our knowledge through rigorous testing with regard to when the use of particular systems are counterindicated. This is particularly important in view of the North American tendency to adulate fashion and thus have some theories in style over others at different times and in different situations.

One other area where in the future it is expected more reflection will be needed, as we move to more permeable boundaries within the profession, is that of interdisciplinary influence. In recent months I have found indications that colleagues in other professions have found the concept of *interlocking theories* to be of interest. If indeed we can open this door wider, a huge wave of useful collaborative activity could be anticipated and hopefully a marked diminution of the seemingly endless turf "skirmishes" that still exist will result.

RESEARCH CHALLENGES

As we continue down the path of increased diversity of theory, accompanied by a demonstrated commitment to accountability, it is clear that increasing efforts need be, and are going to be, put into research. Just as we have welcomed the increasing comfort with plurality in theory and method, we can also observe a similar increasing comfort with diversity in research methodology (Thyer, 1993). In the period of time between the last edition and this one it has been gratifying to see that what appeared to be the emergence of another of our either-or battles between the proponents of quantitative and qualitative research has passed. For the most part researchers are comfortable with the concept that differing research methods are strategies for advancing knowledge; hence all methods are of equal value. One becomes better than the other only in their appropriate application to meet the demands of the challenge at hand (Berlin, 1983).

From the perspective of theory and social work practice there are a number of essential research challenges. One important component of this relates to the aforementioned question of fashion (Shulman, 1993). This question of why some theories are more popular in some parts of the profession and at different times and places is an interesting one. Apart from the sociological impact, the effect on practice of these undulating periods needs to be examined. Related to this is the concomitant question of why some systems have become mainstream and others remain on the periphery of practice. If there were evidence that this was related to specific utility, the question would not be of such importance. But such data do not exist. It appears that the critical variables have not yet been identified. The reality of having some theories differentially in fashion over others means that some clients are deprived of various approaches to therapy based on reasons extraneous to the needs of the presenting situation. In this way clients can be harmed; this makes the quesion one of ethics.

A second research challenge facing us relates to the critical importance of theory in practice. As discussed in Chapter 1, an essential premise of this volume and one that is a major tenet of the profession is that responsible practice needs to be founded on sound theory. We have long proclaimed this and have always acted as if it were so. The task we now face is to demonstrate that this is true. I am particularly intrigued by this question because of discussions I have had in the last few years with several very senior colleagues in clinical practice who challenge me very pointedly on this issue. The persons to whom I refer are recognized by colleagues to be among the leaders in the field of practice but who differ strongly with me on the point of theory. They would argue that theory gets in the way of their practice and limits their spontaneity. In their view what is needed for intervention to be effective is a highly responsive, empathetic, understanding, consistent response to a client. They would say that they practice without theory and advise younger colleagues whom they supervise or teach to do the same.

My view is that indeed these persons are theory-rich as is evidenced when they talk about a client. However, I believe their theory has become so intuitive to them that it is difficult for them to explicate it. As a researcher I have to accept that they may be right, and that my explanations may only be a rationalization to soothe my being challenged in this way.

I have thought about this and related questions and have speculated on the question of how one goes about testing either of these hypotheses as to whether the quality of outcome is related to soundness of theory or skill at empathy.

This conundrum raises a series of potential questions for examination:

1. What theories do persons say drive their practice?
2. How much do persons know about the theories they say they use? That is, does one have to have a strong theory base or is it enough to believe in one?
3. Is it possible to observe differences in the practice of persons related to the theories they profess to use?
4. If this is so, can we see differences in outcomes in cases where different theoretical bases are used?

Of course, these are highly generic questions, each of which would lend itself to a multitude of diverse specific research projects. Until we begin to address the general question of what is the relationship of theory to practice, we need to humbly accept that we do not know and live with the reality that much of what we do in practice rests on the accumulation of practice wisdom and ethical commitment. However daunting the task, we ought not fear it. There is abundant evidence that what we do helps people. Clients are better off as a result of our interventions with them and our ability to help understand and alter their significant environments. But we need to do much more to make precise a further question asked some years ago by Kendell and Butcher: "What intervention, conducted by what therapist, with what clients to resolve what psychosocial dysfunction, produces what effects?" (Kendall & Butcher, 1982). As we have said, the answers to such challenges will not come from one or two breakthrough kinds of studies but through a myriad of small, well-designed, carefully conducted projects that together, in a step-by-step manner, will help us to build this needed further body of tested knowledge.

THE COMPARISON OF THEORIES

One of the premises of this work is that we should make much more effort than we have to date to use our various theories in a differential manner. That is, we need to enhance our efforts to match theory to client, rather than theory to therapist. Since theories have differing value bases and alternate views of what constitutes helping, so too do clients. By having our range of theories analyzed from the perspective of clients it may well be that more effort at matching a client's profile to a theory profile would foster the formulation of a "client friendly" strategy of helping (Souflee, 1993).

However, one of the challenges facing anyone interested in the therapeutic application of our theoretical plurality is how to find a way to compare theories that appear to be so divergent. If we really wish to implement an interlocking perspective, we need to find a way that helps us see where theories are similar and where they are different (Corey, 1995). This is something with which I have long struggled, and in so doing I have formulated a series of conclusions.

It is clear that each system influencing contemporary social work practice in a significant way is attempting to find ways to help individuals, dyads, groups, families, and systems to become more fulfilled and better able to achieve their potential as humans in a manner that fits their values and worldviews. This general thrust can be made more precise in a series of statements, as follows:

1. Each theory has to be looked at from the perspective of its historical origins and path into social work.
2. Each theory has to be looked at from the perspective of the strength of its empirical base.
3. Each theory has to be looked at from the perspective of its specificity or generalizability.
4. Each theory must address the nature of the individual and value assumptions about persons.
5. Each theory must develop a position on the nature and structure of personality, the determinants of personality, and the importance or power of rationality.
6. Each theory must develop a position on the nature of behavior, the nature of change, the determinants of change, and the differential importance of inner and outer influences on persons.
7. Each theory must identify the characteristics of the helping process, including the kind, range, and nature of change agents.
8. Each theory needs to identify the spectrum of its applicability and its limitations.
9. Each system needs to specify the required knowledge and skills of the therapist.

This profile, through its various drafts and reconceptualizations, has proven useful as a basis for comparing theories. As mentioned in the last edition, the then-identified cluster of differentiating factors were used to develop a large chart which compared 21 theories, along 33 variables, subdivided, under the six headings, then identified. This chart has proven to be useful for students, teachers, and colleagues. A modified version of this chart will be forthcoming in the near future. It is hoped that in so doing we will be able to include more theories than before and to cover all of the above items.*

---

*Some discussions have been held with several colleagues about a method of putting this chart into a computer program which would permit us to look for, among other things, a best fit between client and theory. I am planning to turn to this as a next project.

Table 29–1

Classification of Selected Social Work Practice Theories From the Perspective of the Primary Human Activity Focus*

Distinguishing Area of Focus	Relevant Theories†
The Person and His or Her Attributes	
Person as a biological being	Neurolinguistic Programming
Person as a psychological being	Functional Psychoanalytic
Person as a learner	Behavioral theory
Person as thinker	Cognitive
	Constructivism
	Narrative
Person's Use of Attributes	
Person as Contemplator	Meditation
Person as experiential being	Existential
	Gestalt
	Hypnosis
Person as communicator	Communication
Person as doer	Empowerment
	Problem solving
	Task
Person and Society	
Person as individual	Ego psychology
	Client centered
	Crisis
Person as communal being	Feminist Psychosocial
	Transactional Analysis
Person as societal being	Aboriginal
	Role
Person in relation to the universe	Life Model
	Systems

*See *Social Work Treatment,* 3d ed., p. 15.

†As a social work theory, each system needs to address the entire spectrum of a person's bio-psycho-social reality. The differences between and among systems relate to emphasis on focus of the system on discrete aspects of the human condition.

First presented for discussion at a faculty symposium, Columbia University, School of Social Work, Feb. 25, 1985.

IMPLICATIONS FOR PRACTICE

As the above comments indicate, I am comfortable that there is a high degree of consensus between and among the various theories and, more important, the theoreticians and the factors that combine to make up a practice theory. The differences emerge when we put specificity to each factor. If we accept this premise of a higher level of consensus among different thought systems than is usually considered, important questions arise to be addressed related to the nature of practice from an interlocking theoretical perspective. Perhaps the most critical one is to what extent can and should a practitioner be knowledgeable about and comfortable with the range of systems here presented as well as others still to emerge? Several times in this chapter we have raised the question of how strongly practice is linked to theory and have taken the position that they are very strongly linked. But much of this is speculation. It would be cynical in the extreme to suggest that these theories have no influence on practice, but I think it would be equally naïve to impy that practitioners, consciously, deliberately, and consistently formulate their interventive strategies from a specific conceptual base (Reid, 1984).

It is our strong conviction that all of the various theories are important and that it is thus our responsibility to be aware of each, to strive to understand each, and to deliberately attempt to utilize aspects of each system in our practice when appropriate (Hawkins & Fraser, 1981).

I remain strongly committed to this thesis, yet I am aware of the challenge created by such an approach. Too long have we labored under an impression that adherence to one approach to practice by definition excluded others; that there was some component of disloyalty or some quality of Machiavellian manipulation to attempt to move from one approach to another depending on the situation, the setting, the resources, the persons, or the request. One could support this mono-theory approach if it were held that the various theories are mutually exclusive and contradictory. This is much less true if one is committed to the concept of a large element of interconnectedness and interinfluences (Meyer, 1983). The concept of a mono-theory approach is softened, of course, by the current strong interest in a generalist approach. This approach appears to be variously conceived but does seem to imply the possibility of influence from other theories. It is difficult at this point to decide if indeed it is a new system in its own right built on a strong problem-solving tradition.

I am frequently asked by students and practitioners if I really mean that we need to know all of the theories here described. I have pondered this at length and have concluded that the answer is a definitive "yes." We do need to be acquainted with at least the basic parameters of each and, most important, their potential to help and to hurt. In many aspects of our lives we deal with a high degree of diversity. We are able to absorb large amounts of information about many topics in our lives. So too with theories. It is possible to address this diversity in a knowing and responsible way.

As mentioned above, since every theory does address the same questions, once we understand the profile of a theory, and how it addresses these specifics, we can incorporate the profiles of many theories into our armementarium of interventive resources. Colleagues in other disciplines deal with an even greater profile of diversity; so too can we. I am not suggesting that we need to be fully proficient in each system, but we do need to know the dimensions, potentials, and limitations of each. If not, as mentioned elsewhere, we may be depriving a client of access to a form of help that might be of particular benefit because of a goodness of fit between the theory and the client (Smid & Van Kreeken, 1984).

There is a second reason why we need to be informed about all systems and that is because clients expect that we will be resources for them when they are seeking help. For example, a client may be considering a particular type of therapy that has been found to be inappropriate for the kind of person he/she is. With the understanding that we need to respect a client's decision, we also know that our opinions are frequently viewed as all-knowing and all-powerful by many of our clients and our viewpoints about particular systems will be of considerable import to them (Siporin, 1975).

IMPLICATIONS FOR TEACHING

Important as is diversity for practitioners, the question of theoretical plurality has strong and challenging implications for teaching. "And what shall we teach?" was a question put to us by Helen Harris Perlman some years ago. With the immense expansion of the knowledge base of the profession, the challenge as how to address the question of theoretical diversity is indeed an immense one.

"Surely you don't expect a graduate to know all 27 theories that are in this book" is a question I have been and know I will be frequently asked. It is one I formerly found daunting and attempted to respond to evasively. This is no longer so! I think that every graduate today, first, must be aware that this spectrum exists, and second, must know at least in a general way something about the strengths and limitations of each system. This is not as formidable a task as it might seem as long as a student has first been well taught about the nature of practice theory and its role in practice. Accompanying this should be teaching of content of three or four systems, both to equip them for beginning practice and, of equal importance, to equip them with the conceptual tools to incorporate into their practice additional theories as needed as they find themselves ready for, or needing to, expand their repertoire of theory (Saleebez, 1993).

There probably is less than full consensus as to which three or four theories would be the core ones to teach. I have experimented with several approaches and presently am of the opinion that each new graduate should have as a minimum the following theoretical profile: one theory with a biopsychosocial base; one with a cognitive base; one with a short-term profile; and one with a crisis-and-stress-oriented basis. But most important, I believe it is essential that our students of today need to emerge with an understanding of theory, a comfort and respect for diversity, and a commitment to an interlocking and interinfluencing viewpoint.

THE WAY AHEAD

It is difficult to predict with certainty where we are going as a profession from the perspective of theoretical plurality. Clearly we are beyond the point where we have to advocate for it. It is no longer a concept that appears to be "off the wall." Rather there is an appreciation of and wonderment regarding the immense yet exciting challenge that this reality presents (Timms, 1970). This in turn is accompanied by an understanding and acceptance that to translate these convictions to evidenced material will be a long, slow process. But it is one that is worth the prize.

Undoubtedly new theories will emerge. Viewpoints, ideas, and propositions from other parts of the world will enrich us (Imre-Wells, 1984). They will also trouble us as long-cherished beliefs are challenged. Throughout we will continue to learn with wonderment and humility of the complexities and potentials of the human family (Lewis, 1982).

There are many directions in which we can and ought to go. We began this volume with some help from Alice and end in the same vein: *"Alice asked, 'Would you tell me, please, which way I ought to go from here? That depends a good deal on where you want to get to,' said the Cheshire Cat."*

REFERENCES

Berlin, S.B. (1983). Single case evaluation: Another version. *Social Work Research and Abstracts, 19*(1 Spring), 3–11.

Carroll, L. (1871). *Through the looking glass.* London: Collier-Macmillan, 1963.

Caspi, Y. (1992). A continuum theory for social work knowledge. *Journal of Sociology and Social Welfare, 19*(3), 105–120.

Corey, G. (1995). *Theory and practice of group counseling* (4th Ed.) Pacific Grove, CA: Brooks Cole Publishing.

Curnock, K., & P. Hardicker (1979). *Towards practice theory.* London: Routledge and Keagan Paul.

Hawkins, J.D., & Fraser, M.W. (1981). Theory and practice in delinquency prevention. *Social Work Research and Abstracts, 17*(4), 3–13.

Imre-Wells, R. (1984). The nature of knowledge in social work. *Social Work, 29*(1), 51–56.

Kendall, P.C., & Butcher, J.N. (Eds.). (1982). *Handbook of research methods in clinical psychology.* New York: J Wiley.

Lewis, H. (1982). *The intellectual base of social work practice.* New York: Haworth Press.

Meyer, C.M. (1983). Selecting appropriate practice models. In A. Rosenblatt & D. Waldfogel (Eds.), *Handbook of clinical social work* (pp. 731–749.). San Francisco: Jossey Bass.

Mishne, J.M. (1993). *The evolution and application of clinical theory.* New York: Free Press.

Reid, W.J. (1984). Treatment of choice or choice of treatments; an essay review. *Social Work Research and Abstracts, 20*(2) 33–38.

Rubin, A. (1985). Practice effectiveness: More grounds for optimism. *Social Work, 30,* 469–476.

Saleebez, D. (1993). Theory and the generation and subversion of knowledge. *Journal of Sociology and Social Welfare, 20*(1) 5–25.

Shulman, L. (1993). Developing and testing a practice theory: An interactional perspective. *Social Work, 38*(1, Jan.), 91–93.

Siporin, M. (1975). Introduction to social work practice. In *Introduction to social work practice* (Chapters 4 and 5). New York: Macmillan.

Smid, G., & Van Kreeken, R. (1984). Notes on theory and practice of social work: A comparative view. *British Journal of Social Work, 14*(1) 11–22.

Souflee, J.F. (1993). A metatheoretical framework for social work practice. *Social Work, 38*(3, May), 317–333.

Thomlison, R.J. (1984). Something works: Evidence from practice effectiveness studies. *Social Work, 29*(Jan.-Feb), 51–56.

Thyer, B.A. (1993). Social work theory and practice research: The approach of logical positivism. *Social Work and Social Science Review, 4*(1), 5–26.

Timms, N. (1970). *Social work* (pp. 56–57). London: Routledge.

INDEX

712